THE COMPLETE
UP AND DOWN THE EARTH TALES

THE COMPLETE UP AND DOWN THE EARTH TALES

TALBOT MUNDY

SELECT ILLUSTRATIONS BY
JOSEPH CLEMENT COLL
AND DWIGHT FRANKLIN

INTRODUCTION BY
BRIAN TAVES

ACKNOWLEDGEMENTS

For permission to reprint copyrighted material the following acknowledgements are gratefully made:

"Introduction" appears here for the first time. Copyright © 2018 Brian Taves. All rights reserved.

"Oakes Respects an Adversary" originally appeared in the December 3, 1918 issue of *Adventure* magazine (Vol. 19, No. 5). Copyright © 1918 by The Ridgway Company.

"America Horns In" originally appeared in the January 3, 1919 issue of *Adventure* magazine (Vol. 20, No. 1). Copyright © 1919 by The Ridgway Company.

"Jackson Tactics" originally appeared in the February 18, 1919 issue of *Adventure* magazine (Vol. 20, No. 4). Copyright © 1919 by The Ridgway Company.

"Heinie Horns Into the Game" originally appeared in the March 18, 1919 issue of *Adventure* magazine (Vol. 20, No. 6). Copyright © 1919 by The Ridgway Company.

"The End of the Bad Ship *Bundesrath*" originally appeared in the April 18, 1919 issue of *Adventure* magazine (Vol. 21, No. 2). Copyright © 1919 by The Ridgway Company.

"The Ivory Trail" originally appeared as "On the Trail of Tipoo Tib" in the May 3–July 18, 1919 issues of *Adventure* magazine (Vol. 21, No. 3–Vol. 22, No. 2). Copyright © 1919 by The Ridgway Company. This version originally published by The Bobbs–Merrill Company in 1919.

"The Shriek of Dûm" originally appeared in the September 3, 1919 issue of *Adventure* magazine (Vol. 22, No. 5). Copyright © 1919 by The Ridgway Company.

"Barabbas Island" originally appeared in the October 18, 1919 issue of *Adventure* magazine (Vol. 23, No. 2). Copyright © 1919 by The Ridgway Company.

"In Aleppo Bazaar" originally appeared in the January 18, 1920 issue of *Adventure* magazine (Vol. 24, No. 2). Copyright © 1920 by The Ridgway Company.

"The Eye of Zeitoon" originally appeared as "The Eye of Zeitun" in the February & March, 1920 issues of *Romance* magazine (Vol. 1, Nos. 4 & 5). Copyright © 1920 by The Ridgway Company. This version originally published by The Bobbs–Merrill Company in 1920.

THANKS TO

Rebecca Burns, Chris Slembarski & Brian Taves

TABLE OF CONTENTS

"Up and Down the Earth Tales":

The Transition from Experience to Persuasion *by Brian Taves* i

Oakes Respects an Adversary 1

America Horns In 18

Jackson Tactics 34

Heinie Horns Into the Game 52

The End of the Bad Ship *Bundesrath* 84

The Ivory Trail 118

The Shriek of Dûm 299

Barabbas Island 353

In Aleppo Bazaar 402

The Eye of Zeitoon 456

Correspondence 581

Endnotes 590

"UP AND DOWN THE EARTH TALES":

THE TRANSITION FROM EXPERIENCE TO PERSUASION

BY BRIAN TAVES

THERE IS often a temptation to perceive an author's writings through an autobiographical lens, as offering a glimpse of the personal experiences. This is even more pronounced when the author has had such a varied background as those of Talbot Mundy. His African stories in particular drew upon places and people he knew first-hand. However, while it is tempting to read these stories for clues about Mundy's real life, what is more significant is how these details were filtered through the writer's creative process. What finally emerges from his pen will inevitably diverge from those kernels of truth that provided inspiration, as they are rearranged for narrative purposes and the needs of literary formula. As characters emerge on the printed page, they take on a life of their own, leaving steadily further behind those figures who were their progenitor. Nowhere is this shift more apparent in Mundy's writings than in his "Up and Down the Earth" stories, beginning with some of his own encounters with Africa, but finally resolving in a stories set far from anywhere he had visited, and climaxing in a politically-motivated striving for Armenian independence.

TALBOT MUNDY

TALBOT MUNDY was born in London in 1879 as William Lancaster Gribbon and raised according to Victorian standards. The harsh environment of such schools as Rugby could not constrain his free-thinking and non-conformism, and he ran away at age 16. He traveled the Far East, earning his own way, before landing in Africa for four years. Immigrating to the United States in 1909, his second book, *King—of the Khyber Rifles* (1917), told of a fabulous character, Yasmini, who tried to conquer India, and quickly became a classic for its combination of fantastic elements with adventure. Mundy won a reputation as the successor to H. Rider Haggard and Rudyard Kipling—a comparison he found odious, since Mundy opposed Kipling's jingoistic attitude toward colonialism.

Moving to San Diego, California, in 1923 he joined the Theosophical Society centered there. Although occult themes had already appeared in such novels as *Caves of Terror* (1922) and *The Nine Unknown* (1923), H.P. Blavatsky's rendering of eastern teachings combined with Mundy's own experiences as the fantastic increasingly dominated his fiction. While residing at the society, Mundy wrote the novels *Om—The Secret of Ahbor Valley* (1924) and *The Devil's Guard* (1926), about the teachings of the "Masters" in India, especially karma and reincarnation. The theosophical influence was also evident as Mundy tried a new genre, historical novels, producing the classic series, *Tros of Samothrace* (1925–26), *Queen Cleopatra* (1929), and *Purple Pirate* (1935), books that raised a furor at the time for their critical interpretation of Rome and Julius Caesar.

From 1936 until his death, Mundy addressed a new audience, children, when he was hired to composing the daily radio serial *Jack Armstrong—the All-American Boy*. Under Mundy's scripting, his novels were rewritten and heard by millions of children, who absorbed the accounts of mystics, ancient artifacts, and visits to the lamas of Tibet—with the occult implications of such motifs intact. Simultaneously, Mundy continued to write philosophical novels for an adult audience, and *Old Ugly-Face* (1940) placed Christianity in a theosophical context in an epic account of the intrigue surrounding the infant Dalai Lama on the brink of a world war. Talbot Mundy died suddenly at his home in Florida in 1940 from complications related to diabetes.

AN AFRICAN ODYSSEY

IN LATE 1903, Mundy was in Hobart, Tasmania, and, with no prospect of a job, sailed on a three-masted vessel, "bumping bluey"—carrying a form of Australian eucalyptus known as blue-gum piles for a new pier at Delagoa Bay. This ship was nearly wrecked, the entire crew became ill, and they jumped ship at Lourenço Marques, part of Portuguese East Africa in what is today the southernmost part of Mozambique. Ashore, conditions were even worse, without a job or money, a man was jailed, then shipped back to sea, or sent to boss slave labor with himself at the point of a gun.[1] Mundy later described it as the most lawless place in the world, "'where a man was fined only ten pounds for killing a white, and only a pound or two for a black.' "[2]

Mundy was utterly destitute, the climate was dreadful, and in the swamps of the Umbuluzi River he succumbed to a fever. A Chinese laundryman nursed him back to health, then directed him to a good job running a big estate up the Limpopo River at Chai Chai in Gazaland. By Christmas Mundy was ill again, this time with East Coast fever, a malignant form of malaria. A Portuguese trader lent him a bungalow to die in. When the visiting local doctor, Leal, began to help himself to his belongings, Mundy's black servant, Samaki ("Fish"), interfered, and Leal threatened to implicate him in Mundy's death, expected the next day. Instead of simply fleeing, Samaki returned at midnight with a native doctor, and made the nearly delirious Mundy swear to not reveal his treatment. While the doctor danced and hummed a monotonous refrain, four women smeared "quantities of vile smelling greasy stuff" that made Mundy feel like he was being burned alive. However, as daylight came, the pain ceased, and the liquid was sponged off. A few hours later, the fever was gone, and by evening Mundy's appetite returned; on New Year's Day he had completely recovered.[3]

The railway to Lake Victoria had just been completed, and Mundy heard overrated reports that British East Africa was booming. He left at the end of January, 1904, on the steamer *Bundesrath* for Zanzibar and Mombasa. The ship eventually figured in his novelettes "A Transaction in Diamonds," "Heinie Horns into the Game," and "The End of the Bad Ship *Bundesrath*," while the era was documented in his 1925 article, "On the Trail of Sindbad the Sailor." Mundy described Nairobi as "only a corrugated iron frontier town, with one hotel, a cluster of railway bungalows, an Indian bazaar, some government houses and one main street[;] the lions used to enter the town at sunset...." [4]

With no jobs to be found, the only money was in illegally shooting elephants, as he chronicled in his article "Elephant Hunting for a Living" (*Adventure,* July 1912, as Walter Galt). Many of these expeditions were desperate ventures made by luckless, indigent men; in "A Low-Veldt Funeral" (*Adventure,* February 1913), Mundy describes a trip with five Australians into the swamps south of Lake Victoria.

To get out of the government's reach required traveling "up country" and "off the beaten track," at least sixty miles from the Uganda railway. Mundy took a train and hired a native servant just out of jail, named Kazi Moto ("Work like hell"). They put together a safari and slipped into elephant country, joining "a Greek of most blazing amazing courage but very doubtful reputation." [5] Mundy hoped to find the legendary buried ivory hoard of Tippoo Tib, but the terrain and its inhabitants—from lions to tsetse flies to reported cannibals—proved too formidable. At the time, Mundy reflected the conventional belief among his fellow hunters that the law protecting elephants could not be enforced, and that if the white man abstained, the native would take all the plunder; later he would regret the life of the hunter.

With the proceeds, Mundy acquired a herd of 4,000 cattle that bore the brand of an official entitled to only own two.[6] With British officials on his trail, he decided to drive the herd across the border into German East Africa. Near Shirati, on the eastern shore of Lake Victoria, a band of

Talbot Mundy and director Fred Niblo in Hollywood in 1923: Mundy had led the African safaris where Niblo shot the first movies in Africa around 1908.

fierce Masai fought Mundy and his men, taking the cattle. He received a wound in the right leg from a spear dipped in gangrene, and later it took seven men to hold him down while the wound was cauterized with stems of grass heated in a fire. "They were wonderfully loyal and brave to do it, for the treatment is frightful torture;" afterwards, the men left, taking their loads in lieu of pay, recognizing that their employer was now without any other way to compensate them.[7] Mundy and Kazi Moto began a walk to the nearest doctor, 200 miles away in Muanza, where the Germans were inhospitable. Mundy had developed black-water fever, and he was placed in a rat-filled shed where he was expected to die. Kazi Moto stole food for him, and the doctor made brief visits. After a few days, he heard the doctor order a sergeant to bring the chain-gang to dig his grave, and bury him doubled-up.

What happened next changed Mundy and was a crucial turning point in Mundy's life, and an experience that would later fuel his belief in Christian Science. The doctor

> didn't come in that morning, but just looked at me through the door; what he said to the sergeant, though, did me more good than all his physic. Up to that time I had not particularly wanted to get well; I had neither money nor prospects and was feeling much too ill to care, and I haven't the least doubt that if he had said nothing I would have died either that day or the day following. But I hated the man so, and was so utterly disgusted with his treatment of me, that I made up my mind to disappoint him, and from that minute I began to get better. When the chain-gang came with a sack to tie me up in I was sitting up with the aid of Kazi Moto. Two days later I leaned on Kazi Moto's shoulder and walked out to have a look at the grave; I was so weak that I very nearly tumbled into it.[8]

Mundy traveled as far as present-day Uganda to the Ruwenzori Range, the "Mountains of the Moon," 800 miles inland from the coast, on the northeastern border of the Congo, walking as far south as Lakes Tanganyika and Nyasa. Realizing that he could not make enough to live on, he took passage on a dhow for British territory. He did road work and was appointed as town clerk of the frontier village of Kisumu, on the northwest shore of Lake Victoria and situated almost exactly on the equator. He saw two campaigns and mastered several of the local languages.

His interest in indigenous magic began almost immediately after his arrival in Africa, continuing the investigations he had begun in India. Mundy quickly discovered that few whites, especially missionaries, had studied the subject, and fewer still had the opportunity to, since the magicians themselves regarded questions as proof of enmity. While living in Kisumu, Mundy became acquainted with Oketch, a member of the Kakkamegga Kavirondo tribe who made no secret of being a "maganga" (magician).

Mundy was involved in a number of safaris, on one becoming a personal friend of director Fred Niblo who was shooting the first moving pictures in Africa; the contact with Niblo would eventually lead to Mundy's first work in Hollywood in 1923.[9] Another safari was less fortuitous, when he made the acquaintance of the rambunctious, quarrelsome Rupert Cecil Craven, formerly of the Royal Navy. Craven and his party, known as heavy drinkers and gamblers, entered the ivory trade. His wife, 35 year old Inez Broom, was regarded as one of the most beautiful women of her day, and she and Mundy became romantically involved, with the repercussions of the scandal caused them to leave for England, and ultimately the United States.

Talbot Mundy portrait, 1913.

EXPERIENCE INTO FICTION

MUNDY'S EXPERIENCES in Africa would become the basis for a series which had the most autobiographical tone of any of his writing. Delagoa Bay, Lourenço Marques and Chai Chai, capital of Gazaland, along the Limpopo River, areas Mundy had travelled in, were the locales in "A Transaction in Diamonds," in the February 1911 issue of *The Scrap-Book*; the series "Oakes Respects an Adversary," "America Horns In," "Jackson Tactics," "Heinie Horns Into the Game," and "The End of the Bad Ship *Bundesrath*," in the December 3, 1918, January 1, 1919, February 18, 1919, March 18, 1919, and April 18, 1919 issues of *Adventure*, respectively; and *Solomon's Half-Way House*, a four-part serial in the Canadian biweekly *Maclean's* from August 15 to October 1, 1934. This series would climax in the novel, *The Ivory Trail*—which Mundy in turn rewrote into a radio serial spanning months of daily episodes. Although composed over a span of nearly thirty years, all of these told essentially the same narrative, only sometimes changing character names.

"A Transaction in Diamonds," Mundy's very first story, has Charlie Delaguerre as king of the Libomba Hills. Diamonds from the new Premier mine are usually sent through Swaziland and Gazaland by a runner, but unfortunately the shortest route runs past Delaguerre's place, where he robs them. His educated daughter, Marion, is smuggling the diamonds for him to Bombay, in the belief that he will use the profits so they can settle prosperously in Europe.

In *Solomon's Half-Way House*, an out-of-place professor, Elmer Girdlestone, is searching for the gold mines of King Solomon (whom he believes was not an individual, but a dynasty). Girdlestone thinks the gold was transported past Chai Chai across the Libonba mountains. However, he has been preceded in this search by a vicious local outlaw, Charles Dumaurier—Delaguerre by another name. Instead of Marion Delaguerre in "A Transaction in Diamonds," Girdlestone is traveling with his daughter, Doris.

Dumaurier is an even more venal character than he had been previously, having supplied the Germans in Tanganyika during World War I, and once made "a steady income shooting blacks on their way from Kimberley with stolen diamonds for the Hindu buyers in Delagoa Bay." [10] He keeps thirteen huts for his black wives and their uneducated children, and hungers for a new white wife when he sees Doris. Much of the narrative concentrates on the racial milieu, with two Portuguese colonials, one a disreputable trader and the other a courageous policeman. Despite a promising opening, *Solomon's HalfWay House* quickly fizzles, as Doris is abducted by Dumaurier, and the story resolves into a routine and tiresome jungle pursuit. The potentially most interesting aspects, such as the search for Solomon's treasure, and its eventual discovery by Girdlestone under Dumaurier's camp, are all recounted after the event, leaving a disappointing, second-hand flavor.

"Oakes Respects an Adversary," "America Horns In," "Jackson Tactics," "Heinie Horns Into the Game," and "The End of the Bad Ship *Bundesrath*" relate a saga of fortune hunting set before World War I and written in the first person. Together, they formed the beginning of the "Up and Down the Earth Tales," eventually also comprising two long novels and another three novelettes. Premier among the characters is Lord Montdidier (pronounced Mundidger, nicknamed Monty) and earl of Kirkudbrightshire, a middle aged bachelor and unrepentant member of the English old order, quite well aware that he is one of a dying breed. An avid chess-player, athlete, and former colonel of cavalry, he is an aristocrat adventurer whose reading preference runs to dime novels. He hopes to replenish the family treasury, expended over centuries of military service, leaving his hereditary estates heavily mortgaged. Whereas other Englishmen solve the problem by marrying wealthy American heiresses, Monty is determined to succeed on his own.

Slightly older is his lifelong friend, Frederick Joliett Oakes, another English bachelor of a similar build, weighing 240 pounds. Oakes is distinguished halfway through the opening series of stories by his sometimes irritating passion for the concertina, using it to accompany songs of his own devising composed on the spot. He is fluent in a dozen languages and full of humor. He explains his philosophy this way.

> "A hunter hunts, a fisherman fishes, a ship's captain masters the elements. A true adventurer adventures, not specializing so much as embracing all occupations in the one.
>
> "So, you see, I've been soldier, lawyer, hunter, fisherman—you'd be surprised how often a fisherman!—ship's captain on occasion—everlastingly at war with the elements and chance—and I've buried too many good and true men not to have a slice of parson in my make-up.... To me, adventure is life, and life is a succession of adventures. Monotony is death, and the only death." [11]

The narrator (presumably occupying Mundy's role for those stories based on his experiences) joins them, and by keeping him unnamed, this novice outsider doubles as the entry point for the reader into the adventurous existence. In his early 20s, the narrator at first is just a hired associate, hero-worshipping his older comrades, but becomes a full-fledged member after a deed of bravery on behalf of all.

William Simpson Yerkes, often called "America" by Oakes, is added to round out the group. No enthusiast for autocratic government, whether in the colonies or accompanied by nobility, he has to learn respect for Monty, who refuses to allow any questioning if he is to be the leader. The four men cooperate harmoniously, following the classic pattern of Dumas's three musketeers, with the narrator as the initiate d'Artagnan. Monty, Oakes, and Yerkes bring together diverse levels of society in a social mix that dismisses differences of class and caste as each individual must prove himself worthy. Valorous and humane, fulfilling the obligations of duty and selflessness is as much their goal as the search for wealth.

Traveling upriver along the route that King Solomon's adventures came to dig in the hills was also part of "Oakes Respects an Adversary." This time, Charles du Maurier rules Gazaland, through whom the narrator "saw revealed the despicableness of that colonial government." [12] Stoutish, fat-lipped, with cold blue eyes, all fear du Maurier, an expert marksman, who enjoys shooting rats by moonlight. With his eleven brothers and five cousins, and nine wives that ally him with separate tribes, he is stronger than the authorities, and he unhesitatingly lashes any black, or white, he chooses. Moreover, an old Portuguese law gives to the man who married the daughter of a chief title to all his lands upon death, but together they consider du Maurier an asset, and act on his behalf.

The story continues in "America Horns In," in which Yerkes, who has a rubber concession, joins them and they try to prevent du Maurier from either filing or holding the land on which their claims have been made. He falls to his death trying to escape, mourned by his many wives and offspring, too afraid to fetch his corpse but remembering his tyranny too vividly to turn away.

In "Jackson Tactics," his brothers and cousins attack the village in revenge, and Monty lures them to death in an explosion.

In "Heinie Horns Into the Game" and "The End of the Bad Ship *Bundesrath*" Mundy retells other aspects of "A Transaction in Diamonds." As part of the German plan to take over the territory, they claim the du Maurier lands due to the weakness of the Portuguese government. Monty foils the effort, and he and his friends begin a trip up the coast aboard the only vessel available, the filthy *Bundesrath*, that becomes a veritable descent into hell. The ship is running guns and carrying passengers with cholera, before a fire finally sinks it.

At the conclusion of "The End of the Bad Ship *Bundesrath*," Monty, Oakes, Yerkes, and the narrator resolve to go after Tib's treasure. They travel to Mombasa, Nairobi, Kikuyu, Lumbwa, Lake Victoria, Muanza, Ukerewe, and Kisumu, before arriving at Mount Elgon—all places Mundy knew personally, as the African portion of the saga reached its pinnacle in *The Ivory Trail*, originally titled *On the Trail of Tippoo Tib* in its six-part *Adventure* magazine serialization from May to July 1919 (and reprinted in 1953 as *Trek East*). Exciting and well written, it is also a long, sprawling epic, hastily written in a frantic, successful "effort to subscribe for (and pay for) more Liberty Bonds than any mere author ought to be asked to take." [13]

Today *The Ivory Trail* is more than an entertaining adventure, serving as an autobiographical testament of colonial conditions on the continent at the turn of the century and giving the book a documentary flavor. Mundy explained to his publisher at the time, Bobbs-Merrill, that the new stories were reminiscent, an account that only he could tell.

A.L. Burt edition of **The Ivory Trail.**

> I believe I am the only man who saw conditions as they really were in German East before this war, who know and understand British East Africa as well, who have hunted lions and elephants, have held a civil job out there, have fought, sickened, been wounded, recovered and so on all up and down that monstrous land.
>
> Most of the stuff is reminiscent. I am the guy, for instance, who was wounded in the leg with the poisoned spear, whose grave the Germans dug, who was eye-witness of the floggings and hangings, who returned up Lake Victoria Nyanza on the dhow, who saw the cannibals on Elgon, etcetera and so on.... [14]

The colorful descriptions of Africa and the land and animals are beautifully written. In the verses and the book generally, Mundy recognized the need for wildlife conservation, and the most memorable are the songs of the game reserves, as in this excerpt from the prelude to chapter 6.

But who can the paleface people be with red
meat appetites
Who ruled anew what Noah knew—that animals
have rights?

Mundy's verses before each of the eighteen chapters, which he called "Tippoo tiblets," are of variable quality, written at the rate of three a week; but they were of sufficient quality to prompt Bobbs-Merrill to consider publishing a book of Mundy's poetry. Reviews of *The Ivory Trail* were many and favorable; *The Ivory Trail* became Mundy's second great success in book form after *King—of the Khyber Rifles*.

The Ivory Trail is set between the close of the Boer war but while Tippoo Tib is still alive; since he died in 1905, that places the story in the time of Mundy's own African experiences. In chapter 3, Monty and his friends consult the aging great hunter Courtney, who advises them Mount Elgon with its unexplored caves, some inhabited by cannibals, are just the location Tib would have chosen. He sends them his personal gun bearer Kazimoto, who arrives in Chapter 6. Courtney is the name given in the novel to the aging great hunter Frederick Courteney Selous.[15] Selous was probably a childhood hero of Mundy's, having also been at Rugby for two years nearly three decades earlier, and was already a legend by the time Mundy arrived in the continent. The Greek, named Georges Coutlass in the novel, had in fact met a much less merciful death in German East Africa than Mundy provided in the book, and swore so profanely that Mundy had to cleanse his mouth at the request of Bobbs-Merrill.[16] Coutlass "claimed three countries and disgraced each at intervals in turn" but Mundy labels him "a man out of the middle ages, soldierly of bearing, unquestionably bold, and not one bit more venial or lawless than ninety per cent. of history's gallants, if the truth were told." [17]

The treasure hunt of Monty, Oakes, Yerkes, and the narrator for treasure attracts Germans hoping the ivory is on their side of the border. Monty travels to Britain to arrange shares with the various European powers who dispute the area and is absent for most of the novel, while Oakes, Yerkes, and the narrator plunge inland. Possibly the beautiful, arrogant temptress and German agent, the treacherous Lady Isobel Saffren Waldon, is inspired by Inez Broom Craven. Just as she and Mundy lived together as husband and wife before the marriage, so does Waldon agree to pose as the wife of the German villain, Professor Schillingschen. Waldon constantly imposes on the chivalry of the Anglos to escape the consequences of her deeds. She is a sad but entirely selfish figure, exploiting others, even to having her Syrian maid appeal to Coutlass's rough affections. She ends by being burned to death by the German steamer when she steals the dhow from the others.

In Chapter 4, they meet Brown of Lumbwa, a settler who becomes a companion, a friend but never a member of the trio. His drinking is constant but he is also a man of courage; assisting him when his cattle are stolen becomes the catalyst for a long detour amidst the blight of German misrule of East Africa. Following the pattern of Mundy's World War I fiction, the book becoming as much a denunciation of Germany as an adventure in Africa. Certainly the war prompted Mundy to detail the German atrocities he had witnessed. Mundy poured into *The Ivory Trail* all his hatred, acquired as a teenager in Germany and retained through the end of his life with his dismay at the rise of Hitler. The character, Schillingschen, embodies both German science and imperialism, and Mundy is horribly prophetic when he mentions the professor's practice of torturing animals to death, in the name of "science."

Mundy exposes the entire brutality of their colonial rule. The Germans seek to elicit local fear; Oakes and his friend's first sight of such "justice" is seeing the lashing of a black who begged for money after the commandant had made his daughter pregnant.[18] A court practicing "good, sound German law that knows no fear or favor, but governs all alike" becomes a mass of bloody beatings, men and women writhing under the whip.[19] The Teutons turn the same cruelty on each other only as a psychotic game; one officer challenges a fellow German to see who can submit to the most lashes, and relishes the flogging and his victory. As Brown explains, in the British courts the blacks are treated with leniency because they often do not understand

***Full cover of the Big Little Book covering the Mundy's 1937 radio serial version of* Ivory Trail.**

the law, and both races can be condemned for a crime against the other; but in the German court only the African may be guilty.

The natives are herded into villages where they can be controlled, unable to flee. Tib's ivory is to finance Germany's conquest of the continent, through religion, as Waldon explains. German imperialists are not only adversaries for the heroes of the novel, but seek to establish the basis for a pan-Islamic African nation among the Africans, with the Kaiser as its high priest. " 'Germany is planning to conquer the world!—not now, but ten or a dozen years from now! She is getting ready ceaselessly! Part of the plan is to undermine British rule in Africa by means of a religious influence among the natives.... As soon as possible a great native army is to be trained, and thoroughly schooled in the fanatical precepts of Islam.' "[20]

Some *Adventure* readers accused Mundy of pro-British propaganda in his depiction of the German colonial presence. Fred Fleischer of the "Ask Adventure" staff took it upon himself to discover if Mundy's depiction of German practices in Africa was truthful or elaborated. As Fleischer discovered,

> The court scenes, as well as the cruel lashings of the blacks so vividly pictured by Mr. Mundy, are contained almost verbatim—one might take Mr. Mundy's lines as a translation of the German text—in the second volume of Dr. Max Kemmerich's *Kultur Kuriosa*.... These episodes are related to have happened in the year of 1895–96. In addition to this there are several other incidents along the lines depicted by Mr. Mundy.... They are German sources, and, believe me, the Heinies do not publish these things, unless they are quite sure they represent the *absolute, irrevocable truth*.[21]

Adventure readers who had also been in Africa wrote in to "The Camp-Fire" to attest to the truth of the background and conditions as Mundy presented them, and his presentation was praised by the *New York Times* as vivid, detailed, and entirely convincing.[22]

From the perspective of almost a century later, Mundy's own attitude toward the Africans was hardly free of racism, but was certainly enlightened and he unquestionably respected black humanity. Mundy clearly resented white supremacists, and was opposed to imperialism, whether ignorant or evil, respectively, as shown in the characterizations of Brown and the brutal Schillingschen. For the first time, Mundy's anti-imperial sentiment becomes an important theme: the indigenous peoples derive nothing but suffering from their status.[23] Approaching Elgon, the narrator comments that "In every direction were villages, of folk who knew so little of white men that they paid no taxes yet and did no work—marrying and giving in marriage—fighting and running away—eating and drinking and watching their women cultivate the corn and beans and sweet potatoes—without as much as foreboding of the taxes, work for wages, missionaries, law and commerce soon to come." [24]

REWRITING *THE IVORY TRAIL* FOR A NEW MEDIUM

A KEY theme of *The Ivory Trail* is the nature of friendship and the interaction among Brown, Coutlass, and Waldon: who is an ally, who is an enemy, who is seeking their own interest first, and who can be trusted? However, with Coutlass, and to a lesser extent Waldon, constantly changing sides based on their perception of their self-interest at the moment, the novel's episodic quality is enhanced, but this very structure made *The Ivory Trail* suitable for adaptation as a serial for the motion picture screen and for radio, in the latter case scripted by Mundy himself.

By 1932, two of Mundy's early short stories, *The Fire-Cop* and *For Valor*, had been filmed in 1912, and *King—of the Khyber Rifles* had been brought to the screen as *The Black Watch* in 1929, but as a World War I regimental chronicle that used little of Mundy's narrative. In 1930, Metro-Goldwyn-Mayer produced *Trader Horn*, the first major sound film made on location in Africa, which proved extremely popular upon release the following year, and studios quickly followed it up with other jungle adventures. Within this environment, by August 1931, serious interest was expressed in filming *The Ivory Trail*, and the book was finally sold to Universal on March 3, 1932. Mundy's bad luck with the cinema persisted as the movie made from *The Ivory Trail* was transformed and retitled *The Jungle Mystery*, and was adapted as a serial, not a feature, a form considered inherently more juvenile and less respectable, and made on a lower budget, although Universal was one of the most prolific studios producing such adventures. After barely two months of preparation, with Ella O'Neil, George Plympton, Basil Dickey and George Morgan adapting *The Ivory Trail* into twelve episodes of about 20 minutes apiece, the picture went into production in May, 1932, and was quickly completed, with the first chapter going into release on August 5. Mundy's name and *The Ivory Trail* were prominently mentioned in conjunction with publicity for the picture.

Philo McCullough, Carmelita Geraghty, and James A. Marcus were Mundy's villains, George Coutlass (played with a heavy accent and makeup), Lady Isobel Saffren Waldon (here renamed Belle Waldron), and Schillingschen (rechristened Boris Shillov), respectively. The German imperialists of *The Ivory Trail*, too reminiscent of the antagonists in World War I films, considered to have dubious popularity at the time, are conveniently altered in *The Jungle Mystery* to Russians. In the new plot, Monty and Fred are two present-day Americans who fly in quest of big game, but crash their airplane in Africa. Shillov, a South African who is searching for Tippoo Tib's ivory, refuses to aid them, and Monty and Fred encounter a strange half man, half monkey, known as Zungu—the "jungle mystery."

Although retaining much of the plot of *The Ivory Trail*, *The Jungle Mystery*, from its very choice of title onwards, utilized the conventions of serial structure. While the narrative still ostensibly concerned a hunt for the legendary ivory cache of Tippoo Tib that had occupied the novel, *The Jungle Mystery* added to the motivations and number of characters found in the original. These include the romantic subplot and a search for a missing fortune hunter; the standard plot device of a woman imperiled allowed her safety to be threatened at every turn by man and beast.

Since Mundy was in Europe through mid-1933, it is more than possible he never saw *The Jungle Mystery*. However, radio was to offer him the rare opportunity to adapt *The Ivory Trail* to the demands of a different serial form. During the intervening years he had realized audience hunger for information and stories about Africa, writing "Random Reminiscences of African Big Game" (*Saturday Evening Post*, December 7, 1929), "A Jungle Sage" and "Watu" (*Adventure*, March 15 and April 1, 1932, respectively), and "The Things Men Fear" (*Liberty*, February 10, 1934). During these years he went on a lecture tour, often speaking for an hour or more on his colonial experiences in Africa.

In 1936, Mundy was signed to write the daily, 15 minute show, *Jack Armstrong, The All-American Boy*, which he guided to become the top-rated program for youth, with an audience of millions. Jack, a midwestern high school student, and his best friend, the younger Billy Fairfield, travel with Billy's sister, Betty, and are led by Betty and Billy's uncle, Jim Fairfield, a former high-ranking army officer and aircraft manufacturer. In a four-month serial beginning in January 1937, Jack searched for the Elephants' Graveyard with its fabulous ivory treasure.

Although the actual broadcasts are lost, a number of contemporary sources allow a reconstruction of the radio version's plot. In Brazil, after saving a servant the abusive Alonzo Lopez, Jack is given an ivory ring. Kazimoto is a loyal friend and provides minor amusement, more afraid to be left behind, but hardly the pillar of courage presented in the novel, or the man who helped Mundy lead actual safaris. Jack, Billy, Betty, and Uncle Jim meet the magician Booloola, who knew Tippoo Tib and where he buried the map of the place where the elephants go to die. Uncle Jim, flying his aircraft *Silver Albatross* up the Congo River, is pursued by a Belgian hydroplane with Lopez aboard. Lopez is taken aboard the *Silver Albatross* as Uncle Jim navigates by Booloola's directions to a lost city in the jungle where Lopez believes Tib's map has been secreted. In the wild, Jack uses a "mercy gun," armed with bullets that merely put an animal to sleep, rather than killing it—a way for Mundy to inculcate a new generation with a different attitude toward wildlife than he had practiced. A mystical element amplifies this theme; Booloola is known as a Bwana of Beasts, for the influence he holds over wild animals and his ability to speak to them.

While searching a cave, they find the map, showing the Mountains of the Moon, Lake Victoria, and stopping at Kisumu, Jim's old friend Sheik Mohammed invites him to join them in his camp near Mount Elgon. Mohammed shows Jim a more complex parchment map, and the Sheik is abducted by Lopez. A landslide traps them and crushes Lopez; Booloola deliberately blocked the way into the elephant's graveyard to protect it. Mohammed explains that Booloola mistrusts all whites, believing they are merciless in their quest for wealth. Jack tells Booloola that the wealth will not be exploited for private gain but to preserve the elephants, and he will serve on a government commission to control the fund.

TOWARD ARMENIA

THE TEAM of Monty and his friends moved their fortune hunting to the Red Sea, Egypt, and Syria, respectively, in *The Shriek of Dûm*, *Barabbas Island*, and *In Aleppo Bazaar*, which Mundy correctly regarded as no more than three ordinary potboilers. Respectively, these novels appeared complete in the September 3, 1919, October 18, 1919, and January 18, 1920 issues of *Adventure*.

The Middle East was a part of the world of which Mundy had only a tantalizing glimpse in his youth, having visited the Persian Gulf at least once on a tramp steamer nearly two decades earlier. The area's local traits interested him, and had figured in three magazine stories, "The Pillar of Light," in the December 1912 issue of *Everybody's*, and "An Arabian Night" and "MacHassan Ah," in the November 1913 and April 1915 issues of *Adventure*, respectively (all three of which he would choose to include in his 1939 anthology, *The Valiant View*).[25]

In *The Shriek of Dûm*, the tiny port of Dûm was once an active depot of King Solomon's naval trade empire, and the local ruling Shiek, or "Shriek" as he has been dubbed, has a French step-daughter by a marriage to a woman who was once castaway on this distant shore. The use of dynamite serves as a *deus ex machina*, preventing her marriage to another Shiek and accidentally uncovering a cache of gold, making the stopover profitable and allowing the girl to have a proper Western upbringing. *Adventure* readers, in a series of letters in "The Camp-Fire," revealed their primary interest was in comparing Mundy's use of dynamite with their own personal experiences, apparently reading the tale as fiction but equal part fact.

Barabbas Island was also of rather inconsequential caliber, although with a few more virtues, continuing the pursuit of the legendary wealth of antiquity. The premise had potential: the Biblical Barabbas was a much greater robber than he was given credit for, a corsair who raided caravans and the Egyptian coast, whose life was spared by the Romans in the hope of gaining his gold. Subsequently, modern events on his Red Sea island headquarters devolve into routine drama of shipwreck and castaways. Monty and his friends journey to the island on the yacht of a young American heiress, Grace Vandam, a childhood friend of Yerkes's who is hungry for adventure. They discover competitors already arrived, including a bloodthirsty German who has killed the descendants of Barabbas living there.

Monty and his friends move northward for *In*

Late 1920s UK edition of* The Eye of Zeitoon*, published by Hutchinson.

Aleppo Bazaar. The last and perhaps least of the three, this one concerns the rescue of a "half-breed" from marriage to the man who ordered the last Armenian massacre and who desires her property, a crucial piece of land in Germany's proposed Berlin-to-Baghdad rail line. While not predictable, the plot was simultaneously familiar and far-fetched, although it did take the foursome to Turkey, the scene of their next adventure.

The final "Up and Down the Earth" book was nearly the length of these three novels combined. During April 1915, the Turks had ordered the deportation of the Armenian population away from Christian regions to the deserts of Syria and Mesopotamia, resulting in the murder or starvation of up to 1.5 million people. With the defeat of Turkey, the independent Republic of Armenia had been established in mid-1918, but only survived until late 1920, when it was annexed by the Soviet Army. *The Eye of Zeitoon* grew out of Mundy's involvement with the Armenian relief movement as he authored a series of newspaper articles urging the United States to accept Armenia as a League of Nations mandate, believing this was the best way to secure Armenia's independence and peace as a Christian country surrounded by Moslem territories. Unlike Europe, America was regarded as having no territorial intentions in the region, and was respected as having only entered World War I to safeguard democracy.

The title character in *The Eye of Zeitoon,* Kagig, is a leader of his people and veritable "father" of his country, who watches out for their interests and is hence their "eye." Mundy makes Zeitoon a stronghold unconquered by the Turks, to which Kagig urges his fellow Armenians to flee and make their last stand.[26] Kagig had left the Armenian region as a youth, frustrated and embittered by the suspicions of Armenians against one another, a tendency fostered by the Turks for their own ends. He lived prosperously in the United States, but realized he could not leave his homeland permanently. This became especially true when the Turk who had raped and killed his mother arrived to work in the Turkish embassy in the United States. After killing him, Kagig had left America as an outlaw.

The activities of Monty, Fred Oakes, Will Yerkes, and the narrator shifting decisively from fortune hunting to a chivalrous determination to aid the weak and oppressed. Monty and his friends hire Kagig as their guide into Armenia, hoping foreign presence may deter bloodshed—while Kagig plans to use the four as potential hostages. Along the way they encounter another of Mundy's despised Germans, who is fanning the flames of Turkish hatred of the Armenians in order to cement a future German-Turkish alliance: Hans von Quedlinburg (named for the German city that had been Talbot's first stop running away from England in 1895).

In parts of *The Eye of Zeitoon*, Mundy briefly mentions various Turkish tortures inflicted on the Armenians; the Turkish general who attacks Zeitoon singles out Gloria as his personal plunder. However, Mundy's essential purpose is not so much to emphasize Turkish cruelty, but the Armenian's courage, as epitomized by Kagig's notion of "sportman" [sic], a favorite phrase he uses to encompass not only sporting activities but those willing to give all they have, including life and fortune, for friendship and a cause, despite danger. Mundy believed this aspect of the Armenian character that would most appeal to American readers and foster potential future United States assistance for Armenia.

The long journey overland to Armenia, the first two-thirds of *The Eye of Zeitoon,* is long, but the last third of the novel is intense, gripping, and memorable, recounting the arrival in Zeitoon and its defense. As a privy councillor, Monty hopes to secure attention for the Armenian cause, and he discovers his forebear's castle in Zeitoon itself. Besieged inside by the advancing Turks, he flies the Montdidier arms, since there is no Armenian flag. It is a course of action that, should he survive, could mean trial in England, but Mundy compares Monty to Byron in Greece. Recognizing that he, like the castle, is an anachronism, Monty lays down his life in a noble and selfless sacrifice, willingly placing himself under Turkish gunfire and burning the ancestral fortress to win a victory. As a representative of the old order, Monty is laid to rest in a nearby family crypt where the Montdidiers from crusader times were buried.

Leisure Library edition of **The Eye of Zeitoon.**

The comparison of Monty with a medieval knight is reinforced when Kagig announces at the close that he will go into hiding, emerging as a legend to his people when next his country needs him. Although dominating the novel, Kagig is not the only intriguing character. The Rajput Rustum Khan, a Moslem officer who served with Monty in India, and dies simultaneously with him in the battle, fights despite racial and religious animus to the Christian Armenians.

A group of adventurers may only be disbanded by death or marriage, and by the conclusion of *The Eye of Zeitoon,* the foursome of the "Up and Down the Earth" experience both. The novel offers a series of memorable female characters; the Armenian women fight proudly beside their men, and regard it as a historical prerogative. Yerkes's weakness for, and appeal, to women has landed Monty and Oakes in some tricky situations before. Underlying the political conflict in the novel are two very different women. One is the intrepid American college girl, Gloria Vandermann, also traveling in these lands, who eventually wins his heart. Similar to Grace Vandam of *Barabbas Island,* Gloria is as courageous as any of the men, refusing to be "rescued," proud of her wound gained in fighting, and as determined to aid the Armenian cause as her Western companions. One of the factors attracting her to Yerkes is his acceptance of gender equality. The other woman is Maga Jhaere, lovely and wild. Near-savage in some ways, barefoot, wielding a knife and gun, she breaks horses, dances like a force of nature, and has a bloodthirsty streak. She is rabidly jealous of Yerkes and Gloria, but turns out to be Kagig's wife, an Armenian rather than a gypsy. Their relationship was kept secret so she could engage in espionage—one of the novel's least credible developments.

Mundy wrote *The Eye of Zeitoon* for both political and commercial reasons, not only because it was a cause he believed was just, but one he thought would attract a wide readership. He hoped to sell a hundred thousand copies, accepting "inside information" from the head of the Armenian National Committee that President Wilson and the congress were going to support aid to Armenia.[27] Nonetheless, in the novel, Yerkes recognizes that his nation is unlikely to come to Armenia's defense, or even to defend an American imperiled there. As the only Armenian story in recent years, *The Eye of Zeitoon* had no competition, and Mundy had been promised the full backing of the Armenian press, reaching not only the 85,000 Armenians in America, but also as part of a united effort to foment American interest in Armenia, timed for February 1920.[28]

Mundy had expected *The Eye of Zeitoon* would be serialized in the magazine *Asia,* mostly devoted to nonfiction, which would have provided a new, more serious audience, especially appropriate for this novel. Instead, *The Eye of Zeitoon* was serialized (as *The Eye of Zeitun*) in the magazine *Romance,* a Ridgway companion publication to *Adventure,* ostensibly to hasten publication but possibly also because of editor Arthur Hoffman's sensitivity to the propaganda charges already aired in "The Camp-Fire" against the previous "Up and Down the Earth Tales." Hoffman rearranged a whole year's publishing schedule in 1920 for *Romance,* to allow for early serialization of *The Eye of Zeitoon* in order that book publication could be synchronized with pro-Armenian publicity.

Despite Mundy's Armenian contacts promising sales of up to 25,000 copies of the book, in the first three months only 9,000 copies were sold after March 1920 publication by Bobbs-Merrill.[29] *The Eye of Zeitoon* was widely applauded for its message, but the timeliness of the novel was not entirely an advantage; it was turned down by a number of publishers in England (where *The Ivory Trail* had not yet appeared) "on the ground that it gave anyone the blues just to hear the word 'Armenia.' " All of Mundy's personal charm was required during his stop in London in January 1920 when arrangements were made with Hutchinson. Published there in October, sales of *The Eye of Zeitoon* were dismal at first, but Hutchinson persevered and would henceforth handle all of Mundy's books in England.

Despite the initially disappointing sales, *The Eye of Zeitoon* is one of Mundy's most worthy, durable and serious adventure novels, skillfully written, exciting, atmospheric and well characterized. Nor did the discouraging reception dissuade him from writing on behalf of global causes; in 1921, be began a long series of stories in support of Arab independence from British and French colonial dominion, and by a year later, began the stories with a theosophical background that would remain his focus to the end of his life.

CONCLUSION

THE "UP AND DOWN THE EARTH TALES" represent a steady progression, from predominantly reminiscence to political involvement. In rendering into fiction his own experiences, Mundy steadily displayed increasing anti-colonial sentiments, partly facilitated as an America at war was willing to accept such a portrayal of German imperialism. However, Mundy did not stop here; with *In Aleppo Bazaar* and especially *The Eye of Zeitoon,* the autobiographical element and memories of places he had visited was left far behind for overt endorsement of a cause; Mundy the writer became an activist within pro-Armenian organizations. Hence, the "Up and Down the Earth Tales," initially having their origins in his time in Africa, are far more than an instance of using youthful experience in distant locales to spin colorful yarns, but sought to draw therefrom, and apply the framework toward more persuasive, didactic purposes—an end to colonialism, and an independent Armenia.

Brian Taves

Author, *Talbot Mundy, Philosopher of Adventure.* Jefferson, NC: McFarland, 2005.

Editor, *Winds from the East: An Anthology by Talbot Mundy.* Atlanta: Ariel Press, 2006.

OAKES RESPECTS AN ADVERSARY

THE STORIES Fred Oakes can tell of his adventures in all corners of the world are, Heaven knows, numberless. I have known people to doubt that so much could ever happen to one man. But I have known him too long and intimately ever to doubt one word he says, and to my mind the thing to be amazed at is his length of memory. His own explanation is worth recording:

"There's nothing remarkable about it. We get what we look for. Take a parson, for instance: doesn't he dodge devils every day? Is there anything to comment on if a lawyer fights two cases or more a week? Or if a soldier goes to war pretty often? I tell you, a hunter hunts, a fisherman fishes, a ship's captain masters the elements. A true adventurer adventures, not specializing so much as embracing all occupations in the one. Very early in life I decided to adventure; and I qualified to be a prospector with that one end in view.

"So you see, I've been soldier, lawyer, hunter, fisherman—you'd be surprised how often a fisherman!—ship's captain on occasion—everlastingly at war with the elements and chance—and I've buried too many good and true men not to have a slice of parson in my make-up.

"But it's as prospector for minerals that an alert adventurer finds his widest field; and as free-lance writer that he can best keep in touch with opportunity, or feather an empty nest. Those are my two chosen standbys. So, if things hadn't happened to me thick and fast, that would be astonishing. That they did happen is only natural. To me, adventure is life, and life is a succession of adventures. Monotony is death, and the only death. I adventured into the world by being born in a dungeon in the Tower of London. I refuse to say how long ago, and I pray God I may adventure out again when the proper time comes!"

"In a dungeon in the Tower?" I asked. "How can that be?"

"I will tell you some day. Monty could have told you better, for his father and mine were intimate. Good Lord, how the time goes! Think of it—'Didums' went over the border eleven years ago this afternoon!"

We grew silent, he thinking no doubt of a hundred adventures he had shared with the bravest gentleman either of us ever knew, and I of the many I had shared with both of them, playing always a minor part yet generously accorded a greater portion of the credit than was due me. They were strong men in the prime of life when I was a stripling out of college. By their kindness to me they gained a hero-worshiper—which is sometimes not such a useless asset, if you are tolerant—and by my effort to live up to their standard of manliness I gained two friends such as seldom fall to the lot of man.

Thought's processes are swift. Probably Oakes, in the chair that faced me on the club veranda, tugging at his grizzled, upturned mustache reviewed a lifetime. Having less than he to remember, it was naturally I who finished first, and broke the silence.

"Speaking of death and of Didums," I said, "you have never told me why you didn't kill him that time in the Libomba foothills."

Fred Oakes sat up, and his eyes blazed for an instant, as I have seen them do very often when the sight of oppression angered him, or the odds against himself and friends were ten or more to one. Then he laughed at himself, and leaned back.

"I've never told any man," he answered.

"Tell me now."

But he sat silent after that for thirty minutes, and I supposed him unwilling to lay his heart bare.

AS FOR me, who also had loved Monty, those memories were the reverse of terrible—chiefly, I suppose, because they included my own return from nether hell to something more resembling heaven. I hold no brief against college life, but I do maintain that it unfits a man for life before the mast on sailing-ships.

I consider it less to my discredit than a proof of gentle raising, that after a voyage that had led—at the dictates of a nearly crazy skipper—along the arc of a composite grand circle into Antarctic blizzards—after battling for months with wet cotton sails, and ice, and adverse winds, manning the clumsy pumps often for days and nights on end, and eating worse than crow to help line the aforesaid skipper's pocket, I left my wages on board a three-masted British bark at the first chance, and deserted.

At the time it did not look much like the act of God that the port was Lourenço Marques—unless you consider God, as the Vikings did, a very present spell for causing trouble.

It is easy to say at this late day that I had no business in the fo'castle of any such ship, or of any ship at all, and that the experience served me right. But unless, and until you have yourself left college penniless, have seen all your hopes for a career go up in smoke, and have trudged the streets of London city in search of honorable hire, you are not qualified to pass judgment. I had muscle and a good opinion of my pluck. I used them both; and if that particular experience was ugly, it led to my meeting Oakes and Lord Montdidier—an outcome worth the payment, in advance, of any price.

But to get back to the bark: we had not put in, for that would have cost our skipper harbor dues, but lay wallowing in the outer bay while a south wind kept three cables taut ahead of us, and the old blunt-nosed anachronism—named by some one with a gift for irony the *Heatherbell*—scooped up the muddy waves and tossed them over herself like a *must* elephant heaving hay.

However, a Greek boatman will dare anything less than eternity for the sake of unrighteous profit, and it happened that I was made night watchman—deck, not anchor watch. The skipper and mate had a bottle of peach brandy between them in the cabin; and the second mate, who had been snubbed for suggesting we would ride more comfortably higher up the bay, made himself snug in the break of the poop and went to sleep.

Nobody could tell that I had a shore suit under my oilskins, and in my pocket the last of a too lean patrimony in the shape of English gold. I had another suit and some odds and ends in a small bag carefully hidden, and a heart full of rebellion that was much less easy to conceal.

Only one Greek dared the elements that night. He worked his open boat up under our plunging stern, lowered his little sail, and threw me a line very handily, little expecting such swift returns. But I had no choice.

I bent a life-line to the handle of my bag and sent it down to him between waves. Then, before he guessed what was happening I came down the life-line hand over hand, bringing his own line with me. I let go the instant my feet touched the boat bottom, and we were away from under the *Heatherbell's* stern, beam on to a whale of a sea, and in dire need of action, not argument, before the Greek could remonstrate.

When the south winds blow there is no shelter in all that roadstead except the little concrete pier where passengers land and the customs officers take toll. I have seen twenty ships drag anchor there of an afternoon and all go banging and plunging together to the confluence of the Tembe and Umbuluzi rivers.

Until we reached that pier the Greek and I worked like Trojans. Then, in the rain and the dark, each with a hand on the pierwork to keep the little boat from being ground to splinters, we argued out our business problem, while a Portuguese sentry up above the steps regarded us with Sphinx-like disapproval.

The Greek—for his is a garrulous race—wasted the first few plunging moments in explaining that to land anywhere else that night would be stark impossible. I could judge that well enough, without his wet breath in my ear. Then he explained that the sentry was posted there expressly to prevent unauthorized landings—that the immigration of-

ficers were very strict—and that only he, Georgos Aleutherios, had cunning and popularity enough to pass me by. He offered to spiflicate his conscience, take chances, and perhaps even ruin his good standing with the authorities forever, all for the trifling sum of fifty pounds.

We came to terms at last for five pounds, he to pay the sentry; and I learned afterward that I might have bought a lieutenant's services, with half a company of infantry thrown in, for that sum. But rain and wind and darkness—the plunging of a small boat in the lee of a pier—armed sentries—immigration laws—and treaties that call for the surrender to their ships of all deserting seamen, spur youth's eagerness without sharpening youth's wit. A young man afraid and five gold sovereigns are very easily parted, and the Greek could have had the double of it if he had only known.

At any rate, there I stood presently on the rain-soaked sand of Portuguese East Africa, with two good suits of clothes to my name, and ten remaining pounds between me and the fort jail. I had yet to learn to fear that jail, or to know of its existence; but I began with such gratitude to feel steady earth underfoot that no forebodings troubled me.

The first night was spent—what was left of it—trudging the streets; for there were no hotels open, and I did not care to risk being followed into some dry corner by an armed policeman and asked questions in a tongue I did not know. It was a miserable, very hungry, dirty, weary night, but it came to an end, and dawn found me still an optimist.

As soon as doors began opening, and Hindus and Chinese came out to rinse their teeth and hawk, and clean themselves over the gutter, I entered the best hotel in sight, and for the first time since I went to sea had the advantage over a sailor to the manner born; for having removed my oilskins I bore no resemblance whatever to a deserter.

The keeper of that hotel was an Afrikander, not in love with Portuguese, and glad of the chance to unburden himself to ears uncalloused by the constancy of such refrains.

"An Englishman's one chance," he said, "if he goes broke in this place, is to appeal to his consul. He can never do anything for you at the time: there are too many broken Englishmen for the consulate funds to cover a tenth of the cases. But if a ship should put in short of hands he'll get you out of jail and have you sent aboard to work a passage to somewhere else. So, if you go broke, mind you tell him before the Portuguese arrest you as a vagrant."

He little guessed what vinegar he was pouring into open wounds! I was minded to try that jail rather than the fo'castle of the *Heatherbell* again.

"Why talk of going broke?" I asked with the bravest air I could summon. He and I were eating breakfast at the same table, and I was trying to disguise my craving for Christian ham and eggs.

"Because none but a Portugee, or a man on contract, or a merchant with more money than morals can hope to get a living here! I could tell you tales that would make you sick! They'll skin you of your last coin—what they can't steal they'll take in taxes—and then arrest you as a vagrant and throw you in the jail to starve."

"And the cost of living here is—?"

"At this hotel? A pound a day."

I made a swift calculation: Ten pounds=ten days=jail!

"No jobs to be had?" I asked.

He jeered at the notion.

"Black boys?—natives do the menial work. Chinese run the laundries, chickens, eggs, and odds and ends. Indians monopolize money-changing and the larger shops. Bank clerks and business managers are all contract men from home. Greeks do the fishing and run restaurants. Portuguese hold all the official jobs. Where's your chance?"

It looked to me as if my chance of jail was pretty obvious. He had no means of guessing the amount of my resources, but my facial expression must have hinted that his pessimism was sinking into me.

"Get away from here before you're stranded!" he urged. "Book, your passage to British East!"

How should he know that I had not enough to take me up to British East!

"I'll look around first," I said, screwing up courage again.

"Don't say I didn't warn you!" he answered. "Shall you stay here?"

"Let you know later," I told him; and I paid him for the breakfast and went out.

THE FIRST thing I did was to walk all over the town. They were laying the trolley-line in those days, and the street corners were ablock with construction material and gear. While I watched one party at work the English foreman came and tried to sell me an enormous drum of copper wire.

"Yours?" I asked him.

"Of course not! The company's."

"What's it worth?"

"Lord knows! Gimme ten pounds and it's yours to take away!"

By noon, with an unmixed notion of the place's charms I returned to one of the restaurants on the main street that the Afrikander had told me Greeks kept. It was a cheaper place than the hotel. There was nowhere to sit after lunch but in the bar, and the Greek proprietor grew insolent unless one kept a glass at work; but by dint of taking small sips, and pretending to fall asleep at intervals on the shabby plush-covered divan in a corner, it was possible to keep sober, and expenses down to a minimum.

There was nothing for it but to spend some money, for I was tired, and curious besides, to watch and listen, believing I could, perhaps, get a line on opportunity. It was in that way that I met Charles du Maurier, and saw revealed the despicableness of that colonial Government.

I was more actually drowsy than pretending—having had no sleep at all the night before—when I noticed a sudden stir in the street outside, and at the door, and in the café. The men at the bar made room for a newcomer before he appeared on the scene, and three Portuguese officers at a little table on the far side of the door from me ceased talking and looked uncomfortable.

I heard a sharp, disagreeable voice outside, speaking English—nobody except the Portuguese officers spoke any other language in that restaurant—and a moment later a man of middle height strode in, with a hunting-rifle balanced in the crook of his right arm, and a cartridge-bag slung over his shoulder.

"Hello, du Maurier!" said every one at once—except the Portuguese officers. "Glad to see you, du Maurier! Come and have a drink, du Maurier!"

It was obvious that every one desired to have the man's good-will; yet I did not get the impression that he was popular. He was of stoutish build, but looked active as a cat; rather good-looking in a fat-lipped brunette sort of way; and he had cold blue eyes that rested appraisingly on every face in the room in turn. In the course of their casual inspection they fell presently on me.

"Good afternoon!" he sneered, leaning back against the bar and reaching with his free hand for the whisky bottle that the Greek produced without instructions. "How do, stranger? What's your name?"

I did not inform him.

"Ceremonious, eh? Very well—I'll make the introductions. You want to know who I am first, eh? That's natural. But everybody in Lourenço Marques knows me. Still—I'll tell! I'm Charlie du Maurier! Charles du Maurier and I are one and the same individual, and now you know! Now everybody knows, and we're all agreeable!"

He filled his glass with neat whisky, and swallowed half the dose at a gulp. Then his eyes traveled past me to the three officers in uniform, whose conversation had so suddenly damped off. One guessed, without knowing details, that they were hesitating between retreat and dignity.

"Aha!" said the du Maurier person, finishing the whisky at a gulp. He was not in the least drunk. "Here are three gentlemen who know me well! Three Portuguese officers, by ——, swords and all! Why don't you up and arrest me, gentlemen? If it's true there's a warrant out for Charles du Maurier, here he is! You've only to come and take him! I'm Charles du Maurier—afraid of no man, and least of all afraid of the Portuguese Government! Come and take me if you dare! Turn out your garrison and take me!"

The three officers rose and went out, omitting to sign vouchers or pay cash, and the Greek set up a great wail. There was a roar of laughter in which du Maurier joined noisily.

"I'll pay for their *vino tinto!*" he volunteered. "Then they can say they've been drinking with Charles du Maurier. They can go to their commandant and brag to him about it! Ha-ha-ha! That's a good joke! Portuguese officers bragging to their commandant, by ——, that they've had a drink with Charles du Maurier! Oh, Lord, that's a good one!"

I not coming forward, and not joining in the rounds of drinks that his arrival was the excuse for, he paid me no more attention except that every once in a while his cold eye fell on me and I knew I was not out of his mind. He stood at the bar, and drank, or refused to drink, with whom he chose, all that afternoon, continuing as sober as a shark but bragging more and louder as his audience grew drunker and its mood less critical. His bragging was mostly of shooting men.

"I don't encourage the devils myself by paying them money," I heard him say more than once. "But the price, if you'll pay in advance, for killing a white man is ten pounds gold, and do the job yourself. A native costs half. That's thirty miles back from the coast, of course. They say there's a zone near here where the tariff's higher!"

The strange part was that nobody appeared to doubt him. Several men nodded acquiescence. Only one or two shook their heads, and I divined that their objection was to his giving such publicity to the facts, rather than to the facts themselves.

"What are you doing for a living now?" somebody asked him at about supper-time; and he laughed with a hard, dry cackle that made my blood run cold.

The brutality aboard ship had been unalloyed and shameless, but it had been born, one might say, of necessity and took no joy in itself; but this man du Maurier loved cruelty for its own sake, and the very lack of mercy was the essence of a joke to him.

"I'll tell you," he sneered. "Don't say I didn't tell you, now! You've heard of the Premier Diamond Mine? You've all heard of that, haven't you? The big new pipe that's made de Beers look like a four-flush—you've heard of that? Well—they haven't even got it paddocked off with barbed wire yet. There are guards here and there, but there's a lot of clay dug and lying in the open to be weathered. The diamonds are sticking out of it like dew in the morning, and there are nearly as many thieves as stones!

"The plan is to get a bag of diamonds, seal 'em up, and trust 'em to a native. He runs with 'em overland to this place, where an Indian buys 'em for the Bombay market, sending a check back through the mail. The game is to lie up in the bush and watch for natives. If you happen to shoot the right one, you get a fine bag o' diamonds, and the Indian 'ud just as soon buy from you as from anybody else! Ha-ha-ha-ha! Good game, what?"

A man who sat beside me—a nondescript individual—recovering from East Coast fever, and probably on board allowance from the concern that hired him—for he had no money to spend, yet was not destitute—leaned and whispered in my ear.

"If that was really his game, he'd not be telling it," he argued. "But if he hadn't done it he wouldn't trouble to pretend he had—he's that proud and original! It'ud be like him, the cold-hearted swine, to skin all there was in the game and then set others on to trying it! That'ud be like him, that would!"

I WENT to supper, and to bed above the restaurant; and having slept so many months in the *Heatherbell's* abominable fo'castle, it needed more than the babel of that barroom to keep me awake. The clean sheets and the open window were paradise by comparison; and although the morals of the *Heatherbell* seemed, looking back, like those of a Sabbath-school compared to what Lourenço Marques boasted, I reminded myself that corruption came from within and not without a man, and was not troubled much on that score.

My dreams that night were brilliant, and I awoke

a little after dawn feeling under my skin the tingle of unborn happenings. Any one who has chanced his arm must know that tingling. It comes as a rule when hope has no excuse, and invariably presages good fortune. I have known men to own to the tingling, and yet go down, but that was because their courage failed them, not because inspiration lied.

But, although board and bed at that Greek place cost less than half the hotel price, it was obvious enough that yet more economical quarters must be found at once, if I hoped to keep vagrancy and the jail in the offing while I hunted a job of sorts. Life and the talk at sea gives a man strange notions, and after breakfast, and some thinking, no amount of argument could have persuaded me that it was impossible, or even unwise, to camp out on the outskirts of the town.

I saw the man du Maurier at the other end of the long table in the dining-room, and flattered myself that he did not notice me. I managed to slip out without having word with him, and—careless of direction, provided I left the town behind—set out for what are known as Kilos One and Two. Those are fills alongside the harbor, of which the Portuguese are quite inordinately proud—an acre or two of level land where swamps once were, held at enormous prices for factory and dock sites, in the belief that Delagoa Bay was destined to be the greatest, richest, busiest harbor in all Africa. A strange delusion! But all the real estate in that part of the world is held for a fabulous rise on fabulous excuses, and the Governments are as sanguine as the down-and-outs.

It looked a good enough place to camp on, and I spied an old abandoned wagon with broken wheels, whose top was mostly watertight. A little sailor lore, a little luck in finding jetsam—perhaps an old sail, and doubtless some timber along the foreshore—an hour or two's work, and I would have that abandoned wagon fit to live in.

I sat down on its broken tail-board to think out how best to tackle the task, and was growing more and more pleased with the treasure-trove when, to my sudden disgust, I saw the man du Maurier, gun on his arm as usual, sauntering along toward me. There was no use in trying to avoid him. He was coming straight in my direction. I did not doubt he had followed me from the Greek's place.

"Considering things?" he asked as soon as he came within talking distance.

I nodded, and he came and sat beside me on the wagon, chewing tobacco and spitting at remarkably regular intervals.

"See that snake?" he said presently.

I followed the direction of his eyes, and after staring through the glare for a minute or two I could just distinguish a little dark snake upreared above some twigs a hundred yards away.

"Ever see their heads cut off with a bullet?" he asked, and he brought the rather heavy-bored rifle to his shoulder.

He did not aim long, nor did he fire twice. The snake disappeared.

"Go and look at it," he said; and principally because I was glad of the excuse to leave his side I got up and walked to where the snake had been.

Sure enough, its head was severed cleanly and the body lay squirming in the sun.

"Did I hit it?" he called, and I turned to nod to him, only to discover that he was reloading his rifle and had it pointed at me.

There was no cover. Whichever direction I might take he would have a clear view of me against an open background at short range. He had not raised the rifle, but his eye was on me, and the sensation was as mortifying as if he had deliberately taken aim. I decided on the instant to choose the lesser of two evils and call his hand, preferring, if I must be shot, to take it in the face.

So I walked toward him, as casually as I could contrive. I could see his finger on the trigger, and his cold eye never left me for an instant, but he did not shoot, and presently I stood within six feet of him. Then he grinned, rather approvingly, I thought.

"You're a man of nerve!" he said, with his objectionable nasal snarl. "Most men would have made for town as fast as their legs 'ud carry them, beginning slowly for the sake of dignity, but running as soon as the range was in their favor. I wouldn't have shot you! What should I shoot you for? I've nothing against you. I don't want your money!"

It was on the tip of my tongue to tell him I hadn't any money, but some trick of fortune determined me instead to hold my tongue and find out what his game might be. Surely he had not followed me so far for nothing.

"But you're a young fool!" he added. "I've known more than one man to lose his life by turning his back that way on a rifle. Let me tell you something:

when one gentleman has a loaded rifle, another gentleman should walk behind him! When two gentlemen have rifles they walk side by side, or else each sees the other unload! That's bush law. What were you doing out here?"

"As you suggested, considering things," I answered.

"There's mighty little here that's worth considering!" he sneered. "This is no place for a greenhorn. More men without money come ashore here and end up in the jail than in any other port in Africa! Oh, you can't fool me! You've an English university accent, and your kind don't put up at Greek hotels while you've money left!

"You're hoping to find a job. You won't find one, because there ain't any! You can't get away, either, and I'll tell you how I know. Your kind no more like the looks o' this place than a parson likes the breath of hell. If you'd had any money, you'd have gone away again on the same boat. Which boat did you come by?"

To have answered truthfully would have been to put myself entirely in the blackguard's power. He could either have had me arrested then as a deserting seaman, or have held the threat over me. Yet I resented the notion of having to lie to the brute, so I answered nothing.

"None o' my business, eh? All right, you can't offend me. I'm good-natured, I am, and everybody knows it. Charlie du Maurier's not the man to take offense because a gentleman won't answer questions. Let me tell you something, though. You've got no money. Mighty soon the Portuguese 'll find that out Next thing, they'll arrest you. Next, you're in jail! Know what happens after that?"

I was not sure whether or not he was playing with me on the cat-and-mouse plan. He seemed to be amusing himself at my expense, and I did not question that the mere chance of being cruel would be sufficient excuse in his eyes. But there was a suggestion of ulterior motive, and I rather suspected he was probing in his own way for information.

"There are worse towns than this one," I answered, because that was the most colorless statement I could think of.

"Perhaps," he retorted, "and perhaps not!" There was a cold gleam in his eye. "But there are no worse jails than this one! It's lousy, and they starve you, and it's, dark, and it stinks! And when you've been in there a while so that every one has forgotten you, d'you know what they do?"

"Can't imagine," I said, interested against my will.

"They sneak you out in irons at night onto one of their lousy little coastwise steamers and nobody ever hears of you again."

"Drown you at sea?" I suggested, for he waited for me to hazard some kind of guess.

"Drown you at sea!" He laughed like a hyena. "Not they; they're a practical gang. They ship you to the West Coast—the Portuguese West Coast—and put you to work with the coco slave gangs, bossing up natives. Refuse to drive natives and they shoot you!"

I thought I saw through the weakness of that proposition, and was swift to point it out, being yet inexperienced in the practical wisdom of keeping such thoughts to myself.

"Nobody could make a decent fellow do a dirty act by threatening to shoot him. He'd let them shoot and be ——!"

Du Maurier threw his head back and cackled like a champion egg-laying hen.

"You think they're —— fools, don't you? Why you—you chicken! They keep a man everlastingly hoping to escape! They keep him believing each trip with a new gang is his last one! He has to drive the natives to save the natives' lives. And he hopes to get away in order to expose conditions! They work on a bad man's badness, and on a good man's goodness—get you both going and coming. Ha-ha-ha-ha!"

"If this is such an awful place—such a bad Government," I answered, "why do you stay here? Why don't you go to British territory, where law is law, and the king's writ runs, as they call it?"

AT THAT his face darkened as if I had deliberately insulted him, and the steely glint in his cold eyes reminded me—although I can't imagine why—of butchers' shops.

"I guess you don't know I had a little difference with the British?" he said, patting his rifle, and eying me like a chisel.

"I don't know anything about you," I answered frankly.

He judged I was telling truth, and nodded. The storm died as swiftly as it came, and he was all smiles once more—hard, merciless smiles, finding humor in the stones where none was.

"There are tales, and all kinds of tales about me," he said. "Believe 'em or not, as you like. I'll tell you this, though: the Portuguese let me alone! They arrested me once, up in Chai Chai."

"Where is Chai Chai?" I asked him.

"Capital of Gazaland—up the Limpopo a day from here by steamer, or rather a night and part of a day. There's the steamer—look at her!"

He pointed out a small seagoing tug—that lay alongside the nearest quay, busily filling her shallow hold with barrels.

"They wanted me for murder, or so they said. I guess they just wanted me, and the heaviest charge was the best excuse. At any rate, they came and took me by surprise in my tent at dawn, and locked me up in Chai Chai fort. But I had my best natives along, and one of them gave the Portuguese the slip.

"They'd reckoned without my eleven brothers, all living, and five cousins within call. The morning after, all my brothers and cousins rode in from the Libomba Hills—sixteen men. They disarmed the soldiers—burned the fort—loosed me—and tied the fort commandant hand and foot. Then they hitched him to a tree with a rope about his neck, and hauled on the rope until he stood on tiptoe. I was for flogging him, but my brothers said that would bring about counter reprisals; so we left him in that position and rode away.

"Since then the Portuguese treat me with respect. They no more dare take me again than they dare invade British territory with their tin-pot army! I'm King of Gazaland, I am, from the edge of the Lourenço Marques swamps to Pearson's Place, and I'd like to meet the Portugee who dare deny it!"

"Tell me about Chai Chai," I said, since he seemed disinclined to go away.

"It's a rotten hole. Sharks, crocodiles, and hippo—drunken natives, mosquitoes, flies, malaria, mangrove swamps, pineapples, and the worst officials in the country! But it's on the way to my place, if you care to take the longest route. And it's on the way to Inambane and other places. A man can walk from Chai Chai to Inambane in three weeks; and if he hasn't any money or baggage the blacks and Portuguese won't rob him!"

"Anything doing at Inambane?" I asked, and he laughed as if I had made a good joke.

"Less than here, unless you want death and corruption. There's more of those!"

"Does the steamer go there to-day?" I asked, and he laughed again.

"Sure enough. To-day's the day. Say—listen!" He patted his rifle again. "You're broke—I can tell that with half an eye. You're minded to look at Chai Chai—a blind man could see you are. Well—when you get there you'll see I told the truth. From there to my place in the Libomba Hills is roughly a hundred miles. All the natives know my place. Ask them for Charlie du Maurier and they'll point you the way. It's a mean way. It runs 'round the edge of the swamps; and there are lions, and snakes—mosquitoes—flies—all the fun of the fair.

"But if you're a genu-ine white man you can make it! The natives'll let you sleep in their huts, and they'll feed you locusts and wild honey same as John the Baptist ate—there's a famine all through Gazaland and mealies are scarce, but there's plenty at my place. If you dare, and win through you've got guts! If you've got guts, I can use you! If you reach my place in the Libomba Hills I'll put you in the way of making a good living!"

"I'll remember," I answered, turning to go, and he swung along beside me, whistling and nodding in time to the tune as if his thoughts were of Spring-time and merrymaking. Nor could I shake his company.

He walked with me to the Greek's place, and thence to the steamer office, where he roundly abused the Portuguese clerk until that unhappy individual sold me a one-way ticket to Chai Chai at half price. Then he went with me to the little steamer, making one of his own native servants carry my belongings, and he bullied the Goanese steward until I had one of the minute cabins to myself.

"Mind you!" he said again, as they poled the old tug away from the quay. "It's a hundred miles to my place! If you should ever reach there, I'm your friend! I'll give you a week's start, and go the short way up the Tembe River. Bet I'll beat you!" And he stood watching me until he seemed only a speck on a wall in the distance.

It was a weird sensation, being appraised and, so to speak, appropriated by that coldblooded brute. I had no idea of ever seeing him again, and would have walked a thousand miles in the wrong direction rather than deliberately cross his trail. My secret plan was to walk to Inambane, in hope of meeting luck either there or on the way, calculating that the eight pounds odd that I had remaining would in any case take me on from Inambane to Beira, where there would be a different consul, and other ships in the offing than the decrepit *Heatherbell.* But I felt creepy at the thought of having accepted even information from du Maurier, and before we reached the river mouth I had checked up every detail of it by talking with the other passengers.

AND THAT was a weird voyage—a wonderful voyage if only the dread of destitution had not so overhung the venture. We steamed close inshore by mangrove swamps to the shallow Limpopo mouth, and lay for a night there on the thundering bar with the noises of a neolithic age about us. Once a lion roared on the high bluff over the far bank; and from among the mangroves there came crashing, and wild screams, plunging and tearing, ripping and thrashing, and—at intervals—a silence so complete and unexpected that it hurt the eardrums.

The cockroaches drove me out of the cabin, and the mosquitoes sought to drive me in again. Of the two evils I chose the deck and the beauty of moonlight and cool air, and watched until dawn sucked up the mists and showed a military hospital, white and lonely, hugging the shore by the bar. Who chose that site for such a place, and why, is a mystery I never solved.

We dropped a dozen barrels of the stuff they call red wine, and passed on up-river. Great sharks followed us for miles—one followed all the way to Chai Chai, where the hippos thought the water fresh enough and wallowed down to meet him. There were crocodiles in hundreds sunning themselves on rocks and logs, and birds of every color and size and cry perching on mangrove poles, or wheeling to scream abuse at us.

But the chief interest was the atmosphere of mystery. It was up this river that King Solomon's adventurers most likely came to make the old diggings in the distant hills, and the sensation was of being present at the dawn of history. Barring the mangrove stakes set at uncertain intervals to mark the drift of sand, there was no trace of man's handiwork—not a native in sight—not a boat—not a beast.

The other passengers were three hundred Kafirs crowded on the lower deck, on their way back from the Transvaal gold-mines; four Goanese Government clerks, nearly bursting with the pride of having "first-class" cabin berths; and a Portuguese tax-gatherer, with his black wife and a swarm of their half-breed children.

He assured me he was married to the lady, and introduced me to her with punctilious ceremony; but he treated the Goanese as if they were dogs without licenses, and objected loudly to being obliged to eat in the same saloon with them.

He asked me my business, and I wasted an hour in an effort to deceive him without telling out-and-out lies. I might as well have tried to deceive myself as to what the breakfast hash was made of—I, who with my own eyes had seen the poor goat killed.

"I, Eduardo Lopez," he assured me at last, "can tell you more about Gazaland than any other man. There are three authorized occupations for a European who is not an official. Prospector you are not, for you have no license. It is I who sign the licenses. I know. Hunter you are obviously not, for you have no guns, no tent, no servants, and—again, no license! It is also I who sign the hunters' licenses! Trader in mealies you are also evidently not, and for two reasons—it is not the season; there are no mealies. And again, you would require a license, and I—whose business that would be—have issued none! Here is my book of licenses—here is another. Here are yet others. Your name is in none of them!"

"Surely," I said, "a man needs no license to travel and look about him?"

"In Gazaland," he answered smugly, "it is always well to have a permit of one sort or another. It confers a sort of semiofficial standing. It ranks one above the native, and the Indian, and the Goanese. It entitles one to respect, and to a certain measure of confidence. It is presumptive evidence of bona fides.

"Let me issue one to you. My services will cost you nothing, and a trader's permit, let us say, would be only twenty-five pounds—a bagatelle—good for six months. Taxes are payable in Portuguese money, but you may pay me in English gold and I will make the exchange when I return to Lourenço Marques."

I thanked him for the advice, and promised to think it over.

"If you were wise, you would jump at the opportunity!" he answered, with rather a sneer under his black mustache and a mean look in his eye.

"That man du Maurier I saw you with is a low person of very bad reputation. You would better bolster yourself up with semiofficial standing! Englishmen who have no permits are not welcome in Gazaland!"

"I'll think it over!" I assured him, and he sneered again and left me, to go and talk in undertones with the Portuguese captain, who was drunk and steered atrociously. Every time we missed a corner of the winding river by a margin of six inches the Kafirs on the lower deck all laughed, and to the birds we must have seemed a picnic party bent on self-immolation, for their benefit.

They followed and screamed at us as if in haste to get the disaster over, and our bones picked before dark. But the captain, and his half-breed crew, and the tax-collector with his coal-black señora, talked on, and passed a bottle 'round, as if the treacherous river were an open road, and they on metal rails.

Chai Chai came into view beyond a bend at noon, and its excuse for being greeted the nostrils instantly. There is neither mistaking nor forgetting the vile, acrid stench of the barreled stuff the Portuguese call *vino tinto,* that they sell to the natives of that miserable land. Its only resemblance to wine is its murky red color, which may or may not be aniline.

But international law lays down that spirits shall not be sold to natives between certain parallels, and there is more in a name than Shakespeare hinted at. A barrel of the beastly stuff will keep a dozen natives drunk for half a month, and they will work for the sake of it. So three thousand barrels of it went to Chai Chai every thirty days; our tug did a roaring business; and Chai Chai, except for the "fort," was three or four barns of concrete and corrugated iron, all devoted to one purpose.

There were mealie plantations in sight; and two of the planters' houses graced the hillside looking down on the muddy river—cool, they looked, and prosperous; but the locusts had eaten every green thing on either river bank, and the few lean goats and cows licked up and ate the living insects.

The one exception was the pineapples. Fields and roads were all marked out with the prickly plants, and for some reason the locusts scorned those, so that the land was a wilderness of reddish brown, marked with irregular lines of green, and punctuated by the skeletons of leafless trees.

The fort was a mud-walled rectangle down near the river bank, enclosing fifty round, thatched huts and an iron storehouse at one end. In one or two places the ditch had been allowed to fill from neglect. Three or four Portuguese soldiers in ragged uniforms lounged in the shade of a tree, and there was a general air of hungry shabbiness. But the Portuguese flag fluttered bravely from a crooked pole, and the one officer in sight strutted in a uniform whose whiteness was simply dazzling.

For the rest, there were half a dozen Indian stores facing a sandy road—corrugated-iron affairs with open fronts, where matches, thin cotton blankets, and enameled pots were displayed to catch the native eye. And there was a jail—an undoubtable, unspeakable jail, with iron bars, an armed sentry and a smell.

The sun beat down on all this in a splendid effort to melt the iron roofs, and there was only one redeeming spot in sight. The planters' houses, that might otherwise have graced the unlovely scene, only added to the desolation by the insolence of their contrast to all that misery. They were built on the profits of native labor paid for with *vino tinto,* and unexplainably they smirked, and looked, the part.

BUT—AND MY eye fell on these with the instinct that impels a drowning man to grasp at flotsam—beyond the fort, on a little rise by the river bank, were two white tents. They were clean, dazzling, well-constructed tents, with an air about them of self-respect. I reasoned that if they were Portuguese they would almost certainly belong to the Government, and in that case a Portuguese flag would have been in evidence.

But there was no Portuguese flag. Whichever way I looked there was no other pleasant thing in sight, and those tents drew me like a magnet. I walked down the crazy garag-plank and wandered toward them—they were half a mile away—with the sensation of having been reprieved. They were big tents, with awnings out in front, and presently I could see chairs under the awnings, and in one chair a man who, from his dress and attitude, could only have been English.

As I approached within clear view I heard him call to some one in the other tent.

"Monty! Hey, Monty! Didums, d'you hear? Come out, you lazy rascal! I say, Monty—here's an Englishman!"

I walked up to the tent, and he rose to meet me—not so gray then as now, but iron-gray, nevertheless, with the same upturned mustaches, and the same way of standing as if there were a rapier in his right hand. I told him my name, and he told me his was Oakes—Frederick Joliett Oakes.

"Perhaps you've heard of me from the Portuguese?"

But I had not.

"This is Lord Montdidier," he said, as another tall man came from the other tent, as clean-limbed and as cleanly clothed as he, but darker—a gray-eyed man, with a rather heavy, dark mustache, and a neck and shoulders that suggested polo instantly.

He wore a white silk shirt, partly open, showing skin burned to a nut-brown. The rolled-up sleeves showed forearms as lithe and clean as those of the sculptured Hermes. He was a younger man than Oakes, with a rather gentler smile, and the air about him of the English upper class, that knows it is immortal and is far too tactful to be self-assertive.

They ordered a native to bring another chair, and made me sit down facing them.

"You're rather an astonishing apparition!" said Oakes. "You arrive like the god out of a box in the old Greek plays. We weren't exactly praying, and we had given up hope, but we would rather see an Englishman just at this minute than any other unexpected thing we can think of."

"You'll stay to lunch, of course?" said Lord Montdidier.

"I wonder what you're doing here?" said Oakes.

"None of our business, of course," said Lord Montdidier.

"We're prospectors," said Oakes.

"May I order you a drink?" said Lord Montdidier.

"Doing?" I said. "I'm looking for work!"

"Rare!" said Montdidier, shaking his head with a peculiarly gentle smile. "Very rare in these parts!"

"The chance to work seems rare," said I.

"The rarest thing," said Oakes, "is a man who's fit to do what we want done—a reasonably honest man. If there is such a thing in Gazaland, we haven't met him!"

"Shall I shout for the lunch?" said Lord Montdidier.

"How would you like to tell us all about yourself?" said Oakes.

"After lunch," added Lord Montdidier.

"I'd as soon tell you now," said I, but Montdidier shook his head and Oakes yielded the point without demur.

It was easy to see that Oakes was the fiery enthusiast, and Lord Montdidier the more methodical, more patient, rather more formal of the two. Yet they were both men of swift judgment and tremendously strong confidence in their own decisions, as I was destined in the course of years to learn in a thousand ways.

We made a compromise, and I told of myself at the luncheon-table—all spread with snowy linen and white chinaware. The meal was cooked by a Goanese, and served by a Zulu. It could not have been better cooked or served in London town, and as we ate the taint of the *Heatherbell's* fo'castle fell from me, so that I told them of my adventures like a free man to free men, without shame, concealment, or apology.

Then they asked me questions—leisurely questions, seemingly at random, but nevertheless devised to check me up—courteous, shrewd questions that no upright man could take exception to, and no pretender could have answered.

"He's the gift of God!" said Oakes at last, slapping a resonant thigh.

"Suppose we take his own opinion on that point," Montdidier suggested; and forthwith Oakes did the talking while Lord Montdidier sat back and watched us both.

It seemed they had claims staked out in the Libomba Hills—very valuable claims Oakes called them. But in those days the Libomba Hills were a sort of no-man's land, where no Portuguese governor dared show his face, and the iniquitous Charles du Maurier maintained a sort of medieval baron's government from an aerie, that gave him a view of all approaches.

They had licenses to prospect, but their claims must be registered according to law, and they had returned to Chai Chai only to discover that there was no authority in that miserable fort sufficiently exalted to give them papers. It might be necessary to go even as far as Mozambique—possibly to Lisbon, Portugal.

"So I'm going back to hold the claims, while Monty works the oracle," said Oakes.

"And the whole point is," said Lord Montdidier, "that I won't agree to his returning alone. The man du Maurier, who lives in that nest in the hills, has the natives all terrorized and I should imagine would stoop to anything and stop at nothing. How would you like to make the trip with Mr. Oakes? We would pay you a fair thing."

"I'm in no position to refuse any honest job!" I answered. "I'm at your service, and glad to be."

"Can you shoot straight?" Oakes asked me.

"What does that matter?" said Montdidier. "He can learn. A more important point is, will he obey orders?"

"Why ask a seaman that?" laughed Oakes. "I'll tell you my view of it. He can't refuse a job, and we can't refuse him! We've neither of us an alternative! Let's sign him on for a forty a month and found."

"Agreed," said Montdidier.

"Forty what?" said I.

"Pounds," Oakes answered.

"Done!" said I. "I would have come for half—for a quarter of it! But I accept your offer!"

They both laughed, without seeming in the least upset by having missed a bargain. They were unusual men. Later I learned that they would have taken me on their own terms, at their own appraisal, or not at all. Bargains in human flesh and bone were not in their range of vision.

But Montdidier drew a very careful contract with me on a sheet of foolscap paper, and Oakes read it over three times before we all three signed it. By its terms I was limited to my wages, clothing, transportation, food and tent. I was to have no share in the profits of the trip, whatever those might be, or from whatever source. They were business men, as well as generous employers.

From the moment that paper was signed I was treated as a member of the party—apportioned a rifle and a tent, provided with thorn-proof clothes out of their spare kit, given a native servant, and a mule to ride, and in every way magnificently treated.

I told them the man du Maurier had turned up in Lourenço Marques, and that made Montdidier all the more eager to be moving. Next morning with a final charge to me to guard Oakes from harm more carefully than if he were my sweetheart, he ducked the boot Oakes threw at him and boarded the same little steamer that had brought me. We watched him out of sight, and then Oakes went to the fort to take out a license for me, "as if you were my dog," as he remarked; for that colonial Government omitted no means of imposition, and the more degrading the tax the better.

WE STRUCK camp then with the speed of a clipper ship making sail, crossed the Limpopo on a raft—well watched by crocodiles in case the raft overturn, or a mule or a man fall off—and started on a trip that will linger in memory until memory fails. Being my first experience of low veld, or of any veld at all, it was all good going to me. I felt like a boy on a holiday.

Thorns were amusing—even the wait-a-bit thorn that drags the hide from a mule's legs, and strips a man's clothes off him. Lions, roaring around the camp at night, were as fascinating as the low-hung stars and crackling thorn camp-fires. Natives, passed by the way—kraals entered to buy food for our own black following—buck on the short horizon, were all new sources of wonderment to me, and each day's march was crowded full of interest.

I was as happy as the days and nights were long. My ever-rising spirits kept the sun's rays and malaria at bay, and because all natives of Africa are happier when the white man laughs, our boys marched willingly and gave no trouble.

So Oakes was pleased with me. But his own good temper wore thin as march succeeded march. The fever began to threaten him—the low fever of that stricken land, that saps a man's hope and makes his saliva taste in his mouth like aloes. On board ship I had watched the robust good humor of a mate succumb by little notches at a time to the overbearing meanness of a skipper, until the mate himself was the more heartless tyrant of the two.

To some extent I understood how climate, conditions, food and trouble will wear a man's very soul away; but to watch that low-veld loneliness rot into the heart of Oakes was a revelation. Day after day I could see the difference in him, and although he was everlastingly courteous to me I could judge the effort that it cost him now and then. He reached a point where every incident grated on his nerves—every proposal was a lame one—every day's march too long or too short—every night an ordeal to be stoically lived through.

So when we pitched our camp at last under the great cliff in the Libomba foothills, where he and Lord Montdidier had pegged their claims, he was an ailing man, unable to throw off the lassitude of low malaria, yet able enough to torment himself with useless activity. His irritation, manfully though he strove with it, was constantly gaining the upper hand, and at those times our native followers suffered.

One form that his low spirits took more constantly than any other was a sort of morbid interest in the man du Maurier, whose high-perched aerie of a place could just be seen from the opening of his tent.

"That ruffian is as likely as not to thwart us," he prophesied. "He knows well enough there's gold here, and emeralds. He daren't try to work or market it, that's all. He couldn't get even this Government to register a claim in his name, but if he could persuade a more or less reputable citizen to come here and stake, and register, he would try to do business—provided he could first get some sure hold on his partner.

"I suspect he would try to trap his man in some way—plant some disreputable evidence and get ground for blackmail. When we showed up, he rode down here on his mule with three black wives on foot along behind him. He was civil enough in his blackguardly way, but he got no hospitality. He told us we could have title to these claims from himself as King of the Libombas. He cited the old Portuguese law, that having taken to wife the daughter of a chief gives him legal title now to all the land hereabouts since the chief died. He offered us the claims for a thousand pounds, but we didn't trade.

"But he amused Montdidier. Didums was civil to him! 'Pon my soul, if I hadn't been here Didums would have struck a bargain with the brute just for sake of the experience! Strange fellow, Monty—stranger than any man I know! A great reader of character, but a great ass when so inclined! He keeps his hands clean—cleaner than mine are—but he's so interested in freaks of character that he'll go almost any length to get acquainted with a new one! He'll burn his fingers some day—mark my words!"

I began to wonder whether I had been marked down by du Maurier as a possible partner in his claims. At least that would have been a plausible reason for persuading me to wander in search of his dwelling in the hills. But my thoughts were soon diverted from that or any other drift by trouble with our followers.

Oakes was growing bad-tempered and finding too much fault with them. They began deserting one by one; and Oakes, whose malaria increased, found a new vein of ill-humor, grumbling because Montdidier was so long about sending word of his doings.

"We ought to have heard two days ago," he complained to me one morning. "He was to send us word by runner. Where's his runner?"

"I've heard tales of native runners being shot," said I, and I told him what I had heard du Maurier boast of in the bar in Lourenço Marques.

After that Oakes took his favorite rifle from its case and, for all his fever, did such amazing shooting at a dozen different targets that I wondered what his marksmanship could be like with a clear eye and steady hand. Yet his temper grew worse as the days wore on and no news reached us.

At last, I think it was ten days after our arrival on the scene, the spell of that monotony was broken. There was a long shout a little after dawn, and I spied the man du Maurier, with the inevitable rifle over his right arm, riding a mule down the steep path that led from his aerie. There were, however, no black wives behind him and, as far as I could judge, he came alone.

I warned Oakes, and he got dressed in a hurry, in a clean shirt and white sun-helmet, believing no more than Lord Montdidier in appearing ill-clothed before strangers. I took a leaf from his book and snatched a clean shirt from the bagful of reserves.

Du Maurier rode down to our tents and did not offer to dismount, but sat grinning, plainly surprised to see me. Suddenly I remembered Montdidier's warning to guard Oakes carefully. What else was I there for? Yet I sat in a camp-chair like a fool, with no weapon in my lap. I dived into my tent, loaded a rifle, and brought it out.

Du Maurier laughed at me as I resumed my seat in the chair with the rifle across my knees. But I noticed that Oakes had picked up a rifle, too, and that he did not laugh, but glanced approvingly at me. Oakes was in a worse temper than usual, and I think du Maurier suspected it.

"If you had manners you'd get off your mule!" Oakes told him at last.

And without a word du Maurier dismounted. Two of our natives ran out and led the mule away, and du Maurier took a seat on a rock that faced our tents. He had a paper in his hand that I think he wanted us to notice and be perplexed about, for he folded and unfolded it and turned it over.

I am not good at psychology. In fact, Oakes maintains that a Mexican rebel in a good suit could make me believe him honest. But the thought occurred to me that du Maurier's surprise at seeing me was all assumed. I imagined the natives had told him there were two white men in camp, not one; and there were not so many Englishmen in Gazaland that he could not have put two and two together, once he knew—and supposing he did know—that Montdidier had gone to Lourenço Marques by way of Chai Chai.

I suspected the air of surprise was assumed to cover an entirely different attitude. Probably it was designed to throw Oakes off his guard, fever and worry having reduced him to a condition perfectly familiar to men acquainted with that country.

"TWO OF you!" he said at last, letting his rifle fall into the crook of his arm, and pulling out his pipe. "Why didn't you come up to my place on the hill, and treat me as I'd have treated you? Why stand off, as if you and I weren't friends?"

"We're comfortable where we are, thank you," Oakes answered. "I preferred to stay here and keep an eye on our pegs."

"That young man," said du Maurier, pointing a thumb at me, "has a direct invitation to come and stay in my house. He's my guest by rights! He and I had a talk in Lourenço Marques. He and I are friends! He and I have a plan we were to work together. I own all this land hereabouts, you see, and I've been looking for a partner who would register my gold-field. Having a little difference of opinion with the Portuguese, I'm not in position to register claims myself, but that young man and I could work the trade between us."

"Ask him if he wants to go in partnership with you!" said Oakes.

"I ask questions as and when suits me!" du Maurier answered. "I'll ask you one first. What would you do, supposing that young man and I should go in partnership to own these claims you've pegged?"

"I'd shoot him!" said Oakes promptly, and the answer surprised me as much as it did du Maurier.

"Pity to spoil such a nice young gentleman so early!" du Maurier grinned. "What if there's two of us to one of you, though?"

"How d'you mean?" said I.

"I mean," said du Maurier, "that I've a writing here that says—look, it's all done with a typewriter so's nobody can say I wrote it out myself over Lord Montdidier's signature—I've a writing here that says Montdidier is sick in Lourenço Marques, and sick of prospecting, and sick of Gazaland."

He was about to say more, but stopped to watch our faces. He may have read astonishment in mine. In Oakes' he saw exasperation fed by the fever in his veins.

"What would you say," he went on, "if I was to prove to you that Mister Lord Montdidier had registered these claims in Lourenço Marques, and in consideration of a thousand pounds, paid and received in presence of two witnesses, had made over the papers in blank to me, for me to fill in the name of any man I choose?"

Oakes glowered, and did not answer.

"Supposing I showed you the papers, what would you say?"

"You couldn't show them! I wouldn't look at them!" growled Oakes.

"And supposing I showed you here—in writing—all typewritten out and signed—an order by Lord Montdidier to me to take his belongings, and pack and forward them to a certain address he gave me?"

"I wouldn't believe it," said Oakes, in a level voice that was much more impressive than if he had roared.

"Yet here is the order!" announced du Maurier, waving a sheet of foolscap paper on which were several lines of typewriting, and a large seal.

"Touch a thing in this camp if you dare!" said Oakes simply.

"Wait a while!" said du Maurier. "I'm not through yet. There's more explanations due! You don't think your bosom friend Mister Lord Montdidier would do such a thing, but you see, I've played a trick on you. You think you're two to one and could outshoot me, but that young man is already wavering in his mind!" He pointed at me with his thumb again. "He isn't half sure he'd draw a trigger on me to oblige you, seeing he knew me first! And the trick I played on you was a smart one. Mister Lord Montdidier doesn't believe you're his friend any more!"

He lit his pipe nonchalantly, affecting to take his eyes off us, but I was watching him like a hawk and was quite sure that was only a ruse to draw our fire in case we should think of shooting. He was probably confident of being able to outmaneuver the two of us, even at that range and conceding us the drop.

"And as for shooting," he said, throwing away the match and resuming his stare at us with increased insolence, "if you did shoot me—if you could shoot me—I suppose you're not forgetting that the natives hereabouts are mine, and that they'd burn you alive for any harm done me? You shouldn't forget that, for that's a strong point! I've married into nine tribes hereabouts! I've nine wives up the hill there! Their relations consider me the big asset, and they'd surely be resentful of any harm done me. You shouldn't think of shooting me. It wouldn't pay! There'd be no profit in it!"

So far there had been nothing said that in my judgment would make for real trouble. His remarks about me were a joke, due to ignorance. If he chose to suppose me a scoundrel like himself, so much the greater surprise in store for him. I was quite sure Oakes would take no stock in his remarks. But he had not played his trump-card yet.

"You see," he said, "I'm a downy bird, I am. When you came here and pegged, I was willing to make a trade with you, but you refused. Whoever refuses to trade with me on my terms makes his own bed, and lies on it, that's all! I knew one of you 'ud have to go to the coast to try and register; so I went there ahead of you, and waited. Then along comes Mister Lord Montdidier, looking pretty sick. I gave him several days to register the claims, for the Portuguese are slow, and then I called on him. He doesn't think much of you any more, Montdidier doesn't't!"

Now I saw the length and breadth of his position, and really began to tremble for the consequences. How should I know, who had known Montdidier only a few hours, that the swift low fever of the lands had not made a mental wreck of him, as it had nearly made one of Oakes? True, I was sure I would stand by Oakes until whatever the end might be; but how could I know whether Oakes in his heart did not doubt my loyalty. Oakes had not known me long. I was a stranger in a land where neither law nor mercy kept the right-of-way. Unless Oakes, fever or no, should prove adamant, it began to look to me as if du Maurier held a winning hand.

"Maybe you recollect," said du Maurier, "that the day after you got here you sent a runner to the coast with a letter for Mister Lord Montdidier. Well—he didn't go far, that boy didn't, before he fell into my hands, letter and all! Two of my men brought him to Lourenço Marques. He and I had a conference. We arranged between us that I should hold his wife—I had her already in my kraal up there—and he should say what I told him to in case he hoped to get his wife back in condition to be any use to him.

"We came to an agreement pretty soon, and that boy stayed with me in Lourenço Marques—finally coming with me to see Montdidier. Montdidier recognized him, of course, and the boy was word perfect. Between us we told a tale that disgusted Mister Lord Montdidier to the point of saying he'd shoot you at the first sight! I'll tell you what I said, and what that boy confirmed."

Oakes had been pale with the fever, but I noticed now that a dull flush of rage had colored his face, and his eyes would have scared me if I had had to face them. But du Maurier seemed to me to be regarding him as he might a trapped animal, amused at the spectacle of ferocity that could not reach him.

How he was so confident that we two would not shoot was beyond me, until it occurred that he might have a score of blacks in ambush among the rocks behind him, and I began to search for a glimpse of black skin or a spear head, although without avail. I have come to the conclusion since that he was depending entirely on his knowledge of the reluctance of an Englishman to shoot without first giving warning.

"We explained to Mister Lord Montdidier, that boy and I did, that you'd gone! We said you were sick—not very sick in health, but sick of the whole business, and that you'd decided to trek through to Swaziland and leave him to do as he pleased. We said you'd sent that boy to say that Mister Montdidier's things were lying where you'd left 'em on the veld; and I added that I held myself responsible that none of the blacks hereabouts would touch a thing. I promised him that, and that if they did touch anything I'd see he got it back.

"Well—I've seen angry men, but he was the angriest! He didn't believe a word at first, but the native's tale convinced him. I'd drilled that boy until he was word perfect. And finally I bribed a Goanese Government clerk to go to him and say word had come in from the natives that his tent and belongings were left lying on the veld, and what was to be done!

"Oh, we had him convinced all right! And his anger was the terriblest thing I've seen. He swore he will shoot you, and this gentleman here along with you, at the first glimpse he gets; and he's off to Swaziland, by rail to the British border, to look for you!"

He lit his pipe again, that had gone out during that triumphant recital, and watched, for a minute to judge the effect produced.

"What are you going to do about it?" he asked with a leer. "Are you going to get out and leave this gentleman," once more he pointed at me with the appropriative thumb, "and me to strike a bargain between ourselves? My advice to you is to get out of the country, by Inambane or somewhere, before Mister Lord Montdidier gets wind of you and hunts you down! What'll you do?"

"I'll make no terms with you, anyhow!" growled Oakes. "Get out of my sight!"

Du Maurier laughed.

"I'll give you until to-morrow dawn to think it over!" he announced. "Then I'm coming down with my men to take possession of Mister Lord Montdidier's belongings and to pack them, and deal with them as directed! No, I won't take a drink, thanks!" he added sarcastically. "No, thanks, I won't stay to lunch! And if you're man enough to shoot me in the back as I ride away, let's see you do it! I'll have my mule, if your boys are through with admiring it!"

OUR NATIVES, at a shout from Oakes, brought him the mule and he rode away. I sat in silence, for there was very little I could say that would have helped.

"Have you paper and a pencil?" Oakes asked after a few minutes, and I hunted until I had found them. He wrote out a few words, and handed the paper to me.

"Read!" he said.

I read:

> If you want your things come and get them.
>
> FRED OAKES.

"That's a telegram. Take it to Chai Chai," he ordered, "as fast as you can travel. See it dispatched, and make sure it gets there. Then come back!"

It was addressed to Lord Montdidier at the only big hotel.

"I was to guard you," I objected—and then checked myself, remembering that those instructions had been received from Lord Montdidier.

"I suppose I needn't remind you that you receive a salary for obeying orders?" he asked. Then he relented, judging, I suppose, that my objection had been solely on his own account. "You see that rising ground among the rocks?" he asked, and I looked toward a sort of island a half mile from the nearest hill, perhaps fifty feet higher than the level land surrounding it. Judging by the splurge of green below it there was a spring of water, and there was no place within rifle range from which an enemy could snipe. "I shall move camp this morning, and pitch up there. You'll find me there when you return. Don't waste any more time."

I was not afraid of the climate. It takes time for the pestilential low veld to sap a man's strength. I was young, and strong, and scarcely rid of the sea air in my lungs. So I took a mule and one native—to make sure I should not lose myself—and was in the saddle and away within fifteen minutes of receiving orders.

The pace I set was exactly as fast as the native could possibly manage and the mule endure, and I overdid the thing rather than waste time. So that when night shut down on us I had a spent mule and an utterly weary servant, and we were all three utterly grateful for the shelter of a big kraal that lay a little to the right hand of the track. I had turned into it, and the natives were about dragging the brush obstruction across the entrance behind me, when I noticed there was another party of travelers encamped there.

None too pleased—for I thought it might be a Portuguese official party, and that could only mean many questions and delay—I took the mule's saddle off, watered him from a woman's crock, and fed him from the bag I had slung from the saddle. That done, I walked forward to find the head man and get supper for the native and myself. I saw a white man come striding to meet me through the gloom, and stood still, dumb. But as he came on I was compelled to believe my eyes, and when he spoke at last, cheerily, there was no denying him—Lord Montdidier!

Without a word I passed him the telegram. It was growing pitch-dark, so he struck a match and read it.

"Oakes wrote this?" he asked.

"Yes."

"On your way to Chai Chai to send it?"

"Yes."

I thought for a second he was going to ask me for an explanation, but I wronged him.

"My spare mule!" he shouted, and I saw his boys come running out of a hut to do his bidding.

He must have bought new mules at Lourenço Marques and have brought them with him on the tug.

"You're not going tonight?" I asked.

"Going now," he answered.

"But—lions!" I objected.

"Please bring my outfit along to-morrow," he answered. "You'll find cloth and beads—or money if he'd rather—in my bag to pay the head man. Start early, and make it in one day if you can. Good-by!" And he mounted the mule, ordered the obstruction taken from the kraal gate, and was gone—with one faithful native boy trotting with a lantern at his mule's heels.

It took me two days, however, to return, for I had his boys and new purchases to bring along. About three in the afternoon I came in sight of the new camp, and not long after that I made out him and Oakes in two chairs side by side, talking and laughing together as if they had never parted. When I reached them, they were kind to me, but did not refer to what had happened by word or hint; and in those days I was not intimate enough with either man to care to ask personal questions.

IT NEVER did occur to me to ask what happened when they met, until Oakes and I sat together on the club veranda in New York that afternoon and we discussed old times.

"When he showed up, why didn't you shoot him?" I asked, and he sat up with a start, and laughed.

"Because," he said, "I believe in respecting my adversary! I wouldn't stick a pig with a dirty knife, and du Maurier was dirty! I'd made up my mind to ignore every word du Maurier said, and to let Monty pick a fight with me on any ground he chose."

"But Monty was a proud man," I said. "How did he come to forgive your distrust of him?"

"Yes, he was a proud man," Oakes answered. "But there's a Providence looks after fools, and Monty never found me out! Just think of that brute du Maurier inventing all those lies! He never even saw Monty in Lourenço Marques! As soon as Monty showed up, he skunked out, covering his trail! Those documents he had were Lord knows what—some old ones!"

"How did you explain that telegram away?" I asked.

"I didn't. Monty explained it for me. He took it to mean that there was trouble—danger. 'If you want your things, come and get them!' He understood he might not find them if he came too late!"

"All the same," said I, and checked myself.

"All the same, what?" demanded Oakes.

"Nothing," I answered. "I was merely thinking."

I was thinking what would be the use of suggesting to Oakes at that late day that Monty divined well enough that Oakes mistrusted him, but was too splendid a gentleman ever to let the knowledge of the secret out.

AMERICA HORNS IN

THAT LUMPY, rock-littered hillock, scattered with thorn-scrub, stewing in the heat reflected and shut down on it by the western slopes of the Libomba Hills was no heavenly spot to idle in—no place for hesitation, indecision in those fever countries is a sickness worse than the malaria itself.

The climate had already set its teeth into Fred Oakes' leathern constitution, and he lay in his tent shivering with incipient ague, gargling to get the taste of fever from his mouth, and bad-tempered to explosiveness. Some of our best servants had deserted to the enemy; and that was to be expected; yet more were likely to follow them if we lingered, for we, albeit white men, were strangers in the land, whereas Charles du Maurier's bloody name was a byword of long standing all up and down the countryside. If the Portuguese Government dared not try issues with him, who was a next-to-naked Ronga savage that he should do better?

There was only one of us to be depended on, for I was inexperienced, as well as new to the tropics, although still healthy from the fresh air and hard living of a long voyage. But Lord Montdidier, casual and careless though he liked to seem to be, was in fact a very downy bird indeed, and far too alert a counselor to let any situation go from bad to worse.

He could be the most exasperating, noncommittal looker-on who was ever asked to give opinions, and he could say the opposite of what he thought with a cultivated smoothness that bewildered whom he wished. But he was a comforting man to share tight corners with, if only because panic-proof.

"That peculiar scoundrel du Maurier," he said to me, as we washed before our tents, "is probably planning a surprise for us. Suppose we steal a march, and disappoint him—what?"

"I'd like to burn his roost!" said I, squinting up at the aerie fifteen hundred feet above us, from which the self-styled King of the Libombas could see all the trails and any one approaching. One of his thatched roofs was barely visible above the rim of the cliff. "I'll swarm up there and have it out with the half-breed brute alone if you'll give me leave!"

I was no more in love than was he or Oakes with the notion of being blackmailed or hectored by an outlaw, although recent subjection to the mate of an undermanned British bark might have been supposed to give me the submissive habit.

Montdidier looked at me in the lazy way that I was beginning to recognize as the screen behind which he did swift thinking. In that part of the world the men one hires at random, as he and Oakes had hired me, very seldom turn out to be capable of loyalty, or worth much when in difficulties, and I dare say he was wondering how much of my boast was due to anxiety to please, and how much bluff.

"Oakes is in favor of burning all Gaza-land," he answered, "and after that Lisbon and the King of Portugal. Did you hear him throw his tea over the native just now? Scalded the boy. Oakes is full of war. I'm thinking of the claims."

Not very far away in front of us, along the wavering line of the lower foothills, stood long rows of peeled and squared pegs that Oakes and I had remained to watch, while Montdidier went to Lourenço Marques to get registration papers, and a concession to work the mine. I knew nothing whatever of either precious stones or gold in those days, but the other two had assured me there was wealth beneath the parallelograms of barren-looking land sufficient to have made King Solomon of Jerusalem consider himself a pauper; and that was an exciting thought.

But I looked hard at Montdidier. My contract calling for wages by the month and no share of the profits made it easy to take a lofty attitude, and I wondered whether the climate had seeped into his system too.

"If he were really a man, he would scuff that buzzard du Maurier first, and see to the claims later on," thought I. But Montdidier went on talking, telling no more of his thoughts than he saw fit. It seemed impossible to believe that he had been the best polo forward of his day, the keenest, suddenest squadron leader of the Indian army, and a fencer of international fame. Yet Oakes had told me he was all those things. One could understand more easily his playing chess, although I have never been able to beat him at the game, try how I might.

"We'll go from here," he said, eying the breakfast that two Zulu boys were spreading painstakingly. "We've pegged out the pay-dirt du Maurier would never have located but for us, and that may keep the scoundrel quiet. Aren't you sick of the country? What?"

"Not enough to quit without fighting," I answered. "How was it you couldn't get title deeds from the Government? Wouldn't they grant them?"

He smiled as if failure had amused him.

"The Portuguese asked me for money. And after that for some money. And then for some money. And then more money. I bribed them all in suitable amounts, from a man who said he was lieutenant-governor downward. Then they told me the papers would have to go to Lisbon to be signed. So I haven't title. I think we may as well all go to Lourenço Marques."

"Du Maurier will jump the claims the minute your back's turned," I objected.

It exasperated me to think of that half-breed Mauritius-French murderer scoring off any one who paid me wages.

"Let's hope so," he answered, smiling, and I stared.

"Why?" I asked bluntly.

"I detest being sniped on the march. He can't sit on claims and follow us too—eh?—what?"

"What's that, Monty?" Oakes roared from the tent.

He was in a condition the low fever of the country makes familiar, of seeming the one sane man in all the world, the one sorry man; whatever was said by any one was wrong, and his own voice could only be raised in protest—wrong, too, because too feeble. He came out, blinking at the sun through bloodshot eyes, and viewed the breakfast table with disgust.

"What's that I heard you say?"

"Lourenço Marques, Fred."

"Rot, my good man! I won't go!"

But Montdidier showed his strong white teeth in a smile, and pointed to a hammock, already prepared from blankets and a pole. Our four strongest natives were squatting beside it, satisfied to have the personal task of carrying a white man. They will jib at half the dead weight; but to tote a live, bad-tempered human is an honor.

Oakes grinned too, weakly because the fever had hold of him, but none the less determined.

"Monte, you —— fool, if you have me slung in that thing I'll cut the lashings!"

"All right," said Montdidier; "come and eat."

Oakes pecked at tea and biscuits while Montdidier and I made a meal. Then, at a sign the natives raised the hammock, and Montdidier gathered Oakes up as if he were a child—some two hundred and forty pounds of him—went through his pockets—confiscated his knife—and dumped him into the appointed place, the two of them struggling and squealing like a pair of schoolboys.

"Who wins?" Montdidier demanded.

"—— you!" exploded Oakes. "Give me a mule to ride.

But Montdidier, for reasons of his own, had sent the mules to the kraal of a near-by chief to be cared for.

"Get out if you like, Fred! Put me to the trouble of lifting you in again, and I'll take away your boots, socks, and trousers! If that won't work, I'll tie you in!"

BEFORE THE sun was an hour high we had struck camp and were on the march in the inevitable single file, Oakes in advance, blasphemous in the blanket hammock, I on the flank to avoid the smell of loaded porters, that I have never yet grown used to, and Montdidier last, stalking along in football shorts, with a rifle under his arm. How he contrived not to have the skin all shredded from his knees by thorns was a mystery. My own were sore, and bleeding through tough cloth before a mile was passed.

I turned to look back, for the disgust at leaving good, rich claims behind us haunted me, and my eye rose tier by tier, level after level, until it rested on the topmost peak of the ridge above us, and I saw a dark speck that well might be a man. Letting Montdidier overtake me I asked him for his field-glass.

There, sure enough, du Maurier stood, looking like Napoleon at that range, all alone, one hand in his bosom, chin on chest in meditation.

"Look!" said I, and Montdidier took the glasses.

He looked for a minute, and returned the glasses to their case. He almost never laughed aloud, but had a way of throwing his head back and going through the motions that was simply diabolical until one knew him intimately.

Personally I could see no cause for amusement, and it was evident that Oakes agreed with me. Not only was he not amused, he was vehemently discontented. We passed over the long, lean spur of the farthest reaching foothill, and, instead of turning eastward toward the Limpopo River, and Chai Chai where the steamer started for the coast, we swung to the south.

"Where are we going, Monty?" he shouted. "Didums, you —— fool, where are you leading us?"

Montdidier overtook him at a run, to restore equanimity among the bearers; for Oakes had kicked and threatened them into rank disorder.

"To the swamps, old dear—to the swamps. There, that'll do, men—into step again—now, carry on!"

"To the swamps? Are you mad?"

"Not more than usual, Fred."

"Then what in the name of Bedlam is the idea?" Are you saving steamer fares? Are we broke?"

"No, old thing, we've money."

"Then what does this mad maneuver mean?"

"We're in love with solitude."

"Don't be an idiot, Didums! What did you take this cursed way for? We'll be eaten by crocks and mosquitoes! Look at 'em—big as hornets!"

It is not wise to let a man with East Coast fever darken counsel with his everlasting disagreements, but there is a point beyond which it is unsafe to let wrath boil. Montdidier explained.

"Du Maurier's family, you old fathead! The bloodsome Charles has probably asked them to waylay us between the hills and Chai Chai, so behold! We make a circuit!"

"You mean we act like a circus!" Oakes objected. "If they're after us, they'll wait a day, and then get on our trail! Bah! Give me my gruel in the open! Who wants to be tossed to crocks in this blasted swamp?"

"It's all one, old dear," Montdidier answered. "Carry him gently, boys! On the veld hyenas crack your bones and laugh like ghouls!"

"Better than crocks!" swore Oakes, "that lie belly on you in the mud until you're tender! Ough!"

The going as we neared the swamps became abominable, and we two had to walk on each side of the hammock, with a hand to steady it and save the boys from slipping with it sideways into the slimy, scum-covered water. Mosquitoes attacked us until we were a mass of blood, and flies added to the torment. Through gaps in the mangroves I could see that kites were wheeling, doubtless with an eye on us, and many a time I detected the snout of a crocodile, laid between two stumps in the hope that some unwary one might set his foot on it.

But we had a Shangan boy who swore he knew the way, and Montdidier persisted in trusting him. One of his peculiar gifts was the ability to tell good niggers from the bad ones—a trick that Oakes only learned in degree as time went on, and I never learned at all, although there were times when I flattered myself.

The nights in that swamp were the worst part, for then in the noisy darkness—noisy with night-fowl and the plunging crash and cry of half-amphibious beasts—the sensation of being lost was overwhelming. We had Oakes well covered with mosquito netting, but our own pieces were torn all to shreds. If he could have seen us in the dark he would have torn up his own net rather than have the better of either of us, I don't doubt, but those nights were three occasions when we fooled him.

About mid-morning of the fourth day we emerged by way of a dangerous causeway made of half-submerged mangrove poles, into a bay near the mouth of the Limpopo. We were unrecognizable—unclean—and so nearly dead-beat, niggers and all, that another day of it would probably have been the end of us. But we had shaken off the du Mauriers, and that seemed sufficient reward for the moment. The sense of being hunted through the swamps had made me, for one, more wretched than had all the other plagues combined.

There was a rickety dug-out canoe hauled up among the mangroves, and in that we crossed to the Portuguese station at the bar, making nearly a dozen trips before we had all our loads and niggers over. The white-smeared Government hospital—devoid of almost all stores except quinin and castor oil—looked like a palace; and the doctor let us use his genuine imported bath. Then he spread castor oil on our sores, and overdosed us with quinin until the singing in our ears was torment; but, in spite of the medicine, Oakes recovered—very swiftly when a cool sea-breeze blew in and kicked up a big surf on the bar. When the steamer arrived a day late he was well again and quite sweet-tempered, Montdidier now making the worst showing of the three.

The captain of the twin-screw tug that its owners called a "liner"—on the principle that she took the same trip twice a week, and carried far too many passengers—had been drinking brandy this trip in place of *vino tinto,* and was therefore more than usually drunk—anti-English, opinionative, surly. Insulted at the notion of having to carry Englishmen, he ordered the lines cast off from the ramshackle wharf almost before our last loads were on board. Then he sent the mate below for daring to offer advice about the course—rang for full speed ahead with both screws—swung with the flowing tide—and hit the bar head-on at full speed, so hard that we piled up almost clear of the water.

There we had to stay ten days, taking occasional boat trips to the shore to trade the same old yarns with the doctor, fishing for sharks overside, or shooting duck to restock the empty larder. They were dreary, weary days until a Spring tide with a high wind came and lifted us; but we all got well again; and the delay was a godsend in another way besides, although at the moment we were affected by that strange state of mind that resents intrusion even on flattest boredom.

"Plans! Plans! Plans!" Oakes insisted often enough.

Then Montdidier would take his seat on a pile

of old sails and awnings abaft the funnel, and we would begin discussing how to prevent the du Mauriers from taking by force claims that the Government was too corrupt and feeble to protect.

But somehow or other, whenever those conversations started, a chance word or a phrase would set Montdidier to recounting reminiscences, and, for a while at least, the "Thousand and One Nights" became mere dry trash by comparison. But the steamer's captain had sobered up, and presently, when I saw him inventing ways of listening without seeming to, I understood.

IT WAS the day before we finally poled off the bar that another white man came—not a "mean white," but a young man cleaner than ourselves, and as well supplied with tents, guns, and servants. At the first glance he was obviously not an Englishman, even if one could not have seen his rifles, and the pump-gun; but he had picked up something of the Englishman's reserve, no doubt in self-defense. And perhaps we did not look too civilized.

At all events, he did not introduce himself, and it was several hours before he and I got in conversation, he sitting over by the windward rail watching the surf pounding on the steamer's side, or reading. In fact, it was my request that he lend me his book if he was not using it that broke the silent spell.

"I've only an old '*World* Almanac,' he answered, "but it's better than thinking Portuguese!"

He was a prospector like ourselves, only much more homesick.

"Gosh!" he assured me, I'd rather keep chickens for the kosher market in Hoboken than hunt a fortune in this land of thugs. Plain, ordinary murderers 'll look like Y.M.C.A. secretaries after this! I learned Portuguese in Brazil. Thought that might give me an advantage. Nothing to it, though! Riles me in two languages instead of one! I'm no fan for any brand of autocratic Government, but this colonial hold-up is the limit!"

His adventures seemed to be too depressing for discussion; but we got to exchanging personal half-confidences, feeling each other out.

"Tell me some more about your party," he urged after a while. "It's the first time I was close to a member of the House of Lords. He doesn't say 'Haw, don'tcher-know' or wear a monocle. What's the matter with him? Broke?"

"Not at all," I answered. "He's our financier. He has an income too small for his purpose—or so I understand."

"How small?"

"Four or five thousand a year."

"Four or five thousand what?"

"Pounds."

"Twenty or twenty-five thousand dollars? Income? And he chooses to function in this wilderness? What's the matter with the House of Lords that he don't stay home and ride herd on the king? Now he has been below and scraped off the foliage, he doesn't look like a man the police are after."

I told him, for there was never any secret about Monty's ultimate aim; he was always perfectly frank about it to friend or enemy.

"His income is all right so far as financing expeditions goes, but if he were to open up the family seat in the Midlands, it wouldn't pay the gardeners and grooms! So he and Oakes are partners, prospecting for gold and minerals. He finds the capital, and I understand they divvy up two to one. I'm paid wages."

"Have they had any luck?" he asked, and I told him about our claims in the Libomba Hills, and about Charles du Maurier. When I mentioned du Maurier's name he sat up straight and whistled.

"Please introduce me to your lord," he said. "My own name's Yerkes—William Simpson Yerkes. I think I can horn in here without offending."

When I had presented him to Montdidier we all sat cross-legged in the corner where the rotten awning threw its longest shadow, and for a minute or two he and Montdidier studied each other, while Oakes and I looked on.

"This man tells me," he said presently, jerking his head sideways toward me—he did not know yet whether I was footman, foreman, secretary, friend, or combination of all four, for Americans are funny in their non-comprehension of the working of English caste, "that you have some claims you can't get registered, and that you've trouble with a man called Charles du Maurier."

Montdidier nodded gravely, vastly too polite to hint to a stranger that his business was his own. But I caught a swift, sideways glance at me that made me hot and cold all over, and Oakes glared at me.

"I'm aware I'm horning in," said Yerkes. "Perhaps I'd do better to establish my own credentials first. I've papers—references—cast your eye on these."

He drew a long leather wallet from an inner pocket, and passed it to Montdidier, who took it, met the American's eyes, and offered it back again.

"No," said Yerkes. "Be good enough to open that and go through it. Then we'll talk if you see fit."

So Montdidier did as he was asked, and I caught sight of a passport, and what looked like a banker's draft among other things.

"My own passport is with the Standard Bank in Lourenço Marques," said Montdidier, smiling, and handing the wallet back.

"Oh, rot!" Oakes put in. "This isn't a garden party! Say what you like, America, and we'll listen!"

"All the same," said Yerkes, confining his attention to Montdidier with a quiet persistence, but regardful of Oakes' red herring, "I've shown you my papers, and when quite convenient to you I'd like to looks at yours."

"Perfectly in order!" said Montdidier. "You shall. Come to the bank with me when we land."

"Now, America!" said Oakes.

"Well," said Yerkes, "my own tale's a sordid one. "I've a concession—papers applied for—wild rubber near the border of Segokenyan's country, where the Libombas run down toward the low veld. I have my concession all staked out, but there's a bunch of thugs inhabiting those hills, calling themselves white men, who defy the Portuguese and claim the right to levy what they call taxes.

"I refused to pay, and they hunted me off the lot. I had to get out in a hurry, and travel down the seacoast to avoid them. I've seen some Portuguese officials, and they all asked for money, but none offered to do anything. Now—has the du Maurier who troubled you got any relations that you know of?"

Montdidier looked at me. Having talked with the boastful Charles himself in Lourenço Marques, I was an authority, and I felt myself forgiven, by virtue of utility.

"He told me he has eleven brothers and five cousins," I said. They act in concert when there's trouble. When Charles du Maurier was arrested in Chai Chai they burned the fort and rescued him."

"Well," said Yerkes, "I'm not a member of any assassins' union, but I'd join this minute to get the scalps of that gang!"

"Meaning we're its walking delegates?" suggested Oakes.

"Meaning I take you for men who would rather fight than eat crow," he answered.

"Provided we got together," said Montdidier, "and our friend here—" nodding at me—"continued to like his job, there would be four of us—against their seventeen."

"Four white men against seventeen breeds!" said Yerkes.

"Bravo, America!" laughed Oakes.

It was at that point that the steamer's captain began again to show too much interest in us. There was no valid reason why he should have chosen that minute for spreading out his spare shirt on the deck near by, and squatting down to mend it. Besides, the minute we moved away he folded up the shirt and returned it to its lair in an old cigar box.

"Suppose we talk when we reach town?" Montdidier suggested, glancing at the captain.

" 'I go a-fishing,' " said Oakes, and we all got up.

So we fished overside for sharks until the next day's Spring tide lifted us; and until the tug's side pounded on the new quay piles in Lourenço Marques harbor, I think the only further reference any of us made to our affairs was when Oakes gave Yerkes a word of warning.

"The du Mauriers get supplies by this steamer, and pay double to keep the bearings smooth. The captain gets more from them in presents than his salary amounts to. He's their spy."

"Then he'll send them word that we four have met," said Yerkes.

"Maybe," Oakes answered. "I see no way of getting at the brutes."

"Nor I," said Yerkes. "I did, but now I'm cool I don't."

"Nor I," I added. "Four against seventeen men who know the natives, and every inch of the country, is steep odds."

But we were all three reckoning without Montdidier.

ONCE ASHORE we went to the bank first, and Yerkes was accorded his just rights. Then we took up quarters at the one respectable hotel, and while we three talked Montdidier went off on business of his own.

"This man says the House of Lords—" for so he insisted on referring to Montdidier—"is your financier," said Yerkes, after an hour of desultory conversation, and Oakes nodded. Oakes can express more enthusiasm in a nod than some could achieve with the aid of fireworks and a brass band.

The admission seemed to give the American food for thought, and after a time he, too, went off by himself, leaving Oakes and me to our own devices. It occurred to Oakes then that I was being paid for doing nothing, so he sent me down to the hotel storeroom to overhaul the tents and gear; and that took me until supper time.

So I did not see Montdidier come back, or hear the first part of his talk with the other two. But I realized at the first glance, as I took my seat at table, that they had already arrived at some agreement.

Montdidier offered me wine, but it was not so long since I was down and out that I cared to cultivate expensive tastes, and I refused. Yerkes refused too. Tales about Kentucky notwithstanding, I have met more Americans who prefer to campaign on water than any other breed of white man.

"How about it, now?" Montdidier asked me. "Do you like your job?"

"I like you fellows," I said, "if that's what you mean."

"I don't mean that exactly," he answered; and Oakes cut in, as ever impatient of preliminaries.

"Bosh! Tell him the news! America here has joined us—his rubber against our gold. A half-share for Monty, and a quarter each for America and me. Do you accept the situation?"

"Why not?" I asked.

"As before," said Montdidier, "no share of the profits, but we'll raise your salary ten pounds to fifty a month."

"Very generous," said I.

"Generous be—!" said Oakes. "We'll make you work for it!"

"And you understand," said Montdidier, fingering his wine glass, "that before we can work our claims, or even secure them, we shall have to—"

"To put the enemy out of business!" cut in Yerkes.

"Bravo, America!" said Oakes.

"We may have to fight," said Montdidier.

"I'd be glad to fight Charles du Maurier single-handed," said I. "That cold-blooded brute has been above ground too long!"

"And that brings me right to the point." Montdidier fingered his glass again, looking straight at me. "You'll remember saying that, given my leave, you would like to go up alone to his roost and tackle him?"

"Yes," said I, wondering.

"Did you mean that?"

"Certainly," I answered, ceasing to wonder so much, but suddenly feeling lonely.

"We don't doubt you meant it at the time," said Yerkes. "You were feeling right unfriendly then, and hot enough to burn your shadow up. I know that feeling. But a man grows cool after reflection. You've no interest in the property. You'd be justified in calling off your offer. I wouldn't call that backing down."

"You may keep the salary," I said. "I'll join for nothing, to have a crack at Charles du Maurier."

"Piffle!" said Oakes. "What we want to know is, can we count on you, or would you rather tackle something safe?"

"We mean," said Montdidier, "that if you'd rather, we'll give you two hundred pounds, and a steamer ticket to any port in the world you wish." And he leaned back in his chair to watch me. For that matter they all three watched me.

"I've no hesitation," said I. "I stand in with you, on your terms."

"You may be dead in a week!" said Oakes.

"In less than a week!" said Yerkes.

But I know of a dozen things that have always frightened me more than death, and that argument did not turn a hair.

"Supposing I'm shot dead to-morrow," said I. "What of it? I've no dependents—no business—no wife. Barring my possible usefulness to you, I don't know of any one who'd miss me."

"Then you'll remain with us?" Montdidier asked.

"If the choice is mine," said I, "then, yes!"

"All right," he answered. "That's settled. I'm glad. You get fifty a month from to-day."

"We'll write it into your contract, and initial it," said Oakes. "America here shall sign it too."

"Now we may as well make some things clear to you," said Montdidier. "I've seen the governor, and I found him after all he could get and willing to give nothing. But I remembered meeting the captain of their battle-ship lying out there in the harbor, so I took a boat and called on him. The man's a gentleman—a fine fellow—excellent in every way. Has influence, too, of the right kind.

"After a long talk he brought me back in his launch to the governor's palace, and there was straight work in a room alone between us three. He told the governor—in English, so that I could understand, too—that unless he chose to come to terms with me, and stand by his bargain, he would cable to Lisbon certain information he possessed. Blackmail—eh? Can you blackmail a blackmailer? The governor held out for money payments, backing down bit by bit, and we agreed at last. I have it all in writing, witnessed by the navy man."

"The governor is probably in tears," said Oakes. "The poor devil had to buy his job for a four-year term back in Lisbon. Borrowed the money. He has to make enough in four years to repay the loan and interest, support himself and family, and keep him in ease until he dies—hard lines I call it. Monty ought to be ashamed! You ought to have fed him, Didums! You ought to have offered to buy some stamps!"

"The agreement is this," Montdidier went on. "We get registry of our claims at once—our gold and Mr. Yerkes' rubber concession. We also get an official Portuguese member added to our party, who receives a ten per cent, share of any net profit. He is to be appointed by the governor, with full authority to hang—ah—"

"For instance, horse thieves!" put in Yerkes.

"Mule thieves, he means," said Oakes; and it began to dawn on my thought that Montdidier might have planned this all from the beginning. Had he left the mules there for a bait?

"Mule thieves—murderers—outlaws—our official member's authority is to be judicial and executive, and he's to hang them all," he went on. "Our business is to supply the physical force."

"But why can't the Portuguese send half a regiment?" I objected, and they all three laughed.

"The home Government won't stand for the expense," Montdidier answered. "Moving armed men costs money. Besides, they'd need new boots—new tents; and the contractors who have the job of feeding them in barracks would raise Cain."

"Besides," said Oakes, there's a strongly defined hope in the air that we may get the worst of the deal. The du Maurier gang's activities cover up a multitude of official sins."

"And my particular share in the proceedings is what?" I asked.

"What you offered," said Montdidier.

"We've called your bluff," said Yerkes.

"You mean I'm to scuff du Maurier on his hilltop, single-handed?"

"No," said Montdidier. "It's not quite as bad as that. You're to go back and ask that chief for our mules. If they're gone, as we expect, send word up to Charles du Maurier, and ask him for them. If he doesn't answer, or refuses point blank, then go up and interview him in his lair, taking care to leave a good runner to bring us word.

"If you go alone, we don't think he'll kill you. It's a favorite trick of his to hold a prisoner to ransom. If he holds you to ransom, that gives us clear *casus belli* and will make his execution legal under Portuguese law. D'you see the point?"

"And if he shoots you, you're dead!" added Oakes.

"And we'll come and avenge you!" said America.

"But we don't believe he'll shoot," said Montdidier. "If you don't fancy the business, one of us will go. I assure you I'm not sending you on a mission I would not face myself."

"I believe that," I answered. "I'll go."

WE TALKED far into the night, but no amount of talking changed the plan much. Once or twice Oakes and Montdidier had qualms that the governor might find some way of canceling his bargain, once we had done our share. But they pulled out and read again the witnessed agreement, signed with the official seal, promising freehold title deeds as the price of our ridding the Libomba Hills of outlaws. It was plain enough—simple enough.

"It would take a Portuguese to get around it!" said Yerkes.

"Or a Hindu lawyer," added Montdidier.

"Or du Maurier himself!" laughed Oakes.

"Yes, what if we fail?" said I.

"I'll tell you what if we fail!" said Yerkes, placing his clenched fist on the table. "We all go down together if we fail! Well none of us quit until we're each one done for. We'll not leave you scuppered."

"He understands that of course," said Montdidier, and then, on Montdidier's motion, we all went up to bed.

Next day, directly after breakfast, they sent me off, it being agreed that much the wisest course would be to give the enemy no time for preparation. Probably the du Mauriers had heard already through spies of our arrival in Lourenço Marques—or would hear within a day.

"Let's keep on the ball!" said Montdidier.

I did not see our Portuguese official member. He had not yet joined. They three stood and waved me farewells from the quay, having seen to it that I went off well provided, and as we steamed away under the lee of the long, sandy island that almost corks the neck of Delagoa Bay, they were the last three objects that I saw. They surely did look insignificant.

I was the only white passenger on that trip, although there were about two hundred natives on the lower deck, and, with nobody to talk to, and only the mysterious low-lying coast for view, the sheer absurdity of what we four were attempting forced itself on me, until I chuckled and was miserable in turns.

Rotten the Portuguese royal Government might be. Weak it might be. Stupid, inefficient, sordid, out-of-date, absurd it no doubt was. But it was the organized machine of a number of million people, and likely to prove more potent against outlaws than four foreigners could be. Alone, pacing the upper deck of that unclean tug I felt like a fool rushing in where armed authority had feared to tread.

I believe I would have reconsidered my decision, if I could have had the chance, at almost any time before the tug reached Chai Chai.

But as we wound and doubled on our track along the Limpopo's inconvenient course, Chai

Chai hove at last in sight with its painted iron roofs, and acrid smell of barreled so-called wine, the sense of being afoot on high adventure came gradually back, and my three servants, looking up at me from the lower deck, divined enough of my rising spirits to grin and be noisy.

Chai Chai had no charms to hold any one but a money-grubber—and he not careful of the method. I had hired six porters to carry my tent and food, and was up and away from the place within an hour, wishful for one of Montdidier's mules; for on that steamy, smelly low veld there is none of the joy of setting foot to earth that walking on the high veld brings.

Knowledge that the only inducement my porters had for carrying my loads was a barrel of "wine" waiting for them in a Chai Chai factory, helped fire me with a fine self-righteous zeal, that, say what you like, has saved the day for many an adventurer. It was pay-day for the local labor gangs. In sixes, eights, and tens they were clubbing to buy barrels of the fiery filth distilled in Portugal, and colored to resemble grape-juice. A barrel bought, they would tie it between poles and scamper off home with it; and that gang would not return to work until the stuff was finished, the drunk complete, and a burning new desire begun.

The men I got had been fined their whole month's pay for some real or imaginary fault, and jumped at a chance to avoid the next month's slavery and yet get drink. They would not listen to money offers. It was a case of *vino tinto* or no porters; so I had to leave their pay behind in the shape of an order for a full barrel to be surrendered to them only against a letter from me given at the journey's end.

Having made that trip before with Oakes, I had the distances in mind and could make fast going. I cut two days from the schedule, by starting early and continuing late, and though the porters suffered they did it eagerly for sake of the drunk in store, that every stride brought nearer.

We reached the kraal where Monty had sent the mules to be cared for at about half-past five one evening; and although natives loathe to travel at night-time, partly from fear of lions, partly from superstition, and also because of a theory that the night air makes them sick, my porters demanded their order for the barrel and were off like the wind at once.

That left me with my own three men and an appalling sense of helplessness—dependent on the good faith of a Shangan cook whom Monty had assigned as my interpreter. But Monty knows niggers as some men can judge tea, tobacco, horses, wine. That hideous black boy, with three toes missing from his right foot, and nostrils bigger than his eyes, held himself so far superior to any Ronga chief that insolence and undisguised enmity made no impression on him.

Shangans are descended from an *impi* of Chaka's beaten in battle, that did not dare go home; and to be a Zulu among South African natives is like being a tiger in the jungle. One simply is not aware of the claims of other natives to be anything but subordinate.

I sent for the chief, and he came to me, swaggering and smelly in his leopard-skin kaross, with half the kraal behind him to see me rebuked. My cook asked for milk—as civilly as any Shangan can compel himself to speak to any Ronga. There was no milk. A chicken. There were no chickens—although we could hear them clucking in a hut close by. Eggs. There were no eggs. No mention was made of mules yet.

"Sixpence"—that was the Shangan boy's name—his real one was unpronounceable, with three different clicks in it, and two vowels that are not written—carefully removed the rifle Monty had lent me from its japanned steel case, handed it to me, shook my pocket to make sure that I had cartridges, faced the chief again and—without anger—almost impersonally one might say—knocked him down. He had served British soldiers somewhere at some time, for the blow was straight from the shoulder with his weight behind it.

I expected instant reprisals, but I did not know in those days the extent of the low-veld respect for Zulu blood. The chief got up again, and a chicken was produced at once. Then a dozen eggs—all bad ones. Sixpence pelted him with the eggs, and then we permitted ourselves to be supplied with camping ground inside the kraal. It was not until our tents were pitched—a great, big, comfortable thing for me, and a tiny, narrow, single-topped affair for all three boys and kitchen, that I broached the subject of the mules.

The chief promptly denied all knowledge of the mules—said there never had been any; and if there had been, how should he know whose mules they were. He accused me of seeking to plant trouble on him—denied that he ever made a habit of accepting mules even as a gift, let alone in charge for anybody else.

He offered to let me search his kraal, and find mules if I could. How many mules was I looking for? Whose mules? Mine? If they were not mine, why should I look for them at all? Finally he turned his back on me, and went to his own great gloomy hut, to sulk and think up new evasions.

So, having eaten supper, I sent Sixpence after him, and in the pitchy blackness of African night, squatted by the little fire before my tent, he grew more communicative. It was as if the dusk had not been dark enough to hide his fear. He was not so afraid to tell the truth, now that a little shadowy circle about my fire seemed all there was left of the universe.

"Yaaow!" said Sixpence, translating. "He, the chief, say Charrlee come, an' him take mules."

"On whose authority?" I asked.

"He, the chief, say Charrlee big boss heah, not needing ask. He take. He saying give me. Who refuse?"

"Where are the mules now?" I demanded.

"He, the chief, say big boss Charrlee take them mules up along his place. You want to know where mules are now, you better ask Charrlee. Chief, he say no longer his affair."

"Are you afraid to go with a message to Charles du Maurier's place, Sixpence?" I asked.

"Yes!" he answered promptly. "Ja, boss!"

I sent the chief away, and invited Sixpence to tell me all he knew about du Maurier, but went to sleep at last scarcely any wiser. I gathered that du Maurier would shoot, knife, strangle or burn whomsoever, and whensoever he pleased; but I had guessed that much already. The only new discovery was that so far as native assistance was concerned when it came to tackling the dragon in his lair, I might as well look for St. George himself on horseback in shining armor.

MY THREE boys made no secret of their intentions. Sixpence cooked breakfast for me, and they all three sat and watched me eat it as if that were the last chance they expected to have of seeing that particular spectacle. Then Sixpence asked me whether I would take the rifle with me; and he looked visibly relieved when I said "No."

But I had thought that point out thoroughly in bed before dawn, and saw no reason to alter the decision, arguing that even the coldest-blooded ruffian would be less likely to fire on an unarmed man. I told Sixpence, if he should have need to bolt back to Montdidier with a message, to take the rifle with him.

Then I started, the three boys following me at a very discreet distance, and in less than thirty minutes I was standing on one of the parallelograms beneath which Monty and Oakes were so sure lay the wealth of Croesus. I noticed there was a new shaft started. Then I saw that it was being worked, for a shovelful of dirt came flying over the edge.

I looked for Sixpence, to whistle him up and send him investigating, but he and the other two had vanished like yesterday. A minute later a nigger crawled out of the new hole—then another one—and then another. Then came Charles du Maurier himself, rifle in hand, giving the impression of having drunk too much overnight.

He was an awful-looking brute—thick-necked, round-headed—heavy of build, and swart, with a cold blue eye that seemed to know nothing of mercy. But he seemed to know no fear, either, and he did not hesitate before walking toward me. Nor did he trouble to threaten me with his rifle, but carried it slung over his right shoulder.

"Saow!" he snarled, grinning with what he imagined was good humor. "Here's my young friend that was braoke a while agao in Lourenço Marques. Well, I'm bloody well ——! So you've deserted the Montdidier aoutfit, have you, an' decided to come to me after all? Eh? Know which side your bread an butter's jammed on, don't yer, after all? So you've come to join me, eh?"

"I've come to ask you for those mules," I answered, dangerously close to anger.

The most revolting thing about the brute was his insolent assumption that any one with manhood left in him could think of choosing his camp in preference to that of Montdidier and Oakes.

"Mules?" he said. "What mules?"

"Lord Montdidier's mules," said I.

"Haow do you know where the mules are?" he demanded.

"Never mind how I know," I said. "I know."

"You think they're up at my place, eh?"

"I know it," said I.

"—— of a lot you know, don't you!"

I could see he was turning over in his methodically vicious mind the pros and cons of an unexpected situation. He had yellow mud from the digging on his knees and boots—mud on his hands—mud even on his face, and it heightened, if anything, the suggestion of indifference to other human life. It was as if he had come from burying a victim—supposing that such a cynic ever took that trouble.

"You think these claims are Montdidier's, don't you? Well, they ain't, they're mine! I own this country! I'm king o' these hills and the low veld under them! There's gaold here, and it's all mine! Say, who the —— are you anyway, to come here and dictate to me?"

The last thing I wanted was to be shot out of hand, and though the temptation to strike him, or to give him a peppery answer was almost overwhelming, I contrived to keep calm. My business was to give my party *casus belli.* There was no more need for me to die than for the bullock that is tied under a tree at night to bait a lion; nor yet necessarily any greater risk.

"I'm Lord Montdidier's friend," I said, "charged by him to recover his mules. And keep watch on his claims," I added as an afterthought.

The new, cold light in du Maurier's eye betrayed that he had seen the right plan. He no longer hesitated for a second, and he lied as instantly and calmly as another man would breathe.

"Oh, all right, then," he answered. "The claims are mine. I'll sell at my price—reasonable. You tell Lord Montdidier that! But mules—who's crazy enough to think, by ——, that I'd steal mules? What should I want with mules? I've plenty of my own. You think his mules are up at my place? Well, you're wrong. But don't take my word for it. Come along up and I'll show you."

"Very well," I said, "I'd like to see your roost."

He leered at me with an expression that would have made a fox's seem guileless by comparison. The men who act like brutes unconsciously wear brutal masks—I have marked that a hundred times. His face was heavy, round, and dark, yet during the days that followed some swift, slight change made it suggest to me the features of at least a dozen different animals.

"Go ahead!" he said, shouldering his rifle.

"No," said I. "Do you remember telling me on Kilo One in Lourenço Marques that when one man has a rifle the other should walk behind him?"

He laughed—and looked like a hyena.

"I see you've a memory. You and I'll get on all right," he grinned. "Can you shoot a bird with a pistol? Let's see you shoot that weaver bird—see—that one—quick! Shoot him before he's gone."

"I've no pistol," I answered, and he laughed again.

"Which are you—too innocent to walk alone," he asked, "or just rash?"

"I'm looking for mules, not murder," I answered, starting to walk behind him, and praying with all the concentrated fervor I could summon that Sixpence might have me in view from some hiding-place, and might be faithful and swift.

I knew there was a way overland to Lourenço Marques, and supposed he would take it; but I knew, too, that it went through swamps and down along the Nkomati River, and what thousand obstacles might lie in the way to delay or prevent him I could only guess. Knowing something of the swamps, imagination was not comforting.

We climbed up the face of the cliff by a goat track that would have kept goats in splendid exercise. There was a very steep, winding wagon road that we crossed and crossed again, but du Maurier despised it. Aboard ship I had been able to run aloft as actively as any member of the crew, and English school and college training produces men of rather sound wind, able to use both hands and feet; yet that low-living, middle-aged ruffian went up the cliff so fast, jumping and striding from foothold to ledge without ever troubling to reach a hand out to recover his balance, that he distanced me by more than a minute. At the top I was blowing, whereas he stood breathing calmly, smiling at me with a sort of cold amusement.

"How d'you like the look o' my nest?" he asked, almost before I had time to look about me.

The path had led over the edge of a great rock wall, but the wagon road entered a shallow depression at the very apex of the hill by a gate built of squared stone and heavy timber. The whole fort—for such it was—was about two acres in extent and by standing on the surrounding rim one could see to the horizon on both sides, and everything between. At one point I could see the Limpopo River, where it snaked toward us through the heat-haze in one of its long, hairpin bends.

In the center of the cup was du Maurier's own house, a square concern of timber and corrugated iron, with a pole on top supporting a lookout platform. Behind it, in a more or less straight line, was a row of sheds—stores—stables—three wagons, carefully oiled and painted—and a stack of hay. In front, in a spaced-out semi-circle there were fourteen thatch-roofed huts, whose purpose I guessed from rumor, but did not actually know as yet.

There were additional buildings here and there around the inner rim of the depression, the roof of one of which we had just been able to see from below; and a very peculiar wooden post, whose purpose I did not suspect, was planted firmly in the ground about twenty feet in front of the house veranda. The ground all about it was trampled flat.

"IT LOOKS like a comfortable place," said I.

"You bet it's comfortable! You better hope it's comfortable!" he snarled, grinning, and slapping his rifle butt. "You see that shed? That's where Lord Montdidier's mules are. You see that other shed—the stone one without a window? That's where you'll stay on quarter rations if you don't behave! Now you're here, you're here until your friends redeem you! If they don't redeem you—"

He paused, to enjoy my discomfort.

"If they don't redeem me, as you call it, what then?" I asked, deadly curious.

"D'you remember my telling you that time we met on Kilo One in Lourenço Marques about the way of recruiting white men to boss the slave-gangs in Angola? They get some from the jails—sneak 'em by night aboard coasting steamers. But they get some from me. Many a white man I've sent in a boat down the Nkomati River to be thrown aboard a coaster in Delagoa Bay. I get a good price. Your friends 'ud better redeem you quick."

I was soon to learn what the post was for, with the dry earth trampled all about it. He bade me follow to his veranda, and sit beside him in a canvas steamer chair. For a while he smoked in silence, watching the black women and colored children who sunned themselves and were more or less busy about the huts. Then several natives entered the arena through the wagon gate and came toward us with no apparent eagerness. They lined up, seven of them, in front of the veranda, the whites of their eyes showing as they looked anywhere but at du Maurier.

"Well?" he snarled at last. "Where are they? Where are the three niggers who came with this white man?" And since none of them answered he repeated the question savagely in Chironga.

They began an explanation, but he cut them short with an oath.

"Yaow, you swine! You've let 'em get away from you, that's what! I'll teach you! Fetch that sjambok out! Quick, now! No argument!"

He whistled an enormous Zulu from one of the huts, and without as much as asking for instructions the Zulu seized the nearest trembling wretch by the arm, dragged him to the pole, and lashed him there by both hands in such a way that he could dance about the pole but could not fall. Then he flogged him until the blood ran down back, flanks, and legs, using a hippo-hide sjambok more than a yard long.

"Stop!" ordered du Maurier, when the poor wretch fainted. "No use flogging 'em," he said to me, "when the fools can't feel it. "Now the next one!" he ordered.

So the first victim was unleashed and dragged aside, and one by one the others took their torture, until each fainted and du Maurier gave the word *"Longueza"*—that'll do.

When the last one lay unconscious on the trampled earth he filled his pipe leisurely and watched native women come from the huts and drag the victims all away.

"My wives," he said, with an air of being communicative and good-natured. "Black wives for me, my boy! They do as they're told, and you can have as many of 'em as you're minded. Speaking of flogging, though—I don't believe in flogging a white man, not if there's any other way, but the Portuguese—my word, the Portuguese! If your friends don't come and ransom you, and you get sold to the Portuguese for their West Coast plantations, you'll know what flogging means. What you've just seen my niggers get'll be child's play to what the Portuguese'll serve out to you."

I made no comment, and tried not to seem gloomy, but the thought was borne in on me with galling persistence that I had ventured into this trap on no better guarantee than a few weeks' acquaintance with two Englishmen, and a few days' acquaintance with an American.

However brave and honorable these new friends of mine might be, it seemed to me in that hour that I had been every particular species of fool to trust them so implicitly, and depend so entirely on their ability to win where a Government had failed. I think du Maurier divined part at least of my feelings, for he laughed to himself and seemed to enjoy life thoroughly.

We ate stew cooked for us by his wives, and then, while we sat again on the veranda, there was a new diversion. A native entered through the wagon gate, whom I recognized as having been the cabin boy of the Limpopo River steamer. He carried a letter addressed very plainly to me, but offered it to du Maurier, who broke the seal without a second's hesitation. He read it first to himself, and then, grinning, aloud to me.

"From Lord Montdidier," he said. "He's crazy. First the —— fool supposes the captain o' that steamer isn't my stool-pigeon. Then he supposes I'm alone without allies. Hear what he says:

" 'We shall leave here on the fourteenth day from to-day—' that means he'll start in about nine days from now, don't it?—'and in case you've had any trouble with that man du Maurier about the mules we'll take the precaution of bringing with us a Portuguese official, who can settle up about our claims at the same time. Have had a long talk with several prominent officials here, who all assure me there will be no trouble with du Maurier, and no need for offensive tactics. But, in case he should decide to defy us, the Portuguese member of our party, and perhaps a couple of police, and ourselves will be sufficient to bring him to his senses. Meanwhile, please watch the claims, and see that nobody pulls our pegs up.—Montdidier.

" 'P.S.—In order to be sure of getting the upper hand of du Maurier, we have determined to take him by surprise, and have exacted a pledge from the steamer company not to disclose to any one the date of our intended return to Chai Chai. So you would better burn this letter as soon as you have read it.'

"Yah-hah-hah-hah!" du Maurier yelled, shaking the letter up and down. "There's a —— fool for you. There's an intelligent English lord. That's tactics, them are. This lord o' yours is a strategian, by ——. Nine days, eh? Tonight if I summoned 'em—eleven of my brothers and five cousins 'ud be in the kraal o' mine ready to defend it against any one. I'd have 'em here now in advance o' time if they weren't such untamed devils o' hell. I've got my wives to think of. Never fear, I'll have 'em here in lots o' time for Mister Lord Montdidier and his one or two police. You just hope he brings money with him when he comes—else it's West Coast for you."

He was in splendid humor, increased by my obvious discouragement; for I could not for the life of me see any point to Montdidier's letter. It did occur to me several times that it might be a ruse to throw du Maurier off his guard, but the point was drawn from that hope by reflection that the steamer captain would certainly warn du Maurier in advance of any move Montdidier could make, and I walked about his kraal beside the scoundrel, watching and listening to his management, with a feeling that suicide would be the only tolerable outcome.

At night he sat up, drinking, and I got new insight into his psychology. There were two rooms to his frame house, separated only by a curtain on a rod, and a strong man-could have kicked his way through any of the sides without much trouble; but he showed me a trestle bed to which I might retire whenever I saw fit, and told off four strong natives to keep watch all night beside me, making escape unimaginable, for the threat he made of flaying them alive if they let me get away was too sure of fulfilment to be risked.

I lay on the bed for a time, but could not lie still, so got up again, and sat in a Windsor chair across the table from him. He had a small-bore rifle across his knees that I supposed was intended to awe me, until he disillusioned me by showing the big Colt revolver he kept in his pocket on my account.

"I always have a little sport here, nights," he said with a grin. "Sportsman, that's what I am. Can't live without sport—have to have some every day to keep my hand and eye in."

There were two lamps—smoky kerosene affairs, one on the table between us, and one hung on the wall in a metal bracket. Otherwise I would have doused the light and had a try to strangle him. The shadows danced and shifted as the lamp-flames flickered in the draft, and any more unlikely spot for rifle-shooting could not have been imagined. Yet he kept the rifle, loaded, over his knees in readiness, with a handful of cartridges loose on the table at his side. And presently, as we ceased talking and all grew quiet, the manner of his evening sport was shown me.

"THERE GOES one!" he whispered, and the rifle left his knees.

A piece of three-by-four ran all around the inside of the house at about eighteen inches from the top. The lights being lower, the three-by-four threw a shadow upward, and between it and the next timber where wall and roof met was pitchy darkness. His eyes were on that, but I saw nothing.

"Don't you see him?" he asked.

As I did not answer, he fired, and a great black rat fell with a thud to the floor.

"Bring it here," he ordered, and one of the boys told off to watch me carried it to him by the tail.

"Ya-ha-ha-ha!" he yelled in a sort of bestial frenzy. "There's a great black swine for you. There's a whale of a rat. Shot him plop through the head, too—his eyes. Did you see his eyes? His beady little black eyes, squinting down at us? Yah-hah! He thought I didn't see him. Did I see him? Eh? Look out, there's another one."

For hours he shot rats, gloating over each one as a nigger held it up by the tail for inspection, and he certainly made most remarkable shooting. Nor did he seem to tire of the amusement. When the cartridges were used up he went and produced more from an old trunk.

"No gentleman should grudge expense when it comes to sport," he assured me. Having a good time, ain't we, eh? Don't you consider I treat a prisoner pretty decent, amusing him like this, instead of shutting him in a dark hole?"

I assured him his kindness was astonishing.

"But mark you," he snarled, in one of his lightning changes of manner, crashing his clenched fist down on the table until the lamp nearly danced itself out. "Play any dog's tricks on me and I'll treat you like a dog. I'm kind, I am—kind an' considerate; but I'm no man's fool. You beware."

He lay down to sleep at last with his pistol in his right hand, and the little rifle locked away. So I lay down too, for the four natives came and sat so close beside me that the sensation of being watched grew intolerable. When I lay on the bed they were satisfied to squat two at each end of it and I could only hear their breathing, which was better.

At about two in the morning the lights gave out for lack of oil, and the smell of the smoldering wicks was added to the unforgettable kraal smell and the individual personal aroma of my guards. Nevertheless, I am sure I slept, although lightly. Sure of the guards, and heavy from the gin he had drank in tumbler doses, du Maurier slept deeply.

It was dawn that awakened me—the first, cold, dim false-flickering of dawn; but something else that made the goose-flesh rise all up and down my skin. My guards were squatted still at either end of the bed, sleepy, but still faithfully watching me—seeing nothing but me—conscious of nothing but the need of pouncing on me if I tried to get away.

It was a face at the window that stopped my heart beating, and for a moment froze my veins. I could only see it dimly. It was stock still, and I thought I could distinguish a rifle-barrel held up beside it.

There were three windows. I looked at the second, moving nothing but my eyes. There was a face there too, and a rifle.

I looked at the third. There, too, was a face.

My eyes went back to window number one, that faced me as I lay; and as the shock wore off, and the false light strengthened, I saw that the face was no black man's. It was one I did not know—yellow, with a dark mustache and a suggestion of imperial.

"Du Maurier's brothers!" I muttered, and turned over face to the wall in disgust. So, in the fraction of a second that followed, I did not see all that took place.

There came a sudden crash on the door like an explosion, and it burst inward, splintered to bits. My four guards pounced on me and pinned me to the bed, using the blanket more effectually to smother my struggles. I heard du Maurier leap from bed like an avalanche, and the bark of his Colt revolver followed, twice in swift succession.

Through the one window I could see, as I struggled to free myself, the yellow face with the mustache and imperial still stared, almost motionless. I made a spasmodic effort that loosed my captors' hold, and before they could recover it saw du Maurier fire point-blank three times at the face—and miss.

"So much for Hollands by the tumblerful at midnight," thought I.

He only had one shot left, and he fired again. It seemed he hit that time, for the face disappeared. But whose face?

I saw du Maurier reach for cartridges, and wondered whether my turn would not come next. He would almost surely shoot me, I thought, rather than take the chance of losing me. But a voice that I already knew too well to mistake among a thousand—calm, suave, gentlemanly, without a trace of bravado or brag—put a sudden end to that climax, only to produce another one.

"Your game is played. You are covered from four sides. If you put your hands up you shall not be hung without trial."

MY GUARDS fell off me—wrenched off me, I discovered, and I sat up, to see Lord Montdidier with one foot on the splintered door, covering du Maurier with a rifle, and Yerkes the American grinning at me with my blanket in his hand. He had knocked my guards down, for they were sprawling on the floor in four directions.

"Not hurt, I hope?" Montdidier asked, sparing a glance in my direction.

"Look out, Monty, you —— fool!" a voice shouted through the window—another voice I knew well. "That nigger America knocked down last is crawling to get you by the leg. Stand aside and give me a shot at him."

But Yerkes ran forward instead, and kicked the Kaffir's wind out, merciful after a swift fashion of his own.

"How would you like to go and tie that rascal's hands behind him?" Montdidier asked.

So I hunted a rope; and sea-training stood me in good stead, for in two minutes I had du Maurier so trussed that he was helpless. Then a voice called through the doorway.

"You-ah have eem, eh? It ees, ah, safe to enter now?"

"Yes, come along in, Senhor Cadji."

Montdidier, with his eye still on du Maurier, sat down, and through the doorway together with the first yellow rays of real morning Oakes and a Portuguese official entered side by side.

"Didums, you've got no luck." Oakes nodded to me, looked swiftly about him, and sat down too. "If that brute had only refused to surrender we could have shot him and had done with the job. Ough! Who wants to hang him?"

"Oh, as for that," said Senhor Cadji, "the law will run its course in regular manner. But eet will be wise to hasten affairs. This man has brothers—cousins—nephews—uncles—what not. They will come."

"Let's try him, then, and get the job done," growled Oakes.

"Not until after breakfast," said Montdidier; and nobody found fault with that.

He had scarcely said it when Sixpence entered, with a huge and hideous grin for me, and began to spread a white cloth on the only table.

"But wasn't somebody shot?" I asked. "A man with a mustache? Who was at that window?"

"I," said Yerkes.

"But I saw a man with a mustache and imperial shot in the face and collapse."

They all laughed.

"I saw it," said I.

"Go and look," said Montdidier, and I went outside.

In another moment I was laughing too.

By each of the windows was a gourd, stuck on a short stick, and decorated with the crudely moulded features of a man. The first one I picked up had no less than four great holes through it, where du Maurier's soft-nosed expanding bullets had torn their way through.

"There'd have been a fine fat chance of my eating breakfast this morning if I'd pushed my head above that window-sill instead of the pumpkin, eh?" said Yerkes, looking through the window. "It was Monty's idea."

"So you're on good enough terms to be calling him that?" I asked, with a distinct twinge of jealousy.

"Yes," he said, "Monty and I are friends."

Then he came through the door and joined me.

"Gee!" he said, drawing me out of earshot of the house. "I'd hate to horn in again and offer objections. That man Monty's a prince, and I believe he means to hang the prisoner. He'll be right. It's nothing but sentiment that makes me loathe doing it—sickly sentiment. Still—I hate it."

"How about the Portuguese official, Senhor Cadji?" I asked; but he shook his head.

"He'll take the credit for anything we do—that is all."

Montdidier came striding out.

"Did you get my letter?" he asked; and I told him.

"How did you come so soon on the heels of it, and so secretly?" said I.

"The navy man. He couldn't commit his Government or lend us any men. But he sent us up-river in his launch, with a bosun who showed us a short cut to this place that avoided Chai Chai. That Portuguese navy man is like most others of his calling—a good sportsman."

"Didums!" said Oakes, coming out after us, "I

think you're a —— fool to leave that brute in charge of the Portuguee."

"Rot!" said Montdidier. "Come with us and look the place over before breakfast."

"Come and look at his wives," said I. "And the men he thrashed yesterday; and our mules. The sight of the men he thrashed may give us more stomach for hanging him."

Having followed du Maurier all about the place the day before, I made a good guide, and showed them as much in twenty minutes as they could have discovered without me in two hours. Suddenly, as we went for a second look at the mules, Oakes nudged Montdidier and shouted:

"There. What did I say? Look at that, now. That Portugoose of ours has let the blackguard go."

The "Portugoose" was sitting contemplative on the threshold, studiously oblivious. With his arms still lashed behind him—for I had done that job of work Bristol fashion—du Maurier sprang from the window as we looked up, and made at top speed for the notch in the rim of the kraal where the goat path led over to the plain below, Sixpence and all our other boys in noisy, albeit cautious pursuit.

"Well, anyway, we'll have to shoot him now," said Oakes, and we all made after him as fast as we could run.

"Don't shoot yet," I panted, for I knew that steep path he had headed for.

"Why not?" demanded Oakes.

"Wait and see," said I.

"There'll be lots of time," said Yerkes.

He gained the rim thirty seconds ahead of us, and by the time they three had thrown themselves down to get a bead on him, and I had sprung on a rock to get a better view, he was already fifty feet on the way down, leaping from ledge to ledge, from precarious foothold to monkey-grip.

"Don't shoot yet," said I, for I foresaw the outcome.

Once, when he crossed the wagon track he made as if to follow that, and then we should have been obliged to shoot; but he looked up, saw the three rifles pointed at him, and chose the swifter, more dangerous way, leaping—leaping—gaining momentum—at each spring less able to check himself—unable, without the use of arms, to regain balance when he overshot the mark—and at last out of all control, flying downward like something flung from the summit.

He hit a rock with one foot, kicked himself clear of it, began to rotate face-forward like a wheel, and presently was brainless, beaten to a pulp, crushed, dead and done for—still rotating—still hurtling downward. We heard the sickening thud as his carcass brought up at last at the foot of the cliff.

Then a wail went up—a horrible, shrill wail. Unseen by us, his women had come and had watched his fall, from the rim to either hand of where we stood. They cried as if the hero of a thousand splendid deeds had met an unworthy end, beating their breasts and shaking themselves in wordless misery, their little brown-and-yellow brats clinging to them and adding flat cries to the sharp inharmony. And that noise brought the Portugoose.

"He is dead?" said he. "He is already dead? No need of any trial, or any hanging? That is good, then. So I go."

We all looked at him, all, I think, wondering what to say yet none in doubt what to do about it.

"You're the Government official in charge of this kraal," said Montdidier at last. "You're in charge of these women, for instance, and all this property. You stay."

"But the others will come," said Senhor Cadji, "hees brothers—hees cousins—hees nephews—very many."

"Exactly!" said Montdidier. "You'll stay to see the fun. Let's have breakfast—eh? What?" he said, turning to the rest of us.

"It seems I'm everlastingly horning in," said Yerkes, "but haven't we business with this man first?" He nodded in my direction.

"Right you are, America!" said Oakes. "Monty, you —— enigma, tell him. Me tell him? Oh, very well. Your proposal of yourself as a member of this party on shares like the rest of us has been seconded, voted on, and passed."

"My proposal?" I said. "I've never thought of it—let alone—"

"You proposed yourself," said Yerkes, "by volunteering to come up here alone. We did the rest. Now, who's hungry?"

"Oh, and by the way," said Lord Montdidier, striding along beside me, and handing his rifle to a boy, "I'd be awfully glad if you'd cut ceremony, and call me Monty or some such thing. Will you? Thanks. Come on you men, let's eat!"

JACKSON TACTICS

SOMEBODY SHOULD write a great book about breakfast. Not that it has not been attempted, but the opportunities have not been as much as skimmed. Consider Caesar and a hard-boiled egg—why, empires have been lost and won about a breakfast table; and an ear of old corn, roasted in camp-fire coals, to be washed down presently with unclean water, has outweighed—by the inspiration that it brought—many a Lucullan spread.

Supper is good, remarkably good, beneath the singing stars of a frosty high-veld night; but there is something about food at dawn that puts it in another category and goes right to the heart of any true adventurer.

I am thinking now particularly of the breakfast Lord Montdidier, Fred Oakes, Bill Yerkes, Cadji the Portuguese, and I ate in the dead murderer Charles du Maurier's nest in the Libomba Hills. The recent sight of the scoundrel with both hands lashed behind him, leaping and stumbling down a cliff-side until he missed his footing and was brained against the rocks, might be expected to have spoiled our appetite. Not so, however.

The rascal's black wives, and snuff-and-butter-colored young ones, stood on a rock parapet sixty or seventy yards away from us wailing for their dead tyrant, afraid to go down and care for the mangled corpse, but too ridden by memory of his tyranny to turn away. Their ululating howls sent the kites off in startled flight, and stirred the camp curs to emulation. But we ate on—all except Cadji. The Portuguese don't care for early breakfast, or so he said.

A hundred yards away from the women, in a corner behind a shed tucked under the rim of the nearly circular hollow-on-a-hill, that formed the dead robber's lair, some of his Kaffirs sat pounding skin-and-gourd drums, in broken cadences that rose to thunder and died again to a palpitating murmur. Obviously even to the tyro like myself that din was by way of neither mourning nor exultation. It was penetrating—business-like. It had a purpose. Compelling of attention though it was, however, it did not interfere with the thumping noise of women bruising their breasts in token of new widowhood.

"Somebody 'ud better stop that tom-toming," said Yerkes between mouthfuls. "That's their way of sending news."

"Oh, it is nothing—nothing," said Cadji, stroking his imperial and looking at us each in turn.

Montdidier glanced up at once and eyed him searchingly for about a second, but Senhor Cadji was not aware of that.

WE WERE eating at the dead du Maurier's table inside the mean, frame house almost in the exact center of the hollow, its roof about on a level with the camp's circumference—so that by standing on the roof a man could command the whole horizon. Our own clean, white linen had been spread on the unwashed boards, and our own boys served the meal; but the food was taken chiefly from the robber's stores, and it was good food.

Montdidier sat on my right, with a rifle leaning against his knees but with an air, nevertheless, of being in no hurry. Fred Oakes faced him, eating enormously, with the appetite that swift recovery from fever brings, uproarious between platefuls. He had taken a keen dislike to Cadji, and Fred's emotions are not surreptitious; in order to avoid him, the Portuguese sat so close to Yerkes as to make eating for the latter difficult. All the same, Yerkes contrived to demolish ears of corn after the series fashion, in which Americans can do so many wonderful things.

"Great stuff, corn!" he announced with his mouth full. "Only thing that reconciles me to East Africa. I was weaned on it! A man can march, fight, and be merry on corn!"

"We English get along better with wheat," said Montdidier; and I noticed Oakes getting ready a time-worn jest about Americans and corn and hogs and kaffirs.

But the Portuguese interrupted.

"My God, you gentlemen! Oh, my God! You sit here, you joke, you eat, and you discuss! You—what is the expression-you pass the time of day! And the time passes with nothing whatever done to guard against the terrible danger we are all in!"

"Eat, you fool!" Oakes advised him, pushing over a dish of corn. "Fill your belly, and crowd fear out!"

"Pah!" Cadji answered disgustedly. "Who could eat at such a time? Who but a person unaware—one uncomprehending, could as much as swallow? You do not understand! You do not appreciate! You have killed this Charles du Maurier—"

"Pardon me, *senhor,*" Montdidier interrupted, laying down his knife and fork.

We all stopped eating, for it was obvious Monty was going to lead from a strong hand.

"You are the official member of this party, representing your Government. Naturally I put the prisoner in your safe-keeping. You let him escape. So, technically as well as morally, you are answerable for his death. If you had kept him covered with your rifle, he would never have attempted a feat impossible with tied hands. If you had guarded him properly, tried him legally, and hanged him as in duty bound, your Government would have been responsible. As it is, you must accept the blame yourself."

"Oh, my God, *senhor!*" the Portuguese stuttered, his face taking on a shade of blue beneath the yellow. "You don't know what you say! To accuse me of that man's death is to place me at feud with all his fierce relations! I would rather face my Government any day!"

Yerkes burst into a yell of laughter, and Oakes spluttered with a mouth full, but Monty sat unmoved—perhaps a trace more suave—certainly not outwardly amused.

"I understand," he said, finishing his coffee. "I sympathize, and all that kind of thing. But you see, your—ah—Government—at its own price—placed you at our disposal until the completion of—ah—certain duties."

"*Senhor,*" said the Portuguese, "Charles du Maurier being dead, my concern is no longer in these hills. From up above here I can see your claims below this hill. You have staked them properly. I will sign the necessary paper and depart. There is no need for me to pace the boundaries. I go home!"

"Sorry to disagree with you," said Monty. "You've a tenth share, legally assigned to you, in consideration of services yet to be rendered."

"I will sell you back your share," said Cadji, and Oakes and Yerkes set up such a roar of laughter that Monty had to laugh too.

Derision at their own expense is something the Latin races are unable to suffer calmly, and Cadji's mustaches bristled, and his jaundiced eyes expanded until Monty frowned to the others to go slow. It was at Oakes the Portuguese glared most savagely, because Oakes had baited him mercilessly all through breakfast. But it was Yerkes who sprang the next surprise.

"You did not suspect me of knowing Portuguese, did you, Cadji? I learned it in Brazil. I understood when you told the dead man's boys to thump the news out on their drums!"

"You yellow hellion!" said Oakes, smiling pleasantly; and I felt as if a bomb had been exploded.

Monty, however, was calm enough.

"We can imagine," said Monty, "that those claims would not be worth much—to us—if the du Maurier family should come and catch us napping."

"We understand, my saffron sweetmeat," added Oakes, "that your Government would rather see the du Maurier family alive, and us dead, if it has to lose one or the other—"

"As happens to be the case," said Yerkes.

"Shut up, America, and let me talk!" Oakes rapped the table with impatient knuckles. "We know that the du Maurier gang can cover up official crimes, and produce more tribute money than any honestly owned and worked gold-claims. Any fool knows your game now is to leave us to the mercy of the du Maurier gang, and make new terms with them after they've scuppered us! Well—you yellow hellion—your game won't work!"

WITH A prodigious effort the Portuguese official calmed himself and rose from his chair. He had short legs, with the peculiar result that he stood scarcely any taller than he sat. His khaki suit, brownish eyes, and yellow skin were different shades of one hue; even the gold watch-chain dangling in a loop across his breast was part of one objectionable harmony, unrelieved except by dead-black hair, black mustache and little black imperial. From a short distance the wrinkles and freckles on his forehead gave the impression of eyebrows raised in disapproval, but in fact he had scarcely any eyebrows at all. A more disagreeable human it would be hard to imagine, and if it had not been that we four were normally good-tempered men at breakfast I think the explosion would have come sooner.

"You speak of my game!" he said with that savagely restrained utterance which goes with racial loathing. "As if I were a tom-fool, or a child! Game! That is all you English think of! Game! I will tell you how your game stands! This dead man du Maurier's sixteen male relations will come with a host of armed natives to avenge him! You have your four selves, and your unarmed servants! Me you have not got, for I go my way. You dare not restrain me! You dare not prevent my going, for I am of the Government!"

Then Monty did a thing that made us all stare. I would not have questioned him, for they had only that dawn raised me from salaried employment to a partnership in their venture, and I was not yet used to the sensation. Yerkes, too, although a partner from the first, was diffident as yet, and cautious in disagreement. From Oakes, however, I looked for stormy protest. Yet for the moment Oakes kept still.

"I see you have the best of the argument, Senhor Cadji," said Monty. "Of course, we couldn't think of imposing restraint on a Government official."

"Senhor," said Cadji, "I should think not indeed!"

Oakes gasped. But Monty looked at Oakes lazily across the table, without as much as a wink or a smile or quivering eyelid, and that time the explosion died still-born.

"But, of course," Monty went on, looking at Cadji with a frank expression that would have disarmed the suspicion of a panther, "you being a Portuguese officer, and therefore presumably a gentleman—"

Senhor Cadji bowed impressively, not pacified indeed, but mollified.

"You wouldn't accept a share in this enterprise without returning value for it in some shape or another."

"There is nothing I can do for you! Nothing!" said the Portuguese, stiffening again at once. "Your position here is—"

"Pardon me," said Monty. "There is something you can do."

"I will listen," said Cadji stiffly. "But I warn you in advance that you delude yourself!"

"Very good of you, I'm sure," said Monty. "My idea is this: we four can hold this place for some time against half-breeds of the du Maurier stamp. They wouldn't dare come at night. By day we can hold off all comers."

"A flattering thought!" smirked Cadji.

"Since you're so anxious to go," continued Monty, "and Chai Chai is on your way to Lourenço Marques, we should appreciate your calling on the commandant at Chai Chai and telling him of our predicament. You might ask him to send troops to our assistance."

The frown left Cadji's face, and he nodded; more to himself than to us.

"I could do that for you," he said. "Perhaps the commandant would send some soldiers."

"In that case," said Monty, "we would consider your tenth share in our gold-claims paid for."

"Bosh!" exploded Oakes at last. "Why beg favors of him? I say, hold him here! Send a letter by runner to Chai Chai. The commandant wouldn't help us, but he'd have to rescue his Government's official! Kick him into a storehouse and turn the key on him!"

"Second the motion!" said Yerkes, leaning back until his chair swayed dangerously on two legs.

But Monty did not put the motion to a vote.

"You see, you fellows," he said, "our position is not dangerous. The du Maurier gang would never dare attack by night."

Oakes gasped.

"Why the devil not?" he demanded.

"Just when I should imagine they would come," said I.

"They're superstitious," said Monty, "and their native followers still more so. No—by night we're safe. By day we can defend ourselves. Let's let the *senhor* go."

"Monty," said Oakes, "I've seen you drunk on occasion, but I've never known you as bad as this. There's a deep well outside with a bucket and winch. Stick your head in cold water! Get your brain cool!"

But Monty merely smiled.

"Of course," said Yerkes judicially, "Montdidier's a member of the British House of Lords, and they're famous for wisdom! He's a cavalry officer, and the British army's simply notorious for strategy! I was never even in our militia, and don't claim it would have helped much if I had been. But I'm a judge of a blackguard when I see one, and I'd sooner trust a Mexican than this man Cadji. I'll make one to toss him over the cliff after Charles du Maurier, and take the consequences."

"Bravo, America!" roared Oakes, bringing his fist down on the table with a crash. "Monty, it's proposed and seconded that we take this Cadji by his four legs and toss him off the cliff! Put it to a vote!"

"Vetoed from the chair," said Monty, showing his strong teeth in a very friendly smile. One could never believe when Monty smiled that anything could go wrong in the universe. "Shall I ask for a vote of confidence?"

"No, you —— fool!" Oakes answered. "What's your veto for?"

"If it's a question of confidence," said Yerkes, "I'll be a —— fool too rather than stand out."

Monty looked my way.

"Lead on!" I said. "I'd rather get scoughed among friends than save my bacon and lose them."

"Very well," said Monty. "Our claims are the point. One way and another we've a large investment down there on the plain. These du Mauriers are an interlude."

"Interlude?" said Cadji, showing his yellow teeth. *"Senhors,* if they are an interlude, preserve me from a main theme."

"They shall not spoil our sleep," said Monty. "I shall turn in and snore when time to sleep comes. By day I admit there is need of alertness; but if you'll ask that Chai Chai commandant to hurry, that should solve the problem. You may go, Senhor Cadji, if it suits you."

"In other words," said Oakes, "get to —— out of here, and look sharp about it."

CADJI TURNED and faced Oakes, with an expression on his face of loathing, hate, and rage commingled. A Portuguese scoundrel detests the English with the same whole-hearted intensity with which a Portuguese gentleman admires them, and has an almost unique capacity for stirring reciprocal feelings.

"As for you," he hissed between set teeth, "it is well for you a nobleman is of your party. Yourself I would have shot as I would native. You are excr-r-r-uciating! This nobleman, however, obliterates you by his presence. I rejoice to know that when I turn my back I shall have seen your face for the last time.

"These others are Englishmen," he went on, turning to Yerkes. "Everybody knows that to be

English means to have no sense of proportion—no judgment of circumstances. Hypocrisy renders the English blind. The world is peppered over with the bones of Englishmen who did not know enough to run away. But you are American, and should have better sense. You should persuade them to run away at once, sir."

Yerkes had been rude to him too, so it was not likely he was moved by friendliness. He probably thought he detected a weak joint in our armor through which he could inject discouragement.

"Why don't you go with him, America?" jeered Oakes.

"Americans run after the English!" Yerkes answered, and we all laughed, except Cadji.

He sighed with a contemptuous shake of the head.

"I pity you, *senhors,*" he said. "God knows I pity your foolish mirth! You have the gold mania, that makes men deaf, blind, mad. I go to Chai Chai. I shall advise the commandant. In a week his troops may be here—possibly, if all goes well, in time to find such splinters of your bones as the jackals no longer care to lick. I shall spend a little money on masses for your souls. Enough! I go!"

He looked for his rifle, but could not see it anywhere. Monty proceeded to enlighten him.

"We shall keep that, *senhor.* If these du Mauriers are all you say, we'll need spare rifles. Traveling by day, and camping in native kraals, you'll be safe enough. You'll have the satisfaction of knowing too that your rifle is in the hands at last of a man who can shoot straight. Oakes shall have it for his second string."

"This is audacity!" said Cadji, rising to another peak of fury. "Does the English House of Lords condescend to larceny? You are a thief, my lord!"

"You've leave to go!" said Monty, his drawl gone, and his words more like a whiplash.

"Give me my rifle. Then I will too gladly go."

"Fred, if he isn't gone in exactly one minute, will you do the needful?" asked Monty.

Oakes jumped up, and the Portuguese backed away, snarling.

"Who can be sorry for the end of such people?" he sneered. "Who can truly pity you? I shall have masses said for your tormented soul, but—" with a huge shrug of the shoulders—"who can truly pity you?"

We heard him call his own eight porters, and Oakes and I went and watched him down the winding cart-road to the foot of the hill, lest he should try to corrupt our boys before leaving us.

"His sort believe in corruption first and in any event," said Monty, over his shoulder after us. "Better watch him out of sight!"

We watched until he became a little speck amid the hot blue haze on the plain, and vanished finally among the far-spaced thorn-trees, Oakes saying nothing, and I having nothing to say. It was Yerkes who came up behind us and broke the silent spell at last.

"You spoke just now of our House of Lords getting drunk on occasion," he began.

"Almost, you might say he never does," Oakes answered, "except now and then by way of punctuating history."

"Does he suffer from the sun?"

"Not he. Head's like a thatched roof. Even in India the sun couldn't do a thing to him."

"Have fits?"

"No."

"Erratic spells?"

"No," said Oakes, "he's like a compass needle. You can deflect him for a time by side issues, but he always returns to the point."

"Obsessions, then?"

"Only one, and I share it. He's after money enough to open his family seat in the Midlands and live there according to Hoyle. What's your worry?"

"He has asked me to tell you to search this camp for the dead man's favorite servant, and send him with a message to the whole bloodthirsty gang!"

"Um-m-m," said Oakes. "Did he tell you the message? The wording of it?"

"Yes. He's crazy! After eating crow to the extent of asking that Dago to carry our appeal for help to the commandant, what do you suppose? This messenger is to warn the du Mauriers of Cadji's movements!"

Oakes whistled.

"Where is Monty now?" he asked.

"Playing chess with himself on the back veranda."

"A good sign," said Oakes. "When he does that it means he sees the end, and is working out the middle part."

But that did not suit Yerkes.

"That's his message," he said. "I've delivered it.

I'm for an open forum myself, signs or no signs. Just now you yourself were up in the air and arguing with him."

But Oakes scarcely heard.

"Didn't he give you others anything to do?" he asked.

"Yes, but—"

"What?"

"Search for valuable stores—especially ammunition—everything except livestock—and bring it all to the house."

"Well? Why not do it?" snapped Oakes.

"Because—now get this, will you, and tell me whether he's crazy—after we've got everything into the house—especially ammunition, mind—we're to send another boy to the du Mauriers to tell them what we've done!"

"And he's playing chess by himself?" asked Oakes.

"Precisely."

"Good enough! The signs are right!"

"To —— with signs!" Yerkes answered. "I've a right to know what orders mean. So has this man. You bet blindly if you like!"

"Very well," said Oakes. "I always trust him when he plays chess. You two go and heckle him. See what you get!"

And he walked off with a rifle over his shoulder and a native boy behind him, reminding me, for no reason that I could tell, of *Robinson Crusoe* and *Man Friday.* A moment later I heard him questioning Charles du Maurier's natives in a mixture of Cape Dutch, pidgin English, Zulu, Chironga, and Portuguese, with a good-humored skill that would have wrung admiration from the builders of the Tower of Babel.

"Come on," said Yerkes to me. "Let's have this out. Monty's a good man, but I'm going back to know what his game is."

I went, wishing all the way I could think of good ground for refusing. The glamour of Monty's peculiar charm was over me, and his permission, only given that dawn, to address him as Monty, had rather gone to my head. It would have suited me just then to accept orders whatever the consequences; but I understood Yerkes had been first to propose that I be taken into partnership—an argument too subtle to resist.

WE FOUND Monty with his long legs stretched out and a little chessboard on his lap, so absorbed that he did not look up at our approach.

"Like that picture of King Whatsisname playing with a basketful of puppies," Yerkes whispered. "Remember it? *Le roi s'amuse.*"

Monty heard either footfall or whispering, looked up, and eyed each of us swiftly in turn.

"Quite interesting," he said. "Black to move next, and mate in two."

"I told Oakes what you said he is to do," Yerkes began; but Monty was studying the board again.

His bare throat and arms, polo shoulders, and general air of being more at home on horseback than afoot, made the intense interest in a chessboard seem incongruous. The combination should not have suggested effeminacy, or laziness, but to us at that moment I suppose it did.

"Did you?" he said with both eyes on his game. "That's scarcely strange, seeing I asked you to."

"Thought you might like to tell us two something of your plan," Yerkes suggested.

"Hadn't thought of it," he said, still busy with the chess-board.

"We have," said Yerkes.

"Thought what?" asked Monty, still not looking up.

"We ought to be told. We've a right to know."

Bill Yerkes shut his mouth up tight, uncomfortable but resolute. Monty looked up again. The chess-board was one of those folding things with a patent catch, that will hold the pieces in position when a trigger is pressed. He closed up the board, set it on the floor between his feet, and met our eyes.

"Have you a plan of your own to meet the situation?" he asked. I did not detect a trace of rancor or resentment.

"No," said Yerkes. "We want to know yours."

"What for?" he asked. "To criticize it?"

"No," said Yerkes.

"What for then?"

"As a matter of principle."

Yerkes leaned his back against a veranda post in an attitude that said better than words—

"Here's where you and I have this out."

"As a matter of principle," said Monty, "I refuse."

"House of Lords stuff," Yerkes answered.

He smiled, but his eyes were hard. "It doesn't get by me. I like you right well. You're a good leader, but—"

"But what?" demanded Monty.

"We're not hired men."

Monty got up, and offered Yerkes the chair.

"Would you rather lead?" he asked.

"Certainly not!" Yerkes answered.

"I'll resign at once in your favor if you can get the other two to support you," Monty assured him.

"I wouldn't think of suggesting it," said Yerkes, beginning to get rather red behind the ears. "What I'm after is explanation."

"And if you'll take my place as leader, then I'll give it," answered Monty.

"I've not questioned your leadership," said Yerkes.

"You've perfect right to at any time," Monty told him calmly. "But as long as you concede me the right to give them, you must obey orders! I'm leader by election. If the other two will vote for you instead of me, I'll make the vote unanimous."

"Aren't you rather a stickler for your pound of flesh?" Yerkes asked; and Monty, who very rarely laughed aloud, surprised us both by squealing with amusement.

"Speaking of flesh," he said, "if you delay until the sun grows much hotter, my dear chap, you'll lose weight! I imagine there's a lot of stuff that'll need shepherding across the compound. If you don't watch every stick of it the natives 'll steal it all."

"Then I'm to consider myself snubbed?" said Yerkes, grinning with compounded manliness and discontent.

"My dear chap," said Monty with his friendliest smile, "when I feel called on to snub a man he's never in doubt of it. I've refused your request, that's all. Now is it quite clear what I want you both to do?"

"I begin to savvy how kings and lords and similar folk have stayed in the saddle so long!" said Yerkes, walking away beside me.

We stopped a short way off and looked back. There sat Monty, oblivious again of his surroundings, with the chess-board on his knees, and a look on his face that could not by the wildest stretch of imagination be supposed to express resentment, or even victory. The incident had passed utterly out of mind.

"Look at him, will you!" Yerkes murmured, with a sort of grudging, genuine admiration. "That's not put on for effect. That's natural. He'll die in his boots with the same unaffected air of having his own way. You couldn't convert him; he's been educated for a thousand years. You couldn't bribe him. I'd hate the job of trying to teach him. Are the House of Lords all like him?"

"Not by a mile!" said I.

"If they were," said Yerkes with a dry laugh, "autocracy would live forever. Too efficient to dispense with! I'd never have believed I'd let a lord put it all over me. The fact that he is one made me more determined to have it out with him. Gosh! Who'd have thought it? I come away licked, and liking him better! All the same it looks like crazy stuff to me, telling the du Mauriers first of Cadji's movements, and then of what we're doing with the stores. What d'you make of it?"

"Nothing," said I. "Neither head, nor tail, nor middle part—nothing!"

"And how about that boast that the du Maurier gang daren't attack at night? Put yourself in their place. If you had the advantage of numbers and knowledge of the ground, and meant to attack at all, wouldn't you prefer night?"

"Seems so to me," said I.

"I'll tell you one sure thing," said Yerkes. "Monty 'll get less sleep tonight than he supposes! Boss he may be—captain-general—nabob—lord high chancellor, or whatever he cares to call himself. Tonight he stays awake! He keeps a bright lookout, or I wasn't born across the water. But what's that awful noise?"

"Oakes," said I.

"In pain?"

"No," I said. "He's usually silent when it hurts him. He's feeling jolly. He's playing and singing songs."

WE ROUNDED the corner of the longest store-shed, and came face to face with Fred seated on an empty barrel. He must have found Charles du Maurier's favorite servant and dispatched him on the errand, for he had started on our part of the morning's work and had it already under way. I knew him already well enough to be quite sure he would not turn aside or pause until his own job was disposed of.

The three doors of the shed were open wide, and he had set every native he could find to dragging out the sacks of corn and stacking them in readiness to carry across the compound. To encourage them he was making what he calls music, with the aid of the strident, all-too-portable contraption that he has toted with him up and down the length of suffering continents—singing a song in English; that I suppose the blackface minstrels charmed him with when he was a boy in knickerbockers on the sands at Deal.

"Folks say I should be happy,
Oh, the happiest of men;
I am the happy father of
A family of ten.
And they all take after me!
They all take after me!
My peculiaritee seems to run in the familee!
They all take whisky in their tea;
They'd all of 'em rather die than work,
And they all take after me"

"Well, my mutineers?" he grinned, ceasing from his song for lack of breath. "Have you brought the skipper to his senses? In the light of your righteous zeal for explanations does he see light? Or is his belly like a rock, with information frozen in its midst? Was he wax or adamant?"

He struck a wild chord on his infernal instrument and, having some breath to spare again, and natives ayearn for noise to give them courage, proceeded to improvise:

"Puff! Puff! Two men in a huff!
Went to the skipper to grouse at the duff!
Said it was smelly and bad for your belly.
Asked him for plenty of apricot jelly
Instead of that —— indigestible stuff!
The grub wasn't wholesome or tasty enough,
And they told him so pat! But the skipper was gruff!
Gruff, and ungracious, and ugly, and rough!

——! ——! Quicker than ——!
They cut their cackle and ran pell mell!
Their knees were aquiver, their skins all ashiver,
They'd nothing to answer, no nothinsomediver!
The skipper's foot rose, and the skipper's fist fell,
And his language—his language—his language was—well,
It was such as no ladylike singer could tell!
And his wrath neither rum nor tobacco could quell!"

He paused, and was ready with a third verse, but Yerkes picked up a pumpkin that had rolled through the storehouse door, and hove it at him with venomous accuracy. Fred, barrel and concertina went over together in catastrophe, and Yerkes put on the finishing touch with a bucket of water some thoughtful native had left in the shade against thirst-time. They fought, squealed, and rolled each other over like a pair of bear cubs for fifteen minutes after that, reducing natives and every one to such boisterous good humor that the prospect of heavy work in the hot-sun ceased to discourage. So we soon had the corn sacks hurrying in swift procession to the house.

Monty bade us stack them in such manner as to block all the windows except for a peep-hole here and there. The precaution seemed sensible enough, and increased our contentment to the point of no longer worrying about obscure reasons for the rest of his plan. There surely were obscurities.

For instance, we put no store of water in the house; yet nobody troubled himself. We stacked no fuel where it could have been reached without exposure to rifle-fire from the parapet; and nobody worried about that either just at that time.

It was I, nosing among the sheds, who knocked the padlock off an inner compartment and discovered our blasting-powder that Charles du Maurier had stolen out of our cabin on the claims below. I forget how many hundred-weights there were. There was all our fuse as well, and some of the usual prospecting tools, such as picks, crowbars, axes, shovels. Monty took charge of the lot.

Yerkes found du Maurier's ammunition in a chest in another shed. Monty told me to pack it in small parcels ready for mule-back. Whatever was of great value to us, and easy to carry, he seemed to be making ready for a swift exodus. On the other hand, however valuable a thing might be intrinsically, if it was hard to move he had it stowed inside the four walls of du Maurier's house—apparently where the enemy could find it easiest. There was no understanding him.

He instructed the second messenger himself and sent him over the hills to find the du Maurier gang. Yerkes picked out two likely boys, Oakes one, and I two for the purpose, but Monty turned them all down, and, with that uncanny gift of his for understanding natives, chose a limping, skin-and-bone, all-but-naked Ronga savage whom we had overlooked.

First he showed the boy in detail how we had made the house easy to defend, and particularly how the corn and hides, and everything else a native values, had been brought in and stowed. Then he gave him a handful of small coins, and made him promise not to tell the du Mauriers what he had seen. Finally he told him to go and spy on the du Mauriers and bring back word, under penalty of a frightful thrashing if he failed.

"That's where you've missed your guess," said Yerkes. "That's how the Zulu nation spread. Their kings threatened them with death and torture if they failed, so they simply didn't come back. I dare bet you that boy won't return."

"That'll be too bad, then," said Monty, and walked away.

"Stuffy!" said Yerkes. "By ——, he's stuffy! What's the matter with him?"

AFTER THE lame messenger had gone we lined up all the remaining natives in a double row in front of the house, women and brats and all. There and then Monty offered them the unexpected alternative of running away at once wherever they choose, or of obeying all further orders under penalty of death for disobedience.

After some giggling and hesitation, five of the women with their brats, and eleven men elected to go. Monty gave them enough corn for about a week's rations, and chased them away, refusing them time to do more than snatch their few belongings. Yerkes and I watched them depart down the wagon-road and start toward a distant kraal, whose roofs and smoke were just visible like a blot in the heat-haze on the plain.

When we came back it was to find Monty surveying the remaining five of du Maurier's dusky widows, with more than an average of a child apiece, about twenty women belonging to du Maurier's men, and thirty-two of the men themselves.

Especially the women, they stood looking like people who had sold themselves, and to my inexperienced eye they were an awkward problem. But Monty was undisturbed. He summoned "Sixpence," our hideous, wide-nostriled Shangan cook, to interpret, and made a speech to them—a masterpiece of directness, delivered in short, crisp sentences with a pause after each for Sixpence to get his work in. With the African native's incorrigible genius for mimicry, the Shangan multiplied the directness, caricatured Monty, interpreted voice-inflection into gesticulation and turned the stern business into drama.

Nothing makes much impression on the native mind unless the epic, the poetic, the romantic in his nature is appealed to. Natives themselves understand that, and Monty had the knack of choosing natives for his purpose whose special gift was mental quickness.

"Presently there will be fighting," said Monty.

The Shangan, sweeping the huddled assemblage with a fiery eye, flung one bronze arm skyward, shook it as if he held a flaming spear, stamped on the ground-with a right foot from which three toes were missing, and gave utterance to clicks and gutturals that no written form can compass. Monty, himself inspired by the Shangan's mirroring of his own mood, smiled and continued.

"The very bad man Charles du Maurier, who lived on this hill-top and called himself king of the Libombas, is dead. Ye have seen him lie dead. The vultures eat him!"

Snapping fingers, stamping feet, flashing white teeth and an amazing flow of clicks ensued, as Sixpence did that into the Ronga tongue. His pantomime of a vulture descending on a carcass was so realistic that it made the women wail. But the wailing ceased for Monty to speak again.

"All that was Charles du Maurier's is ours now!"

Monty included his party with a gesture; and Sixpence magnified the gesture to mean that we now owned all the earth as far as the horizon, and perhaps beyond.

"But the bad man was born of evil parents, who had other children who are all bad. All the du Mauriers are bad," said Monty.

The face of Sixpence, as he shocked his audience with an announcement of what they all already knew, would have made the angels smile. Accustomed since birth to nothing but outrage and tyranny, they clucked, and clicked, and grunted with pained surprise that such things could be. There is no great fundamental difference between the savage listening to oratory and the white man at a melodrama.

"The du Mauriers will dispute our ownership. They will come soon. There will be fighting."

Mark Antony could doubtless weave spells with his silver tongue; but he never surpassed Sixpence, for Sixpence reached the limit of the humanly attainable, in a language whose chief purpose is to stir emotion. Judging by his frenzy the whole world would presently be at throat-grips.

"But we are much more terrible than they!" said Monty. "So we shall win."

Sixpence interpreted that sentence, stamping as the buffalo treads mud, in token of the utter annihilation of our enemies, his great wide nostrils snorting and his eyes afire with righteous fury. The audience was very visibly impressed.

"It is the custom of conquerors," said Monty, "to do with the goods of the conquered what they will."

Sixpence's outflung arms and rolling eyes expressed the illimitable opportunity thus given us of doing unimaginable things.

"So when the fighting is over," continued Monty, "all the oxen, and all the corn, all the cows; the goats, and pigs, and hens; all the hides and goatskins; all the cut timber, and wire, and beads—" the interpreter's eyes by that time were popping from his head—"the great and little cooking-pots, the old and new blankets, and all else worth taking shall be divided equally among our servants and yourselves—a dower for every woman—a fortune for every man!"

Sixpence paused before he told them that. Then he broke the news in awe-struck tones. Having reached already the ultimate that oratory could attain, he now had to let the amazing fact do its own work.

The response was not quite what might have been expected. Blank incredulity was obvious. One or two of the men and women murmured. They all looked side-wise at one another, some grinning and some afraid to grin, and one man shouted a reply.

"He says," explained Sixpence, "dat —— fool niggah saying, 'You give—come Portuguese an' take away—quick!' "

"Tell them," said Monty, "that I have a letter here from the Portuguese lieutenant-governor, granting to me whatever I find in this robber's lair, in return for my services in ridding the country of him. Tell them that."

Sixpence explained, but it was sight of the sheet of paper produced from Monty's wallet and waved before their eyes, that turned the trick. The more ignorant and raw the savage, the more deeply is he impressed by sight of the written word. Give a native a gun, and he may be afraid to leave his own village; but give him a letter and he will dare travel from end to end of Africa. The written word spells authority. A gun means trouble and stirs resentment.

Faces brightened. The spokesman spoke again.

"Dat niggah saying," explained Sixpence: " 'You giving dem each man letter same time as cows, goats, skins, cooking-pots an' all dem t'ings—dat good. All right. You not giving letter, coming Portuguese and take away!' "

"All right," said Monty; "each man shall have a letter."

Followed a deal of grinning, and speaking behind hands. The spokesman spoke again. Sixpence interpreted.

"Dem niggahs saying, 'Why not you give now?' "

Monty snatched at that opportunity as he would have swooped down on a polo-ball, unerring, swift, and full of a vast good humor.

"Tell them," he said, "there's something to do before I give them letters."

Sixpence, agog with new sense of climax, made the great dish-like hollow ring with that announcement, and the sheepish grins faded.

"And death," added Monty, "for the fool who fails!"

Sixpence interpreted in a voice of tragedy.

"Until dark they are all to stay here and be noisy; to sing, to dance. But no strong drink! There is kaffir beer in a storehouse, but none shall drink it until the fighting shall be over. Let there be tomtoming—thunder of drums, the more the merrier! At dusk I shall give another order. Him who makes not enough noise on the tom-tom all afternoon I shall merely punish with a half-ration for supper. But he who disobeys the order I shall give at dusk shall be thrown to the vultures, and his share of the loot shall be divided among the rest."

IT WAS high noon by the time that speech was finished. The sun beat down on the hilltop, but a wind blew steadily from the west and made life bearable—as it almost never is at midday on the low veld. Having been steadily on the go since dawn, my own inclination was for a solid meal and a long rest in the shade, but, I suppose because I was youngest as well as junior partner, Monty gave me the least assuming work to do.

"I'll send dinner to you," he said. "Just see that they keep together and make lots of noise. There'll be spies sent to look us over. Don't let them doubt we're all here and jubilant."

"Let loose the kaffir beer, then," said I. "Give each of them a quart or two of that, and there'll be any amount of noise."

"Yes," he said, "tonight too, just when I shall want silence. Please do as I say."

My training aboard ship, where work was done in watches Bristol fashion, had left its mark on me and I told off four men to every tom-tom I could find. Then I made a dial of a stick set upright, placing stones to represent the half-hours as nearly as I could guess them. I had to call Sixpence to explain the system of half-hour spells, and it needed patience as well as determination to explain it to him first.

But the game got going at last; and I devised a plan of giving each one a slip of paper as his turn was finished. They, not knowing any more than I what was intended by the slip of paper, stayed close at hand with the paper in their fists to find out. I counted them often, to make assurance doubly sure, but their curiosity had the effect of fetters, and I needed not have troubled.

From time to time Yerkes and Oakes came over to chat with me, but they knew little more than I what was going on in Monty's mind.

"The whole thing's a riddle," I grumbled. "We send Cadji with a request for troops. We send a native at once to warn the enemy of Cadji's movements! We make the house safe against attack, but pay no attention whatever to the outer defenses!"

"Mighty mysterious!" said Yerkes. "You've left out the points that worry me most. Notice; we send Cadji to ask for troops, but carefully insult and enrage him at the last minute! We take his rifle away, to make quite absolutely sure he'll hate us to the limit, after telling him as much of our plans as any of us knows! We send a native to spy on the du Mauriers, after first showing him all our arrangements! We get ready to defend the house after a sort of fashion, but get the mules' saddles and bridles ready for swift departure! Oakes and I have been busy packing the loads for the past two hours. We could saddle the mules in the dark now and be off in a minute. But where to? Why?"

"What has Monty been doing?" I asked. "Playing chess?"

"——, no!" said Oakes. "He packed the box away hours ago. Riddle? Craziness? You two poor simple gallery gods!"

"My life's at stake, and so is yours," said Yerkes. "We've a right to criticize."

"Gallery god," said Oakes. "I flattered you! Can't you understand? Life's no use to Monty unless he can make a play of it. The bally man never grew up. He's younger to-day than yesterday. That's why the fever can't make headway with him. It knocks me down flat every once in so often; it has made Yerkes yellow as a lemon; it'll get you yet, my twenty-one-year-old. But Monty throws it off as a Mexican sheds virtue—it can't find a soft spot to get its claws in! Do you see what he has done now?"

We all went 'round the corner of the shed and looked at the house. On its roof was the platform from which Charles du Maurier had watched all trails on the plain below, on guard against approaching danger. It was a little, round platform, perched on a short, stout pole, and reached by a ladder from the room below. Fixed on the platform now was something I did not recognize at first.

"Our flare!" laughed Oakes.

I remembered then that among our stores, in the shed we had erected on our gold-claims at the foot of the hill, had been a kerosene flare, powerful enough to permit night-time digging on a considerable scale in case the weather or any other contingency should have made that expedient. When Charles du Maurier burst the shed open in our absence and stole everything inside, he had doubtless included that among the loot.

"That," said I, "looks like the limit to me!"

"Limit of what?" said Yerkes.

"Of dramatic skill, Hiram," said Oakes, and Yerkes gave him a playful shove like a grizzly's, that sent him over backward among the tom-tom players. "Hiram," by a sort of tacit understanding between him and Oakes, stood for all that is unsophisticated in the States, and was invariably a signal for horse-play.

"The limit of inconsistency," said I. "If he lights that tonight, the house will be visible from every part of the ramparts. We shall simply look into a wall of black night! There'll be no moon—nothing!"

What I said was absolutely true. The house, standing as it did almost in the exact center of the depression, was commanded from every direction, once an adversary should gain the entrance or swarm over the natural rock parapet that formed the rim, or containing wall. It was true that the only entrance was fairly easy to defend, and that except for the winding wagon-road the sides of the hill were almost unscalable; but between almost and quite there is a great gulf fixed; and there was the equally true, and very disturbing circumstance that Monty bad taken no steps whatever toward defending the ramparts. He seemed obsessed by the importance of the house itself, an importance in our eyes entirely dependent on other considerations.

While we looked at the ridiculous flare that he had lashed to the lookout platform, and, with the possible exception of Oakes—who jeered at Monty to his face and supported him in the teeth of reason behind his back—grew disheartened by the sight, I detected Monty himself crawling out from under the house, where we had stowed the blasting-powder. I called Yerkes' attention.

"Grave-digger stuff!" he sneered. "We'll have an 'Alas poor Yorick' dissertation at supper, I don't doubt! If our case weren't so pathetically serious it 'ud be funny. It's no use squealing, though. If we've cast our lot in with a crazy man, for the love of Mike let's die game!"

"America!" jeered Oakes. "I'll add ten Portuguese spondulix to Cadji's provision for masses for your soul if you'll die slowly in the limelight. I'll take down your last messages in shorthand. Watch—it'll be like this!"

He began to give an imitation of Bill Yerkes crossing the "great divide," but the act was interrupted by the arrival of an obvious spy from the du Mauriers—a bright-eyed young savage with an impudent, leery look, who carried a letter in a cleft stick, but acted as a man might who was taking photographs, turning this and that way to study everything in sight.

Oakes took the letter from him. Yerkes tripped him very neatly, and sat hard on him when he fell. I trussed his hands and feet to a wagon-wheel, and then we all three went to Monty with the letter.

There was no seal—only a thorn stuck through the folded sheet of paper to hold it together; and the writing, done in pencil that had been wetted at frequent intervals, was such a scrawl as would shame a seven-year-old child. Monty read it aloud, and then passed it 'round for us to look at.

It ran:

> To the inglishmun in Charles du Maurier's plac, you hav killed charles, you sonofaguns, and we will kill you onles you maik reckompens. We giv you until day after to-morrow morning early to get to —— out of this and leave five thousand pounds inglish money failing wich we come and let some blood. Put the money on Charleys bed. Leave the mules in stabel. You will get no second warning, du maurier and company, by anatole du M.

"Do you believe a word of that guff?" Yerkes asked.

"Why not?" said Monty with his usual straight face. "Robbers are simple-minded folk."

He took out pencil and paper.

"You're going to answer them seriously?"

Even while he spoke the expression of Yerkes' face changed. I did not understand yet, but I saw that Yerkes divined at least something. If not contented, he was reassured.

Monty wrote in great, bold characters that the enemy would be better able to read than his usual rather illegible hand:

> Your offer under consideration. Will write again in good time.
>
> MONTDIDTER.

He folded the note, ran a thorn through it in the accepted fashion of the country, and gave it to me to give to the spy. So I went and loosed him, with Monty's repeating pistol handy in case of contingencies, and he ran as if all the devils of the murder-fouled Libomba Hills were after him. The tom-toming, that had ceased while he lay bound because of the drummers' curiosity, burst out anew to thunder him farewell, adding wings to his flight; he went almost headlong down the wagon-road, making short-cuts with evident knowledge of the place, gaining speed so fast that long before he reached the plain he certainly could not have stopped himself.

"He's scared," said Yerkes, watching from beside me. "He'll tell them a weird story. He'll say we're preparing to fight like bobcats the day after to-morrow. Good enough!"

And now I began to see a glimmering of light, and suspect that after all Monty was not playing with us for his own amusement. He was amused, no doubt, but that was a by-product.

"Our House of Lords is a downier bird than I thought him," said Yerkes. "D'you get the theory? He tells Cadji he's confident the du Mauriers won't dare attack by night. He makes sure next that they'll capture Cadji; and he takes good care that Cadji hates us so thoroughly as to give us away completely at the first chance. Get that?

"Cadji gloats, and tells the du Mauriers we're easy. Cadji's probably glad to be captured. He makes a dicker with them. Most likely guarantees 'em an indemnity if they come and wipe us out. And he eggs 'em on to attack at night, when we're sure to be off guard!"

"Well and good!" said I.

"We're four to their seventeen—in the dark. What next?"

"Dunno what next," Yerkes admitted, "but I suspicion there's a deep trap laid! We make our play to deceive them into thinking we'll sleep in the house there, with no one on the watch. They send a letter to fool us into the belief that they won't attack until day after to-morrow morning at earliest. We write back kidding them we fall for it. I'll bet you a thousand dollars they come tonight, and that Monty's ready for them. What d'you say?"

"We're not what I'd call ready," I answered. "An enemy could swarm these cliffs at his leisure, jump the parapet, and be in on us without our striking a blow. Why, we haven't even blocked the main gate. They could ride up the wagon-road, and march right in. They couldn't do it in daylight, of course, even with one cool shot stationed at the top, but who's to stop them at night?"

"Search me," said Yerkes. "I don't think they could be stopped. I don't believe Monty wants 'em stopped. I'm beginning to think that it wouldn't be possible to hold this place against seventeen determined men—not at night at any rate—not whatever we did. Tell me, why, d'you suppose, did he take such care to let the du Mauriers know that everything in this camp that's worth plundering has been stowed in the house?"

"How d'ye mean?" I asked.

"That 'spy' we sent, who didn't return and wasn't meant to. Wasn't he shown everything first? He was like Cadji—a free gift to the enemy. Don't I wish Monty would be a mite more trustful, though!

"Here we are, all four of us partners in an enterprise. I bought in; you earned yours. Lord knows which way Oakes got his share, but he and Monty are old friends; I suppose that's the top and bottom of it. What I mean is, we ought to be told what's happening. If we come alive through this I'm going to have a different arrangement, or else pull out."

"What's the sense of all this tom-toming?" said I.

"I expect that's to make the enemy think our natives are drunk. The fake spy is sure to have told them there is plenty of kaffir beer and whisky among the stores.

"I can't see why he didn't send this crowd packing along with the few who elected to leave us," I said. "They are no use. They're only a nuisance, now that the portering's done."

"I suspect Monty didn't care to abandon them," said Yerkes. "Probably those who had anywhere to go went when he offered them the chance this morning. Besides if we had sent them all packing and remained here ourselves, the enemy would surely suspect a trap. This looks like combination charity and business.

"Look at it this way: Charles du Maurier—the one that's dead—lived in this place for years like a king. It's more than likely these have forgotten they ever had homes; they feel they belong here. On the other hand, suppose—gosh! It seems unlikely, but suppose it!—suppose we come out of this on top. The tribes hereabouts, who've looked up to the du Mauriers all these years, 'll likely be out of hand. They won't knuckle under to us right off the bat, and we'll need labor badly to work our gold-claims.

"Oh, I see the thoughtfulness of Monty's moves all right. I see the chess of it! But I'm —— if I see why he should keep it all to himself!"

MONTY GOT very busy that evening about an hour before dusk. We had supper by daylight in the open, Oakes hilarious and poking everlasting fun at Yerkes, Yerkes uneasy, Monty silent and inclined to brood, leaping into life, though, the moment we had finished eating.

"Ready?" he asked me. "Come, then."

He had not been so recklessly contemptuous of accepted strategy after all, for as I walked beside him toward where my crowd was still pounding the drums, some of our own boys, whom I had not noticed all day, came to him through the main gate. He stopped for a minute to question them, and they gave him short, affirmative answers with a great deal of emphasis of nodding heads.

"The enemy's spies have gone back to report," he told me. "We're not watched now—not that they could see us from below, but it's pleasanter to know we're enjoying privacy! Come on."

Close by the great gate, to the right as you faced it with your back to the house, the natural rock parapet was very steep and high—at that point for a distance of fifty yards quite unscalable from within or without. At some time or another a beginning had been made of a wall to enclose a compound there, perhaps for cattle. It ran, about eight feet high, for something like forty feet in a straight line from the gate toward the house, ending abruptly and uselessly, but forming a broad V where it met the rampart.

The sheds were nearly all on the other side of the nearly circular depression, on the left of the house as one faced the gate. Our mules, that du Maurier had stolen, were in one of them. Even while Monty and I approached the gate the dead robber's oxen, cows, and goats came through it toward other sheds, herded by naked boys. When the crack of doom comes the native children will not fail to drive the cattle home!

Monty told me to take some natives and bring our eight mules over into the V. When that was done we brought loads and saddles too, setting each in readiness beside each beast, and feeding them from wooden boxes taken from du Maimer's rough-lumber heap.

"So much for emergency," said Monty. "If the worst happens we can mount the mules and bolt. There's no moon. Any light from inside the camp will help us then."

"Then you do expect to be attacked tonight," I said.

"Who said so?" he answered. "I'm taking precautions. We'll make it hot for marauders, if that's what you mean. Now take all those natives of yours—men, women, and kids, and truss them up 'board-ship style so that they can't stampede at the propitious moment!"

It was a tall order to make that number of humans fast between a quarter after five o'clock and darkness, but I did it. There was fifty fathom of one-inch hempen warp in one of du Maurier's sheds and I used that and some trek-chains, making the chains fast to great iron pegs at each end, and roping them to the chains by the neck. They had to lie down, but I gave them sacks to lie on, and they were not uncomfortable.

Then I tied their hands to their feet, and made their feet fast in line to another chain. I would not have chosen to be bound in that fashion myself, especially before the flies had all quit business for the day, but prisoners can't be choosers. One thing they had to be thankful for—that there were no mosquitoes on the hilltop.

While I was lashing them, and testing knots, Oakes and Yerkes with some of our own boys dragged du Maurier's great trek-wagons into line to form an angle with the unfinished wall of the V, and with the aid of various other bulky things dragged together, including firewood in great bales, boxes, and so on, before dark they had the V fenced off into a triangle.

"Any light from the center now will throw a shadow across most of this triangle," said Monty. "That's good."

Then he sent for Sixpence, and that redoubtable orator was set to work explaining to my trussed prisoners that any one making a sound after the order for silence should be given, would be killed out of hand. Sixpence illustrated the threat by drawing a long cook's knife from his belt and pretending to cut his own throat with the back of it. Monty added to the symbolism by presenting to me very formally his own repeating pistol.

"I shall leave Sixpence with you," he said. "He's to help you keep them quiet, without butcher-work if that can be prevented. Now—one more thing while we're all together."

We stood in a clump between the mules and my lines of prisoners, Monty leaning on his rifle, and I looking into the eyes of each of them with a strange obsession that I must because I might never do it again. Isn't a man foolish! What difference could it possibly have made, supposing we were to be scuppered in the dark, whether or not I had that last look into the faces of my friends? I remember I thought they looked casual—cool—indifferent, and I hoped I looked the same, but did not believe it.

"I want it understood," said Monty, "that whoever sees Cadji, supposing anybody does, is to catch him alive! We can settle with the du Maurier gang, I hope, ourselves. But the only chance I can see of our getting the Portuguese Government to give us real title to our claims is to hold Cadji prisoner. So let's catch him!

"Your business—" he turned to me—"is to keep these natives quiet. If the enemy comes it's a certainty he'll make for the house. Don't open fire unless he breaks in here, or unless he retreats from the house after getting there.

"If you do shoot, remember we others will take that as a signal to join you. Our game will be up then. We shall work our way toward you, jump on the mules, and bolt; that'll be our only chance. So don't shoot unless you absolutely must!"

By the time they three strode back to the house it was almost dark. I saw them reach it—noticed that some sacking had been draped around the platform on the roof, high enough to make a man seated-on a chair up there invisible from below. I saw Oakes, rifle in hand, climb up the ladder to the platform; and then all grew dark.

The great subtropical stars came out, with the million noises of the night that constitute what townsmen think is silence. My prisoners breathed heavily and whispered now and then, but on the whole settled down for the night with fatalistic philosophy. The mules made more fuss than any one, for they had had no recent exercise; but Sixpence had a mulewise way with him, and petted them into more or less repose.

Lamps were lit in the house, for I could see the chinks between the corn-sacks we had piled within. But all was silence over there until at last I heard Monty's voice calling—

"How about it, Fred?"

A moment later Oakes' concertina split the night apart, and Oakes' voice lifted in uproarious song.

Never did a sober man sound drunker! Never did a chorus bellowed by two men from below create a better atmosphere of revelry by night! Never was song more suited to occasion:

"Oh, my name is Johnny Hall, —— your eyes,
—— your eyes!"
"And I hate you one and all, —— your eyes,
—— your eyes!"

A wonder of a song! The chorus, "—— your eyes! —— your eyes!" was accompanied by resounding thumps on the table below, while up above Fred's concertina laughed and carried on in harpy rhapsodies, while the pirate's account of his own forth coming execution unfolded stanza by stanza to the unresponsive night.

"And the parson he will come, —— his eyes,
—— his eyes!
To talk of Kingdom Come, —— his eyes, —— his eyes!
Oh, the parson he will come,
For to talk of Kingdom Come,
And he surely do look glum—oh, —— his eyes!"

I think it was at the parson verse—or perhaps at the point where the sheriff enters, "with all his ugly crew, their dirty work to do," that our own climax arrived. I had climbed into one of the wagons as the best place to see from without being seen, and I kept my eyes busy sweeping the line of the parapet, just visible like a pencil-mark in the velvet gloom.

But our enemy was too cocksure that night to trouble to swarm parapets. He came, all sixteen strong, marching up the wagon-road; and my heart stood still suddenly as I saw a man's full round head in a cowboy hat rise boldly above the level of the gate.

For two or three minutes it kept stock still. The song went on. The concertina raved and wailed. I wondered whether Oakes, singing away behind that sacking, had eyes enough to see as well, for it was a long shot in the dark from house to gate.

The song went on. They hanged Johnny Hall, and danced him over nothing in a noose, and the drunken chorus crashed and bellowed in such convincing style that, had I not known, I too would have suspected there was whisky flowing.

The enemy looked long, listened, and was satisfied. I saw the man with the cowboy hat climb on the gate, and three heads rose on each side of him. For a second then I thought I saw a match struck behind the sacking above the roof—Oakes told me afterward it was a candle he had all ready burning, inside a tin tea-caddy. He was heating the burner of the flare. But the song went on.

Four or five more of the enemy raised their heads above the gate, and at last their chief thought it time for action.

"Stop that —— of-a-noise!" he roared. "Stop it naow! Listen to me!"

The song and concertina music ceased as suddenly as if some one had slammed a lid.

"Come aout an' shaow yerselves! Yer game's up! Ye're covered! I'm Anatole du Maurier, I am! Blood for blood; I'm here for Charlie's price! Come on aout and fight, ye —— *ruineks!"*

One of his gang fired twice, presumably at a chink of light in the nearest window. That was the signal for them all, and they volleyed at random, swearing as they thrust in fresh cartridges. I wondered that the flash of their rifles did not betray my face behind the wagon curtain; but I suppose they were too bent on murder to notice me, just as I was too excited to remember Monty's orders to keep my prisoners quiet.

But for Sixpence, who did not neglect his duty, we might have been done for. He walked up and down between the prone ranks, swinging his naked knife above their faces.

At the fourth or fifth volley the lights inside the house went out—whether shot out or extinguished by Yerkes or Monty I could not guess.

"Come on aout an' fight, ye swine! Ye cattle-thieves!" yelled Anatole du Maurier.

But by that time Fred had the burner hot enough, and the answer was unexpected. The paraffin flare blazed out noisily, bathing the whole amphitheater in ghastly, bright light, dazzling the riflemen. I just caught sight of Fred Oakes clambering down the ladder—and they must have seen him too, for they sent volley after volley at the roof—and I heard the supporting pole splinter as at least a dozen bullets struck it.

But it takes a host of bullets to bring down a nine-inch hard-wood sapling, and the paraffin flare burned on. They began firing at the light itself, but failed to hit it.

There was no answering rifle-fire—nothing but silence from the house; and it began to rattle the du Mauriers.

"Yah! They're dead already! We've bagged 'em!" said a man I could not see.

"Fer the love o' God let's haope not!" sneered Anatole. "Let's haope we catch 'em alive. An' burn 'em alive!" he added with a hard laugh.

"Let's haope that's good liquor the fools were swilling!" said the man at my end of the gate.

"It was Charlie's liquor!" yelled Anatole, with an oath that distanced the angriest effort of any Bluenose bo'sun.

"I'm tired o' waiting, I am! I'm going to see! Remember the agreement—findings, keepings!"

One of the men jumped off the gate, ducked, and began to run toward the house. The slogan, "Findings, keepings!" proved too much for the rest, and they all surged after him, one or two still firing as they ran, and all cursing the yellow flare that showed them in pitiless outline. But there was no answering fire from the house.

It was at that moment that somebody climbed into the wagon beside me. I shut my eyes a dozen times in quick succession to accustom them again to darkness, stared hard, and saw Cadji's face! He did not see me yet. He evidently expected somebody. And somebody came.

"Is that you, Anatole?" he whispered. "It is right not to expose yourself. Let the others risk it! Of what use is a man's dead body?"

There was no answer, although there was certainly some one else in the wagon. I clutched Monty's pistol in a hand that trembled.

"Is that you, Anatole?" he asked again.

"No, my saffron hellion!" the unmistakable voice of Fred Oakes answered.

And that selfsame second Oakes' ten fingers locked with mine on Cadji's neck. We squeezed until I thought we had killed him. Then Oakes sat on him, searching him busily for weapons, finding two pistols and a knife.

"How did you get here, Fred?" I demanded.

"Crawled along the parapet. We all did. Watch!"

"Where's Monty?"

"You'll know presently. Watch!"

He pulled the wagon-curtain right back, and we both leaned out regardless of the risk. The house front door was bolted, and for the past minute the du Mauriers had been thundering on it with feet and hands.

As we watched they stove it in with their rifle-butts, and surged through into the pitch-dark interior. We could hear them cursing as they hunted for lamps, striking matches and getting in one another's way.

"Now for a volley at them, through the open door!" I said excitedly.

"Don't be a fool," Oakes answered. "Watch!"

We did not watch long—perhaps ten seconds longer. Suddenly the hill-top shook—there came a clap like thunder—the house shrugged itself—opened outward like a rotten packing-case, and leaped skyward in fragments amid flame and smoke. Monty had fired our blasting-powder.

The echo of the explosion rattled back from the parapets. There came a ghastly rain of timber, sacks of corn, roofing, and human limbs.

The mules wrenched loose their tethering-stakes,

and stampeded all together in a line, to the awful consternation of my bound prisoners. The cattle in the long sheds lowed. The air became full of soot and particles. Some ruins caught fire, where the house had been, and then all was still again.

"Some little affair," said Yerkes, sticking his head into the wagon. "Where are you, Fred? Are you all right?"

"Right as rain, and I've got that wrong 'un Cadji!" Oakes answered gleefully.

"What's that?" demanded Monty's voice. "You say you've got the Portuguee?"

"Come and look at him! He's beginning to breathe again!" said Oakes.

I lighted a lantern I had stowed in a corner, and Monty looked in, his face smeared and bloody where some part of the house had struck him.

"Cut loose your prisoners," he ordered me. "Set some of them to catch the mules, and the rest to salvaging the corn before the fire spoils it all. Hurry!"

But Sixpence had the mules already rounded up and anchored; and as for the corn, I could no more make those frightened natives salvage it by the light of the smoldering ruins of the house than I could have induced them to run away and leave us before dawn. They would do nothing but sit huddled in a cluster. What corn was not scattered far and near, loose or in parts of bags, was burned, and I went back to the wagon after a half-hour's wasted effort.

WE SLEPT in the wagon, with Cadji tied hands and feet in the midst of us. And we breakfasted in the open at dawn, after I had seen most of the more disgusting mess cleaned up.

It was impossible to tell whether we had caught all sixteen du Mauriers in the trap. Oakes and Yerkes, who had tried to count them as they went in, both thought fifteen was the number. I had made no effort to count, and Monty, who had stayed to light the fuse before running for the parapet, naturally did not know. Cadji refused to throw any light on the matter, declining to say whether he thought Anatole du Maurier might have escaped or not.

"Never mind, senhor," said Monty, offering him a seat at our breakfast table, that Sixpence had improvised from barrels and planks. "We'll deal with you the same way, whether you tell us or not. Only one thing that can help you. When we get clear title to those claims of ours, guaranteed from Lisbon, you go free—not otherwise."

Cadji refused breakfast, although Sixpence had surpassed all previous efforts and produced a spread worthy of a great occasion. Midway through the meal he left us to remove about one-seventh of a man that we had overlooked between two heaps of wreckage. He tossed it over the parapet before Monty could stop him, and a vulture, plunging downward out of empty sky, followed the titbit to earth.

But, as I said before, there is something about breakfast that goes to the heart of all adventurers. If Cadji was no true adventurer, we were; and we made a famous meal.

"—— you, Monty, my boy!" said Oakes, half through it. "That was a top-hole plan! That was the best yet!"

"I rather fancy it worked all right," said Monty modestly.

"Yes, but tell me this," said Yerkes. "Why in thunder, in the name of all that's blue, couldn't you tell a fellow what you aimed to do? Why the secrecy?"

Monty smiled broadly, holding out his cup for Sixpence—the only Shangan who ever made Christian coffee—to fill for the third time.

"Recall jollying me about the British army's reputation for strategic genius?" he asked, and Yerkes nodded.

"Well, the peculiar fact is, my dear chap, that in order to be promoted—I'm a colonel, for instance—we're obliged to study, and are very thoroughly examined in, strictly American—United States American—tactics. We have to study Stonewall Jackson. You might almost say that man's the tutor of the British army. He's almost deified."

"What's that got to do with it?" demanded Yerkes.

He scented a jest at his expense, but Monty was serious enough.

"I expect it's the same with you over there as with us," said Monty. "In the schools they teach you every history except your own. You might say I know nothing about some of our best men, but Stonewall Jackson's a familiar friend. I know pretty well all there is to know about him. I remember things he is reported to have said, that I wouldn't be surprised to know you never heard of."

"Go on," said Yerkes. "I'll be the goat. Out with it."

"Somebody asked Jackson once for particulars of a plan he had in mind. He pointed to the buttons on his overcoat.

" 'If those buttons knew my business,' he said, 'I'd cut 'em off at once.'

"Well, Yerkes, that's my way. I can't for the life of me help copying Stonewall Jackson!"

"Ah!" said Cadji. "Ah! I too know history. Stonewall Jackson was slain by his own men finally, was it not?"

Monty glanced at Yerkes, Yerkes at Oakes and Oakes at me. The Portuguese was standing between the table and the wagons, near a water-butt that I had caused to be filled the evening before for the sake of the mules and my prisoners.

"D'you think he needs a bath?" suggested Monty.

"I found him no nosegay in the night," said Oakes.

"Could we clean out his thinking-gear, d'you suppose?" said Yerkes. "That 'ud be worth an effort."

"In with him!" said I.

"All together then," said Monty.

The Portuguese kicked and screamed. He bit, and spat, and swore. But we brought that breakfast to an end by plunging him head downward into the water-butt, and left him, with short legs gesticulating wildly to an unresponsive sky, for Sixpence to pull out by the pants and wring, madder than a wet hen. Sixpence, of course, being black and a decent Shangan, was proud of the privilege of rescuing a "white" man.

HEINIE HORNS INTO THE GAME

"**SIXPENCE," OUR** Shangan factotum, was out of sight at the moment, although I did not notice it. Four other boys of four tribes and species of ugliness were trying to remove breakfast things without his supervision, yet without breaking plates or cups. Montdidier had got the chess-board out on his knees in the shade of a wagon. Oakes, songful of a morning, had the rest of our personal gang in charge tidying up the compound. Bill Yerkes and I were smoking on the parapet that overlooked all trails to the horizon, as well as our gold claims, staked out on the level and between the spurs of the hill beneath. To look at us a casual observer might have guessed that we were lords of all Gazaland, from the mountains to the sea.

I had one eye on Cadji, the Portuguese official member of our party, and liked the look of him no better than he seemed to like us. Your Portuguese objects as fiercely as any other breed of man to being ducked head-foremost in a water-butt, and, for good cause given, we had done that job thoroughly.

Not that I was seriously considering him. I was speculating rather on the inscrutable quality of destiny, that could bring together into partnership such different types of men as Lord Montdidier, Fred Oakes, Bill Yerkes, and me. I wondered what exactly made clear that sharp distinction between our collective way of looking at the world and Cadji's, notwithstanding we were each as different in temperament as the four winds. What lies behind the racial hatreds, anyway? But the eye I kept on Cadji did not sleep.

"Bill," I said presently. "That rascal would rather make trouble for us than steal money."

Cadji sat in the sunshine, wringing wet garments one by one, meeting no man's eye, not muttering, but exuding adjectives. Yerkes looked him over, filling his pipe slowly.

"Pity he wasn't in there with the outlaws," he remarked, nodding toward the charred props of the house, in which all but one of the sixteen du Mauriers had been blown to smithereens the night before. "It isn't his fault we're alive to look at him! I'm guessing just how far he was obeying Government orders last night, and how far speculating on his own account. Think it over."

I thought it over rather hazily for several minutes, not exactly helped by the antics of Fred Oakes, whose method of making black men work swiftly is to play the outrageous goat for them. He was waking echoes with his concertina and yowling *"killeloo"* at the far side of the compound, imitating a hypothetical witch-doctor doing a never-yet-invented devil-dance—behaving, that is to say, as no dignified Portuguese official would ever dream of doing, but getting the work done. He is not Irish, which accounts for his hilarious success with comic alleged Irish songs.

Already no new arrival on the scene could easily have been persuaded that the bodies of fifteen men mixed up with miscellaneous débris had been scattered all over the hilltop but a few hours back.

"Cadji was loaned to us by his fiasco of a Government," said Yerkes, with that aged expression American young men so readily assume and cast aside, "for two alleged purposes. First, to check up on our gold claims and give us clear title. Second, to hang legally as many of the du Mauriers as we could round up and corral. Cadji's an honest-to-goodness high court judge—little though he looks it! Am I right?"

"So far," said I.

"Well," he went on, "I'm one who saw and heard him try to get away without doing a thing about our claims—although he has a ten per cent. interest by way of payment in advance."

"I bear you out," said I.

"I'm one who saw Charles du Maurier, bound hand and foot, left in his custody."

"It was I who tied him," said I.

"I'm one who saw Cadji look the other way while said Charles du Maurier, with his feet unaccountably free, made a dash for liberty. Did you see that too? How did du Maurier die?"

"Missed his footing, and dashed his brains out against the cliff," I answered.

"You saw that? We all saw it. Cadji saw it. I saw him see it! But I'm one who heard him accuse us afterward of killing Charles du Maurier."

"I heard that, too," said I. "We all heard it."

"I'm one who saw him sneak into this compound last night—after we had let him go, mind you, at his own request—saw him sneak in with the enemy at the time they attacked us. I heard him call to Anatole du Maurier, the gang's leader, in a manner that convinced me he stood in with them to put us out of business. I heard him whisper to some one he thought in the dark was Anatole, to hide until the fight was over."

"He whispered that to me. He mistook me in the dark for Anatole," said I.

"The question is," said Yerkes, "did his Government instruct him to play us false; or did he play traitor on his own account?"

"Who cares for his motives?" said I. "He's caught, tried, and found guilty. What shall we do to him?"

"Would our House of Lords dare hang him?" suggested Yerkes, with a glance over at Monty.

"Scarcely," I said. "The little beast is a Government official. Besides his title and good standing, Monty is a cavalry colonel on half-pay. Cadji's life is probably safe, as far as we're concerned."

"What a pity our Monty isn't a social outcast!" laughed Yerkes. "All the same—hello, what's the program now?"

There was a strange assembly gathering. From the side of the compound where our mules were housed in one of the dead robber's store-sheds, there began to come cattle—oxen, cows, sheep, and goats; also the widows and ex-concubines of the outlaw owner of all that plunder, with their little snuff-and-butter brats, herded in a sort of market bunch by the scoundrel's hirelings, most of whom had chosen to remain with us. Monty had given the order, for he did not look up from his chess, although the noise was prodigious.

Other natives came carrying corn bags. A dozen of them rolled an enormous vat of Kafir beer, whose bung started explosively at every other revolution and had to be replaced. Two of the beer contingent were three-parts drunk already. Natives came running from every shed, carrying-on their heads, or dragging along the ground every conceivable and inconceivable contraption, representing the efforts of fifteen or twenty years by a bandit to grow rich. A history of trading expeditions into Gazaland could have been written from a survey of that heterogeneous junk.

"It seems to me," I said, "there are twice as many natives in the compound as there were at dawn."

"Look!" said Yerkes, and pointed.

I saw three skin-and-boney Rongas climb over the parapet as he spoke, and drop down among the crowd as nonchalantly as the crows alight in a cornfield.

"Who put the countryside wise, I wonder?" Yerkes lit his pipe again and looked at me. "Anatole du Maurier made his getaway. I'll bet he has tipped off every chief for miles around to send men to share the loot. Monty 'll refuse to divvy among new arrivals—sure. Trouble for us! Look at Cadji! See him grin! He's in on this! Where are his four boys? I'll bet in four directions stirring trouble!"

We got down off the parapet and hurried toward Monty, but Monty was still playing chess with himself and undisturbable.

"Hey!" said Yerkes. "Cut your game short and start some real thinking! Every savage between here and the Limpopo is swarming in on us!"

"Of course!" said Monty. "The more the merrier!" And he went on studying the chess-board.

"Dramatic stuff!" said Yerkes disgustedly behind his hand to me. "It makes me tired. It might get across the footlights. It might reassure Tommies. You? Me? It's an insult to our intelligence! If he'd scratch his head and look like a man in doubt, I'd feel more confident."

"But I don't think he is in doubt," I said.

To my mind Monty's attitude toward life's problems was genuine, not assumed.

"I do!" said Yerkes with a wry face. "He has pulled off a lot, I admit. Some was luck, and some good management. But you heard Fred say yesterday that life's no use to Monty unless he can make drama of it. Fred knows him. I'm not acting in a play—I'm after hard cash in deadly earnest!"

"So is he," I answered. "He needs money to take home and keep up the title. He's after millions."

"Believe me," said Yerkes, grinning, "I'll be content with hundreds if we get out of this mess alive."

MEANWHILE, FRED Oakes had joined the round-up and was getting something approaching order out of the chaos savages prefer if left to their own devices. We took a hand, and in half an hour we had Charles du Maurier's black widows with their brats at a table beside Monty, all the male natives in a circle facing us, and the cattle with the other plunder in the midst.

Our own boys, in a group behind us, I thought looked glum—a good, upstanding little company of eleven different tribes—nine-and-twenty coal-black, wooly-headed aborigines, each one uglier than any other imaginable creature, but his neighbor. Well-fed, and having spent most of the early morning laughing under Fred's care, they scarcely seemed to call for sympathy; but a second look at them convinced me they anticipated trouble.

Personally, I expected trouble of the worst kind the moment Monty should call in question the unauthorized arrivals. I brought out my rifle from the wagon in which we slept the night beforehand gave Yerkes his as well.

Monty closed the chess-board at last, and turned his chair so as to face the crowd. There was an instant lull in the babel of voices. The natives recognized him as our chief by a sort of instinct. I suspected then, and do still, that Bill Yerkes would have yielded unquestioning allegiance to Monty sooner, but for that trick of commanding recognition.

Oakes and I were rather proud of him on that account. In Yerkes' case it was not jealousy; but he was raised where the school-books preach against command by right of birth. Cadji, who on the contrary, was autocratic in thought and word and

deed, pulled on his wet clothes and joined us at the table.

"Sixpence!" commanded Monty, and the Shangan appeared from somewhere or other, instantly athrill with the mongrel Zulu's instinct for dramatic crisis.

Few true interpreters are born such, and not very many made; but to an instinct for the business Sixpence had superadded skill, acquired by practise and keen observation of effect. He threw a chest, and with a sweep of flashing eyes—a gesture of out-flung arm—and a stamp of his right foot on the earth, commanded general attention.

Cadji, close beside me, observing another dozen black arrivals drop from the parapet at different points, grinned into my face malevolently. I noticed that Monty saw him grin.

"We have with us," said Monty, "an officer of the Portuguese Government!"

Sixpence, with upflung arm, translated. Cadji shut his yellow teeth with a startled snap. Oakes caught my eye and grinned. Yerkes took a stand rather closer to Cadji as if he expected the little yellow man to make a bolt for it. We were all taken by surprise.

"A judge of the Portuguese high court!" said Monty, and Sixpence threw enthusiasm into that.

If he had been announcing the presence among us of an archangel he could not have been more impressive; but there was no symptom of appreciation by the audience. On the contrary, there grew a kind of restlessness—a shifting from one foot to the other, and resentment a man could feel without knowing how it was expressed.

"He is here," said Monty, "on Government business."

Monty's face was an enigma—Cadji's an exclamation mark.

Sixpence made the announcement in that clicking, clucking lingua franca they all understood, and twenty of the new arrivals, slipping stealthily to the rear, bolted by the way they had come.

"Now ask what they think they stand here waiting for," said Monty, and Sixpence threw an attitude expressing outraged surprise that they should carry no banner having aims and reasons printed on it.

The spoken question was an explosion of contemptuous sounds. Unless to make requests, one seldom asks politely on the high or low veld.

A bold-looking woman was the first to answer, her two naked brats clinging to her. It is not only in educated lands that anti-suffrage is instinctively in the sex. The other women held aloof as from a moral leper; but two men followed her lead, and then in a minute the whole crowd was shouting in a babel that presently evolved itself into repetition of one sentence. Sixpence listened arrogantly, and then held both hands high for silence.

"Them niggahs saying," he translated, "you—big *baas* —making promise yestahday—you giving them to-day all dem tings belonging Charles du Maurier. Them saying—now you give!"

"All right!" said Monty, with a nod in the affirmative that made the assembly gasp. The thing was too good to be true.

"But listen!"

Sixpence checked the rising babel with a gesture of royal impatience.

"The loot was to be divided in equal shares between our servants and du Maurier's. So it shall be!"

Our own boys behind us burst into a cheer, and the ivory gleamed white across nine-and-twenty physiognomies. Gone was depression. But some of the crowd in front looked surly, at the notion of our boys-whom they regarded of course as foreigners—having a finger in the pie. The Shangan and the Ronga are as foreign to each other as the Greek and Esquimaux, and there seemed to me the makings of a first-class fight. But Monty had the situation well in hand.

"Without our good boys," he said, "there would have been no plunder to divide. Du Maurier would have still been tyrant of these hills. But Du Maurier is dead. The plunder lies ready, and our boys shall have first pick!"

Sixpence translated that, like Mark Antony converting the Roman mob to new respect for Caesar. The whole business of victors giving away their plunder was too bewildering, and the promptness too breathtaking for objection to take shape; and Monty wasted no time.

"Sixpence! You choose first!" he ordered, and the Shangan became one avaricious grin.

There was no doubt for a moment what his choice would be. With unanimity born of generations that regarded cattle as the mark of wealth, every man and woman in the crowd singled out the best milch cow and watched him go and take it. Not one hesitated; the selection of the best was made instantly and expertly by every eye.

One by one, each of our boys was given leave to choose, and when they had all done there were cows enough left to give du Maurier's dusky widows one apiece, and a few dry ones remaining.

"Write out deeds of gift," said Monty. "Write that the cow, or whatever the property happens to be, was given by me in pursuance of authority vested in me by contract over the seal of the Portuguese Government."

So I sat at the table and wrote certificates of ownership on slips of paper, passing them to Monty to sign.

"Set your official seal on that!" he ordered, signing the first one, and passing it to Cadji.

"I have no authority!" said Cadji, bridling.

"You have your seal," said Monty.

"But I have no orders!" snarled Cadji.

"D'you mean you didn't hear me give an order?" demanded Monty, in a tone of interested inquiry.

"You can not order me!" snapped Cadji.

"Oh!" said Monty. "Have you seen this?"

He drew out the contract the lieutenant-governor had given him, deeding to him whatever property he might find in the du Maurier lair, as part consideration for ridding the Libomba Hills of outlaws.

"My purpose," he said, flourishing the paper in front of Cadji's face, "is to make this plunder over to the natives in such way that you can't take it away from them. Be good enough to seal the slips!"

CADJI REFUSED. His restless eye sought help where none was, sweeping in vain the sea of dark faces, and the rocky parapet that, from where we all stood, shut off the view of everything beyond but clear blue sky.

"I will go," he said nervously. "Where are my own men?"

"Call them!" suggested Monty.

Cadji raised his voice into that peculiar, rasping shout that the wide world over, marks a mean man. He first used Portuguese, and then, since there was no response, Chironga. Possibly he forgot that Yerkes learned Portuguese in Brazil, and that Monty knew something of the native tongue.

"He is calling for help in the name of his Government! He demands their allegiance!" said Yerkes, and Monty was swift to seize the advantage.

"Senhor Cadji," he said, nodding to Sixpence to interpret, "will take for his own use as porters all those natives who were not here last night! Let them all fall in, between us and the gate."

The answer was an instant stampede. The Government corvée was too well understood in that graft-ridden land for any Ronga in his senses to wait and take a chance. In less than two minutes there was none inside the gate except those who had right there.

"That gets rid of the undesirables, I think," said Monty in an aside to me.

Cadji stood snatching at his little black mustache and shred of imperial, his other hand guarding the hip pocket that bulged with his official seal.

"We shouldn't have ducked the dago," whispered Yerkes.

"Piffle, America!" said Fred Oakes, coming between us. "We ought to have drowned him! Duck him again! Come on!"

"In London or New York, a ducking, or a kick, or a black eye don't much matter," Yerkes went on, "although they'll lock you up for calling names. In Paris, Lisbon, and Madrid offense against the person is the serious crime, say what you like, and no harm done; but kick a pimp, for instance, and they jail you! That's one reason why the English are unpopular abroad—they never understand that."

But Monty was growing impatient, as the sun mounted steadily and the morning wind announced that only about four hours were remaining until noon.

"We're waiting for you to seal those certificates, Senhor Cadji!" he remarked; and once more Cadji's roving eye sought help. "He's expecting somebody," said Fred Oakes.

"There's a card up his sleeve. He's trying to gain time for some reason, or I'll eat my hat!" announced Yerkes.

"He expects help through the gate," said I. "He looks that way whenever he thinks we don't notice."

"I suspect Senhor Cadji had us sold at least twice over before he came away with us from Lourenço Marques," said Monty with a pleasant grin. "While he thought I was playing chess after breakfast he whispered to his own four boys to escape and warn some party to hurry and take us by surprise. I put Sixpence to work at once, and if you care to look you'll find the four boys tied hand and foot in that wagon over there!"

"A shame we ducked him, was it?" Oakes jeered. "We shouldn't have ducked him, eh?"

Yerkes laughed, and Oakes and he eyed the convenient water-butt suggestively, with bursts of laughter that made Cadji splutter and turn even yellower. I think they would have turned suggestion into action had not Monty interfered.

"For the last time—be good enough to seal those certificates, *senhor!*"

Cadji hesitated—glanced furtively to right and left—shrugged his shoulders—and chose discretion, taking a seat at the table with a sidewise glare at Oakes and Yerkes that spoke volumes for his opinion of horse-play. Sealing was merely a matter of squeezing the paper slips between the jaws of a little pocket vice; but it made a prodigious difference to the value the slips would have for their possessors.

One by one, every cow, bullock, goat, sheep, chicken, blanket, cooking-pot, length of iron wire, piece of cheap calico, package of tobacco, bag of corn, knife, ax, leather thong, and what-not was chosen and became the certificated property of some one; until at last the women stood in a group alone, with their brats and their share of the plunder.

All the men had retired to the sheds, to compare luck, make merry, and drink the beer that, as a precaution against total drunkenness Monty ordered distributed by quarts to all and sundry. The women eyed us and their plunder wistfully, chattered—hesitated—made up their minds and took a bee-line for the beer. But Monty called them back.

"Has any one of you fellows a notion what to do with them?" he asked, and Oakes yelled with delight.

"Marry 'em, Monty! You marry 'em! Be King of the Libombas! That's why Charles du Maurier married 'em! Under Portuguese law whoever marries a chief's daughter falls heir to his estates. Take unto yourself some wives! Take an assortment of pretty countesses home to Montdidier Towers! Present 'em at court, Monty! You owe it to the British nation to give 'em a new scandal in high life! Come on—ring the wedding bells—it's proposed, seconded and carried unanimously that Monty ceases to be a bachelor!"

"Why not marry 'em to Cadji?" suggested Yerkes. "That 'd make him King of the Libombas. He'd have to be a what-d'-ye-call-it—a constitutional monarch, with us cabinet ministers. We make decrees; he signs and seals 'em! Are you a bachelor, Cadji?"

"*Senhores,* I have a wife in—"

"In every port!" Oakes cut in. "Shame, Cadji! I'm ashamed of you! Hurry up, Monty, and marry him off. He's got the habit; you may as well give in and let him have his wilful way. Will you marry 'em to him one by one, or all in a lump? Which is the orthodox style? Have to be orthodox, you know!"

Cadji glared about him wildly, in no mood to appreciate a jest. The horse-play type of humor makes no appeal to men whose corrupt politics wear dignity for a disguise; and a joke at his own expense was an insult in any event. Besides, he was not sure about the joke. He more than suspected the proposal might be deadly serious.

Monty, handsome as the devil, leaned back in his chair and laughed silently. His black mustache was waxed into points as carefully as if he were sitting in the House of Lords. The grime and smoke of last night's explosion—the blood from the slight wound on his cheek—the very smell of blasting powder had been washed and groomed away. With bare throat and collar-bones exposed by the open polo shirt, and his general air of athletic manliness, he was just the man to inspire confidence in an Anglo-Saxon; but Cadji lacked the advantage of fair-playing ancestry, and was far from reassured.

"Which will you do?" demanded Monty. "Be married to them, or marry them off officially to men of their own choosing?"

"Neither can be!" Cadji stammered. "They are wards of Government! I claim their property in trust on behalf of my Government!"

"Salary, emoluments and graft," hummed Bill Yerkes brutally, "and the sweetest of these is graft!"

"Aren't you a judge of the high court?" Monty asked.

"Yes!" said Cadji. "I warn you, you tamper with danger, *senhores,* to treat me disrespectfully!"

"We'll treat you like Henry VIII, my saffron Lothario!" grinned Oakes.

"Sixpence!" commanded Monty, and the Shangan came running.

"Ask those women whether they want husbands?"

Sixpence addressed them collectively, in the brusque, abusive manner natives consider dignified toward their womenfolk.

"Them answering 'Why not?' " he announced.

"Call back the men!" commanded Monty.

"Tell them to leave their plunder where it is, and come and stand in a circle."

THERE WAS already a market in full swing, bartering and selling, quarreling and offering for sale. All the new plunder, except the female animals, for they are too valuable ever to part with except in trade for a woman, was changing hands, together with Monty's signed and sealed certificates, as if Monty had set up a stock exchange; and it was only with difficulty that Sixpence broke up the session and persuaded them to shift ground.

"Ask," said Monty, as soon as they were gathered in a ring again, and reasonably still, "which of them would like to marry one of Charles du Maurier's widows."

The widows stood looking foolish, exceedingly self-conscious and abashed, while Sixpence put the astonishing inquiry. A red cotton blanket is not much of a garment in which to seem coquettish, but the native standard is less exacting than the Western, and they did their best.

There was no question of their eligibility. They represented the peak of Ronga chivalry's desire—young women, each with at least one child—and one had three. And were there not the milch cows, deeded one to each in writing, besides other plunder? Nine-hundred-and-ninety-nine times out of a thousand, since the dear old days of intertribal war and marriage by force departed, the black man who wants a wife must work and earn cows with which to pay for her—and the price of wives, like that of most necessities, goes up and up. Yet here were brides free, gratis, with cows thrown in! The meeting was unanimous. There was a forest of upthrown arms, a flash of white ivory, and a yell that left no doubt. Nevertheless, Sixpence did the full measure of his duty.

"Each man demanding whole —— lot!" he translated.

"Tell the married men to fall out!" ordered Monty.

They had left their plunder in the charge of dejected women who were presumably the wives of some of them, but Sixpence's retort was unexpected.

"All them men got one wife—some getting two—some three!"

"Already?" asked Monty, and Sixpence nodded. "Where are the other wives?"

"In the kraals 'round about," said Sixpence. "Them men serving this Charles du Maurier. Some bringing one wife, some none. Some saying him du Maurier liking my wife, him take away."

"Oh, marry 'em all to Cadji and have done with it!" urged Oakes. "Marry 'em all to Cadji, and give 'em each a certificate stamped with Cadji's seal!"

"We'll let the women choose!" said Monty.

Sixpence translated that into the Ronga tongue; and if a bomb had been exploded in their midst those dusky suitors could not have been more astonished. A bird chooses her nest. A pariah dog or a rat may choose which kraal he will infest. But a woman is chosen, to be the chattel of man. There was a new order of things begun that day in Gazaland, whose ultimate culmination, perhaps a century hence, may develop dusky suffragettes and militancy.

Fred Oakes led the ball off like a dancing-master, offering his arm to the senior dame—she with the three offspring. She had not the least idea what he intended—imagined, in fact, at first that she had been spliced to Oakes himself, and was half-pleased, half-embarrassed. Sixpence made matters plain by laying hands on her cow and other loot and shouting the bans of marriage in the shape of a command to all present to stand still and be looked over. Oakes, since she would not take his arm, led her by the hand past all the bucks, pointing out to her in comic pantomime the virtues and probable defects of each.

"Ask this one if he can cook," he ordered, when the woman seemed to hesitate before a more than usually ugly savage.

Sixpence translated. The answer was no, and a roar of laughter followed.

"Him having other cow, bullock, sheep, goat, an' seben wives!" announced Sixpence. "Him rich man. She like him!"

Oakes led her once again around the circle, but none seemed to please her better than the gruesome-looking giant who stood calmly smoking a clay-pipe, as unembarrassed as the day.

"Bring 'em along!" said Monty. "Let's get this over with."

Monty wrote their names down, and declared them married. Yerkes passed the paper to Cadji, and forced him to affix his seal.

"I am entitled to a fee for doing this!" insisted the Portuguese. "There is no legal document without the corresponding fee! Who shall pay me?"

"Wait and see, sweetheart! Wait and see!" Oakes counseled him.

The marrying and sealing of the paper slips went on, Oakes taking one woman after another around the circle and bringing her, hand-in-hand with the buck of her choice to Monty, while the sun rose steadily toward high noon. It grew hot, and the smell of the crowding natives was about intolerable when the last left concubine had picked out for herself the richest buck remaining, and Cadji had unwillingly affixed the legal stamp to Monty's document.

"I go now!" said Cadji, strutting indignantly.

It was his great misfortune, not his fault, that any attempt at dignity only made him look ridiculous. Freckles, yellow skin, gold watch-chain, khaki uniform, brown boots—he was a yellow interrogation mark. He looked about him, forgetting for the moment that his boys were in limbo—hesitated—turned—turned again—and started, baggageless and empty-handed for the gate.

"No, you don't, my saffron proconsul!" Oakes called after him. "Come hither, my Lord Chief Justice!"

Cadji saw fit not to obey, so Fred reached for him with a long, strong arm, took him by the neck, and set him squirming and indignant in front of Monty.

"Awfully sorry to seem pressing, *senhor,* and all that kind of thing, you know," said Monty, with a cheerful eye on the dinner-table Sixpence had begun to construct out of planks and packing-cases. "But we desire your pleasant company at lunch. The last time we let you go you—ah—went in the wrong direction, didn't you? Besides, you have no porters!"

"I need no lunch!" snapped Cadji, his black mustaches bristling. "I eat with no brigands! I go to Chai Chai! I go to Lourenço Marques!"

"I'm just a mite afraid, *senhor,*" said Monty, "that you might fall in with Anatole du Maurier on the way. The last surviving member of the Libomba brigands might make you take lunch with him, and that would be too bad; wouldn't it? Take a seat, *senhor.* Lunch is nearly ready. Sixpence, give the *senhor* a chair."

Sixpence produced a chair and thrust the Portuguese down into it with that peculiarly literal understanding the Shangan exerts when it suits him. Cadji affected to collapse under the sense of outrage.

"Now," said Monty, "what do you say, you fellows? Shall we give 'em leave to go and celebrate the weddings?"

"We'll need labor for the gold claims in a day or two," Yerkes reflected.

"Tell 'em to come back in a week," said Oakes.

"Why not keep them here?" said I. "They'll be smelly, but we'll be sure of them."

Nobody agreed with me, however. Yerkes did not like the theory of keeping black or white man in any place without consulting him.

"How about Cadji?" said I.

"Cadji's under contract to us," Yerkes retorted; and that was true.

Monty had no objection to managing the natives' destiny; he simply did not want the trouble of controling them until ready to begin work on the claims down-hill, and Oakes agreed with him.

"Shall I put it to a vote?" asked Monty. "No? Oh, very well. Sixpence—tell them to go. Where? To their kraals. Take the plunder with them. Come back here in a week. Good wages!"

"Them going—not coming back!" objected Sixpence, with a shake of his head. But if everybody always listened to the voice of experience, the world would be a less alarming place to move about in. Sixpence was abruptly ordered to obey, and presently, at their own disorderly leisure, the natives dispersed through the compound gate and down the zigzag wagon-road.

We ate, under the shade of a wagon-awning stretched on poles, and the meal was excellent. After the fashion of all South African cooks Sixpence had taken unto himself apprentices—youths of the country, naked and unashamed, who did the detail work without wage in return for the education.

This left Sixpence free to do every imaginable thing the mind of Monty could devise, and yet not neglect those artistic touches that make the difference between food and victuals. It is the sign of a good cook in that land that he has time and inclination for whatever else demands attention—the hall-mark of a bad one that he refuses to be dissociated from the pots and pans.

WE WERE half-way through the meal when one

of our boys came over from the parapet with word that a party had pitched camp some miles away and a white man was approaching.

"Alone?" asked Monty.

"Him an' one black man," said the boy, and returned to the parapet to watch.

Cadji pricked his ears at the news, and Monty smiled at him across the table.

"This will be your expected ally," he said genially. "Eat, *senhor,* and try to look at ease."

"I expect nobody!" said Cadji.

"You saffron hellion!" said Oakes, without the least trace of resentment. "You would rather lie than eat!"

"Never mind," said Monty. "Let's wait and see."

So we continued to eat, all, that is to say, except Cadji, who gnawed his nails. Then we smoked for an hour until Oakes at last pushed his stool back and reached for the concertina. No polite person has any dealings with those instruments, or with such as use them. On Fifth Avenue and in Mayfair one does not know how to distinguish concertina from accordion, and only prays to know nothing about either.

But out in the open, where the kites wheel under an azure sky and the conventions are less self-assertive, when Fred Oakes plays on his machine and sings to it, one has to admit that music is not the only attractive noise. The sounds he makes are something different, inelegant, it is true, but now and then refreshing, if unique. And as he generally makes up songs to suit the random tunes, there is an unexpectedness that robs discord of its sting.

He sang now, with legs spread wide, his neatly bearded face upturned to heaven, and the unholy instrument stretching and collapsing in noisy spasms, between hands likelier for driving drills than coaxing music.

"Oh, who wouldn't be a high court judge
On the coast of Africay?
I've no desire, nor need to drudge;
I've jolly well come to stay!
My court shall sit where dicky-birds flit
Beneath the purple sky,
That I may take for tyranny's sake
Whatever may please my eye!
Bribes I accept with an open palm,
And justice takes her course;
I hang the poor, I rob the rich,
My specialtee's divorce!
When dusky co-respondents come
In fear for their skins and pelf,
I settle the hash with a rawhide lash
And elope with the dames myself!

"Chorus, you fellows!"

"I'm a right respectable, dignified
Illustrious high court judge!
I've skill and a will, but that's not all;
I've a cast-iron, brass-bound, bomb-proof gall
No argument can budge!
The law's my tool, and I'm quite corrupt;
I assure you I'm here to stay
Till the money's all mine and the banks are rupt
On the coast of Africay!

"How's that, Monty? How's that, Cadji my saffron Lord Chief Justice? Like it? Listen, there's another verse!"

He was about to begin again when, to Cadji's indescribable relief, a thick-set, big, upstanding man appeared in the middle of the gateway and we all faced toward him. He would have been handsome but for the pouches of fat that hung below his too heavy jaws. The smile on his rather thick lips was arrogant, yet overlaid with a desire to please.

One could guess he had been drilled, although not in recent years, and he carried a rifle German-sportsman style, slung so that the barrel showed perpendicular above one shoulder. He wore a little bunch of hawk's feathers on the side of his brown sun-helmet, and his mustache was of the flowing horse's-tail variety with a tendency to curve upward.

"Lieb Vaterland!" said Oakes in an undertone.

"Milwaukee, by the great horn spoon!" said Yerkes.

Monty and I said nothing, but our eyes met as we both looked at Cadji, who was trying to seem un-self-conscious, although with no conspicuous success.

After a moment's hesitation the German left his one black follower outside the gate and strode toward us, six-feet-one-or-two of him, swinging along like a great automaton. He was not appreciably blown by the steep ascent, for all his full stomach that was ill concealed by the greenish cotton sporting-coat he wore. It occurred to me that he very carefully avoided Cadji's eyes, as he faced the table and removed his helmet with considerable dignity, bowing slightly to Monty.

"My name is Herr Heinrich von Muehlendorff," he announced. "I come to find the Earl of Montdidier."

"Take a chair," said Monty. "I'm Mundidger.

"Pardon me. I asked for the Earl of—"

"Mundidger," said Monty. "Sit down. That's me."

The German took a chair heavily—with his back toward Cadji, I noticed. The Portuguese looked surprised, yet I thought not disappointed. He seemed to me to be smirking to himself.

"I have been told," said the German, "by informants whose authority is indisputable, that you have pegged off certain gold claims near the foot of this hill."

"What about it?" asked Monty noncommittally.

"It is of that matter I would speak with you."

"Go ahead!" said Monty, and we all sat back and lit our pipes—I in order to get a better look at the German from between my hands.

There were pouches under his eyes that suggested animality, but there was nothing particularly furtive in his glance—in fact, rather the contrary. He met our eyes, if anything, too boldly.

"What I have to say, Lord Mun—"

"Mundidger."

"Lord Mundidger, is of a confidential nature. It would be correct to dismiss such of your party as are not of the first standing."

"Thank you," said Monty dryly. "I like to be told what to do!"

"Stick Cadji in the water-butt!" said Oakes, and the Portuguese bridled like a hen in a high wind.

"Sixpence!" called Monty. "Take Senior Cadji, out of ear-shot. See no harm comes to him! Bring him back here when I call!"

The enormous, hideous Shangan beckoned, and tie German laughed aloud as Cadji obeyed. Sixpence herded the high court judge with emotions mixed of equal parts pride and nervousness, that in no way interfered with his obvious intention not to let his charge escape. Cadji seemed strangely meek and unindignant.

"Do you mean that these white men are to hear what I have to say?" asked Herr Heinrich von Muehlendorff.

"If you've anything to say to me these are my friends," answered Monty.

"But what I have to say is of the highest significance!"

"Cough it up!" said Oakes, fingering the concertina.

He looked ready to burst into opprobrious song, but Monty caught his eye.

"Hrrrrumph!" said the German pompously. "My information is not such as to be coughed up! One does not talk of world-matters to the world at large."

"Suit yourself, of course," drawled Monty.

"Who are these other men?"

"Make a noise like a Wienerwurst sandwich, America, and put him at ease!" said Oakes.

"They're my friends," repeated Monty, and introduced us each by name.

The German bowed abruptly to us in turn, standing with heels together, and we annoyed him awfully by remaining in our seats.

"Now," said Monty. "Suppose we hear the news."

"The news is that you have destroyed the du Maurier gang," said the German. "The important fact is that I am commercial attache to the Imperial German consulate in Lourenço Marques."

He said that as if it should carry profound weight, and was visibly disappointed by our obvious lack of interest—imitated in my case from Monty, whom I was watching minutely.

"Never heard of you," said Monty.

"Didn't know your nation had a consulate!" lied Oakes, with a twinkle in his eye.

"YOU DID not know that?" said Herr Heinrich von Muehlendorff. "Then you have much to learn! The largest consulate in Lourenço Marques is the German consulate, also having the greatest number of officials and attaches, of whom I have the honor to be not the least. The largest club in Lourenço Marques is also German. The greatest number of merchants other than Portuguese is German.

The most money in Lourenço Marques is controlled by German interests. The import trade from Germany into Lourenço Marques already is colossal, and is daily growing. Germany has indisputably large interests in this part of Africa."

"Very important, I'm sure," murmured Monty.

"The colonial Government is so corrupt," the German went on, "that it keeps no secrets. I, for instance, became at once aware of the agreement made between you and the governor of Gazaland, that you should have title to these valuable gold claims, and to certain rubber concessions elsewhere, in return for ridding these hills of the outlaw du Maurier gang."

"What of it?" demanded Yerkes. "What of it, Heine? What the —— has it got to do with you?"

"This!" said the German, facing him and showing strong teeth in a smile like a woodchuck's. "The Portuguese Government of this colony is so corrupt it can not govern. The outlaws ruled these hills for years. Theirs was the government of these hills *de facto*. You, having overcome the outlaws, are until some other evolution shall occur the Government of these Libomba Hills!"

Oakes squealed with suppressed delight, and Yerkes laughed aloud, but Monty frowned them into silence.

"I don't see your point yet," he said.

"I arrive at the point," said Herr Heinrich von Muehlendorff. "In my unofficial capacity of private representative of certain German high financial interests, I made an agreement with these du Manners before ever you came on the scene, conceding those alluvial gold deposits to me. The agreement was not registered with the Portuguese Government, on the ground that an impotent Government has no authority. But, you see, I am both official and unofficial. In my official capacity it had been my duty to have the agreement registered among tie archives at the Imperial German consulate."

"I suppose your Imperial German consul is accredited to the—ah—impotent Government?" asked Monty.

"Of course!" laughed the German. "There are certain fictions we all subscribe to for tie sake of appearances!"

"I'm still waiting for the point," said Monty.

"I arrive at it," said Muehlendorff.

"Point—joint—anoint—disappoint—" Oakes muttered.

A song was being born—doubtless irreverent, and very sharp. But it died stillborn in response to Monty's frown.

"By coming up here when you did," said Muehlendorff, "you stole a march on me. You see, I am perfectly frank. Two days after you left Lourenço Marques, the money reached me with which to pay these du Mauriers for the gold concession."

"How much money?" demanded Yerkes, like a sprung trap.

"Ten thousand pounds," said the German.

"I don't believe a word of it!" smiled Oakes.

"Pounds English?" I asked, but Monty said nothing.

"Gold!" said the German. "Gold in the Standard Bank in Lourenço Marques!"

"I still don't see the point," said Monty, yawning.

"The Imperial German Government is disposed to support the commercial claims of its subjects in this or any other foreign country," said Muehlendorff, "whereas it is no secret that your Government, Lord Mun—"

"Mundidger."

"Your Government, Lord Mundidger, never backs up its subjects unless compelled! As for the United States—" he looked hard at Yerkes—"the United States has utterly no influence in Africa!"

"I imagine you're scouting for trouble, Heine!" said Yerkes with a dry grin. "Ignorance can't hurt me! Carry on!"

Herr Heinrich von Muehlendorff chose to ignore the remark.

"My present purpose," he said, "is to establish valid and valuable claims in this country, in my unofficial capacity of commercial representative of those great financial interests at which I hinted. I am willing—" he faced Monty and looked hard in his eyes—"to pay to you the ten thousand pounds for a transfer to me of your claim to the whole property formerly claimed and controlled by Charles du Maurier."

"The devil you are!" said Monty.

"There is no devil about it," said the German. "The gold is in the Standard Bank, and is yours for your signature!"

"You mean you've brought a contract with you?" Monty began to seem interested.

The German drew a single sheet of foolscap from his inner pocket and tossed it on the table.

"It is simple. It is all written on that. There are no deceptions—no riders—no evasions. Ten thousand pounds in gold, in return for your transfer to me of the du Maurier estate."

"Leave it with me. We'll consider it after you've gone," said Monty.

Herr Heinrich von Muehlendorff looked surprised.

"Perhaps I would better call attention to some circumstances," he said, and the tone of his voice took on a subtly triumphant note.

"Say anything you like, as long as it's polite," answered Monty, yawning again.

"Bear me witness, I approached you politely! But observe—this camp—this fort—this hill-top—this outlaw's nest is of no use from a defensive standpoint. The sides of the hill are steep, but climbable. It would need a large force to defend the place, and there are but four of you. In my camp I have two hundred men, many of them armed, and all led by Germans!"

"You mean you propose to drive us out?" asked Monty.

"Shove him in the water-butt!" urged Oakes.

"I thought we'd see your teeth presently!" said Yerkes. "Attack and be —— to you!"

But it was perfectly obvious that, if it were true he had two hundred armed men with German leaders, then he could take the fort when he so chose. He would lose a lot of men, of course, if we defended it, but the conclusion would be foregone. The place never had been put in a state of defence. Charles du Maurier's purpose in choosing it had been to overlook all trails, and have plenty of time in which to run or get ready a flank attack should he descry an enemy.

"Of course I intend no violence," said Muehlendorff. "I only mentioned—"

"Then why mention it?" asked Monty very bluntly.

"Let me present to you some other aspects of the situation," said the German. "I have—not in my pocket, but in safe keeping in my camp below there—certain slips of paper signed by you, and bearing the Portuguese high court seal. I bought them from the natives to whom you gave them an hour or two ago! For the moment let us pass by the peculiar circumstance of Lord Montdidier's signature appearing on any such document!

"Certain of the slips purport to be the marriage certificates of certain women. Those women were the wives of Charles du Maurier. Charles du Maurier claimed title to all these lands by virtue of the old Portuguese law, under which the lands of a chief pass at his death to any white man who may have married one of the chief's daughters. The claim might be made that the lands reverted to the women on Charles du Maurier's death. I might purchase the title from the men to whom you claim to have legally married the women! They are in my camp, and can not get away!"

"Let's hang him!" said Yerkes.

"Hang him and Cadji from one tree!" Oakes seconded.

"Excuse me," said the German, promptly and pleasantly. "My Government will hold to strict accountability whoever assaults my person, as well as the Government permitting such assault!"

"You've some more up your sleeve," said Monty. "Out with it, and save time!"

"You could not work these claims without laborers. "It happens that in my semiofficial capacity I have received authority to visit the chiefs in this district for ethnological research. I am in position to exercise such pressure as will prevent the chiefs from sending you laborers."

MONTY WAS fingering the sheet of foolscap that the German had thrown between them. I noticed that he had read it without seeming to.

"How much does Cadji know about this?" he demanded.

The Germans laughed.

"Why trouble about him?" he sneered.

"How much does he know?" asked Monty.

"It was he," said Herr Heinrich von Muehlendorff, "who interviewed Charles du Maurier on my account, and arranged the terms. He is a mere intermediary. What of him? He is nothing! So!" He snapped his fingers. "He expects a commission from me, and doubtless he demanded a big one from the du Mauriers. But the du Mauriers are dead, and I am dealing with you in person. Let us forget Cadji!"

"What else?" asked Monty, with a sort of abrupt directness that went straight to the mark.

Whatever Yerkes might say—and he said a lot of it very often—about the British aristocracy being a shameless anachronism, there was no denying Monty's ability to command respect. He could draw fire by dint of sheer assumption of superiority, just as easily as he could subdue wrath by his gentle manners. The German, nothing loath when it came to boasting, seized the bait instantly.

"Ha! *Kreutz-Donnerwetter!* You have perspicacity! You perceive that I would not approach you without having first every individual trump card in my hand! That is so! I have them all! Every one, *meine Herren!* I have Anatole du Maurier—ha-ha! The last of the family—the one who alone had any brains—the cousin of Charles—he whom you failed to kill last night—he is in my camp! He expects to make terms with me! Why do I not deal with him? Because you are in possession, and he not! But—make note of it—he remains to make agreements with, should you fail to be amenable!"

"And that's your whole case, is it?" asked Monty.

"That is my case," said the German. "You have until four this afternoon in which to answer!"

"Failing which?" suggested Monty.

"I shall act!"

Herr Heinrich von Muehlendorff replaced a gold watch in the pocket of his ample vest, and rose.

"I will remain out of ear-shot until you make up your minds!" he said condescendingly.

"Take a tip," said Fred, "and keep out of sight, too!"

"Heine," said Yerkes, "be advised, and beat it!"

I had never seen Yerkes so savagely self-restrained. The German caught the war note in his voice and eyed him captiously.

"I am not afraid of all four of you!" he said.

Yerkes half-rose to his feet, but Monty glanced at his wrist-watch and intervened.

"Give you just two minutes, Herr von What'syourname," he said, "to get out of this compound. Stay longer at your own risk! Return at four for your answer if you card to. Good afternoon!"

The German saluted him with a sardonic smile, and a flourish of the hand that was the very peak of insolence.

"Ten thousand pounds by check on the Standard Bank at four o'clock, or nothing—except trouble!" he sneered, turning on his heel.

We watched him swagger out of the compound, with feelings that in my case were unmixed. I could guess what the others thought more or less by their faces, and was surprised to see Monty calm and apparently free from any symptom of resentment.

"This contract he wants us to sign," he said, "is peculiar, under the circumstances. Sixpence!"

The Shangan came at a run, dragging Cadji with him, the little short-legged Portuguese objecting savagely to the indignity of being fetched.

"Baas?"

"Leave Senhor Cadji here. Place two boys where they can watch where that German goes, and report to me. Then come back here."

Sixpence allowed a great grin of comprehension to spread across his flattened physiognomy, made a sort of semi-apologetic grimace at Cadji—for the color-line means more even to the black man than the white—and vanished.

"There's a chance, Senhor Cadji," said Monty, "that your knowledge of law, your experience of Governmental conditions, and all that kind of thing, may—ah—possibly provide you with an avenue of return to our good graces."

The Portuguese looked unpleasant—entirely unwilling to believe us capable of either grace or goodness.

"Take a seat," said Monty. "Look that over, please."

He passed him the sheet of foolscap the German had left on the table.

"What comment occurs to you to make on that?"

The Portuguese frowned over the document, reading it swiftly, considering it slowly, and passing it back. Monty passed it on for us to read in turn.

"It is a joke contract!" said Cadji, with a huge shrug of his shoulders. "It is illegal! It is in fact no contract, *senhores!* It bears no stamps—it—"

"They could affix German stamps at the consulate," said Monty.

"It makes no mention of your agreement with our Government!" said Cadji. "It calls for a transfer of rights that never did exist and that, supposing them ever to have existed, were taken by you by force from men who stole them! A court of law would laugh at it! It is beneath all argument! It is—what shall I say—it is *opera bouffe!"*

"He seems disinclined to deal with your Government, doesn't he?" said Monty. "We having bought the right to prospect here, and title having been promised to us—and he knew about that of course—I suppose he thought it would be no use offering money to the Government."

Cadji shrugged his shoulders.

"Whoever offers money to my Government, *senhores,* will find no hesitation about acceptance! The right to prospect in this district has been sold half a dozen times in my day! It will be sold again, when you are dead or gone away!"

"But why—" Monty's level brows were knitted into a puzzled knot—"why doesn't he offer to buy from us our contract with the Portuguese Government, that conceivably has some value? You see what he says there, you fellows? He asks us to sell for ten thousand pounds rights acquired by us from the du Mauriers—all rights acquired from the du

Mauriers, I think it reads, with no mention as to how we came by them, or when."

"By thunder!" said Yerkes, leaning back in his chair and putting one heel on the table. "I'd send that piece of paper to the British consulate, and await results if I were you!"

"I rather suspect it might arrive too late," said Monty.

Oakes squealed.

"Chess!" he said. "Chess!"

"Yes," admitted Monty. "Chess, I think! Senhor Cadji, you don't forget, I hope, that you hold a ten per cent. interest in our property."

"I am aware of it!" said Cadji, brightening up. "Ten per cent. of ten thousand is a thousand pounds!"

"But, by ——, you shall earn it before you're paid!" said Monty. "You've played us fast and loose in every conceivable way! You sold us to the du Mauriers before this expedition started. You'd sell us to Heinrich von What'shisname if you thought you could make eleven hundred by it. Listen to me now, and remember I'm not joking! When you left Lourenço Marques—" he leaned over the table, strong, dark, and handsome, and his dark eyes seemed to surprise Cadji's thoughts before he could cover them—"were there any unusual political conditions there? Speak!"

Cadji shrugged his shoulders.

"Political conditions?" he said. "They are never what you would call usual. Myself, I am a monarchist. I am for *statu quo.* I am against upheavals of the body politic, which make always for uncertainty."

"Then there are anti-monarchists?" demanded Monty.

"Senhor, there is a very strong undercurrent of republican sentiment in all Portuguese colonies—unhappily in this one also. It meets with my disapproval. Yes, there is republican feeling."

"What else?" demanded Monty, and the Portuguese hesitated.

"It is not proper to discuss the secrets of my Government!" he answered.

"They're no longer secrets if you know them, and if you know them they're for sale!" said Yerkes pointedly.

"Bravo, America!" roared Oakes, thumping him on the back.

"Would you fellows mind keeping quiet a minute?" asked Monty impatiently. "Now, Senhor Cadji. Ten per cent. of ten thousand pounds, as well as ten per cent. of any future profits according to agreement—or out of the compound you go this minute after the German! Choose!"

CADJI HESITATED. It looked as if our terms, although tempting, were not enormously better than what he hoped he might perhaps exact from Muehlendorff. Besides, to the convinced corruptionist a bird in the bush looks twice as good as any in the hand.

"And take your chance of reaching the German alive," added Oakes, with a meaning glance at Sixpence and a rifle.

"We'd duck you again, of course," said Yerkes.

"And then tar and feather you," said I.

"But we'll let you go to Heine if you'd rather," Yerkes added.

"Time's passing," said Monty, and Cadji made up his mind.

"Senhores, there is a feeling among monarchists that—perhaps—who knows?—another monarch—a change of monarchs—might be better."

"You mean revolution?" asked Yerkes.

"Shut up, America!" Oakes thumped him in the ribs and upset him, chair and all. "Go on, Monty!"

"It is those who favor a republic who would bring on revolution," Cadji answered. "Monarchists are against all forms of revolution. We prefer—what should I say?—a *coup d'état.*"

Yerkes, reaching under the table, grabbed Monty's folded chess-board, resumed his seat, and opened it.

"Chess!" he said. "Me for the chess! I don't understand a word. Monty's chessmen may shed light."

He moved a yellow knight to the center of the board.

"Call that one Cadji. Here's Heine von Deutschland."

He moved a rook.

"Take Heine's money—sign the paper—kick Cadji—move down to the claims that belong to us—let Heine take this place that belonged more or less to du Maurier—it begins to look simple to me! *Coup d'état?* What's a *coup d'état* got to do with it?"

Oakes had his foot against Yerkes' chair-leg. At a sign of impatience from Monty he shoved with all his might, and for the second time within two minutes Bill went headlong.

"The *senhores* play the tomfool rather than listen!" sneered Cadji.

The little man's nerves were on edge, what with fear, and intrigue, and the rough handling he had had.

"Never mind them!" said Monty. "Talk to me."

"*Senhor*—my lord—it will make no difference. Should that *coup d'état,* take place, or should it not, the Government will certainly dispute von Muehlendorff's claims under that contract, should you sign it! My advice is—sign, and receive the money!"

Monty nodded, looking puzzled. Watching from one side as I was, with the Portuguese silhouetted against the wagon-flap, I had a chance to see the best of the game. It seemed to me he was in league in some way with the German, although willing to betray him too if worth his while; but from the sudden look of sly satisfaction that crossed his face, I thought he now saw a way of cheating both sides. I tried to signal to Monty, but he did not catch my eye. Cadji leaned toward him and suddenly spoke very earnestly.

"*Senhor*—my lord—you will surely pay me the thousand pounds?"

Monty laughed, but did not answer.

"When will you pay it?"

"Whenever we present the German's check at the bank in Lourenço Marques."

"That is sufficient for me! That is the word of an English gentleman—of an English lord, who is even better than a gentleman! Now listen to me, *senhor!* Pay me that money, and I will pay you further ten thousand pounds, less ten per cent, for my commission! Sign that contract with the German—sign it—sign it! Come with me to Lourenço Marques, I know a syndicate of rich Portuguese merchants who will instantly purchase your real rights for ten thousand pounds! Sell the false, so-called rights that he asks for, to the German. Sell the real rights, for which you have contract from the present Government to my syndicate!"

"What d'you mean by present Government?" demanded Monty.

The Portuguese hesitated.

"Did I say present Government? It was a slip of the tongue. I meant Government, *senhor!*"

Monty turned to us.

"Have you heard, you fellows? What do you say? He proposes that we sell to the German for ten thousand pounds, and again to some Portuguese for another ten."

"The whole thing's a swindle. I say no!" said Yerkes. "To —— with him!"

Fred looked at Monty, and then at Yerkes with an eye that twinkled.

"I vote with Yerkes," he grinned.

It would have been wiser for me to hold my tongue. I had not made my mind rip, but suspected there was some third course not yet obvious.

"All right," I said. "I vote no, too."

"I vote aye!" said Monty dryly. "Three noes to one aye. The ayes have it! *Senhor,*" he said, pushing paper and pencil toward the Portuguese, "do you write German? Just scribble a line to von Muehlendorff asking him to come at once."

And he got up and walked away.

Yerkes fairly gasped, and Oakes roared with laughter. Cadji wrote on the paper with a contemptuous back toward them both.

"America," said Oakes, fingering his concertina, "I wouldn't have voted against you for a million! I'd vote your way every, time, for a sight of your sweet fade when Monty turns the trick. You bally ass! Haven't you realized Monty'll lead from whichever hand suits him as long as the lead's his?"

"Then what in —— did he put the vote for?" demanded Yerkes. "Is he the Kaiser?"

"He might like to know what you were thinking, sweetheart! D'you think he'd ask if he didn't care?"

Cadji folded the paper up and addressed it on the outside to von Muehlendorff.

"Who shall take this?" he demanded.

"I'll sign it first," said Oakes, and reached for it.

"No need," said Cadji. "It is signed already."

Oakes still had his hand out. He and I were facing one way and could both see Monty talking to Sixpence fifty yards away. Monty shook his head violently, and signaled with his hand.

"Oh, very well," said Oakes, and I thought that Cadji smiled.

Sixpence crossed over, took the note from Cadji, and went off with it through the gate, followed by another boy. Presently I saw the boy come back to Monty, who turned his back toward us. After a minute the boy hurried back through the gate again. Oakes undid the clasp of his concertina, tried a dozen haphazard chords, chanced on one that suited him, and sang:

"Consider the brass on the ruddy recruit!
Oh, watch him stand easy, and see him salute!
With the King's Regulations to tell him his rights
He's a barrack-room lawyer, and worse—till he fights!
Oh, but then what a change! You may tread on him then!
Your recruit becomes human—his officers men—
And it's "Stand on my neck, sir!" Oh, anything goes
When the guns are unlimbered and men are at blows!

"Behold the slick voter with topper and cane;
The ballot's his god—good advice is his bane!
Oh, he'll down with the best, and he'll up with the worst,
Putting principle last, and his pocketbook first!
But it's otherwise quite when political schemes
Have corrupted and busted the peace of his dreams;
Then he shouts for dictators! "To —— with the polls!"
One pilot he wants who can steer by the shoals!

"And consider the chief, of priority proud,
How he flaunts a blue ribbon and marshals the crowd;
For ways he's a stickler, on form he insists,
He denounces as damned any rough who resists!
Oh, the route and the time he lays down in advance—
How the banners shall wave and the hired horses prance;
But his pains are all wasted, his tyranny vain—
The procession won't march in the rain—in the rain!"

"It's not often I moralize, America, but the devil drives me now and then! Monty's a democrat when you catch him napping—which is about every third Tuesday in Lent of alternate leap-years! I'm worse than Monty!"

MONTY STROLLED back toward the table casually, and we went to meet him, for Cadji showed a disposition to "listen in," growing alert and attentive; but he could scarcely summon courage to get up and follow us.

"What d'you suppose Cadji wrote in his note to the German?" Monty asked.

" 'All is over between us. I enclose the diamond ring!' " Oakes hazarded.

" 'I have persuaded them. Ten per cent. commission! Come!' " Monty answered.

"Playing both ways from the middle, eh?" said Yerkes.

We strolled together toward the parapet, climbed it, and stood looking over the plain, all blue with haze, blotched here and there with thatch-roofed native kraals. About five miles away we could see the camp the German had pitched, and it looked not at all unlikely there were at least the two hundred more-or-less-armed men of whom he boasted.

Semi-official members of consulates are able to travel in great style in lands where the Government lacks grip. But he had not returned to his camp. Through Monty's glasses I could see him at the foot of our hill, waiting for the answer he doubtless considered inevitable.

With a glance over his shoulder to make sure Cadji was not within hearing, Monty took us more or less into confidence—in his usual way, without prelude or apology.

"As Oakes said, there's chess here! There's an obvious intent to pick a quarrel with the Portuguese Government!"

"I get you!" said Yerkes. "If Heine really wanted title to our claims, he'd offer to buy our contract with the governor."

"Whereas," said Monty, "he particularly avoids that, although well aware of its existence. Without suspecting it, we have—"

"Sat into a crooked game," said Yerkes.

"Von Muehlendorff dealt in the first instance with the du Manners," said Monty. "He admits it. He would never have offered to deal with us, even although we've destroyed the du Mauriers, unless he were in something of a hurry."

"Rot! He has the last-left du Maurier with him," objected Oakes.

"But not the du Maurier who owned this hill and was bully of the Libombas," answered Monty. "He probably prefers our simplicity to Anatole du Maurier's probable treachery. Anatole's only a poor reserve in case of accident. Oh, I don't doubt he's in a hurry."

"But why—for what?" I asked, utterly puzzled.

"If he wants our claims, why not offer to buy them in the ordinary way?"

"He doesn't care a rap for the claims," said Monty.

"Very well," I objected. "Why throw away ten thousand pounds? That's quite a sum of money!"

"For him personally—yes," admitted Monty.

"Then you mean the financial interests he says he represents—"

"Financial jackanapes!" said Monty. "Yerkes had the right idea—see the British consul—see him quickly. D'you recall what von What'shisname said about 'world affairs' not being talked of 'to the world at large'? It's funny, but in all my acquaintance with Germans I've never yet known one who didn't give his own game away—usually through self-importance!" He turned so as to face us three. "By the way, you fellows, I'd like a vote on this."

Yerkes laughed outright.

"Why not have us vote first, and tell us what it's about afterward?"

"This is a question of individual rights," said Monty, perfectly unruffled. "We've got to be unanimous on this or the proposal drops. Do you fellows consider twenty thousand pounds a fair price for our property below there?"

"Sure!" said Yerkes.

"At that price I'm willing to throw in all the malaria—the stink from the swamps—the snakes—the flies—the mosquitos—and a blessing!" said Oakes.

As my share under the partnership agreement would be one-third of a half of that, and never having seen as much as three thousand pounds in one lump in my life, I naturally hesitated. The words would not come.

"Y-yes!" I stammered. "C-certainly!"

"All the same," said Yerkes, "I'd hate to feel that a threatening hog like Heine had put one over on us!"

"But suppose it's the other way 'round, and we fool him?" said Monty.

"Deal me in!" said Yerkes.

There and then we all agreed on twenty thousand pounds as our selling price, but none except Monty saw as much as the next step toward obtaining it.

We went back and amused Cadji by playing football with a bundle of old rope, and him for the unwilling goal, until the German put in an appearance and stalked toward us with a sort of businesslike commercial air.

"So we are agreed?" he said, with helmet off and outstretched hand.

"We'll sell," said Monty, failing to see the strong, thick paw.

"I will write you a check," said the German. But the check he drew from his pocket was already filled out, except for the signature. He sat at the table and wrote his name with a flourish—waved the check in the air to dry it—and pushed it across the table toward Monty. Monty let it lie.

"Now for your signature on the contract! I prefer that all four shall sign!" he said.

"We'll sign when we've cashed that check," said Monty blandly.

The German spluttered indignantly.

"It is unheard of," he asserted, "that the signature on a check of an attache of the Imperial German consulate should be questioned by any one!"

"Senhores," said Cadji in an awe-struck voice, "that check is good! Accept it! How shall an attache of the Imperial German consulate refuse to recognize his own signature? How can the Standard Bank refuse to pay?"

"Couldn't say, I'm sure," said Monty.

Yerkes rubbed his forefinger and thumb together under Cadji's nose.

"Cash!" he said simply.

"But I will guarantee the check!" said Cadji, and excepting Monty we all laughed—even von Muehlendorff.

"Very well," said the German with a shrug of his shoulders. "It is all the same to me. I intend to return at once to Lourenço Marques. Come with me and receive the money!"

"Sure!" sneered Yerkes. "And leave your blackguards below there to occupy this place unopposed! We're simple, we are!"

Monty turned to Cadji. "Will you witness the signature on that check?" he asked and Cadji nodded.

"Will you stamp your official seal on it?"

"Certainly!" said Cadji.

"Do it!" said Monty; and Cadji obeyed.

"Now if you care to give me the check, we'll go to Lourenço Marques," said Monty. "And when we have the money for it, Herr Heinrich von Muehlendorff, we will all four sign that paper!"

"Good!" said the German. "I am satisfied!"

And he certainly looked it.

Monty pocketed the check, and the German rose to go.

"There is beer in my camp," he remarked affably.

"The deuce there is," said Monty.

"Whisky also," said the German.

"You don't mean it!"

"And cigars—imported—from Habana."

"Ah!"

"Will you come?"

"Meet you at our hotel," said Monty. "If you propose to reach Lourenço Marques ahead of us you'll have to travel fast! Good afternoon!"

"What do you mean?" the German demanded. "You must come with me! You must travel with me!"

"Not in the bargain," said Monty. "Meet you at our hotel! Here—have the check back if you like!"

Cadji gasped as Monty drew it from his pocket.

"No!" said the German. "No! I am satisfied. That check has been witnessed. It bears a high court seal. Senhor Cadji knows its purpose. I am content. Besides—the English nobility are well known for honorable dealing. I have no fear you will not keep your bargain."

"Very well, then," said Monty, and the German saluted stiffly, Monty acknowledging it without emphasis.

"**BEGINS TO** look like taking candy from a kid," said Yerkes with glee in his voice.

"But which kid?" said Monty.

And none of us answered. I am sure none of us understood.

"Now then, you fellows!" he said. "Let's shake a leg! The German will go by Chai Chai and the steamer down the Limpopo. He'll probably start at dawn, and won't waste time. We've got to pack, and clear out tonight!"

"*Senhores,* I will not travel at night!" said Cadji. "It is not safe! There are lions! There are disaffected natives! There is malaria! There are mosquitoes! If you do not go by way of Chai Chai you must follow the swamps, and they are impossible!"

"Oh, Lord!" groaned Oakes, whose former journey across the swamps was such as none of us were likely to forget.

Monty ignored them both.

"There's a way down the Tembe River! Charles du Maurier had barges on the Tembe somewhere. He persuaded a Frenchman to put up the money to build them in Lourenço Marques. They loaded them with corn, to trade to the natives in famine time, and towed them up to the nearest point to this place. Charles du Maurier shot the Frenchman as soon as the journey was done, and the barges lie nose to the bank in a backwater—or so I'm told. I'm going to find them!"

"In the dark?" I wondered.

"I will not travel in the dark!" insisted Cadji.

"It'll be daylight when we get there!" answered Monty. "Now, you fellows—pack!"

Most of our loads had been made ready the night before under Monty's orders, in case disaster to us should have necessitated flight when the robbers attacked. It did not take very long to overhaul them, and make the rest ready.

We got the mules out of the shed and set boys to grooming them; they had had a good long rest, and were fit to march furiously. Everything was in order some time before sunset; and as the sun went down beyond the western rim of the parapet we put the unwilling Cadji on a mule and filed out of the gate, with Sixpence leading, carrying an unlit lantern slung over his shoulder on a pole.

I rode last to prick along the stragglers, and had no trouble yet, for there would be a pay-day when we should reach Lourenço Marques and the loaded boys marched with a will.

But the cows that had been our boys' share of the du Maurier loot very soon began upsetting calculations. They objected to traveling at night—were scared by every deep shadow, and of every jackal's whimper—prone to stampede, and willing to go any way but forward. We had not more than descended the steep, zigzag dragon-road and started to march 'round the foot of the hill to place a sheltering spur between us and the German's ramp—we could see his lights glimmering in the distance—than our procession was thrown into disorder; and every effort to remedy matters only made it worse.

Monty rode up and down the length of the line in a fury, threatening to have the cows butchered unless their owners could keep them controlled. Yerkes made a gallant effort to act cowboy, on a mule that would neither wheel nor gallop. Cadji piped incessantly about the madness that impelled us to try to march in the dark.

At last a lion roared in the distance, and the cows became utterly bereft of reason. But for a little disused thorn corral we came on, long abandoned by its native owners and none too well preserved, we should doubtless have lost every one of them.

And if that had happened, nothing was more likely than that our boys would have refused to march until dawn should give them a chance of rounding up what lions and jackals might have left alive. Monty called a halt, and we drove the frantic, foolish beasts into the enclosure.

"If we only had thought of bringing rawhide reams with us!" he said to me. "We could lash them two by two to a chain or a long pole. They couldn't get away from us then."

"I could go back and get the reams and chains from one or two of Charles du Maurier's wagons," I said.

"I wish you would," he answered. Take half a dozen boys with you. Take Sixpence if you like. We shall have to wait here till you catch us up, so hurry!"

We had come further than I thought, and the journey back to the foot of the hill took an interminable time. Half-way up the hill I decided to leave my mule with one of the boys and clamber the rest of the way on foot. Being no horseman, the angle the mule's back made, and his awkward efforts, made me prefer Shanks' mare.

I was ashamed of admitting even to myself that I was a quitter, and made a fuss of pretending the mule was lame, which I suspect did not deceive Sixpence for a moment; but I made him hunt about for a level place and, when he found one at last behind a great rock ten yards to one side of the track, I left the mule there with one of the boys to guard him. It turned out to be a stroke of rare good fortune that I did so.

Sixpence hurried on ahead of me, his black body and dingy blanket part of the night, and his accustomed sinews making nothing of the steep ascent. It was his sharp eyes that saved me from walking straight into a trap. He came hurrying back, silent as a shadow, gesticulating, signaling, doing everything but shout to put me on guard. The other boys lay flat at once wherever it was darkest, and I followed suit.

"Him Anatole," said Sixpence, panting as he crouched in the shadow beside me, "him German, an' many black man—many guns—all up there!"

I lay still and thought the matter out, seeing but one solution of it, and one course to take. We were not very far from the top, and as we all kept silence I heard voices. Men were talking English near the gate. Trying to catch the words was like fishing for something you could see, with a line so short that the hook would scarcely touch—exasperating. I crawled forward, whispering to Sixpence to stay with the others where he was—another stroke of luck. My star was in the ascendant that night.

I crawled carefully, and dare say could not have been heard from a yard away, but my movements made just sufficient noise to increase the difficulty of hearing, and I went up very close to the gate before lying flat at last in the deepest shadow I could find. Then my own heart beat so loud that I seemed for the moment worse off than ever. A singing in my ears made matters worse. But presently I heard footfalls, and saw the figures of two men loom black in the midst of the open gate.

"You must suit yourself," said one of them, and I recognized the voice of von Muehlendorff. "As I told you I will deal with you when you can prove yourself to be the man with whom I should deal! I have helped you. What more can I do?"

"——!" growled the other man. "If I had caught the —— swine napping as you said I could, their throats would be cut by now!"

"In that case I would now be dealing with you instead of them!" said the German.

"You fooled me!" growled the other voice. "You sent me up here on a blind errand!"

"Nonsense!" answered the German, not in the least alarmed, if his voice was any criterion. "They have marched sooner than I thought they would, that is all. You can catch them, can't you? Have you no legs? No courage?"

"Bah! What is the use? If I had caught them here I could have cut all their throats. On the march perhaps I can kill one or two—perhaps not. What is the use?"

"Listen!" said the German, "and don't be a cry-baby!"

"Cry-baby!" snarled the voice. "I'll drink blood tonight! That's the kind of baby I am!"

"Good! Then get on their trail. If you can kill the tall one—him they call Lord Mundidger—Monty—my check is made out in his name, and the others won't have sense enough to do anything—kill him and bring me proof of it, I'll deal with you. I'll buy title from you then. But you'll have to be quick!"

"Give me some more men!" the voice growled. "Give me a pair of your Germans and six more rifles!"

"NO," SAID von Muehlendorff. "Germans must not be mixed in this, and you have guns enough. My other guns are German-made, and might get us all into trouble. Their natives are unarmed. Your ten men are plenty. Even if they shoot wildly and hit nothing, they will cause a stampede. Your rifle will do the real work. My advice to you is, follow them, and get close! Shoot when you get the chance. Shoot them all if you can—never mind their porters—but shoot that man Monty in any case! If you fail, you needn't look for sympathy from me! I don't do business with failures! If you fail I shall deal with them, and you may go to the devil!"

"To the devil, eh?" the voice growled.

"To the devil!" said the German.

"The devil, eh? You don't know who the devil is! I, Anatole du Maurier am the devil! My heart is hell—hell I tell you! What do I care for you? My brothers—my cousins—my nephews—they are dead—an dead—blown to the devil by that pack of blasted Englishmen! My family is all gone to the devil!

"I am alone! I will get them! I will get them! I will cut out their livers! I will bring their livers to you to-morrow at dawn, all warm and bloody! I will squeeze their livers like a sponge with my fingers thus before your tent. And you shall give me the ten thousand pounds, or I will kill you! Go! Get along! Leave me alone! My breast burns! Go, I tell you!"

"Thank you," said the German. "You go first. I prefer to walk behind."

"You first!" growled Anatole.

"No," said the German. "If you care to send your men down first I will walk beside you."

Anatole whistled, and a number of black shapes took form in the night beside him. He said something to them, and in twos, each with a rifle, his gang of natives started down-hill, I praying they might not fall foul of Sixpence and my unarmed contingent.

Then the German and Anatole du Maurier started to walk side by side, Anatole on the side of the track nearest me. In ten strides they were within a yard of me, and I lay crouched as if the very strain of thew and muscle would make me more invisible. They did not see me. They did not suspect me.

In another stride they would have passed when Anatole set his clumsily shod foot unwarily on a loose stone, twisted his ankle, sidestepped to get back his balance, and trod hard on the back of my hand.

"Snakes!" he yelled, jumping a yard high, and coming down with both feet and all his weight on my shoulders.

"——, no! It's a man!"

The pain in my hand was excruciating. I was on my knees in a second and the effort threw Anatole on to his back. The German fired a pistol five times in swift succession, the flash showing me each time, and each shot missing me by smaller margin.

By that time Anatole was on his feet again and the German decided to leave me to his mercy and ran back through the gate. Anatole raised his rifle and aimed at me. I rushed in under it, and closed with him, feeling his ribs crack as I used my whole strength. And that same second I heard several shots ring out on the road below. Sixpence had joined battle with the riflemen!

My fight with Anatole was short and swift. He clubbed his rifle short and tried to brain me, but I drove my head in under his chin and the blows rained less and less heavily on my shoulder. I forced his head back so far that he dropped the rifle and used both hands to wrench and tear at my face.

He was gaining nothing by that, but was doing damage, so I stepped swiftly and changed the grip, getting my right arm over his throat and under his armpit. So we swayed for a minute, he kicking savagely at my shins, and I using all my strength to break his thick neck if I could.

I felt him reach for my eye with the thumb of his left hand, and not being minded to go through the rest of this existence one-eyed put out a terrific effort. The agony of the pressure on his throat frenzied him and be burst free. I swung back and landed with my left fist and all my strength and weight below his breastbone.

He reeled—tottered—staggered—lost his balance—and fell backward over the edge of the road. I could not see, but I remembered that the least drop near that place was a matter of thirty feet, with broken rock to fall on, and I wasted no time wishing him farewell.

Thirty seconds I did waste, though, wondering whether to go after the German next or hurry to the help of Sixpence. Then I heard six shots fired on the road below, and turned and saw the flash of two more. That decided me. I started to run down-hill, and tripped over something Anatole had dropped.

Getting up again, I groped for it, and found a big leather bandolier belt with pouches—by its weight it held two hundred cartridges, and I wondered how many more the men down-hill had between them. Hope told me I had their whole reserve of ammunition.

I picked up my own rifle that lay where I had crouched in the dark-I had actually forgotten it in the struggle—and started to run down-hill, unable to see two yards in front of me. And I was nearly brained by the backward swing of a rifle-butt that missed my nose so nearly that the skin tingled. The weight of the wind it made was like a blow.

There was no doubting the blow either, only happily it did not strike me. It was sweat that gleamed on the broad of Sixpence's naked back in front of me. It was the butt of a rifle he had seized from an enemy that went whistling in the arc of a circle through the blackness. And it was the skull of one of Anatole du Maurier's men that it landed on, with a smack that was simply sickening.

"Dat you, *Baas?"* he panted.

"Yes, Sixpence. Where are the others?"

"One, two, tree man dead—one more man head smash fall over cliff—others run away!"

"Our men, you mean?"

"No, *Baas.* Our men all right."

"Where?"

"One wid mule all the same you left him. Two more gone an' help hold mule. Mule, him afraid."

"Where are the other two?"

" 'Fraid like mule! Dem two hiding!" I looked for them, while Sixpence wiped a beastly mess of brains from the rifle-butt; presently I pulled them out of the shadow where they lurked. The mule was quiet again, so I called two more of the boys and, having found that Sixpence, for all his lion's share of the battle, was unscathed and scarcely winded, started up-hill once more to hunt for Muehlendorff.

But, hunt high and low though we did, I did not find him. For one thing that robbers' lair was a big place, and in the dark there were a thousand spots where even a big man could hide. For another my men were afraid. Even Sixpence, fired with the fury of having slain assailants in the dark, was in no mood to try conclusions with a white man, and I think would have intentionally overlooked him.

We found the chains and reams though, and presently I rode down-hill on the mule with a fine disregard of anything but speech although the bruises Anatole had given me were beginning by then to hurt.

I had a sensation of being aimed at by von Muehlendorff, and rather suspect the mule shared it, for he cantered without urging the moment he set foot on level ground. The rest of that night's journey was and remains a nightmare. We lashed the cows to long poles that somehow or other Monty and the other two had cut in the dark; but even then they rushed about crazy things, and a third of our loads were lost by porters who, rather naturally, jettisoned our property to save their own.

A couple of lions got wind of us and, although afraid to come in close and try conclusions, put in some lusty lung-work at medium range. Each roar was the signal for panic, and even the mules were next to unmanageable.

We got rid of the cows at last by leaving them in a native kraal, whose sleepy owners kept us bargaining outside the gate until Monty in a great rage threatened to fire the roofs, and made a torch in proof of his extermination. Then they dragged away the stake and thorn barrier and, driving our cows in, we left nine men to care for them until the remainder should be paid off and return.

Then we pressed onward through thorn-country, that made the mules' legs bleed, tore our trousers into shreds, and tortured our barelegged men.

The lions, realizing that the cows were safe from them, tagged, along after us and, I suppose in a sort of spirit of revenge, scared us thoroughly whenever specially dark places gave them a chance to rush in without risk. I fired in the dark at real or imaginary yellow eyes a dozen times.

Monty fired less often, but hit nothing either. The mosquitos were a plague. We breathed them. Over and over again I brushed them from my face in handfuls, and my mule's flank to leeward of the scarcely appreciable breeze was a mess of blood.

DAWN FOUND weary and ill-tempered boys, even the usually dauntless Sixpence, clamorous for a long halt and a sleep. Fred was inclined to back them up; he showed signs of another attack of the fever that had wrought such havoc with him on a former march. But Monty laughed all argument aside. He permitted a short halt for breakfast and to feed the mules, then spurred us on toward the Tembe River.

We could see it long before we reached it. The long line of trees on either bank made a mark along the horizon none could miss. And finding the barges proved to be an easy matter because we came on the tracks du Maurier's wagons had made when he hauled the corn bags from the river to his nest among the hills. But we were a worn-out party when we rode down a gully at last and found the barges tied nose to the bank among the reeds. Any one of them was big enough.

But we had to fight then to get the mules on board. The first one jumped in after a fifteen-minute argument with teeth and heels, only to jump out again on the far side into the river. A crocodile seized him promptly, and he disappeared screaming in a pool of blood and mud, which scarcely encouraged the others.

But what with Monty's determination and Yerkes' skill, and the brute force the rest of us exerted, we got them all in at last and lashed them so that the worst they could do was kick one another—which they did on any excuse at all, or none.

Then the worst of the journey for me began. I having served before the mast on a deep-sea-going bark, the pleasant fiction was propounded, and insisted on by all hands, that I was qualified to navigate that load down an uncharted river that was simply perfectly unknown to me.

"So all the rest of us can go to sleep and be happy!" as Fred remarked.

"Call me at Lourenço Marques in time for tea!" Yerkes grinned.

And Monty blandly bade me "up anchor and do the rest!"

There was current enough to keep us moving once we had cast off and, with the probable exception of Monty, boys and all imagined the rest of the trip would consist of a drift down-river. They were swiftly disillusioned.

"Am I skipper?" I asked.

"The captain bold!" said Monty.

"Bo's'n, pilot, engineer, admiral and commodore!" said Yerkes. "Take hold!"

"Be midshipman too!" said Fred. "Be everything! Be happy!"

So I gave Monty a long pole in the stern to steer with, put Fred on the starboard side, and Yerkes to port, each in charge of half the crew with other poles, took a long one in the bow myself for sounding purposes and to fend away from rocks and snags, and nobody got any rest whatever until we reached our destination.

We did not even stop for a meal, for we reached tide-water at the top of the ebb, and Monty agreed with me that the thing to do was to pole along down with the tide to help us. Sixpence cooked up coffee and some sort of stew down among the mules' heels, and we made the quay at Lourenço Marques at dusk.

We got into trouble then that nothing less than gold would quell, by using the Government crane to haul up our mules with. A man in a sword and wideawake hat abused us like pickpockets, we continuing nevertheless; and finally Monty solaced him with a golden English pound. Oakes accused Cadji of backing the man into a shadow and extorting ten per cent, commission on the pound; and the high court judge grew so indignant that the rest of us almost believed the slander.

And then it was dark; and while we got the mules into a livery-stable at the back of the Braganza Arms Hotel and found quarters for our boys, Cadji gave us the slip. We could not have prevented him, of course, now that we were in a city where the law of Portugal had power behind it, but we would rather have known just where to find him later on. I was talking to Monty when the little man came up to us and interrupted.

"You will recollect, Senhor Lord Montdidier," he said in his mincing, insinuating way, "that I did not measure your claims, I did not set foot on them, I did not inspect them, I signed no papers regarding them, and that therefore thus far you have no title to them!"

"You rascal!" said Monty, smiling in a way that would not have reassured me if I had happened to be his enemy.

"Not that I will not sign, *senhor!*" said the Portuguese. "Do not forget you are dependent on me! Ten per cent! Adios!" He raised his helmet with a flourish, stepped into the shadow of the great silent customs shed, and disappeared.

"What next?" said I.

"Bed!" said Monty. "We're two days ahead of the German. We'll steal a march on him again by sleeping peacefully!"

Cordova's is the hotel to go to, away up on the hill above the fever-haunted business section—that is to say, if you can afford the bill. There are real beds, real waiters, real rooms, large and airy, a real cook, and honest-to-goodness food. We rode up in 'rickishas, and were asleep before the scurrying half-bred Zulu boys had dragged and shoved us half the distance. We fell asleep between the dinner courses—snored over the after-dinner coffee—and staggered up to our rooms and sweet oblivion.

But Monty had us all awake and up an hour after dawn, although for all the good that did he might just as well have let us sleep longer. But he seemed ill-at-ease about the check and a point of ethics.

"I suppose you fellows are clear in your minds," he said, "that there's a swindle here somewhere?"

"We haven't robbed anybody yet," said Yerkes sleepily. "Are we in that line of business?"

Monty ignored the question.

"The only thing that makes me willing to sell out to anybody," he said, "is the obvious impossibility of working a mine profitably under this Government. As soon as we reached a profit-paying stage, they would tax or thieve us out of business. That German's money is good but his intention isn't—I'm as sure of that as that I sit here. He knows we're not selling anything that the Portuguese Government would give him title to. Do you get the hang of it?"

"Get the money, and let him get the hang!" said Fred. "Let's all have breakfast!"

"Wait!" said Monty. "As long as we're all clear that the German's eyes are open to what he's doing—and to what we're doing; and Cadji's eyes are open, too—"

"Let's keep that point out from under cover all the time," said Yerkes.

"Oh, cut the cackle," urged Fred. "Come to breakfast! Both sides are trying to double-cross somebody! Let's hope hasn't us! Come and eat!"

"Presently!" said Monty. "We're clear, are we, that we're willing to sell to both sides? Very well. Here's the plan of campaign. Immediately after breakfast-or as soon after that as the Standard Bank opens, we all go down together and present that check. If we get the money, well and good—we transfer it to our own account.

"Then, you, Fred, take a 'rickisha and scoot up to the British consulate. Give the consul my compliments—you'll find he's an army man and a good fellow—and ask him what he knows about local political conditions. Write down what he says if you find yourself getting bushed.

"Yerkes—you go and try to find Cadji. If you succeed, get him to introduce you to his syndicate that he says is so willing to pay us another ten thousand pounds. You handle that end of the business. Bring it as far forward as you can, and pledge our signatures."

He glanced at me. As the youngest, last joined, and least experienced member of the partnership, who could talk no Portuguese and very little Ronga, there did not seem much that I could do that morning.

"You come with me," he said. "We'll call on Captain Rodriguez on the Portuguese cruiser in the harbor, and find out what he knows."

SO WE breakfasted at leisure—the Portuguese are not without understanding of how to serve that meal; and I don't think one of us thought of the overland telegraph from Chai Chai that von Muehlendorff would find at his disposal the moment he should reach that place.

We were outside the bank in high spirits the moment the door opened, and inside it, feeling rather like a gang of hold-ups, before the manager himself arrived. But he came in directly afterward—an Englishman, who of course knew Monty and Oakes at once.

He was accompanied by a squat, broad-shouldered German; and it was at once obvious to every one of us that we were expected. He opened the door of a private office.

"Come in, won't you?" he invited, and we all trooped in, followed by the German and himself.

"Is that a good check?" asked Monty, sitting down.

The manager took the check and frowned.

"The account is good for that amount," he said. "Is the signature in order, Mr. Wilhelmi?"

He showed it to the German.

"Quite all right. That is the signature of Herr Heinrich von Muehlendorff, an attaché of our consulate."

Monty took back the check, endorsed it, drew a slip from the rack on the table, filled it in, and passed both to the manager.

"Credit it, then, to our partnership account," he said; and the rest of us heaved such an obvious sigh of relief that the manager smiled.

"And now a little detail!" said Wilhelmi, coughing to call attention to himself. He was a man with a heavy black mustache that hid his mouth entirely, and almost coal-black eyes that on the contrary scorned concealment. "Herr von Muehlendorff has wired just now from Chai Chai to the effect that you have with you a contract to be signed on receipt of the money. Is that so?"

Monty admitted the fact, and produced the paper.

"Will you sign it, so that the manager of this bank may witness it?"

There being no objection that we could raise, we all wrote our signatures under Monty's at the foot of the paper; the bank manager witnessed them; and Wilhelmi pocketed the deed. But he had scarcely done so—we were scarcely on our feet again—when the door burst open and in came Cadji, all spruced up in a snow-white suit—white shoes—white tie—white sun-hat—his gold watch-chain loaded down with a bunch of seals—and his smile seraphic.

"I trust I am in time!" he said, flourishing a big cigar set in a gold-mounted amber tube.

"In time for what?" demanded Herr Wilhelmi—perhaps a shade too promptly to convince.

"On my way to the court in my 'rikisha I beheld these gentlemen entering the bank. Aware of the probable nature of their business I hastened to assure them—as I now assure you, Senhor Wilhelmi—that the Government will not recognize the transaction. I speak officially!"

"Absurd!" said Wilhelmi. "The money has changed hands! The contract is signed! I have it here!" And he flourished it.

"It has no value," said Cadji.

"I shall apply to the courts this morning!" said the German.

"You will meet with refusal, *senhor!"* said Cadji, with a deep bow.

Curiously—very curiously, I thought—the German did not demand the money back.

"A German working-party is in occupation now," he announced. "The law under which the du Mauriers claimed ownership—"

"Was long ago repealed!" announced Cadji.

"Is fundamental!" said the German. "The Imperial German Government has never been asked to recognize its repeal, even if such were possible. On the contrary, the Imperial German Government did recognize the fundamental law ten years ago, when the land on which the Imperial German consulate building is erected was purchased from a Portuguese who had title to it by marrying a chief's daughter! There will be an official demand made to-day that this contract be stamped by the Portuguese Government and recognized!"

"The demand will be refused!" said Cadji sweetly.

"We shouldn't have ducked that dago!" Yerkes whispered to me. "He has his points! If we had been more friendly, I'd feel less sore about taking sides with him now!"

Wilhelmi stalked out, buttoning the contract in his inside pocket.

"What does this all mean, gentlemen?" demanded the bank manager.

"I thought you fellows were supposed to know everything that's going on," said Monty. "Suppose you explain it!"

"There is nothing to explain!" interrupted Cadji. "You have heard all that there is to hear! *Senhores*—will you follow me?"

We followed the saffron Lord Chief Justice, as Fred Oakes persisted in calling him, to the outer office.

"The next thing to do," he said to Monty in a low voice, "is so to commit the Government that it simply must resist this insolent German claim. A party of my friends is ready to purchase your real rights. I am ready to certify the title to them. They are all men of influence. The money is ready. But first, *senhor,* there is a little formality—the thousand pounds commission—my ten per cent."

Monty wrote out a check and gave it to him.

"It would be gratifying," he said, "and would save trouble, were you to pay me the commission on the next transaction in advance! Another thousand pounds, senhor!"

"Nothing doing!" snapped Yerkes. "Don't you do it, Monty!"

"Oh, for a handy water-butt!" grinned Oakes.

"Thanks. We'll await developments," said Monty. "Mr. Yerkes will go with you, if you're ready, to interview your friends. He has authority to pledge our signatures!"

"Come along, Senhor Yerkes!" said Cadji, as politely as if his wedding were in the wind. "Take a seat in my 'rikisha. I will join you in a moment."

He cashed the check, and I noticed he took the money in Bank of England notes—since time immemorial the approved, and one convenient way of realizing plunder. In another minute he and Yerkes were vanishing up-street as fast as two sinewy 'rickisha boys could hurry them.

"Now!" said Monty. "Lose no time!"

"What d'you suppose is happening?" asked Fred.

"I know what's happening, but I can't prove it! Get to the consulate! Tell them nothing, but try to find out what they know!"

"Consuls are stuffy," objected Fred. "Dukes and ambassadors are gossips compared to 'em. Suppose you give me a little suspicion or two to whisper into the consul's ear—he's more likely then to unbosom himself!"

"Perhaps!" said Monty. "I do wish you'd get a move on!"

"Oh, all right!" said Fred—in rather a huff, I thought.

We parted company at the bank door, and presently Monty and I were in the stern of a small Greek sailing-boat, on our way to the flag-ship anchored in line ahead of two other, smaller cruisers. The flagship was a little enough tub herself and locked like a fixture, but I noticed that smoke was ascending from the third, and smallest, cruiser's one slim funnel.

We were met at the head of the companion-ladder by Captain Rodriguez himself, and if ever a man looked glad to see Monty, that was he.

"Come in!" he urged. "Come into my cabin! Who is your friend, did you say? He is in your confidence? Then come in both of you!"

He took Monty's arm, and led us out. The whole of the rounded stern part under the old-fashioned poop-deck was his stateroom, mighty neat and comfortable, cooled by an electric fan, but far from cool enough to keep Rodriguez calm. We two sat on the red-plush-covered sofa that followed the curve of the stern, but he paced up and down, shaking his fists distractedly at intervals.

A barefooted steward brought in wine, and was sharply ordered out again. The sentry was called in, and told to keep the door closed against all comers.

"Oh, but I am glad you came, my lord!" he exclaimed. "I am glad you came! You can do nothing, but you comfort me!"

He spoke English perfectly, with that ultra-refined accent that is peculiar to educated gentlemen of southern Europe.

"How shall a man serve king and country, when his king is corrupt and his country asleep? Tell me that!"

WHAT COULD one say? It would scarcely have been manners to sympathize with him on his nation's shortcomings. Monty helped himself to wine, which was perhaps the most tactful thing he could have done.

"I have no ammunition on this ship! It have no coal! Yesterday I acquired enough coal at my own expense to bunker the Carlos and send her on a little cruise. She returned at dawn because of leaky boilers! See her behind there—she has steam in one boiler yet. She brought me bad news. Yet, what can I do? What is such a fleet as this with which to honor my king and serve my country?"

Monty sipped the wine again.

"To your king and country, Captain Rodriguez!" he said simply.

Rodriguez stood to attention and bowed—as fine appearing a sailor-man as any one could wish to see.

"Ah, my lord, you are very kind! You can sympathize with me! You can understand me! Perhaps your heart can burn a little too on my king's account!"

He paced up and down, up and down, like a man doing sentry-go, every now and then pausing before a looking-glass to smooth his gray hair that he ruffled between his fingers the next minute.

"You have heard of the republican movement here? You have heard of it? The dogs are not content with their already too terrible corruption, but must seek to dethrone our king! They denounce the unfortunate corruption of the court—but would swallow it in worse corruption of their own!"

"I've been told," said Monty, "that the danger of a republican revolution has been lately growing less."

"True!" said Rodriguez. "True! But why? I will tell you why. Because the monarchists, poor fools, have thought a new king might suit them better. They have appealed to a foreign king—the most unrepublican monarch they could find. Listen, my lord! Listen, gentlemen!"

He came close to us and leaned forward, making a sort of trumpet of both hands as if he were bellowing through a typhoon.

"If there could be found a cause for quarrel—one simple little disagreement at this minute "

"What then?" demanded Monty, upsetting his wine-glass.

"Then Germany would pounce on Lourenço Marques!"

"Oh, nonsense!" said Monty; but I saw that he believed it.

"You seek to reassure me," said Rodriguez. "You are kind, but you are mistaken nevertheless. Yesterday I sent the Carlos on a cruise. This dawn she returns with word that a fleet of great cruisers lies in the offing—three great cruisers and two smaller ones that fly the German flag. And what can I do?"

I stared hard at Monty, and he looked at me. It did not take much thinking then to name the coming ground for an international dispute. The Imperial German Government, the champion of self-righteousness and clattering sabers, would back up its own subjects and the old unrighteous land-title law to the limit. But Rodriguez was too excited and overwrought to notice our mental processes.

"There is a steam-launch tied to the wharf," he said, "a fast one—oil-burning—owned by Germans—manned by Germans. You can see it through this port—look, gentlemen! They have steam up. They have had steam up for two days. Why? Is it not likely they intend to carry word to that fleet of cruisers as soon as an excuse can be arranged? And what can I do?"

"Cable Lisbon," suggested Monty.

Rodriguez laughed bitterly.

"They tell me the cable is not working! There is said to be a fracture out at sea!"

"Why not take the British consul into your confidence?"

Rodriguez bridled.

"My lord, you are no doubt not aware of it, but the British consul and I are not on speaking terms! There is a matter in dispute between us that he has not seen fit to adjust! We are to each other in position of *personae non gratissimae.* I regret the unfortunate fact, but such it is!"

"I could see the consul for you," suggested Monty.

"Ah, my lord, you are kind—you are kind—you are very kind—but—perhaps—might you not already be too late?"

Monty sprang to his feet.

"Put us ashore, old man! Your gig will take us quicker than a Greek's lugger."

"Gig! You shall have my jolly-boat and eight oars!"

He rushed to the door, threw it open, swore at the sentry, and shouted. A subordinate came on the run, buttoning his tunic. A whistle blew. There was shouting—a patter of bare feet—the squeak of blocks—the whine of running sheaves—and a splash.

"All ready!" announced Rodriguez. "Man-o'-war style!" he added.

"Congratulate you! Smart work, Rodriguez! Thanks!"

We were overside in a minute, I utterly content with the rhythmic thump and hum of man-o'-warsmen's oars as our sharp bow split the harbor waves. We reached the shore too soon for me, for that is the finest way in the world to travel, making steam and electricity—aye, and the clattering swagger of armed horse—mere unromantic motion by comparison. But Monty was in no mood to enjoy the means—the end was his concern—and he leaped from the boat to the wharf—and I of course after him—with scarcely a backward glance at the startled midshipman who steered us.

Nor were we alone in a hurry. I had not more than brushed the wharf dust from my knees and looked to see what Monty would do next than I caught sight of a 'rikisha propelled at frantic speed by Oakes, who had a stick in his hand with which to poke the unhappy Zulu in the shafts.

As he came 'round the corner on one wheel he got on his knees on the seat to belabor the sweating stalwart whose task was to shove behind. What with weariness, short-windedness, sweat in his eyes, the sandy track, and Fred's volcanic movements, the man in the shafts took a header and rubbed his broad, black face in the grit for a yard or two.

Then the shafts struck a stone and stopped suddenly. His upthrown feet waving frantically in the air broke Fred's parabolic flight, and a second later Fred was sitting on the Zulu's head, squeezing the sand well home. It cost five shillings and the ministrations of a druggist to subdue the Zulu's wrath.

"Hurry and tell me the news, Fred!"

We left the Zulu in the drug-store and returned to the waterside where we couldn't be overheard.

"News?" answered Fred. "There isn't any! The British consul's away—has been gone for a week, and won't be back for three weeks! The vice is sick—swears he has taken poison—'fraid for his life—don't have any faith in dago doctors—wanted to wire to Johannesburg, of all places, to get a Scotchman who amputated President Kruger's thumb or something-some sort of specialist—couldn't wire! Wire's down! Fact, for I confirmed it!"

"Isn't there a private wire from the consulate to British territory?" demanded Monty.

"Yes, but somebody has cut it! In any case, it leads along the railway just like the others, and the railway wires are cut, too!"

"Where?"

"Lord knows! Anywhere! A dozen places for all I know! Somewhere between here and Umtali—that's as near as I could get for an answer!"

A noise near the wharf made us face about and, as if our own activity had jarred into motion the too-long hidden evil influencesy we saw the German steam-launch cast off and make down-harbor toward the open sea. Her crew of five men were jubilant; they blew their whistle like drunkards, and waved to some longshore sympathizers with as little attempts at secrecy as if they had been off on a birthday trip. They shouted, too, but I could not catch the words.

"There's just one chance!" said Monty.

"What?" demanded Fred.

"Tell us!" said I.

But at that moment Yerkes came, like Fred in a great hurry in a 'rikisha, and even more violent in his efforts to increase the speed. He managed to reach us without mishap, but was obliged to pay the Zulus double to get rid of them. Angry at the extortion, Oakes kicked one of them. That started a fight that very nearly put an end to our usefulness for the day, for two Portuguese policemen appeared and threatened us with all the rigors of their lovely law. Monty had to settle the argument with gold.

WHEN THEY had gone away at last Yerkes, who was bursting with information, began to splutter so, that we could not understand him.

"I've got the money!" he said. "I've got the money! We owe Cadji fifteen hundred pounds, and he's clamoring for it!"

"Why fifteen hundred?" I demanded. "The terms were ten per cent."

"I got fifteen thousand!" answered Yerkes.

There is a cheap hotel not far from the Wharf, and we went to it. Monty ordered drinks for the sake of appearances, and we sat at a table in a corner, where Yerkes grew moderately calm at last.

"You know, you fellows, I'm a Yankee," he said, with a sort of triple-distilled, subacid glee. "That's how I found 'em out!"

"Found whom out? How? What? Where? Hurry up and tell us!"

"I thought of my rubber concession—and that's more than any of you did. Seemed to me I hadn't done much for my share in your gold claims, and I'd just as soon sell my rubber as not. I offered the lot, claims, rubber and all, for fifteen thousand and refused to sell one without the other. You ought to have seen Cadji's jaw drop! He was in a hurry, I soon spotted that. So were his friends!"

"So are we!" declared Monty. "Out with the story, man!"

"Well—no ten Portuguese in a hurry can beat one Yankee at a trade—and the more they argued the tighter I sat. So at last they yielded. And the funny part was that, they had to send to Wilhelmi the German for the extra five thousand! Cadji did not tell them that I know Portuguese. They sent Cadji to fetch Wilhelmi, and while he was gone they talked straight out in front of me! What do you think of it?"

"Oh, hurry, man, hurry!" urged Monty. "Tell us what they said!"

"They're all for selling the colony out—Cadji and all of them—selling out to Germany! We sold the du Maurier so-called rights to Heine von Muehlendorff, and those are what the Germans propose to pick a quarrel over. But they were afraid the Government might yield to the Germans and give 'em whatever they demand, and that 'd spoil the excuse for the high hand.

"So the Germans have put up some Portuguese to pay us this money for the real title, and that'll give them a right to force their Government's hand and compel refusal of the German demands! D'ye see? The Germans don't want peaceful settlement, they want a fight! D'you suppose there's going to be a German revolution?"

"No," said Monty, "I don't. One won't be necessary."

He was biting his knuckles-sweeping the harbor with impatient eyes—impatient, yet uncertain what to do.

"So it's German money we've got! Twenty-five thousand pounds of German gold, less ten per cent, to Cadji!"

"—— it, I know!" said Monty. "Don't rub it in! It's too late to alter it, too! We've as good as sold this part of Africa to Germany! If we offered them the money back now they wouldn't accept it. Oh ——!"

"Just like an Englishman! Didn't I do what you asked, plus fifty per cent?" demanded Yerkes.

"Shut up, America!" growled Oakes. "Who's treading on your corns? I'll compose a hymn about you later on!"

"The —— you will!"

"Yes," smiled Fred Oakes genially. "And sing it over your grave if you don't stop quarreling! Think, you ruffian, think!"

"There's just one chance!" said Monty.

"One's enough if it's good!" grinned Oakes.

"I'll go to the consulate. I'll buy some emetic for the vice on my way up. It's half-past eleven now—phew, but it's hot! An hour and a half from now I'll begin sending a message on the consulate instrument. I'm a poor enough signaler, but I can send faster than receive. I shall keep on sending the same message over and over until I get an answer. Look for the break, and splice it if you can—it's the one slim chance!"

"Better pay Cadji his fifteen hundred," Yerkes advised.

It was not far to the bank. We dashed in there—deposited Yerkes' check for fifteen thousand—drew out fifteen hundred cash—and made for the street again, only to see Cadji's 'rikisha coming at top speed toward us. Yerkes ran and jumped in beside Cadji before it came to a standstill.

"Tell 'em to the railway station!" he ordered, and Cadji obeyed.

"Have you my money?" I heard him ask.

"You bet I have!" said Yerkes. "And you bet you'll earn it!"

Fred and I jumped another 'rikisha, left outside a store by somebody whose boys did not care who paid them. I saw Yerkes shake a fistfull of paper money under Cadji's nose and pocket it again, and then we raced for the station helter-skelter, avoiding collisions and accidents by that most useful article we men possess—the skin of our teeth, and achieving speed by copious bribery. Yerkes got to the station first, for Cadji's 'rikisha boys were thoroughbreds.

Is there anything more dismal in the wide world than the pretentious terminus of a one-train, graft-ridden railway line? Anything more melancholy than the snarled official answer "No train at all to-day!"?

"No train?" demanded Yerkes. "Why not?"

"An accident up the line," was the answer.

"Where? Here, Cadji, you ask him."

"Senhores, there has been an accident. No train can run. The wire is down. No messages can come or go. Who knows anything?"

"You know that unless I get what I'm after you won't get yours!" Yerkes demanded. "You tell that station agent we three men have got to reach British territory somehow in a hurry. You use your influence if you hope to see any fifteen hundred pounds."

There was demur, deliberate delay, dispute, suspicion, and more than a little threatening on our part, but the long and the short of it was that an hour after noon we paid Cadji his fifteen hundred pounds and departed up the single track on a contractor's hand-car, with two natives to work the lever that turned the wheels.

We rode out of sight of the station and then kicked the natives off, manning the lever ourselves with energy born of excitement. But after another few miles Oakes stopped us and insisted on taking along with us a great piece of rusty sheet-iron that he fixed in our bows like a bulwark. We grumbled, and jeered at him, but it turned out to be well that he did it.

Whoever ordered that line cut out had taken small chances on its being repaired from our end. We pumped that disgusting lever until nearly half-past five before Yerkes, who was resting, spied the break in the wire a mile ahead.

"And there's a man there guarding it!" he announced. "The man hasn't seen us yet. He's one lone man with his back this way."

We had a hasty consultation and decided on the strategy. The vote stood two to one. "Monty not being here, the ayes have it!" insisted Yerkes.

They seemed to think that my adventure in the night with Anatole du Maurier entitled me to the post of danger again, and as none of us had any sort of weapon, somebody had to do something desperate.

So I pumped the last mile single-handed, and Yerkes and Fred lay down behind the iron sheet, to make it look as if I were riding alone. The man, who turned out to be a German, saw me when I was a quarter of a mile away, and covered me with a rifle. I pretended not to see him, until I drew within shouting distance and his roared orders made further pretense impossible. Then I began to slow down, but contrived to do it very gradually. When within ten yards of him I was still doing better than walking speed, so that although he aimed now straight for my head I had good excuse for coming about abreast of him before I stopped. And even after I stopped the car rolled forward a turn or two of its own momentum.

"—— you! Vy didn't you stop ven I shout first?" he demanded.

"Who are you, anyway?" I asked him.

"Never you mind who I am! Who are you? You tell me quick!"

"I'm going with a message to meet that other car you see approaching in the distance."

He turned his head to look.

That was the end of him, of course. Fred and Yerkes tumbled out on to the track and, although he almost faced about in time, Yerkes landed with a stone behind his ear and Fred jumped on him with both feet. That left us with a rifle and fifty cartridges to the good, when we had trussed him up and laid him by a culvert where he could crawl to water when he should recover consciousness.

We knew the number of the wire we had to mend—they had all been cut clean through at one place with a hammer and chisel—so we twisted off a section of another wire to splice with; and we had not more than finished splicing when the sound of wheels coming down the line from the direction of the British border warned us that another car was really coming.

"Suppose that's not the only break?" Fred hazarded.

WE HAD no light and it was dark by that time but the oncoming party heard our voices for they began to shout.

"Only break or not, us for the trail!" said Yerkes, and we began to work the lever.

That could be heard, of course, for miles upline. The oncomers stopped to listen, and then renewed their own efforts, overhauling us by dint of strength, numbers, down-grade, and probably because they had a faster car.

Presently they shouted to us again. The next thing a shot splattered and rang off our rusty old iron defense. I answered with our plundered rifle—three shots in swift succession; and whether or not I succeeded in hitting any one—the range was short but it was quite impossible to see—they stopped, and began to return upline.

So we stopped to listen. Within five minutes we could hear the *slam-slam-slammmmm* of blows on the wire we had mended, and a moment later the unmistakable *twang* of the wire as it fell.

"Rather looks as if that was the only break," said Yerkes, "seeing they're in such an all-fired fuss to keep it broken just exactly there. I'll bet you their game is to stand by with some sort of receiving instrument and mend the break at once when they're given the word. Well—if that man Monty is as good as his word—"

"And he's better!" said Fred.

"By a long sight!" said I.

"He'll have got his message through!" said Bill Yerkes, as we pumped the infernal lever and went *ki-bum-ki-bum-ki-bumping* through the dark.

"I wonder what in the world the message is?" said Yerkes.

"Troops!" said I. "British troops down the line from Umtali!"

"Piffle!" said Oakes. "There are no troops! And what right would British troops have in Portuguese territory in any case?"

Being dog-weary of the lever, it was almost midnight before we reached Lourenço Marques—long after midnight when we had rounded up Monty at the consulate. He was smoking on the steps with the vice-consul, slapping mosquitoes and talking in low tones.

"I was poisoned," I heard as we drew nearer. "As sure as we two are sitting here, I was deliberately poisoned!"

"How about it, Monty?" Yerkes demanded. "Did you stick to it? Did you get her through?"

"Yes, I got an acknowledgment shortly after half-past five. The line seemed to be cut again directly after that, but I got the message through."

We slept that night at the consulate, expecting to be wakened at dawn by the whistles of German cruisers summoning the town to pay them homage. But it was afternoon of the next day before we saw their smoke at last; and there had been a fine little fuss in the courts meanwhile, Cadji holding forth from his bench as if no more learned and impeccable judge than he ever held the impartial scales.

The German population of the place seemed, by some uncanny process, to have been stirred to its united depths simultaneously and without advertisement. Some one had alarmed the money-changers, for their booths were closed, and Herr Heinrich von Muelendorff that noon arrived from Chai Chai, drove about town in a 'rikisha looking so important that he overflowed.

But it seemed that even the German Government observed formalities. The great, grim, frowning cruisers came to an anchor in mid-harbor, so nearly afoul of the Portuguese cruiser's chain that Rodriguez had to move.

After that there were official courtesies—calls and return calls—an admiral, all gold lace and pompousness, came ashore and visited the governor. And only after that was a representative of the German population allowed to go aboard and pay his brow-on-the-deck respects. He went in a launch with the German consul and von Muehlendorff.

All that night the cruisers lay there, dumping their garbage and offal in the harbor and fouling the view with smoke. It seemed to add to their commander's sense of his importance to make as much smoke as possible, and the fact that most of it drifted across the clean front of the governor's palace troubled him not at all. All that night they kept five search-lights moving restlessly, so that the town got no sleep. And at nine next morning the next move in the game began.

"Although—supposing that message of mine got through to the man I meant it for—I suspect they may be a wee bit late by now!" said Monty.

"Explain!" demanded Yerkes.

"You see," said Monty, "this fleet sent ashore at Mozambique for mail. I don't doubt for a second that the British consul there notified all our ports by wire."

"But isn't the British fleet probably at Capetown? That's how many hundred miles away?"

"No doubt that's what the German admiral is banking on," said Monty. "He has probably come from the China station in hope of catching our man with his back turned. They'd put into Durban for coal—might coal fast, you know, or they might postpone the business."

"Who should?"

"The British squadron!" said Monty.

The German admiral came ashore again, and this time he was greeted with great uproar, by no less than forty German citizens who lined the wharf to make him a petition. He took the petition grandiosely, and had himself driven to the governor's palace again. It was impossible for us to know what took place within there, but the Germans were jubilant—closed their places of business and sang songs in the hotel dining-rooms. A large section of the Portuguese semi-official politico-merchant class began to make merry with them, and that afternoon we were given to understand that an ultimatum had been handed to the governor. Unless the German demands were complied with in full by midnight, the place would be occupied at dawn next day!

"Good Lord!" said I. "But doesn't that admiral know the British Government would intervene?"

"Of course," said Monty. "But he's counting on the diplomatic value of a *fait accompli.* If he has already occupied the town, it would be an act of war to try to turn him out. He won't care much if the British fleet does come—once he has done what he's here for!"

"Let's hope it comes!" said Yerkes, and we all went into the consulate and had a drink on that.

THAT NIGHT the town was in an uproar, and we went up-hill to the hotel to safeguard our belongings. We got no supper, though. The proprietor informed us that some "gentlemen" had preempted the dining-room, and it turned out that half the officers of the German fleet were being entertained by the local merchants. The songs they sang, and the jests they made were none too agreeable to British ears, even through closed doors, so we went outside on the brow of the bluff at the back of the hotel, that overlooks the harbor, and talked and smoked gloomily.

It was eleven o'clock when I saw a glare under what looked rather like a low-hung cloud not so very far out at sea. At the end of ten minutes we could count five glares—moving very fast in our direction in line ahead. At midnight the German searchlights flashed on number one of an incoming fleet, and were answered by others that out-dazzled them. A few minutes later we heard the rattle of outrunning hawsers. Then Monty led the way back to the hotel.

He brushed the hotel proprietor and half a dozen waiters aside, and threw open the double door of the dining-room. We stood behind him, wondering what next. The diners—sober and drunk—were struck silent, until suddenly one of the officers realized that one or two of us at least were English, and all unarmed.

"Der Tag!" he shouted, holding up his glass, drinking it empty at a gulp, and dashing it in pieces on the floor. There was an united shout in response of *"Der Tag! Der Tag!"* and then all grew still again; for it was obvious that we had not burst open the door merely to see and be seen.

"It was of *'der Tag'* that I came to speak," said Monty. "I invite you all to come outside and see what *'der Tag'* will look like when it comes!"

From the door of the dining-room to the brow of the bluff was about two hundred yards. The night air and the distance sobered some of them. Drunk and sober, they all could appreciate the wonder of the view below—two cruiser fleets at anchor! in a harbor bathed in a flood of electric light.

And though some of them were very drunk indeed, all of the naval officers appreciated that the German fleet was bottled in, and could no more pass the British cruiser fleet without permission than it could fly. They were sober enough, too, to understand the bugle-calls that summoned them from the German flag-ship's deck.

We stayed on the bluff until dawn, and saw the German fleet steam out, the leading British cruisers shifting station to let them by. And when the German fleet was well at sea we saw another ship steam in—a collier, deep-loaded that came in and made itself fast between two British cruisers and promptly began disgorging coal on either side.

"By gad!" laughed Monty, getting up to go. "They postponed it then! My wire must have caught them with nearly empty bunkers, and they took the chance! Bluffed 'em, by gad!"

"I've always heard you Britishers couldn't play poker!" said Yerkes.

"Come along, you fellows. Let's call on the flag-ship!" said Monty. "Her skipper's a friend of mine."

Two days later, with a draft for what seemed a huge sum of money to me in Monty's inner pocket, we booked passages on the only ship available just then up-coast—a German liner called the *Bundesrath.* She was a dirty old beast, with the usual national habits, for though she only lay in the harbor a day the water about her was a stinking mess of floating grease and garbage. Growing greatly daring in the fight of recent happenings the Portuguese authorities complained, and a huge tub full of awfulness was stood amidships, in readiness to be dumped at sea.

The whistles roared farewell to the port—the Germans are great on whistles—and the hawser started clanking home when we espied Heinrich von Muehlendorff in a small boat alongside. He was looking up and waving to attract somebody's attention.

"Cajole him, Monty!" Fred whispered gleefully; and he and Yerkes made in a hurry for the lower deck.

"Here's wishing you a pleasant law-suit for your money, Herr von Muehlendorff!" said Monty

I saw him look up—saw his expression change to one of loathing—and then raced after the other two. From below I could hear Monty again clearly.

"Oh, by the way Herr von Muehlendorff, it was we who sent the message that brought the British squadron!"

"I suspected it, you swindling swine!"

"One!" said Oakes.

"Two!" said Yerkes.

"Three!" said I. "And he's just underneath!"

And we hove the undigested evil from the galley of the *Bundesrath* politely, perfectly, and timely onto Heine in his boat below. The anchor was up by that time, and the *Bundesrath* gaining way. The last I saw of him Heine was removing garbage from his mouth and eyes and ears.

An hour later yet, in our chairs in the after smoking-room, we made a new agreement—oral as always as to intimate details—simple as law would let it be as far as writing went. Yerkes wrote it out, and we signed it, Monty signing last.

"I'm going on with you," said Yerkes, "and I'm glad. I never met three fellows I liked better. I like you, Monty, and agree to what's written there. I agree to what we've said besides. But there's one point I'd like to be wiser on."

"Out with it, America!" roared Oakes. "I'll bet it's about votes for men!"

"Right!" announced Yerkes. "What the —— did you mean, Monty, back there in the Libomba Hills by calling for our vote when you intended all along to take your own line?"

Monty smiled, and leaned back luxuriously, like a handsome, sleek black cat, I thought, that views a bird.

"You suspect that's un-American?"

"Oh, well," said Yerkes, "perhaps not that. The States are a big place. They contain a lot of different sorts of people."

"Who would you call your greatest American?" asked Monty softly.

"Lincoln!" said Yerkes at once.

"I'm inclined to agree with you," said Monty. "I've made quite a study of Lincoln. I've a library of books about him—one of the best in the world, I'm told. Shall we agree that while I'm leader I'm to keep within bounds in future that Lincoln wouldn't have objected to?"

"No one could find any fault if you'd stick to that," said Yerkes.

"Then we'll agree on that," said Monty.

"Fine!" said Yerkes.

"Remarkable man, was President Lincoln," said Monty, and Yerkes agreed.

"D'you remember that occasion when he sat with his cabinet all day and made no headway with them. At last he called for a vote and found they all disagreed with him. Remember what he said? 'The vote stands, seven noes, one aye. The ayes have it!' Then he walked out, you remember. If he had stayed in there and argued, I wouldn't had admired him half as much. Would you?"

"No!" said Yerkes. "They're on me! I admit it! Steward!"

THE END OF THE BAD SHIP *BUNDESRATH*

THE OUT-AND-OUT, admitted tub that pleads guilty to pauper ownership and earns precarious pence along the meaner sealanes—rubbing paint-hungry flanks against comfortless quays, unsaluted, unrespected, unregretted when at last she pounds herself to flotsam on some uncharted reef, is a ship a merry minded man can love.

Even harbor-masters of the less-frequented ports, those sternest of dignitarians, can pity her and concede to her skipper less gusty anchorage of stormy nights. Her very ship's dog, portering fleas ashore for change of diet, finds friendliness in longshore hearts. But your tub that masquerades under a house-flag, carrying passengers at liner rates and pocketing for her owners a fat mail subsidy because they have a pull with powers that think they be, is despicable.

So, therefore, was the *Bundesrath*. As Fred Oakes said of her, she was "six thousand tons of deep-sea-going snob, with an insolent nose and a fat behime-end—simply asking for trouble."

She called her brass-bound mate first officer; the dead goat served in the first saloon was "prime Spring lamb"; the first-class passengers, berthed aft to catch the soft-coal smoke, were supposed to be of other clay than the second and third-class further forward; and all who were foreigners from the German view-point were, except Monty, as dirt beneath the captain's feet. Being Earl of Montdidier and Kirkudbrightshire, as well as cavalry colonel on half-pay, a privy councillor, and certain other things, Monty was addressed by all and sundry as "milor"—*"ja wohl,* milor"—*"sehr gut,* milor"—"olright, milor, oh, yes"—with other perfectly wide-world-comprehending phrases intended to display the speaker's erudition and make Monty feel at home.

Being of his party, we others were accorded seats with him at the captain's table. Monty sat on the captain's right, and we three faced the two of them; so the privilege was ours of seeing the captain wolf his victuals. Having seen and heard, we usually cut our own meal short and fled to the deck, Monty making our desertion an excuse for following.

But the awnings leaked, and the black deck caulking oozed out from the seams. From forward, where the live-stock lingered miserably up among the anchors, and East Indian laborers camped like gypsies amid dirt and sorrow in the waist, came a wholly unlovely smell, unchanging and inescapable. For all the vaunted German discipline, the second, and some of the third-class passengers invaded all decks, sprawling wherever a less shabby section of the awning suggested shelter; but their dirt turned into mud and there was no dry place anywhere.

For the rain had come at last to Gazaland. Famine ashore was in fair way to be ended, and comfort, ashore or afloat, had ceased for the time being to exist. Not that the *Bundesrath* ever had been comfortable, or ever would be. Merely, she was much worse when it rained.

"All the same," said Will Yerkes, sitting upright because a drool from the bridge-deck descended within six inches of him each time the ship rolled to port, "old man Noah was right. I reckon a ship's the place when a flood comes. Even this ship. The ark prob'ly wallowed round in rings. We seem able to keep a course. Ashore the mud'll be waist-deep, bugs keeping 'em company indoors and pestilence stalking abroad. Me for the sea!"

"Right you are!" agreed Fred Oakes. "Noah knew!"

Fred had found and preempted a corner in the lee of the smoking-room, where the awning scarcely leaked at all, and sat nursing his concertina on a camp-stool.

"But, speaking of Holy Writ—we're all in love with the notion of hell for our enemies—specially for this ship's owners—but—d'ye recollect where it says in Revelations there'll be no more sea? I couldn't enjoy a universe without a sea in it."

"The rest of Revelations is light after-breakfast reading, I suppose?" suggested Yerkes.

"You never served aboard ship," said I. "The sea looks fine to all except those who follow it, Fred."

"Fo'castle cynic!" he answered. "Unhappy outcast from sailing tramps! Forget your fo'castle days—they're over!"

"I wouldn't cross a street to be lord high admiral and have to go to sea willy-nilly," said I.

Monty, in a big basket-chair not very far away from us, was deep in a chess problem, with the folding board jammed tight between his knees.

"You're right," he said, glancing up at me. "Yachting's fun, though. It's what ever you've got to do that's ——. If I had to play chess I'd hate it. Fred hasn't got to play the concertina, but it seems we've got to listen! Shut up, Fred! Put that infernal instrument away!"

But the Muse was tickling Fred's larynx and charming his fingers. Some of the third-class passengers recognized the signs of tunes aborning. There were three mean whites in evidence, whose views on music were probably apocryphal, and more than a hundred Sikhs, Punjabees, Goanese, Singhalese, Seychelles boys, and half-breeds of a dozen flavors.

The half-breeds live in a border-world where music, like other things, projects itself, as it were, from both sides into ears attuned to emotion; but pure East Indians scorn Western melody. Nevertheless, they all began to gather about us, reckless of the rain. Misery is seldom in love with itself, and even a flea's high spirits, if not exactly contagious, would attract.

Fred struck a wild chord—corrected a flat into a sharp—changed it—struck another one—and burst into tune. In another moment Monty closed the chess-board, because serious thought is utterly impossible when Fred Oakes sings.

"Oh, I took a trip to a mountain top,
Ah-dee, ah-dee, ah-day!
Where the view should make my heart-beats stop
And chase the blues away.
I climbed where the air was clear and cool
Through a hole in the azure sky,
But the view sat still, and the only fool
Who troubled to move was I!

"Ah-dee, ah-dee again!
Then me for the raging main!
I'd rather the sea in a cockleshell ship
Where combers rise and bulwarks dip
And bellying, thundering topsails rip
Amid the wind and rain!

"Oh, I took a trip to a mountain town,
Ah-dee, ah-dee, ah-day!
Where crags above green valleys frown
I chose a while to stay;
But the food and the folk and the beds were mean
Though the bill and the hill were high,
For they skin you quicker, and close and clean,
The nearer you get to the sky!

"Ah-dee, ah-dee again!
Then me for the raging main!
I'd sooner to sea and be fed salt horse
With fo'castle bread and cockroach sauce
On a punishing, blustering, blistering course
To the Horn and home again!

"Oh, I took a trip 'mid mountain peaks,
Ah-dee, ah-dee, ah-day!
Where the sun-warmed zephyrs kissed my cheeks
The lazy, live-long day!
But the girls o' the mountain passed me by
With haughty stare and cold,
And never a kiss from lips had I
Though I made free and bold!

"Chorus, you fellows!"

"Ah-dee, ah-dee again!
Then me for the raging main,
To labor aloft and reef and furl,
With weatherwise eye and heart awhirl
For a kiss o' the lips of a longshore girl
When I make home again!"

THE THREE mean whites applauded, and the heterogeneous Eastern brethren grinned. Oakes sang until his own long list of compositions was exhausted, and then fell back on stuff remembered from his schooldays or picked up in steamer smoking-rooms and camps the wide world over. But the weather grew worse, until at last the worrying wind and rain damped even Fred's enthusiasm; the mean whites went to the second-class bar to get drunk and the last wet, ragged, homesick Biluchi staggered to his smelly den up forward.

Then, because there was no comfort within or without, but at least air to breathe on deck, we four went out and stood under the navigation bridge, wet to the skin, watching the shore-line and the wonders in between.

Every fresh squall that swept from landward carried with it changing hues of emerald-green and olive. Every low-hung cloud that raced between us and the land flung swifter shadows on a sea already stained by sand and weed and shoals. Minute by minute the weather grew more squally and threatening, great black clouds overhanging the little ones and blotting out the sun entirely except for intervals, when rays like those of a titanic searchlight threw the whole surging waste of water into many-hued relief.

The coco-palms along the low-lying shore bent double, swayed and bent again as if the storm would strip and uproot them. The sea would flatten as if it were semi-liquid stuff and a hand had smoothed it out. Then, as the water rose again in fury in the wake of the squall, the *Bundesrath* would shudder and reel and roll, lifting a third of her ugly length out of a wave and plunging like a leviathan in torment.

It was all fascinating—to anyone who likes that sort of thing. I, who had followed the sea a while for a living and was disillusioned more or less, thought principally of the toil it meant for men on sailing-ships: both watches on deck and all hands half-crazy from lack of sleep. Each squall brought sterner memories.

But Fred Oakes—to whom life is an adventure and death, in any place but bed, at worst a joke—reveled in the wild beauty of the scene, leaning at times so far out over the rail that Monty would grab him nervously. Yerkes, too, was enjoying it.

Like many another Yankee's, his was a deep-sea heritage; grandfather, uncles, cousins, friends had owned or captained those clipper-ships that stole the trade of the world away by dint of swift heels and seamanship. He scarcely knowing why, the sea in her violent moods aroused in him all that was finest. He stood with a hand on the rail, silent and motionless except that his keen eyes quartered the sea without resting.

Monty, on the other hand, was like me, without particular enthusiasm. He stood after a while with his back to the rail and hands in his pockets. I suspected he felt sick, but with that Spartan ability peculiar to men of his breed and raising, would neither own to it, pamper himself, nor yield.

It was Will Yerkes, bright-eyed as a ferret, who had us all by the ears in a moment and, in another second, all staring at one point on our port bow.

"By God, look at that! Can you beat it?"

"What?"

"Who?"

"Where?"

He pointed. A barkentine between us and the shore—eight hundred or a thousand tons—foreign—from a garlic port by the look of her—perhaps out of Bilbao, or Lisbon—was suddenly caught aback by a squall that very nearly swept around the compass. Bad seamanship—inertia—dead weariness maybe—the lightning shift of treacherous wind—and probably ignorance as well combined to make her instantly unmanageable. Sails and two masts were twisted out of her with the speed of an explosion and lay alongside to pound her as she hove her side to meet the howling waves beam on.

She disappeared in a smother of white water to rise only after what seemed an interminable interval and plunge clumsily, a black, dismantled, helpless thing—yet not quite hopeless; for we were black too—easy to see—steaming more or less in her direction, with Lord-knew-how-many thousand horse-power and supernumerary crew to give us mastery.

They saw us; from the rigging of their one remaining mast they presently flew an ensign, jack

downward. I could not recognize the flag, for it fluttered feebly and was twisted in the shrouds by wind and rain; but it seemed to me that then the *Bundesrath* humped herself under us and drove into the boiling sea a knot or so faster. That turned out to have been imagination, but on comparing notes later I found that the others had the same impression at the time.

It certainly at first never entered the head of one of us that we were not headed straight for the stricken ship. It seemed to me that our helm was changed several points. At any rate, our course was such that the crew of the brigantine, seeing us apparently bearing down on them, made little further effort on their own account although their ship seemed not only sinking but drifting, too, toward a boiling reef that would make short work of what remained of her chance of life.

"D'you, calculate we'll lower a boat in that sea—or steam close and send 'em a line?" wondered Yerkes.

"Scarcely," said Monty. "Scarcely a line in this storm—even with a rocket. I think we shall lower a boat. We ought to see pretty seamanship—see what the Germans are good for."

The *Bundesrath* slam-banged along, headed, I thought, another point to port. I suppose we were making fourteen knots at the lowest reckoning—time being an element in most mail subsidies—but I noticed nothing in the way of preparation for the coming rescue work. I thought that cool and admired it.

"I suppose these squareheads have their drill down pretty fine," I said. "On an English ship they'd have had a boat ready before this, with a bucko mate easing his heart of bad language, and everybody nervous."

Yet I knew the reputation of the Germans on the sea. I suppose it was the Englishman's everlasting, foolish habit of imputing sportsmanship to men unable to be guilty of it and conceding the benefit of doubt to hogs undoubtable that blinded me to the already pretty obvious. Monty was soonest undeceived, but said nothing.

I climbed down the companion-ladder and stood in the rain in the waist, facing astern and looking upward to see how Germans shaped at boat drill. From where I clung to a ventilating cowl I could see the rows of life-boats on the bridge-deck—the officers, too—three of them—the junior, apparently in charge. The captain and first officer were watching the wreck through glasses, passing remarks to each other at intervals. I climbed to the saloon deck again.

"They've done nothing yet," I said. "They haven't as much as stripped the covering from a boat. There's no crew up there that could lower away or man a boat. You don't suppose "

"I do!" said Monty grimly.

"What do you mean?" demanded Yerkes.

"Deutschland über Alles!" Monty answered. "However, we'll see—"

Fred Oakes made a grab for him, but missed.

"Didums, you —— fool, come back here!" He had to shout to make himself heard at all, for the storm was increasing. "You ass, they'll clap you in irons! Come back and talk it over!"

But Monty was gone, two steps at a time, up the bridge companion, past the painted board that said *verboten!*

Yerkes leaned toward me and made both hands into a trumpet.

"There'll be a row!" he yelled. "Heinie's a surly brute when you bait him—our man's proud! Stand by to catch when they throw him down!"

He was half-serious, half in earnest, but I took him at his word. Once, on a deep-sea-going British bark, I was elected by the fo'castle to go aft—a delegation of one—to complain of flagrant and intolerable wrongs. Insight received on that occasion into how the "afterguard" review invasion of their sacred deck by uninvited folk had left its deep impression, and I did not suppose Germans would be more tolerant than Englishmen.

I had visions of Monty being hurled backward down the companion-ladder, kicked in the chest most likely—as happened to me. So I hurried after him and the others followed.

BEING WELL used to the deck of a plunging ship, I was only a step or two behind Monty when he reached the top. He did not set foot on the sacred bridge, but stood on the last step, clinging with a hand on either rail and waiting for somebody to turn and see him. I could see and hear, for my head was above the level of the bridge-deck, and the taut, breast-high canvas kept the wind away.

It was the first officer who turned and first saw Monty, and his jaw dropped with astonishment. He did not trouble to call the captain's attention; what is *"verboten"* under the *Vaterland* flag is something to be prevented or undone swiftly by any one in uniform. He made a savage sign with his right arm, as one would order a devil back down into hell, but Monty seemed not to understand. So he left the captain's side and came swiftly—charging, one might say.

"Weg! Go down!" he ordered. *"Dies ist verboten!* It is not allowed! Go below!"

"I'll speak with the captain!" answered Monty, slowly and loud enough for the captain to catch each word.

But that pompous individual was so sure of his subordinate's ability to uphold pride of place that he did not even turn his head.

"Gott im Himmel!" the first officer shouted. "I order you down! Do you not hear?"

"Order your God about all you care to!" answered Monty. "I'll speak with the captain!"

The German then caught sight of Yerkes and Oakes behind me on the ladder, and his hand went to his hip pocket with the blackguard instinct that thinks of violence first and argument occasionally afterward. Monty neither flinched nor even seemed to see the hint.

"What do they say?" yelled Fred from below, behind Bill Yerkes.

"Shut up," I answered, "or I can't hear!"

It may be that the first officer imagined we were counseling a forward move. At all events he decided the situation was too much for him unaided.

"Stay there!" he ordered. "Come no further!"

With two or three nervous backward glances, he hurried to the side of the captain, who seemed annoyed at having to take his eyes away from the spectacle of a helpless ship wallowing toward destruction. He made a gesture of impatience; then stepped briskly to the companion head, brushing the first officer aside.

"Dies is forbidden!" he announced. "Strictly forbidden! Go back!"

But Monty did not move.

"Don't be afraid of him, Didums!" called Oakes from below. "Tell him what you think of him!"

"We're with you, old man!" Yerkes shouted.

Honestly, for the minute I thought we might commit the unforgivable offense and storm the bridge in Monty's wake. I think the captain, too, entertained some foolish thought of that kind, for he followed the first officer's example and touched his right hip pocket.

"Vhat do you vant?" he demanded arrogantly.

He was a big, tub-bellied, pompous man, who took a deal of comfort in his stomach, unlike his lean, nervous second-in-command.

"I call your attention," said Monty, "to a ship in distress over the to port. She's signaling for help!"

"Did you think I saw not?" the German demanded.

"I couldn't account in any other way," said Monty, "for your neglect!"

They were yelling at each other because of the noise of wind and sea and of the engines pounding down below us; it would not have needed much imagination to believe them on the verge of blows.

"What do you mean—neglect?" demanded the German.

"Neglect," said Monty, "of the first principle of decency!"

"Ged down!" the German roared. "Ged off dat ladder! Go to ——! You hear me—yes?"

"Not at all," said Monty. "All hell's yours if you want it! I'm calling attention to that ship in distress. Why don't you send assistance?"

"Who are you to order me? Do you not know this is a German ship?"

"Unfortunately, yes," said Monty. "No English skipper would need to be told his duty!"

"Duty! You tell me! *Donner und Blitzen noch einmal!* You —— English! It is my absolute duty to remofe you from this bridge!"

"Play your game your own way!" Monty answered. "You've been told in the presence of witnesses and of your own subordinate—" the first officer had come to stand beside his chief—"that your duty is to go to that ship's assistance! Unless you do, I shall report your conduct at the first opportunity!"

The German laughed—cynically—brutally—untouched except by a sense of being interfered with.

"Fritz!" he said, turning to the first officer, but shouting in English to make Monty understand. "You order that a live-boat be made retty. Let this English lord and his friends be pud in id. Let them go themselfs and helb that ship! That seddles it! Presto! Get down off this bridge! A boat shall be made retty—you four shall ged into it and go to ——!"

"You've had your attention called and you've been warned!" said Monty, turning his back.

And at that we all came down the ladder in single file, Oakes first.

There was not much to say, but we said it, I, the youngest, first and Monty last.

"Is there nothing we can do?"

"Who'd have believed it?"

"You ought to have knocked him down, Didums!"

"Watch, you fellows! The best we can do now is to be ready to swear to what we've seen!"

We were abreast of the wreck by that time, considerably less than half a mile away, and it was now obvious to the helpless crew that we were passing them without as much as an exchange of signals. Some climbed into the rigging of the one remaining mast and waved shirts—anything—frantically.

"Wave back to 'em!" urged Fred, but I objected.

"Why the devil not?" said Yerkes. "Let 'em know some one on this packet sympathizes!"

"It would raise false hopes," I answered.

"All the same," said Monty, "wave to them. If any get ashore they'll be able to swear they were seen from this ship!"

So we waved hats and handkerchiefs, and, not because we hoped they might hear us but because of rebellion, cheered, too—over and over again until we were hoarse. That called attention to us from the bridge. The first officer leaned over, saw and reported to his chief. The next minute an angry, guttural voice roared through a speaking-trumpet at us:

"Cease—do you hear me! Sdop from doing thad!"

But we only cheered the louder and waved more frantically.

SQUALLS—RAIN—SWIFTLY DRIFTING clouds—and waves that now and then ran cliff-high kept shutting off the wreck from view. It seemed to us that the third mast went by the board. Yerkes, who was keenest-eyed of the four, swore he saw her bottom-up; but after that I was very nearly sure I caught sight of her twice, still right-side-up, but so close to the reef as to seem a part of it. The *Bundesrath's* speed and the weather drew a curtain over the finish. But I went down in the rain to the waist again and, looking up, saw all three officers staring at the wreck, two through binoculars and one through a telescope. They knew all right what happened.

"Did you see the lookout on our fo'castle-head?" asked Oakes.

There was a bearded German seaman, his oilskins glistening with rain and spray, leaning his weight against the rail that penned the suffering goats into the utmost corner of the bow—a Viking by the look of him, blue-eyed, heavily built.

"He watched the whole thing," continued Fred, "as calmly—as calmly—as—"

"As one pig watching another one killed!" said Yerkes. "I know! I went to college at Heidelberg. The whole nation's that way."

We paced the deck, staggering four abreast, for an hour or more, mostly in silence but swearing now and then. At dinner-time we sat down at the usual table, but the captain did not join us. It was six o'clock and time for the evening meal before we had opportunity to carry forward the account. Then, as we sat studying the menu, the captain came and plumped himself in his usual chair next to Monty.

" *'Nabend, meine Herren!*" he grinned.

He intended to be condescending and conciliatory, but there was more than a suggestion of mastery.

Monty turned in the revolving-chair and looked him over as a not very eager buyer regards an animal. The German's lips worked, and I thought there was going to be a row. The others thought the same, and we were all ready in a second to wade into any sort of scrap. But Monty rose leisurely, as no man does who means to start a fight.

"This ship is a sty," he said. "We can't avoid the dirt, but there's no need to sit with the pigs. Care to follow me, you fellows?"

"Vhat do you mean?" demanded the captain.

But we all followed Monty down the saloon to another table at the end. The other first-class passengers were seasick, and we, the captain and two stewards had the whole saloon to ourselves. The captain called to the steward, and we sat waiting.

We waited in vain that evening. No steward would come near us. Our supper was a bad smell from the pantry, and the pickles and olives that Yerkes collected from half a dozen tables.

"Let's smash some crockery!" he suggested.

But that was vetoed.

"He only wants an excuse for putting us in irons," said Monty. "We'd satisfy no one but him that way."

"I dunno," said Yerkes. "I believe I'd be satisfied with one—just one crack at him before he arrested me!"

"He wouldn't arrest you, America. He'd call the crew," said Fred.

"I imagine between us we'd use up the crew—some!" Yerkes answered cheerfully.

"I'm going to sing to him!" announced Fred. "I sing best when I'm hungry. Hold the fort, you fellows, while I run to the cabin and fetch my concertina. I'll sing a song that'll make the fat rascal's belly bitter!"

But Monty talked down that proposal too.

"It's my experience," he said, "that looking for a way to get even with a cad is sheer wasted ingenuity. I'll report him. The papers shall roast him thoroughly, even if nothing worse happens to him. If he were English he'd be broke as a matter of course—might even lose his ticket. Being German, he'll probably be admonished not to get found out again.

"But what I'm driving at is this: a cad invariably fouls his own nest. All we need do is sit tight. He imagines the shoe is on the other foot, and that he should get even with us. Cads always react that way. He considers himself insulted and, in addition, he's more than half-afraid I can do something to jeopardize his prospects."

"But, —— him, at present he's starving us!" objected Fred.

"You're not dead yet, old dear," soothed Monty. "He'll relent by breakfast-time, for sake of the comity of nations. He'll probably try to put us off the ship at Beira. Fading that he's likely to charge us with some serious offense at our first port of call in German East."

"But, —— it!" objected Yerkes. "We've paid our fares to Mombasa! I don't exactly see my name in the Boston papers landed off this tub short of my destination as undesirable!"

Monty smiled amiably.

"As long as we save your reputation," he said, "we others will rest content!"

Fred and I laughed, but Bill Yerkes was not so easily scored off.

"When I joined this partnership the House of Lords achieved new dignity," he answered. "Have a try at living up to it!"

"What do you propose?" asked Monty.

"You think that fat slob feels like putting one over on us. I say put one over on him! Forestall him!"

"How?" asked Fred and I together, but Yerkes betrayed all at once a tendency to dry up, as it were.

"Leave it to me!" he answered.

Monty yawned.

"Sketch out the main lines," I proposed. "Can't you give us a general idea?"

"We'll agree to anything in reason," said Fred cautiously.

"No!" said Yerkes. "I've trusted you fellows time and again. This is my trick!"

Monty yawned again and rose.

"Night, you fellows! I'm off to my cabin—can't stand the smell through that pantry door. Night, night, Yerkes. Let's see you win a trick from Heinie if you can!"

"For a seasick man he is some Indian!" said Yerkes, watching Monty's athletic back disappear through the saloon door. "Almost the only thing I've got against him is his title!"

"The title's been useful," said I, and Fred nodded.

"Then why don't he put it to more use?" wondered Yerkes. "Was he ever married?"

"No," answered Fred.

"He's the sort I wish our girls in the States would sign up with, instead of the aristocratic lemons they do pick! If he's in need of millions to clear the estate and live in style, why in the name of thunder don't he take a trip to N'York or Chicago. He could land a nice girl and a hundred million within a month!"

"Propose it to him, and see what he says!" suggested Fred, with the air of a man anticipating keen enjoyment.

"He's white!" said Yerkes. "He's handsome—healthy—sportsmanlike—I'd be doing the States a good turn—watch and see if I don't do it!"

Then the chief steward came and ordered us insolently out of the saloon. We had fed him when he first came aboard, on the "early and often" principle, and hitherto a more obsequious and flattering purveyor of unwholesome food would have been hard to find anywhere; but word had gone forth from the bridge, and now we were fallen from grace.

"Schon sehr speht!" he said fussily. *"Es wird*—you are required—at vonce you leave the saloon!"

We took our time. It was now Fred's turn to be pugnacious, Yerkes having relapsed into thoughtfulness. Fred's type of physiognomy, with carefully trimmed, pointed, reddish-gray beard—upturned mustaches like a troubador's—the head held jauntily on a strong neck, intolerant of any but the turn-down kind of collar—lends itself to quarrelsome expression, in that way frequently deceiving the elect, to say nothing of those who never see below a surface. Holding his face very close to the steward's, he felt the man's fat ribs for the softest place to punch. And my attitude—I was aching for a crack at somebody—prevented the arrival of reserves in the shape of underlings.

"D'you suppose there was a steward on that wreck we left behind?" demanded Fred through set teeth, prodding at a fat place with one finger.

"I know nothing of any wreck!" said the steward. "Such matters concern the high command!"

"You lie, you dog! I saw you watching from the stern! I hope," Fred selected thoughtfully, "that when a shark gets you at last he'll start in on you just there!"

"Ouch!" exclaimed the steward, all in a sweat with the heat and cold anticipation.

He thought we were going to beat him up, and I saw him, as I left the saloon last, turn savagely on his assistant with the illogical reaction all cowards evince.

THERE BEING so few passengers, we each had a cabin alone, in line; Monty's the end one. Seeing a light in Monty's as I passed, I went with Yerkes as far as the smoking-room and then made an excuse to leave him there a while. Monty's door opened the moment I touched it, but shut again under pressure from Fred's back.

"Let him in, Fred!" ordered Monty. "Now," he said, as the door closed again behind me. "Talk both at once, won't you, and get it over? You both want to say the same thing!"

"Be careful of Yerkes," I said. "He's not a bad fellow, but a Yankee. They have different standards over there. If you allow him a free hand he may get us all into serious trouble. He's our partner. We'd have to see him through."

"Fred has it the other way round," said Monty. "Fred says he's a Yankee, but not a bad fellow!"

"What do you say?" said I.

"I say—suppose you fellows let me sleep—eh? If I never worry more than about what Bill Yerkes leads us into, I shall die in the end of comatose inertia! I suspect he hasn't a plan yet. He's trusting his mother wit to show him one."

Neither of us was satisfied. Fred went to bed, and I returned to the smoking-room to waste an hour or two in a futile effort to pump Yerkes.

"I've yet to meet the German who could put one over on me," was the final sum of the whole of what I got from him.

The following dawn rain had ceased for the time being, but it blew big guns, tearing away the awning all along one side with a noise like the Battle of Waterloo. We took our usual before-breakfast constitutional, reeling arm-in-arm up and down deck in pajamas, and were watched from the bridge with a new air of settled curiosity.

"They've made up their minds what to try to do with us," said Monty. "What interests them now is how we'll take it."

The hatches were closed tight when we came aboard in a hurry in Lourenço Marques, and all our luggage had been stowed in two empty cabins; as we passed along the corridor to breakfast we saw it being brought out and carried to the foot of the main companion. There was an awful pile of it, guns—tents, trunks, ammunition-boxes, saddles, camp-furniture, cases of preserved food—and it all slid back and forth in time to the ship's plunging so that the stewards had their work cut out.

As Monty had anticipated, they gave us breakfast at the table of our own choosing. But the chief steward was more offensively officious than on the night before. When we had finished he came and stood opposite Monty with heels clicked together.

"Orders are given," he said, "that the *Herrschaften* shall leave the ship at Beira. We shall arrive at Beira at about noon. The luggage will be put overboard into a lighter. The Portuguese authorities will be notified of compulsory debarkation of undesirable passengers. You should present yourselves at the purser's office on the main-deck to receive order for reimbursement of the balance of passage-money, payable at our office on shore."

"You have got that nicely by heart, haven't you!" said Fred, admiringly, but the chief steward clicked his heels, turned his back on us, and walked away.

"It 'ud suit my personal convenience," said Monty, "to leave this buzzard of a boat and wait at Beira for the B.I. or the French line. But convenience must go hang until we've taught these pirates a lesson."

"I've a plan for the lesson!" announced Yerkes with a bright eye. "Are you fellows really agreed to stick it out and see this thing through?"

"Waiting for you!" said Monty.

"I'll follow Monty's lead," said I.

"Tell us the plan!" said Fred, but Yerkes laughed.

"Go ashore if you'd rather!" he answered.

"If this were a German port," said Monty, "the rascals 'ud have us at their mercy. Now, why do you fellows suppose they should try conclusions with us here, instead of waiting until we reach Tanga, or Dar es Salaam? We'd have no show at all in one of their own ports. Here we've a British consul and authorities who must at least pretend to be indignant at the German fleet's recent effort to seize Lourenço Marques."

"Quem deus vult perdere," quoted Fred.

He never went to college, but quotes Latin for appearance's sake.

"No," said Monty. "They're not mad yet. That day is coming. This is a day of calculations—every move thought out carefully. There's more in this business than meets the eye."

"A —— of a whole lot more!" agreed Yerkes, and at that we all followed him up on deck, affecting not to notice our mountainous belongings.

There were stewards and a fourth officer hanging about to gloat over our annoyance; so we were aggressively cheerful.

The seasick passengers were on deck, but, besides being seasick, they were anti-English and gave us a wide berth. There was a Herr Professor Liebknecht and a Herr Doktor Kaspari, both with square shoulders and scrawny beards; and there were two beer-consuming representatives of export firms, one fat and the other lean, who showed the Herr Professor marked respect. The professor being evidently some one of importance, it occurred to Monty to go up and speak to him.

"Did you happen to see that ship in distress that we passed yesterday?" he asked.

"Also—wann haben wir uns kennen gelernt?" answered the professor, removing his spectacles to wipe them and blinking at Monty through short-sighted eyes.

He looked as disagreeable as a woodchuck caught away from home.

"He wants to know when you were introduced," Yerkes explained.

"My name's Mundidger," said Monty. "I'm Earl of Mundidger and Kirkoobrisher, and I don't care a —— who you are! Did you see that ship in distress we passed yesterday?"

"I do not care to speak English," snarled the Herr Professor, backing away along the rail.

He was a big Herr Professor, and looked capable for all his spectacles and inadequate whiskers.

"Would you care for a swim?" suggested Monty. "Answer, you reptile, or overboard you go!"

"It is none of your business what I saw!" said the professor in unexpectedly good English.

"You've one more chance!" said Monty. "Your last one!"

"If you mean that we should have stopped in that storm to rescue fools who should have known better than to be caught in distress in such weather—"

"Did you see the ship?" demanded Monty.

"I did see, but—"

"That's what I wanted to know," said Monty. "I'm obliged to you. Thanks!"

The professor hurried off indignantly, what was left of his self-complacency blown away by the wind that hurled him round the corner of the smoking-room and out of sight.

"We've some pleasant companions to finish the voyage with!" Monty laughed. "That's to say, supposing we contrive not to be put ashore."

"That's arranged already," said Yerkes. "I was forward at break of day among the third-class passengers. One look round was enough!"

"Confound you, explain!" urged Fred, but at that moment a steward came, clinging and swinging along the bulwark.

"You should go to the purser at once!" he said, addressing all four of us.

"Tell the purser he may go to ——!" Fred answered genially.

"It is not an invitation," said the steward. "It is an order!"

"Very well," said Monty. "Change our permission into an order. Tell the purser from me that he is ordered to go to ——!"

"I dare not carry such a message!" said the steward.

"Jump overboard, then!" advised Fred.

"Meine Herren, I do not recommend—this is not advisable—it is—will you not please go to the purser?"

"Certainly not!" said Monty. "Tell him to come here if he has anything to say to me!"

THE STEWARD departed in high dudgeon. Later we saw the purser climb to the bridge and hold consultation up there, with the captain probably, for we could already see the low-lying land near Beira—and Germans obey the sort of sea rules that make for safety of their own ships. Presently the purser approached us with something in an envelope outheld.

"Your order for refund!" he announced curtly. "To be presented at our shore office for payment."

He thrust it forward, but Monty, leaning back against the rail, laughed in the wholly exasperating because undoubtedly careless way that the English-speaking nations—and, at that, only the best of them—alone seem able to achieve.

"If you do not take it, you will not obtain the money!" said the purser.

"You don't say so!"

"To which of you shall I then give it?"

He looked from one to the other and finally made up his mind to force it into my hands. I put them behind me. So he thrust it into the breast pocket of a rain-coat I had pulled on in spite of the heat, and before I could snatch it out again the wind performed the office for me. The envelope went whirling and flurrying away astern, and was presently lost like a fleck of foam upon the waste of water.

"There!" said the purser. "There goes your money! You will be set ashore nevertheless! Now your only remedy will be to make application for refund at the company's head office in Hamburg!"

"The devil you say!" said Monty, and the purser walked away.

By that time we were in shallow, calmer water, maneuvering amid the shoals that guard Beira's inhospitable roadstead. A Portuguese pilot clambered aboard and was received contemptuously on the bridge. Monty drew an envelope from his own pocket, and looked about him curiously.

"Something heavy and not too large—the first thing handy!"

Yerkes was quickest. He drew a knife from his pocket and cut away the metal eye-ring, formerly part of the awning, that still hung from the stanchion. Monty enclosed it in the envelope, which I saw then was addressed to the British consul, Beira. Written above the address, very plainly, over Monty's signature were the words—

> Please pay ten pounds or its equivalent to whoever delivers this.

I whispered to Yerkes what I had seen, but he appeared indifferent. Fred, on the other hand, was intensely interested and argued excitedly with Monty as to the best means of getting the message ashore.

"It must get ashore before we drop anchor!" he urged.

I was watching the water and observing the pilot's demeanor.

"The tide'll flow for an hour yet," I said. "I'll bet we don't run in until it begins to make."

"I hope you're right! If the skipper gets word ashore much ahead of mine, we're in trouble!" Monty answered.

But Yerkes grinned—foolishly, I thought.

"Counting your chickens?" I asked him, but he only whistled to himself.

There came alongside presently a neat little

launch with a brass rail and the flag of the Portuguese Government. A man in a white hat and suit on board her shouted and waved his arms until a fat bundle of European magazines and newspapers was dropped from the bridge into the sea, missing him narrowly. His crew and the three passengers up forward under the awning laughed at his short-winded efforts to recover the bundle, and, while that was going on, a seaman in the stern, who held a rope fender between the launch and the ship's side, saw Monty's signals. Monty tossed him the envelope. He caught it—stared at the address, but plainly knew no English—looked up at us for explanations—and was seen from the bridge.

"Send zat letter up here!" the captain bellowed.

It is the exasperating fate of the world-ambitious German merchant fleet that it has to use the loathed English language for a *lingua franca!*

The shout called the man in the snow-white suit's attention and, abandoning all hope of the bundle, which had sunk, he demanded instant surrender to himself of Monty's letter. The seaman gave it up.

"Now we're done for!" said Monty self-accusingly. But Will Yerkes, close beside me with both elbows on the rail, began humming a tune I recognized.

Oh, rustibums and jolly good chums, who live
like royal Turks,
Tee-tum, tee-tum, tee-tiddledy—and
To —— with the man that works!

"It's good to see our House of Lords exerting himself in vain," he said pleasantly.

"Send him down a line!" roared the skipper. "Send me zat letter up here!"

But the man in the white hat and suit could read English as well as hear it, and by that time he had deciphered Monty's order for the payment of ten pounds. He put the letter in his pocket.

"Send it up here!" the skipper roared again, and a hand-line whirled through the air to coil all about him. But he kicked and shook himself free of it.

Ten pounds, payable in gold or exchange at the English consulate, is an unanswerable argument. He gave a sign to the engineer, another to the barefooted Goanese helmsman and in a moment the launch was steaming helter-skelter toward the sand-choked river mouth.

"I'd have hated to be put ashore!" said Monty, but Will Yerkes laughed again.

"What do you think your consul could do for us?" he asked. "He can protest. But what will a protest amount to in the opinion of Heinie up on the bridge there? If the British consul is all you've got up your sleeve we've a fat chance!"

"America, you're simply betraying ignorance!" announced Fred, as usual Monty's instant defender. "You poor Republican ignoramus—you bally ass—don't you realize that the consul will set the cables burning at both ends? Berlin will hear from Whitehall within five hours! Man alive! It 'ud be an international insult to remove a British privy councillor from a ship against his will and in teeth of a consul's protests!"

"Aw, I've heard U.S. senators talk that way," Yerkes answered. "Hot air! Besides—I don't hear Monty boasting. How about it, Monty? Are you willing to call on the British Government to declare war on our account?"

"No need to appear ridiculous," said Monty. "I've invited the British consul to come and dare this captain to put us ashore. You'll find he'll do it!"

"If that's your game," said Yerkes with another chuckle, "I've got it beaten to a frazzle—skinned both ways! Remember—you said, Monty, I was to take the trick from Heinie if I can. You all agreed we'd see this through! Am I right?"

Apparently we were deeper-laden than the coastwise liners usually are, for we had to hang about for four hours until the tide had made enough to lift us over the treacherous, shifting bars. The steward had to feed us again, and did it as ungraciously as Teuton manners permitted. There was still the same sickening smell through the pantry door. Then we went on deck again, to find ourselves in the flat calm of the river mouth and a Portuguese official tugboat coming alongside.

Yerkes left us at once. We three stood on the saloon deck about amidships and watched him go to the gangway forward, where the tug made fast. An officious Portuguese in linen and gold lace placed a sentry on our deck, and Yerkes spoke to the sentry. The sentry pointed, and Yerkes looked wise, with the very owl-like old-man wise look young Americans affect. Presently the gold-laced official, side-by-side with an obvious representative of the steamship company, came aboard and clambered to the bridge.

A perfectly obvious Portuguese doctor followed

up the gangplank and was promptly buttonholed by Yerkes. And then a man who might be anything, neat, lean, and pockmarked, came aboard leisurely and looked about him. He climbed to the saloon deck as if the exercise bored him utterly and looked again—looked at Monty and Fred and me three times—then came toward us.

"I'm Brrritish consul," he announced, as if that, too, were a hardship. "I'm lukin' f'r th' Earrl o' Mundidger an' Krikoobrissher."

"I'm Mundidger," said Monty, offering a hand. "Glad to meet you, Mr.—"

"McAllister. Alan McAllister. Proud to shake han's wi' ye, my lorrd. I knew y'r fayth'r. My fayth'r was bailiff on y'r lorrdship's estate o' Dundromochie—lived six-an'-fifty yearrr there, lad an' mon. That wad be before y'r lorrdship's time. It was through favor of y'r lorrdship's fayth'r I was put in a fair way tae get this poseetion here; an' a sorry, sinful hole it is tae live in, I assure ye! Ye owe me ten pounds, my lorrd."

"Certainly," said Monty and paid him with a ten-pound note.

"Mon—that was an awfu' price to pay for bringin' a wee letter ashore!"

"Cheap at any price," said Monty. "Had to get in touch with you. Fact is I undertook to report the captain of this ship for cowardly neglect of duty in refusing to steam to the assistance of a sailing-ship in distress. His answer to that is to threaten us with compulsory debarkation here as undesirables. That won't do, of course. In case you've forgotten the fact, I'm a privy councillor. Have to consider that, y'know."

"OF COURRSE, of courrse! These Germans are a strange rrace, but here an' there one o' them underrstands the amenities. Their consul here's frequently a friend o' mine when sober, as it happens he is to-day. I dinna doubt that wi' his aid, an' perhaps cigars an' a drrink or two, I c'd perrsuade yon captain tae wrrite ye a verra pretty letter, thankin' ye f'r frenship an' regrettin' 'at his ship isna' fit f'r ye tae trravel in—an' that's the truth! Mon—my lorrd—this is a bad ship ye're in! Have ye no' hearrd o' the recent attempt by the Gerrman navy to seize Lourenço Marques an' proclaim a German protectorate?"

"My friends and myself helped prevent that very attempt," said Monty.

"Then how in God's name d'ye come tae be aboard this *Bundesrath?"*

"En route for British East," said Monty. "She was the first ship making the trip up-coast, so we sent our traps aboard and followed."

"Mon—my lorrd—she was parrt o' the heinous plan! The consul in Durban wired me that from inforrmation received she's simply cram fu' o' guns an' ammunition! Ye know how these liners make the trip, don't ye—they come outward bound from Hamburg down one coast of Africa, an' gang name again up t'other, first ship east, t'other ship west, alternately. This *Bundesrath* came down the west coast so chock fu' wi' guns an' such that she has scorrned to tak' aboard as much as another hundredweight *en route!*

"She has brought a full carrgo all the way down one side o' this grreat continent—an' now apparently she's takin' it home again! Is that natural on the face of it? Listen!" He lowered his voice to a sort of stage whisper, and raised a lean hand to his mouth to heighten the effect. "She has not had a hatch off once, all the voyage, though she's called at twenty porrts!"

"That might account for their stowing our heavy luggage in empty cabins," said Monty.

"Of courrse it does! Of courrse it does! Man, I'm tellin' ye she's loaded full wi' ammuneetion! When was the Gerrman squadron in Lourenço Marques? Eh? Didn't this ship come squatterin' in a matter o' two days later? So I'm inforrmed. Supposin' the coup had not miscarried, would it not have been a most Providential circumstance for the Gerrman admiral to receive ah that extra ammuneetion, to say nothin' o' supplies, in the verra nick o' time? An' listen to this! Here's extra proof f'r ye!

"She's not had a hatch off since she left Hamburg. That's admitted. She's refused profitable business at every port. That's known. Three weeks ago another sinner o' the same house-flag cam' in here down the east coast, an' off-loaded two-hundred cases o' harrdware. Harrdware, mind ye—heavy as ——. They lay in bond here. Now—that coup in Lourenço Marques havin' miscarried, ye remember—this ship—that's refused business at every port—never had a hatch off—puts in here an' consents to take those cases o' harrdware; an' my friend Siegfried Hering, the Gerrman consul here, continues sober an' friendly f'r the space of two weeks, waitin' tae see the business done!

"Oh, but he'll be a drunken man tonight! The harrdware that came from Hamburg is to go back to Hamburg, cases unopened! Would ye call that cirrcumstantial evidence, or not, my lorrd?"

"Looks suspicious," Monty agreed.

"Then listen to this! Oor Government is strictly parrsimonious. I'm allowed no funds to speak of at all—none whatever worth mentionin'—f'r such purposes as procurin' intelligence—nothin' but a very small fund for succorin' distressed British subjects, an' f'r contingencies, etceteries, an' what not—all used up before a year's a month old. Yet I'm curious. An' I'm thrifty. I've money of my own. An' these Portuguese are avarrricious. Mon—I'm tellin' ye—" he raised his scrawny hand again and whispered hoarsely—"I've discovered beyond the risk o' a doubt that the harrdware is naethin' but machine-guns!"

"I don't expect they'll take it all back to Hamburg," said Monty. "Don't you suppose they'll land the lot in German East, Tonga, or Dar-es-Salaam, or Bergamoyo?"

"These cases are reconsigned to Hamburg," said the consul.

"They won't let a little detail of that sort hinder them. I suppose those are the cases coming?"

Monty nodded toward a float that was being warped alongside.

"Aye, yon's they. But if this captain's that anxious tae be rid o' ye, how is it he doesn't begin by orrderin' ye off the ship? There's the tug that sh'ud take ye ashore—the one that brought me. He's dilatory, f'r a man possessed by deterrmination! I'm thinking I'll go speak wi' him. May I understand that ye'll tak' my advice an' leave the ship peacefully—an' wi'out a regret, no doubt—provided I get fr'm him a statement in wrritin' tae the effect 'at he's had a pleasant trip wi' ye an' ye've behaved all the way like baa-lambs?"

"All right, McAllister," said Monty. "Anything to oblige. I guarantee to report him, and to follow it up! But my friends and I will wait here and finish our journey on a French or British ship, provided it's made clear in writing that we do it of our own free will. Otherwise, I'll resist—and let happen what may!"

"Man, man! There'll be no need o' disgracefu' scenes! No captain wi' all that cirrcumstantial evidence under all four hatches—an' the porrts o' all East Africa so thick wi' spies a man c'd scarcely step between 'em—him hurryin' home tae hide the traces o' his Government's failure tae break international law an' treaties an' good faith an' what not—no such captain wad let escape a chance o' avoidin' trouble!

"An' besides—should he deny me—there's Siegfried Hering ashore there, sober, an' fully aware 'at I ken weel what's in those cases! I'll have ye a letter fr'm the captain within twenty minutes. After that, be advised by me an' come ashore!"

The consul walked off in the direction of the bridge, we watching him with feelings of, I think, unmixed relief.

"What'll Will Yerkes say to it?" I asked presently. "We promised him, didn't we?"

"Will's a good fellow," said Monty. "He'll be as glad as the rest of us to leave this buzzard of a boat!"

But Monty was wrong. We all three undervalued Will Yerkes' ingenuity.

Yerkes himself appeared presently, climbing up the accommodation ladder from the deck below.

"What are you grinning about, America?" demanded Fred.

Yerkes certainly did look pleased with himself.

"I've fixed it so that we'll stay on board all right!" he announced. "I lied to the Portuguese doctor, but I told him the truth about that brigantine first. It was the first news he had of it. Seems she was anchored off here all last week—her skipper was Portuguese—friend of the doctor's. Naturally doc was mad enough to eat Germans by the time I'd finished. Then I told him I was a practising physician in the States, with a lot of Brazilian experience of epidemic and endemic diseases. He can't prove I wasn't! Doctors don't flash their diplomas in each other's faces on first acquaintance like two tecs trying to arrest each other.

"Then I told him we've got cholera and bubonic plague aboard! Took him among the third-class passengers and showed him three Indians with bellyaches and a half-breed with a toothache and high temperature. Assured him I knew the symptoms. Now get this and never again call me no diplomatist! If I'd offered my services he might have found me out. But your Uncle Dudley was too wise! I urged him to go ahead off his own bat. 'The discovery is yours,' I said. 'Full credit is due you. Say nothing about me!' "

"Good lord!" groaned Monty.

"You've done it, America!" said Fred with the jaunty air he usually keeps for unexpected trouble.

"What's the matter?" Yerkes demanded.

But there wasn't time just then to unfold the full enormity.

"We've no physician at all on board, have we?" asked Monty. "No one who could contradict the diagnosis?"

"No," said I. "The chief steward told me when we came aboard that the ship's doctor fell overboard off Lagos and was drowned."

"We might go ashore and be quarantined there," suggested Fred, our last-ditch optimist.

But that proposal was exploded even before Yerkes could swallow resentment sufficiently to demand an explanation for our right-about-face. The consul came, hop-skip-and-jumping from the bridge.

"Ye've no call tae worry about bein' set ashore as undesirables!" he announced. "It's quite the contrary! Ye've passages booked for Mombasa by way of Zanzibar, an' ye're refused permission tae land! Not a man may leave the ship! The lieutenant-governor himself—he wi' the gold lace an' white claes up yonder—says as much! I'll be lucky not to be quarantined myself. But his dibs was on the ship too—if they do me, then they shall him!

"Mon, ye've cholera aboard, or so they say—cholera an' bubonic! The captain's been told he may have no further communication wi' the shore on any grounds! Loch! Yon tug's whistlin' f'r all ashore! Goo'-by, my lorrd! Proud to ha' met ye! Glad tae be o' serrvice! Goo'-by, gentlemen! Ou-aye, I'll write the Foreign Office. Goo'-by, goo'-by—I'll be runnin'."

THERE WAS something like a stampede from the ship, headed by the lieutenant-governor. The doctor left last, explaining with great flow of gesticulation how the epidemic should be dealt with, the first officer walking sullenly beside him, receiving the explanation with contemptuous aloofness until, with a foot on the gangplank, the doctor turned to fire a last, unexpected shot.

"But never mind! But never mind! You have a passenger who is a doctor! Your American will tell you—they are skilful, those Americans! Ask him!"

The first officer looked as if a wasp had stung him, but made no answer.

In obedience to orders bellowed from the Government tug, the men in charge of the cases of hardware cast off and let the float drift clear. Bellowing from the bridge betrayed anxiety, shared by a German on the cargo-float, who did his frantic best to make the crew return alongside. But the dreaded word "disease" had gone forth, and no cajolery or threats could outweigh that.

"They're troubled about those cases! Watch the fun!" said Monty.

The Government tug hung around, as if intending to take the float in tow. A conversation in German, Portuguese and English followed, mostly through megaphones and wholly noisy, not ceasing until a man arrived in a fast steam-launch flying the flag of the Imperial German consulate.

Whether or not that was Mr. Siegfried Hering, he certainly had authority. The launch circled the float once, and orders passed in a tone entirely different from the babel that had been. The launch took station then between float and tug, as if to prevent interference, and the totally unexpected took place promptly. The float's crew manned the cases one by one, shoved them to the edge, and dumped them overboard with a splash into the opaque water, beginning along one side first. In ten minutes they had forty cases overboard—then five more—and the float took a list to starboard.

"Watch! Oh, watch!" said Monty, leaning both elbows on the rail.

The German on the float grew alarmed and shouted. The six-man crew clambered to the downward side to obey, and their weight, like a last straw, tipped the balance, The float up-ended leisurely, let cases, crew and angry German slide into the water and righted itself again. We four, leaning on the rail together, cheered and suddenly checked ourselves.

"Well I'll be—!" said Monty.

"Well I'm jiggered!" echoed Yerkes. "Would you believe it?"

"Sweet!" said Fred Oakes. "Sweet and lovely!"

"How dare he, with people looking on?" said I.

The man in the steam-launch gathered the spluttering German from the water with a boat-hook, and promptly steamed away at top speed, leaving the crew of the float to swim or drown as nature and the laws of chance saw fit!

As a matter of fact, they did not drown, for Monty threw one line, and I another, that three of them managed to seize, and the other three clambered back on the float. All six were presently picked up by the Government tug, which took the empty float in tow and turned a hostile back on us. The last we saw of McAllister, he was waving his hat from the stern.

"We've this consolation," said Monty. "The captain knows the British consul came and talked with us. He's likely to take that into consideration."

"But you've done it, America. You've done it!" said Fred with a wry grimace.

"Well, I like that!" exploded Yerkes. "Was the agreement that we'd stay on board or wasn't it?" He turned to Monty. "Did you or didn't you tell me to score off Heinie if I could?"

"Certainly!" laughed Monty. "You scored. The trouble is, though, that we're certainly headed next at top speed for a German port—where we haven't a consul to bless ourselves with! No plague or cholera developing, they scent your practical joke. Having no sense of humor, they retaliate!"

The *Bundesrath* got up her two clumsy anchors very bad-temperedly, wheeled in a muddy circle and made for sea, scarcely slowing down sufficiently to drop the pilot into a lugger that watched for him. Monty proved right about the impression made by our consul's visit; our luggage was returned to the empty cabins, and the under-steward assigned to wait on us—at a table all to ourselves—was the quintessence of servility.

But the four other first-class passengers declared war. Led by Herr Professor Liebknecht, they constituted themselves a board of censorship at the next table, resenting with clucking and sucking of teeth, our outbursts of high spirits. And unless you were a misanthrope it wasn't possible to sit at table with Fred Oakes without laughing nearly all the time.

When supper was nearly finished, the professor went from mere expostulation and being noisily scandalized to the laying down of law to his companions, all of whom—even the Herr Doktor—treated him with utmost deference. Since I sat facing them, I had a good view of the growing rage and indignation.

"There's trouble coming!" I announced.

"Oh, bosh!" said Fred.

But he had his back toward them.

The professor presently began instructing one of the two square-shouldered commercial men—the stouter one, who had a duelling scar on his lower lip—impressing over and over on his mind some formula. Mine was the sort of knowledge of German one learns in an English school and, although I caught occasional sentences, I did not understand.

At last the commercial man seemed primed. He rose and made his way toward us, undignified because of the ship's motion but commanding a deal of arrogance instead.

"Sie!" he said, standing as near Monty as he could come without loosing his hold on the table behind.

"Meaning me?" asked Monty blandly.

The man had what he had to say by heart and said it slowly, without much German accent, accumulating insolence through very absence of all haste.

"You are required in future to take your meals after other passengers have finished! Foreigners permitted to travel on German ships should see to it that their manners are unobjectionable, failing which they can not be permitted to inflict themselves on cultured society! You are notified not to come to table in future until after Herr Professor Liebknecht shall have left the saloon!"

Fred half-rose to his feet, but collapsed again at sight of Monty's face. I was speechless; my one instinct was to punch the man's head, but I, too, divined that Monty had the situation and his own temper well in hand. Will Yerkes laughed outright.

"Would you believe it?" he asked, looking so unqualifiedly amused that my own rage dwindled.

"You object to my manners, do you?" asked Monty.

"Yes!" said the German. "You are notified!"

Monty rose from his chair without haste, and a sort of breathlessness seized every one. I saw the professor wipe his spectacles, and the stewards, coming with dessert, set down what they were carrying. The German would have walked away if his position between Monty and a revolving-chair would have permitted that. As it was, he stood very bolt-upright, looking fierce.

We three knew Monty for the foremost English polo-player of his day—and that was not so long gone—and it is no secret to most people that the muscles of the British upper class are as a rule as well-conditioned as their skins are clean. But, except perhaps for Fred Oakes, who knew him best, I think every one was taken by surprise by what followed.

"You pick your teeth at table!" Monty said quietly. "Neither you nor your professor wash!

You eat like swine! It's a pity to have to touch you, but here goes!"

Divining violence, the German had raised both hands in a sudden, ill-considered posture of self-defense. Monty closed with him so swiftly that one's eye scarcely caught the movement, and the German's gasp was echoed by an explosion of guttural threats and *"Achs!"* from the other table. The other commercial individual aimed a glass at Monty's head, but hit his own man, and the stewards started up-saloon at the double to interfere. But Monty's speed was prodigious.

THE GERMAN gasped as the iron arms crushed him. He beat with his fists at Monty's face and tried to bite when he found he was only beating air. Then he kicked. But Monty shook him, and the fat legs in a second were above table level, scattering dishes, and glasses in all directions. To and fro, faster and faster, higher and higher he shook him, less and less able to think; then suddenly he loosed him like a bag of inert stuff from a catapult. He brought up plump among the dishes on the Herr Professor's table.

Then Monty sat down, not even breathing heavily.

"Steward!" he called. "Bring me some more potatoes!"

"Didums, you —— fool!" said Fred Oakes. "You've done it! Now it's war!"

"War be it!" answered Monty.

"Deal me in!" said Yerkes. "If all the men with titles were like you, Monty, I'd turn monarchist—durned if I wouldn't! I've not seen manhood asserted better even in the States!"

But it was not all over yet at the professor's table. For one thing, the ship was rolling violently. He who was flung broke, as he fell, the wooden fiddle, set to keep dishes and plates from dancing quadrilles; then the ship pitched and he slid with the whole mess into the professor's lap. By the time he had been dragged free he was nearly insane with frenzy and as ready to fight his own crowd as any one. The professor, however, was no longer in love with direct offensive—too bruised—too taken by surprise; he sat clawing colored blancmange from his whiskers, with an air of contemplating worse than murder by subtler means.

The chief steward, fussing like a wet hen, demanded explanations from every one, his blue-jacketed back toward us. Suddenly the man whom Monty had rough-handled recovered breath and wit enough to reassert himself and began blaming the chief steward for the whole business, calling him a *"Schafskopf"* and *"dummer Esel"* for permitting such incidents to take place at all in his saloon.

During that altercation the other commercial man—the lean one—hurled a broken dish at Monty, missed him and hit me. I sprang from my chair to retaliate, when the door at the end of the saloon suddenly swung open and in strode the captain, followed by his fourth officer and two quartermasters.

"Vhat means zis?" he demanded.

Seeing us quiet and the men of his own nation flustered and enraged, he strode down the saloon and began interrogating the professor. All the Germans, including two stewards, talked at once until he angrily demanded silence. Then we heard the professor's voice, like a meat machine mincing words, unmistakably and spitefully denouncing us four.

"He's telling him we began it!" said Yerkes, getting up to interfere.

"Better sit down, Will," Monty advised. "At the first excuse I suspect he'll go the limit!"

"Why don't you horn in, then?" Yerkes demanded. "You don't know what he's saying!"

"As a soldier," said Monty, "I was paid as much as two-pence a day extra for knowing German!"

"But I thought you—"

Monty smiled.

"I don't always tell all I know, Will. Our position's desperate unless we're awfully tactful. I do wish you'd sit down!"

At last the captain turned on us, well backed up by his fourth officer and quartermasters.

"Vill you have meals serfed in your cabins for ze future, or vill you prefer ze second-class? Ze ozzer passengers refuse any longer to eat togezzer vid you! Vun or ze ozzer—choose!"

Monty answered civilly enough.

"You've heard one side only. You've not even asked for our version of what has happened."

"No need!" said the captain. "Vhat has happened has happened! It shall not again! You choose!"

"Certainly not!" answered Monty. "My friends and I have been insulted by the people at that table. You are responsible for your passengers. Do what you see fit—on your own responsibility!"

"Leafe the saloon, then!" the captain ordered. "You four take meals in ze second-class!"

"On your responsibility!" said Monty imperturbably.

"Go at once!"

"Certainly not!" Monty answered. "We'll go when we've finished dinner!"

The quartermasters had revolvers. The captain glanced at them irresolutely, changed his mind and ordered them in German to stand guard over us until we should leave the saloon and not to readmit us. Then, with a bow and a joke to the Herr Professor, he swaggered out, leaving the fourth officer seated at a table near the door to guard against contingencies. The fourth was a very young man, and made a ridiculous exhibition of his pride in owning a repeating pistol.

There came very near to being another fight after that, for the Herr Doktor seemed to think he had been jockeyed out of his fair share of the limelight, and started a tirade against us that lacked nothing of imagination or virulence; it included—according to Yerkes—a dissertation on British rule in India and an assertion that the British themselves are ruled and owned by a German king, financed by German money, fed with German food, clothed with German suits, and Germany's indubitable destined prey. It was Yerkes who stopped him.

"See here, you!" he called to the fourth officer. "If that goes on I'm going to break his jaw! You'd better stop him!"

The fourth did not understand; so Yerkes translated into German and they all got the benefit of the idea. After that there was more or less silence, the chief steward hurrying through the business of laying fresh plates and bringing on the last course. We left the saloon last, at our leisure, dawdling over coffee until the fourth officer, steward and quartermasters looked satisfactorily nervous and exasperated.

"A mere miserable public-house brawl!" said Monty disgustedly, when we got outside the door. "They had the best of it, and we've no remedy!"

"Go and play chess, you old idiot!" said Fred. "Play chess and you'll feel cheerful as an old maid over a cup o' tea by breakfast-time!"

But Yerkes and I were not so sure as Fred of the efficacy of Monty's chess-board and went to our cabins in considerable gloom. They had let us keep the same cabins—I suppose because the German passengers were on the other side of the ship, with a bulkhead between our row of doors and theirs—but I noticed that one of the quartermasters came and stood guard by the saloon door at the end of the corridor.

That was one of the worst nights of a memory that includes more than its fair share of difficult occasions. The over-engined tub, groaning—creaking—throbbing, pitched and rolled to such a tune that one could hardly keep abed by clinging to the hand-rail. Added to that there grew a great and ghastly smell, unchastened by the fact that they had closed all ventilators. The heat between decks grew to be a part of the noise and stink; the whole, with the motion, constituting pure and simple hell. Even the cockroaches seemed distressed, hurrying back and forth across the floor and sheets with something akin to frenzy.

THERE HAPPENED, too, during that night a great rushing back and forward in the corridors. I heard a voice that kept calling, "Herr Doktor! Herr Doktor!" and at last he answered, sleepily—angrily.

"What are they saying?" I called through the grill that separated my cabin from Will Yerkes'.

The Yankees are a remarkable folk. It seemed that he, too, slept.

"Aw—go to ——!" he answered when I finally awoke him.

"Wake up and listen!" said I. "Something's happening. As for ——, we're there!"

He and I put our heads through the cabin doors and heard the Herr Doktor repudiate indignantly a proposal somebody put to him, Yerkes translating to me.

"But I am a Doktor of Psychology, not medicine!" he answered. "I tell you I know nothing at all of medicine! No, no, no!"

Somebody whispered an answer in a hoarse voice—terrified words we could not catch, like the haunting summons of a nightmare.

"I tell you I can do nothing!" repeated the Herr Doktor. "It must be the captain's business! Go to him! Tell him! Consult him!"

The voice insisted he came directly from the captain in obedience to captain's orders. It was reenforced by another voice confirming that, with the added information that orders were to hurry.

"What do I care? I am passenger, not member

of the crew! Tell the captain to manage his own affairs! Go away and leave me!"

There must have been five or six men on that errand to bring the Herr Doktor, for we heard the feet of enough men go hurrying back along the corridor to have carried the Herr Doktor with them, dead or alive. In the comparative silence that followed, I heard Monty being seasick and started to go to him, but the quartermaster on guard by the saloon door aimed his pistol and ordered me back in. So it was morning before we as much as guessed the extent of the trouble, and we had stifling misery enough of our own, meanwhile, to drive most other thoughts out of mind.

They gave us breakfast at the one long, black-oilcloth-covered table in the second-class saloon, together with the three mean whites—all English—who were recovering from being drunk and seasick, but ate omnivorously. They were curious as to the reason of our being there, but Fred turned questions aside, and Monty—I suspect without meaning to—rather overawed them; so the miserable meal was eaten in more or less silence, until the brass-bound first officer came in.

He had white eyelashes, and his great height made bottle shoulders seem all the more inadequate to carry the dignity he claimed. I liked the look of him no more then than on the previous day when we had invaded his privacy on the bridge. And he quite plainly did not like us.

"Which of you is the doctor?" he demanded, holding his chin as the Uhlans do, with those high collars that never permit them a glimpse of less than mightiness.

"No doctor in here, you fool!" snapped Fred. "If there were I'd have him analyze this sausage! Here—look at it—have a smell!"

He held a slice of the atrocious stuff on a fork for close inspection.

"You should behave yourselves!" the first officer answered haughtily. "There is a doctor among you," he repeated. "I know it!"

"The devil you say!" said Fred.

"Which of you is the American?"

"As if you didn't know, you stilted jackass!" Fred retorted. "This man here—" he touched Monty—"is a Scandinavian-Greek-Jew. I'm Hottentot. My friend on my right—" he touched me—"is South-American Eskimo, and the rest of our party is Indo-Chinese. Now what can we do for you, ducky?"

"Good lord!" Yerkes whispered under his breath. "What'll I do? Shall I kid I'm a doctor—"

"Why not be a Yankee!" suggested Monty kindly, leaning forward to whisper as the first officer stepped back to cling to a column for support, for the ship was rolling more than usually badly.

"You mean?"

"Ayez confiance!" as our friends the French say. "If they need a doctor badly we have them where we want them, haven't we?"

"But I'm no doctor!" answered Yerkes.

Monty shrugged his shoulders.

"I've been a blacksmith and a camel's dentist before now!"

"You want me to claim I'm a doctor?"

"I'd let them do the claiming," said Monty. "As for the chance—"

"Oh, all right!" said Yerkes.

Fred began to hum "Yankee Doodle," perhaps under the impression that the tune would improve Yerkes' courage.

"The doctor at Beira—the Portuguese," said the first officer, stepping forward again with some show of impatience, "told me the American passenger is a doctor. It is no use your pretending! You are the American. You are therefore the doctor. Come with me!"

Then Will Yerkes made what the rest of us thought was a mistake. It was certainly not cowardice, for he has too many times stood the uttermost test of five-in-the-morning courage to be challenged on that score. But his peculiar New England conscience now and then tripped and balked him, like a sword on parade between a man's legs.

"I haven't a certificate," he said.

"Who cares!" snapped the German. "If you have forfeited your certificate, you have not forgotten what you know! Come along!"

I met Monty's eyes again; then Fred's. Our momentary gain was lost already. Provision of a doctor in their hour of need was now offset by the hypothetical doctor's lack of caste. Yet for Yerkes to refuse duty now would be to invite such reprisals as desperate men who think they held the whip-hand usually resort to. I, for one, had no faith in the quality of forbearance likely to be extended us on that ship.

Fred seized the mustard, pepper and salt, mixed them all together in the mustard pot and pushed the mess along to Yerkes with a hunk of rye bread.

"There you are, Will!" he grinned. "Make pills out of that. Dose 'em all, beginning with the skipper!"

By this time the three mean whites, already sufficiently solemn after their debauch, grasped the fact that serious trouble was afoot.

"It was true, then," said one of them—he nearest to me.

"Didn't I tell you? Didn't I say I went and looked? You said I was drunk. So I was. But what I seen I seen! Cholera, says I to you! When sailors start chuckin' third-class passengers overboard afore they're properly dead, there's cholera aboard, says I! But you fools wouldn't listen!"

Will Yerkes was listening—with both his ears, and an expression that made all of us except the German laugh.

"It is no use tendering objections!" snapped the first officer. Then he turned from Yerkes to us. "You laugh, but *nun geht es los!*"

His patience being obviously at an end, there was nothing for it but to obey, or else refuse and take the consequences. We were all rather curious to know what the price of refusal would be—how far a German skipper would permit arrogance to take him, yet not willing to court further trouble if Yerkes could be induced to play his part. And, as soon as he realized how Monty felt about it, Yerkes was willing enough. He got up.

"Who's coming with me?" he asked.

"You go," said Monty, nodding to me. "Fred and I will follow if we're wanted."

"No, no! You come alone!" said the German, with a hand on Yerkes' arm.

Will shook off his hand as if it burned him.

"Touch me again and I'll thrash you!" he growled.

"Come to my arms, America!" Fred laughed. "For that you go straight to heaven when you die! Peter will admit you *muy pronto—vous donnera les grande entrée*—only, hit him next time before he paws you!"

"Lead along!" growled Yerkes.

The first officer started for the door, and I followed them. We all three had to cling to door-posts and hand-rails, and at that Yerkes slipped and fell in the slime where sea-water had invaded the passage. Perhaps the second-class and third-class quarters on that ship were cleaned in Hamburg, once every other month, but surely not oftener.

The forward part of the main-deck, open to the sky and sacred to winches, latrines, a jury-galley and third-class passengers, was a slippery, wet wilderness. At every roll waves poured in to boil around number one hatch and escape through a swinging port to leeward. We had to dodge and run for it, clinging to a life-line.

THE FIRST officer was first to reach the dim hole that permitted the ancestor of all stinks to creep out and poison the free air. He stopped and stood aside to let Yerkes pass him; then stepped over the coaming and barred the way.

"You wait here!" he ordered me, with a smirk at the rain and invading waves.

I was already drenched to the knees, hatless, and without any covering against the rain, a fact that he thoroughly appreciated. He turned his back on me and went on in, but the minute I tried to follow a sailor in uniform pushed past him and thrust me backward so suddenly that I hit the coaming with my heels and fell out backward. I was up in a second, in no mood to weigh consequences, and landed with my left fist on the sailor's nose.

"Will!" I shouted. "Hey, there, Will!"

The sailor roared with rage and made a rush at me, but the German is rare who can use his fist to much advantage; and, in full view from the bridge, I held that smelly entrance against him, my back to the air and fight, he no more able to come out than I to enter. Every time the *Bundesrath* pitched or rolled we fell on each other and fought hammer-and-tongs style, he getting the worst of each exchange.

"Herrrrauss!" he roared, making his dozenth rush, and at last Will heard my shouts. He came back three steps at a time up the steep companion-ladder, seized the sailor in the rear, whirled him about and thrust him downward into darkness toward where a couple of electric lights burned like sore, immoral things. They were naked, those lights—naked and ashamed, shedding no rays, except for a space of a few feet. The stench was awful.

There was another row, of course, at the foot of the ladder—fifteen feet below the fo'castle, in the *Bundesrath's* fore-peak.

"Get back!" ordered the first officer.

"Not a bit of it!" said I.

"He stays or I go too," said Yerkes.

"He struck me! They both struck me! This one took me by the neck! He threw me down-stairs!" yelled the sailor in German.

"You shall suffer for this!" said the first officer in English, but whether he meant Yerkes or me or both of us, I never knew.

"Both or neither—which is it?" Will demanded.

"Go on, then—*vorwaerts!"* the German answered between his teeth.

The sailor, still protesting, discovered an electric "trouble-light," with two or three dozen yards of wire attached, stowed under the ladder. He fixed it to a plug and switched it on, revealing such a scene as Chinese treaty-ports, perhaps, and perhaps Calcutta at its wretchedest might rival.

On the floor on mats—on bunks that resembled pantry shelves as much as anything—on a table meant presumably for social amenities—under the table—and slung in hammocks from the smoked and greasy beams, lay human beings of all the national ties that eke out mean existence east of Suez. They were nearly all seasick, but some were evidently stricken by a deadlier foe than that.

There were men, women, children—Chinese, Malays, Hindoos, Singhalese, Somalis, Arabs, Punjabees, Baluchis, Afghans—a score of tongues, religions, habits, smells—one misery—one hopelessness.

I noticed three empty bunks that no one from the foul floor cared to occupy.

Trouble-light held out at arm's length in front of him, the sailor went before us, the smoke and foul air shifting sluggishly in milky streaks. He stopped away up forward, where the sides of the place narrowed rapidly to form the *Bundesrath's* ungainly bow, and thrust the naked light six inches from the face of a man—or the shape of a man—on the lowest, uncleanest shelf of all. It was unclean as cages are.

"Phew!" exclaimed Yerkes.

I pulled out my handkerchief. But the first officer laughed.

"Is he dead or alive?" he asked. "Has he cholera, or is it something else?"

"Has any one offered him a drink since yesterday?" Yerkes demanded, and there seemed no answer to that.

"Is it cholera?" repeated the first officer.

"Am I in charge of this place?" Yerkes demanded fiercely.

"You—a doctor—ask that?" said the German.

"Am I?" demanded Yerkes again.

The first officer made a gesture with hand and shoulder. It was not intended to be commital, nor yet polite. The sailor turned the light on us three, and I never saw such contrast of expressions: Will Yerkes, angry, compassionate, outraged—the first officer arrogant, stupid, but not sure of himself—the sailor simply bovine.

"If that is cholera," said the first officer, "three died in the night—contagious—throw any overboard that seem too bad!"

"What about medicine?" Yerkes demanded. "What have you got?"

"Only a little. Our doctor fell overboard. His quarters are locked up."

"Give me the key! I'll go and look."

"I have no key."

"Then get it! Phew! I'm going on deck! Here, you!" He turned to the man who held the trouble-light. "Get fresh water in a bucket! Offer each of them a drink. Get a move on!"

The man did not understand; so Will translated into German, but he stood like a wooden image, watching the first officer's face.

"You order him, then!" said Will.

The first officer snarled, spat and ordered otherwise.

"Return to the deck, you! *Schnell!"*

He watched him stow the trouble-light and clamber up the ladder.

"Cholera—if this is cholera—is it cholera? The crew can not be spared. You—you care for the sick. Choose an orderly from among them—two—three orderlies—as many as you wish. Make them be useful! That is better for them than to lie like swine in the hold here, dying of dirt and laziness!"

"Me for some air!" said Yerkes, gasping. "Come on!" he called to me.

The first officer was disposed to insist on priority, but we each took a shoulder and flung him back behind us so that he had to climb out last. When we reached the deck, Yerkes and I were sick—no, not seasick. The German was able to make his way below the bridge and shout to the captain.

We could not hear a word of shout or answer, but presently he called us; and there wasn't any good or glory to be had from clinging to a stanchion with water swirling about our feet, so we obeyed. The captain—all brass braid, belly and pomp, came down to the saloon deck to reduce the distance he had to do his cooing from; he had a megaphone under his arm, but did not need to use it.

"Is it what is supposed?" he demanded, holding up a finger and closing one eye semi-confidentially.

"Yes, you fat swab, it's cholera!" roared Yerkes. "Cholera. D'you hear! Cholera!"

The first officer made a jump for the passageway leading aft and stood blocking it. When he shouted over his shoulder, men in uniform came and stood behind him—I could not see how many, but our return toward the cabins was cut off.

"Then you sday dhere!" the captain bellowed, flaring up. "You are infected! You both sday dhere an' care for dhem!"

"You fat blackguard!" Yerkes yelled back at him, pitching his voice against the storm. "That fore-peak's no better than hell! It's inhuman! Your ship's a disgrace! Give me the second-class for a sickbay and I'll take charge of it—otherwise, do your own dirty work!"

THE CAPTAIN answered in German, too enraged by the refusal to be browbeaten, for thought in any language but his own. Will answered him in the same tongue—not grammatically—even I knew that—but in a sort of patois, stuffed and made pungent with Yankee slang. The argument went on minute after minute until the captain turned his back and swaggered out of sight.

"And that means," said Will, turning to me with a wry face, "that you and I are marooned out here, threatened with death if we try to go aft, and ordered to care for the cholera patients! Why didn't you stay with Monty!"

Armed sailors appeared and took station at points of vantage—one, for instance, leaned over the rail of the upper deck with a pistol in his hand. And it seemed there was a speaking-tube to the fo'castle, put to good use already. Out of the fo'castle door firemen and sailors came stampeding, dragging their belongings aft, struggling to be first through the narrow opening, some of them falling, belongings and all, into the filthy water that swished back and forth.

The fo'castle was as empty in five minutes as a loft the rats had left. The whole fore-part of the ship had become an abandoned wilderness. Twenty miserable goats, on the fo'castle-head beyond the anchors, and the stricken third-class crowd below-deck were the only life besides ourselves.

"So now you have your sick-bay!" sneered the first officer, returning to view us from behind the protecting bulk of the armed sentry. "Make yourselves at home! Choose orderlies and make them work! If they will not work, throw them overboard! The doctor's stores shall be brought forward presently. Cooking implements are in the deck galley. You may have the goats for food. Rice, potatoes, coffee, sugar and some canned milk shall be sent."

"How about brandy?" Yerkes demanded.

"There is no brandy."

"You —— liar! What keeps your slob of a skipper's nose that bright cherry red? Send down a case of brandy or I'll show you what real trouble means!"

"No brandy!" he answered.

"Suit yourself!" said Yerkes. "Brandy—or I'll see to it the whole blamed ship's infected!"

The first officer disappeared, and the sailors he left on guard took the bull by the horns in true Teutonic spirit with a threatening display of firearms.

"Monty!" yelled Yerkes. "Oh, Monty! Monty!"

There came a sound of struggling, as bovine bodies barred the way against two determined gentlemen. In another minute Fred Oakes burst between two seamen and emerged into wind and rain. Through the gap thus left strode Monty, looking mightily unconcerned—a sure enough sign he was in fighting trim.

"What's the little game?" he asked.

"Stand back, old man!" said Yerkes, before telling him.

Fred and Monty asked questions simultaneously; Yerkes and I blurted answers, the whole entertainment being interspersed with rough-house business as the seamen struggled to force Monty in again. They did not seem to care whether Fred became infected or not, but that did not prevent Fred from swinging a fist like a club in Monty's cause. It was a funny little fracas, ending in stalemate when Monty became jammed in the passage entrance, unable to advance another foot, yet able to hold his ground, Fred out in the open, covered by a pistol—they seemed anxious not to hurt Monty, but perfectly willing to shoot Fred—and everybody breathless—Yerkes and I with laughter.

"I wish you'd go to my cabin," said Yerkes, "and get my private papers; put 'em with your own."

"Right you are," said Monty, "but—d'you propose to stand the gaff forward there?"

"Nothing else for it!" said Yerkes. "Some one's got to! Seems I'm the goat! But by Gorry! if I don't bring Heinie to book for this, my name's not what I think it is."

"Get even with them, eh?"

"I wish you could have one look at that fore-peak!"

"How about you?" asked Monty, and I laughed.

One point of his mustache had been knocked up and the other down in the struggle, and he looked drunken—before 9 a.m. It did not occur to me to wonder what I looked like.

"I've no papers!" I answered. "Nothing worth rescuing in my cabin."

"How about the cholera?"

"How about Yerkes?" I answered. "Did you suppose I'd leave him—if they'd let me?"

I was young in those days, and Monty, I supposed, recognized extenuating circumstances. At any rate, he withheld the deserved snub for sounding my own horn.

"Anything besides the papers?" he asked.

"Yes," said Yerkes. "Brandy—and then brandy!"

But, as he said that, a steward came staggering down the passage with a case of "Beehive"—low quality export stuff—and shoved it against Monty's legs. One way and another the lot of them contrived to kick it out toward us, where it promptly slid into the scupper. Only the devils of the East Coast stormy season know what prevented the waves from smashing it. I made a slide, rescued it and sat on it to keep it still.

"Anything else?" asked Monty.

"See they send forward any medical books the doctor had in his quarters!"

"That all? See you later, then!"

There was nothing reasonable in my feeling disappointed and discouraged when Monty turned his back and Oakes followed him. All either man need have done by breaking away from the guard and joining us would have been to excommunicate the entire party without any compensating advantage. But one does not reason—one is merely sentimental—in most tight places.

"Come on!" said Yerkes, and he and I carried the case of brandy forward.

We took it into the fo'castle, a fine, big, roomy place divided down the center to keep firemen and seamen separate. We smashed the case open, removed one bottle, hid the rest in a locker, took a stiff drink apiece and were ready to begin. But first and last it was Will Yerkes who led the assault on that situation. I merely obstructed and obeyed him.

"Is it really cholera?" I asked.

We descended again cautiously into the dark fore-peak, I carrying a bucket of fresh water, he the brandy, and both of us coughing and sneezing at the stench.

"Are you sure it's cholera?"

"I wouldn't bet to-morrow's Tuesday," he answered. "My mother's oldest brother was a surgeon in our Civil War. He died before I met him; that's the nearest I ever came to qualifying for a sawbones. But I surmise—eh—what would you say? Whew!"

We dosed out brandy and water—some water, some brandy and some both. There were two stone-dead ones, tossed and stiffening into gargoyle angles, one in a hammock and one in a bunk against the wall. We chose four who were not sick—only numbed and wretched—and made them carry the corpses upon deck, I climbing up the ladder ahead to superintend. A bigger wave than usual met the burial party, and the lot of us, corpses included, went spluttering and rolling down to the scuppers, to the captain's huge amusement.

I could find nothing handy to throw at the brute, and fist-shaking seemed futile and inadequate; so we threw the corpses overboard and he had his laugh out undisturbed. Then I took my gang below, gave them more brandy and saw Yerkes in the gloom sorting out the worst cases from the less appalling ones. Cholera takes hold quickly when it comes.

"Why didn't they stampede for fresh air when the thing began?" I wondered.

"I've asked that," said Yerkes. "There's a Hindoo here speaks English—he's got it badly, though." Conversation was difficult because whenever the ship pitched more than usually wild victims would fall from the knife-board bunks and either he rolling and screaming about the floor,or try to struggle back again, lamenting loudly. "Two of them realized what was happening—had seen cholera before—ran aft—told some officer—driven forward again on the run, kicked down here—door locked on the lot of 'em!

"That's why there was no stampede! Two hours later, he says, somebody came with four sailors and dragged out the worst cases—three—that'll be the three they threw overboard before they were dead. Then they were locked in again—so he says. Then we came!"

I JOINED in the hunt, and, between us, we found a dozen men not evidently sick, although bereft of energy even when physicked with raw brandy. I told them off and we began carrying out the others, for, as Yerkes said, the first thing was to get the poor devils out of hell into the cleaner, roomier fo'castle. I had got to the foot of the ladder with the first case when the opening darkened and I saw a man's leg feeling for the top step. It was a woman I was helping carry—Lord knows her tribe or nation; she and her shriveled husband died that night, and their scrawny young one followed them overboard at dawn. We set the woman down, and a moment later I saw something I recognized.

"For God's sake, Monty," I shouted, "get back out of here! Death's at work in this hole! Keep back!"

Yerkes heard me and came galloping, crashing from side to side of the chamber of horrors and stumbling over prostrate bodies. His voice rose to a squawk like a peacock's.

"You get out o' here, Monty! You've no call in this hole! You belong on the upper deck! Get back up that ladder or I'll knock your block off!"

Monty came on, feeling his way gingerly. I saw legs and heard another voice behind him.

"Didums, you —— fool, d'you expect me to stand all night on these steps holding this dunnage! Go ahead; can't you?"

Between the front and rear fire Monty coolly pursued his way, taking no chances of missing a step; but Fred was less cautious and more unwieldy. It was I who caught the two of them a moment later, collapsing under them and a pile of heterogeneous stuff only just in time to save the woman from a swifter and perhaps more merciful death than the one actually awaiting her.

"Now, you've done it!" said Yerkes, pulling us all up. "You've done it, Monty!"

"Done what?"

"You're defiled!"

"The devil you say! I've brought chocolates—tobacco—cigarets—matches—some books—my chessmen—and a bottle of *eau de cologne*—by gad, it seems to me we're going to need that! There's soap in that package—two dozen cakes—tooth-powder, tooth-brushes—a sponge or two—towels—call that defilement, do you? —— if it looks that way to me!"

"I mean you're infected," said Yerkes. "You shouldn't have come!"

"Fred's got a big box of prunes," said Monty, "and our hair-brushes. Got 'em all—haven't you, Fred? Socks—drawers—clean shirts—and I think the rest is blankets—company's blankets—didn't see the sense of spoiling our own—left 'em in the cabin. I've got your private papers with mine and the gang's in my pocketbook; so now we're all right."

"Didums, you idiot, you've forgotten my concertina!" said Fred.

"No, old dear—it rolled forward there into the dark when we stumbled. Look for it!"

"You shouldn't have taken this chance!" said Yerkes.

"Shouldn't I? Gad but there's a merry little panic aft! The passengers have formed themselves into a sanitary corps! They've hung sheets in the passageways and squirted 'em with alcohol. The doctor person thinks he can brew carbolic out of the bunker coal, and has gone to work. The professor is disinfecting seamen and firemen! It's a pleasant process: the two commercial people make 'em strip in the saloon; the professor doses out alcohol; and the seamen rub one another from head to foot with it. It takes professor and both assistants to keep 'em from drinking the lotion!"

"But what did you come forward for?" demanded Yerkes.

"We're headed for Dar es Salaam," said Monty. "The captain's theory is that if we made Zanzibar first—as of course we should—the British authorities would force friendly help on him—disinfect the ship—and discover what's under the hatches! Any or all kinds of trouble might come out of that! Feel 'em crowding her! Feel the old tub shake! Let's hope her boilers stand the racket!"

"If we reach Dar es Salaam alive," said Yerkes, "they'll quarantine you there and take darned good care you never get away alive to tell of what you've seen! You should have stayed aft and played politics!"

"Let's get ahead with the business, shall we?" Monty answered. "Suppose you give the orders. If Fred don't obey, just tell me and we'll put him down and tickle him. Ever hear Fred scream when he's tickled? Like a dying mule! What's the first trick? Carry 'em out of here, eh? That ought to meet with majority approval! Lead on, then, MacDuff!"

I was MacDuff. I captained the hoisting of the stricken woman up those stairs, and laid her in a clean bunk in the port fo'castle. Yerkes decreed the starboard section was for doubtfuls and convalescents—"s'posin' there be any!" Monty followed next with his unsteady gang and the woman's presumptive husband. Then Fred came, blowing like a grampus, shepherding the resurrection out of Hades of a giant black man of perfectly uncertain origin—perhaps a Seedeeboy. Yerkes brought the one child in his arms, and the game began again.

Some of them could walk up the accommodation ladder. Some could get up with the aid of a little shoving and pulling; but most of them had to be carried, and one actually died in his bearers' arms on the way up, cursing and screaming—vowing we were murdering him. Quite a number of them seemed to think they need expect no mercy.

When at length we had the last one carried up and all sorted as, best we could guess, worst cases to port, not so bad to starboard, Yerkes reeled and slipped aft again to stand below the bridge and shout for jointed pipe, some packing and white lead, and steam on the forward-deck winch. There was a long argument before he got any of it. But Fred and I reenforced him, and while he threatened we actually made shift to open the forward hatch. As that would have let into the hold every wave that passed us the time o' day, and the only way to stop us would have been by shooting, we won the point; thenceforward we held the whip-hand as far as concerned supplies.

They brought us the stores—or at least some of the stores—from the doctor's quarters, and we carried those forward, I nearly breaking a leg when a more than usually heavy wave caught me waist-high and flung me across-deck. Then came the pipes, connected by a universal joint. We were not exactly experts, but all rough-and-ready tinkers in steam—mining prospectors mostly have to be, and, as for me, one learns to humor the steam-winch on pretty nearly any big sailing-ship.

We needed no teaching from Yerkes to disconnect the steam-pipe on the winch and add our new one to it, leading down into the fore-peak. It fell to me to take a handful of waste and go down and scald out the dungeon. I came out after ten minutes, boiled and unable to endure another second of the heat and stench, but I left the belching steam-pipe down there, and we did not signal for steam off until evening.

"Cooked cholera microbes may be as efficient as raw ones, for all I know," said Yerkes, "but at least we've cooked 'em!"

That was the principle we mostly worked on—not at all sure that any of the steps we took were really orthodox. We eschewed the unforgivable offense of doing nothing. Monty, who had commanded a squadron in British India and then served as political "resident" in a native state, was really the most experienced; but—as he said—"experience, don't you know, is mere sight-seeing unless you do it yourself," and Will Yerkes, with his Amazon travels behind him and with his Yankee inventiveness, very rightly kept the lead.

But Monty was a wonder, nevertheless. It was he who kept us good-tempered—he who turned every lament into a joke—Monty who cooked astonishingly appetizing meals in the sheet-iron open-air galley, although I butchered the first goat—the Earl of Montdidier and Kirkubrightshire, P.C., K.C.B., etc., who saw to the fo'castle scrubbing and most of the desperately dirty work. Whenever four jobs turned up at once—or fourteen—or forty-four, as happened oftener—it was always he who promptly took hold of the meanest. And it was he—or rather his example, that presently brought us help from an unexpected quarter.

THE THREE mean whites in the second-class saloon got thoroughly drunk on receipt of the news of cholera. They remained drunk a day and a night, after which liquor supplies were discontinued by captain's orders, and they were sent for to go aft and serve in various capacities. The fallen—or unrisen—Englishman has characteristics which fail to ingratiate him with the world at large. Those three men—Jones, Howard and Hill they said their names were—divided unpleasant ingenuity between efforts to burst themselves on first-class cabin food and to assert unholy pride of race.

Being put on rations because of too monstrous appetite, they forthwith refused to take orders from "furriners" and were finally left to loaf at will, scorned and scornful. So they came and leaned their elbows on the forward rail of the upper deck to smoke and gaze down on us and, after ten or twenty minutes of desultory contemplation, beheld

Monty emptying slops. I was directly underneath them, engaged on certain laundry work that lingers unsweetly on the memory.

The wind had lulled and the sea was falling. Voices, pitched high, fell clearly.

"D'yer mark that?" said one of them—I don't know which.

"What d'yer take me for—a bloody mole? I can see, can't I?"

"An' him an earl!" said the third in awestruck tones. "A perishin' gor-blimy earl a-emptyin' slops!"

"And us a-lookin' on!" resumed the first. "What, oh!"

"Did the Germans make 'im go forrard?"

"Not 'im! If they can't make us do nothin', what price 'is kind? 'E took an' went!"

"Why the ——? Is 'e crazy, or what?"

"Them others are 'is mates."

"Earls? Barons? Baronites? Bunch o' blooming members o' the 'Ouse o' Lords? One's an American, ain't he?"

"Bunch o' nothin'! Pick-ups! 'Im an' them's partners. Germans sent two of 'em forrard an' dared 'em wi' goons to come aft again. 'E goes an' fetches some o' their things from the cabins an' starts forrard too. Germans dares 'im. 'E dares them—I 'eard 'im! Say, that earl's a treat when it comes to 'avin' 'is own way! 'E refuses to talk German to 'em so the captain 'as to talk English, an' I 'eard it all. Cool as a cucumber 'e was. Says the captain, 'You stay aft! Your life is valuable!' Says 'e, 'You go to ——, for yours isn't!'

"Says the captain, 'I forbids you to go forrard.' Says 'e, 'You 'as your bleedin' choice! You permits me to go forrard, or you submits to the mortification o' seein' your 'and forced! I'll not tell you what I'll bloomin' well do,' 'e says, 'but I'll do it, an' you look out! Haw!' 'e says. Then the blinkin' captain tries to mollify 'im. 'Milaw,' 'e says, 'I will gif you leaf to go forrard if you vish, but vy do not ve shake 'an's an' let bygones be bygones?' "

"Go on! Did 'e? What did the earl say to that?"

" 'E says, 'I'd sooner shake 'ands with a vulture than you! I'm goin' forrard,' 'e says. 'Haw!' says 'e. 'An' I'm goin' to kill the swine what tries to stop me,' 'e says, 'an' that's all I've got to say to you until I sees you on a gallows, Captain Fingelmann!' 'e says. An' 'e goes forrard, sure as I'm a standin' 'ere, an' t'other one—'im wi' a beard what plays a concertina—follers 'im, both of 'em loaded down wi' cabin things an' what not."

"An' now 'e's emptyin' slops!"

"That's 'im!"

There followed a long pause. Then—

" 'As them sailors below got goons?"

"Pistols an' rifles!"

"D'yer suppose they'd shoot?"

"What? Meanin' if the earl an' them others was to try an' break back an' bring the cholery aft? You bet they'd shoot!"

Followed another long pause.

"I don't see 'as 'ow an earl's better an' what other folks are!"

"Same 'ere!"

Yet another pause.

"I bet yer I can empty slops as well as 'im!"

"Better!"

"Nor I'm no more afraid nor what 'e is!"

" 'Oo said 'oo's afraid?"

"D'yer suppose them sentries 'ud shoot?"

"What if they do? Bullets or cholery? 'Oo cares?"

"Bullets is quick—cholery 'urts like ——!"

"Maybe we don't get cholery if we stay aft."

Another, longer pause, during which I stirred with a pole in a tub full of suds—and other things.

"We'd need terbaccer along."

"An' blankets!"

"An' liquor if we can get it!"

"But we can't!"

"Well—'oo are we waitin' for?"

" 'Oo's waitin'? I ain't goin' to be outdid by no bleedin' earl—not if I knows it! Let's go to the cabin an' get our things."

"Come on, then. 'Eaps o' terbaccer, mind! Rush the sentries, an' tell the bleedin' earl ——"

"Tell the bleedin' earl nothin'! Rush nothin'! We strolls forward, casual, same as what 'e does. We passes remarks to the sentry, same as 'im. 'Stand to one side,' says we, 'or get yer bloomin' jaw punched!' They stands aside, bein' square'eads an' not 'avin' no specific orders to do nothin' except prevent any one from comin' back aft. We continues forward, 'ands in our pocket casual like—"

" 'Ands in our pockets, an' terbaccer an' blankets an' lord knows what—fat'ead!"

"We strolls forward an' says to 'im, ' 'Ullo! Thought we'd come an' lend a 'and!' says we. 'Thought as 'ow maybe you didn't care to 'og all the blame,' we says. That's the way to do it, dignified an' proper."

" 'Oo's to do the talkin'?"

"You!"

"No, you!"

"Well—let 'Oward do it. 'E's got the gift o' the gab!"

"Garn! You proposed it. Do your own work!"

Whatever they settled—and they left the rail still arguing—it is quite certain something different transpired. In the first place the sentry let them pass with a grin of evil import but no argument, for, just as I had overheard their conversation by dint of keen attention from below, some one on the bridge had very easily overheard it from above them. While they went to their cabin to get things, orders were given to the sentry that left no margin for misunderstanding. They were welcome to go forward whenever they chose, but by no means welcome back again.

Then, dignity was lacking. The rolling of the ship provided for that. One of them stepped on the blanket he was carrying, stumbled, slipped on the wet deck and fell headlong. I suspect he was intended to be spokesman. Monty, by that time smoking on an up-ended bucket outside the fo'castle door, witnessed the whole proceeding without a smile.

Fearfully self-consciously they staggered forward and stood holding to one another in front of Monty, looking exactly like deserters surrendering themselves. Monty surveyed them calmly, at some length.

"So you men have decided to offer your services, have you?" he asked at last.

"Yes, sir."

"Yes, my lord."

"We was ashamed to see you doin' dirty work, my lord!"

"I never did dirty work in my life!" snapped Monty. "God helping me, I never will! Are you all three Englishmen?"

"Yes, my lord."

"Well—we all know that Englishmen are supposed to do their duty. That's what being an Englishman means. You men came very near forgetting what you are—much too near! Twenty-four hours is too long for a man to take considering between shame and duty. England and the United States are standing together here. Go and report yourselves to Mr. Yerkes; we're all taking orders from him."

"Yes, sir! Very good, sir!"

"Yes, my lord!"

"Certainly, your lordship!"

"I hope to see you three men behave creditably. I shall look for courage—exemplary conduct—instant obedience to Mr. Yerkes. I expect to be proud of my countrymen."

"Certainly, my lord!"

"Oh, yes, sir!"

"Yes, indeed, your lordship!"

"Very well. Report to Mr. Yerkes."

I hurried inside on some excuse or other, for I wanted to see the reception. Yerkes was on the starboard side taking temperatures—about an average of one an hour was taken worse and had to be carried to the port side—and that as a rule meant overboard within the day.

"Oh, hello!" he said, continuing his labors.

"Report for duty, sir."

" 'Is lordship's horders to report for duty, sir."

" 'E said—'is lordship said as 'ow—"

"I see," said Yerkes. "I see." He went on taking temperatures. "What are your names?"

They told him.

"Well—I don't see how you men can help. This job's dangerous."

"Beggin' your pardon?"

"I don't understand, sir."

"We wasn't lookin' f'r no birfday party!"

"Now—if I'd anything safe for you to turn your hands to—but—I'd get out of here if I were you; you might catch something!"

"Which what I catches is my own affair!" remarked the first man, with gathering choler.

"Besides, we're short of brandy," said Yerkes. "Can't afford to lose what little we've got!"

"Meanin' as 'ow you suspects us o' wantin' brandy?"

"Meaning brandy is scarce!" said Yerkes. "I've always heard that passengers one meets on these German coastwise ships are—I've been told all kinds of things. Of course, seeing's believing."

"We came forrard free an' willin'!" asserted the man whom the other two addressed as " 'Oward."

"I couldn't make use of timid men," said Yerkes.

"Which it's time to call names when the pitcher's busted!" said he who said his name was Jones.

For reasons none of us could have specified we were all quite sure it wasn't really Jones, but he answered to it, and died under his chosen flag like a gallant man when the time came.

"We're ready an' willing, sir!" announced the third man—Hill.

"I could try you, of course," said Yerkes. "But if the brandy disappeared, or—"

AT THAT moment Fred Oakes pushed his head through the door that communicated between port and starboard sides of the fo'castle.

"Three more of the poor devils dead!" he announced.

The new arrivals flinched perceptibly and turned a ghastly hue.

"Offer them brandy," said Yerkes to me.

"No, sir, no brandy, thanks!"

"None for me neither!"

"Nor me!"

"You'll be wantin' somebody to 'eave them stiffs overside, sir!"

"Come on, mates! Shall we go to work, sir?"

"I'll try you," said Yerkes.

A moment later Jones and 'Oward and 'Ill emerged through the fo'castle door into daylight, carrying a corpse apiece. They looked like devils emerging from the pit to dance a grizzly measure, for the *Bundesrath* rolled and pitched with drunken uncertainty, and the storm, that had lulled but a while ago, was beginning again to shriek through the rigging and funnel stays. Up forward where we were the motion was at its worst.

To waltz and stagger and reel and slide and trip and roll into the scuppers with a yet unstiffened cholera corpse is an adventure to prove or break forever a man's courage. They made the gruesome votive offering to the uneclectic sharks and returned, one behind the other, drawn and scared. I followed again into the fo'castle to see and hear.

"What next, sir?"

"Whatever you say now, sir!"

"Ready f'r anything you say, sir!"

The mean whites had reverted true to type! Yerkes set them to scrubbing. Our orderlies had all curled up with the dread disease and, although, after the swift way of that swiftest, deadliest epidemic, we already had convalescents, they were all too weak both in mind and body to work. Three new unskilful, but unparticular, assistants were a solution, almost, of our worst difficulty.

Thenceforward we had more time for saving life and needed rather less for the disheartening business of jettisoning disused shells of men; but they died, nevertheless, like flies on a poisoned paper, and half that fo'castle was empty before three days were gone.

What little sleep we took was in turns, in bunks on the starboard side, where the not-yet-badly stricken and the few convalescents were. Fred spent some of his short spells of relaxation wringing wild music from the concertina in hope, no doubt, of raising the spirits of the patients; but the effort did not accomplish much, although he raised his own to some extent.

We bellowed choruses, but the bellowing was out of a defiant, not a hopeful, mood; and even on the fifth day out from Beira, when there began to dawn the semblance of a chance that, after all, we might save twenty per cent, of that miserable list alive, including probably ourselves, we were not much encouraged. Gloom had begun to settle down on us. Even Monty, prince, not of optimists, but of last ditch die-hards, found it difficult to keep those waxed ends of his black mustache from drooping.

"I don't see much good in it for us!" said I. "If we reach Dar es Salaam alive, it's more than I can believe that these Germans'll have the gall to let us get away alive with the tale of how they behaved! They'd be ashamed to!"

"I fancy you flatter them!" said Monty gloomily.

"Let's sink the —— ship and be done with it!" urged Fred, more than half-seriously.

I turned in and went to sleep with that proposition of Fred's repeating itself again and again, conjuring up wild and ever wilder pictures in my fevered imagination. It was my "watch below" until midnight, and when Monty called me I went out as usual for a breath of fresh air before going the rounds of gruesome cases to try and guess which would live—which die before morning.

I stood looking aft, accustoming my eyes to the murk of a storm that seemed never-ending, filling my lungs with the wet, warm air. There was no sign of stars or full moon. I could scarcely see the rain that drummed on the swaying deck, and the port, starboard and mast-head lights were like colored pin-pricks in the blackness. Yet it seemed to me there was a sort of luminosity.

The wind—sou'westerly—was on the port quarter, blowing big guns, drowning everything except the thunder of great waves and rattle of rain. Yet once or twice it seemed to me I heard shouting. I looked back into the fo'castle. Monty was sitting beside his bunk, pulling off shoes preparatory to turning in.

"Come and look!" said I, and for a while he came and stood barefooted beside me, sheltered more or less from the downpour by the door he leaned against.

"What d'you make of it?" said I.

"Fire!" said he, and we both sniffed.

It may have been imagination, but I certainly thought I smelled burning more than once, when either the wind or our helm shifted for a moment. But there were no sparks, and the heat was no doubt climatic.

"Call Will," he said; so I fetched Yerkes out of the port side, where he had been spraying brandy on a man's set lips with Monty's hair-restorer bottle. Fred from his bunk saw us making for the door, and followed.

"If it is fire, it's not a big one yet," said Yerkes.

"In this wind, ducky, a one-horse fire would pretty soon make hell look like an iceberg!" argued Fred. And then all at once we all saw sparks burst out away back aft and stream down-wind.

"By Jove, it may be the professor's alcohol sheets!" grinned Monty. "If some body dropped a lighted match or cigaret on one of those—"

"The whole first-class saloon's alight!" said Fred. "Let's get up on the fo'castle head and see better!"

We clambered up to where the miserable goats were cowering under a strip of tight-laced canvas, but even from there we could not be sure. Again and again sparks flew in streams, but after each outburst all grew black again—only with that same peculiar luminous quality I had noticed first.

"If she is on fire," said Monty, bellowing in my ear.

"If she's what?" yelled Yerkes.

"If she's on fire, we've scarcely one chance in a million! No small boat could live!"

My place was inside and I clambered down again off the fo'castle head, but the others stayed up there until dawn. When I awoke our three new assistants at peep o' day to bury the night's grim harvest and went out to watch them heave the poor husks overside, Fred, Yerkes, and Monty were still staring aft; and now there was no question of what the matter might be. A greasy, black column of smoke bathed the ship's whole upper deck and streamed to leeward.

The three no-longer-mean whites performed their allotted task, and halted before Monty, who had climbed down beside me.

"Grim work ahead, men!" he said, and one—he who said his name was Jones—saluted, military style.

All sorts of gestures pass muster for salute the wide world over, but the British military token of respect is unmistakable by any one who knows.

"Deserter or time expired?" I wondered aloud, and Monty heard me.

"We won't question a brave man's past," he said. "I've a notion he'll die as game as any of us!"

"The end isn't yet!" I said. "If this rain holds, it'll squelch almost any fire."

"Almost—but not quite," said Monty. "Look!"

AS HE spoke, the wind changed for a moment in one of those baffling squalls that make of that East Coast no drunken sailor's paradise. The smoke pall shifted and streamed at right-angles to our course, and we could see the whole ship's length for a moment. Near the stem the lower part of the stream of smoke glowed red, and for one second we caught the roar and sizzle of a wetted holocaust.

"This ship is doomed!" said Monty. "Her holds are chock-a-block with ammunition and guns! I suspect the ammunition's forward under this hatch—that'll be why they're not anxious about it yet! See for yourself whether a boat could be launched—let alone live in that sea! Draw your own conclusions!"

The gloomiest speech I had ever heard Monty make! The least resolute! By all odds the most disturbing—for if Monty should lose his poise it seemed to me there was little chance of the rest of us proving masters of all that evil circumstance. Yet to have blamed him would have been rankly unfair, just as it would have been impudence to pity. But a fellow could understand.

I, for instance, had nothing much to lose and a hard time ahead whichever way the cat should jump, for I had my way to make in the world, and nobody but me to worry if I failed to do it. But for a man with a gallant record and a title nearly as ancient as the King of England's to be obliged to die in the cholera ward of a German hell-ship was an ugly fence to face. I began to appreciate what it must have meant to him to sally forward to join Yerkes and me—not that I could imagine him now not doing it.

Whether it was reasoned judgment or just instinct that had warned him, he proved wholly right in the matter of the *Bundesrath*—nor was he the only one to guess how little chance we ourselves had. Captain Fingelmann and his friends carried probability on to the verge of certainty almost as soon as Monty's back was turned. I sat on the step staring aft, fascinated by the billowing smoke and the picture it all made—lumbering, wallowing ship—wild weather-crackle and glare of doom—when men came and began to nail boards across the passageways on each side leading aft.

"Come and look, Monty!" I called, and all six—our three new recruits too—came to see.

Monty laughed dryly.

"It's what I supposed," he said. "The ammunition's forward under this hatch-guns and stores aft. They're trying to put a fireproof bulkhead between them and the explosive stuff. They don't think much of the ship's chance!"

"I guess they're figuring on releasing the sentries for fire-fighting," said Yerkes.

"Or boat drill!" said I. "They're clearing boats away—look!"

"I wish I knew just where we are," said Monty. "I expect they're planning to run in close to some part of the coast where there's a chance to land from small boats. They're counting on keeping the hooker afloat until they're near enough to save their own skins. Then they'll either scuttle her or watch the explosion."

"It's a safe bet they'll leave no boats for us!" said Yerkes.

"I propose we build a raft!" said Monty.

"How can we build a raft," said I, "without being seen from the bridge? They'd probably fire on us!"

"Why the devil didn't we bring our own guns and ammunition aft?" Fred grumbled. "D'you suppose we could take 'em by surprise—swarm to the upper deck (the accommodation ladder had been taken away long ago), storm the bridge—and play general hell until something came of it?"

But general hell came before any one could answer. Very sick men—so sick that they expect death—and especially men sick with the dreadful plagues which haunt the tropics display occasionally what amounts to second sight. Lingering along the borderland between one existence and another, they see, as it were, out of both eyes; such things as partitions, bulkheads, curtains, doors no longer have power to confine their vision. And having determined on death by one route, perhaps having ceased to fear it in the shape that they expect, they resent it—fear it—fight it frantically in any unexpected form.

One of our tortured poor Hindoos on the port side either smelled, heard, or divined the impending holocaust that should rob him of his chosen route across the border. He sat up and screamed. He shouted to the others. He leaped from the bunk, as a corpse might come from a sepulcher at the crack of doom. New fear lent him frenzy—frenzy that breaks all laws except the one law that it must destroy itself. Frenzy gave him strength.

In a moment he was beating on our backs to force a way out into the open. We turned and closed with him, he fighting with the immeasurable efforts of a madman. The poor, weak, tortured thing, that but an hour ago could scarcely lift his head for liquid nourishment, now had all seven of us busy trying to force him back to bed. And that disturbance set most of the rest agog.

There were some too feeble to respond. There were a few too far on the road toward recovery to be influenced by shadows of Death Valley, but the rest leaped into panic as the flames leap out in a jungle-fire.

While we fought with the first man, six others ran for the door. Yerkes, Fred, I and two of the new men rushed out after them, and might as well have tried to catch ghosts on the brink of the pit. The helpless, hopeless human shadows slid, staggered and rolled, until they all lay screaming along the scuppers. One man got up and jumped overboard. Another followed him. Before we could come near enough to pounce on the rest, the fo'castle behind us began to empty itself past Monty.

I saw him trip over the coaming and fall backward. I caught sight of Yerkes, too, thrown off his feet by the rush of the madmen and a staggering blow as the *Bundesrath* shoved her great ugly nose into a sea. The sea seemed to be coming three ways, and the wind to be quartering them all so that we struggled, as it were, above an earthquake. The men out of death-beds had surer feet than we.

The scene that followed under the racing smoke and clouds, amid rain and spray and sparks, lingers in memory like a story of the Inquisition, or of Dante's dream of hell. Some of them, yelling like fiends, jumped overboard. Some—more frenzied and therefore capable of wilder effort than the rest—seized the fallen ones by arms and head and feet and hove them into the sea as if they were corpses. Some leaped and scrabbled at the newly nailed-up boards that shut us off forward. And some of them simply fought—insane—with the fury of animals, not knowing why they fought, or whom.

We were powerless to help or hinder them. If four of us held one man and forced him back through the door, that only left fewer to protect the sane ones; and the moment we took pressure off his limbs the held one would be gone again.

One tortured maniac clambered to the fo'castle head and hove into the sea the few miserable goats remaining. Then he jumped after them, with a yell that pierced through the raging wind and curdled blood already all but frozen by the scene. Three of them attacked me so that I had to use my fists on creatures I had chanced more than an arm to succor. Strangely enough, it did not trouble me. It was like a dream—things happening without connection and passing in review without effect. Even Monty—Yerkes—Oakes—and the formerly-mean white trio—were like specters, and I the only actually living one.

It may be that I would have jumped overboard presently, for when a man gets to that state of watching all about him dispassionately, as if it were panorama passing across a screen, there is no foretelling. But another vision brought me back to the land of the living—to good, sound wrath—to action.

I glanced up at the bridge. Two officers—the captain and another one—were clinging, each with both hands, to the bridge-rail and laughing down at us—roaring with laughter. There was something to turn on and deal with—something I could do! I searched about swiftly—found an iron ring and flung it. The missile was unexpected, and caught the captain full and square in the face. He answered with three prompt pistol-shots, all of which missed me; and then what had been panic became the deliberate storming of the gates of death.

Furor teutonicus or some such malady took possession of the bridge gang, and the two of them opened fire with their pistols on every living thing forward of their bulkhead. We ran for the fo'castle, but the cholera victims tried to tear the hatches off and build something—shelter, perhaps, or a raft. The bullets preventing that, they tried to climb to the upper deck and wreak they alone could guess what vengeance. They were shot down with as little mercy as the stockyard swine expect and get.

STANDING WELL back in the gloom within the fo'castle—they fired whenever one of us approached the door close enough to be visible from the bridge—I saw the great billow of smoke blaze suddenly red and then the whole stern of the ship burst into flame with a roar like artillery. Against that red background I could see the engine-room staff-officers, stokers, oilers and all—swarming among the boats.

"Where's Jones?" asked Monty suddenly, but I did not turn to hunt for him, although I think the others did.

The firing ceased. I suppose there were no more targets. I heard the others behind me rounding up the few poor devils who had not had strength or frenzy enough to run amuck, getting them ready, I suppose, to carry out. I did not see just what good that would do. There was not much choice that I could see between death by explosion, death by cholera, or death by drowning. Only, I did not choose to die with one of that captain's bullets in my brain. I continued gazing aft; so presently I saw Jones—the mean white—he who had saluted. He was crawling backward along the scupper toward me, stopping to sham dead whenever any one on the bridge looked likely to see him. But they were not paying much further attention to us from the bridge—nor to anything except the manning and handling of the boats.

"How did you come to be forward there?" I asked, as Jones slipped into the fo'castle.

"Where's 'is lordship?" he demanded.

So I called Monty, and he came.

"Beg pardon, my lord. I can get us a boat, or I think I can."

"How?" asked Monty.

"I've been up once. I can crawl to the bridge an' climb up by a stanchion an' a line what's 'angin' there. I'd 'a' stayed up an' done what I was minded to, on'y I thought as 'ow you might think I was stampedin' like them poor devils—or takin' sides wi' Germans—or playin' my own 'and, or what not. I wants it known an' understood I'm playin' the game as you'd 'ave me do it, sir!"

"All right, my man," said Monty.

"Then, beggin' y'r leave, my lord, I'd like orders!"

Monty understood.

"What is it?" he asked. "Private—corporal—sergeant?"

"Sergeant-major, sir!"

"Very well, Sergeant-major. Climb up to that bridge and get us a boat if you can! Use your own discretion after you're up there as to how you go about it, but be quick!"

"Yes, sir!"

The man saluted as he had done once before.

"Good-by—Jones!" said Monty, holding a hand out.

I wondered why he called him then by name instead of title. They shook hands.

"Thank you, my lord! I'll get ye a boat, by God! Good-by!"

In a minute he was gone, crawling once more along the scupper.

"Private," said Monty, "is all that fellow ever was! He doesn't look, talk, walk, stand, or think like a sergeant-major! Sergeant-major is probably what the poor chap hoped to be! Well, good luck to him!"

He went inside to help the others, but I was fascinated and stood just within the door, looking aft. The heat from the fire had grown terrific, and they were already trying to swing out two of the boats, waiting for the moment of more or less steadiness between the rollings. I saw one boat full of men smash to pulpwood against the hot steel side, and then I caught sight of Jones going hand over hand up the forward port bridge-stanchion.

Besides that of being seen and shot or kicked on the head, the only great risk he ran yet was of being flung off when the ship plunged in the trough of the waves. For we were lying beam-on now. They must have stopped the engines. I could no longer feel the tremble of the struggling propeller; and every other wave tumbled in over the weather bulwark.

The increased rolling made the work of lowering boats more difficult. There was no panic as yet, but something very like confusion on the boat-deck. I came out and clambered up on the fo'castle head to see better, after one glance inside to make sure that Monty and the others were putting life-belts on both cholera patients and themselves. I caught sight of Jones again in vivid black relief against the crimson flame. There was nobody on the bridge. They were all busy with the boats. He crouched on the bridge, and they did not notice him.

The first boat they lowered having met disaster, they were taking more precaution now and they swung the next one overside with only four men in her, two at each tackle. The *Bundesrath* shook to a more than usually heavy sea and reeled before it, lying right over as if she would bury her very bridge-rail. I saw the captain himself raise both hands and yell to lower away, and then Jones took his chance.

He sprang like a tiger and landed with fists and feet in the outswung boat, knocking one of the four men out of her into the sea. They had begun to lower her, hand over hand, but checked as if bewildered, and the *Bundesrath* hove herself rather more than upright so that the boat's keel clanged on the deck. That frightened the three men thoroughly. As the ship lay over before the thunder of the next oncoming wave Jones sprang at the throat of the one man remaining at the after tackle, and he followed his mate overside.

Then Jones began lowering away, faster and faster, so that the two men at the bow end had either to follow suit or see the boat up-ended. Their weight being greater, they gained speed, and the boat took the water, by the grace of the god of deep-sea accidents, on a fairly even keel. By that time Jones had an oar in his hand, and the two remaining seamen went overboard before they could guess what was happening. I suspect he broke one man's skull. He certainly hit him hard enough.

By that time another boat was smashed to flinders against the ship's side. It began to look as if captain, first-class passengers and crew would all have to go down or blow up. Jones cast off the falls and shoved against the ship's side with an oar with all his might. I looked to see him lifted off his feet and hurled backward into the sea. The captain, on the other hand, saw the only boat that was safely overside in the hands of a man who, whatever else he might do, certainly would not wait there for German passengers. He began shooting—pretty wildly, but fast—and I saw Jones drop his arm as one bullet found a billet.

But the boat was drifting rapidly to leeward. Jones sat and began trying to get steerageway with an oar, but with one arm useless could accomplish nothing. The captain kept on shooting at him and hit him again, for he shook his fist and then drooped.

Meanwhile the dense black smoke and lurid flame prevented me from seeing what else was going on behind the bridge. I saw one great wooden mast go overside with a crash and a roar, but lost sight of all the boats, although figures like black devils kept rushing to and fro as if trying to achieve a dozen impossibilities at once. The boat Jones had stolen drifted my way and would have lost her lee in another two minutes and perhaps been swamped in the raging sea had another miracle not happened. I remembered a lead-line that hung in a rack inside the fo'castle door and went down to get it with a speed born of fear and inspiration coupled.

"Come on, Monty!" I yelled. "Come on, all of you! Bring 'em along!"

I rushed again to the fo'castle head, stood whirling the lead in wide and wider circles and loosed it down-wind, while the captain continued shooting at poor Jones. I expected to have to haul it back and make a second, or third, or fourth attempt, and the boat was drifting all too fast. It was too much to hope that Jones could catch the line and too much to ask that the lead should fall into the boat. But a man hopes and asks for things unprecedented when all the likely things have failed and only the impossibilities remain.

I prayed as the flickering line paid out, and, prayer or no, the lead fell plumb beyond the boat with the line drawn tight across her. Jones grabbed it with his one uninjured hand, and I saw him make it fast to a thwart. Then the captain turned to fire at me—three times again—but missed. He reloaded and fired at Jones again—and hit him.

The question then was whether that flimsy lead-line was going to hold long enough for me to take advantage of it. Haul on it, I simply dared not. Make it fast to something, I must! At that minute Fred Oakes clambered up beside me to bring me one of the clumsy life-belts from the fo'castle rack.

"Put it on!" he said. "All that's left of the cholera kids are out on deck. We're ready!"

"Grab this!" I said. "Play that boat as you would a fish!"

There was a life-line—a new, stout one—coiled by the port anchor. I seized it, made a bowline in the end of it, slipped that over my shoulders and sprang for the lower deck.

"Pay that out after me!" I yelled to Monty, thrusting the coil into his hands. And then I dived for it before he could argue the point. I had only tropical clothes on, and in the lee of that great leviathan there was a chance—if only a chance.

MONTY SAID afterward that then the captain fired at him and succeeded in hitting two more of the cholera cases, but of that I knew nothing. I swam for my own life and the others', praying the slender line might hold. Why it held and how it held is beyond me even to guess. It parted the minute my extra weight was added to the force of wind and drift, and for a minute I clung breathless until Monty had the sense to ease away and take the strain from my shoulders and arms. I had a struggle then to clamber in, for I was tired and half-full of sea water, but I got in at last and rested beside Jones' dead body, that rolled back and forward on the bottom in a pool of bloody water.

It was time then to haul short and be swift about it. Fred Oakes came down the life-line hand-over-hand and took an oar. One of the "mean whites" followed him—Howard, I think it was—and then Monty and Yerkes and the other man began throwing the cholera cases overboard for me to fish for. There were seven, and I rescued all but one, although four more died in the boat within an hour—and little blame to them!

Then—and not till then—I remembered that Monty could not swim! And in the fierce light of the fire I saw the first officer and some sailors make a rush forward to seize the line that held us fast. I yelled. I might as well have yelled at the wallowing *Bundesrath* herself! They came down over the end of the bridge like monkeys, and the next I knew the line was loose. We were drifting, with Monty and Yerkes and Hill marooned behind us, murdered as likely as not.

The oars were going. I took another oar, and, between us, we brought the boat up closer to the ship, but I could not row and see what was happening as well; so, as we wallowed nearer, I started to ship the oar. As I did that, a hand seized it. In another moment I had dragged Yerkes over the side.

"Where's Monty?" I nearly screamed at him.

"Aw—can the excitement—here he is!"

His right hand was over the gunwale. He hauled at something, and I leaned over to help. Between us we dragged in the unconscious Monty, weighted almost beyond recovery by a water-logged cork life-belt of the vintage of Noah or earlier.

"Where's the other man?" I shouted.

"Here I am, sir!" And Hill rose head and shoulders over the gunwale on the other side, to be hauled aboard by Fred.

"Now out oars and row like ——!" said I. We had not shipped the rudder. "Keep her head down-wind and try and race the waves!"

We were none of us oarsmen—not even I, who had "followed the sea." On a British merchant-ship in my day the rule was to stick to the ship until nothing had the slightest chance and then make the best of drowning. The boats were for pigs and chickens, and few but the most enthusiastic second mates could swim. But the knowledge that behind us the flames were racing toward a forward hold supposed to be crammed to the beams with high explosives lent us determination, if not skill.

After a while Monty recovered consciousness, coughed up a lot of water and had pluck enough to ship the rudder. We found it easier after that.

We were more than a hundred yards from the ship when I saw flames burst through the forward end of the bridge. Then men began jumping into the sea. Another boat, dangling from a davit by one fall, smashed itself to smithereens, but at last they did get one into the water, full of men as a tin of sardines. I wondered what they were waiting for—we didn't wait, we rowed a race with death—and then I saw the skipper, all disheveled and blackened in the smoke, stand hesitating, either afraid or unwilling to jump. I could not hear, but I could see them shouting to him.

Then he did jump for it, just as the ship lay over to a sea. He fell between the boat and the ship's side. And, as the *Bundesrath* rose again, her great fat flank upheaving with the force of seven thousand tons, he was caught between ship and boat and squeezed into shapelessness. As the boat turned over and tipped its maddened occupants into the sea I saw the upper half of him—head and shoulders—pinched off and fall over among the rest.

"Fingelmann is dead!" I shouted, straining at my oar.

"Row!" yelled Monty, spitting salt water. "Row, or we'll feed the same sharks! Row, men! Row!"

They say the expected never happens. The flames leaped over the bridge and swallowed it. The wooden deck on the fo'castle head caught fire, and the wooden foremast became a flaring beacon, whose flames were like a great flag in the wind. But the belly of the ship gave never a rumble—never a warning.

We had rowed a full half-mile—perhaps more—when the upper half of the ship along the whole length of her rose, like a box lid hinged at the stern, and stood on end. Flame leaped out of her belly then—savage, white, dazzling flame that hurt the eyes—and a mess of blackened wreck sprang skyward until I thought it would never cease going up—up—up, all in a heap together.

Then, before it fell, there came a thunderclap, louder than all the sounds I ever heard, and the sea in every direction after that was bombarded by the falling débris—metal and wood, but metal mostly. Where the *Bundesrath* had been was nothing but a pall of smoke that mushroomed, rolled over on itself and fled down-wind.

It was the sound of the explosion that brought the Messageries Maritimes S.S. *Natal* reeling and rolling down on us, flying her French ensign like a pretty lady's ribbon. All four classes—the French believe in providing for every purse—cheered us as we struggled toward them across the ugliest sea it has been my lot to witness. We had only one element in our favor—it was warm, not cold.

It was far too rough for them to lower their companion-ladder, but they swung out a boom long before they reached us and hauled us out one by one in a coaling basket, Monty last, he claiming the privilege. I went up first, for somebody had to break the news to our new hosts.

"Cholera!" I yelled, as they hauled the basket in along the boom.

So they kept me in the basket fifteen minutes while the ship's doctor made ready to quarantine us. Monty sent up the cholera victims next, and they lived long enough to make sworn statements, which the captain of the *Natal* wrote down and signed. Those statements must exist somewhere, together with the account we others swore to. If copies of them were ever submitted to the Kaiser's Government, the official comments would make good reading.

The thing that we cared about most, as we looked overside at the *Bundesrath's* boat tossing and rolling along on the merciless sea, was that Monty had saved our papers. The guns, tents, clothes, saddles and supplies were gone.

"But where the passports are there's a key to the door of the future," said Monty.

"Passports be ——!" remarked Fred.

"Where's the money?"

"The drafts are in the package with the passports in my pocketbook. That's the key I referred, to, Fred."

"All the same," said Yerkes, "you'll never get rich enough this way to take up your title and live as you should. Let's go to America next, and hunt up a maid with money!"

Monty laughed.

"Let's try the elephants first in British East. I'll consent to marry pork, or steel, or railways if ivory fails! Let's give the poor woman one last chance! Let's all try British East and ivory!"

THE IVORY TRAIL

THE NJO HAPA SONG

Green, oh greener than emeralds are, tree-tops
beckon the dhows to land,
White, oh whiter than diamonds are, blue waves
burst on the amber sand,
And nothing is fairer than Zanzibar from the
Isles o' the West to the Marquesand.

I was old when the world was wild with
youth.
(All love was lawless then!)
Since 'Venture's birth from ends of earth
I ha' called the sons of men,
And their women have wept the ages out
In travail sore to know
What lure of opiate art can leach
Along bare seas from reef to beach
Until from port and river reach
The fever'd captains go.

Red, oh redder than red lips are my flowers that
nod in the blazing noon,
Blue, oh bluer than maidens' eyes are the
breasts o' my waves in the young monsoon,
And there are cloves to smell, and musk, and
lemon trees, and cinnamon.

I

ESTIMATES OF ease and affluence vary with the point of view. While his older brother lived, Monty had continued in his element, a cavalry officer, his combined income and pay ample for all that the Bombay side of India might require of an English gentleman. They say that a finer polo player, a steadier shot on foot at a tiger, or a bolder squadron leader never lived.

But to Monty's infinite disgust his brother died childless. It is divulging no secret that the income that passed with the title varied between five and seven thousand pounds a year, according as coal was high, and tenants prosperous or not—a mere miserable pittance, of course, for the Earl of Montdidier and Kirkudbrightshire; so that all his ventures, and therefore ours, had one avowed end—shekels enough to lift the mortgages from his estates.

Five generations of soldiers had blazed the Montdidier fame on battle-grounds, to a nation's (and why not the whole earth's) benefit, without replenishing the family funds, and Monty (himself a confirmed and convinced bachelor) was minded when his own time should come to pass the title along to the next in line together with sufficient funds to support its dignity.

To us—even to Yerkes, familiar with United States merchant kings—he seemed with his thirty thousand dollars a year already a gilded Croesus. He had ample to travel on, and finance prospecting trips. We never lacked for working capital, but the quest (and, including Yerkes, we were as keen as he) led us into strange places.

So behold him—a privy councilor of England if you please—lounging in the lazaretto of Zanzibar, clothed only in slippers, underwear and a long blue dressing-gown. We three others were dressed the same, and because it smacked of official restraint we objected noisily; but Monty did not seem to mind much. He was rather bored, but unresentful.

A French steamer had put us ashore in quarantine, with the grim word cholera against us, and although our tale of suffering and Monty's rank, insured us a friendly reception, the port health authorities elected to be strict and we were given a nice long lazy time in which to cool our heels and order new clothes. (Guns, kit, tents, and all but what we stood in had gone to the bottom with the German cholera ship from whose life-boat the French had rescued us.)

"Keeping us all this time in this place, is sheer tyranny!" grumbled Yerkes. "If any one wants my opinion, they're afraid we'd talk if they let us out—more afraid of offending Germans than they are of cholera! Besides—any fool could know by now we're not sick!"

"There might be something in that," admitted Monty.

"I'd send for the U.S. Consul and sing the song out loud, but for you!" Yerkes added.

Monty nodded sympathetically.

"Dashed good of you, Will, and all that sort of thing."

"You English are so everlastingly afraid of seeming to start trouble, you'll swallow anything rather than talk!"

"As a government, perhaps yes," admitted Monty. "As a people, I fancy not. As a people we vary."

"You vary in that respect as much as sardines in a can! I traveled once all the way from London to Glasgow alone in one compartment with an Englishman. Talk? My, we were garrulous! I offered him a newspaper, cigarettes, matches, remarks on the weather suited to his brand of intelligence—(that's your sole national topic of talk between strangers!)—and all he ever said to me was 'Haw-ah!' I'll bet he was afraid of seeming to start trouble!"

"He didn't start any, did he?" asked Monty.

"Pretty nearly he did! I all *but* bashed him over the bean with the newspaper the third time he said 'haw-ah!' "

Monty laughed. Fred Oakes was busy across the room with his most amazing gift of tongues, splicing together half-a-dozen of them in order to talk with the old lazaretto attendant, so he heard nothing; otherwise there would have been argument.

"Then it would have been you, not he who started trouble," said I, and Yerkes threw both hands up in a gesture of despair.

"Even you're afraid of starting something!" He stared at both of us with an almost startled expression, as if he could not believe his own verdict, yet could not get away from it. "Else you'd give the *Bundesrath* story to the papers! That German skipper's conduct ought to be bruited round the world! You said you'd do it. You promised us! You told the man to his face you would!"

"Now," said Monty, "you've touched on another national habit."

"Which one?" Yerkes demanded.

"Dislike of telling tales out of school. The man's dead. His ship's at the bottom. The tale's ended. What's the use? Besides—?"

"Ah! You've another reason! Spill it!"

"As a privy councilor, y'know, and all that sort of thing—?"

"Same story! Afraid of starting something!"

"The Germans—'specially their navy men—drink to what they call *Der Tag* y'know—the day when they shall dare try to tackle England. We all know that. They're planning war, twenty years from now perhaps, that shall give them all our colonies as well as India and Egypt. They're so keen on it they can't keep from bragging. Great Britain, on the other hand, hasn't the slightest intention of fighting if war can be avoided; so why do anything meanwhile to increase the tension? Why send broadcast a story that would only arouse international hatred? That's their method. Ours—I mean our government's—is to give hatred a chance to die down. If our papers got hold of the *Bundesrath* story they'd make a deuce of a noise, of course."

"If your government's so sure Germany is planning war," objected Yerkes, "why on earth not force war, and feed them full of it before they're ready"

"Counsel of perfection," laughed Monty. "Government's responsible to the Common—Commons to the people—people want peace and plenty. No. Your guess was good. We are in here while the government at home squares the newspaper men."

"You don't mean to tell me your British government controls the press?"

"Hardly. Seeing 'em—putting it up to 'em straight—asking 'em politely. They're public-spirited, y'know. Hitting 'em with a club would be another thing. It's an easy-going nation, but kings have been sorry they tried force. Did you never hear of a king who used force against American colonies?"

"Good God! So they keep you—an earl—a privy councilor—a retired colonel of regulars in good standing—under lock and key in this pest-house while they bribe the press not to tell the truth about some Germans and start trouble?"

"Not exactly" said Monty.

"But here you are!"

"I preferred to remain with my party."

"You moan they'd have let you out and kept us in?"

"They'd have phrased it differently, but that's about what it would have amounted to. I have privileges."

"Well, I'm jiggered!"

"I rather suspect it's not so bad as that," said Monty. "You're with friends in quarantine, Will!"

For a quarantine station in the tropics it was after all not such a bad place. We could hear the crooning of lazy rollers on the beach, and what little sea-breeze moved at all came in to us through iron-barred windows. The walls were of coral, three feet thick. So was the roof. The wet red-tiled floor made at least an impression of coolness, and the fresh green foliage of an enormous mango tree, while it obstructed most of the view, suggested anything but durance vile. From not very far away the aromatic smell of a clove warehouse located us, not disagreeably, at the farther end of one of Sindbad's journeys, and the birds in the mango branches cried and were colorful with hues and notes of merry extravagance. Zanzibar is no parson's paradise—nor the center of much high society. It reeks of unsavory history as well as of spices. But it has its charms, and the Arabs love it.

It had Fred Oakes so interested that he had forgotten his concertina—his one possession saved from shipwreck, for which he had offered to fight the whole of Zanzibar one-handed rather than have it burned.

("Damnation! it has silver reeds—it's an English top-hole one—a wonder!")

So the doctors who are kind men in the main disinfected it twice, once on the French liner that picked us out of the *Bundesrath's* boat, and again in Zanzibar; and with the stench of lord-knew-what zealous chemical upon it he had let it lie unused while he picked up Kiswahili and talked by the hour to a toothless, wrinkled very black man with a touch of Arab in his breeding, and a deal of it in his brimstone vocabulary.

Presently Fred came over and joined us, dancing across the wide red floor with the skirts of his gown outspread like a ballet dancer's—ridiculous and perfectly aware of it.

"Monty, you're rich! We're all made men! We're all rich! Let's spend money! Let's send for catalogues and order things!"

Monty declined to take fire. It was I, latest to join the partnership and much the least affluent, who bit.

"If you love the Lord, explain!" said I.

"This old one-eyed lazaretto attendant is an ex-slave, ex-accomplice of Tippoo Tib!"

"And Tippoo Tib?" I asked.

"Ignorant fo'c's'le outcast!" (All that because I had made one voyage as foremast hand, and deserted rather than submit to more of it.) "Tippoo Tib is the Arab—is, mind you, my son, not was—the Arab who was made governor of half the Congo by H.M. Stanley and the rest of 'em. Tippoo Tib is the expert who used to bring the slave caravans to Zanzibar—bring 'em, send 'em, send for 'em—he owned 'em anyway. Tippoo Tib was the biggest ivory hunter and trader lived since old King Solomon! Tippoo Tib is here—in Zanzibar—to all intents and purposes a prisoner on parole—old as the hills—getting ready to die—and proud as the very ace of hell. So says One-eye!"

"So we're all rich?" suggested Monty.

"Of course we are! Listen! The British government took Tippoo's slaves away and busted his business. Made him come and live in this place, go to church on Sundays, and be good. Then they asked him what he'd done with his ivory. Asked him politely after putting him through that mill! One-eye here says Tippoo had a million tusks—a million!—safely buried! Government offered him ten per cent. of their cash value if he'd tell 'em where, and the old sport spat in their faces! Swears he'll die with the secret! One-eye vows Tippoo is the only one who knows. There were others, but Tippoo shot or poisoned 'em."

"So we're rich," smiled Yerkes.

"Of course we are! Consider this, America, and tell me if Standard Oil can beat it! One million tusks I'm told—"

"By whom?"

"One-eye says—"

"You'll say 'Oh!' at me to a different tune, before I've done! One-eye says it never paid to carry a tusk weighing less than sixty pounds. Some tusks weigh two hundred—some even more—took four men to carry some of 'em! Call it an average weight of one hundred pounds and be on the safe side."

"Yes, let's play safe," agreed Monty seriously.

"One hundred million pounds of ivory!" said Fred, with a smack of his lips and the air of a man who could see the whole of it. "The present market price of new ivory is over ten shillings a pound on the spot. That'll all be very old stuff, worth at least double. But let's say ten shillings a pound and be on the safe side."

"Yes, let's!" laughed Yerkes.

"So now suit yourselves!" said Fred, collapsing with a sweep of his skirts into the nearest chair. "I've told you what One-eye says. These dusky gents sometimes exaggerate of course—"

"Now and then," admitted Monty.

"But where there's smoke you mean there's prob'ly some one smoking hams?" suggested Yerkes.

"I mean, let's find that ivory!" said Fred.

"We might do worse than make an inquiry or two," Monty assented cautiously.

"Didums, you damned fool, you're growing old! You're wasting time! You're trying to damp enthusiasm! You're—you're—"

"Interested, Fred. I'm interested. Let's—"

"One thousand million—a billion shillings!" Fred announced. "Fifty million pounds!"

"Two hundred and fifty million dollars!" Yerkes calculated, beginning to take serious notice.

"But how are we to find it?" I objected.

"That's the point. Government 'ud hog the lot, but has hunted high and low and can't find it. So the offer stands ten per cent. to any one who does—ten per cent. of fifty million—lowest reckoning, mind you!—five million pounds! Half for Monty—two and a half million. A million for Yerkes, a million for me, and a half a million for you all according to contract! How d'you like it?"

"Well enough," I answered. "If its only the hundredth part true, I'm enthusiastic!"

"Let's find that ivory and to hell with caution! Why, man alive, it's the chance of a million lifetimes!"

"Well, then," said Monty, "admitting the story's true for the sake of argument, how do you propose to get on the track of the secret?"

"Get on it? I *am* on it! Didn't One-eye say Tippoo Tib is alive and in Zanzibar? The old rascal! Many a slave he's done to death! Many a man be's tortured! I propose we catch Tippoo Tib, hide him, and pull out his toe-nails one by one until be blows the gaff!"

(To hear Fred talk when there is nothing to do but talk a stranger might arrive at many false conclusions.)

"If there's any truth in the story at all," said

Monty, "government will have done everything within the bounds of decency to coax the facts from Tippoo Tib. I suspect we'd have to take our chance and simply hunt. But let's hear Juma's story."

So the old attendant left off sprinkling water from a yellow jar, and came and stood before us. Fred's proposal of tweaking toe-nails would not have been practical in his case, for he had none left. His black legs, visible because he had tucked his one long garment up about his waist, were a mass of scars. He was lean, angular, yet peculiarly straight considering his years. As he stood before us he let his shirt-like garment drop, and the change from scarecrow to deferential servant was instantaneous. He was so wrinkled, and the wrinkles were so deep, that one scarcely noticed his sightless eye, almost hidden among a nest of creases; and in spite of the wrinkles, his polished, shaven head made him look ridiculously youthful because one expected gray hair and there was none.

"Ask him how he lost his toe-nails, Fred," said I.

But the old man knew enough English to answer for himself. He made a wry grimace and showed his hands. The finger-nails were gone too.

"Tell us your story, Juma," said Monty.

"Tell 'em about the *pembe*—the ivory—the much ivory—the *meengi pembe,*" echoed Fred.

"Let's hear about those nails of his first," said I.

"One thing'll prob'ly lead to another," Yerkes agreed. "Start him on the toe-nail story."

But it did not lead very far. Fred, who had picked up Kiswahili enough to piece out the old man's broken English, drew him out and clarified the tale. But it only went to prove that others besides ourselves had beard of Tippoo Tib's hoard. Some white man—we could not make bead or tail of the name, but it sounded rather like *Somebody belonging to a man named Carpets*—had trapped him a few years before and put him to torture in the belief that be knew the secret.

"But me not knowing nothing!" he assured us solemnly, shaking his head again and again.

But he was not in the least squeamish about telling us that Tippoo Tib had surely buried huge quantities of ivory, and had caused to be slain afterward every one who shared the secret.

"How long ago?" asked Monty. But natives of that part of the earth are poor hands at reckoning time.

"Long time," he assured us. He might have meant six years, or sixty. It would have been all the same to him.

"No. Me not liking Tippoo Tib. One time his slave. That bad. By-um-by set free. That good. Now working here. This very good."

"Where do you *think* the ivory is?" (This from Yerkes.)

But the old man shook his head.

"As I understand it," said Monty, "slaves came mostly from the Congo side of Lake Victoria Nyanza. Slave and elephant country were approximately the same as regards general direction, and there were two routes from the Congo—the southern by way of Ujiji on Tanganyika to Bagamoyo on what is now the German coast, and the other to the north of Victoria Nyanza ending at Mombasa. Ask him, Fred, which way the ivory used to come."

"Both ways," announced Juma without waiting for Fred to interpret. He had an uncanny trick of following conversation, his intelligence seeming to work by fits and starts.

"That gives us about half Africa for hunting-ground, and a job for life!" laughed Yerkes.

"Might have a worse!" Fred answered, resentful of cold water thrown on his discovery.

"Were you Tippoo Tib's slave when he buried the ivory?" demanded Monty, and the old man nodded.

"Where were you at the time?"

Juma made a gesture intended to suggest immeasurable distances toward the West, and the name of the place he mentioned was one we had never heard of.

"Can you take us to Tippoo Tib when we leave this place?" I asked, and be nodded again.

"How much ivory do you suppose there was?" asked Yerkes.

"Teli, teli!" he answered, shaking his head.

"Too much!" Fred translated.

"Pretty fair to middling vague," said Yerkes, "but"—judicially—"almost worth investigating!"

"Investigating?" Fred sprang from his chair. "It's better than all King Solomon's mines, El Dorado, Golconda, and Sindbad the Sailor's treasure lands—rolled in one! It's an obviously good thing! All we need is a bit of luck and the ivory's ours!"

"I'll sell you my share now for a thousand dollars—come—come across!" grinned Yerkes.

There was a rough-house after that. He and Fred nearly pulled the old attendant in two, each claiming the right to torture him first and learn the secret.

They ended up without a whole rag between them, and had to send Juma to head-quarters for new blue dressing-gowns. The doctor came himself—a fat good-natured party with an eye-glass and a cocktail appetite, acting *locum-tenens* for the real official who was home on leave. He brought the ingredients for cocktails with him.

"Yes," he said, shaking the mixer with a sort of deft solicitude. "There's more than something in the tale. I've had a try myself to get details. Tippoo Tib believes in up-to-date physic, and when the old rascal's sick he sends for me. I offered to mix him an elixir of life that would make him out-live Methuselah if he'd give me as much as a hint of the general direction of his cache."

"He ought to have fallen for that," said Yerkes, but the doctor shook his head.

"He's an Arab. They're Shiah Mohammedans. Their Paradise is a pleasant place from all accounts. He advised me to drink my own elixir, and have lots and lots of years in which to find the ivory, without being beholden to him for help. Wily old scaramouche! But I had a better card up my sleeve. He has taken to discarding ancient prejudices—doesn't drink or anything like that, but treats his harem almost humanly. Lets 'em have anything that costs him nothing. Even sends for a medico when they're sick! Getting lax in his old age! Sent for me a while ago to attend his favorite wife—sixty years old if she's a day, and as proud of him as if he were the king of Jerusalem. Well—I looked her over, judged she was likely to keep her bed, and did some thinking."

"You know their religious law? A woman can't go to Paradise without special intercession, mainly vicarious. I found a mullah—that's a Mohammedan priest—who'd do anything for half of nothing. They most of them will. I gave him fifty dibs, and promised him more if the trick worked. Then I told the old woman she was going to die, but that if she'd tell me the secret of Tippoo Tib's ivory I had a mullah handy who would pass her into Paradise ahead of her old man. What did she do? She called Tippoo Tib, and he turned me out of the house. So I'm fifty out of pocket, and what's worse, the old girl didn't die—got right up out of bed and stayed up! My rep's all smashed to pieces among the Arabs!"

"D'you suppose the old woman knew the secret?" I asked.

"Not she! If she'd known it she'd have split! The one ambition she has left is to be with Tippoo Tib in Paradise. But he can intercede for her and get her in—provided he feels that way; so she rounded on me in the hope of winning his special favor! But the old ruffian knows better! He'll no more pray for her than tell me where the ivory is! The Koran tells him there are much better houris in Paradise, so why trouble to take along a toothless favorite from this world?"

"Has the government any official information?" asked Monty.

"Quite a bit, I'm told. Official records of vain searches. Between you and me and these four walls, about the only reason why they didn't hang the old slave-driving murderer was that they've always hoped he'd divulge the secret some day. But be hates the men who broke him far too bitterly to enrich them on any terms! If any man wins the secret from him it'll be a foreigner. They tell me a German had a hard try once. One of Karl Peters' men."

"That'll be Carpets!" said Monty. "Somebody belonging to Carpets—Karl Peters."

"The man's serving a life sentence in the jail for torturing our friend Juma here."

"Then Juma knows the secret?"

"So they say. But Juma, too, hopes to go to Paradise and wait on Tippoo Tib."

"He told us just now that he dislikes Tippoo Tib," I objected.

"So he does, but that makes no difference. Tippoo Tib is a big chief—*sultani kubwa*—take any one he fancies to Heaven with him!"

We all looked at Juma with a new respect.

"I got Juma his job in here," said the doctor. "I've rather the notion of getting my ten per cent. on the value of that ivory some day!"

"Are there any people after it just now?" asked Monty.

"I don't know, I'm sure. There was a German named Schillingschen, who spent a month in Zanzibar and talked a lot with Tippoo Tib. The old rascal might tell his secret to any one he thought was England's really dangerous enemy. Schillingschen crossed over to British East if I remember rightly. He might be on the track of it."

"Tell us more about Schillingschen," said Monty.

"He's one of those orientalists, who profess to know more about Islam than Christianity—more about Africa and Arabia than Europe—more about the occult than what's in the open. A man with a shovel beard—stout—thick-set—talks Kiswahili and Arabic and half a dozen other languages better than the natives do themselves. Has money—outfit like a prince's—everything imaginable—Rifles—microscopes—cigars—wine. He didn't make himself agreeable here—except to the Arabs. Didn't call at the Residency. Some of us asked him to dinner one evening, but he pleaded a headache. We were glad, because afterward we saw him eat at the hotel—has ways of using his fingers at table, picked up I suppose from the people he has lived among."

"Are you nearly ready to let us out of here?" asked Monty.

"Your quarantine's up," said the doctor. "I'm only waiting for word from the office."

We drank three rounds of cocktails with him, after which he grew darkly friendly and proposed we should all set out together in search of the hoard.

"I've no money," he assured us. "Nothing but a knowledge of the natives and a priceless thirst. I'd have to throw up my practise here. Of course I'd need some sort of guarantee from you chaps."

The proposal falling flat, be gathered the nearly empty bottles into one place and shouted for his boy to come and carry them away.

"Think it over!" he urged as he got up to leave us. "You might take a bigger fool than me with you. You'd need a doctor on a trip like that. I'm an expert on some of these tropical diseases. Think it over!"

"Fred!" said Monty, as soon as the doctor had left the room, "I'm tempted by this ivory of yours."

But Fred, in the new blue dressing-gown the doctor had brought, was in another world—a land of trope and key and metaphor. For the last ten minutes he had kept a stub of pencil and a scrap of paper working, and now the strident tones of his too long neglected concertina stirred the heavy air and shocked the birds outside to silence. The instrument was wheezy, for in addition to the sacrilege the port authorities had done by way of disinfection, the bellows had been wetted when Fred plunged from the sinking *Bundesrath* and swam. But he is not what you could call particular, as long as a good loud noise comes forth that can be jerked and broken into anything resembling tune.

"Tempted, are you?" he laughed. He looked like a drunken troubadour en déshabillé, with those up-brushed mustaches and his usually neat brown beard all spread awry. "Temptation's more fun than plunder!"

Yerkes threw an orange at him, more by way of recognition than remonstrance. We had not heard Fred sing since he tried to charm cholera victims in the *Bundesrath's* fo'c's'le, and, like the rest of us, he had his rights. He sang with legs spread wide in front of him, and head thrown back, and, each time be came to the chorus, kept on repeating it until we joined in.

There's a prize that's full familiar from Zanzibar to France;
From Tokyo to Boston; we are paid it in advance.
It's the wages of adventure, and the wide world knows the feel
Of the stuff that stirs good huntsmen all and brings the hounds to heel!
It's the one reward that's gratis and precedes the toilsome task—
It's the one thing always better than an optimist can ask!
It's amusing, it's amazing, and it's never twice the same;
It's the salt of true adventure and the glamour of the game!

It is tem-tem-pitation!
The one sublime sensation!
You may doubt it, but without it
There would be no derring-do!
The reward the temptee cashes
Is too often dust and ashes,
But you'll need no spurs or lashes
When temptation beckons you!

Oh, it drew the Roman legions to old Britain's distant isle,
And it beckoned H. M. Stanley to the sources of the Nile;
It's the one and only reason for the bristling guns at Gib,
For the skeletons at Khartoum, and the crimes of Tippoo Tib.
The gentlemen adventurers braved torture for its sake,

It beckoned out the galleons, and filled the hulls
of Drake!
Oh, it sets the sails of commerce, and it whets
the edge of war.
It's the sole excuse for churches, and the only
cause of law!

It is tem-tem-pitation! etc., etc.

No note is there of failure (that's a tune the
croakers sing!)
This song's of youth, and strength, and health,
and time that's on the wing!
Of wealth beyond the hazy blue of far horizons
flung—
But never of the folk returning, disillusioned,
stung!
It's a tale of gold and ivory, of plunder out of
reach,
Of luck that fell to other men, of treasure on the
beach—
A compound, cross-reciprocating two-way
double spell,
The low, sweet lure to Heaven, and the tallyho
to hell!

It is tem-tem-pitation!
The one sublime sensation!
You may doubt it, but without it
There would be no derring-do!
It's the siren of to-morrow
That knows naught of lack or sorrow,
So you'll sell your bonds and borrow,
When temptation beckons you!

Once Fred starts there is no stopping him, short of personal violence, and he ran through his ever lengthening list of songs, not all quite printable, until the very coral walls ached with the concertina's wailing, and our throats were hoarse from ridiculous choruses. As Yerkes put it:

"When pa says sing, the rest of us sing too or go crazy!"

I went to the window and tried to get a view of shipping through the mango branches. Masts and sails—lateen spars particularly—always get me by the throat and make me happy for a while. But all I could see was a low wall beyond the little compound, and over the top of it headgear of nearly all the kinds there are. (Zanzibar is a wonderful market for second-hand clothes. There was even a tall silk hat of not very ancient pattern.)

"Come and look, Monty!" said I, and he and Yerkes came and stood beside me. Seeing his troubadour charm was broken, Fred snapped the catch on the concertina and came too.

"Arabian Nights!" he exclaimed, thumping Monty on the back. "Didums, you drunkard, we're dead and in another world! Juma is the one-eyed Calender! Look—fishermen—houris—how many houris?—seen 'em grin!—soldiers of fortune—merchants—sailors—by gad, there's Sindbad himself!—and say! If that isn't the Sultan Haroun-al-Raschid in disguise I'm willing to eat beans and pie for breakfast to oblige Yerkes! Look—look at the fat ruffian's stomach and swagger, will you?"

Yerkes sized up the situation quickest.

"Sing him another song, Fred. If we want to strike up acquaintance with half Zanzibar, here's our chance!"

"Oh, Richard, oh, my king!" hummed Monty. "It's Coeur de Lion and Blondell over again with the harp reversed."

If Zanzibar may be said to possess main thoroughfares, that window of ours commanded as much of one as the tree and wall permitted; and music—even of a concertina—is the key to the heart of all people whose hair is crisp and kinky. Perhaps rather owing to the generosity of their slave law, and Koran teachings, more than to racial depravity, there are not very many Arabs left in that part of the world with true Semitic features and straight hair, nor many wooly-headed folk who are quite all-Bantu. There is enough Arab blood in all of them to make them bold; Bantu enough for syncopated, rag-time music to take them by the toes and stir them. The crowd in the street grew, and gathered until a policeman in red fez and khaki knickerbockers came and started trouble. He had a three-cornered fight on his hands, and no sympathy from any one, within two minutes. Then the man with the stomach and swagger—he whom Fred called Haroun-al-Raschid—took a hand in masterly style. He seized the police-man from behind, flung him out of the crowd, and nobody was troubled any more by that official.

"That him Tippoo Tib's nephew!" said a voice, and we all jumped. We had not noticed Juma come and stand beside us.

"I suspect nephew is a vague relationship in

these parts," said Monty. "Do you mean Tippoo's brother was that man's father, Juma?"

"No, *bwana.* Tippoo Tib bringing slave long ago f'm Bagamoyo. Him she-slave having chile. She becoming concubine Tippoo Tib his wife's brother. That chile Tippoo Tib's nephew. Tea ready, *bwana.*"

"What does that man do for a living?"

"Do for a living?" Juma was bewildered.

"What does he work at?"

"Not working."

"Never?"

"No.

"Has he private means, then?"

"I not understand. Tea ready, *bwana!*"

"Has he got mali?" Fred demanded.

"Mali? No. Him poor man."

"Then how does he exist, if he has no mali and doesn't work?"

"Oh, one wife here, one there, one other place, an' Tippoo Tib Byumby him giving food."

"How many wives has he?"

"Tea ready, *bwana!*"

"How do they come to be spread all over the place?" (We were shooting questions at him one after the other, and Juma began to look as if be would have preferred a repetition of the toe-nail incident.)

"Oh, he travel much, an' Byumby lose all money, then stay here. Tea, him growing cold."

There is no persuading the native servant who has lived under the Union Jack that an Englishman does not need hot tea at frequent intervals, even after three cocktails in an afternoon. So we trooped to the table to oblige him, and went through the form of being much refreshed.

"What is that man's name?" demanded Monty.

"Hassan."

"Do you know him?"

"Everybody know him!"

"Can you get a message to him?"

"Yes, *bwana.*"

"Tell him to come and talk with us at the hotel as soon as he hears we are out of this."

We did not know it at the time (for I don't think that Monty guessed it either) that we had taken the surest way of setting all Zanzibar by the ears. In that last lingering stronghold of legal slavery, where the only stories judged worth listening to are the very sources of the Thousand Nights and a Night, intrigue is not perhaps the breath of life, but it is the salt and savory. There is a wooly-headed sultan who draws a guaranteed, fixed income and has nothing better to do than regale himself and a harem with western alleged amusement. There are police, and lights, and municipal regulations. In fact, Zanzibar has come on miserable times from certain points of view. But there remains the fun of listening to all the rumors borne by sea. "Play on the flute in Zanzibar and Africa as far as the lakes will dance!" the Arabs say, and the gentry who once drove slaves or traded ivory refuse to believe that the day of lawlessness is gone forever. One rumor then is worth ten facts. Four white men singing behind the bars of the lazaretto, desiring to speak with Hassan, "nephew" of Tippoo Tib, and offering money for the introduction, were enough to send whispers sizzling up and down all the mazy streets.

Our release from quarantine took place next day, and we went to the hotel, where we were besieged at once by tradesmen, each proclaiming himself the only honest outfitter and "agent for all good export firms." Monty departed to call on British officialdom (one advantage of traveling with a nobleman being that he has to do the stilted social stuff). Yerkes went to call on the United States Consul, the same being presumably a part of his religion, for he always does it, and almost always abuses his government afterward. So Fred and I were left to repel boarders, and it came about that we two received Hassan.

He entered our room with a great shout of *"Hodi!"* (and Fred knew enough to say *"Karibu!")*—a smart red fez set at an angle on his shaven head, his henna-stained beard all newly-combed—a garment like a night-shirt reaching nearly to his heels, a sort of vest of silk embroidery restraining his stomach's tendency to wobble at will, and a fat smile decorating the least ashamed, most obviously opportunist face I ever saw, even on a black man.

"Jambo, jambo," he announced, striding in and observing our lack of worldly goods with one sweep of the eye. (We had not stocked up yet with new things, and probably he did not know our old ones were at the bottom of the sea.) He was a lion-hearted rascal though, at all events at the first rush, for poverty on the surface did not trouble him.

"You send for me? You want a good guide?"

The Haroun-al-Raschid look had disappeared.

Now he was the jack-of-all-trades, wondering which end of the jack to push in first.

"When I need a guide I'll get a licensed one," said Fred, sitting down and turning partly away from him. (It never pays to let those gentry think they have impressed you.) "What is your business, Johnson?"

"My name Hassan, sah. You send for me? You want a headman. I'm formerly headman for Tippoo Tib, knowing all roads, and how to manage *wapagazi, safari,* all things!"

"Any papers to prove it?" asked Fred.

"No, sir. Reference to Tippoo Tib himself sufficient! He my part-uncle."

"Ready to tell any kind of a lie for you, eh?"

"No, sir, always telling truth! You got a cook yet?"

"Can you cook?" Fred answered guardedly.

"Yes, sah. Was cook formerly for Master Stanley, go with him on expedition. Later his boy. Later his headman. You want to go on expedition, I getting you good cook. Where you want to go?"

"Are you looking for a job?" asked Fred.

"What you after? Ivory?"

"Maybe."

"I know all about ivory—I shoot, trade ivory along o' Tippoo Tib an' Stanley. You engage my services, all very well."

"Go and tell Tippoo Tib we want to see him. If he confirms what you say, perhaps we'll take you on," said Fred.

"Tell Tippoo Tib? Ha-ha! You want to find his buried ivory—that it? All white men wanting that! All right, I go tell him! I come again!"

"Come back here, you fat rascal!" ordered Fred. "What do you mean about buried ivory? What buried ivory?"

Hassan's face lost some of its transcendent cheek. Even the dyed beard seemed to wilt.

"What you wanting?" he asked. "Hunt, trade, travel—what your business?"

"Fish!" Fred answered genially.

"Samaki?"

"Yes—*samaki*—fish!"

Having no experience of Arabs, and part-Arabs, I wondered what on earth Fred could be driving at. But Hassan wondered still more, and that was the whole point. He stood agape, looking from one to the other of us, his fat good-natured face an interrogation mark.

"I go an' tell *bwana* Tippoo Tib!" he announced, and departed swiftly.

"What's the idea of fish, Fred?" I asked.

"Oh, just curiosity. The way of getting information out of colored folk is to get them so frantically curious they've no time to think up lies. Tobacco would have done as well—anything unexpected. A bird flying, and a black man lying,—are both of 'em easy to catch or confuse unless they know which way they're heading. Let's go and look at the bazaar."

But in order to look one had to reach. We left the great heavy-beamed hotel that had once been Tippoo Tib's residence, but were stopped in the outer doorway by a crowd of native boys, each with a brass plate on his arm.

"Guide, sah!—Guide, sah!—My name McPhairson, sah!—My name Jones, sah!—My name Johnson, sah! Guide to all the sights, sah!"

They were as persistent and evilly intentioned as a swarm of flies, and bold enough to strike back when anybody kicked them. While we wrestled and swore, but made no headway, we were accosted by a Greek, who seemed from long experience able to pass through them without striking or being struck. We were not left in doubt another second as to whether our friend Hassan had dallied on the way, and held his tongue or not.

"Good day, gentlemen! I hear you are after fish! Hah! That is a good story to tell to Arabs! You mean fishing for information, eh? Ha-hah!"

He turned on the swarm of boys, who still yelled and struggled about our legs.

"Imshi! Voetsak! Enenda zako! Kuma nina, wewe!" In a minute he had them all scattering, for only innocence and inexperience attract the preying youth of Zanzibar. "Now, gentlemen, my name is Coutlass—Georges Coutlass. Have a drink with me, and let me tell you something."

He was tall, dark skinned, athletic, and roguish-looking even for the brand of Greek one meets with south of the Levant—dressed in khaki, with an American cowboy hat—his fingers nearly black with cigarette juice—his hands unusually horny for that climate—and his hair clipped so short that it showed the bumps of avarice and other things, said to reside below the hat-band to the rear. Yet a plausible, companionable-seeming man. And Zanzibar confers democratic privilege, as well as fevers; impartiality hovers in the atmosphere as well as smells, and we neither of us dreamed of hesitating, but followed him back into the bar—a wide, low-ceilinged room whose beams were two feet thick of blackened, polished hard wood. There we sat one each side of him in cane armchairs. He ordered the drinks, and paid for them.

"First I will tell you who I am," he said, when be had swallowed a foot-long whisky peg and wiped his lips with his coat sleeve. "I never boast. I don't need to! I am Georges Coutlass! I learned that you have an English lord among your party, and said I to myself 'Aha! There is a man who will appreciate me, who am a citizen of three lands!' Which of you gentlemen is the lord?"

"How can you be a citizen of three countries?" Fred countered.

"Of Greece, for I was born in Greece. I have fought Turks. Ah! I have bled for Greece. I have spilt my blood in many lands, but the best was for my motherland!—Of England, for I became naturalized. By bloody-hell-and-Waterloo, but I admire the English! They have guts, those English, and I am one of them! By the great horn spoon, yes, I became an Englishman at Bow Street one Monday morning, price five pounds. I was lined up with the drunks and pick-pockets, and by Jumbo the magistrate mistook me for a thief! He would have given me six months without the option in another minute, but I had the good luck to remember how much money I had paid my witnesses. The thought of paying that for nothing—worse than nothing, for six months in jail!—in an English jail!—pick oakum!—eat skilly!—that thought brought me to my senses. 'By Gassharamminy,' I said, 'I may be mad, but I'm sober! If it's a crime to desire to be English, then punish me, but let me first commit the offense!' So he laughed, and didn't question my witnesses very carefully—one was a Jew, the other an ex-German, and either of them would swear to anything at half price for a quantity—and they kissed the Book and committed perjury—and lo and behold, I was English as you are—English without troubling a midwife or the parson! Five pounds for the 'beak' at Bow Street—fifty for the witnesses—fifty-five all told—and cheap at the price! I had money in those days. It was after our short war with Turkey. We Greeks got beaten, but the Turks did not get all the loot! By prison and gallows, no! When our men ran before a battle, I did not run—not I! I remained, and by Croesus I grew richer in an hour than I have ever been since!"

"That's two countries," said I. "Which is the third that has the honor to claim your allegiance?"

"Honor is right!" he answered with a proud smile. I, Georges Coutlass, have honored three flags! I am a credit to all three countries! The third is America—the U.S.A. You might say that is the corollary of being English—the natural, logical, correct sequence! The U.S. laws are strict, but their politics were devised for—what is it the preachers call it—ah, yes, for straining out gnats and swallowing camels. By George Washington they would swallow a house on fire! There was a federal election shortly due. One of the parties—Democratic—Republican—I forget which—maybe both!—needed new voters. The law says it takes five years to become a citizen. Politics said fifteen minutes! The politicians paid the fees too! I was a citizen—a voter—an elector of presidents before I had been ashore three months, and I had sold my vote three times over within a month of that! They had me registered under three names in three separate wards! I didn't need the money—I had plenty in those days—I gave the six dollars I received for my votes to the Holy Church, and voted the other way to save my conscience; but the fun of the thing appealed! By Gassharamminy! I can't take life the way the copy-books lay down! I have to break laws or else break heads! But I love America! I fought and bled for America! By Abraham Lincoln, I fought those Spaniards until I don't doubt they wished I had stayed in Greece! Yes, I left that middle finger in Cuba—shot through the left hand by a Don, think of it, a Don! When I came out of hospital—and I never saw anything worse than that hot hell!—I got myself attached to the commissariat, and the pickings were none so bad. Had to hand over too much, though. That is the worst of America, there is no genuine liberty. You have to steal for the man higher up. If you keep more than ten per cent., he squeals. He has to pass most of it on again to some one else, and so on, and they all land in jail in course of time! Give me a country where a man can keep what he finds! There was talk about congressional inquiries. Then a friend of mine—a Greek—who had been out here told me of Tippoo Tib's ivory, and it looked all right to me to change scenes for a while. I had citizenship papers—U. S., and English, and

"The songs of youth, and strength, and health, and time that's on the wing."

a Greek passport in case of accident. Traveling looked good to me."

"If you traveled on a Greek passport you couldn't use citizenship papers of any other country," Fred objected.

"Who said I traveled on a Greek passport? Do you take me for such a fool? Who listens to a Greek consul? He may protest, and accept fees, but Greece is a little country and no one listens to her consuls. I carry a Greek passport in case I should find somewhere someday a Greek consul with influence or a Greek whom I wish to convince. I traveled to South Africa as an American. I went to Cape Town with the idea of going to Salisbury, and working my way up from there as a trader into the Congo. I reached Johannesburg, and there I did a little I.D.B. and one thing and another until the Boer War came. Then I fought for the Boers. Yes, I have bled for the Boer cause. It was a damned bad cause! They robbed me of nearly all my money! They left me to die when I was wounded! It was only by the grace of God, and the intrigues of a woman that I made my way to Lourenço Marquez. No, the war was not over, but what did I care? I, Georges Coutlass, had had enough of it! I recompensed myself en route. I do not fight for a bunch of thieves for nothing! I sailed from Lourenço Marquez to Mombasa. I hunted elephant in British East Africa until they posted a reward for me on the telegraph poles. The law says not more than two elephants in one year. I shot two hundred! I sold the ivory to an Indian, bought cattle, and went down into German East Africa. The Masai attacked me, stole some of the cattle, and killed others. The Germans, damn and blast them, took the rest! They accused me of crimes—me, Georges Coutlass!—and imposed fines calculated carefully to skin me of all I had! Roup and rotten livers! but I will knock them head-over-hallelujah one fine day! Not for nothing shall they flim-flam Georges Coutlass! Which of you gentlemen is the lord?"

We bought him another drink, and watched it disappear with one uninterrupted gurgle down its appointed course.

"What did you do next?" Fred asked him before be had recovered breath enough to question us. "I suppose the Germans had you at a loose end?"

"Do you think that? Sacred history of hell! It takes more than a lousy military German to get Georges Coutlass at a loose end! They must get me dead before that can happen! And then, by Blitzen, as those devils say, a dead Georges Coutlass will be better than a thousand dead Germans! In hell I will use them to clean my boots on! At a loose end, was I? I met this bloody rogue Hassan—the fat blackguard who told me you have come to Zanzibar for fish—and made an agreement with him to look for Tippoo Tib's buried ivory. Yes, sir! I showed him papers. He thought they were money drafts. He thought me a man of means whom he could bleed. I had guns and ammunition, he none. He pretended to know where some of Tippoo Tib's ivory is buried."

"Some of it, eh?" said Fred.

"Some of it, d'you say?" said I.

"Some of it, yes. A million tusks. Some say two million! Some say three! Thunder!—you take a hundred good tusks and bury them; you'll see the hill you've made from five miles off! A hundred thousand tusks would make a mountain! If any one buried a million tusks in one spot they'd mark the place on maps as a watershed! They must be buried here, there, everywhere along the trail of Tippoo Tib—perhaps a thousand in one place at the most. Which of you two gentlemen is the lord?"

"Did Hassan lead you to any of it?" Fred inquired.

"Not he! The jelly-belly! The Arab pig! He led me to Ujiji—that's on Lake Tanganyika—the old slave market where he himself was once sold for ten cents. I don't doubt a piece of betel nut and a pair of worn-out shoes had to be thrown in with him at the price! There he tried to make me pay the expenses in advance of a trip to Usumbura at the head of the lake. God knows what it would have cost, the way he wanted me to do it! Are you the lord, sir?"

"What did you do?" asked Fred.

"Do? I parted company! I had made him drunk once. (The Arabs aren't supposed to drink, so when they do they get talkative and lively!) And I knew Arabic before ever I crossed the Atlantic—learned it in Egypt—ran away from a sponge-fishing boat when I was a boy. No, they don't fish sponges off the Nile Delta, but you can smuggle in a sponge boat better than in most ships. Anyhow, I learned Arabic. So I understood what that pig Hassan said when he talked in the dark with his brother swine. He knew no more than I where the ivory was! He *suspected* most of it was in a country called Rwanda that runs pretty much parallel with the Congo border to the west of Victoria Nyanza in German East Africa, and he was counting on finding natives who could tell him this and that that might put him on the trail of it! I could beat that game! I could cross-examine fool natives twice as well as any fat rascal of an ex-slave! Seeing he had paid all expenses so far, however, I was not much to the bad, so I picked a quarrel with him and we parted company. Wouldn't you have done the same, my lord?"

But Fred did not walk into the trap. "What did you do next?" he asked.

"Next? I got a job with the agent of an Italian firm to go north and buy skins. He made me a good advance of trade goods—*melikani,* beads, iron and brass wire, *kangas,* and all that sort of thing, and I did well. Made money on that trip. Traveled north until I reached Rwanda—went on until I could see the Fire Mountains in the distance, and the country all smothered in lava. Reached a cannibal country, where the devils had eaten all the surrounding tribes until they had to take to vegetarianism at last."

"But did you find the ivory?" Fred insisted.

"No, or by Jiminy, I wouldn't be here! If I'd found it I'd have settled down with a wife in Greece long ago. I'd be keeping an inn, and growing wine, and living like a gentleman! But I found out enough to know there's a system that goes with the ivory Tippoo Tib buried. If you found one lot, that would lead you to the next, and so on. I got a suspicion where one lot is, although I couldn't prove it. And I made up my mind that the German government knows darned well where a lot of it is!"

"Then why don't the Germans dig it up?" demanded Fred.

"Aha!" laughed Coutlass. "If I know, why should I tell! If they know, why should they tell? Suppose that some of it were in Congo territory, and some in British East Africa? Suppose they should want to get the lot? What then? If they uncovered their bit in German East Africa mightn't that put the Congo and the British on the trail?"

"If they know where it is," said I, "they'll certainly guard it."

"Which of you is the lord?" demanded Coutlass earnestly.

"What do you suppose Hassan is doing, then, here in Zanzibar?" asked Fred.

"Rum and eggs! I know what he is doing! When I snapped my thumb under his fat nose and told him about the habits of his female ancestors be went to the Germans and informed against me! The sneak-thief! The turn-coat! The maggot! I shall not forget! I, Georges Coutlass, forget nothing! He informed against me, and they set *askaris* on my trail who prevented me from making further search. I had to sit idle in Usumbura or Ujiji, or else come away; and idleness ill suits my blood! I came here, and Hassan followed me. The Germans made a regular, salaried spy of him—the semi-Arab rat! The one-tenth Arab, nine-tenths mud-rat! Here he stays in Zanzibar and spies on Tippoo Tib, on me, on the British government, and on every stranger who comes here. His information goes to the Germans. I know, for I intercepted some of it! He writes it out in Arabic, and provided no woman goes through the folds of his clothes or feels under that silken belly-piece be wears, the Germans get it. But if a woman does, and she's a friend of mine, that's different! Are you the lord, sir?"

"What do you propose?" asked Fred.

"Help me find that ivory!" said Coutlass. "I have very little money left, but I have guns, and courage! I know where to look, and I am not afraid! No German can scare me! I am English-American-Greek!—better than any hundred Germans! Let us find the ivory, and share it! Let us get it out through British territory, or the Congo, so that no German sausage can interfere with us or take away one tusk! Gee-rusalem, how I hate the swine. Let us put one over on them! Let us get the ivory to Europe, and then flaunt the deed under their noses! Let us send one little tip of a female tusk to the Kaiser for a souvenir—female in proof it is all illegitimate, illegal, outlawed! Let us send him a piece of ivory and a letter telling him all about it, and what we think of him and his swine-officials! His lieutenants and his captains! Let us smuggle the ivory out through the Congo—it can be done! It can be done! I, Georges Coutlass, will find the ivory, and find the way!"

"No need to smuggle it out," said Fred. "The British government will give us ten per cent., or so I understand, of the value of all of it we find in British East."

Georges Coutlass threw back his head and roared with laughter, slapped his thighs, held his sides—then coughed for two or three minutes, and spat blood.

"You are the lord, all right!" he gasped as soon as he could get breath. "No need to smuggle it! Ha-ha! May I be damned! Ten per cent. they'll give us! Ha-ha! Generous! By whip and wheel! they're lucky if we give them five per cent.! I'd like to see any government take away from Georges Coutlass ninety per cent. of anything without a fight! No, gentlemen! No, my Lord! The Belgian Congo government is corrupt. Let us spend twenty-five per cent.—even thirty-forty-fifty per cent. of the value of it to bribe the Congo officials. Hand over ninety per cent. to the Germans or the British without a fight?—Never! Never while my name is Georges Coutlass! I have fought too often! I have been robbed by governments too often! This last time I will put it over all the governments, and be rich at last, and go home to Greece to live like a gentleman! Believe me!"

He patted himself on the breast, and if flashing eye and frothing lip went for anything, then all the governments were as good as defeated already.

"You are the lord, are you not?" he demanded, looking straight at Fred.

"My name is Oakes," Fred answered.

"Oh, then you? I beg pardon!" He looked at me with surprise that he made no attempt to conceal. Fred could pass for a king with that pointed beard of his (provided he were behaving himself seemly at the time) but for all my staid demeanor I have never been mistaken for any kind of personage. I disillusioned Coutlass promptly.

"Then you are neither of you lords?"

"Pish! We're obviously ladies!" answered Fred.

"Then you have fooled me?" The Greek rose to his feet. "You have deceived me? You have accepted my hospitality and confidence under false pretense?"

I think there would have been a fight, for Fred was never the man to accept brow-beating from chance-met strangers, and the Greek's fiery eye was rolling in fine frenzy; but just at that moment Yerkes strolled in, cheerful and brisk.

"Hullo, fellers! This is some thirsty burg. Do they sell soft drinks in this joint?" he inquired.

"By Brooklyn Bridge!" exclaimed Coutlass. "An American! I, too, am an American! Fellow-citizen, these men have treated me badly! They have tricked me!"

"You must be dead easy!" said Yerkes genially. "If those two wanted to live at the con game, they'd have to practise on the junior kindergarten grades. They're the mildest men I know. I let that one with the beard hold my shirt and pants when I go swimming! Tricked you, have they? Say—have you got any money left?"

"Oh, have a drink!" laughed the Greek. "Have one on me! It's good to hear you talk!"

"What have my friends done to you?" asked Yerkes.

"I was looking for a lord. They pretended to be lords."

"What? Both of 'em?"

"No, it is one lord I am looking for."

"One lord, one faith, one baptism!" said Yerkes

profanely. "And you found two? What's your worry? I'll pretend to be a third if that'll help you any!"

"Gentlemen," said the Greek, rising to his full height and letting his rage begin to gather again, "you play with me. That is not well! You waste my time. That is not wise! I come in all innocence, looking for a certain lord—a real genuine lord—the Earl of Montdidier and Kirscrubbrightshaw—my God, what a name!"

"I'm Mundidier," said a level voice, and the Greek faced about like a man attacked. Monty had entered the barroom and stood listening with calm amusement, that for some strange reason exasperated the Greek less than our attitude had done, at least for the moment. When the first flush of surprise had died he grinned and grew gallant.

"My own name is Georges Coutlass, my Lord!" He made a sweeping bow, almost touching the floor with the brim of his cowboy hat, and then crossing his breast with it.

"What can I do for you?" asked Monty.

"Listen to me!"

"Very well. I can spare fifteen minutes."

We all took seats together in a far corner of the dingy room, where the Syrian barkeeper could not overhear us.

"My Lord, I am an Englishman!" Coutlass began. "I am a God-fearing, law-abiding gentleman! I know where to look for the ivory that the Arab villain Tippoo Tib has buried! I know how to smuggle it out of Africa without paying a penny of duty—"

"Did you say law-abiding?" Monty asked.

"Surely! Always! I never break the law! As for instance—in Greece, where I had the honor to be born, the law says no man shall carry a knife or wear one in his belt. So, since I was a little boy I carry none! I have none in my hand—none at my belt. I keep it here!"

He stooped, raised his right trousers leg, and drew from his Wellington boot a two-edged, pointed thing almost long enough to merit the name of rapier. He tossed it in the air, let it spin six or seven times end over end, caught it deftly by the point, and returned it to its hiding-place.

"I am a law-abiding man," he said, "but where the law leaves off, I know where to begin! I am no fool!"

Monty made up his mind there and then that this man's game would not be worth the candle.

"No, Mr. Coutlass, I can't oblige you," he said.

The Greek half-arose and then sat down again.

"You can not find it without my assistance!" he said, wrinkling his face for emphasis.

"I'm not looking for assistance," said Monty.

"Aha! You play with words! You are not—but you will! I am no fool, my Lord! I understand! Not for nothing did I make a friend again of that pig Hassan! Not for nothing have I waited all these months in this stinking Zanzibar until a man should come in search of that ivory whom I could trust! Not for nothing did Juma, the lazaretto attendant tell Hassan you desired to see him! You seek the ivory, but you wish to keep it all! To share none of it with me!" He stood up, and made another bow, much curter than his former one. "I am Georges Coutlass! My courage is known! No man can rob me and get away with it!"

"My good man," drawled Monty, raising his eyebrows in the comfortless way he has when there seems need of facing an inferior antagonist. (He hates to "lord it" as thoroughly as he loves to risk his neck.) "I would not rob you if you owned the earth! If you have valuable information I'll pay for it cheerfully after it's tested."

"Ah! Now you talk!"

"Observe—I said after it's tested!"

"I don't think he knows anything," said Fred. "I think he guessed a lot, and wants to look, and can't afford to pay his own expenses. Isn't that it?"

"What do you mean?" demanded Coutlass.

"I can't talk Greek," said Fred. "Shall I say it again in English?"

"You may name any reasonable price," said Monty, "for real information. Put it in writing. When we're agreed on the price, put that in writing too. Then, if we find the information is even approximately right, why, we'll pay for it."

"Ah-h-h! You intend to play a trick on me! You use my information! You find the ivory! You go out by the Congo River and the other coast, and I kiss myself good-bye to you and ivory and money! I am to be what d'you call it?—a milk-pigeon!"

"Being that must be *some* sensation!" nodded Yerkes.

"I warn you I can not be tampered with!" snarled the Greek, putting on his hat with a flourish. "I leave you, for you to think it over! But I tell you this—I promise you—I swear! Any expedition in search of that ivory that does not include Georges

Coutlass on his own terms is a delusion—a busted flush—smashed—exploded—pfff!—so—evanesced before the start! My address is Zanzibar! Every street child knows me! When you wish to know my terms, tell the first man or child you meet to lead you to the house where Georges Coutlass lives! Good morning, Lord Skirtsshubrish! We will no doubt meet again!"

He turned his back on us and strode from the room—a man out of the middle ages, soldierly of bearing, unquestionably bold, and not one bit more venial or lawless than ninety per cent. of history's gallants, if the truth were told.

"Let's hope that's the last of him!" said Monty. "Can't say I like him, but I'd hate to have to spoil his chances."

"Last of him be sugared!" said Yerkes. "That's only the first of him! He'll find seven devils worse than himself and camp on our trail, if I know anything of Greeks—that's to say, if our trail leads after that ivory. Does it?"

"Depends," said Monty. "Let's talk upstairs. That Syrian has long ears."

So we trooped to Monty's room, where the very cobwebs reeked of Arab history and lawless plans. He sat on the black iron bed, and we grouped ourselves about on chairs that had very likely covered the known world between them. One was obviously jetsam from a steamship; one was a Chinese thing, carved with staggering dragons; the other was made of iron-hard wood that Yerkes swore came from South America.

"Shoot when you're ready!" grinned Yerkes.

I was too excited to sit still. So was Fred.

"Get a move on, Didums, for God's sake!" he growled.

"Well," said Monty, "there seems something in this ivory business. Our chance ought to be as good as anybody's. But there are one or two stiff hurdles. In the first place, the story is common property. Every one knows it—Arabs—Swahili—Greeks—Germans—English. To be suspected of looking for it would spell failure, for the simple reason that every adventurer on the coast would trail us, and if we did find it we shouldn't be able to keep the secret for five minutes. If we found it anywhere except on British territory it 'ud be taken away from us before we'd time to turn round. And *it isn't buried on British territory!* I've found out that much."

"Good God, Didums! D'you mean you know where the stuff is?"

Fred sat forward like a man at a play.

"I know where it isn't," said Monty. "They told me at the Residency that in all human probability it's buried part in German East, and by far the greater part in the Congo."

"Then that ten per cent. offer by the British is a bluff?" asked Yerkes.

"Out of date," said Monty. "The other governments offer nothing. The German government might make terms with a German or a Greek—not with an Englishman. The Congo government is an unknown quantity, but would probably see reason if approached the proper way."

"The U.S. Consul tells me," said Yerkes, "that the Congo government is the rottenest aggregate of cutthroats, horse-thieves, thugs, yeggs, common-or-ordinary hold-ups, and sleight-of-hand professors that the world ever saw in one God-forsaken country. He says they're of every nationality, but without squeam of any kind—hang or shoot you as soon as look at you! He says if there's any ivory buried in those parts they've either got it and sold it, or else they buried it themselves and spread the story for a trap to fetch greenhorns over the border!"

"That man's after the stuff himself!" said Fred. "All he wanted to do was stall you off!"

"That man Schillingschen the doctor told us about," said Monty, "is suspected of knowing where to look for some of the Congo hoard. He'll bear watching. He's in British East Africa at present—said to be combing Nairobi and other places for a certain native. He is known to stand high in the favor of the German government, but poses as a professor of ethnology."

"He shall study *deathnology,*" said Fred, "if he gets in my way!"

"The Congo people," said Monty, "would have dug up the stuff, of course, if they'd known where to look for it. Our people believe that the Germans do know whereabouts to look for it, but dread putting the Congo crowd on the scent. If we're after it we've got to do two things besides agreeing between ourselves."

"Deal me in, Monty!" said Yerkes.

"Nil desperandum, Didums duce, then!" said Fred. "I propose Monty for leader. Those against the motion take their shirts off, and see if they can lick me! Nobody pugnacious? The ayes have it! Talk along, Didums!"

For all Fred's playfulness, Yerkes and I came in of our free and considered will, and Monty understood that.

"We've got to separate," he said, "and I've got to interview the King of Belgium."

"If that were my job," grinned Yerkes, "I'd prob'ly tell him things!"

"I don't pretend to like him," said Monty. "But it seems to me I can serve our best interests by going to Brussels. He can't very well refuse me a private audience. I should get a contract with the Congo government satisfactory to all concerned. He's rapacious—but I think not ninety per cent. rapacious."

"Good," said I, "but why separate?"

"If we traveled toward the Congo from this place in a bunch," said Monty, "we should give the game away completely and have all the rag-tag and bob-tail on our heels. As it is, our only chance of shaking all of them would be to go round by sea and enter the Congo from the other side; but that would destroy our chance of picking up the trail in German East Africa. So I'll go to Brussels, and get back to British East as fast as possible. Fred must go to British East and watch Schillingschen. You two fellows may as well go by way of British East Africa to Muanza on Victoria Nyanza, and on from there to the Congo border by way of Ujiji. Yerkes is an American, and they'll suspect him less than any of us (they'd nail me, of course, in a minute!) So let Yerkes make a great show of looking for land to settle on. We'll all four meet on the Congo border, at some other place to be decided later. We'll have to agree on a code, and keep in touch by telegraph as often as possible. Now, is all that clear?"

"We two'll have all the Greeks of Zanzibar trailing us all the way!" objected Yerkes.

"That'll be better than having them trail the lot of us," said Monty. "You'll be able to shake them somewhere on the way. We'll count on your ingenuity, Will."

"But what am I to do to Schillingschen?" asked Fred.

"Keep an eye on him."

"Do you see me Sherlock-Holmesing him across the high veldt? Piffle! Give America that job! I'll go through German East and keep ahead of the Greeks!"

But Monty was firm. "Yerkes has a plausible excuse, Fred. They may wonder why an American should look for land in German East Africa, but they'll let him do it, and perhaps not spy on him to any extent. It's me they've their eye on. I'll try to keep 'em dazzled. You go to British East and dazzle Schillingschen! Now, are we agreed?"

We were. But we talked, nevertheless, long into the afternoon, and in the end there was not one of us really satisfied. Over and over we tried to persuade Monty to omit the Brussels part of the plan. We wanted him with us. But he stuck to his point, and had his way, as he always did when we were quite sure he really wanted it.

THE NJO HAPA SONG

Gleam, oh brighter than jewels! gleam my
swinging stars in the opal dark,
Mirrored along wi' the fire-fly dance of longshore
light and off-shore mark,
The roof-lamps and the riding lights,and
phosphor wake of ship and shark.

I was old when the fires of Arab ships
(All seas were lawless then!)
Abode the tide where liners ride
To-day, and Malays then;—
Old when the bold da Gama came
With culverin and creed
To trade where Solomon's men fought,
And plunder where the banyans bought,
I sighed when the first o' the slaves were
brought,
And laughed when the last were freed.

Deep, oh deeper than anchors drop, the bones o'
the outbound sailors lie,
Far, oh farther than breath o' wind the rumors o'
fabled fortune fly,
And the 'venturers yearn from the ends of earth,
for none o' the isles is as fair as I!

II

THE ENORMOUS map of Africa loses no lure or mystery from the fact of nearness to the continent itself. Rather it increases. In the hot upper room that night, between the wreathing smoke of oil lamps, we pored over the large scale map Monty had saved from the wreck along with our money drafts and papers.

The atmosphere was one of bygone piracy. The great black ceiling beams, heavy-legged table of two-inch planks, floor laid like a dhow's deck—making utmost use of odd lengths of timber, but strong enough to stand up under hurricanes and overloads of plunder, or to batten down rebellious slaves—murmurings from rooms below, where men of every race that haunts those shark-infested seas were drinking and telling tales that would make Münchhausen's reputation—steaminess, outer darkness, spicy equatorial smells and, above all, knowledge of the nature of the coming quest united to veil the map in fascination.

No man gifted with imagination better than a hot-cross bun's could be in Zanzibar and not be conscious of the lure that made adventurers of men before the first tales were written. Old King Solomon's traders must have made it their headquarters, just as it was Sindbad the Sailor's rendezvous and that of pirates before he or Solomon were born or thought of. Vasco da Gama, stout Portuguese gentleman adventurer, conquered it, and no doubt looted the godowns to a lively tune. Wave after wave of Arabs sailed to it (as they do to-day) from that other land of mystery, Arabia; and there isn't a yard of coral beach, coconut-fringed shore, clove orchard, or vanilla patch—not a lemon tree nor a thousand-year-old baobab but could tell of battle and intrigue; not a creek where the dhows lie peacefully to-day but could whisper of cargoes run by night—black cargoes, groaning fretfully and smelling of the 'tween-deck lawlessness.

"There are two things that have stuck in my memory that Lord Salisbury used to say when I was an Eton boy, spending a holiday at Hatfield House," said Monty. "One was, Never talk fight unless you mean fight; then fight, don't talk. The other was, Always study the largest maps."

"Who's talking fight?" demanded Fred.

Monty ignored him. "Even this map isn't big enough to give a real idea of distances, but it helps. You see, there's no railway beyond Victoria Nyanza. Anything at all might happen in those great spaces beyond Uganda. Borderlands are quarrel-grounds. I should say the junction of British, Belgian, and German territory where Arab loot lies buried is the last place to dally in unarmed. You fellows 'ud better scour Zanzibar in the morning for the best guns to be had here."

So I went to bed at midnight with that added stuff for building dreams. He who has bought guns remembers with a thrill; he who has not, has in store for him the most delightful hours of life. May he fall, as our lot was, on a gunsmith who has mended hammerlocks for Arabs, and who loves rifles as some greater rascals love a woman or a horse.

We all four strolled next morning, clad in the khaki reach-me-downs that a Goanese "universal provider" told us were the "latest thing," into a den between a camel stable and an even mustier-smelling home of gloom, where oxen tied nose-to-tail went round and round, grinding out semsem everlastingly while a lean Swahili sang to them. When he ceased, they stopped. When he sang, they all began again.

In a bottle-shaped room at the end of a passage squeezed between those two centers of commerce sat the owner of the gun-store, part Arab, part Italian, part Englishman, apparently older than sin itself, toothless, except for one yellow fang that lay like an ornament over his lower lip, and able to smile more winningly than any siren of the sidewalk. Evidently he shaved at intervals, for white stubble stood out a third of an inch all over his wrinkled face. The upper part of his head was utterly bald, slippery, shiny, smooth, and adorned by an absurd, round Indian cap, too small, that would not stay in place and had to be hitched at intervals.

He said his name was Captain Thomas Cook, and the license to sell firearms framed on the mud-brick wall bore him witness. (May he live forever under any name he chooses!)

"Goons?" he said. "Goons? You gentlemen want goons? I have the goon what settled the hash of Sayed bin Mohammed—here it be. This other one's the rifle—see the nicks on her butt!—that Kamarajes the Greek used. See 'em—Arab goons—slaver goons—smooth-bore elephant goons—fours, eights, twelves—Martinis—them's the lot that was reekin' red-hot, days on end, in the last Arab war on the Congo, considerable used up but goin' cheap;—then here's Mausers (he pronounced it "Morsers")—old-style, same as used in 1870—good goons they be, long o' barrel and strong, but too high trajectory for some folks;—some's new style, magazines an' all—fine till a grain o' sand jams 'em oop;—an' Lee-Enfields, souvenirs o' the Boer War, some o' them bought from folks what plundered a battle-field or two—mostly all in good condition. Look at this one—see it—hold it—take a squint along it! Nineteen elephants shot wi' that Lee-Enfield, an' the man's in jail for shootin' of 'em! Sold at auction by the gov'ment, that one was. See, here's an Express—a beauty—owned by an officer fr'm Indy—took by a shark 'e was, in swimmin' against all advice, him what had hunted tigers! There's no goon store a quarter as good as mine 'tween Cairo an' the Cape or Bombay an' Boma! Captain Cook's the boy to sell ye goons all right! Sit down. Look 'em over. Ask anything ye want to know. I'll tell ye. No obligation to buy."

There is no need to fit out with guns and tents in London. Until both good and bad, both cowardly and brave give up the habit of dying in bed, or getting killed, or going broke, or ending up in jail for one cause and the other, there will surely always be fine pickings for men on the spot with a little money and a lot of patience—guns, tents, cooking pots, and all the other things.

We spent a morning with Captain Thomas Cook, and left the store—Fred, Yerkes and I—with a battery of weapons, including a pistol apiece—that any expedition might be proud of. (Monty, since he had to go home in any case, preferred to look over the family gun-room before committing himself.)

Then, since the first leg of the journey would be the same for all of us we bought other kit, packed it, and booked passages for British East Africa. Between then and the next afternoon when the British India steamboat sailed we were fairly bombarded by inquisitiveness, but contrived not to tell much. And with patience beyond belief Monty restrained us from paying court to Tippoo Tib.

"The U.S. Consul says he's better worth a visit than most of the world's museums," Yerkes assured us two or three times. "He says Tippoo Tib's a fine old sport—damned rogue—slave-hunter, but white somewhere near the middle. What's the harm in our having a chin with him?"

But Monty was adamant.

"A call on him would prove nothing, but he and his friends would suspect. Spies would inform the German government. No. Let's act as if Tippoo Tib were out of mind."

We grumbled, but we yielded. Hassan came again, shiny with sweat and voluble with offers of information and assistance.

"Where you gentlemen going?" he kept asking.

"England," said Monty, and showed his own steamer ticket in proof of it. That settled Hassan for the time but Georges Coutlass was not so easy. He came swaggering upstairs and thumped on Monty's door with the air of a bearer of king's messages.

"What do you intend to do?" he asked. (We were all sitting on Monty's bed, and it was Yerkes who opened the door.)

"Do you an injury," said Yerkes, "unless you take your foot away!" The Greek had placed it deftly to keep the door open pending his convenience.

"Let him have his say" advised Monty from the bed.

"Where are you going? Hassan told me England. Are you all going to England? If so, why have you bought guns? What will you do with six rifles, three shot-guns, and three pistols on the London streets? What will you do with tents in London? Will you make campfires in Regent Circus, that you take with you all those cooking pots? And all that rice, is that for the English to eat? Bah! No tenderfoot can fool me! You go to find *my* ivory, d'you hear! You think to get away with it unknown to me! I tell you I have sharp ears! By Jingo; there is nothing I can not find out that goes on in Africa! You think to cheat me? Then you are as good as dead men! You shall die like dogs! I will smithereen the whole damned lot of you before you touch a tusk!"

"Get out of here!" growled Yerkes.

"Give him a chance to go quietly, Will," urged Monty, and Coutlass heard him. Peaceful advice seemed the last spark needed to explode his crowded magazines of fury. He clenched his fists—spat because the words would not flow fast enough—and screamed.

"Give me a chance, eh? A chance, eh?" Other doors began opening, and the appearance of an audience stimulated him to further peaks of rage. "The only chance I need is a sight of your carcasses within range, and a long range will do for Georges Coutlass!" He glared past Yerkes at Monty who had risen leisurely. "You call yourself a lord? I call you a thief! A jackal!"

"Here, get out!" growled Yerkes, self-constituted Cerberus.

"I will go when I damned please, you Yankee jackanapes!" the Greek retorted through set teeth.

Yerkes is a free man, able and willing to shoulder his own end of any argument. He closed, and the Greek's ribs cracked under a vastly stronger hug than he had dreamed of expecting. But Coutlass was no weakling either, and though he gasped he gathered himself for a terrific effort.

"Come on!" said Monty, and went past me through the door like a bolt from a catapult. Fred followed me, and when he saw us both out on the landing Monty started down the stairs.

"Come on!" he called again.

We followed, for there is no use in choosing a leader if you don't intend to obey him, even on occasions when you fail at once to understand. There was one turn on the wide stairs, and Monty stood there, back to the wall.

"Go below, you fellows, and catch!" he laughed. "We don't want Will jailed for homicide!"

The struggle was fierce and swift. Coutlass searched with a thumb for Will's eye, and stamped on his instep with an iron-shod heel. But he was a dissolute brute, and for all his strength Yerkes' cleaner living very soon told. Presently Will spared a hand to wrench at the ambitious thumb, and Coutlass screamed with agony. Then he began to sway this way and that without volition of his own, yielding his balance, and losing it again and again. In another minute Yerkes had him off his feet, cursing and kicking.

"Steady, Will!" called Monty from below; but it was altogether too late for advice. Will gathered himself like a spring, and hurled the Greek downstairs backward.

Then the point of Monty's strategy appeared. He caught him, saved him from being stunned against the wall, and, before the Greek could recover sufficiently to use heels and teeth or whisk out the knife he kept groping for, hurled him a stage farther on his journey—face forward this time down to where Fred and I were waiting. We kicked him out into the street too dazed to do anything but wander home.

"Are you hurt, Will?" laughed Monty. "This isn't the States, you know; by gad, they'll jail you here if you do your own police work! Instead of Brussels I'd have had to stay and hire lawyers to defend you!"

"Aw—quit preaching!" Yerkes answered. "If I hadn't seen you there on the stairs with your mouth open I'd have been satisfied to put him down and spank him!"

It was then that the much more unexpected struck us speechless—even Monty for the moment, who is not much given to social indecision. We had not known there was a woman guest in that hotel. One does not look in Zanzibar for ladies with a Mayfair accent unaccompanied by menfolk able to protect them. Yet an indubitable Englishwoman, expensively if carelessly dressed, came to the head of the stairs and stood beside Yerkes looking down at the rest of us with a sort of well bred, rather tolerant scorn.

"Am I right in believing this is Lord Montdidier?" she asked, pronouncing the word as it should be—Mundidger.

She had been very beautiful. She still was handsome in a hard-lipped, bold way, with abundant raven hair and a complexion that would have been no worse for a touch of rouge. She seemed to scorn all the conventional refinements, though. Her lacy white dress, open at the neck, was creased and not too clean, but she wore in her bosom one great jewel like a ruby, set in brilliants, that gave the lie to poverty provided the gems were real. And the amber tube through which she smoked a cigarette was seven or eight inches long and had diamonds set in a gold band round its middle. She wore no wedding ring that I could see; and she took no more notice of Will Yerkes beside her than if he had been a part of the furniture.

"Why do you ask?" asked Monty, starting upstairs. She had to make way for him, for Will Yerkes stood his ground.

"A fair question!" she laughed. Her voice had a hard ring, but was very well trained and under absolute control. I received the impression that she had been a singer at some time. "I am Lady Saffren Waldon—Isobel Saffren Waldon."

Fred and I had followed Monty up and were close behind him. I heard him mutter, "Oh, lord!" under his breath.

"I knew your brother," she added.

"I know you did."

"You think that gives me no claim on your acquaintance? Perhaps it doesn't. But as an unprotected woman—"

"There is the Residency," objected Monty, "and the law."

She laughed bitterly. "Thank you, I am in need of no passage home! I overheard that ruffian say, and I think I heard you say too that you are going to England. I want you to take a message for me."

There is a post-office here" said Monty without turning a hair. He looked straight into her iron eyes. "There is a cable station. I will lend you money to cable with."

"Thank you, my Lord!" she sneered. "I have money. I am so used to being snubbed that my skin would not feel a whip! I want you to take a verbal message!"

It was perfectly evident that Monty would rather have met the devil in person than this untidy dame; yet he was only afraid apparently of conceding her too much claim on his attention. (If she had asked favors of me I don't doubt I would have scrambled to be useful. I began mentally taking her part, wondering why Monty should treat her so cavalierly; and I fancy Yerkes did the same.)

"Tell me the message, and I'll tell you whether I'll take it," said Monty.

She laughed again, even more bitterly.

"If I could tell it on these stairs," she answered, "I could cable it. They censor cablegrams, and open letters in this place."

"I suspect that isn't true," said Monty. "But if you object to witnesses, how do you propose to deliver your message to me?" he asked pointedly.

"You mean you refuse to speak with me alone?"

"My friends would draw out of earshot," he answered.

"Your friends? Your gang, you mean!" She drew herself up very finely—very stately. Very lovely she was to look at in that half-light, with the shadows of Tippoo Tib's old stairway hiding her tale of years. But I felt my regard for her slipping downhill (and so, I rather think did Yerkes). "You look well, Lord Montdidier, traipsing about the earth with a leash of mongrels at your heel! Falstaff never picked up a more sordid-looking pack! What do you feed them—bones? Are there no young bloods left of your own class, that you need travel with tradesmen?"

Monty stood with both hands behind him and never turned a hair. Fred Oakes brushed up the ends of that troubadour mustache of his and struck more or less of an attitude. Will reddened to the ears, and I never felt more uncomfortable in all my life.

"So this is *your* gang, is it?" she went on. "It looks sober at present! I suppose I must trust you to control them! I dare say even tavern brawlers respect you sufficiently to keep a lady's secret if you order them. I will hope they have manhood enough to hold their tongues!"

Of course, dressed in the best that Zanzibar stores had to offer we scarcely looked like fashion plates. My shirt was torn where Coutlass had seized it to resist being thrown out, but I failed to see what she hoped to gain by that tongue lashing, even supposing we had been the lackeys she pretended to believe we were.

"The message is to my brother," she went on.

"I don't know him!" put in Monty promptly.

"You mean you don't like him! Your brother had him expelled from two or three clubs, and you prefer not to meet him! Nevertheless, I give you this message to take to him! Please tell him—you will find him at his old address—that I, his sister, Lady Saffren Waldon, know now the secret of Tippoo Tib's ivory. He is to join me here at once, and we will get it, and sell it, and have money, and revenge! Will you tell him that!"

"No!" answered Monty.

I looked at Yerkes, Yerkes looked at Fred, and Fred at me.

There was nothing to do but feel astonished.

"Why not, if you please?"

"I prefer not to meet Captain McCauley," said Monty.

"Then you will give the message to somebody else?" she insisted.

"No" said Monty. "I will carry no message for you."

"Why do you say that? How dare you say that? In front of your following—your gang!"

I should have been inclined to continue the argument myself—to try to find out what she did know, and to uncover her game. It was obvious she must have some reason for her extraordinary request, and her more extraordinary way of making it. But Monty saw fit to stride past her through his open bedroom door, and shut it behind him firmly. We stood looking at her and at one another stupidly until she turned her back and went to her own room on the floor above. Then we followed Monty.

"Did she say anything else?" he asked as soon as we were inside. I noticed he was sweating pretty freely now.

"Didums, you're too polite!" Fred answered. "You ought to have told her to keep her tongue housed or be civil!"

"I don't hold with hitting back at a lone woman,"

said Yerkes, "but what was she driving at? What did she mean by calling us a pack of mongrels?"

"Merely her way," said Monty offhandedly. "Those particular McCauleys never amounted to much. She married a baronet, and he divorced her. Bad scandal. Saffren Waldon was at the War Office. She stole papers, or something of that sort—delivered them to a German paramour—von Duvitz was his name, I think. She and her brother were lucky to keep out of jail. Ever since then she has been—some say a spy, some say one thing, some another. My brother fell foul of her, and lived to regret it. She's on her last legs I don't doubt, or she wouldn't be in Zanzibar."

"Then why the obvious nervous sweat you're in?" demanded Fred.

"And that doesn't account for the abuse she handed out to us," said Yerkes.

"Why not tip off the authorities that she's a notorious spy?" I asked.

"I suspect they know all about her," he answered.

"But why your alarm?" insisted Fred.

"I'm scarcely alarmed, old thing. But it's pretty obvious, isn't it, that she wants us to believe she knows what we're after. She's vindictive. She imagines she owes me a grudge on my brother's account. It might soothe her to think she had made me nervous. And by gad—it sounds like lunacy, and mind you I'm not propounding it for fact!—there's just one chance that she really does know where the ivory is!"

"But where's the sense of abusing us?" repeated Yerkes.

"That's the poor thing's way of claiming class superiority," said Monty. "She was born into one class, married into another, and divorced into a third. She'd likely to forget she said an unkind word the next time she meets you. Give her one chance and she'll pretend she believes you were born to the purple—flatter you until you half believe it yourself. Later on, when it suits her at the moment, she'll denounce you as a social imposter! It's just habit—bad habit, I admit—comes of the life she leads. Lots of 'em like her. Few of 'em quite so well informed, though, and dangerous if you give 'em a chance."

"I still don't see why you're sweating," said Fred.

"It's hot. There's a chance she knows where the ivory is! She has money, but how? She'd have begged if she were short of cash! It's my impression she has been in German government employ for a number of years. Possibly they have paid her to do some spy-work—in the Zanzibar court, perhaps—the Sultan's a mere boy—"

"Isn't he wooly-headed?" objected Yerkes.

"Mainly Arab. It's a French game to send a white woman to intrigue at colored courts, but the Germans are good imitators."

"Isn't she English?" asked Yerkes.

"Her trade's international," said Monty dryly. "My guess is that Coutlass or Hassan told her what we're supposed to be doing here, and she pretends to know where the ivory is in order to trap us all in some way. The net's spread for me, but there's no objection to catching you fellows as well."

"She'll need to use sweeter bait than I've seen yet!" laughed Yerkes.

"She'll probably be sweetness itself next time she sees you. She'll argue she's created an impression and can afford to be gracious."

"Impression is good!" said Yerkes. "I mean it's bad! She has created one, all right! What's the likelihood of her having double-crossed the Germans? Mightn't she have got a clue to where the stuff is, and be holding for a better market than they offer?"

"I was coming to that," said Monty. "Yes, it's possible. But whatever her game is, don't let us play it for her. Let her do the leading. If she gets hold of you fellows, one at a time or all together, for the love of heaven tell her nothing! Let her tell all she likes, but admit nothing—tell nothing—ask no questions! That's an old rule in diplomacy (and remember, she's a diplomat, whatever else she may be!) Old-stagers can divine the Young ones' secrets from the nature of the questions they ask! So if you got the chance, ask her nothing! Don't lie, either! It would take a very old hand to lie to her in such way that she couldn't see through it!"

"Why not be simply rude and turn our backs?" said I.

"Best of all—provided you can do it! Remember, she's a old hand!"

"D'you mean," said Yerkes, "that if she were to offer proof that she knows where that ivory is, and proposed terms, you wouldn't talk it over?"

"I mean let her alone!" said Monty.

But it turned out she would not be let alone. We dine in the public room, but she had her meals sent up to her and we flattered ourselves (or I did) that her net had been laid in vain. Folk dine late in the tropics, and we dallied over coffee and cigars, so that it was going on for ten o'clock when Yerkes and I started upstairs again. Monty and Fred went out to see the waterfront by moonlight.

We had reached our door (he and I shared one great room) when we heard terrific screams from the floor above—a woman's—one after another, piercing, fearful, hair-raising, and so suggestive in that gloomy, grim building that a man's very blood stood still.

Yerkes was the first upstairs. He went like an arrow from a bow, and I after him. The screams had stopped before we reached the stairhead, but there was no doubting which her room was; the door was partly open, permitting a view of armchairs and feminine garments in some disorder. We heard a man talking loud quick Arabic, and a woman—pleading, I thought. Yerkes rapped on the door.

"Come in!" said a voice, and I followed Yerkes in.

We were met by her Syrian maid, a creature with gazelle eyes and timid manner, who came through the doorway leading to an inner room.

"What's the trouble?" demanded Yerkes, and the woman signed to us to go on in. Yerkes led the way again impulsively as any knight-errant rescuing beleaguered dames, but I looked back and saw that the Syrian woman had locked the outer door. Before I could tell Will that, he was in the next room, so I followed, and, like him, stood rather bewildered.

Lady Saffren Waldon sat facing us, rather triumphant, in no apparent trouble, not alone. There were four very well-dressed Arabs standing to one side. She sat in a basket chair by a door that pretty obviously led into her bedroom; and kept one foot on a pillow, although I suspected there was not much the matter with it.

"We heard screams. Thought you were being murdered!" said Yerkes, out of breath.

"Oh, indeed, no! Nothing of the kind! I fell and twisted my ankle—very painful, but not serious. Since you are here, sit down, won't you?"

"No, thanks," said he, turning to go.

"The maid locked the door on us!" said I, and before the words were out of my mouth three of the Arabs slipped into the outer room. There was no hint or display of weapons of any kind, but they were big men, and the folds of their garments were sufficiently voluminous to have hidden a dozen guns apiece.

"She'll open it!" said Will, with inflection that a fool could understand.

"One minute, please!" said Lady Saffren Waldon. (It was no poor imitation of Queen Elizabeth ordering courtiers about.)

"We didn't come to talk," said Will. "Heard screams. Made a mistake. Sorry. We're off!"

"No mistake!" she said; and the sweetness Monty prophesied began to show itself. The change in her voice was too swift and pronounced to be convincing. "I did scream. I was, in pain. It was kind of you to come. Since you are here I would like you to talk to this gentleman."

She glanced at the Arab, an able-looking man, with nose and eyes expressive of keen thought, and the groomed gray beard that makes an Arab always dignified.

"Some other time," said Will. "I've an engagement!" And he turned to go again.

"No—now!" she said. "It's no use—you can't get out! You may as well be sensible and listen!"

We glanced at each other and both remembered Monty's warning. Will laughed.

"Take seats," she said, with a very regal gesture. She was not carelessly dressed, as she had been earlier in the day. From hair to silken hose and white kid shoes she was immaculate, and she wore rouge and powder now. In that yellow lamplight (carefully placed, no doubt) she was certainly good-looking. In fact, she was good-looking at any time, and only no longer able to face daylight with the tale of youth. Her eyes were weapons, nothing less. We remained standing.

"This gentleman will speak to you," she said, motioning to the Arab to commence, and he bowed—from the shoulders upward.

"I am from His Highness the Sultan of Zanzibar" he announced, a little pompously. "A minister from His Highness." (In announcing their own importance Arabs very seldom err in the direction of under-estimate.) "I speak about the ivory, which I am informed you propose to set out on a journey to discover."

"Where did you get your information?" Yerkes countered.

"Don't be absurd!" ordered Lady Saffren Waldon. "I gave it to him! Where else need he go to get it?"

"Where did you get it, then?" he retorted.

"Never mind! Listen to what Hamed Ibrahim has to say!"

The Arab bowed his bead slightly a second time.

"The ivory you seek," he said, "is said to be Tippoo Tib's own, and he will not tell the hiding-places. It does not belong to him. Such little part of it as ever was his was long ago swallowed by the interest on claims against him. The whole is now in truth the property of His Highness the Sultan of Zanzibar, and whoever discovers it shall receive reward from the owner. His Highness is willing, through me his minister, to make treaty in advance in writing with suitable parties intending to make search."

"You mean the Sultan wants to hire me to hunt for ivory for him?" Will asked, and the Arab made a gesture of impatience. At that Lady Saffren Waldon cut in, very vinegary once more.

"You two men are prisoners! Show much more sense! Come to terms or take the consequences! Listen! Tippoo Tib buried the ivory. The Sultan of Zanzibar claims it. The German government, for reasons of its own, backs the Sultan's claim; ivory found in German East Africa will be handed over to him in support of his claim to all the rest of it. If you—Lord Montdidier and the rest of you—care to sign an agreement with the Sultan of Zanzibar you can have facilities. You shall be supplied with guides who can lead you to the right place to start your search from—"

"Thought you wanted Lord Montdidier to say in London that you know where it all is," Will objected.

She colored slightly, and glared.

"Perhaps I am one of the guides," she said darkly. "I know more than I need tell for the sake of this argument! The point is, you can have facilities if you sign an agreement with the Sultan. Otherwise, you will be dogged wherever you go! Whatever you should find would be claimed! Every difficulty will be made for you—every treachery conceivable practiced on you. Lord Montdidier can get influential backing, but not influence among the natives! He can not get good men and true information by pulling wires in London. The British government once offered ten per cent. of the value of the ivory found. The Sultan of Zanzibar offers twenty per cent—"

"Twenty-five per cent," corrected Hamed Ibrahim.

"Yes, but I should want five per cent. for my commission!"

"This sounds like a different yarn to the one you told on the stairs this afternoon," said Will. "See Monty and tell it to him."

"It is for you to tell Lord Montdidier. He runs away from me!"

"I refuse to tell him a word!" said Will, with a laugh like that of a boy about to plunge into a swimming pool—sort of "Here goes!"

"You are extremely ill advised!"

"Do your worst! Monty'll be hunting for us two in about a minute. We're prisoners, are we? Suit yourself!"

"You are prisoners while I choose! You could be killed in this room, removed in sacks, thrown to the sharks in the roadstead, and nobody the wiser! But I have no intention of killing you. As it happens, that would not suit my purpose!"

We both glanced behind us involuntarily. It may be that we both heard a footstep, but it is always difficult to say certainly after the event. At any rate, while in the act of turning our heads, two of the three Arabs, who had previously left the room, threw nooses over them and bound our arms to our sides with the jiffy-swiftness only sailors know. The third man put the finishing touches, and presently adjusted gags with a neatness and solicitude worthy of the Inquisition.

"Throw them!" she ordered, and in a second our heels were struck from under us and I was half stunned by the impact of my head against the solid floor (for all the floors of that great place were built to resist eternity).

"Now!" she said. "Show them knives!"

We were shown forthwith the ugliest, most suggestive weapons I have ever seen—long sliver-thin blades sharper than razors. The Arabs knelt on our chests (their knees were harder and more merciless than wooden clubs) and laid the blades, edge-upward, on the skin of our throats.

"Let them feel!" she ordered.

I felt a sharp cut, and the warm blood trickled down over my jugular to the floor. I knew it was only a skin-cut, but did not pretend to myself I was enjoying the ordeal.

"Now!" she said.

The Arabs stepped away and she came and stood between us, looking down at one and then the other.

"There isn't a place in Africa," she said, "that you can hide in where the Sultan's men can't find you!

There isn't a British officer in Africa who would believe you if you told what has happened in this room tonight! Yet Lord Montdidier will believe you—he knows you presumably, and certainly he knows me! So tell Lord Montdidier exactly what has happened! Assure him with my compliments that his throat and yours shall be cut as surely as you dare set out after that ivory without signing my agreement first. Tell Lord Montdidier he may be friends with me if he cares to. As his friend I will help make him rich for life! As his enemy, I will make Africa too hot and dangerous to hold him! Let him choose!"

She stepped back and, without troubling to turn away, put powder on her nose and chin.

"Now let them up!" she said.

The Arabs lifted us to our feet.

"Loose them!"

The expert of the three slipped the knots like a wizard doing parlor tricks; but I noticed that the other two held their knives extremely cautiously. We should have been dead men if we had made a pugnacious motion.

"Now you may go! Unless Lord Montdidier agrees with me, the only safety for any of you is away from Africa! Go and tell him! Go!"

"I'll give you your answer now!" said Will.

"No, you don't!" said I, remembering Monty's urgent admonition to tell her nothing and ask no questions. "Come away, Will! There's nothing to be gained by talking back!"

"Right you are!" he said, laughing like a boy again—this time like a boy whose fight has been broken off without his seeking or consent. Like me, he pulled out a handkerchief and wiped blood from his neck. The sight of his own blood—even such a little trickle as that—has peculiar effect an a man.

"By Jiminy, she has scratched the wrong dog's ear!" he growled to me as we went to the door together.

"They're all in there!" I said excitedly, when the door slammed shut behind us. "Hurry down and get me a gun! I'll hold the door while you run for police and have 'em arrested!"

"Piffle!" he said. "Come on! Three Sultan's witnesses and two lone white women against us two—come away! Come away!"

Monty and Fred were still out, so we went to our own room.

"I'm wondering," I said, "what Monty will say."

"I'm not!" said Will. "I'm not troubling, either! I'm not going to tell Monty a blessed word! See here—she thinks she knows where some o' that ivory is. Maybe the government of German East Africa is in on the deal, and maybe not; that makes no present difference. She thinks she's wise. And she has fixed up with the Sultan to have him claim it when found, so's she'll get a fat slice of the melon. There's a scheme on to get the stuff, when who should come on the scene but our little party, and that makes 'em all nervous, 'cause Monty's a bad man to be up against. Remember: she claimed that she knows Monty and he knows her. She means by that that he knows she's a desperado, and she thinks he'll draw the line at a trip that promises murder and blackmail and such like dirty work. So she puts a scare into us with a view to our throwing a scare into him. If I scare any one, it's going to be that dame herself. I'll not tell Monty a thing!"

"How about Coutlass the Greek?" said I. "D'you suppose he's her accomplice?"

"Maybe! One of her dupes perhaps! I suspect she'll suck him dry of information and cast him off like a lemon rind. I dare bet she's using him. She can't use me! Shall you tell Monty?"

"No," I said. "Not unless we both agreed."

He nodded. "You and I weren't born to what they call the purple. We're no diplomatists; but we get each other's meaning."

"Here come Monty and Fred," said I. "Is my neck still bloody? No, yours doesn't show."

We met them at the stairhead, and Monty did not seem to notice anything.

"Fred has composed a song to the moonlight on Zanzibar roadstead while you fellows were merely after-dinner mundane. D'you suppose the landlord 'ud make trouble if we let him sing it?"

"Let's hope so!" said Will. "I'm itching for a row like they say drovers in Monty's country itch for mile-stones! Let Fred warble. I'll fight whoever comes!"

Monty eyed him and me swiftly, but made no comment.

"Bill's homesick!" said Fred. "The U.S. eagle wants its Bowery! We'll soothe the fowl with thoughts of other things—where's the concertina?"

"No, no, Fred, that'll be too much din!"

Monty made a grab for the instrument, but Fred raised it above his head and brought it down between his knees with chords that crashed like wedding bells. Then he changed to softer, languorous music, and when he had picked out an air to suit his mood, sat down and turned art loose to do her worst.

He has a good voice. If he would only not pull such faces, or make so sure that folk within a dozen blocks can hear him, he might pass for a professional.

"Music suggestive of moonlight!" he said, and began:

"The sentry palms stand motionless. Masts move against the sky.
With measured creak of curving spars dhows gently to the jeweled stars
Rock out a lullaby.

"Silver and black sleeps Zanzibar. The moonlit ripples croon
Soft songs of loves that perfect are, long tales of red-lipped spoils of war,
And you—you smile, you moon!
For I think that beam on the placid sea
That splashes, and spreads, and dips, and gleams,
That dances and glides till it comes to me
Out of infinite sky, is the path of dreams,
And down that lane the memories run
Of all that's wild beneath the sun!"

"You fellows like that one? Anybody coming? Nobody for Will to fight yet? Too bad! Well—we'll try a-gain! There's no chorus. It's all poetic stuff, too gentle to be yowled by three such cannibals as you! Listen!

"Old as the moonlit silences, to-night's loves are the same
As when for ivory from far, and cloves and gems of Zanzibar
King Solomon's men came.

"Sinful and still the same roofs lie that knew da Gama's heel,
Those beams that light these sleepy waves looked on when men threw murdered slaves
To make the sharks a meal.
And I think that beam on the silvered swell
That spreads, and splashes, and gleams, and dips,
That has shone on the cruel and brave as well,
On the trail o' the slaves and the ivory ships,
Is the lane down which the memories run
Of all that's wild beneath the sun."

The concertina wailed into a sort of minor dirge and ceased. Fred fastened the catch, and put the instrument away.

"Why don't you applaud?" he asked.

"Oh, bravo, bravo!" said Will and I together.

Monty looked hard at both of us.

"Strange!" he remarked. "You're both distracted, and you've each got a slight cut over the jugular!"

"Been trying out razors," said Yerkes.

"Um-m-m!" remarked Monty. "Well—I'm glad it's no worse. How about bed, eh? Better lock your door—that lady upstairs is what the Germans call *gefaehrlich!* Goo'night!"

THE NJO HAPA SONG

Tongues! Oh, music of eastern tongues, harmonied murmur of streets ahum!
Trade! Oh, frasila weights of clove—ivory—copra—copal gum—
Rubber—vanilla and tortoise-shell! The methods change.
The captains come.

I was old when the clamor o' Babel's end
(All seas were chartless then!)
Drove forth the brood, and Solitude
Was the newest quest of men.
I lay like a gem in a silken sea
Unseen, uncoveted, unguessed
Till scented winds that waft afar
Bore word o' the warm delights there are
Where ground-swells sing by Zanzibar
Long rhapsodies of rest.

Wild, oh wilder than winter blasts my wet skies shriek when the winds are freed.
Mild, oh milder than virgin mirth is the laugh o' the reefs where sea-birds feed,
Screaming and skirling and down again.
(Though the sea-birds warn do captains heed?)

III

THERE IS no public landing wharf at Zanzibar. Passengers have to submit their persons into the arms of loud-lunged Swahili longshoremen, who recognize one sole and only point of honor: neither passenger nor luggage shall be dropped into the surf.

Their invariable habit, the instant the view halloa is raised, is to scamper headlong, pounce on the victim and pull him apart (or so it feels) until fortune, superior strength, or some such element decides the point; and then more often than not it is the victim's fate to be carried between two men, each hold of a thigh, each determined to get ashore or to the boat first, and each grimly resolved not to let go until three times the proper fee shall have been paid. Of only these two things let the passenger assure himself—fight how he may, he will neither escape their clutches nor get wet. Rather they will hold him upside-down until the contents of his pockets fall into the surf. Dry on the beach or into the boat they will dump him. And whatever he shall pay them will surely be insufficient.

But we had a privy councilor of England of our party, and favors were shown us that never fall to the lot of ordinary travelers. Opposite the Sultan's palace is the Sultan's private wharf, so royal and private that it is a prison offense to trespass on it without written permission. Because of his official call at the Residency, and of his card left on the Sultan, wires had been pulled, and a pompous individual whose black face sweated greasily, and whose palm itched for unearned increment, called on Monty very shortly after breakfast with intimation that the wharf had been placed at our disposal, since His Highness the Sultan desired to do us honor.

So when the B.I. steamer dropped anchor in the great roadstead shortly after noon we were taken to the wharf by one of the Sultan's household—a very civil-spoken Arab gentleman—and three English officers met us there who made a fuss over Monty and were at pains to be agreeable to the rest of us. While we stood chatting and waiting for the boat that should row us and belongings the mile-and-a-half or so to the steamer, I saw something that made me start. Fred gazed presently in the same direction.

"Johnson is number one!" he said, as if checking off my mental processes. He meant Hassan. "Number two is Georges Coutlass, our friend the Greek. Number three is—am I drunk this early in the day?—what do you see?—doesn't she look to you like?—by the big blind god of men's mistakes it's—Monty! Didums, you deaf idiot, look! See!"

At that everybody naturally looked the same way. Everybody nodded. Coutlass the Greek, and Hassan, reputed nephew of Tippoo Tib, were headed in one boat toward the steamer, the worse for the handling, but right side up and no angrier than the usual passenger. Following them was another boat containing a motley assortment of Arabs and part-Arabs, who might, or might not be associated with them.

On the beach still, surrounded yet by a swarm of longshoremen who yelled and fought, Lady Isobel Saffren Waldon and her Syrian maid stood at bay. Her two Swahili men-servants were overwhelmed and already being carried to a boat. Her luggage was being borne helter-skelter after them, and another boat waited for her just beyond the belt of surf, the rowers standing up to yell encouragement at the sweating pack that dared not close in on its victims. Lady Isobel Saffren Waldon appeared to have no other weapon than a parasol, but she had plainly the upper hand.

"She has a way with her with natives," said the senior officer present.

"It's a pity," said Monty. "I mean, one scarcely likes to use this wharf and watch that."

"Quite so. Yet we daren't accord her official recognition. She'd be certain to make capital out of it. We're awfully glad she's going. The Residency atmosphere is one huge sigh of relief. We would like to speed the parting guest, but it mayn't be done. However, you'll know there are others not so particular. I imagine her friends are late for the appointment."

"Where's she going?" asked Monty.

"British East Africa."

"Mombasa?"

"And then on. She has drafts on a German merchant in Nairobi."

From that moment until we were safely in our quarters on the steamer Monty's attitude became one of rigid indifference toward her or anything to do with her. The British officers went out to the steamer with us, but all the way Monty only talked of the climate, trade conditions, and the other subjects to which polite conversation of Africa's east coast is limited. Fred kept nudging him, but Monty took no notice. Yerkes whispered to Fred. Then I heard Fred whisper to Monty in one of those raucous asides that he perfectly well knows can be heard by everybody.

"Why don't you ask 'em about *her,* you ass?"

But Monty refused to rise. He talked of the bowed and ancient slaves of Zanzibar, who refused in those days to be set free and afforded prolific ground for attack on British public morals by people whose business it is to abuse England for her peccadillos and forget her virtues.

We reached the ship, and were watching our piles of luggage arrive up the accommodation ladder when the solution of Lady Isobel Saffren Waldon's problem appeared. She arrived alongside in the official boat of the German consulate, a German officer in white uniform on either hand, and the German ensign at the stern.

"Pretty fair impudence, paying official honors to our undesirables, yet I don't see what we can do," said the senior from the Residency.

Yerkes drew me aside.

"Did you ever see anything more stupidly British?" he demanded.

"It's as obvious as the nose on your face that she's up to some game. It's as plain as twice two that the Germans are backing her whether the British like it or not. Look at those two Heinies now!"

We faced about and watched them. After bowing Lady Waldon to her cabin, they approached our party with brazen claim to recognition—and received it. They were met, and spoken to apparently as cordially as if their friendship had been indisputable.

"Did you ever see anything to beat it? Why not kick 'em into the sea? Either that woman's a crook or she isn't. If she isn't, then the British have treated her shamefully, turning their backs on her. But we know she is a crook! And so do they. The Germans know it, too, and they're flaunting her under official British noses! They're using her to start something the British won't like, and the British know it! Yet she's going to be allowed to travel to British territory on a British ship, and the Heinies are shaken hands with! If you complained to Monty I bet he'd say, 'Don't talk fight unless you mean fight!' "

"Monty might also add, 'Don't talk-fight!' " said I.

"Oh, rot!" Will answered. "British individuals may bridle a bit, but their government'll shut its eyes until too late, whatever happens! You mark my words!"

We strolled back toward our party in great discontent, I as much as he, never supposing there was another country in the world that could so deliberately shut its eyes to dog's work until absolutely forced to interfere, by a hair not quite too late.

Coutlass and Hassan traveled second-class—the Arab and half-Arab contingent third—and none of them troubled us, at present, except that Will swore at sight of Coutlass swaggering as if the ship and her contents were all his.

"To bear him brag you'd believe the British government afraid of him!" he grumbled.

But an immediate problem drove Coutlass out of mind. Lady Isobel Saffren Waldon had been given a cabin in line-with ours, at the end of our corridor. Her maid, and her two Swahili servants were obliged to pass our doors to get to her cabin at all. As nearly all ships' cabins on those hot routes do, ours intercommunicated by a metal grill for ventilating purposes, and a word spoken in one cabin above a whisper could be heard in the next.

Fred was the first to realize conditions. He opened his door in his usual abrupt way to visit Monty's cabin and almost fell over the Syrian maid, her eye at Monty's key-hole—a little too early in the game to pass for sound judgment, as Fred was at pains to assure her.

The alarm being given, we locked our cabin doors, repaired to the smoking-room, and ordered drinks at a center table where no eavesdropper could overhear.

"It's one of two things," said Monty. He had his folding board out, and we did not doubt he would play chess from there to London. "Either they know exactly where that ivory is, or they haven't the slightest idea."

"My, but you're wise!" said Will.

Monty ignored him. "They suspect us of knowing. They mean to prevent our getting any of it. If they do know, they've some reason of their own for not getting it themselves at present. If they don't know, they suspect we know and intend to claim what we find."

"How should they think we know?" objected Will. "The first we ever heard of the stuff was in the lazaretto in Zanzibar."

"True. Juma told us. Juma probably told them that we told *him*. Natives often put the cart before the horse without the slightest intention of lying."

"All the same, why should they believe him?"

"Why not? Zanzibar's agog with the story—after all these years. The ivory must have been buried more than a quarter of a century ago. Some one's been stirring the mud. We arrive, unexpectedly from nowhere, ask questions about the ivory, make plans for British East Africa—and there you are! The people who were merely determined to get the stuff jump to the false conclusion that we really know where it is."

"Q.E.D.!" said Fred, finishing his drink.

"Not at all," said Monty. "There are two things yet to be demonstrated. They're true, but not proven. The German government is after the staff. And the German government has very special reasons for secrecy and tricks."

"We four against the German government looks like longish odds," said I.

"Remains to be seen," said Monty. "If the German government's very special reasons were legal or righteous they'd be announced with a fanfare of trumpets."

"Where's all this leading us?" demanded Fred.

"To a slight change of plan," said Monty.

"Thank the lord! That means you don't go to Brussels—stay with us!"

"Nothing of the sort, Fred. But you three keep together. They're going to watch you. You watch them. Watch Schillingschen particularly closely, if you find him. The closer they watch you, the more likely they are to lose sight of me. I'll take care to have several red herrings drawn across my trail after I reach London. Perhaps I'll return down the west coast and travel up the Congo River. At any rate, when I do come, and whichever way I come, I'll have everything legal, in writing. Let your game be to seem mysterious. Seem to know more than you do, but don't tell anybody anything. Above all, listen!"

Fred leaned back in his chair and laughed.

"Didums!" he said. "This is the idioticest wild goose chase we ever started on! I admit I nosed it. I gave tongue first. But think of it—here we are—four sensible men—hitherto sensible—off after ivory that nobody can really prove exists, said to be buried somewhere in a tract of half-explored country more than a thousand miles each way—and the German government, and half the criminals in Africa already on our idiotic heels!"

"Yet the German government and the crooks seem convinced, too, that there's something worth looking for!" laughed Monty. And none of us could answer that.

For that matter, none of us would have been willing to withdraw from the search, however dim the prospect of success might seem in the intervals when cold reason shed its comfortless rays on us. Intuition, or whatever it is that has proved superior so often to worldly wisdom (temptation, Fred calls it!) outweighed reason, and Fred himself would have been last to agree to forego the search.

The voyage is short between Zanzibar and Mombasa, but there was incident. We were spied on after very thorough fashion, Lady Saffren Waldon's title and gracious bearing (when that suited her) being practical weapons. The purser was Goanese—beside himself with the fumes of flattery. He had a pass-key, so the Syrian maid went through our cabins and searched thoroughly everything except the wallet of important papers that Monty kept under his shirt. The first and second officers were rather young, unmarried men possessed of limitless ignorance of the wiles of such as Lady Waldon. It was they who signed a paper recommending Coutlass to the B.I. agents and a lot of other reputable people in Mombasa and elsewhere, thus offsetting the possibility that the authorities might not let him land. (Had we known all that at the time, Monty's word against him might have caused him to be shipped back whence he came, but we did not find it out until afterward; nor did we know the law.)

And at Mombasa we made our first united, serious mistake. It was put to the vote. We all agreed.

"I can come ashore," said Monty, "introduce you to officialdom, get you put up for the club, and be useful generally. That, though, 'll lend color to the theory that you're in league with me—whereas, if I leave you to your own resources, that may help lose my scent. When they pick it up again we'll be knowing better where we stand."

"If you came ashore for a few hours we'd have the benefit of your prestige," said I.

"I admit it."

"I suspect a title's mighty near as useful on British territory as in N'York or Boston," said Will. "We'd bask in smiles."

"Not wholly," said Monty. "There's another side to that. There's an English official element that would rather be rude to some poor devil with a title than draw pay (and it loves its pay, you may believe me!). You'd have friends in high places, but make enemies, too, if I go ashore with you."

"What's your own proposal?" Fred demanded.

"I've stated it. I want you fellows to choose. There's no need of me ashore—that's to say, I've a draft to bearer for the amount you three have in the common fund—here, take it. If you think you'll need more than that, then I'll have to go to the bank with you and cash some of my own draft. I think you'll have enough."

"Plenty," said Will.

"Let's send him home!" proposed Fred.

"How about communications?" We had contrived a code already with the aid of a pocket Portuguese-English dictionary, of which Fred and Monty each possessed a similar edition.

"The Mombasa Bank, Will. You keep them posted as to your whereabouts. When I write the bank manager I'll ask him to keep my address a secret."

So we said good-bye to Monty and left him on board, and wished we hadn't a dozen times before noon next day, and a hundred times within the week. The last sight we had of him was as the shore boat came alongside the wharf and the half-breed customs officials pounced smiling on us. My eyes were keenest. I could see Monty pacing the upper deck, too rapidly for evidence of peace of mind—a straight-standing, handsome figure of a man. I pointed him out to the others, and we joked about him. Then the gloom of the customs shed swallowed us, and there was a new earth and, for the present, no more sea.

The island of Mombasa is so close to the coconut-fringed mainland that a railway bridge connects them. Like Zanzibar, it is a place of strange delights, and bridled lawlessness controlled by the veriest handful of Englishmen. There are strange hotels—strange dwellings—streets—stores—tongues and faces. The great grim fort that brave da Gama built, and held against all comers, dominates the sea front and the lower town. The brass-lunged boys who pounce on baggage, fight for it, and tout for the grandly named hotels are of as many tribes as sizes, as many tongues as tribes.

Everything is different—everything strange—everything, except the heat, delightful. And as Fred said, "some folk would grumble in hell!" Trees, flowers, birds, costumes of the women, sheen of the sea, glint of sun on bare skins of every shade from ivory to ebony, dazzling coral roadway and colored coral walls, babel of tongues, sack-saddled donkeys sleepily bearing loads of coral for new buildings, and—winding in and out among it all—the narrow-gauge tramway on which trolleys pushed by stocky little black men carry officialdom gratis, and the rest of the world and his wife according to tariff; all those things are the alphabet of Mombasa's charm. Arranged, and rearranged—by chance, by individual perspective, and by point of view—they spell fascination, attractiveness, glamour, mystery. And no acquaintance with Mombasa, however intimate or old, dispels the charm to the man not guilty of cynicism. To the cynic (and for him) there are sin—as Africa alone knows how to sin—disease, of the dread zymotic types—and death; death peering through the doors of godowns, where the ivory tusks are piled; death in the dark back-streets of the bazaar, where tired policemen wage lop-sided warfare against insanitary habits and a quite impracticable legal code; death on the beach, where cannibal crabs parade in thousands and devour all helpless things; death in the scrub (all green and beautiful) where the tiny streets leave off and snakes claim heritage; death in the grim red desert beyond the coast-line, where lean, hopeless jackals crack to-day men's dry bones left fifty years ago by the slave caravans—marrowless bones long since stripped clean by the ants. But we are not all cynics.

Last to be cynic or pessimist was Louis McGregor Abraham, proprietor of the Imperial Hotel—Syrian by birth, Jew by creed, Englishman by nationality, and admirer first, last and all the time of all things prosperous and promising, except his rival, the Hotel Royal.

"You came to the right place," he assured us when the last hot porter had dumped the last of our belongings on the porch, had ceased from chattering to watch Fred's financial methods, had been paid double the customary price, and had gone away grumbling (to laugh at us behind our backs). "They'd have rooked you at the other hole—underfed you, overcharged you, and filled you full of lies. I tell the truth to folk who come to my hotel."

And he did, some of it. He was inexhaustible, unconquerable, tireless, an optimist always. He had a store that was part of the hotel, in which he claimed to sell "everything the mind of man could wish for in East Africa;" and the boast was true. He even sold American dime novels.

"East Africa's a great country!" he kept assuring us. "Some day we'll all be rich! Have to get ready for it! Have to be prepared! Have to stock everything the mind of man can want, to encourage new arrivals and make the old ones feel at home. Lose a little money, but why grumble? Get it back when the boom comes. As it will, mind you. As it will. Can't help it. Richest country in the world—grow anything—find anything—game—climate—elevation—scenery—natives by the million to do the work—all good! Only waiting for white men with energy, and capital to start things really moving!"

But there were other points of view. We went to the bank, and found its manager conservative. The amount of the draft we placed to our credit insured politeness.

"Be cautious," he advised us. "Take a good look round before you commit yourselves!"

He agreed to manage the interchange of messages between us and Monty, and invited us all to dinner that evening at the club; so we left the bank feeling friendly and more confident. Later, a chance-met English official showed us over the old fort (now jail) where men of more breeds and sorts than Noah knew, better clothed and fed than ever in their lives, drew endless supplies of water in buckets from da Gama's well.

"Some of them have to be kicked out when their sentences expire!" he told us. "See you at the club tonight. Glad to help welcome you."

But there was a shock in store, and as time passed the shocks increased in number and intensity. Our guns had not been surrendered to us by the customs people. We had paid duty on them second-hand at the rate for new ones, and had then been told to apply for them at the collector's office, where our names and the guns' numbers would be entered on the register—for a fee.

We now went to claim them, and on the way down inquired at a store about ammunition. We were told that before we could buy cartridges we would need a permit from the collector specifying how many, and of what bore we might buy. There was an Arab in the store ahead of us. He was buying Martini Henry cartridges. I asked whether he had a permit, and was told he did not need one.

"Being an Arab?" I asked.

"Being well known to the government," was the answer.

We left the store feeling neither quite so confident nor friendly. And the collector's Goanese assistant did the rest of the disillusioning.

No, we could not have our guns. No, we could have no permit for ammunition. No, the collector was not in the office. No, he would not be there that afternoon. It was provided in regulations that we could have neither guns, sporting licenses, nor permits for ammunition. The guns were perfectly safe in the government godown—would not be tampered with—would be returned to us when we chose to leave the country.

"But, good God, we've paid duty on them!" Oakes protested.

"You should not have brought the guns with you unless you desired to pay duty," said the Goanese.

"But where's the collector?" Yerkes demanded.

"I am only assistant," was the answer. "How should I know?"

The man's insolence, of demeanor and words, was unveiled, and the more we argued with him the more sullen and evasive he grew, until at last he ordered us out of the office. At that we took chairs and announced our intention of staying until the collector should come or be fetched. We were informed that the collector was the most important government official in Mombasa—information that so delighted Fred that he grew almost good tempered again.

"I'd rather twist a big tail than a little one!" he announced. "Shall we sing to pass the time?"

The Goanese called for the *askari,* half-soldier, half-police-man, who drowsed in meek solitude outside the office door.

"Remove these people, please!" he said in English, and then repeated it in Kiswahili.

The *askari* eyed us, shifted his bare feet uncomfortably, screwed up his courage, tried to look stern, and said something in his own tongue.

"Put them out, I said!" said the Goanese.

"He orders you to put us out!" grinned Fred.

"The office closes at three," said the Goanese, glancing at the clock in a half-hearted effort to moderate his own daring.

"Not unless the collector comes and closes it himself, it doesn't!" Fred announced with folded arms.

Will pulled out two rupees and offered them to the sentry.

"Go and bring us some food," he said. "We intend to stay in here until your *bwana makubwa* comes."

The sentry refused the money, waving it aside with the air of a Caesar declining a crown.

"Gee!" exclaimed Will. "You've got to hand it to the British if they train colored police to refuse money."

The *askari,* it seemed, was a man of more than one kind of discretion. Without another word to the Goanese he saluted the lot of us with a sweep of his arm, turned on his heel and vanished—not stopping in his hurry to put on the sandals that lay on the door-step. We amused ourselves while he was gone by flying questions at the Goanese, calculated to disturb what might be left of his equanimity without giving him ground for lawsuits.

"How old are you?"—"How much pay do you get?"—"How long have you held your job?"—"Do you ever get drunk?"—"Are you married?"—"Does your wife love you?"—"Do you keep white mice?"—"Is your life insured?"—"How often have you been in jail?"—"Are you honest?"—"Are you vaccinated against the jim-jams?"—"Why is your name Fernandez and not Braganza?"

The man was about distracted, for he had been unwise enough to try to answer, when suddenly the collector came in great haste and stalked through the office into the inner room.

"Fernandez!" he called as he passed, and the Goanese hurried after him, hugely relieved. There was five minute's consultation behind the partition in tones too low for us to catch more than a word or two, and then Fernandez came out again with a "Now wait and see, my hearties!" smile on his face. He was actually rubbing his palms together, sure of a swift revenge.

"He says you are to go in there," he announced.

So we filed in, Fred Oakes first, and it seemed to me the moment I saw the collector's face that the outlook was not so depressing. He looked neither young nor incompetent. His jaw was neither receding nor too prominent. His neck sat on his shoulders with the air of full responsibility, unsought but not refused. And his eyes looked straight into those of each of us in turn with a frank challenge no honest fellow could resent.

"Take seats, won't you," he said. "Your names, please?"

We told him, and he wrote them down.

"My clerk tells me you tried to bribe the *askari.* You shouldn't do that. We are at great pains to keep the police dependable. It's too bad to put temptation in their way."

Will, with cold precision, told him the exact facts. He listened to the end, and then laughed.

"One more Goanese mistake!" he said. "We have to employ them. They mean well. The country has no money to spend on European office assistants. Well—what can I do for you?"

At that Fred cut loose.

"We want our guns before dark!" he said. "It's the first time my character has been questioned by any government, and I say the same for my friends!"

"Oh?" said the collector, eying us strangely.

"Yes!" said Fred.

"That is so," said I.

"Entirely so," said Will.

"I have information," said the collector, tapping with a pencil on his blotter, "that you men are ivory hunters. That you left Portuguese territory because the German consul there had to request the Portuguese government to expel you."

"All easily disproved," said Fred. "Confront us, please, with our accusers."

"And that Lord Montdidier, with whom you have been traveling, became so disgusted with your conduct that he refused to land with you at this port as he at first intended!"

We all three gasped. The first thing that occurred to me, and I suppose to all of us, was to send for Monty. His steamer was not supposed to sail for an hour yet. But the thought had hardly flashed in mind when we heard the roar of steam and clanking as the anchor chain came home. The sound traveled over water and across roofs like the knell of good luck—the clanking of the fetters of ill fate.

"Where's her next stop?" said I.

"Suez," Fred answered.

Simultaneously then to all three the thought came too that this interpretation of Monty's remaining on board was exactly what we wanted. The more people suspected us of acting independently of him the better.

"Confront us with our accusers!" Fred insisted.

"You are not accused—at least not legally," said the collector. "You are refused rifle and ammunition permits, that is all."

"On the ground of being ivory hunters?"

"Suspected persons—not known to the government—something rather stronger than rumor to your discredit, and nothing known in your favor."

"What recourse have we?" Fred demanded.

"Well—what proof can you offer that you are bona fide travelers or intending settlers? Are you ivory hunters or not?"

"I'll answer that," said Fred—dexterously I thought, "when I've seen a copy of the game laws. We're law-abiding men."

The collector handed us a well thumbed copy of the Red Book.

"They're all in that," he said. "I'll lend it to you, or you can buy one almost anywhere in town. If you decide after reading that to go farther up country I'm willing to issue provisional game licenses, subject to confirmation after I've looked into any evidence you care to submit on your own behalf. You can have your guns against a cash deposit—"

"How big?"

"Two hundred rupees for each gun!"

Fred laughed. The demand was intended to be away over our heads. The collector bridled.

"But no ammunition," he went on, "until your claim to respectability has been confirmed. By the way, the only claim you've made to me is for the guns. You've told me nothing about yourselves."

"Two hundred a gun?" said Fred. "Counting a pistol or revolver as one?" Three guns apiece—nine guns—eighteen hundred rupees' deposit?"

The collector nodded with a sort of grim pleasure in his own unreasonableness. Fred drew out our new check book.

"You fellows agreeable?" he asked, and we nodded.

"Here's a check on the Mombasa Bank for ten thousand, and your government can have as much more again if it wants it," he said. "Make me out a receipt please, and write on it what it's for."

The collector wrote. He was confused, for he had to tear up more than one blank.

"I suppose we get interest on the money at the legal local rate?" asked Fred maliciously.

"I'll inquire about that," said the collector.

"Excuse me," said Fred, "but I'm going to give you some advice. While you're inquiring, look into the antecedents of Lady Isobel Saffren Waldon! It's she who gave out the tip against us. Her tip's a bad one. So is she."

"She hasn't applied for guns or a license," the collector answered tartly. "It's people who want to carry firearms—people able and likely to make trouble whom we keep an eye on."

"She's more likely to make trouble for you than a burning house!" put in Will Yerkes. "If my partner hadn't paid you that check I'd be all for having this business out! I'm going to let them know in the States what sort of welcome people receive at this port!"

"You came of your own accord. You weren't invited," the collector answered.

"That's a straight-out lie!" snapped Will. "You know it's a lie! Why, there isn't a newspaper in South Africa that hasn't been carrying ads of this country for months past. Even papers I've had sent me from the States have carried press-agent dope about it. Why, you've been yelling for settlers like a kid squalling for milk—and you say we're not invited now we've come here! I'm going to write and tell the U.S. papers what that dope is worth!"

"Ivory hunters are not settlers," the collector interjected.

"Who said we're ivory hunters?" Will was in a fine rage, and Fred and I leaned back to enjoy the official's discomfort. "Besides, your ads bragged about the big game as one of the chief attractions! All the information you can possibly have against us must have come from a female crook in the pay of the German government! You're not behaving the way gentlemen do where I was raised!"

"There is no intention to offend," said the collector.

"Intention is good!" said Will, laughing in spite of himself. "There's another thing I want to know. What about ammunition? We're to have our guns. They're useless without cartridges. What about it?"

"The guns shall be sent to your hotel tonight. The provisional sporting licenses—if you want them—will be ready to-morrow morning—seven hundred and fifty rupees apiece—I'll charge them against your deposit. If the licenses should be confirmed after inquiry, I will send you permits through the post for fifty rounds of ammunition each."

Will snorted. Fred Oakes yelled with laughter, and I gaped with indignation.

"I'm going into this to the hilt!" spluttered Fred. "I wouldn't have missed it for a fortune! We three are going to constitute ourselves a committee of inspection. We're going to wander the country over and report home to the newspapers—South African—British—U.S.A.—and any other part of the world that's interested! We won't worry about ammunition. Send us permits for whatever quantity seems to you proper, and we'll note it all down in our diaries!"

We all stood up, the collector obviously uncomfortable and we, if not at ease, at least happier than we had been.

Fred nodded to the collector genially, and we all walked out.

Mombasa is a fairly large island, but the built-over part of it is small, so it was not surprising that we should emerge from the office face to face with Lady Saffren Waldon. She was the one surprised, not we. She probably thought she had spiked our guns in that part of the world forever, and the sight of us coming laughing from the very office where we should have been made glum must have been disconcerting.

She was riding on one of the little trolley-cars, pushed by two boys in white official uniform, dressed in her flimsiest best, a lace parasol across her knee, and beside her an obvious member of the government—young, and so recently from home as not to have lost his pink cheeks yet.

Had there not been an awning over the trolley-car she might have used the parasol to make believe she had not seen us. But the awning precluded that, and we were not more than two or three yards away.

"Laugh!" whispered Fred.

So we crossed the track laughing and the trolley had to pause to let us by. We laughed as we raised our helmets to her—laughed both at her and at the pink and white puppy she had taken in leash. And then the sort of thing happened that nearly always does when men with a reasonable faith in their own integrity make up their minds to see opprobrium through. Fate stepped hard on our arm of the balance.

If built-over Mombasa is a small place, so is Africa. So is the world. Striding down the hill from the other hotel, the rival one, the Royal, came a man so well known in so many lands that they talk of naming a tenth of a continent after him—the mightiest hunter since Nimrod, and very likely mightier than he; surely more looked-up to and respected—a little, wiry-looking, freckled, wizened man whose beard had once been red, who walked with a decided limp and blinked genially from under the brim of a very neat khaki helmet.

"Why, bless my soul if it isn't Fred Oakes!" he exclaimed, in a squeaky, worn-out voice that is as well known as his face, and quickened his pace down-hill.

"Courtney!" said Fred. "There's only one man I'd rather meet!"

The little man laughed. "Oh, you and your Montdidier are still inseparable, I suppose! How are you, Fred? I'm glad to see you. Who are your friends?"

At that minute out came the collector from his office—stood on the step, and stared. Fred introduced us to Courtney, and I experienced the thrill of shaking hands with the man accounts of whose exploits had fired my schoolboy imagination and made stay-at-home life forever after an impossibility.

"I missed the steamer, Fred. Not another for a week. Going down now to see about a passage to Somaliland. I suppose you'll be at the club after dinner?"

"No" said Fred. "We've an invitation, but I think we'll send a note and say we can't come. We'll dine at our hotel and sit on the veranda afterward."

I wondered what Fred was driving at, and so did the collector who was headed across the street and listening with all ears.

"That so? Not a bad idea. They've very kindly made me an honorary member of the club, but I rather expect there's a string to that—eh, Fred, don't you? They'll expect stories—stories. I get tired of telling the same tales so many times over. Suppose I join you fellows, eh? I'm at the Royal. You at the other place? Suppose I join you after dinner, and we have a pipe together on the veranda?"

"Nothing I'd like better," said Fred, and I felt too pleased with the prospect to say anything at all. Growing old is a foolish and unnecessary business, but there is no need to forego while young the thrills of unashamed hero-worship; in fact, that is one of the ways of continuing young. It is only the disillusioned (poor deceived ones) and the cynics, who grow old ungracefully.

We went up-street, through the shadow of the great grim fort. The trolley-car trundled down among the din, smells and colors of the business-end of town. Looking over my shoulder I saw Courtney talking to the collector.

"We're getting absolution, Fred!" said I.

"I'm not sure we need it," Fred answered. "I hope Courtney won't tell too much!" So quickly does a man jump from praying for friends at court to fearing them!

"Courtney looked to me," said Will, "like a man who would give no games away."

Glad you think that of him" said Fred.

"Why?"

"Tell you later, maybe."

But he did not tell until after dinner. (It was a good dinner for East Africa. Shark steak figured in it, under a more respectable name; and there was zebu hump, guinea-fowl, and more different kinds of fruit than a man could well remember.) When it was over we sat in deep armchairs on the long wide veranda that fronts the whole hotel. The evening sea-breeze came and wafted in on us the very scents of Araby; the night sounds that whisper of wilderness gave the lie to a tinkling guitar that somewhere in the distance spoke of civilized delights. The surf crooned on coral half a mile away, and very good cigar smoke (from a box that Monty had sent ashore with our belongings) supplemented coffee and the other aids to physical contentment. Then, limping between the armchairs, and ashamed that we should rise to greet him—motioning us down again with a little nervous laugh—Courtney came to us. Within five minutes of his coming the world, and the clock, and the laws of men might have all reversed themselves for aught we cared. Without really being conscious he was doing it Courtney plunged into our problem, grasped it, sized it up, advised us, flooded us with priceless, wonderful advice, and did it with such almost feminine sympathy that I believe we would have been telling him our love-affairs at last, if a glance at the watch he wore in a case at his belt had not told him it was three A.M.

"There's trouble," he began when he had filled his pipe. "You boys are in trouble. What is it?" he asked, shifting and twitching in his seat—refusing an armchair—refusing a drink.

"Tell us first what's the matter with you," said Fred.

"Oh, nothing. An old wound. A lion once dragged me by this shoulder half a mile or so. At this time of year I get pains. They last a day or two, then pass—Go on, tell me!"

He never sat really still once that whole evening, yet never once complained or made a gesture of impatience.

"I propose," said Fred, with a glance at Yerkes and me, "to tell Courtney everything without reserve."

The little old hunter nodded, watching us with bright blue eyes. I received the impression that he knew more secrets than he could tell should he talk down all the years that might be left him. He was the sort of man in whom nearly every one confides.

"We're after Tippoo Tib's ivory!" said Fred, plunging into the middle of things. "Monty has gone to drive a bargain with the King of Belgium. Do you think it's a wild goose chase?"

Courtney chuckled. "No," he said. "I wouldn't call it that. They've been killing elephants in Africa ever since the flood. Ivory must have accumulated. It's somewhere. Some of it must be so old and well seasoned as to be practically priceless, unless rats have spoiled it. Rats play old Harry with ivory, you know."

"Have you a notion where it is?" demanded Fred.

Courtney laughed. "Behold me leaving the country!" he said. "If I knew I'd look. If I saw I'd take!"

"Can you give us a hint?"

"There are caves near the summit of Mount Elgon that would hold the world's revenues. None of them have ever been thoroughly explored. Cannibals live in some of them. Cannibals and caverns is a combination that might appeal to Tippoo Tib, but there's no likelihood that he buried all that ivory in one place, you know. I suspect the greater part is in the Congo, and that the Germans know its whereabouts within a mile or two."

"How did they discover it?"

"Why don't they dig it out?"

"What keeps 'em from turning their knowledge into money?"

We had forgotten our own troubles. Courtney, too, seemed to forget for the moment that he had began by asking us a question.

"Remember Emin Pasha? When was it—'87—'88—'89 that Stanley went and rescued him? Perhaps you recall what was then described as Emin's ingratitude after the event? British government offered him a billet. Khedive of Egypt cabled him the promise of a job, all on Stanley's recommendation. Emin turned 'em all down and accepted a job from the Germans. Nobody understood it at the time. My own idea is that Emin thought he knew more or less where that hoard is. He didn't really want to come away with Stanley, you know. Being a German, I suppose he preferred to share his secret with his own crowd. I dare say he thought of telling Stanley but judged that the 'Rock breaker' might demand a too large share. The value of the stuff must be so enormous that it's almost worth going to war about, from the point of view of a nation hungry for new colonies. Emin is dead, and it's likely he left no exact particulars behind him. To my personal knowledge the Germans have had a swarm of spies for a long time operating beyond the Congo border."

"Were you looking for the stuff yourself?" I asked.

"Oh, no," he laughed. "But when I'm hunting I look about me. I'll tell you where the stuff may possibly be. There's a section of country called the Bahr el Gazal that the Congo people claim, but that I believe will eventually prove to lie on the British side of the boundary. It was good elephant country—which is to say bad living and traveling for man—since the earth took shape out of ooze. Awful swampy, malarious, densely wooded, dangerous country, sparsely inhabited by savages not averse to cannibalism when they've opportunity. The ivory may be there. If the Germans know it's there they're naturally afraid the British government would claim the whole district the minute the secret was out. Their plan may possibly be to wait until a boundary dispute arises in the ordinary course of time (keeping a cautious eye on the cache meanwhile, of course) and then take the Congo government side. If they can contrive to have it acknowledged as Congo territory, they might then pick a quarrel with the Congo government—or come to some sort of terms with them."

"They've patience," I said, "if they're playing that game!"

Courtney raised his eyebrows until his forehead was a mass of deep wrinkles. Then he blew a dozen smoke rings.

"Patient—perhaps. It's my impression they're as remorseless and persistent as white ants—undermining, digging, devouring everywhere while the rest of the world sleeps. Do you remember there was a mutiny of native troops in Uganda not many years ago? Some said that was because the troops were being paid in truck instead of money, and like most current excuses that one had some truth in it. But the men themselves vowed they were going to set up an African Mohammedan empire."

"What had that to do with Germans?" asked Fred.

"Nothing that I can personally prove" said Courtney. "But I've a broad acquaintance among natives, and considerable knowledge of their tongues. Mohammedanism is spreading among them very rapidly. Over and over again, beside camp-fires, and in the dark when they thought I was not listening, I have heard them talk of missionaries from German territory who spread a doctrine of what you might call pan-Islam for lack of a better name. I said at the time of the Uganda mutiny that I believed Germans were behind it. I've seen no reason to change my opinion since. It's obvious that if the mutiny had by some ill chance succeeded Uganda would have been an easy prey for Karl Peters and his Germans. If that ivory of Tippoo Tib's is really in the Bahr el Gazal at the back of Uganda, then the German motive for stirring up the Uganda mutiny would be obvious."

"But doesn't our government know all this?" demanded Fred.

"That depends on what you mean by the word know," answered Courtney. "I've made no secret of my own opinion!"

"But they wouldn't listen?"

"Some did, some didn't. The Home government—which was the India Office in those days—took no notice whatever. One or two men out here believed, but I think they're dead. When the Foreign Office took the country over I don't suppose they overhauled old reports very carefully. I dare say my letters on the subject lie inches deep in dust."

"England doesn't deserve to keep her colonies!" vowed Fred, caught in a sudden flood of indignation.

Courtney laughed.

"When you've seen as many of the other nations' colonies as I have you'll qualify that verdict! We do our best. God gave us our work to do, and the devil came and made us stupid! Take this country, for instance."

"Yes!" agreed Fred. "Take this country! We came ashore to-day—left Monty on board ship on his way to Europe. Nobody knew a thing about us. A female woman, known to the police in Zanzibar and so notorious in Europe that she's in no hurry to go home—said, too, on every hand to be in the pay of the German government—chose to tell lies about us to the chuckle-headed puppies in charge of Mombasa. Net result—what do you suppose?"

"I know," said Courtney. "I've been told this evening." His eyes changed, and his voice took on the almost feminine note of appeal that came strangely from a big game hunter. "You boys must overlook things. These boys you're angry with are younger than you, Fred. That collector you've contrived to pick a quarrel with has fought Arabs and cannibal troops—odds against him of fifty or a hundred to one, mind you—all across the Congo and back again. He fought in the Uganda mutiny. He's a man. He's a merchant, though, with a merchant's education. He was taken over with the rest of the clerks when the British government superseded the British East Africa Trading Company. He has never had the advantage of legal training. Went to a common school. No advantages of any kind. Poorly paid and overworked. There's no money in the country yet. Nobody to tax. Salaries—expenses and so on come from home, voted by Parliament. As long as that condition lasts they're all going to feel nervous. They know they'll get the blame for everything that goes wrong, and precious little credit in any case. Parliament advertised the country in answer to their complaints of no revenue. Parliament called for settlers. But they're not ready for settlers. They don't know how to handle them. They've no troops—nothing but a handful of black police. How shall they keep in order colonials armed with repeating rifles? They're not ready. The Uganda Railway isn't finished yet; trains get through to Victoria Nyanza once a week, but there's endless work to be done yet on the line, and Parliament grudges them every penny they spend on it. Yet the railway was rushed through by order of Parliament to prevent Doctor Karl Peters and the Germans from claiming occupation of the head-waters of the Nile and so dominating Upper Egypt. You boys must be considerate."

"All right," said Fred. "I'll grant all that."

"But what gets me" Will interrupted, "is that they should condemn us out-of-hand—on sight—untried—on the say-so of this Lady Saffren Waldon. She carries German letters of credit. She's so notoriously in league with Germans that you'd think even these little Napoleons 'ud know it. I'm American myself, thank God, but these two men are their own kith and kin. Why should they judge their own countrymen unheard on the say-so of a woman like that? That's what rattles me!"

Courtney blew six smoke rings.

"You'll have to forgive them, lad. Too many of the Englishmen who have come here were bad bats from the South, so hot-footed that they burned the grass. Then—don't forget that the Germans have a military government to the south of us—all experienced men—a great many of them unmitigated rascals, but nearly all of them clever—students of strategy and psychology and tactics—some of them brilliant men who have had to apply for colonial service because of debt or scandal. They're overmanned where we are under-manned—backed up from home where our boys are only blamed and neglected—well supplied with troops and ammunition, where our police are kept down to the danger point and now and then even without cartridges. The Germans have no railway yet, but they've a policy and they keep it secret. We have a railway, and no policy except retrenchment and economy. I'm convinced the German government has no scruples. We have. So you must sympathize with our young men, not quarrel with them."

"Believe me," I said, "we didn't start out to quarrel with anybody. That woman lied about us. There's no excuse for believing her without giving us a hearing."

"Oh, yes there is. I spoke with her myself this evening," said Courtney. "She's staying at my hotel, you know. She's a match for much more experienced men than our young officials. They've been fighting Arabs, not flirting. She had the impudence to try to flatter me. I don't doubt she's telling a crowd of men tonight that I'm in love with her—perhaps not exactly telling them that, but giving them to understand it. Why don't I stroll down to the club and deny it? For the same reason that you don't openly denounce her! It's semi- or wholly-sentimental chivalry—rank stupidity, if you like to call it that, but it's national, I'm glad to say, and I'm as proud of it as any one."

"Doesn't it look to you," said Fred, "that if she and the German government are so infernally anxious to spoil our chances—and they suspect what we're after, you know—doesn't it look to you as if there may really be something in this quest of ours?"

"Undoubtedly," said Courtney. "There's ivory in it, tons and tons and tons of ivory. Somebody will find it some day."

"Join us then!" said Fred. "Cancel your trip to Somaliland and come with us! I can speak for Monty. I know he'll welcome you into the partnership!"

"I believe I could almost speak for Monty, too," laughed Courtney. "He and I were at Eton together, and we've never ceased being friends. But I can't come with you. No. I'm making a sort of semi-official trip. I shall hunt, of course, but there are observations to be made. The pan-Islamic theory is said to be making headway also in Somaliland."

"Do you feel you have any lien on the Elgon Caves and Bahr el Gazal clues?" Fred asked.

"No. I make you a present of those ideas. I'm sure I hope you find the stuff. I'm wondering, though—I'm wondering."

"I'll bet you a dollar I'm thinking of the same thing," said Will.

"Out with it, then."

"What's to prevent the Germans from making their own dicker with the King of the Belgians or with the Congo government, and rifling the hoard on a fifty-fifty or some such basis?"

"Correct," said Courtney. "I confess myself puzzled about that. But I know no European politics. There may be a thousand reasons. And then, you know, the King of the Belgians has the name of being a grasping dealer. The management of his private zone on the Congo is unspeakable. It's possible the Germans may prefer not to risk putting His Majesty on the scent."

"Well, we've our work cut out," said Fred, laughing and yawning. "That woman has started us off with a bad name."

"That is one thing I can really do for you," Courtney answered. "I've no official standing, but the boys all listen to me. I'll tell them—"

"For the love of God don't tell them too much!" Fred exclaimed.

"I'll tell them you're friends of mine," he went on. "I believe that will solve the sporting license and ammunition problem. As for the woman—if I were in your shoes I would steal a march on her. I wouldn't be surprised if your licenses and ammunition permits were here at the hotel by ten to-morrow morning. I see they've sent your guns already. Well, there's a train for Nairobi to-morrow noon, and not another for three days. I'd take to-morrow's train if I were you. I always find in going anywhere the start's the principal thing. You'll go?"

"We will," we answered, one after the other.

"Good night, then, boys; I'll be going."

But we walked with him down to his hotel—I, and I think the others, full to the teeth with the pleasure of knowing him, as well as of envy of his scars, his five or six South African campaigns, his adventures, and (by no means least) his unblemished record as a gentleman. Merely a little bit of a man with a limp, but better than a thousand men who lacked his gentleness.

THE NJO HAPA SONG

Delights—ah, Ten are the dear delights (and the Book forbids them, one by one)—
The broad old roads of a thousand loves—back turned to the Law—the lawless fun—
Old Arts for new—old hours reborn—and who shall mourn when the sands have run?

I was old when they told the Siren Tales
(All ears were open then!)
And the harps were afire with plucked desire
For the white ash oars again—
For oars and sail, and the open sea,
High prow against pure blue,
The good sea spray on eye and lip,
The thrumming hemp, the rise and dip,
The plunge and the roll of a driven ship
As the old course boils anew!

Sweetly I call, the captains come. The home ties draw at hearts in vain.
Potent the spell of Africa! Who East and South the course has ta'en
By Guardafui to Zanzibar may go, but he, shall come again.

IV

COURTNEY PROVED better than his word. Our Big Game Licenses arrived after breakfast, and permits for five hundred rounds of rifle ammunition each. In an envelope in addition was Fred's check with the collector's compliments and the request that we kindly call and pay for the licenses. In other words we now had absolution.

We called, and were received as fellow men, such was the genius of Courtney's friendship. A railway man looked in. The collector's dim office became awake with jokes and laughter.

"Going up to-day?" he asked. "I'll see you get berths on the train."

We little realized at the moment the extent of that consideration; but understanding dawned fifteen minutes before high noon when we strolled to the station behind a string of porters carrying our luggage. Courtney was there to see us off, and he looked worried.

"I'm wondering whether you'll ever get your luggage through," he said with a sort of feminine solicitude. It was strange to hear the hero of one's school-days, mighty hunter and fearless leader of forlorn campaigns, actually troubled about whether we could catch our train. But so the man was, gentle always and considerate of everybody but himself.

There was law in this new land, at all events along the railway line. Not even handbags or rifles could pass by the barrier until weighed and paid for. Crammed in the vestibule in front of us were fifty people fretfully marshaling in line their strings of porters lest any later comer get by ahead of them; foremost, with his breast against the ticket window, was Georges Coutlass. Things seemed not to be proceeding as he wished.

There was one babu behind the window—a mild, unhappy-looking Punjabi, or Dekkani Moslem. There was another at the scales, who knew almost no English: his duty was to weigh—do sums—write the result on a slip, and then justify his arithmetic to office babu and passenger, before any sort of progress could be made. The fact that all passengers shouted at him to hurry or be reported to big superiors complicated the process enormously; and the equally discordant fact that no passenger—and especially not Georges Coutlass—desired or intended to pay one anna more than he could avoid by hook, crook, or argument, made the game amusing to the casual looker-on, but hastened nothing (except tempers). The temperature within the vestibule was 112° by the official thermometer.

"You pair of black murderers!" yelled Coutlass as we took our place in line. "You bloody robbers! You pickpockets! You train-thieves! Go out and dig your graves! I will make an end of you!"

"You should not use abusive language" the babu retorted mildly, stopping to speak, and then again to wipe his spectacles, and his forehead, and his hands, and to glance at the clock, and to mutter what may or may not have been a prayer.

Coutlass exploded.

"Shouldn't, eh? Who the hell are you to tell me what I shouldn't do? Sell me a ticket, you black plunderer, d'you hear! Look! Listen!"

He snatched a piece of paper from the babu's hand and turned to face the impatient crowd.

"This hell-cat—" (the unhappy babu looked less like a hell-cat than any vision of the animal I ever imagined)—"wants to make out that seventy-one times seven annas and three pice is forty-nine rupees, eleven annas! Oh, you charlatan! You mountebank! You black-blooded robber! You miscreant! Cut your throat, I order you!"

The babu expostulated, stammered, quailed. Coutlass drew in his breath for the gods of Greece alone knew what heights of fury next. But interruption entered.

"There, that's enough of you! Get to the back of the line!"

The man who had promised us berths came abruptly through the barrier, and unlike the babu did not appear afraid of any one. The Greek let out his gathered breath with a bark of fury, like a seal coming up to breathe. Taking that for a symptom of opposition the newcomer, very cool in snow-white uniform and helmet, seized Coutlass by the neck and hustled him, arguing like a boiler under pressure, through the crowd. The Greek was three inches taller, and six or eight inches bigger round the chest, but too astonished to fight back, and perhaps, too, aware of the neighborhood of old da Gama's fort, where more than one Greek was pining for the grape and olive fields of Hellas. With a final shove the railway official thrust him well out into the road.

"If you miss the train, serve you right!" he said. "Babus are willing servants, to be treated gently!"

Then he saw us.

"You're late! Where's your luggage? These your porters? All right—put you on your honor. Go on through. Save time. Have your stuff weighed, and settle the bill at Nairobi. All of it, mind! Babu, let these people through!"

Followed by Courtney, who seemed to have right of way wherever it suited him to wander, we filed through the gate, crossed the blazing hot platform, and boarded a compartment labeled "Reserved." The railway man nodded and left us, to hurry and help sell tickets.

It was an Indian type railway carriage be left us in, a contraption not ill-suited to Africa—nor yet so comfortable as to diminish the sensation of travel toward new frontiers.

Each car was divided into two compartments, entirely separate and entered from opposite ends; facing ours was the rear end of a second-class car, into which we could look if the doors were open and we lay feet-foremost on the berths. The berths were arranged lengthwise, two each side, and one above the other.

It was what they called a mixed train, mixed that is of freight and passengers—third-class in front, second next, then first, and a dozen little iron freight cars of two kinds in front. In those days there were neither tunnels nor bridges on that railway, and there was a single seat on the roof at each end of first- and second-class compartments reached by a ladder, for any passenger enamored of the view. Even the third-class compartments (and they were otherwise as deliberately bare and comfortless as wood and iron could make them) had lattice-work shades over the upper half of the windows.

For the babu's encouragement, and to increase the panic of the ticketless, the engineer was blowing the whistle at short intervals. Passengers, released in quicker order now that a white official was lending the two babus a hand, began coming through the barrier in sudden spurts, baggage in either hand and followed hot-foot by natives with their heavier stuff. They took headers into the train, and the porters generally came back grinning.

"I see through the whistling stunt," Will announced. "My, but that fellow on the engine has faith; or else the system's down real fine in these parts! He won't be back for a week. Those wooly-headed porters are going to save up his commission and hand it to him when he brings the down-train in! The game's good: he whistles—passenger runs—can't make change—pays two, three, four, ten times what the job's worth—and the porters divvy up with the engineer. But good lord, the porters must be honest!"

Presently a pale white man in khaki with a red beard entered our compartment, and Courtney had to make room for him on the seat. He apologized with less conviction of real regret than I ever remember noticing, although the pouches under his eyes gave him a rather world-weary look.

"Not another first-class berth on the train—every last one engaged. Might be worse. Might have had to ride with Indians. Curse of this country, Indians are. I'd rid the land of 'em double-quick if government 'ud pay me a rupee a head—an' I'd provide cartridges! But government likes 'em! Ugh! Ever travel in one compartment with a dozen of 'em? Sleep in a tent with a score of 'em? Share blankets with a couple of 'em on a cold night? No? You be glad I'm not an Indian. One's enough!"

We made room for his belongings, and leaned from the window all on one seat together. The time to start arrived and passed; hot passengers continued spurting for the train at intervals—all sorts of passengers—English, Mauritius-French, Arab, Goanese, German, Swahili, Indian, Biluchi, one Japanese, two Chinamen, half-breeds, quarter-breeds of all the hues from ivory to dull red, guinea-yellow, and bleached out black; but the second-class compartment facing our door remained empty. There was a name on the card in the little metal reservation frame, and every passenger who could read English glanced at it, but nobody came to claim it even when the engine's extra shrill screaming and at last the ringing of a bell warned Courtney that time was really up, and he got out on the platform.

"Good-bye," he said through the window. "I've done what I could to bring you luck. Don't be tempted to engage the first servants who apply to you at Nairobi. If you wait there a week I'll send my Kazimoto to you; he's a very good gun-bearer. He'll be out of a job when I'm gone. I shall give him his fare to Nairobi. Engage him if you want a dependable boy, but remember the rule about dogs: a good one has one master! I don't mean Kazimoto is a dog—far from it. I mean, treat him as reasonably as you would a dog, and he'll serve you well. He's a first-class Nyamwezi, from German East. Oh, and one more scrap of advice—":

He came close to the window, but at that moment the engine gave a final scream and really started. Passengers yelled farewells. The engine's apoplectic coughs divided the din into spasms, and there came a great bellowing from the ticket office. He could not speak softly and be heard at all. Louder he had to speak, and then louder, ending almost with a shout.

"The best way to Elgon is by way of Kisumu and Mumias, whatever anybody else may tell you. And if you find the stuff, or any of it," (he was running beside the train now)—"be in no hurry to advertise the fact! Go and make terms first with government—then—after you've made terms—tell 'em you've found it! Find the stuff—make terms—then produce what you've found! Get my meaning? Good-bye, all. Good luck!"

We left him behind then, wiping the sweat from his wrinkled, freckled forehead, gazing after us as if we had all been lifelong friends of his. He made no distinction between us and Fred, but was equally anxious to serve us all.

"If that man isn't white, who is?" demanded Will, and then there was new interest.

We had left the ticket office far behind, but the train was moving slowly and there was still a good length of platform before our car would be clear of the station altogether. We heard a roar like a bull's from behind, and a dozen men—white, black and yellow—came careering down the platform carrying guns, baggage, bedding, and all the paraphernalia that travelers in Africa affect.

First in the van was Georges Coutlass, showing a fine turn of speed but tripping on a bed-sheet at every other step, with his uncased rifle in one hand, his hat in the other, an empty bandolier over one shoulder and a bag slung by a strap swinging out behind him. He made a leap for the second-class compartment in front of us, and landed on all fours on the platform. We opened the door of our compartment to watch him better.

Once on the platform he threw his rifle into the compartment and braced himself to catch the things his stampeding followers hurled after him—caught them deftly and tossed them in, yelling instructions in Greek, Kiswahili, Arabic, English, and two or three other languages. It may be that the engineer looked back and saw what was happening (or perhaps the guard signaled with the cord that passed through eyeholes the whole length of the train) for though we did not slow down we gained no speed until all his belongings had been hurled, and caught, and flung inside. Then came his traveling companions—caught by one hand and dragged on their knees up the steps. They were heavy men, but he snatched all three in like a boy pulling chestnuts from the fire.

The first was a Greek—evil-looking, and without the spirit that in the case of Coutlass made a stranger prone to over-look shortcomings—dressed in khaki, with rifle and empty bandolier. Next, chin, elbow, hand and knee up the steps came a fat, tough-looking Goanese, dressed anyhow at all in pink-colored dirty shirt, dark pants, and a helmet, also with rifle and empty bandolier. I judged he weighed about two hundred and eighty pounds, but Coutlass yanked him in like a fish coming overside. Last came a man who might be Arab, or part-Arab, part-Swahili, whom I did not recognize at first, fat, black, dressed in the white cotton garments and red fez of the more or less well-to-do native, and voluble with rare profanity.

"Johnson!" shouted Fred with almost the joy of greeting an old acquaintance.

It was Hassan, sure enough, short-winded and afraid, but more afraid of being left behind than of the manhandling. Coutlass took hold of his outstretched arm, hoisted him, cracked his shins for him against the top step, and hurled him rump-over-shoulders into the compartment, where the other Greek and the Goanese grabbed him by the arms and legs and hove him to an upper berth, on which he lay gasping like a fish out of water and moaning miserably. Their compartment was a mess of luggage, blankets, odds-and-ends, and angry men. Coutlass found a whisky bottle out of the confusion, and swallowed the stuff neat while the other Greek and the Goanese waited their turn greedily. There was nothing much in that compartment to make a man like Hassan feel at home.

"Those Greeks," said our red-bearded traveling companion as we shut the door again, "are only one degree better than Indians—a shade less depraved perhaps—a sight more dangerous. I sure do hate a Punjabi, but I don't love Greeks! The natives call 'em *bwana masikini* to their faces—that means Mister Mean White y'know. They're a lawless lot, the Greeks you'll run across in these parts. My advice is, shoot first! Walk behind 'em! If they ain't armed, hoof 'em till they cut an' run! Greeks are no good!"

We introduced ourselves. He told us his name was Brown.

"There's three Browns in this country: Hell-fire Brown of Elementaita, Joseph Henry Brown of Gilgil, and Brown of Lumbwa. Brown of Lumbwa's me. Don't believe a word either of the other two Browns tell you! Yes, we're all settlers. Country good to settle in? Depends what you call good. If you like lots of room, an' hunting, natives to wait an' your own house on your own square mile—comfortable climate—no conventions—nor no ten commandments, why, it's pretty hard to beat. But if you want to wear a white shirt, and be moral, and get rich, it's rotten! You've a chance to make money if you're not over law-abiding, for there's elephants. But if you're moral, and obey the laws, you haven't but one chance, an' she's a slim one."

"Well," said Fred, genially, "tell us about the only one. We're men to whom the ten commandments are—"

"You look it!" Brown interrupted. "Well, what's the odds? You'll never find it, and anyhow, everybody knows it's Tippoo Tib's ivory. I mean to have a crack at spotting it myself, soon as I get my farm fenced an' one or two other matters attended to. Gov'ment offers ten per cent. to whoever leads 'em to it, but they can't believe any one's as soft as that surely! They'll be lucky if they get ten per cent. of it themselves! Man alive, but they say there's a whale of a hoard of it! Hundreds o' tons of ivory, all waiting to be found, and fossicked out, an' took! Say—if I was some o' those Greeks for instance, tell you what I'd do: I'd off to Zanzibar, an' kidnap Tippoo Tib. The old card's still living. I'd apply a red-hot poker to his silver-side an' the under-parts o' his tripe-casings. He'd tell me where the stuff is quicker'n winking! Supposin' I was a Greek without morals or no compunctions or nothin', that's what I'd do! I don't hold with allowin' any man to play dog in the manger with all that plunder!"

"Have you a notion where the stuff might be?" Fred wondered guilelessly.

"Ah! That 'ud be tellin'!"

We had crossed the water that divides Mombasa from the mainland. Behind us lay the prettiest and safest harbor on all that thousand-league-long coast; before us was the narrow territory that still paid revenue and owed nominal allegiance to the Sultan of Zanzibar, although really like the rest of those parts under British rule. We were bowling along beside plantations of coconut, peanut, plantain and pineapple, with here and there a thicket of strange trees to show what the aboriginal jungle had once looked like. When we stopped at wayside stations the heat increased insufferably, until we entered the great red desert that divides the coastland from the hills, and after that all seemed death and dust, and haziness, and hell.

At first we passed occasional baobabs, with trunks fifteen or twenty feet thick and offshoots covering a quarter of an acre. Then the trees thinned out to the sparse and shriveled all-but-dead things that struggle for existence on the border-lines between man's land and desolation. At last we drew down the smoked panes over the window to escape the glare and sight of the depressing desolation.

The sun beat down on the iron roof. The heat beat up from the tracks. Red dust polluted the drinking water in the little upright tank. Dust filled eyes, nostrils, hair. Dust caked and grew stiff in the sweat that streamed down us. Yet we stopped once at a station, and humans lived there and a man got off the train. A lone lean babu and his leaner, more miserable native crew came out and eyed the train like vultures waiting for a beast to die. But we did not die, and the train passed on into illimitable dusty redness, leaving them to watch the hot rails ribbon out behind our grumbling caboose.

There began to be carousing in the second-class compartment next ahead of us. Our own Brown of Lumbwa produced a stone crock of Irish whisky from a basket, imbibed copiously, offered us in turn the glistening neck, looked relieved at our refusal, and grew voluble.

"Hear them Greeks an' that Goa. You'd think they were gentlemen o' breeding to hear 'em carryin' on! Truth is we've no government worth a moment's consid'ration, an' everybody knows it, Greeks included! You men lookin' for farms? Take your time! Once you get a farm, an' get your house built, an' stock bought, an' stuff planted—once you've got your capital invested so to speak, they've got you! Till then you're free! Till then they'll maybe treat you with consideration! Till then you leave the country when you like an' kiss yourselves good-bye to them an' Africa. Till then they've got no hold! The courts can fine you, maybe, but can they make you pay? It's none so easy if you're half awake! But take me: Suppose I break a reggylation. What happens? They know where to find me—how much I've got—where it is—an' if I don't pay the fine, they come an' collar my cattle an' sticks! D'you notice any Greeks applyin' for farms? Not no crowds of 'em you don't! I don't know one single Greek who has a farm in all East Africa! Any Goas? Not a bit of it! Any Indians? Not one! So when a few extry elephants get shot, I get the blame—down at Lumbwa, where there ain't no elephants; an' the Greeks, Goas, Arabs an' Indians get fat on the swag! It's easy to keep track of a white man; the natives all know him, an' his name, an' where he lives, an' report everything he does to the nearest gov'ment officer. But Greeks an' Goas an' Indians an' Arabs ain't white, so the natives make no mention of 'em. They do the lootin'; we settlers get the blame; an' the whole perishing country's going to blazes as fast as a lump of ice melting in hell—but not so fast as I'd like to see it go. Have some o' this whisky, won't you?"

I was scarcely listening to him, but he seemed to get drunk just "so far and no further," and Fred found him worth attention. It happened that Fred, Will and I were all thinking of the same thing. Will put a hand to his neck and stroked the little scar the Arab knife had made in Zanzibar.

"What sort of a country's this for women?" Fred demanded.

"Which women?" Brown asked in sort of mild amazement.

"White women?"

"Rotten! Leastwise, there aren't any. Yes, there's three. Two officials' wives, an' Pioneer Jane French. Heard o' her? Walked from South Africa, Jane did—hoofed it along o' French, bossed his boys, drove the cattle, shot the meat, ran the whole shootin' match, an' runs him, too, when he's sober an' she's drunk. When they're both drunk everybody ducks. She's scarcely a woman, she's sort of three-men-rolled-into-one. Give her a horsewhip an' she'll manage the unruliest crowd o' savages ever you or she set eyes on! Countin' her as one, an' the two officials wives, an' her on this train, there's four!"

Our eyes met. I awoke to sudden interest that startled our informant and made him curious in turn.

"On this train?"

"On this train. Didn't you see her? She was watching you chaps through the window slits like the Queen o' Sheba keepin' tabs on Solomon. Say, what's she doing in this country anyhow? I made a try to get a seat in her carriage, but she ordered me out like Aunt Jemima puttin' out the cat the last thing. She's got a maid in with her, but the maid ain't white—Jew—Syrian—Levantine—Dago—some such breed. She's in this compartment next behind."

Our eyes met again. Fred laughed, and Will leaned forward to whisper to me: "She heard what Courtney said to us about the way to Mount Elgon!"

"D'you know her name?" asked Brown.

"No!" we all three lied together with one voice.

"I do! I seen it on the reservation card. Lady Isobel Saffren Waldon! Pretty high-soundin' patronymic, what? Lady Isobel Saffren Waldon!" He repeated the name over and over, crescendo, with growing fervor. "What's a woman with a title doin' d'you suppose? The title's no fake. She's got the blood all right, all right! You ought to ha' heard her shoo me out! Lummy! A nestin' hen giving the office to a snake weren't in it to her an' me! Good looker, too! What's she doin' in East Africa?"

We made no shift to answer.

"The officials' wives," he went on, "are keen after Tippoo's ivory, but, bein' obliged to stay in the station except when their husbands go on *safari,* an' then only go where their husbands go, they've no show to speak of. Pioneer Jane's nuts on it, an' she's dangerous. Jane's as likely to find the stuff as any one. She's independent—go where she blooming well pleases—game as a lioness—looks like one, too, only a lioness is kind o' softer an' not so quick in the uptake. My money's on Jane for a place. But d'you suppose this Lady Saffren Whatshername's another one? Them Greeks ahead of us I'm sure of; all the Greeks in Africa are huntin' for nothin' else. But what about the dame?"

"Going to join her husband, perhaps," suggested Fred to put him off.

"There's no man o' that name in British East or Uganda. I know 'em all—every one."

"Father—brother—uncle—nephew—oh, perhaps she's just traveling," said Fred.

"Just traveling my eye! Titled ladies don't come 'just traveling' in these parts—not by a sight, they don't—not alone!"

He helped himself to more whisky, but had reached the stage where it had no further visible effect on him.

"Anyhow," he said, wiping the neck of the jar with his hand, "if she kids herself she'll be let go where she pleases—why, she kids herself! It takes Pioneer Jane to trespass where writs don't run! Jane goes where her husband don't dare follow. The officials don't say a word. Y'see there's no jail where they could stow a white woman and observe the decencies. So she goes over the borderline whenever she sees fit. The king's writ runs maybe for thirty miles north o' this railway. Once over that they can't catch you. But unless you're a black man, or Pioneer Jane, the natives tip the gov'ment off an' gov'ment rounds you up afore you get two-thirds the way. They'll take less than half a chance with her ladyship or I'm a Dutchman. Why! How would it look to have to bring her back between two native policemen? She'll not be allowed five miles outside Nairobi township!"

He up-ended his whisky again, consumed about a pint of it, and settled down to sleep. We took him by the legs and arms and threw him on the upper berth to stew in the cabined heat under the roof.

"It's good Monty's not with us," said Fred. He sat down and laughed at our surprise that he should state such heresy. "Monty mustn't break laws, but who cares if we do?"

"Laws?" said Will disgustedly. "I don't care who makes, or breaks the laws of this land! Let's beat it! Let's join Monty in London and make plans for some other trip. Everybody's after this ivory. We haven't a look-in. Even if we knew where to look for it we'd be followed. Let's take the next train back from Nairobi, and the next boat for Europe!"

Fred rubbed his hands delightedly, and stroked his beard into the neat point it refuses to keep for long at a time in very hot weather.

"Let's stay in Nairobi," he said, "at least until Courtney sends that boy he promised us. We can put in the time asking questions, and then—"

"What then?" grumbled Will.

"There may be truth in what Brown of Lumbwa says about a dead-line."

"Dead-line?"

"Beyond which the king's writ doesn't run."

"Betcherlife there's truth in it!" Brown mumbled from the upper berth.

Will exploded silently, going through the motions of reeling off all the bad language he knew—not an insignificant performance.

"He's really asleep now," I said, standing on the lower berth and lifting the man's eyelid to make sure.

"Who cares?" said Will. "He's heard. We've given the game away. The woman heard Courtney shout about how to reach Mount Elgon. So did this sharp. Now he hears Fred talk about dead-lines and the king's writ and breaking laws! The game's up! Me for the down-train and a steamer!"

We smoked in silence, rendered more depressing by the deepening gloom outside. With the evening it grew no cooler. What little wind there was followed the train, so that we traveled in stagnation. Utter darkness brought no respite, but the fascination of flitting shadows and the ever-new mystery of African night. The train drew up at last in a station in the shadow of great overleaning mountains, and the heat shut down on us like hairy coverings. We seemed to breathe through thicknesses of cloth, and the very trees that cast black shadow on the platform ends were stifling for lack of air.

"One hour for diner!" called the guard, walking limply along the train. "Just an hour for dinner! Dinner waiting!"

He was not at all a usual-looking guard. He was dressed in riding breeches and puttee leggings, and wore a worn-out horsey air as if in protest against the obligation to work in a black man's land. In countries where the half-breed and the black man live for and almost monopolize government employment few white men take kindly to braid and brass buttons. That fellow's contempt for his job was equaled only by the babu station master's scorn of him and his own for the station master. Yet both men did their jobs efficiently.

"Only an hour for dinner, gents—train starts on time!"

"Guard!" called a female voice we all three recognized—"Guard! Come here at once, I want you!"

We left Brown of Lumbwa snoring a good imitation of the Battle of Waterloo on the upper berth, and filed out to the dimly-lighted platform. A space in the center was roofed with corrugated iron and under that the yellow lamplight cast a maze of moving shadows as the passengers swarmed toward the dining-room. The smell of greasy cooking blended with the reek of axle and lamp oil. At the platform's forward end shadowy figures were throwing cord-wood into the tender, and the thump-thump-thump of that sounded like impatience; everything else suggested lethargy.

"Guard!" called the voice again. "Come here, guard!"

He stopped in passing to close our windows and lock our compartment door against railway thieves.

"There's a man asleep in there," I said.

"The 'eat 'll sober 'im!" he grinned, slamming the last window down. "What'll you bet 'er 'ighness don't want me to fetch dinner to 'er? She was in the train in Mombasa two hours afore startin' time, an' the things she ordered me to do 'ud have made a 'alf-breed think 'e was demeaning of 'imself! I 'aven't seen the color of 'er money yet. If she wants dinner she gets out and walks or 'er maid fetches it—you watch!"

Coutlass, the other Greek and the Goanese staggered out beside us on to the platform, drunk enough not to know whether Hassan was with them or not. He came out and stood beside them in a sort of alert defensive attitude.

"Guard!" called the voice again. "Where is the man?"

We followed the last of the crowd through the screened doors, and took seats at a table marked "First Class Only!" There were four men there ahead of us, two government officials disinclined to talk; a missionary in a gray flannel shirt, suffering from fever and too suspicious to say good evening; and a man in charge of that section of the line, who checked the station master's accounts and counted money in a tray between mouthfuls. Between us and the second-class tables was a wooden screen on short legs, and beyond that arose babel. Second-class is democratic always, and talks with its mouth full. In addition to our privilege of paying more for exactly the same food, we enjoyed exclusiveness, a dirty table-cloth, and the extra smell from the kitchen door. (The table-cloth was dirty because the barefoot Goanese waiters invariably stubbed their feet against a break in the floor and spilt soup exactly in the same place.)

We had scarcely taken our seats when Coutlass swaggered in, closely followed by his gang. Inside the door he turned on Hassan.

"Black men eat outside!" he snarled, and shoved him out again backward. Then he came over to us and stood leering at the framed sign, "First Class Only," avoiding our eyes, but plainly at war with us.

"Gassharamminy!" he growled. "You think you're popes or something! You three would want a special private piece of earth to spit on!" He raised his voice to a sort of scream. "I proclaim one class only!"

At that he lifted his foot about level with his chest and kicked the screen over. The crash brought everybody to his feet except the two officials and the railway man. They continued eating, and the railway man continued counting copper coins as if life depended on that alone.

"Sit down all!" yelled Coutlass. "You will eat with better appetite now that you can behold the blushes of these virgins!" Then he swaggered over to the long table, thrust the other Greek and the Goanese into chairs on either side of him, and yelled for food. It was the first time we had been referred to publicly as virgins, and I think we all three felt the strain.

The Goanese manager—a wizened old black man with perfectly white hair—came running from the kitchen in a state of near-collapse, the sweat streaming off him and his hands trembling.

"What shall I do?" he asked, almost upsetting the railway man's tray of money. "That man is crazy! He came in once before and broke the dishes! Twice he has come in here and eaten and refused to pay! What shall I do?"

"Nothing," said the railway man. "Go on serving dinner. Serve him too."

The manager hurried out again and the running to and fro resumed. Then in came the guard.

"First-class for two on trays!" he shouted.

The railway man beckoned to him and he winked as he passed by us.

"When you've seen to that, and had your own meal, I want you," said the railway man.

"Thought you said the lady's maid would have to come and fetch the food?" I said maliciously as the guard passed my chair a second time.

"So I did. But if you know how to refuse her, just teach me! I told her flat to have the maid fetch it. She let on they're both too frightened to cross the platform in the dark! Never saw anything like 'em! Tears! An' dignified! When I climbed down they was too afraid next to be left alone. Swore train-thieves 'ud murder 'em! I had to leave 'em my key to lock 'emselves in with until I come back with the grub! What d'you think of that?"

But our soup came, and one could not think and eat that stuff simultaneously. The railway man looked up for a moment, saw my face, and explained in a moment of expansiveness that meat would not keep in that climate but was "perfectly good" when cooked.

"Besides," he added, "you'll get nothing more until you reach Nairobi to-morrow noon!"

That turned out to be not quite true, but as an argument it worked. We swallowed, like the lined-up merchant seamen taking lime-juice under the skipper's eye.

The guard grew impatient and went into the kitchen, but had scarcely got through the door when a scream came from the direction of the train that brought him back on the run. No black woman ever screams in just that way, and in a land of black and worse-than-black men imagination leaps at a white woman's call for help.

There was a stampede for the door by every one except the Greeks and Goanese and the railway man. (He had to guard the money.) We poured through the screen doors, the guard fighting to burst between us, and, because with a self-preserving instinct that I have never thought quite creditable to the human race, everybody ran toward his own compartment, it happened that we three and the two officials and the guard came first on the scene of trouble.

Brown of Lumbwa was still drunk-affectionate, it seemed, by that time.

"You've no call to be 'fraid of me, li'l sweetheart!" The door was open. Within the compartment all was dark, but every sound emerged. There came a stifled scream.

"Li'l stoopid! What d'you come in for, if you're 'fraid o' poor ole Brown? I won't hurt you."

The guard passed between us and went up the step. He listened, looked, disappeared through the open door, and there came a sound of struggling.

"Whassis?" shouted Brown. "An interloper? No you don't! This is my li'l sweetheart! She came in to see me—didn't you, Matilda Ann?"

The woman apparently broke free. The guard yelled for help. Fred and one of the government officials were nearest and as they entered they passed the woman coming out. I recognized Lady Saffren Waldon's Syrian maid, with the big railway key in her fist that the guard had left with her. By that time there was a considerable crowd about our car, unable to see much because it stood in the way of the station lamp-light. She slipped through—to the right—not toward Lady Isobel's compartment, and I lost sight of her behind some men. I ran after her, but she was gone among the shadows, and although I hunted up and down and in and out I could find her nowhere.

When I returned to our car Brown of Lumbwa was out on the platform with his hair all tousled and a wild eye. The guard was wiping a bloody nose and everybody was inventing an account of what nobody had seen.

"Scrag him!" advised some expert on etiquette.

"What the hell right has anybody got," demanded Brown with querulous ferocity, "to interfere between me and a lady? Eh? Whose compartment was she in? Me in hers or her in mine? Eh? Me. I'm sleeping. Hasn't a gent a right to sleep? Next thing I know she's fingerin' my whiskers. How should I know she's not balmy on red beards an' makin' love to me? What right's she got in my compartment anyhow? Who let her in? Who asked her? What if I did frighten her? What then?"

"Who was she?" demanded the official. "Had anybody seen her before?"

"The maid attending the lady in the next compartment," said I.

"Are you sure?"

"Positive."

"Very well. Guard! See who is in there!"

The guard wiped blood from his nose and obeyed orders. We clustered round the steps to hear.

" 'Ow many's in here?" he demanded.

There was no answer. He tried the door and it opened 'readily.

" 'Scuse me, but is there two of you? I can't see in the dark."

"Oh, is that our dinner?" said Lady Saffren Waldon's Voice.

"No ma'am, not the dinner yet."

"Why not, pray?"

"There's folks accusin' your maid o' enterin' the next compartment an'—an'—"

"Nonsense! My maid is here! You kept us so long waiting for dinner we were both asleep! Ah! There's light at last, thank heaven!"

Two native porters running along the roofs were dropping lamps into the holes appointed for them, and the train that had been a block of darkness hewn out of the night was now a monster, many-eyed.

"They're both in there, so 'elp me!" the guard reported, retreating backward through the door and leering at us.

There remained nobody, except the still indignant Brown of Lumbwa to levy charges, and the crowd remembered its dinner (not that anything could be expected to grow cold in that temperature).

"The train will start on time!" announced the babu station master, and everybody hurried to the dining-room. Brown came with us, bewildered.

"How did it happen?" he demanded. "When did we get here? Why wasn't I called for dinner? How did she get in? Where did she go to?"

"Oh, come and eat curried cow, it's lovely!" answered Will.

Fred overtook us at the door, and whispered:

"Our things have been gone through, but I can't find that anything's missing."

Within the dining-room was new ground for discontent. The British race and its offshoots wash, but disbelieve with almost unanimity in water as a drink. Every guest at either table had left at his place a partly emptied glass of beer, or brandy and soda, or whisky. Each looked for the glass on his return, and found it empty.

"Those Greeks!" exclaimed the Goanese manager, with a fearful air, and shoulders shrugged to disclaim his own responsibility.

Coutlass and the other Greek were sitting at a table with a gorged look, glancing neither to the right nor left, yet not eating. I looked at the railway official, who had not left his seat. It struck me he was laughing silently, but he did not look up. The crowd, after the manner of all crowds, stormed at the Goanese manager.

"What can I do? What shall I do?" wailed the unhappy little man. "They are bigger than I! They were greedy! They took!"

All those charges were evidently true, and stated mildly. Coutlass rose to his feet.

"Gassharamminy!" he thundered, and his stomach stuck out over the table it was so full of various drinks. "Why should we not take? Who isn't thirsty in this hell of a place? Who leaves good drink deserves to lose it!"

"What shall I do?" wailed the Goanese manager.

"Take the orders for drinks again," said the railway man, glancing up from his figures. "Bring the account to me."

The waiters ran to fill orders, and a babel of abuse at the second table was hurled at Coutlass and his friends; but they lid not leave the table because there was another course to come, and, as the manager had said, they were greedy. Then in came the guard, his face a blood-and-smudgy picture of discontent.

"Say!" he yelled. "Ain't I goin' to get those two first-classes on trays?" He came and stood by us. "Did you ever 'ear the likes of it? They swear neither of 'em was out of the compartment. They call me a liar for askin' for my key back! They swear I never gave it to 'em, 'an they never asked for it, an' their door was never locked, nor nothin'!"

He passed on to the railway man.

"I'll have to borry your key, sir. Mine's lost. Can't open doors until I get one from somewhere."

The railway man passed him his key with a bored expression and no remark.

"Don't forget that I want you presently," be ordered. "Be quick and get your own dinner."

"I'm in love with this ivory hunt!" Fred whispered to us across the table. "If she's sure our pockets are worth going through, I'm sure there's something to look for!"

"Are you sure the maid went through our things?" asked Will.

"Quite. I left my shooting jacket hanging on a hook. Everything was emptied out of the pockets on to the berth."

"I think I'll make you a confession presently," said I, with a look at Will that just then he did not understand.

"Never confess before dessert and coffee!" advised Fred. "It spoils the appetite."

THE SLAVE GANGS

Our fathers praised the old accustomed things,
The privilege of chiefs, the village wall
Within whose circling dark Monumme sings
O' nights of belly-full and ease and all
They taught us we should prize and praise
(Only of dearth and pestilence should be our fears;)
And now behind us are the green, regretted days.
The water in the desert is our tears.
Then ye, who at the waters drink
Of Freedom, oh with Pity think
On us, who face the desert brink
Your fathers entered willingly.

Our fathers mocked the might of the Unseen,
Teaching that only what we saw and felt
Was good to fight about—what aye had been,
Old-fashioned foods that their forefathers smelt,
Old stars each night illuming the old sky,
The warm rain softening ere women till the ground,
The soft winds singing, only ask not why!
And now our weeping is the desert sound.
Oh ye, who gorge the daily good,
Unquestioned heirs of all ye would,
Spare not too timidly the blood
Your fathers shed so willingly.

Our fathers taught us that the village good was best.
Later we learned the red, new tribal creed
That our place was the sun—night owned the rest
Unless their treasure profited our greed!
But now we gather nothing where our fathers sowed,
For harvest grim the vultures wait in rows
As, urged by greedier than us with gun and goad,
Yoked two by two the slave safari goes.
Oh ye, who from true judgment shrink,
Nor gentleness with courage link,
Be thoughtful when the cup ye drink
Your fathers spilled so willingly.

V

THE GUARD procured his trays at last, delivered them at a run, returned in a hurry and swallowed his own meal at a side-table. Then, with his mouth full, he reported for orders to the railway official, who was still checking figures. The room was beginning to grow empty. Coutlass and his Greek friend and the Goanese sat almost alone at the far end of the other table, finishing their pudding. I had not noticed until then that the guard was a singularly little man. He stood very few inches taller than the seated official. I suppose that hitherto in some way his energy had seemed to increase his inches.

"Are there handcuffs in the caboose?"

"Yes, sir."

"Fetch them."

In spite of Brown of Lumbwa's protests, who wept at the notion of having to eat alone, we were in the act of settling our bills and going. But mention of handcuffs suggesting entertainment, we lit cigars and, imagining we stayed for love of him, Brown cooed at us.

"I've the darbies in my pocket, sir!"

I thought the guard looked more undersized than ever. He would have made a fair-sized middle-weight jockey.

"Tell that Greek—Coutlass his name is—to come here."

With his tongue stuck into his cheek and a wink at us the guard obeyed.

"He says for you to go to 'ell, sir!" he reported after a moment's interview.

"Very well. Arrest him!"

"He'll need help," I interrupted. "My two friends and I—"

"Oh, dear no," said the official. "He is fully up to his work."

So we moved our chairs into position for a better view.

The guard advanced fox-terrierwise to within about six paces of Coutlass.

"Up with both your 'ands, Thermopylae!" he snapped. "Your bloomin' reckonin's come!"

Coutlass showed tobacco-stained teeth for answer, and his friends rutched their chairs clear of the table, ready for action. Yet they were taken unawares. With a terrier's speed the guard pounced on Coutlass, seized him by the hair and collar, hurled him, chair and all, under a side-table, and was on the far side of the table kicking his prostrate victim in the ribs before either Greek or Goanese—likewise upset in the sudden onslaught—could gather themselves and interfere.

The Goanese was first on his feet. He hurled a soda-water bottle. The guard ducked and the bottle smashed into splinters on the wall. Before the sound of smashing glass had died the Goanese was down again, laid out by blows on the nose and jugular. Then again the guard kicked Coutlass, driving him back under the table from which he was trying to emerge on all fours.

The second Greek looked more dangerous. His face grew dark with rage as the lips receded from his yellow teeth. He reached toward his boot, but judged there were too many witnesses for knife work and rushed in suddenly, yelling something in Greek to Coutlass as he picked up a chair to brain the guard with. He swung the chair, but the guard met it with another one, dodged him, and tripped him as he passed. In another second it was his turn to be kicked in the ribs until he yelled for mercy. (An extra large dinner and all those assorted drinks in addition to what they had had in the train made neither man's wind good.)

No mercy was forthcoming. He was kicked, more and more violently, until the need of crawling through the door to safety dawned on his muddled wits and he made his exit from the room snake fashion. By that time Coutlass was on his feet, and he too elected to force the issue with a chair. The guard sprang at the chair as Coutlass raised it, bore it down, and drove his fist hard home into the Greek's right eye three times running.

" 'Ave you 'ad enough?" he demanded, making ready for another assault. The Goanese had recovered and staggered to his feet to interfere, but Coutlass yielded.

"All right," he said, "why should I fight a little man? I surrender to save bloodshed!"

"Put your 'ands out, then!"

Coutlass obeyed, and was handcuffed ignominiously.

"Outside, you!"

A savage kick landed in exactly the place where the Goanese least expected and most resented it. He flew through the door as if the train had started, and then another kick jolted Coutlass.

"Forward, march! Left-right-left-right!"

With hands manacled in front and the inexorable bantam guard behind, Coutlass came and stood before the railway official, who at last condescended not to seem engrossed in his accounts.

" 'Ere he is, sir!"

"I suppose you know, my man, that I have magisterial powers on this railway?" said the official.

Coutlass glowered but said nothing.

"This is not the first time you have made yourself a nuisance. You broke dishes the last time you were here."

"That is long ago," Coutlass objected. "That was on the day the place was first opened to the public. There was a celebration. Every one was drunk."

"You broke plates and refused to pay the damage!"

"Officials were drunk. I saw them!"

"The damage amounted to seventeen rupees, eight annas."

"Gassharamminy! All the crockery from Mombasa to Nairobi isn't worth that amount! I shall not pay!"

"Now there's another bill for those drinks you and your friends stole when passengers' backs were turned. I saw you do it!"

"Why didn't you object at the time?" sneered Coutlass.

"Here is the bill: twenty-seven rupees, twelve annas. Total, forty-five rupees, four annas. You may make the manager a present of the odd sum for his injured feelings, and call it an even fifty. Settle now, or wait here for the down-train and go to jail in Mombasa!"

"Wait in this place?" asked Coutlass, aghast.

"Where else? There'll be a down passenger train in a week."

"I pay!" said the Greek, with a hideous grimace.

"Take the irons off him, then."

The guard unlocked the handcuffs and Coutlass began to fumble for a money-bag.

"Give me a receipt!" he demanded, thumbing out the money.

"You are the receipt!" said the official. "An Englishman would have been sent to jail with a fine, and have paid the bill into the bargain. You're treated leniently because you can't be expected to understand decent behavior. You're expected to learn, however. Next time you will catch it hot!"

"All aboard!" called the guard cheerfully. "All aboard!"

"Tears, idle tears!" said Brown of Lumbwa, taking my arm and Fred's.

"Thass too true—too true! They'd have jailed an Englishman—me, f'rinstance. One little spree, an' they'd put me in the Fort! One li'l indishcresshion an' they'd jug me for shix months! Him they let go wi' a admonisshion! It's 'nother case o' Barabbas, an' a great shame, but you can't change the English. They're ingcorridgible! Brown o' Lumbwa's my name," he added by way of afterthought.

"Take advice and get under blankets afore you go to sleep, gents!" warned the guard. All windows were once more opened wide, and every one was panting.

"A job on this 'ere line's a circus!" he grinned. "I'm lucky if there's only one fight before Nairobi! 'Ave your blankets ready, gents! Cover yourselves afore you sleep!"

That sounded like a joke. The sweat poured from every one in streams. The hot hair cushions were intolerable. The dust gathered from the desert stirred and hung, and there was neither air to breathe nor coolness under all those overhanging mountains.

"Get under your blankets, gents!" advised the guard, passing down the train; and then the train started.

I had the upper berth opposite Brown's, where it was hottest of all because of the iron roof. Drunk though he was, I noticed that the first thing Brown did after we had hoisted him aloft was to dig among the blankets like a dog and make the best shift he could of crawling under them. With one blanket twisted about his neck and shoulders and the other tangled about his knees he remarked to the roof that his name was Brown of Lumbwa, and proceeded to sob himself to sleep. He had made the journey a dozen times, so knew what he was doing. I drew on my own blankets, and stifling, blowing out red dust, remembered a promise.

"Will!" I said. "Tell Fred what happened to us in Zanzibar while he and Monty viewed the moon!"

"We agreed not to," he answered, but it seemed to me he might arouse his own enthusiasm if he did tell.

"Who's afraid of Fred?" said I.

That settled it.

"One of you shall tell before you sleep!" Fred announced, sitting up. "Who feareth not God nor regardeth me will blench before the prospect of a sleepless night! Speak, America!"

He took out a cleaning rod from his gun-case, and proceeded to stir Will's ribs and whack his feet. In a minute there was a rough-house—panting, and bursts of laughter—cracks of the cleaning rod on Will's bare legs—the sound of hands slipping on sweaty arms—and

"Murder!" yelled Brown of Lumbwa, waking up. "Murder! Oh, mur-durrr!"

"Shut up, you fool!" I shouted at him. But he only yelled the louder.

"I knew these tears were not for nothing!" he wailed. "It was premonition! Pass me the whisky! Pass it up here! Oh, look! They're at each other's throats! Murder! Oh, mur-durrr! Pass the whisky or I'll come down and kill everybody in self-defense! Murrrrr-durrr!"

They stopped fooling because his idiotic screams could be heard all down the train.

"There," said Brown, "you see, I've saved two worthless lives! Very foolish of me! Pass the whisky! See that I save a little for the morning!"

At that he fell asleep again; and because Fred threatened to start new commotion and wake him unless Will or I confessed at once, Will took up the tale, I leaning over the edge of my berth to prompt him. Fred laughed all through the story, and finally crawled under his blanket again to lie chuckling at the underside of Brown of Lumbwa's berth.

"I don't see what we've scored by telling him," said Will to me. "We've merely given him a peg to hang jokes on!"

But I knew that now Will had told the story he would not, for very shame, withdraw from the venture until we should have demonstrated that no Lady Saffren Waldon, nor Sultan of Zanzibar, nor Germans, nor Arabs could make us afraid. And it seemed to me that was sufficient accomplishment for one night.

The train's progress slowed and grew slower. The panting of the engine came back to us in savage blasts. We were climbing by curves and zigzags up the grim dark wall of mountains. And as we mounted inch by inch, foot by foot, the air freshened and grew cooler—not really cool yet by a very Jacob's ladder of degrees, but delectable by comparison.

There was something peacefully exhilarating in the thought of rising from the red dead level of that awful plain, littered with the bones of camels and the slaves whom men pinned into the yokes to perish or survive in twos. As we mounted foot by foot we fell asleep. Later, as we mounted higher, we shivered under blankets. There is a spirit and a spell of Africa that grip men even in sleep. The curt engine blasts became in my dreams the panting of enormous beasts that fought. A dream-continent waged war on itself, and bled. I saw the caravans go, thousands long, the horsed and white-robed Arab in the lead—the paid, fat, insolent *askaris,* flattering and flogging—slaves burdened with ivory and other, naked, new ones, two in a yoke, shivering under the *askari's* lash, the very last dogged by vultures and hyenas, lean as they, ill-nourished on such poor picking.

Then I saw elephants in herds five thousand strong that screamed and stormed and crashed, flattening out villages in rage that man should interfere with them—in fear of the ruthless few armed men with rifles in their rear. Whole herds crashed pell-mell through artfully staged undergrowth into thirty-foot-deep pits, where they lingered and died of thirst, that Arabs (who sat smoking within hail until they died) might have the ivory.

And all I saw in my dream was nothing to the things I really was to see. None of the cruelty of man, none of the rage and fear of animal have vanished yet from Africa. Some of the cruelty is more refined; some of the herds are smaller; some good is making headway but Africa is unchanged on the whole. It is a land of nightmares, with lovely oases and rare knights errant; a land whose past is gloom, whose present is twilight and uncertainty, but whose future under the rule of humane men is immeasurable, unimaginable.

In my dream din followed crash and confusion until the engine's screaming at last awoke me. My blanket had fallen to the floor and I was shivering from cold. I jumped down to recover it and realized it was dawn already. We were bowling along at a fine pace past green trees and undulating veldt, and I wondered why the engine should keep on screaming like a thing demented. I knelt on Fred's berth to lean from the window and look ahead. We were going round a slight curve and I could see the track ahead for miles.

Three hundred yards away a full-grown rhinoceros stood planted on the track, his flank toward us and his interest fixed on anything but trains. He was sniffing the cool morning, looking the other way.

"Wake up, you fellows!" I yelled, and Fred and Will put their heads through the window beside me just in time to see the rhino take notice of the train at last. When the engine was fifty yards from him he wheeled, took a short-sighted squint at it, sniffed, decided on war, and charged. The engineer crowded on steam.

"He's a game enough sport!" chuckled Fred.

"He's a fool!" grinned Will.

He was both, but he never flinched. He struck the cow-catcher head-on and tried to lift it sky-high. The speed and weight of the engine sent him rolling over and over off the track, and the shock of the blow came backward along the train in thunderclaps as each car felt the check. The engineer whistled him a requiem and a cheer went up from fifty heads thrust out of windows. But he was not nearly done for.

He got up, spun around like a polo pony to face the train, deliberately picked out level going, and charged again. This time he hit the car we were in, and screams from the compartment behind us gave notice that Lady Saffren Waldon's maid was awake and looking through a window too. He hit the running-board beside the car, crumpled it to matchwood, lifted the car an inch off the track, but failed to disrail us. The car fell back on the metal with a clang, and the rhino recoiled sidewise, to roll over and over again. This time the impetus sent him over the edge of a gully and we did not doubt he was dead at the bottom of it.

The guard stopped the train and came running to see what the damage amounted to.

"Any gent got his rifle handy?" he shouted. "The

train's ahead o' time. There's twenty minutes for sport!"

We dived for our rifles, but Coutlass had his and was on the track ahead of us, his eye a ghastly sight from the guard's overnight attentions, his face the gruesome color of the man who has eaten and drunk too much, but his undamaged eye ablaze, and nothing whatever the matter with his enthusiasm.

"Give me a cartridge—a cartridge, somebody!" he yelled. "Gassharamminy! He's not dead! I saw him kick as he went over the edge legs upwards! Give me one cartridge and I'll finish him!"

By that time every male passenger was out on the track, some in night-shirts, some in shirts and pants, some with next-to-nothing at all on, but nearly all with guns. Somebody gave Coutlass a handful of cartridges that fitted his Mauser rifle and he was off in the lead like a hero leading a forlorn hope, we after him. We searched high and low but lost all trace of the rhino, and at the end of half an hour the engine's whistle called us back. There were blood and hair all over the engine—blood and hair on our car, but the rhino had been as determined in defeat as in attack, and if he died of his wounds he contrived to do it alone and in dignity.

"That leaves Coutlass with six cartridges," said I, overtaking Fred. "Let's hope their owner asks for them back."

The owner did ask for them. He stood with his hand out by the door of the Greek's compartment.

"You didn't use those cartridges," he said.

"But I will!" sneered Coutlass. "Out of my way!"

He sprang for his door and slammed it in the man's face, and the other Greek and the Goanese jeered through the window. I caught sight of Hassan beside them looking gray, as unhappy black men usually do. Will saw him too.

"The cannibal's ours," he said, "supposing we want him and play our cards kind o' careful."

The next thing to delay the train was an elephant, who walked the track ahead of us and when the engine whistled only put on speed. Hypnotized by the tracks that reached in parallel lines to the horizon, with trunk outstretched, ears up, and silly tail held horizontally he set himself the impossible task of leaving us behind. The more we cheered, the more the engine screamed, the fiercer and less dignified became his efforts; he reached a speed at times of fourteen or fifteen miles an hour, and it was not until, after many miles, he reached a culvert he dared not cross that he switched off at right angles. Realizing then at last that the train could not follow him to one side he stood and watched us pass, red-eyed, blown and angry. He had only one tusk, but that a big one, and the weight of it caused him to hold his head at a drunken-looking angle.

"Stop the train!" yelled Coutlass, brandishing his rifle as he climbed to the seat on the roof. But the guard, likewise on the roof at his end of the train, gave no signal and we speeded on. We were already in the world's greatest game reserve, where no man might shoot elephant or any other living thing.

We began to pass herds of zebra, gnu, and lesser antelope—more than a thousand zebra in one herd—ostriches in ones and twos—giraffes in scared half-dozens—rhinoceros—and here and there lone lions. Scarcely an animal troubled to look up at us, and only the giraffes ran.

Watching them, counting them, distinguishing the various breeds we three grew enormously contented, even Will Yerkes banishing depression. Obviously we were in a land of good hunting, for the strictly policed reserve had its limits beyond which undoubtedly the game would roam. The climate seemed perfect. There was a steady wind, not too cold or hot, and the rains were recent enough to make all the world look green and bounteous.

To right and left of us—to north and south that is—was wild mountain country, lonely and savage enough to arouse that unaccountable desire to go and see that lurks in the breast of younger sons and all true-blue adventurers. We got out a map and were presently tracing on it with fingers that trembled from excitement routes marked with tiny vague dots leading toward lands marked "unexplored." There were vast plateaus on which not more than two or three white men had trodden, and mountain ranges almost utterly unknown—some of them within sight of the line we traveled on. If the map was anything to go by we could reach Mount Elgon from Nairobi by any of three wild roads. Fred and I underscored the names of several places with a fountain pen.

"And say!" said Will. "Look out of the window! If we once got away into country like that, who could follow us!"

"But you can't get away!" said a weary voice

from the upper berth. "I'm Brown of Lumbwa. That's my name, gents, and I know, because I tried! Thought I was sound asleep, didn't you! Well, I weren't! Listen to me, what happens. You start off. They get wind of it. They send the police helter-skelter hot-foot after you—native police—no officer—Masai they are, an' I tell you those Masai can make their sixty miles a day when they're minded an' no bones about it either! Maybe the Masai catches you and maybe not. S'posing they do they can't do much. They've merely a letter with 'em commanding you to return at once and report at the gov'ment office. And o' course—bein' ignorant, same as me, an' hot-headed, an' eager—you treat that contumelious an' tip the Masai the office to go to hell. Which they do forthwith. They're so used to bein' told to go to hell by wishful wanderers that they scarcely trouble to wait for the words. Presently they draw a long breath an' go away again like smoke being blowed downwind. An' you proceed onward, dreamin' dreams o' gold an' frankincense an' freedom."

"Well, what next?" said I, for he made a long pause, either for reminiscence or because of headache.

"Whisky next!" he answered. "I left a little for the morning, didn't I? I almost always do. Hold the bottle up to the light—no, no, you'll spill it!—pass it here! Ah-h-h—gug-gug!"

He finished what was left and tried to hurl the empty bottle through the window, but missed and smashed it against the woodwork.

" 'Sapity!" he murmured. "Means bad luck, that does! Poor ole Brown o' Lumbwa—poor ole fella'. Pick up the pieces, boys! Pick 'em up quick—might get some o' poor ole Brown's bad luck—cut yourselves or what not. Pick 'em up careful now!"

We did, and it took ten minutes, for the splinters were scattered everywhere.

"Next time you do a thing like that you shall get out an' walk!" announced Fred.

"That 'ud be only my usual luck!" he answered mournfully. "But I was tellin' how you notify the Masai police to go to hell, an' they oblige. It's the last obligin' anybody does for you. Every native's a bush telegraph—every sleepy-seemin' one of 'em! They know tracks in an' out through the scrub that ain't on maps, an' they get past you day or night wi'out you knowin' it, an' word goes on ahead o' you—procedes you as the sayin' is. You come to a village. You need milk, food, Porters maybe, an' certainly inf'mation about the trail ahead. You ask. Nobody answers. They let on not to sling your kind o' lingo. Milk—never heard o' such stuff—cows in them parts don't give milk! Food? They're starving. It isn't overeating makes their bellies big, it's wind. Porters? All the young men are lame, an' old 'uns too old, an' the middle 'uns too middle-aged—an' who ever heard of a native woman workin' anyhow. Who tills the *mtama* patch, then? It don't get tilled, or else the women only 'tend to it at tillin' time. Nobody works at anythin' about the time you come on the scene, for work ain't moral, pleasin' nor profitable, an' there you are! As for the trail ahead, lions an' cannibals are the two mildest kind of calamities they guarantee you'll meet."

"You don't have to believe them," I argued. "No man in his senses would start without porters of his own—"

"Who *never* run away, an' *never, oh never* go lame o' course!" said Brown.

"Porters enough and to spare," I continued. "And food for a month or two—"

"How are you going to get away right under their noses with food for a month or two?" demanded Brown. "You've got to live off the country after a certain distance. The further you go, the worse for you, for they'll sell you nothing and give you less. By and by your porters get tipped off by the natives of some village you spend a night at. You look for 'em next mornin' and where are they? Gone! There are their loads, an' no one to carry 'em! You've got to leave your loads an' return, an' the police you told so stric'ly to go to hell meet you with broad grins and lead you to the gov'ment office. There the collector, or, what's worse, the 'sistant collector, gives you a lecture on infamy an' the law of doin' as you'd be done by. You ask for your loads back, an' he laughs at you. An' that's all about it, excep' that next time you happen to want a favor done you by gov'ment you get a lecture instead! No, you can't get away, an' it's no use tryin'! If you was Greeks maybe, or Arabs, yes. Bein' English, the Indian Penal Code, which is white man's law in these parts, 'll get you sure!"

Brown of Lumbwa sighed at recollection of his wrongs, turned over, and went to sleep again. The train bowled along over high veldt, cutting in half magnificent distances and stopping now and then at stations whose excuse for existence was unimaginable. We stopped at a station at last where the Hindu clerk sold tea and biscuits. The train disgorged its passengers and there was a scramble in the tiny ticket office like the rush to get through turnstiles at a football game at home, only that the crowd was more polyglot and less good-natured.

Coutlass, his Greek friend and the Goanese being old travelers on that route were out of the train first, first into the room, and first supplied with breakfast. Fred and I were nearly last. Brown of Lumbwa refused to leave his berth but lay moaning of his wrongs, and the iniquity of drink not based on whisky. I missed Will in the scramble, and although it was nearly half an hour before I got served I did not catch sight of him in all that time.

I counted eleven nations taking tea in that tiny room and there were members of yet other tribes strolling the platform, holding themselves aloof with the strange pride of the pariah the wide world over.

When Will came in he was grinning, and his ears seemed to stick out more than usual, as they do when he is pleased with himself.

"Didn't I say fat Johnson was ours if we'd play our cards right?" he demanded.

"You mean Hassan?"

"He'd had no breakfast. He'd had no supper. He had no money. The Greeks took away what little money he did have on the pretext that he might buy a return ticket and desert them. They seem to think that a day or two's starvation might make him good and amenable. I found him trying to beg a bite from a full-blooded Arab, and say! they're a loving lot. The Arab spat in his eye! I offered to buy him eats but he didn't dare come in here for fear the Greeks 'ud thrash him, so I slipped him ten rupees for himself and he's the gratefulest fat black man you ever set eyes on. You bet it takes food and lots of it to keep that belly of his in shape. There's a back door to this joint. He slipped round behind and bribed the babu to feed him on the rear step, me standing guard at the corner to keep Greeks at bay. He's back in the car now, playing possum."

"Let's trade him for Brown of Lumbwa," suggested Fred genially. "Call him into our car and kick Brown out!"

"Trade nothing! I tell you the man is ours! Call him, and he'll bargain. Let him be, and the next time the Greeks ill-treat him he'll come straight to us in hope we'll show him kindness."

"Swallow your tea quickly, Solomon!" Fred advised him. "There goes the whistle!"

It was fresh tea, just that minute made for him. Will gulped down the scalding stuff and had to be thumped on the back according to Fred. With eyes filled with water he did not see what I did, and Fred was too busy guarding against counter-blows. The most public place and the very last minute always suited those two best for playing horse.

"Thought you said Johnson was asleep," said I.

"Possuming," coughed Will. "Shamming sleep to fool the Greeks."

"Possuming, no doubt," I answered, "but the Greeks are on. He has just come scurrying out of Lady Saffren Waldon's compartment. The Greeks watched him and made no comment!"

We piled into our own appointed place and sat for a while in silence.

"All right said Will at last, lighting his pipe. "I own I felt like quitting once. I'll see it through now if there's no ivory and nothing but trouble! That dame can't thimblerig me!"

"We're supposed to know where the ivory is," grinned Fred. "Keep it up! They'll hunt us so carefully that they'll save us the trouble of watching them!"

"I'm beginning to think we do know where the ivory is," said I. "I believe it's on Mount Elgon and they mean to prevent our getting it."

"If that turns out true, we'll have to give them the slip, that's all," said Fred, and got out his concertina just as Monty always played chess when his brain was busy, Fred likes to think to the strains of his infernal instrument. One could not guess what he was thinking about, but the wide world knew he was perplexed, and Lady Saffren Waldon in the next compartment must have suffered.

After a while he commenced picking out the tunes of comic songs, and before long chanced on one that somebody in the front part of the train recognized and began to sing. In ten minutes after that he was playing accompaniments for a full train chorus and the seared zebra and impala bolted to right and left, pursued by Tarara-boom-de-ay, Ting-a-ling-a-ling, and other non-Homeric dirges that in those days were dying an all-too-lingering death.

It was to the tune of *After the Ball* that the engine dipped head-foremost into a dry watercourse, and brought the train to a jaw-jarring halt. The tune went on, and the song grew louder, for nobody was killed and the English-speaking races have a code, containing rules of conduct much more stringent than the Law of the Medes and Persians. Somebody—probably natives from a long way off, who needed fuel to cook a meal—had chopped out the hard-wood plate on which the beams of a temporary culvert rested. Time, white ants, gravity and luck had done the rest. It was a case thereafter of walk or wait.

"Didn't I tell you?" moaned Brown of Lumbwa. "Didn't I say walkin' 'ud be only just my luck?"

So we walked, and reached Nairobi a long way ahead of Coutlass and his gang, whose shoes, among other matters, pinched them; and we were comfortably quartered in the one hotel several hours before the arrival of Lady Saffren Waldon and those folk who elected to wait for the breakdown gang and the relief train.

It was a tired hotel, conducted by a tired once-missionary person, just as Nairobi itself was a tired-looking township of small parallel roofs of unpainted corrugated iron, with one main street more than a mile long and perhaps a dozen side-streets varying in length from fifty feet to half a mile.

He must have been a very tired surveyor who pitched on that site and marked it as railway head-quarters on his map. He could have gone on and found within five miles two or three sightlier, healthier spots. But doubtless the day's march had been a long one, and perhaps he had fever, and was cross. At any rate, there stood Nairobi, with its "tin-town" for the railway underlings, its "tin" sheds for the repair shops, its big "tin" station buildings, and its string of pleasant-looking bungalows on the only high ground, where the government nabobs lived.

The hotel was in the middle of the main street, a square frame building with a veranda in front and its laundry hanging out behind. Nairobi being a young place, with all Africa in which to spread, town plots were large, and as a matter of fact the sensation in our corner room was of being in a wilderness—until we considered the board partition. Having marched fastest we obtained the best room and the only bath, but next-door neighbors could hear our conversation as easily as if there had been no division at all. However, as it happened, neither Coutlass and his gang nor Lady Saffren Waldon and her maid were put next to us on either side. To our right were three Poles, to our left a Jew and a German, and we carried on a whispered conversation without much risk.

She and her maid arrived last, as it was growing dusk. We had already seen what there was to see of the town. We had been to the post-office on the white man's habitual hunt, for mail that we knew was non-existent. And I had had the first adventure.

I walked away from The post-office alone, trying to puzzle out by myself the meaning of Lady Saffren Waldon's pursuit of us, and of her friendship with the Germans, and her probable connection with Georges Coutlass and his riff-raff. I had not gone far either on my stroll or with the problem—perhaps two hundred yards down a grassy track that they had told me led toward a settlement—when something, not a sound, not a smell, and certainly not sight, for I was staring at the ground, caused me to look up. My foot was raised for a forward step, but what I saw then made me set it down again.

To my right front, less than ten yards away, was a hillock about twice my own height. To my left front, about twelve yards away was another, slightly higher; and the track passed between them. On the right-hand hillock stood a male lion, full maned, his forelegs well apart and the dark tuft on the end of his tail appearing every instant to one side or the other as be switched it cat-fashion. He was staring down at me with a sort of scandalized interest; and there was nothing whatever for me to do but stare at him. I had no weapon. One spring and a jump and I was his meat. To run was cowardice as well as foolishness, the one because the other. And without pretending to be able to read a lion's thoughts I dare risk the assertion that he was puzzled what to do with me. I could very plainly see his claws coming in and out of their sheaths, and what with that, and the switching tail, and the sense of impotence I could not take my eyes off him. So I did not look at the other hillock at first.

But a sound like that a cat makes calling to her kittens, only greatly magnified, made me glance to the left in a hurry. I think that up to that moment I had not had time to be afraid, but now the goose-flesh broke out all over me, and the sensation up and down my spine was of melting helplessness.

On the left-hand hillock a lioness stood looking

down with much intenser and more curious interest. She looked from me to her mate, and from her mate to me again with indecision that was no more reassuring than her low questioning growl.

I do not know why they did not spring on me. Surely no two lions ever contemplated easier quarry. No victim in the arena ever watched the weapons of death more helplessly. I suppose my hour had not come. Perhaps the lions, well used to white men who attacked on sight with long-range weapons, doubted the wisdom of experiments on something new.

The lioness growled again. Her mate purred to her with an uprising reassuring note that satisfied her and sent my heart into my boots. Then he turned, sprang down behind the hillock, and she followed. The next I saw of them they were running away like dogs, jumping low bushes and heading for jungle on the near horizon faster than I had imagined lions could travel.

That ended my desire for further exercise and solitude. I made for the hotel as fast as fear of seeming afraid would let me, and spent fifteen aggravating minutes on the veranda trying to persuade Fred Oakes that I had truly seen lions.

"Hyenas!" he said with the air of an old hunter, to which he was quite entitled, but that soothed me all the less for that.

"More likely jackals," said Will; and he was just as much as Fred entitled to an opinion.

While I was asserting the facts with increasing anger, and they were amusing themselves with a hundred-and-one ridiculous reasons for disbelieving me, Lady Saffren Waldon came. She had, as usual, attracted to herself able assistance; a settler's ox-cart brought her belongings, and she and her maid rode in hammocks borne by porters impressed from heaven knew where. It was not far from the station, but she was the type of human that can not be satisfied with meek beginnings. That type is not by any means always female, but the women, are the most determined on their course, and come the biggest croppers on occasion.

She was determined now, mistress of the situation and of her plans. She left to her maid the business of quarreling about accommodations; (there was little left to choose from, and all was bare and bad); dismissed the obsequious settler and his porters with perfunctory thanks that left him no excuse for lingering, and came along the veranda straight toward us with the smile of old acquaintance, and such an air of being perfectly at ease that surprise was disarmed, and the rudeness we all three intended died stillborn.

"What do you think of the country?" she asked. "Men like it as a rule. Women detest it, and who can blame them? No, comfort—no manners—no companionship—no meals fit to eat—no amusement! Have you killed anything or anybody yet? That always amuses a man!"

We rose to make room for her and I brought her a chair. There was nothing else one could do. There is almost no twilight in that part of East Africa; until dark there is scarcely a hint that the day is waning. She sat with us for twenty or thirty minutes making small talk, her maid watching us from a window above, until the sun went down with almost the suddenness of gas turned off, and in a moment we could scarcely see one another's faces.

Then came the proprietor to the door, with his best ex-missionary air of knowledge of all earth's ways, their reason and their trend.

"All in!" he called. "All inside at once! No guest is allowed after dark on the veranda! All inside! Supper presently!"

"Pah!" remarked Lady Saffren Waldon, rising. "What is it about some men that makes one's blood boil? I suppose we must go in."

She came nearer until she stood between the three of us, so close that I could see her diamond-hard eyes and hear the suppressed breathing that I suspected betrayed excitement.

"I must speak with you three men! Listen! I know this place. The rooms are unspeakable—not a bedroom that isn't a megaphone, magnifying every whisper! There is only one suitable place—the main dining-room. The proprietor leaves the oil-lamp burning in there all night. People go to bed early; they prefer to drink in their bedrooms because it costs less than treating a crowd! I shall provide a light supper, and my maid shall lay the table after everybody else is gone up-stairs. Then come down and talk with me. Its important! Be sure and come!"

She did not wait for an answer but led the way into the hotel. There was no hall. The door led straight into the dining-room, and the noisy crowd within, dragging chairs and choosing places at the two long tables, made further word with her impossible, even if she had not hurried up-stairs to her room. "What do you make of it—of her? Isn't she the limit?"

The words were scarcely out of Will's mouth when a roar that made the dishes rattle broke and echoed and rumbled in the street outside. The instant it died down another followed it—then three or four—then a dozen all at once. There came the pattering of heavy feet, like the sound of cattle coming homeward. Yet no cattle—no buffaloes ever roared that way.

"Now you know why I ordered you all inside," grinned the ex-missionary owner of the place. I divined on the instant that this was his habit, to stand by the door before supper and say just those words to the last arrivals. I had a vision of him standing by his mission door aforetime, repeating one jest, or more likely one stale euphuism night after night.

"Lions?" I asked, hating to take the bait, yet curious beyond power to resist.

"Certainly they're lions! Did you think you were dreaming? Are you glad you came in when I called you? Would you rather go out again now? Make a noise like a herd of cattle, don't they! That's because they're bold. They don't care who hears them! The day is ours. It used to be theirs, but the white man has come and broken up their empire. The night is still theirs. They're reveling in it! They're boasting of it! Every single night they come swaggering through like this just after sunset. They'll come again just before dawn, roaring the same way. You'll hear them. They'll wake you all right. No trouble in this hotel about getting guests down-stairs for early breakfast!"

"I'll get my rifle and settle the hash of one or two of them before I eat supper!" announced Will, turning away to make good his words. But the proprietor seized him by the arm.

"Don't be foolish! It has been tried too often! I never allowed such foolishness at my place. A party up-street fired from the windows. Couldn't see very well in the dark, but wounded two or three lions. What happened, eh? Why the whole pack of lions laid siege to the house! They broke into the stable and killed three horses, a donkey, and all the cows and sheep. There weren't any shutters on the house windows—nothing but glass. It wasn't long before a young lion broke a window, and in no time there were three full-grown ones into the house after him. They injured one man so severely that he died next day. They only shot two of the lions that got inside. The other two got safely away, and since that time people here have known enough not to interfere with them except by daylight! They'll do no harm to speak of unless you fire and enrage them. They'll kill the stray dogs, or any other animal they find loose; and heaven help the man they meet! But the place to be after six P.M. in Nairobi is indoors. And it's the place to stay until after sunrise! Hear them roar! Aren't they magnificent? Listen!"

The noise that twenty or thirty lions can make, deliberately bent on making it and roaring all at once, is unbelievable. They throw their heads up and glory in strength of lungs until thunders take second place and the listener knows why not the bravest, not the most dangerous of beasts has man aged to impose the fable of his grandeur on men's imagination.

We were summoned to the table by the din of Georges Coutlass rising to new heights of gallantry.

"Gassharamminy!" he shouted, thumping with a scarred fist. With a poultice on his eye he looked like a swashbuckler home from the wars; and as he had not troubled to shave himself, the effect was heightened. "What sort of company sits when a titled lady enters!" He seized a big spoon and rapped on the board with it. "Blood of an onion! Rise, every one!"

Everybody rose, although there were men in the room in no mind to be told their duty by a Greek. Lady Saffren Waldon walked to a place near the head of the table with a chilling bow. As usual when night and the yellow lamplight modified merciless outlines, she looked lovely enough. But she lacked the royal gift of seeming at home with the vulgar herd. She could make men notice her—serve her, up to a certain point—and feel that she was the center of interest wherever she might choose to be; but because she was everlastingly on guard, she lacked the power to put mixed company at ease.

Only the ex-missionary at the head of the table seemed to consider himself socially qualified to entertain her. She was at no pains to conceal contempt for him.

"You honor my poor hotel!" he assured her.

"It is certainly a very poor hotel," she answered. "Do you expect to remain long, may I ask?"

"What right have you to ask me questions? Tell that native to go away from behind my chair. My own maid will wait on me!"

Whether purposely or not, she cast such a chill upon the company that even Georges Coutlass subsided within himself, and, though he ate like a ravening animal, did not talk. Almost the only conversation was between the owner and the native servants, who waited at table abominably and were noisily reprimanded, and argued back. Each reprimand increased their inefficiency and insolence. Natives detest a fussy, noisy white man.

Bad food, indifferent cooking, and no conversation worthy of the name produced gloom that drove every one from table as soon as possible. Even the proprietor, with insatiable curiosity exuding from him, but no spirit for forcing issues, departed to a sanctum of his own up somewhere under the roof. The boys cleared the tables. The smell of food spread itself and settled slowly. A half-breed butler served countless orders of drinks on trays, and sent them upstairs to bedrooms. Presently we three sat alone in the long bare room.

"Shall we wait for her?" I asked. "Haven't we had enough of her?"

Fred laughed. "She can scarcely cut the throats of all three of us!"

"I said we'd never hear the last of it!" said Will, with a scowl at me.

"Shall we wait for her?" I repeated.

My own vote would have been in favor of going upstairs and leaving her to her own devices. I could see that Fred was afire with curiosity, but guessed that Will would agree with me. However, the point was settled for us by the arrival of her maid, who smiled with unusual condescension and produced from a basket an assortment of drinks, nuts, cigarettes and sandwiches. She spread them on the table and went away again.

We sat and smoked for an hour after that, imagining every moment that Lady Saffren Waldon would be coming. Whenever we yawned in chorus and rose to go upstairs, a footstep seemed to herald her arrival. To have passed her on the stairs would have been too awkward to be amusing.

At last we really made up our minds to go to bed; and then she really came, appearing at the bend in the stairs just as I set my foot on the lower step, so we trooped back to our chairs by the window. She was dressed in a lacy silk negligee, and took pains this time to appear gracious.

"I waited until I felt sure we should not be disturbed," she said, smiling. "Won't you come and sit down?"

We brought our chairs to the table, she sitting at one end and we together at one side, Fred nearest her and I farthest away. She made a sign toward the wine and sandwiches, and offered us cigarettes of a sort I had never seen. Without feeling exactly like flies in a spider's web, we were nervous as schoolboys.

"What do you want with us?" asked Will at last.

She laughed and took a cigarette.

"Don't let us talk too loud. You three men are after the Tippoo Tib ivory. So is the Sultan of Zanzibar. So is the German government. So am I!"

She gave the statement time to do its own work, and smoked a while in silence. The strength of her position, and our weakness, lay in there being three of us. Any one of us might let drop an ill-considered word that would commit the others. I think we all felt that, for we sat and said nothing.

"You answer her, Fred," I said at last, and Will nodded agreement.

So Fred got up and sat on the other side of the table, where we could see his face and he ours.

"You haven't answered Mr. Yerkes' question," he said. "What do you want with us, Lady Saffren Waldon?"

"I want an understanding with you. I will be plain to begin with. We all know you know where the ivory is. Lord Montdidier is not the man to connect himself with any wild goose chase. We don't pretend to know how you came by the secret or why he has gone to London, but we are sure you know it, perfectly sure, and for five or six reasons. We are willing to buy the secret from you at your own price."

"Who are 'we'?" asked Fred pointedly, helping himself to nuts.

"The German government, the Sultan of Zanzibar, and myself."

Fred smiled. "Between you you probably could pay," he remarked.

"I will tell you a few hard facts," she said, "now that the ice is broken. You will never be allowed to make full use of your own secret. You have arrived at an inopportune moment, for you and for us. Our plans have been on foot a long time. Our search has been systematic, and it is a mathematical certainty we shall find what we look for in time. We do not propose to let new arrivals on the scene spoil all our plans and disappoint us just because they happen to have information. If you go ahead you will be watched like mice whom cats are after. If you find the ivory, you will be killed before you can make the discovery known!"

"We seem up against it, don't we!" smiled Fred.

"You are! But you can save us trouble, if you will. Name your price. Tell me your secret. Go your way. If your story proves true you shall be paid by draft on London."

"Are you overlooking the idea," asked Fred, "that we might tell the secret to the British government, and be contented with our ten per cent. commission?"

"I am not. You are expressly warned against any such foolishness. In the first place, you will be killed, at once if you dare. In the second place, how do you know the British government would pay you ten per cent.?"

"I've had dealings with the English!" laughed Fred.

"Bah! Do you think this is Whitehall? Do you think the officials here are proof against temptation? When I tell you that in Whitehall itself I can bribe two officials out of three, perhaps you'll understand me when I say that all these people have their price! And the price is low! Tell them where the ivory is—lead them to it—and they'll swear they found it themselves, so as to keep the commission themselves! And as for you—you three"—she sneered with the most sardonic, thin-lipped smile I ever saw—"there are lions out here, and buffalo, snakes, fevers, native uprisings—more ways of being rid of you than by choking you to death with butter!"

"Do you suppose" asked Fred, "that Lord Montdidier has no influence in London, that he—"

"I know he *had* influence. I should have told you first, perhaps. Lord Montdidier was murdered on board ship. A telegram reached Mombasa yesterday at ten A.M. from up-coast saying that the body of an unknown, Englishman had been picked up at sea by an Arab dhow, with the face too badly eaten by fish to be recognizable. You may take it from me, that is Lord Montdidier's corpse."

The calm announcement was intended to surprise us, and it did, but the result surprised her.

"You she-devil!" said Will. "If you and your gang have murdered that fine fellow I'll turn the tables on you! You go up-stairs, and pray he isn't dead! Pray that corpse may prove to be some one's else! If he's dead I'll guarantee you it's the worst day's work you ever had a hand in! Go up-stairs!"

He flung away the cigarette she had given him and knocked his chair away.

"Sit down, you young fool!" she said. "Don't make all that noise!"

But Will had none of the respect for titles acquired by marriage that made most men an easy mark for her.

"Leave the room!" he ordered. "Go away from us! Just you hope that's a lie about Monty, that's all!"

"Sit down!" she repeated. "I admit I am a little previous. The story is unconfirmed yet. Sit down and be sensible! Something of the sort will happen to all of you unless you three men get religion!"

But Will began to pace the floor noisily, stopping to glare at her each time he turned.

"Is there any sense in protracting the scene?" asked Fred.

"No," she admitted. "I see you are too hot-headed to be reasoned with. But it makes little difference! Fever—animals—climate—sun—flood—accident—natives—there are excuses in plenty—explanations by the dozen! I will say good night, then—and good-bye!"

"Yes, good-bye!" growled Will, facing her with his back to the stairs. "You take us for men with a price, do you?"

"All men have a price," she smiled bitterly. "Only it is no use offering flowers to pigs! We must treat pigs another way—pigs, and young fools! And fools old enough to know better!" she added with a nod toward Fred, who bowed to her in mock abasement—too politely, I thought.

Will got out of her way and she went up-stairs with the manner of an empress taking leave of subjects. Fred swept her food and wine from the table and stowed it in a corner, and we sat down at the table again.

"The whole thing's getting ridiculous," he said.

"Why don't we hunt up some official in the morning," I proposed, "and simply expose her?"

"No use," said Will. "She never followed us up here and tried that game without being sure of her pull. Besides—what kind of a tale could we tell without letting on we're after the ivory? I vote we see the game through to a finish."

"Good!" said Fred. "I agree!"

"The only clue we've got," said I, "is Courtney's advice about Mount Elgon."

"And what Coutlass said in Zanzibar about German East," added Will.

"Tell you what," said Fred, rapping the table excitedly. "Instead of falling foul of this government by slipping over the dead-line, why not run down to German East—pretend to search for the stuff down there—and go from German East direct to Mount Elgon, giving 'em all the slip. Who's got the map?"

"It's up-stairs," I said. "I'll fetch it."

There was nothing like silence in the rooms above. Men were smoking and drinking in one another's rooms. Some doors were open to make conversation easier across the landing, and nobody was asleep. But I was surprised to see Georges Coutlass leaning against the door-post of the room he shared with the other Greek and the Goanese, obviously on guard, but against whom and on whose behalf it was difficult to guess.

"Are you off to bed?" he asked, piercing me with his unbandaged eye. "Why don't the others go, too?"

It dawned on me what he was after.

"Take the wine if you want it," I said. "None of us will prevent you."

He went down-stairs in his stocking feet, leaving his own door wide. I glanced in. The other Greek and the Goanese were asleep. Hassan lay on the floor on a mat between their cots. He looked up at me. I did not dare speak, but I smiled at him as friendly as I knew how and made a gesture I hoped he would interpret as an invitation to come and attach himself to our party. Then I hurried on, for Coutlass was coming back with a bottle of wine in each hand.

I was five minutes in our bedroom. In a minute I knew what had happened. We had left the door locked, but the lock was a common one; probably the keys of other doors fitted it, and there was not one thing in the room placed exactly where we had left it. Everything was more or less in place, but nothing quite.

I returned empty-handed down-stairs, locking the bedroom door behind me.

"Listen, you chaps!" I said. "While we waited for that woman she and her maid went through our things again!"

"How d'you know it was she?" asked Fred.

"No mistaking the scent she uses. Where's our money?"

"Here in my pocket."

"Good. The map's gone, though!"

Will showed big teeth in the first really happy smile for several days.

"Good enough!" he said. "Let's go to bed now. I'll bet you my share of the ivory they're poring over the map with a magnifying-glass! D'you remember the various places we underscored? They'll think it's a cryptogram and fret ever it all night! Come on—come to bed!"

THE SONG OF THE GREAT GAME RESERVE

Noah was our godfather, and he pitched and caulked a ship
With stable-room for two of each and fodder for the trip,
Lest when the Flood made sea of earth the animals should die;
And two by two he stalled us till the wrath of God was by.
But who in the name of the Pentateuch can the paleface people be
Who ha' done on the plains of Africa more than he did at sea?

A million hoofs once drummed the dust (Kongoni led the way!)
From river-pool to desert-lick we thundered in array
Until the dark-skin people came with tube and smoke and shot,
Hunting and driving and killing, and leaving the meat to rot.
And we didn't know who the hunters were, but we saw the herds grow thin
That used to drum the dust-clouds up with thousand-footed din.

We were few when the paleface people came—scattered and few and afraid.
Fewer were they, but they brought the law, and the dark-skin men obeyed.
The paleface people drew a line that none by dark or day
Might cross with fell intent to hunt—capture or drive or slay.

But who ran the paleface people be with
red-meat appetites
Who ruled anew what Noah knew—that animals
have rights?

And now in the Athi Game Reserve—in a
million-acre park
A million creatures graze who went by twos into
the Ark.
We sleep o' nights without alarm (Kongoni, prick
your ear!)
And barring the leopard and lion to watch, and
ticks, we've naught to fear,
Zebra, giraffe and waterbuck, rhino and ostrich
too—
But who can the paleface people be who know
what Noah knew?

VI

THE LIONS awoke us a little before dawn as the proprietor had promised. They seemed to have had bad hunting, for their boastfulness was gone. They came in twos and threes, snarling, only roaring intermittently—in a hurry because the hated daylight would presently reverse conditions and put them at disadvantage.

I grew restless and got up. The air being chilly, I put my clothes on and sat for a while by the window. So it happened I caught sight of Hassan, very much afraid of lions, but obviously more afraid of being seen from the hotel windows. He was sneaking along as close to the house as he could squeeze, his head just visible above the veranda rail.

For no better reason than that I was curious and unoccupied, I slipped out of the house and followed him.

Once clear of the hotel he seemed to imagine himself safe, for without another glance backward he ran up-street in the direction of the bazaar. I followed him down the bazaar—a short street of corrugated iron buildings—and out the other end. Being fat, he could not run fast, although his wind held out surprisingly. If he saw me at all he must have mistaken me for a settler or one of the Nairobi officials, for he seemed perfectly sure of himself and took no pains whatever now to throw pursuers off the track.

It soon became evident that he was making for an imposing group of tents on the outskirts of the town. As he drew nearer he approached more slowly.

It now became my turn to take precautions. There was no chance of concealment where I was—nothing but open level ground between me and the tents. But now that I knew Hassan's destination, I could afford to let him out of sight for a minute; so I turned my back on him, walked to where a sort of fold in the ground enabled me to get down unseen into a shallow nullah, and went along that at right angles to Hassan's course until I reached the edge of some open jungle, about half a mile from the tents. I noticed that it came to an end at a spot about three hundred yards to the rear of the tents, so I worked my way along its outer edge, and so approached the encampment from behind.

I had brought a rifle with me, not that I expected to shoot anything, but because the lion incident of the previous afternoon had taught me caution. It had not entered my head that in that country a strange white man without a rifle might have been regarded as a member of the mean white class; nor that anybody would question my right to carry a rifle, for that matter.

The camp was awake now. There were ten tents, all facing one way. Two of them contained stores. The central round tent with an awning in front was obviously a white man's. One tent housed a mule, and the rest were for native servants and porters. The camp was tidy and clean—obviously belonging to some one of importance. Fires were alight. Breakfast was being cooked, and smelled most uncommonly appetizing in that chill morning air. Boys were already cleaning boots, and a saddle, and other things. There was an air of discipline and trained activity, and from the central tent came the sound of voices.

I don't know why, but I certainly did not expect to hear English. So the sound of English spoken with a foreign accent brought me to a standstill. I listened to a few words, and made no further bones about eavesdropping. Circumstances favored me. The boys had seen I was carrying a rifle and was therefore a white man of importance, so they did not question my right to approach. The tent with the mule in it and the two store tents were on the right, pitched in a triangle. I passed between them up to the very pegs of the central tent from which the voices came, and discovered I was invisible, unless some one should happen to come around a corner. I decided to take my chance of that.

The first thing that puzzled me was why a German (for it was a perfectly unmistakable German accent) should need to talk English to a native who was certainly familiar with both Arabic and Kiswahili. When I heard the German addressed as *Bwana* Schillingschen I wondered still more, for from all accounts that individual could speak more native tongues than most people knew existed. It did not occur to me at the time that if he wished not to be understood by his own crowd of boys he must either speak German or English, and that Hassan would almost certainly know no German.

"A good thing you came to me!" I heard. The accent was clumsy for a man so well versed in tongues. "Yes, I will give you money at the right time. Tell me no lies now! There will be letters coming from people you never saw, and I shall know whether or not you lie to me! You say there are three of the fools?"

"Yes, *bwana.* There were four, but one going home—big lord gentleman, him having black m'stache, gone home."

There was no mistaking Hassan's voice. No doubt he could speak his mother tongue softly enough, but in common with a host of other people he seemed to imagine that to make himself understood in English he must shout.

"Why did he go home?"

"I don't know, *bwana.*"

"Did they quarrel?"

"Sijui."

"Don't you dare say *'sijui'* to me!"

"Maybe they quarrel, maybe not. They all quarreling with Lady Saffunwardo—staying in same hotel, Tippoo Tib one time his house—she wanting maybe go with him to London. He saying no. Others saying no. All very angry each with other an' throwing *bwana masikini,* Greek man, down hotel stairs."

"What had he to do with it?"

"Two Greek man an' one Goa all after ivory, too. She—Lady Saffunwardo afterwards promising pay them three if they come along an' do what she tell 'em. They agreeing quick! Byumby Tippoo Tib hearing bazaar talk an' sending me along too. She refuse to take me, all because German consul man knowing me formerly and not making good report, but Greek *bwana* he not caring and say to me to come along. Greek people very bad! No food—no money—nothing but swear an' kick an' call bad names—an' drunk nearly all the time!"

"What makes you think these three men know where the ivory is?" said the German voice. It was the voice of a man very used to questioning natives—self-assertive but calm—going straight each time to the point.

"They having map. Map having marks on it."

"How do you know?"

"She—Lady Saffunwardo go in their bedroom, stealing it last night."

"Did you see her take it?"

"Yes, *bwana.*"

"Did you see the marks on it?"

"No, *bwana.*"

"Then how do you know the marks were on it? Now, remember, don't lie to me!"

"Coutlass, him Greek man, standing on stairs keeping watch. Them three men you call fools all sitting in dining-room waiting because they thinking she come presently. She send maid to their room. Maid, fool woman, upset everything, finding nothing. 'No,' she say, 'no map—no money—no anything in here.' An' Lady Saffunwardo she very angry an' say, 'Come out o' there! Let me look!' And Lady Saffunwardo going in, but maid not coming out, an' they both search. Then Lady Saffunwardo saying all at once, 'Here it is. Didn't you see this?' An' the maid answering, 'Oh, that! That nothing but just ordinary pocket map! That not it!' But Lady Saffunwardo she opening the map, an' make little scream, an' say, 'Idiot! This is it! Look! See! See the marks!' So, *bwana,* I then knowing must be marks on map!"

"Good. What did she do with it?"

"Sijui."

"I told you not to dare say *'sijui'* to me!"

"How should I know, *bwana,* what she doing with it?"

"Could you steal it?"

"No, *bwana!*"

"Why not?"

"You not knowing that woman! No man daring steal from her! She very terrible!"

"If I offered you a hundred rupees could you steal it?"

"Sijui, bwana."

"I told you not to use that word!"

"Bwana, I—"

"Could you steal it?"

"Maybe."

"That is no answer!"

"Say that again about hundred rupees!"

"I will give you a hundred rupees if you bring me that map and it proves to be what you say."

"I go. I see. I try. Hundred rupees very little money!"

"It's all you'll get, you black rascal! And you know what you'll get if you fail! You know me, don't you? You understand my way? Steal that map and bring it here, and I shall give you a hundred rupees. Fail, and you shall have a hundred lashes, and what Ahmed and Abdullah and Seydi got in addition! The hundred lashes first, and the ant-hill afterward! You're not fool enough to think you can escape me, I suppose?"

"No, *bwana.*"

"Then go and get the map!"

"But afterward, what then? She very *gali* woman."

"Nonsense! Steal the map and bring it here to me. Then I've other work for you. Are you a renegade Mohammedan?"

"No, *bwana!* No, no! Never! I'm good Moslem."

"Very well. Back to your old business with you! Preach Islam up and down the country. Go and tell all the tribes in British territory that the Germans are coming soon to establish an empire of Islam in Africa! Good pay and easy living! Does that suit you?"

"Yes, *bwana.* How much pay?"

"I'll tell you when you bring the map. Now be going!"

Hassan went, after a deal of polite salaaming. Then boys began bringing the German's breakfast, and unless I chose to confess myself an eavesdropper it became my business to be in the tent ahead of them. So I strode forward as if just arrived and purposely tripped over a tent-rope, stumbling under the awning with a laugh and an apology.

"Who are you?" demanded the German without rising. He had the splay shovel beard described to us in Zanzibar—big dark man, sitting in the doorway of a tent all hung with guns, skins and antlers. He was in night-shirt and trousers—bare feet—but with a helmet on the back of his head.

"A visitor," I answered, "staying at the hotel—out for a morning shot at something—had no luck—got nothing—saw your tents in the distance, and came out of curiosity to find out who you are."

"My name is Professor Schillingschen," he answered, still without getting up. There was no other chair near the awning, so I had to remain standing. I told him my name, hoping that Hassan had either not done so already, or else that he might have so bungled the pronunciation as to make it unrecognizable. I detected no sign of recognition on Schillingschen's face.

The boys reached the tent with his breakfast, and one of them dragged a chair from inside the tent for me. I sat down on it without waiting for the professor to invite me.

"I'm tired," I said, untruthfully, minded to refuse an invitation to eat, but interested to see whether he would invite me or not.

"Have you any friends at the hotel?" he asked, looking up at me darkly under the bushiest eyebrows I ever saw.

"I've got friends wherever I go," I answered. "I make friends."

"Are you going far?" he demanded, holding out a foot for his boy to pull a stocking on.

"That depends," I said.

"On what?"

"On whether I get employment."

I said that at random, without pausing to think what impression I might create. He pulled the night-shirt off over his head, throwing the helmet to the ground, and sat like a great hairy gorilla for the boy to hang day-clothes on him. He had the hairiest breast and arms I ever saw, hung with lumpy muscles that heightened his resemblance to an ape.

"I might give you work," he said presently, beginning to eat before the boy had finished dressing him.

"I want to travel" I said. "If I could find a job that would take me up and down the length and breadth of this land, that would suit me finely."

"That is the kind of a man I want," he said, eying me keenly. "I have a German, but I need an Englishman. Do you speak native languages?"

"Scarcely a word."

To my surprise he nodded approval at that answer.

"I have parties of natives traveling all over the country gathering folk lore, and ethnographical particulars, but they get into a village and sit down for whole weeks at a time, drawing pay for doing nothing. I need an Englishman to go with them and keep them moving."

"All well and good," I said, "but I understand the government is not in favor of white men traveling about at random."

"But I am known to the government," he answered. "I have been accorded facilities because of my professional standing. Have you references you can give me?"

"No," I said. "No references."

I thought that would stump him, but on the contrary he looked rather pleased.

"That is good. References are too frequently evidence of back-stairs influence."

All this while he kept eying me between mouthfuls. Whenever I seemed to look away his eyes fairly burned holes in me. Whenever food got in his beard (which was frequently) be used the napkin more as a shield behind which to take stock of me than as a means of getting clean again. By the time his breakfast was finished his beard was a beastly mess, but he probably had my features from every angle fixed indelibly in his memory. The sensation was that I had been analyzed and card indexed.

"I pay good wages," he remarked, and then stuck his face, beard and all, into the basin of warm water his boy had brought. "Where did you get that rifle?" he demanded, spluttering, and combing the beard out with his fingers.

It was on the tip of my tongue to say "At Zanzibar," but, as that might have started him on a string of questions as to how I came to that place and whom I knew there, I temporized.

"Oh, I bought it from a man."

"That is no answer!" he retorted.

If I had been possessed of much inclination to play deep games and match wits with big rascals I suppose I would have answered him civilly and there and then learned more of his purpose. But I was not prepossessed by his charms or respectful of his claim to superiority. The German type super-education never did impress me as compatible with good breeding or good sense, and it annoyed me to have to lie to him.

"It's all the answer you'll get!" I said.

"Where is your license for it?" he growled.

The game began to amuse me.

"None of your business!" I answered.

"How long have you been in the country!"

"Since I came," I said.

"And you have no license! You have been out shooting. A lucky thing you came to my camp and not to some other man's! The game laws are very strict!"

He spoke then to a boy who was standing behind me, giving him very careful directions in a language of which I did not know one word. The boy went away.

"The last man who went shooting near Nairobi without a license," he said, "tried to excuse himself before the magistrate by claiming ignorance of the law. He was fined a thousand rupees and sentenced to six months in jail!"

"Very severe!" I said.

"They are altogether too severe," he answered. "I hope you have killed nothing. It is good you came first to me. You would better stand that rifle over here in the corner of my tent. To walk back to the hotel with it over your shoulder would be dangerous."

"I've taken bigger chances than that," said I.

"If you have shot nothing, then it is not so serious," he said, disappearing behind a curtain into the recesses of his tent.

He stayed in there for about ten minutes. I had about made up my mind to walk away when four of his boys approached the tent from behind, and one of them cried *"Hodi!"* The boy to whom he had given directions across my shoulder was not among them.

They threw the buck down near my feet, and he came out from the gloomy interior and stared at it. He asked them questions rapidly in the native tongue, and they answered, pointing at me.

"They say you shot it," he told me, stroking his great beard alternately with either hand.

"Then they lie!" I answered.

"Let me see that rifle!" he said, reaching out an enormous freckled fist to take it.

I saw through his game at last. It would have been the easiest thing in the world to extract a cartridge from the clip in the magazine and claim afterward that I had fired it away. Evidently he proposed to get me in his power, though for just what reason he was so determined to make use of me rather than any one else was not so clear.

"So I shot the buck, did I?" I asked.

"Those four natives say they saw you shoot it."

"Then it's mine?"

He nodded.

"It's heavy," I said, "but I expect I can carry it."

I took the buck by the hind legs and swung

myself under it. It weighed more than a hundred pounds, but the African climate had not had time enough to sap my strength or destroy sheer pleasure in muscular effort.

"What's mine's my own!" I laughed. "You gave me something to eat after all! Good day, and good riddance!"

The boys tried to prevent my carrying the buck away.

"Come back!" growled the professor. "I will take responsibility for that buck and save you from punishment. Bring it back! Lay it down!"

But I continued to walk away, so he ordered his boys to take the carcass from me. I laid it down and threatened them with my butt end. He brought his own rifle out and threatened me with that. I laughed at him, bade him shoot if he dared, offered him three shots for a penny, and ended by shouldering the buck again and walking off.

Meat was cheap in Nairobi in those days, so the owner of the hotel was not so delighted as I expected. He reprimanded me for being late for breakfast, and told me I was lucky to get any. Fred and Will had waited for me, and while we ate alone and I told them the story of my morning's adventure a police officer in khaki uniform tied up his mule outside and clattered in.

"Whose buck is that hanging outside the kitchen?" he demanded.

"There's some doubt about it," I said. "I've been accused of being the owner."

"Then you're the man I want. The court sits at nine. You'd better be there, or you'll be fetched!"

He placed in my hand what proved to be a summons to appear before the district court that morning on the charge of carrying an unregistered rifle and shooting game without a license. Two native policemen he had with him took down the buck from the hook outside the kitchen door and carried it off as evidence.

We finished our breakfast in great contentment, and strode off arm-in-arm to find the court-house, feeling as if we were going to a play—perhaps a mite indignant, as if the subject of the play were one we did not quite approve, but perfectly certain of a good time.

The court was crowded. The bearded professor, his four boys, and two other natives were there, as well as several English officials, all apparently on very good terms indeed with Schillingschen.

As we entered the court under the eyes of a hostile crowd I heard one official say to the man standing next him:

"I hope he'll make an example of this case. If he doesn't every new arrival in this country will try to take the law in his own hands. I hope he fines him the limit!"

"Give me your hunting-knife, Fred!" said I, and Fred laughed as he passed it to me. For the moment I think he thought I meant to plunge it into the too talkative official's breast.

First they called a few township cases. A drunken Mohammedan was fined five rupees, and a Hindu was ordered to remove his garbage heap before noon. Three natives were ordered to the chain-gang for a week for fighting, and a Masai charged with stealing cattle was remanded. Then my case was called, very solemnly, by a magistrate scarcely any older than myself.

The police officer acted as prosecutor. He stated that "acting on information received" he had proceeded to the hotel. Outside of which he saw a buck hanging (buck produced in evidence); that he had entered the hotel, found me at breakfast, and that I had not denied having shot the buck. He called his two colored *askaris* to prove that, and they reeled off what they had to say with the speed of men who had been thoroughly rehearsed. Then he put the German on the stand, and Schillingschen, with a savage glare at me, turned on his verbal artillery. He certainly did his worst.

"This morning," be announced, after having been duly sworn on the Book, "that young man whose name I do not know approached my tent while I was dressing. The sound of a rifle being fired had awakened me earlier than usual. He carried a rifle, and I put two and two together and concluded he had shot something. Not having seen him ever before, and he standing before my tent, I asked him his name. He refused to tell me, and that made me suspicious. Then came my four boys carrying a buck, which they assured me they had seen him shoot. I asked him whether he had a license to shoot game, and he at once threatened to shoot me if I did not mind my own business. Therefore, I sent a note to the police at once."

His four boys were then put on the stand in turn, and told their story through an interpreter. Their words identical. If the interpreter spoke truth one account did not vary from the next in the slightest degree, and that fact alone should have aroused the suspicion of any unprejudiced judge.

Having the right to cross-examine, I asked each in turn whether the rifle I had brought with me to court was the same they had seen me using. They asserted it was. Then I recalled the German and asked him the same question. He also replied in the affirmative. I asked him how he knew. He said he recognized the mark on the butt where the varnish had been chafed away. Then I handed the hunting knife I had borrowed from to the police officer and demanded that he have the bullet cut out of the buck's carcass. The court could not object to that, so under the eyes of at least fifty witnesses a flattened Mauser bullet was produced. I called attention to the fact that my rifle was a Lee-Enfield that could not possibly have fired a Mauser bullet. The court was young and very dignified—examined the bullet and my rifle—and had to be convinced.

"Very well," was the verdict on that count, "it is proved that you did not shoot this particular buck, unless the police have evidence that you used a different rifle."

The policeman confessed that he had no evidence along that line, so the first charge was dismissed.

"But you are charged," said the magistrate, "with carrying an unregistered rifle, and shooting without a license."

For answer I produced my certificate of registration and the big game license we had paid for in Mombasa.

"Why didn't you say so before?" demanded the magistrate.

"I wasn't asked," said I.

"Case dismissed!" snapped his honor, and the court began to empty.

"Don't let it stop there!" urged Will excitedly. "That Heinie and his boys have all committed perjury; charge them with it!"

I turned to the police officer.

"I charge all those witnesses with perjury!" I said.

"Oh," he laughed, "you can't charge natives with that. If the law against perjury was strictly enforced the jails wouldn't hold a fiftieth of them! They don't understand."

"But that blackguard with a beard—that rascal Schillingschen understands!" said I. "Arrest him! Charge him with it!"

"That's for the court to do," he answered. "I've no authority."

The magistrate had gone.

"Who is the senior official in this town?" I demanded.

"There he goes," he answered. "That man in the white suit with the round white topee is the collector."

So we three followed the collector to his office, arriving about two minutes after the man himself. The Goanese clerk had been in the court, and recognized me. He had not stayed to hear the end.

"Fines should be paid in the court, not here!" he intimated rudely.

We wasted no time with him but walked on through, and the collector greeted us without obvious cordiality. He did not ask us to sit down.

"My friend here has come to tell you about that man Schillingschen," said Fred.

"I suppose you mean Professor Schillingschen!"

The collector was a clean-shaven man with a blue jowl that suffered from blunt razors, and a temper rendered raw by native cooking. But he had photos of feminine relations and a little house in a dreary Midland street on his desk, and was no doubt loyal to the light he saw. I wished we had Monty with us. One glimpse of the owner of a title that stands written in the Doomsday Book would have outshone the halo of Schillingschen's culture.

I rattled off what I had to say, telling the story from the moment I started to follow Hassan from the hotel down to the end, omitting nothing.

"Schillingschen is worse than a spy. He's a black-hearted, schemer. He's planning to upset British rule in this Protectorate and make it easy for the Germans to usurp!"

"This is nonsense!" the collector interrupted. "Professor Schillingschen is the honored friend of the British government. He came to us here with the most influential backing—letter of introduction from very exalted personages, I assure you! Professor Schillingschen is one of the most, if not the most, learned ethnologists in the world to-day. How dare you traduce him!"

"But you heard him tell lies in court!" I gasped. "You were there. You heard his evidence absolutely disproved. How do you explain that away?"

"I don't attempt to! The explanation is for you to make!" he answered. "The fact that he did not succeed in proving his case against you is nothing in itself! Many a case in court is lost from lack of proper evidence! And one more matter! Lady Isobel Saffren Waldon is staying—or rather, I should say, was staying at the hotel. She is now staying at my house. She complains to me of very rude treatment at the hands of you three men—insolent treatment I should call it! I can assure you that the way to get on in this Protectorate is not to behave like cads toward ladies of title! I understand that her maid is afraid to be caught alone by any one of you, and that Lady Saffren Waldon herself feels scarcely any safer!"

Fred and I saw the humor of the thing, and that enabled us to save Will from disaster. There never was a man more respectful of women than Will. He would even get off the sidewalk for a black woman, and would neither tell nor laugh at the sort of stories that pass current about women in some smoking-rooms. His hair bristled. His ears stuck out on either side of his head. He leaned forward—laid one strong brown hand on the desk—and shook his left fist under the collector's nose.

"You poor boob!" he exploded. Then he calmed himself. "I'm sorry for your government if you're the brightest jewel it has for this job! That Jane will use everything you've got except the squeal! Great suffering Jemima! Your title is collector, is it? Do you collect bugs by any chance? You act like it! So help you two men and a boy, a bughouse is where I believe you belong! Come along, fellows, he'll bite us if we stay!"

"Be advised" said the collector, leaning back in his chair and sneering. "Behave yourselves! This is no country for taking chances with the law!"

"Remember Courtney's advice," said Fred when we got outside. "Suppose we give him a few days to learn the facts about Lady Isobel, and then go back and try him again?"

"Say!" answered Will, stopping and turning to face us. "What d'you take me for? I like my meals. I like three squares a day, and tobacco, and now and then a drink. But if this was the Sahara, and that man had the only eats and drinks, I'd starve."

"Telling him the truth wouldn't be accepting favors from him," counseled Fred.

"I wouldn't tell him the time!"

That attitude—and Will insisted that all the officials in the land would prove alike—limited our choice, for unless we were to allay official suspicion it would be hopeless to get away northward. Southward into German East seemed the only way to go; there was apparently no law against travel in that direction. On our way to the hotel we passed Coutlass, striding along smirking to himself, headed toward the office from which we had just come.

"I'll bet you," said Will, "he's off to get an ammunition permit, and permission to go where he damned well pleases! I'll bet he gets both! This government's the limit!"

We laughed, but Will proved more than half right. Coutlass did get ammunition. Lady Saffren Waldon's influence was already strong enough for that. He did not ask for leave to go anywhere for the simple reason that his movements depended wholly on ours—a fact that developed later.

At the hotel there was a pleasant surprise for us. A squarely built, snub-nosed native, not very dark skinned but very ugly—his right ear slit, and almost all of his left ear missing—without any of the brass or iron wire ornaments that most of the natives of the land affect, but possessed of a Harris tweed shooting jacket and, of all unexpected things, boots that he carried slung by the laces from his neck-waited for us, squatting with a note addressed to Fred tied in a cleft stick.

It does not pay to wax enthusiastic over natives, even when one suspects they bring good news. We took the letter from him, told him to wait, and went on in. Once out of the man's hearing Fred tore the letter open and read it aloud to us.

> "Herewith my Kazimoto," it ran. "Be good to him. It occurred to me that you might not care after all to linger in Nairobi, and it seemed hardly fair to keep the boy from getting a good job simply because be could make me comfortable for the remainder of a week. So, as there happened to be a special train going up I begged leave for him to ride in the caboose. He is a splendid gun-bearer. He never funks, but reloads coolly under the most nerve-trying conditions. He has his limitations, of course, but I have found him brave and faithful, and I pass him along to you with confidence.
>
> "And by the way: he has been to Mount Elgon with me. I was not looking for buried ivory, but he knows where the caves are *in which anything might be!*
>
> "Wishing you all good luck,
>
> Yours truly,
>
> "F. Courtney"

For the moment we felt like men possessed of a new horse apiece. We were for dashing out to look the acquisition over. But Will checked us.

"Recall what Courtney said about a dog?" he asked. "We can't all own him!"

Fred sat down. "Ex-missionaries own dice," he announced. "That's how they come to be ex! You'll find them in the little box on the shelf, Will. We'll throw a main for Kazimoto!"

"I know a better gamble than that!"

"Name it, America."

"Bring the coon in and have him choose."

So I went out and felt tempted to speak cordially to the homeless ugly black man—to give him a hint that he was welcome. But it is a fatal mistake to make a "soft" impression on even the best natives at the start.

"Karibu!" I said gruffly when I had looked him over, using one of the six dozen Swahili words I knew as yet.

He arose with the unlabored ease that I have since learned to look for in all natives worth employing; and followed me indoors. Will and Fred were seated in judicial attitudes, and I took a chair beside them.

"What is your name?" demanded Fred.

"Kazimoto."

"Um-m! That means 'Work-like-the-devil.' Let us hope you live up to it. Your former master gives you a good character."

"Why not, *bwana?* My spirit is good."

"Do you want work?"

"Yes."

"How much money do you expect to get?"

"Sijui!"

"Don't say *'sijui'!"* I cut in, remembering Schillingschen's method.

"Six rupees a month and *posho,"* he said promptly. *Posho* means rations, or money in lieu of rations.

"Don't you rather fancy yourself?" suggested Fred with a perfectly straight face.

"Say two dollars a month all told!" Will whispered to me behind his hand.

"I am a good gun-bearer!" the native answered. "My spirit is good. I am strong. There is nobody better than me as a gun-bearer!"

"We happen to want a headman," answered Fred. "Have you ever been headman?"

"Would you like to be?"

"Yes."

"Are you able?"

"Surely."

"Choose, then. Which of us would you like to work for?"

"You!" he answered promptly, pointing at Fred.

It was on the tip of the tongue of every one of us to ask him instantly why, but that would have been too rank indiscretion. It never pays to seem curious about a native's personal reasons, and it was many weeks before we knew why he had made up his mind in advance to choose Fred and not either of us for his master.

His choice made, and the offer of his services accepted, he took over Fred forthwith—demanded his keys—found out which our room was—went over our belongings and transferred the best of our things into Fred's bag and the worst of his into ours—remade Fred's bed after a mysterious fashion of his own, taking one of my new blankets and one of Will's in exchange for Fred's old ones—cleaned Fred's guns thoroughly after carefully abstracting the oil and waste from our gun-cases and transferring them to Fred's—removed the laces from my shooting boots and replaced them with Fred's knotted ones—sharpened Fred's razors and shaved himself with mine (to the enduring destruction of its once artistic edge)—and departed in the direction of the bazaar.

He returned at the end of an hour and a half with a motley following of about twenty, arrayed in blankets of every imaginable faded hue and in every stage of dirtiness.

"You wanting cook," he announced. "These three making cook."

He waved three nondescripts to the front, and we chose a tall Swahili because he grinned better than the others. "Although," as Fred remarked, "what the devil grinning has to do with cooking is more than anybody knows." The man, whose name was Juma, turned out to be an execrable cook, but as he never left off grinning under any circumstances (and it would have been impossible to imagine circumstances worse than those we warred with later on) we never had the heart to dismiss him.

After that, Will and I selected a servant apiece who were destined forever to wage war on Kazimoto in hopeless efforts to prevent his giving Fred the best end of everything. Mine was a Baganda who called himself Matches, presumably because his real name was unpronounceable. Will chose a Malindi boy named Tengeneza (and that means arrange in order, fix, make over, manage, mend—no end of an ominous name!). They were both outclassed from the start by Kazimoto, but to add to the handicap he insisted that since he was a headman he would need some one to help look after Fred at times when other duties would monopolize his attention. He himself picked out an imp of mischief whose tribe I never ascertained, but who called himself Simba (lion), and there and then Simba departed up-stairs to steal for Fred whatever was left of value among Will's effects and mine.

We had scarcely got used to the idea of once more having a savage apiece to wait on us when Kazimoto turned up at the door with a string of porters and a Goanese railway clerk. We had left our tents and heavy baggage checked at the station, but had said nothing about them to our new headman; however, he had made inquiries and worked out a plan on his own account. The railway clerk asked to know whether he should let Kazimoto have our things.

"Why?" demanded Fred.

"This hotel no good!" announced Kazimoto. "No place for boys. Heap too many plenty people. Pitching camp, that good!"

"All right," said Fred, and then and there paid our baggage charges.

Presently Brown of Lumbwa, who had spent most of the daylight hours in The little corrugated iron bar run by a Goanese in the bazaar, came lurching past the township camping ground, and viewed Kazimoto with his gang pitching our tents. He asked questions, but could get no information, so came along to us.

"Where you chaps going?" he demanded, leaning against the wall. Fred took advantage of the opportunity and examined him narrowly as to his knowledge of German East and ways of getting there. He was in an aggravating mood that made at one moment a very well of information of him, and at the next a mere garrulous ass.

"Come along o' me t' Lumbwa," was his final word on the matter. "I'll put you on a road nobody knows an' nobody, uses!"

We spent that night under canvas and talked the matter out. The usual way to reach Lumbwa was to wait for a freight, or construction train and beg leave to ride on that, for as yet, no passenger trains were running regularly on the western section of the line. But there was no rule against traveling anywhere south of the equator, and it was our purpose to march down into German East without any one being the wiser.

The next morning we imagined Brown was sober and sorry enough to hold his tongue, so, without going into details with him, we agreed to go with him "some of the way," and Fred spent the whole of that morning in the bazaar buying loads of food and general supplies. Will and I engaged porters, and with Kazimoto's aid as interpreter, had fifty ready to march that afternoon.

The whole trick of starting on a journey is to start. If you only make a mile or two the first day you have at least done better than stand still; loads have been apportioned and porters broken in to some extent; you have broken the spell of inertia, and hereafter there is less likely to be trouble. We made up our minds to get away that afternoon, and I was sent back to the hotel to find Brown, who had gone for his belongings.

If Brown had stayed sober all might have been well, but his headache and feeling of unworthiness had been too much for him and I found him with a straw in the neck of a bottle of whisky alternately laying down law to Georges Coutlass and drinking himself into a state of temporary bliss.

"You Greeks dunno nothin'!" he asserted as I came in. "You never did know nothin', an' you're never goin' to know nothin'! 'Cause why? 'I'll tell you. Simply because I am goin' to tell! I'm mum, I am! When s'mother gents an' me 'ave business, that's our business—see! None o' your business—'ss our business, an' I'm not goin' to tell you Greeks nothin' about where we're off to, nor why, nor when. An' you put that in your pipe an' smoke it!"

I sat in the dining-room for a while, hoping that the Greek would go away; but as Brown was fast drinking himself into a condition when he could not have been moved except on stretcher, and was momentarily edging closer to an admission of all he knew or guessed about our intention, I took the bull by the horns at last—snatched away his whisky bottle, and walked off with it.

He came after me swearing like a trooper, and his own porters, who had been waiting for more than an hour beside his loads, trailed along after him. Once in our camp we made a hammock for him out of a blanket tied to a pole, and made him over to two porters with the promise that they would get no supper if they lost him. Then we started—uphill, toward the red Kikuyu heights, where settlers were already trying to grow potatoes for which there was no market, and onions that would only run to seed.

To our left rear and right front were the highest mountain ranges in Africa. Before us was the pass through which the railway threaded over the wide high table-land before dipping downward to Victoria Nyanza. On our left front was all Kikuyu country, and after that Lumbwa, and native reserves, and forest, and swamp, and desert, and the German boundary.

We made a long march of it that first day, and camped after dark within two miles of Kikuyu station. Most of the scrub thereabouts was castor oil plant, that makes very poor fuel; yet there were lions in plenty that roared and scouted around us even before the tents were pitched.

Nobody got much sleep that night, although the porters were perfectly indifferent to the risk of snoozing on the watch. Kazimoto produced a thing called a *kiboko*—a whip of hippopotamus-hide a yard and a half long, and with the aid of that and Will's good humor we constituted a yelling brigade, whose business was to make the welkin ring with godless noises whenever a lion came close enough to be dangerous.

I made up a signal party of all our personal boys with our lanterns, swinging them in frantic patterns in the darkness in a way to terrify the very night itself. Fred played concertina nearly all night long, and when dawn came, though there were tracks of lions all about the camp we were only tired and sleepy. Nobody was missing; nobody killed.

We never again took lions so seriously, although we always built fires about the camp in lion country when that was possible. Partly by dint of carelessness that brought no ill results, and partly from observation we learned that where game is plentiful lions are more curious than dangerous, and that unless something should happen to enrage them, or the game has gone away and they are hungry, they are likely to let well alone.

If there are dogs in camp—and we bought three terrier pups that morning from a settler at Kikuyu—leopards are likely to be more troublesome than lions. The leopards seemed to yearn for dog-meat much as Brown of Lumbwa yearned for whisky.

The journey to Lumbwa is one of the pleasantest

I remember. We took Brown's supply of whisky from him, locked up with our own, sent him ahead in the hammock, and let him as work as guide by promises of whisky for supper if he did his duty, and threats of mere cold water if he failed.

"But water rots my stomach!" he objected.

"Lead on, then!" was the invariable, remorseless answer. So Brown led.

Until we reached Naivasha with its strange lake full of hippo at an elevation so great that the mornings are frosty (and that within sight of the line) there was never a day that we were once out of sight of game from dawn to dark. When we awoke the morning mist would scatter slowly and betray sleepy herds of antelope, that would rise leisurely, stand staring at us, suddenly become suspicious, and then gallop off until the whole plain was a panorama of wheeling herds, reminding one of the cavalry maneuvers at Aldershot when the Guards regiments were pitted against the regular cavalry—all riding and no wits.

Although we had to shoot enough meat for ourselves and men, we never once took advantage of those surprise parties in the early morning, preferring to stalk warier game at the end of a long march. The rains were a thing of the past, and we seldom troubled to pitch tents but slept under the stars with a sensation that the universe was one vast place of peace.

Occasionally we reached an elevation from which we could look down and see men toiling to build the railway, that already reached Nyanza after the unfinished fashion of work whose chief aim is making a showing. Profits, performances were secondary matters; that railway's one purpose was to establish occupation of the head waters of the Nile and refute the German claim to prior rights there. At irregular intervals trains already went down to the lake, and passengers might ride on sufferance; but we deluded ourselves with the belief that by marching we threw enemies off the scent. It was pure delusion, but extremely pleasant while it lasted. Where Africa is green and high she is a lovely land to march across.

Brown grew sober on the trip, as if approaching his chosen home gave him a sense of responsibility. His own reason for preferring the march to a ride in a construction train was simple:

"Every favor you ask o' gov'ment, boys, leaves one less to fall back on in a pinch! Ask not, and they'll forget some o' your peccadillos. Ask too often, and one day when you really need a kindness you'll find the Bank o' Good Hope bu'sted! And, believe me, boys, that 'ud be a hell of a predicament for a poor sufferin' settler to find himself in!"

The approach to Lumbwa was over steep hilly grass land, between forests of cedar—perfect country, kept clean by a wind that smelt of fern and clover.

"You can tell we're gettin' near my place," said Brown, "by the number o' leopards that's about."

We had to keep our three pups close at heel all the time, and even at that we lost two of them. One was taken from between Will's feet as he sat in camp cleaning his rifle. All he heard was the dog's yelp, and all he saw was a flash of yellow as the leopard made for the boulders close at hand. The other was taken out of my tent. I had tied it to the tent pole, but the stout cord snapped like a hair and the darkness swallowed both leopard and its prey before I could as much as reach my rifle to get a shot.

"Splendid country for farmin'," Brown remarked, "Splendid. Only you can't keep sheep because the leopards take 'em. You can't keep hens for the same reason. Nor yet cows, because the leopards get the calves—leastways, that's to say unless you watch out awful cautious. Nor yet you can't keep pigeons, 'cause the leopards take them too. I sent to England for fancy pigeons—a dozen of em. Leopards got all but one, so I put him in the loft above my own house, where it seemed to me 'tweren't possible for a leopard to get, supposin' he'd dared. Went away the next day for some shootin', an' lo and behold!—came back that evenin' to discover my cook an' three others carryin' on as if Kingdom Come had took place at last. Never heard or saw such a jamboree. The blamed leopard was up in the loft; and had eaten the pigeon, feathers and all, but couldn't get out again!"

"What happened? Nothin'! I was that riled I didn't stop to think—fixed a bayonet on the old Martini the gov'ment supplies to settlers out of the depths of its wisdom an' generosity—climbed up by the same route the leopard took—invaded him—an' skewered him wi' the bayonet in the dark! I wouldn't do it again for a kingdom—but I won't buy more pigeons either!"

"What do you raise on your farm, then—pigs?" we asked.

"No, the leopards take pigs."

"What then?"

"Well—as I was explainin' to that Greek Georges Coutlass at Nairobi—there's a way of farmin' out your cattle among the natives that beats keepin' 'em yourself. The natives put 'em in the village pen o' nights; an' besides, they know about the business.

"All you need do is give 'em a heifer calf once in a while, and they're contented. I keep a herd o' two hundred cows in a native village not far from my place. The natural increase o' them will make me well-to-do some day."

The day before we reached Brown's tiny homestead we heard a lot of shooting over the hill behind us.

"That'll be railway men takin' a day off after leopards," announced Brown with the air of a man who can not be mistaken.

Nevertheless, Fred and I went back to see, but could make out nothing. We lay on the top of the hill and watched for two or three hours, but although we heard rifle firing repeatedly we did not once catch sight of smoke or men. We marched into camp late that night with a feeling of foreboding that we could not explain but that troubled us both equally.

Once or twice in the night we heard firing again, as if somebody's camp not very far away was invaded by leopards, or perhaps lions. Yet at dawn there were no signs of tents. And when that night we arrived at Brown's homestead we seemed to have the whole world to ourselves.

Brown's house was a tiny wooden affair with a thick grass roof. It boasted a big fireplace at one end of the living-room, and a chimney that Brown had built himself so cunningly that smoke could go up and out but no leopards could come down.

He got very drunk that night to celebrate the home-coming, and stayed completely drunk for three days, we making use of his barn to give our porters a good rest. By day we shot enough meat for the camp, and at night we sat over the log fire, praying that Brown might sober up, Fred singing songs to his infernal concertina, and all the natives who could crowd in the doorway listening to him with all their ears. Fred made vast headway in native favor, and learned a lot of two languages at once.

Every day we sent Kazimoto and another boy exploring among the Lumbwa tribe, gathering information as to routes and villages, and it was Kazimoto who came running in breathless one night just as Brown was at last sobering up, with the news that some Greeks had swooped down on Brown's cattle, had wounded two or three of the villagers who herded them, and had driven the whole herd away southward.

That news sobered Brown completely. He took the bottle of whisky he had just brought up from the cellar and replaced it unopened.

"There's on'y one Greek in the world knew where my cattle were!" he announced grimly. "There's on'y one Greek I ever talked to about cattle. Coutlass, by the great horn spoon! The blackguard swore he was after you chaps—swore he didn't care nothing about me! What he did to you was none o' my business, o' course—an' I figured anyway as you could look out for yourselves! Not that I told the swine any o' your business, mind! Not me! I was so sure he was gunnin' for you that I told him my own business to throw him off your track! And now the devil goes an' turns on me!"

He got down his rifle and began overhauling it, feverishly, yet with a deliberate care that was curious in a man so recently drunk. While he cleaned and oiled be gave orders to his own boys; and what with having servants of our own and having to talk to them mostly in the native tongue, we were able to understand pretty well the whole of what he said.

"You're not going to start after them to-night?" Fred objected. But he and Will were also already overhauling weapons, for the second time that evening. (It is religion with the true hunter never to eat supper until his rifle is cleaned and oiled.) I got my own rifle down from the shelf over Brown's stone mantelpiece.

"What d'you take me for?" demanded Brown. "There's one pace they'll go at, an' that's the fastest possible. There's one place they'll head for, an' that's German East. They can't march faster than the cattle, an' the cattle'll have to eat. Maybe they'll drive 'em all through the first night, and on into the next day; but after that they'll have to rest 'em an' graze 'em a while. That's when we'll begin to gain. The tireder the cattle get, the faster we'll overhaul 'em, for we can eat while we're marchin', which the cattle can't! You chaps just stay here an' look after my farm till I come back!"

"You mean you propose to go alone after them?" asked Fred.

"Why not? Whose cattle are they?"

He was actually disposed to argue the point.

"Man alive, there'll be shootin'!" he insisted. "If they once get over the border with all those cattle, the Germans'll never hand 'em over until every head o' cattle's gone. They'll fine 'em, an' arrest 'em, an' trick 'em, an' fine 'em again until the Germans own the herd all legal an' proper—an' then they'll chase the Greeks back to British East for punishment same as they always do. What good 'ud that be to me? No, no! Me—I'm going to catch 'em this side o' the line, or else bu'st—an' I won't be too partic'lar where the line's drawn either! There's maybe a hundred miles to the south o' their line that the Germans don't patrol more often than once in a leap-year. If I catch them Greeks in any o' that country, I'm going to kid myself deliberate that it's British East, and act accordin'!"

At last we convinced him, although I don't remember how, for he was obstinate from the aftermath of whisky, that we would no more permit him to go alone than he would consider abandoning his cattle. Then we had to decide who should follow with our string of porters, for if forced marching was in order it was obvious that we should far outdistance our train.

We invited Brown to follow with all the men while we three skirmished ahead, but he waxed so apoplectically blasphemous at the very thought of it that Fred assured him the proposal was intended for a joke. Then we argued among ourselves, coaxed, blarneyed, persuaded, and tried to bribe one another. Finally, all else failing, we tossed a coin for it, odd man out, and Fred lost.

So Brown, Will Yerkes and I, with Kazimoto, our two personal servants, and six boys to carry one tent for the lot of us and food and cooking pots, started off just as the moon rose over the nearest cedars, and laughed at Fred marshaling the sleepy porters by lamplight in the open space between the house and barn. He was to follow as fast as the loaded porters could be made to travel, and with that concertina of his to spur them on there was little likelihood of losing touch. But the rear-guard, when it comes to pursuing a retreating enemy, is ever the least alluring place.

"You've got all the luck," he shouted. "Make the most of it or I'll never gamble on the fall of a coin again!"

That pursuit was a journey of accidents, chapter after chapter of them in such close sequence that the whole was a nightmare without let-up or reason. I began the book by falling into an elephant pit.

Before we had gone a mile in the dark we stood in doubt as to whether the most practicable trail went right or left. Brown set his own indecision down frankly to the whisky that had muddled him. Even Kazimoto, who had passed that way three times, did not know for certain. So I went forward to scout—stepped into the deep shadow of some jungle—trod on nothing—threw the other foot forward to save myself—and fell downward into blackness for an eternity.

I brought up at last unhurt in the trash and decaying vegetation at the bottom of a pit, and looked up to see the stars in a rough parallelogram above me, whose edge I guessed was more than thirty feet above my head. I started to dig my way out, but the crumbling sides fell in and threatened to bury me alive unless I kept still. So I shouted until my lungs ached, but without result. I suppose the noise went trumpeting upward out of the hole and away to the clouds and the stars. At any rate, Will and Brown swore afterward they never heard it.

I was fifteen minutes in the hole that very likely had held many an elephant with his legs wedged together under him until the poor brute perished of thirst, before it occurred to me to fire my rifle. I fired several shots when I did think of it; but we had agreed on no system of signals, and instead of coming to find me at once, the other two cursed me for wasting time shooting at leopards in the dark instead of scouting for the track. I used twenty cartridges before they came to see what sort of battle I was waging, and with the last shot I nearly blew Brown's helmet off as he stooped over the hole to look down in.

Then there were more precious minutes wasted while someone cut a long pole for me to swarm up, and at the end of that time, when I stood on firm ground at last and wiped the blood from hands and knees, we were no wiser about the proper direction to take.

The next accident was a little before midnight. Will Yerkes was leading, I following, next the boys, and Brown bringing up the rear (for in those wild hills there is never a good track wide enough for two men to march abreast. Even the cattle proceed in single file unless driven furiously.) Will came on a leopard devouring its kill, a fat buck, in the midst of the track in the moonlight, and the brute resented the interruption of his meal. It slunk into the shadows before Will could get a shot at it, and for the next two hours followed us, slinking from shadow to shadow, snarling and growling. It plainly intended murder, but which of us was to be the victim, and when, there was no means of guessing, so that the nerves of all of us were tortured every time the brute approached.

We wasted at least thirty cartridges on futile efforts to guess his whereabouts in velvet black shadows, and Brown went through all the stages from simple nervousness to fear, and then to frenzy, until we feared he would shoot one of us in frantic determination to ring the leopard's knell.

At last the brute did rush in, and of course where least expected. He seized one of our porters by the shoulder, his claws doing more damage than his teeth. I shot him by thrusting my rifle into his ear, and although that dropped him instantly his claws, in the dying spasm and by the weight of his fall, tore wounds in the man's arm eighteen or twenty inches long.

One of the things we did have with us was bandages. But it took time to attend to the man's wounds properly by lamp and moonlight, and after that he could neither march fast, nor was there anywhere to leave him.

So just before dawn Fred came up with us, and was more pleased at our discomfiture than sympathetic. He told off two men to carry the injured porter to a mission station more than a day's march away, and redistributed the loads. Then we went on again, once more placing rock, hill, and cedar forest between us and our supply column, this time with Fred's counsel ringing in our ears.

"Better send for nursemaids and perambulators, and have yourselves pushed!"

At noon that day we found the track of the driven cattle, and soon after that came on the half-devoured carcass of a heifer that the Greeks had shot, presumably because it could not march, and perhaps with the added reason that freshly-killed meat would draw off leopards and hyenas and provide peace for a few miles.

Once on the trail it would not have been easy to lose it, except in the dark, for the Greek marauders were bent on speed and the driven cattle had smashed down the undergrowth in addition to leaving deep hoof-prints at every water-course.

The first suspicion that dawned on me of something more than mere freebooting on the part of Coutlass, was due to the discovery of hoof-prints of either mules or horses. I was marching alone in advance, and came on them beside a stream that was only apparently fordable in that one place. After making sure of what they were I halted to let Will and Brown catch up.

"Did Coutlass have money enough to buy mules for himself and gang?" wondered Will.

"That robber?" snorted Brown. "When Lady Saffren Waldon refused him tobacco money in the hotel he tried to borrow from me!"

"Where could be steal mules?" Will asked.

"Nowhere. Aren't any!"

"Horses' then?"

"He'd never take horses. They'd die."

"What are they riding, then?"

"Unless he stole trained zebras from the gov'ment farm at Naivasha," said Brown, "an' they're difficulter to ride 'an a greasy pole up-ended on a earthquake, he must ha' bought mules from the one man who has any to sell. And he lives t'other side o' Nairobi. There are none between there and here—none whatever. Zachariah Korn—him who owns mules—is too wide awake to be stolen from. He bought 'em, you take it from me, and paid twice what they were worth into the bargain."

"Then he bought them with her money!" said Will.

"If not Schillingschen's," said I.

"Or the Sultan of Zanzibar's" said Will, "or the German government's."

"But why? Why should she, or they, conspire at great expense and risk to steal Brown's cattle?"

"They'll figure," said Will, "that Brown is helping us, and therefore, Brown is an enemy. Prob'ly they surmise Brown is in league with us to show us a short cut to what we're after. If that's how they work it out, then they wouldn't need think much to conclude that putting Brown on the blink would hoodoo us. Maybe they allow that that much bad luck to begin with would unsettle Brown's friendly feelings for us. Anyway—somebody bought the mules—somebody stole the cattle—cattle are somewhere ahead. Let's hurry forward and see!"

We did hurry, but made disgustingly poor time. Once a dozen buffalo stampeded our tiny column. Our five porters dropped their loads, and the biggest old bull mistook our only tent for our captain's dead body and proceeded to play ball with it, tossing it and tearing it to pieces until at last Will got a chance for a shoulder shot and drilled him neatly. Two other bulls took to fighting in the midst of the excitement and we got both of them. Then the rest trotted off; so we packed the horns of the dead ones on the head of our free porter (for the tent he had carried was now utterly no use) and hastened on.

Once, in trying to make a cut that should have saved us ten or fifteen miles between two rivers, we fell shoulder-deep into a bog and only escaped after an hour's struggle during which we all but lost two porters. We had to retrace our steps and follow the Greek's route, only to have the mortification of seeing Fred and our column of supplies coming over the top of a rise not eight miles behind us.

Determined not to be overtaken by him a second time and treated to advice about nursemaids, we dispensed with sleep altogether for that night, and nearly got drowned at the second river.

We found a native who owned a thing he called a *mtungi*—a near-canoe, burned out of a tree-trunk. He assured us the ford was very winding (he drew a wiggly finger-mark in the mud by way of illustration) but that his boat would hold twice our number, and that be could take us over easily in the dark. In fact he swore he had ferried twice our number over on darker nights more than twenty or thirty times. He also said that he had taken the cattle over by the ford early that morning, and then had crossed over in the boat with two Greeks and a *bwana* Goa. He showed us the brass wire and beads they gave him in proof of that statement, and we began to put some faith in his tale.

So we all piled into his crazy boat with our belongings, and be promptly lost the way amid the twelve-foot grass-papyrus mostly—that divided the river into narrow streams and afforded protection to the most savagely hungry mosquitoes in the world. Our faces and hands were wet with blood in less than two minutes.

Presently, instead of finding bottom for his pole, he pushed us into deep water. The grass disappeared, and a ripple on the water lipping dangerously within three inches of our uneven gunwale proved that we were more or less in the main stream. We had enjoyed that sensation for about a minute, and were headed toward where we supposed the opposite bank must be, when a hippo in a hurry to breathe blew just beside us—saw, smelt, or heard us (it was all one to him)—and dived again.

I suppose in order to get his head down fast enough he shoved his rump up, and his great fat back made a wave that ended that voyage abruptly. Our three inches of broadside vanished. The canoe rocked violently, filled, turned over, and floated wrong side up.

"All the same," laughed Will, spluttering and spitting dirty water, "here's where the crocks get fooled! They don't eat me for supper!"

He was first on top of the overturned boat, and dragged me up after him. Together we hauled up Brown, who could not swim but was bombastically furious and unafraid; and the three of us pulled out the porters and the fatuous boat's owner. The pole was floating near by, and I swam down-stream and fetched it. When they had dragged me back on to the wreck the moon came out, and we saw the far bank hazily through mist and papyrus.

The boat floated far more steadily wrong side up, perhaps because we had lashed all our loads in place and they acted as ballast. Will took the pole and acted the part of Charon, our proper pilot contenting himself with perching on the rear end lamenting the ill-fortune noisily until Kazimoto struck him and threatened to throw him back into the water.

"They don't want a fool like you in the other world," he assured him. "You will die of old age!"

The papyrus inshore was high enough to screen the moon from us, and we had to hunt a passage through it in pitch darkness. Then, having found the muddy bank at last (and more trillions of mosquitoes) we had to drag the overturned boat out high and dry to rescue our belongings. And that was ticklish work, because most of the crocodiles, and practically all the largest ones, spend the night alongshore.

Matches were wet. We had no means of making a flare to frighten the monsters away. We simply had to "chance it" as cheerfully and swiftly as we could, and at the end of a half-hour's slimy toil we carried our muddied loads to the nearest high ground and settled down there for the night.

It would be mad exaggeration to say we camped. Wet to the skin—dirty to the verge of feeling suicidal—bitten by insects until the blood ran down from us—lost (for we bad no notion where the end of the ford might be)—at the mercy of any prowling beasts that might discover us (for our rifle locks were fouled with mud)—we sat with chattering teeth and waited for the morning.

When the sun rose we found a village less than four hundred yards away and sent the boys down to it to unpack the loads and spread everything in the sun to dry, while we went down to the river again and washed our rifles. Then we dried and oiled them, and without a word of bargain or explanation, invaded the cleanest looking hut, lay down on the stamped clay floor, and slept. It was only clean-looking, that hut. It housed more myriads of fleas than the air outside supported "skeeters;" but we slept, unconscious of them all.

At four that afternoon we had the mortification of being roused by Fred's voice, and the dumping of loads as his sixty porters dropped their burdens inside the village stockade. He had scorned the ferry and crossed the ford on foot, making a prodigious splash to keep crocodiles away, and was as full of life and fun as a schoolboy on vacation.

"Wake up, you vorloepers!" he shouted. "Wake up! Shake off the fleas and come, and I'll show you something."

He had already had the tale of our night's misfortune in detail from the owner of the only canoe (who claimed double pay on the ground that we had lost no loads in spite of over-turning. "The last really white man who crossed lost *all* his loads!" he explained).

"Come and I'll show you something you never saw before, you scouts!—you advance guard!—you line of skirmishers!"

Will hurled a lump of earth at him, and chased him to the river, where they wrestled, trying to throw each other in, until both were breathless. Then, when neither could make another effort:

"Look!" gasped Fred.

There was an island in mid-stream below where we must have crossed. The stream was straight, and from where we stood we could see more than half a mile of alluvial mud with an arm of the river on either side. The mud was white, not black—so white that it dazzled the eyes to look at it.

"Know what it is?" Fred panted.

We did not know, and it was no use guessing. It looked like burned lime, or else the secretions of about a billion birds; and there were no birds to speak of.

"Crocodile eggs!" said Fred.

We did not believe that. Even Brown did not believe it. There was no time to spare, but Brown out of curiosity agreed, so we took the absurd canoe and poled down to investigate. As we came nearer the solid white broke up into a myriad dots, and Fred's tale stood confirmed.

They were as long as two hens' eggs laid end to end, or longer. They lay in the sun in batches in every stage of incubation, and from almost every batch there were little crocodiles emerging, that made straight for the water. What worse monster preyed on them to keep their numbers down, or what disease took care of their prolixity we could not guess. Perhaps they ate one another, or just died of hunger. The owner of the boat vowed there were no fish left in the river, and that the crocodiles did not eat hippo unless it were first dead.

We took another tent from among Fred's loads, changed two of our porters for stronger ones, and went forward that evening; for it began to be obvious that the speed had been telling on the cattle. We passed two more dead heifers within a few miles of the river bank, and there were other signs that for all our long sleep we were gaining on them.

Perhaps the Greeks thought they had shaken off pursuit. Judging by the compass they were headed for the shore of Victoria Nyanza, where the grazing would be better, food for men would be purchasable, and the number of villages closely spaced would make the task of night-herding vastly easier. There isn't a village in that part of Africa that is not proud to be a host to anybody's cattle, if only because the ownership of so much living wealth casts glory on all who come in contact with it.

There was no means of telling whether or not we were over the German border. The boundary line had not been surveyed yet, and on the map the part where we were was set down as "unexplored," although that was scarcely accurate; the route was well enough known to Greeks and Arabs, and other had characters bent on smuggling or in some other way defeating the ends of justice.

We marched that night until midnight, slept until dawn, and were off again. At noon we reached rising ground, and Kazimoto ran ahead of us to the summit. We saw him standing at gaze for three or four minutes with one hand shading his eyes before he came scampering back, as excited as if his own fortune were in the balance.

"Hooko-chini!" he shouted. *"Hooko-chini—mba-a-a-li sana!"* (They're down below there, very far away!)

We hurried up-hill, but for many minutes could see nothing except a plain of waving grass higher than a man's head and almost as impenetrable as bamboo-country that carried small hope in it for man or beast, that would be a holocaust in the dry season when the heat set fire to the grass, and was an insect-haunted marsh at most other times. However, path across it there must be, for the Greeks had driven Brown's cattle that way that very morning, and Kazimoto swore he could see them in the distance, although Brown, and Will, and I—all three keen-sighted—could see nothing whatever but immeasurable, worthless waving grass.

At last I detected a movement near the horizon that did not synchronize with the wind-blown motion of the rest. I pointed it out to the others, and after a few minutes we agreed that it moved against the wind.

"They're hurrying again," said Brown, peering under both hands. "There's no feed for cattle on all this plain. They're racing to get to short grass before the cattle all die. Come on—let's hurry after 'em!"

For the second time on that trip we essayed a short cut, making as straight as a bee would fly for the point on the horizon where we knew the Greeks to be. And for the second time we fell into a bog, nearly losing our lives in it. We had to pull one another out, using even our precious rifles as supports in the yielding mud, and then spending equally precious time in cleaning locks and sights again.

After that we hunted for the cattle trail and followed that closely; and that was not so easy as it reads, because the trampled grass had risen again, and cattle and mounted men can cross easily ground that delays men on foot.

The heat was that of an oven. The water—what there was of it in the holes and swampy places—stank, and tasted acrid. The flies seemed to greet us as their only prospect of food that year. The monotony of hurrying through grass-stems that cut off all view and only showed the sky through a waving curtain overhead was more nerve-trying than the physical weariness and thirst.

We slept a night in that grass, burning some of it for a smudge to keep mosquitoes at bay, and an hour after dawn, reaching rising ground again, realized that we had our quarry within reach at last.

They were out in the open on short good grazing. The Greeks' tent was pitched. We could see their mules, like brown insects, tied under a tree, and the cattle dotted here and there, some lying down, some feeding.

"At last!" said Brown. "Boys, they're our meat! There's a tree to hang the Greeks and the Goa to! When we've done that, if you'll all come back with me I'll send to Nairobi for an extra jar of Irish whisky, and we'll have a spree at Lumbwa that'll make the fall of Rome sound like a Sunday-school picnic! We're in German territory now, all right. There's not a white man for a hundred miles in any direction—except your friend that's coming along behind. There's nobody to carry tales or prevent! I'm no savage. I'm no degenerate. I don't hold with too much of anything, but—"

"There'll be no dirty work, if that's what you mean," said Will quietly.

Brown stared hard at him.

"D'you mean you'll object to hanging 'em?"

"Not in the least. We hang or shoot cattle thieves in the States. I said there'll be no dirty work, that's all."

"Shall we rest a while, and come on them fresh in the morning?" I proposed.

"Forward!" snorted Brown. "Why d'you want to wait?"

"Forward it is!" agreed Will. "When we get a bit closer we'll stop and hold council of war."

"One minute!" said I. "Tell me what that is?"

I had been searching the whole countryside, looking for some means of stealing on the marauders unawares and finding none. They had chosen their camping place very wisely from the point of view of men unwilling to be taken by surprise. Far away over to our right, appearing and disappearing as I watched them, were a number of tiny black dots in sort of wide half-moon formation, and a larger number of rather larger dots contained within the semicircle.

"Cattle!" exploded Brown.

"And men!" added Will.

"Black men!" said I. "Black men with spears!"

"Masai!" said Kazimoto excitedly. He had far the keenest eyes of all of us.

We were silent for several minutes. The veriest stranger in that land knows about the feats and bravery of the Masai, who alone of all tribes did not fear the Arabs, and who terrorized a quarter of a continent before the British came and broke their power.

"Mbaia cabisa!" muttered Kazimoto, meaning that the development was very bad indeed. And he had right to know

He explained it was a raid. The Masai, in accordance with time-honored custom, had come from British East to raid the lake-shore villages of German territory, and were driving back the plundered cattle. None can drive cattle as Masai can. They can take leg-weary beasts by the tail and make them gallop, one beast encouraging the next until they all go like the wind. For food they drink hot blood, opening a vein in a beast's neck and closing it again when they have had their fill. Their only luggage is a spear. Their only speed-limit the maximum the cattle can be stung to. On a raid three hundred and sixty miles in six days is an ordinary rate of traveling.

Just now they did not seem in much hurry. They had probably butchered the fighting men of all the villages in their rear, and were well informed as to the disposition of the nearest German forces. There were probably no Germans within a hundred miles. There was no telegraph in all those parts. To notify Muanza by runner and Bagamoyo on the coast from there by wire would take several days. Then Bagamoyo would have to wire the station at Kilimanjaro, and there was no earthly chance of Germans intercepting them before they could reach British East.

Nor was there any treaty provision between British and German colonial governments for handing over raiders. The Germans had refused to make any such agreement for reasons best known to themselves. The fact that they were far the heaviest losers by the lack of reciprocal police arrangements was due to the fact that most of the Masai lived in British East. The Masai would have raided across either border with supreme indifference.

"Masai not talking. Masai using spear and kill!" remarked Kazimoto.

"One good thing our gov'ment's done," said Brown. "Just one. It has kept those rascals from owning rifles! But lordy! They've got spears that give a man the creeps to see!"

He began looking to his rifle. So did Will and I.

"Now this here is my fight," he explained. "Them's my cattle. They're all the wealth I own in the world. If I lose 'em I'm minded to die anyhow. There's nothing in life for a drunkard like me with all his money gone and nothing to do but take a mean white's job. You chaps just wait here and watch while I 'tend to my own affairs."

"Exactly!" Will answered dryly. "I've a hundred rounds in my pockets. That ought to be enough."

While we made ready, leaving our loads and porters in a safe place and giving the boys orders, I saw two things happen. First, the Masai became aware of the little Greek encampment and the two hundred head of cattle waiting at their mercy; and second, the Greeks grew aware of the Masai.

The Greeks had boys with them; I saw at least half a dozen go scattering to round up the cattle. The tents began to come down, and I saw three figures that might be the Greeks and the Goanese holding a consultation near the tree.

"And now," remarked Will, "I begin to see the humor in this comedy. Which are we—allies of the Greeks or of the Masai? Are we to help the Greeks get away with Brown's cattle, or help the Masai steal 'em from the Greeks? Are your cattle all branded, Brown?"

"You blooming well bet they are!"

"Masai know enough to alter a brand?"

"Never heard o' their doing it."

"Then if the Masai get away with them to British East, if you can find 'em you can claim 'em, eh?"

"Claim 'em in court wi' the whole blooming tribe o' Masai—more'n a quarter of a million of 'em—all on hand to swear they bought 'em from me; an' the British gov'ment takin' sides with the black men, as it always does? Oh, yes! It sounds easy, that does!"

"But if the Greeks get away with 'em," argued Will, "you've no chance of recovering at all."

"I'll not take sides with Masai—even against Greeks!" Brown answered grimly, and Will laughed.

"If we attack the Greeks first," I said, "perhaps they'll run. We're nearer to them than the Masai are. The Masai, will have to corral their own cattle before they can leave them to raid a new lot. We can open fire at long range begin with. If that scares the Greeks away, then we can, round up Brown's cattle and drive them back northward. We may possibly escape with them too quickly for the Masai to think it worth while to follow."

Brown laughed cynically.

"We can try it," he said. "An' if the Greeks don't run pretty quick they'll never run again—I'll warrant that!"

Nobody had a better plan to propose, so we emptied our pockets of all but fifty rounds of ammunition each, and gave the rest to Kazimoto to carry, with orders to keep in hiding and watch, and run with cartridges to whoever should first need them.

Then, because instead of corralling their cattle the Masai were already dividing themselves into two parties, one of which drove the cattle forward and the other diverged to study the attack, we ducked down under a ridge and ran toward the Greeks. The sooner we could get the first stage of the fighting off our hands the better.

It proved a long way—far longer than I expected, and the going was rougher. Moreover, the Greeks' boys were losing no time about rounding up the cattle. By the time they were ready to make a move we were still more than a mile away, and out of breath.

"If they go south," panted Brown, throwing himself down by a clump of grass to gasp for his third or fourth wind, "the Masai'll catch 'em sure, an' we'll be out o' the running! Lord send they head 'em back toward British East!"

He was in much the worst physical condition because of the whisky, but his wits were working well enough. The Greeks on the other hand seemed undecided and appeared to be arguing. Then Brown's prayer was answered. The Greeks' boys decided the matter for them by stampeding the herd northward toward us. They did not come fast. They were lame, and bone-weary from hard driving, but they knew the way home again and made a bee line. Within a minute they were spread fan-wise between us and the Greeks, making a screen we could not shoot through.

"Scatter to right and left!" Brown shouted. "Get round the wings!"

But what was the use? He was in the center, and short-winded. I climbed on an ant-hill.

"The Greeks are on the run!" I said. "They are headed southward! They've got their boys together, and have abandoned the cattle! They're off with their tent and belongings due south!"

"The cowards!" swore Brown, with such disappointment that Will and I laughed.

"Laugh all you like!" he said. "I've a long job on my hands! I'll have revenge on 'em if it takes the rest o' my life! I'll follow 'em to hell-and-gone!"

"Meanwhile," I said, still standing on the ant-hill, "the Masai are following the cattle! They're smoking this way in two single columns of about twenty spears in each. The remainder are driving their own cattle about due eastward so as to be out of the way of trouble."

"All right," said Brown, growing suddenly cheerful again. "Then it'll be a rear-guard action. Let the cattle through, and open fire behind 'em! Send that Kazimoto o' yours to warn our boys to round 'em up and drive 'em slow and steady northward!"

Kazimoto ran back and gave the necessary orders. He lost no time about it, but returned panting, and lay down in a hollow behind us with cartridges in either fist and a grin on his face that would have done credit to a circus clown. I never, anywhere, saw any one more pleased than Kazimoto at the prospect of a fight.

We let the cattle through and lay hidden, waiting for the raiders. They were in full war dress, which is to say as nearly naked as possible except for their spears, a leg ornament made from the hair of the colobus monkey, a leather apron hung on just as suited the individual wearer's fancy, a great shield, and an enormous ostrich-feather head-dress. They seemed in no hurry, for they probably guessed that the cattle would stop to graze again when the first scare was over; yet they came along as smoke comes, swiftly and easily, making no noise.

Suddenly those in the lead caught sight of our boys getting behind the cattle to herd them northward. They halted to hold consultation—apparently decided that they had only unarmed natives to deal with—and came on again, faster than before.

"Better open fire now!" said Brown, when they were still a quarter of a mile away.

"Wait till you can see their eyes!" Will advised. "An unexpected volley at close quarters will do more havoc than hours of long-range shooting.

"This ain't a long range!" Brown objected. "As for unexpected—just watch me startle 'em! My sight's fixed at four hundred. Watch!"

He fired—we wished he had not. The leading Masai of the right-hand column jerked his head sidewise as the whistling bullet passed, and then there was nothing for it but to follow his lead and blaze away for all we were worth. If Brown had been willing to accept Will's advice there is nothing more likely than that the close-quarter surprise would have won the day for us. We would have done much more execution with three volleys at ten-yard range. As it was, we all missed with our finest shots, and the Masai took heart and charged in open order.

The worst of it was that, although we dropped several of them, now the others had a chance to discover there were only three of us. Their leader shouted. The right-hand column continued to attack, but changed its tactics. The left-hand party made a circuit at top speed, outflanked us, and pursued the cattle.

Supposing my count was right, we had laid out, either wounded or dead, seven of the crowd attacking us. This left perhaps fourteen against us, to be dealt with before the others could come back with the cattle and take us in the rear.

Will brought another man down; I saw the blood splash on his forehead as the bullet drilled the skull cleanly. Then one man shouted and they all lay prone, beginning to crawl toward us with their shields held before, not as protection against bullets (for as that they were utterly worthless) but as cover that made their exact position merest guesswork.

I fell back and took position on the ant-hill from which I had first seen them, thus making our position triangular and giving myself a chance to protect the other two should they feel forced to retire. The extra height also gave me a distinct advantage, for I could see the legs of the Masai over the tops of their shields, and was able to wound more than one of them so severely that they crawled to the rear.

But the rest came on. Kazimoto began to be busy supplying cartridges. In that first real pinch we were in he certainly lived up to all Courtney had said of him, for without the stimulus of his proper master's eye he neither flinched nor faltered, but crawled from one to the other, dividing the spare rounds equally.

The Masai began to attempt to outflank us, but my position on the ant-hill to the rear made that impossible; they found themselves faced by a side of the triangle from whichever side they attacked. But in turning to keep an eye on the flank I became aware of a greater danger. The cattle were coming back. That meant that the other Masai were coming, too, and that in a few moments we were likely to be overwhelmed. I shouted to Will and Brown, but either they did not hear me, or did not have time to answer.

I fired half a dozen shots, and then distinctly heard the crack of a rifle from beyond the cattle. That gave matters the worst turn yet. If one of the raiders had a rifle, then unless I could spot him at once and put him out of action our cause was likely lost. I stood up to look for him and heard a wild cheer, followed by three more shots in quick succession. Then at last I saw Fred Oakes running along a depression in the ground, followed at a considerable distance by the advance-guard of his porters. He was running, and then kneeling to fire—running, and kneeling again. And he was not wasting ammunition. He was much the best shot of us all, now that Monty was absent.

The terrified cattle stampeded past us, too wild to be checked by any noise. Seeing them, and sure now of their booty, the party attacking us hauled off and took to their heels. Will and Brown were for speeding them with bullets in the rear, but I yelled again, and this time made myself heard. Those who had got behind the cattle and were driving them were coming on with spears and shields raised to slay us in passing. The other two joined me, and we stood on the ant-hill three abreast. They charged us—seven or eight of them. Three bit the dust, but the rest came on, and if it had not been for two swift shots from Fred's rifle in the very nick of time we should have all been dead men.

As it was, one seized me by the knees and we went over together, rolling down the ant-hill, he slashing at me with his great broad-bladed spear, I hold of his wrist with one hand, and with the other fist belaboring him in the face. He was stronger than I—greasier—sweatier—harder to hold. He slipped from under me, rolled on top, wrenched his wrist free, and in another second grinned in my face as, with both knees in my stomach, be raised the spear to kill. I shut my eyes. I had not another breath left, nor an effort in me, I thought I would deny him the pleasure of watching my death agony. But I could not keep my eyes shut. Opening them to see why he did not strike, I saw Kazimoto with my rifle in both hands swing for his skull with the full weight of the butt and all his strength. Kazimoto grunted. The Masai half turned his head at the sound. The butt hit home—broke off—and my face and breast were deluged with blood and brains.

When I had wiped off that mess with Kazimoto's help I saw Fred and Will and Brown pursuing the retreating Masai, kneeling to shoot every few yards, at every other shot or so bringing down a victim, but being rapidly out-distanced. Cattle are all the Masai care about. They had the cattle. They had hold of tails and were making the whole herd scamper due east, where they no doubt knew of a trail not in maps. They made no attempt to defend themselves—left their dead lying—and ran. I saw two or three wounded ones riding on cows, and no doubt some of those who ran holding to the cows' tails were wounded, too.

I was useless now, as far as fighting was concerned, for the butt of my rifle was broken clean off at the grip, but I ran on, and heard Brown shout: "Shoot cattle! Don't let the brutes get away with them all!"

He was shooting cows himself when I came up, but it was Fred who stopped him.

"Never mind that, old man. We'll follow 'em up! Our time's our own. We'll get your cattle back, never fear. Dead ones are no use."

Brown stopped shooting and began to blubber. Whisky had not left him manhood enough to see his whole available resources carried away before his eyes, and he broke down as utterly as any child. It was neither agreeable nor decent to watch, and I turned away. I was feeling sick myself from the pressure of the Masai's knees in my stomach. That, and the sun, and the long march, and hunger (for we had not stopped to eat a meal that day) combined in argument, and I hunted about for a soft place and a little shade. It happened that Fred Oakes was watching me, although I did not know it. He suspected sunstroke.

I saw a clump of rushes that gave shade enough. I could crush down some, and lie on those. I hurried, for I was feeling deathly sick now. As I reached the grass my knees began giving under me. I staggered, but did not quite fall.

That, and Fred's watchfulness, saved my life; for at the moment that my head and shoulders gave the sudden forward lurch, a wounded Masai jumped out of the rushes and drove with his spear at my breast. The blade passed down my back and split my jacket.

He sprang back, and made another lunge at me, but Fred's rifle barked at the same second and he fell over sidewise, driving the spear into my leg in his death spasm.

The twenty minutes following that are the worst in memory. Kazimoto broke the gruesome news that the spear-blade was almost surely poisoned—dipped in gangrene. The Masai are no believers in wounded enemies, or mercy on the battlefield.

We doubted the assertion for a while—I especially, for none but a hypochondriac would care to admit without proof that gangrene had been forced into his system. Kazimoto grew indignant, and offered to prove the truth of his claim on some animal. But there was no living animal in sight on which to prove it. We asked him how long gangrene, injected in that way, took to kill a man.

"Very few minutes!" he answered.

Then it occurred that none of us knew what to do. Kazimoto announced that he knew, and offered to make good at once if given permission. He demanded permission again and again from each one of us, making me especially repeat my words. Then be gathered stems of grass a third of an inch thick from the bed of the tiny watercourse, and proceeded to make a tiny fire, talking in a hurry as he did it to several of Fred's string of porters, who were now arriving on the scene.

While I watched with a sort of tortured interest what he was doing at the fire, five of the largest boys with whom be had been speaking rushed me from behind, and before I could struggle, or even swear, had me pinned out on my back on the ground. One sat on my head; one on my poor bruised stomach; the others held wrists and ankles in such way that I could not break free, nor even kick much, however hard I tried.

Then Kazimoto came with glowing ends of grass from the fire, blowing on them to keep them cherry-red, and inserted one after another into the open spear-wound. I could not cry out, because of the man sitting on my face, but I could bite. And to the everlasting glory of the man—Ali bin Yema, his name was—be it written that he neither spoke nor moved a muscle, although my front teeth met in his flesh.

I do not know how long the process lasted, or how many times Kazimoto returned to the fire for more of his sizzling sticks, for I fainted; and when I came round the agony was still too intense to permit interest in anything but agony. They had my leg bandaged, how and with what I neither knew nor cared. And it was evident that unless they chose to leave me in camp where I was they would have to abandon all thought of pursuing Masai for the present. Even Brown saw the force of that, and he was the first to refuse flatly to leave me there.

For a while they hunted through the grass for more wounded men, but found none. There must have been several, but they probably feared the sort of mercy from us that they habitually gave to their own enemies, and crawled away—in all likelihood to die of thirst and hunger, unless some beast of prey should smell them out and make an earlier end.

Then there was consultation. It was decided a doctor for me was the most urgent need; that Muanza, the largest German station on Victoria Nyanza, was probably as near as anywhere, and that German East being our immediate destination anyway, the best course to take was forward, roughly south by west. So I was slung in a blanket on a tent-pole, and we started, I swearing like a pirate every time a boy stumbled and jolted me. (There is something in the nature of a burn that makes bad language feel like singing hymns.)

Our troubles were not all over, for we passed through a country where buck were fairly plentiful, and that meant lions. They did no damage, but they kept us awake; and one night near the first village we came to, where our porters all quartered themselves with the villagers for sake of the change from their crowded tents, the fires that we made went out, and five lions (we counted their foot-prints afterward) came and sniffed around the pegs of the tent in which Fred and I lay, we lying still and shamming dead. To have lifted a rifle in the darkness and tried to shoot would have been suicide.

Then there were trees we passed among—baobabs, whose youngest tendrils swung to and fro in the evening breeze like snakes head-downward. And taking advantage of that natural provision, twenty-foot pythons swung among them, in coloring and marking aping the habit of the tree. One of them knocked Fred's helmet off as he marched beside me. They are easy to kill. He shot it, and it dropped like a stone, three hundred pounds or more, but the sweat ran down Fred's face for half an hour afterward.

(Since then I have seen pythons kill their prey a score of times. I never once saw one kill by crushing. The end of their nose is as hard as iron, and they strike a terrific blow with that, so swift that the eye can not follow it. Then, having killed by striking, they crawl around their prey and crush it into shape for swallowing.)

But the worst of the journey was the wayside villages—dirty beyond belief, governed in a crude way by a headman whom the Germans honored with the title of sultani. These wayside beggars (for they were no better)—destitute paupers, taxed until their wits failed them in the effort to scrape together surplus enough out of which to pay—were supplied with a mockery of a crown apiece, a thing of brass and imitation plush that they wore in the presence of strangers. To add to the irony of that, the law of the land permitted any white man passing through to beat them, with as many as twenty-five lashes, if they failed to do his bidding.

On arriving at such a village, the first thing we did was to ask for milk. If they had any they brought it, not daring to refuse for fear lest a German sergeant-major should be sent along to wreak vengeance later. But it was always too dirty to drink.

That ceremony over, the headman retired and the village sick were brought for our inspection. Gruesome sores, running ulcers, wounds and crippled limbs were stripped and exposed to our most reluctant gaze. There was little we could do for them. Our own supply of medicines and bandages was almost too small for our own needs to begin with. By the time we passed three villages we scarcely had enough lint and liniment left to take care of my wound; but even that scant supply we cut in half for a particularly bad case.

"Don't the Germans do anything for you?" we demanded, over and over again.

The answer was always the same.

"Germani mbaia!" (The Germans are bad!)

They were lifeless—listless—tamed until neither ambition nor courage was left. When their cattle had brought forth young and it looked as if there might be some profit at last, the Masai came and raided them, taking away all but the very old ones and the youngest calves. The Germans, they said, taxed them and took their weapons away, but gave them no protection.

At one place we passed a rifle, lying all rusted

by the track. At the next village we asked about it. They told us that a German native soldier had deserted six months before and had thrown his rifle away. Since that day no one had dared touch it, and they begged us to send back and lay it where we found it, lest the Germans come and punish them for touching it. So we did that, to oblige them, and they were grateful to the extent of offering us one of their only two male sheep.

I forget now for how many days we traveled across that sad and saddening land, Fred always cheerful in spite of everything, Will more angry at each village with its dirt and sores, Brown moaning always about his lovely herd of cows, and I groaning oftener than not.

My leg grew no better, what with jolting and our ignorance of how to treat it. Sometimes, in efforts to obtain relief, I borrowed a cow at one village and rode it to the next; but a cow is a poor mount and takes as a rule unkindly to the business. Now and then I tried to walk for a while, on crutches that Fred made for me; but most of the time I was carried in a blanket that grew hotter and more comfortless as day dragged after day.

At last, however, we topped a low rise and saw Muanza lying on the lake-shore, with the great island of Ukerewe to the northward in the distance. From where we first glimpsed it it was a tidy, tree-shaded, pleasant-looking place, with a square fort, and a big house for the commandant on a rise overlooking the town.

"Now we'll wire Monty at last!" said Fred.

"Now we'll shave and wash and write letters!" said Will.

"Now at last for a doctor!" said I.

But Brown said nothing, and Kazimoto wore a look of anxious discontent.

THE DARKNESS COMPREHENDED IT NOT

When Kenia's peak glows gold and rose
A dawn breeze whispers to the plain
With breath cooled sweet by mountain
snows—"The darkness soon shall come
again!"
Stirs then the sleepless, lean Masai
And stands o'er plain and peak at gaze
Resentful of the bright'ning sky,
Impatient of the white man's days.

Oh dark nights, when the charcoal glowed and falling hammers rang!
When fundis forged the spear-blades, and the warriors danced and sang!
When the marriageable spearmen gathered, calling each to each
Telling over proverbs that the tribal wise-men teach,
Brother promising blood-brother partnership in weal and woe—
Nightlong stories of the runners come from spying on the foe—
Nights of boasting by the thorn-fire of the coming tale of slain—
Oh the times before the English! When will those times come again!

Oh the days and nights of raiding, when the feathered spearmen strode
With the hide shields on their forearms, and the wild Nyanza road
Grew blue with smoking villages, grew red with flaring roofs,
Grew noisy with the shouting and the thunder of the hoofs
As we drove the plundered cattle—when we burned the night with haste—
When we leapt at dawn from ambush—when we laid the shambas waste!

Oh the new spears dipped in life-blood as the women shrieked in vain!
Oh the days before the English! When will those days come again!

Oh the homeward road in triumph with the plunder borne along
On the heads of taken women! Oh the daughter and the song!
Oh the tusks of yellow ivory—the frasilas of beads—
And, best of all, the heifers that the marriageable needs!
The yells when village eyes at last our sky-line feathers see
And the maidens run to count how many marriages shall be—
Ten heifers to a maiden (and the chief's girl stands for twain)—
Oh the days before the English! When will those days come again!

Now the fat herds grow in number, and the old
are rich in trade,
Now the grass grows green and heavy where the
six-foot spears were made.
Now the young men walk to market, and the
wives have beads and wire—
Brass and iron—glass and cowrie—past the limit
of desire.
There is peace from lake to mountain, and the
very zebra breed
Where a law says none may hurt them (and the
wise are they who heed!)
Yea—the peace lies on the country as our herds
o'erspread the plain—
But the days before the English—when shall
those days come again!

When Kenia's peak glows gold and rose
A dawn breeze whispers to the plain
With breath cooled sweet by mountain
snows—"The darkness soon shall come
again!"
Stirs then the sleepless, lean Masai
And stands o'er plain and peak at gaze
Resentful of the bright'ning sky,
Impatient of the white man's days.

VII

WHAT FIRST looked like a pleasant place dwindled into charmlessness and insignificance as we approached. There was neatness—of a kind. The round huts were confined to certain streets, and all inhabited by natives. Arabs, Swahili, Indians, Goanese, Syrians, Greeks and so on had to live in rectangular huts and keep to other streets. On one street, chiefly of stores, all the roofs were of corrugated iron. And all the streets were straight, with shade trees planted down both sides at exactly equal intervals.

But the German blight was there, instantly recognizable by any one not mentally perverted by German teaching. The place was governed—existed for and by leave of government. The inhabitants were there on sufferance, and aware of it—not in the very least degree enthusiastic over German rule, but awfully appreciative.

The first thing we met of interest on entering the township was a chain-gang, fifty long, marching at top speed in step, led by a Nubian soldier with a loaded rifle, flanked by two others, and pursued by a fourth armed only with the hippo-hide whip, called *kiboko* by the natives, that can cut and bruise at one stroke. He plied it liberally whenever the gang betrayed symptoms of intending to slow down.

Those Nubians, we learned later, were deserters from British Sudanese regiments, and runaways from British jails, afraid to take the thousand-mile journey northward home again, scornful of all foreign black men, fanatic Mohammedans, and therefore fine tools in the German hand. They worked harder than the chain-gang, for they had to march with it step for step and into the bargain force it to do its appointed labor. The chain-gang kept the township clean—very clean indeed, as far as outward appearance went.

The boma, or fort, was down by the water-front and its high eastern wall, pierced by only one gate, formed one boundary of the drill-ground that was also township square. Facing the wall on the eastern side of the square was a row of Indian and Arab stores. At the north end was the market building—an enormous structure of round stucco pillars supporting a great grass roof; and facing that at the southern end were the court-house, the hospital, and a store owned by the Deutsch-Ostafrikanische Gesellschaft, known far and wide by its initials—a concern that owned the practical monopoly of wholesale import and export trade, and did a retail business, too.

We went first to the hospital. Fred and Will lifted me out of the hammock, for my wound had grown much worse during the last few days, and the door being shut they set me down on the step. Then we sent Kazimoto into the fort with a note to the senior officer informing him that a European waited at the hospital in need of prompt medical treatment.

The sentry admitted Kazimoto readily enough, but he did not come out again for half-an-hour, and then looked glum.

"Habanah!" he said simply, using the all-embracing native negative.

"Isn't any one in there?" we demanded all together.

"Surely."

"How many?"

"Very many."

"Officers?"

He nodded.

"Is a doctor there?"

He told us he had asked for the doctor. A soldier had pointed him out. He had placed the note in the doctor's hand.

"Did he read it?" we asked.

"Surely. He read it, and then showed it to the other officers."

"What did they say?"

"They laughed and said nothing."

It seemed pretty obvious that Kazimoto had made a mistake in some way. Perhaps he had visited the non-commissioned officers' mess.

I'll go myself," announced Will. "I can sling the German language like a barkeep. Bet you I'm back here with a doctor inside of three minutes!"

He strode off like Sir Galahad in football shorts, and was passed through the gate by the sentry almost unchallenged. But he was gone more than fifteen minutes, and came back at last with his ears crimson. Nor would he answer our questions.

"Shall I go?" suggested Fred.

"Not unless you like insolence! We passed the camping-ground, it seems, on our way in. We've leave to pitch tents there. We'd better be moving."

So we trailed back the way we had come to a triangular sandy space enclosed by a cactus hedge at the junction of three roads. There were several small grass-roofed shelters with open sides in there, and two tents already pitched, but we were not sufficiently interested just then to see who owned the other tents. We pitched our own—stowed the loads in one of the shelters—gave our porters money for board and rations—and sent them to find quarters in the town. Another of the shelters we took over for a kitchen, and while our servants were cooking a meal we four gathered in Fred's tent and began to question Will again.

"They've got a fine place in there," he said. "Neat as a new pin. Officers' mess. Non-commissioned officers' quarters. Stores. Vegetable garden. Jail—looks like a fine jail—hold a couple of hundred. Government offices. Two-story buildings. Everything fine. The officers were all sitting smoking on a veranda.

" 'Is one of you the doctor?' I asked in German, and a tall lean one with a mighty mean face turned his head to squint at me: but he didn't take his feet off the rail. He looked inquisitive, that's all.

" 'Are you the doctor?' I asked him.

" 'I am staff surgeon,' he answered. 'What do you want?'

"I told him about your wound, and how we'd marched about two hundred miles on purpose to get medical assistance. He listened without asking a question, and when I'd done he said curtly that the hospital opens for out-patients at eight in the morning.

"Well, I piled it on then. I told him your leg was so rotten that you might not be alive to-morrow morning. He didn't even look interested. I piled it on thicker and told him about the poisoned spear. He didn't bat an eyelid or make a move. So I started in to coax him.

"I did some coaxing. Believe me, I swallowed more pride in five minutes than I guessed I owned! A ward-heeler cadging votes for a Milwaukee alderman never wheedled more gingerly. I called him 'Herr Staff Surgeon' and mentioned the well-known skill of German medicos, and the keen sense of duty of the German army, and a whole lot of other stuff.

" 'To-morrow morning at eight!' was all the answer I got from him.

"I reckon it was somewhere about that time I began to get rattled. I pulled out money and showed it. He looked the other way, and when I went on talking he turned his back. I suspect he didn't dare keep on lookin' at money almost within reach. Anyhow, then I opened on him, firin' both bow guns. I dared him to sit there, with a patient in need of prompt attention less than two hundred yards away. I called him names. I guaranteed to write to the German government and the United States papers about him. I told him I'd have his job if it cost me all my money and a lifetime's trouble. He was just about ready to shoot—I'd just about got the red blood rising on his neck and ears—when along came the commandant—der Herr Capitain—the officer commanding Muanza—a swag-bellied ruffian with a beard and a beery look in his eye, but a voice like a man falling down three stories with all the fire-irons.

" 'What do you want?' he demanded in English, and I thanked him first for not having mistaken me for one of his own countrymen. Then I told him what I'd come for.

" 'To-morrow at eight o'clock!' he snapped, after he'd had a word with the medico. 'Meanwhile, make yourself scarce out of here! There is a camping-ground for the use of foreigners. You and your party go to it! If you do any damage there you will hear from me later!'

"I didn't come as easy as all that. I stood there telling him things about Germany and Germans, and what I'd do to help his personal reputation with the home folks, until I guessed he had his craw as near full as he could stand it without having me arrested. Then I did come—whistling *Yankee-doodle.* And say—Fred! Where's that concertina of yours?"

Fred patted it. His beloved instrument was never far from hand.

"Why don't you play all the American and English tunes you know to-night? Play and sing 'em, *Britannia Rule the Waves—Marching Through Georgia—My Country, 'Tis of Thee—The Marseillaise—The Battle Hymn of the Republic*—and anything and everything you know that Squareheads won't like. Let's make this camp a reg'lar—hello—see who's here!"

Fred had begun fingering the keys already and the first strains of *Marching Through Georgia* began to awake the neighborhood to recognition of the fact that foreigners were present who held no especial brief for German rule. The tent-door darkened. Brown leapt to his feet and swore.

"Gassharamminy!" said a voice we all recognized instantly. "That tune sounds good! I've lived in the States! I'm a United States citizen! A man can't forget his own country's tunes so easily!"

Cool and impudent, Georges Coutlass entered and, without waiting for an invitation, took a seat on a load of canned food. Brown grabbed the nearest rifle (it happened to be Fred's)—snapped open the breach—discovered it was loaded—and took aim. Coutlass did not even blink. He was either sure Fred and Will would interfere, or else at the end of his tether and indifferent to death.

"Don't be an ass, Brown!"

Fred knocked the rifle up. Will took it away and returned it to the corner.

"All very easy for you men to take high moral ground and all that sort of rot," Brown grumbled. "It's my cattle he took! It's me be's ruined! What do I care if the Germans hang me? Let me have a crack at him—just one!"

"Use your fists all you care to!" grinned Will.

But Brown was no match for the Greek without weapons—very likely no match for him with them. Coutlass sat still and grinned, while Brown remained in the back of the tent, glaring.

"Bah!" sneered Coutlass. "Of what use is being sulky? I found cattle in a village. How should I know whose cattle they were? Why blame me? The Masai got the cattle, not I! They took them from me, and they'd have taken them from you just the same! You lost nothing by my lifting them first! Gassharamminy! By blazes! We're all in the same boat! Let's be friendly, and treat one another like gentlemen! We're all in the power of the Germans, unless we can think of a way to escape! I and my party are under arrest. So will you be by to-morrow! I shall tell a tale to-morrow that will keep you by the heels for a month at least while they investigate! Wait and see!"

"Get out of this tent!" growled Fred in the dead-level voice he uses when he means to brook no refusal.

"Presently!"

Fred made a spring at him, but Coutlass was on his feet with the speed of a cat, and just outside the tent in time to avoid the swing of Fred's fist. He withdrew about two yards and stood there grinning maliciously.

"You'll be glad to make terms with me by this time to-morrow!" he boasted. "By James, you'll be glad to have me for a friend! Listen, you fools! Make terms with me now; let us all go together and unearth that Tippoo Tib ivory, and I can arrange with these Germans to let us go away! Otherwise, you shall see how long you stop here! By the Twelve Apostles! You shall rot in a German jail until your joints creak!"

His Greek friend and the Goanese, supposing him in trouble perhaps, came and stood in line with him. Very comfortless they looked, and of the three only Coutlass had courage of a kind.

"They stole the cattle on the British side of the border," Will said sotto voice. "No earthly use threatening them with German law."

"Keep away from our camp," Fred Ordered them, "or take the consequences! Mr. Brown here is in no mood for pleasantries!"

"That drunkard Brown?" roared Coutlass. "He is in no mood for—oh, haw-hah-hee-ho-ha-ha-ha-ha! Drunkard Brown of Lumbwa wants to avenge himself, and his friends won't let him! Oh, isn't that a joke! Oh, ha-ha-ha-hee-hee-ha-ho-ho!"

His two companions made a trio of it, yelling with stage laughter like disgusting animals. Fred took a short quick step forward. Will followed, and

Brown reached for the rifle again. But I stopped all three of them.

"Come back! Don't let's be fools!" I insisted. "I never saw a more obvious effort to start trouble in my life! It's a trap! Keep out of it!"

"Sure enough," Will admitted. "You're right!"

He returned into the tent and the Greeks, perhaps supposing he went for weapons, retreated, continuing to shout abuse at Brown who, between a yearning to get drunk and sorrow for his stolen cattle, was growing tearful.

"They got here first," I argued. "They've had time to tell their own story. That may account for our cold reception by the Germans. He says they're under arrest. That may be true, or it may be a trick. It's perfectly obvious Coutlass wanted to start a fight, and I'm dead sure he wasn't taking such a chance as it seemed. Who wants to look behind the cactus hedge and see whether he has friends in ambush?"

"Drunkard Brown is on the town—on the town—on the town!" roared Coutlass and his friends from not very far away.

"Oh, let me go and have a crack at 'em!" begged Brown. "I tell you I don't care about jail! I don't care if I do get killed!"

Fred kept a restraining hand on him. Will left the tent and walked straight for the gap in the cactus hedge by which we had entered the enclosure. It was only twenty yards away.

Once through the gap he glanced swiftly to right and left—laughed—and came back again.

"Only six of 'em!" he grinned. "Six full-sized Nubians in uniform, with army boots on, no bayonets or rifles, but good big sticks and handcuffs! If we'd touched those Greeks they'd have jumped the fence and stretched us out! What the devil d'you suppose they want us in jail for?"

"D'you suppose they think," I said, "that if they had us in jail in this God-forsaken place we'd divulge the secret of Tippoo's ivory?"

"Why don't we tell 'em the secret!" suggested Will, and that seemed such a good idea that we laughed ourselves back into good temper—even Brown, who had no notion whether we knew the secret, being perfectly sure we would not be such fools as to tell the true whereabouts of the hoard in any case.

"I want to get even with all Africa!" he grumbled. "I want to make trouble that'll last! I'd start a war this minute if I knew how! If it weren't for those bloody Greeks laughing at me I'd get more drunk to-night than any ten men in the world ever were before in history! Yes, sir! And my name's Brown of Lumbwa to prove I mean what I say!"

After a while, seeing that no trouble was likely, the Nubian soldiers came out of ambush and marched away. We ate supper. The Greeks and the Goanese subsided into temporary quiet, and our own boys, squatting by a fire they had placed so that they could watch the Greeks' encampment, began bumming a native song. Their song reminded Fred of Will's earlier suggestion, and he unclasped the concertina.

Then for three-quarters of an hour he played, and we sang all the tunes we knew least likely to make Germans happy, repeating *The Marseillaise* and *Rule Britannia* again and again in pious hope that at least a few bars might reach to the commandant's house on the hill.

Whether they did or not—whether the commandant writhed as we hoped in the torture of supreme insult, or slept as was likely from the after-effect of too much bottled beer with dinner—there were others who certainly did hear, and made no secret of it.

To begin with, the part of the township nearest us was the quarter of round grass roofs, where the aborigines lived; and the Bantu heart responds to tuneful noise, as readily as powder to the match. All that section of Muanza, man, woman and child, came and squatted outside the cactus hedge. (It was *streng polizeilich verboten* for natives to enter the European camping-ground, so that except when they wanted to steal they absolutely never trespassed past the hedge.)

Enraptured by the unaccustomed strains they sat quite still until some Swahili and Arabs came and beat them to make room. When the struggle and hot argument that followed that had died down, Indians began coming, and other Greeks, until most of the inhabitants of the eastern side of town were either squatting or standing or pacing to and fro outside the camping-ground.

At last rumor of what was happening reached the D.O.A.G.—the store at the corner of the drill-ground, where it seemed the non-commissioned officers took their pleasure of an evening. Pleasure, except as laid down in regulations, is not permitted in German colonies to any except white folk. No less than eight German sergeants and a sergeant-major, all the worse for liquor, turned out as if to a fire and came down street at a double.

They had *kibokos* in their hands. The first we heard of their approach was the crack-crack-crack of the black whips falling on naked or thin-cotton-clad backs and shoulders. There was no yelling (it was not allowed after dark on German soil, at least by natives) but a sudden pattering in the dust as a thousand feet hurried away. Then, in the glow of our lamplight, came the sergeant-major standing spraddle-legged in front of us.

He was a man of medium height, in clean white uniform. The first thing I noticed about him was the high cheek-bones and murderous blue eyes, like a pig's. His general build was heavy. The fair mustache made no attempt to conceal fat lips that curled cruelly. His general air was that most offensive one to decent folk, of the bully who would ingratiate by seeming a good fellow.

" 'nabnd, meine Herren!" he said aggressively, with a smile more than half made up of contempt for courtesy. *"Ich heisse* Schubert—Feldwebel Hans Schubert."

"Was wollen Sie?" Will asked. He was the only one of us who knew German well.

But Schubert, it seemed, knew English and was glad to show it off.

"You make fine music! *Ach!* Up at the D.O.A.G. very near here we *Unteroffizieren* spend the evening, all very fond of singing, yet without music at all. Will you not come and play with us?"

"I only know French and English tunes!" lied Fred.

"Ach! I do not believe it! *Kommen Sie!* There is beer at the D.O.A.G.—champagne—brandy—whisky—rum—?"

"I'm going, then, for one!" announced Brown, getting up immediately.

"Cigars—cigarettes—tobacco," the sergeant-major continued. "There is no closing time." He saw that the line of argument was not tempting, and changed his tactics. "Listen! You gentlemen have not too many friends in Muanza! I speak in friendship. I invite you on behalf of myself and other *Unteroffizieren* to spend *gemuthlich* evening with us. That can do you no harm! In the course of friendly conversation much can be learned that official lips would not tell! *Kommen Sie nun!"*

"Let's go!" I said. "My leg hurts like hell. If I stay here I can't sleep. Anything to keep from thinking about it! Besides, some one must go and look after Brown!"

"Who'll watch those Greeks?" Fred demanded. "They'd as soon steal as eat!"

"We'd better all stay here together," said Will, "and take turns keeping watch till morning." He said it with a straight face, but I did not think he was in earnest.

"Ach!" exclaimed Schubert. "That is all *ganz einfach!* You shall have *askaris!"*

He turned and shouted an order. A non-commissioned officer went running back up-street.

"You shall have three *askaris* to guard your camp. So nothing whatever shall be stolen! Then come along and make music—*seien Sie gemuthlich!* Yah?"

Brown had already gone, jingling money in his pocket. We waited until the Nubian soldiers came—saw them posted—and then walked up-street behind the sergeants, Schubert leading us all, and I limping between Fred and Will. They as good as carried me the last half of the way.

The sergeants marched with the air peculiar to military Germans, of men who are going to be amused. They said nothing—did not smile—but strode straight forward, three abreast, swinging their *kibokos* with a sort of elephantine sporty air. They were men of all heights and thicknesses, but each alike impressed me with the Prussian military mold that leaves a man no imagination of his own, and no virtue, but only an animal respect for whatever can make to suffer, or appease an appetite.

The D.O.A.G. proved a mournful enough lounging place in which to spend convivial evenings. However, it seemed that when the sergeant-major had decreed amusement the non-commissioned officers' mess overlooked all trifles in brave determination to obey. They marched in, humming tunes (each a different one, and nearly all high tenor) and took seats in a room at the rear of the building with their backs against a mud-brick wall that was shiny from much rubbing by drill tunics.

Down the center was a narrow table, loaded with drinks of all sorts. A case of bottled beer occupied the place of pride at one end; as Schubert had boasted, nothing was lacking that East Africa could show in the way of imported alcohol. Under the table was an unopened case of sweet German champagne, and on a little table against one wall were such things as absinthe, chartreuse, peppermint, and benedictine. Soda-water was slung outside the window in a basket full of wet grass where the evening breeze would keep it cool.

"Now for *Gesang!"* shouted Schubert, knocking the neck off a bottle of beer, and beginning to sing like a drunken pirate.

A man whom he introduced as "a genuine Jew from Jerusalem" came out from a gloomy recess filled with tusks and sacks of dried red pepper, and watched everything from now on with an eye like a gimlet, writing down in a book against each sergeant's name whatever he took to drink. They appeared to have no check on him. Nobody signed anything. Nobody as much as glanced at his account.

"What is the use?" said Schubert, noticing my glance and interpreting the unspoken question. "There is just so much drink in the whole place. We shall drink every drop of it! All that matters is, who is to pay for the champagne? That stuff is costly."

They all took beer to begin with, knocking the necks from the bottles as if that act alone lent the necessary air of deviltry to the whole proceedings. A small, very black Nyamwesi came with brush and pan and groped on the floor all night for the splinters of glass, sleeping between times in a corner until a fresh volley of breaking bottle necks awoke him to work again.

"Die Wacht am Rhein!" yelled Schubert. "Start it up! Sing that first!" He began to sing it himself, all out of tune.

Fred cut the noise short by standing up to play something nobody could sing to a jangling clamor of chords and runs on which he prides himself, that he swears is classical, but of which neither he nor anybody knows the name. Then he drank some beer and sang a comic song or two in English, we joining in the choruses.

Meanwhile, Brown was soaking away steadily, taking whatever drink came first to hand, and having no interest whatever in anything but the task of assuaging the thirst he had accumulated in the course of all that long marching since he left home. He had forgotten his cattle already—the Greeks who stole them—the Masai who stole from the Greeks. He paid for all he took, to the Jew's extreme surprise and satisfaction, and grumbled at the price of everything, to the Jew's supremest unconcern.

"An' my name's Brown o' Lumbwa, just in proof of all I say!" he informed the room at large at intervals.

When Will had exhausted all the American songs he knew, and Fred had run through his own long list there was nothing left for it but to make up accompaniments to the songs the sergeants had been raised on. Fred made the happy discovery that none of them knew *The Marseillaise,* so he played that as an antidote each time after they had made the hard-wood rafters ring and the smoke-filled air vibrate with Teutonic jingoism. The Jew, who probably knew more than he cared to admit, grew more and more beady-eyed each time *The Marseillaise* was played.

There was a pause in the proceedings at about ten o'clock, by which time all the sergeants except Schubert were sufficiently drunk to feel thoroughly at ease. Schubert was cold-eyed sober, although scarcely any longer thirsty.

A native was brought in by two *askaris* and charged before Schubert with hanging about the boma gate after dark. He was asked the reason. The Jew, sitting beside me with his book of names and charges, poured cool water over my bandages and translated to me what they all said. He spoke English very well indeed, but in such low tones that I could scarcely catch the words, drawing in his breath and not moving his lips at all.

The native explained that he had waited to see the *bwana makubwa*—the commandant. He had nowhere to go and no money with which to pay for lodging, so he proposed to wait outside the gate and watch for the coming of the commandant next morning. He would intercept him on his way down from the white house on the hill.

He was asked why. To beg a favor. What favor? Satisfaction. For what? For his daughter. He was the father of the girl whom the commandant had favored with attentions. She had been a virgin. Now she was to have a child. It would be a half-black, half-white child. Who would now marry a woman with such a child as that? Yet nothing bad been given her. She had been simply sent back home to be a charge on her parents and an already poverty-stricken village. Therefore he had come to ask that justice be done, and the girl be given at least a present of money.

The sergeants roared with laughter, all except Schubert, who seemed only appalled by the impudence of the request. He sat back and ordered the story repeated.

"And you dare ask for money from the *bwana makubwa?"* he demanded. "You dog of a Nyamwesi! Is the honor not sufficient that your black brute of a daughter should have a baby by such a great person? You cattle have no sense of honor! You must learn! Put him down! Beat him till I say stop!"

There was no need to put him down, however. The motion of the hand, voice inflection, order were all too well understood. The man lay face-downward on the floor without so much as a murmur of objection, and buried his face in both hands. The *askaris* promptly stripped him of the thin cotton loin-cloth that constituted his only garment, tearing it in pieces as they dragged it from him.

"Go on!" ordered Schubert. "Beat him!"

Both the *askaris* had *kibokos.* The longest of the two was split at the nether end into four fingers. The shortest was more than a yard long, tapering from an inch and a half where the man's fist gripped it to half an inch thick at the tip. They stood one each side of their victim and brought the whips down on his naked skin alternately.

"Slowly!" ordered Schubert. "Slowly, and with all your strength! The brute doesn't feel it when you beat so fast! Let him wait for the blow! Don't let him know when it's coming! So—so is better!"

Not every blow drew blood, for a native's skin is thick and tough, especially where he sits. But the blows that fell on the back and thighs all cut the skin, and within two minutes the native's back was a bloody mass, and there was blood running on the floor, and splashes of blood on the whitewashed wall cast by the whips as they ascended.

I made up my mind the man was going to be killed, for Schubert gave no order and the *askaris* did not dare stop without one. The victim writhed, but did not cry out, and the writhing grew less. Even Brown sobered up for a time at the sight of it. He came and sat between me and the Jew.

"It's a shame!" he grumbled. "Up in our country twenty-five lashes is the masshimum, an' only to be laid on in the presence of a massishtrate. *You* beat a black man an' they'll fine you first offense, jail you second offense, an' third offense God knows what they'll do! Poor ole Brown o' Lumbwa! They fined me once a'ready. Nessht time they'll put me in jail! Better get quite drunk an' be blowed to it!"

He staggered back to his chair by the farther wall, leering at Schubert as he passed.

"You're no gentleman!" he asserted aggressively. "You're no better 'n a black man yourself! You ought-to-be-on-floor 'stead o' him! Dunno-how-behave-yourself! Take your coat off, an' come outside, an' fight like a man!"

Schubert gave the order to stop at last. The *askaris* stood aside, panting from the effort.

"Get up!" ordered Schubert.

The miserable Nyamwesi struggled to his feet and stood limply before Schubert, his back running blood and his face drawn with torture.

"Don't you know how to behave!" demanded Schubert.

The native made no answer.

"If you don't salute properly I'll order you thrown down and thrashed again!"

The native saluted in a sort of imitation of the German military manner.

"Now, will you lie in wait for the *bwana makubwa* to trouble him with your pig's affairs again?"

"No."

"Will you go back home?"

"Yes."

"You've learned a lesson, eh?"

"Yes.

"Then say thank you!"

"Thank you!"

"Rrruksa!"

The poor wretch turned and went, staggering rather than walking, to the door and disappearing into outer darkness without a backward glance.

"Now for some more songs and a round of drinks!" Schubert shouted.

But Fred was no longer in mood to make music, or even to be civil. He shut the concertina up, and asked the Jew how much he owed. The sergeants went on singing without music, and while we waited for the Jew to reckon up Fred's score Schubert came over to us, sat down between me and Fred, and proceeded to deal with the new situation in proper German military manner, by direct assault.

"Always you English criticize!" he began. "Can you never travel without applying your cursed standards to everything you behold? I tell you, we Germans know how to rule these black people! We understand! We employ no sickly sentiment!

We give orders—they obey, or else suffer terribly and swiftly! In that manner we arrive at knowing where we are!"

"Are you well loved by the people?" Fred asked him politely.

"Bah! *Sie wollen wohl beliebt werden!* Not I! Not we! Of what value is the love of such people? Their fear is what we cultivate! Having made them afraid of us, we successfully make them work our will! But why should I trouble to explain? In a few years there will only be one government of Africa! One, I tell you, and that German! You English are not fit to govern colonies! You are mawkishly sentimental! You think more of the feelings of a black man and of the rights of his women than of progress—advancement—*kultur!* Bah! I tell you they have no feelings a real man need consider! They are only fit for furthering the aims of us Germans! And their women have no rights! None whatever! You know, I suppose, that it is the policy of the German government to encourage the spread of Mohammedanism in Africa? Well, under the Mohammedan law as given in the Koran women have no souls! That is good! That is as it should be! No women have souls!"

"How about your own mother?" Fred suggested.

"She was a good Prussian! She was a superwoman! Not to be mentioned in the same breath with women of any other race! Yet even she—the good Prussian mother—could not hold a candle to a man! Her business was to raise sons for Prussia, and she did it! I have eight brothers, all in the army, and only one sister; she has four sons already!"

"Strange that your nation should breed like that!" said Fred.

"Not strange at all!" answered Schubert. "We are needed to conquer the world! Think, for instance, when we have conquered the Congo Free State, and taken away East and South Africa from England—to say nothing of Egypt and India!—how many Prussian sergeant-majors we shall want! *Donnerwetter!* Do you think we Germans will long be satisfied with this miserable section of East Africa that was all the English left to us on this coast? We use this for a foothold, that is all! We use this to gain time and get ready! You think perhaps I do not know, eh? I am only *feldwebel*—non-commissioned officer, you call it. Well and good. I tell you our officers talk all the time of nothing else! And they don't care who hears them!"

The Jew gave Fred his bill, scrawled on a piece of wrapping paper. Schubert snatched it away and crumpled it into a ball.

"Kreuzblitzen! You are my guests to-night! I invited you!"

"Thanks," Fred answered, "but we don't care to be your guests. Here," he said, turning to the Jew, "take your, money!"

Schubert said nothing, but eyed the Jew with a perfectly blank face, as if he watched to see whether the man would damn himself or not.

"Take your money!" repeated Fred. But the Jew turned his back and busied himself with bottles at the side-table.

"He knows better!" Schubert laughed. "He understands by this time our German hospitality!"

"All right," answered Fred. "We'll go out without paying!"

"Not at all," retorted Schubert. "The mess shall pay bill in full! You stay here until I have said what I have to say to you! The rest of your party may go, but you stay! You can explain to the others afterward."

He leaned forward, reached a bottle of beer off the table, knocked off the neck, and emptied the contents down his throat at a draught. Behind his back we exchanged glances.

"I'll listen," said Fred.

"You alone?"

"No, we all stay. All or none!"

Schubert made a contemptuous gesture with his thumb toward Brown, who had fallen dead drunk on the floor.

"Will that one stay, too?"

"He is not of our party really," Fred answered. "He knows nothing of our affairs."

"You men are in trouble—worse trouble than you guess!"

Schubert looked with his cruel blue eyes into each of ours in turn, then stared straight in front of him and waited.

"I don't believe it," Fred answered. "We have done nothing to merit trouble."

"Merit in this world is another name for chance!" said Schubert.

"What are we supposed to have done?" demanded Fred.

Schubert at once assumed what was intended to be a sly look, of uncommunicable knowledge.

"None of my business to tell what my officers

know," he answered. "As for that, time will no doubt disclose much. The point is—trouble can be forestalled."

"Aw—show your hand!" cut in Will, leaning in front of Fred. "I've seen you Heinies fishing for graft too often in the States not to recognize symptoms! Spill the bait can! There's no other way to tell if we'll bite! Tell us what you're driving at!"

"Ivory!" said Schubert savagely and simply, shutting his jaws after the word like a snap with a steel spring. It would have broken the teeth of an ordinary human.

"What ivory?"

We all did our best to look blank.

"You know! Tippoo Tib's ivory! It belongs to the German government! Emin Pasha, whom that adventurer Stanley rescued against his will, agreed to sell the secret to us, but we never agreed on a price and he died without telling. *Gott!* He would have told had I had the interviewing of him! It was known in Zanzibar that you and a certain English lord shared the secret. You have been watched. You are known to be in search of the stuff."

"The deuce you say!" Fred murmured, with a glance to left and right at us.

"If you were to go to the office to-morrow, and tell our commandant what you know," said Schubert, "you might be suitably compensated. You would certainly be given facilities for leaving the country in comfort at your leisure."

"Who told you to promise us that?" Fred demanded, turning on him.

The *feldwebel* did not answer, but sat with his legs straight out in front of him, his heels together, and the palms of his hands touching between his knees. The sergeants were all singing, smoking and drinking. The Jew was back at his old post, watching every one with gimlet eyes.

"Think it over!" said Schubert, getting up. "There is time until morning. There is time until you leave this building. After that—" He shrugged his square shoulders brutally.

There was no sense in going out at once, as we had intended, with that combination of threat and promise hanging over us.

"Why not do what we said—admit that we know what we don't know—and put 'em on the wrong scent?" Will whispered.

"I wish to God Monty were here!" groaned Fred.

"Rot!" Will answered. "Monty is all you ever said of him and then some; but we're able to handle this ourselves all right without him. Tell 'em a bull yarn, I say!"

Fred relapsed into a sort of black gloom intended to attract the Muse of Strategy. He was always better at swift action in the open and optimism in the face of visible danger, than at matching wits against something he could not see beginning or end of.

"Tell 'em it's in German East!" urged Will. "Offer to lead them to it on certain conditions. Think up controversial proposals! Play for timer!"

Fred shook his head.

"What if it turns out true? Monty's in Europe. Suppose he should learn while he's there that the stuff is really in German East—we'd have spoiled his game!"

"If the stuff should really be in German East," Will argued, "we've no chance in the world of getting even a broker's share of it, Monty or no Monty! Take my advice and tell 'em what they want to know!"

Meanwhile an argument of another kind had started across the room. Schubert had related with grim amusement to Sergeant Sachse, who was sitting next him, our disapproval of the flogging of the father of the commandant's abandoned woman.

"At what were they shocked?" wondered Sachse. "At the flogging, or the intercourse, or because he sent the female packing when she proposed to have a child? Do they not know that to have children about the premises would be subversive of military excellence?"

"They were shocked at all three things," grinned Schubert, "but chiefly, I think, at the flogging."

"Bah! Such a tickling of a native's hide doesn't hurt him to speak of! Wait until they see our court in the morning!"

It was that that raised the clamor. Even Schubert, who might be supposed to have won promotion because he could stay sober longer than the others, was beginning to grow noisy in his speech and to laugh without apparent reason. The rest were all already frankly drunk, and any excuse for dispute was a good one. They one and all, including Schubert, denied Sachse's contention that a flogging did not hurt enough to matter.

"I bet I could take one without winking!" Sachse announced.

Schubert's little bright pig-eyes gleamed through the smoke at that.

"Kurz und gut!" he laughed. "There is a case of champagne unopened. I bet you that case of champagne that you lie! That you can not take a flogging!"

There was an united yelp of delight. The sergeants rose and gathered round Sachse. Schubert cursed them and drove them to the chairs again.

"Open that case of champagne!" he roared, and the Jew obeyed, setting the bottles on the table in two rows.

"I bet you those twelve bottles you dare not take a regular flogging, and that you can not endure it if you dare try!"

"I can stand as much as you!" hedged Sachse.

"Good! We will see! We will both take a flogging—stroke for stroke! Whoever squeals first shall pay for the champagne!"

Sachse could not back out. His cheeks grew whiter, but be staggered to his feet, swearing.

"I will show you of what material a German sergeant is made!" he boasted. "It is not only Prussians who are men of metal! How shall it be arranged?"

The arrangement was easy enough. Schubert shouted for an *askari,* and the corporal who was doing police duty outside in the street came running. He had a *kiboko* in his hand almost a yard and a half long, and Schubert examined it with approval.

"How would you like to flog white men?" he demanded.

"I would not dare!" grinned the corporal.

"Not dare, eh? Would you not obey an order?"

"Always I obey!" the man answered, saluting.

"Good. I shall lie here. This other *bwana* shall lie there beside me. You shall stand between. First you shall strike one, then the other—turn and turn about until I give the order to cease! And listen! If you fail once—just one little time!—to flog with all your might, you shall have two hundred lashes yourself; and they shall be good ones, because I will lay them on! Is it understood?"

"Yes," said the corporal, the whites of his eyes betraying doubt, fear and wonder. But he grinned with his lips, lest the *feldwebel* should suspect him of unwillingness.

"Are the terms understood?" demanded Schubert, and the sergeants yelped in the affirmative.

"Then choose a referee!"

One of the sergeants volunteered for the post. Schubert lay down on the floor, and Sachse beside him about four feet away. The corporal took his stand between. He was an enormous Nubian, broad of chest, with the big sloping shoulder muscles that betray double the strength that tailors try to suggest with jackets padded to look square.

"Nun—recht feste schlagen!" ordered Schubert. Then he took the sleeve of his tunic between his teeth and hid his face.

"One!" said the referee. Down came the heavy black whip with a crack like a gun going off. Schubert neither winced nor murmured, but the blood welled into the seat of his pants and spread like red ink on blotting-paper.

"One!" said the referee again. The corporal faced about, and raised his weapon, standing on tiptoe to get more swing. Sachse flinched at the sound of the whip going up, and the other sergeants roared delight. But he was still when it descended, and the crack of the blow drew neither murmur nor movement from him either. Like the *feldwebel,* he had his sleeve between his teeth.

"Two!" said the referee, and the black whip rose again. It descended with a crack and a splash on the very spot whence the blood flowed, this time cutting the pants open, but Schubert took no more notice of it than if a fly had settled on him. There was a chorus of applause.

"Two!" said the referee. Again the corporal faced about and balanced himself on tiptoe. Sachse was much the more nervous of the two. He flinched again while waiting for the blow, but met it when it did come without a tremor of any kind. He was much the softer. Blood flowed from him more freely, but his pants seemed to be of sterner stuff, for they did not split until the eight-and-twentieth lash, or thereabouts.

From first to last, although the raw flesh lay open to the lash, and the corporal, urged to it by the united threats and praise of all the other sergeants, wrought his utmost, Schubert lay like a man asleep. He might have been dead, except for the even rise and fall of his breathing, that never checked or quickened once. Nine-and-forty strokes he took without a sign of yielding. At the eight-and-fortieth Sachse moaned a little, and the referee gave the match against him.

Schubert rose to his feet unaided, grinning, red in the face, but without any tortured look.

"Now you can say forever that you have flogged two white men!" he told the *askari.*

"Who will believe me?" the man answered.

Sachse had to be helped to his feet. He was pale and demanded brandy.

"What did I tell you?" laughed Schubert. "A Prussian is better than any man! Look at him, and then at me!"

He shouted for his servant, who had to be fetched from the boma—a smug-faced little rascal, obviously in love with the glory reflected on the sergeant-major's servant. He was made to produce a basin and cold water—he discovered them somewhere in the dim recesses of the store—and sponge his master's raw posterior before us all. Then he was sent for clean white pants and presently Schubert, only refusing to sit down, was quite himself again.

Sachse on the other hand refused the ministrations of the boy—was annoyed by the chaff of the other sergeants—refused to drink any of the sweet champagne he would now have to pay for—and went away in great dudgeon, murmuring about the madness that takes hold of men in Africa.

Meanwhile, while Schubert strutted and swaggered, making jokes more raw and beastly than his own flogged hide, the Jew came and poured more cool water on my hot bandages, touching them with deft fingers that looked like the hairy legs of a huge spider—his touch more gentle—more fugitive than any woman's.

"You should not tell zat dam *feldwebel* nozink!" he advised in nasal English. "Nefer mind vat you tell heem he is all ze same not your frien. He only obey hees officers. Zey say to cut your troat—he cut it! Zey say to tell you a lot o' lies—he tell! He iss not a t'inker, but a doer: and hees faforite spectacle iss ze blood of innocence! Do not effer say I did not fell you! On ze ozzer hand, tell no one zat I did tell! Zese are dangerous people!"

He resumed business with his account book, and I whispered to Fred and Will what advice he had given. Seeing us with our heads together, Schubert crossed the room, beginning to get very drunk now that the shock of the flogging had had time to reinforce the alcohol. (The blows had sobered him at first.)

"What have you decided?" he asked, standing before us with his legs apart and his hands behind him in his favorite attitude—swaying gently back and forward because of the drink, and showing all his teeth in a grin.

"Nothing," Fred answered. "We'll think it over."

"Too late in the morning!" he answered, continuing to sway. "I can do nothing for you in the morning."

"What can you do to-night?" Fred asked.

He shrugged his shoulders. "I can report. The report will go in at dawn."

"You may tell your superiors," Fred answered, rising, "that if they care to make us a reasonable offer, I don't say we won't do business!"

Schubert leered.

"To-morrow will be too late!" he repeated.

It was Fred's turn to shrug shoulders, and he did it inimitably, turning his back on Schubert and helping Will support me to the door. The *feldwebel* stood grinning while I held to the doorpost and they dragged Brown to his feet. He made no offer to help us in any way at all, nor did any of the sergeants.

There was no getting action from Brown. He was as dead to the world as a piece of wood, and there being no other obvious solution of the problem, Will hoisted him upon his back and carried him, he snoring, all the way home to camp. Fred hoisted and carried me, for the pain of my wound when I tried to walk was unbearable.

We reached camp abreast and were challenged by the sentries, who made a great show of standing guard. They took Brown and threw him on the bed in his own tent—accepted Fred's offer of silver money—and departed, marching up-street in their heavy, iron-bound military boots with the swing and swagger only the Nubian in all the world knows just how to get away with.

I lay on the bed in Fred's tent, and then Kazimoto came to us, hugely troubled about something, stirring the embers of the fire before the tent and arranging the lantern so that its rays would betray any eavesdropper. He searched all the shadows thoroughly, prodding into them with a stick, before he unburdened his mind.

"Those *askaris* were not put here to guard our tents," he told us. (The really good native servant when speaking of his master's property always says our, and never your.) "As soon as you were gone the Greeks and the Goa came. They and the *askaris* questioned me. It was a trick! You were drawn away on purpose! One by one—two by two—they questioned us all, but particularly me."

"What about?" Fred demanded.

"About our business. Why are we here. What will we do. What do we know. What do I know about you. What do you know about me. Why do I serve you. How did I come to take service with you. To what place will we travel next, and when. How much money have we with us. Have we friends or acquaintances in Muanza. Do you, *bwana,* carry any letters in your pockets. Of what do you speak when you suppose no man is listening. *Bwana,* my heart is very sad in me! Those Greeks tell lies, and the Germans stir trouble in a big pot like the witches! I know the Germans! I am Nyamwezi. I was born not far from here, and ran away as soon as I was old enough because the Germans shot my father and let my mother and brothers starve to death. I did not starve, because one of them took me for a servant; but I ran away from him. My heart is very sad to be in this place! They ask what of a hoard of ivory. I tell them I do not know, and they threaten to beat me! This place is bad! Let us go away to-night!"

There was no sleep that night for any of us. My wound hurt too much. The others were too worried. By the light of the lantern in Fred's tent we cooked up a story to tell that we hoped would induce the Germans to let us wander where we chose.

"Sure, they'll watch us!" Will admitted. "But as our only real reason for coming down here—leaving Brown's cattle out of the reckoning—was to throw people off the scent, in what way are we worse off? The lake is big enough to lose ourselves in! What is it—two hundred and fifty miles long by as many broad? D'you mean we can't give their sleuths the slip? We can't beat that for a plan: let 'em keep on thinking we know where Tippoo hid the stuff. If we succeed in losing 'em they'll think we're at large in German East and keep on hunting for us—whereas we'll really be up in British East. Let's send a telegram in code to Monty!"

Then Fred thought of an idea that in the end solved our biggest problem, although we did not think much of it at the time.

"They may refuse to take a telegram in code," he said. "It's likely they'll open letters. (We can try the code, of course. They'll probably take our money, and put their experts on deciphering the message. They'll say it was lost if there are any inquiries afterward.) I propose we send a straight-out cablegram advising Monty of our whereabouts (they'll let that go through) and warning him to ask for letters at the Bank in Mombasa before he does anything else."

"Yes, but—" Will objected.

"Wait!" said Fred. "I haven't finished. Then write two letters: one full of any old nonsense, to be sent in the regular way by mail. They'll open that. The other to go by runner. Kazimoto can find us a runner. He knows these Wanyamwezi. He can pick a man who'll get through without fail."

We could think of nothing to say against the plan. The argument that the German government would scarcely stoop to opening private mail did not seem to hold water when we examined it, so we wrote as Fred suggested—one letter telling Monty that we hoped to make some arrangement with the Germans, and at all events to wait in German East until he could join us—and the other telling him the real facts at great length, laboriously set out in the code we had agreed upon.

We sealed the second letter in several wrappers, and sewed it up finally in a piece of waterproof silk. Then we sent for Kazimoto and ordered him to find the sort of messenger we needed.

"Send me!" he urged. "I will start now, before it is light! I will hide by day and travel by night until I reach the British border! Give me only enough cooked food and my pay and I will take the letter without fail!"

We refused, for he was too useful to us. He begged again and again to be sent with the letter, promising faithfully to wait for us afterward on the British side of the border at any place we should name. But we upbraided him for cowardice, ordered him to find another messenger, and promised him he need have no fear of Germans as long as he remained our servant.

Before high noon we would each have given many years of Kazimoto's pay if only we could have recalled that decision and have known that he was speeding away from Muanza toward a border where white men knew the use of mercy.

Just as the first peep of dawn began to color the sky Schubert came swaggering down-street to us, wiping his mouth with the back of his hand.

"How have you slept?" he asked us, laughing.

We answered something or other.

"I did not trouble to sleep! I stayed and finished the drinks. I have just swallowed the last of the beer! Whoever wants a morning drink must wait for it now until the overland *safari* comes!"

We displayed no interest. Brown, the only one likely to yearn for alcohol before breakfast, snored in his still.

"What of it now? I go drill my troops. Parade is sharp! There remain twenty minutes. Come with me tell your secret at the boma now, before it is too late!"

"Explain why it would be too late after breakfast!" demanded Fred.

"All right," said Schubert. "I will tell you this much. There will come a launch this morning from Kisumu in British East. There will be people on that launch, one of whom has authority that overrides that of the commandant of this place. The commandant desires to know your information—and get the credit for it—before that individual, whose authority is higher, comes. Is that clear?"

"Perfectly," Fred answered.

"See if this is clear, too!" cut in Will. "You go and ask your commandant what price he offers for the secret! Nothing for nothing! Tell him we're not afraid of him!"

"It is none of my business to tell him anything," sneered Schubert, spitting and turning on his heel. He swaggered out of the camping-ground and up-street again, leaving the clear impression behind him that he washed his hands of us for good and all.

"Let's watch him drill his men," said I. "I'll wait on the hospital steps until they open the place."

So we ate a scratch breakfast and Fred and Will helped me up-street, past where the Jew stood blinking in the morning sun on the steps of the D.O.A.G. He seemed to be saying prayers, but beckoned to us.

"Trouble!" he said. "Trouble! If you have any frien's fetch them—send for them!"

"Can you send a letter for us to British East?" Fred asked him.

"God forbid!" He jumped at the very thought, and shrugged himself like a man standing under a water-spout. "What would they do to me if I were found out?"

"What is the nature of the trouble?" Fred asked him.

"Ah, who should tell! Trouble, I tell you, trouble! Zat cursed Schubert sat here drinking until dawn. I heard heem say many t'ings! Send for your friens!"

He turned his back on us and ran in. There was a lieutenant arrayed in spotless white with a saber in glittering scabbard watching us all from the boma gate. A little later that morning we knew better why the Jew fled indoors at sight of him.

Schubert was standing in mid-square with a hundred *askaris* lined up two-deep in front of him. There were no other Germans on parade. The corporals were Nubians, and the rest of the rank and file either Nubian or some sort of Sudanese. He was haranguing them in a bastard mixture of Swahili, Arabic, and German, they standing rigidly at attention, their rifles at the present.

Not content with the effect of his words, he strode up presently to a front-rank man and hit him in the face with clenched fist. In the effort to recover his balance the man let his rifle get out of alignment. Schubert wrenched it from him. It fell to the ground. He struck the man, and when he stooped to pick the rifle up kicked him in the face. Then he strode down the line and beat two other men for grinning. All this the lieutenant watched without a sign of disapproval, or even much interest.

Meanwhile the chain-gang emerged from the boma gate, going full-pelt, fastened neck to neck, the chain taut and each man carrying a water-jar. The minute they had crossed the square Schubert commenced with company drill, and for two hours after that, with but one interval of less than five minutes for rest, he kept them pounding the gravel in evolution after evolution—manual exercise at the double—skirmishing exercise—setting up drill—goose-step, and all the mechanical, merciless precision drill with which the Germans make machines of men.

His debauch did not seem in the least to have affected him, unless to make his temper more violently critical. By seven o'clock the sun was beating down on him and dazzling his eyes from over the boma wall. The dust rose off the square. The words of command came bellowing in swift succession from a throat that ought to have been hard put to it to whisper. If anything, he grew more active and exacting as the *askaris* wearied, and by the time the two hours were up they were ready to a man to drop.

But not so he. He dismissed them, and swaggered over to the marketplace to hector and bully the natives who were piling their wares in the shade of the great grass roof. Then he went into the boma to breakfast just as a sergeant in khaki came over and unlocked the hospital door. I followed the sergeant in, but he ordered me out again.

"I have come to see the doctor," I said. "I need attention."

He was not one of the sergeants who had been drunk in the D.O.A.G. the night before, but a man of a higher mental type, although no less surly.

"It will be for the doctor to say what you need when he has seen you!" he answered, turning his back and busying himself about the room. Will translated, and I limped out again.

By and by the doctor came, and passed me sitting on the steps amid a throng of natives who seemed to have all the imaginable kinds of sores. He took no notice of me, but sent out the sergeant to inquire why I had not stood up as he passed. I did not answer, and the sergeant went in again.

Fred by that time was simply blasphemous, alternately threatening to go in and kick the doctor, and condemning Will's determination to do the same thing. Finally we decided to see the matter through patiently, and all sat together on the steps watching the activity of the square. There was a lot going on—bartering of skins and hides—counting of crocodile eggs, brought in by natives for sake of the bounty of a few copper coins the hundred—a cock-fight in one corner—the carrying to and fro of bunches of bananas, meat, and grain in baskets; and in and out among it all full pelt in the hot sun marched the chain-gang, doing the township dirty work.

By and by Schubert emerged from the boma gate followed by natives carrying a table and a soap-box. He set these under a limb of the great baobab that faced the boma gate not far from the middle of the square. I noticed then for the first time that a short hempen rope hung suspended from the largest branch, with a noose in the end. The noose was not more than two feet below the branch.

Schubert's consideration of the table's exact position, and the placing of the soap-box on the table, was interrupted by the arrival of Coutlass, his Greek companion and the Goanese arm in arm, followed closely by two *askaris* who shouted angrily and made a great show of trying to prevent them. One of the *askaris* aimed his rifle absurdly at Coutlass, both Greeks and the Goanese daring him gleefully to pull the trigger.

They purposely came close to us, not that we showed signs of meaning to befriend them. They were simply unable to understand that there are degrees of disgrace. To Coutlass all victims of government outrage ought surely to be more than friendly with any one in conflict with the law. Personal quarrels should go for nothing in face of the common wrong.

"There is going to be a hanging!" Coutlass shouted to us. "They thought we would remain quietly in camp with that going on! Give us chairs!" he called to Schubert. "Provide us a place in the front row where we may see!"

Schubert grinned. He returned to the boma yard and presumably conferred with an officer, for presently he came out again and gave the Greeks leave to stand under the tree, provided they would return to camp afterward. Later yet, Brown came along and joined us on the steps, looking red-eyed and ridiculous.

"Goin' to be a hangin," he announced. "I been askin' natives about it. Black man stole the condemned man's daughter an' refused to pay cows for her accordin' to custom or anythin'—said he could do what the white men did an' help himself. Father of the girl took a spear and settled the thief's hash with it—ran him through—did a clean job. Serve him right—eh—what? Germans went an' nabbed him, though—tried him in open court—goin' to hang him this mornin' for murder! How does it strike you?"

We were not exactly in mood to talk to Brown—in fact, we wished him anywhere but with us, but he thought self perfectly welcome, and rambled on:

"Up in British East we don't hang black men for murder unless it's what they call an aggravated case—murder an' robbery—murder an' arson—murder an' rape. Hang a white man for murderin' a black sure as you're sitting here, an' shoot a black man for murderin' a white; but the blacks don't understand, so when they kill one another in such a case this, why we give 'em a short jail sentence an' a good lo lecture, an' let 'em go again. These folks have it t'other way round. They never hang a German, whether he's guilty or not, but hang a poor black man, what doesn't understand, for half o' nothin'!"

A great crowd began gathering about the tree, and was presently driven by *askaris* with whips into a mass on the far side of the tree from us. Whether purposely or not, they left a clear view from the hospital steps of all that should happen. Evidently warning had been sent out broadcast, for the inhabitants of village after village came trooping into town to watch, each lot led by its sultani in filthy rags and the foolish imitation crown his conquerors had supplied him at several times its proper price. The square was a dense sea of people before nine o'clock, and the *askaris* made the front few hundreds lie, and the next rows squat, in order that the men and women behind might see.

Then at last out came the victim with his hands tied behind him and a bright red blanket on his loins. He was a proud-looking fellow. He halted a moment between his guard of German sergeants and eyed the crowd, and us, and the tree, and the noose. Then he looked down on the ground and appeared to take no further interest.

The sergeants took him by the arms and led him along to the table between them. Out came the commandant then, in snow-white uniform, with his saber polished until it shone—all spruced up for the occasion, and followed by a guard of honor consisting of lieutenant, two sergeants, and six black *askaris.*

There was a chair by the table. At sight of the commandant the sergeants made their victim use that as a step by which to mount the table and soap-box, and there he stood eying his oppressors as calmly as if he were witnessing a play. A murmur arose among the crowd. A number of natives called to him by name, but he took no notice after that one first steady gaze.

"They're sayin' good-bye to him," said Brown, breathing in my ear. "They're telling him they won't forget him!"

The crack of *askaris'* whips falling on head and naked shoulders swiftly reduced the crowd to silence. Then the commandant faced them all, and made a speech with that ash-can voice of his—first in German, then in the Nyamwezi tongue. Will translated to us sentence by sentence, the doctor standing on the top step behind us smiling approval. He seemed to think we would be benefited by the lecture just as much as the natives.

It was awful humbug that the commandant reeled off to his silent audience—hypocrisy garbed in paternal phrases, and interlarded with bunkum about Germany's mission to bring happiness to subject peoples.

"Above all," he repeated again and again, "the law must be enforced impartially—the good, sound, German law that knows no fear or favor, but governs all alike!"

When he had finished he turned to the culprit.

"Now," he demanded, "do you know why you are to be hanged?"

There was a moment's utter silence. The crowd drew in its breath, seeming to know in advance that some brave answer was forthcoming. The man on the table with his hands behind him surveyed the crowd again with the gaze of simple dignity, looked down on the commandant, and raised his voice. It was an unexpected, high, almost falsetto note, that in the silence carried all across the square.

"I am to die," he said, "because I did right! My enemy did what German officers do. He stole my young girl. I killed him, as I hope all you Germans may be killed! But hope no longer gathers fruit in this land!"

"Ah-h-h-h!" the crowd sighed in unison.

"Good man!" exploded Fred, and the doctor tried to kick him from behind—not hard, but enough to call his attention to the proprieties. His toe struck me instead, and when I looked up angrily he tried to pretend he was not aware of what he had done.

Under the trees the commandant flew into a rage such I have seldom seen. Each land has a temper of its own, an the white man's anger varies in inverse ratio with his nearness to the equator. But *furor teutonicus* transplanted is the least controllable, least dignified, least admirable that there is. And that man's passion was the apex of its kind.

His beard spread, as a peacock spreads its tail. His eyes blazed. His eyebrows disappeared under the brim of his white helmet, and his clenched fists burst the white cotton gloves. He half-drew his saber—thought better of that, and returned it. There was an *askari* standing near with *kiboko* in hand to drive back the crowd should any press too closely. He snatched the whip and struck the condemned man with it, as high up as he could reach, making a great welt across his bare stomach. The man neither winced nor complained.

"For those words," the commandant screamed at him in German, "you shall not die in comfort! For that insolence, mere hanging is too good!"

Then he calmed himself a little, and repeated the words in the native tongue, explaining to the crowd that German dignity should be upheld at all costs.

"Fetch him down from there," he ordered.

Schubert sprang on the table and knocked the condemned man off it with a blow of his fist. With hands bound behind him the poor fellow had no power of balance, and though he jumped clear he fell face-downward, skinning his cheek on the gravel. The commandant promptly put a foot on his neck and pinned him down.

"Flog him!" he ordered. "Two hundred lashes!"

It was done in silence, except for the corporal's labored breathing and the commandant's incessant sharp commands to beat harder—harder—harder. A sergeant stood by counting. The crack of the whip divided up the silence into periods of agony.

When the count was done the victim was still conscious. Schubert and a sergeant dragged him to his feet, and hauled him to the table. Four other men—two sergeants and two natives—passed a rope round the table legs. Schubert lifted the victim by the elbows so that his head could pass through the noose, and when that was accomplished the man had to stand on tiptoe on the soap-box in order to breathe at all.

"All ready!" announced Schubert, and jumped off with a laugh, his white tunic bloody from contact with the victim's tortured back.

"Los!" roared the commandant

The men hauled on the rope. Table and soap-box came tumbling away, and the victim spun in the air on nothing, spinning round, and round, and round—slower and slower and slower—then back the other way round faster and faster. They say hanging is a merciful death—that the pressure of rope on two arteries produces anesthesia, but few are reported to have come back to tell of the experience. At any rate, as is not the case with shooting, it is easy to know when the victim is really dead.

For seconds that seemed minutes—for minutes that seemed hours the poor wretch spun, his elbows out, his knees up, his tongue out, his face wrinkled into tortured shapes, and his toes pointed upward so sharply that they almost touched his shins. Then suddenly the toes turned downward and the knees relapsed. The corpse hung limp, and the Crowd sighed miserably, to the last man, woman and child, turning its back on what to them must have symbolized German rule.

They left the corpse hanging there. It was to be there until evening, some one said, for an example to frequenters of the market-place. The crowd trailed away, none glancing back. The pattering of feet ceased. The market-place across the square resumed its hum and activity. Then a native orderly came down the steps and touched me on the elbow. I struggled to my feet and limped after him up the steps.

Practically at the mercy of the doctor, I made up my mind to be civil to him whether that suited me or not. I rather expected he would come to meet me, perhaps help me to chair, and I wondered how, in my ignorance of German, I should contrive to answer his questions.

But I need not have worried. I did not even see him. He had left by the back door, and the orderly washed the wound and changed my bandages. That was all. There was no charge for the bandages, and the orderly was gentle now that his master's back was turned.

"Didn't he leave word when he would see me?" I asked.

"Habanah!" he answered—meaning, "He did not—there is not—there is nothing doing!"

IPSOS CUSTODES

We were an ignorant people. Out of a gloom we came
Hungering, striving, feasting—vanishing into the same.
Came to us your foreloopers, told us the gloom was bad,
Spoke of the Light that might be—simply it could be had—
Knowledge and wealth and freedom, plenty and peace and play,
And at all the price of obedience. "Listen and learn and obey,"
We were told, "and the gloom shall be lifted. Ignorance surely is shame."
We listened to your foreloopers till presently Cadis came.

We were an ignorant people. Our law was "an eye for an eye,"
And he who wronged should right the wrong, and he who stole should die—
Bad law the Cadis told us, based on the fall of man;
And they set us to building law-courts on the pan-Germanic plan—
Courts where the gloom of ages should be pierced, said they, with Light
And scientific theory displace wrong views of Right.
The Cadis' law was writ in books that only they could read,

But what should we know of the strings to that?
'Twas gloom when we agreed.

We were an ignorant people. The Offiziere came
To lend to law eye, tooth, and claw and so enforce the same.
Now naught are the tribal customs; free speech is under ban;
Displaced are misconceptions that were based on fallen man,
And our gloom has gone in darkness of the risen German's night,
Nor is there salt of mercy lest it sap the hold of Might.
They strike—we may not answer, nor dare we ask them why.
We sold ourselves to supermen. If we rebel, we die.

VIII

I **SAT** down once more on the hospital steps, and listened while Fred and Will relieved themselves of their opinions about German manners. Nothing seemed likely to relieve me. I had marched a hundred miles, endured the sickening pain, and waited an extra night at the end of it all simply on the strength of anticipation. Now that the surgeon would not see me, hope seemed gone. I could think of nothing but to go and hide somewhere, like a wounded animal.

But there were two more swift shocks in store, and no hiding-place. The path to the water-front led past us directly along the southern boma wall. Before Fred and Will had come to an end of swearing they saw something that struck them silent so suddenly that I looked up and saw, too. Not that I cared very much. To me it seemed merely one last super-added piece of evidence that life was not worth while.

Plainly the launch had come from British East, of which Schubert had spoken. Hand in hand from the water-front, followed by the obsequious Schubert, all smiles and long black whip (for the chain-gang trailed after with the luggage, and needed to be overawed), walked Professor Schillingschen and Lady Isobel Saffren Waldon. They seemed in love—or at any rate the professor did, for he ogled and smirked like a bearded gargoyle; and she made such play of being charmed by his grimaces that the Syrian maid fell behind to hide her face.

None of us spoke. We watched them. Personally I did not mind the feeling that the worst had happened at last. I was incapable of sounding further depths of gloom—too full of pain bodily to suffer mentally from threats of what might yet be. But the other two looked miserable—more so because Fred's bearded chin perked up so bravely, and Will set his jaw like a rock.

Not one of us had said a word when the biggest *askari* we had seen yet strode up to us—saluted—and gave Fred a sealed envelope. It was written in English, addressed to us three by name (although our names were wrongly spelled). We were required to present ourselves at the court-house at once, reason not given. The letter was signed "Liebenkrantz—Lieutenant."

The *askari* waited for us. I suppose it would not be correct to say we were under arrest, but the enormous black man made it sufficiently obvious that he did not intend returning to the court without us. The court-house was not more than two hundred yards away. As we turned toward it we saw Lady Saffren Waldon being helped into the commandant's litter, borne by four men, the commandant himself superintending the ceremony with a vast deal of bowing and chatter, and Professor Schillingschen looking on with an air of owning litter, porters, township, boma, and all. As we turned our backs on them they started off toward the neat white dwelling on the hill.

The court was a round, grass-roofed affair, with white-washed walls of sun-dried brick. For about four-fifths of the circumference the wall was barely breast-high, the roof being supported on wooden pillars bricked into the wall, as well as by the huge pole that propped it up umbrella-wise in the center.

The remaining fifth of the wall continued up as high as the roof, forming a back to the platform. Facing the platform was the entrance, and on either side benches arranged in rows followed the curve of the wall. There was a long table on the platform, at which sat the lieutenant who had summoned us, with a sergeant seated on either hand. The sergeants were acting as court clerks, scribbling busily on sheets of blue paper, and in books.

Behind the lieutenant, in a great gilt frame on the white-washed wall, was a full-length portrait of the Kaiser in general's uniform. The Kaiser was depicted scowling, his gloved hands resting on a saber almost as ferocious-looking as the one the lieutenant kept winding his leg around.

All the benches were crowded with spectators, prisoners, witnesses, and litigants. Outside, at least two hundred Arabs, Indians, and natives leaned with elbows on the wall and gazed at the scene within. The lieutenant glared, but otherwise took no notice of our entry; he gave no order, but one of the two sergeants came down from the platform and kicked half a dozen natives off the front bench to make room for us.

We were mistaken in supposing our case would be called first, or even among the first. The floor in the midst of the court was clear except for a long single line of natives and six *askari* corporals, each with a whip in his hand. It was evident at once that these natives were all ahead of us, even if those on the benches were not to be heard and dealt with before our turn came.

"Look at the far end of the line!" whispered Fred.

Lo and behold Kazimoto, looking rather drawn and gray, but standing bravely, looking neither to the right nor left. I judged he knew we were in court—he could hardly have failed to notice our coming in—but he sturdily refused to turn his head and see us.

"What has he done?" I wondered.

"Nothing more than told some Heinie to go to hell—you can bet your boots!" said Will.

The lieutenant was in no hurry to enlighten us. Our boy stood at the wrong end of the line to be taken first. The lieutenant called a name, and two great *askaris* pounced on the trembling native at the other end and dragged him forward, leaving him standing alone before the desk.

"Silence!" the lieutenant shouted, and the court became still as death.

He had a voice as mean as a hyena's—a voice that matched his face. The insolent, upturned twist of his fair mustache showed both corners of a thin-lipped mouth. He had the Prussian head, shaped square whichever way you viewed it. There was strength in the jaw-bones—strength in the deep-set bright eyes—strength in the shoulders that were square as box-corners without any padding—strength in the lean lithe figure; but it was always brute strength. There was no moral strength whatever in the restless fidgeting—the savage winding and unwinding of his left foot around the saber scabbard, or the attitude, leaning forward over the table, of petulant pugnacity. And the cruel voice was as weak as the hand was strong with which he rapped on the table.

He questioned the boy in front of him sharply—told him he stood charged with theft—and demanded an answer.

"With theft of what thing, and whose thing?"

The answer was bold. The trembling had ceased. Now that he faced nemesis the strength of native fatalism came to his rescue, bolstering up the pride that every uncontaminated Nyamwezi owns. He was not more than seventeen years old, but he stood there at last like a veteran at bay.

"Put him down and beat him!" ordered the lieutenant. "Impudent answers to this court shall always be soundly punished! Call the next case while that one is being taught good manners.

A woman was stood in front of the line, fidgety with fear, in doubt whether to lay her suckling baby on the bench before she faced military justice. She laid it on the floor at her feet, hesitated, and then picked it up again and wrapped it in a corner of the red blanket that constituted her only dress.

"Take that brat away from her!" the lieutenant ordered. "She must pay attention to me. With that in her arms she will only think of mothering!"

An *askari* seized the baby by the arm and leg and gave it with a laugh to another woman to hold, its mother whimpering with fright until she saw it safely nestled.

"Quick, now! What about this one?"

It seemed there was no charge against her. The two sergeants searched through the piles of blue sheets in vain.

"Then what the devil is she here for? What do you want, you?"

The trembling woman pointed to her baby, but was dumb. It needed courage to answer that lieutenant, and the crack—crack—crack of a thick *kiboko* descending at measured intervals on the naked back of the boy who had answered boldly was no help toward reassurance.

"Speak!" the lieutenant ordered, "or I shall have you compelled to speak!"

She burst into sudden volubility. The dam once down, she poured forth a catalogue of wrongs that seemed endless, switching off from one dialect to another and at intervals inserting, apropos apparently of nothing, the few words of German she had picked up. The lieutenant yelled for an interpreter, and a Nyamwezi who knew German rose from the front bench and came and stood beside her.

"That baby is a white man's," he explained.

"What does she want?"

"She says the white man is the *bwana daktari* (the doctor!)."

"Oh! Then I am glad she came here. It is time these loose women were taught a lesson! They tell the same tale. They say a white man passed through the village, gave their father a present, and carried them off. Is that her tale, too?"

"Yes."

"Well—what of it? The father agreed at the time when he accepted the present, didn't he? The consequence is a baby—not for the first time! Instead of going back to her village, she comes here and tries to blackmail the officer! She is young. It's the first time she has been in this court. This time I will be lenient. One hundred lashes!"

The interpreter translated, and the woman screamed. An *askari* seized her by the shoulders. She clung to him, but he threw her to the ground, and another one tore off the blanket that would have deadened the blows to some extent. She begged, and clung to their feet, but the blows began to rain on her, and presently she lay still, her breasts flattened against the earth floor, her mouth full of dust, and her naked body paralyzed by fear of the descending lash.

"Now bring up number one again!" the lieutenant ordered.

The *askaris* ceased from flogging him. One of them kicked him to his feet, and he resumed his stand in front of the lieutenant, looking up at him as proudly as ever, for all that his back was bruised and bloody.

"Did you steal or did you not?" asked the lieutenant.

"Steal what from whom?"

"Oh, go on beating him! Next case!"

The next man escaped the whip, but his witnesses were less fortunate. He brought two men and a woman with him to prove an alibi on a charge of attempted theft, and the glibness of their answers convinced the lieutenant they were lying. In the absence of all evidence for the prosecution except the unsupported word of a police *askari* who admitted a personal grudge against the defendant, the lieutenant resorted to the whip to change the witnesses' convictions, but without avail.

The woman yelled under the lash like a demented thing, but, far from withdrawing her statements, tried to spit in the lieutenant's face when jerked to her feet and stood again before him—an impossible feat because the platform on which he sat at the table was too high. He had her beaten a second time for spitting.

The next man was a fat Baganda from British territory, charged with trading without a license. He pleaded ignorance of the law, and denied having traded. He was flogged for telling lies in court, and changed his testimony under the lash, whereat he was promptly sentenced to a hundred and fifty lashes and a month on the chain-gang. Under the lash a second time, he recanted—swore that his first statements had been true and that he had done no trading—a mistake in tactics that only caused the tale of lashes to be increased by fifty and the term on the chain-gang to be doubled.

"You must learn that the methods taught you on British territory are of no use here!" remarked the lieutenant.

By the time Kazimoto was called and stood out alone in front of him the lieutenant was in a boiling rage, and the floor of the court was actually crowded by prone natives being beaten. Extra *askaris* had been sent for in order that proceedings might not be delayed, and the audience could scarcely hear the evidence and sentences because of the crack of whips and the moans of victims. (Not that they all moaned by any means. By far the most of them submitted to the torture in grim proud silence: but the few who did make a noise—especially the women—made lots of it.)

As Kazimoto faced the lieutenant he turned once and looked at us. His eyes sought Fred's.

"Oh, *bwana!*" he said—and now for the first time we learned why he had chosen Fred to be his particular master. "I have been faithful! Stroke, then, that beard of yours as *Bwana* Courtney, my former master, used to stroke his. Then we shall both know what to do!"

Fred stroked his beard promptly, for the man needed comfort, not ridicule: but the concession to his superstition did none of us any good.

"Face this way!" the lieutenant shouted at him. "You are charged with being a deserter from German service. Also with giving information to foreigners. Also with serving foreigners in their effort to exploit the country, and with refusing to give proper answers when questioned by those in authority. Do you understand?"

"No," said Kazimoto in the most melancholy tone I ever heard from him.

"Are you a Nyamwezi? Now don't dare to lie to me!"

"Yes."

"You were born in this country?"

"Yes."

"Then you belong in this country!"

"I belong where my master takes me. My spirit is good. I am a true man," Kazimoto answered.

"Your spirit is rotten! You are a traitor! What do you mean by talking to me of your master, you reptile! Your master is the German government, of which His Majesty the Kaiser is supreme overlord! There is a picture of your master!" He pointed with a thumb over his shoulder to the full-length atrocity in oils behind him. "Salute it!"

The boy obeyed.

"Answer now! Who is your master?"

Kazimoto hesitated.

"Answer, I order you!"

He turned and pointed a finger at Fred, who nodded.

"That English *bwana* is my master," he said stoutly. It was a forlorn hope, though. He did not seem to believe that the statement of fact would do him any good.

Fred jumped to his feet.

"That is perfectly correct," he said in English. "The boy is my servant, engaged on British territory, under a contract for wages to be paid in English money. He is to be paid off in British East at the end of my journey."

"Who asked you to speak?" demanded the lieutenant angrily, sitting up like a startled scorpion. "Do you not know this is a court?"

"It looks like a shambles!" Fred answered, glancing to right and left and indicating the victims of the whip writhing in the name of German justice.

"Shut up, you fool!" counseled Will in a stage whisper, but either Fred did not hear him, or was too worked up to care.

"Silence! Sit down!"

"I warn you!" Fred answered. "That boy has claimed British protection. I shall see he has it!"

Then he sat down. The lieutenant glared at Kazimoto, the glare changing to a cold grin as he realized how fully we were all at his mercy for the moment.

"You are sentenced," he said, "to two hundred lashes for making impudent answers to the court, and to six months on the chain-gang for deserting from this country and entering foreign service. Further evidence against you will be assembled in the meanwhile, and other charges against you will be tried on completion of the chain-gang sentence!"

"I protest!" shouted Fred, jumping up again. "I give notice of appeal to whatever higher court there is. I am ready to give bonds!"

"What does this delay mean?" snapped the lieutenant. "Put him down at once and lay the lashes on!"

The unfortunate Kazimoto was pounced on by two *askaris* and thrown face-downward on the floor. One of them tore off his clothes, ripping up his good English jacket.

"Did you hear my protest?" shouted Fred. "Did you hear my notice of appeal?"

"I did," said the lieutenant. "Appeals are heard at the coast. You must give notice by mail, and receive an acknowledgment from the higher military court before I grant stay of execution. Lay on the lashes!"

"I will hold you personally liable for this outrage," Fred told him, "if it costs me all my money and all the rest of my years! I defy you to continue!"

"You have yourself to blame!" the lieutenant grinned. "But for your uninvited interruption the Nyamwezi would have had a better hearing! Lay those lashes on harder and more slowly!"

Kazimoto was taking his gruel like a man. Two *askaris* were beating him. The blows fell at random anywhere below the neck and above the heels, raising a great welt where they did not actually cut the skin. He had buried his face in his forearms, and Will had gone to stand near him, stooping down to encourage him with any words at all that might seem to serve.

"Stick it out, Kazi! We'll stand by! We won't leave you down here! Remember you've got friends who won't desert you!"

Probably in his agony Kazimoto did not understand a word of it, but the lieutenant did,—and swiftly took steps to interfere.

"Call the Europeans' cases next!" he shouted, and promptly the German sergeants stepped down from the platform to marshal us in line. The lieutenant went through the form of studying the blue papers, and called out our names. That of Brown was included, but Brown was not in court and we were kept standing there until he had been fetched from his tent. He had retired immediately after the hanging to sleep off the effects of his debauch, and being now deprived of that luxury arrived between two *askaris* in a volcanic temper. He insulted the lieutenant to begin with.

"A diet o' beer an' sausage don't seem to have filled you full o' good manners, do it?"

The lieutenant scowled, but for the moment chose to ignore the pleasantry.

"You people are charged," he said, "with entering German territory otherwise than by a regular road and without reporting at a customs station. Further, with intending to defraud the customs—with carrying and possessing arms without a license—with being in possession of ammunition without a permit—with shooting game without a license—with filibustering—with intentional homicide, in that you shot and killed certain men of the Masai tribe within German territory—with wandering at large without permits and with felonious intent; and last, and this is the most serious charge, with being spies within the military meaning of that term. Do you plead guilty or not guilty?"

We were dumb. Even the crack of the heavy whips on poor Kazimoto's skin ceased to make impression on us. Suffering already from my wound to the point of nausea, I actually reeled before this new deluge of trouble, and had to hold on to Fred and Will. They each put an arm under mine. It was Brown who spoke and stole from our sails what little wind there might have been.

"Decline to plead!" he shouted boisterously. "You're no judge, you're a pirate! You're not fit to try natives, let alone white men! You're a disgrace, that's what you are! All you're fit for is to make a decent fellow glad he needn't know you!"

"Silence!" roared the lieutenant, banging on the table with his open palm—then with his fist—then with a mallet.

"Silence yourself!" retorted Brown as soon as the hammering ceased. "You ought to be ashamed o' yourself! Your court's a bally disgrace, an' you're the worst thing in it! You and your Kaiser can go to hell, and be damned to both of you!"

"One month in jail for contempt of court and *Majestätsbeleidigung!*" snapped the lieutenant. "Take him away!"

Quite clearly that was not the first time that a white man had been imprisoned in Muanza. There was no hesitation about the way in which an *askari* seized Brown's wrists or a sergeant snapped the handcuffs. He was hustled out expostulating, kicked on the shins by the sergeant when he faced about to argue, and shoved into a run by both sergeant and *askari*.

"You others would better be careful what you say!" said the lieutenant.

"I've a mind to share Brown's cell!" said Will, but the lieutenant affected not to hear that.

"Since you refuse to plead in this court, you shall be held until the arrival of Major Schunck from the coast. Your arms and ammunition are to be handed over to the *askaris,* who will be sent to the rest-camp to receive them. The *askaris* will search your belongings thoroughly to make sure they have all your weapons. You are ordered confined within the limits of this township, and if you are detected making any attempt to trespass outside township limits you will be confined as the Greeks are within the rest-camp under observation. The porters you brought into the country are all to be paid their full wages by you until Major Schunck shall have dealt with you; the porters are refused permission to leave Muanza, being needed as witnesses. Next case!"

He scrawled his signature at the foot of each sheet of blue paper, and made a motion with his arm that we should leave court. But we sat down and waited until the two Nubian giants had finished flogging Kazimoto, and when they dragged him to his feet Will and Fred walked over to give him a few words of comfort. That act of ordinary kindness threw the lieutenant into another fury.

"Bring the Nyamwezi here!" he ordered, and the *askaris* hustled him up in front of the table.

"What do you do? Have you no manners? Return proper thanks for the lesson you have received!"

Kazimoto stood silent.

"For God's sake—" Will began.

"Say 'Thank you' to him, Kazimoto!" Fred whispered.

There is no native word for "Thank you"—only a bastard thing introduced by tyrants from Europe who never understood the African contention that the giver rewards himself if his gift is worth anything at all.

"Asente," said Kazimoto meekly.

"Why don't you salute? Don't you know where you are?"

"For the love of God salute him!" Will almost shouted.

Kazimoto obeyed.

"Take him and put him on the chain-gang!" ordered the lieutenant. "You Europeans leave the court!"

"I'm no European!" Will shouted back. "Thank the Lord I was born in a country you'll never set foot in!"

"Take them away before I have to make an example of them!" the lieutenant ordered.

Obediently the *askaris* gathered about us and hustled us out into the open, poking at my bandaged wound to get swifter action, and going as far as to threaten us with their hippo-hide whips. I trod on the naked toe of one of them with sufficient suddenness and weight to deprive him of the use of it for all time, and luckily for me he did not see who did it. The *askari* next to him had boots on, and got the blame.

The black men who were to search our belongings tried to induce us to hurry, but we insisted on seeing the iron ring riveted to Kazimoto's neck. The ring had a shackle on it, and through that they passed the long chain that held him prisoner in the midst of a gang of forty men. Nobody washed the wounds on his back. We bought water from a woman who was passing with a great jar on her head, and did that much for him. He was naked. His clothes that the *askaris* had torn from him had been thrown outside the court, and some one had stolen them. Later they gave him a piece of cheap calico to bind round his waist, but during all that hot afternoon he had nothing to keep the sun from his tortured back; nor would they permit us to give him anything.

The mortification of having one's private belongings gone through by black men in uniform was made more exasperating still by the fact that Coutlass and the other Greek and the Goanese were spectators, amusing themselves with comments that came nearer to causing murder than they guessed.

The real motive of the search was evident within two minutes from the commencement. The *askaris* could not read, but they showed a most remarkable affinity for paper that had been written on. They took the guns and ammunition first, but after that they emptied everything from our bags and boxes on to the sand, and confiscated every scrap of paper, shaking our books to make sure nothing was left between the leaves.

They even took away our writing material in their zeal to find information likely to prove useful to their masters. But they forgot to search our pockets, so that they overlooked the letter we had written in code to Monty and had not yet sent away by messenger.

That letter became our most besetting problem. How to find a runner who would take it to British East and mail it for us up there without betraying us first to the Germans was something we could not guess. Even Fred grew gloomy when we realized there was probably not a native on the whole countryside with sufficient manhood left in him to dare make the attempt. The first overture we might make would almost certainly be reported to the commandant at once.

"What fools we were not to send Kazimoto with it when he begged us to!"

"What worse than fools!"

"What brutes! Think what we might have saved him!"

We were unanimous as to that, but unanimity brought no comfort, until we all together hit on a notion that did ease our feelings a trifle. Coutlass and his two friends were sitting on camp-stools in the open where they could have a full view of our doings. Assuming the camping-ground to be equally divided between their party and ours, they were well within our portion. We decided their curiosity was insolent, declared inexorable war, and there and then felt better.

Fred went out with a tent-peg and scored in the sand a deep line to denote our boundary, the Greeks watching, all eyes and guesswork.

"Over the other side with you!" Fred ordered when he had finished.

They refused. He charged at them, and they ran.

"Whichever of you, man or servant, sets foot on our side of that line shall be a dead-sure hospital case!" Fred announced. "We'll reciprocate by leaving your side of the camp to you!"

"Who made you men rulers of this rest-camp?" Coutlass demanded.

"We did," Fred answered. "We've lost our rifles just as you have. We'll fight you with bare hands and skin you alive if you trespass!"

"Gassharamminy!" shouted Coutlass. "By hell and Waterloo, you mistake me for a weakling! Wait and see!"

We had to wait a very long and weary time, but we did see. In the days that followed, when my wound festered and I grew too ill to drag myself about, Fred and Will were able to leave me alone in the camp without any fear of a visit from the Greeks. It was not that there was much left worth stealing, but a mere visit from them might have had consequences we could never have offset. Alone, unable to rise, I could not have forced them to leave, and their lingering would surely have been interpreted by the guard, who always watched them from the corner of the road, as evidence of collusion of some sort between them and us.

Just at that time Coutlass, as it happened, would have liked nothing better in the world than the chance to persuade the Germans that he was in our councils. Fred's mere irritable determination to divide the camp in halves saved us in all human probability from a trap out of which there would have been no escape.

"SPEAK YE, AND SO DO"

Oh Thou, who gavest English speech
To both our Anglo-Saxon breeds,
And didst adown all ages teach
That Art of crowning words with deeds,
May we, who use the speech, be blest
With bravery, that when shall come
In thy full time our hour of test—
That promised hour of Christendom,
We may be found, whate'er our need,
How grim soe'er our circumstance,
Unwilling to be fed or freed,
Or fame or fortune to enhance
By flinching from the good begun,
By broken word or serpent plan,
Or cruelty in malice done
To helpless beast or subject man.

Amen.

IX

THERE WAS method, of course, behind the difference in treatment extended to us and to the Greeks. The motive for making Coutlass sell his mules and stay within the miserable confines of the rest-camp was to make sure be had money enough to feed himself, and to cut off all opportunity for swift escape. Not for a second were the Germans sufficiently unwary to admit collusion with him.

The real ownership of the three mules was left in little doubt when they were sold at public auction and bought in by Schillingschen. Fred and Will attended the auction the day following our scene in court, and extracted a lot of amusement from bidding against Schillingschen, compelling him finally to pay a good sum more than the mules were worth.

Coutlass was in a strange predicament. The looting of Brown's cattle had been a bid for fortune on his own account. Yet by causing us to give chase he had brought us into the German net more handily than ever they had hoped. So it was reasonable on his part to suppose that if he could betray us more completely still, he might get rewarded instead of treated as a broken tool.

Yet he did not dare to approach our camp, for fear lest Fred should carry out his threat and fight. The fight would certainly be reported by the *askari* on watch at the crossroads, and that would destroy his chance of making believe to be in our confidence. So he kept sending notes to me when the others were absent, even the native boy who brought them—not daring to enter our camp, but fastening the message to a stone and throwing it in through the tent door.

They were strange, illiterate messages, childishly conceived, varying between straight-out offers to help us escape and dark insinuations that he knew of something it would pay us well to investigate.

It was an English missionary spending three days in Muanza on his way to Lake Tanganyika, who came to see what he could do for my wound and cleared up the mystery quite a little by reporting what he had heard in the non-commissioned mess, where he had been invited to eat a meal.

"The Greek," he said, "is trying to curry favor by pretending he knows your plans. If he succeeds in worming into your confidence and persuading you to make plans to escape with him, they will feel justified in putting you in jail—and that, I understand, is where they want you."

"Will you do me a favor?" I asked.

He hesitated. It was kindness that had sent him down to ease my pain, if possible, not anti-Germanism; it was part of German policy to pose as the friend of all missionaries, and if anything he was prejudiced against us—particularly against Brown, whom he had visited in jail, and who assured him the only hymn he ever sang was "Beer, glorious beer!"

"That depends," he answered.

"We are quite sure any letters we write will be opened," I said.

He answered that he could hardly believe that.

"If we could send a letter unopened to British East it would solve our worst problem," I told him. "If you know of a dependable messenger who would carry our letter, I would contribute fifty pounds out of my own pocket to the funds of your mission."

I made a mistake there, and realized it the next moment.

"What kind of letter is worth fifty pounds?" he asked me. "Isn't it something illegal that you fear might get you into worse trouble if opened and read?"

I argued in vain, and only made my case worse by citing as an instance of German official turpitude the staff surgeon's neglect of me.

"But be tells me you refuse to be treated by him!" he answered. "He says you enter his hospital and are insolent if he happens to be too busy to attend to you at once. He says you refuse to let a native orderly dress your wound!"

He had been entertained to one meal at the commandant's house on the bill, and regaled by awful accounts of our ferocity. I did not succeed in inserting as much as the thin end of a different view until he asked me how a man's name could be professor Schillingschen and his wife's Lady Isobel Saffren Waldon.

"I don't understand about titles," he said. "Shouldn't she take his name, or else he hers, or something?"

I assured him that marriage had never as much as entered the head of either of them.

"They're simply living together," I said. "He's a cynical brute. She's a designing female!"

The missionary mind recoiled and refused to believe me. But after he had thought the matter over and seen the probability, he swung over to a sort of lame admission that a few more of my statements might perhaps be true.

"I will take your letter and guarantee its delivery in British East, provided I may read it and do not disapprove of its contents," he volunteered.

"That's not unreasonable," I said, "but the letter is in code."

"I should have to see it decoded."

I told him to find Fred and Will. He came on them sitting smoking under the great rock near the waterfront that bad been inset with a bronze medallion of Bismarck, and startled them almost into committing an assault on him, by saying that he wanted our secret code at once. They had been trying to get tobacco to Brown, and sweetmeats to Kazimoto, had failed in both efforts and were short-tempered. He explained after they had insulted him sufficiently, and they walked down to the camp one on either hand, apologizing all the way. I imagine they had criticized missions of all denominations pretty thoroughly.

In the end he decided not to read the letter at all.

"I have reached the conclusion you three men are gentlemen," he said, "and would not take advantage of me. I will take your letter to Ujiji, and send it to the south end of Lake Tanganyika, to be put in the British mail bag for Mombasa by way of Durban. It will take a long time to reach its destination—perhaps two months; but I will have it registered, and it will undoubtedly get there."

That he kept his word and better we had ample proof later on, but I did not bless him particularly fervidly at the time, for he went straight to the doctor and repeated my complaints. He left for Ujiji the next day, and the net result of his friendly interference was that the doctor refused me any sort of attention at all—even a change of bandages.

Fred and Will did their best for me, but it was little. I read in their faces, and in their studied cheerfulness when speaking in my presence, that they had made up their minds I was going to lose the number of my mess. They went to the commandant and the lieutenant besides the doctor in efforts to secure for me some sort of consideration, but without result; and they wrote at least six letters to the British East African Protectorate government that we ascertained afterward never reached their destination. They tried to register one letter, but registration was refused.

"Why don't they jail us simply, and have done with it?"—Will kept wondering aloud.

"They will when it suits their books," said I. "For the present they scarcely dare. Word might reach the British government. They're breaking no international law by holding us here and keeping tabs on us."

Before many days I grew unable to leave the hard cork mattress on the camp-bed in Fred's tent. They went again to the commandant, this time determined to force the issue.

"I will send some one," he told them, and they came away delighted that strong language should succeed where politeness formerly had failed.

But all the commandant did send was an *askari* twice a day, to lean on his rifle in the tent door, leer at me, and march away again.

"He comes to see if I'm dead," said I. "It would be inconvenient to have me die in jail; there might be inquiries afterward from British East. After I'm dead and buried they'll jail you two healthy ones, and keep you until you 'blab'!"

"Why don't we straight out tell 'em we don't know a thing about the ivory?" wondered Will.

"Because they wouldn't believe us!" Fred answered.

Seven days after the sentry's first call the doctor took to coming in person to look at me. He never except once stepped inside the tent, but was satisfied to give me a glance of contempt and go away again, once or twice taking pains to inspect the Greeks' camp before leaving. He usually had Schubert trailing in his wake, and gave him stern orders about sanitation which nobody ever carried out. The sanitary conditions of that rest-camp were simply non-existent until we came there, and we had gone to no pains on the Greeks' account.

But the Greeks did us an unexpected good turn, though it looked like making more trouble for us at the time. They began to complain of lack of exercise, and to grow actually sick for want of it. Because of that, and jealousy, they raised a clamor about our freedom to go anywhere within township limits as against their strict confinement to the camp. The commandant came down to the camp in person to hear what they had to say, and being in a good humor saw fit to yield a point. Being a military German, though, he could not do it without attaching ignominious conditions.

There was a band attached to the local company of Sudanese—an affair consisting of four native war-drums and two fifes. They knew eight bars of one tune, and were proud of it, the fifers blowing with beef and pluck and the drummers thundering native fashion, which means that the only difference between their noise and a thunder-storm was in the tempo.

Day after day, twice a day, whether it rained or shone, it seemed to be the law that this "band" should patrol the whole township limits, playing its only tune, lifting the tops of men's heads with its infernal drumming, and delighting nobody except the players and the township urchins, who marched in its wake rejoicing.

The Greeks and the Goanese were given leave to march with the band twice a day for the sake of exercise. They refused indignantly. The commandant flew into the rage that is the birthright of all German officials, but suddenly checked himself; he had a brilliant idea.

He withdrew the permission and changed it to an order that Coutlass and his two friends should march with the band twice daily for the sake of their health, on pain of imprisonment should they refuse.

"And I will prove to you," he said, "that the good German rule is impartial. All aliens awaiting trial and confined within the township limits shall march with the band if they are able!" As an afterthought he added magnanimously: "Those in the jail, too, provided they have not been sentenced for serious crimes!"

So Coutlass, his Greek friend, the Goanese, Fred, Will, and Brown of Lumbwa marched about the town twice daily, at seven in the morning and three in the afternoon, a journey of five miles, Fred and Will making no objection because it gave them a chance to talk with Brown. There were strict orders against talking, and four *askaris* armed with rifles marched behind to enforce the rule as well as keep guard over Brown. But the drums were so thunderous and the shrill fifes so lusty that the *askaris* could not hear conversation pitched in low tones.

"Brown says," said Fred, returning from the first march, "that he sleeps with only a sheet of corrugated iron between him and the ward where the chain-gang lies. He can talk with Kazimoto when be happens to be at that end of the chain. They've nothing but planks to lie on, any of them. He says Kazimoto seems determined to kill the lieutenant who sentenced him, and as soon as he's off the chain we'd better grab him and hurry him out of the country."

"Six months!" said I. "Splendid advice! How many of us will be alive or at liberty six months from now? Not I, at any rate!"

"How d'you suppose they discipline the chain-gang?" Fred asked, ignoring my growing hopelessness.

"With the lash," said I. "I've seen!"

"That's by day," said Fred. "They've better ways at night. One plan is no supper or breakfast; but the champion scheme is the doctor's. On complaint by the *askaris* that a man on the chain has shirked his work, or answered back, or been obstreperous, the doctor serves him out a handful of strong pills and sees him swallow them. They don't unchain them at night. D'you get the idea?"

"Not yet."

"Every time the man has to go outside he must wake the whole gang and take them with him! They're weary after working twelve hours at a stretch. After the second or third time up they begin to object pretty strenuously. After the third or fourth time he's so unpopular that he'd almost rather die than wake them. Imagine the result, and what he suffers!"

Despondency began to have hold of me, and I no longer wished to live. The doctor's momentary daily visits increased my loathing for the crew who tyrannized there in the name of Progress, and I could see no way of retaliating. I became seized with a sort of delirious conviction that if only I could die and be out of the way my friends would be far better able to contrive without me. There is no convalescence in a mood of that sort, and each morning found me nearer death than the last. Then malaria developed, to give me the finishing touch, and although strangely enough I grew less instead of more delirious, Fred and Will at last made no secret of their belief that I was doomed.

I myself was as sure of death as they were of dinner, and had better appetite for my fate than they for the meal, when one morning the doctor came earlier than usual. He had Schubert with him, and they both peered through the tent door. I was alone, for Fred and Will were in the other tent. The doctor stepped inside and examined me closely, drawing up the mosquito net to see my face. I did not trouble to speak to him, or even to open my eyes after the first glimpse. He spoke to Schubert in German, let the net fall again, and went away. Schubert spat and rubbed his hands, and swung along after him.

Then I heard Will and Fred arguing.

"Don't be a fool!" That was Fred's voice.

"I tell you I'll tell him!"

"Fine thing to tell a poor devil that's dying! Let him die in peace!"

"No. He has guts, for I've seen him use 'em. I shall tell him. You wait here!"

But they both came in, and sat one on either side of my bed.

"Did you hear what that doctor person said to the sergeant-major?" asked Will.

"I don't talk his beastly language," I answered.

"He said you'll be dead by this evening! He told Schubert to go and get the chain-gang and have them dig your grave at noon instead of laying off for dinner. He added they'll have you buried and out of the way by four or five o'clock. Then Schubert asked him—"

"No need to tell him that!" Fred objected. But Will was watching my face keenly, and went on.

"Schubert asked him who was to say whether you are dead or not. What d'you suppose the answer was?"

Fred objected again, but Will waved him aside.

"The answer he gave Schubert was: 'Once he is covered with two meters of earth, I shall not hesitate to sign a certificate!'—So now you know what to expect!"

Will smiled as he watched me. His face was as keen and calm as Fred's was troubled.

"Take more than his guesswork to put you where he'd like to have you—eh?" he laughed. And I sat up.

Fred began to grin too. "You were right, Will!" he admitted.

It was not anger that swept over me and gave me new strength. Anger, I think, would have hastened the end. It was sudden recognition of my own superiority to the devils who knew so little mercy. It was simple inability in the last recourse to admit myself able to be their victim. Even my leg felt better. I demanded food; and by the time they returned from their morning march around the township I had made my boy dress me and was sitting up.

We dated the turn of the tide of our fortunes from that hour. Certainly from that day we began to prosper—at first gradually, but after a while in the old swift way that had made all our ventures with Monty such amazingly amusing work

We saw the chain-gang—Kazimoto last, with a shovel over his shoulder—march away at noon to dig me a grave in the sand close to where they burned the township refuse. Fred and Will went and watched them a while, contriving to slip a paper of snuff into Kazimoto's hand while he rested and let the pick-men labor. (Snuff to a Nyamwezi is as comforting as an old sweet pipe to nine white men out of ten.)

When Schubert came that evening at five with an old sack to put my body in, and plenty of *askaris* to help decide disputes, I was standing up. He could not very well make even himself believe that a man who could speak and walk was dead, but he could be immensely enraged by what he was pleased to call my *schweinespiel.* He cursed me in every language he knew, including several native ones, and ended by threatening to make sure of me before going to so much trouble a second time.

We enraged him still further by laughing at him, and Fred got out his concertina that for many days past had lain idle. The first few notes of it made me realize more than any other thing could have done what depths of despondency we must have plumbed, for hitherto, for as long as I had known Fred, he had always been able with that weird instrument of his to rouse his own spirits and so stir the rest of us. He resumed old habits now, and gloom departed.

That evening I went to bed like a new man, and for the first night for long weeks slept until dawn, awaking hungry. My leg began to mend. We all saw the absurdity, if nothing else, of the treatment meted out to us, based on no better grounds than our supposed possession of a secret. Laughter brought good hope. Hope gave us courage, and courage set Fred and Will hunting for a means of escape. We decided there and then that to wait for this Major Schunck to come from the coast and pass judgment on us was a ridiculous waste of time as well as highly dangerous.

The first discovery Fred and Will made was that there were footholds cut in the great granite rock in which the Bismarck medallion was set. They climbed it, and discovered that from the summit they could see all Muanza harbor from the shore line to the island in the distance. Sitting up there, they presently spotted a native dhow drawn up with bow to the beach with the indefinable, yet unescapable air of rather long disuse.

Resisting the first temptation to hurry along the shore and examine it, they returned to camp to tell me of the find, and sent Simba, Kazimoto's understudy, to find out whose the dhow was and why it lay there. They explained it was a fairly big dhow, and might be laid up there on account of leakiness.

But Simba came back grinning with the news that the dhow belonged to an Indian from British East who had been jailed for smuggling. The dhow had been sold to pay his court fine, and was now owned by a Punjabi who had bought it as a speculation and repented already of his bargain, because the Germans would grant him no license to use it and nobody else would buy.

They went off again to have another distant view of it and to try and invent some means of inspecting it closely without betraying their purpose. I was already able to walk with the aid of a stick, although not fast enough to keep up with them, and curiosity taking hold of me I called two of our servants to give me a supporting arm and limped off to see the grave the chain-gang had recently dug for me.

It was a struggle to get there, but it seemed to me the trip was worth it. I found the grave about a foot too short, but otherwise commensurate, and sat down on a stone beside it to consider a number of things. A convalescent man sitting beside his own grave may be forgiven for amusing himself with a lot of near-philosophy, and if I trespassed over the borders of common sense on that occasion I claim it was not without excuse.

My meditations were disturbed by the arrival on the scene of the very last man I expected. We had been told that Professor Schillingschen had gone out on a journey, leaving his "wife" in the care of the commandant; yet I looked up suddenly to see him standing on the other side of the grave with both hands in the pockets of his knickerbockers and a grin of malevolent amusement showing through the tangled mass of hair that hid his lower face.

"Yours?" he asked.

I nodded.

"A close call! I have seen closer! I have stood so close to the brink of death that the width of an eyelash would have damned me!"

"Piffle!" I answered rudely. "How can the already damned be damned again?"

He laughed.

"You are sick still. You are petulant. Never mind. I was coming to call on you. I watched you leave the camp from the top of that hill behind you, and followed. It is better. We can talk here without being overheard. Send those natives away!"

"Certainly not!" I answered, but I reckoned without the professor and the fear his hairy presence instilled in them.

"Go!" he said simply in the native tongue; and although I ordered them at once to stay by me they ran back to the camp as fast as their legs could carry them.

"How do you feel now?" the professor asked.

I stared at him, wondering just what he meant.

"I mean, without a pistol!"

I saw the point. The rest-camp was not far away, but as far as I could judge we were quite out of sight from it, and unless there should happen to be some one hiding among the rocks at the foot of the hill behind me we were quite alone, unless, as was probable, he had placed one or two of his own hangers-on in hiding within call.

"This grave should be a lesson to you!" he grinned.

"It has been," I answered.

"An illustration," he suggested.

"A period," said I.

"To your youth?" he asked maliciously. "To the age of folly?"

"To the time," I said, "when any man could blackmail me. I would go into that grave ten times rather than tell you what you want to know!"

"There are worse places than the grave!" he said, beginning to leer savagely. His eyes glittered. He could scarcely find patience for argument. The thin veneer of his first mock-friendliness was gone utterly.

"I imagine that German colonial life is far worse than death," said I.

"German will be the only rule in Africa," he answered. "You fools of English have set your hopes on the Christian missionary. No weaker-backed camel could exist! The German Michael is wiser! Islam is the key to the native mind—Islam and the lash—they understand that! In a few years there will be nothing in Africa that is not German from core to epidermis! As to whether you shall live to see that day or not depends on yourself, my young friend!"

Being quite sure that he had a plan in mind that nothing would prevent him from unfolding, I did not waste effort or words on prompting him, but sat still. My silence and apparent lack of curiosity disturbed him; there is nothing your bully likes better than to force his victim into a war of words.

"I will be short and blunt with you!" he began again. "I know your history! You were in Portuguese Africa with Lord Montdidier. There he came in possession of the secret of Tippoo Tib's ivory; how, I do not yet know, but you shall tell me that presently! You and your friends came with him to Zanzibar, where you made certain inquiries—sufficient to set the Sultan of Zanzibar by the ears. You left Zanzibar for Mombasa, and for some reason that you shall also tell me presently, Lord Montdidier did not leave the ship at Mombasa but continued the voyage toward London. Certain individuals decided that it would be better not to permit Lord Montdidier to reach Europe alive. There were agents charged with the duty of attending to that. It was considered safest to throw him overboard into the Mediterranean; men were ordered by cable to board the ship at Suez. Yet when the ship reached Suez nobody knew anything about him! Tell me where he left the ship, and why!"

He glared with eyes accustomed to extorting facts from savages, depending on physical weakness so to undermine my will that I would give my secret away, perhaps without knowing it.

I lowered my eyes, not being minded to match the strength of my eye-muscles against his. The news that Monty had not reached Suez as a matter of fact made me feel physically sick. If it were true, it meant most likely that he had been the victim of foul play, for that steamer was not scheduled to stop anywhere before reaching the Suez Canal. As for the people on the ship knowing nothing about him they no doubt preferred not to talk to strangers. That sort of news is easily kept under cover for a while. Schillingschen grew angry at my silence, and changed his tactics.

"Where did he leave the ship?" he shouted—suddenly—savagely.

I did not answer. He came round to my side of the grave, and laid a heavy clenched fist on my shoulder. It seemed to weigh like lead in the weak condition I was in.

"You shall tell me what Lord Montdidier is doing now, or that grave shall resemble in your imagination a bed of roses!"

He seized my neck in a grasp like iron, and squeezed it. I rose suddenly and struck him in the stomach with my elbow. Strength had returned more swiftly than I had guessed, or perhaps it was indignation at the touch of his fingers. At any rate he staggered clear of me, and I thought he would assault me now in real earnest; but perhaps he suspected me of having weapons concealed somewhere. Instead of rushing at me like an angry bull he calmed himself and laughed.

"You are strong for a man they thought of burying!" he said. "Never mind! You shall see reason presently! It is well understood that you and your friends know where Tippoo Tib's ivory is hidden. You imagine you can keep the secret. If you keep it, you shall never make use of it, my young friend! If you choose to tell, you shall be suitably rewarded! Come now—I thought you were going to look for it down in these parts. I admit you fooled me. You simply made a false move to draw attention off from Lord Montdidier. Tell me where he is and what he does—and—or—"

"And what? Or what?" I demanded, as insolently as I knew how. I saw no sense in answering him gently.

"I will show you!"

I had begun to feel weak again, but he offered me an arm, and since he seemed in no hurry I was able to struggle along beside him. We took to the main road and when we reached the D.O.A.G. he called for a hammock and some porters. Being carried in that way was sheer luxury after the walk in my weak state, and I lay back feeling like a tripper on vacation. I saw Fred and Will climbing down from their observation post on top of the Bismarck monument, but he did not notice them.

Every German sergeant, and every *askari* we passed saluted us with about twice as much respect as I had ever seen them show the commandant; and Schillingschen returned salutes much less carefully than he, merely by a curt nod, or one raised finger. Apparently the military feared him, for when we passed the commandant, who was personally superintending the flogging of two natives in the market-place for not saluting himself, he took several paces forward to make sure Schillingschen should see his act of homage. The professor merely nodded in return, and I began to I wonder whether there was a rift in the lute of Muanza's official good relations. Surely I hoped so. Anything calculated to set the Germans' garrison life at odds looked to me like the gift of heaven!

Schillingschen, striding beside the hammock, directed our course along the shore-front under palm-trees, planted in stately rows with meticulous precision. He kept far enough to one side to avoid the charge of being seen walking with me, but from time to time tossed me remarks calculated to keep my nerves on edge.

"What I shall show you is by way of warning!" was a remark he repeated two or three times. Then:

"A native can always be made to talk by flogging him. Some white men need sterner measures!"

We left the commandant's house on the hill far behind and followed the curve of the lake shore, toward a rocky promontory with a clump of thick jungle behind it. Fear began to get its work in, until the thought came that what he most desired was to make me afraid; then I managed to summon sufficient contempt for him and his tribe to regain my nerve and once more almost enjoy the promenade.

He halted the hammock bearers at a spot about three hundred yards away from the promontory and, leaving them standing there, turned inland with a hand on my arm to give me support and direction. We followed a path that was fairly well marked out and trodden, but rough, and several times I should have fallen but for his help. My legs still refused any sort of strenuous duty.

"The staff surgeon at this station is a man of ideas," he announced as we rounded a big rock and passed down a narrow glade in the jungle. "He is original. He is not like some of our official fools. He studies."

I refused to seem curious, and walked beside him in silence.

"He studies sleeping sickness. If he can find the key to the solution of that scourge it will mean promotion for him. He has noticed that the sleeping sickness is always at its worst beside the lake, and putting two and two together like a sensible man has reached the conclusion that the disease may be propagated in some way in the blood of these things."

We emerged into a clearing in which a pool more than a hundred yards long and nearly as many wide was formed naturally by a hollow in the surface of a great sheet of granite. The pool was fed by a trickle of water from a jumble of rocks at one end. At the other end the bottom of the pond sloped upward gradually, so that a ramp of smooth rock was formed, emerging out of shallow water. A stone wall had been built about three feet high to enclose that end of the pond, and all the way along both sides the granite had been broken and chipped until the edges were sheer and unclimbable.

"Look!" he said, pointing.

I looked and grew sick. On the ramp, half in the water and half out lay about a hundred crocodiles basking in the sun, their yellow eyes all open. They were aware of us, for they began to move slowly higher out of water as if they expected something.

"You see that post?" asked Schillingschen.

The stump of a dead tree that he referred to stood up nearly straight out of a crack in the rock, and a few yards above water level. The crocodiles all lay nose toward it, some of them twelve or fourteen feet long, some smaller, and some very small indeed, all interested to distraction in the dead tree-trunk.

"That is where he feeds them," Schillingschen announced. "He has tested them for hearing, smell, and eyesight. By making fast a living animal to that post be has been able to convince himself that from about nine in the morning until five in the afternoon their senses are limited. Only occasionally do they come and take the bait between those hours. They are hungriest in the early morning just before daylight. Recently a large ape tied to the post at midday was not killed and eaten until four next morning, and that is about the usual thing, although not the rule. Now my proposal is—"

He stepped back and eyed me with the coldest look of appraisal I ever sickened under. I blenched at last—visibly suffered under his eye, and he liked it.

"—that you tell your secret or be fastened to that post from noon, say, until the crocodiles make an end of you!"

He stepped back a pace farther, perhaps to gloat over my discomfort, perhaps from fear of some concealed weapon.

"You have not much time to arrive at your decision!"

He took another pace backward. It occurred to me then that he was looking for some one he expected. Nobody turning up, he began to gather loose stones and throw them at the reptiles, driving them down into deep water, first in ones and twos and then by dozens. Most of them swam away to the far side of the pool, and hid themselves where it was deep.

Then, panting with having run, there came a native who looked like a Zulu, for he had enormous thighs and the straight up and down carriage, as well as facial characteristics.

"You are late!" shouted Schillingschen in German, "*Warum?* What d'ye mean by it?"

The man opened his mouth wide and made grimaces. He had no tongue. Schillingschen laughed.

"This is a servant who does no tattling in the market-place!" he said, turning again toward me.

"He and I can tie you to that post easily. What do you say?"

There was nothing whatever to say, or to do except wonder how to circumvent him, and nothing in sight that could possibly turn into a friend—except a little tuft of faded brown that out of the corner of my eye I detected zigzagging toward me in the direction from which we had come. A moment later I knew it really was a friend. "Crinkle," a mongrel dog that Fred bad adopted the day after our arrival, breasted the low rise, saw me, gave a yelp of delight and came scampering.

The dog sniffed my knee to make sure of me, and then trotted over to sniff Schillingschen. The professor stooped down to pat him, rubbed his ear a moment to get the dog's confidence, and then seized him suddenly by both hind legs. I saw what he intended too late.

"Stop, or I'll kill you!" I shouted, and made a rush at him. But he swung the yelping dog and hurled him far out into the pool.

A second later my fist crashed into his face and be staggered backward. A second later yet the dumb Zulu pinned my elbows from behind and set his knee into the small of my back with such terrific force that I yelled with pain. Then Schillingschen approached me and began to try to drive my teeth in with unaccustomed fists. He loosened my front teeth, but cut his own knuckles, so began looking about for a stick.

Strangely enough my own attention was less fixed on Schillingschen than on the wretched "Crinkle" swimming frantically for shore. Dog-like he was making straight for me, and there was no possibility whatever of his being able to scramble up the steep side. I shouted to call his attention, and tried to motion to him to swim toward shallow water, but the Zulu would not let my arms free, and the dog only thought I was urging him to hurry.

Schillingschen found a stick and came back to give me a hammering with it just at the moment when a crocodile saw "Crinkle." A blow landed on my head, cut my forehead, and sent the blood down into my eyes at the same moment that I heard the dog's yelp of agony; and next time I looked at the pond there was a tiny whirlpool on the surface, slightly tinged with red.

"You swine!" I shouted at Schillingschen, trying to break loose and attack him. For answer he raised his cudgel in both hands and stood on tiptoe to get leverage. If that blow had landed it must have broken something, for he was strong as a gorilla; but somebody shouted—I recognized Fred's voice, and in another second he and Will charged down on us. Schillingschen turned about to strike Fred instead of me, but Will's fist hit him on the ear and split it. The professor staggered backward, and a moment later Fred had felled the Zulu. I reeled from weakness and excitement, and nearly fell down.

"Throw him to the crocks, you men!" I urged madly. "He threw Crinkle in. Throw him! Nobody'll ever know! He'd have dared throw me in! Nobody comes here! Throw him in and trust the crocks to leave no trace!"

"Shut up, you fool!" growled Fred.

"Did you see him throw that dog in?" I retorted.

"No," he answered, "but I saw him strike you. That's enough! I'll deal with him!"

I suppose Fred intended to knock the professor down and belabor him with the same stick be had used on me, but the plan died stillborn. Schillingschen bethought him of his hip-pocket, produced a repeating pistol, and leveled it.

"Any nonsense, and I shoot you all!" he announced.

That ended the battle as far as we were concerned. We had no firearms. Schillingschen wasted no time on explanations, but beckoned his Zulu and walked off, striding at a great pace and only looking back over his shoulder once or twice to make sure we were not in pursuit.

Fred and Will lent me an arm apiece and we followed slowly, I recounting as fast as I could all that had happened, and they trying to chaff me back into a sensible frame of mind.

"That was a decent dog!" I insisted. "He slept on my bed those nights when I had fever!"

"I know it," Fred answered. "Will and I lay and scratched, while you rested, with proper flea-food for protection! Don't worry, we'll find you another dog!"

Schillingschen's consideration for my wound had vanished with the chance of making use of me. As we emerged into the open we saw him in the distance lolling in the hammock he had brought me in.

"Never mind!" grinned Will. "I'll bet the brute has an earache!"

"And teeth-ache!" added Fred.

"And I'll bet he has gone to prepare us a hot reception!" said I. "He owns this town!"

But nothing happened immediately on our return into the town. Actually Fred and Will had been outside township limits and could be arrested; suspecting foul play as soon as they saw me with Schillingschen, they had followed at once. They were as mystified as I when no swift vengeance lit on them. We saw Schillingschen carried in the hammock up the steep path leading to the commandant's house; but no one came down again. After we got back to camp we spent all the rest of the day waiting for the vengeance we felt sure was overdue, but none came. Toward evening we even began to grow hopeful again and to talk about the dhow. Fred and Will had examined it through field-glasses from the top of the rock, and were optimistic 'regarding its size and general condition.

"Even if it leaks rather badly," said Will, "we could reach some island, and beach it there, and caulk it."

"How about that launch, that brought the professor and Lady Saffren Waldon?" I asked.

"What about it?"

"Couldn't they follow us with that?"

"You bet they could!" said Will. "We've either got to spike the launch's boilers, or give them the complete slip on a dark night!"

"We might steal the launch!" suggested Fred, but that was too wild a proposal to be taken seriously. The launch was the apple of the German governmental eye, and the engine crew slept on it always.

The prospect was unpromising as ever, yet I went to bed and listened to the strains of Fred's concertina in the next tent with less foreboding than at any time since reaching Muanza, and fell asleep to the tune of *Silver Hairs Among the Gold,* a melancholy piece that Will liked to sing when hope or courage stirred him.

I was awakened near midnight of a moonless black night by a hand on my bedclothes and the light of a lantern in my eyes.

"Hus-s-s-h!" said some one. "Don't speak yet! Listen!"

It was a woman's voice, and it puzzled me indescribably, for a sick man's wits don't work swiftly as a rule when he lies between sleeping and waking.

"Listen!" said the voice again. "I must come to terms with you three men! You are the only hope left me! I have no friends in Muanza—and none whom I trust! Those Greeks and that Goanese would sell me to the first bidder, and these Germans are worse than dogs!"

"But who are you?" I asked stupidly.

For answer she held the lantern so that I could see her face. Her hand trembled, and the unsteady light threw baffling shadows, but even so I could see she looked drawn and aged.

"Where is your maid, then, Lady Waldon?" I asked, for it seemed to me that was one friend who had served her through thick and thin.

"Ask the commandant!" she answered. "The poor foot thinks he will marry her! Little she knows of the German method! I am alone! I have not even a servant any longer! I have walked through the shadows from the commandant's house, only lighting this lantern after I was inside the hedge. Nobody knows I am here. One watchman was asleep; the others did not see me. All you need fear is those Greeks. As long as they don't suspect I am here we can talk safely."

I tumbled out of bed on the far side, and went to waken the other two. After a hurried consultation we decided my tent was the best for the interview, because of the light that had burned in it nearly always while I was so deathly ill. We wrapped ourselves in blankets, and Fred went and shook Simba awake.

"Watch those Greeks!" he ordered him. "If they show signs of life, come and give the alarm!"

Then we set Lady Waldon's lantern on the ground in the back of my tent, closed the tent up, and foregathered. There was one chair. We three sat on the bed.

"Before we begin," said Fred, "we'd like some kind of proof, Lady Waldon, that your overture is honest! I've no need to labor the point. Until now you have been our implacable enemy. Why should we believe you are our friend to-night?"

She sighed. "I don't expect friendship," she answered. "You and I are in deep water, and must find a straw that may float us all! If I can help you to escape out of the country I will. If you can help me, you must! If you don't escape there are worse things in store for you than you imagine! If you tell your secret now, they intend to prevent your telling it to any one else afterward! And unless you tell they intend to take terrible steps to compel you! As for me—they have discovered that after all I know nothing, and am of no further use to them! They have not said so, but it is very clear to me how the land lies. Professor Schillingschen is drunk to-night; he came home with his car and mouth bleeding, and has plied the whisky bottle freely ever since until he fell asleep an hour and a half ago. He boasted over his cups. They are simply using this long wait for Major Schunck, who is supposed to be coming from the coast, to gather additional evidence against you. They have men out following your trail back by the way you came, and if they can find no genuine evidence they will invent what they need; the purpose is to get you legally behind the bars; and if you ever come out again alive that would not be their fault!"

"What do you propose?" asked Fred.

"Escape!" she answered excitedly. Then another thought made her clench her fists. "Is it possible you told Professor Schillingschen your secret to-day? Did one of you tell him? Is that why he is drunk?"

She saw by our faces that that fear was groundless, but a greater one, that she might not be able to convince us, seized her next and she made such an excited gesture that the shawl she wore over her head and shoulders fell away and her long hair came tumbling down like a witch's.

"Listen! There is nothing that you men from your point of view could say too bad about me! I know! I have been in the pay of Germany for many years, but what you don't know is how they got me in the toils and kept me in, dragging me down from one degradation to another! They have dragged me down so far at last that I am not much more use to them. If we were in British territory they would simply expose me to the British government and save themselves the trouble of ending my career. They did that to Mrs. Winstin Willoughby, and Lord James Rait, and fifty others; it was so easy to put incriminating evidence against them in the hands of the public prosecutor. Lord James Rait died in Dartmoor Prison—a common felon. I shall not! But believe me—I am certain as I sit here that they only wait for my return to British East! To have me murdered here might start inconvenient rumors that would lead to unanswerable questions! It was proposed to me to-day that I should return to British East on the launch!"

"Then why talk about escaping?" Fred wondered. "Why not go?"

"Because," she hissed emphatically, "don't you see, you stupid!—if they send me back it will be to my doom! My one chance is to escape from their clutches—get into touch with British officials—and save the situation by telling my own tale first!"

Fred was in no hurry to be convinced. I was already for accepting her story and helping her out; but that was perhaps because I was a sick man, too recently recovered from the gates of death to care to be hard on any one.

"I still don't see your danger," Fred told her. "In all my life I fail to recall a single instance of the British courts passing a severe sentence on a spy. If you'll excuse my saying so, your story about Lord James Rait is incorrect. I recall the case well. He got a twenty-year sentence for forgery."

"True!" she answered. "And Mrs. Winstin Willoughby was sentenced to fifteen years for theft! Lord James did forge—in the way of business for the German government! Jane Winstin Willoughby did steal—for the same blackguard masters! Do you think they will expose me as a spy? That would be too clumsy, even for such bullies as they are! Do you suppose they could have dragged me down to this without some sword held over me? They can prove that I committed a crime in England several years ago. Oh, yes, I am a criminal! I raised a check. It was a check on a German bank, given to me by a German on behalf of a countryman of his. I needed money desperately, and the man who brought the check to me suggested I should raise it! Since then I have tried to repay that money with interest a dozen times, but they have always laughed and told me they preferred to leave matters as they are."

"What would be the use of returning to British territory, then?" asked Fred. "If they hold that over you, they can denounce you at any time."

"Not they!" she answered. "Not if I get there first! I know too much! I can tell too much! I can prove too much! If I were once arrested on the charge of raising that check, no government in the world would listen to me. But if I can tell my story first, and confess about the check, and explain why the charge is likely to be brought against me, then there will be Downing Street officials who know how to whisper to the German Embassy words that will frighten them into silence! I can prove too much against the German government, if only I can tell my tale before they crush me!"

"Why not write it?" asked Fred, and it seemed

to me there was humor in his eye, but she only detected stubbornness, and laughed scornfully.

"My own maid even gave them the letters written to me by my sister! If I should be suspected of writing they would never rest until they had the letter!"

"Give me your letter to mail!" suggested Fred maliciously.

"Deluded man!" she sneered. "All the letters you have written since you came to Muanza lie in a drawer in the commandant's desk! I myself have read them!"

In the dark, with shifting shadows thrown by the cheap trade lantern, it was difficult to judge what was going on behind that beard of Fred's. I had begun to suspect he was coming over to my way of thinking and would yield to her presently, but he returned to the attack—very directly and abruptly.

"What is it you know against the German government?" he demanded, and sat with his jaw in the palm of his hand waiting for her answer.

"Why should I tell you? Why should I put myself completely in your power?"

"Why not?" asked Fred.

"What would prevent you from stealing my thunder, and telling my story as your own—leaving me at the Germans' mercy?"

"Something very potent that I think you would not understand if I talked of it," Fred answered. "Listen to me now a minute. I haven't conferred with my friends here, as you know. Whatever I tell you is subject to their agreeing with me. The only condition on which I, for one, would consent to taking part with you in anything—after all our experience of you!—would be that you should put yourself so completely in our power that we could feel we had your safekeeping. On those terms I would be willing to do my best to help you out."

"I agree to that like a shot!" said Will; and I nodded.

"You mean—?"

"All or nothing!" Fred insisted.

"You mean that you also, just like these Germans, must have a sword to hold over me?"

"I thought you wouldn't understand!" Fred answered. "What we demand, Lady Saffren Walden, is proof that you really do give us your confidence. Without that we have nothing to say to you, and nothing to do with you!"

She broke down then and cried a little, tearing herself with sobs she hated to release. Suddenly she raised her head and glared at us wildly, dry-eyed; not a tear had accompanied the sobbing.

"If I tell you—if you fail me after that—I shall kill myself in such way that you shall know—my blood is on your heads!"

Fred laughed. It was no doubt the best thing to do, but I wondered how he managed it.

"Suppose you begin by telling us," he said. "We can discuss the blood-stains afterward!"

Then she suddenly burst into her tale, as if she had rehearsed it a hundred times in readiness to pour into the ears of the first British official who had power enough to shield her. She told it dramatically, in few words, wasting no breath on side-issues, and without once pausing to explain, letting her words smash down the barriers of unbelief and pave their own way for explanations afterward.

"Germany is planning to conquer the world!—not now, but ten or a dozen years from now! She is getting ready ceaselessly! Part of the plan is to undermine British rule in Africa by means of a religious influence among the natives. That is the special duty of Professor Schillingschen. As soon as possible a great native army is to be trained, and thoroughly schooled in the fanatical precepts of Islam. But the German people are too heavily taxed already, and refuse to vote money for this miserable colony, where the great beginning must be made because it is only here that they can work unsuspected. So funds must be found in some other way!"

She paused for breath. No woman pleading at the bar of justice could have seemed more in earnest. Of one thing I was quite sure: she had found it worth her while to convince us if that were possible. She was playing no half-hearted game.

"Do you begin to see now why the Germans are so set on finding Tippoo Tib's hoard of ivory? Do you begin to understand why they are determined, not only to prevent your finding it, but to learn your secret? If rumor is one-half true, the Arab buried somewhere enough ivory to finance this plan of theirs! They have been going about the search systematically, and sooner or later they feel they must stumble on it. They will not let you forestall them!"

She paused again. Her very earnestness exhausted her more than the walk through the dark in danger had done.

"Take your time," Fred advised her. "We're all listening!"

"When I told you in Nairobi that Lord Montdidier had been murdered, I believed I was so near the truth that you would never know the difference. I knew the order had been given to have him killed on board ship—given by men who are accustomed to be obeyed—who do not excuse failure on any ground. They feared he might be going to divulge the secret of the ivory to his government in London. Oh, I tell you they stop at nothing! To-day London is the ivory market of the world, but they have their arrangements made for transferring that center of trade to Hamburg! They mean first to crush competitors, and then monopolize! They hope the ivory is in this country. In that case their task will be easy. But if it should be found in British East, they are all ready with the necessary men of influence to apply for a mining or agricultural concession, and they will fence that place off so thoroughly that no one will ever be the wiser until they have carried the ivory out of the country!"

"Let's do our part."

"They could never get it out of British East without the government knowing," objected Fred; but she laughed at him.

"If worse came to the worst, they are ready with an offer to exchange ten times the territory elsewhere for just that small section of the country. They would give up German New Guinea, or Southwest Africa—anything! They have fooled the French and Russian governments until they are ready to bring pressure to bear on England diplomatically to induce her to make almost any bargain of that kind that the Germans want. They are even willing to concede to England the whole of Abyssinia, which nobody owns yet, and to back her up against the claims of France and Italy! Why should they not be willing to make temporary concessions, when all Africa is to be theirs in ten years' time! They will give to-day, and with the help of the money that ivory will bring they will create an army that shall take away to-morrow!"

"But how can you prove all this?" Fred asked her.

"How? I know the names of the men who are preaching Germany's sermons all through British East! I know all Schillingschen's secrets! Why should I not? I have suffered enough! He is a drunken brute nearly always after the sun goes down, and his caresses are disgusting; I have endured them until I know all he knows! Now he realizes that I know his secrets and have none of my own to tell, so he hopes to send me to my doom at the hands of the government I have betrayed too many times! What is the use of my pretending to be better than I am? I am a spy—a traitress—a divorced woman with worse than no reputation! I am not a person likely to be shown much mercy! I never would have recanted unless the end of my rope had come! Now I know I must buy my pardon—I must earn it—I must pay for it with solid value! Luckily I can do that! I do not ask you men for mercy. I know what is in store for you if you do not escape! I offer to help you to escape, in exchange for helping me!"

"Better be more precise!" suggested Fred. "Exactly what is in store for us?"

She pointed her finger at me. "You went out of bounds to-day with Schillingschen! Well and good; he was with you. But you, and you—" She pointed at Fred and Will, "—went without permission. Why do you suppose they over-looked such a splendid chance of jailing you legally? Schillingschen came up to the commandant's house in a towering passion, demanding the immediate arrest and close confinement of all three of you. He was only persuaded to wait a few days longer because a runner has come in with word that the bodies of several Masai whom you shot on this side of the German border have been found! The bones—the bullets found among the bones—and cartridge cases that will fit your rifles are being brought to Muanza! After that—the deluge, my friends! That is why Professor Schillingschen gets drunk and sings himself to sleep in spite of your being still at liberty! Either escape before that evidence reaches Muanza, or make up your minds for the worst! It is growing late—answer me—do you agree?"

Fred glanced once at each of us. We both nodded.

"We agree with reservations," he said.

"What are they? Man—don't be a fool! Don't fritter the lives of all of us away!"

"They're simple. We've a friend in the jail here. His name's Brown."

"That drunkard? Leave him! He's worthless!"

"We've a servant on the chain-gang. His name is Kazimoto."

"A nigger? You'd risk another day in this place for a nigger? How absurd! They're never grateful. They don't see things from the white man's standpoint. They don't expect ideal treatment. Leave him his wages and tell him to follow when they let him off the chain!"

"And we have a string of porters," Fred continued. "We will not leave Muanza without the porters, our man Kazimoto, and Mr. Brown of Lumbwa!"

"You are mad! You are crazy!"

"We are the men you have invited to trust you," Fred answered kindly. "Those are our conditions. We will not 'bate one iota! Take 'em or leave 'em, Lady Waldon!"

IN HOC SIGNO VADE

Lean, loveless, hungry lanes are these!
The longest has an end.
Ill luck tasted to the bitter lees
Soonest shall mend.
From out the foe's ranks if Heaven please
Shall come your friend.

X

WE CAME to no fixed decision that night, although we knew there was no alternative. She held out, in the vain hope of making us agree to leave Kazimoto and Brown behind. The porters, she agreed, might come in very handy, although it was at least doubtful that we should be able to slip out of Muanza by land. The Germans had taken latterly to counting our porters every morning, to supplying them with ration money once every day, and to sending the bill to us by an *askari,* who waited for the cash. At any rate, she conceded the porters, provided we would leave the two others behind. And of course we were adamant.

She left us an hour and a half before dawn, we letting her return alone because of the greater danger of detection if we had tried to escort her. It was after she had gone, while we sat listening for the sound of a challenge that would have ruined all her hopes, if not ours, that Will conceived the bright idea which finally saved us.

"The Heinies don't know that we're wise to their game," he said cheerfully. His ears were sticking out from his head and he had the naughty boy look that always presaged wisdom. "Why don't we play that card for all it's worth?"

"We need five cards to make even a poker hand," Fred objected.

"Will a full house suit you—aces and queens?" he answered. "I've named you one ace already. Ace number two is the fact that these German officials are brutes pure and simple—brutes who don't understand how to be anything else, with brutal low cunning and no other cleverness."

"That sounds like the joker!" said Fred.

"It's ace number two, I tell you! The third is the fact that Brown of Lumbwa can talk with Kazimoto in the night through that corrugated iron partition! Three aces—count 'em—one, two, three! Queens? One of 'em left a few minutes ago! The other's the dhow! We'll call that blessed boat the *Queen of Sheba* for luck! The *Queen of Sheba* got to her journey's end, and found more than she expected, and by the lights of little old Broadway, so shall we! I've dealt the cards—is it up to me to play them?"

"Your hand, America! Talk it over first, though! There's an awful lot hangs on the game!" said Fred.

I fell asleep while they argued over the points of Will's strategy. Africa is a land of sudden death and swift recoveries, but for a convalescent man I had been through a strenuous day and had right to be tired out. It was broad daylight when I awoke, and breakfast was ready. Fred and Will had returned from their march around the township with the native band, and to my surprise the commandant was standing in front of their tent, talking with them. I threw on a jacket and joined them at table.

"I don't understand you," said the commandant. "Either talk German or speak more slowly!"

Will took a purchase on his stock of patience and began again.

"If our porters run away, you'll blame us. We don't care to be blamed for what is none of our fault. So if you don't put 'em all on a chain and lock 'em up nights, we're going to discontinue paying for their keep. That's flat! You can work 'em if you like. Let 'em help keep the township clean. We'll pay their board and wages as long as you're responsible for their not escaping! And say! If you want to get real work out of 'em I'll give you a tip. There never was a savage like that Kazimoto of ours for getting results out of that gang. Put him on the same chain with the lot of 'em, and we'll all be satisfied! I don't presume to be running your jail, but I'm telling you facts that'll hurt nobody. Those porters 'ud be a darn sight better off with plenty of exercise."

"Do I understand you to ask that your porters be made prisoners?" asked the commandant.

"You get me exactly!" said Will.

The commandant grunted, nodded, waited for us to get up and salute him, grunted again with disgust when we did nothing of the sort, turned on his heel, and walked off. We spent an hour on tenterhooks, and I began to believe the German had simply become more suspicious than ever and would keep closer watch on us without troubling at all about the men. But at the end of an hour we saw the porters rounded up, and a chain fetched out that was long enough to hold them all. They disappeared within the boma wall. Ten minutes later suddenly Will pointed toward the southward.

"Look! See what happens when the roofs of shanty-town take fire!"

Flames went up from the dry grass roof of one of the rectangular Swahili huts. Within thirty seconds the *askaris* on guard at the boma began firing their rifles in the air as fast as they could pull the trigger and reload. Within two minutes the chain-gang was headed for jail, where it was locked behind doors, in order that every *askari* in Muanza might be free to pile arms and hurry to the fire. It was not only *askaris;* the whole township turned out as to the circus, with Schubert and his long *kiboko* ruling the riot. The other sergeants were in evidence, but quiet, imperturbable men compared to their *feldwebel*, plying their *kibokos* without wasting words, stirring the whole world within their reach into action—if not orderly and purposeful, action, at least.

Schubert climbed on a roof well to windward and safe from the sparks, and directed proceedings in a voice that out-thundered the mob's roar and crackling flames. To illustrate his meaning he seized handfuls of the thatch on which he stood and tore them out, to the huge discontent of the owner. The crowd saw what he wanted and began at once tearing off roofs in a wide circle around the fire so as to isolate it, Schubert demonstrating until scarcely a handful of thatch remained on the roof he honored and he had to stand awkwardly on the crisscross poles, while the owner and his women wept.

Within ten minutes after the commencement of the fire there was under way a regular orgy of roof pulling. Whoever had an enemy ran and tore his roof off, and there were several instances of reciprocity, two families tearing off each other's roofs, each believing the other to be at the fire.

Muanza was a furious place—a riot—a home of din and tumult while the fire lasted, and when it was put out it took another hour to stop the fights between victims of the flames and unofficial salvage-men.

"D'ye get the idea of it?" asked Will. "D'ye see the Achilles heel?"

In that second, I believe, Fred Oakes and I betrayed ourselves genuine adventurers. Any fool could have talked glibly about setting the town on fire; any coward could have yelped about the danger of it, and improbability of success. It needed adventurers to size up instantly all the odds against the idea, recognize the one infinitesimal chance, and plump for it. And we were there!

"It's the only chance we've got!" agreed Fred. "I'm for it! Lead on America!"

"I believe we can pull it off!" said I. "I'm game!"

After that it seemed like waste of time to talk, yet every single detail of our plan had to be thought out beforehand and mentally rehearsed, if we hoped to have even the one slim chance we built on. Luckily Professor Schillingschen continued drunk, which meant that he would sleep early and give Lady Waldon another chance to pay us a nocturnal visit. One of our boys told us that according to market gossips the commandant was drinking with him and the two of them were watching a sort of prolonged native nautch they had staged in seclusion on the hill.

The next day we learned there was to be a murder trial of no less than nine men—an event likely to keep the whole garrison's attention drawn away from us. And after the trial would come the hanging (it would have been impossible to convince any one, German or native, that the verdict and sentence were not foregone conclusions). The stars in their courses appeared to be on our side. For several nights to come the worst the moon could do would be to show a sliver of silver crescent for an hour or two.

Lady Waldon came earlier that night. When we outlined our plan to her roughly she argued against it at first—and it was impossible far-fetched—ridiculous. She insisted again on our simply sneaking away by night with her. But Fred wasted no time on argument, and took the upper hand.

"Take us or leave us, Lady Waldon, as we are! We've an unwritten rule that none of us has ever thought of breaking, that binds us to obey the member of the party whose plan we have adopted. On this occasion we have agreed to Mr. Yerkes' plan, and you've got to obey him implicitly if you want to have part with us! We will not leave our men or Brown of Lumbwa behind, and we will not change the plan by a hair's breadth! Will you or won't you obey?"

She yielded then very quickly. It seemed a relief to her at last to subject her views to those of men whose purpose was merely honest. Will took up the reins at once.

"We've talked over buying the boat," he said, "but that's hopeless. The more we paid for it the louder the owner would brag. The Germans would be 'on' in a minute. We've simply got to steal it. It's up to you to find out the man's proper name and address, and we'll send him the money from the first British post-office we reach."

"Don Quixote de la Mancha!" she said critically. "Well—we steal the boat and you pay for it afterward. The owner will think you are crazy, and if the Germans ever discover it they will take the money away from him by some legal process. But go on!"

"We've plenty of money," said Will, "so there's no need to worry about too many supplies to begin with. But we'll need scant rations for ourselves and all our men until we reach some place where more are to be bought. And we've got to get them on board the dhow secretly. The first question is, how to do that."

She told us at once of a path going round by the back of the hill behind us, that would make the trip to the dhow in the dark a matter of over two miles, but that avoided all sentries and habitations. We agreed that all three of us should climb to the top of the hill, which was not out of bounds—and study the track next morning. On the fateful night we must take our chance, just as she had done, of avoiding the sleepy-eyed sentry who kept watch over the Greeks.

"We'll talk to Brown of Lumbwa on the morning and afternoon march around the township," Will went on. "Brown must whisper to Kazimoto through the corrugated iron partition in the jail at night, and have them all ready to break loose at the signal and bring him along with them. We must be careful to show Brown just where the dhow is. He has been sober quite a while. Maybe he'll remember if we direct him carefully."

"What is to be the signal?" she asked.

"Just what I'm coming to," said Will. "A fire-alarm on the first windy night! The next question is, who is to start the fire? We'll need a good one! Yet if we do it, we're likely to be caught by the crowd coming running to deal with it."

"Coutlass!" she answered suddenly. "Coutlass and his two friends!"

"You'll perhaps pardon me," Fred answered, "but none of us would trust those Greeks as far as a hen could swim in alcohol!"

"Yet you must! Leave them to me! They don't know that the sand in my glass has run down. Let me go to them presently, pretending that I went direct to them and am afraid of being seen by you. I will tell them that the Germans want a good excuse for putting you three men in jail and that they will he sent away free as a reward if they will start a fire and charge you afterward with arson! I will tell them to choose the first windy night, so as to have a really spectacular blaze worth committing perjury about!"

"Better arrange a signal," Will advised. "They might otherwise fire before we were ready!"

"Very well. You men give me the word at midday of the day of the start, and I will spread red, white and blue laundry on the roof of the commandant's house for the Greeks to see."

"Good enough!" agreed Will. "Now one more stunt! We simply must have firearms. The Germans have taken ours away and locked them up. At a pinch I suppose we could manage with one rifle, provided we had lots of ammunition. We would rather have one each. In fact, the more the merrier. One we must have! What about it?"

She thought for several minutes. At last she told us that one of the commandant's rifles and one of Schillingschen's stood leaning in a corner of the living-room beside a book-case. Whether she could make away with one or both of those without detection she did not know, and she would have to use her wits regarding ammunition. It was always kept locked up.

"Why not kill an *askari* and take his rifle and cartridges?" she asked. "The sentry on duty watching the Greeks will be in the way. Knock him on the head from behind!"

"Thank you!" grinned Will, exchanging glances with us. "We shall have about enough on our consciences setting fire to half the township. We'll not kill except in self-defense."

"But you won't set the town on fire! The Greeks will do that!"

"Don't let's argue ethics!" Fred interrupted, for Will's cars were getting red. "Can you tell us for certain, Lady Waldon, whether *all* the *askaris* and German sergeants really run to a fire? Or do a certain number remain in the boma?"

"Oh, I know about that," she answered. "Until the prisoners are all locked in—that is to say, in case of fire in the daytime—six or eight *askaris* remain inside the boma. The minute they are locked in, if the fire is serious, and in case of fire by night, they all go except two, who stand on the eastern boma wall, one at each corner. From there they are supposed to be able to see on every side except the water-front. Nobody guards the water-front; I don't know why, unless it is that the gate on that side is kept locked almost always and the wall runs along the water's edge."

"As a matter of fact," said I, "those two sentries on the wall will be too busy staring at the fire, if the Greeks really make a big one, to see anything else unless we march by under their noses with a brass band."

"Bah!" sneered Lady Waldon. "If I get that rifle I would dare shoot them both for you myself!"

"If you overstep one detail of Will's plan, I guarantee to put you ashore on the first barren island we come to!" said Fred. "Leave shooting to us!"

The next problem was to draw away from the Greeks the attention of the *askari* at the cross-roads. We could not see him, for it was one of those black African nights when the stars look like tiny pin-pricks and there are no shadows because all is dark. To go out and look what he was doing would have been to arouse his suspicion. Yet there was always a chance that he might be patrolling down near the Greek camp; doubtless acting on orders, he had a trick of approaching their tents very closely once in a while.

So when Lady Waldon had slipped out into the darkness we lit half a dozen lamps and started a concert, Fred playing and we singing the sort of tunes that black men love. He took the bait, hook, sinker, and all; in the silence at the end of the first song we heard his butt ground on the gravel just beyond the cactus hedge in front of us; and there he stayed, we entertaining him for an hour. By that time we were quite sure that Lady Waldon had passed along the road behind him; so Fred went out and gave him tobacco.

"It's time you went and looked at those Greeks again!" he advised him. "You would be in trouble if they slipped away in the night!"

Now that a plan of campaign was finally decided

on, there seemed much less to do than we had feared. Mapping out in our minds the way round the back of the hill to the dhow was perfectly simple; we went and smoked on the hilltop, and within an hour after breakfast had every turn and twist memorized. Fred drew a chart of the track for safety's sake.

Persuading Brown of Lumbwa proved unexpectedly to be much the most difficult task. Added to the fact that the *askaris* who marched behind and the Greeks who marched in front were unusually inquisitive, Brown himself was afraid.

"We'll all be shot in the dark!" he objected.

"Would you rather," Will asked, "be shot in the dark with a run for your money, or fed to the crocks in the doctor's pond?" And be told him about the crocodiles to encourage him.

"They'll have to let me out of jail at the end of the month," Brown argued.

"Don't you believe it! In less than a week from now we'll all be in on one and the same charge of filibustering! They'll not let you go back to British East to tell tales about their treatment of the rest of us," Will assured him.

But Brown proved tinged with a little streak of yellow somewhere. It was not until the afternoon march that Fred and Will, one on either side of him, by appeals to his racial instinct and recalling the methods of the military court, induced him to do his part. Once having promised he vowed he would see the thing through to the end; but he was the weak link; he was afraid; and he disbelieved in the wisdom of the attempt.

It was Kazimoto in the end who kept Brown up to the mark, and shamed him into action by superior courage. Fred found a chance to speak to him as the long string rested at noon under the narrow shade of a cactus hedge, and warned him in about fifty words of what was intended. (The *askaris,* almost as leg-weary as the gang, were sprawling at the far end of the line, gambling at pitch-and-toss.)

"Be sure you sleep as near to the partition as you can. Get details of the plan from Mr. Brown, and then drill the porters one by one! Don't let them tell one another. You tell each one of them yourself!"

Then he walked down the line and ordered the porters in a loud voice to obey the *askaris* implicitly, and to work harder in return for the good food and care they were getting, winking at the same time very emphatically, with the eye the *askaris* could not see.

The night work was the hardest, because, although we were quite sure about direction, even in the dark, it was another matter to feel our way and carry unaccustomed loads. By day we decided what to take and what to leave behind, and we cut down what to take with us to the irreducible, dangerous minimum. Then we broke that up into thirty-or forty-pound packages, so that when we all three made the trip to the dhow the most we took at one time was about a hundred pounds' weight. In the condition I was in I could take not more than one trip to the others' two; after the first it was agreed that I would better stay behind and keep an eye on the *askari.* The minute he showed symptoms of becoming inquisitive I was to invent some way of keeping his attention; so all unsuspected by him I lay in the sand by the roadside within three yards of him, while the ants crawled over me and he dozed leaning on his rifle. Once a long snake crawled over my wrist and my very marrow curdled with fear and loathing; but except for mosquitoes, who were legion and sucked their fill, there was no other contretemps. I don't know what I would have done if the *askari* had taken alarm and set off to investigate. I trusted to intuition should that happen.

The work of arranging the stuff in the dhow was the most difficult of all, because we dared not light a lantern, yet we also dared not stow things carelessly for fear of confusion when the hour of action came. The space was ridiculously small for ourselves and all those men, and every inch had to be economized. In addition to that the dhow had to be worked backward off the mud far enough to be shoved off easily, and then made fast by a rope to the bushes in such way as not to be noticeable. Most of the ropes turned out to be rather rotten, and we could only guess at the condition of the sails; the feel of them in the dark gave us small assurance. But fortunately we had a couple of hundred feet of good half-inch manila in camp with us, and that Fred and Will took out and stowed in the hold the night following.

We bought such things at the D.O.A.G. as we could without arousing suspicion, as, for instance, a quantity of German dried pea-soup—not that the porters would take to it kindly, but it would go a long way among them at a pinch. Live stock we did not dare buy, for fear of the noise it would make; but we laid in some eggs and bananas. Most of the thirty-pound loads were rice.

It troubled us sorely to leave our good tents, beds, and equipment behind, yet all we could take was the blankets and one Gladstone bag packed with clothes for us all. Kettles and pots and pans were a noisy nuisance, yet we had to have them, and blankets for all those porters, who would escape from jail practically naked, were an essential; but fortunately we had a sixty-pound bale of trade-blankets among our loads.

Not one word did we exchange all this while with Coutlass and his friends. Not one overture did we make to them, or they to us. But there was no doubt of their intention to do their worst. They gloated over us—eyed us with lofty disdain and scornful superior knowledge. They were so full of the notion of having us jailed for their misdeed that they positively ached to come and jeer at us, and I believe were only saved from doing that by the shortness of the time.

At last, three days after decision had been reached, we threw our blankets with a red one uppermost over the top of both tents in the sun; and within thirty minutes after that Lady Saffren Waldon had spread on the commandant's roof a blue cotton dress, a white petticoat, and a blazing red piece of silken stuff. There and then the Greeks and the Goanese pledged one another out in the open with copious draughts in turn from the neck of one whisky bottle, and we began to pray they might not get too drunk before night. Judging by their meaning glances at us, they considered us their mortal and cruel enemies whom it would be an act of sublime virtue to bring to book.

The trial of the natives for murder had taken place, accompanied by the usual amount of thrashing of witnesses and the usual stir throughout the countryside. These were charged with having murdered an *askari* near their village—a big bully sent to arrest a man, who had taken leave to help himself to more than rations, and had made a lot too free with the village women. So German military honor had to be upheld exemplarily. Condign vengeance was sure and swift. The execution was to take place on the drill-ground on the day we chose for our departure.

There was no risk of investigations that day. Had we known it, we could have gone away in all likelihood in broad daylight, so busy was the garrison in marshaling into place and policing the swarms of villagers brought in from as far as sixty miles away to witness German justice. Even the customary parade of the band was canceled for that occasion, and that was our only real ground for uneasiness, for it prevented our having a last talk with Brown of Lumbwa and assuring ourselves that courage would not fail him in the pinch.

We worried in plenty without cause, as it seems that humans must do on the eve of putting plans, however well laid, to the test. We had a thousand scares—a thousand doubts—and overlooked at least a thousand evidences that fortune favored us. Toward the end our hearts turned to water at the thought that Kazimoto would probably fail to do his part, although why we should have doubted him after his faithful record, and knowing his hatred of German rule, we would have found it hard to say.

Several times that morning we showed ourselves about the town, with the purpose of allaying any possible suspicion and saving the authorities the trouble of asking what we were up to. With the same end in view we attended the execution in the afternoon, and sincerely wished before it was over that we had stayed away.

On this occasion even the chain-gangs were included among the spectators, in the front row, on the ground that, being proved criminals, they needed the lesson more than the hempen-noose-food not yet caught and tried and brought to book.

The same sort of sermon, only this time more fiery and full of ranting humbug about German righteousness, was preached by the commandant. The miserable victims had received a simple death sentence, but he explained that in virtue of his superior office be had seen fit to add to it. "Death" he explained, "would certainly rid the German protectorate of such conscienceless scalawags as these, but might not be enough to discourage the bad element that disliked German rule. Natives must be taught that the very name of all that is German must be reverenced, and that German punishment is as terrible and sure as the German arm is long! And be sure of this!" he continued. "The ear of the German government is as far-reaching as its arm! In your villages—in your homes—in your families—there is always an agent of the government listening! Your own brother—your wife—your child may be that agent of the government! Now, watch carefully and see what happens to men with bad hearts—aye, and to women with bad hearts, who conspire against German rule!"

What followed was more impressive because of the determination we had heard of to bring all Africa under the German yoke. In vain should the wretched natives in after years escape by the hundreds northward in the hope of living under British government. The fools—the "easy people"—the "folk who gave without a price"—the "truth tellers"—the "men who wish to forget"—the unwise, cocksure, cleaner-living, unbelievably credulous, foolishly honest British officials would be all gone. The *pickelhaube* and the lash, blackmail and coercion would take the place of generosity. Africa would better be back under the Arabs again, for the Arabs had no system to speak of and were inefficient. Some Arabs have a heart—some a very soft heart.

The crowd grew bright-eyed, little children straining forward between their elders in the bull-fight frenzy—that same intoxication of the senses that held the Roman freemen spellbound at the sight of suffering.

One at a time, that the last might see the torture of the first, the victims were noosed by the heel (one heel)—thrown with a jerk—hauled heel-first to the overhanging branch—and flogged into unconsciousness with slow blows, the lieutenant standing by to reprove the *askaris* if they struck too fast, for that would have been merciful. Not until the victims ceased to struggle were they lowered and thrown on the ground, to lie bleeding, awaiting their turn to be hanged.

The last two—supposed to have been the culprits who actually held the spear that pierced the marauding *askari's* heart—were hauled up heel-to-heel together, and hanged presently in the same noose, the commandant laughing at their struggles and Professor Schillingschen studying their agony with strictly scientific interest.

When the last had ceased struggling Schillingschen permitted himself one more pleasure. He strolled over to us and blocked Fred's way, standing with hands behind him and out-thrust chin.

"You flatter yourself, don't you!" he sneered. He was just drunk enough to be boastful, while thoroughly sure of what he was saying. "You expect to tell a fine tale! I know the psychology of the English! I know it like a book! Let me tell you two things: First, your English would not believe you. They are such supremely cocksure fools that they can not be made to believe that another so-called civilized nation would act as they, in their egoism, would be ashamed to act! Civilization! That is a fine word, full of false meanings! Civilization is prudery—sham—false pride—veneer! Only the Germans are truly civilized, because they alone are not afraid to face naked animalism without its mask! The British dare not! They hide from it—shut their eyes! The fools! If you could tell them their story they would never listen!

"Second: You will never tell the story! Being English, you were such dull-witted fools that you did not even hide the cartridge cases, or the bones of the Masai you shot! Bah-ha-ha-ha-hah! You can escape hanging yet by telling your secret. Jail you can not escape! Try it if you don't believe me! Try to escape—go on!"

He turned on his heel and left us, striding heavily with the strength of an ox and about the alertness of a traction engine, turning his head every once in a while to enjoy the spectacle of our discomfort.

We judged it best to appear concerned, as if that was indeed our first realization of the extent of the case against us and the nature of the evidence. But we did not find it difficult. We were all three startled by the fear that in some way he had got wind of our plans, and that he meant to play with us cat-and-mouse fashion.

That night it stormed—not rain, but wind from east to west, blowing such clouds of dust that one could scarcely see across the narrow streets. Every element favored us. Even the *askari* at the cross-roads, supposed to be watching the Greeks, turned his back to the wind, and what with rubbing sand in and out of smarting eyes and fingering it out of his ears, heard and saw nothing. It was scarcely sunset when we saw both Greeks and the Goanese sneak out of the camping place in Indian file with their pockets full of cotton waste. They had soaked the stuff in kerosene right under our eye that afternoon.

There ought to have been a sliver of moon, but the wind and dust hid it. Fifteen minutes after sundown the only light was from the lamps in windows and the cooking fires glowing in the open here and there. Thirty minutes later there began to be a red glow in three directions. Less than one second after we saw the first indications of the holocaust a regular volley of shots broke out from the boma as the sentries on duty gave the general alarm. Less than five minutes after that the whole of the southern, grass-roofed section of the town was going up in flames, and every living man, black, white, gray, mulatto, brown and mixed, was running full pelt to the scene of action.

We waited ten minutes longer, rather expecting the Greeks to double back and begin denouncing us at once. In that case we intended to stretch them out with the first weapons handy. I sat feeling the weight of an ax, and wondering just how hard I could hit a Greek's head with the back of it without killing him. Fred had a long tent-peg. Will chose a wooden mallet that our porters carried to help in pitching tents.

But the Greeks did not come, and there streamed such a perfect screen of crimson dust, sparkling in the reflected blaze and more beautiful than all the fireworks ever loosed off at a coronation, that it was folly to linger. We each seized the load left for that last trip (Fred's included the hammer, Pincers, and cold chisel for striking off the porters' chain) and started off quietly round the hill, not beginning to hurry until the hill lay between us and the burning town.

There was not much need for caution. The roar of flames, the shouting, the excitement would have protected us, whatever noise we made, however openly we ran. Over and above the tumult we could hear Schubert's bull-throated bellowing, and then the echo to him as the sergeants took up the shout all together, ordering "Off with the grass roofs! Off with the roofs!"

The white officials were more than interested, and had no time for anything but thought for the blaze. As we crossed the shoulder of the far side of the hill we could see them standing on the drill-ground all together, clearly defined against the crimson flare. Schillingschen was with them.

There was no sign of what had happened at the boma. The gang would have to emerge from a little-used gate at the northern end, provided they could break the lock or secure the key to it; otherwise their only chance was to climb the wall by the cook-house roof and jump twenty feet on the far side. I was for running to the little gate and bursting it in from the outside, but Fred damned me for a mutineer between his panting for breath, and Will, who was longer-winded, agreed with him.

"Have to leave their end of the plan to them! Let's do our part right!"

As it turned out, we were last at the rendezvous. We heard the chain clanking in the dark just ahead of us, and try how we might, could not catch up. Then, near the boat bow, Kazimoto suddenly recognized Fred and nearly throttled him in a fierce embrace, releasing all his pent-up rage, agony, resentment, misery, fear in one paroxysm of affection for the man who cared enough to run risks for the sake of rescuing him. Fred had to pry him off by main force.

"Into the boat with you!" Will ordered them. "Chain-gang first! Get down below, and lie down! The first head that shows shall be hit with a club! Quickly now!"

Clanking their infernal chain like all the ghosts from all the haunted granges of the Old World, they climbed overside and disappeared. There were more figures left on shore then than we expected. Brown we could make out dimly in the dark: he was chattering nervously, and admitted that but for Kazimoto he would not be there. The faithful fellow had broken down the corrugated iron partition and had dragged him out by main force. He was rather resentful than grateful.

"Hauled here by a nigger—think of it!"

We ordered Brown on board and below, pretty peremptorily. Lady Saffren Waldon stepped out of the darkness next, holding a rifle and two bandoleers so full of cartridges that she could hardly raise her arms. We took the load from her, and helped her overside. Fred took the rifle and succumbed to the hunter's habit of opening the breach first thing. It was a German sporting Mauser, with a hair trigger attachment and magazine, as handy and useful a weapon as the heart of man could wish. He had scarcely snapped the breach to again when a voice we all recognized made the hair rise on my neck. Fred jumped and raised the rifle. Will swore softly—endlessly.

"Gassharrrrammminy! You men took us for damned fools, didn't you? You thought to get away and leave us! By hell, no! We go or you stay! Birds of a feather fly together! One of you is American—I am American! Two of you are English—I am English, and can prove it! My friends come with me!"

Fred leveled the rifle at him.

"About face! Off back to town with you!" he barked.

"Not on your tin-type!" Coutlass yelled. "I'm no man's popinjay! Shoot if you dare, and I'll spoil the whole game! Help! He-e-e-lp! He-e-e-e-lp!"

The other Greek and the Goanese joined in the shout, the dark man setting up such an ululating screech that the very storm dwindled into second place in comparison. It was true, the unearthly yelling was carried out over the water, and very likely not a sound of it reached twenty yards inland; but it rattled our nerves, nevertheless. The skin grew prickly all up and down my backbone, and the men on the chain-gang inside the hull began shouting to know what the matter was.

Will remembered then that he was captain for the day, and made virtue of necessity.

"In with you!" he ordered. "Quick!"

With a grin that was half-triumph, half-cunning, and wholly glad, Coutlass helped his companions over the bow, and had the civility to stand there with hand outstretched to help us in after him. We sent him below with his friends, but be came up again and insisted on leaning his weight on the poles with which we began shoving off into deeper water. It was hard work, for with her human cargo and several hundred gallons of water that had leaked through her gaping seams, the dhow was down several inches. Her hull had just begun to feel the wind and to rise and fall freely, when a white figure ran screaming down toward the water's edge and stood there waving to us frantically.

"Leave her!" said Lady Waldon excitedly, clutching my arm. I was up on the bow, just about to lay the pole along the deck and haul on the halyards. She spoke very slowly right in my ear. "That, is my maid Rebecca. The faithless slut—"

Coutlass began to shout, trying to pole the dhow back to land single-handed.

"We can't leave that woman behind there!" Fred shouted, hardly making himself heard against the wind.

"Can't we!" shouted Lady Waldon. "Give me that rifle, and I'll solve the problem for you!"

But Coutlass solved it in another way by jumping overboard, over his head in deep water, taking our hempen warp with him (I had made one end of it fast to the bitts, meaning to be able to find it in the dark).

There was quite a sea running, even as close inshore as that, and for a moment I doubted whether the Greek would make it. By that time it was all we could do to see the woman's white figure, still gesticulating, and screaming like a mad thing. Presently, however, the warp tightened, and then by the strain on it I knew that Coutlass was trying to haul us back inshore. Failing to do that, for the strength of the wind was increasing, he seized the Syrian woman by the waist and plunged into the water with her. I saw them disappear and hauled on the warp hand-over-hand with all my might, Lady Waldon leaning over to strike at my hands until I shouted to Fred to come and hold her. Then she begged Fred again for the rifle, promising to kill the two of them and reduce our problem to that extent if we would only let her.

Will and I hauled the dripping pair on board, and Coutlass carried the maid to the stern. She had fainted, either from fright or from being half-drowned, there was no guessing which. Then in pitch blackness with Will's help I got the ship beam to the wind and began to make sail.

Now danger was only just beginning! I was the only one of them all who knew anything whatever about sails and sailing. I was too weak to get the sail up single-handed, had no compass, knew nothing whatever of the rocks and shoals, except by rumor that there were plenty of both. There appeared to be no way of reefing the lateen sail, which was made of no better material than calico, and I was entirely unfamiliar with the rigging.

Behind us, as we payed before the gaining wind, was brilliant blaze that showed where Muanza was. Against the blaze stood out the lakeward boma wall. I stood due east away from it, and discovered presently that by easing on the halyard so as to lower the long spar I could obtain something the effect of reefing.

I set Fred and Will to making a sea-anchor of buckets and spars in case the sail or rotten rigging should carry away, leaving us at the mercy of the short steep waves that fresh-water lakes and the North Sea only know. The big curved spar, now that it was hanging low, bucked and swung and the dhow steered like an omnibus on slippery pavement. Luckily, I had living ballast and could trim the ship how I chose. They all began to grow seasick, but I gave them something to think about by making them shift backward and forward and from side to side until I found which way the dhow rode easiest.

When Fred had finished the sea-anchor he got

out the tools and began striking off the iron rings on the porters' necks through which the chain passed. The job took him two hours, but at the end of it we owned a good serviceable chain, and a crew that could be drilled to take the brute hard labor off our shoulders.

Coutlass meanwhile was busy on the seat in the stern beside me making Hellenic inflammatory love to Lady Waldon's maid, whom he had wrapped in his own blanket and held shivering in his arms. Lady Waldon herself sat on the other side of me, affecting not to be aware of the existence of either of them. The other Greek and the Goanese had been driven below, where they started to smoke until I saw the glow of their pipes and shouted to Will to stop that foolishness. He snatched both pipes and threw them overboard. The thought of being seen from shore was almost incitement enough for murder. They refused to turn a hand to anything that night, but sat sulking below the sloping roof of reeds and tarpaulin that did duty for a deck, wedged alongside of seasick Wanyamwezi.

It was Kazimoto who chose the least disheartened of the gang, beat them and stung them into liveliness, and set them to bailing. There was a trough running thwartwise of the ship into which the water had to be lifted from the midship well. It took the gang of eight men, working in relays, until nearly dawn to get the water out of her; and to keep her bottom reasonably dry after that two men working constantly.

I knew vaguely that the great island of Ukerewe lay to the northwestward of us. Between that and the mainland, running roughly north, was a passage that narrowed in more than one place to less than a hundred yards. That would have been the obvious course to take had we not been afraid of pursuit, had we dared get away by daylight, and provided I had known the way. As it was I intended to add another hundred miles to the distance between us and the northern shore of the lake, by sailing well clear of and around Ukerewe, trusting to the less frequented water and the wilder islands to make escape easier.

I judged it likely that the moment we were missed, the launch would be sent off in search of us, and that the Germans would search the narrow passage first. They would expect us to take the narrow passage, as the shortest, and depend on their ability to steam a dozen miles an hour to overhaul us, even should we get a long start on the outside course.

With gaining wind, a following sea, a little ship crowded to suffocation, and a sail that might blow to shreds at any minute, it was not long before I began to pray for the lee of Ukerewe, and to stand in closer toward where I judged the end of the island ought to be than perhaps I should have done. It was lucky, though, that I did.

In making calculations I had overlooked the obvious fact that, steaming three miles to our one, the launch could very well afford to take the outside course to start with. Then they could take a good look for us in the open water next morning, and, failing to find us, steam all around Ukerewe, come back down the inside passage, and catch us between two banks.

It was Lady Saffren Waldon on my left hand, looking anywhere but at her maid and sweeping the dark waste of water with eyes as restless as the waves themselves, who gave the first alarm.

"What is that light?" she asked me.

Following the direction of her hand I saw a red glow on the water to our left, not more than a mile behind.

"Reflection from the burning town," I answered, but I had no sooner said it than I knew the answer was foolish. It was the glow that rides above hot steamer funnels in the night.

"Fred!" I shouted, for fear took hold of the very roots of my heart, "for the love of God make every one keep silence! Show no lights! Don't speak above a whisper! Keep all heads below the gunwale! That cursed German launch is after us!"

We were in double danger. I could hear surf pounding on rocks to starboard. I did not dare to come up into the wind because nobody but I knew how the spar would have to be passed around the mast, and in any case the noise and the fluttering sail might attract attention.

"Look out for breakers ahead!" I ordered. "I'm going to hold this course and hope they pass us in the dark!"

"SO DAVID PREVAILED"

(1. SAMUEL 17:50)

Be glad if ye know the accursed thing
And know it accurst, for the Gift is yours
Of Sight where the prophets of blindness sing
By the brink of death. And the Gift endures;
Ye shall see the last of the sharpened lies
That rivet privilege's gripe.
Be still, then, ye with the opened eyes,
Come away from the thing till the time is ripe.

Be glad that ye loathe the accurséd thing,
It is given to you to foreknow the end.
But they who the unwise challenge fling
Shall startle foe at the risk of friend
As yet unready to endure—
And can ye fend Goliath's swipe?
The slowly grinding mills are sure,
Let terror alone till the time is ripe.

Be glad when the shout for the spoils, and the glee,
The hoofs and the wheels of the prophets of wrong,
Out thunder the warning of what shall be;
Be still, for the tumult is not for long.
The Finger that wrote, from a polished wall
As surely the closed account shall wipe;
The accurséd thing ye feared shall fall
To a boy with a sling when the time is ripe.

XI

IF THE dhow had been seaworthy; if the crew had understood the rigging and the long unwieldy spar; if we had had any chart, or had known anything whatever of the coast; if nobody had been afraid; and, above all, if that incessant din of surf pounding on rocks not far away to starboard had not threatened disaster even greater than the Germans in the steam launch, our problem might have been simple enough.

But every one was afraid, including me who held the tiller (and the lives of all the party) in my right hand. Lady Saffren Waldon disguised fear under an acid temper and some villainously bad advice.

"Steer toward them!" she kept shouting in my ear. "Steer toward them! Ram them! Sink them!"

Coutlass, on my other hand, made feverish haste with his love-affair, fearful lest discovery by the Germans should postpone forever the assuaging of his hungry heart's desire.

"Steer toward shore!" he urged me. "Who cares if we run on rocks? Can't we swim? Gassharamminy! Take to the land and give them a run for it!"

He seized the tiller to reinforce the argument, and wrenched at it until I hit him, and Fred threatened him with the only rifle.

"Get up forward!" Fred ordered; but Georges Coutlass would not go.

"Gassharamminy!" he snarled. "You want my girl! I will fight the whole damned crew before I let her out of the hollow of my arm.

"All right, touch that tiller again and I'll kill you!" Fred warned him.

"Touch my girl, and you kill me or get out and swim!" Coutlass retorted.

Will was up forward with Brown, looking out for breakers through the spray that swept over us continually. I watched the glow that rode above the launch's funnel, marveling, when I found time for it, at the mystery of why the cotton sail should hold. The firm, somewhere in Connecticut, who made that export calico, should be praised by name, only that the dye they used was much less perfect than the stuff and workmanship; their trademark was all washed out.

Suddenly Will dodged under the bellying sail, throwing up both hands, and he and Brown screamed at me: "To your left! Go to your left! Rocks to the right!"

The Germans had passed us, but not by much, for the short steep seas were tossing their propeller out of the water half the time. Because of the course I had taken the wind was setting slightly from us toward them, and I could have sworn they heard Will's voice. Yet there was nothing for it but to put the helm over, and as I laid her nearly broadside to the wind a great wave swept us. At that the Greek, the Goanese, and all the natives in the hold set up a yell together that ought to have announced our presence to the Seven Sleepers.

I held the helm up, and let her reel and wallow in the trough. Now I could see the fangs of rock myself and the white waves raging around them. See? I could have spat on them! There was a current there that set strongly toward the rocks, for a backwash of some sort helped the helm and we won clear, about a third full of water, with the crew too panicky to bail.

"Hold her so!" yelled Fred in my ear. "Don't ease up yet! If we get too close and they see us, I've the rifle! They haven't seen us yet!"

"Rocks ahead again!" yelled Will. "To the left again!"

We were in the gaping jaws of a sort of pocket, and it was too late to steer clear.

"Throw the anchor over!" I roared, "and let go everything.

Will attended to the anchor. Fred was too anxious for the safety of the only rifle to trust it out of hand, and he hesitated. Georges Coutlass saved the day by letting go the shivering Syrian maid and slashing at the halyard with his knife. Down came the great spar with a crash, and as the dhow swung round in answer to anchor and helm, Fred, Will and Brown, between them, contrived to save the sail, Brown complaining that we were the first sailors he ever heard of who did not have rum served them for working overtime in dirty weather.

So we lay, then, wallowing in the jaws of a crescent granite reef, and watched the red glow above the German launch move farther and farther away from us. We waited there, wet and hungry, until dawn dimmed the flame from the burning roofs of Muanza, Lady Isobel Saffren Waldon loudly accusing us all at intervals of being rank incompetents unfit to be trusted with the lives of fish, and Coutlass afraid of nothing but interruption. The things he said to the maid, in English—the only language that they had apparently in common—would have scandalized a Goanese harbor "guide" or a Rock Scorpion from the lower streets of Gib. He did not mention marriage to her, beyond admitting that he had half a dozen wives already, and had been too bored by convention ever to submit to the yoke again. The maid seemed enraptured—delirious in the bight of his lawless arm, forgetful of her wetting, and only afraid when he left her for a minute.

We dared not try to cook anything, even supposing that had been possible. Forward was a box full of sand to serve as hearthstone, but the little scraps of fuel we had brought with us were drenched and unburnable, even if the risk of being seen were not too great. Lady Saffren Waldon told us we were "toe-rag contrivers." In fact, now that she was out of reach of the men she feared and hated most, she reverted to type and tried to domineer over us all by the simple old recipe—audacious arrogance. Luckily, she slept for an hour or two.

A little before dawn, when it began to be light enough to let us see the outline of the shore, we sent Kazimoto aloft to reeve our hemp rope through the hole that did duty for block, and by the time the sun had pushed the uppermost arc of his rim above the sky-line we once more had the sail set.

The wind was still blowing a gale; the seamanlike precaution would have been to lie where we were at anchor until fairer weather; but daring is forced on the fearfullest, and there was nothing for it but to study out the method by which the unwieldy spar should be made to pass the mast when tacking, drill Fred, Will, Brown and Kazimoto, and then haul up the anchor and sail away before people on shore could see us.

We had to tack toward Muanza for a quarter of a mile with fear in our arms to make them clumsy before I dared believe we were clear of the reefs; but when I put the helm down at last there was neither launch in sight nor any other boat that might contain an enemy. The southern spur of Ukerewe stuck out like a wedge into boiling water not many miles ahead, and once around that we should be sheltered. The only fly in the ointment then was the probability that the launch would be waiting for us just around the spur, or else under the lee of another smaller island in the offing to our left, but what we could not see in that hour could not upset us much.

Every one clamored for food. The porters, already forgetful of the chain that had galled them, and the whips that had flayed them day and night, demanded to be set ashore to build a fire and eat. Lady Saffren Waldon awoke to fresh bad temper, and Coutlass, too, grew villainously impatient. His Greek friend, from under the shelter of the leaky reed-and-tarpaulin deck, offered him Greek advice, and was cursed for his trouble. One curse led to another, and then they both had to be beaten into subjection with the first thing handy, because when they fought Lady Saffren Waldon egged them on and the maid tried to savage the other Greek with a brooch-pin, which brought out the Goanese to the rescue. That crowded dhow was no place for pitched battles, plunging and rolling between the frying-pan of Muanza and the fire of unknown things ahead.

"One more outbreak from you, and I shoot!" Fred announced, patting the rifle. But, he did not mean it, and Coutlass knew he did not. The English temperament does not turn readily on even the most rascally fellow beings in distress. Besides, it was an indubitable fact that we all much preferred Coutlass, with his daring record, and now a most outrageous love-affair on hand, to the other Greek or the Goanese, who were now disposed to bid for our friendship by abusing him. Georges Coutlass was no drawing-room darling, or worthy citizen of any land, but he had courage of a kind, and a sort of splendid fire that made men forget his turpitude.

We were a seasick, cold and sorry company that rounded the point at last and came to anchor in a calm shallow bay where fuel grew close down to the water's edge. Having no small boat, we had to wade ashore and carry the women, Coutlass attending to his own inamorata. Lady Saffren Waldon's picric acid rage exploded by being dropped between two porters waist-deep into the water. It was her fault. She insisted one was not enough, yet refused to explain how two should do the work of one. Sitting on their two shoulders, holding on by their hair, she frightened the left-hand man by losing her balance and clutching his nose and eyes. She insisted on having both men flogged for having dropped her, and Fred's refusal was the signal for new war, our rescue of her being flung at once on to the scrap heap of her memory.

She counted with cold cynicism on our unwillingness to leave her again at the mercy of the Germans, and had no more consideration of our rights or feelings than the cuckoo has for the owner of the nest in which she lays her eggs.

"Beat those fools!" she ordered. "Beat them blue and give them no breakfast!"

"Do you see that rock over there, Lady Waldon?" Fred answered. "Go and spread your clothes to dry. When we've cooked food we'll send Rebecca to you with your share."

"If you send that slut to me I will kill her!" she answered, flying into a new fury.

"Whom do you call slut?" demanded Coutlass (and he had no compunctions of any kind—particularly none about women, and calling names. He was simply feeling gallant after his own fashion, and alert for a chance to show off.) Lady Waldon backed away from him.

"Of course," she sneered, "if you loose your bully at me, I am no match at all!"

Fred promptly kicked Coutlass until he ran limping out of range, to sit and nurse his bruises with polyglot profanity. The Syrian Rebecca went over to comfort him, and eying the two of them with either malice or else calculation (it was impossible to judge which) Lady Waldon retreated toward the rock that Fred had pointed out.

We cooked a miserable meal, neither daring to make too great inroad into our stores before making sure we could replenish them, nor caring to make more smoke than we could help. We hoped to escape being seen even by natives, but Lady Waldon upset that part of our plan by setting up such a scream when she saw three islanders crossing a ridge three hundred yards away, that they could not help hearing her, and came to investigate. She was forced to dress faster than ever in her life before, and came running to demand that we flog all three "to teach them manners." She had perfectly absorbed the German attitude toward all black men.

From the natives we learned that there was no telegraph wire along that coast, and that the only German settlements were semi-permanent camps where they were cutting wood, for fuel for their own launch and for the steamers the British were building to serve the lake ports, Muanza included.

With that good news for encouragement we made the three natives a small present in the vain hope that they might be induced not to talk about us, and put to sea again. The weather was fairer and growing intolerably hot. Even before the sun grew high the dhow was a comfortless indecent thing, more crowded than anything Noah can have had to tolerate: and we lacked Noah's faith in omniscient guidance, in addition to sailing in a hotter latitude, and having more fleas on board than the pair he is reported to have carried.

As we crept up-coast, leaning to this or that side when the gusts of wind varied, the only enviable ones were the three in the bow, posted there to keep a look-out for the launch or any other enemy. They had room enough to sit without touching one another, and air to breathe that mostly had not been tasted half a dozen times. Fred, Will and Brown took turns commanding the foredeck look-out, keeping it awake and its units from quarreling. The rest of us found no joy in life, and not too much hope even when Fred's concertina lifted the refrain of missionary hymn-tunes that even the porters knew, and most of us sang, the porters humming wordless melancholy through their noses. (When that happened Lady Saffren Waldon's scorn was something the arch-priests of Babylon would have paid to see.)

There was never room on the tiny after-deck for more than six people sitting elbow to elbow and back to back or knee to knee. Lady Waldon simply refused to yield her corner seat on any account at any time to any one. Coutlass refused to leave his new sweetheart, for the freely-voiced reason that then Brown might make love to her; and we did not care to send both of them below for obvious reasons. That reduced open-air accommodation to a minimum, because the reed-and-tarpaulin deck was scarcely strong enough to bear the weight of two men at a time, and we did not care to throw the whole deck overboard for fear of rain.

And by-and-by the rain came—out of season, but no less violent because of that. It rained three days and nights on end—three windless days and starless nights, during which we had to linger alongshore close to the papyrus. In order to keep mosquitoes out we had to light a smudge in the sand-box below. The smudge added to the heat, and the heat drove men to the open air to gasp a few minutes in the rain for breath and go down again to make room for the next in turn.

Sleep on shore was impossible, for thereabouts were crocodile and snake swamps, fuller of insect life than dictionaries are of letters. Poling was next to impossible, because the soft mud bottom gave no purchase. And the oars we made out of poles were clumsy affairs; there was not room for more than two boys to try to use them at a time, even if the deck would have stood the strain of more feet, which it certainly would not have done.

Lady Waldon slept seated in her corner, with her head wrapped in a veil over which the mosquitoes prospected in gangs. Coutlass and his lady-love endured rain and insects in the open, too, but suffered less, because of mutual distraction. The rest of us took turns with the natives below, lying packed between them, much as sardines nestle in a can, wondering whether the famous Black Hole of Calcutta was really such a record-breaker as they say. Brown was of the opinion that the Black Hole was a nosegay compared to our lot—"Besides which, they probably had rum with 'em!" he added.

Some of the porters grew sick under the strain of heat, fear, excitement and inactivity. The native suffers as much from unaccustomed inconvenience as the white man, and more from close confinement. The third night out the man next me began coughing, shaking my frame as much as his own as he racked himself, for we were wedged together with only the thickness of his blanket and mine between us, and I was jammed tight against the ship's side. Toward morning he grew quiet—grew colder, too. When dawn came we found that he had coughed up the most of his lungs on my white English blanket.

I gave them the blanket to bury him in, and we poled the *Queen of Sheba* inshore to find a place to dig a hole, leaving the body stretched on some tree-roots while we prospected. We should have known enough by that time to leave four or five men on guard close by; as it was, when the men still on board the dhow began kicking up a Babel, Fred and I came running and jumping back through the marsh just in time to see a crocodile wriggle off into the water, with the corpse in his jaws feet first. Fred fired a shotted salute, but missed, and that ended that funeral.

By day we passed villages on higher ground, where we might have procured more food if we had dared run the risk of meeting Germans. It was likely enough the villagers were so used to dhows that they would not trouble to report having seen us in the distance; but it was perfectly certain that if we paid them a visit they would pass word along from mouth to mouth with that astonishing, undiscoverable ease that is at once the blessing and bane of governments.

So Fred wasted hot hours with the only rifle, trying to hunt meat on a shore where all the four-legged game had been ran down by the natives, or butchered by the German machine-guns long ago (for to teach Sudanese mercenaries the art of rapid fire in action their officers marched them out to practise on herds of antelope. There was game in plenty away from the lake, but none where the German officer could conveniently practise his profession.)

We tried to shoot ducks and geese; but a rifle at long range is not the best weapon for that sport. We shot very few, and then only to discover the invincible repugnance natives have to eating "dagi" as they call all birds. We kept ourselves alive, but did not solve the problem of the ever-diminishing supplies of rice for our men.

Somebody thought of fishing. We found hooks in a crevice in the *Queen of Sheba's* bow, and made lines from a frayed rope. But although the shore was lined with traps in which the inhabitants no doubt took fish in proper season, all that we caught was one miserable finny specimen, all head and mouth and tail, that the natives said would poison any one who ate it. The truth was, of course, that they preferred rice to anything, and, African native-like, would eat nothing else as long as rice was to be had, having no earthly notions of economy. When the rice was all gone on the fifth day out of Muanza they raided a banana plantation before we knew what they were up to, and came back gorged, with bunches enough to feed them for two or three more days.

The fat was in the fire then, of course. We paid the owners handsomely, giving them their choice of money or blankets when they bore down on us in long canoes demanding vengeance. They voted for blankets and money, but vowed they would far rather have the bananas, because now their own people would be on short commons to make up for the surfeit of ours.

We left them never doubting that they would send word to the nearest German officer. (They told us there was a wood-cutting station within a "few hours," and we prayed he might be only a non-commissioned man in charge of it, but knew that prayer was too sweetly reasonable to be answered where the German *Gott* makes war on foreigners.) Kazimoto assured us he heard them telling one another they would make complaint against us within the day.

It remained, then, only to guess where that steam launch might be. We were approaching the northern end of Ukerewe, not a day's sail, if the light wind held, from the narrow mouth of the channel between Ukerewe and the mainland. That was the likeliest place for the launch to lie in wait; it was where we would have waited had we been pursuers and they the pursued. So we decided after a council of war to put the helm over and sail almost due westward, hoping to meet with an island where we might stop for a few days, catch fish and dry them, and caulk the leaky dhow, without the risk of letting the Germans know our whereabouts. (It is a peculiar fact that whatever the native secret system of transferring messages may be, it does not work across water.)

Not all the little gods of Africa were fighting for the Germans, although it began to seem so. An hour after putting up the helm we sighted a school of hippopotami—fifty at least, and for half a day we chased them, Fred trying to shoot one until Will and I objected to further waste of ammunition. A dead hippo would have provided us with meat enough for a month for the whole ship's company. We could have towed the carcass ashore somewhere and dried the meat in slabs. But the glare on the water made shooting very nearly impossible (Fred's eyes were sore from it); and if we should meet the Germans those remaining cartridges would be our only hope. But the diversion took us out of sight of land, and that stood us in better stead presently than tons of fresh meat.

Whether the Germans heard us, or were merely quartering that part of the lake in wait, we never knew. Probably they heard the shooting in the distance and gave chase. At any rate, within ten minutes of Fred's last wasted shot Coutlass caught sight of smoke and announced the fact with his favorite oath.

"Gassharamminy! The launch!"

At first we were all in a stew because there was no land near, where we might have beached the dhow and scattered. It was an hour before our advantage of position dawned on us, and all the while the launch approached us leisurely. She had plenty of fuel; the wood was piled high above her gunwale in a stack toward the stern; but those on board her seemed to take more pleasure in contemplation of our defenselessness than in speed. She steamed twice around us slowly before closing in; and then we made out Schillingschen's hairy shape, leaning against the cord-wood with a rifle between his hands.

"Shoot him! Shoot him, by Jiminy!" urged Coutlass, but Fred was not so previous as that. We were not yet on the defensive. We counted five rifles, in addition to Schillingschen's protruding above the launch's side, and we all took cover in the hope either that they might decide we were not the dhow they waited for, or else that they might come very close out of curiosity. For Fred had a plan of his own. Rifle in hand, he crawled under the hot tarpaulin and lay flat on the reed deck, Will crawling after him to snatch the rifle in case Fred should be hit.

"Steer straight toward 'em!" Fred called to me, as soon as it was evident that the launch did not intend to pass us by. "Keep headed toward them!"

That was not easy in the light wind, until Schillingschen tired of staring at us and gave an order to the engineer. Then they laid the launch broadside on to our bow at about two hundred yards' range, and without a word of warning opened fire on us from all six rifles, Schillingschen devoting his first attention to myself at the helm.

Our lone rifle cracked in reply, but they could not see Fred and did not guess where to shoot in order to search him out. They came no nearer, but circled slowly around us, only Schillingschen's bullets appearing to come anywhere near the target, until a yell from below showed what their real plan was and I understood why the sail was not ripped and no bullets whistled overhead. They were shooting through the planking of the dhow, endeavoring to massacre the helpless crowd below, and no doubt to sink her and drown us as soon as she was full enough of holes.

A wounded Nyamwezi came scrambling on deck, spouting blood from his neck and crazed with fear. He jumped overboard and tried to swim toward the launch, but one of the Germans hit him in the head at the third shot and he disappeared. Then one of Schillingschen's elephant bullets slit my sleeve, and the next one pierced my helmet.

"Put one into Schillingschen, Fred!" I shouted, but Fred did not answer. He kept up a very steady succession of shots that were doing no good at all that I could see.

Another German bullet found its mark below deck in the thigh of the Goanese. He might have known enough to lie quiet, having some alleged white blood in him, but instead he, too, came struggling to the after-deck, bellowing like a mad-man. Coutlass knocked him back below with a blow on the chin, and he there and then threw the whole crowd into a panic by screaming and kicking. They all began to try to swarm together through the narrow opening, and those in the rear tore at the reed deck.

Into that pandemonium went Coutlass, armed with nothing but Hellenic fury, thoughtful of nothing but his lady-love—surely reckless of his own skin. He beat, kicked, bit, scragged, banged their foolish heads together, cursed, spat, gouged, and strangled as surely no catamount ever did. Brown leaped in to lend a hand, and into the midst of that inferno three more bullets penetrated, each wounding a man. Lady Waldon, mad with some idiotic strategy of her own sudden devising, seized the tiller and tried to wrench it from my hand. The Syrian Rebecca, imagining new treachery and fearful for her Greek lover, tried to prevent her with teeth and nails. The Germans raised a war-whoop of wild enjoyment. And just at the height of all that, Fred's three-and-twentieth shot went home.

There was a loud report, followed by instant nothing except stampede on the part of the Germans to get out of reach of something. Then the something grew denser; invisible hot vapor became a pall of steam that bid the launch from view, three more shots from Fred's rifle finding the proper mark by sheer accident, for there was another explosion; the cloud increased and the launch stopped dead.

"That gray sheet of metal wasn't her boiler at all!" Fred shouted back to me. "The first shot pierced the boiler when I found out where to aim! I think three of them are scalded badly—hope so!—high pressure steam—superheated—did you see? Now leave 'em to find their own way home!"

"See if you can't get Schillingschen!" said I.

But Schillingschen was invisible in the white cloud, and Fred refused to waste one of the half-dozen cartridges remaining. The light wind that bore us away from the launch also spread the screen of steam between us and them. A shot or two from Schillingschen's rifle proved him to be still alive, and still determined, but missed us by so much that we began to dare to sit upright. Then Fred went below to sort out wounded men, plug holes in the dhow, and stop the panic, and we all prayed for wind with a fervor they never exceeded in Nelson's fleet.

When Will had gone below to help Fred, the panic had ceased, two dead men had been thrown overboard, and six of the crew had been set to work bailing in deadly earnest to keep ahead of the new leaks, there was time to consider the position and to realize how hugely better off we were than if the launch had caught us somewhere close inshore. Now we could sail safely northward, every puff of wind carrying us nearer to British water and safety, whereas unless they could mend that high-pressure boiler, they would have to lie there for a week, or a month—die unless some one came in search of them. Had we holed their boiler near the shore they would have been able to take to the land until they found canoes. Good canoes, well manned, could have overhauled us hand over fist like terriers after a rat.

"Our lone rifle cracked in reply."

It was fifteen minutes yet before we were out of rifle range, and Schillingschen tried to make the most of them when the steam thinned, exposing his beefy carcass recklessly. But by the time it had thinned down sufficiently to let him really see us we were too far away to make sure shooting. He slit the sail, giving us half a night's work to mend it, and made three more holes in our planking, but hurt nobody.

That was the only launch the German government had on the lake in those days, an almost perfect toy with an aluminum hull and more up-to-date gadgets on her machinery than a battleship's engineer could have explained the purpose of in a watch. They had lavished a whole appropriation on one show. From the minute we were out of range of Schillingschen's big-bore elephant gun we ran risk of starvation, and perhaps surprise, but no longer of pursuit, and we headed the *Queen of Sheba* as nearly as we could guess for British East with feelings that even Lady Waldon shared, for she grew distantly polite again, and complimented Fred on his cool nerve and accurate shooting.

We should have suspected treachery, for she

made no attempt to retaliate on Rebecca for scratching her face. Unnatural inaction should have put us on our guard. She even went so far as to compliment the maid on "finding such a great, strong, brave man as Coutlass to cherish her." The Greek simply cooed at that—threw out his great chest and rearranged with his fingers the whiskers that had almost totally disguised him.

(There was not one of us but looked like a pirate by that time. The natives of that part of Africa shave every particle of hair from their bodies whenever they get the chance, and prefer their heads as shiny and naked as any other part of them. But the German prison system, devised to break the spirit of whoever came within its clutches, included prohibition of shaving, so that we had the woolliest crowd of passengers imaginable.)

We found it impossible to help being sorry for Lady Waldon, or even for the maid, who suffered in spite of Coutlass's kisses and strong arms. The obvious fact that the dhow was no place for a woman made us overlook the conduct of both of them over and over again, shutting eyes and ears to Lady Waldon's meanness and the maid's increasing impudence.

Lady Waldon actually began to set her own cap at Coutlass, encouraging him to boast to the porters, and pretending to admire the gift with which he told them tales in Kiswahili that would have made even her blush if she had understood the half of them. At intervals the maid grew jealous, and had to be kissed back to serenity by Coutlass, who was no less in love with her because of any mere addition to the number of his interests. He could have made hot love to six women, and have enjoyed it. There were times when he really flattered himself that Lady Waldon admired his looks and fine physique.

Food was now the chief concern. We trailed a fishing line behind us, but caught nothing. Brown said there were too many crocodiles for fish to be plentiful, but on the other hand, Kazimoto, who surely should have known, swore that the water was full of big fish, and that the islanders lived on little else. Whatever the truth of it, we caught nothing; and when we reached an island whose shore was lined with fish-traps made of stakes and basket-work we searched all the traps in vain. The natives we saw in the distance all ran away from us, and there were no crops that we could see of any kind, which rather bore out Kazimoto's story.

"Crocks' eggs are what those savages eat, I tell you!" Brown insisted. "They're wholesome and don't taste worse than a rotten hen's egg." We offered him his own price if he would eat one himself in the presence of us all; but hungry though we were all beginning to be, he refused, and we needed his example.

After that first island we began to sail among a regular archipelago, most of them scarcely better than granite rocks on which the crocodiles could crawl to sun themselves, but some of them a half-mile long, or longer. Nearly all of them were barren, but at last, when we judged ourselves well inside the British portion of the lake, we came on a very large one that had a mountain in the middle of it, and contained a fair-sized village hidden among trees.

It was dark, and we were all famished when we reached it, so when we had poled the dhow into a little bay between granite boulders big enough to hide her, mast and all, we went ashore, made fires, and served out the last handfuls of rice, skimping our own allowance to increase those of the porters, whose larger stomachs afforded vaster yearning power. They were pitiably meager rations—a mere jest—an insult to hungry men; but we found before we had cooked and finished them that we had witnesses who thought us fortunate.

They came so silently that even the porters did not notice them at first—gaunt black shadows flitting in the deeper shadows, and coming presently to squat outside the edge of the circle of firelight, until a tribe, men, women and little children, were all gathered around us burning up the darkness with their eyes.

They were hungrier than we! Our food, that looked so scant to us, to them was a very feast of the gods! They all had pieces of leather or plaited grass drawn tight around their middles to lessen the pangs of hunger, and the chief, who sat rather apart from the rest, gnawed at a piece of bark.

None of them wore any clothes. Those that had goat-skin aprons had them on behind, and they were as free from self-consciousness as the trees in winter. Some of them had spears, and they all had knives, yet none offered violence, or as much as begged. There were three or four hundred of them, at the lowest reckoning, yet they allowed us to finish our meal in the dark in peace.

There was nothing to say when we had finished. We knew what the matter was, and they knew we knew. We had nothing to share with them, and they knew that, for they could see the empty rice bags that the porters had shaken and beaten to get out the very dust. We did not know their language; even Kazimoto professed himself ignorant of any dozen words that could unlock their understanding.

Presently, under the eyes of all of them, Fred got out the rifle from its wrappings and proceeded to clean and oil it carefully, as every genuine hunter should before he sleeps.

Then it was evident at once that new hope for some reason had been born among that silent crowd. The chief, uninvited, drew nearer and watched every detail of Fred's husbandry with glittering eye.

"Give him the oily rag to suck!" suggested Brown, but that proved not to be the key to his interest, for he thrust the rag back into Fred's hand and motioned to him to continue cleaning.

Finally Fred examined the last handful of cartridges carefully one by one, and filled the magazine. Then, after making sure the sights were in order, he began to wrap the rifle again.

But at that the chief held out a lean long arm and stopped him. Coutlass sprang to his feet in a hurry, imagining that was a signal to attack at last, but Fred ordered him to sit down, and Lady Waldon, who seemed possessed for the once by uncanny calmness, asked him to give her an arm to the dhow, where she proposed to try to sleep. Coutlass felt flattered, and obeyed. The maid got up and followed them both in a fury of jealousy, and they three were lost to view in a moment among the shadows cast by our four flickering fires. The other Greek got up and followed them, leaving the Goanese already snoozing by the fire.

Then, just as the half of a brilliantly pale moon rose above the papyrus, the chief came a pace nearer and touched Fred's hand. Then he beckoned. Then he touched the hand again and retreated backward. Glancing around I saw the shadows that were his tribe leaning toward us in strained attention, with eyes for nothing but their chief and Fred. Understanding there was something that the chief desired him to go and do, Fred passed the rifle to Will and rose to his feet.

With patience that was simply pathetic the chief shook his head and tried to explain something in weary-motioned pantomime. Fred took the rifle back from Will. The chief nodded. Fred started to follow him, and then the whole tribe sighed, with a sound like the evening wind rustling through the papyrus.

It being clear now that he was to shoot something, Fred took the wrappings off the rifle, threw them to me, and walked into the dark, the chief trotting ahead like a phantom and glancing back to beckon about once a minute. Not caring to miss the play, we followed in Indian file, I bringing up the rear.

The whole tribe rose at once and flitted along beside us on our landward side. We could not hear a footfall, or a breath. They passed through dry grass without rustling, neither stumbling nor crowding one another, but all so governed by one all-absorbing thought that they acted in absolute unison. That the thought was food did not, even in their starving state, make them forget the crowning need for silence. We with our leather boots made more noise than all they together.

We passed along the lake shore for half a mile, until suddenly the chief, looking tall as a stripped tree in the pale uncertain light, threw up an arm and waved it in a circle. Instantly the whole tribe vanished. It was as if a puff of wind had blown them; or as if they had been figures thrown on a screen by a magic lantern and suddenly switched off at the performer's whim. Then the chief continued forward, we marching more carefully.

Now he turned to the half-right and followed a narrow track across a neck of land that jutted out into the lake. We approached a low rise, and as he drew near the top of that he went down on hands and knees, crawling up the last few yards so cautiously that I had to stare hard to be sure he was there at all.

As soon as Fred came near he made frantic signals to him to get down and crawl too; so we all knelt down and crawled behind Fred, striving to make no noise and filling the unhappy chief so full of fury at the noise we did make that he writhed in nervous torment.

On top of the rise Fred stopped and in imitation of the chief thrust his head forward very gradually. One by one we followed suit until, lying prone in line along the ridge within thirty paces of the water, we saw at last what we were after.

Bathed in the moonlight, head and shoulders

clear of the mirror-like water, a great bull hippopotamus surveyed the scenery, drinking in contentment through his little placid eyes. Out there nothing troubled him, as for instance the mosquitoes troubled us. He had eaten his fill, for some sort of green stuff hung from his jaws; and he was beginning to feel sleepy, for be opened his enormous mouth and yawned straight toward us—three tons of meat on the hoof, less than a hundred yards away, stock-still, and unsuspicious!

The chief began whispering unintelligible warnings in a voice so low that it sounded like the drone of insects. Fred thrust the rifle forward inch by inch and, taking his time about it, settled himself comfortably for the shot. It was no easy shot in that uncertain light at a downward angle. The glare of the sun on the lake had troubled his eyes during the last few days. The shimmer of the moonlight was deceptive now. I wished he would pass the rifle to Will, or even to Brown of Lumbwa, who was digging his fingers into the earth beside me in almost uncontrollable excitement. But Fred was unperturbed, and the chief, who was nervous enough to detect the slightest sign of nervousness in Fred, did not seem to mistrust him for one second.

Three times I saw Fred breathe deeply, as if about to squeeze the trigger, but each time he was only *"makkin' sikkar,"* and eased his lungs again. The target a hippo offers to a Mauser rifle bullet is not much more than half the size of a man's hand, including only the ear and eye and the narrow space between them. By daylight at a hundred yards that is nothing for a cool shot to complain about, but in half-moonlight, at that angle, it is none too much. I swore silently, wishing again and again that Fred would pass the rifle to Will, or to Brown—or to me! Yet if he had passed it to me I should have trembled worse than any one.

Visions began to haunt me of what would happen if Fred should miss! What would the effect be on wild folk tortured by hunger and keyed to the pitch of frenzy by suspense? Then, even while we watched, another problem added itself. Over on the water there began to come a wind, driving ripples and little waves in front of it. The moment those came near the hippo be would vanish from view, for they only care for moonlight when they can see it mirrored on a perfectly still surface

I cursed Fred between set teeth, almost loud enough for him to hear me; for the hippo did move. His head was a foot nearer water-level; he had seen or heard something that alarmed him. He was in the act of sinking under water when Fred made sure of the sights at last and the rifle spoke, ringing out into the still night like the crack of Judgment Day, more startling because we had waited so long for it in such suspense.

Instantly the amazing happened. A yell burst out behind us that split the night apart. Where stilly blackness had been, now four or five hundred crazy shadows leaped and danced, murdering the silence with marrow-curdling noises intended to express joy.

Out on the water the stricken hippo pitched head downward and plunged like a mountain of meat gone mad, thrashing up great waves that were darkened with his life-blood. A whole herd, several hundred strong, emerged shoulder-high from the water to take one swift look at him and flee. The arriving wind overswept the little whirlpools they all made in the moonlight, as they dived to seek seclusion somewhere and no doubt to choose themselves a new bully after terrific fighting.

Our quarry plunged a last time, and stayed under. Now was new anxiety. In twenty minutes or half an hour he should rise to the surface again, but no man could guess where, and the wind and currents would very swiftly hide his great carcass somewhere amid the acres of papyrus unless sharp eyes were alert.

But the papyrus was friend as well as foe. In a space of time to be measured by seconds the yelling young men of the tribe had uncovered three canoes, hidden from marauding enemies among the more-than-man-high reeds, and the rest of the tribe—men, women and young ones—scattered along the shore to watch from between the stalks.

In less than fifteen minutes some one yelled, and even the very old men, who had stayed beside us to gape at Fred's rifle and our clothes and boots, began running like hares toward the sound. In twenty minutes after that, with the aid of grass ropes and leather thongs, they had hauled the huge carcass to the shore and rolled it out of the water, where it lay glistening in moonlight, stumpy, foolish, legs uppermost.

The butcher's work—the feast—did not begin yet. There was time-honored custom to obey, which Kazimoto knew all about even if those ignorant *wachenzie* would have fallen to without ceremony. He drove them off. A white man had slain that animal; therefore the white man's choice of meat was first, and he very leisurely and skillfully cut out the enormous tongue for us and fifty pounds of meat for our following before he would let them as much as touch the carcass with a dagger.

Then, though, the tribe fell to, naked, with little naked knives—tearing off the thick hide in foot-wide strips, and hacking the red flesh into lumps that they ate, raw and quivering, while they worked. The little bits of children, each chewing raw bloody meat, brought baskets for the overflow, dragging them to wherever they could find a space between the legs of struggling men, the women emptying the baskets almost as fast as the children filled them, and chewing until their jaws ran blood.

Nothing was wasted. The blood was caught in pools in part of the hide, spread like an apron on the earth, and lapped up by whoever could get to it. The very guts were gathered up in baskets to be cooked. And where the last little soft iron dagger had done its work, the blood had been drunk, and the last scrap of hide bad been cut into strips, to be chewed when the meat and its memory were things of the past, the enormous ribs lay glistening in the moonlight like those of an abandoned wreck, picked as clean as if the kites had done it.

"Have we done a commendable thing?" laughed Fred, looking at the crowd's distended paunches. "There's a good bull hippo the less. We've saved the lives for a time of several hundred gluttons. They know neither grace nor gratitude."

But he was wrong. They did. They brought Fred a woman—their fattest, ugliest; which means she was skin and bone and uglier than Want, also she was more afraid of Fred than Satan is said to be of shriving. The chief led her by the hand, she hanging back and hiding her face under one arm (which left the rest of her nakedness unprotected). He seized Fred's hand and put the woman's in it.

"Now you're spliced!" Brown explained. "Married to the gal forever in presence of legal witnesses!"

Kazimoto confirmed the fearful news.

"Married in regular form an' accord with tribal custom!" Brown continued, nodding solemnly.

"Divorce me—soon and swiftly, somebody!" Fred demanded.

We appealed to Kazimoto for information, but only threw him into a quandary, and he proceeded to add to ours. The usual price for a woman, it seemed, was cows—many or few according as she was lovely or her father rich. In case of divorce, custom decreed that the cows with their offspring should be given back. The objection to any other property than cows changing hands to bind or loose in wedlock was that food, for instance, when eaten was not returnable.

"Married to the gal for good an' all!" Brown grinned, nudging Will and me to note Fred's consternation. "You'd better stay here an' take the chief's job when he kicks the bucket—possibly you can speed the day by overfeedin' him!"

"Some men's luck," Will murmured, but stopped in mid-sentence, for interruption came in the form of a weird figure, gesticulating like a windmill, stumbling and careening through the gloom, shouting as it came. Not until it was thirty yards away did an intelligible sound explain at least who the apparition was.

"Gassharamminy! Give me that gun!"

Coutlass burst in among us so out of breath that he could not force through his teeth another rational syllable, but he made his intentions partly clear by snatching at Fred's rifle, persisting until Will and I pulled him off.

"The dhow's gone!" he panted at last. "Give me that rifle, or come yourself! Hurry! There's a wind! You'll be too late!"

"You're dreaming or drunk!" Fred answered, but Coutlass refused to be disbelieved, and in another moment we were all running as fast as we dared through the darkness toward the camp-fires, where we had left the Goanese snoozing and the dhow snugly moored among the rocks.

The chief and his followers far outdistanced us in spite of their gorged condition—all except the woman, who jogged dutifully, although unhappily, behind Fred. When we reached the campfires they were standing gazing out on the lake, where we could just make out the bellying sail of the *Queen of Sheba* leaning like a phantom away from the gaining wind. The distance was not to be judged in that weak uncertain light. We all shouted together, but there came no answer and we could not tell whether the sound carried as far as the dhow or not.

"Gassharamminy!—why don't you shoot!" shouted Coutlass, dancing up and down the bank in frenzy. "Give me that rifle! I'll show you! I'll teach them!"

I believe I would have fired if the rifle had been in my hands. Brown, last to arrive and most out of breath, joined with Coutlass in angry shouts for vengeance. Will offered no argument against sending them a parting shot. Fred set the butt of the rifle down with a determined snort, walked over toward the fire, stirred the embers, threw on more fuel, and looked about him when the dry wood blazed.

"If she has left as much as one blanket among the lot of us, I don't see it anywhere!" he said, taking his seat on a rock.

"A blanket?" sneered Coutlass. "She has even your money! Worse than that—she has my woman! You were a gum-gasted galoot not to shoot at her!"

Fred patted the bulging pocket of his shooting jacket.

"Most of the money is here" he said quietly, and we all sighed with relief.

"Take canoes and chase them!" shouted Coutlass, beginning to dance up and down again.

"There's time enough" Fred answered. "We know the winds of these parts well enough by this time. This will blow until midnight. Then calm until dawn. After dawn a little more wind for an hour or two, then doldrums again until late afternoon. They'll run on a rock in all likelihood. If they do we can catch them at our leisure, supposing we can get these islanders to paddle. If it should blow hard, then we can't catch them anyhow. Sit down and tell us what happened, Coutlass!"

The Greek cursed and swore and pranced, but all in vain. Fred was inexorable. We others grew calmer when the problem of who should paddle the canoes solved itself suddenly with the arrival of fourteen of our own men. Discovering themselves left behind, they had run along the bank in vain hope of catching the dhow somehow—perchance of swimming through the crocodile-infested water, and returned now disconsolate, to leap and laugh with new hope at sight of us and of the red meat that Kazimoto had thrown on the ground near the fire. They came near in a cluster. Will hacked off a lump of meat for them, and they forthwith forgot their troubles, as instantly as the birds forget when a sparrow-hawk has done murder down a hedge-row and swooped away.

Not everything was gone after all. Kazimoto found the pots we had cooked the rice in, and started to boil the hippo's tongue for us.

"Come, Coutlass—sit down before we eat and tell us what happened," Fred suggested.

The Greek paced up and down another time or two, and at last calmed himself sufficiently to laugh at Fred's woman, who had squatted down patiently in the shadow behind him.

"Easy for you!" he grinned savagely, squatting on the far side of the fire. "You have a woman! Mine is God knows where! She said to me—that hell-damned Lady Saffren Waldon said to me—we sat all three together in the stern of the dhow, I with my arm around Rebecca, and she said to me—"

"I'll see if I can't make a dicker for the chief's canoes," Will interrupted. "We can hear the Greek's tale any old time."

"Trade my woman for them!" Fred suggested cheerfully. "Go on, Coutlass!"

The Greek gritted his teeth savagely. "She said—that hell-damned Lady Saffren Waldon said, as we sat there in the dhow, 'How about the kicking Fred Oakes gave you on the island, Mr. Coutlass? Where is your Greek honor?'—Do you see? She worked on my bodily bruises and my spiritual courage at the same time—the cunning hussy! 'That Fred Oakes will win this Rebecca away from you very soon!' she went on. 'I have watched him.' "

Fred smiled about as comfortably as a martyr on the grid. The presence of the dusky damsel, confirmed by her smell behind him, made him touchy on the subject of sex.

"Presently she said to me, 'I have my own affairs that will adjust themselves all the better for their absence when I get to British East. As for you, they will simply report you to the authorities for raiding those cattle of Brown's. Can you imagine that creature Brown forgiving you? He will have you thrown in jail! Why wait? But we must not leave the Goanese or the other porters, and we must hurry! You go,' she said, 'and send the Goanese and the rest of the porters on board!'

"So I did go. I kicked de Sousa awake, and he cursed me, because my toe landed once or twice on his thigh where the bullet wounded him. I drove him on board, and she put him to work with Kamarajes getting up the sail. Then I went off to get those cursed porters. I could not find them! The dogs had gone to the village, to find women

I don't doubt! I tell you what I would do to them if they were mine!"

"Never mind that!" Fred cut in. We could all guess what form the punishment would take. "Get on with the tale! You couldn't find the porters. What next?"

"I decided to leave the dogs behind, and serve them right! I went back to the dhow in a great hurry. She was gone! Vanished! Disappeared as if the lake had opened up and swallowed her! I could just see the sail in the distance. I shouted! No answer! I shouted again. I heard Rebecca call to me! Then I heard laughter—Lady Isobel Saffren Waldon's laughter! Gassharamminy! I will run red-hot skewers into that woman when I catch her! Do you see how she has vengeance on Rebecca? Do you see now why she took sides between me and Kamarajes and de Sousa? Do you see how she has plotted? What will she do now? What Will she do?"

He began to pace up and down again furiously, shaking both fists at the unresponsive stars.

"She will do Rebecca an injury! She will give that girl to de Sousa or to that old Kamarajes! We shall never catch them! Gassharamminy! Oh, Absalom! You should have fired when I told you! That she-dog has a trick of some kind up her sleeve yet! How shall we catch her? Why do we wait? Give me that rifle! I will take a canoe and go after them alone! You do not know what Greek spirit is! I am American sometimes—English when it suits me—always Greek when I am wronged!"

"You certainly have been put upon" Fred answered. "Tell us how your Greek spirit justified deserting us."

"Why not?" snarled Coutlass. "Do you love me? What would you do to me if you could get me to British East in your power? You would hand me over as a cattle thief!"

"You bet I will!" admitted Brown of Lumbwa. "You dog, you've ruined me!"

"What did I tell you?" demanded Coutlass. "Why, then, should I not look out for myself?"

"I think we'd better leave you on this island," Fred told him quietly. "We can't trust you out of sight. The only way to prevent you from stealing this rifle and murdering us all would be to lie awake in turns."

"Bah!" grinned the Greek, striding back toward the fire. "How many cartridges have you left? Five, eh? After I had murdered all of you, how many would remain?"

"You'll have to think of a better argument than that," smiled Fred, and for the first time I suspected he was speaking in deadly earnest. Coutlass suspected it, too, and grew still. The sweat burst out on his face, and his eyes bulged from their sockets.

"You will leave me here?" he stammered.

Fred nodded, smiling up at him.

"You see, you're such on all-in scoundrel!" Brown assured him.

"You! You poor drunkard!" Coutlass turned his back on Brown, and faced Fred squarely. "You are a man, Mr. Oakes! I can speak to you as to my brother."

Fred smiled blandly.

"I will speak to you God's truth!"

Fred grinned.

"I will tell you where the ivory is!"

Fred threw his head back and laughed outright.

"I speak to you on my honor! That mother of misery, Lady Saffren Waldon, stole a map from Schillingschen. Before I would agree to set the town on fire I made her give me that for a hostage, lest she should prove treacherous and leave me behind after all! I have it now! It is marked with a circle to show where Schillingschen believes the stuff must be, because he has searched everywhere else!"

"If that map is worth anything," Fred countered, "how did Lady Saffren Waldon care to leave you behind with it?"

"The harridan forgot it!" answered Coutlass. "She was so delighted to get vengeance on Rebecca by taking her away from me that she did not care for anything else! She hates you! She hates me! She hates Rebecca! Those who hate—as I can hate!—would rather have revenge than all the riches of Africa! Do you think I would hesitate between money and revenge on her?"

"All right," Fred answered. "The map, then—what about it?"

"Take me with you and the map is yours!"

"Show it to me, then!"

"I must have a share of the ivory!"

"Show me the map first!"

Coutlass searched inside his flannel shirt—swiftly—more swiftly—angrily. His jaw dropped. Even between the fire-light and the moonlight one could judge that his color changed—and changed again.

"Show me the map before we bargain!" Fred insisted. "Hurry, man! There's Mr. Yerkes with the canoe. We can't wait here all night!"

"It is gone!" admitted Coutlass. "Some one stole it!"

"I could have told you that in the first place," Fred informed him, rising to his feet. "I have the map in my pocket."

"You stole it?" Coutlass gasped.

"Certainly not. Rebecca stole it while she was supposed to be sleeping in your arms!"

"Gassharamminy! I might have known it! Those Syrians—she meant to give us all the slip and find the ivory herself!"

"Nothing of the Sort!" said Fred. "She stole it from you, to give it to Lady Saffren Waldon! Kazimoto saw her do it—saw where Lady Waldon hid it—and stole it from her while she slept to give to me, believing it to be something of mine. Here it is!"

Fred let the end of a folded map protrude from his inner pocket just far enough for Coutlass to recognize it by the fire-light. The Greek turned on his heel.

"All right!" he said ruefully, swinging suddenly round again. "If you were alone I would fight you, my knife against your rifle! I can not fight all four of you! Go away then, and be damned! I have nothing to offer. There is nothing I can do. Leave me, and I will look after myself!"

"Now you're talking like a man," said Fred.

"Leave me that woman of yours, and go to hell, all of you!" laughed the Greek.

Fred seemed suddenly possessed of a bright idea. He turned to the woman and beckoned her to rise. Then in unmistakable pantomime he went through the motions of presenting her to Coutlass. The woman gasped—stammered something that was positively not consent—stared with frightened eyes at Coutlass—shook her shaven head violently—and ran away into the darkness, pursued by roars of laughter that speeded her on her way.

"A clear case of desertion!" announced Fred judicially. "You men are witnesses!" Then he turned once more to Coutlass. "I don't think we'll leave you to raise Cain on this island. It depends on you whether we find you a lonelier island—turn you loose or hand you over to the authorities in British East!"

"Good!" Coutlass shouted. "By Jingo, you are a gentleman! You are the best man in the world! I will treat you as my brother!"

"Thanks!" said Fred dryly.

"Aren't you men ever coming?" asked Will, striding out of the shadows. "I've made the dicker—found a man who'd been on the mainland and knows Swahili. The chief's agreeable to loan us two canoes in place of deeding you the woman. I took your name in vain, Fred, and consented to that while your back was turned—kick all you like—the deed is done! Four of his savages come with us as far as we want to go, we feeding 'em meat and paying 'em money. It's agreed they're to eat just as often as we do. They paddle the canoes back home when we're through with them. Are you all ready? Then all aboard! Let's hurry!"

"MANY THAT ARE FIRST SHALL BE LAST; AND THE LAST FIRST"

When the last of the luck has deserted and the
least of the chances has waned,
When there's nowhere to run to and even the
pluck in the smile that you carry is feigned;
When grimmer than yesterday's horror to-mor-
row dawns hungry and cold,
And your faith in the coming unknown is denied
in regret for the known and the old,
Then you're facing, my son, what the Fathers
from Abraham down to to-day
Have looked on alone, and stood up to alone,
and each in his several way
O'ercame (or he shouldn't be Father). So ye
shall o'ercome: while ye live,
Though ye've nothing but breath and good-will to
your name ye must stand to it naked, and give!

Ye shall learn in that hour that the plunder ye
won by profession is naught—
And false was the aim ye aspired with—and
dross was the glamour ye sought—
The codes and the creeds that ye cherished were
shadows of clouds in the wind,
(And ye can not recall for their counsel lost
leaders ye dallied behind!)
Ye shall stand in that hour and discover by
agony's guttering flame
How the fruits of self-will, and the lees of
ambition and bitterness all are the same,
Until, stripped of desire, ye shall know that was
death. Then the proof that ye live

Shall be knowledge new-born that the naked—
the fools and the felons, can give!

Then the suns and the stars in their courses
shall speedily swing to your aid,
And nothing shall hinder you further, and
nothing shall make you afraid,
For the veriest edges of evil shall challenge your
joy, and no more,
And room for the right shall shine clear in your
vision where wrong was before.
Then the stones in the road shall be restful that
used to be traps for your feet,
Then the crowd shall be kind that was cruel
before, and your solitude sweet
That was want to be gloomy aforetime and
gray—when the proof that ye live
Is no longer the pain of desire, but the will—and
the wit—and the vision, to give!

XII

THE CANOES were the usual crazy affairs, longer and rather wider than the average. The bottom portion of each was made from a tree-trunk, hollowed out by burning, and chipped very roughly into shape. The sides were laboriously hewn planks, stitched into place with thread made from papyrus.

Some of the men left behind were our personal servants. Counting them and Kazimoto, there were twenty natives remaining with us, making, with the four men lent us by the chief, an allowance of twelve to each canoe. If we had had loads as well it would have been a problem how to get the whole party away; but as Lady Saffren Waldon had left us nothing but three cooking-pots, we just contrived to crowd the last man in without passing the danger point, Fred taking charge of the first canoe with Brown of Lumbwa and Kazimoto, and leaving Coutlass with the other canoe to Will and me. We agreed it was most convenient to keep the Greek and the rifle separated by a stretch of water.

There is one inevitable, invariable way of starting on a journey by canoe in Africa. Somebody pushes off. The naked paddlers, seated at intervals down either side, strain their toes against a thwart or a rib. The leading paddler yells, and off you go with a swing and a rhythmic thunder as they all bring their paddles hard against the boat's side at the end of each stroke. Fifty—sixty—seventy—perhaps a hundred strokes they take at top speed, and the passenger settles down to enjoy himself, for there is no more captivating motion in the world. Then suddenly they stop, and all begin arguing at top of their lungs. Unless the passenger is a man of swift decision and firm purpose there is frequently a fight at that stage, likely to end in overturned canoes and an adventure among the crocodiles.

Our voyage broke no precedents. We started off in fine style, feeling like old-time emperors traveling in state; and within ten minutes we were using paddles ourselves to poke and beat our men into understanding of the laws of balance, they abusing one another while the canoes rocked and took in water through the loosely laid on planks.

The fiber stitching began to give out very soon after that, because when not in use the canoes were always hauled out somewhere and the dried-out fiber cracked and broke. We had all to sit to one side while some one re-stitched the planking. Later, when a wind came up and the quick short sea arose peculiar to lakes, we were very glad we had done that job so early.

It was only the first mile that as much as suggested enjoyment. Never accustomed to much paddling in any case, our own men had suffered from hunger and confinement in the reeking hot dhow. Then, hippo meat needs hours of cooking to be wholesome (our own share of it was still in the pot, waiting to be boiled more thoroughly at the next halting place). They had merely toasted their tough lumps in the camp-fire embers and gobbled it. The result was a craving for sleep, noisily seconded by the chief's four men, who had eaten the stuff without cooking at all, and in enormous quantities.

We began with a keen determination to overhaul the dhow, that dwindled as we had time to think the matter over; wondering what we should do with two such women in case we should capture them, and how we should prevent Coutlass in that case from acting like a savage.

"Why don't we leave 'em to make their own explanations?" I proposed at last. "We can claim our few belongings at any time if we see fit." But the suggestion took time to recommend itself.

That night until nearly morning we fretted at every rest the paddlers took—drove them unmercifully—ran risks of overturning on the slippery shoulders of partly submerged rocks—took long turns ourselves to relieve the weary men, Coutlass working harder than the rest of us. It would have been a bad night's work if we had overhauled the dhow and loosed him to do his will.

"Think of the baggage!" he kept shouting to the night at large. "Lying in the arms of Georges Coutlass, kissing and being kissed, simply to rob him—Coutlass—me! Think of it! Only think of it. She lay in the hook of my right arm and only thought of how to win back the favor of the other she-hellion! And I was deceived by such a cabbage! Wait though! Nobody ever turned a trick on Georges Coutlass more than once! Wait till we catch them! See what I do to them! I don't forget Kamarajes either, or that bastard de Sousa, also pretending they were friends of mine! Heiah! Hurry! Drive the paddles in, you lazy black men!"

It was more his hunger for revenge than any other one thing that tipped the scales of indecision and called us off the chase. A little before morning, at about that darkest hour, when the stars have seen the coming sun but the world is not yet aware of it, Fred called to us to turn in toward a barren-looking hill of granite that rose almost sheer out of the water but at one corner offered a shelving landing place. There we all clambered out to stretch cramped muscles and make a fire to cook the hippo's tongue, Coutlass cursing us for letting what he called idleness come between us and revenge.

Kazimoto had scarcely more than gathered an armful of wood, thrown it down, and gone to hunt for more; one of the other boys had struck a match, and the first little flicker of crimson fire and purple smoke was starting to curl skyward, when Fred jumped on it and stamped it out.

"Silence!" he ordered. "Keep still every one!" and repeated it twice in Kiswahili for the natives' benefit.

We could not see at first which way he was staring through the darkness. It was more than two minutes before I knew what had alarmed him, and then it was sound, not sight that gave me the first clue. There came a purring from the lake; and when I had searched for a minute for the source of it I saw the glow we had watched from the dhow in the storm the first night out—the telltale crimson stain on the dark that rides above a steamer's funnel, and at intervals a stream of sparks to prove they were burning wood and driving her at top speed.

"It can't be the German launch," said I.

"Why not?" demanded Fred irritably. He knew I knew it was the German launch as certainly as he did.

"How can they have patched her boiler?" I asked.

"How many beans make five? They've done it, and there she goes! No other launch on the lake can make that speed! I've heard the British railway people have a launch or two, but they're small enough to have traveled down the line on ordinary trucks. That's the German launch and Schillingschen as surely as we stand here!"

We waited there until dawn, arguing at intervals, not daring to light a fire, nor caring to sleep, Coutlass sitting apart and laughing every now and then like a hyena.

"If the men weren't so dead beat I'd be for carrying on, said Fred.

"What's the use?" argued Brown. "We can't catch the bally launch, can we? Soon as it's daylight they'd see us, like as not. I hope to get drunk once more before I die! Schillingschen 'ud run us down, an' good-bye us!"

"I'd say follow them if the men could make it," Will agreed. "But what's the odds? It's us they're after. They'll dare do nothing to the women on the dhow—in British waters."

"That's so," I agreed, not believing a word of it, any more than they. One had to calm one's feelings somehow; the men were too weary to drive the canoes another mile at anything like speed. Coutlass, who had heard every word of the argument, burst out into such yells of laughter that Fred threw a rock at him. "Curse you, you ghoul!"

Coutlass changed his tone from demoniacal delight to quieter, grim amusement.

"They will do nothing, eh? It is I, Georges Coutlass, who need do nothing! I have my revenge by proxy! Wait and see!"

Fred threw a second rock, and hit him squarely.

"Gassharamminy!" swore the Greek. "Do you know that rock is harder than a man's head?"

Fred let the boys light a fire when the sun had risen high enough to make the little blaze not noticeable. Most of the men were asleep, but though our eyes ached with the long vigil we could not have copied them. About three hours after daylight we breakfasted off slices of hot boiled hippo tongue and cold lake water, without salt or condiments of any kind, and with discontent increased by that unpleasing feast we aroused the boys and drove them into the canoes.

We forced the pace again, and picked up smoke on the sky-line an hour before noon, but it was not from a steamer's funnel. It was lazy, flat-flowing, spreading smoke with a look of iniquity about it that sent our hearts to our mouths. We paddled toward it with frenzied energy, and long before any of us could make out details Coutlass, standing balancing himself amidships, told us what we knew was true and flatly refused to believe.

"It's the *Queen of Sheba* burning to the water-line!"

"Sit down, you fool, or you'll upset us!"

"She's gutted already—the flame is about finished! nothing now but smoke!"

"Sit down, you lying idiot, and hold your tongue!"

"I can see the smoke of the German launch now! Don't you all see it? Straight ahead beyond the smoke of the dhow! They've burned the dhow and steamed away! I'll bet you a million pounds they've killed everybody—shot 'em, or burned 'em alive, or drowned 'em!"

"Did you hear me tell you to sit down? I'll tip you overboard and make you swim for shore—d'ye see those crocodiles? Ugh! Look at the brutes! In you go among the crocks if you don't sit down at once!"

Coutlass took no notice of the threat, but rocked the canoe recklessly as he stood on tiptoe.

"Think of their gall! By Bacchus, they're steaming for British East! I bet you five million pounds to a kick they think they've drowned the lot of us! They're going to steam in and report the accident!"

We got him to sit down at last by ordering the paddlers nearest him to throw him overboard, but nothing would stop his evil croaking any more than flat refusal to admit the truth of what he gloated over lessened our real conviction.

Long before we reached the dhow there was no room left for unbelief. The stern planks were charred, but stood erect, unburned yet, and the blue and white paint smeared on them was surely that of the *Queen of Sheba*. When we came within fifty yards the water was full of loathsome reptiles; our paddles actually struck them as they swarmed after the prey, snapping at one another and at our canoes—long, slimy-looking monsters, as able to smell carrion in the distance as kites are to see.

There were garments on the water—blankets—and one soaked, torn, lacy thing that certainly had been a woman's. More than a dozen crocodiles fought around that. We tried to go close enough to see whether there were dead bodies in the dhow's charred hull, but as if the very ripple from our paddles were the last straw, the wreck dipped suddenly ten feet from us and plunged, the crocodiles following it down into deep water with lashing tails—swifter than fish.

We paddled about for an hour in the blistering sun, searching stupidly for what we knew we could never find; crocodiles remove traces of identity more swiftly than kites and crows.

"I'll bet you they thought we were on board!" gleed Coutlass. "I'll bet you they opened fire, and when we didn't answer came to the conclusion we had no ammunition. Then they steamed close enough to throw kerosene on board and light it! I bet you they steamed round and round and watched the people jump as the flames drove them overboard! Or d'you think they shot them all, and then threw them overboard and fired the dhow? No—then they'd have known we weren't on the dhow; they'd have steamed back then to find us; they thought we were in the dhow!" They thought we were hiding below deck! They're going to British East to take their Bible oaths they saw us burn and drown! Isn't that a joke! Isn't that a good one! Gassharamminy! But I'd give my hope of heaven to know whether they shot the women first or watched them jump among the crocodiles when the heat grew fierce!"

We paddled to another rocky island—one that had trees on it, and rested through the heat of the day when we had killed all the snakes that had forestalled us in the shade. There, after again eating hippo-tongue unseasoned and ungarnished, we held a council of war, and Fred produced the map that Rebecca stole from Coutlass.

"If we make for a township now—Kisumu is the nearest—about five and twenty miles away," said Fred, "we can give ourselves the pleasure of surprising Schillingschen, and of course we can get a square meal and some clothes and soap and so on—incidentally perhaps some rifles and ammunition. But we can't prove a thing against Schillingschen, and he has enough pull with British officials to make things deuced unpleasant for us, for a time at least. Consider the other side of it. Suppose we don't make for a station.

Schillingschen reports us dead. Nobody looks for us—unless perhaps out on the lake for a hat or some scrap of clothing by way of corroborative evidence. Suppose we paddle out of this gulf and take to shore somewhere along the north end of the lake. We've no food, no tents, only one gun, next to no ammunition, nothing but money and a purpose. We don't know what chance we have of getting supplies, and particularly rifles, without letting any one know where we are, but we do know we've a clear field and a straight mark for Elgon, where rumor says—and Courtney said—and Schillingschen thinks—and this map says the ivory ought to be! The odds are against us—climate—starvation—wild beasts—savages—last and not least, the government, if they ever get wind of our being beyond bounds. Are we willing to take the chance, or are we not?"

We talked it over for an hour, Coutlass listening all ears to most of what we said, although we drove him to the farthest limit of the shade trees. We were in two minds whether or not it mattered if he listened, and made the usual two-minds hash of it. Finally we put it to a vote, letting Brown have a voice with the rest of us. He was in favor of anything that offered prospect of a gamble; and we remembered the letter in code we had given the missionary to mail to Monty. We had told him in that that we should make tracks for Elgon, and we all voted the same way.

"In other words" grinned Fred, "we're perfect idiots, and ready and willing to prove it! Good! If you fellows had voted the other way I'd have gone forward to Elgon alone!"

It was then that Georges Coutlass took a hand in the game again. He came striding through the trees with something of his old swagger, and sat down among us with an air.

"Count me in!" he demanded.

"D'you mean in the lake?" suggested Fred.

"In on the trip to Mount Elgon!"

"We've had nearly enough of you!" Fred answered. "I know what's coming! If you don't come with us you'll tell tales? Blackmail, eh? Well, it won't work! We'll set you ashore on the mainland, and if you dare show yourself to Schillingschen or any British official, we'll run that risk cheerfully!"

But Coutlass was imperturbable for once. He laid a hand on Fred's knee, and changed his tone to one of gentle persuasion between friend and friend.

"Ah! Mr. Oakes, I know you now too well! You are not the man to leave me in the lurch! These others perhaps! You never! You know me, too. You have seen me under all conditions. You are able to judge my character. You know how firm a friend I can be, as well as how savage an enemy! You know I would never be false to a friend such as you—to a man whom I admire as I do you!"

Will Yerkes, who had tried to keep a straight face, now went off into peals of laughter, rolling over on his back and rocking his legs in the air—a performance that did not appear to discourage Coutlass in the least. Brown was far from amused. He advised throwing the Greek into the lake.

"Remember those cattle o' mine!" he insisted.

"Yes!" agreed Coutlass. "Remember those cattle! Consider what a man of quick decision and courage I am! How useful I can be! What a forager! What a guide! What a fighting man! What a hunter! What a liar on behalf of my friends! What a danger for my friends' enemies! What are the cattle of a drunkard like Brown—the poor unhappy sot!—compared to the momentary needs of a gentleman! Ah! By the ordeal! I am a gentleman, and that is the secret of it all! You, Mr. Oakes, as one brave gentleman, can not despise the right hand of friendship of Georges Coutlass, another gentleman! I know you can not! You haven't it in you! You were born under another star than that! I have confidence! I sit contented!"

"You good-for-nothing villain!" Fred grinned. "I'll take you at your word!" and Brown of Lumbwa gasped, the very hairs of his red beard bristling.

"I knew you would!" said Coutlass calmly. "These others are not gentlemen. They do not understand."

"If your word is good for anything," Fred continued.

"My word is my bond!" said the Greek.

"And you really want to prove yourself my friend—"

"I would go to hell for you and bring you back the devil's favorite wife!"

"I will set you on the mainland, to go and recover those cattle of Mr. Brown's from the Masai who raided them! Return them to Lumbwa, and I'll guarantee Brown shall shake hands with you!"

"Pah! Brown! That drunkard!"

"See here!" said Brown, getting up and peeling off his coat. "I've had enough of being called drunkard by you. Put up your dukes!"

But a fight between Brown and the Greek with bare fists would have been little short of murder. Brown was in no condition to thrash that wiry customer, and we in no mood to see Coutlass get the better of him.

"Don't be a fool, Brown! Sit down!" ordered Fred, and having saved his face Brown condescended readily enough.

"What you said's right," he admitted. "Let him get my cattle back afore he's fit to fight a gentleman!"

And so the matter was left for the present, with Georges Coutlass under sentence of abandonment to his own devices as soon as we could do that without entailing his starvation. We had no right to have pity for the rascal; he had no claim whatever on our generosity; yet I think even Brown would not have consented to deserting him on any of those barren islands, whatever the risk of his spoiling our plans as soon as we should let him out of sight.

From then until we beached the canoes at last in a gap in the papyrus on the lake's northern shore, we pressed forward like hunted men. For one thing, the very thought of boiled meat without bread, salt, or vegetables grew detestable even to the natives after the second or third meal, although hippo tongue is good food. We tried green stuff gathered on the islands, but it proved either bitter or else nauseating, and although our boys gathered bark and roots that they said were fit for food, it was noticeable that they did not eat much of it themselves. The simplest course was to race for the shore with as little rest and as little sleep as the men could do with.

However, we were not noticeably better off when we first set foot on shore. There was nothing but short grass growing on the thin soil that only partly hid the volcanic rock and manganese iron ore. Victoria Nyanza is the crater of a once enormous, long ago extinct volcano, and we stood on a shelf of rock about a thousand feet below what had been the upper rim—a chain of mountains leading away toward the north higher and higher, until they culminated in Mount Elgon, another extinct volcano fourteen thousand feet above sea level.

It was not unexplored land where we stood, but it was so little known that the existence of white men was said to be a matter of some doubt among natives a mile or two to either side of the old *safari* route that passed from east to west. We could see no villages, although we marched for hours, the loaned canoe-men tagging along behind us, hungrier than we, until at last over the back of a long low spur we spied the tops of growing kaffir corn.

At sight of that we broke into a run and burst on the field of grain like a pack of the dog-baboons that swoop from the hills and make havoc. We seized the heads of grain, rubbed them between our hands, and had munched our fill before we were seen by the jealous owners. A small boy herding hump-backed cattle down in the valley watched us for a minute, and then deserted his charge to report to the village hidden behind a clump of trees. Ten minutes after that we were surrounded by naked black giants, all armed with spears and a personal smell that outstank one's notions of Gehenna.

We had nothing to offer them, except money, for which they obviously had not the slightest use. None of us knew their language. From their point of view we were thieves taken in the act, all but one of us unarmed as far as they knew, to be judged by the tribal standard that for more centuries than men remember has decreed that the thief shall die. They were most incensed at the four unhappy islanders, probably on the same principle that dogs pick on the weakest, and fight most readily with dogs of a more or less similar breed.

It was Coutlass who saved that situation. He instantly went crazy, or the next thing to it, wrinkling up his black-whiskered face into a caricature, yelling a Greek monologue in a refrain consisting of five notes repeated over and over, and dancing around in a wide ring with one leg shorter than the other and his arms executing symbols of witchcraft.

The chief was the biggest man—not an inch less than seven feet—black as ebony, from the curly hair, into which his patient wives had plaited fiber to hang in a greasy lump over his neck, all down his naked body to the soles of his enormous feet. Each time he came in front of that individual Coutlass paused and executed special finger movements, like the trills of a super-pianist, ending invariably in a punctuation point that made the savage shiver.

The fifth time round, to avoid the accusing fingers, the giant dodged behind a smaller man, who dodged behind a woman, who promptly turned and ran, swinging in the wind behind her a bustle like a horse's tail that was her only garment. Her flight was the touch that settled the decision in our favor. We all began to do a mumbo-jumbo dance around Coutlass, and in five seconds more the whole armed party was in full retreat, holding their spears behind them as some sort of protection against magic.

"After that," said Coutlass proudly, "will you still dismiss me from your party, gentlemen?"

"You've got to go and find Brown's cattle and return them to him!" Fred answered firmly. But we none of us felt like sending him packing until he was better fed and some provision could be made for his safety on the road. It was wonderful, the number of excuses that flocked through my mind for befriending the ruffian, and later on I found it was the same with Fred and Will. Brown, on the other hand, affected indignation at his being allowed to go with us another yard.

"Make a rope o' grass an' hang the swine!" he grumbled.

We decided to march on the village, retreat being obviously far too dangerous, and the only likely safe course being to follow up the chance success. Sleep another night in the open among the mosquitoes and wild beasts, besides making us wretched at the mere suggestion, was likely to bring us all down with fever. We preferred the thought of fever to the loneliness; for man is unlike all other nomads, and that is why the dog takes kindly to him; he must have a home of his own—a portable one, if you will—a tub like Diogenes—a Bedouin's tent—a cave, or a hole in the ground—something, so be he may rent it or own it or know for a fact he may sleep there when night comes. Life in the open is only good fun when there is cover to take to at will.

All the way along the winding foot-track leading in every imaginable direction except toward the village, and only turning suddenly toward it when we had grown disgusted and decided to leave it and try to find another, Brown kept pointing out trees with suitable overhanging arms to which we might hang Coutlass. The Greek, with eyes for nothing but the fat, hump-backed village cattle in the distance, seemed to think only of them, until Will commented on the fact, and Fred saw fit to drop a hint.

"Steal as much as a young calf, Coutlass, and we'll let Brown choose the tree! Try it on if you don't believe me!"

The villagers closed their gate against us by dragging great piles of thorn across the gap in the rough palisade, but, as Coutlass pointed out, they would have to open it up again to let the cattle in before dark, so we sat down and ate the remaining fragments of the hippo tongue—no ambrosia by that time; it had to be eaten, to save it from utter waste!

Then Coutlass once more did a first-class devil dance backward and forward this time before the gate, putting genius into it and fear into the hearts of the defenders. Kazimoto helped even more than he by discovering a native within the palisade who could speak a common tongue.

Their villagers held a very noisy council on their side of the thorn obstruction, under the apparent impression that it was sound- and bullet-proof. It was beginning to be pretty obvious that a man who advised volleying through the crevices with spears was winning the argument when Kazimoto detected familiar accents and raised his voice. After that the barricade was dragged aside within ten minutes and we entered, if not in honor, at least in temporary safety.

Luxury is a question of contrast. That evening in a hut assigned to us by the chief, squatting on the trodden cow-dung floor, leaning against the dried-mud sides, with a little fire of sticks in the midst to give us light and keep mosquitoes at a distance at the expense of almost unbearable heat, we ate porridge made from *mtama,* as they call their kaffir corn, and washed it down with milk—good rich cows' milk, milked by Kazimoto into our own metal pot instead of their unwashed gourds. Lucullus never dined better.

The feast was only rather spoiled by two things: we all had chiggers in our feet—the minute fleas that haunt the dust of native villages and insert themselves under toe-nails to grow great and lay their eggs. (Nearly every native in the village had more than one toe missing.) And the chief felt obliged to insert his smelly presence among us and ask innumerable idiotic questions through the medium of his interpreter and Kazimoto. He received some astonishing answers, but would not have been satisfied with anything more reasonable. We wanted him satisfied, and gave our interpreter free rein.

The main trouble was we had nothing of value to offer him. Money was something he had no knowledge of. He wanted beads of a certain size and color; for two handfuls of them he expressed himself willing to be our friend for life. We had to educate him about money, and Kazimoto assured him that the silver rupees Fred produced from a bag were so precious that governments went to war to get them away from other governments.

But the impression still prevailed that we were *wasikini*—poor men; and that is a fatal qualification in the savage mind.

"Why have you only one gun?"

In vain Kazimoto assured him that we had dozens of guns "at home"—that Fred's landed possessions were so vast that two hundred strong men walking for a month would be unable to march across them—that Fred's wives (Fred seemed to live under a cloud of sexual scandal in those days) were so many in number they had to be counted twice a day to make sure none was missing.

The chief had eighteen wives of his own to show. He could prove his matrimonial felicity. Why had Fred left his behind? How did he dare? Who looked after them? Had he left the guns behind to guard the women? Why did such a rich man travel without food for his men? The chief had seen us with his own eyes devour porridge as if we were starving.

To have told him the truth would have been worse than useless. To have mentioned such a thing as shipwreck would only have stirred the savage instinct to prey off all unfortunates. Failing evidence of wealth in our possession, the only feasible plan was to claim so much that he might believe some of it, and it was Coutlass, drawing a bow at a venture, who ordered Kazimoto to tell him that we expected a party in a few days bringing tents, provisions and more guns.

"There will be blue-and-white beads of the sort you long for among those loads," added Kazimoto on his own account; and that eased the chief's mind for the night. Fred gave him a half-rupee, and promised him to exchange it when the loads should come for as many of the beads as he could seize in his two fists. The chief went out to brag to the village, opening and closing his fists to see how huge their compass was; and later that night his wives had to be beaten for fighting. They were jealous because the fattest and the youngest new one had both been promised double shares.

There was another fight because our porters emerged from their hut and demanded that a barren cow out of the village herd be butchered. They made their meaning perfectly clear by taking the cow by the horns and tail and throwing her on her back. Fred decided that argument with a thick stick about four feet long.

The unusual spectacle of some one taking sides against his own men, whatever the rights or wrongs of it, so affected the chief that he entered our hut next morning disposed to hold us up for double promises of beads. It was evident we had to deal with a born extortioner. He would increase his demands with every fresh concession.

"Oh, what's the odds!" laughed Coutlass. "Promise him anything! The only loads likely to come along this way for a year or two are Schillingschen's!"

Fred told the chief he would think the matter over, and chased him out of the hut. Coutlass had given us all a new idea in an instant, and he was the only one who did not see its point—he, the only one who did not give a snap of the fingers for the laws of any land!

"D'you suppose—"

"Too good to hope for!"

"If he thinks we're dead—?"

"And if he believes in that map—"

"He'll not need the map. He'll have memorized it. There's only a circle drawn on it to mark the Elgon district. All the old pencil marks have been rubbed out as he searched the other likely places and drew them all blank."

"He'll travel without military escort?"

"Sure! He won't want witnesses! He'll make believe it's a scientific trip. Remember, he's a professor of ethnology. That's how he puts it all over the British and goes where he pleases without as much as by-your-leave."

"Say, fellows! It's a moral cinch that when we broke away from Muanza he made up his mind in a flash to return to British East and destroy us on the way. He thinks he made a clean job of that. I'll bet he loaded the launch down with stuff for a long *safari*, and thinks now he has a clear run and can take his time!"

"If that's how the cards lie, the game's ours!"

Coutlass saw the point at last and offered himself on the altar of forgiveness and friendship.

"Make me your partner, gentlemen, and if he travels within a hundred miles of this I will crawl into that Schillingschen's tent in the night and slit his throat! I would murder him as willingly as I eat when I am hungry!"

"Your job has been assigned you!" answered

Fred. "When Mr. Brown's cattle are back in Lumbwa perhaps we'll give you something else to do!"

Nevertheless, Coutlass had outlined in a flash the limits of the plan. We would draw the line at murdering even Schillingschen, but must help ourselves to his outfit as our only chance of re-outfitting without betraying our presence in British East. But the plan was not without rat-holes in it that a fool could see.

"Schillingschen's boys will escape and run to the nearest British official with the story!"

"And the British official will be so full of the importance of Schillingschen and the need of protecting his beastly carcass—to say nothing of the everlasting disgrace of letting him be scoughed on British territory—and the official reprimand from home that's sure to follow—that he'll come hot-foot to investigate!"

"We'll have to provide against that," said Fred, and we all laughed, including Coutlass. Talk of provisions is easy when you have no means out of which to provide. It did not occur to include Coutlass in the calculations, or to dismiss him from them; but without exchanging any remarks on the subject it was clear enough to all of us that no such plan could hope to succeed with the Greek at large, at liberty to spoil it. We saw we should have to keep him in our party for the present.

"Don't forget," said Coutlass, more accustomed than we to seizing the strategic points of desperate situations, "that Schillingschen will have his own boys with him from German East."

"I didn't see any with him on the launch," I objected.

"He would never have come without them" Coutlass insisted. "He made them lie below the water-line out of reach of bullets at the only time when you might have seen them! He wouldn't trust himself to British porters. My word, no! That devil knows natives! He knows some of them might be British government spies! He'll have his own boys,—if they can't carry all his loads he'll buy donkeys at Mumias; there are always donkeys to be bought at that place, brought down from Turkana by the Arab ivory traders. Do donkeys talk?"

At any rate, we talked, and made no bones at all about including Georges Coutlass in the conversation. It was his suggestion that we should send natives to look out for Schillingschen, and Fred's amendment that reduced the messengers to one, and that one Kazimoto. Any of the others might decide to desert, once out of sight, and we could scarcely have blamed them, for their path had not lain among roses in our company.

Kazimoto had a million objections to offer against going alone on that errand, as, for instance, that the chigger fleas would invade our toe-nails disastrously without his cunning fingers to hunt them out again. He also prophesied that without him to interpret there would swiftly be trouble between us and the chief; but we saw the other side of that medal and rather looked forward to an interval when the chief should not be able to talk to us at all.

At last, on the second morning after our arrival at the village, Kazimoto wrapped an enormous mound of cold *mtama* pudding in a cloth and went his way, prophesying darkly of murder and sudden death lurking behind rocks and trees, as unwishful to be alone as a terrier without a master, but much too faithful to refuse duty.

The chief saw a side of the medal that we had not guessed existed. He came and sat beside us like an evil-smelling shadow, satisfied that now we could not dismiss him, he being under no obligation to understand gestures. Curiosity was the impelling motive, but he was not without suspicion. Fred said he reminded him of a Bloomsbury landlady whose lodgers had not paid their board and rooming in advance.

Will solved that problem by taking the rifle, and one cartridge that Fred doled out grudgingly, and after a long day's stalking among mosquitoes in the papyrus at the edge of the lake five miles away, at imminent risk of crocodiles and an even worse horror we had not yet suspected, shooting a hippopotamus. Forthwith the whole village, chief included, went to cut up and carry off the meat, and there followed revelry by night, the chiefs wives brewing beer from the *mtama,* and all getting drunk as well as gorged. Coutlass and Brown got more drunk than any one.

Will came back with flies on his coat—three large things like horse-flies, that crossed their wings in repose, resembling in all other respects the common tsetse fly. He said the reeds by the lake-side were full of them.

Remembering tales about sleeping sickness, and suspicion of conveying it said to rest on a tsetse fly that crossed its wings, I went out the following day and walked many miles east-ward, taking with me the only two sober villagers I could find. They came willingly enough for five miles, thinking, I suppose, that I intended to follow Will's example and kill some more meat (although, as I did not take the rifle with me, they were not guilty of much dead-weight reasoning).

At the bank of the fifth stream we came to they stopped, and refused to go another yard. Thinking they were merely lusting after the meat and beer in the village, I took a stick to drive them across the stream in front of me, but they dodged in terror and ran back home as if the devil had been after them.

I crossed the stream and continued forward alone about another mile toward a fairly large village visible between great blue boulders with cactus dotted all about. There was the usual herd of cattle grazing near at hand, but the place had an unaccountable forlorn look, and the small boy standing on an ant-hill to watch the cattle seemed too listless to be curious, and too indifferent to run away. The big brown tsetse flies, that crossed their wings when resting, were everywhere, making no noise at all, but announcing themselves every once in a while by a bite on the back of the hand that stung like a whip-lash. They seemed to have special liking for coat-sleeves, and a dozen of them were generally riding on each side of me. One could drive them off, but they came back at once, as horse-flies do when poked off with a whip.

When I drew near the village nobody came out to look at me, which was suspicious in itself. Nobody shouted. Nobody blocked the way, or dragged thorn-bushes across the gateway. There were black men and women there, sitting in the shadows of the eaves, who looked up and stared at me—men and women too intent on sitting still to care whether their skins were glossy—unoiled, unwashed, unfed, by the look of them—skeletons clothed in leather and dust, desiring death, but cruelly denied it.

One man, thin as a wisp of smoke, rushed at me from the shadow of a hut door and tried to bite my leg. The merest push sent him rolling over, and there he lay, too overcome by inertia to move another inch, his arm uplifted in the act of self-defense. Nobody else in the village stirred. There were more huts than people, more kites on the roofs than huts. Some of the littlest children played in the hut doors, but nearly all of them were listless like the grown folk. The only sign of normal activity was the big black earthen jars that witnessed that the women performed part at least of their daily round by bringing water from the lake.

I returned late that afternoon, walking, as it were, out of a belt of tsetse flies. On one side of a narrow stream they were thick together; to the west of it there were scarcely any, although the wind blew from east to west.

"There's no fear of news about us reaching any government official," I announced. "There's a curtain of death between us and the government that even suspicion couldn't penetrate!"

THE SLEEP THAT IS NO SLEEP

Ten were the plagues that Israel fled, and
leaving left no cure,
Whose progeny self-multiplied a million-
fold remain,
The cloak of each one ignorance, idolatry its
lure,
And death the goal till, clarion-called, lost
Israel come again.
Till then that loaded lash that bade the tale of
bricks increase
(Eye for an eye, and limb for limb!) shall
fail not though ye weep;
The conqueror's heel for Africa!—The fear that
shall not cease!—
Desire, distrust, the alien law!—The sleep
that is no sleep!

XIII

KAZIMOTO WAS gone five days, and then came preceded by proof of the news he brought. He came in the evening. In the morning, unaccountably from the northward, instead of from the westward where Uganda lay, avoiding the regular *safari* route and the belt of sleeping sickness villages, came a genial, sleek, shiny Baganda, arrayed in khaki coat, red fez, and bordered loin-cloth, gifted with tongues, and self-confident beyond belief.

He knew nothing of us at first, for we sat in our hut with a smudge going, nervous about flies, even Coutlass, reckless as a rule of anything he could not see, and perfectly indifferent to death for others, now fidgety and afraid to swagger forth.

One of our Nyamwezi porters suddenly made a great shout of *"Hodi!"* and came stooping through the low door, standing erect again inside to await our pleasure. We could hear others outside, listening under the eaves. When we had kept him waiting sufficiently long to prevent his getting too much notion of his own importance, Fred nodded to him to speak.

"Is it true, *bwana,*" he asked, "that the Germans will come soon and conquer this part of Africa?"

"Certainly not!" said Fred.

"There is one out here, a Baganda, who says they will surely come. He says the religion of Islam will be preached from end to end of everywhere, and that the Germans are the true priests of Islam. They will come, says he, when the time is ripe, and call on all the converts of Islam to rise and slay all other people, including all white folk, like the English, who do not accept that creed. If that is true, *bwana,* whither shall we go, and whither shall you go, to escape such terrible things?"

"Does the Baganda know there are white men in this village?" Fred asked.

"Not yet, *bwana.*"

"Don't tell him, then, but bring him in here. Tell him there are folk in here who say he is a liar."

The Nyamwezi backed out, and we heard whispering outside. There is precious little performance in Africa without a deal of talk. At the end of about ten minutes the porter again shouted *"Hodi!"* and this time was followed in by the stranger, seven other of our own men, uninvited, bringing up the rear.

"Jambo!" said the Baganda, with a great effort at bravado, when his eyes had grown accustomed to the gloom and the first severe surprise of seeing white men had worn off. He was a very cool customer indeed.

"Whose pimp are you?" demanded Fred, without answering the salutation.

The man fell back on insolence at once. There is no native in Africa who takes more keenly to that weapon than the mission-schooled Baganda.

"I am employed by a gentleman of superior position," he answered in perfectly good English.

"In what capacity?" demanded Fred.

"I am not employed to tell his secrets to the first strangers who ask me!"

"Do you obey him implicitly?"

"I do. I am honorable person. I receive his pay and do his bidding."

"Is his name Schillingschen?"

The Baganda hesitated.

"All right," said Fred. "I know his name is Schillingschen. You have boasted that you do what he orders you. These men tell me you have said that the Germans are coming to conquer the country and destroy all people, including the English, who have not accepted Islam!"

The man hesitated again, glancing over his shoulder to discover his retreat cut off by our porters, and eying Fred with malignity that reminded one of a cornered beast of prey. He could control his face, but not his eyes.

"Oh, no, sir!" he answered after swallowing a time or two. "How could they tell such lies against me! I am a person born in Uganda, now a British protectorate and enjoying all blessings of British rule. I am educated at the mission college at Entebbe. How should I tell such a tale against my benefactors?"

"That is what you are here to explain!" Fred answered. "No! You can't escape, you hellion! Squat down and answer!"

"All this stuff is pretty familiar," Will interrupted. "In the States there are always people going the rounds among our darkies preaching some form of treason. Over there we can afford to treat it as a joke—now and then an ugly one, and on the darkies!"

"This is an ugly joke on a darkie, too!" grinned Fred.

The Baganda made a sudden dive and a determined struggle to get through the door, but our porters were too quick and strong for him.

"Confession is your one chance!" said Fred.

"Put hot irons to his feet!" advised Coutlass. (The native beer had left him villainously ill-tempered.) "Gassharamminy! Leave me alone with that fat Baganda for half an hour, and I will make him tell me what is on the far side of the moon, as well as what his mother said and did before she bore him!"

"Shall I hand you over to this Greek gentleman?" suggested Fred.

"Oh, my God, no!" the Baganda answered, trembling. "Hand me over to the *bwana* collector! He will put me in jail. I am not afraid of British jail!

It will not be for long! The English do not punish as the Germans do! You dare not assault me! You dare not torture me! You must hand me over to the *bwana* collector to be tried in court of law. Nothing else is permissible! I shall receive short sentence, that is all, with reprieve after two-thirds time on account of good conduct!"

"Make him prisoner in the sleeping sickness village you told us about!" advised Coutlass, lolling at ease on his elbow to watch the man's increasing fear.

"Oh, no, no! Oh, gentlemen! That is not how white Englishmen behave! You must either let me go, or—"

He made another terrific dive for liberty, biting and kicking at his captors, and finally lying on his back to scream as if the hot irons Coutlass had recommended were being applied in earnest.

"What shall we do with the beast?" asked Fred. The hut was so full of his infernal screaming that we could talk without his hearing us.

"Tie him up," I said. "If we let him go he'll run straight to Schillingschen."

"Leave him here with Coutlass and me!" urged Brown. (He and Coutlass had grown almost friendly since getting drunk together on the native beer.)

"I recommend," said Will, "that we take the law in our own hands—"

The Baganda ceased screaming and listened. For some reason he suspected Will of being the deciding factor in our councils—perhaps because Will had said least.

"—take the law in our own hands, and thrash him soundly. Later on we can report what we have done to the British government, and ask for condonation under the circumstances or pay whatever piffling fine they care to impose for the sake of appearances. The point is, there's no court of law in these parts to hand him over to, and he needs punishing."

"I agree," said Fred. "Let's thrash him to begin with."

"Let's thrash him," went on Will, "as thoroughly as we've seen his friends the Germans do the job!"

"Both sides!" agreed Brown.

"Oh, no, no, no! You can not do that, gentlemen!"

"Lay him out!" ordered Fred. "Let's begin on him. Who shall beat him first?"

At a nod from Fred our porters stretched him face downward on the dry dung floor, and knelt on his arms and legs. One of them staffed a good handful of the dry dung into his mouth to stop his yelling.

"Of course," said Will, rather slowly and distinctly, "if he told us about Schillingschen, we'd have to let him off. Let's hope he holds his tongue, for I never wanted to flog a man so much in all my life!"

The most palpable absurdity at the moment was that there was nothing in the hut to beat him with. There were dozens of strips of the recently shot hippo hide hanging in the sun outside to dry, with stones tied to the end of each, to keep them taut and straight, but nobody made a move to bring one in.

"Take off his loin-cloth!" ordered Fred. "It won't hurt him enough with that thing on!"

The Baganda spat the cow-dung from his mouth and struggled violently.

"Oh, no, no!" he shouted. "I will tell! I will tell everything!"

"Too late now!" said Will jubilantly.

"No, gentlemen, no! Not too late! I tell all—I tell quickly! Only listen! *Bwana* Schillingschen will shoot me if he knows! He is very bad man—very *kali*—very fierce—and oh, too clever! You must protect me!"

He could hardly get the words out, for the knees of our porters pinned him down, and his chin was pressed hard on the floor.

"I ordered that loin-cloth removed!" was all Fred commented. One of the porters attended to the task, and the Baganda hurried with his tale, drawing in breath in noisy gasps like a man with asthma because of the weight of his captors on him and the strained position of his neck.

"*Bwana* Schillingschen is sending me and many other men—not all Baganda, but of many tribes—to go through all parts and say Islam is the only good religion—all Germans are high-priests of Islam—soon the Germans are coming with great armies to destroy the British and all other foolish people who have not accepted Islam as their creed! All are to get ready to receive the Germans."

"Where is Schillingschen now?" demanded Fred.

"Beyond Mumias."

"How far beyond Mumias?"

"Who knows? He is marching."

"In which direction? What for?"

"To Mount Elgon. I do not know what for."

"How do you know he is going to Mount Elgon?"

"He told me to go there and find him after my work is done."

"How long were you to continue at what you call your work?"

"A month or five weeks."

"So he expects to stay a long time up there?"

"Yes."

"Why?"

"I do not know."

"Has he many loads with him?"

"Very many provisions for a long time."

"Guns?"

"Several. I do not know how many. He gives guns to some of his men when he gets to where the government will not know about it."

"How many men has he?"

"Not many. Ten, I think."

"How can they carry all those loads?"

"He brought a hundred porters from Kisumu to Mumias, and there bought more than forty donkeys, sending the porters back again."

"Then are the men he has with him his own?"

"Yes."

"From German East?"

"Yes."

"What orders did he give you besides to tell these lies about German conquest?"

"None.

"Pass me that whip!" ordered Fred. There was no whip, but the Baganda could not know that.

"He gave the same order to all of us," he yelled. "We are to stay out a month or five weeks unless we meet white men. If we meet white men we are to discover the white men's plans by talking with their servants, and then hurry to him and report."

"Ah! How many other spies has he out in this direction?"

"None."

"Why don't you pass me that whip when I ask for it?" demanded Fred.

"None! None! None, *bwana!* I am the only man in this direction! He has sent them north, south, east and west, but I am the only one down here."

"He has a lot more to tell yet," said Coutlass. "Let me put hot irons on his feet!"

Fred demurred. "He couldn't march with us if we did that!" he said with a perfectly straight face.

"Who cares whether or not he marches!" answered Coutlass. "To tell all he knows is his business! Wait while I heat the iron!"

The Baganda began to scream again, babbling that he knew no more. He assured us that Schillingschen had set the closest watch along the old caravan route, and toward his own rear in the direction of Kisumu, whence officials might come on chance errands.

"All right," said Fred. "Truss him up tight and keep him prisoner among our men in their hut."

"Our men are likely to get drunk tonight," warned Will.

"Let me watch him!" urged Coutlass. "Leave me with him alone!"

To the Greek's disgust we decided to trust the prisoner with our own men, and to keep very careful watch on them, threatening them with loss of all their pay if they dared get drunk and lose him—a threat they accepted at its full face value, but resented because of Brown's and the Greek's behavior the night before. They begged to get a little drunk—to get half as drunk as Brown had been—half as drunk as Coutlass had been—not drunk at all, but just to drink a little. We were adamant, and Brown added to their resentment by preaching them a sermon in their own tongue on the importance of being respectful toward white folk.

Kazimoto came in toward dark, foot-weary, but primed with news, and most of what he had to say confirmed the Baganda's story. Schillingschen, he said, was making for Mount Elgon in very leisurely stages, letting his loaded donkeys graze their way along, and spending hours of his time in questioning natives along the way on every subject under the sun.

Besides the fact of his leisurely progress, which was sufficiently important in itself, we learned from Kazimoto that Schillingschen's own ten boys were unable to speak the language of the country beyond a few of the commonest words—that they all slept in a tent together at night, usually quite a little distance apart from Schillingschen's—and that the donkeys were usually picketed between the two tents in a long line. He also told us the ten men had five Mauser rifles between them, in addition to the German's own battery of three guns, one of which he carried all day and kept beside his bed at night; the other two were carried behind him in the daytime by a gun-bearer.

That was good news on the whole. Coutlass went out on the strength of it and began to drink beer from the big earthenware crock in which the women had just brewed a fresh supply. Brown joined him within five minutes, and at the end of an hour, they were swearing everlasting friendship, Coutlass promising Brown his cattle back, and Brown assuring him that Greece and the Greeks had always held his warmest possible regards.

"Thermopylae, y'know, old boy, an' Marathon, an' all that kind o' thing! How many miles in a day could a Greek run in them days? Gosh!"

They two drank themselves to sleep among the gentle cattle in the circular enclosure in the midst of the village, and we—going out in turns at intervals to make sure our own boys were not drinking—matured our plans in peace.

We were too few to dare undertake the task in front of us without the aid of Brown and the Greek. It was a case of who was not against us must be for us, and the end must justify both men and means. We tried to work out ways of managing without them, but when we thought of our Baganda prisoner, and the almost certainty that both he and Coutlass would race to give our game away to Schillingschen if let out of sight for a minute, the necessity of making the best, not the worst, of the Greek seemed overwhelming.

Early next morning, before the village had awakened from its glut of beer and hippo meat, we shook Coutlass and Brown to their feet none too gently, and, with the Baganda firmly secured by the wrists between two of our men, started off, Fred leading.

The village awoke as if by magic before we bad dragged away the thorns from the gate, and the chief leaped to the realization that the beads he had promised his women were about as concrete as his drunken dreams. He and a swarm of his younger men followed us, begging and arguing—mile after mile—growing angrier and more importunate. It was by my advice that we crossed the stream into the sleeping sickness zone and left them shuddering on their own side. Our own men did not know so much about the ravages of that plague, and in any case were willing to dare whatever risks we despised. But we took a long bend back and crossed the stream again higher up as soon as the chief and his beggars were out of sight. It was a pity not to keep exact faith and give them the promised beads, if only for the sake of other white men who might camp there in the future; but more than two tons of hippo meat was not bad pay for their hospitality.

We wished we had as good price to offer at the villages on our way, for sleep under cover we must, if we hoped to escape the ravages of fever; and the primitive savage, at least in those parts, had the principle down fine of nothing whatever for nothing. Yet as it turned out, the very man whose company we looked on as a nuisance proved to be a key to all gates. We marched along the track the Baganda had taken. The chiefs of all villages knew him again; and the men who dared take such a prophet of evil prisoner were looked upon as high government officials at least.

We accepted that description of ourselves, letting it go by silent assent, and explained our lack of tents and almost every other thing the white man generally travels with as due to haste. Heaven only knew what lies Kazimoto told those credulous folk, to the perfectly worthy end of making our lot bearable, but we were fed after a fashion, and lodged after a worse one all along our road. And who should send in reports about us—and to whom? Obviously white men with a prisoner, marching in such a hurry toward the north, were government officials. Who should report officials to their government? As for the tale about our having left our loads behind—are not all white people crazy? Who shall explain their craziness?

From being a nuisance the Baganda became a joke. When it dawned on his fat intellect that we were hurrying toward Schillingschen with only one rifle among us and no baggage at all, he jumped at once to the conclusion we must be Schillingschen's friends; and his fear that we intended to hand him over to that ruthless brute for summary punishment was more melting to his backbone than the dread of our imaginary whip, that had caused him to give Schillingschen away.

He tried to bite through the thongs that held him, but Will twisted for him handcuffs out of thick iron wire that we begged from a chief, who had intended to make ornaments with it for his own legs. We did not dare let the man escape, nor care to prevent our men from using force when he threw himself on the ground and wept like a spoiled child.

"I will tell you" he said at last, deciding he might as well be hanged for mutton as for lamb, "what *Bwana* Schillingschen is searching for! I will tell you who knows where to find it! I will tell you where to find the man who knows! Only let me run away then to my own home in Uganda, and I will never again leave it! I am afraid! I am afraid!"

But that was only one more reason for keeping him with us, and no ground at all for delay. He would not tell unless we loosed his hands first, so we pressed on, camping late and starting early, until about noon of the fourth day we caught sight of Schillingschen's tents in the distance, and gathered our party at once into a little rocky hollow to discuss the situation.

Behind us the land sloped gradually for thirty or forty miles toward a sharp escarpment that overlooked the level land beside the lake. At times between the hills and trees we could glimpse Nyanza itself, looking like the vast rim of forever, mysterious and calm. In front of us the rolling hills, broken out here and there into rocky knolls, piled up on one another toward the hump of Elgon, on which the blue sky rested. In every direction were villages of folk who knew so little of white men that they paid no taxes yet and did no work—marrying and giving in marriage—fighting and running away—eating and drinking and watching their women cultivate the corn and beans and sweet potatoes—without as much as foreboding of the taxes, work for wages, missionaries, law and commerce soon to come.

Schillingschen was more than taking his time, he was dawdling, keeping his donkeys fat, and letting his men wander at pleasure to right and left gathering reports for him of unusual folk or things. We came very close to being seen by one of them, who emerged from a village near us with a pair of chickens he had foraged, followed by the owner of the luckless birds in a great hurry and fury to get paid for them.

Schillingschen's tent could fairly easily be stalked from the far side in broad daylight, and I was for making the attempt. There was the risk that one of our porters might grow restless and break bounds if we waited, or that the Baganda might take to yelling. We gagged him as soon as I talked of the danger of that.

Coutlass and Brown, however, were the only two who would agree with me. Like me, they were weary to death of *mtama* porridge, with or without milk, and the sight of Schillingschen's distant campfire with a great pot resting on stones in the midst of it whetted appetite for white man's food. They and I were for supping as soon as possible from the German's provender, and sleeping under his canvas roof.

But Fred and Will insisted on caution, claiming reasonably that surprise would be infinitely easier after dark. It was unlikely that Schillingschen would post any sentries, and not much matter if he did. His knowledge of natives and natural air of authority made him quite safe among any but the wildest, and these were a comparatively peaceful folk. In all probability he would sit and read by candle light, with his boys all snoring a hundred yards away. There was no making Fred and Will see the virtue of my contention that a sudden attack while his boys were scattered all about among the villages would be just as likely to succeed; so we settled down to wait where we were with what patience we could summon.

It was a miserable, hungry business, under a blazing hot sky, packed tightly together among men who objected to our smell as strongly as we to theirs. It is the fixed opinion of all black people that the white man smells like "bad water"; and no word seems discoverable that will quite return the compliment. That afternoon was reminiscent of the long days on the dhow, when nobody could move without disturbing everybody else, and we all breathed the same hot mixed stench over and over.

We posted two sentries to lie with their eyes on the level of the rim and guard against surprise. But there was so little to watch, except kites wheeling overhead everlastingly, that they went to sleep; and we were so bored, and so sure of our hiding-place and Schillingschen's unsuspicion that we did not notice them. I myself fell asleep toward five o'clock, and when I awoke the sun was so low in the west that our hollow lay in deep gloom.

Fred was lying on his elbow, sucking an unfilled, unlighted pipe. Will lay on his side, too, with back toward both of us, ruminating. Coutlass and Brown were both asleep, but Coutlass awoke as I rolled over and struck him with my heel. Nearly all the porters were snoring.

It was a sharp exclamation from the Greek that caused me to sit up and face due westward. The others lay as they were. It was the gloom in our hollow—the velvety shadows in which we lay with granite boulders scattered between us, and no alertness on our part that saved that day, although Coutlass acted instantly and creditably, once awake.

Schillingschen stood there looking down on us, with his feet planted squarely on the rim of the hollow, and Mauser rifle under one arm. His great splay beard flowed sidewise in the evening wind. One hand he held over his eyes, trying to make out details in the dark, as stupid as we were. He stood with his back to the setting sun, exposing himself without any thought of the risk he ran, his huge, filled-out head refusing stubbornly to take in the truth of what had happened. Once convinced, the Prussian mind is not readily unconvinced. He had assured himself long ago that our party was at the bottom of Victoria Nyanza.

The second he did make out details he was swift to act, but that was already too late, although he did not know it at the moment. He threw up his rifle and laughed—a great deep guffaw from the stomach, that awoke every one.

"So, so!" he gloated. "So Mr. Oakes and his fellow escaped convicts are alive after all! Ha-ha-ho-ho! So you followed me all this way, only to forget that kites are curious! A fine comfortless journey you must have had, too! There were twenty kites wheeling over you. I counted, and wondered. Curiosity drove me to come and see. The first man who moves a finger, Mr. Oakes, will die that instant! Let your rifle lie where it is!"

It would be no use pretending the man had not courage, at all events of the sort that glories in the upper hand of a fight. He chuckled, and reveled in our predicament, taking in, now that his eyes had grown accustomed to the darkness of our hollow, the utter lack of comforts or provisions, and enjoying our disappointment. He certainly knew himself master of the situation.

"I suspect you have a man of mine down there with you!" he announced presently. "Is not that my Baganda? Is he gagged? Is he bound? Loose him, Mr. Oakes, at once!" I say at once! Otherwise you die now!"

He pointed his rifle directly at Fred, and the next second fired it, but not intentionally. Coutlass sprang from behind him, having crawled out through a shadow, and hit him so hard with a stone on the back of the skull that he loosed off the rifle and pitched head-foremost down among us. The Greek promptly jumped on top of him with a yell like a maniac's, failing to land with both heels on his backbone by nothing but luck. As it was, he lost balance and sat down so hard on Schillingschen's head that there was no need of the energy with which we all followed suit, piling all over him to pin him down like hounds that have rolled their quarry over.

The German was stunned—knocked into utter oblivion—breathing like a sleeping drunkard, and bleeding freely from the nose. Coutlass jumped off him and began to execute a war dance up and down, yelling like a madman until Fred threatened him with the rifle and Will gagged him from behind.

"Do you want his armed men down on us, you ass?"

"Gassharamminy!" he laughed. "I forgot about them! Let us go and eat their supper!" He spoke as a man who had full right now to be considered a member in good standing. We all noticed it, and exchanged glances; but that was no time for argument about men's rights.

Brown was already over the rim of the hollow and making in the direction of the tents. We called him back and compelled him to stay on guard over the prisoners, to his awful disgust, for he suspected there was whisky among Schillingschen's "chop-boxes." But so did we! We left all our boys with him except Kazimoto, threatening them with hitherto unheard of penalties if they dared as much as show a lock of hair above the rim of the hollow while we were gone.

Then the rest of us, with Fred leading and Kazimoto last of all, crept out and sought the lowest level along which to reach the camp. Will had taken Schillingschen's rifle and went next after Fred. Coutlass followed so close on my heels that more than once he trod on them, and once so nearly tripped me that Fred called a halt behind some bushes and cursed me for clumsiness.

But it turned out to be easy hunting. The ten boys had tied the donkeys up to a rope in line and sat crooning while their supper cooked at a long bright fire. We came up to Schillingschen's tent from behind, crept around the side of it, and in a moment had three more good weapons, I taking the big-bore elephant gun that had dealt with us so savagely on the lake, Coutlass seizing another Mauser, and Kazimoto adopting the shot-gun.

The rest was child's play. We marched out of the tent all abreast and called on the ten boys to surrender, making them put up their hands until Coutlass had found their five rifles and ammunition. They were too astonished even to ask questions. Accustomed to Schillingschen's despotic orders, they obeyed ours silently, showing no symptoms of trying to bolt, having nowhere to bolt to; but we took precautions.

Kazimoto ran back to bring our party, and we took a coil of iron wire from Schillingschen's trade goods and fastened every prisoner's hands firmly behind his back, including the unconscious German's. That done, we ate the meat, beans and vegetable supper that the ten had cooked.

Brown and Coutlass found Schillingschen's whisky after that, and under its influence again swore ceaseless friendship beneath the non-committal stars. While they feasted we took Coutlass' rifle away as a plain precaution.

PARCERE SUBJECTIS?

When the devil's at bay
Ye may kneel down and pray
For a year and a day
To be spared the distress of dispatching him,
But the longer ye kneel
The more squeamish ye'll feel
'Cause the louder he'll squeal,
And at brotherly talk there's no matching him.
Discussion's his aim,
And as sure as you're game
To give heed to the same,
You regarding extremes with compunction,
You may bet he'll requite
Your compassion with spite,
Knifing you in the night
With much probonopublico unction.

XIV

FOR A while we looked like having trouble with Coutlass. We gave Brown a rifle, and distributed the other Mausers among Kazimoto and our best boys, but we did not dare trust the Greek with a weapon he might use against us, and be resented that bitterly. He had an answer to Fred's subterfuge that as a white man he would need a license before daring to carry firearms. "I dare do anything! I care nothing for law!" he argued, and Fred nodded.

That night we reveled in luxury, for after the life we had led recently it took time to reaccustom any of us to the common comforts. Schillingschen traveled with every provision for his carcass and his belly; and we plundered him.

We put the prisoners and our own porters in a hut in the nearest native village (less than half a mile away) under the watchful eye of Kazimoto and the shot-gun, dividing Schillingschen's two large tents between ourselves. The others offered me the camp-bed as a recent invalid, but I refused, and Will won it by matching coins. We divided the blankets in the same way, and all the spare underwear. Brown and Coutlass had to be satisfied with cotton blankets from a bale of trade goods; but when they had rifled enough to build up good thick mattresses as well as coverings, there were still two apiece for our boys and all the porters.

The chop-boxes were a revelation. The man had with him food enough for at least a year's traveling, including all the canned delicacies that hungry men dream about in the wilderness. Before we slept we ate so enormously of so very many things that it was a wonder that we were able to sleep at all.

We all hoped Schillingschen would die, for it was a hard problem what to do with him. He had no papers in his possession, beyond a diary written in German *schrift* that even Will could not make head or tail of, for all his knowledge of the language; and a very vague map bearing the imprint of the British government, filled in by himself with the names of the villages he had passed on his way. There was no proof that we could find that would have condemned him of nefarious practices in a British court of law.

"And believe me," argued Will, sprawling on the plundered bed, blowing the smoke of a Melachrino through his nose, "your local British judges would take the word of Professor Schillingschen against all of ours, backed up by simply overwhelming native evidence! They're so in awe of Schillingschen's professorial degree, and of his passports, and his letters of introduction from this and that mogul that they wouldn't believe him guilty of arson if they caught him in the act!"

"Something's got to be done with him pretty soon, though," answered Fred from the floor, lying at ease on a pillow and a folded Jaeger blanket, smoking a fat cigar.

Coutlass and Brown were singing songs outside

the tent and I sat in a genuine armchair with my feet on a box full of canned plum pudding. (Nobody knows, who has not hungered on the high or low veldt—who has not eaten meat without vegetables for days on end, and then porridge without salt or sugar—how good that common, export, canned plum pudding is! To sit with my feet on the case that contained it was the arrogance of affluence!)

"We have his stores and his papers," said I. "We have his Baganda; and as time goes on, and his other spies begin to come in, we shall have them, too, if we're half careful. Why don't we let him go, to tell his own tale wherever he likes?"

"Maybe he'll die yet!" said the optimist on the camp-bed, blowing more cigarette smoke.

"Suppose he doesn't. We've done our best to keep him alive. He's quit bleeding. Suppose we let him go, and he lays a charge against us. Suppose they send after us and bring us in. We've his diary and his men—evidence enough," said I.

"You bally ass!" Fred murmured.

"Cuckoo!" laughed Will.

"I don't believe he'd dare approach a British official with his story," said I.

"Incredible imbecile!" Fred answered. "He has the gall of a brass monkey."

"And magnetism—loads of it," Will added. "He'd make the Pope play three-card monte."

"To say nothing," continued Fred, "of the necessity of not letting the government know we're here! Rather than turn him loose, I'd march him into Kisumu and hand him over. But, as Will says wisely, our proconsuls would believe him, and put us under bonds for outraging a distinguished foreigner."

"Well, then," said I, "what the devil shall we do with him? Offer something constructive, you two solons!"

"Have the four men we borrowed from the island bolted home yet?" wondered Will.

"They hadn't this evening," I answered. "I don't believe they'll venture home until we stop feeding them. They were hungry on their island. Our shortest commons then seemed affluence. Now they're in heaven!"

"Their canoes must be where they left them in the papyrus."

"Sure. Who'd steal a canoe?"

"Whoever could find them," Fred answered. "But they're skillfully hidden. Why don't we put Schillingschen and his ten pet blacks into those canoes, with a little food and no rifles—and show them the way to German East?"

"Because," said I, "they wouldn't go. They'd turn around and paddle for Kisumu, to file complaint against us."

"Don't you suppose," suggested Will, "that Schillingschen's own men 'ud insist on going home? Out on the water, ten to one, without guns or too much food, they wouldn't have the same fear of him they had formerly."

"That chance is too broad and long and deep," said Fred. "Altogether too bulky to be taken. Let's sleep on it. This cigar's done, and I'm drowsy. Are you quite sure Schillingschen's hands are fast behind him? Then good night, all!"

The problem looked no easier next morning, with Schillingschen recovered sufficiently to be hungry and sit up. There was a look in his eye of smoldering courage and assurance that did not bode well for us, and when we untwisted the iron wire from his wrists to let him wash himself and eat he looked about him with a sort of quick-fire cunning that belied his story of headache.

He was much too astute a customer to be judged superficially. I whispered to Fred not to shackle him again too soon, and sat near and watched him, close enough for real safety, yet not so close that he might not venture to try tricks. He said nothing whatever, but I noticed that his eye, after roving around the tent, kept returning again and again to a chop-box that stood near the foot of the bed.

Now I had unpacked that chop-box and repacked it the previous night. I knew everything it contained—exactly how many cans of plum pudding. It was the box I had rested my feet on. I felt perfectly sure he knew as well as I what the box contained, and to suppose he would sit there planning to recover canned food, however dainty, was ridiculous.

Wherefore it was a safe conclusion he was trying to deceive me as to his real intention. I put my foot on the box again, and he frowned, as much as to say I had forestalled his only hope. Pretending to watch the box and him, I examined every detail of the tent, particularly that side of it opposite the box, away from where it seemed he wanted me to look.

The human eye is a highly imperfect piece of mechanism and the human brain is mostly grayish slush. It was minutes before I detected the edge of his diary, sticking out from the pocket of Fred's shooting coat that itself protruded from under the folded blanket on which Fred had slept. It was nearer to Schillingschen than to me. After watching him for about fifteen minutes, during which he made a great fuss about his headache, I was quite sure it was the diary that interested him.

I stooped and extracted it from the coat pocket. The grimace he made was certainly not due to headache.

"Fred!" I called out, and he and Will came striding in together.

"That diary's the key," I said. "It's important. It holds his secrets!"

Will was swift to put that to the test.

"What will you offer?" he asked Schillingschen.

"We want you to go back direct to German East. Will you go, if we give you back your diary?"

Schillingschen blundered into the trap like a buffalo in strange surroundings.

"Ja wohl!" he answered. "Give me that, and you shall never see me again!"

At that Fred threw himself full length on his blanket and took one of Schillingschen's cigars.

"Of course," he said, "you would give anything for leave to take those words back! You needn't try to hide the wince—we fully appreciate the situation! What do you say, you fellows? How about last night's idea? Who mooted it? Shall we send him back by canoe to German East, with a guarantee that if he doesn't go we'll hand over diary and him to our government?"

"Better send the book to the commissioner at Nairobi, or Mombasa, or wherever he is," suggested Will. "Then if the 'prof' here doesn't get a swift move on he's liable to be overtaken by the cops, I should say."

"Let's make no promises," said I. "I vote we simply give him time to get away."

At that the German saw the weak side of our case in a flash.

"If you dared give that diary to your government," be growled, "you would do so without bargaining with me! Why do you propose to let me go? Out of love for me? No! But because you dare not appeal to your government! Give me that diary, and I will go at once to German East, not otherwise! It is only a diary," he added. "Nothing important—merely my private jottings and memoranda."

Fred turned toward me so that Schillingschen could not see his face.

"Are you willing to start for Kisumu at once with that book?" he asked, and I nodded. He winked at me so violently that I could not trust myself to answer aloud and keep a straight face.

"Very well," he said. "Suppose you start with it to-morrow morning. At the end of a week well turn the professor home to follow his own nose!"

Schillingschen shrugged his shoulders and refused to be drawn into further argument. We gave him a good meal from his own provisions, and then once more made his hands fast with wire behind him and left him to sleep off his rage if he cared to in a corner of the tent.

Later that morning we sent for the Baganda—gave him a view of Schillingschen trussed and helpless—and questioned him about the man he boasted he knew, who could tell us what Schillingschen was after. He was so full of fear by that time that he held back nothing.

He assured us the German was after buried ivory.

There was a man, who had promised to meet Schillingschen, who knew where to find the ivory and would lead the way to it. He did not know names or places—knew only that the man would be found waiting at a certain place, and was not white.

"How did you get that information?" Fred demanded.

"By listening."

"When? Where?"

"At night, months ago, in Nairobi, outside the professor's tent. I lay under the fly among the loads and listened. The man came in the dark, and went in the dark. I did not see him. I did not hear him called by name. He must have been an old man. Speaking Kiswahili, he admitted he knew where the ivory is. He said he saw it buried, and that he alone survives of all men who buried it. He promised to lead the professor to the place on condition that the Germans shall release his brother, and his brother's wife, and two sons whom they keep in prison on a life-sentence. The professor agreed, but said, 'Wait! There are first those people who also think they know the secret. Perhaps they do! Wait until after I have dealt with them. Then you shall take me to the place! After that your criminal relations shall be pardoned! Here is money. Go and wait for me at the place we spoke of when we talked before.' "

We each cross-examined him in turn, but could not make him change his story in any essential. He merely exaggerated the parts that he guessed might please us, and begged to be allowed to run before Schillingschen could break loose and get after him.

By noontime, when we gave him his second meal, Schillingschen had made up his own mind that his case was desperate and called for heroic remedy.

"All right," he growled. "I need that diary. Hand it to me and I'll tell you how to find what you're after!"

"You mean about the man who's to meet you?" suggested Fred blandly.

Schillingschen started as if shot.

"One of your men is an eavesdropper," Fred assured him with a cheerful nod. "That plug has been pulled already, Professor!"

"Let's play the cards face up!" Will interrupted impatiently. "Listen, Schillingschen. You're an all-in scoundrel. You're a spy. You're a bloody murderer of women and defenseless natives. If we could prove that we wouldn't argue with you. We know you burned that dhow with the women in it, but we've got no evidence, that's all. We know the German government wants that ivory, and we know why. We also want it. Our only reason for secrecy is that we hope for better terms from the British government. We've nothing to fear, except possible financial loss. If you prefer to come with us to Kisumu and have the whole matter out in court, all you need do is just say so. On the other hand, if you want to get out of this country before your diary can reach the hands of the British High Commissioner—you'd just better slide, that's all!"

"You've only until dawn to think it over," remarked Fred. "You poor boob!" continued Will. "You imagine we're criminals because you're one yourself! The difference between your offer and ours is that you're bluffing and we know it, whereas we're not bluffing by as much as a hair, and the quicker you see that the better for you!"

"Oh, rats! Let's take him in with us to Kisumu!" said I, and at that Professor Schillingschen capitulated.

"Very well," he said. "*Kurz und gut.* I will leave the country. Permit me to take only food enough, and my porters, and one gun!"

"No guns!" said Fred promptly.

Schillingschen sighed resignedly, and we went out of the tent to talk over ways and means. In spite of our recent experience of Germany's colonial government we were still so ignorant of the workings of the *mens germanica* that we took his surrender at face value.

The problem of getting him down to the lake shore safely was none too simple. I was soft hearted and headed enough to propose that we should loose his hands, now that he had surrendered, and permit him reasonable liberty. Will—least inclined of all of us to cruelty—was disposed to agree with me. We might have overborne Fred's objections if Coutlass and Brown, returning from walking off their overnight debauch together, had not shouted and beckoned us in a mysterious sort of way, as if some new discovery puzzled them.

We walked about a hundred and fifty yards to where they stood by a row of low ant-hills. Neither of them was in a sociable frame of mind. It was obvious from the moment we could see their faces clearly that they had not called us to enjoy a joke.

They stood like two dumb bird-dogs, pointing, and we had to come about abreast of them before we knew why we were summoned.

There lay five clean-picked skeletons, one on each ant-hill. One was a big bird's; one looked like a dog's; the third was a snake's; the fourth a young antelope's; and the fifth was certainly that of a yellow village cur, for some of the hairs from the tip of its tail were remaining, not yet borne off by the ants.

The skeletons lay as if the creatures had died writhing. There were pegs driven into the earth that had evidently held them in position by the sinews. Most peculiar circumstance of all, there was a camp-chair standing very near by, with its feet deep in the red earth, as if a very heavy man had sat in it.

I went back to the camp and told Kazimoto to bring one of the professor's men. Kazimoto had to do the talking, for we did not know the man's language, nor he ours.

Yes, the professor always did that to animals. He liked to sit and watch them and keep the kites away. He said it was white man's knowledge (science?). Yes, the animals were pegged out alive on the ant-hills, and the professor would sit with his watch in his hand, counting the minutes until they ceased from writhing. It was part of the duty of the ten to catch animals and bring them alive to him in camp for that purpose. No, they did not know why he did it, except that it was white man's knowledge. No, natives did not do that way, except now and then to their enemies. The professor always made threats he would do so to them if they ran away from him, or disobeyed, or misbehaved. Certainly they believed him! Why should they not believe him? Did not Germans always keep their word when they talked of punishment?

We decided after that to let Schillingschen lie bound, whether or not the iron wire cut his wrists. We did not trouble to go back to inquire whether he needed drink, but let him wait for that until supper-time. The remainder of that afternoon we spent discussing who should have the disagreeable and not too easy task of taking the professor to the lake and sending him on his way. We sat with our backs against a rock, with the firearms beside us and a good view of all the countryside, very much puzzled as to whether to leave Coutlass behind in camp (with Brown and the whisky) or send him (with or without Brown) and one or two of us on the errand. He was a dangerous ally in either case.

Evening fell, and the good smell of supper came along the wind to find us still undecided. We returned to the tent thinking that perhaps something Schillingschen himself might say would help us to decide one way or the other.

"Better see if the brute wants a drink," said Fred, and I went in ahead to offer him water.

He was gone! Clean gone, without a trace, or a hint as to how he managed it! I called the others, and we hunted. The sides of the tent were pegged down tight all around. The front, it is true, was wide open, but we had sat in full view of it and not so much as a rat could have crept out without our seeing. There were no signs of burrowing. He was not under the bed, or behind the boxes, or between the sides of the tent and the fly. The only cover for more than a hundred yards was the shallow depression along which we had come to the capture of the camp, and that was the way he must have taken. But that, too, had been practically in full view of us all the time.

We counted heads and called the roll. Coutlass was close by. It did not look as if he had played traitor this time. Brown was sleeping off his headache in the shade. Kazimoto and all the boys were accounted for. The prisoners were safe. No donkeys were missing—no firearms—and no loads. The earth had simply opened up and swallowed Schillingschen, and that was all about it!

He had not made off with his pocket diary. Fred had that. There and then we packed it in an empty biscuit tin and buried it under a rock, Will and I keeping watch while Fred did the digging and covering up. It was too likely that Schillingschen would come back in the night and try to steal it for any of us to care about keeping it on his person.

It was too late to look far and wide for him that evening. A hunter such as he could have lain unseen in the dark with us almost stepping on him. Gone was all appetite for supper! We nibbled, and swore, and smoked—locked up the whisky—defied either Brown or Coutlass to try to break the boxes open—and arranged to take turns on sentry-go all that night, Will, Fred, and I—declining very pointedly offers by the other two to have their part in keeping watch. In spite of lack of evidence we suspected Coutlass; and we knew no particular reason for having confidence in Brown.

THE SONG OF THE DARK-LORDS

Turn in! Turn in! The jungle lords come forth
Cat-footed, blazing-eyed—the owners of the dark,
What though ye steal the day! We know the worth
Of vain tubes spitting at a phantom mark
With only human eyes to guide the fire!
Tremble, ye hairless ones, who only see by day,
The night is ours! Who challenges our ire?
Urrumph! Urrarrgh! Turn in there! Way!

Ye come with iron lines and dare to camp
Where we were lords when Daniel stood a test!
Where once the tired safaris used to tramp
On noisy wheels ye loll along at rest!
Tremble, ye long-range lovers of the day,
'Twas we who shook the circus walls of ancient Rome!
The dark is ours! Take cover! Way there! Way!
Urmmph! Urrarrgh! Take cover! Home!

XV

THE MAN who tries to explain away coincidences to men who were the victims of them is likely to need more sympathy than he will get. The dictionary defines them clumsily as *instances of coinciding, apparently accidental, but which suggest a casual connection.*

Lions paid us a visit that first night after Schillingschen's escape—the first lions we had seen or heard since landing on the north shore of the lake. We prayed they might get Schillingschen, yet they and he persisted until morning—they roaring and circling never near enough for the man on guard to get a shot—he also circling the camp, calling to his ten men, whom we had transferred from the native village to the second tent under guard of Kazimoto and our own men as a precaution.

Our boys slept as if drugged, but not his. He called to them in a language that even Kazimoto did not understand, and they kept answering at intervals. Once, when I was listening to locate Schillingschen if I could, the lions came sniffing and snuffing to the back side of the tent. I tried to stalk them—a rash, reprehensible, tenderfoot trick. Luck was with me; they slunk away in the shadows, and I lived to summon Fred and Will. We tried to save the donkeys, but the lions took three of them at their leisure, and scared the rest so that they broke out of the thorn-bush boma we had made the boys build (as a precaution against leopards, not lions). Next morning out of forty we recovered twenty-five, and wondered how many of them Schillingschen got.

Remembering how we ourselves had managed, without ammunition or supplies, we did not fool ourselves with the belief that Schillingschen, with his brutal personal magnetism and profound knowledge of natives, would not do better. The probability was he would stir up the countryside against us.

He had been doing missionary work; it might be the natives of that part were already sufficiently schooled to do murder at his bidding.

We decided to leave at once for a district where he had not yet done any of his infernal preaching.

"You should set a trap and shoot the swine!" Coutlass insisted. Will was inclined to agree with him, but Fred and I demurred. The British writ had never really run as far as the slopes of Elgon, and we could see them ahead of us not very many marches away. If Schillingschen intended to dog us and watch chances we preferred to have him do that in a remote wilderness, where our prospect of influencing natives would likely be as good as his, that was all.

Part of our strategy was to make an early start and march swiftly, taking advantage of his physical weariness after a night in the open on the prowl; but after a few days in camp it is the most difficult thing imaginable to get a crowd of porters started on the march. It was more particularly difficult on that occasion because none of our men were familiar with Schillingschen's loads, and the captured ten, even when we loosed their hands and treated them friendly, showed no disposition to be useful. We gave them a load apiece to carry, but to every one we had to assign two of our own as guards, so that, what with having lost the fifteen donkeys, we had not a man to spare.

It was after midday when we got off at last. We had not left the camp more than half a mile behind when I looked back and saw Schillingschen where his great tent had stood, cavorting on hands and feet like an enormous dog-baboon, searching every inch of the ground for anything we might have left. We three stood and watched him for half an hour, sweating with fear lest he chance on the place where his diary lay buried in the tin box. We began to wish we had brought it with us. I said we had done foolishly to leave it, although I had approved of Fred's burying it at the time.

"Suppose," I argued, "he sets the natives of that village to searching! What's to prevent him? You know the kind of job they'd make of it—blade by blade of grass—pebble by pebble. Where they found a trace of loosened dirt they'd dig."

"Did you bury something, then?" inquired a voice we knew too well. "By the ace of stinks, those natives can smell out anything a white man ever touched!"

We turned and faced Coutlass, whom we had imagined on ahead with the *safari.* If he noticed our sour looks, he saw fit to ignore them; but he took an upperhanded, new, insolent way with us, no doubt due to our refusal to shoot Schillingschen. He ascribed that to a yellow streak.

"I was right. Gassharamminy! I could have sworn I saw two of you on watch while the third man dug among the stones! What did you bury? I came back to talk about Brown. The poor drunkard wants to head more to the east. I say straight on. What do you say?"

We told him to go forward. Then we looked in one another's eyes, and said nothing. Whether or not the original decision had been wise, there was no question now what was the proper course.

Instead of tiring out Schillingschen we made an early camp by a watercourse, and built a very big protection for the donkeys against lions—a high thorn enclosure, and an outer one not so high, with a space between them wide enough for the two tents and half a dozen big fires. Before dark we had enough fuel stacked up to keep the fires blazing well all night long.

Neither Coutlass nor Brown had had a drink of whisky that day, so it was all the more remarkable that Coutlass lay down early in a corner of the tent and fell into a sound sleep almost at once. We were thoroughly glad of it. Our plan was for two of us to creep out of camp when it was dark enough, and recover the contents of that tin box before Schillingschen or the blacks could forestall us.

The lions began roaring again at about sundown, but they love donkey-meat more than almost any except giraffe, and it was not likely they would trouble us. We were so sure the task was not particularly risky that Fred, who would have insisted on the place of greater danger for himself, consented willingly enough to stay in camp while Will and I went back.

Our original intention was to take Schillingschen's patent, wind-proof, non-upsettable camp lantern to find the way with and keep wild beasts at bay; but just as Will went toward the tent to fetch it (Fred's back was turned, over on the far side where he was seeing to the camp-fires) we both at once caught sight of Coutlass creeping on hands and knees along a shadow. We had closed the gap in the outer wall of thorn, but he dragged aside enough to make an opening and slipped through, thinking himself unobserved.

To have followed him with a lantern would have been worse than my crime of stalking lions in the dark. Will ran to tell Fred what had happened while I followed the Greek through the gap, and presently Will and I were both hot on his trail, as close to him as we could keep without letting him hear us.

"Fred says," Will whispered, "if we catch him talking with Schillingschen, shoot 'em both! Fred won't let him into camp again unless we bring back proof he's not a traitor!"

We were pursuing a practiced hunter, who at first kept stopping to make sure he was not followed. He took a line across that wild country in the dark with such assurance, and so swiftly that it was unbelievably hard to follow him quietly. It was not long before we lost sound of him. Then we ran more freely, trusting to luck as much as anything to keep him thinking he had the darkness to himself.

Our short day's journey seemed to have trebled itself! We were leg-weary and tired-eyed when at last we reached, and nearly fell into a hollow we recognized. Will went down and struck a match to get a look at his watch.

"There ought to be a moon in about ten minutes," he whispered. "We're within sight of the place. Suppose we climb a tree and scout about a bit."

It was not a very big tree that we selected, but it was the biggest; it had low branches, and the merit of being easy to climb.

When the pale latter half of the moon announced itself we could dimly make out from the upper branches all of the flat ground where the camp had been. There was no sign of Coutlass. None of Schillingschen. A lioness and two enormous lions stood facing one another in a triangle, almost exactly on the spot where the larger tent had stood, not fifty yards from us.

"Gee!" whispered Will excitedly. "We nearly stumbled on 'em!"

"Shoot!" I whispered. My own position on the branch was so insecure that I could not have brought my rifle into use without making a prodigious noise. Will shook his head.

"I can see Coutlass now! Look at that rock—he's hiding behind it—see, he's climbing! And look, there's Schillingschen!"

Neither man was aware of the other's presence, or of ours. They were out of sight of each other, Coutlass on the very rocks against which we had leaned to watch the tent the afternoon before, and neither man really out of reach of anything with claws that cared to go after them in earnest.

The arrival of the dim moon seemed to give the lions their cue for action. The lioness turned half away, as if weary of waiting, and then lay down full-length to watch as one lion sprang at the other with a roar like the wrath of warring worlds. They met in mid-air, claw to claw, and went down together—a roaring, snarling, eight-legged, two-tailed catastrophe—never apart—not still an instant—tearing, beating—rolling over and over—emitting bellows of mingled rage and agony whenever the teeth of one or other brute went home.

Even as shadows fighting in the shadows they were terrible to watch. They shook the very earth and air, as if they owned all the primeval bestial force of all the animals. And the she-lion lay watching them, her eyes like burning yellow coals, not moving a muscle that we could see.

Iron could not have withstood the blows; the thunder of them reached us in the tree! Steel ropes could not have endured the strain as claws went home, and the brutes wrenched, ripped, and yelled in titanic agony. Their fury increased. Wounds did not seem to enfeeble them. Nothing checked the speed of the fighting an instant, until suddenly the lioness stood erect, gave a long loud call like a cat's, and turned and vanished.

She had seen. She knew. Like a spring loosed from its containing box one of the lions freed himself in mid-air and hurtled clear, landing on all-fours and hurrying away after the lioness with a bad limp. The other lion fell on his side and lay groaning, then roared half-heartedly and dragged himself away.

The second lion had hardly gone when Coutlass descended gingerly from the rock, peering about him, and listening. He evidently had no suspicion of our presence, for he never once looked in our direction. It was Schillingschen, not lions, he feared; and Schillingschen, clambering over the top of another rock, watched him as a night-beast eyes its prey. Another one-act drama was staged, and it was not time for us to come down from the tree yet.

Satisfied he was not followed and that Schillingschen was elsewhere, Coutlass crept from rock to rock toward the little cluster of small ones where, by his own confession, he had seen Fred bury the box. Schillingschen stalked him through the shadows as actively as a great ape, making no sound, as clearly visible to us as he was invisible to Coutlass.

There was not a trace of mist—nothing to obscure the dim pale light, and as the moon swung higher into space we could see both men's every movement, like the play of marionettes.

Down on his knees at last among the small loose rocks, Coutlass began digging with his fingers—grew weary of that very soon, and drew out the long knife from his boot—dug with that like a frenzied man until from our tree we heard the hard point strike on metal. Then Schillingschen began to close in, and it was time for us to drop down from the tree.

We made an abominable lot of noise about it, for the tree creaked, and our clothing tore on the thorny projections of limbs that seemed to have grown there since we climbed. To make matters worse, I stepped off the lowest branch, imagining there was another branch beneath it, and fell headlong, rifle and all, with a clatter and thump that should have alarmed the village half a mile away. And Will, not knowing what I had done but alarmed by the noise I made, jumped down on top of me.

We picked ourselves up and listened. We could hear the short quick stabs of the knife as Coutlass loosed and scooped the earth out. Among the myriad noises of the African night our own, that seemed appalling to us, had passed unnoticed—or perhaps Schillingschen heard, and thought it was the injured lion dragging himself away. (Nobody needed worry about the chance of attack from that particular lion for many a night to come; he would ask nothing better than to be left to eat mice and carrion until his awful wounds were healed.)

Reassured by the sound of digging we crept forward, knowing pretty well the best path to take from having seen Schillingschen stalking. But it was more by dint of their obsession than by any skill of ours that we crept up near without giving them alarm. Coutlass was still on his knees, throwing out the last few handfuls of loose dirt. Schillingschen stood almost over him, so close that the thrown dirt struck against his legs.

We took up positions in the shadow, one to either side, almost afraid to breathe, I cursing because the rifle quivered in my two hands like the proverbial aspen leaf. The prospect of shooting a white man—even such a thorough-paced blackguard white as Schillingschen—made me as nervous as a school-girl at a grown-up party.

At last Coutlass groped down shoulder-deep and drew the box out.

"Give that to me!" Schillingschen shouted like a thunder-clap, making me jump as if I were the one intended.

The moonlight gleamed on the tin box. Coutlass did not drop it but turned his head to look behind him. Schillingschen swung for his face with a clenched fist and the whole weight and strength of his ungainly body. He would have broken the jaw he aimed at had the blow landed; but the Greek's wit was too swift.

He kicked like a mule, hard and suddenly, ducking his head, and then diving backward between the German's legs that were outspread to give him balance and leverage for the fist-blow. Schillingschen pitched over him head-forward, landing on both hands with one shoulder in the hole out of which the box had come. With the other arm he reached for the knife that Coutlass had laid on the loose earth. Coutlass reached for it, too, too late, and there followed a fight not at all inferior in fury to the battle of the lions. Humans are only feebler than the beasts, not less malicious.

Will reached for the tin box, opened it, took out the diary, closed it again, put the diary in his own inner pocket, and returned the box; but they never saw or heard him. The German, with an arm as strong as an ape's, thrust again and again at Coutlass, missing his skin by a bait's breadth as the Greek held off the blows with the utmost strength of both hands.

Suddenly Coutlass sprang to his feet, broke loose for a second, landed a terrific kick in the German's stomach, and closed again. He twisted Schillingschen's great splay beard into a wisp and wrenched it, forcing his head back, holding the knife-hand in his own left, and spitting between the German's parted teeth; then threw all his weight on him suddenly, and they went down together, Coutlass on top and Schillingschen stabbing violently in the direction of his ribs.

Letting go the beard, Coutlass rained blows on the German's face with his free fist. Made frantic by that assault Schillingschen squirmed and upset the Greek's balance, rolled him partly over and, blinded by a very rain of blows, slashed and stabbed half a dozen times. Coutlass screamed once, and swore twice as the knife got in between his bones. The German could not wrench it out again. With both hands free now, the Greek seized him by the throat and began to throttle him, beating with his forehead on the purple face the while his steel fingers kneaded, as if the throat were dough.

We were not at all inclined to stop Coutlass from killing the man. We came closer, to see the end, and Coutlass caught sight of us at last.

"Shoot him!" he screamed. "Gassharamminy! Shoot him, can't you, while I hold him!"

As he made that appeal the German convulsed his whole body like an earthquake, wrenched the knife loose at last, and as Coutlass changed position to guard against a new terrific stab rolled him over, freed himself and stood with upraised hand to give the finishing blow. Then suddenly he saw us and his jaw dropped, the beastly mess that had been his well-kept beard dropping an inch and showing where the Greeks fist had broken the front teeth. But that was only for a second—a second that gave Coutlass time to rise to his knees, and dodge the descending blow.

I made up my mind then it was time to shoot the German, whatever the crimes of the Greek might be; but Coutlass had not grown slower of wit from loss of blood. As he dodged he rolled sidewise and seized my rifle, jerking it from my hand. He jerked too quickly. The German saw the move and kicked it, sending it spinning several yards away. We all made a sudden scramble for it, Schillingschen leading, when the German turned as suddenly as one of the great apes he so resembled, tripped Will by the heel, wrenched the rifle from his right hand, pounced on the empty tin box, and was gone!

Too late, I remembered my own rifle and fired after him, emptying the magazine at shadows.

Will's rage and self-contempt were more distressing than the Greek's spouting knife-wounds.

"By blood and knuckle-bones! Give me that gun of yours, will you! I go after the swine! I cut his liver out! Where is my knife? Ah, there it is! Stoop and give it me, for my ribs hurt! So! Now I go after him!"

We held Coutlass back, making him be still while we tore his shirt in strips, and then our own, and tried to staunch the blood, Will almost blubbering with rage while his fingers worked, and the Greek cursing us both for wasting time.

"He has the box!" he screamed. "He has the rifle!"

"He has no ammunition but what's in the magazine," said I; and that started Will off swearing at himself all over again from the beginning.

"You damned yegg!" he complained as be knotted two strips of shirt. "This would never have happened if you hadn't sneaked out to steal the contents of the box!"

Suddenly Coutlass screamed again, like a mad stallion smelling battle.

"There he is! There the swine is! I see him! I hear him! Give me that—"

He reached for my rifle, but I was too quick that time and stepped back out of range of his arm. As I did that the blood burst anew from his wounds. He put his left hand to his side and scattered the hot blood up in the air in a sort of votive offering to the gods of Greek revenge, and, brandishing the long knife, tore away into the dark.

"I see him!" he yelled. "I see the swine! By Gassharamminy! To-night his naked feet'll blister on the floor of hell!"

We followed him, enthralled by mixed motives made of desire and a sort of half-genuine respect for the courage of this man, who claimed three countries and disgraced each one at intervals in turn. We did not go so fast as he. We were not so enamored of the risks the dark contained.

Suddenly there came out of the blackness just ahead a marrow-curdling cry—agony, rage, and desperation—that surely no human ever uttered—roar, yelp of pain, and battle-cry in one.

"Help!" yelled Coutlass. "Help! Oh-ah! Ah!"

We raced forward then, I leading with my rifle thrust forward. A second later I fired; and that was the only time in my life I ever touched a lion's face with a rifle muzzle before I pulled the trigger! The brute fell all in a heap, with Coutlass underneath him and the Greek's long knife stuck in his shoulder to the hilt. The lion must have died within the minute without my shot to finish him.

Coutlass lay dead under the defeated beast that had crawled away to hide and lick his wounds. We dragged his body out from under, and in proof that Schillingschen, the common enemy, lived, a bullet came whistling between us. The flash of my shot had given him direction. Perhaps he could see us, too, against the moon. We ducked, and lay still, but no more shots came.

"He's only got four left," Will whispered. "Maybe he'll husband those!"

"Maybe he knows by now that box is empty!" said I. "He'll stalk us on the way back!"

"Us for the tree, then, until morning!" said Will.

"Sure!" I answered. "And be shot out of it like crows out of a nest!"

But Will had the right idea for all that. He was merely getting at it in his own way. After a little whispering we went to work with fevered fingers, stripping off the bloody bandages we had tied on the Greek's ribs—stripping off more of his clothes—then more of ours—tying them all into one—then skinning the mangled lion with the long knife that had really ended his career, tearing the hide into strips and knotting them each to each. In twenty minutes we had a slippery, smeary, smelly rope of sorts. In five more we had dragged the Greek's dead body underneath the tree.

Then I went back to the vantage point among the rocks and waited until Will had thrown the rope with a stone tied to its end over an upper branch. Presently I saw Coutlass' dead body go clambering ungracefully up among the branches, looking so much less dead than alive that I thought at first Will must have tangled the rope in the crotch of the tree and be clambering up to release it.

The ruse worked. Georges Coutlass served us dead as well as living. Out of the darkness to my

"I felt the fear that turns the heart to ice."

to bury a body that the brutes would dig up again within five minutes of our leaving it.

"Schillingschen has three cartridges," said Will. "One each for you, me and Fred Oakes! I'll stay and trick him some more. I'll think up a new plan. I don't care if he gets me. I'd hate to face Fred without my rifle, and have to tell him the enemy is laying for him with it through my carelessness."

It was my first experience of Will with hysteria, for it amounted to that. I remembered that to cure a bevy of school-girls of it one should rap out something sharply, with a cane if need be. Yet Will was not like a school-girl, and his hysteria took the pseudo-manly form of refusal to retreat. I yearned for Fred's camp-fires, and Fred's laugh, hot supper, or breakfast, or whatever the meal would be, and blankets. Will, with a ruthless murderer stalking him in the dark, yearned only for self-contentment. All at once I saw the thing to do, and thrust my rifle in his hands.

"Take it," I said. "Hunt Schillingschen all night if you want to. I'm going back to tell Fred I've lost my rifle, and was afraid to face you for fear you'd laugh at me. Go on—take it! No, you've got to take it!"

I let the rifle fall at his feet, and he was forced to pick it up. By that time I was on my way, and he had to hurry if he hoped to catch me. I kept him hurrying—cursing, and calling out to wait. And so, hours later, we arrived in sight of Fred's fires and answered his cheery challenge:

"Halt there, or I'll shoot your bally head off!"

Lions had kept him busy making the boys pile thornwood on the fires. He had shot two—one inside the enclosure, where the brute had jumped in a vain effort to reach the frantic donkeys. We stumbled over the carcass of the other as we made our way toward the gate-gap, and dragged it in ignominiously by the tail (not such an easy task as the uninitiated might imagine.)

left there came a flash and a report. I did not look to see whether the corpse in the tree jerked as the bullet struck. Before the flash had died—almost before the crack of the report bad reached my ear-drums I answered with three shots in quick succession.

"Did you get him?" called Will.

"I don't know," I answered. "If I didn't, he's only got three cartridges left!"

We left the Greek's body in the tree for Schillingschen to shoot at further if be saw fit; it was safer there from marauding animals than if we had laid it on the ground, and as for the rites of the dead, it was a toss-up which was better, kites and vultures, or jackals and the ants. We saw no sense that night in laboring with a knife and our hands

Once within the enclosure I left Will to tell Fred his story as best suited him, Fred roaring with laughter as he watched Will's rueful face, yet turning suddenly on Brown to curse him like a criminal for laughing, too!

"Go and fetch that Mauser of yours, Brown, and give it to Mr. Yerkes in place of what he's lost! Hurry, please!"

It was touch and go whether Brown would obey. But he happened to be sober, and realized that he had committed the impermissible offense. Fred might laugh at Will all he chose; so might I; either of us might laugh Fred out of countenance; or they might howl derisively at me. But Brown, camp-fellow though he was, and not bad fellow though he was, was not of our inner-guard. He might laugh *with,* never *at,* especially when catastrophe brought inner feelings to the surface.

"Take the shot-gun if you care to," Fred told him, as he passed Will the rifle. "I'll unlock the chop-box presently, and let you have some whisky!"

This last was the cruelest cut, but it did Brown good. When Fred kept his promise and produced a whole bottle from the locked-up store Brown refused to touch it, instead insulting him like a good man, cursing him—whisky, whiskers, whims and all, using language that Fred good-naturedly assured him was very unladylike.

Before dawn the boys, peering through the gaps between the camp-fires, to distinguish lions if they could and give the alarm before another could jump in and do damage, swore they saw Schillingschen, rifle in hand, stalking among the shadows. Nothing could convince them they had not seen him. They said he stooped like a man in a dream—that big beard was matted, and his shirt torn—that he strode out of darkness into darkness like a man whose mind was gone. We purposely laughed at their story, to see if we could shake them in it. But they laughed at our incredulity.

"My eyes are good eyes" answered Kazimoto. "What I see I see! Why should I invent lies?"

It was not pleasant to imagine Schillingschen, mind gone or not, with or without three cartridges and a rifle, prowling about our camp awaiting opportunity to do murder.

"Come to think of it," said Fred, "we've no proof he hasn't a lot more than three cartridges. It's hardly likely, but he might have cached some in reserve near where we found his camp pitched. More unlikely things have happened. But the bally man must go to sleep some time. He seems to have been awake ever since he escaped. We'll be off at dawn, and either tire him out or leave him!"

"I'll bet he's got one or more of those donkeys," I answered. "He'll not be so easy to tire."

"Suppose you and Will go and sleep," suggested Fred. "Otherwise we'll all go crazy, and all get left behind!"

There did not remain much time for sleeping. The porters, being used to the tents and their loads now, got away to a good start, heading straight toward the frowning pile of Elgon that hove its great hump against a blue sky and domineered over the world to the northward.

There were plenty of villages, well filled with timid spear-men and hard-working naked wives. Now that we had trade goods in plenty there was no difficulty at all about making friends with them. They had two obsessing fears: that it might not rain in proper season, and "the people" as they called themselves would "have too much hunger;" and that the men from the mountain might come and take their babies.

"Which men, from what mountain?"

"Bad men, from very high up on that mountain!" They pointed toward Elgon, shuddered, and looked away.

"Why should they take your babies?"

"They eat them!"

"What makes you think that?"

"We know it! They come! Once in so often they come and fight with us, and take away, and kill and eat our fat babies!"

All the inhabitants of all the villages agreed. None of them had ever ventured on the mountain; but all agreed that very bad black men came raiding from the upper slopes at uncertain intervals. There was no variation of the tale.

One thing puzzled us much more than the cannibal story. We heard shooting a long way off behind us to our right—two shots, followed by the unmistakable ringing echo among growing trees. Had Schillingschen decided to desert us? And if so, how did he dare squander two of his three cartridges at once—supposing he were not now mad, as our boys, and his, all vowed he was? His own ten men began to beg to be protected from him, and the captured Baganda recommended in best missionary English that we seek the services of the first witch doctor we could find.

THE SONG OF THE ELEPHANTS

Who is as heavy as we, or as strong?
Ho! but we trample the shambas down!
Saw ye a swath where the trash lay long
And tall trees flat like a harvest mown?
That was the path we shore in haste
(Judge, is it easy to find, and wide!)
Ripping the branch and bough to waste
Like rocks shot loose from a mountain side!
Therefore hear us:

(All together, stamping steadily in time.)

'Twas we who lonely echoes woke
To copy the crash of the trees we broke!
Goad, nor whip, nor wheel, nor yoke
Shall humble the will of the Ivory Folk!

Once we were monarchs from sky to sky,
Many were we and the men were few;
Then we would go to the place to die—
Elephant tombs that the oldest knew,—
Old as the trees when the prime is past,
Lords unchallenged of vale and plain,
Grazing aloof and alone at last
To lie where the oldest had always lain.
So we sing of it:

(All together, swinging from side to side in time, and tossing trunks.)

'Twas we who lonely echoes woke
To copy the crash of the trees we broke!
Goad, nor whip, nor wheel, nor yoke
Shall govern the strength of the Ivory Folk!

Still we are monarchs! Our strength and weight
Can flatten the huts of the frightened men!
But the glory of smashing is lost of late,
We raid less eagerly now than then,
For pits are staked, and the traps are blind,
The guns be many, the men be more;
We fidget with pickets before and behind,
Who snoozed in the noonday heat of yore.
Yet, hear us sing:

(All together, ears up and trunks extended.)

'Twas we who lonely echoes woke
To copy the crash of the trees we broke!
Goad, nor whip, nor wheel, nor yoke
Have lessened the rage of the Ivory Folk!

Still we are monarchs of field and stream!
None is as strong or as heavy as we!
We scent—we swerve—we come—we scream—
And the men are as mud 'neath tusk and knee!
But we go no more to the Place to die,
For the blacks head off and the guns pursue;
Bleaching our scattered rib-bones lie,
And men be many, and we be few.
Nevertheless:

(All together, trunks up-thrown, ears extended, and stamping in slow time with the fore-feet.)

'Twas we who lonely echoes woke
To copy the crash of the trees we broke!
Goad, nor whip, nor wheel, nor yoke
Shall humble the pride of the Ivory Folk!

XVI

WE HAD laughed at Fred's suggestion that Schillingschen might have ammunition cached away. Fred had sneered at my guess that the German might ride donkey-back and not be so easily left behind. Now the probability of both suggestions seemed to stiffen into reality.

Day followed day, and Schillingschen, squandering cartridges not far away behind us, always had more of them. He seemed, too, to lose interest in keeping so extremely close to us, as we raced to get away from him toward the mountain.

If he was really crazy, as his trembling boys maintained, then for a crazy man blazing at everything or nothing he was shooting remarkably little. On the contrary, if he was sane, and shooting for the pot, be must have acquired a big following in some mysterious manner, or else have lost his marksmanship when Coutlass bruised his eyes. He fired each day, judging by the echo of the shots, about as many cartridges as we did, who had to feed a fairly long column of men, and make presents of meat, in addition, to the chiefs of villages.

It began to be a mystery how he carried so much ammunition, unless he had donkeys or porters.

Soon we began to pass through a country where elephants bad been. There was ruin a hundred yards wide, where a herd of more than a thousand of them must have swept in panic for fifteen miles. There were villages with roofs not yet re-thatched, whose inhabitants came and begged us to take vengeance on the monsters, showing us their trampled enclosures, torn-down huts, and ruined plantations. They offered to do whatever we told them in the way of taking part, and several times we marshaled the men of two or three villages together in an effort to get a line to windward and drive the herd our way.

But each time, as the plan approached development, ringing shots from behind us put the brutes to flight. It became uncanny—as if Schillingschen in his new mad mood was able to divine exactly when his noise would work most harm. Our fool boys told the local natives that a madman was on our heels, and after that all offers of help ceased, even from those who had suffered most from the elephants. We began to be regarded as mad ourselves. Efforts to get natives to go scouting to watch Schillingschen, and report to us, were met with point-blank refusal. Rumor began to precede us, and from one village that had suffered more than usually badly from passing elephants the inhabitants all fled at the first sign of Brown, leading our long single column.

We followed the herd. Its track was wide, and easier than the winding native foot-paths; and we were willing enough to jettison loads of trade-goods if only we could replace them with tusks. The chase led up toward Elgon, over the shoulder of an outlying spur, and upward toward the mountain's eastern slopes.

As long as we kept in the wake of the herd the going presented no difficulties. We knew by the state of the tracks and the dung that the herd was never far ahead. Frequently we heard them crashing through trees in front of us. Yet whenever we came so close as to hope for a view, and a shot at a tusker, invariably a regular fusillade from the eastward to our rear would start the herd stampeding with a din like all the avalanches.

Streams by the dozen flowed down from the mountain's sides, their banks crushed into bog where the elephants had crossed. Our donkeys grew used to being tied by the head in line and hauled across (for in common with all herds of donkeys, there were a few of them that swam readily, and many that either could not or refused). The flies in the wake of the elephants were worse than the tsetse that haunted the shore of Nyanza.

We had no trouble now from our boys. We could even let the Baganda's hands loose. They feared the cannibals of the higher slopes, but were much more afraid of the madman to our right rear. Our difficulty lay in compelling them to keep a course sufficiently to eastward, and in calling a halt each day before men and animals were too utterly tired out. Yet for all their hurry, we did not gain on the man who made them so afraid.

Elephants, once thoroughly seared, will ran away forever. Our boys openly praised the herd in front for its speed and stamina, hoping it would continue on its course and oblige us to keep the madman with the rifle at a safe distance to our rear. But it seemed he had an easier line than we, or else his frenzy gave him seven-league boots, for he even began to gain on us, keeping along our right flank at a distance of several miles, and driving us nearly mad in the frantic effort to keep our column from turning and running away to the westward. If we had relaxed our vigilance for a moment they would have broken line and fled.

It was old volcanic country we were marching through, densely wooded, virgin forest for the most part, with earth so warm at times that it was not easy to believe the crater of Elgon quite extinct. Even at that low level we came on blow-holes nearly filled in with dirt and trash, serving as fine caves for beasts of prey. We went into one for about three hundred paces before it narrowed into nothing, and would have camped in it but for the stink. It smelt like a place where the egg of original sin had turned rotten. Fred said that was sulfur, with the air of a man who would like it believed that he knew.

At last the enemy must have made a night march, for he passed us, and the following dawn we heard him shooting to our right in front. That morning it was simply impossible to make the boys break camp. They swore that the ghost of Schillingschen had gone in league with the elephants to destroy us, and they preferred to be shot by us rather than murdered by witchcraft.

Beyond doubt they would have bolted and left

us had that camp not been an almost perfect one, on rising ground with two great wings of rock almost enclosing it, and a singing brook galloping through the midst. There was only one gap by which elephant or man could enter (unless they should fall from the sky), and they closed that by rolling rocks and dragging up trunks of trees.

After a useless argument, during which we all lost our tempers and they were reduced to the verge of panic, we decided to leave them there in charge of Brown and those porters, except Kazimoto, who had rifles. The armed men promised faithfully to die beside Brown in the only place of exit rather than permit a man to pass out; and the rest all agreed it would be right to shoot them if they attempted to desert; but we left the camp together—Fred, Will, I, and Kazimoto, with Will's personal servant and mine bringing up the rear—wondering whether we should ever see any member or part of the outfit again. It felt like going to a funeral—or rather from it—more than likely Brown's.

Kazimoto and the other two should have been carrying spare rifles; but Brown had refused to remain behind unless we left him all but the one apiece we absolutely needed. We took the boys more from habit than for any use they were likely to be; and my boy and Will's bolted back to the camp almost before we were out of sight of it, Kazimoto begging us to shoot them in the back for cowards.

"Huh!" he grunted. "They are afraid of death. Teach them what death is!"

We heard Brown challenge them as they approached the camp, and hoped he thrashed them soundly. But it turned out he did not. He himself had grown afraid; for the fear of a crowd is contagious, and spreads nearly as readily from black to white as from white to black. He broke open a chop-box and consoled himself with whisky.

Forcing our way through vegetation that crowded around a spur of volcanic rock, it soon became evident that the whole of the huge herd was breakfasting not far in front of us, tearing off limbs of trees, and crashing about as if noise were the only object. We climbed and attempted to look down on them, only to discover that the part of the forest where we were consisted of a narrow belt, with a mile-wide open space beyond it between us and the elephants. The wind was from them toward us, but that did not wholly account for the amount of noise that reached us. It was the fact that the herd was twice as big as we imagined. There were elephants in every direction. We could see and hear branches breaking with reports like cannon-fire.

Kazimoto was as steady as an old soldier, a great grin spreading across his ugly honest face, and his eyes alight with enthusiasm. This was the profession he had followed when he was Courtney's gun-bearer, and he kept close to Fred with a handful of cartridges ready to pass to him, whispering wise counsel.

"Get close to them, *bwana!* Go close! Go close! Wind coming our way—smell coming our way—noise coming our way—elephant very busy eating—no hurry! No long shooting! Go right up close!"

It was easier said than done. The elephants had spread broadcast through the forest, and there was no longer one well-defined swath to follow, but a very great number of twisting narrow alleys through elastic undergrowth between great unyielding trees. We had to separate, to gain any advantage from our number, so that we emerged into the open more than a hundred yards apart, with Fred at the far left and Will in the center. Fred, with Kazimoto close at his heels, was more than fifty yards in front of either of us.

And crossing that mile of open land was no simple business. It was a mass of rocks and tree-roots, burned over in some swift-running forest fire and not yet re-seeded, nor yet rotted down. There were winding ways all across it by the dozen that the elephants, with their greater height and better woodcraft, could follow on the run, but great stumps and rocks higher than a man's head (that from a distance had looked like level land) blocked all vision and made progress mostly guesswork.

However, the latter half-mile was more like level going—I emerged from between two boulders, wondering whether I could ever find my way back again, and envied Fred, who had found a better track and had the lead of me now by several hundred yards. Will was as far behind him as I, but had gone over more to the left, leaving me—feeling remarkably lonely—away in the rear to the right.

Kazimoto followed Fred so closely, stooping low behind him, that the two looked like some strange four-legged beast. They were headed for the forest in front of them at a great pace, increasing their lead from Will, who, like me, was more or less winded. I stooped at a pool to scoop up water and splash my face and neck. When I looked up a moment later I could see none of them.

At that instant, when I could actually smell the great brutes crashing in the forest, unseen within a hundred yards of me, and would have given all I had or hoped for just to have a friend within speaking distance, a shot rang out in the forest ahead, and rattled from tree to tree like the echo of a skirmish. It was not from Fred's gun, or Will's. It was the phantom rifleman at work again. Schillingschen—Schillingschen's ghost—or whoever he was, he could not have timed his fusillade better for our undoing. The first shot was followed by six more in swift succession. And then chaos broke loose.

Toward where I stood, from every angle to my front, the whole herd stampeded. No human being could have guessed their number. The forest awoke with a battle-din of falling trees and crashing undergrowth, split apart by the trumpeting of angry bulls and the screams of cows summoning their young ones. The earth shook under the weight of their tremendous rout. I heard Fred's rifle ring out three times far to my left—then Will's a rifle nearer to me; and at that the herd swung toward its own left, and the whole lot of them came full-pelt, blind, screaming, frantic, straight for me.

There was no turning them now. None but the very farthest on the flank could have turned, given sense enough left to do it. It was a flood of maddened monsters, crazed with fear, pent by their own numbers, forced forward by the crowd behind, that invited me to dam them if I could! As they burst into the open, more shots rang out in the forest to lend their fury wings!

I glanced behind, to right and left, but there was no escape, I had come too far into the open to retreat! There were big rocks to the rear to have scrambled on, but there was no time. There was one big rock in front of me that divided their course about in halves; to pass it they must open up, although they would almost surely close again. I took my stand in line with that, as a man on trial for life takes refuge behind an unestablishable alibi.

They talk glibly about men's whole lives passing in review before them in the instant of a crisis. That may be. That was a crisis, and I saw elephants—elephants! I remembered some of what Courtney had told us—some of the mad yarns Coutlass spun when liquor and the camp-fire made him boastful. All the advice I ever heard; all my previous imaginings of what I should do when such a time came, seemed to be condensed into one concrete demand—shoot, shoot, shoot, and keep on shooting! Yet my finger, bent around the trigger, absolutely would not act!

The oncoming gray wave of brutes split apart at the rock, as it must do, some of them screaming as they crashed into it breast on and were crushed by the crowd behind. In the van of the right-hand wing, brushing the rock with his shoulder, charged an enormous bull with tusks so large that the heavier had weighed down his head to a permanent rakish angle. He caught sight of me—trumpeted like a siren in the Channel fog—and came at me with raised ears and trunk outstretched. I heard shooting to the left, and more shots from the forest, where the very active ghost or madman was keeping up a battle of his own. I felt the fear, that turns a man's very heart to ice, grip hold of me—felt as if nothing mattered—imagined the whole universe a sea of charging elephants—accepted the inevitable—and suddenly received my manhood back again! My forefinger acted! I fired point-blank down the throat of the charging bull. And it seemed to have no more effect on him than a pea-shooter has on a railroad train!

I had left Schillingschen's heavy-bored elephant gun behind with Brown, considering it too cumbersome, and was using a Mauser with flat-nosed bullets. I fired four shots as fast as I could pump them from the magazine straight down the monster's hot red throat; and he continued to come on as if I had not touched him, hard-pressed on either flank by bulls nearly as big as he.

Perhaps the reason why my past history did not flash review was that my time was not yet come! I continued to see elephant—nothing but elephant!—little bloodshot eyes aflame with frenzy—great tusks upthrown—a trunk upraised to brain me—huge flat feet that raged to tread me down and knead me into purple mud! I kept the last shot with a coolness I believe was really numbness—then felt his hot breath like a blast on my face, and let him have it, straight down the throat again!

He screamed—stopped—quivered right over me—toppled from the knees—and fell like a landslide, pushed forward as he tumbled by the weight behind, and held from rolling sidewise by the living tide on either flank. I tried to spring back, but his falling trunk struck me to earth. On either side of me a huge tusk drove into the ground, and I lay still between them, as safe as if in bed, while the herd crashed past to right and left for so many minutes that it seemed all the universe was elephants—bulls, cows and calves all trumpeting in mad desire to get away—away—anywhere at all so be it was not where they then were.

Blood poured on me from the dead brute's throat—warm, slippery, sticky stuff; but I lay still. I did not move when the crashing had all gone by, but lay looking up at the monster that had willed his worst and, seeking to slay, had saved me. Those are the moments when young men summon all their calf-philosophy. I wondered what the difference was between that brute and me, that I should be justified in slaying; that I should be congratulated; that I should have been pitied, had the touch-and-go reversed itself and he killed me. I knew there was a difference that had nothing to do with shape, or weight, or size, but I could not give it a name or lay my finger on it.

My reverie, or reaction, or whatever it was, was broken by Fred's voice, flustered and out of breath, coming nearer at a great pace.

"I tell you the poor chap's dead as a door-nail! He's under that great bull, I tell you! He's simply been charged and flattened out! What a dog I was—what a green-horn—what a careless, fat-headed tomfool to leave him alone like that! He was the least experienced of all of us, and we let him take the full brunt of a charging herd! We ought to be hung, drawn and quartered! I shall never forgive myself! As for you, Will, it wasn't half as much your fault as mine! You were following me. You expected me to give the orders, and I ought to have called a halt away back there until we were all three in touch! I'll never forgive myself—never!"

I crawled out then from between the tusks, and shook myself, much more dazed than I expected, and full of an unaccountable desire to vomit.

"Damn your soul!" Fred fairly yelled at me. "What the hell d'you mean by startling me in that way! Why aren't you dead? Look out! What's the matter with the man? The poor chap's hurt—I knew he was!"

But that inexplicable desire to empty all I had inside me out on to the trampled ground could no longer be resisted, that was all. The aftermath of deadly fear is fear's corollary. Each bears fruit after its kind.

To my one tusker Will and Fred had brought down five and six respectively. That made twenty-three tusks, for one was an enormous "singleton." We sent Kazimoto back alone to try to persuade some of our porters to come and chop out the ivory with axes, bidding him promise them all the hearts, and as many tail-hairs as they chose to pull out to keep witches away with. Then, since my sickness passed presently and left me steady on my legs, Fred made a proposal that we jumped at.

"Let's go and lay Schillingschen's ghost! If that was Schillingschen shooting in the forest, we've a little account with him! If it wasn't I want to know it! Come along!"

We advanced into the forest and toiled up-hill along the tracks the stampeding elephants had made, amid flies indescribable, and almost intolerable heat. The blood on my clothing made me a veritable feeding-place of flies, until I threw most of it off, and then began to suffer in addition from bites I could not feel before, and from the sharp points of beckoning undergrowth. My bare legs began to bleed from scratches, and the flies swooped anew on those, and clung as if they grew there.

Will climbed a huge tree, at imminent risk of pythons and rotten branches, and descried open country on our right front. We made for it, I walking last to take advantage of the others' wake, and after more than an hour of most prodigious effort we emerged on rolling rocky country under a ledge that overhung a thousand feet sheer above us on the side of Elgon. To our right was all green grass, sloping away from us.

There was a camp half a mile away pitched on the edge of the forest—a white man's tent—a mule—meat hanging to dry in the wind under a branch—two tents for natives—and a pile of bags and boxes orderly arranged. We could see a man sitting under a big tent awning. He was reading, or writing, or something of that kind. He was certainly not Schillingschen. We hurried. Fred presently broke into a run; then, half-ashamed, checked himself and waited for me, who was beyond running.

When we came quite close we saw that the man was playing chess all by himself with a folding board open on his knees. He did not look up, although by that time he surely should have heard us. Fred began to walk quietly, signaling to the camp hangers-on to say nothing. We followed him silently in Indian file. As he came near the awning Fred tip-toed, and I felt like giggling, or yelling—like doing anything ridiculous.

He who played chess yawned suddenly, and closed the chess-board with a snap. He got up lazily, smiled, stretched himself like a great good-looking cat, faced Fred, and laughed outright.

"Glad to see you all! Did you get many elephants?" he asked.

"Monty, you old pirate—I knew it was you!" said Fred, holding a hand out.

Monty took it, and forced him into the chair he had just vacated.

"You damned old liar!" he said, nodding approvingly.

"THEY TOIL NOT, NEITHER DO THEY SPIN"

Now for opulence and place
And the increment unearned
We will thieve and stab and cover it with perjury,
Contemptuous of grace
And the lesson never learned
That the Rules are not amenable to surgery.
We will steal a neighbor's tools
In the quest for easy cash,
Aye, jump his claim and burrow to the heart of it,
But the innocents and fools
Get all the goods, and we the trash,
And that's the most exasperating part of it!

XVII

NOBODY IN camp slept that night. When the tusks had been chopped out, and our camp carried across and pitched beside Monty's—ivory weighed—lion-proof boma built—and elephant-heart portioned out to the men, who gorged themselves on it in order that their own hearts might grow great and strong; when all the myriad matters had been seen to that make camping in the tropics such a business, then there were tales to be told. We demanded Monty's first; he ours; and because his was likely to be much the shortest we won that argument.

"Wait one minute, though," he insisted. "Before I begin, have you any notion who a man with a beard could be—bruised face-broken front teeth—Mauser rifle—big dark beard cut shovel-shape—enormously powerful by the look of his shoulders and arms? I came on him three, no, four days' march back."

"Schillingschen!" we exclaimed with one voice.

"Show me Schillingschen!" echoed Brown, who was very drunk by that time, nearly ready to be put to bed. "Show me Schillingschen, an' I'll show you a corpse!"

"He's right," nodded Monty. "The man's dead. Blew his brains out with his last cartridge. Looked to me to have lost himself. Slept in trees, I should say. Clothing all torn. Hadn't been dead long when some of my boys came on him and drove away the jackals. Had he been in a fight, do you know?"

But we would not tell him that tale until we had his own.

"Mine's short and simple," he began. "Some ruffians boarded my ship at Suez, who made such eyes at me, and so obviously intended to do me damage at the first opportunity, that I talked it over with the captain (giving him a hint or two of the possible reason) and he agreed to slip me off secretly at Ismailia. It was easy—middle of the night, you know—had the doctor isolate the ruffians on the starboard side while the ship anchored—some cooked-up excuse about quarantine—and kept 'em out of sight of what was happening until the ship went on again. Very simple."

"Go on, Didums—we'll be all night talking—what did you do with the King of Belgium?" Fred demanded.

"Nothing. Didn't go near the King of Belgium. I was quarantined at Ismailia on wholly imaginary grounds for fourteen days; and who should come smiling into the same lazaretto on the last day but Frederick Courtney—a very old friend of mine!"

"He was to go to Somaliland," I said.

"So he told me. He's on his way there now. Decided for reasons of his own to enter the country by way of Abyssinia. Told me of the advice he'd given you fellows, and assured me he'd seen King Leopold himself on the very matter scarcely a year before. Of course, he said, I might succeed where he failed, using influence and all that sort of thing, but he assured me Leopold was hard to deal with, and difficult to tie down. His advice was, go back to Elgon, and hunt for the stuff there."

"That's what he kept advising us," said Will. "But why should he give away his information free? And if it's good, where did he get it?"

"Courtney's no dog in the manger," Monty answered. "He told me of this man Schillingschen. Said he had sent in a report about him to the Home Government, but couldn't for the life of him get documentary evidence with which to back up his charges."

Will whistled, and drew out the diary he had rescued from the tin box. Fred nodded. Will threw it to Monty, who caught it.

"He told me this Schillingschen had searched the whole country over for the stuff—had it straight from Schillingschen's boys—I dare say you know how Courtney can make a native tell him all he knows. Schillingschen, he said, had eliminated pretty nearly all the likely places until Mount Elgon was about all there is left. Courtney said, too, that there were always so many thousands of elephants near Elgon that Tippoo Tib probably gathered a harvest there. We discussed probabilities, and agreed it wasn't likely he would carry the stuff far in order to hide it. It seemed likely to both of us, too, that if the quantity the old man hid was anything like what rumor says, then there were probably half a dozen hiding-places, not one. Most of the stuff may be in the Congo Free State, and we'll do well to leave that to Leopold of Belgium and his pet concessionaires. Some of it may be near here. I stayed in the lazaretto an extra day with Courtney, talking it over. One other thing he remembered to tell me was that Schillingschen had hunted high and low for Tippoo Tib's old servants, and had finally managed to have the relatives of that man Hassan—I remember, Fred, you called him Johnson in Zanzibar—thrown in jail in German East for some alleged offense or other."

Monty stopped to scrape out a faithful pipe, fill it, press down tobacco with a practiced thumb, and reach toward the campfire for a burning brand. Then he smoked for two minutes reflectively.

"I offered Courtney a share should we find the stuff. Knew you fellows would agree." Pause. "Courtney wouldn't hear of it." Pause. "Said good-bye to him, and took a coastwise trading steamer back to Mombasa. Delightful trip—put in everywhere—saw everything. Saw a lot of the Galla—fine tribe, the Galla."

"Suppose you cut the travelogue stuff until later on!" suggested Will.

"Landed at Mombasa, and learned the first day that you fellows had managed to make more enemies than friends. Put in a number of days on heavy social labor—lingered at the club—drank too much of their infernal gin-and-black-pepper appetizer—but made you fellows right, I think."

"We're not interested in the slumming. Go on and tell us what you did!" urged Fred.

"That is what I did—and undid. I made friends. Soon I had all the other junior officials in a state of mind to help me if they could. Then I began to inquire for Hassan. They drew the dragnet tight, and discovered him at Nairobi! A young assistant district superintendent of police, who will rise in the service, I hope, before long, discovered a woman—who was jealous of a man—who was just then making love to the dusky damsel particularly favored by Hassan; and in that roundabout way we discovered that Hassan intended to take a trip very soon toward Mount Elgon, where, if you please, he was to take part in Professor Schillingschen's ethnological studies. On condition that he held his tongue until I gave him leave to talk, I promised that young policeman—to put him *en rapport* with Schillingschen's doings as swiftly as may be. Then I returned to Mombasa, and got your code letter saying you would head this way. It all fitted in like a game of chess."

"How in the world did you get that letter so soon?" demanded Fred. "The missionary chap was to mail it in Ujiji, via Salisbury, Rhodesia."

"I suppose he simply didn't do that, that's all," Monty answered. "The bank manager told me he received it in the mission mail bag—from Ujiji, yes, but by way of Muanza, Tabora, and Dar es Salaam. It reached me in the nick of time. I must have been marching nearly parallel with you chaps for about a week!"

"If coincidence of evidence means anything," said Will "we're all on a red-hot scent! That Baganda we have in our outfit is our prisoner. One of Schillingschen's pet pimps. He swears Hassan—or rather some old native whose name he doesn't know—was to meet Schillingschen in these parts and lead him to where he actually helped bury the ivory, years ago!"

"We may have difficulty finding him," said I. "Mount Elgon's big!"

"What about Brown?" asked Monty. "I hope you haven't made him partner? I agree, of course, if you have, but I hope not!"

"Nothing doing!"

"No. Why should we?"

"Brown's all right, but a present ought to satisfy him."

We began to tell Monty about Brown's cattle that Coutlass stole, and the Masai looted from Coutlass and us.

"Were they branded?" asked Monty.

"Branded *and* hoof- *and* ear-marked," said I.

"Then they ought to be traceable, even among the huge herds the Masai have. I think I've influence enough by this time with this government to have those cattle traced and returned to Brown."

"They're his only love!" said I. "Do that for him, and he'll never wait to receive a present!"

Dawn found us still recounting our adventures and Monty alternately laughing and frowning.

"I regret Coutlass" he said, shaking the ashes from his pipe at last when Kazimoto brought our breakfast. "I regretted having to throw him out of the hotel in Zanzibar. I wish he could have escaped with his life—a picturesque scoundrel if ever there was one! I'd rather be robbed by him than flattered by ten Schillingschens or Lady Saffren Waldons. I suppose if I'd been with you I'd have killed him. It's well I wasn't. I might have regretted it all my days!"

"What de we see?" we called down.

We buried our newly won ivory under a tree, locating the spot exactly with the aid of Monty's compass, and broke camp, starting sleepless up the mountain. As Monty said:

"No use meandering around the mountain. Hassan might be higher up or lower down. If he *is* there you may depend on it he's tired of waiting. He's looking for a *safari*. Let's climb where we can be seen from miles away."

So climb we did, thousand after thousand feet, until the night air grew so cold that the porters' teeth chattered and they threatened to desert us. They grew afraid, too, remembering the tales the villagers had told them down below.

"Wow! You are not fat babies!" Kazimoto told them. "Who would eat such stringy meat as you?"

We came to caves that none of the men dared enter—vast, gloomy tunnels into the mountain through which the chill wind whistled like a dirge. Yet the caverns were warmer than the wind, and not bad camping-places if we could have persuaded the boys to take advantage of them.

The earth, too, all over the mountain and the range to eastward of it was warm in spite of the wind. In places there were warm springs bubbling from the rock, and at night and early morning a blanket of white mist that was remarkably like steam covered everything. It was a land of thunderless lightning—lightning from a clear sky, flashing here and there without warning or excuse. On the high slopes there was little or no game, and no signs whatever of inhabitants, until late one afternoon the porters shouted, and we saw an old man racing toward us along the top of a ridge.

He held his hands out, and shouted as he ran—a round-faced, big-bellied man, although not nearly so fat as when we saw him last; unclean, unkempt, in tattered shirt and crushed-in fez—a man with one desire expressed all over him—to see, and touch, and talk with other men. He ran and threw himself at Monty's feet, clasped his legs, and blubbered.

"Oh *bwana!* Oh, *bwana!* Oh, *bwana!*"

"Get up, Johnson!" Fred took him by the arm and raised him. "Tell us what's the matter."

"Men who eat men! Men who eat men! I had three porters to carry my tent and food. Now I have none. They have eaten them! Now they hunt me!"

"Well, you're safe," said Monty. "Calm yourself."

"But you are not *Bwana* Schillingschen! I am here to wait for him. Have you seen him? Where is he?"

Fred answered him. "Dead!"

Hassan threw himself on the ground again at Monty's feet.

"Oh, what shall I do?" he blubbered. "I am an old man. Who shall take my people out of jail? Who shall go to Dar es Salaam and make Germans give them up?"

"If you're willing to show us what you intended to show Schillingschen," said Monty, "I'll do what I can for your relations."

"What can you do? Oh, what can you do? No man but a German can make these Germans cease from punishing!"

Monty beckoned to the Baganda who had once done Schillingschen's dirty work.

"D'you see this man? This is a German spy. The German will be willing to hand over your relations in exchange for a promise not to make a fuss about this man. Wait a minute, though! Are your relations criminals?"

"No, *bwana!* No, *bwana!* My relations honorable folk! Formerly living in Zanzibar—going to Bagamoyo to serve in German family by invitation of person attached to German Consulate—no sooner landed than thrown in jail on charges they know nothing whatever about. Then Schillingschen he finding me, and say to me, 'You show where is that Tippoo Tib's ivory, and your relations shall go free!' And Tippoo Tib, he say to me, 'You take first step to show any man where is that ivory, and you shall be fed to white ants by my faithful people!' And Schillingschen he catch two of them faithful people, and feed 'em to white ants when nobody looking that way! Schillingschen terrible! Tippoo Tib terrible! What shall do? Tippoo Tib, he one time making me go long trip with *Bwana* Coutlass, very bad Greek, *Bwana* Coutlass wanting ivory—me pretending showing him—leading him wrong way. Coutlass very bad man, beating me *ngumu sana.* All the same, me more afraid of Tippoo Tib and *Bwana* Schillingschen. Not long ago Tippoo Tib sending me with *bwana* Coutlass second time, making bad threats against me if I not lead him wrong. Then Schillingschen he send for me and making worse threats! Oh, what shall do! Oh, what shall do!"

"You shall show us where that ivory is!" Monty answered him. "Stop blubbering! Get up! Look here! See this! (Get me that diary, Will.) If the Germans won't release your relations from jail on account of this Baganda, this is a written book that will make them do it! In this book are the names of men who have broken treaties and the law of nations. When the Germans know the British Government in London has this book under lock and key, they will think it a little thing to release your relations for the sake of avoiding trouble!"

"Promise me, *bwana!* You promise me!"

"I promise I will do my best for you."

"Word of an Englishman—promise!"

"Word of an Englishman—I promise to do my best!"

That was a proud enough moment on the shoulder of a mountain, with wilderness in every direction farther than the highest eagle in the air above could see, to have that helpless, hopeless ex-slave, part Arab, part *machenzie,* put his whole stock-in-trade—his secret—all he had on earth to bargain with for those he loved—in the balance on the promise of an Englishman. It was a tribute to a race that has had its share, no doubt, of bad men, but has won dominion over half the earth and pretty much all the sea by keeping faith with men who could not by any means compel good faith.

"Then I tell!" said Hassan. "Then I show!"

But now a new fear seized him, and he clung to Monty, trembling and jabbering.

"The men who eat men! The men who eat men!"

"Pah! Cannibals!" sneered Fred. "They're always cowards!"

"Tippoo Tib, he afraid of nothing—nobody! He is hiding the ivory where men who eat men can guard it and none dare come!"

"Lead on, McDuff!" Fred grinned, shouldering his rifle.

All of us except Monty had beards by that time that fluttered in the wind, and looked desperate enough for any venture. Considering the rifles and our uncouth appearance, Hassan took heart of grace. He insisted on an armed guard to walk on either side of him, and nearly drove Kazimoto frantic by ducking behind rocks at intervals, imagining he saw an enemy; but he did not refuse any longer to show the way.

It seemed that in expectation of Schillingschen's early arrival he had camped within a mile of the place where the stuff was hidden, taking unreasoning courage from the bare fact of having the redoubtable Schillingschen for friend. But the cannibals (who must have been a hungry folk, for there were no plantations, and almost no animals on all those upper slopes) had pounced on his three lean porters, missing himself by a hair's breadth.

In hiding, he had watched his three men killed, toasted before a fire in a cavern-mouth, and eaten. Then he had run for his life, following the shoulder of the mountain in the hope of meeting Schillingschen, munching uncooked corn he had in a little bag, hiding and running at intervals for a day and a night until he chanced on us. For an old man almost sick with fear he was astonishingly little affected by the adventure.

We took longer over the course than he had done, because he wanted to find cannibals, and teach them, maybe, a needed lesson. Fred's theory was that we should surprise them and pen them into a cavern, discovering some means of talking with them when hunger brought them out to surrender and cringe.

So we threw out a line of scouts, and pounced on cave-mouths suddenly, entering great tunnels and following the course of them in ages-old lava until sometimes we thought ourselves lost in the gloom and spent hours finding the way out again.

Time and again we found bones—bones of wild animals, and of birds, and of fish; now and then bones that perhaps had been monkeys, but that looked too suspiciously like those of the fat babies mothers mourned for in the villages below for the benefit of the doubt to be conceded without something more or less resembling proof. But never a human being did we see until we rounded the northeastern hump of the mountain in a bitter wind, and spied half a hundred naked men and women, thinner than wraiths, who scampered off at sight of us and volleyed ridiculous arrows from a cave-mouth. The arrows fell about midway between us and them, but threw Hassan into a paroxysm of fear, out of which it was difficult to shake him.

"Those are the people who ate my men! That is the cavern where Tippoo Tib hid the ivory! That is where my men's bones are! See—they have torn my tent for clothing for their naked women!"

We put Hassan under double guard for fear lest he bolt again and leave us. And all that day, and all the next we hunted for cannibals through mazy caverns that seemed to extend into the mountain's very womb. There were times when the stench was so horrible we nearly fainted. We stumbled on men's bones. We collided with sharp projections in the gloom—fell down holes that might have been bottomless for aught we knew in advance—and scrambled over ledges that in places were smooth with the wear of feet for ages. Everlastingly to right, or left of us, or up above, or down below we could hear the inhabitants scampering away. Now and then an arrow would flitter between us; but their supply of ammunition seemed very scanty.

At night we camped in the cavern mouth to cut off all escape, and resumed the hunt at dawn. But the caverns were hot—hotter by contrast with the biting winds outside; and when in the afternoon of the second day we all came out to breathe and cool off the running sweat, we saw the whole tribe—scarcely more than fifty of them—emerge from an opening above, whose existence we had not guessed, and go scampering away along a ledge like monkeys. Some of them stopped to throw stones at us—impotent, aimless stones that fell half-way; and Fred sent three bullets after them, chipping bits from the ledge, after which they showed us a turn of speed that was simply incredible, and vanished.

"Now for the great disillusionment!" laughed Will. "Hassan! Go forward, and show us where that hoard of ivory ought to be!"

We all expected disillusionment. Brown, who was under no delusion as to his share in the venture, scoffed openly at the idea of finding anything buried, in a land where every living "crittur," as he put it, was a thief from birth. But Hassan led on in, fearless now that the cannibals were gone, and positive as if he led into his own house and would show his house-hold treasures.

He stopped before a black-mouthed chasm, two or three hundred yards along the smallest subdivision of the cavern, and called for lights and a rope. We lit lanterns, and he showed us men's bones lying everywhere in grisly confusion.

"Tippoo Tib his men!" he remarked. "They throwing ivory in here, then byumby men who eat men kill and eat them. I alone living to tell! Plenty men who eat men in those days—all mountains full of them!"

He tied a lantern to a rope and lowered it down what looked like an old vent-hole in the lava. But the little light was lost in the enormous blackness, and we could see nothing.

"Send a man down!" he counseled.

We leaned over the edge and sniffed. There was a faint smell of what might be sulfur, but not enough to hurt.

"Who'll go?" asked Monty, and I thought he was going to volunteer himself.

"I go down!" announced Kazimoto cheerfully, and promptly proceeded to divest himself of every stitch of clothing.

We made our stoutest line fast under his armpits, gave him a lantern and lowered him over the edge. For fifty or sixty feet he descended steadily, swinging the lantern and walking downward, held almost horizontally by the slowly paid-out rope. Then he stopped, and we heard him whistling.

"What do you see?" we called down.

"Pembe!" (Ivory.)

"Much of it?"

"Teli!" (Too much!) "Oh, *teli, teli! Teli, teli, teli, TELI!"*

His voice ended with the very high-pitched note that natives use when they want to multiply superlatives. Then he whistled again. Next he called very excitedly.

"Very bad smell here, *bwana!* Pull me out quickly!"

L'ENVOI

The dry death-rattle of the streets
Asserts a joyless goal—
Re-echoed clang where traffic meets,
And drab monotony repeats
The hour-encumbered role.
Tinsel and glare, twin tawdry shams
Outshine the evening star
Where puppet-show and printed lie,
Victim and trapper and trap, deny
Old truths that always are.
So fare ye, fare ye well, old roofs!
The siren warns the shore,
The flowing tide sings overside
Of far-off beaches where abide
The joys ye know no more!
The salt sea spray shall kiss our lips—
Kiss clean from the fumes that were,
And gulls shall herald waking days
With news of far-seen water-ways
All warm, and passing fair.
They've cast the shore-lines loose at last
And coiled the wet hemp down—
Cut picket-ropes of Kedar's tents,
Of time-clock task and square-foot rents!
Good luck to you, old town!
Oh, Africa is calling back
Alluringly and low
And few they be who hear the voice,
But they obey—Lot's wife's the choice,
And we must surely go!
So fare ye, fare ye well, old roofs!
The stars and clouds and trees
In place of you! The heaped thorn fire—
Delight for the town's two-edged desire—
For thrice-breathed breath the breeze!
For rumble of wheels the lion's roar,
Glad green for trodden brown
For potted plant and measured lawn
The view of the velvet veldt at dawn!
Good-bye to you, old town!

XVIII

IF ALL is well that ends well, and only that is well, then this story fails at the finish, for we never caught the cannibals, so never taught them the lesson in housekeeping and economics that they needed. But there is no other shortcoming to record.

It is no business of any one's what terms we made in the end with the Protectorate Government; but thanks to Monty's tact and influence, and to their sense of fair play, we were treated generously. And if, when the world war at last broke out and the Germans undertook to put in practise the treachery they had so long planned, there was a secret fund of hugely welcome money at the disposal of the out-numbered defenders of British East, its source will no doubt be accounted for, as well as its expenditures, to the proper people, by the proper people, at the proper time and place.

But those who are curious, and are adept at unraveling statistics might learn more than a little by studying the export figures relating to ivory during the years that preceded the war. They say statistics never lie; but those who write them now and then do, and it may be that camouflage was understood and went by another name before the great war made the art notorious and popular.

Some of the ivory in that huge hole was ruined by the heat that still lives in Elgon's womb. Some of it was splintered by the fall when yoked slaves tossed it in. Rats had gnawed some of it, to get at the soft sweet core.

But the men who keep the keys of the bursting ivory vaults by London docks could tell how much of it was good, and what huge stores of it reached them. For some strange reason they are not a very talkative breed of men.

We did not haul the ivory out ourselves. That would have been too public a proceeding. But any one who attempted during the years that followed nineteen hundred to make a trip to Elgon can truthfully inform whoever cares to know, how jealously and wakefully the Protectorate Government guarded those lonely trails. And there are folk who saw the hundred-man *safaris* that came down from that way every week or so, carrying old ivory, said to be acquired in the way of trade. But that is really all government business, and looks impertinent in print.

We did not make enough money to establish Monty in the homes of his ancestors at Montdidier Towers and Kirkudbrightshire Castle; for that would have been an unbelievable amount; it takes more than mere affluence to keep up an earldom in the proper style. But we all got rich.

Brown received his cattle back after a long wait, as well as a present of money that set him up handsomely for life. And certain dissatisfied Masai were fined so many cows and sheep for raiding across the border that they talked of migrating out of spite to German East—but did not do it.

A youthful red-headed assistant district superintendent of police was unaccountably alert enough to round up and bring into court more than a dozen natives who had preached sedition. And, being lucky enough to secure convictions in every case, he was promoted. The last I heard of him he was fighting in the very heart of German East in command of a whole brigade. So it is advantageous sometimes to do favors for stray noblemen, provided you are clever enough, and man enough to make good when the favors are repaid.

And while on the subject of favors, the four homesick islanders who had lent us their canoes and came with us all that journey, were sent back to their island followed by a launch towing two barges full of corn—free, gratis, and for nothing—*"burre tu,"* as the natives say, meaning that the English are certainly crazy and giving away food without a pull-back to it simply and solely because "the people" have too much *nja*. *Nja* is the nastiest word in all those languages. It means the one thing everybody dreads—the thing that only the English seem to know charms against—want—emptiness—HUNGER.

At our expense, but by the favor of the government, there went to that island food enough in boxes and strong sacks—and seeds, treated against insects—and tools with which the wives could chop the soil up (for you can't expect the owner of a wife to work) to keep that island and its friendly folk from hunger for many a day.

THE SHRIEK OF DÛM

SOMEBODY UP on the stilt-legged bridge gave a monosyllabic command that sounded like a bored remark. Somebody else, who wore boots on the high, hot fo'c'stle-head lest his feet be broiled, struck iron with a hammer; it sounded like a pole-ax blow in a lonely abattoir where they kill one beast a day. The rusty anchor splashed into water nearly warm enough for cooking. The rustier chain-cable roared through the hawse-pipe—checked—coughed—had a spasm—and was still.

Somebody else made another remark devoid of all enthusiasm, and the French tramp-steamer *Jean Marie* lay at anchor, three miles off shore. Then the sharks that had fled like lightning flashes came back to inspect the ground-tackle suspiciously and wait about for jetsam, as visible in the blazing sunlight as if they swam in air, not water.

Between ship and shore lay a line of irregular fanged reefs, in among which the oily sea sucked and ejected itself. Land was a dazzling wilderness of whitish-yellow sand, but, if one stared long enough through puckered eyes, a darker blur grew recognizable. The glasses showed distinctly a semicircular drab maze of flat-roofed dwellings packed closely between the beach and the barren cliffs behind.

"Enfin," said the captain of the *Jean Marie,* "what in name of sacred absurdity persuades you, *messieurs,* to go ashore at this polluted place? I am devour' of curiosity. *Voilà*—the voyage is over. Remains nothing but to explain to me the reason of it."

He did not look curious, except perhaps for the brown eyes that were as sympathetic as a dog's. He was a very hairy man, bearded and whiskered like most French sea-captains, and his shoulders, even in that hot climate under the soiled white jacket, gave the impression of being protected by several shirts at least. Yet they were perfectly mobile; their shrug in the direction of Dûm, the three-mile distant port, was liquid eloquence. Just as he had the softest, hairiest mustache, he had the whitest teeth imaginable, and his smile redeemed the landscape as he stood with a hand on either hip and his back to the bridge-ladder.

Monty smiled down on him from a shaven, smooth six feet, his black mustache waxed out to needle-points and his manner cool and good-natured in spite of the heat, There was never a great deal in common until recent years between the British aristocracy and members of the French class that manned Villeneuve's guns and yards previous to throwing kings into the discard—perhaps nothing whatever except mutual admission of each other's right to unintelligible points of view, and a simply splendid courage. But each race adores politeness in its own way, and each prefers above all things to be gentle and to please—also, be it noted, wholly in its own way.

"We haven't told any one our intentions, *mo'sieur,*" Monty answered. "You might say they're vague. Can't tell you what we don't quite know ourselves, don't you know."

The captain laughed.

"Eh, bien. I come here because I am paid to—a most prodigious, unreasonable price or I would not have come. I go away again the minute after

you are safely landed, just as fast as this slow old *Jean Marie* can take me with trembling boiler and quivering sides! That is because I know Dûm. It must be because you do not yet know it that you visit such a place—*hein?"*

"Undoubtedly," grinned Monty, and Fred Oakes, tossing a cigar overboard because tobacco in that temperature tasted like straw, came and leaned against the hot side of the chart-room—or whatever the French call the den where the ship's officers play cards of afternoons. A shark came and swallowed the cigar. Fred swore explosively and stood away from the paintwork. It had blistered him.

"If you'd told us you'd been to the place, Captain, we'd have told you all we know willingly, in exchange for what you know," he said. "Didums, you oyster, limber up your French and explain to the cappy what we've come for."

"Why do you call him Didums?" asked the captain, vastly preferring his own English to our attempts at French. "Is that not what the English call baby-talk? He is so unlike a baby, that great, strong, tall, good-looking one, that so to name him is to laugh. Explain to me."

Whether or not because Fred was like himself, bearded—although not nearly so hairily—the captain liked him best of us four. He might have been expected to prefer Will Yerkes; French and Americans are ever friends in theory. But Will's swift summaries of the *Jean Marie's* defects had produced a sort of strained feeling that his offer to the engineer "to go over the old hooker and find some way of putting pep into her" had by no means relieved. But it was Will, with both hands in the pockets of colored flannel pants and a helmet pushed to the back of his head, who came to his assistance now and explained intricacies that are as Greek to the rank and file of either nation.

"Didums is short for Kirkoobrisher," he explained. "You spell that M-a-r-j-o-r-i-b-a-n-k-s and pronounce it Mundidger except on Tuesday and Friday afternoons. He's an earl, you know."

"Mon Dieu!" remarked the captain.

The Earl of Montididier and Kirkudbrightshire extracted the bulky cigar case from Will's side pocket, emptied its expensive contents into the captain's hands and returned the case to Will.

"It's perfectly simple," he said.

"That name is simple? *Mon Dieu!* I call that—"

"No, *mo'sieur.* I mean the reason of our being here."

"Then tell it to me, *mo'sieur* the Earl of Didums and Kirkoobreeches. I am in a mood to understand only very simple matters."

"Have you heard of King Solomon?" asked Monty.

"The gentleman who ruled Jerusalem?"

"Precisely."

"Mo'sieur, I have done more. I have pitied him. To have one wife is perhaps a privilege, at all events for the lady—but a thousand—*quel chaos!"*

"No doubt you recall," said Monty, "that King Solomon sent his men and his navies to some place then known as Ophir."

"But Dûm is not Ophir," said the captain. "Dûm is *Oh phui!* Very many bad smells to make a man spit and screw his nose up!"

"The legend we have heard," said Monty, "is that Solomon's navies used Dûm for a depot. The camel-trains are supposed to have come down here by routes long since vanished under blown sand, to meet the fleets with gold and ivory and spices. In case the legend is true, there ought to be discoverable traces."

"Sacré nom de Dieu! You will look for the traces of Solomon's mercantile marine?" He touched his forehead significantly. "You do not need money, for you have paid for the use of this ship like men to whom money is a bagatelle. You look for adventure? Permit me to observe that an expedition down the sewers of Paris or of London would provide danger more amusing and less insanitary! You look for discoveries—archieological—architectural—historical—cultural? Let me tell you, *messieurs.* These people of Dûm, if they ever had any history, are too much like animals—like great apes—to remember it!

"If these people of Dûm had ever any ancient architecture, then they have certainly pulled it down in order to make sides for cesspools or platforms for drying fish! If they ever had culture, it was that of vice, and believe me, they still pursue that with avidity! Discoveries? You will discover more different kinds of insects than your healthy imaginations permitted you previously to believe existed in all the universe. You will discover them, gentlemen, all in this one place—this place without a conscience, without scenery, without virtue, without happiness—this sink—this modern Sodom

and Gomorrah combined in one—this Red Sea port of Dûm! I wish you joy of your adventures, gentlemen."

"Sounds appetizing," grinned Will. "Who runs the place?"

"Pardon, it does not run. It stands still. It knows neither progress nor retrocession, having reached the dead-level bottom of all iniquity."

"I mean, who owns it? Who governs it? Who rules it?"

"THREE DIFFERENT questions, *mo'sieur.* The devil owns it! Turkey pretends to rule it. A sheik governs it, in the name of Allah, by permission of the Turkish Government because the Turks have no means of preventing him."

"Tell us about the sheik, won't you?"

"His name is Abdul bin Mahmoud. He calls himself also 'The Wrath and the Flail of God,' and 'The Lord of the Limits of Decency.' They say his mother was a Persian, which accounts for the extravagant self-esteem. He has many wives—how many, it is possible he himself has quite forgotten. One of them was French, which accounts for my former visit to the place at a time when she expended the remnants of her fortune by mail in the Paris shops and caused the cases and bales of merchandise to come to her by steamer.

"She had a daughter—a pretty little daughter, perhaps at that time nine or ten years old, who spoke both French and English as well as Arabic and was so loved by the sheik that he would willingly have had me, for instance, burned alive for her sole amusement. The little girl was chic, sweet, amusing, lovely. The mother was a little faded. I interviewed the mother through a sort of window breast-high—so—with great armed guards uglier than Satan standing close to me for fear lest I run off with her and compromise the sheik's conjugal renown. The mother was a leetle more than faded, but not without a certain charm.

"As for papa the sheik, *messieurs,* if I should have to make choice between taking supper with him or in a den of untamable lions, I would hasten to find a forceps with which to pull lions' teeth; that is all! In making choice I would not hesitate a moment."

"How old would the daughter be now?" asked Will.

"Oh, perhaps sixteen—seventeen."

Will whistled, and the captain opened his mouth wide like a man confronted with proof of his own wrong-doing.

"Oh, là, là! See what folly to talk too much. Intending to offer wise advice, what have I done! I should never have mentioned Rosalie."

Will whistled again.

"Cappy," he grinned, "it's more than three years of wandering in unpleasant places since I set eyes on a genuine skirt. You say she talks English?"

"Yes—she did—a little—not very well."

"And her name is Rosalie?"

"Ah, I will say no more of her!"

"Too late, Cappy! I'd go and lamp the lady if I had to swim!"

"No need to feed sharks," laughed the captain. "Look."

A fleet of small craft was headed toward us from the shore, paddling for lack of wind enough to fill their ragged sails.

"Was she pretty when you saw her all those years ago?" asked Will.

"She was the loveliest, *mo'sieur,* the prettiest, the sweetest little mistress of a whole city on whom my eyes ever rested—so lovely that the sheik would have slain any one so rash as to disobey her whims. Even the mother I think he would have slain."

"She must be a half-breed, though," said I, knowing Will's racial prejudice along that fine.

"Probably married long ago to a fat Greek trader or an Arab chief," added Monty. "They marry 'em young, you know, east of Vienna."

"As for marriage," said the captain with a shrug that expressed refusal to try to investigate the workings of destiny, "who can know? She was a little girl of spirit who would have her own way in all matters. But she was not half-breed—oh no, never!"

"Didn't you say the sheik was her father?" I asked. "We call a half-breed a person in whom the blood of the East and West is mingled."

The captain nodded.

"She is not half-breed. She was born in France or perhaps on board ship on the way from France. There was a *naufrage*—how do you call it—shipwreck, and this is no merciful coast for sinking ships. I do not know who the husband was; it is not always wise to inquire regarding such matters. Perhaps he was drowned on the ship—perhaps murdered—perhaps not. Who knows? The lady, the little Rosalie's mother, was made prisoner, and either she was compelled to marry the sheik or perhaps she made love to the sheik and persuaded him to marry her. Again who knows?

"Marriage is not a question of—what do you call it—red tape—in these parts. There is little ceremony. The lady steps behind a curtain, and if any other man ever sees her again it is either, as I saw this one, in the presence of armed guards on strictest business or else because the husband has grown too tired of her. Marriage is easy—divorce easier—murder easiest of all. Remain on my ship, gentlemen, and permit me to take you to safety in Suez—Alexandria—Marseilles."

"What was the color of Rosalie's eyes?" Fred inquired mischievously.

Will had turned his back to us and was gazing through the glasses toward shore.

"Blue!" said the captain. "Bluer than the sky in France in Summer time!"

Will faced about impatiently.

"Hair?" Fred inquired.

"Ah, I am growing old; I do not remember. I think it was of a certain shade between gold and brown."

"Just the very shade Will adores above all others!" Fred announced. "No, Captain, we decline your offer of a voyage toward safety, I'm afraid. Mr. Yerkes has made up his mind to go ashore. We have to look after him, be witnesses at the wedding, give evidence at the divorce-trial later on and all that sort of thing."

THE CAPTAIN threw all our affairs, and all responsibility attached to them, from off his shoulders with a more, expressive shrug than ever and walked aft to where an equally hairy mate was boring himself in attendance on the noisy winch. Our belongings—and they were very many—for the wise man does not travel too light to ports where no mail-steamers touch—were coming up from the after-hold and being deposited on the iron deck ready to be swung overside. The engine-room crew and the black cook emerged to stare and remark on our imbecility in French they probably imagined we could not understand. And presently the first of the oncoming shore craft grated alongside, its crew yelling for a rope and trying to find purchase for their fingers.

The captain ordered the hose got ready at once, a precaution the boatmen seemed to understand thoroughly.

"They have all the discommodities," he explained. "Smallpox—insects—sores—a bad smell—everything—as well as being bad thieves and expert at using the knife. No, they are not allowed on my ship!"

So a bargain was struck after a fashion I never saw before or since. Fred—our linguist—master of at least a dozen tongues and all their combined derivatives—was slung in a bosun's chair and lowered from the derrick until his legs were just out of reach of the boatmen's up-stretched hands. From that point of vantage he argued, bartered, swore, expostulated, abused, commanded, quoted the Koran, threatened not to come ashore at all and finally chartered a fleet of five crazy-looking boats to take us and our luggage at a price, in Maria Theresa dollars, that should have been sufficient to purchase the whole lot outright, crews and all.

Terms made, the captain wasted not another minute but ordered our things overside. Fred was hove inboard still exchanging insults with the boatmen, and Monty—always the most careful, as he was the least talkative or ostentatious of us—took his stand where he could overlook proceedings without annoying the mate, who was touchy regarding supervision.

Fred, once free of the bosun's chair, went to shooting craps with the colored cook by way of making him a present; he owed him gold in next to no time, and the cook's smile as he pouched the coin was more than "much fine gold." For that matter so was Fred's, who, when his guileless diplomacy chances to succeed, prefers that the world should know it.

Will and I paced the deck at the captain's right and left hand, he rather bored with us and we determined to extract from him the last few shreds of information.

"Parbleu!" he exclaimed, throwing his hands up after about the tenth question. "I have told you all I know. It is a devil of a place, this Dûm, hot, dry, unwholesome. No man in his senses would visit it except for business reasons."

"But why does anybody stay there?" I insisted.

"Mon Dieu, what a question!"

"The sheik must like it. He must have some way of keeping his subjects interested. What does he do? How does he get his revenues?"

"Revenues? He steals them!"

"From whom? From his subjects? Then where do they get wealth for him to steal?"

"Sacré, nom! He was desirous even to make me—me understand—pay an import duty on the merchandise I was bringing to his own wife! If there were nothing else to steal they would remove the golden glimmer from the ripples on the sea."

"Is there no trade here?" Will asked.

"None any more. They have destroyed the oyster-beds that gave them pearls. What else have they to trade with?"

"Have they no cattle?"

"A few mangy camels. A few oxen that draw water from the wells—such lean oxen that they look like hungry dogs! A few lean goats. A very few sheep. Some chickens."

"And how many people?"

"That is the astonishing part—that so many disreputable characters can be found to submit to existence in such a spot—such a dirt-spot! There were at least five thousand people when I was there last."

"Do they take in each other's washing?" suggested Will.

"Mon Dieu! They never wash! None but the sheik and his wives and immediate entourage—and they only because the act causes trouble for the servants who must carry water! Therefore they wash very often and wear white clothes!"

"Linen?" Will suggested.

"Linen—fine cotton—silks."

"Where do they get them?"

"Oh, I suppose occasional steamers—now and then dhows—ships perhaps from Turkey or from Aden."

"How do they pay for them, if they have no more pearls and no wealth of any kind?"

"Sacré nom d'un question, how should I know? *Voilà!* Look! See! There the place lies, and there it stinks. There are the boats to take you ashore, *messieurs.* I wish you *bon voyage et bonne fortune!* It is only to be hoped you shall not be like the ladies who go to get married—a step behind a curtain—*poof*—good-by—oblivion!"

"Come along," called Monty. "They've only

dropped one case into the sea so far, and that was tinned soup."

"Are the guns and ammunition safe?" Will asked.

"Yes. So's the dynamite. If we hadn't packed the guns in wooden boxes to look like anything but what they are, I suspect those boatmen would have bolted with them and left us to follow if we dared. Is your pistol where you can reach it in a hurry?"

Fred, Will and I patted the place where each preferred to keep his weapon.

"All right, then—down the rope one at a time—who goes first? I? Oh, very well. By-by Captain! *Au revoir!* See you again some day!"

"Au revoir I hope, *messieurs!* They say the good God cares especially for those who have not too great discretion!"

II

SO WE landed on the evil-smelling beach of Dûm, although not without preliminary incident. In the first place the boatmen claimed their craft were too heavily loaded already to permit our traveling together in one. Rather than waste time arguing in the hot glare with a hand on the rope and a foot on an unsteady boat's broken gunwale, we yielded the point. And, having separated us, they imagined us completely in their power.

Boatmen never were original. There were always good ones, always bad ones; not even pirates ever invented a new way of drowning passengers. No sooner clear of the ship's side and out of reach of possible rifle-shot than these ceased paddling and began to try to extort double the sum they had bargained for, with payment in advance, pointing significantly at the sharks that swarmed around us and actually nosed the boats.

Of course it was only a matter of pointing pistols at them—utterly unexpected pistols of a sort they had never seen—and then explaining what the pistols were. I shot a shark in the nose and, when that failed to kill him, again in the spine. Forthwith my boatmen became so eager to get the shark-meat before the other ravening monsters could tear and gorge it all that they nearly upset the boat. I snatched a paddle and, threats failing, had to begin actually to knock the nearest man overboard before he and the rest of them saw the point and consented to stick to business.

Then the men in the fifth canoe, having no passengers, imagined they could make away with the baggage and took a course almost at right-angles to ours. Moreover, our crews refused to give chase and head them off. For some reason they all doubted the length of range of Colt's repeaters.

So they had to be convinced. Will was our best shot with a pistol, but the sun was in his eyes. Intending to knock the paddle out of a man's hand on the deserting boat, he barked the skin of his breast and back with two shots. That was sufficient. The deserters elected to behave and paddled back among us, we taking station north, south, east and west of them to prevent any further tricks.

We came through a gap in the fangs of the reef by a miracle, the sharks crowding through after us, inconvenienced nearly as much as ourselves by the tidal suction in the shallow opening, "like a run of monstrous salmon," as Monty put it. And we landed on the filthy beach without any miracle at all by the simple process of upsetting everything and everybody into the surf and then racing to salvage the baggage before the undertow could suck it out of reach forever.

"There was a stone pier here once on a time," said Monty. "Look."

Great blocks of tough rock worn smooth by sea and sand lay half-covered, in positions clearly indicative of some long-ago forgotten purpose. The stuff resembled granite, although there was no sign of quarry or of anything but sand in the hills behind the town.

But we had no time then for archeology. We were pounced on by the riffraff of the town, who seized our belongings and bore them off with no regard whatever for our threats. Pistols pointed at them only made them laugh, and, as Fred said, "it would probably queer the luck if we began our activities in Dûm with murder." There was nothing for it but to follow with as much dignity as we could summon, picking our way gingerly amid the unspeakable filth of a Red Sea beach. The original Gehenna of the Jews can not have been more fly-inflicted.

From the steamer's deck the town had seemed to lie down by the water's edge, but actually there was almost a quarter of a mile of loose sand between the sea and the nearest dwellings. It was toward those that our possessions were being borne at top speed—a motley collection of flat-roofed, windowless shacks built all about a more pretentious building that boasted two rude towers and a sort of medieval fortification guarding the main door.

It was not the sheik's palace we were headed for, because that was perfectly obvious half a mile away—bigger and better built, with the Turkish crescent banner flying from the roof. Our destination proved to be a sort of punctuation mark at which all the straggling streets and alleys of Dûm came to an end, and, judging by the dirty, trampled condition of the sand, it was a more than ordinarily busy quarter of the town.

As we approached, a string of lean, solemn camels emerged from a gap in the wall of the largest building and betrayed the fact that the main entrance was either dummy or else kept closed. The gap in use was simply a break that had never been repaired; those who used it had even been too lazy to remove the débris, and the camels had to climb over it clumsily.

It was through that gap that our belongings were hurried: so through it we followed, to find ourselves in a great courtyard with a deep veranda along the greater part of all four sides and a broad open space in the midst of which the camels had been stabled. Our luggage was set down in a heap where the camels had been; we all four began counting the loads aloud at once, but could not determine whether anything was missing. Most important of all, though, perhaps, the guns and ammunition were there in their deceptive white-pine boxes.

ALL OF the verandas but one were screened, for the most part with shabby-looking black cloth, although here and there was a touch of faded color. On the only open one stood four chairs that suspiciously resembled fittings from a ship's saloon, and toward those a nondescript individual motioned us with gestures that were half-insolence and half-obsequious salaam.

He was the dirtiest-looking scarecrow I had ever seen anywhere, although he wore a clean white cloth wrapped several times around his middle. The rest of his clothes, from the red fez stuck on the back of his head at an angle to the goatskin sandals, were almost falling from him with age and filth.

"You gents English?" he asked, with a sidewise, half-impudent glance at Monty.

We sat down, grateful for the shade, and stared at him. The men who had brought us ashore and the men who had carried our luggage squatted in the sun staring at us, waiting to be paid and clamorous with reasons why no sum anybody named could be enough.

"Are you?" demanded Monty.

"Hi was once. Hi ain't nothink now. Nobody's nothink in these parts," he added insolently.

"How do you come to be here?"

The man drew himself up and removed the twisted cigaret from behind his ear in a partly conscious effort to achieve dignity. He spoke slowly, giving the impression of having learned what he had to say by heart in preparation for just such a contingency.

"Hi come 'ere of me own free will, same as any man's entitled to. Hi stays 'ere to suit meself, an' it ain't no bus'ness o' nobody's. Hi've me rights, the same as any man."

"Why do you wear that fez?" demanded Monty.

He had evidently planned to create a great impression on all strangers, and being put through his paces visibly annoyed him. Given time he might have attained to a lofty arrogance, but just at the moment birth, education, memories, old habit and perhaps the remnants of wholesome shame had him all bewildered, and he answered like a culprit in the dock.

"Hi've a right to adopt hany religion I please! What diff'rence does it make whether you calls Gawd, Gawd or Allah? It's all one to me, and I takes no stock in the argyment 'at Gawd gives a —— one way or the other. Hi'm a Mohammedan, that's what Hi am—as good as any Christian or better."

"How long were you in the army?" asked Monty, with a slight change of inflection that ever so subtly suggested friendlier interest.

"Hi never was in no army."

The man assumed a very deliberate, entirely unconvincing slouch.

"The whole world seems to be peppered over with the British army's relics!" said Will.

"It is," Monty agreed. "No better men breathe than the good ones. There are no worse blackguards than the broken ones; no worse liars—sots—thieves—tramps—idlers. But there's good in them all."

"Of course," nodded Will. "Every man has good in him. We all know that."

"That's not what I mean," said Monty. "These

men who have been in our army have something more—something the army gave them in return for service rendered. The worst cases I ever met have always redeemed themselves when shown an opening."

If proof were needed that this man lied in denying he had ever served in any army, it was there in the manner of his standing—speechless while two other men discussed him like the commanding officer and a subordinate in an orderly-room.

"What do you do here?" asked Monty.

"Me? I works for Mr. Snoblauch."

It was on the tip of my tongue to ask who he might be and what he did, but Monty saw fit not to appear ignorant.

"In what capacity?"

"Ho, I'm a sort o' gen'ral manager—anything what turns up—anything what nobody else won't do or ain't able to do. I keeps a heye on all an' sundry."

"You're not well dressed for a man with responsibility," said Monty. "Doesn't your master pay you?"

" 'Im?" said the nondescript, bridling visibly. " 'E ain't my master! Hi don't call no man me master, let alone no old German 'uckster! Hi'm me own master!"

"I've a suit of English clothes in one of my boxes," said Monty, "that very likely might fit you with a bit of alteration here and there. Don't you think it would become you better than those rags you're wearing? More in line with self-respect, wouldn't it be? More in keeping with your race, and your past? It's not good for an old army man to slouch about in your garb."

"Hi tell you I weren't never in no army!" the man retorted.

"Polish up your memory," suggested Monty. "Think the offer over. I won't withdraw it for the present."

" 'Tention all. This'll be Snoblauch," whispered Fred.

The nondescript faced about very much at his leisure with the deliberate purpose of asserting disrespect, and we all glanced across the courtyard toward where another individual was emerging through a gap between two shabby cloth curtains.

He came hurrying toward us with the tassel of an almost new red fez dangling over one eye, dressed in a suit of tweeds made in Europe donned in a great hurry—for one end of his suspenders dangled down behind—and carpet slippers that lent him an otherwise unexplainable air of benign senility.

He was a man of not more than middle age, although his beard and mustache were nearly white. His stomach gave notice of four meals a day and naps in the shade of afternoons, and he walked like a man unaccustomed to much exercise.

HE WAS all smiles that increased as he drew nearer, and he fairly ran across the last few yards of camel-desecrated compound.

"Velcome, *meine Herren!* Velcome, shentelmen! Vot a treat! No, no; sit down! My man here shall fetch me a chair. Go, Villiam—bring me at vonce a chair, *ja!*"

"Your brace is 'anging down, you old fool," announced the man addressed as Villiam. " 'Ere, I'll show yer."

He seized the offending article and jerked at it so violently that it came away in his hand. He held it up, roaring with laughter until, seeing that no one else joined in, he ceased suddenly and stalked off with less than his usual slouch.

"Zat man is no good—terrible—but what can you expect to find in Dûm? Tell me your names, please. My own is Snoblauch—Walter Snoblauch, merchant, importer and perhaps Imperial German consul."

Villiam came back carrying the chair, an old cane-bottomed thing, swinging it aloft in one hand and whirling it to show at one and the same time indiscipline, strength of wrist and independence. He slammed it down behind Snoblauch and went and stood at a little distance, whistling.

We announced our names, Monty giving his as Montdidier, *tout court* without the handle, and Snoblauch addressed him thenceforward as *Herr* or else Mr. Mundidger, assuming for some inscrutable reason that I was the aristocrat of the party, perhaps because I said least, having least to say. In the days that followed he several times addressed me as "your lordship."

"And vy are you here?" he asked.

We told him.

"Archeology?" His eyes hardened. "There is none here. None whateffer!"

"We have already seen traces of a very ancient stone pier," I answered, but Monty promptly kicked my shin with his heel.

The change in the German's manner was astonishing. From garrulous hospitality he went to silent suspicion at a bound. One recognized the physical act of closing up his mind against us lest anything he might say should serve our purpose. And he set himself to study what our purpose might be with the sort of cunning of a child denied the key of a cupboard.

"Vy have you come?" he asked again. "Vhat are in those boxes? Vhat steamer brought you? Vhither has it gone? And vhen vill you go?"

"We'll go all right when we're ready," said Will. "Where can we get board and lodging?"

The German did not answer him but came over and stood in front of me.

"You tell!" he insisted, leveling a finger at me. "Tell me why you come and vhen you go."

I took a leap in the dark, so to speak, nervous lest Monty accuse me of telling too much again, yet judging it good policy to put our host at ease. And I accomplished the exact opposite of what I hoped, yet did no harm.

"We've some presents for Rosalie," I said. "We'll go away when we've Rosalie's permission."

"Rosalie?" he answered. *"Oh, Mein Gott! Mein Gott! Mein Gott! Wass für unsinn!"*

He snapped his fingers, made impatient noises through his teeth, paced up and down in front of us a time or two without saying a word and then went straight back across the dung-littered courtyard and disappeared between the shabby curtains. From behind them we could hear him denouncing somebody—us perhaps—in what sounded like mixed Arabic and German.

"And nothing said about dinner," remarked Fred.

"But Rosalie's in the land of the living," Will answered. "We've made sure of that."

"No, we haven't," said Monty. "Perhaps the idea of our bringing presents for a girl who is dead or gone away is what upset him."

Vlliam the unclean, with snowy whiteness still about his middle and his fez at a more than ever impudent angle, came near and leaned against a veranda-pole that looked remarkably like a ship's spar. He stuck both hands deep in the pockets of his baggy Turkish pants, in hope of establishing by illustration how unmartial his past had been, and proceeded to prove what a fine sense he had of responsibility.

"The old fool's gone in to sulk an' study out a plan," he announced. "You've busted 'is schemes for fair!"

Nobody answered. It was hardly our business to prevent him from telling the secrets of the man whose salt he ate; so he continued.

"Soon as 'e seed you acomin' in the boats, 'e sets me to scarin' up natives to go an' grab your things an' bring 'em 'ere. 'E's got two ideas, 'e 'as, and 'is 'ead won't 'old no more. One is to be made the German consul 'ere—which they ain't got no consulate, nor no trade, nor nothin' at all, 'xcept a lot o' schemes, an' as long as 'e'll do their dirty work wi'out pay they'll let him, an' I've told 'im so a thousand times."

"What's the other?" I interrupted.

He seemed likely to wander off into accounts of his own long-sightedness.

"T'other's Rosalie! But she's too wide awake, besides bein' a judge of a man if ever I see one. The old fool thinks 'e can twist 'er round 'is little finger. Fact is she twists 'im. She'd 'ave 'ad the sheik scrag the old fossil long ago, on'y 'e gets books an' clothes an' pictures for 'er from Europe, an' she knows no other way o' gettin' 'em. 'E'd two reasons for 'avin' me set all the boys to grabbin' your things on the beach.

"One was to get you all 'ere afore Rosalie or 'er pa could 'ave first chin with you. T'other was to keep 'em all too busy to go a-runnin' to 'er wi' early inf'mation. But don't you worry. I sent a runner to 'er straight away quick—with orders! Now, about that suit o' clothes you was mentionin', sir—"

"About the sheik," said I. "Tell us about him."

"HI CALLS 'im the shriek—the shriek o' Dûm! 'E's a shriek for fair, an' no argyment. 'F 'e weren't Rosalie's pa—or so 'e will 'ave it, although 'e ain't really nothin' o' the kind—I'd 'ave left this 'ole long ago. But, bein' as 'ow she's 'ere an' got no friends of 'er own color an' persuasion, why I stays 'an' puts up wi' the shriek an' old Snoblauch. When the shriek wants to 'ave me crucified or fed to the sharks or buried alive for gettin' 'alf-cocked an' singin' songs outside Rosalie's windows, she interferes.

"An', when Snoblauch seeks to 'ave me jailed for one thing or another, she interferes again. Which that's no trifle. You just ought to see the jail! Rosalie's no perishin' sister o' mercy, but, if it weren't for 'er, the shriek 'ud skin the devil an' make hell look like a drorin'-room! The shriek's the jimdandiest son of a rotten tomater ever I see! Now about that suit o' European clothes as you was speakin' of—"

The truth of a part of his story was established that very second by the arrival of messengers, who entered breathless through the gap without ceremony and without more than a glance in our direction began to order our unpaid boatmen and porters to shoulder our effects once more and follow them. They seemed to take it for granted we would not let our luggage out of sight.

"It's the same principle," said Fred, "that the chuckers-out use in London music-halls. Ever see them at work? They each take a tail of a man's dress-coat and haul on it; the second he hears the coat ripping up the back the very drunkest lunatic begins to come quietly!"

Monty laughed.

"The last time I drove to the Derby we passed a dozen donkey-carts whose 'mokes' were being persuaded to trot by a bunch of carrots on the end of a stick. Same idea! Well—what do you say? Shall we follow them and see?"

He got up from his chair to lead the way, but a big brute who looked about half-Somali, black as ebony and stronger than a bull, swaggered over to us and began jabbering orders at a great pace.

"What does he say is the matter with him?" asked Will.

"That's Rosalie's chief eunuch," announced Villiam. " 'E says for you to come 'is way."

Monty sat down again promptly.

"Nothing to be gained by forgetting what is due to one," he said. "Tell that eunuch to take back word to his mistress that distinguished visitors are here, who expect distinguished treatment."

"What's the use?" demanded Villiam. "All 'e'll do is carry away your goods an' leave you flat."

"Did you hear what I told you to tell him?" Monty demanded, and Fred began in much too good Arabic to try to make the eunuch understand.

Seeing the job of interpreter being thus snatched from him, Villiam made all haste to translate the answer into the villainous patois that passed current for local speech. The eunuch instantly grew civil. By gesture more than words he sought to make us understand that we were invited, not commanded, to follow him, but Monty took no more notice than of the crows that perched along the roof. We took our cue from Monty and lighted cigars.

So the eunuch, looking worried and all in a shiny sweat with sense of responsibility, went off with our belongings, and we sat feeling like unwise virgins, as Fred described it, yet much more masters of the situation than we guessed.

"If we had followed that rascal," said Monty, "we'd have been given the raw end of everything until we leave town."

"We'll talk about leaving town," said Will, "after we've seen the baby-doll!"

As soon as our porters had vanished through the gap in the wall vainly clamoring for their pay, Snoblauch came slippering out again, no particle less suspicious but apparently convinced it was wisest to get on our soft side.

"Mein Gott!" he exclaimed, shaking two fists in the air. "Vat did zat man threaten you? Zat was Rosalie's eunuch. Did she send for you and you not go? You must be crrrrazy. I must make peace for you. I must interfere. I must protect your property and your persons. It is known I am to receive the appointment of imperial German consul. My authority is sufficient on that ground to save your situation. I vill go. I vill expostulate. You vait here."

Before we could offer him any remonstrance he had gone slippering back to the veiled mystery of his private quarters, muttering and arguing to himself, with a hand held up as if to ward off impending disaster while he figured out a way to prevent it at its source. We heard him shout for a camel, but the camels were all gone. He roared for his donkey to be brought, but, although the donkey stood munching straw in dusty solitude in a corner of the courtyard, there seemed nobody to saddle and bring the beast.

He yelled for his sunshade, his smoked glasses and his elastic-sided boots—now in German, now in Arabic, now in English. Nobody obeyed him, although there were undoubtedly plenty of people behind the scenes, for we heard their voices.

"The old fool's in one of 'is tantrums," explained Villiam. "Later on 'e'll come an' threaten to 'ave me 'orse-whipped—which I'd like to see 'im dare try! 'E won't be fit to speak to until after Rosalie 'as give 'im a piece of 'er mind, an' then 'e'll cringe. Now, about that suit o' clothes as you was speakin' of. They've been an' took everything. Lord knows when you'll see a single thing again. If you was to mention to me in which o' those there packages the suit o' clothes was, maybe I might manage to swipe it and anything else you particularly fancied for yourselves at the same time. 'Ow would that be?"

But Monty was in unresponsive mood.

"You'll have to wait and see, my man," he answered.

Besides what we had in our pockets the only thing left to us was Fred's new concertina, obtained by parcels-post from London but a day before we started on the trip and considered so precious that he kept it within reach of his hand by day and night. It had not even been wetted when the boats turned over in the surf, for he held it high in the air.

HE UNDID the clasp now and began to while the time with music reminiscent of the London music-halls, of "smokers" in Cape Town and Johannesburg, of the Lisbon quays, of Paris cabarets, and of unauthorized, unadvertized entertainments in those strange parts of the world where, in times of stress, the King of England's junior officers forgather. There is absolutely no end to Fred's musical resources, just as there is no known port where you can land him and not find him unearthing friends within the hour.

Now he proceeded to make friends, there being none available of the vintage of other years. Villiam recalled old evenings in canteen and, speechless from reminiscence, strutted to and fro amid the camel dung posturing ridiculously, his baggy pants extended like a circus clown's and his feet pattering out the long-forgotten steps of jigs and breakdowns.

There began to be movement too behind the shabby curtains. Every once in a while a female head appeared—by no means always the same one—to be jerked back instantly in response to force applied from behind. A man with a long stick came to do guard duty in front of the curtains but became so enraptured by the music that he forgot to strike at outthrust female heads. We became on nodding terms with all the old German's harem, and Snoblauch came out himself at last, having discarded European clothes and arrayed himself in Arab dignity that suited him far better.

He seemed better able to enforce respect in that garb. Even Villiam ceased step-dancing and obeyed him, picking up camel's dung to throw at every female who dared discover herself.

"Oh, play somezing of Wagner," he begged. "It is longer since I heard somezing of Wagner than is good to remember!"

But Fred is no Wagnerian enthusiast and said so.

"Play, then, from Beethoven."

"Can't," said Fred.

"Play, then, *'Die Fruekling.'* No? You do not know that? Play, then, *'Die Wacht am Rhein.'* "

Fred broke promptly into "Rule Britannia" and, since Will was considerate enough to hum the tune, followed it with "Yankee Doodle." Snoblauch paced up and down shaking his head.

"Zat 'Yankee Doodle' zing is not so insupportable," he said when Fred had finished. "Von of these bright days the United States is going to vake up and be German; zen zat tune vill be a German tune, and all is well. It is bright. It is lifely. It is not bad. But that zing 'Rule Britannia'—*phui!* Such jingoismus! I assure you that within a few years ze only connection British ships shall have vith the sea vill be to lie rrro'ting under it! Vait and see! Play somezing else!"

But Fred did not get the opportunity. Astonishing interruption intervened in the shape of Rosalie on camel-back, surrounded by hot, yelling natives, headed by the eunuch, who had run all the way through the sand and were one and all determined to get their effort's worth if not in entertainment, then in trouble. A more truculent, abominably noisy crowd surely never burst through a hole in a wall; nor was there ever a more refreshingly unconventional lady than their mistress.

She was not veiled, except for a gauzy brown affair to keep the sun from her face that she used artfully as an edge to loveliness. Amid a babel of yells the camel kneeled, and in little silken slippers and a dress that combined the East's appetite for coolness with Western love of freedom Rosalie stepped down and stared at us.

She answered faithfully to the French captain's description of her. Delight at the novelty of meeting strangers brightened her blue eyes and lent color to pale cheeks. The Red Sea coast is no complexion-maker, but protection from sun and wind had preserved her natural creamy whiteness. If her lips were not rouged, then she had stolen the color from the reddest Persian roses and kept it by some magic of her own.

Leaning back against the kneeling camel to get a better look at us four, she clapped her hands—little exquisite white hands, loaded with barbaric rings.

Her little bare feet in the pale-blue slippers began to dance excitedly.

"Oh!" she exclaimed. "Oh! Oh!" glancing from one to another of us.

Suddenly she laughed like a child and ran to Monty—threw both arms around him and upset the immaculate points of his mustache by kissing him repeatedly on the mouth. Before he could recover from surprise she had left him and was kissing Fred—then me.

"Oh, 'ow different you all schmell!" she exclaimed, looking at us admiringly.

Then she attacked Will and kissed him half a dozen times.

Monty accepted his dose philosophically enough, adjusted his mustache ends and was himself again. As the oldest of us—colonel of cavalry, politician, privy councillor—he might be expected to have his nerve under control and he had. Fred blushed like a schoolboy and giggled like a girl. I decline to record my own sensations. Will was the only one of us' who acted like a man of flesh and blood. He stood up and gave her back more kisses than she had bargained for.

"Oh, you!" she laughed, pointing a finger at him as he set her down.

Except that his ears stick out, Will is a handsome young man, without Monty's dignified presence but with an ever-exuding glow of human spirits. She loved him on the instant, and we groaned as we watched.

"COME AGAIN, Rosalie!" he said and held his arms out.

She flung herself into them, and they clung lip to lip for half a minute.

"Vy arre you 'ere? Vot you come for? 'Ow long you stay?" she demanded, dropping her aitches after the manner of Villiam and murdering her consonants something after Snoblauch's way.

Will took her hand in his.

"We've brought you presents, sweetheart," he said, stealing my thunder without blinking.

"Where? Where?"

"In the baggage your savages took from us."

"Terry arre not safagees! They took nozzing! All zings haf been taken to a 'ouse beside my 'ouse. Vat else 'you come for?"

"We're just travelers, sweetheart—inquisitive people—come to have a look-see."

"Vot is zat—sweet'eart?" She flashed a look of indignant rebuke at Villiam, who winced under it. "You nevair told me, Villiam, vot is sweet'eart!"

"You bet yer life I didn't," he grumbled. "If old Snoblauch 'ad over'eard me a-tellin' yer what sweet'eart means, 'e'd 'a told yer pa, the shriek, an' I'd ha' been faced wi' a fine 'owdydo!"

"You tell me!" she coaxed, turning her back on the indignant henchman and looking into Will's eyes.

"Not here!" he laughed. "Later—somewhere else—when you know me better."

Nobody took the slightest notice of Snoblauch, who had slippered across the courtyard and was standing scandalized before us, his eyes ablaze with fury and his fists trembling with the vain, prodigious effort to suppress his feelings.

"Just at present—sweetheart," said Will, squeezing her hand and having his own squeezed in return, "we're anxious about board and lodging. We don't like these quarters. Is there a caravanserai?"

She laughed—just like a child at a party, pushing at his breast with both hands.

"Zere is ze 'ouse next to my 'ouse. You vill all come at vonce."

At that point Snoblauch saw fit to intrude objections and began a regular tirade in guttural Arabic. But she cut him short.

"Malaish!" she said—an Arabic word that means simply "it doesn't matter"—but that can be made to mean a very world of insolence besides.

He resumed his flow of rhetoric, but she cut him short again by the swiftly simple expedient of spitting in his face three times. At that the ineffable Villiam set up a yelp of laughter, and all the black men jeered in chorus. Snoblauch exploded, shook both fists at the universe, rubbed the spittle from his face and backed away.

"Bah!" exclaimed Rosalie, spitting at him again. "Now I need you no longer to tich me Inglees, old *vache!* Now I nevair marry to your old Bedouin sheik of Urza! As for you yourself, you go to ——, as Villiam say it! I shall tell my papa you are no good—Germanee sausage, like Villiam also say it—cheat—tomfool—son-of-a ——"

Will placed a hand over her mouth, and she made her teeth nearly meet in his finger by way of reprisal. He winced but refused to release her until the outraged German had departed in high dudgeon to his holy of holies. Will had kissed those red lips too recently to care to hear gutter-language flow from them.

"I hope she uses much worse words than that!" Fred whispered to me. "Let's pray she disgusts him utterly before tonight!"

But she was nothing less than charming as she turned away and began giving orders to the crowd, among whom we recognized the rascals who had paddled us ashore as well as those who pounced on our belongings. It occurred to Monty at that minute to commence paying them, sufficient time having elapsed to make them aware that their likes and dislikes were not the most pressing or important matters in the universe. But she commanded him to stop with a gesture that was positively regal, and the meekness, with which that swarm of Red Sea pirates submitted to being deprived of pay they had earned was the best proof we had had yet of her power in the land.

It seemed she had brought donkeys for us to ride. She ordered them now brought in through the gap in the wall—fine, white Arabian beasts, saddled and bridled with fancy leather and not lean like Snoblauch's camels or his own particular donkey that munched straw in the corner. These were fit mounts for a journey home from Mecca.

"Again!" she said and held her arms out.

Will picked her up and kissed her to her heart's content—no meagerly measured dole! Then she sprang on her camel and commenced kicking and thumping while her uproarious following yelled to the beast to rise. We had to mount our donkeys in a hurry then, for they kicked and plunged to be off, and the men who were holding them let go to give chase to the camel. In another minute we were leaping and scrambling through the gap in the wall in full gallop after the camel, and he was a genuine riding-beast with speed and a gift for kicking up a cloud of dust behind him. White men striving to combine dignity with donkey-back and too-short stirrups are a sight for the god of practical jokes, and each could hardly ride for laughing at the other.

We rode through the streets of Dûm like a troop of marauders, followed by yelling fiends who ran with outspread toes and by all the yelping curs that are the only sewerage system Red Sea Arabs understand. Our course was through a maze of narrow, winding, human rat-runs, with no pretense at paving. Nor was the slightest effort made to avoid collision with the presumably lawful loiterers before the doors. Whoever heard or saw us coming ran for his life, taking no chances.

THERE WERE no windows overlooking the street. Perhaps from the superior height of camel-back Rosalie could see at times over a flat low roof and into a courtyard, but all we saw were everlasting blank walls and doors that slammed before we reached them. Even the mosque we passed was closed against us. Three men who sat cross-legged on a platform by the door of a coffee-house, stumbled inside one after the other; a moment later a swarm of dusky customers pushed their heads and rifle muzzles out into the street again, but we galloped too swiftly round a turn to offer the leisurely aim an Arab likes.

Up past the sheik's great, four-square, squat pile of buildings we galloped, passing an armed guard well enough trained to keep the hammers of the long trade muskets cocked but too scornful of woman, or else too surly, to salute Rosalie. She spat as she passed them, which seemed significant, for all through the East the act of spitting is the pluperfect expression of contempt. The guard took no notice of the act whatever—tall, wiry-looking, solemn men in soiled white burnooses and flowing robes, as silent as the disgusting vultures perched on a wall nearby.

The sheik's "palace" proved to be the northern limit of the town. Beyond it was a wilderness of baking, blazing sand. Around its other three sides was an almost princely generous open space, kept comparatively clear of rubbish. Facing toward that were the town's best houses, if that is a house which has no windows, and if it can be said to face at all. All the roofs were flat, and some were surrounded by a breast-high parapet. One place was stables—camel and cow and donkey by the smell. One was the " 'ouse near my 'ouse" to which Rosalie was leading us.

She stayed outside on camel-back, not venturing as far as the threshold. Perhaps some stray figments of convention held her after all.

"You go in zere!" she ordered. "You stay in zere! In zere you are all olright! My papa, Sheik Abdul bin Mahmoud, is letting you alone, or I mak' for heem a grreat trouble. Food is bring you zere—all your zings arre zere—you stay zere. Bye and bye you 'ear from me again, and you gif me ze presents—yes? Goo'-by!"

She laughed and hit the camel a crack with a leather thong she had knotted on her wrist. The beast swung into a league-long trot at once, and we watched until she vanished round the palace corner, followed at full pelt by her black attendants.

"You'd think they'd stay for their pay now at least," wondered Monty.

"Don't worry—they'll come for it," said Fred. "We've a worse trouble on our hands than that!"

We did not waste words asking what he meant. The red tips of Will's ears were proof that he knew what worried us. There was no use in either blinking facts or overstating them. We had to solve a brand-new problem—Will Yerkes and a woman—our problem as much as his, and his as much as ours, with no label of instructions attached to it from either end.

We entered in silence through the high, narrow opening in the wall and dismounted in a sandy courtyard not much unlike Snoblauch's, except that it was cleaner and the curtains of the surrounding verandas were much less shabby. All our loads appeared to be piled indescriminately in the midst, with guns in their white-pine boxes on top and the dynamite underneath everything.

We unsaddled the donkeys, and they went to scratching themselves against the loads while we explored the house—a foursquare series of parallelograms, each room leading into the next—fairly clean, high-ceiled, comparatively cool and gloomy as the home of mystery. Only a little light crept past the veranda curtains and the narrow, barred windows, until Monty went out and threw all the curtains up on the veranda roof.

Then we could see the furniture—every individual item of it plundered from a luckless ship. There were one or two steamer deck-chairs that might have been blown overboard in a storm and washed ashore, but the benches had been torn out bodily from wrecks, and the beds were the spring-steel bunks from sailing-ship cabins, refitted into frames made from longshore jetsam and perched on plundered wooden stanchions.

There were no bed-clothes. In Dûm it was conventional for guests to bring their own. The kitchen was hung with cooking-pots from ships' galleys, and the pitchers were enormous copper things in which stewards had collected slops and carried water to the cabins. The only table had had its legs sawed off until it stood about a foot high off the floor, and close to that was a divan taken from a high-sea smoking-room, deep enough for the friends of Allah to squat cross-legged on, and long enough for nearly a dozen of them.

Monty sat down on it, set his feet on the low table-edge and lit a cigar.

"I propose," he said, "that one of us shuts and bolts the gate. Then the rest of us sit here and smoke while Will Yerkes carries in all our loads from the courtyard and unpacks them, including the dynamite, in this room. If that exercise is not enough to cure his infatuation, I propose he be given two pockets full of dynamite and permission to jump from the roof!"

"Second the motion!" said Fred.

"Agree to it!" said I.

"Aw!" Will jeered, throwing himself back next to Monty on the cushioned seat and lighting a cigaret, "you unattractive guys are jealous! It must be —— to sit back and watch a wide-awake chicken choose."

It was Monty who went out and closed the gate. Will flatly refused.

III

THERE WAS no use in disputing Will's claim. He held our hand now and must play it. But the lead was Rosalie's.

"Instead of questioning a girl's right to kiss whom she pleases as often as she pleases, suppose you plain-faced guys get down to considerin' what presents you'll give her? A handful o' sticks o' dynamite might make a deeper kink in her regards than trade blankets, f'r instance! Get out the inventory, somebody."

Monty produced his pocketbook and read down the long list in a voice that was sufficient comment. We had fitted out that expedition after sleepless nights and days-long arguments with a view to being prepared against any contingency likely to arise on an Arab coast. We had thought of almost everything from compass to reserve can-opener, including an Arabic-English dictionary and blue for washing clothes, but who could be blamed for not thinking of diamond necklaces for the foster-daughter of a sheik? Woman, dead or alive, black, white or snuff-colored, was the one and only thing we had all felt sure before we started that we need not make provision for meeting on this trip!

Fred suggested giving her some canned soup.

"Rot!" said Monty. "She's probably fanatically Moslem—most likely won't eat meat she didn't see killed. Besides, the soup fell overboard."

"Haven't we some chocolate?" said I, with the air of a man who has solved the problem.

"Rats!" remarked Will. "Give her chocolate, of course, but candy to a girl isn't presents; it's her birthright. What she expects to get from us is something lawless, and the costlier the better!"

"A repeating-pistol is all we've got that's likely to interest her," Fred grumbled. "Whose shall it be?" he added with an air of resignation.

"Will's, of course!" decreed Monty without hesitation. "I'll polish it and pack it in my silk scarf with some chocolate and a hundred rounds."

Monty went out into the courtyard and dug out his scarf from a steel trunk. He would take no refusal regarding the pistol.

"I'll match you," Will laughed ruefully. "Yours or mine, and the winner to pay the loser what the pistol cost!"

"Just hope your pistol is all this amusement costs you," Monty answered and presently sat polishing the metal-work with canned milk gun-oil and his handkerchief.

Then there came a thundering on the locked gate, and I climbed up on the roof to investigate. It was Villiam, using fists and heels, and his wandering eye detected me as soon as I leaned over the parapet.

"Let me in!" he shouted. "I've news for yer!"

There being nothing we wanted more than news, I went down and admitted him.

"You've yer bits o' sticks, I see," he said, glancing at the heap of luggage. "So Hi can 'ave me suit o' clothes now, can't I?"

"Depends on your news," said I, balancing, all inadvertently, the mistake I had made before in saying too much. The suit of clothes had assumed exaggerated value in his mind, and thenceforward the problem as concerned him was only to keep him down to hard facts. I led him in, and he squatted like an Arab in front of us, hesitating everlastingly between obsequious respect for Monty and extremes of self-assertion.

"Soon as you was gone," he announced, "Snoblauch tells me to saddle the donkey, an' off 'e rides fast as 'e can lick for the shriek's palace. The shriek ain't full of 'ospitality of afternoons; 'e's asnoozin' in 'is 'arem an' what not. But Snoblauch considers the tune's near enough ripe to take a chance. The donkey's not fed so's 'e'll gallop, an' I'm that lean I can run like the wind. Hi gives 'im a start an' then doubles. An' I sees 'im go in through the palace gate, the guards a-givin' 'im a great argymint and 'im not listenin'."

"Have you any idea what he proposes to say to the sheik?" Monty asked.

"Any idee? Well, I should say! The old fool talks aloud to 'isself when 'e's upset, an' me wantin' that suit o' European clothes, an' you wantin' to know the news, thinks I to meself I'll listen. This is what 'e says. You've seen 'im. You've 'eard 'im. You know 'ow 'e be'aves. A-shakin' 'is fist at 'eaven and a-trottin' up an' down in carpet slippers. '*Donnerwetter!*' 'e says. 'A man who is to be Imperial German consul must 'ave sharp vits! It is evident these newcomers vill so act on Rosalie's mind zat no ozzer influence over her vill remain! Zey must be put a stop to! Zey must be made to convict zemselves! Zey can not be allowed to interfere!'

"The old fool's so busy a-cudgelin' of 'is wits that 'e don't know whether 'e's talkin' German, English or Arabic. Off 'e rides as soon as I've put the donkey's bridle to rights—which I weren't in any 'urry to do as long as 'e was talkin' out 'loud to 'isself. And now 'e's in the sheik's presence chamber, accusin' you gents of Gawd knows what."

"What are these plans of his that he is so anxious we should not spoil?" Monty asked.

"Ho, 'e's full o' plans, 'e is. Chiefest, 'e wants to be consul, and 'e believes if 'e can get Rosalie safe an' sure married to the sheik of Urza—who's a sort of a Bedouin settled down an' by all accounts a great believer in Germans as the comin' lords o' the earth—if 'e can only get 'er safe an' sure married to 'im so's the sheik of Urza can make out a claim to succeed this old tiger, why then 'e thinks the German Gov'ment 'll be that grateful they'll create 'im Imperial consul out of 'and! 'E's everlastingly a-gassin' to me about 'ow Germany means to cut loose an' conquer the earth. 'E kids 'isself 'e's one o' their advance agents greasin' the skids for 'em. Which it's my belief they'll skid down-'ill when they start, if 'e's the kind o' specimen they plots with! Nor they don't use 'im right neither.

"The poor old fool 'as 'is own money all locked up in a business 'ere what can't be made to pay, an' they don't contribute no thin'. 'E as a 'arem what breaks 'is 'eart as well as 'is bank-account, all for the sake o' knowin' what's bein' said be'ind the scenes. One of 'is wives is a sister to one o' the shriek's wives. Snoblauch 'ears from 'er what's goin' on, an' it fair drives 'im crazy! Now, about that suit o' clothes, sir?"

BEFORE MONTY could reply to that there came another prodigious hammering at the gate, and Villiam leaped to his feet as if a whip had cracked.

"That's 'er!" he announced with a grimace. "If she catches me 'ere, she'll charge me wi' tellin' tales! Hi'm an orphan, Hi am!"

He did not wait on ceremony but ran like a shadow from the room, swarmed up a post to the roof, vaulted the parapet and dropped to earth outside the wall without as much as "by-your-leave" or hesitation. And in proof of the accuracy of his judgment Rosalie's voice began to make itself heard in extremely unladylike objurgations above the thunder of blows on wood and the shouts of her followers. With a laugh at our looks of concern Will made haste to admit her.

She came in with the eunuch in attendance and half a dozen servants bearing hot food. Another dozen ruffians stayed outside to gape at our belongings. In her own hands she carried chin-high a great dish of steaming curry—"like John the Baptist carrying Salome's head," as Fred remarked, too excited to care which was martyr and which miscreant.

"See!" she said, laughing like a child at a party, "I am gifing presents first. Now you shall eat. Zen you shall gif me your presents!"

Ordering the dishes spread on the low table, and us on to our heels in front of them, she flung herself on the long seat with a squeal of delight and yelled with laughter when Fred burned himself. With a mouthful of something hotter than the hinge of Tophet he had either to swallow or spit, tried both at once and exploded. When she had recovered her breath, she assured us the heat was wholly due to excellence.

"Nothing has been poison! Everyzing I 'ave tasted first! See—look!"

With a spring she was beside Monty-snatched a liberal handful of the hot stuff from the dish in front of him—stuffed it into her own mouth and was gone again with the springs of the long seat dancing under her.

"All very good food—much better than my papa, Sheik Abdul bin Mahmoud, is eating!"

There were no knives, spoons or forks, and we had not unpacked our own. The only way was to roll up balls of rice in our fingers and mop up the meat and gravy, and it takes the civilized man longer to learn the methods of his tribal ancestors than the barbarian needs to acquire the tricks of Mayfair and Tooting Beck. We made a most unholy mess of faces, fingers and table-cloth and had to take little less than a bath in the basin the eunuch brought to each of us afterward in turn, amid the jeers of Rosalie.

Then she summoned Will to sit beside her and what with kissing and hugging him was too busy for a while to remember what else she had come for. She did not in the least mind our witnessing the love-affair and was vastly amused at our embarrassment.

Suddenly, however, she did remember and cut short a kiss in the middle.

"My presents—ze presents for me!" she shouted, clapping her hands. "Vhere arrre zey?"

So Monty produced the pistol and chocolates wrapped in the silk scarf with the best grace he could assume, and for a moment she was so disappointed that I thought she would hit him or break into tears. She pouted, and her eyes flashed. But Will called her "sweetheart" again, and she permitted him to show her how the pistol worked and to peel the tin-foil from a cake of chocolate.

Then for a while, munching with dark brown smears on either corner of her mouth, she was fascinated while Will loaded and unloaded the pistol before her eyes, explaining its mechanism. At last, when he had loaded it for about the fiftieth time, she snatched it from him suddenly, jerked at the trigger and put three shots in succession through the table, smashing a dish that had survived both storm and shipwreck before we ate from it.

"Oh! Oh! Oh!" she shouted. "It ees good! Yes, it ees good! My papa, Abdul bin Mahmoud, has not such a pistol! I vill use it to shoot Villiam tonight! He vas in here just now vizout my perrmission! Tonight 'e vill come to sing under my vindow, and I vill shoot 'im!"

She fired two or three more shots, sending the eunuch and the rest of them scattering for cover, and then demanded that Will reload the new toy, which he did. Monty made faces to prevent him, but he was too busy to see, and a man can't be expected to do much cool thinking with the chocolate from such a damsel's otherwise red lips smeared all over his own. Fred went near and kicked him savagely, but Rosalie saw that and misinterpreted.

"Oh! Oh! You arre jealous! Zey arre all jealous! Zat is why zey look unhappy vhen you and I embrace. Oh, *mon ange! Mon beau, brave homme*—I dare not leave you 'ere viz zese jealous people any longer. You must come with me to my 'ouse!"

It was at the point that Will finally glimpsed through the mist of his infatuation that all was not going perhaps exactly according to Hoyle. But by that time the pistol was loaded, and she had it again.

"—— young fool!" swore Monty between set teeth, and Rosalie heard that.

She misinterpreted again.

"Who is —— fool?" she demanded. "Me? I? Me? I vill show you!"

Will made a belated move to join us, but she said something below her breath very swiftly in the local patois to the eunuch, and he repeated it louder and yet more swiftly. In an instant every one of the servants had closed on Will, and she stood between them and us, with the pistol pointed at us and a look on her beautiful face that betrayed ungovernable passion and unbridled will.

We had pistols, although she may not have known it, and, whatever her delusions on the subject, it would have been ridiculous to suppose ourselves unable to rescue Will. But, on the other hand, to shoot one's hostess and her servants in her own house on any pretext less than sheer necessity was a proposition to give the coolest adventurer pause. And to add to our confusion Will begged us to let things take their course.

"If you interfere with her," he warned, "you'll have the whole tribe down on the lot of us!"

I ran to the outer gate and bolted it. Guessing what I had done, Rosalie came hurrying out at the head of her contingent with Will held firmly in their midst. Fred and Monty followed them, and in the long shadow by the gate we had another altercation.

"You open!" ordered Rosalie.

NOT DARING to draw my own weapon for fear lest the sight of it should start her off shooting at random, I stood still with my back to the gate doing my best to look calm and confident. Monty and Fred proceeded to create a diversion from the rear in hope of something turning up, and Rosalie turned on them in towering fury, abusing them in Arabic, French and English simultaneously, mixing similies, metaphors and tongues into one hot-breathed babel of vituperation.

Under cover of that I managed to get word with Will.

"Make a dash for it!" I advised. "If we four once get back to back together, they'll not be able to get us apart again. Break back toward Fred and Monty suddenly!"

But he had not yet quite conquered the fascination of the unknown adventure in store. He had realized how serious we considered the predicament and was willing to concede our right to call the game, but he still believed soft words and caresses could turn the trick.

"Aw, what's the use?" he answered. "Suppose she makes me prisoner for a while—why, it's a joke! As long as she's partial to me she won't hurt me, will she? And she won't care to get my goat by making trouble for you three. Open the door. I'll take the chance."

At about that moment Fred said something or other in Arabic to which the eunuch took exception. The black ruffian promptly drew a knife and aimed for him, only to drop it with a roar as Monty struck his wrist a terrific blow from his pistol-butt. Rosalie backed up her own man by aiming pointblank at Monty, but I made a spring and knocked up her hand from behind in the nick of time. Then I pinned both her arms to her sides, she yelling as if I were killing her, and a free-for-all fight began that was about the briskest I ever took part in.

Fred got the pistol away from Rosalie while I held her, but that was only the beginning of things. She broke free from me with the strength of a wildcat and went after Fred and the pistol. Will took the cue to make a fight for liberty and went down under a tangle of legs and arms. Once they had him down, it took but three of them to hold him so that when I closed in to kick them off him they easily spared two of their number to tackle me, and the remainder, including the eunuch, followed Rosalie in her assault on Monty and Fred.

Having all the firearms once more in our possession, there would have been no sense in not making at least a bluff with them. Monty leveled a pistol at the eunuch's head. Fred followed suit with his two, pointed straight at Rosalie. I broke loose from my two assailants and held them at bay with the fourth.

"Tell your men to let our friend get up!" Fred ordered, as Rosalie backed away.

"Call your men off our man on the ground!" Monty growled at the eunuch, who had both hands up.

"Make another kick for it, Will!" I shouted, and the convulsions of the heap of men on top of him proved that he had heard. I got near enough to kick one or two of his captors off him, and he had risen to his knees, when there came a new sound of thundering on the gate and every one, Rosalie included, stopped in midact.

There were shouts as well as the din of rifle-butts on the stout wood. The words were all Arabic—the voices arrogant—and the number of men by the sound was a score or more. Rosalie began to laugh. Will made a last effort and broke free.

"Slip me that gun!" he said, taking his stand between Monty and Fred.

Rosalie began answering the men outside, mocking them and evidently calling their courage in question.

"Back to the veranda!" ordered Monty. "Come on, now, all four together!"

But we did not execute that maneuver. Rosalie laughed louder than ever and made a signal toward the roof. We all looked up and saw that Arabs had swarmed the wall on three sides and were covering us with firearms. I pocketed my own weapon quickly, being minded to have it to use on some occasion when the drop should be mine and not the other men's. Rosalie began laughing and talking at top speed, the men on the roof answering never a word but betraying plenty of interest, and the eunuch unbolted the gate.

It was thrown wide instantly by pressure from without, and a dozen men rushed through the opening. But Rosalie was quicker than they were and gave less explanation. She went like a flash through the gate with a hop, skip and jump and was gone! The men on the roof came down close to the edge and covered us at close range then. To have fired a shot would have been simple suicide.

It was now I who stood alone, cut off from Monty and Fred and Will by a distance of a dozen paces and as many armed men. The eunuch was too busy talking sixteen to the dozen, telling the newcomers what hellions we were and how brave he himself, to pay any attention to what was happening. A man on the roof gave a sudden, sharp order and followed it with a string of brimstone Arabic by way of emphasis. All Rosalie's men, eunuch included, promptly took to their heels, leaving the recent arrivals to attend to business.

It was scarcely surprising under the circumstances that they should mistake their man and pounce on me instead of Will. Their speed and determination did them credit. With a whirl that took me off my feet breathless, they swept through the gate and slammed it behind them, while the men on the roof covered my friends. I shivered, expecting to hear shots by way of protest and reprisal and then, being human, and a prisoner and helpless for the moment, grew indignant because neither Monty nor Fred nor Will was fool enough to ruin the chances of all of us in the heat of the moment.

At least fifty men were taking part in the capture. Some remained on the roof. A dozen stayed outside the gate to prevent pursuit, and a dozen more dragged me across the open ground toward the sheik's palace. Evidently there were strict orders not to harm any of us, for, when Monty climbed to the roof and shouted after me, the roof-guard only pointed rifles at his head and did not molest him.

"You know what our resources are!" he shouted. "We won't let the night go by without an attempt at rescue!"

I saw him turn his back and leave the roof and ran on between my captors wondering what in the world he meant by resources. I knew as well as he did what was in our luggage, but, even supposing he and Fred and Will should be clever enough to save that from being plundered, our little arsenal would be a flea-bite in that armed land. More than a dozen times I had experienced Monty's resourcefulness and ingenuity in what had seemed impossibly tight places, but what he could do to solve this problem seemed likely to prove even beyond his power to guess.

And that question, being remoter of the two, was dwarfed into insignificance beside the mystery of what would happen when Rosalie should discover they had captured the wrong man—and what steps that fiery young woman would take to remedy the error!

As they hurried me along the palace wall in the long, purple shadow of late afternoon, I looked up and saw what must be Rosalie's quarters. Near the top of a tower at one end of the palace was the only window in Dûm that faced outward. Beneath that no doubt Villiam sang songs that so enraged the "shriek," and there she had coolly proposed to murder him tonight if only we had not deprived her of the pistol! There was white stuff fluttering behind it—doubtless the sleeve or handkerchief of Rosalie herself, on watch.

IV

THE INTERIOR design of that palace was after the fashion of Hampton Court maze, cross-bred with a mole-hill and a rat-run. It was nearly dark when my captors went through the form of satisfying the men on guard at the main gate that they were not strangers sprung out of the earth or from the sky.

As they let us pass, a *muezzin* began to announce the hour of evening prayer, his clear voice rising and falling more musically than a bell. The sun in those parts seems always to perform the last few leagues of his day's journey in a special hurry; he plunged under the sky-line just as the heavy gate clanged behind us, and, Dûm being one of those feckless places not yet blessed by Mr. Edison—there was not even a brass-lunged phonograph in all the town—we marched forward into darkness that my eyes could not penetrate, although my captors seemed to know the way by ear and sense of touch.

We advanced and turned to right and left, swung around corners apparently leading back toward the main gate—turned again sharply and mounted half a dozen steps, on which I stumbled and barked my shins—passed through three doors and under a curtain of heavy, dusty cloth, before we came to a square antechamber where an old tin kerosene lantern burned dimly on a stool. A man with the longest rifle I ever saw stood guard beside it.

My captors spoke with him in cautious undertones, I for comfort's sake feeling all the while at the pistol under my jacket. There was nothing suggestive of ritual about the interchange of words; it sounded more like small-talk. But after a minute or two the man on guard saw fit to slap the door noisily three or four times with the flat of his open palm. Then he flung it open suddenly, and my captors thrust me through.

They remained outside. The door slammed behind me, and I stood and blinked at six oil lamps with colored glass lenses—very pretty and impressive. There was a carpet on the floor, perhaps twenty feet by thirty, and as likely as not priceless, but I was in no mood at that minute to appraise what Will calls "dry-goods."

I faced a divan, cushioned with bright colors and long enough to seat a dozen men, although only one man was on it—a gray-bearded, hook-nosed ancient in snowy white linen, smoking a water-pipe through a very long silver mouthpiece. Below him on the floor Snoblauch squatted, noticeably ill-at-ease, and facing Snoblauch sat two other men, both apparently Arabs. They smoked cigarets through amber tubes, and the air of the place was filled with layer on layer of blue aromatic smoke. Through the dim light I could not see any of the walls except the one I faced, but I was aware of movement to my left and suspected a screen that concealed women.

The old man on the divan stared at me like an owl without blinking but said nothing, continuing to puff at his water-pipe at arithmetically even intervals. Suddenly one of the two Arabs who faced Snoblauch spoke in almost perfect English, and the surprise nearly scared me out of my wits.

"Make obeisance to Abdul bin Mahmoud, the Excellent, the Servant of the Most High, the Wrath and the Flail of Allah, the Lord of the Limits of Decency, the Sheik of Dûm!"

I made a gesture with my right hand indicative of admission that I stood with dusty shoes on an Arab's carpet—a mere mannerly salute.

"Make obeisance!" boomed the voice again.

I bowed, as stiffly as a man can who has race, color and creed in mind as well as other good ground for resentment.

"Lay your forehead on the carpet!" the voice commanded, but I stiffened and stood still.

"Goodness gracious, *mein Herr!*" Snoblauch protested in his high-pitched, worried way. "Why not do as he tells you? I always make obeisance. Why anger him merely for the sake of jingoismus?"

I did not answer Snoblauch.

At last the sheik spoke, grumbling and mumbling into his gray beard but not moving a fraction of an inch one way or the other. Only his hand that held the pipe-stem rose toward his mouth at the everlasting measured intervals. The man with the booming voice interpreted.

"Who are you who come apparently from nowhere, for no reason, and behave scandalously with one who is the greatest gem of all the sheik's gems?"

It would not have been good Arab manners to name even such a veil-despising young lady as Rosalie in front of me, a foreigner, a prisoner.

Remembering Monty's words that had made such effect on the ennuch I answered at once.

"I am a distinguished visitor, expecting distinguished treatment. Is this your Arabian manner of treating strangers?"

"For God's sake, *mein Herr,*" cut in Snoblauch, "do not say anything to aggravate him!"

"On what steamer did you come?" was the next question, and in answer I reeled off the ship's name and her captain's, as well as the owners' names and place of business, the tonnage, nature of cargo, port of departure and destination.

To my surprise the information was received with deep interest and translated word for word to the sheik, he nodding after each item.

There followed twenty or more searching questions, directed chiefly to fix the responsibility for the ship's remaining outside the reef. Presumption of guilt apparently rested on me, and the crime appeared to be very serious, judged by local standards. At last the sheik said something that the other man translated to me—not a question this time but a statement of fact so couched as to amount to condemnation.

"Had the ship taken on board one of our pilots and come through the opening in the reef, all that good cargo and all the ship's fittings would have been divided already!"

THERE WAS a rustle in the darkness to my left hand in proof that the judgment had been heard by others—and no doubt considered just. The sheik spoke again, the interpreter letting his cigaret burn away to gray ash untasted.

"This man—" the interpreter nodded in the direction of Snoblauch, who began to look uneasier than ever and to try to look extremely confident—"says you and the three other men have come purposing treachery. There is marriage contemplated between the Sheik of Urza and one whom this great sheik holds in honor. This man says you four men come seeking to prevent this marriage. Why?"

"We came," I answered, "bearing presents for the Sheik of Dûm and seeking permission to explore in his neighborhood for ancient stones and buildings. We have been prevented from offering the presents, first by this man, Snoblauch, whose men by his orders carried off our belongings when we landed on the beach, and secondly by another person whose name is held in honor by the sheik."

"Where are the presents?" came the almost instant answer.

"They are like the old stones and the ruins of ancient buildings," said I. "They are not things to be withheld from unoffending people."

"You shall give the presents to-morrow," was the prompt answer. "What would you do with ancient stones and ruins of buildings? He who carries off old stones has sweat for his reward, but how much else? What profit is there for any man in the ruins of buildings?"

I thought of the vanity that induced this Red Sea wrecker-sheik to call himself "Lord of the Limits of Decency" and decided to tell just as much of the truth as would flatter him:

"We have heard," said I, "that the servants of the great King Solomon came formerly to Dûm. We came to find proofs of that; to find traces of the buildings that the servants of Solomon erected; to prove, if that is possible, that the great Sheik Abdul bin Mahmoud, Wrath and Flail of Allah, Lord of the Limits of Decency and Sheik of Dûm, is the direct descendant of King Solomon or, if not that, then at least the descendant of the chief among Solomon's servants."

There was a long pause when that had been translated. The sheik sat puffing at the silver mouthpiece no faster and no more emphatically, not blinking his eyes any oftener or moving anything except his right hand. Yet it was perfectly clear that he was blinking furiously and that neither the interpreter nor the other Arab nor Snoblauch knew any better than I what form his answer would take. When it came after several minutes, it was entirely surprising and logical after the fashion of the East that sidesteps nothing except essential facts.

"You are a very great liar! If your story were true and you really came here to discover whether this sheik is not the descendant of the great King Solomon, then you would have been so full of respect and worship for this sheik that you would have touched the floor with your forehead on entering this room!"

Floored for the moment by the unexpectedness of that assertion I stood silent.

"You are condemned by your lack of words!" said the sheik.

Compelled to make some sort of defense, I took refuge in the sheik's own trenches.

"It is not the fashion among the men of my land," I said, "to make obeisance to sheiks whose lineage is not yet proven, for, if we did make too ready obeisance, then those sheiks whose ancestry was proven might say that our salute was worthless, being given at random to men of no birth or merit!"

It was the sheik's turn to reflect again, this time for several minutes. He made the interpreter repeat my argument at the end of that time and reflected once more. Finally he postponed his verdict but contrived to leave me with food for grim reflection on my own account.

"To-morrow you shall give the gifts. There is a man condemned to be flayed alive in the sun with salt water thrown on him at intervals. After receiving the presents, Abdul bin Mahmoud, the Merciful, the Servant of the Most High, the Wrath and the Flail of Allah, the Lord of the Limits of Decency, the Sheik of Dûm, will decide whether you shall be flayed alive likewise or given leave to search for old stones!"

There was a ship's bridge-bell—a beautifully modeled thing of engraved brass—suspended from a metal bracket on the wall by the sheik's shoulder. He rang it sharply by the leather thong made fast to the end of the tongue, and I heard a door open in the darkness to my right.

After a pause during which the sheik neither spoke nor moved but Snoblauch stared into the darkness fascinated and I endured the sensation of being studied thoroughly by men whom I could not see, four very tall Arabs, whose wrist sinews were like violin strings, emerged out of the gloom and made me prisoner anew, one to the left, one to the right, one behind to drive me forward and the fourth in front of me lest I go too fast.

The man behind growled in my ear, so close that his whisker tickled me. We started forward in step in quick time, I discovering too late that the floor on which I had stood was but a platform and falling a matter of two feet on to a lower floor, throwing my guard into disorder—an offense for which they cuffed me mercilessly.

Reaching a door in the wall we changed formation to what the navy calls "single line ahead," two of them in front in single file and two behind me. A boy seated on the floor by the door pulled a string and made it slide in grooves, disclosing a parallelogram of utter blackness out of which a warm smell emerged. He was a peculiar-looking boy, as naked as Truth is usually said to be, except for an enormous turban, and he gave me a look as I passed that made me shudder more than all the "shriek's" cross-examination.

THE SMILE that was merely grimace, the eyes full of interest that was not curiosity, the matter-of-fact way of sitting and pulling at the thong, seemed to suggest that he had seen a hundred men go that way and well knew what fate befell them. He did not speak. He made no sign of recognition. The door closed behind us with the same uncanny calm with which he opened it, and the man in front of me reached back to drag me to the left. It was more than a minute before I realized that the two men behind me had remained on the other side of the door.

I began to hang back then, remembering that I had a pistol and going over in mind with the speed of a drowning man the chances of hiding it somewhere before I should be searched, or of using it to advantage before I could be secured for the night behind lock and key. And while I conjectured, groping along a pitch-dark narrow passage after my captors, warm arms were suddenly thrown around my neck, and warm lips kissed mine until my breath was lost.

Rosalie did not know yet that they had taken the wrong man, and neither darkness nor I disillusioned her!

"Oh! Oh! Oh!" she whispered. "Oh! *Mon ange! Mon beau, brave homme!"*

But she was not content with whispering. One hand left my neck and sought so swiftly among my pockets that mine could not follow fast enough to catch and hold it, and on tiptoe with lips to mine she found the precious pistol. She let go of me and made off with it then with a speed suggestive, perhaps, that kissing my face would have been pleasanter had I shaved more recently.

"Mon dieu!" she called back from behind the

cover of blind darkness. *"Sois heureux maintenant*—zey would 'ave taken eet! Moi—I can use eet to bettaire purpose! First I shoot Villiam! Zen I shoot zose three ozzer men who no like me! Zen I marry you, an' ve togezzer make my papa be'ave! *Au revair!"*

Strange that she should have balked at shooting the sheik as well! Perhaps she was considering the number of cartridges the pistol held and with the practical spirit of her sex confining her calculations for the present to what she possessed the means to undertake—hereditary Gallic thrift asserting itself even amid those surroundings!

Suddenly the two guards either realized that I had fallen too far behind or else were aware that Rosalie had done her will, for they came pouncing back on me and shook me like a rat, now shoving me along in front of them, their iron fingers driving into my flesh like clamps, and I too disappointed from loss of the pistol to make more than a half-hearted effort to break loose.

The passage seemed endless as well as utterly devoid of light. There was scarcely room in it for the three of us to go abreast with their bare elbows rubbing along the sun-dried brick wails. Without being able to see them, I was aware of the beams within a foot of my head, and the earthen floor was so full of pitfalls that but for the men who hustled me along I should have fallen twenty times.

We reached a corner at last, however, around which a dim light penetrated, and turned at a right-angle into the dazzling glare of a common ship's tin hurricane-lantern, hung on an iron spike in the wall opposite a door with a grating in its upper half.

Under the lantern they two now started to search me, but I had had about enough of that for one night and put up a stiffer fight than they bargained for. They tore my clothes to rags but got nothing for their pains except a bloody nose apiece and crushed feet—for I had boots on, and they nothing but sandals.

However, their strength was that of leopards, and finally they hurled me through the door into darkness and locked it on the outside. Then for revenge one of them went and fetched a jar of water, lifted it for me to look at through the bars, invited me to drink and lovingly poured it all out on the dry floor, holding the jar high enough for me to see the lamplight shining through the stream.

When that was done, he smashed the earthen jar as a sort of extra suggestion of drought, blew the lantern out and called his friend away. In darkness that felt like the night before the universe was made I heard their retreating footfalls punctuating ghoulish laughter, until at last even the echoes of that ceased and all was still.

I began to remember then what the French captain had said about insects. First in dozens, then in squadrons, then in myriads they began to crawl on me, and, although not all of them appeared possessed of teeth and claws, there were several special sorts that made up for the others' deficiency—and those that did not bite compensated for that by being much more restless.

After scratching until I realized that it only spurred the vermin to greater effort, I began to explore my prison, feeling the way cautiously around the walls. It was nearly four-square, and after making the circuit three times I guessed the dimensions at thirty feet by twenty-five. The walls, except in one place, were apparently of coral rock, and overhead I could just touch stout beams with the tips of my fingers when I stood on tiptoe.

That much ascertained, I made an inventory and found that I had a pocket-knife, a few coins, a very good gold watch, whose ticking sounded in that silent waste of darkness like the reassuring counsel of a friend, some matches in a safety match-box and a pocket note-book containing more than a hundred leaves. Everything else had been snatched or spilled from my pockets in the effort to search me.

I discovered there were only nine matches and did not dare strike one for the present. I sat for a while with my back against the rock wall, because in that position I could crush a great number of insects without too great effort, and while in that position thoughts began to haunt me of Villiam going to sing songs under Rosalie's window and being shot down without warning. I wondered why I should feel so anxious on that ruffian's account.

Then of my three friends being attacked from the roof at night—vivid mental pictures of Rosalie's walking up to each one with my pistol and blowing his brains out while Arabs held him. Then arrived visions of what would be likely to happen to me when the lady should discover the wrong man was under arrest. I thought of the threatened death by flaying and wondered whether that could after all be much worse than the present ordeal by insects.

IT WAS the thought that Rosalie would almost certainly not choose to leave the man she considered her lover in such an infernal predicament for longer than she could help that finally set me to doing something instead of wasting time. Of all the disagreeable probabilities my frightened brain could conjure up, the least acceptable was to be rescued by Rosalie and discovered as my own true self, not Will. I had about as much confidence in that young lady's fund of forgiveness as in the mercy of the insects.

So I made a lot of spills out of sheets torn from my note-book and sacrificed a match. By burning both match and spills to the very last fraction, and my fingers incidentally, I made a complete survey of the cell, and before my eyes had grown accustomed to the dark again I was at work furiously with the pocket-knife on a part of one wall made of big, flat, sun-dried bricks that looked as if it had been breached by somebody else at some time or other, rather carelessly filled up and forgotten.

The bricks, what with the pressure on top of them and the dryness, had grown almost as hard as the coral, but not quite, and I was spurred to greater violence by the sight I had had of the insects swarming over me. I broke one blade of the knife but had better luck with the other, and after what seemed like an hour's digging I could get my arm almost up to the shoulder into the hole I had made.

Then I struck another match, looked at my watch, examined the hole and continued—beginning to suffer by that time from thirst as well as weariness and bleeding hands. I worked until my head swam and then had to lie still, panting, for what seemed a week; then I sacrificed a third match, looked at my watch again and discovered that only fifteen minutes had passed since I looked at it last.

That brought me to my senses. I took command of myself again and began to work steadily and systematically. At the end of about another half hour my effort was rewarded by feeling my fist break through on the far side of a wall that was more than four feet thick. I did not dare strike a light then but lay listening, and hearing nothing I began to enlarge the hole until I could crawl through it.

Once I made the attempt too soon and so nearly stuck half-way that deadly terror seized me and I rubbed all the skin from my elbows and knees in the belief that the weight of the wall above was crushing me. But I had the hole big enough at last and struggled through into a fresher-smelling, perfectly dark passage.

After lying still for a long time, I heard distinctly the noise a sleeping camel makes when he disapproves of his dreams. Nobody could hear that sound once and ever again mistake it. Crouching and crawling on hands and knees for what seemed an interminable time, I turned a corner and rammed my head into a wooden door, part of one of whose lower panels were missing. I could see the stars through that when I got my face near enough to the floor. I had reached the sheik's private camel stable, and at once the thought that servants might be sleeping in among the brutes sent new cold chills all through me.

However, there was nothing else for it. The door was locked, and the framework solid. Like almost every other fitting I had noticed in the whole town, this, too, was a relic of some shipwreck, and the panels had never been designed to let full-grown men go through them. I must have made enough noise while forcing my too solid body through that needle's eye to have awakened ordinary sleepers fifty feet away. And yet, when I struggled through at last and walked away over dust-dry camel dung, I all but set my booted foot on the face of a sleeping black man! The camels, some standing, some lying, all saw me but did not take alarm. Five or six attendants lay on the ground among them, snoring, all of them naked except for the thin trade blankets that the East has come to think as necessary to its skin, and that gave me an idea.

I stripped off my own verminous clothing, left it for whoever cared to associate with its countless new inhabitants, tore off a corner of the shirt and did up my valuables in that and proceeded on my way stark naked, trusting to the night to make my whiteness look like blackness and to soften down the awkward gait of the white man unaccustomed to bare feet.

In a corner was a tank at which the camels drank. I got into it and washed off the last of the insects, drinking, too, sparsely and with vast repugnance. The walls on three sides were but partitions of sun-dried brick separating the camel quarters from some other divisions of the palace. Close by the outer wall lay a camel asleep, not tied. And near to the tank in which I bathed lay a bundle of old heel-ropes, mostly rotten.

I knotted the ropes together into one long one and, all glistening wet in the starlight, got on to the sleeping camel's back and waked him with heels and rope, not hitting him hard enough to hurt but trying to rouse him gently. The brute let out a yell as if I had murdered him, and, jumping up in a panic, began to run about the yard, frightening the other tied beasts and so nearly treading on the man I had almost stepped on myself a few minutes before that for a moment I thought he had done it. But camels are forever having nightmares, and it needed more than one stampeding creature to disturb Arabia's calm.

The man awoke and swore lustily in vile Arabic for about a minute. Another man not far from him sat up and joined in the hallelujah chorus. Hearing their voices, the camels decided there was nothing to be afraid of after all and settled down to finish their night's sleep. My own chosen mount went back grumbling to his favorite place and proceeded to try to get rid of me by scratching me off against the wall.

I would have asked him nothing better, except perhaps a little less haste. Trying to get his teeth round to bite my knee, he put his head through the noose I had made for him. I pulled it nearly taut enough to throttle, lest he slip it off too easily, then stood up on him and jumped for the top of the high wall, just reaching it.

AFTER THAT I was over the top in less than a second and lowering myself knot by knot on the far side. I had just begun to congratulate myself on my safety for the present and to speculate on whether it would be safest to try to join my friends at once or to wait until daylight, when a voice from below me challenged in gruff Arabic.

I looked down and saw a man in burnoos and flowing white garments, armed with a long gun, about fifteen feet below me and exactly underneath. Wondering what to do and whether he would shoot, I checked my downward course, and the camel chose that moment either to chew through the rope or to break its rotten strands by struggling. At any rate, the rope broke, and I fell, crupper first, on the face of the man below.

Whether or not I broke his neck I never ascertained. I am not even sure that the accident killed him. But he lay like a log, and I lay beside him for about ten minutes, watching to see whether anybody else would come on sentry-go below the wall. When I had made up my mind at last that this man was not a sentry after all but a mere curious individual promenading by night on lawless errands of his own, the moon rose over the walls across the open square and bathed everything in silver light.

That made further drastic action of some sort imperative. A white man walking naked under the full moon would have aroused the active curiosity of folk less easy to pique than Arabs.

I am told that since the great war ran its course the mere putting on of dead men's garments has become an ordinary act to men obliged to do it. That may be; war is the father and mother of calloused feeling. But that was my maiden effort at anything of that kind, and, whether that Arab was really dead or not, the pulling on one after another of his none too sweetly smelling clothes made my flesh creep more than the insects had done.

I left his naked body there at last and started across the open ground with the best attempt I could make at Arab stateliness, cursing the sandals that slipped back and forward and the moon that was putting forth a very passable imitation of sunlight. Nothing was more certain now than that I was actually being seen by keen eyes from the palace roof and towers. Yet I could not for the life of me remember how an Arab carries his rifle when not on the war-path, or whether in stooping to adjust the clumsy sandals I ought to bend my back, one knee, both knees or every joint in my body. It is little details of that kind that take on greater importance than ammunition in tight places, for by them a man is saved or damned.

I soon had proof that the palace guard was wide awake. A rifle barked on the parapet, and a bullet whistled close enough to my ear to fill me with profound respect for the fellow's shooting. That propounded another problem in local etiquette. How was I to know whether a local gentleman returning, say, from paying court to the wife of an absentee would or would not return the compliment by wasting a cartridge on the roof-guard? It well might be that the shot was intended as mere pleasantry—a sort of "Ah, you gay dog, I see you!" prophetic of verbal chaff to follow in the coffeehouse next day.

I solved the problem by facing about shaking my rifle in the general direction of the roof and not answering the shrill shout that greeted the pleasantry. What the shout meant I could not guess, but what the incident meant was this, that, if I hoped to gain access to my friends without the whole sheik's palace full of rascals knowing it, then I must invade the " 'ouse near my 'ouse" from the flank or rear.

I half expected to see guards posted like sleepy vultures along the roof, but apparently there was none. Whether or not they were sleeping in the rooms below or posted in the courtyard, it would have been much too risky for me to do any shouting or hammering on the door to wake my friends. Yet to try to climb the wall would have scarcely commended me to any one on watch, and, supposing the guards were gone away, as of course might be the case, Monty or Fred or Will would have been perfectly justified in firing on a man in Arab garments crawling over the wall. I could easily imagine any one of them doing it and making better shooting than the Arab on the palace did.

The fact remained, though, that that afternoon the sheik's men had swarmed up our wall from the outside with no delay or difficulty. That sort of feat, of course, is very much easier to numbers of men than to one, but recollection of it set me to feeling along the wall, my side of it being, of course, in shadow. When I had turned the corner and entered the little passageway between our high wall and the next, I found holes where the sun-dried bricks had been pulled out to give purchase for fingers and toes.

Everything became easy then except climbing with a long, heavy rifle in my hands, but by using the rifle as a prop against the opposite wall I managed it at last and lay on the top full-length, looking and listening.

Half of our courtyard was in light, half of it in shadow. The donkeys lay sleeping close to their saddles. Our luggage, apparently almost untouched, still lay piled in a great heap. There were no lights in the windows—no guards that I could see—no sound of snoring and nothing whatever to suggest that anything was wrong or anybody not at ease. I dropped down on to the roof, crept to the edge and lay still again. I could neither hear a sound nor see any living being, except the donkeys. So I slipped down one of the rounded posts and looked about me. All was still.

I walked to the door of the apartments and struck it with my rifle-butt—then again—then louder—then as loudly as I dared. There came no answer. I pulled at the latch-string, and the door swung open by its own weight. There was no light within, nor any sound of breathing. I went in and struck one of my scanty supply of matches, nearly jumping out of my skin at sight of my own gaunt shadow on the wall. There was nobody in the room where we had received Villiam and Rosalie.

I found a lantern and lit it—then began a search of the whole house, trembling in anticipation of finding my friends' dead bodies lying somewhere. But I found neither trace of them nor sign of fighting. There was no disorder; nothing was overturned; the plates they had eaten from that evening lay on the table unwashed, and the pots they had cooked a simple meal in were still warm on the kitchen hearthstones, but of Monty or Fred or Will there was no more trace than if the sands of Dûm had opened up and swallowed them. I went out to the gate and tried it. It was bolted on the inside!

V

THAT WAS a night of very strange adventure. The first thing I did was to bathe again, using the crocks of water Rosalie had ordered stacked in the rack outside the kitchen. Then I hunted by moonlight for Christian clothes among the luggage and put them on with a feeling of having changed my luck as well as my appearance.

I had scarcely done that when a knock came on the gate, stealthy and several times repeated. Pretending not to notice it, I hurried to open a white pine case and take out my rifle. I had opened an ammunition-box, too, and filled my pockets with cartridges when a figure I thought I recognized came over the wall by the route I had taken and dropped on the roof on all fours.

"For Gawd's sake, don't shoot!" he whispered raucously.

A moment later Villiam came spinning down a veranda-pole and begged me with almost tears in his voice to admit him into the house, where none could see us.

"Where are my friends?" I demanded.

"I'll tell," he said. "Let me in!"

He elbowed past me and threw himself on to the long divan with an air of unaccustomed luxury.

"Your friends is in 'ookey!" he told me with a

grin. "Got any smokes? Got anything better than water to drink?"

I gave him a cigar.

"Mr. Monty told me as 'ow you 'ad some whisky," he announced.

"Either he lied, or else you do," I answered.

There certainly was whisky—Monty always carried some, but that was neither time nor place for a spree, any more than he was the man to drink with.

"Sure," he said. "I'm a liar! Hi thought maybe as 'ow I'd get a drink, that's all!"

"Where are my friends?" I demanded again.

"In the palace," he answered, "along o' Rosie! It's known you've escaped. They sent me with a message."

"What message?"

"As 'ow you're to bring the presents for the shriek as soon after dawn as you can sort 'em out and carry 'em over!"

I tapped the rifle that I held across my lap.

"You don't get out of here," I said, "until you've told me the truth! You had better begin, hadn't you?"

"I'm tellin' yer the Gawd's truth! You 'adn't been gone out of 'ere much more than a hour afore your friends decided they'd go and get yer or never come back no more, amen! Them's friends, that kind is. They 'as a powwow first as to whether one of 'em shan't stay an' keep an eye on the guards what the shriek's men left be'ind, but finally they makes it up all to go together, and sure enough, soon as they starts—the guard ups and follows 'em.

"They takes the sole military precaution o' boltin' the gate from the inside and departin' by way o' the wall. Rosalie 'as given stric' orders long ago as 'ow the luggage ain't to be touched on no account, not even if the shriek says different, but they couldn't know that. They kisses 'emselves good-by to it, takin' nothing with 'em except Fred's concertina. They laughed at 'im, but 'e wouldn't leave that."

"Wait," I said. "How do you find out all this?"

"Easy as spittin'. You seen me make my 'asty adieus when Rosalie showed up? All I did was duck be'ind the wall and wait there. Soon as she an' the shriek's men 'ad slung their 'ooks, taking you along with 'em, I pops back over the wall an' lies doggo, watching for whisky an' listenin' for tips. When they ups and 'ops it, I stays be'ind. I was that thirsty—same as I am now—that I'd 'ave found the whisky, on'y for coming oversentimental an' letting my feelin's 'ave the better o' my judgment. Hi ups and 'ops after 'em, and, when they reaches the palace gate, I'm along."

"You mean you went into the palace with them?"

"Not so 'asty! Not so 'asty! There was a guard outside the palace, most of twenty strong, some of 'em the same what 'ad put up the scrap and collared you, and they 'ad stric' orders not to admit nobody. But say, that feller named Monty is a hot 'un and no kid! 'E walks about twenty paces one way and twenty more t'other, an' then 'e ups an' says to me, 'That window up there, facing outward from the tower—isn't that hers? Haw!' says 'e. 'Answer me!' And I tells 'im as 'ow 'e's guessed accurate. There was a light behind the window, burning dim. Swift as winkin' then 'e pulls out 'is pistol an' puts a shot slick through the window!"

"Hit anybody?" I asked.

"Not 'im! 'E shoots too 'igh. 'Tweren't 'is purpose to 'it nobody. Two or three 'eads moves about be'ind the bars pretty middling soon after that. They can't see who we are, 'cause it's dark, an' we can't make them out for the same reason, but they've been give notice as 'ow things of interest is taking place outside. It's my belief that Rosalie's not there but only a few of 'er women."

"I'm sure of it," I said. "She certainly wasn't there. I know where she was. Carry on."

"Well, we 'as to wait there a —— of a long time, stampin' an' fussin' an' smokin' cigarets. By and by Snoblauch comes out, an' Mr. Monty catches 'im by the scruff o' the neck, demanding by the great 'ornspoon to know where you are and what about yer—'im callin' you Yerkes, which I take it ain't your right name. It's Yerkes that Rosalie is sweet on, ain't it?

"Well, Snoblauch says 'e don't know, and Monty takes an' shakes 'im until the feller with the beard you all call Fred begs mercy for 'im for the 'arem's sake—which, if 'e'd only known it, the 'arem don't need no mercy! Them wives of 'is can comb the old man's 'air out proper. Monty gives Snoblauch a kick be'ind that delivers 'im mighty close to the 'alf-way post on the road 'ome, and we settles down to wait again. We waits a long time, too.

"It's my private impression we waits until Rosalie can finish bamboozling the shriek and is quite sure the coast's clear. At any rate, when she comes at last, she brings the eunuch with 'er, 'im 'aving 'is wrist tied in a cloth and no love in 'is craw whatever! The eunuch gives the orders, and we're all admitted, me included."

"Into the palace, to see the sheik?"

"NOT SO 'asty! Not so 'asty! Believe it or not, that's the first time I've been inside the palace since I came to Dûm eight years ago! Rosalie beckons, sort o' mysterious, and we goes along in single file through all sorts o' passages, me walking last and the real Mr. Yerkes in front o' me. Finally we brings up at the corner tower and climbs up steps what was once a ship's companion into a room with windows facing inward, underneath 'er room what 'as the window facin' the street that Mr. Monty fired through.

"I never seen such another room in all my born days. Luxury ain't the word! Velvets—plush—crimson silks—satins an' carpets an' curtains—books on shelves—divans what come close to swallowin' a man when 'e sits down—cunning little glass lamps—Lord! I never seen such a sight!

"The lights was all lit. Soon as she gets into the room, she turns sharp round and gets a good look at Mr. Yerkes. You should 'ave 'eard 'er scream! Gawd! You'd ha' thought she was balmy! The eunuch comes up close an' shows 'is teeth, thinking maybe one of us was threatening 'is mistress. But she grabs 'old o' Mr. Yerkes by the arm and stares in 'is face as if 'er eyes 'ud burn 'im up.

" 'You?' she says. 'You?' And she kisses 'im slap on the mouth.

"Yerkes, 'e looks foolish an' kisses 'er back, but she cuts that part o' the performance short and stands clear to take another look at 'im.

" 'You was in ze cell!' she says. 'Me, I see you put into ze cell! Me, I kiss you in ze passage! 'Ow did you get out? Zat cell is all rock—*solide!'*

"It's pretty clear by that time to any one with 'alf an eye that neither Yerkes nor the other two knows what to say. They're took by surprise as much as she is. She makes us all sit down, me included, and calls for a little swine of a naked Arab named 'Assan, what never wears nothin' but a turban and 'ates me worse than cobras—"

"I think I know him," I said. "Go on."

"She sends 'im to go surreptitious and peep in through the cell door, her passing round cigarets meantime and cussing out the women something awful for not 'aving coffee all ready and piping 'ot. Along o' the cigarets she makes love to Mr. Yerkes a while, me blushin' all among the roots of my 'air—which I'm no believer in conventionalities myself! Presently that little beast, 'Assan, comes back with the news that the cell's empty and a big 'ole dug through the wall."

"Was she savage," I asked, "when she found out she had kissed the wrong man in the dark?"

"Not so 'asty! Not so 'asty! She goes into a rapture! She accuses this feller Yerkes of working miracles! She says 'e's the only genuine 'ero what ever come 'er way. A man, she says, what can dig 'is way out o' that dungeon an' come back looking clean and handsome wi' neither dirt nor blood on 'is hands, an' clean clothes an' what not, 'e's 'er feller, she says.

" 'Were you a-goin' to leave me in there alone all night?' 'e asks 'er, and that starts 'er to making love to 'im all over again from the beginning.

"Under cover o' that, this 'ere Mr. Monty lays 'is 'ead next to Fred's, me fair makin' my ears twitch wi' trying to catch what 'e says.

"They agrees between 'em that the odds is a million to one you've come straight back to this place. But they also agrees that the wisest game is to keep Rosalie thinking as 'ow 'er version of the tale is right. Likewise they reaches the Solomon-wise conclusion that the right an' proper thing to do is communicate wi' you as quick as may be. Then I sees you when I comes in, but I says nothing."

"Did Rosalie know yet what the sheik's decision was regarding the man he thought was Yerkes?" I asked.

"Not so 'asty, mister! Not so 'asty! She asks Yerkes what the shriek 'ad said to 'im, and Yerkes gets out o' that by bidding 'er ask the old 'un 'imself. But at that 'Assan dips an oar in. The little beast's been listening all the while, and, though 'e don't know no English, 'e's sharper than what 'e looks. He begins to proceed to say that this ain't the same gent what was sentenced by the shriek. But 'e don't get far.

"I catches Monty's eye and promptly 'its 'Assan over the fish-trap that 'ard 'e won't eat no more fish for a month o' Sundays! O' course Rosalie wants to know what I done that for. I tells 'er 'Assan was makin' faces—which, if 'e weren't doin' it before I 'it 'im, 'e did afterwards; so I told no lie. 'Assan couldn't speak no more. All the little beast could do was yell fit to bust 'isself, and she sends 'im below till 'e gets better.

"The eunuch follows 'Assan down the stairs to get the truth from 'im, but that eunuch always was a stoopid, and 'Assan can't be made to say it plain 'cause o' cut lips. All o' the story 'e gets is that there's to be a great givin' o' presents to-morrow morning and 'im what was sent to the cell was to suffer for it if the presents ain't up to dick.

"That sets Rosalie in another whirl. She says when the shriek talks that way 'e means business and there ain't no stoppin' of 'im. And, that bein' the Gawspel truth, I confirms what she says—which she'd 'ave shot me, like as not, if I 'adn't, but it was the Gawd's truth all the same. A present to the shriek is something almost better than a ship in trouble.

" 'You must give 'im presents!' says Rosalie. 'You must give my papa very many good presents—much better presents than this foolish one that you gave me!' And she pulls out the repeating pistol.

"For about a minute I thought as 'ow she'd shoot me where I squatted on the floor. Mr. Monty thinks so, too, and motions to me to get be'ind 'im, which I does. Then Mr. Fred, 'e ups and says, 'Princess,' 'e says—'e calls 'er princess like 'e knew she was born to the purple, an' she fairly purrs at 'im—'we left one of our friends be'ind,' 'e says. 'We'd better send word to 'im about those presents!'

"Now, weren't that smart? 'E takes a chance on your bein' back 'ere already. And Monty jumps into the opening quick and says, 'Yes, Princess; we ought to send word to our friend about the presents, We had better send this man,' meaning me.

"She likes that, if only because it's an excuse to keep the real Yerkes in the palace until morning. She tells Monty and Fred they can go with me and 'elp take the message, but Monty puts on a last-ditch look and refuses. I reckon he's scared on account o' what might 'appen to Yerkes's morals! She's picked up one or two notions about Arab 'ospitality and don't see 'er way clear to turning 'em out into the moonlight; so the long and the short of it is that Monty turns to me and bids me cut and run.

" 'Tell 'im to do 'is best,' 'e says, 'and to use 'is ingenuity.' Them was his very words.

"**SO 'ERE** I be! And 'ere I stays until mornin' doth appear, only wishin' there was whisky! There'll be porters waitin' outside the gate to carry the presents as soon after first call for prayer as the echo is after the shot. So now you know!"

He settled himself into a corner of the couch and reached for another cigar, the fez tip-tilted over one eye giving him a drunken look in spite of enforced sobriety.

"And while you're 'unting presents," he remarked, "suppose you look up that suit o' reach-me-downs for me—them as Mr. Monty said 'e'd give me?"

I cross-examined him for a while but could not shake his story or get much more out of him. Whisky and a suit of clothes were the only ideas left in his head, and he talked of those until I ordered him to stop on pain of no more cigars.

Then, oppressed by the almost insuperable drowsiness that haunts the breathless Red Sea nights, I sat down at the other end of the divan to think the problem out. And be it written that I slept. I slept deep, and so did Villiam!

There is rightly no mercy for the soldier who sleeps at his post, and surely I was entitled to none, with my friends and myself at the mercy of a savage sheik and his ungovernable foster-daughter and that message "to use my ingenuity" still almost ringing in my ears. But men do fall asleep on post in spite of the penalty, and as for me, the limit of human endurance seemed to have been reached. The consolation was that Villiam slept, too; it would have been awful to be put to shame afterward by him.

And, whatever my deserts, sleep brought the solution of what to choose by way of presents for the "shriek."

Of all the explanations of dreams that I have read and listened to, none ever satisfied. Once, the night before going to the Derby, I dreamed the winner. I saw the crowd running along inside the railing and heard the shout, "Sir Visto wins! Sir Visto wins!" Next day courage failed me to bet on such a rank outsider. I plunged on the favorite. But Sir Visto did win, and I lost.

Once again on the high seas on a hell-ship I dreamed that the third mate fell overboard. Nobody loved him, but in the dream I threw him a line, which he missed, although it fell all about his shoulders, and the next wave smothered him forever. I told him of the dream at dawn. He called me a name they use frequently on such ships and struck me in the teeth. But it happened exactly as I dreamed it. I threw him a line. He missed it and was drowned.

Now again, in a corner of the cushioned sofa torn from the big stern cabin of some tall ship, I lay and dreamed so clearly that no actual adventure could have been more sharply impressed on my mind. It was not uncanny, nor yet terrifying. It was not as if anybody told me what was going to happen but simply as if I lived through the hours in advance, rehearsing, as it were, the parts we all should play.

When I awoke, as the strange way of dreams is, most of the details vanished from mind, but the salient points remained. The details came back to me afterward at the time of their actual happening, like memories of a former life.

I awoke with a start and a guiltier feeling than I had ever known. Leaving Villiam still snoring in his corner of the long seat, I went on the roof to shake off drowsiness and con my surroundings. There seemed to be a breath of air coming in from the west, and I stood for several minutes gazing seaward and filling my lungs. At the end of that time I saw three red rockets go roaring skyward and remembered they had done the same thing in my dream!

There was nothing to see but the rockets—no shadowy ships—no lights. When their flare had faded, there was only darkness where they had been. The strangest part was that I could not connect them up with the rest of the dream or fit the salient parts of the dream together in any way.

It was very nearly morning; so I went down into the courtyard, opened one of our largest chests, transferred some of the contents to my pockets, closed the chest again and wrapped it carefully in unbleached calico. Then, instead of waiting for the promised porters, I awoke Villiam and persuaded him with some difficulty to help me load the chest on the back of a donkey.

The donkey resented the imposition. For one thing, we had no pack-saddle; for another, he was a riding-donkey, unaccustomed to the ignominy of commercial loads.

"What's in the perishin' box?" demanded Villiam as I made a dive for the dozenth time and saved it from donkey-wreck.

"Breakables," I answered. "For God's sake, don't drop it!"

"D'ye mean whisky?" he asked. "Oh, crickey! Lord lumme, you're the wise one! Give the shriek a case o' whisky, and 'e'll be your friend till the jag wears off! But say, there must be two dozen in this 'ere case—why don't me an' you split a quart between us first? If we closes up the chest careful afterward, nobody'll never be no wiser!"

I would not yield, nor would he abate his demand. It was a matter with him of no whisky no performance now, and in the end the best terms I could make was to promise him one bottle for himself to be given him together with the suit of clothes after delivery of the whole case to the sheik. And at that I had to produce an odd bottle from Monty's hand-bag and let him see where I stowed it again so that he could come and fetch it in case of anything happening to me. He was not very sanguine of the party's chances, now that he had slept off the excitement and the novelty.

The time we had getting that donkey across the open space to the palace gate was busy, even considering the known characteristics of the donkey tribe and allowing for reasonable reluctance to leave his companions. Time and again one or other of us just contrived to save the case from destruction. Once the donkey tried to roll on it. And everlastingly Villiam begged me to let the brute smash it.

" 'Cause then, dontchersee, we'll 'ave a good excuse for emptying one bottle! 'Ow's the shriek to know 'ow many bottles was in there?"

If I had not been carrying the rifle and had not threatened freely to use it, Villiam would have let the case drop on purpose. But something or other had given him the wholly false impression that I was the party's fire-eating member, and he chose to believe I would carry out the threats unless he behaved himself.

NEAR THE end of the short journey the donkey began to gallop, hoping to break away and reach the palace well ahead of us, where he could get rid of his unwelcome load by the time-honored method of scraping along the wall. We only prevented him by the proverbial skin of our teeth and arrived at the main gate breathless about three minutes after dawn, before the last sounds of the *muezzin's* call to morning prayer had died away.

Of course there was no admitting us until the pious gate guard had said prayers, using sand unctuously instead of water for the ceremonial washing—to save trouble—and going through all the genuflections that the faithful are so sure will frank them into lustful paradise. To my disgust, Villiam joined them. Watching him do those acrobatics went against the grain, and having to hold that infernal donkey single-handed only added fuel to the fire of prejudice.

"Get up, you hypocrite! Cut that humbug out!" I ordered, trying in vain to force the donkey closer to him.

But all I got for my trouble was a kick from the brute myself and a smirk from Villiam when he had finished. He shrugged his shoulders with a gesture that included in its survey all the guard.

"You've been and gone and done it now!" he said.

He spoke the truth. I had merely called attention to my own abstinence from morning prayer, and the guard got off its knees with fanatical disapproval added to its normal distrust of any one with white skin.

"Giaour!" they growled at me and spat.

Who is always wise in a crisis? I have read of such people in books—and particularly in the books for boys that were inflicted on the youth of England in the early eighties. But I found that the tighter the case the more surely will the man's own normal, underlying nature emerge from the shell—which is only added reason for the sternest self-discipline at all times. It was my intolerance—contempt for what I did not approve of—racial pride and other traits even less admirable that prevented me then from entering the palace peacefully. They had orders to let me in and doubtless would have done it if I had received their abuse in silence. Instead of doing that, I kicked the man who called me *"giaour."*

It is necessary to see a faithful follower of the prophet kicked before appreciating the enormity of that act. He fired at me promptly but was so close that I knocked his rifle up, and he only singed my forehead. The remainder of the guard, not having been kicked in person but only included in the general blanket-insult to their creed and race, were satisfied to loose off their rifles all around me, snapping their fingers under my nose and prancing like marionettes on elastic strings.

None of that would have mattered very much; I had my rifle; I knew I was expected inside the palace alive, not dead. And, if the man I had kicked proposed to reload and have a second shot, I was ready for him. But their *feu d'affront* put a finish to the donkey's scant store of tractability. The brute bit through the leather rein, kicked up his heels and broke away.

"Presents!" yelled Villiam, forgetting in his excitement what tongue he was talking. He seized the nearest Arab and yelled in his ear, "Them's the presents for the shriek!"

Then he remembered and translated into Arabic.

In a moment all the guard except the rascal I had mistreated were scattering in full flight after the donkey, displaying vast experience in the art of heading him, but small skill in coming close. Whenever a more than usually swift pursuer made a dash to seize the broken rein, the animal spun on his forefeet more swiftly than a zebra—lashed out two or three times—and was gone again.

"If I'd only had the sense," I groaned, "not to disturb the contents of the chest!" I forgot that Villiam was close enough to hear.

"Took a bottle out, did you?" he demanded. " 'Ere, what did you mean then by refusing me a drink?"

I think he would have struck me, he was so indignant, but the follower of the prophet, who had not dared reload yet because that would have necessitated taking eyes off me, was so obviously in love with the prospect of seeing two white men at blows that Villiam found the temptation to disappoint him the greater of the two.

The Arab urged him to strike me—offered him a knife and nudged him. If I had been cool-headed enough at the time to appreciate it, the appeal of race to Villiam's deliberately calloused conscience ought to have exceeded all other interests. As it was, instead of striking me he turned on the Arab fiercely and in the end it was he who caught the donkey. They chased the brute our way, and he sprang and caught the broken rein.

Then somebody within the palace threw open the great iron-studded door, but it was not our time to enter yet. There came a procession of camels bobbing their heads across the desert from the north. One of the guards promptly backed me against the palace wall; another held the donkey, and the remainder formed themselves into a double line with suddenly reacquired dignity. Villiam came and stood beside me.

"This bloke what's coming," he said, "is the

Bedouin Sheik of Urza, what wants to marry Rosalie. 'E's a swine for fair!"

They did not look like bridal camels. Surely no statelier, shabbier robber gang ever paraded across a desert! There were twenty camels—twenty riders—every one armed to the teeth and every camel's patchy hide showing through holes in the flowing saddle-cloths.

They did not seem to have come far. Probably they camped a little way outside the town on purpose to enter as soon after dawn as possible.

"How is it there's no crowd running along to gape at them?" I asked Villiam.

"Gawd knows!" he answered.

That was the only really remarkable thing about them. They were ordinary enough Bedouins, turning up in the ordinary way on business that, if not ordinary, was at least easy to explain. But why a sheik with twenty camels should be allowed to enter Dûm without a crowd of curious lookers-on was a mystery, when one considered that Dûm existed as it were from wreck to wreck, with only occasional thefts and murders in between.

The procession halted before the gate, and the camels kneeled after the usual harsh objurgations. Only two men stayed to mind them. The leader was a tall man, mean and solemn-looking, able to take in every detail on either side of him without moving his head—swarthy—straight as an arrow—lean as a man must be who wrings his living from Arabia's deserts.

HE STRODE in through the open gate with his followers close at his heels, all kicking off their sandals at the threshold but none of them shedding a weapon. They looked more like men going in to loot the place than peaceful suitors for a maiden's hand. Not a man spoke. Not a man looked to right or left of him. They strode straight in with the gait of conquerors and the smoldering eyes of lust.

Then the guard permitted Villiam and me to enter, leading the donkey between us, and just as I turned to go through the gate I saw Snoblauch emerge on donkey-back from the end of the street. He was kicking the beast along at something between a trot and a walk and looked hurried. I called Villiam's attention.

"Ho!" he jeered. " 'Oose wives 'ad to saddle the moke this morning? 'E must ha' knowed this 'ere Urza sheik was coming—'ence the 'urry. 'E kids 'isself the Bedouin's 'is pal. 'E's building on being a court favorite after Urza marries Rosalie and the old 'un's underground. Poor old swizzlebrain!"

I had expected to be obliged to leave the donkey outside and had dreaded the indignity of perhaps being compelled to carry in the chest myself. The picture I had in my mind was of the dark inner chamber of the night before, and I expected to be led along the corridors again to that door and thrust through into "the presence."

However, nobody hustled or bothered us, and the donkey's presence caused no more comment than our own, even when he kicked out in random rebellion, making the contents of the chest rattle ominously. Instead of taking the mazy way of the night before, we followed Urza and his party straight down the middle of the building, out past a latticed screen into a courtyard of the usual sort with draped verandas on every side of it but one—the eastern, and that was high blank wall.

The courtyard was open to the sky, but in the center was a covered platform with a canvas canopy on four posts—the nearest thing I had seen in Dûm to a pleasance of any kind.

There were some shriveled flowers of a sort I did not recognize eking out a shriveled, dwarfed existence in the sandy soil on three sides of the platform. And on the platform were cushions and the inevitable water-pipe. It was obviously the place where the "shriek" took the morning air, and betrayed pitiful vestiges lingering in his breast of a belief that somewhere nature might be lovely.

The Bedouin chief of Urza sat down on a mat before the platform and curled his legs under him. His followers promptly began squabbling for other mats, each striving to be nearest to him and he rebuking them sharply to avert actual blows. At last they all settled down to wait patiently, Urza himself staring meditatively straight in front of him, but his following, like myself, all eyes to see between veranda curtains if that were possible. They were a drab, dusty, shabby-looking lot.

Nothing happening, and, nothing being visible—although I eyed every tear and every gap—I got Villiam to rise by threatening him with my rifle-butt and made him help me unload the donkey. I was puzzled what to do with the chest I had brought so as to show it off to best advantage. In giving gifts to an Arab chief there is no sense whatever in undervaluing them, even when life does not hang in the balance.

The Sheik of Urza had placed himself on the west side of the platform. Doubtless he considered that the most fashionable and dignified. I thought at first of choosing the side directly opposite for my own activities, but, as that would have entailed the "Shriek" of Dûm's turning his back to me whenever he noticed the Sheik of Urza, and I wanted all the notice I could get, I decided on the south side so that when the old man came he could sit if he chose and watch us both at once.

So I tied my rifle to me by a piece of string—not daring let go of it with all those desert-thieves, to say nothing of Villiam, within reach—and helped Villiam place the chest in the center exactly facing the platform's southern side. And, after arranging the calico covering to look as decent as might be, I stood well back, with the idea of giving the present a suggestion of greater importance. I stood farther back than I really intended, and Villiam came along with me until we stood closer to the southern veranda than I realized. In a moment I heard Monty's voice.

"Don't look round! I'm standing behind the curtain at your back. The position's pretty ticklish. We've been all night in Rosalie's quarters, and the 'shriek' has just found it out. He pretends to be utterly outraged. That man who has just come is the Sheik of Urza, expecting to arrange a wedding between himself and Rosalie. Rosalie objects, but Snoblauch has contrived to talk the 'shriek' 'round to his way of thinking. Now, to please Urza, Rosalie has been carried off and made to play the veiled lady. We're close prisoners. We were pounced on from the rear an hour ago, tied and searched. Now that they've got our pistols, our hands are free again."

"You see I've a rifle," said I.

"Lord send you wit to use it to advantage!" Monty answered. "Fred has been singing and playing for Rosalie all night; his throat is played out. Will's frightened Rosalie swears he's hers, and he's seeing visions of himself on Fifth Avenue with her on his arm. It seems Will's folk in the States move in very polite society, and he can't for the life of him see how to sidestep the issue either. Says he'd be a cad to leave the girl to the mercy of Urza and a bigger cad to take her home. I tell him not to worry—he'll be lucky if he lives the day out!"

"What would three red rockets mean out at sea an hour before dawn?" I asked over my shoulder.

"A wreck," said Monty. "They talk of a wreck outside the reef. They say the whole population has taken to the boats to go and plunder, and but for Urza's arrival the 'shriek' would be out there, too."

"If there's a wreck," said Villiam, "then Lord help the lot of us! They'll butcher the crew, and that'll give 'em blood-lust. Mark me—they'll come back and put the 'ooks into us double-quick!"

"Have you any plan?" asked Monty.

"Part of one," said I. "Tell Fred to turn the music on whenever he judges the time's ripe. It may create a diversion—who knows? If you fellows see me raise the rifle to fire, get as near me as you can. I funk being flayed alive. Let's die together!"

"Righto!" answered Monty cheerfully. "What did you bring the old devil for a present?"

AT THAT minute I noticed movement behind the curtains at the northern end and took a quick step forward rather than arouse suspicion by standing so close to where my friends were known to be. Villiam did the answering for me.

"Whisky!" he answered.

"Oh, Lord!" I heard Monty groan. "I was hoping—"

"Oh, Lord, my eye!" retorted Villiam. "Whisky's the one stuff the shriek 'ud rather 'ave than news of a wreck! Wait till the old card's drunk 'isself proper spiffed and then see!"

Snoblauch came in in his Arab clothes, barefooted like the rest of them and looking very benign and dignified with his snowy linen and respectable gray beard. He went straight to the Sheik of Urza and sat beside him, offering platitudes that met with very slight response. Urza was plainly in no mood for small-talk. Snoblauch saved his face by motioning me and coming over toward me. He paid no more attention to Villiam than if his former jack-of-all-trades had not been there.

"Gott im Himmel, mein Herr!" he began as soon as he was near enough to address me without being overheard by any one except Villiam. "This iss a bad predicament I vind you in! You haf escaped, eh? You come back with a rifle, eh? You haf the nerve to bring yourself the presents, and you think that nerve vill safe the day for you, eh? Let me tell you, you are totally wrong, my friend.

"You vill only succeed in annoying the Sheik

of Dûm by appearing vith a rifle in his presence when you are supposed to be prisoner! Gif me that rifle, please! I vill take it and pretend it belongs to me. In that vay it may be ve shall deceife the sheik and turn away from you a little of the calamity."

The man actually had the conceit to think I would do what he asked. He held his hand out to take the rifle from me. Something in my manner, I suppose, arrested his attention and stopped him before he touched the weapon. It is impossible to say what I would have done had he not withdrawn his hand as if a wasp had stung him. I was half minded to discover which way the "shriek" liked rum better—dead or alive.

" 'It 'im, sir! 'It 'im in the teeth!" advised Villiam quite loud enough for Snoblauch to hear, but the German continued to ignore him.

"Are those your presents for the sheik?" he asked, pointing toward the calico-covered chest. "You should not lay them there. It is better for you that I gif them to him vith a suitable vord of explanation. I take them and set them beside vhere I shall sit—*ja*."

He walked over to the box, and I did nothing until he started to try to lift it. Then I coughed suddenly, and he looked back—as straight into my eye along the barrel of the rifle as eye to eye can see.

"Oh, vell," he said, straightening himself, "it is heafy. Maybe after all I leafe it there and let you take your chances."

He would have sat down very near it then, only that I continued to aim at him and would not set the rifle down until he had removed himself to the far side of Urza's party.

Then I heard Rosalie's voice, loudly protesting, using English swear-words that would have procured her arrest along the London docks and Arabic argument that only did not break rocks by its violence because there were none to withstand it.

Before she had finished, the "shriek" came in, leaning on the arm of the man who had interpreted to me the night before and looking very spruce indeed in bright red Morocco slippers. Never was linen whiter than that he was wearing. Nowhere surely was more perfect cloudy amber than the lumps he wore strung round his neck on silver wore. He took his seat on the cushions on the platform with a dignity simply sublime, reminding one more of a Christian bishop about to conduct a commination service than of anything else I could think of. Although I was sure he had seen me and at any rate perfectly sure that he knew I was there, I could detect no sign of annoyance or recognition.

Urza and his following stood up and gave him very stately salutation, calling on Allah, the Most High, the Merciful, to bless him and his household, at which the old rascal bowed his head with simply benign humility.

After that there was silence for about five minutes, broken only by one long shrill complaint from Rosalie. Then the "shriek" glanced at me. Then there was conversation tossed back and forward from mat to platform—sheik to "shriek." Then a glance at me again. Then the man who had interpreted the night before, who sat on cushions beside the "shriek," stood up and addressed me, rather as if he were speaking to a black slave.

"The noble Sheik of Urza has announced," he said in the educated English Mohammedans may learn at Cairo University, "that he brings to Abdul bin Mahmoud, the Renowned, the Magnificent, the Wrath and the Flail of God, the Lord of the Limits of Decency, the Sheik of Dûm, presents of five riding-camels fully caparisoned! What do you bring?"

"Hundreds of presents!" I answered.

"Where are they?"

"There!"

I pointed to the box I had so carefully draped with calico, and all eyes were instantly focussed on it.

"What d'yer mean by tellin' 'im 'undreds and 'undreds o' presents?" grumbled Villiam in my ear. " 'E'll only get mad as a wasp when 'e finds out you're lying! Oh—I see, though! Aren't you the bright one! 'Undreds o' special sensations to the quart. I get yer! 'E'll see the point o' that!"

The "shriek" gave an order that I did not catch, and four men came out from behind the veranda curtains to carry the box closer to him.

"Stop!" I shouted. "I've something to say before the gifts change hands!"

A bomb could not have produced greater sensation.

"You are a strange giver of gifts!" sneered the Arab who interpreted, and the old "shriek" began to rock himself back and forward.

" 'E's working up a tantrum," Villiam whispered.

"I'll give no presents to any enemy!" I said.

"There were words last night about my being flayed alive."

"Oh, Gawd!" groaned Villiam. "Pacify 'im, can't yer? Pacify 'im!"

At that point Rosalie broke bounds, all smothered up in a great black veil reaching nearly to her feet. She burst through the curtains with the eunuch after her, shouting in English at the "shriek":

"You shall not kill nobody! You ole stiff! You big —— fool!"

SHE HAD the repeating pistol in her hand and pointed it at every quarter of the compass, not by any means omitting the "shriek" himself, who lost his temper thoroughly at last and began to jump about and scream like an angry parrot. At that Rosalie tore the veil off, and there followed a game of tongue-lashing in Arabic and French and English that made mere Billingsgate sound like politeness by comparison.

The Sheik of Urza sat quite still, although his followers moved and whispered. Snoblauch got up from the carpet he was sitting on and joined in the argument in fluent Arabic, stamping his feet and shaking both fists for emphasis.

"What's he saying, Villiam?" I asked.

" 'E's tellin' the shriek to exercise authority and 'ave 'er muzzled and bastinadoed, prior to marryin' 'er to Urza, who'll know just 'ow to keep 'er in order. That's what Mr. Snoblauch says."

The German's persistent repetition of his argument began to tell at last. The "shriek" grew silent in order to think and regain his breath. Then he began to shout again, and this time in obedience to his orders four men came running out, seized Rosalie and pinned her arms to her sides. One of them threw a hand over her mouth, forcing her head back by main force and laying bare her beautiful white throat. It was pretty obvious that something a white man doesn't care to see was going to take place there and then before the lot of us.

"Stop!" I shouted at the top of my lungs, and for the second time my impudence succeeded where mere rightful authority would probably have failed.

"Shoot the swine! Make 'em let go of 'er!" urged Villiam.

I took my right hand from my pocket, and held it high with something in it.

"Translate!" I said to the man on whose arm the old "shriek" leaned, and every one in the courtyard grew as still as death.

"I hold one of the presents," I said, "in my hand. A box full of them lies in front of me. I will show first what this present is. Then there shall be a conference. After judging the worth of this one, if the Sheik of Dûm agrees, he shall have the others all at once!"

While the man translated that loud enough for all to hear so that the blackguard took his hand away from Rosalie's mouth and everybody gaped with interest—except the Sheik of Urza, who sat very still and dignified—I looked swiftly about me. The donkey who had carried the gifts gave me the right idea. He was scratching himself against the wall opposite, and I owed him neither love nor gratitude for the dance he had led me since dawn.

But in the second following that I experienced more sorts of sickening fear than any one man has right to. Memory of the donkey's caperings and kicks robbed the idea of all its brightness. He had jolted that case sufficiently to have smashed two dozen of whisky into wet glass fragments and strong-smelling straw! Wherefore, then, was there any donkey left? I clutched the stick of dynamite I held tightly enough to explode it, almost. Was anything wrong with the stuff? Would it fail to go off? If it did—but I dared not think of that. The interpreter finished interpreting, and every eye was on me.

I hurled the stick of dynamite with all my strength against the wall a yard above the middle of the donkey's back. And it did its duty!

The shock was greater than I hoped; the noise, being unexpected, scared the whole crowd utterly out of its wits. Why the whole box did not go off from the concussion I neither knew at the time nor can guess now, beyond that many people have told me dynamite is temperamental stuff.

The donkey simply disappeared, as did a section of the mud-brick wall behind him. Then a great slab from higher up sat down into the gap, and the whole wall split so that an enormous V stretched skyward. Rosalie shrieked with laughter; in fact, that was the first sound I grew conscious of after the din of the explosion and the crash of falling masonry, until I heard Monty's quiet voice beside me and found that he and Fred and Will had made a run for it and escaped their frightened guards.

"That was very well done indeed!" he said. "Don't let the effect wear off, though. Carry on!"

"Do zat again!" shouted Rosalie.

I raised my hand. Promptly, as if I had given them a prearranged signal, the shabby Sheik of Urza and his men started for the entrance at a run, sweeping by in front of me with only one thought—who should reach the camels first! I waited until the noise of their hurrying footsteps had died before I raised my voice. Then:

"Interpret again!" I shouted. "Here in my hand is another present. In my pockets are more of them! If I throw this one at the wall, the wall will fall down! If I throw it at the box, however, all the other presents like this one that are in the box will explode together, and all of you will go together to hell, the same as that donkey did!"

The man interpreted at length. Having been to Cairo and doubtless having seen dynamite in quantity at work, he knew I was not exaggerating. So he himself did exaggerate very thoroughly.

"Or if," said I when he had finished, "I should shoot at the box with this rifle I hold, then it would be the same thing. Choose ye!"

I made as if to throw the second stick, and Rosalie shrieked. Snoblauch began to make tracks for the entrance, but I ordered him back again, and he went as close as he dared to the "shriek" and whispered to him. I made as if to hurl the stick of dynamite at both of them, and the "shriek" capitulated, holding up both hands.

"Now, Monty," I said, "you take the hand and play it!"

"Not a bit of it," he answered. "You're doing famously."

"What'll I do next?" I asked, beginning to feel at a loose end—hysteria, no doubt.

"Get us our pistols back!" Fred answered promptly. "Didums, you —— fool, why don't you tell him what to say?"

Villiam was lying on the ground all that time, screeching with satanic laughter, holding his sides and rolling over, slobbering at the mouth and growing purple, amused and agonized—victim of all the emotions the renegade white alone knows how to suffer from.

"Gawd!" he kept yelling. "Gawd! Koko-Gawd—an' I thought it was wuwu-whisky!"

Rosalie's captors had let go of her, and now she came running over to throw her arms around Will and cling to him.

"Our pistols back first!" I shouted at the "shriek," and this time it was Snoblauch who translated.

"I am telling him," he called back to me, "zat he need not fear reprisals from you if he only vill do ze reasonable zings you ask him! I am telling him to leave zis matter in my hands to make arrangements—*ja?"*

"Pistols!" I answered.

"Ha! I 'ave von of zem! I gif it not up!" laughed Rosalie.

But the other pistols were forthcoming. Somebody threw them, and they fell in the sand at my feet. Then Rosalie began to cajole Will.

"Now I nevaire marry to zat old Sheik of Urza! Now I marry to you! Now you and I togezzer make ze sheik, my papa, be'ave 'imself. Now you and I, we rule' zis place and grow veree rich. Ve kill ole Snoblauch. He no good. Ve shoot Villiam. He no good; he not teaching me good English same as you spik it. Yes? You and I. You promise me? Promise me—now—quick!"

"Oh Lord!" moaned Will. "If only you'd got a mother to take you to!"

"Mother? My mother is dead. She say to me, 'Some day a man is coming from France and shall marry with you!' And then she is dead, and zey take away and bury her. You are ze man from France."

"No," said Will despairingly, "I'm not from France."

"You arre not from France? You vill not stay and marry vid me?" she demanded.

I DID not catch Will's answer to that, supposing he made one. A rifle-bullet whizzed by me from between the veranda curtains to our right rear—that is to say, from somewhere behind the latticed screen. I turned and hurled the second stick of dynamite straight to where the bullet came from, and whoever was responsible for that shot had fired his last one. That end of the veranda ceased to be, together with a ton or two of roof and party walls.

Loads of the stuff, including a twisted rifle barrel and part of a human leg, fell all about us, and there was panic over on the far side of the courtyard. But the "shriek" sat still. He would have had too far to run; I had a third stick ready, and he watched my hand like a dog watching a bone.

In a way the old man's inactivity was rather masterly, for all his world was crumbling about him, and now Rosalie, the apple of his eye and one trump-card for diplomatic purposes, was seceding in public to the enemy. Whatever he might have done would almost certainly have been the wrong thing, whereas by sitting still and saying nothing he left the next move up to us and stood an even chance with us of Fortune tipping the balance.

And the jade Fortune did, giving him apparently the best of it at first. There came a surging, panting, sweating crowd of fifty men through the entrance, and the din they left behind them gave notice that the women of Dûm were also up and doing, even if etiquette did not allow them to follow their menfolk into the palace.

These newcomers were too full of their own news to pay attention to us or even to notice the destruction the dynamite had done. They swarmed round the "shriek," all yelling at him together, and under cover of that the sly old rascal ducked and ran for the seclusion of his harem—they close on his heels, unwittingly forming a screen that protected him completely unless I cared to be ruthless and blow the lot of them to smithereens. Villiam was all for ruthlessness. So was Rosalie.

"Now's your chance, sir!" went into my ear on one side.

"T'row zem all a present!" chuckled the fairer temptress.

It was Monty, cavalry leader and born seizer of opportunity, who gave the order then that finally won us the game. I was for bolting for the open. Fred was for discussion. Will was too embarrassed by Rosalie's embraces to have any wit left for decision.

"Come on, now," said Monty, leading the way at a run. "Up with the box of dynamite and follow me."

He led the way; Fred and Villiam carried the chest; I took a strategic position on the flank with the rifle and a stick of dynamite, and Will brought up the rear with Rosalie.

And Monty led us straight toward the harem. Cavalry-fashion, unexpected as the devil, sudden as thunder, full pelt into the enemy's unprotected vitals!

Snoblauch had been borne along with the crowd when the fifty pursued the "shriek." He found himself now on the edge of the forbidden harem veranda, between the devil and the deep sea—between them and us. He hesitated—changed his weak mind—changed it again—and chose. Joining us, he was swept forward under the veranda curtains, through a short passage, into a hall in the very heart of Islam's inner stronghold, where slavery of woman makes forever for the slavery of man.

"Oh, là, là! See the women! See zem run! See zem hide!" laughed Rosalie.

"Meine Herren!" protested Snoblauch. "Let me advise you. Let me guide you. Leave that box of presents here—zey vill never dare to touch it—and come, run avay out of zis vith me!"

"Easy all," said Monty. "Put the chest down. This 'll do for the present!"

VI

"M*EINE HERREN!"* Snoblauch calmed himself with a prodigious effort. He looked very much like a native of the country in those voluminous Arab garments, except that his stomach protruded too much. The Red Sea coast is a land of lean kine and leaner people. That is why obesity in woman is considered the rarest beauty.

"Listen to me now! Be advised by me! You are in ze one place zat is utterly forbidden both by custom and religion. Villiam here vill confirm what I say."

"Aw—go to ——!" sneered Villiam.

"Rosalie—she vill tell you. An intrusion into ze harem of an Arab is never forgiven. I am Orientalist, and I know. You may commit any ozzer crime against ze Arab, and perhaps he vill forgive—but zis offense never! Is zat not so, Rosalie?"

For answer Rosalie leaned across Will's protecting bosom and spat with astonishing precision in the old man's face.

"Go to your own wives and let zem pull your 'air out—old fool!" she answered.

Meanwhile Monty's restless eye had been making survey, and now we were due for the benefit of that. The babel of low-bred Arabs outside the veranda, all calling to the "shriek" at once to come and lead them on some mad errand, was a fine diversion that prevented the palace minions from paying us undivided attention yet. Invasion by our small party was bad enough, Allah knew!

But the danger of being overrun by the quarrelsome fifty was too awful to contemplate, and every available servant was marshaled to line the veranda. We were watched but for the present unmolested. Monty leaned over—took Rosalie by the shoulder—and drew her toward him.

"Let me go, you!" she pouted, slapping at his wrist and trying to break back to Will's side.

But that was the wrong time for opposing Monty's will.

"What other way out of the harem is there except across this hall and into the courtyard?" he demanded. "Answer me!"

His manner, his voice and the unyielding clench of his fingers on her shoulder frightened her thoroughly. She glanced at Will—saw that he had no intention of coming to her rescue—and raised the pistol. I don't know who struck it out of her hand; Fred, Will and I all struck together. Snoblauch picked the pistol up, and I took it from him. Rosalie began to whimper.

"Answer me!" Monty demanded.

"Zere is none—no ozzer vay out!"

"Are you sure—positive?"

"Of course I am positive. Do I not know zis place, who haf' run in and out of it since I vas little?"

"Then to get out, your papa, the sheik, must cross the hall?"

"Yes, I tell you! Yes! Let go of me, ol' fool!"

"All right," said Monty. "Up those stairs then. Leave the dynamite where it is. Now—all together again!"

The stairs were to the right of the entrance. They were steep and narrow and led to a narrow balcony that ran the full width of the hall—about thirty feet.

"Vhat of me? I do not dare go up zere!" called Snoblauch. "If I trespass in a harem, vhat guarantee is zere zat nobody shall invade mine?"

" 'Ear 'im," grinned Villiam. " 'Why, the old fool's 'arem is the coffee-shop of 'alf the town! Soon as 'is back's turned, there ain't one of 'is wives but—"

"Oh, listen to him! Oh, hear him!" shouted Snoblauch, coming running up after us. "Who are you, you vermin, to say such an untruth, vhen it is you who should have earned your pay by guarding my premises?"

"Pay?" grinned Villiam. " 'Ark at 'im! Fish for dinner an' all the money ever I gets was what 'is perishing wives paid me for 'olding of my tongue!"

"Hold it, then," snapped Monty, as we all lined out along the balcony, with Rosalie as usual clinging to Will.

There was a door in the middle of the wall, and I stepped through it, pushing aside curtains on the other side.

"There's a bigger hall through there," I said, "with a much wider balcony than this overlooking it."

Monty went and saw for himself how the ground lay.

"Is there any other way from that hall into this one than through the door below this balcony?" he demanded, and Rosalie shook her head, slinking away from him.

She was unaccustomed to be mastered by any one and wondered whether to be meek or impudent.

"You see, you fellows," he said, "we command the situation. The window at that end overlooks the whole courtyard. This balcony commands the only exit into the courtyard, and the balcony behind us commands the harem. Couldn't ask anything better. I want volunteers now to go down and distribute the dynamite strategically."

Everybody except Snoblauch volunteered. Both Rosalie and Villiam were particularly eager, but Monty chose to keep Rosalie within reach and Will to keep her quiet.

Fred and I quickly went down—tore off the calico—reopened the chest—filled our pockets with sticks of dynamite—left a neat pile of the stuff on the floor where the box had stood—and carried more than half the chest-full through the lower door into the next hall, where we placed it conspicuously and came away.

After that we divided forces to some extent, Monty and I taking the inner balcony and leaving the others to guard the only door to the courtyard. The crowd of yelling Arabs had gone away, and all was quiet again.

"Now's the time for music, I believe," said Monty, and to Rosalie's immeasurable joy Fred unclasped his concertina and began to play.

Snoblauch crouched and shivered. He had lived long enough in Dûm to understand how recklessly we were heaping offense on unforgivable offense. Centuries might lapse, and Dûm would still remember how the sheik's harem had been invaded. But to endure the added desecration of that unrighteous music—the music of unbelievers—the riotous, loud-lunged, unintelligible din such as white men make in taverns, was worse than the roar of a conquering army.

A conquering army—in that land—would have cleaned up everything, leaving none to weep and none to be ashamed, but Dûm would have to live with the memory of our invasion, and every note of the raucous concertina was a nail in the sarcophagus of Arab pride!

"You see," said Monty to me, as we both leaned over the rail and looked down on the sparsely furnished inner hall. There were many cushions and some carpets and brass trays and ornaments, but very little else, and our box of dynamite was far the most conspicuous thing. "The whole point is to keep things moving. Give tham half an hour for more or less calm reflection, and they'll very likely think of some way of scuppering us. At any rate, time would give them courage. But the music is likely to bring their indiscretion uppermost."

FRED PLAYED "Killaloe" with all his might and then "The Wearing of the Green." He was half-way through the "Marseillaise" when a door moved at the far end.

"Ah! Here they come," said Monty. "That'll do for the present, Fred."

The music ceased on a crashing chord, and the wry face of Rosalie's eunuch emerged out of shadow. He stepped forward—eyed the box of dynamite—and retired again until his back was against the door. In that position he began jabbering in the local patois at such terrific speed that Fred, with his head through the door between the two balconies, could not follow him. Will pushed Rosalie through to help us out.

"He is saying," she translated, "what do you all want? He is saying, 'You should go outside and my papa ze sheik vill hav' somezing to say to you."

"Tell him," said Monty, "we'll talk with the sheik or nobody! Tell him to take that answer and be quick about it!"

Rosalie translated and evidently added insults of her own. The eunuch retorted savagely and backed out.

"Resume the music, Fred."

The strains of "Onward, Christian Soldiers" began to ring through the halls, and there was noise of much disturbance beyond the wall we faced—the wall through which the eunuch had come and gone again.

"I'm only a cavalryman," said Monty to me. "There's only one side to my vision. The first maxim of cavalry tactics is, 'Keep the enemy guessing.' The second is, 'If you bother him enough, he'll make mistakes.' The third is, 'Take advantage of the enemy's mistakes to redeem your own!" I haven't a notion what will happen next. Have you?"

I had not. But we had not long to wait. The door at the far end opened again gingerly, and the eunuch reappeared, followed by two others of his pitiable profession. Last came the "shriek" himself, leaning on an ebony walking-stick with a silver handle.

"All right, Fred," called Monty, and the music ceased in mid-career.

Seeing us apparently unwarlike, the "shriek" sent the eunuchs back and faced us alone.

"Oh, là, là!" laughed Rosalie and began to talk Arabic sixteen to the dozen, until Will came through and put his hand on her mouth.

"Somebody 'd better watch the outer door," warned Monty, and Will went back again.

Then the "shriek" raised his head and, pointing with the ebony stick at Rosalie, commenced a tirade that for dignity and emphasis could only be compared to the sermons on Sinai in Bible days. His eye flashed, and his hand that held the walking-stick trembled with fury rather than feebleness. Rosalie giggled and flushed in turns and, for the first time since we had seen her, exhibited symptoms of remorse.

"What is he saying?" demanded Monty.

"He is saying I am veree bad woman. He is saying he no forgive me nevaire. He is saying he cast me out. He is saying he take me in formerly and love me and mak' pet of me and give me everyzing, and all I bring him is zis shame on 'is gray 'ead. Oh, I am afraid. I am sorree. Oh! Oh!"

She burst into tears and threw herself down on the floor of the balcony, sobbing as if her heart would break. Monty frowned and set his teeth as the old sheik came to an end of his rhetoric and stood grimly dignified, waiting for our reply.

" 'Ow would it be if Hi was to talk with 'im, sir?" asked Villiam, coming forward to the rail.

"Very well," said Monty. "Call his attention to that box of dynamite. Explain that we can blow up the whole palace and everybody in it whenever we care to."

Villiam commenced, throwing his arms about like a demagog speaking from the forum. The "shriek" interrupted him with an outburst of venomous Arabic.

"What does he say?" demanded Monty.

"He says truly," answered Snoblauch, "zat zis

man Villiam is a low fellow and he vill not demean himself by listening to him. Permit me, *mein Herr,* to do ze honors."

"Very well," said Monty. "Tell him what I told the other man to say."

Snoblauch began in his floweriest manner, using both hands in wheedling gestures and evidently prefacing his remarks with prolonged apology. The "shriek" interrupted him, too, curtly, abruptly, with a snarl.

"What does he say now?" asked Monty.

" 'E says," answered Villiam promptly, "this 'ere ole German's belly is a bag o' wind and 'e won't listen to no such noises!"

"Fred," said Monty, "you're our last! chance. Do the talking."

Fred came and leaned across the balcony rail, stepping gingerly lest he put his foot on the sobbing Rosalie. He began to speak in pure Arabic, but the "shriek" interrupted him, too.

"He says I'm an infidel," laughed Fred. "He won't talk with infidels."

"Call him a —— ship-wrecking old murderer!" snapped Monty.

Fred did, Villiam holding his sides the while with irrepressible excitement. And the effect was just opposite of what any of us expected. The "shriek" took it for a compliment!

PERHAPS HE misunderstood the exact meaning of Fred's scholarly Arabic, his own detestable patois being a conglomerate of other tongues with altered shades of meaning to many of the more familiar words. At all events his face brightened for the first time since entering the hall, and he looked at Fred with the appraising eye of a sportsman who has found his like at last! He began talking swiftly and emphatically.

"He wants me to go down there and chin with him!" Fred announced.

"Don't you," advised Monty. "Tell him to say what he has to say out aloud!"

"Oh no! Go down and talk vith him!" insisted Snoblauch. "I can assure you he vill not harm you. Vonce *der alte Herr* has gifen his vord of honor there is no further necessity for caution. If you go down and talk with him, I accept full responsibility."

Monty smiled.

"You are afraid?" asked Snoblauch. "Zen I go instead. Oh yes, I go. I go down and talk viz him in your name—*ja?"*

Rosalie looked up with tear-stained, swollen eyes and shook her head violently.

"Zat ole man is playing treeck," she warned. "Zis ole fool, Snoblauch—trust 'im also not at all!"

"Carry on, Fred," said Monty, and Fred began again with his scholarly Arabic, speaking very slowly, repeating whatever the "shriek" appeared to fail to understand and waiting patiently while the "shriek" talked back at him in a language that was almost unintelligible.

Long before the linguistic duel was finished, Snoblauch had grown beside himself with excitement, and Villiam scarcely less so.

"What's it all about?" I whispered.

"Just you wait till you 'ear, that's all," grinned Villiam. "There's a proposition bein' broached as 'll make your 'air stand on end."

At last the conversation ceased, and the "shriek" sat down on a pile of cushions so that Fred could confer with us.

"I began by telling him," said Fred, "that we came ashore here to look for traces of King Solomon and for no other reason and that we're scandalized and all that sort of thing by his disgraceful treatment of us. He cut me short by saying that we're bigger pirates than he is, and he knows it because otherwise why should we travel with such a box of lightning-maker! I told him the explosive is for exploration purposes, and his answer to that was, 'Then why should we offer to give it to him?' He's convinced we're born pirates and that we've come here to steal his girl; so he makes us the following offer. Now hold your breath, all of you!

"There's a steamship in the offing, outside the reef. Been there since midnight. Sent up rockets an hour before dawn, supposed to be signals of distress. Practically every able-bodied man in town took to the boats at once and put out to plunder, but on arriving at the ship they find she is not anchored and not on the rocks but able to move up and down just fast enough to keep them at a safe distance. They've tried all the tricks they know to get her to run on the reef, but nothing's doing.

"So the 'shriek' proposes that one of us should go out to the ship and, being a white man, get aboard. He promises, if one of us will induce the captain to try to bring his ship inside the reef, he will give Rosalie to Will here and show us the cellars of Solomon. He says some of his men have already been to our quarters and taken every stick we own. We can have everything back by way of reward after the wrecking is over. What shall I answer him?"

"Let me tell you vhat to answer him!" said Snoblauch.

"You should tell him 'yes.' You should tell him zat you delegate me to go and speak viz ze captain of zat ship. Zen I vill arrange some vay of your being rescued!"

"No! No!" urged Rosalie, shaking her head violently. "Vhen zat ole zing go—oh, no, no—Villiam, you tell!"

Snoblauch glared at Villiam with the sort of look lion-tamers are supposed to depend on for safety.

"None of your tricks now," he said meaningly, but Villiam snorted.

"I ain't afraid o' you no more," he answered. "Listen, you gents. The last wreck there was on this shore, Snoblauch 'e goes out in a boat an' talks about bein' German consul an' persuades the captain to come in through the reef. The 'shriek's' men does the dirty work that night, but Snoblauch, 'e gets 'is dividend same as the rest of 'em!"

"Is that true?" demanded Monty.

"No, *mein Herr!* Vould you take ze vord of a low-down beach-comber such as Villiam against my vord?"

"It is true! It is! It is!" shouted Rosalie.

"Ask the 'shriek'!" ordered Monty.

Fred leaned over the rail and put the question slowly and distinctly. The "shriek" shrugged his shoulders and answered at some length.

"He says it is true," Fred turned and told us. "Only he adds that Snoblauch has tried so many times since to blackmail him on account of it, by threatening to write to Germany and to Turkey and to England and all sorts of places, that he's weary of the man and won't employ him any more!"

Monty turned on Snoblauch coldly and addressed him without rancor in a level voice.

"I shall kick you down those stairs," he said, "unless you go of your own accord at once. If I ever catch sight of you again, that will be at your risk. Go!"

"Do you judge me on ze strength of Villiam's vord and zat pirate's?" Snoblauch demanded.

"Thank God, I'm not your judge!" Monty answered.

"Zen vhy do you order me to go?"

"Because I'm judge of my own actions and inactions. Shall I count ten? Or will you go like a free man?"

Snoblauch turned away.

"Come along, Villiam," he called. "Zis is no place for us. Come at vonce—zat's a good boy."

" 'Ark at 'im!" jeered Villiam. "Hive worked for that old devil acause o' Rosalie and there not bein' no other means o' living on this beach. Along o' 'is talk I becomes Mo'ammedan. Hi've done dirty work for 'im. But I knows gents when I sees gents, and me and 'im ain't 'itting it no more—not if Hi knows it!"

SNOBLAUCH WENT down the stairs with more speed than dignity, backward glances betraying fear lest Monty's toe prove less judicial than his words. He slunk out into the courtyard, and where he went after that we neither knew nor cared.

"Now whatever we are, Fred, we've got to pretend we're cowards," said Monty. "There's no other way of establishing communication with that ship. We've got to do that or die in this hole. Make terms with the old scoundrel. Ask him first where all those men are who came storming into the courtyard a while ago."

Fred put the question, and the "shriek" replied.

"On the beach," Fred told us. "They went away because the 'shriek' had the nerve to promise them without consulting us that he'd send one of us to board the ship to fool the captain!"

"So he thinks things are reversed, does he? Thinks we're at his mercy, not he at ours?"

"You bet he does," Fred answered. "Our best course is to dynamite the palace and die in it. Suppose one of us goes to the ship. That one's safe, but how about the others? Who shall rescue them?"

"Observe the Nelson touch," said I. "The treacherous old wrecker depends confidently on our man bringing the ship in to destruction rather than leave his friends behind."

Monty nodded.

"Tell him," he ordered Fred, "that we agree to his plan in general principle but are still talking over the details. Add that at the slightest hint of treachery on his part we'll blow this whole place to ——! He looks too pleased with himself to satisfy me!"

While Fred was translating that into Arabic, Monty addressed himself to Rosalie.

"Get up, Rosalie!" he said with that unimpassioned voice of his that even angry women would obey.

She rose to her knees, looked at him rebelliously and then got up and faced him with sullen disrespect.

"You need to think now," he told her. "We're going away. You're a white woman, and your place is not here among these savages. You must choose whether you will take the risk of trying to escape with us, or whether you will stay here."

"And 'e? Does 'e go?" she asked, pointing at Will.

Monty nodded.

"Zen I go, too!"

"You may have to leave all your belongings behind."

"I go if zat man go!"

"You will have to obey absolutely—to hold your tongue—to make believe what you are told to make believe—and—you have read the Koran?"

She nodded.

"Not me read—no. I 'ave 'eard it read."

"You know the story of Lot's wife?"

She nodded vehemently.

"You must not dare look back!"

"Oh, olright," she said with a sigh. "I obey everyzing."

" 'Ow about me?" demanded Villiam. "I ain't goin' to stay be'ind if she goes. She's all I've lingered 'ere for any'ow."

"Shut up!" snapped Monty.

But Rosalie had heard, and soft sentiment refused to be denied.

"Oh, Villiam," she exclaimed, "you are after all not so veree bad. I forgif you. I am glad I not shoot you. Some good games ve 'ave ad', *n'est ce-pas?* I vill not go vit'out you!"

Villiam turned away with a tear in his eye, and Monty addressed Will Yerkes.

"Listen to me, Will," he said. "I want no back-talk! Take that girl to the ship, while we three stay and throw the bluff. One reason why you're the man to go is that the girl will go with you without argument. Another is that you're the last-joined member of the party. A better reason yet is that we three men are English. It wouldn't be decent to give the only non-British member of the firm anything but the best end of the deal. The best reason of all is that I was elected captain of the party, and I order you. Now—no back-talk! Tell the girl you're going, while Fred informs the 'shriek'!"

Will looked at him for a moment with a queer, half-humorous, wholly appreciative twinkle in his eye.

"There's only one other breed of man talks that way in a tight place," he said. "We do it in the States. I talk your language. I'll go. If there's any way on earth of coming back for you men, count on me. But the girl goes to Europe. Is that it?"

Monty nodded. So did we all. Then Fred once more gave his attention to the "shriek."

"Tell him," said Monty, "that the only sure way we know of to tempt a European skipper to let passengers on board is to have a woman in the boat. Say that, unless Rosalie goes along to make the trick feasible, we won't have anything to do with it."

Fred interpreted that slowly and distinctly, and once again the "shriek" astonished us with a wholly unexpected point of view. He rose to his feet and stormed at our balcony, where Rosalie slunk out of his sight behind Will and trembled in horrid fear of the curses he hurled at her.

It seemed that the only thing she did not have was his permission to remain in the palace a day longer. He was done with her. He condemned her. He cast her out. She had caused him to be put to open shame before the Sheik of Urza and his men, and the tale of that would go all up and down Arabia until the very dancing-women would sing it in the coffee-shops. He cursed her by every ancestor he owned, including in the commination all her possible future offspring.

And he ended by vowing that, unless she did make herself useful by going out to the ship and helping trick the captain, he would forbid her ever to set her foot again on the streets of Dûm. It did not enter his crazy head that any woman who had once learned Dûm's delights would ever elect to leave the place. No Arab woman would dream of leaving it. Then why should Rosalie?

He was out of breath when he had finished, and then Fred nearly took our breath away by translating what he had said. There remained very little after that but to make the final dispositions as swiftly as possible. We gave Will two pistols and several sticks of dynamite—in case of trouble with the pirates on the beach—and even Villiam shook him by the hand.

ROSALIE WAS much too excited to think about the things that would have troubled any ordinary woman. She never had troubled for to-morrow and did not propose to begin at that interesting moment. She kissed Villiam good-by with a fervor that would have been less displeasing if she had not insisted on doing the same to us immediately afterward. The sensation was of having kissed the beach-comber by proxy! He wiped his mouth with the back of his hand and grinned like a man at a fair pulling faces through a collar for a prize.

"That's the fu'st perishing time she ever done that to me—strike me pink if it ain't!" he remarked to the balcony at large and then wiped his mouth a second time to find out whether or not the flavor lingered.

"If we can manage it," said Monty, "we'll be waiting for you on the beach, Will, when you return with a ship's boat. If you can't come, you're forgiven in advance. If you do come and don't find us waiting, come here—provided there's any palace left. Good-by, old chap! The best of luck!"

Will went down the stairs with Rosalie on his arm, and Villiam actually blubbered until Monty saw fit to put him to work, as much for our own peace of mind as for the beach-comber's benefit.

"There's too much dynamite in that case," he said. "It would kill us all as well as the enemy. Go down, William, and carry the greater part of it up here."

"Crickey!" said Villiam, clowning again in his voluminous, filthy-looking Turkish pants. "What if I was to drop some and if goed off?"

Monty rounded on him like a whiplash.

"Look here, my man! You've been in the British Army. No use trying to deny it. I never make a mistake on a point like that. You've handled explosives by the gross and seen them dealt with by the ton!"

"Not dynamite, sir, no, sir. Didn't 'ave no dynamite, sir. I weren't in the sappers, I was—"

"I don't want to know your secrets!" Monty answered, cutting him short. "Go down and bring up that dynamite in handfuls. Keep on doing it until I tell you it's time to stop."

Villiam proceeded to obey, with rather a stiffer back than usual, whistling to himself and seeming at last to take comfort for obedience' sake.

"I put half a case-full there for the 'shriek' to see at first," said Monty to Fred and me, "because the main point was to terrify him. We still need him afraid, but it stands to reason the edge of his fear is wearing off, and we'll need ammunition if he decides to take chances. A few sticks left down there in the bottom of the box will be enough."

We heard Will's strong boots go clumping out across the "shriek's" veranda, with Rosalie chattering on his arm. We heard her voice still laughing as they reached the latticed screen and the passage leading out to the main gate. And we drew the safe conclusion that nothing untoward occurred before they reached the open, because neither pistol-shot nor dynamite awoke the echoes.

After that there seemed nothing left to do but to watch the "shriek" and wait. He was as interested as we were in Villiam's trips up and down, and he eyed the fast emptying box with a look of increasing comfort, until Fred assured him there were plenty of sticks remaining to blow him backward through his harem wall. After that he grew fidgety.

At the end of half an hour he announced his intention of retiring through the door behind.

"Tell him no!" said Monty, and Fred did.

But the door behind him opened, and the eunuch who had been Rosalie's came through, and whispered to him from behind. After that there was more than a little movement behind that door, and every now and then it was pushed ajar. On those occasions the "shriek" pricked his ears so obviously that we could not fool ourselves no whispering was going on.

"What's to prevent the eunuchs or the women of the harem from talking and making signals to people on the veranda or in the courtyard?" I asked.

"Nothing," said Monty. "It's, being done. I suspect there's a plan on foot to creep along the veranda in force and take us by surprise."

I went to the window at the end of our balcony, tore the curtain down and looked out.

"There are men gathering around the thing with a roof over it that the 'shriek' sat on in the courtyard," I said. "There are more than twenty already, and they're beckoning to others."

"All right," said Monty. "They may not mean murder. Wait until we're sure of them. Will that window open?"

I wrenched at it.

"Yes," I said. "It gives."

"Be sure. If it won't, be ready to break every atom of glass on the instant."

"It's ship's glass," I answered, "tougher than metal. All right—the frame moves—I've got it open. We command the courtyard through it!"

"Have you dynamite ready? Stand by there, then," said Monty. "Fred, old chap, what do you say to another tune? It might possibly make the 'shriek' too bad-tempered to use his wits!"

A moment later the strains of one of Albert Chevalier's ditties burst forth and made the palace harem ring again.

"What cheer!" all the neighbors cried.
"Oo are you goin' to meet, Bill? 'Ave you bought the street, Bill?"
Laugh! I thought I should ha' died,
When I knocked 'em in the Old Kent Road!

VII

AS A matter of fact our position was hugely worse than it appeared at first sight, although first sight was bad enough. The present checkmate in which we held the "shriek" depended entirely on his belief that we would be unscrupulous enough to explode the dynamite in front of him and blow up his harem with himself.

We would have blown him up without compunction if we could have done it without risk to the women behind the wall at his back. He simply was not civilized enough to suspect us of qualms on the women's account.

If the old pirate had but known it, his very safest trick would have been to bring his wives and concubines up close behind that party wall and prove to us that they were there. Even immediate personal danger of life could never have induced us then to risk that massacre.

Under the circumstances, what he did decide to do was fairly sportsmanlike, for him, but much the best riling for us. Perhaps Fred's music unhinged his judgment.

"Suppose Will and the girl reach the ship safely," said I. "Suppose Will persuades the captain to risk sending a boat, or boats, and suppose the boats, with armed crews, reach the beach. There'll be a whole town-full of disappointed Arabs to deal with. Can we fight all Dûm?"

"I told you before," Monty answered. "Our only chance is to take advantage of the enemy's mistakes. By my reckoning, supposing everything goes well, it should take Will between two and three hours to reach the ship—three hours probably by the time he has had his parley and been hoisted aboard. Allow him an hour for confab and persuasion. Two hours to return—European crew, presumably, with oars—quicker, you know. We might hear from Will again by three this afternoon. Plenty of time for the 'shriek' and his followers to make mistakes. Suppose you pay more attention to watching from that window."

It was well I did. For a short time past there had come a sound of thumping not easy to account for. It had seemed to come from the harem wall, perhaps under the veranda, and at any rate from a spot out of my line of vision unless I should push my head and shoulders through the window—an obviously unwise thing to do.

There was no crash of falling masonry, but a constant thumping, as of a crowbar striking stone. Presently the thumping ceased, and then at last I saw the key to the solution. Two men, eunuchs presumably, carried out a large lump of stone and laid it carefully on the courtyard sand. Then somebody shouted, and all the collected ruffians by the little roofed-over platform in the center turned their backs.

"They've made a hole in the harem wall and are transferring the women," I said.

"Thank the Lord!" grinned Monty. "Now I can tell you their next move. Their first is into our hands."

Fred clasped up his concertina.

"Come on!" he said. "Hazard your conjectures, Solomon!"

"They'll divide forces," said Monty. "One party will enter the harem through the hole they've made. The other will cut off our way of escape to the rear. It's likely they've brought up men who did not see the dynamite behave. Their plan will be to attack from front and rear simultaneously. The 'shriek' hasn't the slightest idea of keeping faith, you know. He thinks Will is safely on the way to trick the steamer captain, and he'll argue we're only a nuisance, the sooner out of the way the better! He sits there thinking we're wholly unsuspicious of fresh treachery."

I began to see the women now. There was a party wall across the veranda at one place, which obliged them at that point to come into the open and accounted for the men in the midst of the courtyard turning their backs. A positive stream of them began to curve out and in again in single file—a dismal-looking, slowly-moving procession, hidden from crown to heels in brown or black and shepherded by sexless brutes who would have wrung the necks of a dozen of them with no compunction whatever at the chance whim of their master. Surely Rosalie, with her Europe-born rebellious contempt for veil and its pseudo-sanctity, had enjoyed a better lot than theirs! Not, though, that they would have admitted it!

"Come and look!" said I. "There were twenty-two before I lost count, and they're still coming!"

But Monty refused to leave his post. He was standing facing the "shriek," with his back to the door between the two balconies and Villiam on his left. Fred and I had the narrow balcony above the outer hall to ourselves.

"There goes the last of 'em," I announced. "Yes, you're right—there's a gang of cutthroats armed for the most part with long knives, but four or five have rifles, starting to go in through the hole the women came out of!"

"Let 'em," said Monty.

"What's the 'shriek' doing?" I asked.

"Working back toward the door behind him by inches at a time! When I threaten him with a pistol, he stays still for several minutes. Then he begins again."

"Why not fire just once by way of argument?" said I. "Don't hurt him—scare him!"

"It might be the signal for the scrap to begin," Monty answered. "It's better to leave them to work up their own courage and give their own signal—I think."

But he was wrong that time. I heard Villiam urging him in whispers to "shoot and not care nothin' for that ole swine!" It was an entirely gentlemanly, wholly impractical dislike of the idea of firing on an elderly unarmed man that kept him hesitating, unfaithful to the cavalry tactics he so loved and well understood.

"There's another party of them now beginning to make tracks for the veranda to my right!" I warned. "Twenty—twenty-five—thirty—thirty-five—forty of them! Once they're under the veranda, they'll be out of sight. I could blow up the lot of 'em now with one stick of dynamite. Say the word!"

He made a sudden exclamation.

"Ah!" it sounded like.

Then his pistol barked once. I sprang back from the window and crashed into Fred as we both tried to see through the door what was happening. The "shriek" was gone. Monty's bullet had splintered the top panel of the door too late. The old rascal must have jumped like a man of less than half his years.

"Back to your posts!" Monty ordered.

The first glance through the window was enough to show me that the enemy had acted while I looked away. Not one was in sight, but the loose veranda curtain bulged and bellied in evidence of an advancing hidden wave of men.

"I'm going to open fire," said I.

"Go ahead," said Monty. "Here comes the other gang through the door."

I HURLED a stick of dynamite. It fell short but exploded and broke a veranda-post. How many men it killed or injured I had no means of guessing, for the curtain merely blew inward without tearing, as before a gust of wind, and settled among the débris. Then part of the mud roof collapsed on top of all. The greater part of the oncoming enemy took to their heels across the open, and my second stick completed their rout, blowing four of them to pieces and leaving three more lifeless on the ground.

Monty began his work with a pistol, but I suppose they came too fast for him through the harem door. At any rate I heard six shots and then the crash of dynamite. He told me afterward that it was Villiam who hurled the explosive, but that was not until we had first found Villiam and dragged him out, bruised but living, from among the débris of floor and walls and roof.

And Fred and I had to find Monty first. In order to do that, we had to clamber down cautiously into a chasm where the harem hall had been.

The great, thick wall between the two balconies saved Fred and me—and the rest of the dynamite—although a blast of wind came through the opening that knocked both of us off our feet. Villiam's stick of dynamite exploded in the midst of the savages swarming through the door and detonated the remainder in the chest! It rained building stuff and bloody bits of Arab for what seemed minutes.

It was a marvel there was any palace left at all! All that did go were the outer walls and roof and floor of that one section. But the reason for that was obvious as soon as the dust and fumes had cleared away and we could see down into the yawning chasm. There had been nothing underneath to offer resistance; instead of driving its full fury up and outward, the dynamite had squandered half its force. The harem hall had been built above a cavern. The floor-beams—mostly the ribs and beams of martyred ships—were a bridge!

Deaf from the concussion, dazed by the stupefying noise and fumes, Fred and I stared down through the gap in the wall for several minutes before either of us could think of a way of getting down to look for Monty. Then Fred thought of the carpet in the outer hall—a long, narrow strip—and went down to fetch it. In two minutes after that I was hanging on to it while he lowered himself down into the abyss. When he reached bottom he shouted to me to stay up there with the rifle and guard against attack.

But attack was out of the question. There was nobody left within the four outer walls of that great building with nerve enough to attack a stray dog. And Fred had to call me down after all, for he discovered Monty with a fallen beam pinning him down and could not lift it single-handed.

So I tore strips from the carpet and lashed it fast to the balcony-rail—then came down, rifle and all, and added my strength to Fred's. By a miracle the beam had pinned Monty down without harming him. Most of its weight was upheld by the end of another lump of wood, and the moment our combined effort raised the beam a fraction of an inch he was able to crawl free, not much the worse except for a dozen bruises and a cut above the eye. It was he who insisted on hunting for Villiam before starting anything else.

We located the beach-comber by his groans, by which we judged, too, that he was far less hurt than frightened. He was lying in a corner under a pile of débris with his left leg forced nearly round his neck and his mouth full of dry dust.

"D'yer mean to tell me, gents, as I ain't dead?" he demanded when we had dragged him loose and he had spat most of the dust out. "Gawd! I thought I was dead and in 'ell!"

It was an extraordinary place in which we found ourselves, shaped something like the hull of an old-time ship—a hollow partly natural and partly hewn out of the rock, with shelves or ledges near the top on which to rest floor-beams. Now that both the floor and the roof above that had vanished and blue sky poured down hot light, we could see into nearly every nook and cranny, and presently I spied three huge holes like the ends of sewers at the farther end. They had been covered with wood, but the explosion had reduced the doors, or lids, or whatever they were, to splinters.

"Tunnels!" I said, pointing. "Three of 'em!"

We made our way through the débris leisurely until the sound of groaning lent us wings. A moment later, in the mouth of the middle hole, we came on the "shriek" in a sitting posture rubbing his naked head and his elbows alternately. At sight of us he grew silent at once, his sensations smothered by a new one.

The hole he was in turned out to be a short tunnel that led to the floor above and was closed at its upper end by an enormously heavy trap-door. The trapdoor was either bolted or else loaded down with weights, for my utmost efforts failed to move it. The "shriek" suddenly took a fancy to the tunnel in spite of, or perhaps because of, its darkness and scurried along it, we following.

When we were all in the tunnel except Villiam, he showed a disposition to talk terms and began jabbering his bastard Arabic, until it dawned on him that Villiam had deserted us. Then he gave his hand away. He had decoyed us up the tunnel of set purpose, for he scurried out past us like an eel—turned sharp to the right at the mouth—glanced down that hole—doubled back across the tunnel mouth to the other hole—looked into that—drew an enormous knife—and flung himself at Villiam!

Not that we knew he had found Villiam until yells for help brought us racing to the rescue. There, at the end of the short hole, the knife was going like a flail, with Villiam's both hands hold of the "shriek's" wrist and more curses flying to the minute than a cat-and-dog-fight ever loosed. I missed sheathing the knife in my stomach by sheer good fortune as I brought the "shriek" to ground and sat on him, while Monty took the knife away. Then I clapped my hand to my pocket, and, if I swore, I had excuse.

"What's the matter?" asked Monty, striking a match. "Are you hurt?"

For answer I removed my hand from the hip pocket and showed a stick of dynamite! Why I had forgotten I had it there—why it had not exploded and blown me and "shriek" and cave and every one to smithereens, were mysteries. It detonated finely later when the right time came to use it.

MONTY'S MATCH showed what the "shriek's" anxiety and change of mind were all about. Villiam's tattered clothes were leaking gold coin! There was an old wooden chest on the floor of the cave with its lid burst open. I kicked it, but the bullion it still contained was so heavy it did not move. Fred went down on his knees and dipped both hands in, lifted them up and poured back gold coin in a ringing shower.

"Bring some of that to the light!" ordered Monty.

I stayed behind to watch the "shriek," who was about as full of planless fury as a cow robbed of her calf.

"What is it?" I asked, and Fred answered:

"Gold coin! Loot from the cabins of merchant-ships!"

"Old stuff?" I asked.

"Old and new."

"Come back in here," I said. "The old pirate is squinting after something in the corner."

They returned and rummaged. Presently I heard the ringing clink that no man hears and forgets—suggestive of infinite opulence—unmistakable.

"More than a hundred ingots!" said Monty's voice.

"Gold?" I asked, although I knew.

"Count 'em!" said Fred, suddenly grown practical.

"A hundred and ten!" announced Monty.

We did not wait to see what further treasures the cavern held, for faces began to peer down from above. I threw the stick of dynamite that had so strangely not exploded. This time it went off like a cannon and sent a hundred-weight or two of courtyard sand down in among us. It certainly "cleared decks."

Then we found the "shriek's" turban—a most voluminous affair—crumpled and soiled among the dynamited rubbish. He claimed it at once, but Monty had a better use for it than to comfort his iniquitous, bruised cranium. There were thirty yards of it of finest silk. With one end he tied up the wooden chest. Then he and I dragged and shoved and heaved and carried it over beams and débris to where the carpet still hung. Fred followed, carrying ingots.

Then, looking very sheepish and clinking like an old bell-wether because of stolen coin secreted in his clothing, Villiam did the same. Then we all went back and carried ingots. Finally Fred and Monty drove the "shriek" along in front of them, and I climbed up by the carpet with the end of the silken turban tied to me.

By the time we had all come up by that route and had hauled the coin and ingots after us—Villiam simply shedding money as an honest man yields sweat—there was a new crowd assembling in the courtyard, accompanied now by women, and dozens more were pouring in through the main entrance. The "shriek" began haranguing them, but Fred put a hand over his mouth and a knee in the small of his back besides. Then I went into the outer hall for more dynamite, and while I was gone on that errand several shots were fired in our direction by the crowd.

When I returned and flung three sticks at the canopied platform in the center, blowing it to bits, there began a new stampede, but it was still touch and go whether we could make good our escape or not. Those behind, who had not felt the sharp shock or seen men dismembered in a fraction of a second—and especially the women—were disposed to stay and see the matter through.

But Monty took charge again. He tied the "shriek's" hands with the loose end of the turban—drove him in front and set us all to climbing—up along a broken wall that rose like zigzag steps against the sky, to the nearest undamaged roof.

There we left the "shriek" in charge of Villiam, putting that disheveled beach-comber on his honor, for lack of a safer expedient, and returned to carry the plunder, I volleying again with dynamite to create a diversion and gain time. The crowd replied with rifle-fire; so I hurled a stick right into the midst of them, and after that they gave us respite. Carrying that booty was almost the hardest job I ever bent back to, and made worse by the scorching sun and myriads of flies and doubly difficult by reason of precarious foothold.

Having reached the first roof at last with the bullion, Villiam and I were sent back for the rest of the dynamite, and by the time we had that on the roof, Monty had made progress toward one of the four square corner towers. We entered that through one of the windows facing inward, to find ourselves in Rosalie's luxurious quarters that Villiam had described to me before dawn.

There was nobody in there. A huge, stout door made us safe—except for the route along the roof—from anything less than battering-rams. We had dynamite with which to break the roof up if we must, and it was not easy to see how a ram could be swung round the curve of the narrow entrance steps. Short of fire and drought, we could hold out for a week.

Leaving the loads where they were, but driving the "shriek" up in front of us, we emerged on the roof of the tower with a full view at last of the sea, and we all gasped—sighed—filled our lungs—and laughed. Faithful to the last to his fiendish instrument of music, Fred had the concertina tied round his neck with a torn pocket-handkerchief. He would have loosed it and made music there and then, but Monty did not want attention called yet to our whereabouts.

"That ship looks familiar," he said, as we all gazed out across the molten glare.

"Most merchant-ships look alike," Fred answered with a deprecating frown.

"Except to men like us," said Monty, "who have watched ships up and down seven seas. I've seen that ship before."

"So have I," said I.

"I admit it," said Fred.

But we none of us voiced what memory was telling us for fear sight might be playing tricks. He who has seen the Red Sea desert mirage mistrusts eyesight, doubts his ears, has lost taste—because of dreadful food—discredits touch—where nearly all things are too hot to lay a finger on—and puts faith only in smell. But smell is overworked! It would have been ridiculous to say we smelled that ship's peculiar aroma. So we all kept still.

NOT SO the "shriek" however. He was voluble and no longer in mood to refuse Villiam's service as interpreter. He had not yet got it through his shiny, bone-bald skull that Will and Rosalie had no intention of tempting the ship's captain to destruction on the reef. It was only bit by bit, as question followed question and fact, that the horrid realization dawned, not only that Rosalie had run away from Dûm forever, but that the ship would go, too, presently.

Sight of that rich prize so near and yet so far away from clutching fingers saddened him more than the damage we had done his palace and the loss of the marriageable Rosalie. For a while after that he would not talk, until we threatened, unless he did, to go down again and search among the débris in the cavern for things we might have overlooked. That loosed his tongue.

"Where did you get this gold?" demanded Monty, touching the heap of bars.

" 'E says it's ole King Solomon's!" announced Villiam. " 'Im what 'ad the million wives and wrote the Bible."

But historical accuracy was not the "shriek's" long suit. As Monty pointed out, gold bars in Solomon's day were not cast in wedge-shaped molds and did not have their weight stamped on each in latter-day Christian figures.

"Where did you get the coins?" asked Monty.

"Got 'em in trade, 'e says."

"What trade does he have with Greece—Peru—China—United States—Italy—Denmark—the Argentine—Guatemala?" asked Monty, picking up gold coins at random.

"Aw—what's the use?" grumbled Villiam. " 'E'll only tell yer them's Solomon's if yer press 'im too 'ard. 'E got 'em out o' the strong-boxes o' ship's captains, that's where the ole crook got 'em from! 'E changes 'em into Maria Theresa dollars whenever 'e gets the chance."

"Ask him about the hole we found the money in," said Monty.

" 'E swears by the Koran that 'ole was made by King Solomon's captains to stow their stuff in while they waited 'ere for camels to come an' carry it away. 'E says it's true by 'is beard and 'is father's honor. It's likely the ole liar means it."

"Ask him how he knows that."

" 'E says the marks the captains made are down there. And when 'is grandfather first fell down the 'ole an' discovered it there was chests and some very old gold."

"Gad!" exclaimed Monty. "I'm antiquarian enough to go down again and see those marks! Who's coming with me?"

But none of us did go. I was positive that minute that I saw a flash like a rifleshot out at sea, close by the ship that was not at anchor but moving slowly up and down. A minute later we certainly all saw a flash, and then—in one of those strange gaps in the glare that gunners bless and no one understands—we saw the fleet of pirate shore-boats scurrying away like flies.

"D'you suppose Will used some dynamite?"

"Looks mighty like it."

"If it's so—if he's on board, using rifles and dynamite from the ship's deck—then he'll be heading for shore again in half a jiffy!"

"Watch for him," said Monty. "I'll attend to business here. William—pay attention to me, please!"

The first thing he demanded of the "shriek" was all our belongings that had been looted from "the 'ouse near my 'ouse" Rosalie had lent us. The "shriek" promptly denied all knowledge of them, in spite of the fact that he had admitted possession less than an hour ago. Monty sent me down to the room below at once for dynamite and ordered a stick thrown on the roof above the general living-quarters. The "shriek" capitulated before I could throw the stuff and admitted he knew where all our loads were.

"Order them laid outside the wall at the foot of this tower, where I can count them from up here!" ordered Monty. Turning to me he added, "Throw dynamite at the palace without the slightest hesitation if he fails to do as he's told!"

The "shriek" stood accordingly on the edge of the tower, rather like a *muezzin,* except for his bare head, and sent out an ululating call that carried like a jackal's—an astonishing, shuddersome shout from such an old man.

It was answered from below, and then the "shriek" gave his orders, twice repeated, Villiam listening carefully to make sure no treachery was spatchcocked into the conversation. Fifteen minutes later our loads began to be carried on men's heads, and within thirty minutes the last of them lay below us. It was perfectly obvious even from where we were that several of the larger cases had been rifled of their contents, but we had more than sufficient plunder to compensate for that. The guns were there, unsuspected in their white pine boxes, and most of the really valuable things.

"Will's on the way!" said Fred suddenly, peering under cupped hands. "Two boats have left the ship. They're rowing like the devil!"

"Excellent!" Monty rose to his feet. "I'm hungrier than a shark, but we'll not go supperless. Tell him, William, to shout down for women—women, mind—his own harem if he can't get others—to carry those loads to the beach—and what we've got here as well!"

Suspiciously obedient, the "shriek" returned to the edge of the tower and yelled the required commands. He knew what the effect would be. The novelty of the thing—the outrageous impropriety of requiring wives of the faithful to carry loads for foreign unbelievers—brought out men instead of women to crowd around the tower and shout at us. Several bullets, aimed as a hint to the "shriek" to reform his ways, whistled over our heads. One rebellious ruffian pounced on a package of ours and began to make off with it.

"Dynamite!" said Monty, and I flung some, hurling it as far out as possible.

I had the luck to kill nobody and followed it with two more sticks that completed the panic without doing injury. We were left once more masters of the solitude but with neither men nor women to do porterage. The "shriek" looked pleased. He began to suspect a new basis for bargaining and treachery. His were not cavalry tactics.

"Say, you chaps, they're coming like ——!" shouted Fred. "Take a look! Rowing like the royal navy! Can you see through the glare? The shore-craft are giving chase—after 'em like a swarm of flies! Oh God, for a Maxim! Why aren't prayers answered nowadays?"

MONTY TURNED on the "shriek" and began to introduce that gentleman to what the little British army calls "brute force and bloody ignorance." He crammed the point of a pistol in his ear—seized him by the scrawny neck—shook him—and proceeded to throw a bluff that was pure and without any sort of leg to stand on if it had not worked. But he who can pride himself on keeping more than thirty women in a harem can believe the worst of any one.

"Tell him what I say now, William!"

The nondescript stood close, screwing his face into a frown and thrusting out his jaw, for he sensed they were not to be pleasantries that he would have to render into longshore Arabic.

"His eunuchs and the women of his harem are to carry our loads!"

Villiam himself was shocked by the revolutionary nature of the demand and swallowed twice before he could muster what he deemed a suitably villainous voice.

"He has no time allowed him to decide! He must give the order at once!"

Villiam did that into the argot.

"If he disobeys, he shall see his women dynamited before his eyes!"

Villiam grinned, and the "shriek" winced as

that decree went into Arabic. Neither Villiam nor the "shriek" paid Monty the compliment of disbelieving. In fact it was Villiam's faith in the genuineness of the threat that enabled him to convince the victim.

"The whole palace shall be blown up, together with everybody in it!"

The "shriek" began to make motions of submission with his hands, muttering prayers to himself in Arabic.

"But he shall not be killed!" added Monty—inspired for the occasion by the height of our necessity. "He shall live and be taken away with us, to be drowned at sea after shame has had time to gnaw his heart!"

Monty turned away, for he could not keep a straight face. I went to rearranging the remaining heap of dynamite to help Villiam carry conviction.

"The boats are through the gap in the reef!" Fred shouted. "The shore-craft are hot and hard after 'em—all choked together in the gap now—good! Some one's standing in the stern of one boat shooting into the mess with a pistol in each hand! Bet you a thousand it's Will! I can see the paddlers falling! Gosh! Did you see that? Did you hear? He flung a stick of dynamite plunk into the middle of the crowded boats—blew a —— of a lot of 'em to Kingdom Come! Good boy, Will! Well done, sir! Well played, America!"

" 'E says please to give 'im back the gold bars and 'is money, sir," said Villiam, removing his ear from the lips of the mumbling "shriek."

Monty made a sign to me. The "shriek" looked up. I took aim very deliberately with a stick of dynamite for the only part of the palace that looked large enough to house thirty women and their attendant maids and eunuchs. The "shriek" held a hand up to prevent me. I made a motion as if to throw. He rose and went to the edge of the tower and began to raise his ululating howl.

After about a minute eunuchs came into the open through a gap in the veranda curtain and listened with gaping incredulity. Not by ten words, or by a thousand, is real revolution brought about in Moslem lands. The authority of custom was stronger than that of the autocratic "shriek." They answered, demanding explanations. Every word of their retort—every second lost was a new spike in our chance of winning free. Monty took the whip hand again.

"You shout to them," he ordered Villiam. "Say that, if orders aren't obeyed before I count a hundred, sticks of dynamite will begin to rain on the roof!"

The eunuchs went in, to confer presumably.

"Lob dynamite into the courtyard by way of hint!" ordered Monty, and I threw one stick that landed beyond the destroyed center platform and scattered sand and stones all over the veranda roof.

That had an instant effect. The same eunuchs ran out and made signals of surrender.

"Tell 'em to march the women out, or we'll do that again and do it nearer," Monty ordered, and Villiam's impudent Cockney voice made the building ring.

They capitulated. Within thirty seconds a woman veiled from crown to heels in dull black emerged into the open, and others followed.

"Shall we take a chance on the main gate?" I asked, wondering how much safety there would be in the dark passage between it and the courtyard.

"Not at all!" said Monty. "This corner is nearest the sea. William, explain to the women that this is to show them what will happen if they're disobedient. Tell 'em nobody 's going to be hurt—yet!"

Villiam explained at length, delighting in the exercise of terrorism pure and simple. Not for nothing had he himself been terrorized for years by the "shriek" and Snoblauch—probably by every Arab in the whole of Dûm—and by Rosalie in her own peculiar way. He was getting a little of his own again. The women shuddered and clung together in a crowd, forgetting jealousies, the eunuchs squatting on the ground between them and the door they had emerged through, to watch and cut off retreat. There were eight eunuchs in all—big, well-fed, burly customers with eye and attitude that sang aloud of license—intrigue—lust.

"Now make a hole through the wall below!" Monty ordered. "No, not that side—you'll cover our loads with débris. That's better!"

But it isn't so easy as it sounds to make a practicable passage through a wall of rock and plaster with sticks of dynamite thrown at an angle from an elevation. I wasted six sticks before the seventh made a gap in the proper place, and then it required three more, thrown very carefully, to finish the task and clear a passage from the courtyard to the open.

By this time the women, grown indifferent to the noise, were all agog with excitement, standing on tiptoe to see the effect and laughing in shrill chorus when extra large lumps of stone and roofing stuff were hurled toward them. The "shriek" was frantic, grieving for his property; the eunuchs were frankly afraid; the women enjoyed the spectacle. They marched forward at the word of command over the débris and through the gap, not, it is true, as their European sisters might have done in semi-military fashion, but giggling—squealing like schoolgirls—higgledy-piggledy—anyhow—three-parts scared out of their skins—wholly excited—having the time of their lives and not at all too careful of the law that decrees no woman shall let her face be seen by strangers.

We were able to form a very poor opinion of the "shriek's" taste. With all those Red Sea ports to raid and batter in and all Dûm for his own, he had picked for himself the ugliest swarm of shrews that ever a prophet's faithful follower kept under lock and key!

THE MINUTE they were through the gap and looking in consternation at the loads they were to carry—for the "shriek's" harem did not have to carry water and grow muscular like ordinary Dûm drabs—we started down the tower one by one, carrying armfuls of booty—gold coin tied into bags made from sections of the "shriek's" silk turban—gold bars done up in the same way—and last and not least, dynamite.

Fred was the last to come, driving the "shriek" in front of him—for we did not dare leave the ruler of Dûm behind us to reassert lost prestige with his townsmen and contrive our undoing at the last.

"The boats are close inshore now!" Fred shouted. "There's a crowd running down to the beach to receive them, and the canoes are scarcely a quarter of a mile behind! We're all done for if we don't hurry!"

And who could make women hurry, whose only training was in laziness and coquetry? Even the eunuchs, driven to the peak of frenzy by fear of Monty's pistol and the feel of Monty's toe in their fat "behimes," could not persuade them to pick up the loads one by one and walk with them. They had to cackle and giggle and argue and pretend they couldn't and declare they wouldn't and waste more time than if the fight on the beach would take place to-morrow and to-day was holiday. We could have carried loads ourselves and abandoned everything but the gold and dynamite, but for wanting both hands free.

Finally it was Fred who thought of the solution. He tied what was left of the "shriek's" turban round the old rascal's neck and threatened to hang him to a beam that stuck out from the shattered wall unless the women went to work at once. And, if they didn't love their old tyrant, at least they looked to him for luxuries. When Fred had made the threat in pure Arabic and Villiam had rendered it impurely but more intelligibly, they screamed and made haste at once.

Once on the way they showed speed and stamina far beyond anything we had hoped. We abandoned the biggest, heaviest cases because those had been looted of some of their contents. Some of what were left weighed sixty pounds, but we made the fat eunuchs shoulder those. And we only had to halt three times between the palace and the beach, where we could hear Will's pistols cracking busily.

The two boats, with only four rowers in each, were lying off-shore at exactly that point where the undertow balanced the onshore current and established equilibrium, the oars dipping once and again to keep position. Behind them, trying to dodge Will's pistols, thirty or forty native boats formed a screen that cut off retreat toward the ship. And on the beach practically the whole of Dûm waited with something almost like patience until they should be forced to land.

In spite of the din we had made destroying walls, and the surely obvious fact that the boats had come to establish communication with us, our arrival from the rear was a complete surprise. What that town of sea-robbers lacked was generalship. Perhaps we had their only general prisoner!

It would not have been generalship to wait for their attack. We took the risk of the women stampeding—picked a place in the crowd where men—and only men—seemed to stand thickest—and fired, all four of us, Monty, Fred, Villiam and I, lobbing sticks of dynamite in swift succession that blasted a hole a company of camels could have marched through in open order. There was panic—prompt and dire. All but the women and the children, who watched from a little distance, took to their heels and fled.

Will hailed us with a glad yell from the nearest boat and shouted instructions we could not catch. We expected our women to have bolted, but the harem beauties proved to be of sterner stuff and went forward with their burdens, down between the ghastly mangled fragments of the victims of our dynamite, with little else than curiosity. Blood and viscera spread on the sand did not trouble them one iota.

It was the "shriek" who bolted. Villiam yelled too late to warn us. The old rascal doubled back like a rabbit at our first shot—ducked low—crawled along a sand furrow for fifty yards as swiftly as a hunting snake and then took to his heels toward the town. I could have hit him with the rifle, but, as Monty said:

"What's the use? We've taken toll of him!"

I wished I had shot him, though, within ten minutes. He reached the street and rallied his followers. Then, utterly regardless of the safety of his wives, whom he thought perhaps defiled by our use of them as porters, he opened a scattering fire on us. One wife was hit in the foot, and a eunuch was shot dead.

We let the wives go—made them throw down the loads and sent them running toward the palace to be out of harm's way. Then Villiam and I made a shelter of bags and boxes, and I lay down behind it to return the fire while the others waded waist-deep through the treacherous undertow and carried first the loot and then our own things to the boats. For they did not dare bring the boats inshore for fear of their turning turtle on the beach.

By the time they had everything on board the boats—except a few loads dropped into the sea and not recoverable in that state of haste—and they had begun yelling for me to make haste and wade out to them, the "shriek's" men had summoned courage sufficient to attempt a rush. They came charging down on the beach a hundred strong, brandishing spears and some of them firing long-barreled rifles as they ran.

In my hurry I dropped a dozen sticks of dynamite in one place on the sand, and could not stop to pick them up. As I jumped into Will's boat, they were pounced on.

"Now we're done for!" said I.

BUT WILL had one shot left in one pistol. Monty held a stick of dynamite, by some miracle not lost overboard or exploded in the hurry. Pistol-shot followed missile as with one thought and landed simultaneously, leaving doubt as to which had detonated the twelve sticks on the sand—but very little else in that near neighborhood! The shock of the explosion knocked me back head over heels into the water, where I was sucked under by the ground-swell and would have been drowned but for Monty's strong arms and a most infernally sharp boat-hook that left a scar in my left side that I wear to-day in memory of it and him.

They kept up the shooting from the beach, but their aim was rotten. One of the rowers had his knuckles barked, and there were several holes in both boats, but there was no serious damage done. Will's ammunition was gone, but I had plenty for the rifle, and, being hungry, weary and wet, I passed the weapon to him. In between potting at the fleet of small craft that fought with rashness that did their crews' courage credit but not their wit, he told us what had been happening at his end.

"You noticed the name on the bow of the boats?"

"Sure. *Jean Marie!* How did she come to turn back?"

The crews who manned the oars and the bearded third mate in the other boat had nodded to us like old friends. Headed for a rusty-plated tramp that we had left the day before with sighs of thankfulness, we felt like wanderers coming home again.

"It's the queerest tale ever you heard! Look out! Those three boats on the right are coming for us all together! See—they've lashed 'em side to side like a raft!"

"Hand me a stick of dynamite," said Monty grimly. "There! That settled 'em, I think. William, you take the rest of the dynamite and repel boarders! Continue the story, Will."

"Well—we'd no sooner left the ship and she was under way again than the first mate—you recall he was a stoutish, rather elderly, bearded man—went to the skipper and questioned him about things he'd overheard us say but particularly about things he thought he'd heard the captain say to us.

"Seems when he was in Cochin China years ago his wife and little daughter were to come out and live with him but were shipwrecked in the Red Sea. He was never able to get near the scene of the wreck—poor man, you know—had to go where ships' owners sent him, but he heard rumors, and one was that a little French girl and her mother had been made prisoners by the coast Arabs.

"Then he heard another story, to the effect that there was a European merchant at this place, who could be reached by mail once in three months or so by way of Constantinople. Name of merchant—Snoblauch, if you please!

"So he wrote to this man, Snoblauch, to ask if the story about the woman and the child were true, stating that the woman was his wife and the child his daughter and promising on receipt of a reply in the affirmative either to come to Dûm in person or persuade his Government to send a cruiser to bring the women away.

"What do you suppose friend Snoblauch does? I've seen the letter. He wrote back after thinking the thing over for a month or two and said there was no truth whatever in the story: that there was no white woman and no white child in Dûm, nor ever had been! Consider the old beast? What d'you know about him, eh? So full of his own scheme to marry the girl to a Bedouin chief that he sent that heartless lie to her father!

"Well—talk led to talk, and one thing led to another until the captain had told the story he told us about delivering goods to the rather faded mother, and they were both sure to the point of conviction that mother and girl would still be found in Dûm. They piled on the weight of argument by letting 'emselves get nervous on our account. And then the captain figured that we were generous sort of men who'd settle up with the owners for extra coal and time lost and so on. So they steamed back, and here we are!"

"And where's Rosalie?"

"In the arms of papa!"

"Recognize him?"

"Of course not. But she's crazy about him—simply crazy. Dotes on his whiskers and fat stomach and blue uniform. She has cultivated the Arab standards of beauty, you know."

"So you're left in the cold, are you?"

He made a wry face.

"She has told pop she means to marry me at once!" he answered.

We left the disheartened crews of the longshore boats behind, but one canoe—or rather ship's boat driven by paddles—approached us at an angle and persisted, reaching the steamer abreast of us. Two hundred yards before we came within hailing distance we knew it was Snoblauch perched in the stern with his feet on luggage and his European tweeds put on tidily.

"Where are your wives?" Monty called to him, as he bade his paddlers wait and let us up the companion-ladder first.

"Oh, I leaf zem! Zey are nozzing but safages! Zey vill find zemselfs anozzer hosband! It is nozzing. Later I explain to you on board the ship."

"Of course you will!" Will Yerkes stood on a thwart and shouted. "Mr. Anatole Molyneux! Oh, Mr. Molyneux!"

The hairy first mate put head and shoulders over the bridge rail.

"This is Herr Snoblauch of Dûm, who wrote you that letter! Mr. Snoblauch, this is Mr. Anatole Molyneux, father of Rosalie Molyneux, first mate of this steamer. Won't you step aboard?"

"Venez, mo'sieur!" said the Frenchman, leaning over. *"Je suis prêt!"*

An impudent and very lovely girl's face thrust itself past his and spat three times in swift succession.

"Go back to your vifes, an' zey comb your 'air, ole Germanee sausage!" she shouted.

And Snoblauch went, sixteen to the dozen, screaming at the paddlers to take him swiftly out of rifle-range.

VIII

THE TRAMP-STEAMER *Jean Marie,* with trembling boilers and every loose gadget on her rattling like a brass band, accomplished seven full knots northwestward toward Suez, and the grim east coast of the Red Sea faded in the glare. She knew a new regime at last, that old frequenter of half-forgotten ports. There was brand-new life on board her; thought was all of whimsicality, and, because the French lack reverence for Mrs. Grundy, to speak was to laugh.

Outrageously attired in Turkish trousers, and little blue Morocco slippers on bare feet, with odds and ends of shore-going frippery looted from drawers and chests to complete the array, Rosalie danced on the deck, swearing in awful detail in coast Arabic whenever the fancy seized her, but for the most part making jokes.

Villiam—down on the ship's papers now as "Mr. William Hodges, passenger, rescued at sea"—sat a great deal alone and puzzled over gold coins that he extracted from various folds of a dirty old pair of baggy trousers. He still wore a fez at an impudent angle, but Monty had given him the "suit o' Europe reach-me-downs" his heart desired, and now the old beach-combing clothes were luggage.

"Mister," he asked me on the morning of the first day out. " 'As the price o' public 'ouses riz since Hi left 'ome? Can a man still take a nice little pub in the country who's got a couple o' hundred to 'is name? If that's so, Hi means to 'ave one!"

"What 'll you call it?" I asked. "The Shriek of Dûm?"

"No, guv'nor! No; you're laughing at me. I ain't joking. I'm going to 'ave a little dinky public 'ouse and call it 'Roses on the Lee' in mem'ry o' her once kissing me! Can't you see it—nice, pretty signboard—picture of a rosebush—red roses on it all ablooming—underneath in big black letters, William 'Odges, Proprietor! Blimy! Can't they make this 'ooker crawl faster? I'm in a 'urry!"

So much for Villiam. Each to his taste, and water to its level. Rosalie was not such an easy problem, nor her ambitions so easy to fulfil. We held a consultation about her in the unspeakably stuffy cabin next the chart-house, while the second mate stood watch so that the skipper and first could both be present. She herself superintended and passed remarks through the open window, smoking a cigaret and dividing her attentions between Pop Molyneux and Will.

One thing was extremely easy to decide. Including bullion and gold coins we had brought away with us a capital sum sufficient, when carefully invested, to make her extremely well off from the standpoint of a young, unmarried woman.

"Vhat diff'rence zat make?" she demanded. "Vill Yerkes he marry me an' take all back!"

It really looked very serious for Will. Pop Molyneux—ridiculously proud of the girl and satisfied with her "dot," as only a thrifty French papa knows how to be, but scared to death of the prospect of taking care of her ashore—was lavish of his praise of Will and all in favor of the match. It never entered Rosalie's head that Will might prefer to choose his own mate or that he might balk at the prospect of marrying an orphan rescued from a Red Sea beach. And he was much too fine a chap to hurt her feelings.

From joking about him, poking fun at him and taking imaginary strolls with him and his bride down Bond Street, in the Bois, or up Fifth Avenue, we began to share his gloom. It was not until we passed through the Suez Canal and all took train with Pa Molyneux and Rosalie to Alexandria to buy her Christian clothing, while the *Jean Marie* took on coal and waited for orders, that Rosalie herself found the only true solution of it all.

Will is a presentable young chap. If it were not that his ears stick out he would be handsomer than ninety-nine men out of any hundred. And because Fred, who was born into fine society but loathes it, never can be induced to do anything conventional in cities and because it fell to my lot to hunt with Pop Molyneux and Rosalie among the shops—the money not being settled on her yet, and Molyneux himself greatly admiring our persistence in overseeing expenditures until proper legal papers had been drawn and signed—it followed that Monty and Will went about a great deal together and were seen in the hotel together at all hours of the day.

They were altogether too good-looking to escape recognition. Monty had not signed his proper name and title on the hotel-register, but it was only a matter of hours before Mrs. John Calvert sent her servant with an invitation to take tea in her room and bring his friend. And all the world knows who she is. Not royalty refuses when she invites.

She took quite a fancy to Will. Women do, especially the women who have been and seen and who have successful grownup sons. By the second day he was riding in her carriage, and that evening at dinner, she being what she is and knowing half the honorable secrets of more cabinets than one, he had unbosomed himself to her about the whole business.

"Bring the girl to me. Let me see her," was the only comment.

We had been keeping Rosalie in a private room and taking her about in hooded carriages, for obvious reasons.

So Rosalie was produced and left with Mrs. John Calvert, who had nothing particular to do just then because her husband was up the Nile making treaties with unknown tribes or some such matter. In an hour Rosalie was her sworn slave. Within a day the whole process of acquiring a wardrobe had been rearranged, with Mrs. John Calvert in charge and Mrs. Calvert's private carriage taking the place of our beastly, stuffy, hooded, hired victorias.

Once made presentable—and, heavens, what a change it was—Rosalie was taken to call on interesting folk, with that astonishing story of hers to tell and her naive manners—or lack of them—to make her entertaining. In that way she met some of the nicest people—French as well as British—in Alexandria.

It was on the fifth, or the sixth day, that she confronted Monty and me and Will in the hotel lobby. We had been strolling. Fred was making concertina music to three steamer-captains, Pa Molyneux, a fat policeman and a Chinese mandarin in the red room up-stairs at Bill's—and, if you never heard of Bill's, it's time you traveled. Rosalie had just come in from driving with Mrs. Calvert and was looking lovely in her new dress with dark red roses at her waist.

"I no marry you!" she told Will frankly.

"Why?" he had the nerve to ask.

"Oh, because! I 'ave seen too many ozzer ladies. You should 'ave a lady like zem—like zis one, Madame Calvert! I no marry you! I go to school! I learn! Madame Calvert, she is arranging everyzing. By and by, maybe I forget you!"

"I hope not!" we all answered fervently.

At that she kissed us each in full view of every one in the lobby. Mrs. Calvert looking away to hide tears or laughter, I don't know which.

"I never forget you—none of you—never! I love you all always! But now I am one voman! One year more—two year more—and I know not now what I choose zen! Tell Papa Molyneux I go viz Madame Calvert! Tell 'im come say me good-by!"

BARABBAS ISLAND

"BILL'S," AT Alexandria, is one of those strange places dotted here and there about the world so well known to some men that mention of them brings surging reminiscence, and utterly unknown to everybody else.

The very name of the place makes, for instance, certain brands of missionary blink, including even those who have been inside. On the other hand, there is a bishop—whom half the world agrees to honor—who always spends an hour or two up-stairs at Bill's on the occasions when he visits Alexandria.

But he, in addition to being a friend of man, plays chess. In spite of the lurid lies ignorant untraveled and malignant traveled tell, in spite of appearances and some history, chess made Bill's famous. It was chess that brought Monty there—in the rather dim front room above the noisy bar.

A strange setting undoubtedly for a privy councilor of England, Earl of Montdidier and Kirkudbrightshire, ex-colonel of cavalry. But chess levels ranks and respects no persons. Monty sat with waxed mustache-ends pricked to la qui vive and his long legs stretched apart, face to face with a Chinese mandarin—in exile but receiving ample funds from mysterious sources—who played a subtle game, yielding as it were before the wind of Monty's swift attacks, gentle, smiling, losing a game very seldom.

Superficially at least, the atmosphere of Bill's suited Fred Oakes vastly better. He sprawled in the opposite far corner, suggestive of the roistering swordsmen of a bygone age with his neat beard, frankly awake eyes and attitude of hips and shoulders that only campaigning gives a man. He made music troubadour fashion on his concertina to a motley gathering of men of many nations—for you can do what you like and when you like at Bill's, whatever the chess-players have to say about it.

Every once in a while Monty glanced across and damned him for being noisy. Then the mandarin sought with a deprecating smile to preserve the peace, not understanding that English friendship is in danger only when the friends grow too polite. At each remonstrance Fred laughed.

"Thank your stars I take my pleasures soberly!" he shouted in reply to one of Monty's fierce rebukes. "I've known friends of yours, Didums, carried to bed in the middle of convivial afternoons. Thank the Lord I am not as other men are—or even as this Egyptologist!"

He touched with his toe the recumbent form of a man better known as authority on Gizah than as a drinker, yet a drinker of strange, strong drinks for all that.

There was remarkably little drunkenness up-stairs at Bill's, although the bar below is the usual longshore lush-house with the stains all gilded over and the mirrors screened from flies. Anybody down-stairs could get drunk as deeply and often as he pleased and take his chance with the police. But up-stairs only the favored few forget themselves, and they are protected; it is thoroughly understood that any police officer who treads the shabby, narrow strip of carpet leading to the rooms above does so with official eyes shut.

So, although Prof. Grogan Guthrie's head lay on a

footstool close by the heels of Samson—and a blind man could have recognized him for a policeman, by the air with which he tried to seem soldierly and civil at the same time—there was no risk of any consequences but a headache, and that was certainty, rum mixed with Van der Hum would make a tile roof throb.

After a while Will Yerkes came in, looking blithe and unscarred by circumstance, and very handsome except for his protruding ears. It is strange that a bishop should look in place in Bill's upper room, and a Yankee gentleman adventurer like some strayed angel. But so it was. Will had already killed his man in fair fight more than a dozen times; yet the bishop, whose flies, and even fleas, were killed for him, would have been shocked to see him there, without troubling much on Prof. Grogan Guthrie's score. There are a number of things in this world that it takes fools to explain.

Will came over and sat by me and we both watched Monty's game during several moves, until the mandarin castled his king and Monty made a cavalry swoop with his queen's bishop, taking a pawn.

"Check!" said Monty sternly.

"The Chink has him in three all the same!" Will whispered.

"Excuse me, in two!" smiled the mandarin, overhearing what was not intended for him, as is the way of some quiet men.

Monty frowned over the board and began twisting one end of his mustache.

"Cut it, Monty!" Will advised him.

"Cut what? The game?"

"No, the mustache. Pulling it out by the roots is going to hurt too much."

Monty retired his bishop. His opponent moved a knight.

"Checkmate, I believe," said the mandarin politely.

"Thanks," said Monty. "Very good game."

"No," smiled the mandarin. "Very feeble game. You were thinking all the time of whether professors of Egyptology need more time than other men in which to grow sober. Impatience is not a proper frame of mind in which to approach the chess-board."

"Join my friends and me in a drink," Monty invited him.

"And become as the Egyptologist?" He smiled with the peculiar inscrutable humor that is the birthright of his race. One could not guess whether he approved or disapproved of drunkenness. "We Chinese have different failings. I will eat with you."

MONTY STRUCK a table bell.

"Sandwiches!" he ordered the dark-skinned nondescript who appeared out of a corner like the jinnee of Aladdin's lamp. "What racial failing do you admit?" he asked the Chinaman.

"We are garrulous."

We all expressed surprise.

"You've a national reputation for keeping secrets," said Monty.

"In my country," said Will, "we've a police custom known as the third degree. It's highly civilized—guaranteed efficient or your money back. Nobody believes a Chinaman has feelings, so his feelings aren't spared. Yet nobody ever found out the facts about a Tong war yet!"

The mandarin smiled.

"Perhaps there are no facts," he suggested. "We are garrulous. I myself am very garrulous. It was I who told Prof. Grogan Guthrie the story that has made you gentlemen so anxious to see him sober."

"Excuse me. How did you come to hear it yourself?" Monty asked him, and the Chinaman smiled again, as some folk smile at children who ask questions.

I realized for the first time why as a boy I always loathed my teachers. It was not superior wisdom—one could respect that. Nor was it low cunning—this mandarin was a gentleman, as very many teachers are. It was pride in the great gulf fixed between him and us; and, whereas I did not loathe him, I lost all desire to know him better. I suppose I showed it. Monty, schooled in diplomacy and strategy and tactics, was urbane.

"Pass me your watch," said the mandarin, looking at me.

Mine happens to be an heirloom—one of those examples of marvelous workmanship on which our grandfathers liked to lavish money. I unhooked it from the chain and passed it to him, not without pride of ownership.

"You observe?" His voice was as unemotional as when he explained a deep move to his opponent after a game of chess. "He passes me his priceless thing. Yet he would not give me his confidence even should we sit land talk forever. I would not lend my watch to him, although it is an inexpensive one. Am I to tell him what is in my mind?"

"You must do as you like," said Monty. "He is a friend of mine. I vouch for him."

"In China," said the mandarin, passing my watch back, "we once had an emperor who was invited to vouch for the good faith of his son. What do you suppose he answered? 'When I can prove the good faith of you who ask and am satisfied with the purity of my own purpose in answering, then it will be time to speak about my son.' I respect your loyalty to your friend but am unconvinced by it, having lived to witness disappointment. I am garrulous. Why should I trust another not to talk?"

"You may speak out," I said. "I will repeat nothing without your permission."

"Is your friend an English gentleman?" he asked, and Monty nodded.

"Then the only risks I should run in making him confidences would be that he should become drunk, or be enamored of a woman, or confess to a priest, or turn sentimental on his death-bed. The English consider the approach of death releases from obligation to keep secrets!"

"Not at all," said Monty.

"If it were not so," the mandarin continued calmly, "few of your novels, almost none of your melodramas and some of your best plays could not have been written! The English make death-bed confessions. It is a national disease!"

"You shouldn't take the playwrights seriously," Monty answered, getting a little hot behind the ears I thought.

"But I do! They know! It was deathbed confession by an Englishman that put me in possession of the secret which you are so eager to know that you offer to vouch for a friend, over whose tongue you have no control whatever!"

"The point is this," said Monty, casting diplomacy to the winds and falling back on the British army's everlasting strategy—"brute force and —— ignorance."

"There are four of us—Mr. Oakes over there, Mr. Yerkes, this gentleman and myself. It's a case of all or none of us. Prof. Guthrie invited me to help finance and to take part in an expedition. Then he, ah—"

"Fell off the wagon," suggested Will.

"Excuse me," said the mandarin. "There was no wagon. He is not injured bodily. It is a case of—"

"Under the weather," said I.

"No, no," said the mandarin. "Drunk. He is drunk."

"That's what I meant," I said. "There is one Englishman for you who doesn't tell when drunk. We couldn't get a word out of him."

"That is because he is Scotch," said the mandarin. "He tells when he is sober. He had no permission from me."

"Perhaps you would rather we withdrew?" suggested Monty, who is also, of course, Scotch in every fiber of his being, unless you go back so many hundred years that you prove him Norman.

"It is I who should withdraw, seeing it is my secret," said the mandarin. "Yet it was told me by a man so foolish as to imagine death made it of no further value to himself. We Chinese, you know, extract exquisite humor from the practice of taking secrets with us beyond the grave, whence no amount of ingenuity can bring back anything but vain desire. Seeing that you have met me mind to mind over the chessboard, I will take you into confidence, accepting promises."

"Good of you, I'm sure," said Monty.

"Promises conditional on human failings! If that gentleman gets drunk, or grows enamored of a woman, or is sentimental on his death-bed, my secret shall be spread to the four winds! I recognize and accept that risk!"

I ROSE to my feet. One does not need almond eyes in order to feel racial prejudice. I had heard about enough of his candor.

"Sit down, please!" he begged me, instantly cordial.

I would have walked away, but Monty made me a signal with his eyebrows. The mandarin's next question staggered all three of us.

"Do you ever read the Bible?"

"I think I've read most of it," Monty admitted, "or heard it read at one time or another."

"They made me read parts of it at school," said I.

"My mother drilled it into me," admitted Will, smiling far away, as if he saw New England in the distance.

"Some day," said the mandarin, "we Chinese will send missionaries to England and America. The English and Americans send Bibles to the East but never read the book themselves. We enjoy it. Some day we will come and teach you to enjoy it. Do you remember who Barabbas was?"

Monty nodded.

"When I was at Oxford, there was a dean who couldn't say his Rs. I made a point of attending chapel when he read the lesson. 'Now Bawabbas was a wobber!' Yes. Go on."

"Did you know there is an island named after Barabbas?"

"No."

"It lies in the Red Sea. It is so small and thought to be so worthless and so far away from the ordinary track of ships that it appears only on the most carefully compiled British charts. On those it is called by another name. But the real name is Barabbas Island."

"How do you know that?" demanded Monty.

"Have I not said that an English gentleman made to me a death-bed confession? Does one English gentleman doubt the word of another?"

"I'm an American myself," said Will, "better able to doubt a Chink's word than maybe you'd believe!"

The mandarin blinked.

"Has the island's real name been confirmed from any other source?" asked Monty.

"The Turks own it," said the mandarin. "In the course of my studies of all nations I have found that the Turks when they conquered nearly always changed the names of places—but not quite always. There are rare exceptions. This is one of them. If you watch at this port or at Port Said or at Suez for a steamer flying the Turkish flag and ask to see the captain's charts, you will find, if you can read the Turkish characters, that the island is there marked Barabbas. Let us be thankful because Turks left something as they found it. Very well!"

"I know where I can see a Turkish chart," said Monty. "Go ahead. Tell the story, and we'll listen."

The mandarin coughed. It would be exaggeration to say he smiled, but he conveyed the impression of being secretly amused.

"I have said I am studying all nations," he began. "Nations—even the Swiss are of more than one class. Therefore, besides conversing with many members of the English House of Lords, I have visited the jails—finding incidentally a lord or two confined in them. I study high and low—the Prussian military caste, which is immensely amusing, the French peasant, the priest, the merchant, the fisherman, the lawmaker, who saddens me. So, when I found an English gentleman suffering severely from an unknown disease in Shepheard's Hotel at Cairo, I studied him too."

"How did you get introduced to him?" I asked, not without intentional edge to my voice.

"His fellow countrymen at the hotel were all afraid of the disease," he answered. "He was glad to see me. Oh yes, there was a doctor. He signed the death certificate and called it 'general debility' on account of the hotel's reputation. Selection of that name for the disease precluded an autopsy. He was extremely inquisitive to see the man's inside. Oh yes, and there was a nurse also—a volunteer—a lady of title; but she was a most homely lady, with pronounced views on religion and most other things, and the sick man was extremely pleased to talk to me."

"Did you learn his name?" asked Monty.

"Dent—Charles Dent—the son of a well-to-do London merchant. He told me about himself. His father sent him to a university—Oxford—Cambridge—I forget which—intending him for one of what you so humorously call the learned professions. But nothing interested him except travel—and history as it is not written in the text-books. So he and his father quarreled."

"Cut him off?" I asked, with a twinge of fellow feeling.

"No. He hid money. But he left home. His father desired him to become famous, but his treatises on the politics of ancient Judea were read by nobody except a critic or two, who denounced him for a humbug. They even became out of print, his publisher not caring for the stigma of being connected with such harebrained stuff. So from nosing among old manuscripts Charles Dent came abroad to investigate old places. One trail led to another. He made friends with the Turkish officials. He was shown ancient court records recovered from ruins that may have been those of Herod's palace. A Turk refused money for them. Think of that! One of them related to the trial of the man Barabbas, who seems to have been a much greater robber than he is given credit for."

"What became of the manuscripts?" demanded Monty.

We were all on the *qui vive* now, race prejudice forgotten. Not that Monty had once forgotten manners.

"The Turk sent them by Turkish mail to his father in Constantinople, hoping to secure a fortune, and they went down with the ship in a storm."

We swore with unanimity and vehemence that made the mandarin jump. He thought for a moment that we were going to accuse him of making away with priceless historic records.

"Go on!" said Monty, grimly.

"IT SEEMS Barabbas was a corsair—an adventurer—a pirate on a great scale, who owned an island. On land his men looted the caravans, waylaying them as they passed between Jerusalem and Egypt. At sea they plundered the coasts of Upper Egypt. They always escaped to the island when hard pressed, but they were not pressed hard very often, because Barabbas understood how to bribe to advantage. Finally he seems to have tried too rashly to exercise influence on politics, and Herod's men captured him.

"But the Romans did not allow him to be executed. They wanted to 'squeeze' him first, as I think the civilized nations describe the process. These court papers that have so unhappily been lost through a Turk's too great cupidity took the form, I believe, of letters from Herod to the Romans and from the Romans to Herod, regarding the probable amount of the hoarded plunder, the prospects of securing all or part of it, the division of it and the means to be employed."

"Well?"

We all spoke at once. The pause was intolerable.

"That is all."

"All?"

We eyed one another as the dogs do when they think a bone has been stolen, each looking for a hint of the solution in the other's eyes.

"The Turk had no other papers. There was no record of what happened to Barabbas. There was no account of the division of the spoil."

"There wouldn't be," said Will. "Politicians leave no traces when they divvy up the swag."

"Charles Dent reasoned," said the mandarin, "that since Barabbas is known to have been released from prison by the Romans, perhaps there was no division of the booty. Perhaps the island was never visited by Herod's men or Roman guards. He decided to go to the island."

"Well?"

"He did. He was afraid to go alone. The island is inhabited by very fierce savages, descendants of the original followers of Barabbas. So he took a certain professor into confidence—a German, by name Schindler, and they went together and lived on the island. They found many traces but no treasure."

"What happened to Schindler?"

"That is a question. Perhaps he is on the island now. Charles Dent was quite convinced treasure will be found, and the German no less. But Dent fell ill and the German inoculated him with some preparation that he said would render him immune from tropical disease. He became more ill, was obliged to come away. Finally he fell to pieces—literally."

"Well?"

"That is all. I told the story to Prof. Grogan Guthrie. It affected him. Look! See! Behold!"

"Are you going to the island?" I asked.

"My young Christian friend," said the mandarin, "I could no more be persuaded to go there than you could now be prevented—you and your friends. I recognize symptoms. I wish you better fortune on the journey than I think is likely to befall you. Charles Dent told me it is a devil of an island."

II

BILL'S NEVER shuts its doors, and nobody except the man too drunk to come away sleeps there. The mandarin departed smiling to unknown quarters in a part of town the English rarely visit. Other, noisier guests went out; less sober ones came in, and other deadly sober men with hungry eyes intent on midnight chess.

We laid Professor Guthrie on cushions under a table where he would be quite safe, put a note in his pocket telling him where to find us when he should come to himself, collected Fred Oakes—who objected, because he was listening to tales about the Frijiloffs from two ex-sealing captains—and tramped back to our hotel by the longest route, along the sea front, to get real air into our lungs.

"They assure me," said Fred, "that, when the seals come back in Spring to breed—"

"Shut up!" growled Monty.

"To —— with seals!" said Will.

"But what on earth could any man ask for better," objected Fred, "than to steam out to lonely islands and explore?"

Three hours later, when we had thrashed out the problem of Barabbas Island, sitting in Monty's armchair and on Monty's bed, confusing each other with absurd arguments and viewing the thing from every angle except the unimaginable one of letting the whole thing drop, Fred yawned and reversed himself.

"Islands are no good!" he asserted. "Better try the mainland. D'you mean to tell me that you—"

"Ginks," suggested Will.

"That you Homeless Katies honestly intend to go down that bleeding Red Sea again? We four again alone? Offer to take Guthrie with us? All right. I make one stipulation."

"Name it and let us get to sleep," said Monty.

"If we catch Barabbas, that we cage him and put him on view in Bond Street at half a guinea admission! Hang it, I've got to have some hope to draw me forward! Now go to sleep. I'll round up Guthrie and pour black coffee into him. Will, please put the Castile soap in Monty's mouth if he snores. Night-night, everybody!"

An hour after dawn he was back again, all sluiced and spruced, with Grogan Guthrie in tow, and the professor did not look much the worse for his night's debauch—not much worse—nor very self-conscious. The things one does in Bill's are cast in no man's teeth. His hand trembled a little. He was a shade too cordial. But he could not guess from our manner that his own was not perfect.

"Lord Mundidger, I'm deelighted. Yes, deelighted. Yes, your friend Mr. Oakes has told me everything. I'm willing to go with you. In fact, I'm eager to go with you. In fact, I couldn't consent to be left behind! My period, you know! My pet study! Jerusalem—the Red Sea—Israelites—Great Pyramid—fascinating! This story of Barabbas makes me simply wild—wild, I assure you! I suppose you'll let me tag along?"

The evening before, until unconsciousness crept over him like night over the day, it had been he who was persuading us to go with him. His eyes darkened while I watched him as disturbing memory danced out of reach.

"Rum mixed with Van der Hum works wonders," Fred whispered. "Just now a cocktail's raising counter-revolution."

"I don't like this guy!" remarked Will in the sort of stage whisper that carries farther and produces more conviction than a shout.

Monty frowned.

"Have you any plans or information beyond what we learned from Hi Ying Lang?" he asked.

"Hi Ying is a rascal!" snapped Guthrie, dropping his ingratiating manner like a glove. Elusive memory was pinned at last. "He had no business to tell you anything. He promised to keep the whole thing secret! I remember now! Oh, yes, I remember now! Hi Ying was to have financed me—I've spent my available funds, you know, taking measurements of Gizah. Hi Ying was to have lent me a thousand pounds, to be repaid out of the proceeds, if any, of the expedition. He had no right to tell you people a word!"

The change from solicitude to mean resentment was so swift that we had no answer ready. It was Fred, proud of reconstruction work, who took up cudgels for him and made further negotiations possible.

"He feels," he said, "as we might if Hi Ying had sold us."

"That is so," said Guthrie. "I feel indignant."

"It was you who first told me of the thing," said Monty bluntly. "We propose to go and see. We can finance a trip, and we're willing to take you with us. You may have any literary credit accruing from it. You may give the story to the world afterward, if you see fit, without competition."

"Will you put that in writing—in writing?" snapped Grogan Guthrie, pacing up and down the floor with bright eyes and snapping fingers.

Monty laughed.

"Put your own terms on paper and let me see them," he said.

Guthrie sat down by the window and wrote eagerly, as if he had already considered every point. Will took my elbow.

"Are you going to wait to see Monty turn him down or will you come with me?" he asked.

"Come where?"

"To send a telegram."

The walk to the telegraph office was a scant three hundred yards along a drab street. I was not interested. Will Yerkes departed alone, whistling "There'll be a hot time—"

Grogan Guthrie, with a gleam in his eye that would have done credit to a professional duelist, got up from the rickety writing-desk and offered a half-sheet of paper to Monty.

"Roughly, those are my terms," he said. "I should employ a lawyer, of course, to draw the real contract."

Monty read, laughed and passed the paper back without a word of comment.

"You said you would sign!" snapped Guthrie.

"You're mistaken, professor. If you are looking for some one to finance you, guard you on your journey, guide you, work for you, obey you, give you all the credit—and the profit—and say nothing to any one about it forever afterwards without your leave, you'd better try elsewhere."

"Step off the earth and try the next world!" Fred suggested.

"You will not sign that?" said Guthrie. "Then I serve you notice, Lord Mundidger, that I shall make other arrangements."

"You're welcome," said Monty cheerfully.

"And that the secret of that island is rightly mine!"

"Not, for instance, Hi Ying's?" suggested Monty.

"Not at all! The rascal gave it to me! If you should dare try to forestall my expedition to that island, I shall denounce you publicly as a dishonorable adventurer, Lord Mundidger!"

"Very well," said Monty, lighting a cigaret.

"Out you get! Out into the sun with you!" said Fred. "I held the brute's head in these two hands while he catted out the Van der Hum. One hand should have held a strainer. I might have caught the modesty and spread it out to dry! Good-by forever, Grogan Guthrie! No, don't stammer. Nobody will tell tales out of school! We shall deny all knowledge of you! You're thumbs downed! Don't give me excuse for picking a new bone with you, that's all!"

Guthrie went out with a fine rage boiling in his vitals and conviction of the justice of his own case stiffening his back.

"IF HE is determined," said Monty, "he has friends who believe in him. He can get money."

"This time to-morrow," I said, "he'll repent and go back to his pyramid."

"I'd find it hard to rejoice about him even if he did," said Monty.

"Repent!" said Fred. "He's the same man who claimed sole right to explore Egypt for traces of the Exodus. I've heard Lord Cromer offered to file his application for a monopoly of hell! We'll hear from him again."

"Poor fellow!" said Monty.

"Good riddance!" said I. "I'll bet we've seen the last of him!"

Then in came Will Yerkes, cheerier than ever, smoking a fearful thing he calls a stogie that he buys by the thousand even in Egypt, where they make real cigarets.

"Asked for the earth, didn't he? I've met up with his brand! Did he go or was he pushed? Went? What's come over you fellers? We leave for Port

Said at noon. Not more than time to pack. You'd better get a move on!"

"Isn't this sudden?" asked Monty.

"You bet it is! So's the Vandam sudden! Met her yesterday while Monty played chess with the Chink. Hadn't seen her since I sat on one seat in school with her. She and her aunt. The old man's dead. I'm told the estate paid taxes on eighty million. Gracie's the only child. Doing the world on a yacht like a young Cunarder and bored already plum through to the middle—says she's tried every way to get in trouble and simply can't; nothing goes wrong. They wouldn't even arrest her for flirting with young British officers at Gib! Says she could have learned all their naval secrets in a week but they didn't have any! Grade is some live wire. The yacht's at Port Said, coaling. She joined it this morning. I've wired her we're coming with a red-hot plan for real adventure, and she's to wait for us. Hurry, you fellers, hurry!"

The old Greeks knew what they were doing when they made a god jump out of a trap and adjust things at critical moments in the play. They were dealing in truth—life as it really is. We were only one more instance of a pack of ingrates looking fortune's gift horse in the mouth. We actually dared to doubt. It was minutes before Fred seized all the things on Monty's dressing-table and threw them on the bed in rank confusion.

"Pack, Didums!" he shouted and ran to his own room, where we heard him hurl a trunk against the wall.

Doubt was still uppermost in my mind. Something else, probably experience, cautioning against adventures with young women, dulled the edge of Monty's enthusiasm. But the unwritten code compelled. Will Yerkes was one of us. At our call—Monty's or Fred's or mine—he had chanced his arm already a hundred times. Unbelieving, he had flung himself into ventures of ours for simple friendship's sake, arguing always, ridiculing almost always, but unswervingly with us to the end. We had neither right nor will to back out from his arrangement now.

So high, hot noon saw us sweating under the roof of a first-class reserved compartment, while Fred—acting cashier for the day—accused the station baggage-clerk of nameless crimes on account of the size of our bill for excess luggage.

The heat in the end got the better of both of them. Fred paid and got in panting five minutes before the train started The baggage-clerk withdrew into a shadowy corner with the stigma of seven separate and distinct insults unanswered.

"I forgot to mention his deceased wife's sister," Fred admitted self-accusingly. "But never mind—I damned his family in heaps. He'll never be able to look at one of them again without thinking of things I told him. Think of it! Fifteen pounds, sixteen and sixpence for toting four men's luggage from Alexandria to Port Said!"

"Was it fair to soak that poor devil for the administration's sins?" Will wondered.

"Of course not!" Fred retorted. "Did you ever know me jump seriously on the right man?"

"Out with it!" grinned Monty. "What's the meat under the crust?"

"I tipped the pig half a sovereign. He pouched it and then weighed even my walking stick! I'll get out and mention his deceased wife's sister!"

But the train wailed and screamed and started. Fred forgot all baggage-clerks while listening to Will's accounts of Grace Vandam. All the way to Port Said we speculated on what sort of offer to make the lady. Even Will was with us in determination to have a clear understanding with her before starting for anywhere on board her yacht.

"We're previous," I objected.

"Don't you believe it," said Will. "Gracie will jump at us."

And so she did, if not exactly as Will prophesied or she intended.

We left our heaps of luggage on the platform at Port Said for strategic reasons, meaning to be free to decline all offers and retreat with dignity should we desire. And we walked through the sandy streets because our legs were stiff from sitting in the torture-box they called a train.

We were followed, of course, by eleven beggars—three of them blind, two indescribably diseased and the rest too well to work; also by a donkey-boy, proclaiming loudly to the universe the virtues of his beasts by name and his unbelief in the virtue of white men who soiled their shoes.

Close to the main street another swarm of beggars joined us, so that we were a pretty fair-sized party as we turned at a right-angle and headed toward the quay, along a street that passed the prison. Opposite that we saw a lady dressed in creamy, expensive stuff, who stepped toward the bars to peer at the criminals inside.

"That's Gracie," said Will.

The six-foot six-inch coal-black sentry motioned her away. She argued with him. He talked back in a jargon resembling Arabic, not a word of which she understood, as he well knew. He said things that a polyglot Levantine dandy loafing near at hand understood perfectly, for he waved his cigar with a very jaunty air and came up close, leering and saying things in English with fat, unwholesome lips. She slapped his face.

IN A minute there was a crowd, arrived from nowhere like the fleshless motion-picture people but stinking in proof of reality. The brute hit her back and received a blow in the eye that staggered him. Gracie had not shared schooling with boys for nothing. There went up a roar like the loosing of riot. We began to charge down-street, blocked at every cross-street by the hurrying, yelling natives of the place. A policeman blew a vilely shrill whistle and Gracie screamed. We could not see her any longer.

I snatched a club from a policeman who was arguing with the crowd from the rear—a lovely thing, twice as long as a New York policeman's night-stick. Monty used his fists. Fred upset a money-changer's stand and seized the legs it stood on. Will went through the crowd in the style of an American line-plunging full-back—bucked it—the swiftest piece of rescue work I ever saw—and we crashed along behind him.

So the crowd opened up. The Levantine and two others let go of Grace Vandam. She saw Will and Monty and jumped—was between them—in their arms—in a twinkle, nothing the worse excepting a bruise where the Levantine landed with his knuckles on her cheek-bone.

"I said Gracie 'ud jump at us!" laughed Will.

Fred and I reached the fat Levantine simultaneously and his screams for the next three minutes would have convinced any one three blocks away that he was being flayed alive, which was not at all the case. The club did not break the skin much. And about six minutes after that we were all under arrest, on the way to the police station, with hot, uniformed United States Americans from the *Daisy*—the Vandam yacht—hurrying to the rescue from four directions. We had utmost difficulty in preventing them from renewing the fight.

Luckily the magistrate had seen the whole thing from the roof of the hotel. He came down to the police court, heard the case at once and discharged everybody.

"That ends it," he told us, "provided you all get out of Port Said before they can go over my head. Civil suits for damages for assault will be the next in order. Be advised!"

"The *Daisy* is coaled," said Miss Vandam.

"And the *Daisy's* officers and crew are unanimous against your staying ashore in this hole, miss," put in the yacht's second mate.

"You take some men and go and bring these gentlemen's baggage, Smith," she answered. "They'll tell you where it is. Be quick!"

We fooled the waiting crowd, which would have started things all over, by having cabs fetched. The horses, fed chiefly on sand and date straw, could just about trot, and the *Daisy's* crew made a rear-guard. In twenty minutes we were sitting in deep basket chairs beneath the *Daisy's* snowy awning, drinking long drinks out of frosty glasses and eyeing Port Said and its squalid pretentiousness as if it and we had not even dislike in common.

"Explain the telegram," Grace Vandam demanded, sitting down in front of us.

A darky maid had already rouged and powdered the bruise out of sight.

She was pretty enough in all conscience. Will did the talking. I took stock of her—the first nice American girl I had seen at close quarters. She was an eye-opener. I wondered why Will left the States, until Aunty Elmira Vandam came out; middle-aged, dressed to look thirty or thirty-five and in love with vivacity. One realized at once that roses had thorns in the United States also.

"Aunty, we're going to Barabbas Island!"

"Mercy, child, where's that?"

"Nobody knows."

"I'll have to know who I'm going with before I start off on that trip!"

Will realized he had not introduced any one. He began at once with Monty and it dawned on the dazzled aunty that she sat next a member of the House of Lords. She did not get anybody else's name and never overcame the impression that the rest of us were in the footman class.

Our luggage came aboard before Monty quite succumbed under the flow of aunty's gush and he seized the excuse to stand by the gangway and count things. I went and stood by him. Grace Vandam stepped between us.

"Poor aunty suffers dreadfully from heat," she said. "She lies in her stateroom and pants when the glass goes over eighty-five. Is the Red Sea very hot? I've heard so."

We did not let our luggage go below yet. There was a simple man, with one simple rule of life and the courage to follow it, to be interviewed first. Captain John McGraw knew nothing whatever of English lords except by hearsay and reading of their peccadillos in the Portland, Maine, Sunday papers; so he kept his cabin on the bridge-deck, and we had to go to him there, like schoolboys bearding the head-master.

"Never heard o' Barabbas Island. It's not on the chart."

But Monty had procured a Turkish chart from somewhere and had persuaded somebody to underscore the names with the corresponding English characters. Careful comparison of charts showed where Barabbas Island was.

"I'll not go there! A savage coast—uncharted water—hot—unhealthy—you tell Miss Vandam to go get another captain if she wants to make that trip!"

"Nonsense, John!" Grace Vandam stepped in, through the open door and took a seat on the captain's desk-chair. "I'll not listen to your croaking. To hear you talk one would think I was a child in arms."

"You're little better!" he grumbled.

"To be told what to do, where to go, what to eat, when to go to bed, instead of owner of this yacht! Just because you were father's captain and he gave in to you in every little thing is no reason why you shouldn't obey me! This yacht is going to Barabbas Island and you're to take her there!"

"Listen to me, miss!"

"I've done nothing but listen to you all the voyage! I've had no fun at all! You've turned a joy-ride into a funeral procession! Not allowed to go ashore without two men in attendance, just as if papa were still giving orders."

"What happened, miss? Is your face bruised? Had your own way to-day, I think. As for your pa still giving orders, he and I spoke last afore he died. I've kep' my word and I'll keep it!"

Her eyes sparkled and his grew worried. Simply he had promised. Simply he spoke now. And he blundered simply and was aware of it, with sailor simplicity that recognized a fact but could not help itself.

"Will you find me another captain?" she asked him.

"No, miss."

He looked away.

"Papa knew I would make this trip."

"Not to no Barabbas Island I'll bet he didn't!"

"He didn't care where I went as long as you promised to go with me. Dear John—all I want is a good time—something really exciting—just to get away from the street signs and keep-to-the-rights for once! Besides, where's the danger? You know how to navigate. If anything goes wrong with you, there's Arthur, and then Smith; they've both got certificates. And if there's trouble with natives, what fun! Let's get that quick-firer out from under the hatch and mount it!"

"No, miss. We've no letters of marque against pirates."

"D'you mean that in case of attack you wouldn't defend the yacht?"

"I don't say a word o' that, miss." He shut his shaven lips with a grim snap. "What I do say is Barabbas Island is no place to take yachts or young ladies to!"

"We ought to back out," whispered Monty behind his hand.

"Leave me alone with him, please!" the girl demanded, and we trooped out on to the bridge.

Being last, I heard her first words.

"Now, John, are we friends or enemies?"

"We ought to back out," Monty repeated, not with much regret I thought.

"If we do," said Will, "she'll go without us. I know her of old!"

FIVE MINUTES later she emerged triumphant from the captain's cabin and called us in to further conference. With fine generalship she had yielded to the captain's native honesty and overridden his rebellious mood by accepting a precaution we would have insisted on anyhow. Paper, pens and ink lay ready on the table and John McGraw sat ready to draw the terms.

"Whatever you and he agree to, I will sign!" she said, starting below with a gay laugh. "John is an old bear, but he takes commissions and credits them to me to keep expenses down! Beat him if you can!"

But we could play at that game. We left Monty to do our bargaining and followed her down to the long armchairs beneath the awning.

"Let's hope your man proves easy," said Will.

"Why?" she asked naively. "Do you need money?"

"Monty does."

"Oh! Is he poor?"

"He's our financier."

"Then what in the world—"

"The poor chap has only about thirty thousand a year of private income."

"Pounds?"

"No, dollars. He needs a fortune to reopen the ancestral towers in proper style. So many of his people have been soldiers that the estate's plumb impoverished. 'Tween you and me, he's not half so keen as we are. We like him awfully well. We want to see him—"

"What? You too?"

"Why not? I'm nuts on seeing him make millions!"

She jumped up and clapped her hands.

"Hurrah! Splendid! Then that's settled! We'll go to the island, find the treasure and give it all to him to run his earldom with! Stay here while I run up and tell John what to put down on paper!"

But Monty met her on the way, coming down the ladder with a folded paper in his hand.

"That didn't take long," he said, laughing. "Your captain is a man of sound principle, Miss Vandam. Anything we find is to be divided in three thirds, after the expenses from this port and back again have been charged against the whole. One third to the owner. One third to the officers and crew pro rata. One third to us. Nothing could be fairer."

"Nothing could be meaner, you mean! Give me that paper! Whoever heard of such a thing! What? You won't let me change the terms? Oh, very well, I shall simply give you my share, that's all! I won't hear of having the expenses charged! This is a pleasure trip! You're my guests!"

"When do we start?" asked Monty with a nervous glance toward the quay.

"We shall have to wait our turn through the ditch," said our hostess. "Are you seeing ghosts?"

"Worse than a ghost! I've seen Grogan Guthrie. He stood on the quay there. No mistaking him. Hullo! Here comes a boat."

A smart launch hissed alongside and a note was passed up for the Earl of Montdidier and Kirkudbrightshire, P.C. Monty tore it open and read it twice.

"That magistrate's a very decent chap," he said. "He writes to-day that Guthrie came by the same train we did—didn't see him, Fred, did you?—that he saw the fracas we were in and has already wired to Cairo for the best lawyer he can get to come and make trouble for us. Meanwhile he has engaged a local man to apply, in the names of twenty of the inhabitants, for a writ preventing us from leaving, pending damage suits. Philosopher he may be. Cad he is. We'd all better go ashore again, Miss Vandam; otherwise they'll arrest the yacht and hold you, too."

"Nonsense!" She jumped up and stamped her foot. "Steam is up." She caught sight of the first mate leaning over the bridge-rail. "Are all hands on board?" she asked him.

"Yes, miss."

"Then get up anchor and steam back into the Mediterranean!"

But the process was not quite so simple as she thought. The yacht had to get clearance papers. Captain or owner had to go ashore to get them.

So Captain John McGraw tumbled into the steam tender and I went along with him to send a cautionary telegram to the banker at Alexandria who held the bulk of our united funds. The very first man I recognized after we had made our way through the swarm of longshore guides, beggars and mountebanks was the mandarin. Like Guthrie, he must have traveled on our train. He was coming down the hotel steps with the bowed head and introspective manner that he affected without in the least reducing his powers of observation.

He saw me before I saw him—changed his course so as to pass me close enough to be heard—and turned into a tobacco store.

"I wish to speak to you," he said as if thinking aloud.

Nobody else could have guessed he meant the remark for me. Captain McGraw was quite unsuspicious.

"We've no time for buying cigarets, sir!" he objected as I turned to follow the Chinaman. "Besides, the yacht's stores include more luxuries o' every kind than twice our number could get through in a year."

"All the same—" I said and turned into the shop.

McGraw followed me in, very suspicious of Port Said shops but mindful that he had a guest of Miss Vandam's in tow. I got the impression that nothing less than personal responsibility for my safety would have induced him to darken the door.

JUST INSIDE, where the shadow was deepest, the Chinaman waited, and McGraw was almost startled into striking him.

"If life is so dangerous for you," said the Chinaman, smiling ironically, "consider my condition. Your fist looks heavier than any weapon I might be supposed to have. To do the first kindness seems riskier than to strive the first blow. I have advice for you."

"I've got along for fifty years without much Chink advice," McGraw answered impatiently.

The Chinaman ignored the pleasantry and turned to me.

"Prof. Guthrie," he said, "has set his heart on being first at Barabbas Island. The magistrate of this place can be dilatory when he chooses but I imagine there are limits. He is besieged at present by witnesses who clamor for legal action, and Guthrie is paying the lawyer's bill. The lawyer has been to the bank to ask whether you have funds in this place. You would better hurry!"

I stood irresolute. I could not imagine what the Chinaman's purpose could be.

"You want us out of your way," I said. "Why?"

"Y, my young friend, is a letter of your English alphabet," he answered. "Standing alone, it means as nearly nothing as anything in this world can. I have told you of Barabbas Island. That yacht to take you there— Oh, you should take swift advantage!"

"What if the yacht isn't going there?" I countered, and for a moment he eyed me curiously.

At the end of that time I was aware that he was not in the least deceived.

"If you should appear to steam toward Europe," he said, "there would be a lapse of hue and cry."

He terminated the interview then by turning his back on us and walking toward the counter. More than ever mystified as to his purpose, I followed McGraw to the shipping office, where he found an American captain, who promised to send the telegram I signed with a code signature, thus completely throwing the enemy off that trail. Half an hour later we were back on board and the anchor chain was coming in noisily.

"Lapse of hue and cry is sheer buncombe!" said Monty when I had told what happened ashore. "There's no understanding Chinamen. But that particular mandarin believes too little in the genuineness of human motives to be anything but a schemer himself. If we steam away and return, we simply give them time. When we come back they'll be ready for us and we'll know nothing of what they've cooked up for us in the meantime."

"Let's go ashore, then, and see the trouble through," suggested Will. "Running away is no way to win games."

"No?" says Monty. "If you'd played chess with that mandarin you'd change your mind."

It was at that point that Gracie Vandam came to the rescue with wholly United States vision—seeing the thing in its broadest aspect possible.

"Isn't Africa an island?" she demanded.

We all laughed.

"Counting the Suez Canal as sea," said Monty, "I suppose it is. Have you any idea how large it is?"

"No. Who minds the size! Can't we steam right round it? Can't we come up to this Barabbas Island from the other side?"

"Weeks and weeks!" said Monty, shaking his head.

"Are you so old that a little matter of weeks disturbs you?" she retorted. "Won't Mundidger Towers stand until you come?" One does not feel the force of great decisions while they are making, and we discussed that tremendous proposal from the mouth of a twenty-three-year-old girl without the least attempt at gravity. Only Aunty Vandam took the prospect seriously.

"I'll be all out of everything I need before we're half-way!" she insisted.

But nobody minded her necessities.

The Port Said mole slid past us, with its statue of Lesseps introducing West to East. We gained speed as we cut clean water, and a little launch that might or might not carry a detention warrant gave up the pursuit. A rather pompous darky steward came and thundered on a deep gong the command to dress for dinner.

"And my hair will take hours!" said aunty, running off, whereat we blessed her hair, wordlessly unanimous.

"It amounts to this," said Fred Oakes, and I knew which way he would vote by the way he reveled in the enormity of the whole thing. "We stand invited to steam all the way round a continent on this young lady's yacht, with a pretty probable fight at the far end—"

"Sure!" said Will. "Guthrie will think we've flunked. He'll get there first. When he finds we weren't afraid after all he'll be riled worse than Mount Vesuvius!"

"And the merest shadow of a tale of treasure to tempt us," said I. "The unlikeliest tale four men ever listened to. Are we game? We are? We accept? We do! Then I vote we go and dress!"

"Hurry!" urged Grace Vandam. "The chef gets furious if anybody's late!"

III

SO WE four, who had thought ourselves heirs to earth's rough quarters, whose luxuries of late had been reduced to odd days in unspeakable hotels, entered on eight long weeks of what Fred diagnosed as "La-di-da."

I had bought a dress suit in Alexandria and the others had theirs—of ancient vintage—packed in steel cases with the creases of accumulating years grown almost permanent. We dressed for dinner, changed our clothes between meals and lay abed as long as we wanted to. It was astonishing how soon and strongly that demoralizing habit grew.

The *Daisy* was unlike anything whatever in the world except the yacht of a United States millionaire. She was the ultimate of everything, comfort included. Twin, quadruple expansion engines could send her through the water just about one knot faster than the Cunard's latest crack. She had a vast refrigerating-plant and every kind of bath the skin of hot humanity could yearn for and the mind of engineers invent.

There were push-buttons all along the deck, in order that enervated passengers might ring for a steward and refreshments without troubling to rise. And the library of seven thousand volumes contained only editions de luxe.

There was a grand piano in the music room and a little balcony above the dining saloon from which the yacht's orchestra of six very fair musicians discoursed at meals. The wines were excellent, the tobacco better and the cooking best of all, for an enormous black expert from Maryland tyrannized over the galley and wrought miracles thrice daily. Not that there were only three meals a day; there was food served hot whenever anybody thought of it.

If we had only had fine weather it would have been a voyage such as a man should make but once, to look back to and keep in mind as his standard of heaven on earth. But between Alexandria, where we ran in to withdraw funds from the bank, and Cape Town, where we spent a week ashore, there were exactly three days when they did not rig fiddles on the saloon table. From Cape Town to Durban there were none. After Durban we ran into a typhoon, and that was scarcely more than herald to our serious adventures.

There is a well-defined belief among buyers of Cook's excursion tickets that the Mediterranean is a sun-warmed mill-pond, incapable of wrath. We stood alternately on nose and heel all down the length of it until cylinders primed because of racing propellers and the engine-room staff discussed birth-control and suicide at meals.

Through the Straits of Gibraltar we pitched like a Deal lugger coming in with a storm against the tide. And outside the Strait we met a genuine sou'wester, come all the way from America without meeting anything to squander fury on. We took that on our beam.

Down past Madeira we rolled gunwale under—enjoyed a three-day respite in the neighborhood of Teneriffe—and then bucked our beautiful nose into a skin-rasper fresh from the antarctic and wallowed into Cape Town with blistered funnels and white spars, two boats washed away and the shovels snarling on the bunker floors to scrape up the last few hundredweights of coal.

Captain John McGraw took stern delight in it all—not that he liked the beastly weather or the incessant watch and risk, but he hoped to give his young mistress more than enough of it, believing the weeks of discomfort would change her mind. And never in the world did a man miscalculate more wildly.

With the storms her courage grew. Aunty Vandam spent the whole trip in her stateroom and as chaperon was about as useful as the awnings rolled up and ready for warm, calm days that never came. But Gracie was not the girl to need a chaperon. The United States is the only land that raises boys and girls together and so turns out women honestly incapable of understanding why they are not safe among their equals of either sex.

There was not even the seed of a flirtation sown on all that trip, nor—excepting the day when Gracie fell down the main companion and lay stunned for an hour or two—one dull minute. Perhaps the wildest sprees were the theatricals, held with the ship rolling thirty-five degrees and the whole of the watch below impressed for audience.

She acted Romeo for choice, with a false moustache, to Fred's Juliet—beard and all. When a specially 'wild roll brought Fred down headlong from the balcony in the middle of the love scene, there was nothing lacking, not even Fred's language, to make joy complete.

She had the gift of laughter. Not the conventional sort that grows noisy at the ordinary, cut-and-dried jokes. Conventional humor could not hold her attention. But the unexpected jest—quaint, unplanned reversals of the usual—unpremeditated, chance things that tickled imagination—and burlesque of the rowdiest type had power to reduce her to squeals and giggles like those of a child being tickled.

Fred Oakes, born to the social summit and whole-souled loather of his birthright as a rule, was in an element here that he liked. His concertina out-brayed the grand piano, overrode the clang of the engine-room at times and even jerked out tortured music in the belly of the bunkers, when the coal came down in avalanches from the upper shelves and a brave man's life was worth a second's purchase. Then, grimy with dust and grease, he would return to the saloon and act clown, unwashed, to Grace Vandam's King Solomon.

Ninety per cent, of our high spirits were born of sure knowledge that she was getting what she came for. When the ship pitched and rolled too wildly for any one to keep his feet, we sat in the music room and spun yarns she unbelieving at first, and after that—when she realized we had seen and done too many things to need invent—almost beside herself with all the emotions that combine into go-fever. When go-fever fastens on to courage there is no holding down the victim.

Cape Town after that was bathos. We dug out aunty and took her ashore to recover. There we were all known—even Grace was known by name—and they got up a round of labeled gaiety while the yacht was coaled and something or other was fitted in the engine-room—well-meant, expensive, social-conscious stuff that made Fred sick at heart.

We were only all merry together once, when we left aunty with the social gang and climbed old Table Mountain, with a man and his wife who knew the tracks to guide us—spending a night on top with a scanty camp-fire to keep feet from growing numb—a red ring of burning mountain-flank below us and the naked, swinging stars for company. Little we thought of Barabbas Island that night, or of mandarins or professors of Egyptology. Yet we were within closer touch of all of them than we guessed.

WHEN WE came down from the mountain, it was to find a man at the Mount Nelson who fingered a cablegram nervously and eyed us one by one as if he did not like his job.

"I am an attorney. I am instructed to say," he began, "er—I have a long cablegram here—to say that Prof. Grogan Guthrie has already been to er—I think it says Barabbas Island—some such place—and has returned to Suez on an Egyptian Government steamer with everything worth bringing away. I am to say your yacht was reported passing Gibraltar and your purpose to steam round Africa was guessed. Everything has been done to make your trip useless. A hot reception from the natives, in the event of your continuing the voyage, is a moral certainty."

"Do you believe a word of that yourself?" asked Monty.

The man laughed.

"I have been retained by cable by the other side," he said, "to deliver the message. That is now done. If you want to retain me to give an opinion, legal or merely human, my office is on Adderley Street!"

"Very well," said Monty. "I suppose you'll send word you've delivered the message?"

"Within ten minutes. After that I am free to serve you, if you wish."

"All right. Send your own wire first. Then send this: 'Yacht needs repair. Party's original intentions abandoned. Warning came too late to make any difference.' "

The lawyer charged ten pounds in addition to the rate per word for sending that truthful if deceptive telegram. They were ten pounds thoroughly well spent. After that we drove down to the docks to find out whether the needed repairs were yet finished and, finding they were, we steamed next day into the teeth of an antarctic wind that raised the thunders on Greenpoint rocks and buried us in icy spray.

We rolled, bucked and kicked our way to Durban through perpetual storms that ceased only when we lay alongside and took coal from the blunt-bowed floats. And in that sun-warmed, trim little harbor Grace Vandam met and weathered a storm of another kind.

John McGraw's lips and eyes were growing stern again, and it was quite clear that the mates and engineers stood with him, although theirs were dumb protests, expressed chiefly in surly answers to chance questions and averted eyes.

"I had hoped, miss," said the skipper bluntly at lunch three days after we tied up the Durban quay, "that you'd be tired o' the foolishness afore this."

She had asked him how long it must be before we pressed forward.

For answer she mocked him, jeered at him, laughed him to shame that a sea-dog should quail where a girl dared go on eagerly.

"Any fool dares when he's ignorant o' what he's up against!" he growled. "Settin' aside uncharted water an' the reefs near Barabbas, you've a sullen crew and discontented officers. That's no makin's o' success."

"It seems I've a scare-cat on the bridge!" she retorted hotly.

"I'm not afraid o' bein' called names!" he answered. "A fool's way is a fool's way, and that's no other than the course you're orderin' me to lay!"

She sat at the head of her own table with the air of a woman who had done the same for twenty years instead of about that many weeks, but for a moment I thought she was going to appeal to Monty on her right. John McGraw seemed to think he had beaten down her rash spirit at last.

"It's no womanly thing to do," he said, "to risk this yacht and the lives aboard her, all for a whimsy!"

"Very well," she answered, rising to face him. He had stood by her chair on the way from his own table to the companion. "You shall have your way. I'll risk neither yacht nor your precious skin. Take the yacht back to the States and lay her up."

"Ah!" he said. "That's better, miss! But no need to lay her up. Take a cruise across to Rio. Steam around the Horn if you will."

"Take her back and lay her up, I say! These gentlemen and I will charter some kind of boat here for our purpose and go on without having to suffer every day or two from your nerves and the crew's cold feet! Take the *Daisy* to New York now and lay her up!"

"No, miss!" he answered. John McGraw was not made of the stuff that runs away, whatever his expressed opinions. "Get ye a new captain if that's the lay of it. I'll not leave you! If ye're set, then so'm I. But I've warned ye. There'll come trouble of it!"

"Bah! Trouble!" she answered. "Show me some!"

So John McGraw submitted and began there and then to bulldoze mates and crew into acquiescence. We steamed out of Durban with the nearest approach to unanimous good temper the ship's company had known for very many days.

The weather promised fair at last. Fred's concertina set to work vibrations that stirred echoes in men's breasts, so that even the second engineer, who was made up mostly of mock-dignity and disagreeable remarks, did a step dance. Probably all would have gone thenceforward as smoothly as a wedding but for the lost typhoon.

McGRAW SAID it was a "lost" one because it "weren't the typhoon season, nor yet that the track of 'em." It was a crazy, unannounced, unrighteous thing strayed out of the China Seas, born out of time and doubly wrathy. The glass began falling suddenly, as if inches were ten-thousandths, and the thermometer rose at about the same pace. Then, before half the loose deck-gear could be lashed, in heat that had us pouring sweat and gasping like caught fish, the fury burst on us.

Sudden darkness made the world seem a tiny sphere of whirling black cloud and water. Walls of sea rose high above us on either hand—sea that screamed and was smooth in places like polished marble because of the weight of wind.

Then our motion ceased to bear any resemblance to that of a ship and all sound became swallowed in the womb of Noise, all sight in chaos, and three men went overboard, blown like the rags of the awnings. It would have been more nearly possible to bridle the typhoon with bit and rein than to save those deck-hands.

One by one the boats went; first those in the davits, then the bigger ones that rode on blocks on the upper deck, ripped away like weightless things. Next the foremast went overboard, snapped off a foot above the deck, and lay alongside, pounding at every plunge like the hammer of Thor. Fred, Will and I took the place of the three lost deck-hands and fought for our lives with the tangled rigging, cutting it clear at last.

And then the mainmast went in a smother of sea that boiled on the funnel until the stays drew taut as a knife-edge. We went down again, this time with Monty and four seamen, led by the second mate, and cut that spar free while the ship did her best to turn turtle.

None of us knew how we won our way back to the upper deck and comparative safety. I remember how I blessed my luck, waist-deep, clinging for dear life to a stanchion, as I heard a crash and felt the tremor of coal shifting in the bunkers, and thought of the fellows below. It is better to see the teeth of death than to wrestle between steel walls in the dark. None could go below to help them. None could come up through the locked steel hatches. Hell knows more torments than the water-cure.

Grace Vandam saw the fight through from the upper bridge, strapped to a stanchion from which the canvas shield had been blown away by the first fury of wind. After what seemed a million years I worked my way along and tried to yell to her to crawl into the chart-house, but the storm snatched the words out of my teeth, and I had to cling, as the horse-breaker grips leather, to save myself from crashing into her and breaking perhaps the wet, straining strap around her waist and her hold as well as mine.

She looked like a wild woman with her hair to all four quarters and a man's torn oilskins snapping in yellow streamers from her in the wind. There was not in attitude or expression as much as a hint of fear. She clung to the stanchion with determination—excitement—almost with delight—her white teeth set in a grin that was more than three parts courage.

I have observed since then many a time that it is not woman who is afraid of the material elements. She fears and screams at things that to men seem not realities at all. It is men who know the grisly price the elements exact, who fear them even while they fight—woman who exults in the savagery.

There are decadents of either sex—fewer than some profess to think, and yet too many; but I speak of the women and men who are each their own stern judges—the decent folk—the fellows we can strive with without rancor or contempt and the women whose opinion of us makes us search our hearts in secret.

Grace Vandam no more feared that typhoon than she could have faced without whimpering the thought of being cut off from kith and kin. Sometime sailor before the mast, contented with disinheritance, I shivered in ghastly fright with every side-sweeping plunge of the ship and at each new screaming wall of smoke-gray water. She, who might have flinched at terrors I should laugh at defiantly, herself laughed where I feared.

Aunty Vandam, on the other hand, a decadent, clung to her cabin bed and died ten deaths a minute, lamentably, noisily.

We did not find the ever-to-be-recommended, too elusive center of the typhoon, where stillness is said to reign because the chaos needs a vortex around which to hurl itself. Rather we battled through the fiercest, swiftest rage, the twin propellers flogging up the spume to mingle with shrieking clouds, scarcely our superstructure—scarcely our thick funnel visible through smothering water for more than a minute at a time.

The havoc on deck, was a bagatelle to what took place below, but of that we knew nothing until after the typhoon had spent itself and left us stricken on a heaving waste. They kept the engines turning by dint of unimaginable courage and resource and so made possible John McGraw's forlorn hope—to stand away from reefs and shoals into the open sea.

But the next day we buried, in sewed-up canvas hammocks with fire-bars to their feet, seven of the engine-room contingent, three scalded beyond recognition, one mangled in the moving steel and the others crushed. A day later we dug a flattened body out from under an avalanche of shifted coal.

There was scarcely a man below decks who had not an injury to show. The galley fires were scattered on the cooks. The fire-extinguisher broke loose and fractured a steward's leg. The unbruised in the engine-room were scalded and the wounds men got in the bunkers varied all the way from a broken arm to cuts from a dead man's shovel.

We became a floating hospital with pumps that clacked interminably while the less seriously injured and the merely bruised made shift to get us under way again. It was three days before the sea ceased raging—five before they had rebushed a main-shaft bearing and restuffed a dozen wheezing valves. By that time we had drifted to somewhere near the middle of the Indian ocean and it became a problem which port to make for, to refit and sign new men.

We decided on Bombay after long discussion of the pros and cons and were all gloomy all the long way there, wheezing an unsteady thirteen knots, Grace Vandam depressed because we laughed no longer and Aunty Elmira in a state of strident mutiny against everything and everybody not United States American.

She vowed it was our nationality—the crimes of England and the curse of kings that had brought down vengeance on us from the skies. She bewailed the *Daisy's* injuries as Rachel bewailed her children and, reversing her adoration of Monty, refused to speak to him—except that she talked at him nasaly and noisily whenever chance brought them near enough.

JOHN McGRAW was perhaps the least troubled. He left the first mate on the bridge one morning and came to where Monty was standing on deck with Fred and Will and me, smiling with a sort of horse-trade expression that would have put a born fool on his guard.

"Bombay very soon now," he said, addressing the remark to all of us.

So we all four grunted noncommittally and left him with the conversation still to open. But that did not disconcert him. He opened it like an oyster, by main force applied with a sharp instrument to the proper spot without unnecessary preface.

"I've been studyin' the contract," he said, facing us all with both hands behind him.

"You're late in the day, if your idea is to change it," Monty answered.

"Naw," he said dryly. "We're agreed on that then. Changin' is barred out. She stands as written."

"Stands as spoken," said Fred. "If you've lost your copy you may look at ours, and if that goes overboard we'll live up to every line of it!"

"Good enough!" remarked John McGraw dryly. "Good enough! Then you'll not gainsay that lawful expenses o' this trip are to come out o' your pockets!"

"I take issue there," said Monty. "Expenses are to be charged according to contract against the total proceeds before making division. Is that what you mean?"

"I do not! Ye took no typhoons into reckonin', but I did! I made the stipulations, and I dare bet there are lawyers ashore as 'll take my view! Ye're liable, accordin' to what ye've signed, for yer pro rata share o' the cost o' these repairs in Bombay."

He waited more than a minute for the full enormity of that announcement to sink in, but no one answered him.

"Repairs—accordin' to my way o' sizing it up—are goin' to cost a heap o' money—likely twice as much in Bombay as they would in New York. She'll need a through an' through overhaul. Ye've got to foot y'r full third o' that bill!"

We did not answer. It would have been Monty's place to do that, and it was never his plan to check the discovery of what an enemy intended.

"Miss Vandam can well afford it," McGraw continued, pretty obviously stopping what he considered the worst hole in his own argument; "but writing 's writing and law's the law. Ye've one chance, and only one."

"I don't see any chance," said Monty, unstopping the hole again. "Who would take advantage of our hostess?"

"Oh yes, ye've one. The contract reads we're to voyage to Barabbas Island. If we shouldn't, then the contract 'ud be broken and you couldn't be held to the terms of it. So now, gents, if you'll take my side in the argument with Miss Vandam and help me talk her out o' this Barabbas foolishness, ye'll save y'rselves a heap o' money!"

Monty laughed and pulled out his cigar-case.

"Take one!" he said. "I wouldn't bet on your law half as confidently as on your navigation. As you say—typhoons aren't mentioned in the contract. We never thought of them. But my friends and I propose to foot half, not a third, of these repairs, As for continuing the trip, we'll stand neutral. If Miss Vandam goes forward, we'll go. If you can talk her out of it, we'll release her from the contract. Are you satisfied?"

"No," he said grimly. "Not yet. But I'll name ye. Ye're gentlemen! Here comes Miss Gracie herself. Mind—ye promise to stand neutral. Mark what I say to her."

"Morning, John! "she nodded cheerfully. "I was looking for you to tell you what my plans are."

"Here's hoping ye've changed 'em, miss," he answered, making shift to put on a paternal air.

"I have. You'll stay at Bombay and see to the

repairs and refitting. These gentlemen may stay or come with me as they see fit. I'm going to hire a smaller steamer in Bombay and make the Barabbas trip while the *Daisy* is being fixed. Now, don't look at me in that way, John! You may go back home if you'd rather, and now you know!"

"Now wouldn't that beat the measles!" muttered John McGraw, turning away dejectedly with both hands in his pockets.

IV

IT WAS one of Grace Vandam's strongest and most likable characteristics that she was willing to change details of her strategy at a second's notice without ever losing sight of the main idea or relaxing determination.

The minute we stood on the stonework of the Apollo Bunder in Bombay we were in a sphere where Monty could command whatever prestige and influence can do for a man—in a land where the one begets the other and both take precedence of mere ambition.

The clubs were ours. All officialdom was at our service. The Royal navy knew a hundred ways of making yacht repairs less costly and more thorough. And there were officers in the Royal navy—very bright-eyed, soft-speaking gentlemen, made lean by fevers and alert by responsibility—who knew strange tales of stranger seas and would tell, if they liked you well enough.

Most of them fell in love with Grace Vandam, it being a British navy privilege to lose its gallant heart as often as lovely woman heaves in sight, and Monty, simply by being what he was, held the key to their silences.

Fred Oakes, too, was a man after the British navy's heart—a wandering maker of unclassic music—singer of uncensored songs—gently bred and roughly weaned adventurer, with deeds to his credit that would stand unctuous hair on end and a wholly honest distaste for praise or for any reference to his virtues. Will Yerkes and I sat in, as it were, being unknown quantities, accepted without reserve for sake of the men who introduced us.

Those were days—and nights and mornings even, when we sat on the old *Magdala's* deck and watched the paling stars—of unconfined imagination and unrestrained romance. There was not a tale they tell in all those seas that we did not hear three versions of; not a chart they did not let us pore over; not a rare, dim photograph we were not shown; not a torn, thumbed, folded letter we were not allowed to read. Sons of hanged Red Sea pirates were sent for and given lawless un-Islamic drinks, that they might tell us in the dim light under awnings what they knew or had heard or guessed of Barabbas Island.

Grace Vandam grew feverish with the boundless fascination, and it is not the Royal navy's way to quench approved desire or to pour cold water on good courage.

"Only one stipulation I make," she insisted again and again. "We're to go there! We're to get there! How I don't care! Go I will!"

So Monty was not limited by too explicit orders as to local steamers and native crews. Aunty Elmira was handed over to a fat, debt-laden sub-lieutenant—for his sins—to be shown the official sights and do the social round, while we searched strange water-fronts together and held converse with the captains of unusual, mainly unpainted craft.

In the end we took the advice of a navy man whose intimate knowledge of those ships and seas was keen enough to compel the respect of Arabs—and that is harder to win than the viceroy's cup or a Hugli pilot's certificate. He led us down to a smelly wharf in an ancient part of town, where a rakish two-masted sailing-ship lay on the mud between green stone walls.

"She can show heels to many a steamer," he told us. "Her skipper and owner is Osman bin Omar, part Arab, part Turk, part Seedeebay, with a dash of something; else—sportsman all ends up—particular according to his lights, which are red and green. That's to say he'd rather die than not cheat a landsman but he'll play straight cricket if he's sure you know the sea. His ship was a French yacht once. I don't know how he came by her. He changed the rig and name and gets a living with her in devious ways; but he keeps out of jail, and the little ship's bottom is as clean as his own prayer mat. I'm told he prays five times a day—three times to Allah and twice to the devil of the Christians. See if you can't come to terms with him."

To our surprise Osman bin Omar talked English, after a terse fashion of his own. He stuck to English, especially after Fred surprised him with a rich flow of Arabic, seeming to prefer to fight out the bargain on our domain rather than his. He showed us over the little ship with the manner of a prince, his bright brown eyes glittering appreciation of what he had to offer. And each of us, Grace Vandam included, took a turn at knocking lumps from the sum he named as his minimum per month for charter.

Eastern bargains, alongshore or on land or sea, are not made in an hour or two or overnight. We stuck to him for two hours and then withdrew and stayed away, sweating anxiety, for three days, until Osman bin Omar himself threw caution to the dogs and came to call on us at the hotel. Then the war of words began again, Will Yerkes commencing with the statement that we did not want to buy the —— ship.

"She ship not ——; she blessed, she not for sale!" he answered. "Barabbas —— bad place; get big price."

In the end we beat him down to half his original demand and, still loudly calling him a thief, led him in triumph to the naval man who had introduced us. Under his wise eye a Parsee lawyer drew a contract. Osman bin Omar disputing every point with threats of suicide because of our exceeding exactions and seeking persistently to write in shameless extortions of his own—as for instance, that we should pay the crew's wages in addition to the charter price, he having already stipulated that the fabulous price agreed on was inclusive.

"He fights now," said our mentor, "but he'll live up to the terms agreed on if I know him."

Finally, when we had fought out every clause of the agreement word by word and the Parsee had almost finished writing two fair copies of it all, the navy man sprang a surprise that reduced Osman bin Omar to the verge of speechlessness.

"Write now," he ordered the Parsee, "that the party of the second, part, shall take along ten U.S. seamen chosen from the crew of the yacht *Daisy*, who shall not be required to work ship or obey the orders of the party of the first part but may do so if so requested and if so ordered by the party of the second part."

"Why you want 'em?" demanded Osman when outraged caution permitted speech to escape him.

"None of your business!" said the navy-man. "It goes in or we charter some other ship!"

OSMAN STORMED and argued. We were adamant. From our point of view ten white sailors were none too many to take our part against the sixteen nearly naked sons of pirates who would man the Arab's yards. In the end, however, he refused pointblank, vowed there was no room on his ship for that many extra passengers and took himself off in a fury.

"Don't let that worry you," said our mentor. "No; don't send after him, Miss Vandam. Come and dine and dance on the *Magdala*. He'll be back to-morrow morning."

And so he was—too early, causing us to be aroused from the delicious deeps of slumber that follow on dancing in Bombay's hot humidity until the peep o' day.

"I allow you two sailor-man, not one —— man more!" he announced.

Gracie was "tickled to death with him"—wanted to offer him breakfast—hot coffee at least—and to agree there and then to his condition. But we were a trifle more experienced in driving Eastern bargains and added to our tale, demanding that twelve men come with us instead of ten. The discussion that followed might easily have been mistaken by the uninitiated for a difference between umpire and the bleachers at a dog-fight.

Aunty Elmira Vandam came down and demanded that Grace come away from listening to such awful language. Fingers snapped. The "damns" and "blasts" and other words that help make the longshore English language picturesque exploded regardless of folk at breakfast or the bishop's chaplain vainly attempting to read the *Times*. We accused Osman bin Omar of nameless intentions on the high seas, and he us of crimes and habits that he did not hesitate to name.

And finally—suddenly—we all agreed on five men as the only number of U.S. sailors any one in his senses would dream of taking and sent for the Parsee lawyer with mutual expressions of admiration and good-will. After that the only question left to be disputed was which side should pay the lawyer. Osman bin Omar, like a good sportsman, offered to toss coins for it. We agreed. He won. It was weeks before we learned that he beat us with a double-headed English penny.

Picking the five men we should take with us was easy. Grace Vandam did it in twenty minutes. With one stroke she eliminated all the married men, because, as she explained in an aside, that shut out John McGraw, the mates and the engineer officers.

Then with wisdom like Solomon's she asked which unmarried men would rather be discharged and free to seek active employment than loaf in harbor while repairs were made.

Replies were fairly equally divided. There were nine who did not like the prospect of laziness. She eliminated four by having a British naval doctor pass on them and signed on the remaining five at double pay for the sailing trip. They were fine young fellows, three New Bedford men and two from Portland, Maine, all about as free from the sin of cowardice as birth and schooling can make a man.

After that we had to put the *Samaki*—the word means fish—in shape to carry two women passengers, stock her with civilized comforts and provisions and exchange Aunty Elmira Vandam for a chaperon less likely to be a Jonah. Persuading aunty proved impossible. She wept, railed and sent cablegrams to United States relatives. And nobody would take her in exchange. So in the end we left her flat, with leave to use her quarters on the yacht or do anything else she liked in reason, and took along the widow of a British officer—India is full of them—to whom a trip of any sort spelt blessed relief from pensioned pauperdom. Her name was Alice Ellis and she turned out trumps.

After that speed became sole object. We bought cabin fittings from a ship-breaker and constructed quarters for the women that were less intolerable than our portion of canvas hammocks swinging under beams. Will thought of rat-poison at the last minute and brought along a ten-pound can.

It was Monty who remembered bug-bane and brought a large drum of some foul-smelling compound on which a dozen sorts of insect pests were destined to grow strong and fat.

My last-minute contribution to the general weal was zinc ointment in a gallon jar—and faith we needed it before that voyage was through. Fred went aboard the night before we started and concealed canned kippered herring where no lascar prowling in search of something to give flavor to his curry would be likely to pounce on them.

We got away before dawn, too early for club folk and the idly curious but not for the *Sphinx* and her commander. That nearly-ready-to-be-superannuated gunboat steamed ahead of us with squattering paddles and sent us on our way at last with rousing cheers and waving helmets.

She was the last we saw of India. When we lost sight of her we settled down, Monty to everlasting chess by himself under a burlap awning and the rest of us to books, while the polyglot crew sang songs to the god of fair winds in time to the squeak and strain of the lateen spars.

We had found an astonishing number of books in Bombay on the subject of Biblical history, and some of them included guesses at who Barabbas might have been that, if not so wild as ours, had the merit of being based on study on the spot. Added to ours, they helped make up a story sufficiently romantic to offset even our discomfort in such a ship on such seas.

Ten days out from Bombay, when the heat and the glare across oily water had reduced us to speechless ill-temper that bug-bites did nothing to soothe and Fred's concertina could only irritate, storms became our lot again.

At first we blessed them, for they filled our bellying sails and sent us boiling northwestward out of sight of Aden. But after the third day of wind there came a sandstorm—clouds of dry dust as sharp and hard as emery, ripped by the wind from the barren hills and hurled on pilgrims of the sea like one of Egypt's plagues.

The first storm left us and we shoveled sand off deck by the hundredweight. We ate two meals that did not make our gums bleed with the grinding grit. Then a second swept down, and a third. Sight became a matter of chance and snatched seconds. Watery eyes full of sharp sand and skin rendered raw by the blast are no aids to navigation.

Grace Vandam and Alice Ellis kept to the stove-hot cabin and knew only the misery of bugs, uncleanliness and prickly heat. I heard them laugh in spite of all those things.

Out in the driving sand we others leaned outboard and lent our aid to the keen, skinned Arab eyes, doing little good except to keep ourselves from "nerves," as men call panic. Time and again we knew that Osman bin Omar, the redoubtable, had lost himself. Time and again we saw him, by dint of luck, dead reckoning, chance glimpses of some shore mark or sight of a steamship driving through the storm, guess his position again.

Compass he had, but he did not use it much. The thing swung back and forward like a high volt electric indicator, demanding Art, with a capital A, to interpret its maneuvers. If he had any other navigating instruments he never produced them, and he thought more of the stars than all the other aids to seamen put together.

But one could not see the stars on those sandstormy nights except for a glimpse now and then when bright blue planets seemed to race across black gaps in the dusty clouds. Once in the night we struck a reef and jumped clean over it, Osman shoving the helm hard over with the remark that that was "—— bad place." After that our seamen from the *Daisy* took turns at the helm, two together, not that they could see any better or knew anything about the course, but it gave us all more courage, themselves included—that being part of the white man's heritage.

Then there was mutiny. Nothing more serious at first than a mournfully couched demand by the native crew that we turn about and run for Bombay.

"They are saying bad ship, bad wind, bad grub, bad luck, bad journey," explained Osman.

"And you?" we asked him. "What do you say?"

"——!" was the answer. "Bad place ahead. Not good. Go back worse. Shipwreck—folk on Barabbas cut 'um throat. Not shipwreck—bad spirits come—maybe Christian devil—make of a time! Me brave man!"

CERTAINLY HE was braver than his crew. He seemed to fear neither wreck, evil spirits, crew nor us. The native crew must have heard us talking of our destination, for the name of the place was on our lips everlastingly, but our pronunciation of it perhaps conveyed no meaning to their ears.

When Osman bin Omar said the word the nearest man snatched it up and passed it on. Within five minutes they were clamorous to know whether we were truly making for Barabbas. When the answer was yes, with a bunch of explosive oaths to drive it home, they mutinied there and then.

Mutiny is a strange passion with a lawlessness all its own, not governed by precedent or swayed by any motives of farsightedness. The first thing that occurred to any of them was to throw the two ladies overboard. I heard screams and entered the cabin through the poop hatch without waiting for invitation.

Grace Vandam and Alice Ellis were struggling in the grip of four sinewy lascars, fighting to keep themselves from being dragged on deck—to what fate they could scarcely guess. I being as much of a surprise to the lascars as they had been to the women, the rest of that session was one-sided. The nearest weapon was a chair; I broke it on the first man's head and laid out the three others with the remnants.

After that we got out firearms from the boxes in the hold and served out a repeating pistol each to our five New England seamen. We had not done that before because Osman bin Omar had assured us that sight of firearms would only whet cupidity, and his men were expert thieves. But now we set regular watches, and those of us not in the watch below became whips, as it were—the fist, flail and threat with which Osman could bully his crew.

The men I had brained with the chair-leg did not die, which was a mercy under the circumstances, for they went about with bandaged heads for an example to the others, the groans their throbbing aches gave rise to so far quelled the mutiny that Grace Vandam dared go alone and change the victims' bandages. But subjection is one thing, obedience another.

One man, when the storm lulled in the nighttime, climbed aloft and, standing on the main yard with a hand on the mast, so that he looked crucified, jabbered about devils at the limit of his lungs, urging us all to die—so Osman said—before the evil spirits of Barabbas Island could catch us and carry us to hell forever. Then he set the example by plunging overboard with a scream that made the hearer's marrow creep within the spine.

Another man jumped after him over the stern and a third ran amuck, charging in the dark along the swaying deck, slashing at imaginary bogies with a long knife until Monty's fist took him neatly under the jaw-bone and he went overboard to join his friends.

Although the wind had dropped, the sea ran high. We wallowed without headway and the crew swore the drowned men were swimming around us, calling. We did hear the cry of sea-birds once or twice and the goose-flesh rose at the sound.

The lull in the storm gave Osman bin Omar his bearings again, for dawn showed land—high hot cliffs and boiling reefs. He swore he knew every fang protruding out of the swell and hugged the shore so close that we shuddered and grew ill with anxiety. There were sharks in hundreds all about us, and no ship could have lived long enough, once on the rocks, to have given passengers a chance.

Several times Fred tried to raise our spirits with mad music, but we only abused him for it. Monty dropped a hook and stout line overboard and caught a shark. The crew—who normally would have eaten shark greedily—denounced him for a bringer of bad luck. We hauled the line short, cut it through with an ax and let the shark go—proof enough that our nerves were getting frayed, although we made a bluff of seeming reckless.

Grace Vandam was as nervous by that time as any of us, but the need of seeming bold before the other woman kept her chin stiff. And of course we were not going to show a white feather in front of either of them.

"Is the sea around Barabbas anything like this?" I asked Osman by way of seeking comfort.

"—— sight worse!" he answered tersely.

"How far away is it?" I demanded.

For answer he puckered his eyes and after a long stare to the northward pointed to a scarcely visible prong of rock notched against the far horizon. It looked like part of the mainland.

"That sharp rock one side—worse shore-reefs other side—bad passage in between—come Barabbas!" he announced and then spat repeatedly with fervor.

I told the others. We all crowded forward to watch the island of our destiny lift out of distant glare. There returned to us something of the fascination. Our lateen spars and sails all golden in the sun were not, perhaps, so very much unlike those unremembered ones that rose over that horizon in the dawn of history. We forgot reefs, currents and the too unwilling crew—until the storm came down again like baffled hatred from the hot cliffs to the west.

It blew as Osman swore he had never known it, and the crew vowed all the devils of hell were combining to drive us back. The sea rose and the reefed sails ripped, until we anchored to try and ride it out. Then the anchor-cable parted where a sullen Arab mate forgot the parceling. When we let go the other anchor it fouled and dragged.

Osman bin Omar was a sailor from crown to heels—head, eyes and hands, as they say, but his crew was on fire with fear. Our five New England seamen built a drog for him out of a spare sail and spars and got it overboard in time to save us from wallowing on to the seaward line of reefs. That held our nose up-wind a while and steadied the rate of drift, providing us an hour or two to spare instead of minutes. Then Osman showed what he was made of.

He produced an old revolver and a whip of twisted wire, threatening with the one and with the other sparing neither kith nor kin. Like all Eastern skippers he had relatives in the crew and he struck them first and hardest. He made the blood squirt and his victims scream. Then, in the storm with the decks awash and the little ship rolling like a mad thing, he produced his contract and addressed himself to Grace Vandam.

"—— —— mess!" he shouted, shaking the contract under her nose. "You —— party of second part! You so permit!"

"Yes!" she answered. "Yes! I understand! Mills! Perkins! Hammond! Constable! Hewitt! Take his orders—do you hear me?"

"Aye, aye, miss!"

New England ran up to windward handily and Osman bin Omar laughed—a rare event with him. With oaths and blows, by dint of sheer brute hauling, we recovered the drog and got sail reset. Osman did not dare run and risk being pooped in those short, steep seas. He did the only thing a bold man could do—shoved his ship's nose right into the mess and beat up for the passage between mainland and Barabbas. We tacked a hundred times in ten miles—and tacking is no joke on a lateen-rigged ship—New England hauling on the sheets and putting enthusiasm into the laggard crew.

We made a great lagoon between the reefs ten minutes before dark and then, in proof of Osman's seamanship, paid off down a long narrow lane between sharp rocks toward where we could see Barabbas looming grim and unfriendly.

Night shut down on us as we raced through crazy seas toward a haven protected by a curving arm of rock. The cliffs of Barabbas loomed above us, blacker than the night. White water hissed and boiled on every hand. Somebody screamed "Oh—Allah!" in a voice like a drowning horse's.

"Hard over!" yelled one of the New England seamen, but Osman held the helm straight. Next, somebody close to me said—

"Oh, my God!"

Then the ship rose like a horse at a railing and we struck, in a smother of water and a noise like doomsday.

V

IT IS the looker-on who must describe a shipwreck. We were participants—victims, thrown down in the dark on a bucking deck amid the crash of rocks and sea and splintering timbers. We had two boats, but they were gone by the board more quickly than the thought that turned to them. Every man of the native crew stampeded overside, and we never again saw as much of one of them as a mangled limb or rag of clothing. They were pulped on the rocks and devoured by pirate sharks and sea-birds when the storm went down.

Only Osman's courage in holding a steady helm and piling her on to the rocks nose first saved any of us. Memory is unreliable of moments when death's fingers seem to clutch and his chill breath blows, but I think there were five minutes between the first crash and the last gulp when the broken ship slid back into the waves and disappeared.

Within a minute both masts went overboard, one to either side—and that was sheer Providence. I saw Monty rush to the women's cabin and emerge with a suitcase. Fred brought another. I started to try to save some more of their things, but they and the women struck me, and Monty cursed me for a lunatic.

"Get forward!" he yelled. "The ship's bow's ashore!"

But I went below in the dark and found some pistol ammunition and an overcoat, not ceasing search for other things until the hull slid with a sickening lilt and water arose knee-deep around me. Then I rushed for the deck and carromed into Will with his arms full of blankets.

"Monty's got the women safe!" he shouted in my ear. "These ought to keep 'em warm!"

We went forward together, slipping and scrambling through tangled rigging on the heaving deck. When we reached the bow, there was nobody, nor any sound from shore except the roar of surf on rocks. Fumbling about, I found a rope over the bows and pulled on it. It was loose and came in freely. Then Will yelled in my ear again.

"The mast! It makes a bridge! One end's on land!"

So we hauled the loose rope in—there was not more than fifty or sixty feet of it—and, making it fast again to one of the wooden bollards, clung to it and tried to walk ashore along the mast. I could have done it if Will had not slipped and snatched at me. But with those blankets to encumber him he did the only thing he could to save himself.

We fell one on each side of the mast, holding arms over it while wild surf wrenched at us and pounded our legs on the jutting ledge. In the effort to get back on the mast we broke our grip. Will let go of everything except the blankets but I caught him as he fell.

The surf rolled us over and whirled us round like tops, wrapping three coils of the rope about us both. I gave up then. I heard the ship go scraping, creaking, splintering down off the ledge, and shut my eyes.

Yet I breathed—air, not water. I felt myself turning slowly, like a corpse on a gibbet. Will yelled in my ear and kicked until the wet rope cut into my flesh. I awoke to the fact that the ship had gone down to Davy Jones but not the mast, whose upper end was jammed in a crevice of the rock, and we were hanging like two fish caught on one pole. One more slow turn and we would both have been loose again and down among the dead men in the waves.

I don't remember how we got ashore. We twisted the rope about ourselves again and hung for a time, daring neither to let go nor try experiments. Then it dawned on both of us at once that our united weight, acting like a pendulum as the waves pushed us to and fro, was loosening the mast, and we began to make frantic efforts.

I remember an agony of piercing, bruising rock and the disgusting smother of salt water, and the next I knew I was lying on my back in a low cave with one of Will's blankets under my head and the pistol cartridges out of my pockets spread to dry all about me. It was beginning to be dawn and the sea was raging twenty yards away as if it hoped to climb and seize us in spite of all.

"I guess you're not so dead as you look!" said Will, peering down at my face. "There's sweet water near. I'll fetch you some in my folding cup when you say the word. It's all you'll get for breakfast, feller!"

"Where's Monty?" I asked weakly.

"Blessed if I know. Don't know where Gracie is, or any of 'em. I've climbed all over the cliff in the dark, but I didn't find a soul."

"Are they drowned?"

"Search me! Let's hope not!"

The utter, blank hopelessness of the thought that

we might be the sole survivors aroused me to a sort of dogged, quarrelsome-defiant mood that served us both, for I staggered up and with that defiance in place of strength set out to supplement Will's search. He followed me and presently shot a great sea-bird with his pistol.

"He'll taste like Standard Oil," he said, "but I've got matches and I'll bet we eat! Keep an eye lifting for driftwood."

The first weak efforts made me vomit, but when I was about empty of salt water I drank like a colt at the rain-water pool Will had found and felt better. Then we went up the cliff-side together, three or four hundred feet, by a track so suspiciously easy that I swore once or twice the grades were no accident.

Will said the smoothing of the rock was due to weather, but I showed him ancient pick-marks that the weather had only half obliterated and indentations where we clambered around a rock-face that bore man's mark as unmistakably as tracks used yesterday.

It was no wonder that he had not found our party or any traces of them in the dark. From the top of the cliff we could see such a toothed and serried maze of treeless rock as recalled more than anything one of those Japanese landscapes where the hills are all but perpendicular and all the narrow valleys run in curves.

As far as the eye could see there was not a patch of level or a dwelling or a stream or anything to rest the eye. Within five yards of us a hundred people could have hidden easily. Ten thousand could have peopled the ravines within a quarter-mile and we have been none the wiser.

We shouted, but all that came back was echoes and the screams of sea-birds. We sat down and searched the sea for traces of the wreck. Beyond that the birds appeared more busy between some waves than others, we detected nothing.

"D'you suppose the natives live in caves?" Will wondered. "Old Osman said something pleasant about their cutting throats. D'you suppose they're cannibals? Say—I'd hate to be eaten in a cave, wouldn't you? Me for the open! Me for a picnic out o' doors!"

"I'm ravenous," I answered. "I'll eat that bird raw unless we find fuel soon!"

So we set out in search again, exposing ourselves against the sky-line as much as possible in order that Monty or any of the others might see us. But no shouts came to announce friends, and after a time we lost all memory of the track back to our cave and wandered uselessly for hours looking for it, until the sun made the blazing rock unbearable and I grew too weak from hunger to go another yard.

Then we plucked what Will was pleased to call the pigeon—gutted him with our fingers and a piece of a sharp rock—gathered tufts of dry grass from places where time and the sea-birds had deposited seed and some dust in which it could germinate—and went through the farce of singeing the oily carcass. It was the most revolting meal I ever ate. Memory of it has power to spoil appetite to-day.

"Let's listen a while." Will suggested. "If Fred got ashore, it's a cinch he had his concertina along. He'd rather be drowned than lose it! If they're all ashore, they'll be just as badly off as we are and probably mourning for us into the bargain. Fred'll make music to cheer 'em up. Let's listen, and maybe we'll hear him!"

But that forlorn hope bore no fruit either. We sat still under the shade of an overhanging rock with ears alert, until the strain of that added to the previous exhaustion sent me off again, either into sleep or a dead faint. Will said afterward it was sleep, to reassure me, but I doubted him. It was growing dark again when I awoke, and we set out at once in an effort to find our first cave and the blankets and cartridges we left there.

IT WAS a useless effort. We could not even find sweet water again, and when the sun went down in an angry red haze we were glad to take shelter on a ledge, in a place like the hollow of a giant's hand, fifty feet below the summit of a sharp crag that we climbed to try to get a view. Nothing but a bird's-eye view, however, would have been the least use. All we got and remembered all night was a picture of jumbled granite, planless and barren—the teeth of chaos carved in gray, imperishable stone.

We were both growing spiritless by that time, reverting to the child's hunger for caresses, as the strongest men do when death looks near and lonely. We sat first back to back and then with an arm about each other, and I suppose Will thought of faraway New England meadows and the tidy, elm-lined streets. I tried to think of London and its good, bold roar—of the clatter of hoofs when the hansom cabs go spinning through the lighted squares—and the din of spoons and dishes behind the swinging doors the waiters come and go through.

But another sound kept breaking in on the reverie—a sound that at first seemed a part of it all, because I suppose we were both too numb mentally to separate the pictures we imagined from the sounds we really heard. But all at once Will sat bolt upright and gripped my leg until I swore at him. "Did you hear that?" he asked hoarsely. There was a scream, high pitched and long, like that of a woman undergoing torture. After an interval, during which the whole earth seemed to pause and listen, there came another one.

"D'you suppose that's Gracie?" asked Will. "D'you suppose some darned natives have caught her and—"

"No," I said, "Gracie's voice is different. I heard her scream once—more like a boy."

"Alice Ellis, then!"

"No," I said. "Mrs. Ellis couldn't scream so loud."

"Nobody could tell how loud she'd scream until there was excuse for it," he answered.

Then we heard it again and it made the blood run cold. I thought there was grief in it as well as pain, but pain was uppermost. I wasn't sure it was a woman's cry.

"Was it Fred's concertina, d'you suppose?" Will hazarded. "Fred's always up to tricks."

"Don't be an ass," I said. "Could it be a wild animal?"

"What sort?"

"How should I know?"

The cry was repeated—surely a woman's, we both thought, full of agony and hopelessness, finishing crescendo as if the pain increased.

"I can't sit here!" said Will. "I can't stand it! That may be Gracie or Alice Ellis. Either of them would take a chance in the dark for either of us!"

That was true. Yet I did not see how the truth of it would help us find footing in uncharted blackness. We both had pistols, so that the danger of attack by animal or human was one we need not hesitate about. But we had both seen the landscape from the top of the crag at sundown.

"Did you ever hunt for needles in the hay?" I said. "Let's try for the top of the crag again and sit and watch a while."

He agreed to that, and by dint of striking more of his precious matches than was wise and by feeling out every hand and foothold, we gained the summit, tired and breathless. Just as we reached the top the scream pierced the darkness again, louder and shriller than ever, and we lay side by side, shuddering, staring downward into blue gloom out of which the shadows of a hundred other summits gradually grew and formed a solid ring around us.

"Might as well look for ice in hell!" said Will. "Look up—there's stars. Look down—there's night. We couldn't see an army down there!"

"Hsssh!" said I. "Look! Listen!"

I had seen a spark. It might have been imagination that suggested the woodpecker tapping of flint on steel.

"Which direction?"

I did not answer. We both lay still as mice and my eyes ached with trying to pierce the dark. Then—and it may again have been imagination—I thought I heard once more the tap-tap-tapping of a flint. Sound carries unaccountably. A moment later we both saw several sparks. Then a little blue flame. The blue flame grew—grew redder—and bent away before the unsteady puffs of some one blowing with his mouth. There was not a doubt of it.

"Shall I shout?" Will whispered.

"No," I said. "Mark the bearings carefully, and then let's stalk him. He or she, if it's a member of our crowd, well and good. If not, let's take precautions. It might be Osman bin Omar," I suggested, "imagining himself sole survivor and mourning his little ship!"

"Gee!" said Will. "I never thought of that! If he has a pistol—and that may be—and we came on him too suddenly, he'd shoot! But I don't believe Osman could scream like a woman."

"Osman was a strange old scout," said I. "How about bearings? Have you got them? Come on, then."

If the climb up had been difficult the descent into blackness was a thousand times worse. Luckily there were not very many loose stones and we made no noise that would alarm a person not deliberately listening for us; but I twisted an ankle rather badly and Will fell twice and bruised himself so that he could hardly bear to touch knees or elbows. And that was before we had reached the foot of the crag with which we were already to some extent familiar.

Once at the foot of that we groped our way into the sheer unknown, not daring to strike matches or to speak or to take one step without first stooping and feeling the way along. Though we rounded our crag at once we could see no sign of the fire; there were other, rather lower saw-tooth ridges between it and us.

But from time to time the agonizing cry came over to us, to make us sure that someone lonelier and more wretched than we ourselves was still bivouacking near.

Far from growing used to the tortured voice, we grew more and more afraid of it. Each interval between the cries was torture of drawn-out anticipation that was only rendered more acute when the cry did come.

Whoever it was had more fuel than we had been able to find, for as we crawled along the bottom of a fissure between high granite walls we saw the glow of a good-sized fire reflected on the darkness above the next ridge in front of us. With that glow to give us direction the last part of the stalk bade fair to be the easiest.

But when we came to climb the ridge we found it all but straight up-and-down, without a cranny that we could find to drive fingers into. We had to make another dark circuit of perhaps a quarter of a mile and come up from the far side over a broken ramp that cut our knees and bruised my feet through the shoe-soles.

We lay at last side by side again in a niche on the sky-line, fifty feet above and a hundred and fifty feet away from a big square granite rock, like a pagan high altar, that stood bold and lonely in the midst of a nearly level space within the circumference of saw-tooth crags. The fire was on top of that rock, in the midst of it not such a very big fire after all, but burning bright because of the sea salt in the driftwood it was made of.

THE PERSON who had built the fire stood by it, erect against the night, motionless, betrayed by the hot flame as distinctly as if by sunlight.

She was a woman—rather young—not very dark-skinned, as far as we could judge by firelight—almost entirely naked but with jewels on her neck and fingers that I could see from where we lay. One great gem in a ring on her right hand sparkled in the firelight as if it were the source of light itself.

She seemed to be standing in an attitude of prayer; but prayer was not bringing her much consolation, for while we watched she threw her head back and sent her wild, weird grief-cry echoing among the crags.

"If she does that again I'll yell too!" Will whispered. "You see if I don't! There are some things a feller can stand about just so much of!"

The moon got up at last over a ring of rock wall and bathed her in lemon light. She looked at it for several minutes and then struck her breast defiantly—the most magnificently contemptuous, cruel gesture I ever saw. Then she cried again, but Will kept command of himself, although I felt him shivering as violently as I did.

She looked rather like an African woman, only taller than the ordinary—clean-limbed and supple like a Galla, but with longer hair. The hair looked thick and reached to her shoulders, being cut off at that length evenly. I guessed her to be of mixed Asian and African descent, probably of good, proud blood on either side.

Presently, as she turned away from the moon, I saw that her upper right arm was bandaged tightly. It looked badly swollen under the rags, and one or two gestures she made toward the bandage with her other hand suggested that she was in acute pain.

"Will!" I whispered. "What'll you bet me her clothes haven't all been used up for bandages?"

"What'll you bet me she isn't shipwrecked like ourselves?" he answered.

"She seems in no fear of being seen," said I.

"It begins to look bad to me," said Will. "If she has been wandering about, why hasn't she come across Monty and the rest of our crowd? If they're alive, she'd either be with them by now or else afraid of being seen by them, you'd think."

"I suppose if we discover ourselves she'll run?"

"Maybe," he answered. "Yet we've got to do something. If she's wounded, at least we can give her a shirt to make bandages of. Which shall we do—call to her from here or try to go closer before she sees us?"

The question was answered for us by the woman herself. Her keen ears caught the sibilant note that makes human whispering the least secret of all communications—even a shout blends better with the natural sounds. She glanced swiftly once in our direction, with the enviable gift, denied to men from towns, of locating sound unerringly, and was gone with a leap like a leopard's, springing down from the altar rock and vanishing in shadow.

We clambered and slid clumsily down into the level place and hunted for her like idiots, probing the shadows and calling in what we imagined were reassuring tones. At last Will saw the folly of that proceeding and called me off. We both went and sat on the altar rock in the fire-light and I put my hand on something sticky. I held my hand to the fire to examine it.

"Will," I said, "that woman left a little pool of blood behind!"

He came and examined it.

"Splashes!" he said. "See—and here. There's another where she jumped from the rock—it's wet. We can track her."

"Let's try to find the blankets first and take her one," said I. "If she's wounded as badly as that we can afford to give her a long start. Let's wait for morning and hunt first for our cave."

"Look for food now!" said Will. "Didn't she mean to cook something at the fire? Perhaps she dropped it before she ran."

But we hunted in vain.

Whatever her purpose in building a fire on that square rock, cooking had not been included in it.

"D'you suppose she was making a signal?" said Will.

"To whom?" I objected. "Why should she signal and then run the minute she heard a whisper?"

"Why should she build a fire and yell and yell and yell—and then run at the first whisper, if not because she was hoping to decoy an enemy?" he retorted.

"In that case," I said, "we'd better look out for the enemy, too!"

He was sitting on the edge of the square rock, clearly outlined by the blazing fire. I was in shadow below him. He got down and sat beside me and had scarcely done so when a lump of granite whizzed in a parabola past where his head had been and broke in pieces on the rock.

"She's less than twenty yards away," I said.

The stone was too big for any one to have thrown it much farther than that.

We listened intently and heard the sound of bare feet retreating swiftly.

"She crept close and hurled it and ran!"

"I guess she saw only me," Will hazarded.

"And mistook you for some one else."

"D'you suppose," he said, "that the stone arrived soon enough after I ducked for the person who threw it to think I was hit?"

"You may have saved some one's life," I answered. "If she thinks she hit you, the person she wanted may escape."

"Maybe it wasn't she who tossed the rock!" he said suddenly. "Maybe it was some ope gunning for her! Say—if I'm sitting all hunched up on the edge of this rock in the fire—and moonlight, could you or any one mistake me for a woman without clothes on?"

"From some angles you'd look just like some one's shadow," I answered.

But we abandoned that theory, because surely an enemy who imagined he was pelting the woman would have continued throwing and then have come closer to investigate. We lay in the shadow until nearly dawn, but no one came and no other sound broke the stillness. I think Will slept for a short time, but he denied it indignantly and swore he had been puzzling out the problem.

"My final guess," he said, "is that the woman threw that rock at me, mistaking me for some one else; that she knows she missed; that she was afraid of reprisals and ran; and that she's on the watch now like a mountain goat."

I did not agree with him. His denial of having fallen asleep annoyed me and I would not have agreed with him whatever he said. But his guess turned out accurate. Perhaps he got the clue to the puzzle in his dreams.

WHEN DAWN did come at last, we found the path to the cave and the cave itself far more easily than we expected. The surf was still raging among the rocks and we stood and watched it for a little while for wreckage or dead bodies. But suddenly Will made an exclamation that brought me hurrying into the cave.

"There were three blankets!" he said.

One was left. The one my head had rested on was still folded in the same place.

"How many cartridges did you have loose in your pockets?" he asked.

I did not know.

"I left them spread all about the floor of the cave in twos and threes and sixes. Look!"

Some one had gathered them all together, as if

meaning to carry them off, and had then thought better of it, for they lay in a heap in one place.

"And here's blood!" said Will.

If it was the woman—and we did not doubt it—she had rested for a while with her back against the rock wall, for there was a blood-smear exactly where the bandage on her right arm would have touched. There was a great splash of blood, too, on the threshold of the cave, scarcely yet dry, as if she had left the place in a hurry when she heard our approach.

We were growing famished and first we went to the water-hole to drink. She had been there ahead of us. The water was tinged where she had washed her wound.

"Maybe I'll drink here about this time to-morrow," said Will, "provided we find no other drinking-hole meanwhile!"

I feeling the same about it, we chose small slips of granite to suck and took up the trail there and then; not troubling very much about concealment, because we argued that in spite of increasing hunger our strength must be greater than hers with that wound, and pursuit would wear her down.

"She has a mate somewhere," I said. "Else why did she take two blankets?"

"A man would have taken all three," said Will. "She took what she needed. I'll bet you she's wearing 'em both! Come on—I see the way she went—look! Quick, man! There goes the tail end of a blanket over that ridge!"

She was going like the wind and we hunted her like clodhoppers, stumbling and clattering over rocks that she took in her stride. But washing her wound had not stanched the bleeding, nor did the blankets altogether soak up the flow, for we kept-finding crimson traces that made it comparatively easy to follow her line, although we did not catch sight of her again.

We had overestimated our strength and under-rated hers. At the end of an hour we lay panting, with swimming eyes, and tried to nerve ourselves to climb a hillside that was already glimmering in heat strong enough to cook by and that owned as far as eye could measure not one level plane to stand on.

At it we went, after a five minute respite and after twenty minutes of sickening effort we lay down again, with a view beneath us of almost all the island. One thing and one only gladdened our eyes—water, sweet, splashing, unmistakable, cascading from a split crag half a mile in front.

With that sole exception—for we could not yet see the solitary tree that flourished with its roots deep down in crevices into which the water had carried infinitely tiny particles of food for it for centuries—the whole panorama was one of hideous battlements—naked, hot rocks, blue in the sunlight—raw, grim valleys leading nowhere, looking like the scars left by fighting Titans—and all around in dim, hazy obscurity, the merciless sea. Away in the distance to the right, through a gap between two horrid crags, we could see surf plunging sky-high.

"If Barabbas ever lived in this place," Will murmured, "jail must have looked like heaven to him! Even a Jerusalem jail!"

There was only one way the woman could have taken—along a narrow ridge like the working edge of a twisted saw that led to another pile of granite lumps like the one we lay on. But we had given up the thought of chasing her. The sight of water falling like a spray of diamonds drove every other consideration out of mind. The one remaining thing worth while was to lie and gather strength to reach the precious stuff.

But we were weaker than we knew. Reaction at the sight of what we needed sickened us, and for an hour it would have been impossible to crawl a dozen yards. So we lay and cursed the sun that beat down on our backs, turning this and that way like tortured martyrs on a grid, only swearing as the martyrs are said never to have done.

There was not a square foot of shadow within reach. Every boulder seemed to be either a wedge or a cone with its smallest angle uppermost. The crevices, all open to the sun, took in the heat, redoubled it and cast it forth again to tremble and shimmer in hot tides.

"So this is hell!" said Will, trying to force humor where there was none, and failing bravely. The remark was too true to draw a smile.

"There's another man in it!" said I after a short while. "D'you suppose that's the devil walking up the valley?"

The heat played tricks with our eyes, so that we could see pretty clearly one minute and not at all the next. But the new excitement had the effect of banishing fatigue. First one of us, then the other, made out the figure of a man clad in khaki, with a battered green helmet, and a rifle slung behind his shoulder, walking pretty leisurely along the ravine below us in our direction.

He disappeared at intervals behind tumbled rocks but was taking no precautions to conceal himself. Every now and then we could hear his foot-fall as distinctly as a hammer-stroke.

WE COULD see he was a ragged-bearded man; but that was to be expected in such a place. He was broad-shouldered, too, and powerfully built, although to judge his height from that angle was impossible. There were a dozen or more dark blots within sight that looked like cave-mouths, out of any one of which he might have come; but he was leaving the cascade of water behind him and his object was simply unguessable in walking in that heat along a comfortless ravine-bottom leading nowhere.

"Shout to him!" said I, for my own throat was too parched.

For one wild moment I thought he was Fred. Then I remembered that all the rifles must have gone down with the ship and that Fred's neat beard could not have grown to that length in two days. Will shook his head.

"Remember the woman!" he said. "She was afraid of some one. Some one wounded her!"

Then, for the first time since we reached that dreadful place, there flashed across my memory the story the mandarin had told at Bill's. This might be Prof. Grogan Guthrie, still here in spite of his cablegram. Or it might be the German professor, said to have inoculated young Charles Dent against disease—the strange disease that killed him.

And while we watched and wondered just what was best to do it became evident that some one else saw the man. A rock as big as the one that had missed Will so narrowly went hurtling out from behind a boulder on the side of the ravine and broke in pieces just behind him.

He had his rifle free in a second and sent a bullet back by way of answer. I caught a momentary glimpse of one of our stolen blankets fluttering. So did he, for he sent three shots straight at it. And then we heard again that hideous, grief-laden cry that had made our marrow creep in the night. In the silence that followed it we heard the man laugh. The blanket fluttered again, and again he fired at it.

"Here's where I interfere!" said Will.

"She attacked first," said I; not that I really believed that, but I wanted to gain time and think.

"Maybe she had cause," he answered.

"She pelted us with a rock that would have killed a bullock," I argued. "You saw her pelt him. I don't see what claim she has on our help."

I would not have said that if I had believed for a second that Will would listen to it; but I had a sort of delirious idea that time was the thing to gain—time—time.

"I'll not see murder done," he answered. "He'll have to let me try the case if he wants my leave to shoot that woman. Hey there! Hello there! Below there! Hey!"

The man with the rifle jumped as if something had hit him and Will stood up to let him see who challenged.

"Cover him with your pistol!" he said. "He's almost out of range, but fire if he fires at me!"

The man drew a bead on Will so suddenly and fired so instantly that the bullet struck the rock between us sooner than Will could duck. My own answering pistol bullet went utterly wild but the noise of it brought him to his senses. He set the butt of his rifle down and waved his hand.

Instantly then, in proof that the woman was still on the war-path and not so injured that she could not seize swift advantage, another lump of rock went whizzing down at him, and he only jumped away in the nick of time to avoid it. He raised his rifle to reply.

"Stop that!" Will roared. "Fire, and I fire on you!"

The man put up his rifle again. Promptly another stone came spinning down at him, heavier and as accurately aimed. That was too much for him. He fired three answering shots. Promptly Will made good his own threat and fired twice with his pistol, coming so near the target that I saw a chip fly within two feet of the man. So he lowered the butt of the rifle again and shouted something gutturally that we could not catch.

Plainly the woman was in no mood for any armistice. Her ammunition was limitless. She began to rain down rocks on him so fast and with such sure aim that he had to dodge incessantly.

"Run for cover, you fool!" yelled Will, standing up again. "Come up here out of reach! If you fire at her I'll shoot you sure as ——!"

Whether the man understood all that or not, he did start to clamber up the difficult slope toward us; and the first few yards put so many boulders between him and the woman that he was out of her range. But then he changed his mind suddenly, turned and ran back the way he had come, she getting in four more shots at him as he passed her.

"Will you bet with me which is the guilty one?" asked Will.

VI

PURSUIT OF neither the man nor the woman tempted us one particle. Our one obsession was the water cascading half-a-mile away and we climbed down toward it, reckless of having made enough noise with our pistols to draw the attention of all the inhabitants the island might contain.

The man with the rifle might turn on his tracks and stalk the pair of us for all we cared. Our tongues were swelling. Sight of the water in the distance robbed us of all desire except that one, to drink. Death would have been a cheap price to pay for it.

I remembered, as we scrambled down-hill and stumbled along the bottom of the boulder-strewn ravine, that every one who had mentioned Barabbas Island had mentioned fierce inhabitants. A sort of fatalistic resignation settled on me, born of the thought that Grace Vandam and Monty and the rest of our party had been murdered. I supposed our turn was next and did not care, provided I could reach the water and die wet, not parched.

So we heard nothing except the music of the sparkling, tumbling stream that was too far away to be heard really, and the way to it seemed down a very valley of fire, growing longer instead of shorter as we hurried. We each fell a dozen times, tearing our clothes and bruising ourselves so badly that later, when we had drunk and sanity returned, each thought the other had been fighting.

When we reached it at last we were like men in a dream, but we had learned enough self-control, adventuring up and down the earth, not to drink too deeply even in that first frenzy of quenching thirst so that within ten minutes of the touch of water to our lips we were ourselves again, weak from hunger now, but masters of our own free will and able to laugh at the scarecrow figure each cut.

Then we saw the tree and our tired eyes yearned to it. It was the only spot of green, the only touch of friendliness and peace, in all that island—a great, gnarled monstrous thing, with roots like prehistoric Titan snakes and only a few dull olive leaves among the twisted black branches. It bore fruit, though, and we walked unsteadily nearer to discover what kind, rubbing sun-tortured eyes and refusing to believe them.

The tree stood in the midst of a cup-like amphitheater about three hundred yards across and we came right under it before we yielded to the evidence and knew those bleached, awkwardly poised things on the up-turned ends of branches were human skulls. But there was no doubt of it then, for the rocks underneath were littered with human bones and other broken skulls that had fallen like apples in a wind-blow.

"Where did all these guys live?" demanded Will.

"Caves," I suggested.

"They can't have killed one another and hung one another's bones to dry! Where are the murderers?"

"That's easy!" I said. "Where would you and I be if we had overcome our enemies on such an island? We'd be gone as fast as boats could take us! Nobody could live here permanently. What could they eat?"

"That's easier," he answered. "Fish. See the bones. There has been a regular shore lunch under the tree, either before the murder fest or else by way of celebration afterward! Look—clam-shells—shark bones—all kinds o' fish-bones—and here are date-stones—lots of 'em scattered all over the place. Dates, fish and water—an islander in these parts would thrive on that diet. Dates are imported, of course. We've no proof whatever that the people have gone."

I squinted up at the skulls on the tree and took leave to doubt that. Circumstantial proof can never hold a candle to intuition; I could not escape from the thought that the fish had been eaten by the owners of those skulls before they died.

"There's a rib-bone here," I said, "with a bullet mushroomed on it from the inside! It must have passed clear through the body and broken the far rib before it stopped."

Then Will found another flattened piece of lead between two fractured vertebra and I found a skull with a hole in it and a mushroom of lead inside.

"Whoever did the job comes here to drink," said Will. "Stands to reason he must if he's on the island. Even if there are other springs, or rain pools, sooner or later he'll come here. If I weren't so all-fired hungry I'd wait."

"No need to wait long," I answered. "Duck, man—quick! Here comes a native!"

The easiest thing to do anywhere on that island was to hide at a moment's notice. We dropped where we stood between the rocks and tree-roots, within twenty feet of a shallow hollow where the water from the cascade formed a pool between us and the man who was coming warily toward us. It was a marvel that he had not seen us, but by good luck the trunk of the tree had partly concealed us and his own fear did the rest, for he looked behind him oftener than before.

It seemed to me there was something familiar about him, but eyesight was playing strange tricks that day. He had a pan in his hinds, and when he struck it inadvertently against a rock he jumped at the sound as if frightened out of his senses. For a minute after that he stood stock still, facing back the way he came, as if in two minds whether to return empty-handed or go forward.

At last, however, he recovered courage and came and dipped up water, washing the pan pretty carefully and then himself. Then he prayed, going through all the Moslem ritual, and after that he filled the pan again and started back with it, balancing it carefully.

"Osman!" Will called after him then. "Oh, Osman bin Omar!"

It was certainly he, and equally certainly the pan was something he had never brought ashore with him. But the sound of a friend's voice had the opposite effect to that intended. He spilt the water and ran for dear life, glancing back in terror over his shoulder and running the harder when he saw us standing erect among the tree roots.

"He fancies we're ghosts," said I.

"So we shall be, unless we eat soon!" Will answered. "That old rascal has had a bellyfull. He'll show me where he got it or I'll know why! Come on!"

So we left the tree with its gruesome fruit behind us and set off in pursuit, reckless again of the man with the rifle, or the woman with her well-aimed lumps of rock. And because appetite was whip and spur and thirst no longer made us imbecile, we kept him in view and were hard on his heels when he dodged down a narrow defile and disappeared.

WE WENT down the defile after him like terriers after a rat—up over a jumble of rocks where we heard his metal pan banging—and brought up short at a small, dark cave-mouth that nobody less than a madman would have dared charge into without first taking precautions. The opening was less than half a man's height and the entrance sloped at an angle of forty-five.

But we made sure there was another opening somewhere, because it was not quite dark inside; and when we withdrew a little way and looked up we saw smoke coming in a very thin column from a crevice. We had started to climb to investigate that when I heard voices.

So Will kept watch with his pistol cocked and pointed, while I crouched beside the mouth of the cave to listen.

"They're talking English!" I whispered presently.

And then neither he nor I could hold ourselves in a second longer. We both yelled together:

"Monty! Oh, Monty! Fred, you old skate, come out and show yourself! Good lord, Didums—come out and show us where some food is! Hey, below there! Come out! Come out!"

But there was no answer, and when I listened again I could hear nothing. After we had waited a minute or two Will chose a good-sized stone and hurled it through the opening, only to discover that the passage turned sharply ten or twelve feet down, presenting a blank wall to bullets, stones or any other missiles.

"All right!" he said. "What shields them shields me. I'm going down!"

I tried to dissuade him, for that was sheer recklessness, but he shook my hand off.

"I tell you I'm going to eat real eats within the hour or pick a fight!" he answered. "I'm in no waiting mood!"

Nor was he in a mood to take things leisurely. He went through that opening feet first with a run and a jump, and I heard his feet strike hard against the rock where the passage turned. I could think of nothing whatever for me to do but to follow him, but I lacked his skill in sliding bases and in similar imitations of the elusive eel that boys learn at school in America; he was out of sight before my own heels hit the rock more gently.

When I entered the cave, which was really not dark inside at all, he was sitting on Osman bin Omar. Another man, whom I did not know from

Adam, was sitting up on a bed of dried seaweed, staring in speechless fear.

Light came in from three directions. The roof of the cave appeared to be formed by two enormous rocks caught together in the jaws of a hole. The chinks between the rocks served for light and air holes, although not nearly so efficiently for letting out the smoke, clouds of which coiled round and round and made my eyes smart.

There was a pretty big pile of driftwood in a corner, but the fire was of economical proportions, laid on a flat stone in the middle of the cave.

The only other furniture noticeable at first was a numerous collection of empty tin cans in the comer opposite the driftwood-pile, which gave the cave an air of dump-heap melancholy. Both Will and I stared at the empty cans with sour distaste. Something about our appearance seemed to reassure the man on the seaweed bed at last.

"I have to keep a fire smoking, you see, or they would bring too many flies," he said apologetically in a weak voice. "Yet I am always in fear that he will see the smoke."

"Why not throw them outside, then?" suggested Will, getting off Osman at last.

"Because then he would see the cans and that would be certainly fatal! Since he captured my rifle my one hope lies in concealment. How did you discover me?"

Osman answered that question.

"I go for water. You —— fool sending me in —— daylight! —— man see me! Running —— fast, but he catch!"

The old sea-rover did not seem to bear the least resentment on account of Will's rough handling, although he could scarcely breathe yet.

"Where are the others?" Will asked him. "Where are Miss Vandam—Mrs. Ellis—Lord Montdidier—Mr. Oakes—and the five sailors?"

"Damfiknowathing!" answered Osman, especially adept at concertina words when he wanted to express the unlimited negative.

The man on the seaweed bed forced himself on to his knees with a motion of extreme excitement. His hair was long and his beard so I straggly and ill-kempt that he resembled a scarecrow. His clothes bore out the resemblance. Our beards, too, had a few days' growth and our clothes were torn, but we were immaculate dudes compared to him.

"Do you mean to tell me you are of that party?" he demanded. "Do you mean to tell me you came here on the yacht, in spite of the cablegram I received about you from Cape Town?"

"Who are you?" demanded Will, by way of retort courteous.

"My name is Prof. Grogan Guthrie!"

Will whistled.

"Is the yacht wrecked?" demanded Guthrie.

"Not that I know of," Will answered. "But your larder will be, professor, unless I and my friend here eat eats right soon! We're famishing!"

"You'll find food under that flat stone," said Guthrie.

We both hurried at once to lift it. Underneath was a coffin-shaped space, rather shallow and narrow, but long, very nearly filled with cans of soup and bully beef and jam and all the other makeshifts for a square meal that travelers have to digest. There was a kettle in there, too, and we took two cans of soup because we could prepare that quickest.

"Ah—er—I hope you appreciate—ah—I—er—carried all that stuff two or three at a time on hands and knees! You—ah—distinctly owe your dinner to—ah—my patience and resource!"

"Obligation placed on record hereby," said Will, opening both cans with his pocket-knife, cutting the metal in quick, firm strokes toward him, as whittlers cut wood. "Tell us about yourself, prof. You don't look thrifty!"

He emptied both cans into the kettle and a wondrous savory smell that was able to suggest white napkins, silver cutlery, music and all the trimmings began to pervade the cave. Personally, I wished he would not invite the man to talk about himself until the infinitely more important food had been discussed. But Will seemed to take delight in tantalizing both himself and me.

"ABOUT MYSELF?" said Guthrie. "Ah—well—you see—it is obvious—I am sick. I doubt my chance of recovery. I have a disease. I permitted that blackguard German to inoculate me. This man—you say his name is Osman?—wandering about in search of water, so he said, discovered me in a fainting condition by the tree where the skulls are, near the—ah—waterfall. We made a bargain there and then. He brings the water. I feed him while the food lasts. Judging by his appetite, it will not last very long! He—ah—assisted me to reach the cave again and I—ah—very much doubt that I shall—ah—ever leave it! The disease has hold of me. In time I shall fall apart!"

"You're cheerful, aren't you!" Will murmured, stirring the soup with the blade of his pocket-knife and secretly enjoying my impatience.

"No, my friend, I am the reverse of cheerful."

"You don't mean it!" said Will. "Tell us about the German?"

"Curse him! What can I tell of him? Who would believe?"

"I'm not one of those incredulous guys," said Will. "I can believe 'most anything of a German, professor. S'pose you out with it?"

"Suppose you out with that soup," said I. "It's hot enough!"

There seemed to be no plates, but Will had his folding drinking-cup and we took turn about with that, the professor talking while we ate.

"If I were well," he said, "I would never yield to you—never! The secret of this island is rightly mine. You have no business here. If the rest of your party has come to grief trying to make a surreptitious visit without my permission, I am not sorry for them! It serves them right! Understand that, please—first, last, and all the time!"

"Memo made of it," said Will, swallowing hot soup.

"The Chinaman in Alexandria—Hi Ying Lang is his rapscallion name, the yellow rascal!—gave the secret first of all to me, and mine it is! This German devil Schindler was here first, but he is an outrageous criminal and beneath consideration morally, although a legion in himself when it comes to ousting him, as I daresay you will find! Such a conscienceless hellion as he has no rights of any kind—unless death by the shortest route is a right. If you kill him you will earn my gratitude. Unless you kill him he will kill you!"

"Some one else might get him first," suggested Will, wiping his mouth with the back of his hand.

"No!" said Guthrie, his eyes blazing. "No, no, no! He has killed every one else! He has killed all the islanders!"

"I know of one he hasn't got yet," Will answered.

"Eh? Eh? You mean to say that wretched woman is still on the prowl? Eh? How does she do it? How in the lord's name does she do it? She was wife of the chief of the island. Most of them he inoculated with his serum. All those died. He told them—as he told me and poor Charles Dent before me—that the serum would protect them against the low malaria that haunts the place. Those who would not take his serum he set against one another, causing a sort of civil war. Whenever either side could catch a prisoner or kill a man, they set his head on the tree. There's only one tree on the island. They worship it in some pagan fashion. Both sides used it to hang trophies on, going there in the night so that the enemy could see the new horror at break of day. Sometimes both sides would hang up a new head during the same night. In that way more than fifty islanders met their death."

"How many were there to start with?" I asked.

"I am not sure. I think the population varied. I think there was a lot of travel to and fro, especially to get wives from the mainland, until the island got such a bad name."

"Who gave it a bad name?"

"He did—Schindler! He intended that immigration should stop until he could get his schemes developed. If you've done with that kettle, please give it to the man you call Osman to take away and wash before it attracts the ants; they came and drove me out of the cave once and I can't afford to be rendered homeless in my condition!"

Will gave the kettle to Osman, who went outside with it. Then he put the empty soup can in the flames to burn out all traces of anything ants could eat. Grogan Guthrie cleared his throat. Although he obviously resented our being there he seemed to appreciate the luxury of unbosoming his story.

"When I came there were less than a hundred islanders, though there had been many more."

"For the land's sake, where did they live?" demanded Will.

"In caves. Caves like this one, and better than this. There are many. The less-than-a-hundred remaining islanders were troublesome. I came in a sailing-boat and landed with six men. Schindler pretended to welcome me, saying I could help him with the native problem. We lived in a large cave together. One of my men became sick very soon. He said something bit him in the night, and he certainly had a nasty place on his arm, but Schindler said it was the malaria and persuaded me to be inoculated. I have never been well since. It was quite a while before the poison he put into me really took hold, but I felt ill from the first, and he watched me with the delight of a connoisseur, Oh, that man is a fiend incarnate!"

"Where did he get his serum from?" I asked.

"God knows! I have suspected him of preparing it on the island from the carcases of fish. It wash shortly after I came that he brought about the civil war among the islanders who refused to be inoculated. I rather approved at first. The islanders were a fierce and implacable breed, extremely proud, wholly without gratitude and prone to treachery. I thought of the ancient Roman maxim—*divide et impera.* But when I saw how he played fast and loose, first with one side and then the other, I remonstrated. I told him a white man can't play the dark man's game and still claim the white man's privileges."

"How did he take the advice?"

"**I WILL** tell. He pretended to see the point. He pretended to agree with me and to be mortified by his own impropriety. He promised to make peace between the contending parties. That woman—then the chief's wife—was the intermediary. I don't know I'm sure what she thought she saw in him, but the fact is that there was an affair between them of which the chief knew nothing.

"She used to come and see him in the dead of night, and one night he persuaded her to talk her husband into calling a meeting between both parties for the purpose of eating a banquet of fish under the tree—the time-honored way of cementing an agreement.

"Negotiations took a day or two. At last a day was agreed on. Both sides caught enormous quantities of fish and carried them to the tree. And if I told you what took place there you would not believe me."

"If I don't I'll tell you," said Will, "so go ahead!"

"It doesn't matter whether or not you believe me! I shall be—ah—going soon to a Tribunal where truth is sifted from the lies. I prefer to tell, but it doesn't in the least matter whether you believe. This happened: that cursed villain Schindler stole my two guns and my pistol, with the ammunition. He loaded them, and loaded his own, and went and hid in a place where he had command of all the space around the tree.

"With my two guns and his three, and the two pistols, I have calculated that he had fifty shots ready to fire without reloading. He had more cartridges in their clips where he could reach them instantly. And he is what you call a dead shot. That is to say, he never misses at close range when the light is good."

"I've seen him miss," said Will. "He missed me for one."

"Ah! That may be, of course. Let us hope his nerve is going. He missed nothing on that day, though. He did not shoot them all, of course, for some ran, but most of them were so taken by surprise that they stood up to be slain! I did not see it. I was ill. But he came back and told me a wild story about their attacking him, and his brave fight in self-defense. I might have believed it, but one of my four fellows—an Egyptian *fellah*—a great good-natured oaf—came in and told me the truth. He overheard and promptly shot the man. Then he shot my three remaining servants and I think he would have shot me if he had not been so sure that I was dying. He preferred to see me die by disease."

"How long ago was that?" asked Will.

"About three weeks. He took to hunting the men and women who had escaped him, driving them up into the higher crags like goats and potting them at long range. They used to throw rocks at him. Once the woman came in the night, pretending to resume the old relation, and tried to murder him. Her scream when he awoke in time and turned on her is something I shall never forget. He told me next evening that he had wounded her at long range and that he expected her to die from loss of blood. But I have seen her once or twice since then myself."

"What were you doing all this time?" I asked.

"Living in the same cave with him. I did not dare pull out before I was ready. I needed to provision this cave, and I made use of the hours when he was hunting to crawl here with the canned food, and that kettle, and this seaweed for my bed. Ever since I came to the island he had been living off my provisions."

"Why on earth—"

"I will tell that too. He has discovered the secret of this island. There is a cave with God knows what in it—probably wealth enough to satisfy the dreams even of his avarice, to say nothing of antiquities too precious to imagine. He stored his own provisions in that cave long ago. When I came he was afraid to visit the cave, even in the dead of night, lest I or my men follow him and learn the secret.

"So we had to tell me a cock-and-bull story about a relief ship he expects before long. He expects no relief ship. His purpose is to make himself sole possessor of the secret and then to exploit it. I don't doubt he feels now that he has murdered so many people that he must finish the gruesome business before he dares to take the next step!"

"Did "you contrive to remove all the provisions?" I asked.

"No. How could I? Unless I had left a lot of cans carefully arranged so as to make a good showing he would have suspected instantly and that would have been the end of me! On the last day I loaded myself almost to the breaking point, but I left behind even then sufficient to keep him in three meals a day for a number of days. Unless he has been very, careful with the food—and that would not be like him; he is wasteful of whatever is not his—he should be very short by this time. About now he should begin to be thinking of his own hidden supplies. But I don't think he will visit them, unless absolutely obliged, before he believes me dead.

"He has been stalking me of late. He nearly got me one day when I went to drink. We played puss-in-the-corner among the rocks all the rest of that afternoon and evening. I dared return here only after dark, nearly dead with exhaustion. I was beginning to lose heart when this man Osman came and assured me he was sole survivor of a shipwreck. I named him Joe and let him go for water after that! Believe me, I was glad to have him!"

Will sat still for a long time, scratching with his finger in the ashes on the cave floor. Grogan Guthrie, apparently exhausted, dropped back on the seaweed and lay still. Osman bin Omar came back with the washed-out kettle and a look of having been fearfully afraid again. At last Will delivered judgment.

"Well," he said, "I'm not going to believe your unsupported word. I don't like you. You've acted like a pig from the first about this hell-hole of an island. You'd be welcome to it for all of me, but I've got friends and I don't believe they're dead yet. Now—supposing what you say is all true—supposing I should meet up with this German professor guy, and him and me differed, and he 'et' crow—what about the cave with the treasure and the antiquities? Whose d'you claim they'd be?"

Grogan Guthrie sat up again and blinked. He seemed no less inclined than Will to side-step that issue.

"I do not—ah—see," he said, "that any set of circumstances could be held to change your condition. You are robbers! You have no earthly right here! I am not in a position to prevent you, that is all!"

WILL'S STARE and attitude betrayed interest devoid of all irritation or resentment.

"Tell us your private opinion," he said, "of the man who sent a lying, cablegram to Cape Town."

"Meaning me?" suggested Guthrie. "I sent no cablegram at all."

"Who did, then?"

"I suspect my lawyer had some communication with you. I told the man to take any step likely to balk your intentions."

"And you think that what he did does not reflect on you?"

"Certainly not! Any step was legitimate in dealing with men who refused to respect my prior claims. What law could I appeal to? There are no courts here. I had tried appealing to Lord Montdidier's sense of honor but discovered that was altogether lacking. So I instructed my lawyer to find some way of checkmating you. I imagine he sent you a cablegram. I saw the untruthful reply to it."

Will rested his chin between both hands and thought.

"You can't horsewhip a man as sick as he is," I said.

"Horsewhip him?" he answered. "Can't we save him alive and take him a tour through the States in vaudeville? I'd like my country to know what humor is! Osman," he continued, "will you wait here and watch this heavenly-minded gent until we two come back? He'll bear watching mighty close, mind! If he leaves the cave, follow him. I'd like an exact account of every move he makes."

"All right," answered Osman. "Keep —— eye peel."

With that highly satisfactory arrangement made to guard our rear we wasted no further time but crawled out of the low opening and set off in search of traces of our friends. We felt enormously better after the soup; but strangely enough the taste of physical ease, small though it had been, had increased our dread of the outer savagery. The heat and glare seemed to smite us more than ever and the bruises we had won in scrambling over rocks reasserted themselves until the torture was almost unbearable.

Will conceived the idea that a cold bath might alleviate the pain; so, when we had taken very careful bearings of the cave—whose smoke was invisible in the simmering atmosphere the moment we left it twenty yards behind—we started off for the cataract.

But whereas on our way to the cave we were reckless of danger, we found that since we had established even such a graceless substitute for a home as Grogan Guthrie's cave we were inclined to be much too cautious. We could hardly force-ourselves forward without elaborate preliminary scouting.

Another view of the skulls and bones did nothing to rearouse courage. We washed in turn, the other standing guard, and wished sincerely five minutes later that we had done nothing of the kind; for the sun seemed to exert more strength than ever after that, and although the first evaporation of the wet skin through our clothing cooled us the reaction almost immediately afterward was overwhelming. Instead of pressing forward with strength renewed we took cover on a ledge under an over-jutting rock that gave us a considerable view while protecting us from the sun when we hugged the wall closely enough.

"I guess like a poker-player," said Will. "I'm doing it all the time. What I know don't keep me awake, but what the other fellow knows and I don't makes me curious. I'm figuring on where that secret cave can be. S'posing what that Guthrie says has ten cents worth o' truth in it, then the German professor guy ought to be running short of canned eats. Get me?"

"So far; but I don't see where it leads."

"His violent exercise, tramping these gosh-awful rocks and hunting folk—who must hold life mighty precious to cling to it in this place—folk able to keep him hustling, ought to have given him an appetite, supposing such a bloodthirsty gink has any human traits remaining. Get that?"

"Yes."

"Let's suppose he has an appetite. Let's suppose a square meal of bully beef and canned tomatoes, with a piece of cheese and some pineapple, is more to him at the moment than discretion. He's thinking o' those private stores o' his. He's figuring he can maybe make the secret cave without Guthrie being any wiser, specially since he knows the man's sick and maybe isn't sure he's even alive any more. How about it? Do you see the point?"

"No."

"My! Aren't you astute! Suppose he's hungry—and thinking of the cave—and actually making for it when we first saw him. Suppose the reason he changed his mind and ran, after starting to climb up toward us, was that he didn't propose to give utter strangers a line on where the treasure is? Wouldn't you deduce that the entrance to his treasure cave is somewhere near where we stood when he fired at us and we fired back at him?"

"I've been thinking along a different line," I answered. "Do you remember—or were you saying your prayers with eyes shut?—that when Osman bin Omar turned the ship toward the island he seemed to be running for a sort of haven, protected by a curving arm of rock? We struck to the south of that arm, if I remember rightly. My idea is that we'd do well to explore in the direction of the haven. There may be anything there—might find our crowd there—they'd be likely to cling to the beach and eat fish."

"I'm for the cave, you're for the haven," said Will. "Let's match for it!"

I agreed to anything that would add a suspicion of the mildest possible sporting interest to a dilemma, either prong of which was hopeless, and we searched our pockets. Neither of us had a coin.

"Nothing to toss with! How shall we decide it?"

"Here!" said a gruff voice that frightened us nearly out of our sunburned skins. "I got a coin. I toss!"

OSMAN BIN OMAR'S turbaned head appeared around the rock and he favored us with one of his rare grins, more full of mischief than a boy's.

"You old scoundrel!" said Will. "You promised to keep an eye on the man in the cave."

"That —— man promise me fifty —— pound to come keep eye on you two! No more ship, fifty —— pound a heap o' money!"

"How do you know," I demanded, "that he isn't following the three of us?"

"I make —— sure!" he answered.

"How?"

"Tie um feet!"

"But what proof have you he'll give you the money?" asked Will.

Osman fumbled in his garments and produced a clean, crisp fifty-pound Bank of England note.

"He talk. Me take!" he answered grimly.

"Let's decide our question," I said. "Lend us the coin, Omar."

"You head—he tail—I toss," he stipulated.

"Not a bit of it," Will answered. "Give me the coin. You've a scheme of some sort up your sleeve. My friend can call and I'll do the tossing."

"He call heads," said Osman. "Heads—go look for —— cave!"

"Give me the coin then. I don't care which he chooses."

Reluctantly Osman unfolded a coin from his belt and passed it to Will, who spun it in the air without a glance at it. It rang on the rock heads uppermost. Osman reached out his sinewy hand to snatch it back, but something made Will suspicious. Not that there was anything suspicious in a man of Osman's caliber being nervous on account of his own money, but he tried too hard to look innocent, and Will picked up the coin too quickly for him. He turned it over, laughed and showed it to me.

It was the double-headed English penny with which the old rascal had beaten us out of the lawyer's fee in Bombay when we drew the contract.

Will gave it back to him with the air of a king bestowing a decoration on the field of battle.

"Why are you so anxious we should look for the cave?" he asked.

"—— man promise me hundred pound s'posing you find it and me tell him!"

Then I thought of a bright idea.

"Did you get the hundred yet?" I asked.

"Me tie urn legs. Me take!"

"I don't believe it. Show me!"

He fumbled, and produced a hundred-pound note, new and neatly folded like the other one.

"Will," I said triumphantly, "this old ruffian is honest according to a standard of his own. He wouldn't have taken that money if he hadn't more than a notion where the cave is!"

"Is that right, Osman?" Will demanded. "Do you know how to find the cave?"

"You —— bet I do!"

"Go ahead, then! Lead the way!"

"How much you —— give me?" he retorted.

"Not one —— cent, you pirate! I hold you to contract! You're to pilot us to the best of your ability to any place on earth we name! Lead on to the cave in question!"

"All right," said Osman bin Omar. "You pay me, —— fool; no pay me, all right!"

"Are you sure it's the right cave?" I asked. "How did you come to find it?"

Before answering he spat half-a-dozen times and looked cautiously about him, as if he thought the rocks had ears.

"Come ashore—hungry—look for grub—climb—walk—sit down. Man come with rifle—man see me—shoot—run —— quick—duck—hide—stop—look-see—man watch—me watch—me wonder what —— man shoot for—why he watch—what —— thing there he no want me to know about—me, —— eyes very good indeed—watch like ——. Soon see place in among stones he not wanting me to know about—wait a —— long time—byumby he go away—creep closer, —— careful, —— slow—take a look-see—dark place—me afraid—run away —— quick—man see me run—shoot—miss—so I take you there an' you learn whether I tell lies. I truthful feller."

After reeling off that Odyssey he grew impatient and started down the rocks without waiting for us.

"Very —— hot now," he called back. " —— man he keep quiet in shadow somewhere. Byumby getting cool, —— man coming out and look-see—catch um—shoot um—better you hurry!"

It sounded like good advice. If the murderer took any rest at all it was likely he would choose the hottest part of day for it. Will and I made haste to follow Osman, finding endurance easier now that we had a colored man to remind us of the white man's privilege. He suffered more than we, for his feet were bare and the hot rocks roasted them; but the desire to earn the hundred pounds he had taken in advance outweighed discomfort, or else, like ourselves—and it was just as likely—he was conscious of the color line and refused to sing small.

It was we who called a halt first. The man had a compass under that thick skull of his and never hesitated, until at last we yelled to him and threw ourselves down in the shadow of a boulder. Above us I recognized the crag on which we had stood when we saw the bearded German have his duel with the woman.

He beckoned to us, but we refused to move another yard until we had rested. Watching his impatient gestures, I saw beyond him. Up on a high crag, close beside the one I recognized, outlined against the brazen sky, I saw the woman again.

Osman did not see her. She was standing erect with our two blankets wrapped about her and held a large stone poised in both hands above her head. I nudged Will and he looked up. We both saw her hurl the stone—almost straight downward with all her might—and then stoop over to see what harm she had done. Then we heard two rifle-shots in quick succession. At the second she pitched forward silently and fell headlong out of sight.

"So he has got her at last!" we said both together.

And then a sight that was not horrible at all, but that made the hair on the back of my head rise by its total unexpectedness, changed the whole prospect in an instant.

A hand—freckled and adorned with curly, long, red hairs—not by any stretch of imagination to be mistaken for a colored man's or woman's—lifted itself cautiously above a rock not far from us and was followed by a khaki helmet.

Then, one eye at a time, the upper part of a sunburnt face appeared—then a hairy upper lip—then a smile—then the other hand—and Perkins, one of our five seamen I from the *Daisy,* hoisted himself to the tops of the rock, peered about him and lay flat.

"Psssst!"

HE NO more needed to call our attention than if he had been a serpent and we birds within his power, but he went through the form of it with the gusto of a boy playing a game.

"You're in the way, gents! You're lying on the very line the guy's supposed to take! Come out o' the way, please, or Miss Gracie'll raise Cain! We'll have it to do all over if you head him back!"

We beckoned Osman, who seemed horribly disappointed until he, too, caught sight of Perkins. Then his face wrinkled up into one vast grin and he followed us at top speed. Perkins led over a maze of tumbled rocks that were hotter than the fabled lid of Tophet, stopping at last on a square one that provided room for all of us to lie abreast—albeit not in shadow.

"Let yourselves be seen now," he advised. "His shooting's wild. He got the poor girl a minute ago, but she was a target nobody could miss, standing like that against the sky-line!"

"For the land's sake, explain!" said Will. "We're not mind-readers!"

"Oh, is this the first you've seen of our party? Well now! I made sure you'd met up wi' Miss Gracie earlier and she'd set you to driving. No? Mr. Monty took charge o' the drive at first, but—"

"Then is Lord Montdidier safe?"

"Yes, only we've taken to calling him Mr. Monty. So is Mr. Oakes and Mrs. Ellis and the rest of us. We all got safe ashore. We started first to look for you gents and this affair developed out of it. As I was saying, Mr. Monty had charge o' the drive at first, but then Miss Gracie, she got impatient and so-to-speak superseded him—not that he minded, he just laughed. We're after a man wi' a great beard and a rifle, who was hunting that poor bit of a girl in the mountains like she was a pantheress or something!"

"Tell us the plan," I said.

I was lying next him, with Will next to me straining to listen and Osman on the outside. Osman was not paying any attention to the talk.

"Well, sir, Miss Gracie, she's furious. We all got a sight of the poor girl close up and we tried to catch her, so's to tame her, I suppose. And we all saw the man wi' the long beard shoot at her. And in less than no time we was spread all around in a circle to round him up and bring him to book for his conduct—wi' strict orders from Miss Gracie not to hesitate to pistol him in case he proves obstreperous. She'll be glad you've come. Three extra, supposing you count the colored gent, will be a godsend to help out the line; we're all too few."

"But where have you been staying?"

"Didn't you know that, sir? Well, we doped it out—at least Miss Gracie and Mr. Monty and Mr. Fred did—that the cave we're staying in belongs to the guy with the gun that we're all after. We came on it the very first thing the morning after we got ashore. Mr. Fred was scouting for something to shoot—you know what a fine shot Mr. Fred is—and thought he recognised the marks where a man had clambered over the rocks with boots on. He followed the track and took a chance, being as fearless as they make 'em. Presently he came back and took us to the cave, and there was food in there—lots of it—and a great stone cistern full o' sweet water. But wait till you've seen it!

"The theory is that the man must be hungry and ought to be heading up about this time for his store o' provisions. We're keeping him on the run. We don't think he knows we've occupied his cave. The entrance to it is not much more than fifty feet from where you lay when I came on you!"

"D'you mean you want him in the cave?"

"That's the idea! Once he's in we figure we can

smoke him out again pretty well whenever we see fit. We've heard him do a lot o' shooting in the short while we've been on the island and we've seen more human bones than is right or proper. He has had a crack at more than one of us. Miss Gracie herself included, and we're minded to ask him what he has to say for himself face to face, in a manner of saying."

"Listen!" said Will.

"Look!" whispered Osman, whose eyes had been very busy all the time we talked.

There came a sound of something dragging among the rocks, and heavy breathing. Osman on the outside could see down lower than we. He grinned sardonically.

"Me tie um—good sailor-fashion!" he said in a low voice full of contentment.

The dragging sound continued, accompanied by the short, sharp panting of a human struggling with all his might. I crept a few inches further forward and peered over the edge of the rock. One look was enough and I drew back. Will did the same.

Underneath us was Grogan Guthrie, with his legs tied, dragging himself along by painful inches on his hands and knees toward the opening between two boulders, fifty yards beyond which Perkins had told us the cave mouth was.

"Got to give it to him," Will whispered. "He sure is some persistent sleuth!"

"Me follow you—him follow me—money mine all right!" announced Osman in a loud voice.

But Guthrie down below us was in no condition to hear anything. He was pressing forward with the obsession of a maniac, oblivious of all except his goal and too close to death to be concerned about bleeding knees and hands and elbows.

He had no hat. How the sun had failed to put an end to him was mystery. He must have taken the full force of it on the back of his head and his neck and back all along that hot, hard trail. No sane man could have done that. No sane man would have dared crawl forward into such a trap without taking any precaution.

He passed us and rounded a boulder out of sight. We heard him scuffling along until at last a laugh like a wild beast's, sounding hollow in the cave mouth, announced that he had reached his goal. The laugh died in a gurgle as he crawled into the cave.

Soon after that we heard shouts behind us and I thought I recognized Monty's voice. Then I was quite sure I heard Gracie's.

"There they are!" grinned Perkins.

"Hard behind him! They figure he'll take no chances on doubling back as long as they're so close and there's that hiding-hole in front of him! Gee, but they must have sweated to throw the line all around that way! I've had the best end of it lying here!"

A LITTLE while after that we heard another sound among the rocks below, swifter and more stealthy than the scuffling made by Guthrie. We held our breath and lay so flat along the rock that our eyes could barely see down over its rim. A moment later the man with the rifle came into view whom Will and I now knew for Schindler; more than six feet tall, he was broad and deep and wiry, with a brown beard down to His middle and the stride of a man who had stalked game all his life.

He seemed to make no effort to move quietly and yet made less noise with leather-soled feet than Guthrie had made on all-fours. He was coming fast, but his breathing was even and he did not once look behind him, as a hunted man might be expected to do.

It entered my head then that the one thing was to save Grogan Guthrie from the Nemesis hard on his heels. The mental picture of a sick man, with his legs tied, at the mercy of that bearded fiend was too strong for discretion or any other thought. I slipped down from the rock, only to find that Osman bin Omar had conceived some thought that produced an exactly similar effect, for he was running along ahead of me at a speed I could not hope to emulate.

He could not have done me a more signal service, though neither he nor I knew that at the minute. His bare feet made very little sound on the rock, so that when Schindler heard my heavier footfall and faced about at last to do more murder his enemy was nearer than he imagined, and the too ready rifle missed its aim.

The report of the rifle rattled among the boulders. I redoubled my efforts. Will raced after me—Perkins after him, all making noise enough by that time to awake the island's echoes. Emerging into an open space about thirty feet across, I saw a nearly round, black hole in the rock-wall. I did not realize at first that I saw it between Schindler's outstretched legs.

He was standing with his back to the hole, with Osman bin Omar gripped in both hands and swung up above his head to be brained like a puppy. He had dropped the rifle and had our old captain paralyzed and helpless in the grip of his iron fingers. As he saw me he raised Osman's body another inch higher, to dash him and smash him on the rock. Not knowing what I did, I spurted and ran in under, receiving the full force of Osman's descent on my back and shoulders.

The wonder was that it did not stun me. It knocked me down like a pole-axed bullock but left me with strength and sense enough to grip the German's legs, and haul on them with all my might. A second later I heard Will's battle-shout and then felt a huge spasm pass down the German's frame as both Will and Perkins closed with him. But that did not finish the fight by a long way.

He wrenched, tore himself almost loose and backed into the cave-mouth, we clinging to him like hounds to a hunted boar. In another moment we were rolling on the floor of a dark cavern, fighting like maniacs, the German bellowing with agony as Osman twisted lengths of the flowing beard about his wrist and hauled at it as if he were trying to up-anchor in a tide rip.

Never was such berserk fury as that German's since the day when the Viking pirates harried Britain's coasts and were brought to bay along some lonely beach. Again and again in the dark he flung us from him, only Osman managing to cling to the twisted beard. Over and over again we all went down together in a struggling confusion of arms and legs, to be borne to our feet again on top of the man's enormous strength and flung to all four quarters of the compass.

Again and again we closed—always excepting Osman, who clung to the beard and swung there like a bull-dog—and were received by fists that beat through the dark like flails. The weight of his blows was like the concussion of wooden clubs; his speed was unbelievable. I believe he would have killed the lot of us but for a sudden blaze of light that dazzled him. Somebody had come into the cave, struck a match, lit a lamp and was holding it now above his head.

Blinded by the glare, the German struck out a dozen times before he realized that the darkness had been his chief ally. Our eyes grew accustomed to the light as soon as his, and in a second more we should have mastered him. But he realized the situation in the nick of time and devoted all his colossal strength to one supreme spasm of fury. Even Osman was hurled on his face on the ground, a yard of brown beard in either hand, and we were thrown off like chips from a wheel.

He made a dash for the opening but that was darkened by more people hurrying in, one behind the other. He might have killed the first one with his enormous fist, but that would have left another, and another; and we were behind to have interfered with that performance. So he ran around the cave like a three-quarter-back at Rugby football carrying the ball over the opponents' goal-line, and took refuge in the shadows among a pile of boulders in the rear.

Then at last we turned to look at the man who held the lamp. It threw one side of him in shadow, but a man half-blind could have recognized Monty from the stature, attitude and general air of being perfectly at ease whatever the circumstances. It was the face that was unbelievable—the long mustache-ends drooping instead of waxed, and the dark beard, half-a-week old.

The spirit was unchanged, for his hand did not tremble and his smile was reassuring, but his clothes were as torn as ours; he was as dirty as we and as battered about the knees and elbows; he looked on the surface more like a tramp than an English nobleman. We were too out of breath to speak to him and he too bent on holding the lamp so that light would reach into the farthest corner of the cave to speak to us.

"Didums, you look like the devil!" said a cheery voice we all knew well, and Fred Oakes entered, getting up from all fours with the grace of a kangaroo.

He had his concertina with him, strapped across his shoulder like a knapsack. He took one long look at us, laughed and threw his arms out. In another second he was hugging us like the Scriptural she-bear, we cursing him for torturing our bruises.

Fred did not look particularly disheveled, but that was the advantage of always wearing a beard. Close inspection proved him to be as battered and torn as anybody else but possessed of a more boisterous spirit that conquered all appearances. He made as much fuss of Osman bin Omar as of us and was perfectly in his element, much happier there than in any place where conventions ruled.

Then Alice Ellis came in and was shyly pleased to see us. Then the four other New England seamen; Monty told two of them to stand close by the opening and prevent the German's escape. Last of all Gracie Vandam came in, hot but radiant, illustrating the everlasting miracle of how some women can look lovely where unlovely man collapses into disarray.

Her dress was torn and a bleeding bare knee showed through a gap in skirt and stocking. Convention had nothing whatever to do with the way her hair was disarranged. Her sun-helmet was broken. One of her hands was bleeding from chafing on the hot rocks. But nobody could have possibly mistaken her for anything but a lady, and a wealthy, well taught one at that.

"Boys!" she said, laughing at us by the light of Monty's lamp.

She took the lamp away from him and held it so as to see us better. Then she gave it back to him and discovered whiskered places that the German had not bruised with his huge fists and kissed us both.

"I'm more glad to see you than if you were gold and silver!"

I judged by that they had found no bullion in the cave.

Then, because she did not know just what to do about Osman but surely wished to express delight at seeing him, she took him by the hands and began to dance him round. Monty passed the lantern to a seaman and in a moment we had all joined hands and were dancing "Ring-around-the-rosy" in spite of wounds and weary feet.

Osman bin Omar seemed to imagine it was some sort of religious exercise and went at it sanctimoniously, until we all dropped from sheer exhaustion, except Monty, who found more lamps and lit them.

THEN WE all began to talk at once, all asking questions, and then more questions before the first were answered, until suddenly a new alarm reduced us to silence. A noise between a roar of rage and scream for help recalled our attention to the fact that an enemy was in the cave. The three seamen who were not on guard by the entrance raced all together to the far end of the cavern and we could see that they pounced on something.

A swift struggle followed among the shadows and they came back dragging something between them. One of the seamen had a hand to his eye, where a fist like a sledge-hammer had landed. The thing they dragged groaned and gasped.

"Grogan Guthrie!" said Will. "Grogan Guthrie with his legs still tied!"

We laid the dying man on the floor between us and made Osman bin Omar unlash the legs he had secured so cunningly, yet with so little avail.

"Don't let that incarnate fiend escape you!" Guthrie exploded, forcing himself into a sitting posture. "A minute ago he tried to murder me, because he knew I would tell you about him otherwise. Shoot him! He is like a rat in a trap now! Show him no mercy!"

Monty walked without hurry toward the corner whence the seamen had rescued Guthrie. Fred, who was the next least battered of us, followed. Monty told Fred to keep behind him; yet I noticed that he was not holding his pistol in his hand or prepared for a fight in any other way that I could see.

"Come out of that!" he ordered, directing his voice into the shadows. "If you don't, you shall be tied and dragged out feet first. If you come, you shall have decent treatment."

I had begun to suppose the German was a raving maniac, but the reason of Monty's quiet ultimatum appealed to him at once and he came striding out of the dark corner like an ogre in a picture out of a fairy book. It was only then that I realized what damage we had done him. His clothes were torn and he was a mass of bruises. One eye was altogether closed. His beard that Osman had thinned by handfuls was matted with blood from his nose; and for all the swaggering pride of strength expressed in his stride, he limped.

"That'll do," said Monty. "Stand there."

He stood in the midst of us, eying us balefully, scanning each of us in turn with unhurried deliberation.

"English—uh!—Americans—uh!—and one Asiatic—uh! None of you have jurisdiction over me!" he announced at last.

At that Guthrie recovered waning strength again, like a candle burning down into the socket.

"The fiend!" he screamed. "Whoever lets that fiend incarnate live another day shall answer to God for it! He has murdered three hundred men and women! He has murdered me! He murdered

Charles Dent! He tried to murder me again just now, as if once were not enough!"

"You shut up!" growled the German. "You hear what he says. The man is raving. He is mad."

"Counting Osman bin Omar and not counting the accuser, we are twelve men and women," said Monty grimly.

"What of it?" the German snorted.

"Have you heard of trial by jury?"

"Women on a jury!" the German answered with a laugh of such whole-souled scorn that I began again to believe him mad.

"I could not sit on the jury in any case," said Grace Vandam. "I am a witness against him. I saw him with my own eyes shoot that poor wild woman. I went to the foot of the crag and found her broken body, with a festered bullet wound in the arm and a newly made one in the breast. I, too, charge him with murder!"

"You saw her?" yelled the German. "You found her? Where is the ring, then? What have you done with the ring she was wearing?"

"Did you think I would strip a corpse?" asked Grace in amazement.

"You fool!" the prisoner thundered. "You double-dyed, sentimental fool! Go and get the ring—or let me go and get it! The setting is worth a Kaiser's ransom and the stone is a rose diamond as big as the Koh-i-noor! Oh, you double ——, blind asses! Don't you know a fortune when you see it?"

"I don't know just what administration this island falls under," said Monty, "but I am a privy councillor of England, and I dare assume responsibility under the circumstances. If the Indian Penal Code covers this territory, then I rely on the former authority granted me as official resident at Palanpur, which included powers of a first-class magistrate."

"I repudiate your alleged authority!"

"You'll have right of appeal, of course," said Monty blandly.

"Rot!" I said. "Let's kick the brute into the sea and let the sharks attend to him!"

The German eyed me with swift concern, but Monty ignored the remark.

"I impanel a jury," said Monty. "The greatest number obtainable at the time and place."

"I can tell these are Americans," the German retorted. "You have no authority over Americans nor have they any right to try me on British territory!"

Monty smiled.

"Several times," he answered, "I have seen United States Americans—missionaries, for instance—impaneled against their will on British juries. They have invariably given close attention to the case and a fair verdict, which I have seen upheld by the courts of appeal. Mrs. Ellis—will you kindly get the pens and paper we found in the box in the cave? I appoint you clerk."

"My pens and paper!" the German snorted.

"There shall be no compulsory panel on this occasion," said Monty. "Any one unwilling to serve on the jury may leave the court."

No one moved or objected.

"Very well, then. Fred, you're foreman. You and Will, and you five seamen, raise your right hands and swear to give a true and honest verdict in this case according to the evidence."

We did as ordered, he making sure we each spoke.

"Very well, then. Write down the names of the jurymen, Mrs. Ellis."

VII

THE TRIAL would have gone on there and then, had not Guthrie, our most important witness, been seized with a fainting spell.

"Can't we do without his evidence?" said I.

"No," said Monty sternly. "Circumstances oblige us to live on this island, for all we know for the rest of our lives, and we find this person already in occupation. But no law of God or man can compel us to tolerate a murderer in our midst. Our plain duty is to arrive at the facts and then to do justice in the name of the law that we all agree to honor."

There was nothing to do under the circumstances but to adjourn. Fred, as foreman, suggested an interval for lunch, and that was agreed to. Grace Vandam went and cooked canned meat and vegetables for all of us over a fire in the corner.

"That's all gammon about staying here all our lives!" she asserted. "You'll all see the *Daisy* in the offing before long!"

"I heard you tell Captain McGraw to take her back to New York," said I.

"D'you think he'll obey me?" she asked with an air of surprise. "That man doesn't believe a woman has the right to sign her own check, let alone direct a yacht's destinies. He'll elect to go to New York through the Suez Canal and turn aside to see what has happened here or my name is Jezebel!"

That being the most hopeful opinion any one had voiced yet and its accuracy seeming fairly likely on reflection, Osman bin Omar was appointed a committee of one, to choose himself a lookout post and to occupy it at fixed, short intervals. Then Fred took Will and me to look at the treasures the cave contained and, seeing us so occupied, the German flew into a new passion.

"What do you fools know of such things? Leave them alone! Don't touch them!"

There were four seamen guarding him or he would have flung himself at us and put up another fight.

"I was here first! I braved the islanders single-handed! I made myself king of them in all but name! How dare you late-comers have the insolence to take my booty away? —— you, put those down! Did you have the hardihood to make love to a savage chief's lawful wife and so win this secret? No! Then put those treasures down! You skulking thieves! Have you labored for years on this hell of an island, with only one end in view? No! You came late, by an accident! Then do justice, that you brag about, and go away and leave my treasures to me! Those are things whose worth such fools as you aren't able to imagine! Put them down, I say!"

His language became so abominable that Monty threatened to have him trussed up and laid on a rock in the sun to wait until Guthrie should recover consciousness. The threat of the physical discomfort did not seem to disturb him but he suffered at the thought of what we might do to the treasures in his absence and kept his language for a while within the confines of common decency.

Candidly, neither Will nor I was able to appraise the value of the treasure at all. There was a stone chest nearly full of manuscripts, written in strange characters on parchments so ancient that they cracked if they were touched.

There was one brass box of jewelry that looked rather crude to me, for the stones had lost long ago whatever sheen and brilliancy they once had. Then there was a case full of ancient weapons and the stone water-cistern that Monty vowed was priceless but that could not possibly be removed from the cave by any means at our disposal.

But the treasure of treasures—the thing that made the German curse and swear and clench his fists whenever one of us touched it—was a model of a building about two feet by three, made of gold and silver and so heavy I could scarcely move it. It was doubtless as old as the manuscripts in the stone chest, for it bore the marks of age—of knocks made during transportation, and the stains of time.

"Contemporary model of the Temple at Jerusalem," said Fred.

"How in the world was it preserved?" I wondered, as Will and I stooped to examine the wonderful details.

"Maybe the islanders worshiped it," said Fred. "Don't you suppose that Barabbas may have seen the value of religion to hold his followers together and that perhaps he brought this model back from one of his raiding trips with that idea? They might easily miss the real meaning of it; within two or three generations respect for the symbol would degenerate into idol worship. The existence of that thing would account then for such a devil of an island continuing to be inhabited; they'd come to associate the place with the thing. But think what the antiquarians are going to say about it!"

The thing was perfect. Even the costumes of the miniature priests who stood on the steps were worked out in minutest detail. We set a lamp near and examined it until Guthrie began to recover. Then he, too, demanded to see the prize that had cost him his life in a vain effort to obtain. We helped him close to it, and he pawed it with trembling fingers; but he seemed to think the old cracked manuscripts were more precious and wanted to dig among them.

Strangely enough, sight of the man, who never would be able to exploit them, touching and fondling the treasures seemed to enrage Schindler even more than our possession of them. Perhaps it was the knowledge that Guthrie could estimate the stuff's real value. He could be jealous of the professional mind, whereas he was merely indignantly contemptuous of us.

At any rate he suddenly became beside himself with passion, burst free from his guards and landed with both feet on the small of Guthrie's back. Monty's swift fist struck him under the jaw and knocked him down too late. Guthrie was done for.

Finding himself free, the German sprang to his feet, dodged his captors again and ran around the cavern. Monty made a bee-line for the opening. Will and I were too stiff and bruised to make any swift movements at all. Seeing Monty in the way between him and outer freedom, Schindler lowered his head and charged with a roar like a bull's.

Monty stood his ground and the two went down together in the jaws of the opening. They became jammed there by Schindler's struggles, so that to loosen them we had to drag Monty toward us by the heels. And then, with a vicious kick that missed Monty's head by a hair's breadth, the German broke through into the open and was gone.

We had taken his ammunition from him, but his rifle was outside, leaning against a rock where one of the seamen had picked it up and left it. He snatched it as he went by.

"And likely as not he's got a cavefull of cartridges somewhere!" shouted Will.

"After him, then!" said Monty. "Catch him or kill him before he can arm himself! We've all seen him do murder!"

We poured out of the cave in a stream, the women last, for they had pistols and there was no need of any one to stay on Guthrie's account. He had gone to his reckoning with both hands full of the parchments the lust to obtain which had made such a huckster of him.

It was useless to try to follow along the narrow fissures and bottoms of ravines, for we were in pursuit of a man who had lived years on the island and in all probability knew by heart every track. We had to make for the higher levels in the hope of seeing him whenever he crossed from hole to hole or shinned along a ridge. Will and I, being more sorely bruised than any one, were given stationary posts on nearby prominences, to watch for him and shoot him should he try to double back.

SO WE sat and heard the hue and cry go rising and falling away from us, making the sea-birds wheel in curious curves and stirring all the echoes of the rocks. Then, when the pursuit had taken the party almost out of hearing, both Will and I saw a man's back at the same time and both of us fired. The man promptly disappeared and we, standing on our rocks and jumping in the effort to see down between the boulders, began shouting with all our might to turn the pack again.

Presently we saw the man and fired again, but we both missed. Pistol shooting in the glare on granite rocks is far from easy when you are tired and bruised. The man was heading in the direction of the place where Will and I had landed, or a little to the north of that, and we were tempted to leave our posts and go after him.

But then I thought I saw him again a long way to the right of where he had been, so that he seemed to be making a zigzag course. Will could not see him, although I gave him the new direction and we both sent a shot down among the rocks in the hope of a lucky hit. Then we yelled and yelled again. Grace Vandam was the first to hear us.

Being last to start, she was nearest, on the left end of the line. She shouted to the others and headed back at once. Several times I saw her scrambling over the granite ledges or jumping from one rock to the next. Once or twice I saw the others, scattered in an irregular line that had become much too drawn out.

Suddenly I caught sight of Schindler and realized that he, too, had seen Gracie. He was well out of range of Will's pistol and mine. Between us and him was a mass of saw-tooth rocks that would have taxed the ingenuity of a wildcat to hurry across. He was lurking under the shoulder of a comparatively small rock in Grace's path. His intention was perfectly obvious.

We could not make her stop. We could not make her see him. We did not dare shoot, because at that long range the shots would surely have gone wild and Grace Vandam would more likely have been hit than the German. We simply danced and yelled. And the more we yelled, the more she believed we were urging her to hurry, and she scrambled along toward the man at her utmost speed.

Too late we began to clamber off our rocks and try to scramble to other vantage points from which to shoot at a wider, safer angle. She was too near Schindler before we started. By the time I had swarmed up to another pinnacle fifty yards away she was standing directly over him, peering this way and that for a view.

I yelled again, for I saw him begin to crawl toward her rear. She stared in exactly the opposite direction from that I intended and Schindler took full advantage of that. Desperate, at last I fired at him and missed. But the bullet struck the rocks to his right and, hearing that, Grace faced about.

At that very second Schindler sprang at her. I heard her scream—and it was as different from the other woman's who had cried by night as a sea-gull's is from an eagle's. I saw the flash of her pistol just as he seized her in his huge arms but heard no report and judged by that he must have stopped the bullet from a muzzle pressed against his body. The last I saw of them they were falling, with Grace on top, and Will and I began running, without breath and without plan, not hoping exactly but simply unable to stay where we were until we knew the worst.

At that we were not the first to reach the spot. When we had clambered over the last ridge we found Monty there ahead of us, offering Grace his absolutely last cigaret with the air of a man who gives absolutely nothing. The German's dead body lay beside them. Grace took no more notice of it than if it had been a bundle of rags.

"She didn't kill him," said Monty casually. "The blighter fell under her and broke his neck."

"Didn't her bullet go into the brute?" I asked.

"No. Passed through the coat and never touched him!"

"I wish I had shot him all the same!" said Grace. "I'd have counted it for that poor woman he was hunting over the hills!"

The party rejoined us one by one. We searched Schindler's body for information as to further treasure but found nothing more than a map of the island done very carefully and cleverly on tracing paper. The cave where we had found treasure was marked with a large cross and several other caves were indicated, in one of which no doubt he had lived with Guthrie off Guthrie's provisions.

We started back to the treasure cave, meaning to look over that again and discuss some sort of plan, when I began to puzzle over what Will and I had seen from our two rocks while the rest were hunting in line.

"Do you believe it was possible," I asked Will, "for that man Schindler—that great, heavy, hull of a man, to appear in two places so far apart at such short interval?"

"I thought it all right at the time," he answered.

"So did I at the time," I said, "but think again. Was it possible? We have crossed that ground since, on our way here. You know now what it's like. Could any man have been in those two places within that number of seconds?"

"No!" said Will. "Now I think of it, he couldn't!"

"Then there's another man on the island!" I said.

"Osman bin Omar!" said somebody.

"No," said I. "Osman's coat is a dingy brown. The man whose back I saw was wearing washed-out khaki, the same as Schindler's."

"Right," said Will.

"Good lord! We've no proof the island isn't still full of murderers!" grumbled Fred. "Are we to spend the rest of our days in guerilla warfare with men who shoot women like cats on a roof?"

"Back to the cave!" ordered Monty. "Whoever knows about the treasure will come there sooner or later. Any one ignorant of what's in there isn't so likely to be an enemy. Come on!"

So we headed back cautiously, once more spaced out in line, with Monty and three of the New England seamen well to the rear to guard against surprises. So it was only in keeping with all the happening of that eventful day that surprise should come, but from the front—the unexpected quarter.

It was Grace Vandam who saw a man's head and shouted to us all.

"I thought he was a white man!" she called to us. "Don't shoot, any one, until we're positive!"

The prospect of a new hunt across the blazing rocks after all that exhausting excitement did not please any of us much—Grace, I think, least of all; but nobody cared to display a white feather and we wheeled our line half-right at Monty's word without remonstrance. But it was a slow, dispirited maneuver.

IT WAS very soon evident that the two women had reached their limit of expended effort. There was not anything even remotely resembling a foot-path in the direction we had to take, and the strongest of us was so nearly exhausted that a fight of any sort was likely to prove a farce. So Grace Vandam and Alice Ellis were sent back to the treasure cavern, protesting but resigned.

Ten minutes later Will and I threw up the sponge. Will had to be lifted out of a hole into which he had fallen and I was in scarcely better plight. I could no more climb the smooth granite slope in front of me than I could drag out Will single-handed. Yet Monty shouted that he had seen the man we were pursuing scramble over the top of the slope and there was no easier way around.

So they sent Will and me back to join the women, with the comforting advice to lie still in case we got stuck and could not help ourselves. They promised to look out for us on their way back and carry us home if need be.

And the word "home" was not such an empty jest as it sounded. That cavern, with Guthrie's broken body in it and the treasure and the food and the cistern full of tepid water was headquarters, whatever its other associations. It was the best we had and likely to be the best for many a long, hot week to come. But added to that it sheltered two women and, whatever the explanation of that, the fact remains that even the primitive cave man regards as home the place where the women of his party happen to be.

So it was easy enough to retrace our steps. A foundered horse, a dog with a broken leg, the spent fox whom the hounds have over-run, can generally limp home, even if home is a barrel or a draughty lean-to shack. We found we had actually strength to spare and curiosity enough to wonder how and why Osman bin Omar had managed with his sharp eyes not to see the man in khaki and give the alarm.

Curiosity grew. We sat down to look for him, examining the heights one by one without success. Finally we screwed up sufficient extra energy to hunt for him awhile along the less difficult ravines. And we came on him at last below the crag from which the woman of the island had pitched headlong when Schindler shot her.

The old sea-rover saw us first and made believe to be doing anything but looting a corpse. But we remembered Schindler's anxiety to get the woman's jewelry, and that Osman bin Omar had been present in the cavern with ears cocked. The body was crushed almost out of recognition and the birds had already begun their task of scavenging. But the birds did not explain the outstretched arm and the finger that was cut off cleanly.

"Come here, Osman!" said Will.

The man of the sea demurred.

"No —— ship no more," he shouted. "Got to buy 'nother —— ship!"

"Which is it to be?" Will demanded. "Peace or war?"

"I go keep —— look-out!" he answered, starting off at once to climb the peak.

"See here," said Will, sitting down on a rock and covering Omar with his pistol. "If we ever get away from this island, you'll get your full contract price for your services in cash. You're not entitled to anything else. You hand over what you've got there!"

Osman showed his knowledge of human nature, or at least of Will's good nature, by ignoring the aimed pistol and proceeding on his way. He climbed the peak with the same agility he showed on shipboard, where he habitually went up the masts to make sure his crew had done their work well.

Deciding to postpone the argument until Monty should have a chance to use his influence, we turned back and gathered stones with which to build a cairn over the woman's body. That took us a long time. We had not finished when shouts and jubilant yells from the peak of the crag above us made us suddenly stop work.

Osman bin Omar was dancing on the summit like a lunatic, undignified for the first time since we met him, capering like a six-year-old, clapping his hands and hooting like a steam-engine.

We shouted to know what the matter was but could not make him hear. Instead of taking notice of us he set out at top speed toward the cavern by another route, along ridges that he could see from his superior eminence but that were beyond our ken. We had to take the humbler, longer way by bottoms of ravines. When we reached the cavern at last he had been in there a long time.

He was still jubilant—still unable to behave like a true follower of the Prophet—still snapping his fingers at intervals and jumping up without apparent excuse to dance, as if he stood on hot plates and could only cool his feet by furious motion.

"What's the matter with him?" we asked with one voice.

"Oh, nothing," said Alice Ellis.

"Nothing," said Grace.

"Then what's the matter with you two?"

If ever two women were stiff with self-restraint and nearly bursting with excitement, those were they.

"Nothing's the matter," said Grace. "Why have you two turned alarmists?"

We could not stand any longer. We sat on the stone chest that contained the ancient parchments and grew angry, as most men do when women affect superior wisdom.

"I suppose Osman gave you the ring he bit from the dead woman's finger," suggested Will. "I surely would hate to gloat so over a poor dead native's jewelry! I'd be ashamed!"

"You mean you're jealous?" said Grace.

Will turned toward me.

"And they want us to let 'em vote!" he said disgustedly.

"I didn't know Osman had any ring," said Grace. "He certainly hasn't shown it to me."

"Then what are you crowing about?"

"I'm a prophet!"

"Gosh!"

"A true prophet!"

"Say, Gracie, I'm not in a fit state to guess conundrums. I couldn't walk to that cistern and stick my head in to cool it off. Have a heart! Spill the news!"

"You'll know very soon," she answered.

"Here comes the gang back," said I. "Let's hope they've caught their man. Keep an eye on Osman. Don't let the old rascal leave the cave until Monty interviews him."

We could hear voices outside and the tramping of many feet; but only one man at a time could come in through that low opening and it was quite a long time before the hole darkened and somebody crawled through.

He was a bulky-looking man—one of our five seamen I thought at first, only with an air of authority they did not usually assume.

"Miss Gracie is here?" he asked, blinking this way and that.

I knew his voice then.

"Hello, John!" she said, getting up to shake hands with him. "Why didn't you come sooner?"

He fairly gasped.

"I suppose ye mean why did I come at all! I'd orders to take the yacht home as soon as repairs were completed!"

"If I were going to disobey orders I'd blow the lid right off, John," she answered. "I'd do it so fast that the devil and his angels couldn't stop me."

"Wait till you see the *Daisy's* funnel," he answered grimly. "It has been red-hot from Bombay to here. You'll need a new one. As for disobeying orders—I obeyed your dad's, miss. A mere matter o' his being dead don't make any difference to me that I can see."

"I knew it wouldn't!" she answered. "I'd have betted on it! What's that on your cheek, John? No, the other one."

He turned his face to the light and she promptly hugged and kissed him, to his huge embarrassment.

"Haven't done that for fifteen years, have I, John? Now catch Osman for me. Turn him upside down and take that ring away."

VIII

THE WORK of getting that stone chest and the heavy gold and silver model of the Temple from the cavern to the yacht was performed with prodigious labor and cunning by the *Daisy's* mates and crew. The stone chest weighed a quarter of a ton and had to be hauled over pathless ridges to the beach, where it was lashed to planks between two boats and rowed to the yacht three miles away. For Captain John McGraw had taken no chances with the saw-tooth rocks.

So cautious had he been that he had equipped six of the crew and one mate as a sort of expeditionary force, with rifles for self-protection but strict orders not to shoot unless cornered. It was one of those men whom we had seen and hunted, and he led the pursuers straight toward the beach, where Captain John McGraw was standing guard beside the boats.

There was not a piece of earth anywhere to dig a grave in nor did the sharp sand on the beach appeal to us as suitable; so we emptied the water from the cistern in the cave and laid Guthrie's body in that. There, when they have dragged away the boulders that the whole crew jacked and rolled into place before the entrance to the cavern, antiquarians will some day find his skeleton. And doubtless they will imagine that the cistern is a sarcophagus, and that the bones are those of Barabbas himself—especially if the ants shall have been busy with the clothing in the meanwhile.

After that—and when we had all scrubbed ourselves clean again in the various sorts of baths the *Daisy* was fitted with—the ship's log grew into a thing of blots and a joy forever. For after John McGraw had written in his version of what happened, we each took a turn and wrote on page after smudgy page—ink runs where it meets the drops of sweat—our individual account.

Before we reached Alexandria we had the records—from that of Lord Montdidier and Kirkudbrightshire down to the youngest of the five seamen's—of our impressions of what had taken place and what we saw and heard, set down as nearly at the time as might be, for any one to read who had the right. And there were many, who had no right at all, who tried to move heaven and earth and the consulates to get a look.

Ashore at the hotel we argued long over a settlement, for Grace Vandam insisted on selling all the booty and giving the proceeds to Monty for the support of his estates. And Monty simply laughed at her.

"You're a good girl, Grace," he told her. "A —— nice girl, if I may say so! I'll come to America and dance at your wedding when that time comes, in proof that I mean what I say. But you don't understand."

If there is anything on earth a nice girl hates it is being told she doesn't understand a question of ethics.

"You're simply dirt-proud!" she answered, so that Monty laughed again.

"I'll try to tell you," he answered; for he liked her frankly.

And for the first and last time I heard Monty discuss his own unbending rules of conduct. He died, when his time came, fighting grimly in accordance with the rules, without troubling to explain them or caring in the least whether friend or enemy understood them or not. It took a nice girl, as he had called her, and she of a nation that in those days preferred to regard itself as entirely alien, to get an explanation from him.

"My estates, you know, are held in trust. They're entailed. They go with the title. I didn't ask for the title. I'd have refused it if I could, but it fell to me. It's my duty, worse luck, to try to leave those estates in better shape for the next man, so that he can play the game better. The old order's changing and I don't regret it. Some day, perhaps, there won't be any such estates, but that day isn't yet. The cards in my hands are the ones I have to play, not those to be dealt out later.

"I'd like a million or two to invest in improvements—roads, drains, fences, stock, houses for the tenants and all that kind of thing. But money that came the wrong way would be worse than useless. That's not sentiment, it's iron law.

"My people were never robber barons. The first earl of the line was a statesman and the rest have been soldiers. It's creed with us that a man should leave the world better than he found it. And none of us has flinched.

"So if there's to come a million or two or three from anywhere to shore up the Montdidier estates it'll have to do the world good first before I touch it. A goldmine, for instance. This sort of treasure trove that was stolen very likely in the first place and surely belongs to-day to humanity at large is not what I need for my purpose."

"And this ring?" she asked.

"Should be worn by a beautiful young woman, if the world is to get the most good from it!"

Of course, that did not much more than begin the argument. She agreed to present all the manuscripts and the Temple model to the British Government; but there was the crew of the *Daisy* to settle with—entitled to their one-third share of the total after deducting expenses. Nobody cared to suggest to them that they should do without their profit, for the simple reason that it would not have been decent to do it. Furthermore, we insisted on our right to pay our share of the cost of the trip.

It was Alice Ellis who suggested the solution of the difficulty. She and Grace Vandam took train to Cairo and interviewed a jeweler. The value he set on the rose-pink diamond in its ancient setting was so tremendous that Grace refused to accept it, on the ground that its sale would have made the rest of us rich.

However, we went into accounts then. The crew of the *Daisy* were very well satisfied with fifty pounds a man, and officers in proportion. We bought a new lateen-rigged little ship for Osman bin Omar. After counting all the other expenses for coal and repairs and so on, there was enough balance remaining to offset the diamond to make a very handsome money gift to Alice Ellis, who certainly deserved it, having risked her life as cheerfully as any one, and who needed it beyond a doubt.

So Grace Vandam paid the bills out of her affluence and took the ring; and when you see pictures of the ring in its ancient setting in the New York Sunday papers you will know now that it is not true that she bought it for a million in the rue de Rivoli. This also sets forever at rest that other absurd tale that she bought the ring from Lord Montdidier in order that he might pay his debts. He had not any debts—except mortgages. And they still encumber the estate.

THAT NIGHT—THE night of the final settlement—we all sat until nearly dawn in Monty's bedroom while Will Yerkes laid down the law.

"You need the money!"

"I admit it."

"Isn't she a darned nice girl?"

"Of course she is."

"Then why don't you marry her? She'd have you like a shot!"

"I don't propose to marry and I don't believe that's true."

"Bonehead! One o' these durned ginks with a title and no morals is going to get her if you don't!"

"I think not," said Monty. "Grace is a very wise young woman."

"Don't you consider her good enough to be a countess?"

Monty laughed.

"Too good!" he answered. "This is final, Will. She is young. I am nearly fifty. I wouldn't consent to inflict myself on a young girl and I'm too confirmed a bachelor to choose an old one. Marry her yourself and I'll come and be best man!"

"Oh, Gracie 'ud never marry me," said Will.

"Good night!" growled Monty. "Get out and let me sleep. Fred, put that cursed concertina away."

THERE WAS one point left to be settled. We went next evening to Bill's at about the hour when Monty had usually met his most redoubtable opponent at chess. On time like a phase of the moon, the mandarin smiled himself in. We left him to make the approaches.

"You are back? You are well? You are prosperous?" he said, rubbing his hands one above the other. "And Mr. Grogan Guthrie, how is he?"

"Dead," said Monty.

"Ah? Did he die—ah—pleasantly?"

"He died like a dog in a ditch, poor chap."

"Ah. Indeed. Dear me. Dear me."

The mandarin sat back on the plush cushions and seemed to absorb satisfaction through his nostrils. Never was a should-be mourner more indecently contented.

"You sent him to his death!" said I.

The mandarin blinked.

"My dear young Christian friend," he said after a minute, "I have lived up to the letter of your Christian rule. That man did me an evil—a great evil. In return I told him all he wished to know. He asked me for the secret of Barabbas Island and I told him. I withheld nothing. I even told him of the nature of the priceless manuscripts that Charles Dent believed could be recovered there. Did he ever mention, I wonder, that he felt grateful to me for the information I gave him freely?"

"He called you a —— infidel rapscallion less than an hour before he died," said Fred, and the mandarin blinked again.

"Yet I lent him the money with which he hired the men who took him to Barabbas," he said reminiscently.

"What harm did he ever do you?" asked Will.

The mandarin shook his head.

"I never talk of the evil that men do me," he answered. "But tell me this; in your experience, who is most likely the debtor—he who says nothing or he who calls names?"

"I begin to see at last through the theory of your game of chess," said Monty.

"Ah! Let us play a game!"

"Thanks; I think not."

"It is not safe to believe you understand my theory until you have put it in practice on the board. It is like all precepts—like all religions—like honor; until you have turned theory into accomplishment you are not—"

"Not guilty!" said Monty. "Yes, I know. It's the same way with murder and revenge—not guilty till you got your man. Well—you got yours. I'm sorry to say that Guthrie came to a miserable end. It was clever—deuced clever! Next time we meet I'll thank you to forget the short acquaintance! Are you fellows ready?"

"Now wouldn't that beat poker!" murmured Will, following the rest of us out—reluctantly, I think.

He wanted to stay and thrash the Chinaman.

Hi Ying Lang watched us leave the room and descend the narrow stairs with eyes that were gentle and magnanimous. His attitude, upright on the cushions, was of unassuming forgiveness and benevolence for all mankind.

IN ALEPPO BAZAAR

"ONE O' these days there's going to be a —— of a war!—oh, a whale of a war!—a war to make all the others put together look like a fish-wife argument!"

A bull voice, bellowing above the hum of Bill's upper room in Alexandria, exulted in the glory of the awful wrath to come without disturbing anybody's peace; for Bill's has this peculiarity, that although down-stairs in the long bar with its three subdivisions you may say what you please at your own risk exactly as anywhere else, up-stairs, where the initiate sit, entire tolerance is the rule, and nothing whatever that you say or think or do is held against you provided it does not impinge on the like privilege of others.

That is why the dingy place, with its narrow stairs and cheap plush furniture, is visited by such strangely assorted folk as bishops, sea-captains, camel-traders, Greek smugglers and Senussi pirates, to mention only a few of them. The right to play chess there at all hours of day or night was what first brought the soberer of earth's adventurers; something or other in the atmosphere that made the owners of deep scars—mental and physical—talk at random kept listeners coming. And out of that grew a democratic spirit that is loathsome to the loathly ones who strive always so bitterly to impose their vices on the world; that spirit strains the visiting list as through a fine-meshed sieve, without need of other Cerberus or censorship.

Drunkenness, for instance, is permitted in Bill's upper room out of charity, but not insisted on. Get drunk down-stairs, and they throw you in the street for the police to deal with for the sensualist you are; up-stairs they will lay you under a table and put feet on you and, by way of being one's brother's keeper, not a man will say a word about the matter afterward. So drunkenness up-stairs is very rare.

Fred Oakes was far from drunk, although the songs he was singing and the raucous braying of his concertina might have misled the casual onlooker. Monty was, as always, stone-cold sober, playing chess, as it happened, with the chief engineer of a Cardiff collier, who would have been beside himself with nervousness had he known he sat *vis-à-vis* to an earl.

Will Yerkes was sitting telling tales of a New England village to a Jesuit priest from Ooticamund on his way to a Soudan flea-and-fly patch where he said he expected to remain until he died. I sat near them until the roar of other voices made Will's difficult to catch, and then crossed the room to the table where the man with the bullfrog throat was holding forth to fifteen nationalities. Not one of them was English, but they talked English because that is the tongue the ages have decided shall wipe out the curse of Babel, interspersing it with oaths like the edge of a rusty file, compounded of all the spite of the Levant.

He who roared had British blood in him. Not by a host are all the Anglo-Saxons who leave home observers of even half the Commandments—the Seventh perhaps least of all. His mother might have been part Greek, and there was a dash of black as well as Syrian in his make-up. Although he used the language, he professed a hatred of England.

"When the big war comes," he bellowed, "then we shall know who is to be master!"

He had money or the evidences of it. His fat fingers were carefully manicured—a very rare circumstance in the Levant unless the owner of them was raised in luxury. Two huge gold rings rather gave the lie to soft schooling, however; that on his right hand was set with an enormous emerald, that on his left with a ruby, and the combination produced a suggestion of ships, sailors and the sea that there was no escaping. Nor could he have picked up his phraseology—the educated slang, the tarry oaths and Western metaphor—without traveling in places where luxury, such as the East aspires to, is reckoned contemptible because impractical, or else a deadly sin. He sipped imported French champagne with the air of an epicure and ate sliced, raw German sausage with a noise like an ill-packed plunger-pump. A black-haired, thick-necked, low-collared, puppy-eyed, stocky, heavy mixture of a man.

He seemed to take delight in prophesying evil for the English. My nationality was written all over me—skin, clothes, attitude, angles—and he took advantage of the law of tolerance governing that upper room to direct the full force of his own intolerant spleen at me, knowing that nobody would support me in case I should object.

"Those cursed English own the sea-lanes because the world was asleep and let them take. They're a rotten lot of pirates, that's all! Gibraltar—Egypt—Aden—India—think of the plunder going to England every week in ships stuffed full to the hatches that 'ud have to sneak round the Cape o' Good Hope if it weren't for those well-chosen forts along their course. Well, that isn't going to last long!"

He sipped at his champagne half a dozen times, as if sampling the flavor of a fine revenge, while his audience cracked jokes that would pass muster in Fenian circles—tolerant of everything except England's friendliness.

"Not long, by the blood of a dog, not long! Any one who knows Aleppo could know that. There's going to be a railway-station at Aleppo—a junction. Lines running north, south, east and west. A railway all the way from Europe into Persia and Afghanistan! Where will the English right of way be then? Tell me that! Who'll hold the shortest road to India when that time comes? Eh? And it's not far off, gentlemen; I myself have seen the men with instruments who mark off the place where the station shall be when the time comes."

That last sentence placed him at any rate. Anything can come out of Aleppo—even such an incongruous wealthy one as he. If he had seen what he said it was likely he had lived there; and since he was so vehement it was possible his own pocket might feel the heaping values when land in Aleppo should be bought up for railway purposes, for thus self-interest doth make apostles of us all. You couldn't affect to love England and boom the Bagdad Railway at the same time—not in those days.

HIS TALK soon grew boresome and I went over to watch Monty at his chess. Later Monty and I went out together to get mail—the exiled Anglo-Saxon's endless pilgrimage. On our return I was annoyed to see Will Yerkes sitting in very close conference with the owner of the bull voice. A whisper was beneath the compass of the Levantine, but he could lower his voice to a point where its rumble swallowed up the words and only the nearest man could understand. The whole room was aware they were discussing something, but the subject was obscure and Will's answers quite inaudible.

"I'll bet you that brute has discovered Will is American," said I, "and that he thinks the War of 1812 is still rankling in Will's bosom. He's proposing to twist the old lion's tail."

"Let's go and see whether you're right," said Monty and we crossed the room and sat beside them, to the Levantine's immediate and unconcealed disgust.

"This man has introduced himself to me by the name of Achmed McNamara," said Will. "The name sounds fishy but the business listens good."

The Levantine had sharper ears than Will imagined.

"Fishy?" he demanded. "My name is fishy? What do you mean?"

"Haven't you heard the saying that every time you eat fish you bite into a Scotchman?" Will answered.

Achmed McNamara laughed like a storm among loose doors and shutters, although he did not see the point. Nobody minds being called Scotch, or Irish, or Welsh, or Cornish, or even British. The

English get the blame for others' virtues. Scotch, Welsh, Irish are excused for England's sins; and if you don't believe that try it.

"My grandfather was a Scotch general in the British army that fought in the Crimea," said Achmed McNamara proudly.

"D'you suppose he means general servant?" wondered Monty behind his hand and again the Levantine's sharp ears caught what was not intended for them.

"I had an English valet once," he said with a fat sneer. "I dismissed the man for pilfering."

At that moment he saw Fred Oakes making his way through the crowded room toward us. He spat at sight of him, and eased his stomach cautiously out from between the bench and table.

"I am not particular," he said. "I can stand almost anything. But not that man!"

Most people smile on Fred and his concertina, and make room for him with shouts of welcome. Runaways at sight of him are rare.

"What have you done to the fat rascal, Fred?" I asked.

"Merely made a song about him—nothing very libelous. Achmed McNamara is too tempting—rhymes with Sahara—goes with a deuce of a lilt—couldn't overlook it. I don't think he liked the verse about his ancestor who made love to the dusky damsel of the Soudan oasis. Never mind him; let's talk about food."

"Wait!" insisted Will. "Achmed McNamara has a scheme, and if you ginks hadn't interrupted I'd have the whole of it down pat by now. He's a crook all right, but that doesn't mean necessarily that this particular bit of business hasn't meat in it."

"I wouldn't be found dead in partnership with that brute!" I said.

Monty looked at me sharply and raised his eyebrows.

"Neither would any of us. Do you say that sort of thing when you're hungry, or thirsty, or what? Go on, Will."

"He's nutty about the Bagdad Railway. He says it's going to put Aleppo on the map in two-inch letters."

"So it will," said Monty. "Aleppo will be as big as London some day."

"He says property is already being bought up along the line the railway 'll have to take, but there's one piece lying right across the route, almost in the middle of the city, that the speculators can't get. He says that, counting what the railway people can be made to pay for their piece in the middle of it, and the natural increase in value of the remainder, there's a profit of about a million pounds to be made by any one who can get title."

"That 'ud be half a million for you, 'Didums'!" Fred could never see any proposition except from the viewpoint of Monty's needs. Left to himself Monty might have shrugged his splendid shoulders free of the burden of his mortgaged estates and have enjoyed life simply. But Fred, who would have died of ennui at Montdidier Towers and would have given Monty no peace until he had dragged him away on new travels, would never let his friend lose sight of the altruistic goal. "Half a million 'ud build new barns for all the tenants as well as make roads and fences and care for a mortgage or two!"

WILL SLAPPED the palm of his hand on the table.

"Listen!" he said. "Achmed McNamara didn't know you and I are acquainted. He saw me talking to the U.S. consul and found out from him that my credentials are O.K. On the strength of that he came across with a proposal which you interrupted before he reached rock. Roughly it's a plan to get that strip of real estate and sell it for all it'll fetch. He says it's no earthly use his going after it because he's known. All the other men who know its potential value are stalling along in hope of buying cheap; some of them are trying to get together on a syndicate to bear the market and then buy the strip between 'em. Achmed McNamara proposes to snap while the snapping's good and get rich quick."

"Doesn't the present owner know the value of the piece?" asked Monty.

"The present owner is a woman!"

"And we're to go and plunder the lady!" Fred grinned genially. "Achmed McNamara, I misjudged you. I shall have to change the song!"

"Hurry up and tell us, Will," Monty urged. It was obvious he would not waste time and breath just before dinner on any such proposal as that.

"Achmed McNamara had the gall to suggest to me that I, being young and handsome, as he kindly put it, and of whole white ancestry, as he observed, should go to Aleppo and make arrangements to marry the dame. She's of proud, mixed family and it seems her sort never marry beneath 'em. Always aiming to breed toward the white and away from Asia. Seems the property is in her name and would still be hers under Mohammedan law even should she marry, but he thinks a trifle like that shouldn't trouble a bright young man like me. Once a woman is married, he says, to get her signature to title deeds is easy."

"Where would Achmed McNamara find his little honorarium?" asked Fred. "And how much?"

"Fifty-fifty was his idea—me to give promissory notes, properly witnessed, in advance; he to work the introductions and hoodwink the Turkish governor, who has to be in on everything, murder included."

"If that's all let's go to dinner," said Monty, "and if we pass Achmed McNamara on our way let's kick him where he hides his sentiments."

"It isn't all. The lady's name is Thabita—Syrian, I suppose for Tabitha. That's her given name; he hadn't come to the family name when you broke up the meeting. Thabita is all of a clue we've got."

"Clue to what?"

All three of us asked that question in one disgusted voice.

"To the lady's identity. But there ought to be only one strip of real estate to correspond with the story. We should be able to pick up the trail all right."

"What trail? Are you mad?"

"He tells me there are other marriageable scions in the market. In fact, the speculators are divided into two camps—those in favor of outright purchase—they have to be most cautious, he says, because the Turks 'ud swoop down and tax 'em into the poor-house if they suspected 'em of having money—and those in favor of acquiring title by marriage. The marriage boosters, he says, are all split up among themselves in favor of different candidates."

"What about the girl?"

"Not in love! Believes in female franchise—education—cigarets—and outdoor exercise. 'Just the wife for an American,' said Achmed McNamara."

"What's the point of all this?" demanded Monty. "You're surely not fool enough to be caught with a Syrian woman for bait?"

" 'In vain the net is spread in the sight of any bird,' " Will quoted.

"What d'you mean, Will?"

"Where they spread a net there's something doings—"

"Said the fish!" smiled Fred.

"I'm fond of bucking a crooked game myself as long as I know it's crooked. I'm for going to Aleppo."

"You're mad, Will!"

"America, I shall include you in the amended song of Achmed McNamara!" announced Fred contentedly.

"Why shouldn't we go? What are we doing here? I'm weary of this place. Types and tales don't interest me any longer worth a nickel. What's the matter with Aleppo anyway? Why don't you go and look at it? If there turns out to be nothing in this yarn, aren't we as likely to start another rabbit running there as here? Are we any worse off after we get there, barring the few dollars for transportation? My theory is that while the forty thieves are plotting to steal the estate from Thabita we all can come by it fair and square. Why not make an honest dollar when we get the chance? The last two ventures have turned out punk as far as profit was concerned."

"Will," said Monty, "I've lived most of my life in the East, old fellow. When I wasn't in the cavalry I was political resident in native Indian states, and when I wasn't that I was traveling. If I've learned one thing it's this: The surest and generally the swiftest route to deadly trouble is through the harem door. Let women alone!"

"Aw—quit preaching! When did you see me fooled by a woman?"

We all laughed loud at that. Will's respect for any kind of woman is a joke—at any rate east of Sable Island. That very morning he had thrashed a man in the street for insulting a woman through her window, quite regardless of the fact that ladies able to appreciate an insult are not visible through windows in Alexandria. The resultant row had led to the call on the United States consul and indirectly, therefore, to this very Aleppo madness, supposing it were really true that Achmed McNamara had decided to trust him on the consul's word.

"I'll bet Achmed McNamara is half-uncle on his mother's side to the second cousin of the man you thrashed this morning and they've cooked up a plan between them to fleece you to the bone for it. I'm off to dinner now," said Fred, "if I have to go alone. Aleppo and Jemima of the real estate can await!"

WE ALL followed Fred down the dingy, narrow stairs and out into the clean night air that sweeps the Alexandria sea-front. The stars were out. Men dine at the Christian hour of eight or nine o'clock in those wise latitudes.

We strolled along the sea-front toward our hotel in the blissful condition of free men with appetites and money in the bank, oblivious of everything except whatever—stars, scenery, sea air, cigars—tended to subserve the mood.

Monty and Will walked arm-in-arm in mute disclaimer of the unbidden thought that either might have been offended by what the other said. It was I who first noticed we were followed.

"There's either a footpad, a beggar or a spy keeping pace with us twenty yards behind," I said.

"Piffle! What would a spy want?" Fred asked.

"Let's see," said Monty. "Wait for him."

So we faced about, and in a minute the man was at arm's length—very bulky-looking in the dim light—none other than Achmed McNamara.

"Good evening, gentlemen," he said, nervous, yet deadly determined to go through with it.

"What do you want?" asked Monty.

"From you nothing. From this man—" he pushed a fat forefinger out and touched Will—"a promise."

"You're getting sensibler," grinned Fred. "It was promissory notes an hour ago."

Achmed McNamara spat savagely and showed the beautiful, regular teeth between his coarse lips.

"From you I want silence!" he barked. "From you with your songs and your barbarous instrument I have had more than I mean to endure without reprisal. I have warned you. I shall get you. Unless you run away you shall pay through the snout for that song you made!"

"I always run away to save my snout from overtaxation!" Fred laughed. "It's habit. Go on—let us know what you want from my friend."

Achmed McNamara turned sideways so as to face Will squarely and pointed again with the fat forefinger.

"Your consul told me you were a gentleman. I hope that is true. I made you a proposal between gentlemen, not knowing at the time that you were connected in any way with these other persons." What volumes of slander that meek word "persons" can imply on the lips of an accuser! "It happens, though, that what I said was only said to test you. The real proposal was to follow, after I had satisfied myself of your bona-fides. Consequently you know nothing at all about my affairs really—only a little that is vague and meaningless."

"I'm sure I feel overwhelmed with concern," said Will.

"You said something about a promise," I put in. "Why the promise?"

He ignored me entirely. I was as dirt beneath his patent-leathered feet.

"However—as between gentlemen—I expect you to promise me to let the matter drop."

"What the devil do you mean?" demanded Will.

The flint of his voice struck fire on the steel of the Levantine's insolence.

"This—that you would better keep your silly fingers out of fire! I saw you talking to these persons. I know you were telling them what I told you. I warn you to let the whole thing alone. If you don't, you take the consequences!"

"Meaning just him, or all of us?" asked Monty.

The man detected the amusement underlying Monty's calm inquiry and flew into a rage.

"All —— four of you! Go to Aleppo if you dare! Forget you ever saw me—that is wisest. I will make the earth too hot to hold you if you interfere with me. You Englishmen! You swagger about the world and poke your noses into anybody's business. This time you poke into a hornet's nest! Get away! Keep away! Go to —— and mind your own affairs! It is a pity this American is in your company."

"That'll do for you!" said Will, and we all stood ready to prevent him in case he should mean violence. The Levantine could have hired a hundred police-court witnesses within an hour to swear to anything. But Will was more amused than angry.

"I'm going to kick you in the belly if you stand there, McNamara. And if you can't run faster than me I'm going to duck—you in the nice salt water over yonder. Now then—at the word three! One! Two!—"

So we four hunted Achmed McNamara along the shore front at Alexandria, whooping like lunatics, and were out of breath as well as hungry when he ran like a hurried hippopotamus across the street, and we lost him at a corner, a minute or two away from our hotel.

"I tell you what, Will," said Monty, panting between bursts of laughter, "I'm beginning to believe there's something in this view halloo of yours. That Levantine is a shade too anxious to throw us off the scent of something."

"I said let's go to Aleppo and look," said Will. "I say it again. What's the matter with going and looking?"

"I'm willing," said Monty. "How about you, Fred?"

"You're two utter idiots!" he answered. "Didums knows better, and Will ought to. But I've squeezed all the juice out of Alexandria. I'll go with you under protest."

"And you?"

"I'm outvoted already," said I, "but I'll make it unanimous."

"There's just one thing to make sure of first," said Monty. "Are we undertaking this because the Levantine said we shouldn't or because we think there's something in it?"

"You mean are we taking a dare? That greasy half-breed couldn't dare me into eating dinner! I chose to go and I go," said Will. "He can neither stop nor send me."

"Suppose we see how we feel about it in the morning," Monty suggested, but that was more than Fred's high spirits could endure.

"Didums, you croaker, you're getting old. My protest is withdrawn. I insist on seeing Will make love to the fair Jemima. He and I start for Aleppo on the first boat going that way if I have to wheel him on board in a barrow. Now then—dinner! Do you hear me? Dinner!"

So we went and tubbed ourselves, donned stiff-fronted shirts and ate eight courses in a gilded dining-room as earnestly as men who have never stepped a yard beyond the boundaries of London Town.

II

DINNER WAS good and the moon saw us after dinner on the roof, optimistic and smoking exquisite cigars. But daylight again brought Monty to his senses, if not the rest of us.

"Aleppo if you like," he said. "I've always wanted to explore Mesopotamia. All caravan routes end at Aleppo, but no monkeying with married or unmarried Syrian women!"

The rest of us, even including Will, were glad to have him to blame for vaccillation. In the calm, sweet light of the Mediterranean morning we did not view the prospect of speculation in Syrian real estate with quite the same gusto. To wander off into the Mesopotamian desert proffered no hope of swift financial success but smacked more of sanity for all that.

So Fred and Will went down to the hotel store-room to inspect our mounds of camping-kit and hunting-gear, while Monty and I strolled to the steamship offices to make the round and find when a ship would start. Besides the regular lines there are several small fleets of tramps that earn ingratitude in the Levant, and we were lucky enough to find one of a fleet of four, belonging to one owner, that was loading and would sail next day for Alexandretta—Aleppo's nearest port.

She had accommodation, labeled first class, pooped up high at the stern where the cabins could catch the smoke. The lone clerk in the office showed us a diagram, but we preferred to know the worst in advance and strolled down to the dock—followed rather closely, I observed, by a limping, wizened little cripple in brown rags, who, without perceptibly improving its condition, had been cleaning the office window when we arrived on the scene.

The cabins turned out to be less unsanitary and the galley and bathroom less unclean than anticipated, so we returned to the office—followed again by the cripple in brown rags. By that time, of course, we were quite sure that Achmed McNamara had employed him to look out for us and report. It did occur to me to wonder why McNamara's spy should have the right to wash steamship office windows and I said something to Monty about it, but he was busy examining change for worthless paper money and, by the time he had obliged the clerk to make good three suspicious bills, the other suspicion was clear out of our heads.

Being of the Alexandrian slums—which is to say, so utterly without shame as not to be aware of its existence—the spy begged of us as we emerged through the office door. I gave him a shilling and his astonishment was so unfeigned at the sight of all that money all his own that we again forgot suspicion, this time in laughter. At the time I thought he ran away anxious to get the money spent before he should wake up and discover it was not real. Within half an hour we knew he had run to warn Achmed McNamara, but the last thing we intended was to change our minds on the Levantine's account and it did not even enter our heads to book passage later on another ship.

Discovery that I had left a couple of novels behind in the steamship office was what brought enlightenment. I went back to get them. Achmed McNamara saw me first. He dodged round a corner but I recognized his back and it occurred to me to ask the clerk what he knew about him.

"He is part-owner of the line," he answered. "For some reason he has decided to return to Aleppo on the ship to-morrow."

So we were not surprised when we went on board and found the fat-lipped Levantine, with his port and starboard rings in place, in full enjoyment of the glory that goes with ownership. He and we were the only passengers, and, although the voyage was unlikely to be long, it was obvious from the first that either we should know one another vastly better by the end of it, or else turn what he called his "liner" into a "hell-ship." For he made a dead set at us from the start—refused to be snubbed—utterly ignored all cause for enmity, quite freely offered him, and turned the steward loose on cases of special canned food solely for our benefit.

There was only one table in the saloon, nor more than room for one. He sat at the head of it and kept meals waiting until we joined him. Then he had all the plates taken out and rewarmed, and no medical major domo at a fashionable cure ever cared for his patients' digestions more studiously than he for ours.

When sheer, downright snubbing failed to discourage him—and Monty on social stilts could make an iceberg seem like June sunshine—Fred Oakes sang the song again that had given such offense in Alexandria:

"Oh, Achmed McNamara, oh, tarara, oh, tarara,
Left his home in the Sahara for the far Sahara's good."

It was a wholly opprobrious song, intended to reach down among the victim's sensibilities and scarify them. Yet the victim laughed! The man who could do that was not going to be held at a distance with anything less than blows, and those delivered with a marlin-spike or some similar aid to emphasis.

"All the decencies disdaining, he was warned against remaining;
"It was no use his explaining that he wasn't understood."

Verse after verse, each less sparing than the last, swelled under the low saloon beams and let the ship's crew know of McNamara's alleged impious history. And finally McNamara himself suggested an incident or two that threw all Fred's imaginations into shade. There was simply no way of outraging him. Yet ashore the same man had flown into a tantrum at half as much.

"I wasn't understood. That's the key of it. You men don't understand me, gentlemen all. You don't know the East. You are trying to apply your Western rules of conduct to me, by Allah! You might as well try to measure a round ball with a straight yardstick!"

"You're mistaken," said Monty, "we're not interested in you in the least."

Achmed McNamara laughed at that rejoinder as if it had been a merry effort to amuse him. His great coarse guffaw made the dishes rattle.

"All right, gentlemen all," he answered, "that only adds proof of how East and West are different. I've East enough in me to know the ropes, and West enough to be interested in four fine men when I see them. Four fine men, I said. I've made inquiries since you hunted me along the esplanade. I know how much money you had in the bank at Alexandria. I know what your business is—prospectors, gold-miners, explorers. I know what you want more money for. I've friends on back-stairs who can report what Lord Montdidier says to other lords and ladies. I know all about you. What do you know about me?"

"We don't want to know about you!" Monty answered.

"There you are," said McNamara, "that is an instance of the West's indifference toward the East."

"Not at all," Monty answered, "it's simple dislike for a bounder!"

The man's amusement at that, if laughter meant anything at all, was titanic. He leaned back in his chair to let the buffalo mirth escape.

"You're going to like me," he gasped, "before you're finished." Then, as the steward left the saloon: "Liking has to have roots. You have to build on something. Can't build on air. Can't build on acquaintance scraped in a place like Bill's. Money's the stuff to build on! I'm going to put money your way, gentlemen all. Money talks!"

"If it talked as loud as you do," said Monty, "no self-respecting man would touch it!"

But there was no repressing him at all. And the dinner was good, although our host ate like an animal and the liquids sought to wander abroad because of the semicircular gyrations of the ship's stern. We did not care to leave before the end of it.

"You think that because I made a shady proposition to your American in Bill's that evening, that I'm not to be trusted. Now isn't that so?"

"Marvelous!" said Monty. "Your insight is simply marvelous!"

"Well, you don't know the East."

"As you keep saying."

"I use Eastern methods."

"Or any other, I should say, that suits your purpose!"

"I was simply finding out whether the American would take me up on a shady proposition."

"You found out," said Will. "If you need any more convincing just make me another, that's all!"

"Aha! Oho! Oo-uh-ho-ho! Not me! Not Achmed McNamara. I've found out to my complete satisfaction that you four men are true blue. I'd be willing to trust you with my money. I feel sure of you."

Will leaned back and blew smoke rings while we waited for the pudding course.

"You make me tired," he said, looking sideways at the man from under lowered eyelids. "You couldn't work a con game that way on the kindergarten grade where I come from. Get out your pea and shells; you'll find that easier."

"You think I want your money. I don't! I have more than all you four together!"

"Then what the deuce are you after?"

"I have discovered that you are not to be frightened easily. I tried to keep you away from Aleppo with threats. You were not to be intimidated. You are just the men I want for my honorable purpose. I can introduce you straight away into the heart of an Aleppo business into which you could not break otherwise with the aid of a thousand influential English friends."

PARTLY FOR sake of the amusement, for the man's persistence in itself was entertaining, partly because his dinner was good, but mainly because there was no preventing him, we sipped our coffee and let him roar out his confidences in what he thought a whisper. Once yet Monty interrupted him:

"You're talking nonsense. Aleppo has always been an English trading-ground. My bankers can supply me with the key to any decent commercial circles in Asia Minor. I don't need your interference."

But it was hopeless. Every argument against him seemed only to strengthen his case in his own eyes. He lolled back in his chair at the head of the table and laughed again until our ears were full of the abominable noise.

"Imagine me going to London to make a million pounds within a month on the strength of my banker's introduction! Oah-ha-ha-ha! Besides—if I could make two million pounds without sharing it with you, d'you suppose I'd as much as mention it? D'you take me for a fool?"

"No, for a bounder," said Monty.

"I'm too well known in Aleppo—"

"To the police?" suggested Fred.

"To everybody! The police of Aleppo, gentlemen all, are Turkish; that is sufficient description of them. What they do not actually steal they accept in the form of bribes. We have nothing to do with the police in this case, nor they with us. We have nothing to do with the Turkish governor, either, and that is the whole point. When I told this American that the property I am after is owned by a lady named Thabita, I made use of the simple truth, but not all of it. The lady in question is my sister."

That was certainly something of a bombshell to drop among four after-dinner dullards, and we suddenly took more interest—as he noticed with those fat, ox eyes of his—although none of us could have given a reason why the sister of such a man should interest us more than the man himself. She was probably fat like himself and greasy, with a voice that would raise a roof. The same thought passed across Will's mind, for I saw him shudder.

"My sister is not single."

Our eyes met. Complications!

"She acquired the property by marriage."

"Why not say she's a widow and have done with it?" asked Fred.

"Because she is not a widow—not exactly."

"You suggested I should marry her, a night or two ago," Will reminded him.

"Ah! That is because you are American. You understand such matters. I am told the Mormons of America—"

It was Will's turn to laugh now and he did it with

the high-pitched squeal the U.S. keeps in stock for the Old World's misinterpretations of the New.

"A small minority has seceded," he said. "At least one per cent, of the States now are non-Mormon, if you count the women and kids."

"Never mind!" said Achmed McNamara. "The point is that you will understand the situation readily and meet it with open mind. These others—these English—are too —— conventional; they will be shocked. It is to America that we must look for open-mindedness."

"Cut the compliments and spill the beans," said Will. "I want to go on deck."

when the widow claimed the protection of Moslem law and denounced the husband's cruel murderers as fratricides—slayers of one on whom they had conferred the strongest brotherhood there can be, that of religion—the governor of Aleppo was in something of a quandary. But he desired that property nevertheless.

"So what did he do but seize my sister, the widow of that rich Mohammedan Armenian, and put her in his own harem!"

"And so endeth this lesson," said Fred impiously. "Between us four and harems is a great gulf fixed!"

"Then listen! My sister—she is my only sister, much younger than I—became the wife, and the only wife, observe, of a wealthy Armenian—a very wealthy Armenian. He owned all that land I speak of. He became a Mohammedan for the sake of safety, but it did not save him because he was so wealthy that when there was an Armenian massacre he was one of the first to be butchered in order that his property might be acquired. But recollect! My brother-in-law, the Armenian, had changed his religion and had become Mohammedan. There was no doubt of it. His wife had proof.

"That placed her, of course, under the protection of the Moslem law. That gave her the absolute right, as widow, to the deceased husband's property under the terms of the testament. The Turks will do anything to a Christian, or to any non-Moslem, but they are careful of their own religionists to a certain extent. That is why I am a Mohammedan. I do not believe in being a Christian on Turkish territory. A man's religion is what he lives by, as we say in the East, and we should cut our coats accordingly.

"It happened that it was the governor of Aleppo who had his eye on my brother-in-law's estate. So

"It was very far from being ended! Excuse me, but it is I who am telling this story, not you!"

Achmed McNamara was very far from laughing now. His bull voice had taken on a sort of leather-mallet tone, such as the ultra-sensual keep to talk religion with and love.

"If he could have married my sister, then it would have been ended."

"Then why the devil didn't he? Can't a Turkish governor do as he pleases?"

"He already had four wives. The law allows him four only!"

"But what about concubines?"

"As many as he pleases."

"Well then?"

"He does not acquire control of the property of a concubine. With her death it would pass to her heirs, not to him. At my sister's death that property would pass to me. Therefore her life is safe in Aleppo, and mine is not. As long as I live my sister will not sign any paper altering the disposition of the property, even supposing that the religious court would recognize such a document. Therefore as long as I live that governor and his friends will seek to murder me!"

"Why did you tell me, then," demanded Will, "that there is a party in Aleppo in favor of acquiring that property by marriage, and that the party is all divided up in favor of different candidates?"

"I told the truth, but only part of it. There are two parties. One is representing German financiers; they would acquire the property from the governor by purchase. They propose to bribe him handsomely and leave the means of obtaining my sister's signature to the necessary title deeds to him.

"But the other party, which is very influential behind the scenes, objects to playing so simply into the hands of foreigners. They recommend marriage; they have at least a dozen candidates who are bidding against one another. The girl is young and beautiful. They would accept a very small share of the estate; then the syndicate could sell the rest of the estate outright to the Germans.

"That is all very simple, of course. But there enters in this complication. One of the governor's four legal wives is old and in ill-health! If she should die, then he could marry my sister, and there would be no need to share the plunder with any one. So he is pursuing dilatory tactics. They say that the doctor, whom he permits to attend his old wife at intervals, has lost some suspicious cases."

"WHY DON'T he use the bow-string?" demanded Will. "I've always heard that Turks throttle the wives they're tired of, sew 'em in a sack and drop 'em down a well, or in the Bosphorus or something."

"Ah, these stories about Turks! Some of them are true. Most of them no doubt are true—at one time or another. But for the governor of a province to murder his wife with such an obvious motive would be too outrageous altogether. He would simply submit himself to so much blackmail on that account that all the taxes of the province would never be enough to pay it. Why, there would be a stampede to Stamboul of eunuchs and hangers-on, all seeking to be first to lay the information where it would fetch the highest price. Some high court official would then proceed to turn the screws and the governor of Aleppo would become a very poor man—bit by bit. No, no! The thing is not so simple. Judges can be bribed in Turkey. So can everybody else. Massacres can be arranged at wholesale; there are so many guilty ones in that event that the blame can not be brought home. But there are limits to what even the governor can do without paying a price for it."

"Well, what's your proposal?" Monty demanded.

"That you should help me rescue my sister."

"Gee!" from Will.

"The devil you say!" from Monty.

"First explain this," I said, "before we turn your offer down finally. How is it that you couldn't abuse England and the English violently enough the other day at Bill's, and yet you invite us now to undertake this delicate mission?"

"Ah!" he answered. "Who likes England? To do good business, deal with England; to be sure of your pay, deal with Englishmen; if you want to know the truth about a thing, then read the English papers; if you want a good time, value for your money, sport, fun, good food, toleration—go to London, England. But to —— with England! I deal with the English because they play straight, but I hate them! —— them! Everybody hates them! This man is American, which is a different matter.

"I invite you three because you are men of integrity and courage; him I invite because of his nationality. My sister desires above everything to go to America and live there. She has no use for the estate in Aleppo. She would be very well satisfied with a draft on New York for a million dollars as her share. We would divide the rest—you four and I. But the simplest, the safest, the easiest course would be, would it not, for this young American to marry her?"

"I'll hand it to you," laughed Will, "you're an optimist. You think I'm a Mormon because I hail from the States, and a Mormon's the same as a Turk in your judgement, eh? You guess I'd marry 'em fast as they come, if they'd money. But what if the lady wouldn't have me?"

"Not have you? Yuh-ho-ha-ha! She'd jump through a top window into your arms!"

"Some fairy!" Will murmured. "What does she weigh?"

"Ah! You laugh! You do not believe! Her late husband—my brother-in-law—the wealthy Armenian, took her with him more than once to the United States on business. She loves New York. She idolizes the Americans. As to her weight? You think that because I am heavy— Wait! Wait until I show you her photograph! Wait here!"

While he was gone we sat looking at one another in silence, smiling but saying nothing. None wanted to be first to admit that the fat-lipped mongrel had told at least a plausible story. None cared to scoff, lest some strange twist of fortune should eventually prove the weird tale true and the scoffer no wiser than all scoffers are. Even Fred Oakes, the irrepressible, to whom we all looked for a first opinion, averted his eyes and blew cigar-smoke rings up between the beams. Not one word had passed between us when the Levantine came back.

He unwrapped the photograph from half a dozen sheets of pink and tinsel paper, his fat fingers shaking with emotion.

"Judge for yourself!" he said, passing it to Will.

Will took it, judged and passed it on. It was the faded likeness done in New York of a girl not more than eighteen or nineteen, dark-haired as the Levantine himself, but slender, with an almost perfect figure and hands as unlike his pudgy paws as chalk is unlike cheese. She had the Armenian nose but the rest of her features would have passed for Western.

"She can't be your sister," said I.

"Oh, yes! She is my sister by my father's second wife. My mother was a Jewess from Greece, hers an Armenian from Tarsus."

"Well," said Monty, glancing in turn at the photograph and passing it back to its owner, "your story may be true and that may be your sister, but it doesn't interest me. We have no right, legal or moral, that I know of, to break into any Turk's harem and carry off a woman from it. If she were English or American the case might be different."

"It isn't even as if she had appealed to us herself," said I.

"Or even as if we liked our host," added Fred maliciously.

"If I were looking for a wife," said Will, "I'd have to be very drunk and destitute before I'd choose a widow, sight unseen."

"But, gentlemen all!" The Levantine threw back the heavy locks of oily hair from off his forehead with a gesture of almost magnificent appeal. "What if the lady herself should address her appeal direct to you? What then? I do not ask you to believe me. I do not ask anything for my own sake—"

"Not a whopping big percentage of the loot, for instance, eh?" asked Will.

"Yes. I will take my share—my full share—that is true. But at that you know all about me. I have no other stipulations up my sleeve. A man is a fool who lets wealth slip past him. What is he, gentlemen all, when he refuses to rescue a lady in distress?"

We met eyes again and did not answer him. Florid—extravagant—absurd—nevertheless, his appeal had weight to it, and I for one would not have committed myself to a flat refusal—not until he should have a chance to prove his statements. He seemed able to read something of our change of mind—a legacy with which his eastern ancestors had blessed him.

"What if Thabita, my sister, should herself appeal to you direct? Would you then refuse her? Listen! There is not a man in all Aleppo to whom I can appeal. To the Greeks? To the Syrians? To the Armenians? To the Jews? To the Georgians? To the Turks? To the Arabs? To the Circassians? Any one of those would sell the information promptly for a very small sum to the governor! Then to the English? They would laugh at me! To the French? They would ask me whether the woman was not well provided for? To the Germans? They would take the matter up, no doubt, but in their own interest; it is likely they would cause me to be arrested. You do not know what goes on in Turkish prisons. Once in a Turkish prison—I am a big, strong man, gentlemen all; the bigger and stronger, the worse for me. I am not weak but I would sign anything if they once put the torture to me in a Turkish prison. Ugh! I have seen the bodies brought out for burial."

IF WE had had anything else to occupy our time with, except Monty's perennial chess-board—and that interested only him, not us—it is practically certain we should have dismissed the man's proposal without ceremony. It was not in its favor, for instance, that he frankly disliked three of us and that we were unanimous in our distaste for him. We did turn him down flat for the time being and went on deck to pace back and forth under the stars.

But time came to retire to the stuffy little cabins and then each of us had only four walls very close at hand instead of the illimitable sky. Sleep refused to come to me and, as I tossed on the hard bunk, imagination played strange tricks. Utmost efforts at concentration on twenty other problems in turn failed to banish from mind the picture of a widow in the hands of that scoundrelly Turk, pleading in vain through iron bars for ordinary human charity.

The creaking of the woodwork became the footfall of assassins or the whispering of schemers. The noise of an overworked pump somewhere down in the bilge transformed itself into a woman's sobs. When I did fall asleep at last, a Turk came in my dreams and explained in excellent English that I had no legal right whatever to interfere and that the woman would be dropped into the Bosphorus at dawn; yet all the while a voice there was no locating insisted that any gentleman would know what to do and would do it swiftly without reference to his own convenience.

At breakfast I found that the others' experience had been similar. We had all dreamed about the business in one form or another and, although we were the last men to be influenced in our decision by "such stuff as dreams are made of," we recognized the dreams as evidence that the Levantine's strange story had got down deeper into our thoughts than his personality had into our regard.

And then came bad weather, to keep us in the saloon with nothing to do but read uninteresting books, tell oft-repeated tales, play chess or cards and think. Thought brought back that story of the woman in the governor's harem and, although reflection on the subject set us more on guard than ever against Achmed McNamara's blandishments, curiosity increased.

"Can't you go with your story to the missionaries?" we asked him the third night at dinner.

"Missionaries!" He puffed out his cheeks and held his hands palms uppermost. "Everybody goes to them with tales. Most of them believe the lies and disbelieve the truth. But suppose they did believe me; what could they do? They can't interfere in a purely domestic issue between Mohammedans. I'm Mohammedan—so is my sister—so is the Turkish governor. And if you can point to a single infringement of Turkish law or custom, even down to the kidnaping of my sister, that's more than anybody else can. Suppose you can prove she was kidnaped—what then? Shall the missionaries imitate the Turks and burst the governor's harem open?"

"Then how do you propose we should go about the rescue?" Monty asked him.

"Ah! Ask me another. You are offered the half of a property worth two million pounds; do you imagine you are offered that for nothing? That is the price of American ingenuity and English bulldoggedness to be applied to the problem. If I knew how to do it, I would do it. If I could put the million pounds I offer you into my own pocket, I would multiply my little fleet of liners until all the Mediterranean—and perhaps even other seas—should know my house-flag."

"Your house-flag is a yellow dog, isn't it?" Fred asked him blandly.

"No, sir! That animal is a golden fox."

The more his little liner pitched and wallowed in the trough of the great waves crowding before the west wind into that shallow gulf, the more we studied the proposition and the more we threw deliberate cold water on it, the less illusory it seemed. Long before Iskanderun came in view—to give the port its true, historic name instead of the uglier modern one—we had made up our minds that there really was a woman beleaguered in a harem against her brother's will, even if not against her own.

As for getting her out, that was another matter. To make any sort of business deal with Achmed McNamara was a dangerous proceeding in itself. As Monty was careful to point out, if we should set the terms down on paper they would have to include the rescuing of the lady, and what court in the world could be expected to enforce a contract that included among its provisions the crime of harem-breaking?

Fred proposed drawing on Achmed McNamara for a million pounds and obliging him to accept the note before we would undertake anything. But, as Monty again pointed out, supposing that Achmed McNamara intended playing a trick on us—as was only too probable—our possession of any such note might be taken as proof of our complicity in some nefarious scheme. He might be able to represent us as the chief beneficiaries in some other crime he was contemplating and about which we actually knew nothing at all.

"It's an old trick all through the East," he warned us, "to prepare a scapegoat in advance in case of failure."

"Why don't we just carry out the original intention," I proposed, "and simply go and see Aleppo? Then, if anything turns up to corroborate McNamara's yarn, we'll be there on the spot to judge of it."

That was what we agreed upon. We sighted Iskanderun late in the evening and lay to, the captain preferring to keep his offing until dawn. That night Achmed McNamara surpassed himself. The force of his appeal at times was almost poetic. Reckless of our opinion of himself, he swept the strings of all the emotions he supposed us conceivably heirs to, touching on our pride of race, avarice, ambition, religion, superstitions, curiosity, generosity, sportsmanship, charity, good luck and courage, among a host of others.

"Think when you shall come to die, gentlemen all. Dare you look back then and remember this chance that you missed of doing a good deed and at the same time feathering your own nests?"

WHAT CONVINCED us finally that this extraordinary man was telling at least part of the truth and really had set his fat heart on employing us to crack a governor's harem open was his insistence on a full half-share of the profit from the sale of the estate—half and no more, no less. If he had been a trickster out-and-out, merely decoying us into some miserable confidence game, he would certainly have offered us a larger share than half when we stood out so long against him. Had he been deceiving us he could safely have offered us all the loot and no doubt would have done it. He might have pretended to be satisfied with the rescue of his sister. But he stuck vociferously to his first proposal of a half-and-half division, so that we grew convinced that there was really something to divide.

Finally Monty half satisfied him with a promise that had the merit of taking the wind out of his sails for the present without committing us to anything too outrageous.

"All right," he said, "if you can prove us to us that your sister is really in the governor's harem against her will and wants to be released, then we'll talk the matter over in Aleppo. But I warn you, before we would consider taking any kind of action, we should require an unquestionably authentic appeal addressed to us by the lady herself. We would listen to that. Without it we wouldn't even consider the matter."

"I will satisfy you, entirely."

"Mind you, McNamara!" Fred warned, "let us get as much as an impression that you're playing tricks, and we'll use all our ingenuity in making things hot for you!"

"As for that," said McNamara, "I can care for myself. At present business is business. I forget about that song you made regarding me. I swallow my pride. I laugh at it. I am good-natured—a good sport. That is because we shall engage in this business together. After that, I shall resume my displeasure as I put on a glove, and you shall be sorry about that song."

"Excellent!" laughed Fred. "I'll add some verses."

"I'm a man of my word!" frowned the Levantine. "Good night, gentlemen all; if your word is as good as mine we are already as good as partners, for a time."

Although we still had no faith in his promises, we liked him a lot better for his manner of making them.

III

ISKANDERUN—ALEXANDRETTA—IS A long way from being the hideous pest-hole some guide-books make of it and there is a hotel there that can give points and a beating to many a well-known European hostelry. True, at meal-times a Turkish guide takes you by the hand and leads you through twisted streets to a restaurant half-way down a hidden alley, where they feed you *kabobs* on skewers with the cinders sticking to them, but that is a small price to pay in the East for a clean bed and flealessness.

We had all our belongings brought to the hotel under the curious eyes of fifty or sixty Turkish officers billeted there and prepared to stay a week while we got ready for a protracted journey inland. But we had reckoned without Achmed McNamara, our host on his ship and now self-constituted host ashore.

He was not to be denied, nor were his myrmidons. However great his fear of the Turkish government, he seemed to have local influence; even the officers lounging in doorways treated him with genial, half humorous respect.

He sent us servants with a note apiece in English extolling their virtues, until it looked like a tribe that lurked for us in the hotel compound. Then, the second day, he began sending horses, and they were by no means bad ones. No less than thirty arrived for us to choose from, and when we had picked two each and got ready for the time honored Turkish bargain that takes no account of time except to squander it, it was only to learn, to our amazement, that there was nothing at all to pay and only a present to make to the dragoman.

It was not at all agreeable to us to accept valuable presents from McNamara, yet there was no way of making that clear to him, for he himself kept carefully out of our way, after his first visit to make sure we had found comfortable quarters. We refused to accept the horses, but those we had picked out were stabled at the hotel, nevertheless, and fed at some one's expense, certainly not ours. And when we sent out word that we desired to buy other horses on our own account, none came.

So, on the third day, Will Yerkes paid his habitual visit to the United States consul to ask questions, prophesying disappointment all the way, but he came back grinning.

"He says McNamara is a good sport," he announced. "Says he'd trust him."

Thereafter Monty called on the British consul and received much the same report, although he added—

"They do say the man is a clever smuggler."

Learning that we proposed to ride to Aleppo, the British consul applied for a *kavass* for us—a Turkish soldier to act as escort and lend the semi-official touch that would keep away robbers and perhaps even stand off the beggars. No sooner had the soldier turned up with his hungry-looking mount than we made up our minds to surprise McNamara by starting that very afternoon.

Yet it was we who were taken by surprise, for he came round himself, magnificently mounted, and begged us to not delay any further, but to start immediately and keep only far enough behind him to create an impression of independence.

"If it once gets out that I belong to your party—" he began, but Fred cut him short.

"You're not of our party! We'll deal with any one who brings that charge against us."

"And about our horses," Monty cut in. "Let us have the bill for them, will you?"

"They are not your horses!" he retorted, sitting his own restive mount with a very fine seat for such a stout, squat lump of a man. "I lend them to you because you are proceeding to Aleppo on my business."

Then he did an almost Homeric thing. The sweat of sheer anxiety was streaming down his temples. Most of the horse's restiveness was due to a sense of the rider's uneasy state of mind. Yet he turned at bay, as it were, threw caution to the winds, dismounted, gave the reins to a ragged attendant and strode up close to Monty.

"If you're afraid," he said, "say so now! If you're willing to give me a chance to prove my story is true, come on. If you're not willing—blast and shiver it—own up now, and I'll give the four of you a free trip on my steamer back to where you came from."

Monty laughed like a boy out of school. It was rare to have any one, particularly out of the Levant, impute that sort of motive to our indecisions.

"We intend to go to Aleppo," he said, "at our own expense. We'll give you the chance there you ask for. We're ready to start as soon as we've settled for the horses."

"Curses!" thundered McNamara. "Allah made the English stiff-necked in order that all other men might hate them. It is too late. You must pay me at Aleppo. I will make out the bill when I get there and present it to you on arrival. But for the love of fire and food, make no more excuses!"

That arrangement being perfectly satisfactory, we told him to ride on and gave orders to our own crowd of followers to load our belongings on the weird thing they called an *araba,* which resembled a wagon in two respects: it had wheels and, moreover, it was drawn by horses.

An hour, almost to the minute, after McNamara had ridden away post-haste, we rode out of the courtyard after him, reckless of the future, free as the delicious air we breathed—for it is not true that no healing breezes come to blow away Alexandretta's smells—aware of the green delights of Mesopotamian Spring and light of heart accordingly—as we should not have been had we permitted McNamara to pay our expenses. Stiff-necked the British are no doubt, in spots, but that is mainly because they know from sweet experience what the fruits of independence are.

McNamara, from a varying distance of a mile to a dozen miles ahead of us, exhausted ingenuity in trying to make us hurry over the seventy-mile road that crosses a mountain range and links Aleppo with the sea. But for the very reason that it was a good road through a lovely countryside, well used by a host of men of every nationality, trade and rank, with whom talk in half a dozen tongues was good, who sat by the wayside gratefully to exchange remarks with strangers, we lingered.

The more he stormed and sent back messages, the keener our delight became in side-excursions to view historic monuments.

THERE WAS the pillar, for instance, on which St. Simeon Stylites marooned himself for a tale of years, less than a day's march out of Aleppo but reached by a by-road over the flower-strewn hills, close to the village of Termanin. Wild horses could have borne us past that turning, but not our tame and tired ones, nor any impatient arguments scrawled by McNamara on slips of wrapping-paper and sent back by a ragged runner.

We turned off, singing to Fred's concertina, followed by our own gang and four times their number of unattached wayfarers, who did not recognize the noise as music but liked it nevertheless, if only because it testified to that priceless gift, good spirits. Some of them, no doubt, attached themselves to us because of our Turkish soldier—one lone, lean, ragged veteran on a horse nearly as old as he was. Such is the power of a sword in its scabbard and a uniform in tatters to drive men's fears away. But the most came because Fred sang. For aught they knew he was some new sort of religious fanatic, glad instead of gloomy, and our side-trip to the ruined chapel of Simeon Stylites confirmed that explanation.

There we camped for the third night, scorning the government post-house with its dirt and fleas, out in the open with the ruins of chapel and pillars in full view, bathed in moonlight, with the riffraff of Asia Minor asleep under our tent-flies, squatting around our camp-fires, getting in the cook's way, commenting on our equipment and commissariat, curious and kind, and wholly unselfconscious. Nothing less emphatic than whips and goads could have persuaded them that their room could be preferable to their company.

So, when we had eaten supper, it pleased us to decree a great feast of rice and grease and spices, at which all who cared might fall to and eat their fill. Nobody who had not seen could ever believe what quantities of boiled rice the Syrian wayfarer can eat nor the gentleness with which he can be grateful afterward, Moslem or Christian.

We fell asleep amid an atmosphere of mixed blessings and wood smoke. And because we slept well and liked the spot and rather preferred to see the historic place without our uninvited following, we chased the crowd away soon after dawn and spent the whole day loafing at Termanin.

So to Termanin came Achmed McNamara, back from Aleppo on horseback in a prodigious passion, with a three-day beard outstanding from his swarthy cheeks.

"Is this your English way of making haste?" he thundered, for all the world as if we had taken his pay.

What he would have said and done had we cared to travel at his expense was beyond imagination. He roared at us like a lime-juicer boatswain in a hurry to get sail off. So, to calm him a little, Fred sang the offensive song.

"You men would sing while your mothers roasted!" he bellowed at us, believing, perhaps, that his voice was within bounds.

Like some animals, he did not seem to realize that the thunders had their home in him. All ears had to listen when he spoke above a whisper. But Fred's concertina had no ears nor modesty and dinned him down. Rage how he would, McNamara had to bide his time until the chapel of St. Simeon of the Pillar had echoed to the legend of his infamy in rime.

Achmed McNamara, oh, tarara, oh, tarara,
Left his home in the Sahara for the far Sahara's good.
All decency disdaining, he was warned against remaining.
It was no use his explaining that he wasn't understood.
His utter lack of virtue was the element that hurt you—
The vacuum of goodness that no sermoning would fill.
They'd have tolerated vanity or stood for sheer insanity,
But Mac's unmixed satanity made far Sahara ill.
So they banished McNamara, oh, tarara, oh, tarara,
And the ladies of the desert now no longer know the thrill
Of the battle-cry announcing that a watchful hubby's pouncing,
And the screams behind the tent as McNamara foots the bill!

At that stage of the song's development there were already seven verses, and Achmed McNamara had to listen to them all before he could get us to pay any attention to his business. The enforced pause did him good. It enabled him to calm himself and get some measure of self-control. When Fred had finished, and the echoes of the last chorus had gone galloping down the valley, he got off his lathered horse and came and stood almost meekly by the camp-fire.

"Gentlemen all!" he pleaded—something like a ballyhoo man vainly laboring to fill an empty tent. "There is no time for enjoyment. This is serious. This is—oh, my ——! How shall I tell you? How shall I make you see? Listen, then—I will tell you all, from the beginning."

He flung himself down before the fire and began blubbering with great sobs, like a bullock with its throat cut, and the convulsions of his big frame seemed likely to shake the meat from the bones. If he was acting then, or anything but elemental, I, for one, was deceived about him.

"GENTLEMEN ALL, I searched Aleppo—I searched Antioch—I searched Alexandretta for Turk, Greek, Jew, Arab, Frenchman, Englishman—for any one who dared help me release my sister. I found nobody! Some were cowards—some not to be trusted—all were hopeless—no use! Twice I traveled to Alexandria in hope of finding cutthroats there—men I could hire—who would not be known—who could cross on my steamer—go to Aleppo swiftly—do murder in the dark—seize my sister—escape again! I found none! I found none! Plenty of cut-throats—none to be trusted! Then I found you!"

At that unintended bull we lay back in our chairs and roared with laughter until the village dogs awoke and set up a chorus of barking.

"Oh, my ——! Gentlemen all!" he implored us. "For the love of God listen to me! If it is Allah's will that my sister be released—and we lie here letting opportunity pass by us—then what are we? Listen! I went to Aleppo. I engaged accommodation for you there, making believe you were great travelers intending to proceed later to Mosul to view the remains of Nineveh. Then I sent word by a sweetmeat seller to the assistant of the eunuch who has charge of that part of the harem where my sister is, saying I had come. She sent back word to me that within a week the governor will give her to be the wife of a Turk named Mustapha Kamil. That man Mustapha Kamil is a monster, gentlemen all, no less! It is he who gave the word for the last great massacre—he who ordered the warehouse burned in which two hundred Armenians had taken refuge—he who cut the fingers from living women in order to get their rings! Two of his wives have died—Allah knows of what complaint. Now he is to take my sister—and all that property—and I am told he has threatened to take me, if he can find me, because my sister in despair screamed through a window to men in the street to find me in Alexandretta and bring me to her.

"Gentlemen all, if that man Mustapha Kamil catches me, the things that will be done to my poor body are worse than hell could ever be! A week from now—one week, gentlemen—and it will be too late to save my sister and all that property!"

Monty drew a bow at a venture—better acquainted with the East than any of us, and so more likely to chance on the key to any situation.

"Suppose we let the property go hang?" he suggested. "Suppose that instead of attempting any harebrained rescue we interview this governor of Aleppo and make a bargain with him—the property against your sister's freedom? Surely you're rich enough to support your sister afterward—in America or anywhere else."

"Oh, no! Oh, no! But yes! Yes! Oh, no! Gentlemen all, how could you propose to me to let a million pounds of money slip through my fingers? You do not know the circumstances—you can not know, or you would not make such proposals. I am not bankrupt but I am trembling on the brink. My fleet of liners is all mortgaged—the interest eats up the profits—I have no money for the repairs that should be made. Unless I get that property, I am ruined!"

"D'you mean," Monty asked him, "that unless you can get the property you don't care what happens to your sister?"

"Oh, no!" he answered gloomily. "Let us go and rescue my sister by all means—by any means. I would rather Mustapha Kamil should have me than her!"

"Now you're talking!" said Will, and I knew by the way he shoved his lower lip out and puckered his eyes as if peering into the future that he was won over to the man's cause—not that Will would necessarily have admitted it yet.

"But I tell you this—I warn you," sobbed McNamara, "that the governor will laugh at you. Why should he make bargains about what is already in his hands? Why should he let my sister escape to America to tell about Turkish rule? Can he not hand her over to Mustapha Kamil and make a friend of his powerful enemy?"

"The man's right," said Will, blowing smoke rings.

"All that will happen, if you try to bargain with the governor," continued McNamara, warming to his tale and forgetting a little of his grief in the process, "is that he will throw me in prison. Ow! Have you seen a Turkish prison?"

"We can easily avoid that," said Monty. "My servants are under British protection as long as they are in my service, do you understand me?"

"M-n-yes," said McNamara' doubtfully.

"Do you care to enter my service?"

"Effendi, if I do it makes no difference. The governor of Aleppo will do as he sees fit, not as the law says he shall."

"Yes or no?" demanded Monty.

"Yes!"

"Then I engage you as my dragoman."

McNamara sighed heavily.

"Very well," he said, "but what is the use? They will ask what an owner of ships is doing in the part of a dragoman and will point to it as proof of intended wrongdoing. My only hope is that I may not be recognized."

"Recognized? Take that thick mustache off!"

"Ah, what is the use? These servants—for one piastre any one of them would tell."

"Let them all return to Alexandretta, then," Monty answered. "We can send the *kavass* back in charge of them with an order on the consul for their pay at the other end. You can drive the *araba* with our luggage."

At that proposal Achmed McNamara recovered from the depths of gloom sufficiently to smile.

"I have always said the English have I good sense," he commented. "Which of you is the gentleman who will lend me a razor?"

To the almost riotous disgust of all the servants, we sent them packing on the homeward road that night. The *kavass* was the only philosophic one; it was all the same to him which road he took, at what unseemly hour, provided he was paid double for the journey and provided with good food. He coerced the rest, but not without blows.

NEXT DAWN we were in the saddle, riding down-hill toward Aleppo, the heavily loaded *araba* laboring along behind us in charge of a fat man with fat lips and an absurdly boyish-looking face. Whoever should recognise Achmed McNamara in that guise and garb, using those expostulations to the horses, would have needed the eyes of a hawk and more suspicion than even the Near East cuddles in its bosom.

So, each leading a spare horse, and with a plausible tale ready of servants who deserted in the night because of some fancied grievance, we came in sight of the ancient Saracenic wall with seven gates and the huge citadel some idiots say was built by Abraham—of the Kuwaik River with its miles of gardens on either bank—and the spreading, wealthy-growing suburbs through which we had to pass.

McNamara had seen fit not to engage quarters for us in New Azizieh, the suburb, where most of the Europeans live, nor in any of the *Khans*—the great barrack-like buildings where travelers, merchants with wares especially, may rent space and care for themselves. He had rented a small house for us at the bottom end of a short blind alley, in the densest part of the native town, without the wall.

"Here," he said, "not one single person except the beggars will care a continental who you are, or anything about you. Lock the gate then, gentlemen all, and keep the beggars outside."

What he said was likely enough true. If we had come clattering in with a host of retainers behind us and a *kavass* to shout for right of way, there would have been limitless curiosity to meet. As it was, the only persons interested in the sober-looking party of four dusty foreigners with one fat servant were the chance-met urchins whom the said fat servant hired to lead away the horses to some stable of which he knew a furlong away. We carried the luggage ourselves and left the *araba* horseless in the street.

The house was big enough for twice our number. Like most Turkish houses, its only outer windows were narrow slits in the wall of the upper story. The entrance was through a high door into a small courtyard and the other windows and the house door proper all opened on to that.

It was not the sort of place in which to stand a siege or to hide, once hue and cry were raised, but it was a mooted point whether concealment could help us in any event. We should have to come out into the open to do anything about McNamara's sister and in the event of trouble our only sensible or safe course would be to appeal to our consuls—British and American—immediately.

The speed with which travelers can make empty quarters comfortable, both to look at and to live in, is their sign of experience the wide world over. We set up our chairs and camp-beds, constructed a table out of a broken American export packing-case, spread a cloth over that, unpacked our bags, drove nails and hung hats and rifles on the walls, had a bath in the place beyond the kitchen where the water ewers stood in a row and decided we were at home.

Then, before we had rested in Aleppo half an hour, McNamara returned with new servants and a cook who could do unrighteous things to bits of meat on skewers, as well as make thin, flat cakes and boil rice. When evening fell we were all four suffering from indigestion but otherwise in shape for happenings.

"What's Aleppo like by night?" Will wondered.

"Like any other smelly dark place, unless, you've a wise guide," Monty answered. "Nothing to do but sit indoors and twiddle thumbs, Will. Remember, this is the place that invented the word assassin. The Assassins were a tribe of murderers who waylaid strangers in the Middle Ages. They tell me the town has lost none of its old flavor."

Presently Achmed McNamara returned bearing five hurricane lanterns and dressed, with a red sash round his fat stomach, in the garb of the sort of venial coast-hireling who hunts the ports and preys off well-to-do foreigners. The breed is unmistakable and he looked and acted the part so well that Fred added a verse to the song, describing papa McNamara's former means of livelihood and reasons for escaping from the Levant to the Sahara—outrageous, unholy reasons that made even McNamara, beside himself with nervousness, laugh so that he could not light the lanterns.

"Now, gentlemen all," he said in his best bull showman voice, "we are going within the ancient city wall to a place that might be said to correspond to a London club—the Carlton, let us say, or perhaps rather the Bachelor's, except that membership is not required. It is where the more important citizens come together of an evening. It will be quite in order for your dragoman to enter with you, to explain what you see and to give your orders in Turkish. It is the only place where one can be really sure to see the governor and his friends."

So we armed ourselves very carefully with repeating pistols and a good, stout stick apiece and followed McNamara out into the pitch-dark streets, each carrying a lantern. And, as if they had known and were waiting on purpose, all the miserable street dogs in Asia seemed to emerge out of the night and yap at our heels. It was useless to try to beat them off or kick at them; that only started reprisals and the teeth of those street curs are too unclean for a man to laugh at the idea of being bitten. There was nothing to do but walk gingerly, with a trail of green, glowing eyes and snapping fangs behind.

There were no lights worthy of the name except our own. Here and there a glint like the point of a dagger would betray itself through a keyhole or under a door-jamb, but there were no sounds of indoor revelry to contrast with the outdoor gloom, nor even Turkish music—that antithesis of the glad and beautiful—in proof that life of any kind was being lived.

The dogs did us one good turn. They called attention to us, which was just exactly what we did not want, but, when a pair of presumable footpads rushed out from a dark corner with long blades gleaming in our lantern-light, they tripped over the curs and fell among the pack.

The ensuing fight lacked any kind of glamour. We did not care to shoot, partly for fear of killing the men, mainly for sake of our own privacy; street brawls are no man's business after nightfall, but a shot in the dark gives that touch of modernity that breaks the ancient spell and brings the curious hot-foot. So we beat at the dogs with our sticks; and what with that, and the bitten victims' knives, there was some disgusting work done. Finally the two men, torn to rags, staggered up and ran for cover with a pack snarling viciously behind them. After yelping at us for a minute or two, most of the rest of the curs stayed behind to consider the disposal of their dead and wounded comrades.

AFTER THAT we eyed every dark corner—and Aleppo is full of them—as if it surely held armed footpads. We went like stage villains on the prowl, led by a fat man more afraid than any of us, until Fred, who came last and saw the humor first, called a halt and leaned against a door to yell with laughter. Somebody who lived in the house and doubtless thought our attentions were meant for him began to pelt us with sticks and lumps of hard mortar from the roof, breaking the glass of Will's lantern with a lucky shot.

"I'm going back," Fred announced, "to find some of those dead dogs and toss them on the rascal's roof."

But Monty would not hear of that and McNamara, urging us to hurry, preached a breathless sermon about the depths of unseemliness associated with a dead dog in the Eastern mind.

"My proposal was to act unseemly," answered Fred. "I want to make the liver and lights of the owner of that house turn into gristle with rage."

"For such an insult he would follow you to the ends of the earth and, if he died, then his son and his grandson after him," said McNamara.

But Fred was in one of his irresponsible moods and affected to care nothing for the Near East's sense of values. We walked on, he always last, in the wake of McNamara until a gaunt man with a great sword, in the shadow of the gate in the wall, challenged us. Fred asked to see the sword and the man let him handle it. We passed on.

There was a lantern by the gate-side and in its dim rays Fred and the sentry looked like a picture of the present talking to the past. Fred offered to buy the weapon and to his own astonishment was taken up. A minute later he came clanking after us with the long sword at his waist; we inclined to rail at him for wasting time on foolishness, not at all suspecting what influence the bought sword was to have on our immediate future. If we had stopped to think, a night-stick bought or stolen from a New York policeman or a saber taken in trade from the life-guard sentry at Whitehall might be expected to produce results of some sort, but in Turkey in Asia one has left the rules of proportion behind.

We passed along the streets ever narrower and narrower, by turnings ever darker, with only the stars overhead and now and then a graceful, slender minaret upreared against the sky to give us reassurance that it was a great city through which we made way. But for the stars and those rare glimpses of tower and roof, it might have been a jungle gorge—interminable, deep, with wild dogs hunting us.

At last we swung down the narrowest, darkest side alley of all, where an enormous black man with a candle-lantern and a rifle leaned against the wall and looked us over. Seeing us to be Europeans, decently clad and with a servant to light us along, he let us pass, muttering something that ended in Allah.

"What's he there for?" demanded Monty.

"None pass him by night who ought not to enter the place we shall visit," said McNamara.

"What if some one drove a sword through him?" Fred asked.

"You shall see!" said McNamara.

A dim light burned at the end of the alley in a stone niche in the lintel of a very narrow door. Without a word or sign to us McNamara turned in there, his bulky figure filling the opening. We followed in single file. Six paces down the passage we were aware of eyes in the dark that glanced us over, and four black men, bigger than he who had stood alone in the street, took shape out of the gloom. They all had knives and one held a coiled cord in his hand.

"Now you know what would happen," laughed McNamara.

A door slammed behind us and shut off our line of retreat. I nearly jumped out of my skin at the sound of it. Then another door opened in front and our eyes were dazzled by a blaze of light—soft enough really but torture for a moment after so long in the outer dark. At a word from McNamara we set our lanterns down on the floor and followed in.

Immediately the inner door shut fast behind us.

WE FOUND ourselves in a long, wide, stone-walled room, whose vaulted roof was supported on a double row of pillars. There was a feeling of being underground, caused, no doubt, by the crypt-like construction of the place. Little colored glass lamps hung down from the center of each section of roof and stained with a dozen mingled hues the rings of smoke rising from cigarets and Turkish water-pipes.

On benches along the wall, comfortably cushioned in bright red, on seats built around each supporting pillar, on carpets on the floor and on piled-up cushions at the farther end sat men of twenty nationalities. A hum of conversation had died down as we entered, and they all stared at us in silence, continuing to smoke, continuing to sip coffee out of ridiculously tiny cups, but letting fall no word either of greeting or comment.

There were men there of nationalities none of us had ever seen, besides Turks, Armenians, Greeks, Persians, Syrians, Kurds, Germans, Italians and Serbs, and in a moment, after a long, deliberate stare at us, they were all again talking in a babel of low-grumbling tongues, none raising his voice, perhaps because of the echoing vaulted roof—perhaps, too, because a man's friends are mostly dead men and his enemies live too alertly, as the proverb says.

It was clear at the first glimpse that this was no political society. Nor was it a place like Bill's at Alexandria, where democratic principles are practiced if not preached. These men were all divided into little groups, each group distinct and on guard against confusion with the rest. Men of a nation sat together. Turks sat with Germans, and Armenians with any one at all; but the others were exclusive, each to his tongue and clan. Only something one could not at first lay a finger on seemed to hold all the groups in one thrall.

Near the center of one long wall was a low table unoccupied, if that is rightly a table whose legs are a foot high. Cushions were heaped between it and the wall and we sat down on them, curling up unaccustomed legs as best we could, Fred tossing his bought sword on the table with the clatter of a cavalier born to the swashbuckling trade. By the tilt of his trim beard and the laugh in his eye, anything except inaction would amuse him that night. Achmed McNamara took his seat on a cushion on the floor at one end of the table and eyed Fred with furtive anxiety.

"Men have been killed for presuming too far in this place," he announced.

"The deuce you say!" Fred answered. He had his concertina strapped over his shoulder like a camera and by the way his fingers danced along imaginary keys it was evident that, whatever the night-owls of Aleppo might think was seemly, his mood was for music.

Nor was it Monty's way to restrain him. Those two, mutually licensed critics of each other's plans and walks in life, invariably faced the unknown with sublime indifference to the direction of the cat's jump. Monty's was the cavalry leader's frame of mind that secretly approves of anything unconventional because it may lead to opposition and developments. Fred had a sort of schoolboy love of throwing a mocking hat into the ring for Monty to fetch out again.

Presently a Turk of the brand-new Turkish type, with his fez cocked at an angle and his pants out of an export bale from Birmingham—a little, pale-faced, spry-footed shrimp with a very neatly waxed mustache—came mincing over to us from some sort of den behind a screen in the farthest corner and asked for our orders. Achmed McNamara ordered coffee and cigarets without consulting us and the Turk repeated the order to a thick-lipped savage in turban and red pantaloons.

"This is the proprietor," announced McNamara and the shrimp smirked. He appeared inclined to indulge the curiosity that exuded from him like a smell.

"For what is the sword?" he asked, making a motion toward it with his smoking cigaret.

"To cut with," Fred announced.

"To cut what?" He spoke quite good English, although he was plainly not of that Turkish class that is always Anglophil.

"Knots. I am a man of scant patience."

"What kind of knots?"

"Nots of any kind," Fred answered, grinning. "I never take no for an answer. Stand here and tell us who the gentry are who dislike one another so, yet come here to breathe the same tobacco smoke. Who are they all?"

Achmed McNamara made violent gestures of warning which Fred studiously affected not to see. Achmed in Bill's at Alexandria had been a thundering bully; here he was a panicky scareling, rolling side-wise on a cushion in wordless anxiety.

The Turk threw an air of cheap importance.

"It would be unwise to attract attention," he said, facing us squarely with his legs apart, "but if you will look behind me you will see no less than the governor of Aleppo sitting cross-legged on the seat against the wall. He is the man with the water-pipe. He to the right of him is Mustapha Kamil Bey, smoking the cigaret in an amber tube. You are keeping good company tonight."

The coffee came and a small box of Turkish Regie cigarets. Fred tossed money on the table.

"I'm not interested in them," he said. "Tell me about some of the others."

"Oh, there are German financiers, engineers, merchants, concession hunters of many nationalities, Turkish officers—all men of active minds. They come to this place, like yourselves no doubt, to learn what is going on in the world."

"The world consisting of Aleppo?"

"Scarcely. The world all leading to Aleppo."

"Show me a German financier."

"That one—the man in a black suit sitting against the pillar, in the direction in which my right elbow is just now pointing. They tell me he could write a check for fifty million Turkish pounds."

"Who would cash it?" Fred asked and the Turk laughed thinly.

"His name is Griffenhahn," he answered. "Doubtless you have heard of him. It is his habit to buy what he desires. Should he desire one of you gentlemen, for instance, he would buy you outright—if not directly, then indirectly; if not with money, then with the aid of a woman or a horse or social benefits or, perhaps, the jail. I can assure you the jail is entirely at his disposal."

"Does he know your price?" Fred wondered blandly.

The Turk laughed with apparently genuine good humor.

"If not, that is not for lack of being told," he answered, turning to leave us. "But why should he pay my so great a price until I can make him a suitable return? Patience is a virtue. Each man has his moment of maximum usefulness, even in Aleppo. The thing is to be awake at the proper moment and clear as to the value of one's services."

HE SWAGGERED away with the annoying strut that seems to be the outward sign of inward mental indigestion—a very fair example of the Asiatic who has done with the old order because it restrained his appetites and has wholly misunderstood the new. Impudent assertion of venality was his attempt at frankness. Airing his rank opinions to strangers in his coffee-shop, he thought, proved him man of the world.

I leaned back to look around a pillar and observe Griffenhahn—a fine figure of a man, although with the too square German shoulders padded to look clumsier than they naturally were. He looked as if he would stand more than six feet high. He had the unmistakable swordsman's wrist and a depth and breadth of head that advertised the thinker. The color of his hair and eyes at that distance in that multicolored light was unguessable, but his mouth was good-humored, although too firm at the corners, and his general air was of culture and intellect. There was a German on either side of him, both of whom lacked his evident personal charm. They looked meaner than perhaps they were, by strength of the contrast.

Achmed McNamara leaned over the table and unbosomed himself of terror.

"For the love of Allah, gentlemen all, be careful what you say and to whom you say it! It is true that that is the governor of Aleppo. It is true that is Griffenhahn. It is true that is Mustapha Kamil Bey who is to have my unhappy sister given him. That idiot Feyamil—the unwhapped dog who owns the place—has told the truth, hoping perhaps to see amusement. Nothing delights his heart so much as to see strangers in difficulty. He knows how likely you English and you, an American, are to blurt out what you know. Yet to call a man by name in this place, or to pretend acquaintance afterward on the ground of having met in here, is to pass the unforgivable insult. That man Feyamil is like a scorpion; he bites and stings without waiting to be tickled."

"What the devil did you bring us in here for?" demanded Monty.

"To see! To observe! In order that you might judge of the men against whom you must pit your wits. Look at that Mustapha Kamil Bey! Did ever you see a meaner, more miserable looking man?"

The description fitted perfectly. The bowed, brown-bearded, hollow-eyed man sitting next the governor looked as if meanness had entered into his very stomach and replaced the generous gastric juice with gall. The hand that held the amber cigaret-tube shook like a leaf in the wind.

"That man Griffenhahn," continued McNamara, dropping his voice to the drone that was his closest possible approach to a whisper, "is he who is buying land. Who ever shall acquire my sister's property, whether the governor or Mustapha Kamil Bey or even you and I, must eventually sell to him. He buys on behalf of the Bagdad Railway. They say the German government finances him. He is one of this world's great ones."

"Oh, what rot!" said Monty. "If he's as great as all that, what brings him squatting in this place?"

"Ah, there is entertainment here."

"There's going to be entertainment before I leave, you mean," Fred grinned.

"For the love of Allah, make no rash foolishness! Think, gentlemen all! To arouse the least suspicion is to make success impossible! Yet what hangs on success? My sister's liberty—that valuable property—my steamship line! Oh, be cautious!"

"I don't see that this view of the villains of the piece brings us any nearer to the issue," said Monty. "This stuffy hole doesn't amuse me. As for Griffenhahn and the governor, I can be introduced to both of them to-morrow morning if that should seem worth while. You forget that, before we consent even to consider taking action, your sister must appeal to us direct."

"That shall happen! Oh, be reasonable, my lord! Surely it is obvious that to stand on ceremony and pay a call on the governor is to insure failure of our purpose. Having accepted the hospitality of the governor or of Griffenhahn, can you thereafter interfere in the private affairs of either? Blast and shiver it, no! You —— English have the faults of your infernal virtues! I knew what I was doing when I proposed to put my case in your hands. I took the best that Allah sent my way. You can not pay a call on them and then act the enemy.

"And can you speak to the governor of his harem? No! Ten thousand times no, blast and shiver it! That is the crime unforgivable in Turkey—the rudeness that means enmity for ever and ever!"

All this while Will sat frowning with his head against the wall behind and an expression of settled gloom about his mouth and shoulders.

"Rotten business!" he whispered to me. "No head or tail to it!"

"Monty has his hand on the way out," I answered. "That stipulation that the sister must appeal to us personally can't be fulfilled—you'll see."

"Rats!" Will answered. "Monty's a man! I know him! He'll no more leave that woman in dutch without a —— hard fight than he'll take money for his honor. He's playing for time, that's all, and conning points. Presently he'll see a way clear—which is more than I can."

"I hope you're right," said I. "My impression is that the case is hopeless and Monty knows it."

"Nothing's hopeless! Next thing you know, Monty 'll turn Fred loose to play the fool. Anything may come of that."

"Even your wedding," I answered sourly.

Optimism without visible foundation from a man with a frown on his face suggestive of sympathetic pessimism is bad for the temper.

Will looked hard at me with a sort of fear behind his eyes.

"D'you know," he said, "I've often wondered just how far I'd go to protect a woman."

"If she were pretty," I said, "you'd go simply as far as she'd let you."

That was slander by inference. Will is as susceptible to good looks as any man in the world, but the veriest hag has only to beckon him to help her out of difficulties. We knew that to our cost. It was the debit side of Will's account, dwarfed to insignificance by the credits that included faithful friendship.

"Why not tell McNamara you'll marry the woman," I grinned. "Then all we've got to do is kidnap the Grand Turk, torture him, make him sign the marriage papers and pack you off on your honeymoon to the States."

Whether or not Monty was playing for time, as Will suggested, time certainly played for us and disclosed, incidentally, the fact that Achmed McNamara, however scared, could keep his own counsel and withhold reasons.

"I still can't see your point in bringing us to this place," Monty repeated.

Instead of answering, McNamara drummed his fingers on the table and nodded toward the far end of the room where there was a screen that hid the kitchen door and the servants only knew what other offices.

Then, if not Achmed McNamara's reasons, at least those of the cosmopolitan guests for being there danced from behind the screen on tiptoe—three of them.

"Straight off a pack of cigarets," Will described them in a whisper to me.

Two of them were not more than ordinarily attractive dancing girls, plump, as the Asiatic likes them, not at all too warmly clothed and adorned with the usual cherry-red lips and glistening teeth that men the world over seem willing to accept as the symbols of pleasure. They danced with tambourines in the style that is taught in the cheap schools by the Marseilles water-front—mock-Oriental, mock-anything but modest.

The third was otherwise. She was plump too—bare-footed, impudent, red-cheeked like the others. But she entered with the air of entering paradise and laughed with the ring of real pleasure in the game before her.

It was perfectly obvious to any man in his ordinary senses that no clever woman could extract whole-souled satisfaction from the prospect of dancing, even divinely, before that congregation of sensualists.

Yet she was a clever woman or I never saw one. It was not belladonna that made her eyes bright or the praise of the mixed mongrels of Aleppo that put life into her movements and her laughter. Nor was it wholly deviltry that gave her joy in what she did.

"That woman can think," said I aloud.

"She is all the hope we have," groaned Achmed McNamara.

IV

"AH!" SAID Monty. "At last there's something slightly interesting. Tell us about her."

We all leaned toward McNamara, but the woman was at least equally interested in us. She fulfilled what appeared to be routine by circling the pillars more or less on tiptoe and making mock-profound obeisance to the worthies, but her bright eyes sought us every moment, from every ingle.

"Gee!" murmured Will. "She'll wring her own neck!"

"Tell us her name, for instance," said Monty.

McNamara shrugged his shoulders and pouted his fat lips until they looked like a pig's snout.

"Name?" he said. "It changes. Here, just now, she calls herself Fatima. In Algiers she was Gabrielle. Before that, in Marseilles, I have been told she was the daughter of Old Man Larilly whom they all called Coeur de Chat. He was famous for the hare soup he sold in the Rue de la Croix de Malte, but they do say no hare meat entered into it. She had left home before I saw Larilly and he never spoke of her, but the sea-captains who frequented that dining-room used to swear by their wheels and anchors that the old man sold her outright to a Moor."

"Would the French government permit that?" I asked, with all the accumulated innocence of three-and-twenty years.

McNamara snickered.

"There is a law against such sales in every country I was ever in," he answered; "laws also against theft, usury, extortion, drunkenness, lese-majesty, Sabbath-breaking and I know not what else. There is also a theory in all those countries that the women do not wish to be sold, the drunkards do not wish to drink, the thieves would rather get what is humorously called an honest living, the extortioners would rather not extort, and that the majority prefers to keep the Sabbath. Why, blast and blizzard, if a woman wishes to be sold, the only man in Europe who can keep her from it is the Turk! He locks her up!"

Daughter or not of Old Man Larilly of Marseilles, this girl who chose to call herself Fatima and once was Gabrielle knew the trick of focusing attention on herself. Hers was not the sort of daring that displays itself diamond-wise, to best advantage in a splendid setting; the other girls were awkward buffoons compared to her, content to squander improprieties of speech and gesture on owl-eyed, unresponsive men who expected it of them and rewarded them for it with blunt ingratitude. She did the unexpected always, choosing to contrast her will-o'-the-wispishness with their too evident ambition to be caught.

She sang in French when it suited her and only when it suited her, at first without accompaniment—little snatches of song, ending as likely as not in the middle of a verse—as she skipped around another pillar to avoid devouring eyes and tantalize new ones. It became quite clear to us before long that every move she made, however apparently unstudied, was really with the purpose of assuaging her curiosity regarding us.

Presently she waltzed and pirouetted over to the German, Griffenhahn, tossed him a jest or two and was rewarded with a swift-witted retort. She asked him questions about his own country in irreverent colloquial French; for instance whether it was true, as some men said, that the German nation was to adopt the Mohammedan religion.

"We are Moslems to a man at heart already," he answered.

"Then do the Germans have harems?"

"In the good German manner, yes."

"Then I know how Germany is ruled. But are they real harems—legal—under one roof?"

"Ah!" he answered. "As in Turkey, so in Germany the principal objection to that is the expense. But every true German has a hotel heart with never less than a hundred rooms in it. To be a German is to be *gemütlich,* that is to say, to love hugely and at random."

"I do not believe, you," she answered, escaping the sweep of his arm.

"Try me!"

"Ah! Ah! Allah gave men noses. I smell before I buy. I will ask first about Germany."

So she had her excuse to come dancing over to us as naively as if that had not been her fixed intention from the first. Her bright eyes had a very shrewd gleam at closer quarters and she took in every detail of our appearance before she came to a stand in front of the low table and, for lack of better introduction, helped herself to a cigaret from our box.

"Alumette?"

Will held up his own cigaret for her to light hers from, no more able to withhold response to a woman's blandishments than a skinned eel can keep from squirming.

Already Achmed McNamara rolled back and forward on his cushions in the throes of scenting danger. He had had no chance as yet to learn what we knew of the length, depth and utterness of Will's platonic worship of a whole sex. For that matter the rest of the denizens of the place were in like predicament, so that Achmed's uneasiness, was not quite unfounded. Without knowing any of the languages—and we all knew more than a smattering of several—that were rising and falling—*staccato—scherzo—andante*—in a devil's orchestra, it was quite easy to observe that the fair Fatima's attention to us was disturbing equanimity. No pointed remarks were addressed at us; nothing was said aloud that had particular reference to her or us, but there was an atmosphere.

CONSIDERING THAT she had broken the last possible barriers of reserve between strangers, she sat down on the table and proceeded to quiz Fred in the sort of French that he could rattle off as fast as she, she playing with the sword-hilt as she laughed at his quick retorts—rather in the French style, rebellious against convention. He amused her more than any of us—far more than Will with his too obviously respectful gallantry. And Fred, being in mood for mischief, chose to revel in the rest of the room's resentment, Monty not at all restraining him but rather seeming to approve and smiling rather grimly under his pointed, waxed mustache.

I began to share Achmed McNamara's nervousness, for I could see no possible advantage in beginning our adventure with a riot. Achmed reached past me to call Fatima's attention by plucking at the fullness of her gauzy Turkish trousers. Catching her eye, he said something to her in Turkish and she turned on him in a flash, arrogantly reckless.

"Poltron!" she jeered at him. *"Vous mefiez—"*

Then she changed into jargon English for our benefit and perhaps to balk other ears, for French in the Levant is more often than not the *lingua franca* that the name implies.

"You ssink zat I not know you? You —— ole fool, Achmed McNamara! You shave off mustache—poof! All same you get in a hole and pull ze hole in after you! Any woman whatever she know you once, she know you again in —— viz your visage all entirely *gâché* by ze devil! Such a man as you 'e can not 'ide 'imself, not from a woman!

"You warn me to be cautious? *Poof!* You zink I not know you bring zese new foreigners for somezing vairee special? You own steamboats and you shave off your mustache and come 'ere like a fat, stupid dragoman all for nothing, eh? You zink me fat 'eaded, eh? Poof! All because your sister is in ze governor's 'areem!"

That last proof of her incisively good guesswork reduced Achmed to a state of cold sweat and collapse. She had no patience with such easily pricked balloons and turned to Fred again.

"Zat! What is zat? Give it 'ere! Show me!"

But Fred never lets that precious concertina out of his own hands, supposing he is conscious and can by any means help it. He took it off the strap and unclasped it.

"Oh, my ——, gentlemen all!" groaned McNamara. "Such a thing as this has never happened here!"

If his deliberate purpose had been to spur Fred to the commission of social sin, he could not have chosen his words better.

"Oh, am I breaking rules?" he inquired with his head at a bird angle and his laughing lips visible between mustache and beard.

Monty was the only one who could have restrained him then, but Monty laughed with the bark of a hound who has winded his quarry.

Fred's arms stretched outward and the yard-long leather bellows drew a mammoth breath. Then, with a crash that sounded like the bells of Bedlam, he wrung out a dozen wild chords just—as he expressed it afterward—to let 'em all know the fat was in the fire. Then he dropped into two-four time and *Swanee River.*

Will began to sing, of course. Nothing on earth but unconsciousness can stop him whenever the tunes of his native land break forth, and he has a voice that totally lacks what has been labeled "concert quality" while full of such United States elements as vim and pep. The vaulted ceiling took up the sweet refrain and echoed it against the floor and walls in clamorous protest against all things new.

Instantly in rushed Feyamil, the elegant owner of the place, spluttering with indignation.

"Stop! What is this?" he demanded.

But he was too late. Whether by accident of taste and fancy, or genius and design, she who chose to call herself Fatima had taken fire. Fred's crude, unholy music stirred in her veins feelings foreign to her since she had sold fish at a street stall where the polychromatic swarm surges on Sunday mornings toward the Cannabiere, Marseilles. It was out of Marseilles the Marseillaise came and the spirit that gave it birth still lives there, by no means trimmed of teeth and claws.

Fatima seized the heavy, curving saber that Fred had acquired illegally from the guardian of the wall, drew it with all the fire and abandon of red-capped rebellion, leaped to the floor and flung herself into a frenzy of unrestraint.

In vain Feyamil rushed at her to put an end to such irreverent upsetting of Turkish decorum. She whirled the whistling saber over his head and drove at him with the heavy scabbard until he fled like a cat before the cook. Then Fred changed into a cake-walk measure and the eyes of Asia Minor learned what fire may underlie the olive skin and gentle eyes of folk of the opposite coast.

It was not any kind of regular performance. None but the gamins of the French streets or March hares or lambs in April ever dreamed of such amazing steps or did them with such spirit of revelry. Her burning cigaret that she had in her scabbard-hand she flung away from her. It fell in the lap of Mustapha Kamil Bey, who wriggled from it like a vulture suffering from fleas. Her hair, ribboned in tidy sheafs of gold on either shoulder, awoke into burnished waves that knew no law but motion. Beads, ribbons, ornaments fell from her and were scattered among the audience like chaff under the flail. And, if the audience was scandalized, it nevertheless could no more have removed its eyes than the fabled bird can from the python's hunger dance.

Again and again Fred changed the tune. She leaped from strength to strength, frenzy to wilder frenzy. She was tireless, fed, instead of taxed, by violence, borne up, not by music, not by exultation at a row of outraged eyes, but by memory of better days, when whiter men with perhaps the merest modicum of more respect for woman clapped hands at her outbursts. The birthright, too long disregarded, now roused her to rebellion against the slavery she despised.

The two other women did not despise their slavery. They read their master's disapproval—solemn, glowering silence and eyes afraid to wander lest a neighbor detect embarrassment—and became themselves dutifully scandalized. More than once they ran with outspread arms to stop her in mid-course, only to be swept aside like weeds by the wind.

Yet, Fatima being human after all and her physical way of life redeemed from deadliness only by the obligation to dance often, the thing had to have an end. The tide of lower sense, swept back for a little while by her volcanic uprising, returned for revenge and overwhelmed her in womanly weakness. She stood swaying, dropped the scabbard to cover swimming eyes with her hand, dropped the saber with startling clatter of steel on stone, turned once or twice in delirious effort to overtake the whirling panorama and collapsed, sobbing for breath and maybe other things, on the milk-white tiles.

IT WAS illustrative of the spell she had fought against and for a few mad minutes overcome, that none of the worthies made a move to pick her up and the other girls did not dare. She lay, heaving and sobbing, within five feet of the German Griffenhahn and he watered her with the interested smile of the savant viewing an experiment. It was wonder he did not take his watch out and time the battle between breath and death.

It was Will, idolizer of Woman in abstract and swiftest gallant who ever flung his decency into a ring to fight for it against whatever odds, who was first to go and comfort her. I went with him because Will was our true friend and a blind man could have seen that the racial, religio-fanatical gorge was rising. Besides, the girl was heavy; the Grand Turk loves his dancing women by the hundredweight.

Between us we gathered her off the floor and carried her, still sobbing with great gasps, to the cushions we had sat on. There Will sat beside her so that she might have manhood between her and the crowd. I got between Monty and McNamara.

"That is the end of my affairs," said McNamara very sadly. "Oh, but blast and shiver it! To think that my sister's fate and my own fortune should be sealed by a dancing girl in this place!"

But nobody sympathized very much just then with McNamara. We had too many rising interests of our own in addition to a woman—on our hands for all we knew—whose company and past associations were not likely to shed glamour on us.

The reactions of other men have always interested me a lot more than my own emotions and it amused me just then to observe that Monty, who alone of all of us might be expected to suffer socially should tales about him and this dancing woman get abroad, was the least concerned. McNamara, on the contrary, who had no social caste to lose, nor much of anything if his tale about mortgages were true, was more upset by the thought of ruin at a dancing girl's fell touch than at loss of sister and estate—little though he liked the latter prospect.

The thing of first concern, likely to lead to swiftest difficulty, was the saber. We had left it where she dropped it, having arms full enough without the cutlery and heads too excited for discretion. I jumped up and overturned McNamara in sudden determination to get the weapon and scabbard off the floor before anybody else should think of it.

But I was too late. There were two men ahead of me, both Turks. Feyamil, owner of the place, now returning like a runaway cockerel to crow and strut, picked up the scabbard. Another, younger, even loathlier-looking upstart, who wore much too valuable linen, pounced on the saber and examined it.

"What shall I do?" I asked, returning to the table. "What do you say? Shall I go and demand the thing and take it if he refuses? Or shall we deny all knowledge of Fred's trophy?"

"I don't know yet," said Monty with a soft of grim amusement flickering on his lips. "Sit down! Wait and see!"

The younger of the two Turks—he with the lingerie—reached out a manicured hand and demanded the scabbard. Feyamil refused. Promptly the younger man cuffed and kicked him and in the scuffle that followed snatched the thing away, striking him with it over the face and shoulders half a dozen times.

"Oh, Allah, All-merciful!" groaned McNamara. "That young devil is Haroun, son of the governor! Look how the old man beams on him! Apple of the dissolute old eye—scourge of Aleppo!"

It was certainly true that the governor approved of this young weed and was at pains to show it. Like many an old Turk, whatever his private lusts and public tyrannies, he wore his rank with dignity and looked, with gray beard and sober mien, preeminently decent. Probably the weak worship of degenerate sons is only proof of parental viciousness the wide world over, but he was a perfect picture of age that claims honor for itself and condones dishonor in its son, more than condones—protects, approves.

He chuckled at the slaps with the scabbard that raised welts on Feyamil's face. He rocked on his cushions in grim amusement as the youngster kicked at his retreating victim and pricked him to rout with the saber-point. Then he called for the saber and examined it himself, all eyes in the room turning at once to us, presumably owners of the weapon.

"Looks as if I bought trouble for us all when I paid a few shillings for that thing," Fred admitted, grinning. "I'm willing to be scapegoat."

"Down one, down all!" Will answered across Fatima's body. She was still sobbing, with her head on his shoulder and his arm around her, but was recovering fast. His dark jacket was a mess of rouge and powder. This gang doesn't pass the buck to one member, not while I belong to it."

"If the governor charges one of us with crime in connection with the ownership of that sword," said Monty, with every trace of amusement vanished from the firm line of his lips, "I shall very likely have to claim privilege. I detest the thought of announcing myself, a privy councilor of England, in connection with a brawl in this place. But I shall lead with the ace if I'm forced to trump."

"I don't believe he will—in here," said I. "McNamara told us it was the unforgivable sin to call a man by name in here. Surely the governor won't name himself!"

"He is right," said McNamara, gloomy as a man

with both legs in the grave, "we still have that chance left us."

It was evident in a minute that the governor recognized the saber as city property, or perhaps as his own personal belonging, for it was quite as likely as not that he pocketed the public funds and armed a private guard for private purposes with weapons of his own selection. It was also as clear as daylight that he chose to pigeonhole the excuse for applying screws to us, for future use if need be. He returned the sword to the scabbard, looked piercingly at us across the room through the eddying layers of tobacco smoke and rose to go, saber in hand.

Before he left he glanced to left and right of him, as if to challenge disloyalty. At once every man in the room who might presumably believe himself beholden to the governor for leave to prosper got up and followed him, not one man stopping to pay his score or make excuses to the unhappy Feyamil, lost between self-commiseration and rage at us, the authors of his trouble.

THE EXODUS left the room almost empty except for Haroun, the governor's son, only a few nondescripts on cushions here and there continuing to smoke and sip. Griffenhahn, after a minute's counsel with himself, avoided Haroun's polite overtures by stretching his tall frame and striding over to us.

"Where are you from?" he asked. "What are you doing here?"

Moved by some intuition beyond the grasp of the rest of us, Monty took pencil and the back of an envelope and wrote down the address of the house McNamara had rented for us.

"That is where we are staying," he said.

"Names?" asked the German.

"Not in this place!"

"Hah! My own is Heinrich von Trottrich Griffenhahn. You see I am not afraid to mention it!"

"Fear is rather an ugly word," said Monty quietly; "discretion is free for all."

The German changed his tactics.

"I have seen you before," he said, "somewhere."

"You've no invitation," Monty answered, "but you have permission to see me again, if that should suit you."

Again the German switched.

"I'll give you a piece of advice. That woman—she belongs to the house, you know. Better let her alone and avoid trouble. Young Haroun has a notion to buy her from Feyamil. Feyamil is in debt and daren't refuse. Be advised and keep her at arms' length! If you don't know who is Heinrich von Trottrich Griffenhahn, you soon will. Come and call on me. All Aleppo knows where I live."

"Not at all," Monty answered. "If you're as big as you seem to think, you should know more of the world. You'll call first or keep your distance!"

"Well," the German laughed, "you're used to society at any rate. Take my advice about that girl. Give her the cold shoulder. Good night."

He swaggered out in time to be counted as having followed the governor's lead, yet not too soon to preserve his own name for independence. Haroun scowled after him, snapping thin, vindictive fingers behind his own back. The instant the door had slammed behind Griffenhahn's retreating figure, Haroun came and sat on the broad seat nearest us, looking toward us with his back propped against a pillar—one of the eight that supported the vaulted roof. Fatima was quite recovered by that time, physically at any rate, but clung to Will's shoulder like seaweed to a rock, fearful of letting go the only refuge in sight.

Haroun watched her with glittering eye, sitting quite still with his legs crossed on the seat. Feyamil, owner of the place—of anything except self-confidence just then—watched Haroun furtively. The two other dancing girls made the best of a bad evening's business by posturing and giggling for the very few remaining visitors, most of them Kurds and Albanians. There was one Japanese, blandly indifferent to everything except his cigaret and coffee, for Aleppo's boast is not vain that all roads lead to her.

Presently Fatima listened to the voice of reason warning her that there must be limits even to Will's strong patience. She opened her eyes and looked about, doubtful whether to smile for friendship or weep again for sympathy.

Instantly Haroun's lean forefinger crooked itself and beckoned. He said not one word. He made no other signal. But he beckoned and grinned with the diabolical confidence of one who knows he must not be disobeyed.

Fatima shuddered in every inch of her being and smothered a scream.

"Don't be a fool," Will counseled. "Don't go to him—you don't have to!"

Haroun beckoned again—wordless, shameless, perfectly confident of the outcome.

"Oh, my ——! You not know! Zat *canaille* of a 'Aroun, 'e know all about it! If I not go to 'im, zen 'e buy my debts from Feyamil. Zen 'e own me! Oh, my ——!"

"How much do you owe Feyamil?" demanded Will, the instant *preux chevalier,* and Monty caught my eye and laughed.

" 'Ow should I know? Feyamil, 'e know! Feyamil, 'e writing down always double. Once I pay 'im in full. Feyamil, 'e saying zen I owe 'im more as ever."

Haroun kept on beckoning, patient in only one particular, as a cat is patient with a mouse.

"What is use?" Fatima wailed. "I go to 'im. Better go now zan wait and make 'im angry."

"You don't have to go," said Will, and she turned her head to look into his eyes, conning them with the hunted, doubtful keenness peculiar to women of her class. The act broke the spell of Haroun's evil eye, as that individual was quick to realize. He got to the floor and swaggered over to where the discouraged proprietor sat brooding over an unlighted cigaret.

"Zere! I told you! 'E go now an' buy my debts from Feyamil. Zen you see what 'appen."

For that once at any rate she was at sea regarding the brute's method. Knowing no Turkish, and too far away to have heard in any case, I was perfectly sure that no offer of money changed hands. He was content to make threats and Feyamil was eager to submit. Presently the two came toward us, one swaggering and smirking, the other with hands crossed in front of him in the attitude of unconditional and not responsible obedience.

"Now you see!" sneered Fatima, scornful of fate and all optimism.

HAROUN HAD picked up his riding-whip from the floor, where it had lain all evening—one of those imported, whalebone things, more than a yard long, bound with gold around the leather handle. He played with it jauntily, in illustration of his relish over our coming discomfiture. At a halt, with legs apart in front of us, he nudged Feyamil, who spoke at once with the rapid delivery of extreme distaste combined with insolence.

"That woman belongs to this place. She is to come away at once." He added some thing for Fatima's benefit rapidly in Turkish.

But Fred Oakes, past master of Arabic, knows Turkish enough to pass the time of day and to understand much more than is meant for him. He sat bolt upright suddenly.

"You scullion!" he barked. "You dirty little squirt! Out of my sight before I whip you!"

He jumped to his feet and Feyamil fled across the room. Haroun, however, stood his ground, sure of the immunity that hovers over sons of Asian governors.

"She is to be mine. I order her to come with me," he announced in mincing English. At that stage of proceedings Achmed McNamara entirely lost his nerve and whatever of common sense was left him.

"Gentlemen all!" he bellowed in his huge bull voice, tremulous with fear and vanished hope. "In the name of Allah the compassionate, don't offend this important personage! This gentleman before you, this nobleman, this son of a high official should be greeted with *salaams* of respect. Not to rise and greet him is an insult. Only ignorance excuses your attitude. Now you are not ignorant. Rise in your places, gentlemen all, and show him respect."

We did not rise, of course. In fact, in the absence of any immediate obvious danger, we were all more interested in the new quirk of McNamara's mind than in the obviously contemptible indecency of Haroun. Seeing his prayer for social observance ignored, poor McNamara threw all wisdom to the winds and clasped Haroun about the knees.

"Mercy!" he bellowed. "Forgiveness!"

Forgetting whether he spoke Turkish, French or English, he let the fear flow out of him in bellowing agony, doubtless with pictures before his mind of fat men like himself whose tortured bodies he had seen thrown out of Turkish prisons for the crows to finish off.

"They do not know! They are foreigners! How should they understand, *effendi,* that the great ones of the earth are to be fawned upon. Take your woman and go, *effendi!* Go and forget us all! Let your shadow lengthen until San Sophia throws the lesser one—only go away and leave me to argue with these fools."

Fawning on Haroun had exactly the effect that it always does have on his type of degenerate of whichever continent. He spurned McNamara away from him and swelled with windy insolence. The whip that lay across his open palms seemed like sudden inspiration. He closed his fingers and cut at McNamara twice as a reminder that he had touched an aristocrat with unbidden, unblessed fingers and should not offend a second time.

I saw Fred Oakes slip the concertina strap from off his shoulder, a thing he never does unless he feels the fighting blood flow hot behind his ears. But Monty frowned at him. My own opinion was that Achmed McNamara had earned a whipping and it did not much matter whose whip did the work.

"I grow impatient," announced Haroun. "I have said that woman is to come with me.

Nobody answered him. McNamara crouched belly downward on the floor with his great jaws agape; even the woman seemed to sense at last that all she need do was acquiesce, one way or another. Let her choose the Turk and we would let her go with him—choose not to go and we would make a stand for her, capable beyond her imagining.

"Tell 'im to go to ——!" she said suddenly—slowly, as if seeing a new, dim, distant light.

"No need to tell him that," laughed Fred. "Hell is his sure, near destiny."

Haroun began to realize that his presence lacked any kind of awe for us. Where a white man would have flushed, he darkened as if the shadow of a cloud had covered him. He was a very ill-bred pup. Men's mothers are not chosen in Turkey for their probable effect on the race and they do their best in the curtained stupidity of harem life to rob young sons of the slightest trend to manliness. But there was no excuse for him.

Will was the nearest to the girl. Impatience told him Will was the impediment between him and desire. He leaned over the table and struck Will smartly on the wrist with the whalebone riding-whip.

"You hear me?"

McNamara sent up a bellow of unbelieving agony of fear. Feyamil, the proprietor, emptied his shrill lungs in a shout for servants. Fred tried to be first to avenge the impudence, but he was between Monty and the woman with his knees thrust under the edge of the low table. He and I were both left like common dawdlers by Monty's lightning flash. Will was hampered by Fatima, who clung to him as if he were the only rock and she overtaken by the deluge. Besides, he was taken by surprise and not quite so swift as we to appreciate the depth of the creature's insolence.

I HAVE witnessed many a thrashing, but none the peer of that. Once I saw a Chinaman lambasted by the cook of a British lime-juicer for stealing his false teeth. Another time I narrowly missed being the victim when a bluenose boatswain hunted for and found the man who had set a light to cotton waste in the forepeak. That came close to being murder. Then, I saw a two-year-old retriever whaled for sucking pheasant eggs. That last was the nearest in point of physical resemblance to what Monty did.

He jumped for him as nobody in the world would believe a man could jump who had not seen red, racial war. I thought for a second he would break the Turk's neck, but he took him with his left hand by the scruff off it and with his right reached leisurely for the whalebone whip.

With a yell that betokened dawning enlightenment as to what he might expect, the Turk unwisely fought for the whip for a moment. That cost him a twisted wrist and saved him nothing of the punishment to come.

Servants—thick-lipped and woolly-headed—leather-skinned and woollier-witted—Turk, Ethiopian and mixed Armenian—ran in at the proprietor's call to interfere. But Fred, Will and I saw fit at just that juncture to draw pistols and stand them off.

"Ah-h-h!" sighed Fatima luxuriously then.

Pistols meant more to her than all the assurances of four unknown casual guests in that den.

"Ow-aie-ow!" screamed the Turk, flailing with both hands to fend off the descending whip but only driving Monty to attack new surfaces. "Ow-yow-ah-rrgh!"

Swish! Swish!

The thin, supple whip rose and fell with that sincere appreciation of the minute details and broad aspects of a task that comes so close to being art. Monty had seen something more than half a hundred Summers and the Turk not twenty-five, but the life of a British cavalry officer, toughened by pig-sticking, polo and tiger-hunting in the Rajputana Hills, has some advantages in the scale against the high life of young Turkey.

The Turk was not flabby exactly; he could kick

and fight sufficiently to elevate the incident from mere routine to the ranks of minor indoor sport. He had imagination in plenty to suffer with and a cheap class pride, based on nothing better than effrontery, that helped him to hate the indignity. But he had no earthly chance of defending himself or of shortening the experience of a minute. He kicked mostly at random, although he did find Monty's shins a time or two. But he could not bite because Monty's steel-wire fingers gripped his scruff and shook him by it like a puppy.

The Turk's yells were exceeded all the while the thrashing lasted by McNamara's bellowings.

"Have pity on him! Oh, gentlemen all, you sign your own death sentences! His father will put us all in jail, and then—oh Allah! Let him be! Oh! Oh! Oh! You will kill him! Be wise! Be wise! Have discretion now! Oh! Oh! Cease for a minute—set him on his feet and make a bargain with him—immunity for you, mercy for him. Gentlemen all—can you others not stop him? This is going to be the end of all of us! That man's father is the most powerful governor in all Asia!"

On the other hand, Feyamil, the proprietor, and his servants, now that we commanded the situation with our pistols, looked on in philosophic calm not unmingled with appreciation. The accepted manner of avenging the minor, and even some major insults, throughout all Turkey is by beating. Their tales are full of such incidents; scarcely a street story-teller sends a crowd away without recounting how the hero of the piece gave some one else a beating. There was nothing new about this, except the splendid thoroughness with which the whalebone was laid on. The fact that the whip was the victim's heightened the onlookers' sensations. When Monty at last flung the Turk away into a corner and the whip after him, they let him lie.

But then came Feyamil, all arrogance again, now that the bully lay incapable of anything but agony. If there was any advantage to be snatched from the situation, he proposed to have it, and he pounced on the bone of contention astutely enough. He ordered Fatima, in Turkish, to get up and leave the room.

"Don't you do it!" advised Will. He and I kept our pistols well in evidence. Fred put his away in order to be free to use his fists, having a notion to fight and no hope of it, as long as he showed a weapon.

Feyamil leaned over the low table and reached out a hand to seize the girl but froze to immobility while yet half-way—one eye down a pistol muzzle, one on Fred's fist.

"She belongs to the house!" he asserted.

"By what right?" asked Monty calmly.

"Let her pay her debts," the Turk sneered, recovering position and deciding that after all Monty, guilty of the violence, was the one to be browbeaten. Some men have no luck in judgment.

"What debts—to whom?"

"The money she owes me. By Allah, you ought to pay it! You come here and empty my place by the mere offensiveness of your presence! Not satisfied with that, you fight in here—"

"Pardon me," Monty interrupted with his merriest smile, "admonish is the word. Not satisfied, I admonish. Pray continue."

"You make the woman valueless by causing her to be the center of disturbance. It is you who should pay every piastre she owes."

Will's eyes blazed at that, every fiber of his altruism thrumming to the tune.

"Do you want to have your debts paid?" he demanded and the girl looked at him for a minute in dumb wonder.

Feyamil began to see a triumphant ending to the night's misfortunes and stood with legs apart and arms folded on his breast.

"To pay the woman's debts is your only chance to escape imprisonment," he announced, deciding that a cigaret would add to his air of authority.

He stooped to help himself from our package. I was just in time to strike the box away from under his hand and send it spinning, scattering its contents.

"Dogs of your type feed from the floor. Help yourself!" I said and he grinned at me with that peculiar malice men reserve for the unexpected absolute affront.

"You pay him?" wondered Fatima stupidly. "You buy me? Which of you?"

Will snorted. Then he laughed, remembering Achmed McNamara and the Mormon argument.

"Slavery ceased some years ago where I come from. Besides, we shouldn't know what to do with you. No, if we pay your debts, you go free."

"Free? I? In Aleppo? Oh la, quelle innocence! But Feyamil would cheat you. Feyamil is all lies. You agree to twenty, 'e say forty. You agree to 'undred, 'e say thousand. You agree to ten t'ousand, 'e say million. Pay 'im until 'is *portemonnaie* it burst Feyamil 'e go an' fetch a sack to put much more in."

I CALLED Monty's attention then to the armed guard in the passage between the two outer doors. They had entered and were clearing the room quietly of other guests. One of them had a revolver as big as a highwayman's horse-pistol and they were all heavily armed.

Promptly, and without a word to me, Monty made another of his lightning moves. In a second he had Feyamil by a leg and an arm and had dragged him down between himself and Fred, forcing him so hard against the wall behind that the astonished rascal belched all the wind out of his lungs and sat there gasping like a fish.

"And so," exclaimed Monty in his level, admonishing tone of voice, "if we've any trouble with your armed servants, you'll be the first to suffer. Advise them to keep their distance, won't you?"

As soon as he had his breath back, Feyamil decided that was not the time to try conclusions with us and said something to the armed guard that sent them to the cushions by the far wall.

"Keep an eye on them!" said Monty to me; so I could not watch what followed at our end of the room, although I heard every word of it.

"We're in no hurry," said Monty. "The streets before dawn don't tempt me. Too many dark corners and long knives. Let's take our time."

"Gentlemen all!" exploded McNamara, recovered at last from speechlessness. His bull voice was almost like a bomb. "Go now! Get out of here! See that Haroun—look at him! He recovers—he will go presently! Do you think he will go to prepare for you a bed of roses? Leave that Fatima; this is her place! Let her pay her own debts, gentlemen all! If, you take her away, what can you do with her? If you let her go, she will be in this place or in another like it within the day, for what else can she do? Where can she hide? They will simply track her down and take her. Yet, will you keep her yourselves?"

"Oh, shut up," ordered Fred. "Nobody can even think when you open your mouth."

"This is no time for thinking, gentlemen all. This is time to run away. There is only one thing at all to do. By Allah, we must run! Come back to the house! Wait there twenty minutes while I bring the horses. Gallop for the coast!"

"McNamara," said Monty, "your advice would be perfect if it weren't for the certainty of pursuit."

"Oh, Allah! Oh, All-merciful, All-wise—"

His prayer was interrupted by the sudden, noisy arrival of three men in Turkish costume who entered the room at a run, shouting words we could not understand but that included the word Haroun several times repeated. Seeing the governor's son sprawling with his head on the pillow to which he had dragged himself, they ran and pounced on him, lifting him not at all tenderly, but accompanying the act with great shouts of "Oh-oh!" and angry grimaces at us.

At Haroun's command they lifted him between them and carried him past us with his feet barely touching the floor, stopping just long enough in front of us for him to say ten words to Feyamil.

"There!" announced Feyamil when they had borne him out of the room. "You heard what he said to me? Fatima is to await his pleasure. You shall not fail to feel the heel of his displeasure."

"Oh, Allah!" groaned Achmed McNamara.

Then in a sudden random recovery of the former bombast, he stood up and thundered at us with both fists clenched, gesticulating like some barrel-pounding preacher of the wrath to come.

"Come with me, you —— fools! To —— with the estate! My sister must take her chances; she will at least be married and have property of her own! Leave that Fatima and come away!"

"Be still, you idiot!" said Monty. "I will not be still! I adjure you! I order you! I—"

"You'll exhaust my patience in a minute. Do you think we have come so far only to turn back with nothing accomplished? You are an able dragoman but a poor sportsman, Achmed. Will, have you found out whether Fatima wishes to leave this place?"

"She'll come sure enough," said Will. "But does she want to come? That's the point."

"I come quick as ——!" announced Fatima. "I come anywhere. You all get kill—zen me too!"

"All right," said Monty. "Feyamil, listen to me! If that girl owes you money, make out a proper bill to-morrow, have it witnessed and certified by some one in whom we can have a little confidence and present it to me. Then I'll pay it."

"But how shall I find you?" grumbled Feyamil.

"Ask that German fellow Griffenhahn. He has my address. He'll tell. You fellows," he said, turning to us, "I'll be dashed if I don't see daylight through this business. Let's use it instead of real daylight to go home with. Somebody see that Fatima gets some sort of covering."

Will attended to that. He drew his pistol again and made one of the other women bring a flowing cloak and black *yashmak* from behind the scenes. In two minutes Fatima was a figure of black mystery.

"Now!" said Monty. "McNamara, you go first!"

"Oh, Allah, I am afraid! Knives in the dark, my lord!"

"Do you hear me? Go first! Stop and light the lanterns at the door. You fellows walk one each side of Fatima and one behind. I'll follow behind McNamara to lend him courage. Are we ready? Then forward all!"

We did not get away, though, without a demonstration by the enemy. The guards of the outer door, seeing Feyamil released from between us and imagining their master to be master of his house again, intercepted us with their backs to the exit and a great show of loosening hilts. But Monty was too quick for them. He pushed McNamara at a run in front of him and they divined McNamara's condition of mind too well to take that danger seriously. They were satisfied to call on him to halt at two yards' distance, and he did.

Then Monty sprang and the rest was fist work, swift and skilful. Two were knocked down and the rest were sent reeling backward before they could draw their weapons. The next event was the slamming of two doors in turn behind us and our emergence into starlight and the comparatively speaking clear air of the alley.

"But we shall be murdered in the streets!" moaned McNamara. "We shall not reach home alive!"

V

WE HAD laughed at ourselves as we came because of the figure of prowling night adventure that we cut. Now we proceeded to laugh ourselves home again, not so loudly, because of the genuine danger, but with even more appreciation of the humor of it all.

Fred Oakes was for marching in front with the concertina going full blast. Since Monty did not want to keep our destination secret, Fred could see no sense in anything but noise and vowed that a tune or two would far more likely keep our enemies away, for fear we were decoying them, than attract them toward us. He may have been right, but Monty would not listen and Fred had to content himself with such tomfoolery as stalking shadows spider-fashion and pouncing on them with a yell.

"You know the story of the missionary and the tiger?" he explained. "Tiger crouched. Missionary crouched. Missionary recalled the text about the devil fleeing from you if you're bold. Missionary sprang first. Couldn't see the tiger's tail for dust and stones."

Even Achmed McNamara laughed at him between paroxysms of chattering teeth and cold sweat. Only Fatima, draped like the figure of death and awfully respectful of the Moslem law denying laughter or any self-advertisement to women in the streets, kept silence, staring straight ahead through the tiny *yashmak* eyeholes.

It was she who really saw the figure of a man go slinking into shadow ten yards ahead of us and passed the alarm. McNamara fled incontinently, set a foot in a puddle of Aleppo sewage and fell into it, bawling his sorrow to high heaven, whereat somebody pelted him from a roof. Presently he rejoined us, smelling atrociously and too busy spitting to speak or swear.

Nobody was in time to stop Fred. The spirit of mischief was still working in him and an anecdote suggestive of unexpected action scarcely off his lips. He began to creep along the right-hand wall with the knee-action of a murderer in pantomime and had reached the shadow down which the man had slunk before Monty or any one could prevent. There he crouched. There he unslung his concertina and removed the catch.

There are sudden noises of a cat-fight in the dark that remotely resemble, in wealth of hatefulness and snarled in harmony, the war cry of a concertina with its keys all touched at once. Only the concertina is immensely louder and richer in suggestiveness of war.

Fred pounced and touched off his clanging instrument, emptying the bellows with all the strength of both arms, shaking them to throw a sort of demon laugh into the din.

Three men rose out of the same shadow and cut and ran for dear life, scampering down-street as if the grave-yards had given up revengeful dead.

"What did I tell you?" he demanded, bowing to complete the performance, but his nerves in fact on end and his very beard bristling with excitement.

A moment later he stooped and picked up something.

"Look here!"

We gathered around him with our lanterns and McNamara bellowed with new fear.

"What did I warn you, gentlemen all? If that is not the same sword you bought from the city watchman, it is another like it. That is the property of the governor of Aleppo. We are all dead men!"

"Can a dead man feel?" asked Will. "I'm going to kick you, McNamara!"

"Oh, Mr, Yerkes, no! Allah! This is no time for horse-play!"

"Play nothing! There—ere—ere! Take that! Next time you open your fool mouth I'll drive my foot into it up to the heel! D'you understand me? Don't dare answer!"

Under the compelling spell of violence the Levantine controlled himself. But he was so afraid to walk alone that each of us in turn was hampered to exasperation by the treading of his toes upon our heels or his elbow searching out our ribs. At last we made him walk beside Fatima—to protect her, as Will explained. I heard her threaten to raise the veil and spit on him for crowding her into a pool of mud, but if she had to serve as scapegoat at least that left us free to scout and skirmish.

Most of the skirmishing was with the street curs that awoke out of invisible lairs and flew at us savagely. Fred slew more than one with the captured saber. But we took two more human shadow-lurkers by surprise and hunted them until they were lost down by-lanes. If they, too, had been sent by the father of the wastrel Monty whipped, to waylay us and pay the reckoning, they probably took back an account of our numbers and prowess that made their masters pause and think.

When we reached our house at last and slipped in through the creaking door in the I wall, we could not be sure whether we had been followed home or not.

"Not that it matters," as Monty was quick to assert.

"Why not?"

The sheer impossibility of defending our fortress, or of escaping from it unseen should that seem the way of discretion, rather took heart out of us now that we stood within the wall.

"That German Griffenhahn knows where we are and before long they'll know he knows. They won't dare force the door to do murder for fear of the excuse it would give him for blackmailing. He'd be likely to make them pay too high for holding his tongue."

Achmed McNamara, presuming the embargo on mournful utterance to be removed now that we were within walls, went to a corner of the courtyard and prayed noisily, not without gigantic sobs. His prayers were to Allah, but the tongue was English and the form was of a litany built of fragments from at least three Christian rituals. He offered candles to the Mother of God and vowed there was no god but God, nor any prophet but Mohammed, in one breath.

We went in and left him to his litanies. The problem on our hands was how to dispose of Fatima—a problem distinctly ours, not hers. She, with the *yashmak* off again, was all agog with a Marseillaise spirit of mischief and unrighteous curiosity to know what four, single men would do with her. The last thing she seemed to expect or desire was solitude behind a closed door.

"Who shall defend me then from Achmed McNamara?" she asked, perplexed.

The situation could have become tragic at any minute if we had dared lose sight of its humor. The woman was so used to being preyed upon, the chattel of any fulsome cad with money enough to free her masters, that it took time to convince her she was in clean hands.

We parried her puzzled questions with jokes, ignored her astonishment, refused to let her dance for us, behaved as if nothing at all was serious in a world entirely meant for laughter and she no more than a common occurrence—one more bright planet spinning across our orbit in the night. At last it dawned on her that we asked no price for the risk we had shouldered on her account.

Then came three wretched minutes when she asked to give, since we were not disposed to take. Three more minutes of abject grief, when it seemed to her that all she had to give us was refused as not good enough. Then more beweilderment—and at last the dawn.

The first soft twitter of birds and the first faint color of the coming sun entered through our open window with the dawning understanding that in so far as manhood gave us any power at all we gave her back full womanhood. Women are quicker than men to understand, when the process has once begun with the entering wedge, and she understood then, without our saying it, that life for her might begin anew that minute, if she cared. The past might clutch, but it could only hate and hurt, not hold or kill.

We got her to go to sleep after that on a camp-bed in the little kitchen place, without a qualm for McNamara, although his snores from our pile of saddlery, where he had made himself a comfortable nest, were self-assertive as a storm at sea. Then three of us slept for an hour or so, Monty sitting on guard with his perennially absorbing chessmen out in front of him. When we awoke we held council of war.

"OUR TRUMP card, as I told you," said Monty, "is my identity."

"It 'ud look lovely in the papers," Fred assured him. "The Earl of Montdidier and Kirkudbrightshire, P.C., K.P., D.S.O., etc., arrested in Aleppo for eloping with a favorite of the governor's son. Released from jail on representations made by the Foreign Office. Splendid! Fine! We've got to see this thing through on the soles of our shoes, Didums—no appeals to Cæsar."

"Say!" said Will. "You guys have hold of this stick by the wrong end. I'm the goat. I insisted on coming to Aleppo; I befriended the girl; I eat crow if anybody does. You can't be allowed to scandalize your folks and ruin your own good rep., Monty old man, not by a darned sight. If any one of us has to toe the line, I'm it!"

"Dashed good of you, Will," said Monty, "but we'll see it through the way we started it—in partnership. As I was saying, my name is our one trump card. I hardly expect to have to play that. Developments are likely to be quick. Don't let's forget that we came to Aleppo with an object."

The rest of us had overlooked that in the excitement of this new turn of events. Even McNamara seemed to have forgotten it in his one all-shadowing desire to flee.

"It's a very good cavalry maxim to beat the objective in mind and keep after it. Many a battle has been won by refusing to swap purposes."

"But, good Lord, Didums!" Fred objected, "we haven't a leg left to stand on." McNamara's spine has turned to water. The woman is a loadstone that'll bring half the cutlery in Aleppo around us in half no time. I'm for action myself, attacking when the odds look tall and all that kind of thing, but —— it, we can't take all Aleppo by the beard, not we four, and pull till they pay us a million."

"When Achmed McNamara wakes," Monty answered, "I propose to compel him to attend to business. Retreat 'ud be too dangerous. We've got circumstantial proof that some of the governor's men were sent last night to waylay and murder us. Let's accept that as proof that the enemy is rattled and rattle him more yet."

"Aw!" said Will. "You're talking rot now! I'm pretty sure there's a U.S. consul in this place. I'll go and tell him the thing from start to finish. He'll know the best way out."

"How about McNamara's sister?" I objected.

"Aw! You heard Mac himself, say she'd be well fixed if Mustapha Kamil makes her his wife."

I laughed at that and Will colored. There was not any need to argue the point or to remind him who was the *Don Quixote* of our party.

"Well—what's to stop you ginks from carrying on with the McNamara business, while I play safe by getting the U.S. consul's ear?"

The fear that had Will by the heart was caused by thinking himself to blame for our predicament, and we knew that. A man more lion-hearted than he in any kind of fight, by day or in the darkness, did not live. But the bravest have hysteria at times and the most unselfish then are likely to have it worst. Hysteria in any of its hydra-headed forms needs scotching swiftly. Monty was the man.

"You may do that over my dead body, Will! If you'd rather back down and run for the coast while the road is open, kindly hold your tongue and give the rest of us a chance!"

"Me? Back down?"

Monty nodded.

"Say, if you hadn't proved yourself a friend of mine twenty times over, I'd punch your head for that!"

"Have a try," laughed Monty.

Then he leaned behind me, tipped up the cot on the end of which Will was sitting, and sent him sprawling on the floor. The schoolboy rough-house that followed—gasps and barks of explosive laughter, yells of impartial encouragement from Fred, upsetting beds and scattering furniture—awoke McNamara and Fatima, in addition to banishing

Will's fit of nerves. So the number of councilors grew, McNamara squatting on the floor Turk fashion near Fatima's feet, she appearing older and strangely better looking since she had washed the rouge and powder off, but full of her new beginnings, although the costume hardly indicated that.

"Have you any plans?" Monty asked her.

"Plans? She?" sneered McNamara in his solemn, booming bittern note. "By nine this morning Feyamil, the Turk, will have sold her debts. By ten she will be arrested. By this evening she will be back at her trade in some other place."

Fatima nodded.

"Where would you go if you had your way?" Monty demanded.

"Ah! Europe! Marseilles! Oh!"

"Then you shall. Are you willing to work for your freedom?"

"Anyzing! Everyzing! Yes! You order me! You shall see!"

"You would be paid for your services."

"Ah! No, no! I work free! You are my friends—I charge you nozzing!"

"Enough money to pay off your debts, provide traveling expenses and leave you with a fair sum over to start life again with."

"Oh! You fool me—yes? You ——"

"Never more serious," Monty assured her.

"DIDUMS WAS playing chess while we slept," said Fred with a wise nod to me.

Will and I were inclined to be scornful of the sedentary game but Fred regarded Monty's folding box of pieces with almost superstitious veneration and always believed their inspiration to Monty was infallible.

"I do anyzing whatever what you order me," vowed Fatima who once was Gabrielle, the daughter of old man Coeur de Chat of the Rue de la Croix de Malte, Marseilles. One could actually feel the stages by which her mind was groping its way back to Europe and new beginnings.

"Very well! Can you write?"

She nodded.

"Compose a letter to Haroun, son of the governor. Write it in French. Tell him you are afraid of us men. Tell him you regret the unfortunate occurrences last night. Suggest to him that you are willing to be punished—the beast will snap at that bait if he doesn't take the other—if he will only take you to his bosom, or some such piffle. Give her pen and ink, somebody."

"Wait!"

Her own quick wit was swifter than ours to detect what Monty intended and she knew Aleppo inside out, as we did not.

"Zere is a better place as zis. Zis is nowhere. I write—zen 'Aroun is coming 'ere viz ten men and 'e make grreat fight. No, no! 'Ere 'Aroun suspect. I know some place where 'e no suspect."

"Name it!" ordered Monty.

But she could not name it. The intricacies of Aleppo streets lend themselves to no swift directions. She tried for a few minutes, Achmed McNamara booming interruptions that only helped confuse because none of us knew any of the landmarks by which they sketched a course. Then she gave it up.

"I write ze letter. Zen I go. McNamara, 'e come too, to carry ze letter. One of you is wearing Arab dress and coming also. Later zat one come back 'ere and tell where I am. I write ze letter so as 'Aroun come tonight, because 'e will be lying in 'is bed all day groaning on account of 'ow much you strike 'im. If I tell 'im come alone, zat no good, because 'e is suspicious. If I tell 'im bring too many men, 'e think maybe zere will be a bad fight, zen 'e is coward and not come at all. No, no! I tell 'im come viz two—t'ree men to overcome one man. You four can overcome t'ree men—yes?"

"Him and three? I fancy so," said Monty.

McNamara objected sturdily with fifty arguments, first against trusting Fatima, second against putting faith in any plan that included forecast of Haroun's movements, third against sending himself with the letter.

"Blast and shiver it, gentlemen all, they will simply pounce on me and lock me up letter and all. Then they will torture me for information. If you should ever see my poor carcass again, crows and vultures would be picking it."

It seemed about time to deal with McNamara drastically unless we proposed to let him spoil everything, including his own prospects.

"You are to carry that letter," said Monty sternly, "and give it to somebody else to deliver at the door, standing to watch the person who delivers it and bringing back word to me here after you have seen it with your own eyes handed to the porter. If you are not prepared to do that, you shall be thoroughly beaten immediately and then kicked out of doors. Choose!"

"Oh, all right, I will go with it," he answered sulkily.

"Go first, then, and buy Arab clothing for all four of us. Answer no questions, mind, and be quick!"

The cook whom McNamara had procured for us the day before had deserted, suspicious, perhaps, on account of our late hours. I had to go and scratch our breakfast together out of odds and ends of camp provisions and took so much time about it that when I had it all spread on the packing-case table at last they had pegged the plan down pretty fine, Fatima suggesting most of the trickier details, as indeed she had to.

Immediately after breakfast Monty took command again.

"Fred, you're least like an Arab. You stay with me. Will, you're leanest and easiest to disguise. You go with Fatima and bring back word of the hiding-place."

He did not consider sending me because I knew least Arabic of all four and if challenged would have had an impossible task to escape detection.

Very soon after that came Achmed McNamara with a bundle and the news that he believed police spies were watching the house from several vantage-points—a likely enough tale in all conscience, but not to be allowed to frighten us from our purpose, although McNamara trembled in his shoes and vowed noisily that he was mad when he made us his proposal on board ship.

Fatima wrote her letter in none too classic French, in a round, bold hand like a washerwoman's, well adorned with blots.

"It is to punish me ze little beast vill come," she asserted, sealing the envelope under Monty's eye.

Will was dressed very carefully to look like an Arab and schooled in the not-so-easy art of walking like one. Then, in Indian file, McNamara first, then Fatima, indistinguishable in the *yashmak,* then Will, they started out and were nearly knocked down by a pair-horse, mud-splattering carriage with a footman on the box and a runner in front to whip stray dogs and people out of danger. They dodged under the horses' heads and Will swore lustily in Arabic, spitting and scowling to act the part.

What with the carriage blocking the end of the alley, our *araba* obstructing some of the view, McNamara's obvious native blood and costume and Will's good acting, they managed to get away without being recognized by any one as belonging to our party.

THE NEW arrival by carriage was in no mood to be recognized either. He came hurrying down the alley, jumping and skipping from one dry spot to another between the pools of slime, preceded by the runner, who beat on our gate with the end of his long whip.

I opended to him and admitted, rather to my astonishment, none other than Heinrich von Trottrich Griffenhahn, our new acquaintance of the night before.

"Are you all here?" he asked and started for the house ahead of me without waiting for an answer.

Monty met him at the inner door and stopped his impetuous course by the simple process of not making way for him.

"So you've come?" he said.

"Yes. Let me in and tell me your name now!"

"What have you come for?"

"Not here! We might be overseen from roofs. Who knows who is watching! Let me in!"

Monty stood aside when it suited him and not before, smiling with amusement that appeared rather to unstiffen the German's air of importance.

"I suppose you realize what a mess you're in?" he suggested, after a swift glance at everything in the common room. We had not much to look at, but what we did have was such as no fly-by-nights would travel with—expensive guns, expensive camping-gear. "This is not all of you. Where are the others?"

"Don't make so much noise," said Monty. "Shut that bedroom door, Fred!"

The inference was that Fatima, at any rate, was sleeping. The German might draw any other conclusions he liked.

"Oh, well—" He shrugged titanic shoulders and smiled immoral tolerance as he took the seat I offered him. "I'll be brief. You're in an awful fix. I heard the whole story while I was shaving and came to see you at once. Let me tell you that however well the whipping you gave Haroun was deserved, it was very unwise. His father idolizes him. The little wretch can practically have his own way in Aleppo. He is more toadied to than the governor himself, for the simple reason that the governor gives him anything he wants and he sells in turn to the highest bidder—concessions—court decisions—anything."

"What has all this to do with you and me?" asked Monty calmly and the German laughed.

"I see you are not easily disturbed. Well, this is an occasion when you can afford to forget *sang-froid.* You are in very serious danger."

"As you remarked once before, I believe."

"Haroun is certain to demand revenge. As soon as he gets out of bed he is quite sure to go to his father and insist on your arrest. You are likely to be bastinadoed first and tried afterward, should you survive the operation. There is only one way of forestalling him that I can see."

"I'm listening."

Monty took out his cigaret case and helped himself. I wondered at his not offering it to the German first; yet I noticed that Fred did not remedy the oversight, although he was watching with wide-awake eyes and missing nothing. Yet hospitality had always seemed Monty's first rule.

"Haroun is a peculiar scoundrel. He has strange obsessions. His latest has been that girl Fatima. He could simply reach out and take her at any time, of course, but it has amused him to act the part of fisherman and angle leisurely. I know him so well that I would stake my reputation on the statement that, until the next bait tantalizes him, Fatima is his one supreme desire."

"And you propose?"

"That you hand the girl over to me. I am told you have her here."

Monty's face did not change. He lit the cigaret and eyed the glowing end of it with a sort of thoughtful interest.

"I am quite sure that if I went to him and said I have that girl in my possession, I could persuade him to overlook even the whipping you gave him last night, I would bargain *quid pro quo.*"

Monty flicked off the first quarter-inch of ash. Fred began to grow a little restless.

"And what do you get out of this?" asked Monty, looking at the ground for a moment and then quite suddenly into the German's eyes.

"Nothing!"

Still Monty's face did not change. He blew three smoke rings.

"For a man who expects to get nothing, you are almost in a hurry, aren't you?"

"What the —— the do you mean?"

"Even in Germany, do—ah—men of some social position propose to—ah—use an unfortunate woman's living body for purposes of barter unless they expect to get something out of it?"

The German's eyes changed and glittered. He did not seem exactly to let a mask fall, but his features hardened.

"I am not a suitable person to insult," he said coldly.

"I take it you came to talk business," said Monty and I noticed Fred get ready for anything at all in the way of violence.

Heinrich von Trottrich Griffenhahn had lost his grip on the situation. Fully expecting to find us at our wits' end and as anxious to clutch straws as the proverbial drowning man, he was made nervous by the surprising discovery that Monty could see through him. He was obviously inclined by instinct to bluster and bully his way out of the situation, yet afraid to do that for fear of meeting more than his match and being sent away empty-handed.

And the more he hesitated to use his natural methods, the more sure Monty knew that he had found the key to our problem.

"Come," said Monty, crossing his knees and knocking off more ash. "There is something you want to get out of Haroun. What is it?"

The German's lips grew hard, and he pressed his wrists down firmly on the chair-arms.

"Why should I tell you?"

"Because," said Monty, "without my help you won't get what you're after."

"If you can tell me what I am after, then I will lay my cards on the table and admit you into partnership."

"I have sufficient partners," Monty answered and to judge by his leisurely air of enjoying the cigaret nobody could have guessed his intention of risking all our prospects on a dozen words and their probable effect. "You are after a certain piece of land for the Bagdad Railway. You know it's going to slip out of your grasp if Mustapha Kamil Bey ever marries the Armenian woman in the governor's harem. Mustapha Kamil would make you pay through the nose for it. You came here hoping to get possession of Fatima in order to bribe Haroun to persuade his father to find some way of conveying the woman's property to you. Isn't that so?"

"How did you know?"

"Never mind. How much will you pay me for the property?"

"I can not say off hand."

"Oh, if you're not interested I beg pardon. It'll be quite easy to sell elsewhere."

"It's not worth much."

"How much?"

"Ten thousand pounds, Turkish."

"IT'S WORTH much more than ten times that sum to me," said Monty casually. "Let us understand each other. I know quite well you want it. I know who else wants it. I have no particular desire to sell to you, but I shall sell to somebody before this time to-morrow. I am giving you first offer because you happen to be here and, unless you care to make me what I consider a reasonable bid, this is the last chance you will get."

"Ridiculous!" sneered the German. "Prove to me that you own the property or can control the sale of it. You can't!"

"If you don't believe me, you have only to walk out and close the door behind you," answered Monty, reaching for another cigaret.

I knew that the superhuman calmness was as a glove he had drawn on, but the German could not be expected to know that.

"Why should I believe you? You have not told me your name yet."

"The omission was intentional."

"Are you ashamed of your name?"

"Merely ashamed to bandy it in certain circles."

"I don't believe a word you say!"

"Good morning, then. Show him out, Fred!"

Fred was on his feet in a moment and he did not look like a man to be lightly defied, for all the German's weight and obvious muscularity.

"This way!" he said.

The German shrugged shoulders and turned to go. He was half-way to the door when he faced about suddenly.

"You refer, of course, to the *Hamidieh* property?"

That was an obvious trap. With a sudden tingle of goose-flesh I realized that Achmed McNamara had never once mentioned to us the name of the property, supposing that it had a name. He had described it often enough.

"I refer to the single piece of land that the promoters of the Bagdad Railway need in order to complete their right of way through Aleppo."

"If I offer you a quarter of a million pounds Turkish for it, what proof do you offer that you can deliver the title?"

"Make the offer in writing and sign it," Monty answered

"Then what?"

"Take it and see!"

"Bah! A common baazar trick! You hope to show my written offer in order to get a higher price from somebody else."

"Good morning," answered Monty. "Show him out, Fred!"

Once more the German turned to go. Again he paused before he reached the door and faced about.

"If I had any reason for believing your bare word was worth listening to, I'd write you that offer," he said.

"Too bad," said Monty, striking a match with an air of such utter boredom that the German was convinced against his will of one thing: we were at least in no hurry and not over-anxious to make terms.

"Tell me your name."

Monty shook his head.

"You might tell other people. That would be disagreeable."

The German looked keenly again at every one of our cases and trunks—at the guns on the wall—then at me—then at Fred—then at Monty.

"Somewhere I have seen you once before," he said, searching his memory for time and place. "Not these others, but you—yes, you!"

He shrugged his shoulders again, this time with the air of a man who bets at random.

"All right! You are obviously of the class that plays cricket, as you English say. I will write my offer of a quarter of a million pounds, Turkish, for that property, sign it and leave it with you, provided you tell me your name in return. And as long as you keep my offer to yourself I shall not mention your name to any one."

Monty smiled.

"How long is that agreement to last?" he asked.

"For a month, if you like. I am not a talker. It is likely I should never tell it. I only want to know for the sake of convincing myself you are no common adventurer."

"Write your offer," said Monty. "Then write another note giving me your word of honor not to disclose my name in connection with this business.

In case of your breaking your word I would use that document against you."

"All right!"

The German came back and sat down at our table. I passed him paper. He wrote two separate notes, signed them, waved them in the air to dry and passed them both to Monty. Monty read them carefully, folded them up and passed his own card to Griffenhahn. The German whistled.

"I don't believe you!"

Monty felt in an inner pocket and produced his passport, signed by the Prime Minister of England and vised by so many notables that it would be worth a good round sum to the hunters of autographs.

"So that's it, eh? *Kreutz blitzen!* Fooled, am I? So the English Foreign Office was not so fast asleep as I supposed."

"You're mistaken," Monty answered. "Our Foreign Office has nothing to do with this whatever."

"Oh, no, no! Of course not! Nevertheless—as between ourselves—tell me—oh, I see!" He whistled again. "Do you suppose your government will thank you for this? Of course, they wouldn't like to see a man of your standing in a Turkish jail, with all the ensuing publicity, but—well—that's your affair. It's understood I say nothing provided you take up my offer within—"

"Twenty-four hours," said Monty.

"I shall expect the title deeds properly transferred by the Turkish authorities."

"You can attend to the transfer yourself. Have the money ready to bring to me—"

"Here?"

"To whatever place I shall name by messenger, at whatever hour I send for you. What cities do you draw on?"

"Berlin."

"Won't do."

"Vienna."

"No good at all."

"Paris—London."

"Either of those. Say a draft on Paris, then, for the equivalent of two hundred thousand pounds, Turkish, at the daily rate of exchange—then a draft on Alexandria or Cairo for fifteen thousand and another for ten thousand on the same place."

"Payable to you?"

"No, to bearer."

"Very well. I hope you will live up to your part of the contract, Lord—"

"No names, please."

"All right! But understand me! If you don't toe the mark and deliver that title to me to-morrow I shall let the cat out of the bag. Until this time to-morrow I shall use my influence to save you from arrest for last night's foolishness. After this time to-morrow, let us hope you will have earned the right to my continued services."

FRED SHOOK his fist as the house door slammed after the man's athletic back. Monty laughed silently and then aloud when the outer gate slammed too.

"Observe the workings of the cultivated German mind," he said. "I'll pay any one a thousand pounds for proof that he has convinced that man that I'm not betraying our Foreign Office. He imagines now he is blackmailing me. He'll probably try to blackmail me afterward. Do you see his point? He supposes I'm a Foreign Office agent, sent to spoil the German Bagdad Railway plans. He jumps to the conclusion that I've succeeded, but that I'm willing to sell the prize to him in order to get out of our last night's scrape. My stipulation for three drafts for odd amounts probably confirmed his judgment in some cross-grained way. Perhaps he thinks I'm planning to return the government's money by the way it came—or perhaps he thinks I'm stealing it."

"But is our government trying to spoil the German Bagdad Railway plans?" I asked.

"Not in any underhanded way," he answered. "I've been told of negotiations and diplomatic *pourparlers,* but you may be quite sure there's no plotting of the kind he suspects. We don't use the German method, I'm glad to be able to say."

We sat for a long while after that, waiting for Will to return with news of Fatima's hiding place and for McNamara to bring word of the safe delivery of the letter. At noon I scraped up an indifferent luncheon, and it was not until after we had eaten that, that we became at all nervous. We ceased talking—ceased smoking; Fred ceased fingering the concertina keys; Monty closed the chess-box with a frown. There was neither sign nor sound of them, nor a way that we could think of by which to discover their whereabouts.

By two in the afternoon we had begun to blame

ourselves savagely for letting Will go off on such a dangerous venture alone.

"Letting him," grumbled Fred. "We made him do it. I'll never forgive the three of us if harm has come to that boy. America is the only one of us with genuine idealism. We're three wizened, worldly-wise men. Will is a boy out of a book."

We each had our individual way of liking Will but none had ever guessed before how much we liked him. The thought that we might have sent him to his death in that old city of assassins made silence unbearable. Yet there was nothing whatever to say. We scarcely gave a thought to McNamara or to Griffenhahn, who would have to wait in vain for title deeds. Once or twice we did think of Fatima, but without consolation.

"We should never have trusted that woman," said Fred, and Monty and I both nodded.

"I can't sit still here any longer," I said at last. "Let's do something—anything!"

Monty looked at his watch.

"I'll go to the consul, show my papers and claim official protection for Will," he said.

"I'll go with you."

"So will I."

"One of us ought to stay here."

But nobody would agree to stay. We filed out into the courtyard and locked the house door behind us.

"What's that?" demanded Monty suddenly. "It sounds like some one at the outer door. Listen! Might have been making that noise for an hour—we'd never have heard it. Open the gate gingerly, Fred—be careful now!"

Fred tried to look through the keyhole first but failed, so he pulled the squeaking spring-latch back and opened the narrow gate by inches. Then suddenly he threw it wide, admitted a bundle of dark-brown rags and slammed it shut again.

She was about the most frightened little female I ever saw, who unwrapped the dirty covering from her shaven head and disclosed two jewel-bright brown eyes. She covered her face again instantly, as if virtue at her age and the sight of three grown men were things incompatible. She could not have been more than ten years old and the little, thin fingers with which she held the rags over herself trembled with terror. Apparently she knew no English—French—Arabic or any language we could speak.

At the end of two or three minutes of seductive questioning by Fred, our champion linguist, she suddenly seemed to remember her mission and produced from somewhere underneath her clothing a folded, soiled envelope. It bore no address.

"How did she find us, I wonder?"

Monty led the way back into the house and we brought the terrified messenger between us, she as fearful of us as we were that she might slip between our hands and cut and run.

We followed Monty in, locked the door to prevent the child from giving us the slip and stood twitching with excitement, watching Monty open the envelope. He did it with the dilatory, deliberate patience of a man who will not let himself betray his galloping nerves, examining every corner of the envelope and holding it up to the light before inserting his little finger and tearing cautiously.

Inside was a scrawl in French on half a sheet of ruled exercise paper in Fatima's bold hand, adorned with a hundred blots and signed with only one initial.

"After dark this little one will lead you to my place," it ran, roughly translated. "Your fat dragoman is no good. He delivered the letter. They arrested him. He squealed. Inside ten minutes they had come and seized Will—" She did not know any but the first names by which we addressed one another—"I do not know where they have put Will, but my confidante sends word they have beaten the dragoman to make him talk. Do not move before dark, and then come disguised. F."

For one long minute we were silent. Then we swore in unison.

"If they arrested Will at her place, what's the use of our going there to be pounced on, too?" demanded Fred.

"Question is," said I, "is it wise or not, for you to find a consul and demand help?"

Monty did not answer. He tried instead with a hundred wiles and smiles—with bribes of small change, candy, fruit—then with stern, firmness—to persuade the small messenger to talk.

"Is Fatima at the same place or has she gone to another place?" he asked in five languages in succession.

But the ridiculous mite merely nodded. She did not cry at his sterner tactics, being presumably used to severity in far worse forms than any of us would dream of using, but retired into her brown shell turtle fashion, the rags coming over her head again.

"Feed her!" said Monty at last with a sigh that admitted failure.

SO I took the little creature by the arm and introduced her to our stock of camp provisions. Biscuits out of a tin and jam and raisins seemed to comprise her notion of heaven, but talk even then she would not, although she had a tongue, for she stuck it in the jam-pot.

When I pulled her away from the feast for fear she might burst, Monty and Fred were still in deep conclave. Fred was for seeking out a consul at once and demanding to know what had become of Will. Nobody cared a continental about poor McNamara.

"The letter doesn't say he was arrested; it says seized," he insisted. "If he were simply arrested, I'd say all right, let him lie among the lice a while until we work our scheme; the jail's accessible. But seized may mean that he's being tortured or garroted now. Maybe he's dead."

"If the poor chap is," said Monty, "we can't help him. I say let us stick to the objective. Carry on! I know a little of the East. The motive underlying everything a Turk does is fear. He eats for fear of starving. He locks his women up for fear of other men. If they have seized Will for sake of revenge, they will do nothing to him yet for fear of us. They'll wait to get the rest of us before they dare apply torture or kill. I don't believe Haroun has told his father or any other official, of the seizure of Will, or even of McNamara, for fear political reasons might induce them to interfere—as they almost certainly would. He expects to catch one of us tonight and he'll go on that expedition himself for fear Fatima might give him the slip after all. But it's my belief he'll send more of his men down here to seize the other two simultaneously for fear the other two might go in search of number one and raise ructions. Let's leave lights burning on the upper floor, so that they'll show through the slits of windows from the road, and go with this little messenger the minute it gets dark."

We argued it out, Fred sticking to his plea that "the only thing a decent chap could do" was to throw our own plans to the wind and invoke the full force of ex-territorial consular jurisdiction. Finally we put it to a vote and I took Monty's side, reasoning that if the worst had happened to Will, it had happened already and that Fatima had likely enough taken thought before she wrote to us what to do.

So Fred went up-stairs to see about the lights and, what with, arranging a draft to keep the naked flame of several candles dancing—cutting the silhouette of a man's face out of wood and balancing it with a paper sail so that every stronger gust would move it—and arranging a steady drip from a bucket of water into a small tin can, so that one of the candles would move several feet along a board and perhaps be upset and be extinguished—he contrived a very fair after-dark appearance of occupancy for spies to watch.

Monty and I, meanwhile, explored for some other means of exit than the front gate. To climb walls or run along roofs would have been too risky. But we found out that our courtyard adjoined another one and, although the house next door was occupied, we preferred the chance of outraging a neighbor and being mistaken for burglars to the prospect of being followed all through the streets by Haroun's spies. So we got out our little prospecting picks and cut away the thick dividing-wall of sun-dried bricks until nothing was left in one place but a film a man could kick through with his foot. After that we all got into our Arab dress and bewailed the shaving-glass, too small to let us see how nice we looked.

Then we sat down again to wait for darkness; and of all the interminable, miserable watches we three ever spent together that one was the worst. Twenty times our whole plan appeared sheer craziness. Ten times, at least, we began to talk of changing it and were only prevented from undermining our tottering courage in that way by Monty's vigorous bad language.

"Better make mistakes—go ahead and make 'em," he said, "than change a plan at the eleventh hour. The enemy 'll make mistakes too. Everybody makes 'em. The one safe way is to have an objective and stick to it through thick and thin."

"—— it! We ought to have gone to the consul!" grumbled Fred.

"Well and good!" said Monty. "But we decided not to. If we had gone we'd have saved our own bacon but not our reputations. And we'd have left McNamara and his sister in the lurch!"

"—— McNamara!"

"Very well, —— him! But don't let vacillation —— us!"

SO THE time passed and darkness at last put an end to conversation that toward the end was growing too polite for friendship and maddening because useless in any case. Fred went up-stairs and set his deceptive lights to work. Monty and I kicked a hole through the courtyard wall and, because we had previously thinned the earthen bricks, very little dry dirt fell on the far side and there was almost no noise. Inspection showed that the family was indoors. Gloaming and the blackness of long shadows favored us, helped out by Turkish theories on dogs that precluded any chained friend of man to bark alarm.

So we crossed the courtyard, one at a time, Monty leading the child by the hand and each of us hugely comforted by the dead weight of a loaded repeating pistol and the heft of a thick stick in his hand. The door in the wall leading out of the courtyard was locked and the key nowhere to be seen, but Fred worked swiftly with clasp-knife and trembling fingers and unscrewed the iron casing of the lock. After that it was a second's work to lift the tumbler and slide the bolt back.

Our guide seemed lost for a minute, inclined to head first up-street and then down. Then, with the gamin bump of locality that is the heritage of poverty in crowded streets, she turned definitely up-street and led the way without once again hesitating.

She did not take us at all the way we had gone under McNamara's leadership the night before. She led us instead toward the great bazaar—so great that it dwarfs the notorious, enormous one of Stamboul. Bagdad is a small affair compared to it. Through everlasting, winding, narrow streets she hurried so fast that we were troubled to keep pace, the dogs snarling and yapping at us strangers but ignoring her.

We had only one lantern with us. She carried it, reckless of the light reflected in the green eyes of a dozen dogs or of the fangs bared within three feet of it. Yet she had feared us three who had not between us as much as one tendency to harm a child of her age. And we feared those clattering fangs worse than the devil.

Who shall tell of Aleppo Bazaar who plunges into it by night in the wake of a hurrying girl-guide so small that any shadow could swallow and lose her? Monty kept hold of her, but a false step, a stumble or a jerk would have ripped the rotten garment in his fingers. If she had not feared retribution more than she did us, she could have lost us in a minute.

We hurried under echoing stone roofs, past countless dark side-passages where trades as old as man's dispersal made night clamorous—they know no labor laws where the Turkish code has sway. The beasts of burden seemed to recognize a law of day and night; some we saw stalled in the dark side alleys and one sleeping camel blocked the main thoroughfare we hurried down, so that we had to climb over him, at risk of his waking suddenly and rising in a panic.

Each quarter to a trade and there were a thousand quarters. Each passage to a branch of a trade appeared to be the rule. Each owner of a stall his own provider of dim light or shuddery dark. Candles, naked or sheathed in cheap imported glass, candles in twenty-colored globes, oil lamps, oil-flares, patent acetylene lights that threw a corpsy whiteness over half an alley, saucers of vegetable oil of a make and smell more ancient than the tongues of men who bargained in among them—all these gave a little light and illustrated darkness.

The smells of all the ancient trades greeted us, blended with the next and passed. Stinks announced that corruption underlay and overlay the whole bazaar—trade, methods, morals, merchandise—we could see the rats that ate the heart out of the best, leaving the rinds for less picksome plunderers, and other creatures more evil than rats.

Once and again there came out of the dark the friendly, raw smell of carpets. Those seemed the wealthier, safer streets where most of the shutters were up by night and the men who lingered spoke in quieter tones and wore clean garments. But next-neighbor to a mart that drew its wares from all the honest East would be a cheap-jack alley again, with snatches of obscene song lifting where the pipe-smoke curled around tin hurricane lights.

Not once did our small guide hesitate. She did not once fear to turn down a reeking dark alley or take a short-cut under echoing tunnels. Darkness, lurking humans, shadows that shook with unimaginable evil—nothing frightened her except our company and Monty's grip on her dirty, decaying garment. Stalking in the guise of Arabs where Arabs caused no more comment than the smells, we sweated with fear at every black lurking-place, maintaining dignity and self-command only by act of will. Safe as any of the rats that knew each hole and corner, she feared only the three men who would have fought for their honor's sake rather than see her struck.

We came at last to a passage under stone vaults, a little less smelly and a little more illuminated than most of the rest had been. She turned and hurried down it, we close after her, past open doors where women sat with their veils not arranged with that complete dishonor of man's eye that the Moslem code decrees. There was music of the Turkish sort that is neither harmony nor melody, within those precincts.

Then we turned sharp to the left down a tunnel, past a coffee-shop where men of a dozen nations sat on rugs that had seen a hundred skies and entered a door half-way down the tunnel on the right-hand side, that strangely opened before one of us touched it and shut again behind us with a slam and the click of a spring lock.

WE STOOD in a long, narrow stone passage with four oil lamps burning at intervals on brackets along the wall. At the end, in the middle of another door, stood Fatima, arrayed in such gorgeous tinsel-and-muslin finery as surely was never before seen but of fairy-tales, holding a lamp over her head and laughing with the glee of brewing deviltry.

"My little Josephine, she bring you nicely, yes? No, 'er name is not Josephine, but I call her so because of old times. You gave 'er to eat, yes? Zen she go right away now to my ozzer place where zey come and seize Will. Zat pig 'Aroun will be zere soon. She must take 'im by ze 'and and show 'im ze vay 'ere. Go, Josephine—go, *cherie—vite!*—vairee qvick!"

Apparently not in the least tired, the wordless guide wrapped her minute self more carefully in the ragged cloth and departed through the door we had come in by, Fatima jerking at a cord to draw the latch. We walked into a room furnished with mats and cushions and one half-couch. There were mats on the walls as well as floor, producing an effect of smothering warmth and silence. Fatima laughed and drew a mat back, disclosing a door in the wall, close beside the doorway she was standing in when we first entered from the street.

"Zat is vhere you vait for 'im," she laughed.

But we were in no mood to joke about prospects until we had heard all she knew about Will.

"McNamara, 'e is no good," she announced with a shake of the head in answer to the questions we all three fired at her at once.

"But Will—what about Will?"

" 'E is vairee good!"

Evidently she proposed to tell us in her own way and not be hurried. We sat down on the three-thick carpets and pretended we were calm. She produced cigarets and we helped ourselves, she with sparkling eyes contributing to the game of make-believe, pretending she thought us what we tried to seem.

Whether or not her father, Coeur de Chat of the Rue de la Croix de Malte, had sold her to the Moor as McNamara said he did, the reason of her undoing had been appetite for lawless intrigue. If any one was in danger now, surely she was—if not of life, then of being seized for debt and dragged into worse slavery than we had snatched her from. Yet she was dressed for a wedding and sipping lazily at the danger as if it were wine in a glass.

"Will, 'e walk wiz me," she continued in her own good time, talking over her shoulder to us as she prepared coffee at a little brazier, "an' McNamara, 'e come along too. McNamara by-and-by is afraid—not willing to take ze letter. Will, 'e go along and make 'im, kicking 'im be'ind in ze street as no Arab kick anozzer man, making me laugh so. Presently I follow zem both because no one in street is knowing me through ze *yashmak.* I want to see. Zey go to 'Aroun's palace. McNamara is thump on ze door, and a eunuch open. McNamara is so afraid zat ze eunuch, 'e suspect 'im—give a shout—t'ree ozzer men come—zey all seize McNamara and pull 'im inside.

"Zey shut ze door. Will, 'e is much disturb'. 'E walk up an' down outside, like no Arab ever be'ave. Vairee bad. Me, I go close an' tell 'im make different be'avior. Veree crosslee 'e tell me go to ——. I go away—no use woman in *yashmak* standing arguing with Arab in Aleppo street—I go away, quick. Presently ze door is opening again and same t'ree men come running out. Will 'e walk up cool as cucumber, maybe to ask zem where is McNamara. Zey seize 'im quick. Will, 'e fight vairee good, same as a lion. 'E tear all zeir clothes off and knock 'em down two—t'ree time. Zen two more men come out and all zey five carry 'im in and shut ze door. Zen I find my frien', and she make inquiry by back door to ze 'areem. Afterward I write you zat leetle letter and send it by Josephine."

"Have you any more news of Will?" we all demanded.

She clapped her hands. Another mat swung on the wall and a good-looking gipsy type of woman, with the world-over gipsy swing from the hips, came out of an unexpected door to take the cups away.

"She is taking message by-an'-by," she announced. "She is vairee dependable as long as you pay good. You pay 'er first, zen she take message."

"All right! Tell us about Will."

"My frien', she go to 'Aroun's 'areem to manicure ze ladies' 'ands and she learn everyzing. McNamara is telling all 'e know because zey whip 'im on ze feet, but not very bad because 'e is telling all before zey can 'it 'im often. Will is lock up in dark room in cellar. By-and-by 'Aroun's men are going to your 'ouse to kill two of you zere. Also 'Aroun is coming to see me because of zat letter I sent 'im, and after 'e is finding me and killing ze ozzer one of you, zen 'e is no longer afraid to go back and torture Will. 'E is going to torture him zen like ze devil. Maybe 'e torture me too. So it is good if you t'ree men are not letting 'Aroun escape. 'E is going first to ze place where 'is spy saw Will and McNamara take me. Zen Josephine she find 'im and bring 'im 'ere. Only, if 'e 'ave more zan t'ree man wiz 'im, Josephine will come back alone."

"Um-m-m!" remarked Monty. "I'm not what you'd call keen on doing murder, but if Haroun comes to this place he'll not escape alive without my leave."

Fatima nodded.

"Now you go and 'ide!" she ordered, drawing the mat to one side and pushing us through. "I will tidy ze room so 'Aroun may not suspect. Leave zat door open, only let ze mat 'ang down. Soon as zey come though ze ozzer door, use pistol—stick—anyzing. Only be vairee qvick!"

We took her advice about the door, because the mat hung down copiously over the opening. There was just room for the three of us to stand together in the passageway, in pitch darkness in which we could hear one another's heart-beats. Monty's fingers, clenching and unclenching on the stick he held, irritated me to the verge of unendurance. Fred, breathing in time to an imaginary tune, picked at the catch of the concertina slung, as ever, about his shoulder, until I could have brained him with the thing.

VI

I **COUNTED** pulse-beats—then breaths—then took out my watch and tried to keep tale of seconds. Then I whispered—

"How long have we waited?"

Fred and Monty answered raucously with one voice—

"Shut up, you idiot!"

They made ten times as much noise answering as I did with the harmless question. Fatima drew the mat back and held a warning finger to her lips.

"There, what did I tell you, you ass!" hissed Fred.

We had gone from the stage of having nerves on end to the deadly dangerous point of numbness, when a sound of distant thumping—one two, then one two three, repeated three times, warned us of Haroun's approach. Evidently that signal had been agreed on with Josephine to mean that not too many armed followers accompanied the governor's son, for we distinctly heard Fatima jerk the cord to admit them.

Instantly loud Turkish voices filled the passage, and we heard Josephine begging for silence.

"She's telling 'em you are asleep—that's you, Didums, you profligate," whispered Fred.

After that they came tiptoeing down the passage—in single file we knew, because of the narrowness. Fatima, bowing to admit them, backed against the mat that blocked our view, we cursing her in silence for spoiling whatever prospect we might have had of taking Haroun by surprise. But she judged her maneuver by what she could see, not by what we thought in the dark was wisest. It transpired that Haroun sent his two men ahead of him, with knives in their hands, to do any necessary killing; it was not until they had reported all clear and Haroun himself had ventured gingerly into the room that she shut the door firmly enough to signal us, stepping away at the same time from the hanging mat and pulling it down with a jerk.

So surprise was the essence of the business after all. The two men were stout rascals, one a Greek and the other an Arab. Fred and I beat their knives down with our sticks, since they showed fight, and the hanging mats smothered any yell they made. After that, when we leveled pistols at them, they capitulated readily enough.

Haroun, having had a taste of Monty's whip the night before, still smarting from it, sore to the touch in a hundred places and no brave man at the best of times, slunk away from his first onslaught and cowered with hands over his head, begging for mercy.

Fred got carefully between our captives and the tiny table in the middle of the room and laughed aloud.

"Won't you share the joke?" said I, but Monty had seen it already and laughed with him.

"The only lighted lamp is this on the table behind me," he answered. "One kick and any one of the three could have turned the odds against us. Lucky the fools didn't think of it, or bigger fools would have lost tonight's game."

At Fatima's call the gipsy woman came out from under a hanging mat with coils on coils of good hemp rope and the other two watched while I put into use a little of the lore I learned at sea, trussing all three captives so that no ingenuity or restlessness of theirs could have freed them as long as the rope should hold together. Haroun yelled at the bite of the cord on his well-whipped muscles, but the condition of his flesh was his affair; he who goes adventuring in Aleppo tunnels after dark should go in training.

When all three were bound, we gagged them, giving them wads of folded cloth to bite on. Then we laid the two hired bullies in the dark place that had hidden us and hung up the mat in its place. Haroun we left for the present on his back in the midst of the room, having use for him.

"Did he only bring two men?" I asked.

"T'ree," said Fatima.

"The other?"

"Zey left 'im outside to keep a guard."

"How do you know?"

"I heard 'Aroun give ze order. 'E is to stay zere. If 'e 'ear shouts 'e is to come in but 'e is not to let ozzers enter."

"What shall we do? Go out and lasso him? He'll likely see us first, run and give the alarm," said I.

But disposal of the third man was easy, it happened, without such clumsy means as pursuit and a thrown noose, which no doubt would have brought the whole warren of night-prowlers down on us.

"Vous êtes fou!" snorted Fatima. "I send ze jipsee. She show ze teeth at 'im. Zat one outside is Mahmoud—a fat fool who always stays outside 'ouses to mind shoes and makes love to ze shadow of everee ole woman in a *yashmak*."

So we concealed ourselves again, and the gipsy went out to open the door and say that Haroun the worshipful needed his faithful servant Mahmoud. There followed a question or two that we could hear—a deep base voice and an impudent answer. A moment later the door slammed shut and a heavy footfall pursued a light one. There was a stifled scream and a struggle, for the Turkish servant is no light-handed dallier in the toils of love; the gipsy burst into the room, followed by Mahmoud at soberer gait; trying to seem unconnected with the disturbance.

He stood for a second to gaze in the doorway and we realized at once we had made a mistake in not hiding Haroun out of his sight. With a bellow of mingled fear and fury he started back down the passage to escape.

I was first after him. I caught him by the neck. He tossed me forward over his shoulders with the strength of a bull and the skill of the public porter he once had been, hurling me against the door at the end with almost force enough to burst it open. Perhaps that was his intention. At any rate, I fell, half-stunned, across the doorway, and while he wrenched at the latch and kicked at me in Berserker rage Fred came up. Fred used a stick to begin with—more, as he said afterward, for the sake of saving my ribs than because he thought himself and Monty unequal to the task.

But even when he had hit the man a blow on the pate that would have cracked an ostrich-egg Mahmoud put up a ten-times better fight than the others had all together. He turned and drew a knife and when they knocked that out of his hand he fought like a bear with his fists and feet, bellowing and charging.

We were all three the worse for wear when we had him trussed at last. Even then, like a newly caged panther that tests each separate bar, he strained at the cords until they cut him. After we had him gagged, he lay with flaming eyes and jaws that worked tirelessly to chew the cloth wad into pulp, so that he might swallow it and use his teeth on the lashings. We respected Mahmoud—regretted the pain he obliged us to inflict on him. Ten of his master rolled into one would not have made half of him.

But we had him safe at last and stowed him away in a dark, locked hole at the far end of a tunnel at the back of Fatima's strange quarters, to make assurance doubly sure. Rooms and passages with long octopus arms reached out for more than fifty yards toward the rear into the heart of Aleppo Bazaar, none of them having any other access to a street than the one narrow door through which we had all entered that evening. It was simply a disused storehouse, planned for use in a city in which law and order is an unknown luxury, and plunder by force of arms has been yesterday's story and to-morrow's prospect for fifteen hundred years. Fatima did not tell us how it came to be unoccupied or how she had acquired possession. Probably the gipsy could have answered that question better than she.

OUR FIRST idea after we had rubbed the hurts Mahmoud gave us was to write a letter to the governor and send it by the hand of the gipsy. But Fatima, whose stake was as great as ours, claimed the right to advise.

"Zat Mahmoud is beating out all your wits, eh?" she sneered. "You write a letter, eh? What say ze governor? 'E say 'Fetch ze English consul; he and I go and see zis affaire togezzer.' English consul, 'e come 'ere, and what you say zen? What you do zen? No, no, no!"

There was no denying her contention. Should the governor appeal to the British or the American consul, or to both of them, we should almost certainly bring about Will's release forthwith, but McNamara, being a Turkish subject, would remain in durance vile and his sister in condition even viler. After which we should have explanations to make to the consuls, who had ex-territorial jurisdiction and would want to know what we meant by taking the law into our hands.

"Zat miserable 'Aroun, 'e shall write ze letter to 'is papa!"

Monty set his teeth. The part of the business he fancied least would be the dirty work of making Haroun obey orders. But Fatima was used to dirty work and no shirker at all.

"You loose 'is one 'and. Zen you sit over zere and let me manage."

So we unbound his right hand as she directed, she summoning the gipsy to chafe it where the cord had numbed the wrist. Then we sat in a row on mats against the wall and watched while she worked on his fear and made him do her will.

The little brazier at which she had made our coffee was her unanswerable argument. She had tongs with which to select the choicest morsels of cherry-red charcoal and the mere mention of applying those to the more tender parts of his soft anatomy, blanched his face white. Monty had told less than the truth when he said a Turk's motives are based on fear; Haroun's were nothing but fear.

She was not unwise enough to tell him that we three would apply the torture unless he obeyed her will, for the Turks know the English. But she told him we had passed our word not to interfere with her; and the worse liar a Turk is, the more respect he has for the word of an Englishman.

Then she ordered him to take pen and ink and write to his father that he was a prisoner; that he was held to ransom; that his ransom could only be effected by his father in person; that unless his father and not more than two attendants should come with the guide at once, he—Haroun—would be burned about the right foot and the right foot sent to papa for evidence of good faith on the captors' part. Moreover, that if papa should try any tricks, such as ordering a body of men to follow him, or should attempt anything except exact compliance with the spirit of the summons, torture would begin forthwith and death would put an end to any possibility of rescue. Torture, she made him add by way of footnote, was to commence in any case one hour before midnight unless papa should have put in an appearance before that time.

Haroun wrote it all out in Turkish and the paper was passed to Fred for consideration. He ordered it written out again, with the wording changed in places, and watched the process of rewriting and the signature with hawk eyes for tricks. Not that Haroun was the type of individual likely to be proficient in cryptic writing at high speed, but the risk was too grave for taking chances even with that spoiled product of Turkish rule. Finally Fred ordered sealing-wax and insisted on Haroun sealing the letter with his thumb-mark. The man's intense distaste for that task was sufficient proof in itself that his father would be likely to regard the thumb-mark as evidence conclusive.

"Without that the old card might try tricks," Fred grinned. "But these strange folk have a fatal regard for the personal touch. There's no logic in it, but there's very little logic in anything under the stars. The governor will recognize that thumbprint and come with two attendants as required."

Monty nodded. Between them those two were more than a match for the Eastern mind. What one did not know, the other did, intuition piecing out the blanks.

"Who shall take the letter?"

Fatima had considered that problem beforehand in all its bearings. She was the only one who was to sit idle in that room; the rest of us were to go to work at once. The gipsy brought out Josephine from the inner room and they two went off with the letter, hand-in-hand.

"Josephine, she is to deliver it. Anybody know it is no use to ask her questions. Zat child 'as more silence as appetite. Josephine, she deliver it and say nozzing. Zat woman—" she never once mentioned her name, perhaps for fear lest we might grow familiar and transfer our regards—"shall watch Josephine from long way off. One of you watch zat woman from long way off—anozzer one watch 'im—ze ozzer one watch ze second one. Zen, when Josephine is coming out, zat woman run and tell 'ow many men come and all about it. Ze man what watch 'er, 'e run—zen ze second man, 'e run—zen ze third man run and tell me. And all t'ree men and ze woman is getting back 'ere long before ze governor, because ze governor is 'ave to walk with Josephine and she come slow on purpose.

"If everyzing is olright, Josephine she shall not fall down; but if Josephine fall down and get up again, zen zat woman is making signal so and everybody know it is no good and we all make —— quick escape. But it will be all right and Josephine shall not fall down. You wait and see!"

The plan was simple enough, and as hole-proof as any plan could be under the circumstances. Desperate men have to take desperate steps, and the thought of Will locked up in Haroun's cellar inclined us toward anything rather than inaction. Dressed as Arabs, we were highly unlikely to excite suspicion by loitering in the dark bazaar tunnels. Speech with strangers could be declined at night without risk of arousing curiosity. The only danger I could see was of losing our way in the dark, or losing touch.

They sent me on ahead to watch the woman, as having the youngest eyes. Mahmoud had torn and soiled my Arab clothes, but that merely served to strengthen the disguise and further protect me from questions; men do not dally in Aleppo's dim passageways at night to cross-examine tall, lean Arabs with the marks of fighting on their persons.

FOR MORE than a mile I followed the woman and the girl at a short distance, making mental notes of turnings and the marks that should guide me back again. Then, after passing down a wide, arched street, we reached the open, and I fell to the rear. Even then I could not content myself with keeping the woman in sight. I had to see the place where Will was imprisoned and when the gipsy halted and hid in a shadow I drew near enough to watch the wide, iron-studded door, outside which two sentries stood looking lonely and solemn. They had told me that Haroun's rented house stood next beyond the governor's, but I could not make out its outlines in the dark.

Josephine was seized by a soldier as she tried to approach the door. I saw him raise a hand to hit the girl but could not determine whether he struck her or not before she made the nature of her errand clear. He rang a bell and struck the door with his rifle-butt. After an interminable wait the door was opened and Josephine was pushed inside.

There followed a half-hour of torture as keen in its way as the murderous bite of hot coals. Absurdity danced in the shadows and claimed itself mother of plans. Imagination pictured Josephine, questioned by eunuchs, silent under the lash and the torturing twisted thongs, breaking down at last and telling all she knew. Conscience whispered of the law of England and the consul in residence, sworn to apply it without fear or favor to all British subjects disrespectful of that law—as were not we? The ticking of my watch and singing heartbeats told of time that passed too slowly to be borne, yet too swiftly for our purpose. Surely the dragging—no, the swiftly hurrying—no, the dragging minutes meant that another plan was being laid in that dark house to spring surprises and defeat us.

I forgot in that drawn-out anxiety that Haroun, the dissolute, had made himself so many enemies in Aleppo as to make the present situation seem likely enough to his parent. I forgot, too, Fatima's remark to the effect that the father would think himself lucky to get off with payment of a good, round sum, cash blackmail.

" 'E 'as paid so often 'e is used to it!" she had told us.

In the governor's eyes, according to her, it would merely mean the nuisance of a night adventure and the awkward necessity of wringing extra taxes from an already outraged townsfolk. But one does not remember the optimism of a woman of her past when a child's fate hangs on a Moslem's credulity behind iron-studded doors in the dark. Ten times over I started along the street to go and demand admittance. Ten times I drew back again at sight of the gipsy woman lurking in a shadow. She straightened each time I went near her and, for fear of her scorn, I did not go near enough to speak.

Then, at last, as I battled with impatience and a million self-accusing fears, the great door opened and three men emerged, one of whom was unmistakably the governor—big, heavy-bearded, his head bowed forward, striding manly. The other two were members of his official household by the look of them, well armed but without the air of servants. I thought at first Josephine was not with them. Then I saw that the man on the left was dragging her by the hand. He dragged her so violently that she stumbled and recovered. I stood two-minded in a corner shadow, wondering whether she had not passed the signal that meant warning against trickery. The woman, lurking in her dark place, made no move and gave no signal. I wondered whether Fred, who was supposed to be watching me, could see me and whether I ought to run or not and pass along the alarm.

But I did not run. Fascination held me rooted there and the gipsy woman proved herself owner of nerve and good judgment. She lay until Josephine passed so close as almost to touch her skirts. They must have exchanged a whisper, for no sooner were they ten yards past her than she rose out of her shadow and gave me the signal agreed on as meaning "all safe."

So I turned and sped toward the nearest arched passage of the great bazaar, expecting every second—in spite of reason and common sense—to hear a bullet whiz after me or to hear the footsteps of an armed Turk in hot pursuit. An Arab runs rarely through city streets and when he runs does so desert-fashion. None seeing me that night would have been fooled for an instant by the headgear and flowing garments. Fred said afterward that I galloped down the tunnels like a churchyard ghost.

At any rate, he saw me in time, which was the principal thing. And if I ran like a ghost, he did so like a friar in orders—brown, beefy and short-winded, with his skirts hauled up around him and his strong, stout legs dancing a caper underneath. He held on in full career until Monty made sure of the signal and put some dignity into the proceedings by really running with the Arab stride. Then Fred let me overtake him and he and I arrived together at Fatima's door, only to be refused admission and sent up and down street to hide again in shadows and keep watch.

So I crouched where a dead dog awaited the scavenging clan and the rats in odoriferous unsanctity, wondering how the governor of a province should be able to pass along such streets at night without attracting crowds. In Europe—in America—wherever the white man plays the out-and-indoor game of spotting motes in neighbors' morals, there would have been reporters—idlers—merely curious—maliciously inquisitive—and a host of political enemies watching, none too secretly, to learn the outcome. But in Turkey and Turkey in Asia the governor's business on a dark night is very likely shared only by a victim and he who has the ill luck to run across him carefully averts his eyes or wisely runs. Whoever else saw the governor and his two attendants, with a little child leading them by the hand, we were the only ones who chose to admit it that night.

They hesitated at the entrance, muttering one to the other, Josephine tugging at the end man's hand but saying never one word. They faced her suddenly and asked her questions in savage whispers. But she only pointed at the door and covered her face with the dirty brown cloth she honored with the name of clothing.

Our business was to watch and make sure there was no cohort of armed men coming to wind up the night's proceedings with an all-around arrest. I did not see what good it would do us at that late stage to know that avenues of escape were all cut off and that men might pounce on us at their leisure, but it was part of the plan to continue looking out for the worst that might possibly happen and we did so.

But no footfalls ringing along the tunnels, no figures flitting swiftly from dark to dark, advised us of failure and presently we saw the gipsy woman come out of a shadow to stand bold and graceful in a stream of yellow lamplight and repeat the "all's well" signal.

The governor and his two friends did not see her. They were calling on reserves of fear and courage—fear for Haroun's soft carcass and courage to take them forward. The door opened a little while they hesitated and a voice suspiciously like Fatima's said things in Turkish that one of the governor's friends answered arrogantly.

But arrogance did not pay. The voice behind the door laughed merrily. Knowing no Turkish, I could guess, nevertheless, the nature of the threats she made, chuckling and swinging the door a little back and forward, suggestive of invitation.

Finally the governor made his mind up and strode forward sturdily, the two other men hanging back and remonstrating still, doubtless by way of establishing a "told you so" position in case of ill success.

He kicked at the door, but it opened in front of him without any effort. The force of the kick was squandered at cost to his dignity. Then in he strode, swift and burly, in no mood to play with caution or to waste time once the die was cast. His friends followed him, each objecting to be last for fear of knives in the dark, compromising finally by dragging Josephine behind them.

We gave them just sufficient time to get well down the passage before we headed for the door ourselves. Then we ran in, Fred leading and the gipsy woman last but least breathless, closed the outer door behind us with a snap that made the governor's two attendants jump two feet in air.

"Go on in," Fred urged them cheerily. "The dog don't bite. Nobody's going to hurt you."

But only the governor marched in like a man.

VII

FATIMA HAD placed more lamps about the room. It would have needed more than a chance kick now—more than one man's unsupported effort to overwhelm us in darkness. Haroun—the lure, the only argument, the one trump card—was nowhere to be seen.

Monty had charge of the situation, seated in a chair, of all things unexpected, looking incongruous in waxed mustache and Arab headdress, but too obviously sure of his ground to raise a smile.

"Be seated," he said in English, motioning toward the row of cushions by the wall. But the Turks preferred to stand.

The governor said something abrupt and to the point in Turkish, but Monty felt out of his depth in that tongue. He answered in Arabic, and thenceforward the conversation took place in a language he knew fairly well, and Fred knew perfectly.

Fred and I leaned against the wall on either side of Monty, with pistols drawn and cocked. His own pistol was pretty obvious, bulging ready to his hand.

"My son sent for me," announced the governor. "Where is he?"

"On the contrary, I sent for you," corrected Monty.

"Where is my son?"

"He is in this place."

"I do not believe you. Let me see him."

"You shall believe in good time," Monty answered gravely.

"Insha Allah!" said the Turk—If God wills! i.e., Let us hope so!—a fairly insolent retort.

The gipsy woman came into the room then, locking the door behind her and disappearing under a hanging mat into one of the octopus-like passages. The governor shrugged his manly shoulders at the shot bolt, as much as to say that no threats could frighten him.

"First," said Monty, "there shall be an explanation."

"I need no explanation!" he snorted. "This is blackmail! Name the sum of money and produce my son! The sum of money shall be paid."

"That is where you are mistaken, my friend," Monty answered. "This is not blackmail."

"Then what is it? Show me my son!"

"In good time. I am aware, excellency, that the subject of a man's harem is not one he cares to discuss."

The firm line of the old Turk's lips grew stiff as iron and his companions froze into immobility.

"But circumstances alter cases and this is an occasion when, in spite of custom, your harem must not only be brought under consideration, but actually laid in the scale against your son's—ah—what shall we say—well-being."

The Turk did not answer. Monty had broached the unmentionable subject; committing the unforgivable, proclaiming himself thus the enemy of Moslem manhood. By using his heaviest artillery first, he produced consternation in the enemy's ranks and caused all subsequent proposals and demands to seem, by comparison, mere bagatelles. The Turk, in spite of a gift of silence on occasion, wears his emotions on the surface, so that even he who runs may read.

"You have in your harem—"

"I will not speak of it!"

"—the widow of a rich Armenian, sister of Achmed McNamara, who owns the Golden Fox Line of steamers sailing out of Alexandria. You have no right to that woman or her property. You are to hand her over tonight, with all her belongings, including the papers proving her title to all the real estate in Aleppo that belonged to her late husband, the Armenian."

"I will not hear! I will not speak of it!"

For answer to that, Monty clapped his hands. At once the wall-hanging to our right was pulled aside, disclosing Haroun trussed and gagged, Fatima stooping over him with tongs holding red-hot charcoal in her hand.

"You see your son!" said Monty and the old Turk bowed his head.

"Nor is that all," Monty continued after a suitable pause.

"This only son of yours has a household of his own—servants of his own. He has even set up a prison of his own."

"No, no! That is not so!"

"Not so! Not so!" echoed the companions. "Such irregularities ceased long ago when the foreign consuls represented—"

"Silence!" growled the governor.

"A prison and a torture chamber of his own," Monty continued calmly. "He has made prisoner an American and a Turkish subject—the American a friend of mine and a partner; the Turkish subject my servant, entitled to protection of British law."

"Let the law take its course. I have nothing to do with that. Release my son and a sum of money shall be paid."

"The Turkish subject has been beaten."

"Doubtless he deserved it! My son, I hear, was beaten. He, too, deserved it! Nothing shall be said of beatings. Money shall be paid. Deliver him!"

"Do you play the game of chess?" Monty asked him.

The governor nodded.

"You are in check! You have only one course—to comply with my demands in every particular. Money payments can effect nothing. If you wish to have your son tonight, whole and alive, you must deliver first that widow woman with her property, that Turkish subject and that American."

There followed a good deal of whispering between the three Turks, the governor doing most of the listening.

"I have nothing to do with my son's household," the governor said at last.

"You are governor of Aleppo," Monty answered.

There was no sense in denying that, so the three men whispered again.

"The American has escaped," announced one of the companions.

"Who knows what may have happened in the streets to such a brawler since his escape?" asked the other.

Fred and I glanced at Monty and my own heart sank into my boots. In check the governor might be, but the savor of all our purpose was lost if harm had come to Will. Self-accusation returned in a flood. I was the one who had voted against Fred, to let Will wait in durance.

BUT TRAINED cavalry leaders who can play the game of chess are not so easily defeated by mere statements of alleged fact. And check is check, with no gainsaying it.

"If that's so," said Monty, "you'd better be quick and find him, for Haroun's safety depends on his. The woman, the Turkish subject and the American—all three in our hands, with the woman's property, against your son, excellency! Time flies, let me remind you! I will not sit and argue forever!"

"The Turkish subject is already dead," announced the other of the governor's companions. He said it without consultation, but with the abrupt manner of a man who lets the truth escape him because the truth will out.

"How do you know that?" demanded Monty.

The Turk did not answer. It was a fine kettle of fish for us, if true. In the first place, McNamara being a Turkish Mohammedan subject, no consular law could be made to touch his case. In the second place, without McNamara we would be helpless to identify the sister who was also a Turkish subject, amenable to Turkish law. But again Monty was not to be defeated by mere assertions.

"It will be all right, in that case, if you produce his body," he said pleasantly. "By the way, this conversation is growing too prolonged. I shall set a time limit. I give you ten minutes in which to reach a decision. At the end of ten minutes your son's voice from behind the hangings shall inform you of what is happening. The gag shall be removed from his mouth for your benefit."

Doubtless, if we ourselves had been bending over

Haroun, the governor would have held out. He was too shrewd to mistake us for mean whites. Mean whites would have demanded a money ransom and would have behaved altogether differently. Moreover, even the meanest of mean English or Americans would shrink from torturing a tied man, as all Turks know. But Haroun lay at the mercy of a woman who had felt the heel of Turkey's white-slave tyranny, and that was different.

They whispered again, evidently not yet without hope of winning by trickery.

"It shall be done," said the governor at last.

Then in a flash I saw the danger of our situation. What should prevent the rearrest of McNamara and his sister, once Haroun should be given up? And what was to prevent our murder by way of reprisal? But Monty saw that too—in fact already had foreseen it.

"Then understand me. You, excellency, are not a prisoner here, of course. You came under flag of truce. But your son's—ah—comfort and condition, let us say, depend on your remaining. Leave if you wish, but with that understanding. McNamara and his sister and the American, Mr. Yerkes, are to be taken to the United States consulate at once and a receipt for their bodies and for the title deeds to the sister's property, signed by all three of them and by the consul, is to be brought back here to me.

"One of your companions may go at once and attend to that. One of my friends may go with him if you wish. While he is absent, I'll get you to be good enough to write out and sign a full discharge of the girl Fatima's debts. I don't care who pays them, but I want a clear discharge signed by you and written permission from you for her to leave the country."

The governor made no argument about that. Signing a discharge in full of debts payable to Feyamil, keeper of the coffee-house, was too much like grim pleasantry to cause him the least concern. He took Monty's fountain pen and began to write at once.

"Send your man, then, with my man," he said simply and I saw him slip his signet ring to the man who was to do the errand, by way of conferring visible authority that eunuchs would recognize.

I had hoped I was to go on the trip to rescue Will, but Monty sent Fred, not because he resembled an Arab in appearance in the very least, but because of his ability with the language. It did not much matter, in tow of a Turkish official of the governor's household, whether his disguise should fail or not. As a matter of fact, the English trousers he had pulled above his knees were down about his ankles again and he walked off in that shape, frankly indifferent to curious eyes, his inseparable concertina dangling openly by a shoulder-strap.

The ensuing wait was boredom rendered concrete and intolerably long. Having yielded all along the line, the governor had no further interest in anything except the release of his contemptible son and heir. And he was not so pleased with himself and the night's work that he cared for conversation, nor yet so unwise as to doubt our intentions, since we had dared drag in the U.S. consul. Turkish phlegm, so called, is akin to torpor and existent only when there is no danger to apprehend. Governor and companion sat with crossed legs and folded their arms, saying nothing and, as far as we could judge, thinking less.

There was only one interlude to break the spell of heavy breathing silence. Monty and I were sitting with ears pricked for indications of treachery from outside, when I caught unexplainable sounds much closer at hand than any plan from which any calculable danger could arrive. After waiting for a minute in the stupid, sweating fear that small sounds produce on people in dangerous places, I jumped for the wall-hanging next beside the entrance and dragged it aside.

I was just in time to pounce on Mahmoud before he could emerge into the room and start a fresh fight. How he had managed it was mystery. We had bound him as they cat the anchors—immovably. We had thrown him in a cupboard of a place and locked the door. He had only partly loosed himself, and that by inches, but he had broken the door down without making noise enough to startle us and had come like a crippled snake to wage new war for his master. I would have been gentler with him if I could, but nothing less than new ropes and tying him upright to a stone pillar at a distance down one of the passages—tying him so that a match could not pass between any portion of him and the stone—would have the least effect.

That accomplished, I returned to keep vigil beside Monty, who had covered the two Turks ostentatiously with his pistol while the excitement lasted, not that they made any effort or showed the slightest inclination to take advantage of the situation. The governor had simply given up the game—thrown down his hand—quit.

IT WAS an hour after midnight when Fred came back at last, without the governor's attendant but with no less than three armed men from the U.S. consul's guard to escort us to the consulate.

"The consul didn't want to wake up—didn't want to have anything to do with us—didn't want to admit us at such an hour," he announced, "but Will knew just how to tackle him and the consul turns out to be a good fellow. Yes, Will is all right. So is McNamara—a trifle cut and bruised about the feet—doesn't walk with any comfort, but otherwise in fine shape. The lady Thabita, his sister, has ceased to be slim or very youthful but is glad to be at liberty and makes us the personal appeal for help that we insisted on. What are you waiting for?"

Monty was writing busily on a page of his pocket-book.

"Somebody must take this to Griffenhahn, the German," he said, folding the note and discovering an envelope. He had foreseen everything.

So one of the consular guard was sent off post-haste to find the German's house, get him out of bed and place Monty's messages in his hands. Then Fatima was called out and presented with her discharge and permission to travel.

"What's the use?" she said simply. "I've no money."

"Have you paid that gipsy woman or Josephine for the night's work?"

"I had nothing to pay them with."

Monty always carries money. Time and again we have found that inviolable rule of his worth more to us in a tight place than all the passports, guns, pluck and permits we could muster. I did not see how much he gave either the gipsy or Josephine, but I did see Josephine's round eyes and the gipsy's racial ecstasy at the feel of money.

"Are we ready?" he asked and we filed out, leaving the governor and his companion to untie Haroun and the servants.

On the way Fatima told us that the mats and meager furniture of the place belonged to an absent merchant who had another place of business in Damascus. The gipsy had stolen the key from the wife of the man who had charge of it and would return it before morning. It would be no use for the governor to try to visit vengeance on the owner of the storage-vault, for he had too good an alibi. Moreover, all the furnishings, rugs included, were scarcely worth official seizure.

At the United States consulate the only shock in store for us was the condition of McNamara's feet, which was worse than Fred had intimated. They had continued to beat the unfortunate man after his confession, probably for the sake of making him retract and so justifying further torture. But luckily for him he had merely blabbed out all the truth and stuck to it.

Thabita—fat and homely, less like a bride to look at than the mother, or even the grandmother, of the woman in the photograph that McNamara showed us on his steamer—had bound up the tortured feet and was making a fuss over him, McNamara not at all objecting.

Monty, in the consul's presence, called her to the table.

"You wish us to help you in this matter?"

She nodded. He named the sum he had agreed on with Griffenhahn.

"Will you be satisfied with that price for your property?"

She nodded again. It was not likely she would refuse any price at that time and under those circumstances.

"McNamara—how about you?"

"No, sir! No! It is worth two million if a penny! She shall not take less!"

"Two million?" the consul snorted. "Man, you're crazy! A quarter of a million Turkish pounds is half as much again as it is worth!"

"I'm glad to hear you say that," said Monty. "That, I take it, is disinterested evidence. It's the best we can get under the circumstances. McNamara, you shall permit your sister to accept that price or we'll turn you loose to play your own game with the Turks."

"But blast and shiver it! I've got to share with you! How much will be left me? How much will you have the face to demand for your share?"

"Now we come to a question," said Monty, "that I am not competent to decide alone. My friends and I are a partnership. I propose that each of us shall write on a slip of paper what he considers ought to be our joint share. The average of the sums named should be the sum to agree on."

"I don't agree! I don't agree!" yelled McNamara. "I need money for my ships! How shall I lift my mortgages if you get your unconscionable share? I will never agree!"

"All the same," said Monty, "suppose you fellows write."

So we wrote down our individual opinions on little slips of paper and passed them to Monty, who did not look at them, but added his own slip and passed the four to the consul.

"I don't agree! I don't agree!" bellowed McNamara, his voice beginning to resume a little of its former bullying note.

The consul examined the slips of paper and laughed.

"The top one is blank," he said. "The second contains the word 'Nothing.' The third reads 00000. And the fourth says 'The money is hers, not his. Tell her to keep it all and keep control of it."

"I'll bet that last one was Fred's," said I.

"No, it wasn't," said Will.

"It states the case," said Monty. "One more thing—Fatima did the ticklish work in this affair. She is fully entitled to payment for it."

"Oh," said McNamara grandiosely, "anything in reason. Treat the girl liberally. Fifty—a hundred pounds—"

"Ten thousand!" said Monty.

Fatima giggled in a corner of the room. McNamara flew into a passion.

"Blast and shiver it! Whose money do you think you give away? Shall I go through all this torture and danger to see my money squandered on a—"

"Ten thousand!" Monty answered firmly. "And that's enough from you. If your sister agrees, then that settles it."

Thabita agreed very swiftly when the consul had explained to her exactly what was meant. Then we all sat down to wait, in varying stages of sleepiness, for Griffenhahn, on whose respect for his own written promise the rest of the night's work depended.

He arrived almost at the peep of dawn and swaggered into the room as if he expected to have to fight his way out again. He laughed uproariously at our disarranged disguises but drew no response in kind.

"Have you brought those drafts with you?" asked Monty.

"Yes. I got them ready yesterday afternoon, but I don't believe you have the *quid pro quo.*"

Monty pointed to papers on the table.

"Those are evidence of title to the property you want. Examine them. The consul is willing to witness the sale. You can see to registration yourself at any time."

"But why the American consul?" asked the German. "Oh, I understand—ha-ha!—of course!—a little sense of delicacy—wouldn't do, would it, to drag the British consul in?"

Monty said nothing in reply to that, but looked on quietly while McNamara's sister signed the transfer of the title, and most of us witnessed the signature. Then Heinrich von Trottrich Griffenhahn tossed the drafts on the table. The consul examined them, passed that for ten thousand pounds to Fatima and handed the others to McNamara's sister.

"Take my advice and keep control of the money," he said simply.

Then Monty turned to Heinrich von Trottrich Griffenhahn and smiled his blandest.

"As you remarked," he said, "I was anxious not to drag the British consul in. But as soon as I've shaved and breakfasted I'm going to call on him and tell him the whole story, including your share in it, and how you've paid half as much again as the property is worth. Would you care to meet me at the consulate and share the fun?"

BUT GRIFFENHAHN did not put in an appearance at the British consulate, although he saw us leave there for the coast with our party, riding McNamara's horses once again, but provided for the journey with four consular guards guaranteed to prevent Turkish reprisals on the way—not that we expected any. The Turks lose fairly gentlemanly.

The story that went the rounds of Europe afterward about the Earl of Montdidier and Kirkudbrightshire becoming involved in Asia Minor with some woman of the underworld was set in motion by the fact that we four set Fatima on board ship for France and her gratitude to Monty was witnessed by two missionaries' wives.

The same identical ladies told most unrighteous stories about Fred, for they were scandalized by the last verse of the song he made and yowled for the benefit of all who did not plug their ears:

"Achmed McNamara, oh, tarara, oh, tarara,
Returns to the Sahara where the old zariba
stood.

Sick of needless night alarums in the land of
guarded harems
Where a sound at night will scare 'em, he
is going home for good.
He will love the dusky ladies where the sand is
hot as Hades
And the far horizon beckons the Don Juan
who can run.
Oh, it's not so much locality, or climate, or
morality—
He's sickened of formality—the eunuch
with the gun!
So it's home for McNamara—oh, tarara, oh
tarara,
Where a man of merry manners may
employ a zest for life.
Where if bad luck should befall him, then the
prospect won't appall him
'Cause the husbands who would maul him
have no weapon but a knife."

THE EYE OF ZEITOON

SALVETE!

Oh ye, who tread the trodden path
And keep the narrow law
In famished faith that Judgment Day
Shall blast your sluggard mists away
And show what Moses saw!
Oh thralls of subdivided time,
Hours Measureless I sing
That own swift ways to wider scenes,
New-plucked from heights where Vision preens
A white, unwearied wing!
No creed I preach to bend dull thought
To see what I shall show,
Nor can ye buy with treasured gold
The key to these Hours that unfold
New tales no teachers know.
Ye'll need no leave o' the laws o' man,
For Vision's wings are free;
The swift Unmeasured Hours are kind
And ye shall leave all cares behind
If ye will come with me!
In vain shall lumps of fashioned stuff
Imprison you about;
In vain let pundits preach the flesh
And feebling limits that enmesh
Your goings in and out,
I know the way the zephyrs took
Who brought the breath of spring,
I guide to shores of regions blest
Where white, uncaught Ideas nest
And Thought is strong o' wing!
Within the Hours that I unlock
All customed fetters fall;
The chains of drudgery release;
Set limits fade; horizons cease
For you who hear the call
No trumpet note—no roll of drums,
But quiet, sure and sweet—
The self-same voice that summoned Drake,
The whisper for whose siren sake
They manned the Devon fleet,
More lawless than the gray gull's wait,
More boundless than the sea,
More subtle than the softest wind!

Oh, ye shall burst the ties that bind
If ye will come with me!

I
PARTHIANS, MEDES, AND ELAMITES

IT IS written with authority of Tarsus that once it was no mean city, but that is a tale of nineteen centuries ago. The Turko-Italian War had not been fought when Fred Oakes took the fever of the place, although the stage was pretty nearly set for it and most of the leading actors were waiting for their cue. No more history was needed than to grind away forgotten loveliness.

Fred's is the least sweet temper in the universe when the ague grips and shakes him, and he knows history as some men know the Bible—by fathoms; he cursed the place conqueror by conqueror, maligning them for their city's sake, and if Sennacherib, who built the first foundations, and if Anthony and Cleopatra, Philip of Macedon, Timour-i-lang,

Mahmoud, Ibrahim and all the rest of them could have come and listened by his bedside they would have heard more personal scandal of themselves than ever their contemporary chroniclers dared reveal.

All this because he insisted on ignoring the history he knew so well, and could not be held from bathing in the River Cydnus. Whatever their indifference to custom, Anthony and Cleopatra knew better than do that. Alexander the Great, on the other hand, flouted tradition and set Fred the example, very nearly dying of the ague for his pains, for those are treacherous, chill waters.

Fred, being a sober man and unlike Alexander of Macedon in several other ways, throws off fever marvelously, but takes it as some persons do religion, very severely for a little while. So we carried him and laid him on a nice white cot in a nice clean room with two beds in it in the American mission, where they dispense more than royal hospitality to utter strangers. Will Yerkes had friends there but that made no difference; Fred was quinined, low-dieted, bathed, comforted and reproved for swearing by a college-educated nurse, who liked his principles and disapproved of his professions just as frankly as if he came from her home-town. (Her name was Van-something-or-other, and you could lean against the Boston accent—just a little lonely-sounding, but a very rock of gentle independence, all that long way from home!)

Meanwhile, we rested. That is to say that, after accepting as much mission hospitality as was decent, considering that every member of the staff worked fourteen hours a day and had to make up for attention shown to us by long hours bitten out of night, we loafed about the city. And Satan still finds mischief.

We called on Fred in the beginning twice a day, morning and evening, but cut the visits short for the same reason that Monty did not go at all: when the fever is on him Fred's feelings toward his own sex are simply blunt bellicose. When they put another patient in the spare bed in his room we copied Monty, arguing that one male at a time for him to quarrel with was plenty.

Monty, being Earl of Montdidier and Kirkudbrightshire, and a privy councilor, was welcome at the consulate at Mersina, twenty miles away. The consul, like Monty, was an army officer, who played good chess, so that that was no place, either, for Will Yerkes and me. Will prefers dime novels, if he must sit still, and there was none. And besides, he was never what you could call really sedative.

He and I took up quarters at the European hotel—no sweet abiding-place. There were beetles in the Denmark butter that they pushed on to the filthy table-cloth in its original one-pound tin; and there was a Turkish officer in riding pants and red morocco slippers, back from the Yemen with two or three incurable complaints. He talked out-of-date Turkish politics in bad French and eked out his ignorance of table manners with instinctive racial habit.

To avoid him between meals Will and I set out to look at the historic sights, and exhausted them all, real and alleged, in less than half a day (for in addition to a lust for ready-cut building stone the Turks have never cherished monuments that might accentuate their own decadence). After that we fossicked in the manner of prospectors that we are by preference, if not always by trade, eschewing polite society and hunting in the impolite, amusing places where most of the facts have teeth, sharp and ready to snap, but visible.

We found a khan at last on the outskirts of the city, almost in sight of the railway line, that well agreed with our frame of mind. It was none of the newfangled, underdone affairs that ape hotels, with Greek managers and as many different prices for one service as there are grades of credulity, but a genuine two-hundred-year-old Turkish place, run by a Turk, and named Yeni Khan (which means the new rest house) in proof that once the world was younger. The man who directed us to the place called it a *kahveh;* but that means a place for donkeys and foot-passengers, and when we spoke of it as *kahveh* to the *odabashi*—the elderly youth who corresponds to porter, bell-boy and chambermaid in one—he was visibly annoyed.

Truly the place was a khan—a great bleak building of four high outer walls, surrounding a courtyard that was a yard deep with the dung of countless camels, horses, bullocks, asses; crowded with *arabas,* the four-wheeled vehicles of all the Near East, and smelly with centuries of human journeys' ends.

Khans provide nothing except room, heat and water (and the heat costs extra); there is no sanitation for any one at any price; every guest dumps all his discarded rubbish over the balcony rail into the courtyard, to be trodden and wheeled under foot and help build the aroma. But the guests provide a picture without price that with the very first glimpse drives discomfort out of mind.

In that place there were Parthians, Medes and Elamites, and all the rest of the list. There was even a Chinaman. Two Hindus were unpacking bundles out of a creaking *araba,* watched scornfully by an unmistakable Pathan. A fat swarthy-faced Greek in black frock coat and trousers, fez, and slippered feet gesticulated with his right arm like a pump-handle while he sat on the balcony-rail and bellowed orders to a crowd mixed of Armenians, Italians, Maltese, Syrians and a Turk or two, who labored with his bales of cotton goods below. (The Italians eyed everybody sidewise, for there were rumors in those days of impending trouble, and when the Turk begins hostilities he likes his first opponents easy and ready to hand.)

There were Kurds, long-nosed, lean-lipped and suspicious, who said very little, but hugged long knives as they passed back and forth among the swarming strangers. They said nothing at all, those Kurds, but listened a very great deal.

Tall, mustached Circassians, with eighteen-inch Erzerum daggers at their waists, swaggered about as if they, and only they, were history's heirs. It was expedient to get out of their path alertly, but they cringed into second place before the Turks, who, without any swagger at all, lorded it over every one. For the Turk is a conqueror, whatever else he ought to be. The poorest Turkish servant is race-conscious, and unshakably convinced of his own superiority to the princes of the conquered. One has to bear that fact in mind when dealing with the Turk; it colors all his views of life, and accounts for some of his famous unexpectedness.

Will and I fell in love with the crowd, and engaged a room over the great arched entrance. We were aware from the first of the dull red marks on the walls of the room, where bed-bugs had been slain with slipper heels by angry owners of the blood; but we were not in search of luxury, and we had our belongings and a can of insect-bane brought down from the hotel at once. The fact that stallions squealed and fought in the stalls across the courtyard scarcely promised us uninterrupted sleep; but sleep is not to be weighed in the balance against the news of eastern nights.

We went down to the common room close beside the main entrance, and pushed the door open a little way; the men who sat within with their backs against it would only yield enough to pass one person in gingerly at a time. We saw a sea of heads and hats and faces. It looked impossible to squeeze another human being in among those already seated on the floor, nor to make another voice heard amid all that babel.

But the babel ceased, and they did make room for us—places of honor against the far wall, because of our clean clothes and nationality. We sat wedged between a Georgian in smelly, greasy woolen jacket, and a man who looked Persian but talked for the most part French. There were other Persians beyond him, for I caught the word *poul*—money, the perennial song and shibboleth of that folk.

The day was fine enough, but consensus of opinion had it that snow was likely falling in the Taurus Mountains, and rain would fall the next day between the mountains and the sea, making roads and fords impassable and the mountain passes risky. So men from the ends of earth sat still contentedly, to pass earth's gossip to and fro—an astonishing lot of it. There was none of it quite true, and some of it not nearly true, but all of it was based on fact of some sort.

Men who know the khans well are agreed that with experience one learns to guess the truth from listening to the ever-changing lies. We could not hope to pick out truth, but sat as if in the pit of an old-time theater, watching a foreign-language play and understanding some, but missing most of it.

There was a man who drew my attention at once, who looked and was dressed rather like a Russian—a man with a high-bridged, prominent, lean nose—not nearly so bulky as his sheepskin coat suggested, but active and strong, with a fiery restless eye. He talked Russian at intervals with the men who sat near him at the end of the room on our right, but used at least six other languages with any one who cared to agree or disagree with him. His rather agreeable voice had the trick of carrying words distinctly across the din of countless others.

"What do you suppose is that man's nationality?" I asked Will, shouting to him because of the roar, although he sat next me.

"Ermenie!" said a Turk next but one beyond Will, and spat venomously, as if the very name Armenian befouled his mouth.

But I was not convinced that the man with the aquiline nose was Armenian. He looked guilty of altogether too much zest for life, and laughed too boldly in Turkish presence. In those days most Armenians thereabouts were sad. I called Will's attention to him again.

"What do you make of him?"

"He belongs to that quieter party in the opposite corner." (Will puts two and two together all the time, because the heroes of dime novels act that way.) "They're gypsies, yet I'd say he's not—"

"He and the others are *jingaan,*" said a voice beside me in English, and I looked into the Persian's gentle brown eyes. "The *jingaan* are street robbers pure and simple," be added by way of explanation.

"But what nationality?"

"*Jingaan* might be anything. They in particular would call themselves Romany. We call them Zingari. Not a dependable people—unless—"

I waited in vain for the qualification. He shrugged his shoulders, as if there was no sense in praising evil qualities.

But I was not satisfied yet. They were swarthier and stockier than the man who had interested me, and had indefinite, soft eyes. The man I watched had brown eyes, but they were hard. And, unlike them, he had long lean fingers and his gestures were all extravagant. He was not a Jew, I was sure of that, nor a Syrian, nor yet a Kurd.

"Ermenie—Ermenie!" said the Turk, watching me curiously, and spitting again. "That one is Ermenie. Those others are just dogs!"

The crowd began to thin after a while, as men filed out to feed cattle and to cook their own evening meal. Then the perplexing person got up and came over toward me, showing no fear of the Turk at all. He was tall and lean when he stood upright, but enormously strong if one could guess correctly through the bulky-looking outer garment.

He stood in front of Will and me, his strong yellow teeth gleaming between a black beard and mustache. The Turk got up clumsily, and went out, muttering to himself. I glanced toward the corner where the self-evident gypsies sat, and observed that with perfect unanimity they were all feigning sleep.

"Eenglis sportsmen!" said the man in front of us, raising both hands, palms outward, in appraisal of our clothes and general appearance.

It was not surprising that he should talk English, for what the British themselves have not accomplished in that land of a hundred tongues has been done by American missionaries, teaching in the course of a generation thousands on thousands. (There is none like the American missionary for attaining ends at wholesale.)

"What countryman are you?" I asked him.

"Zeitoonli," he answered, as if the word were honor itself and explanation bound in one. Yet he looked hardly like an honorable man. "The *chilabi* are staying here?" he asked. *Chilabi* means gentleman.

"We wait on the weather," said I, not caring to have him turn the tables on me and become interrogator.

He laughed with a sort of hard good humor.

"Since when have Eenglis sportsmen waited on the weather? Ah, but you are right, *effendi,* none should tell the truth in this place, unless in hope of being disbelieved!" He laid a finger on his right eye, as I have seen Arabs do when they mean to ascribe to themselves unfathomable cunning. "Since you entered this common room you have not ceased to observe me closely. The other sportsman has watched those Zingari. What have you learned?"

He stood with lean hands crossed now in front

of him, looking at us down his nose, not ceasing to smile, but a hint less at his ease, a shade less genial.

"I have heard you—and them—described as *jingaan,*" I answered, and he stiffened instantly.

Whether or not they took that for a signal—or perhaps he made another that we did not see—the six undoubted gypsies got up and left the room, shambling out in single file with the awkward gait they share in common with red Indians.

"Jingaan," he said, "are people who lurk in shadows of the streets to rob belated travelers. That is not my business." He looked very hard indeed at the Persian, who decided that it might as well be supper-time and rose stiffly to his feet. The Persians rob and murder, and even retreat, gracefully. He bade us a stately and benignant good evening, with a poetic Persian blessing at the end of it. He bowed, too, to the Zeitoonli, who bared his teeth and bent his head forward something less than an inch.

"They call me the Eye of Zeitoon!" he announced with a sort of savage pride, as soon as the Persian was out of ear-shot.

Will pricked his ears—schoolboy-looking ears that stand out from his head.

"I've heard of Zeitoon. It's a village on a mountain, where a man steps out of his front door on to a neighbor's roof, and the women wear no veils, and—"

The man showed his teeth in another yellow smile.

"The *effendi* is blessed with intelligence! Few know of Zeitoon."

Will and I exchanged glances.

"Ours," said Will, "is the best room in the khan, over the entrance gate."

"Two such *chilabi* should surely live like princes," he answered without a smile. If he had dared say that and smile we would have struck him, and Monty might have been alive to-day. But he seemed to know his place, although he looked at us down his nose again in shrewd appraisal.

Will took out tobacco and rolled what in the innocence of his Yankee heart he believed was a cigarette. I produced and lit what he contemptuously called a "boughten cigaroot"—Turkish Régie, with the scent of aboriginal ambrosia. The Zeitoonli took the hint.

"Yarim sa' at," he said. *"Korkakma!"*

"Meanin'?" demanded Will.

"In half an hour. Do not be afraid!" said he.

"Before I grow afraid of you," Will retorted, "you'll need your friends along, and they'll need knives!"

The Zeitoonli bowed, laid a finger on his eye again, smiled and backed away. But he did not leave the room. He went back to the end-wall against which he had sat before, and although he did not stare at us the intention not to let us out of sight seemed pretty obvious.

"That half-hour stuff smacked rather of a threat," said Will. "Suppose we call the bluff, and keep him waiting. What do you say if we go and dine at the hotel?"

But in the raw enthusiasm of entering new quarters we had made up our minds that afternoon to try out our new camp kitchen—a contraption of wood and iron we had built with the aid of the mission carpenter. And the walk to the hotel would have been a long one, through Tarsus mud in the dark, with prowling dogs to take account of.

"I'm not afraid of ten of him!" said I. "I know how to cook curried eggs; come on!"

"Who said who was afraid?"

So we went out into darkness already jeweled by a hundred lanterns, dodged under the necks of three hungry Bactrian camels (they are irritable when they want their meal), were narrowly missed by a mule's heels because of the deceptive shadows that confused his aim, tripped over a donkey's heel-rope, and found our stairway—thoroughly well cursed in seven languages, and only just missed by a Georgian gentleman on the balcony, who chose the moment of our passing underneath to empty out hissing liquid from his cooking pot.

Once in our four-square room, with the rags on the floor in our especial honor, and our beds set up, and the folding chairs in place, contentment took hold of us; and as we lighted the primus burner in the cooking box, we pitied from the bottom of compassionate young hearts all unfortunates in stiff white shirts, whose dinners were served that night on silver and laundered linen.

Through the partly open door we could smell everything that ever happened since the beginning of the world, and hear most of the elemental music—made, for instance, of the squeal of fighting stallions, and the bray of an amorous he-ass—the bubbling complaint of fed camels that want to go to sleep, but are afraid of dreaming—the hum of human voices—the clash of cooking pots—the voice of a man on the roof singing falsetto to the stars (that was surely the Pathan!)—the tinkling of a three-stringed instrument—and all of that punctuated by the tapping of a *saz,* the little tight-skinned Turkish drum.

It is no use for folk whose finger-nails were never dirty, and who never scratched themselves while they cooked a meal over the primus burner on the floor, to say that all that medley of sounds and smells is not good. It is very good indeed, only he who is privileged must understand, or else the spell is mere confusion.

The cooking box was hardly a success, because bright eyes watching through the open door made us nervously amateurish. The Zeitoonli arrived true to his threat on the stroke of the half-hour, and we could not shut the door in his face because of the fumes of food and kerosene. (Two of the eggs, like us, were travelers and had been in more than one bazaar.)

But we did not invite him inside until our meal was finished, and then we graciously permitted him to go for water wherewith to wash up. He strode back and forth on the balcony, treading ruthlessly on prayer-mats (for the Moslem prays in public like the Pharisees of old).

"Myself I am Christian," he said, spitting over the rail, and sitting down again to watch us. We accepted the remark with reservations.

When we asked him in at last, and we had driven out the flies with flapping towels, be closed the door and squatted down with his back to it, we two facing him in our canvas-backed easy chairs. He refused the "genuine Turkish" coffee that Will stewed over the primus. Will drank the beastly stuff, of course, to keep himself in countenance, and I did not care to go back on a friend before a foreigner, but I envied the man from Zeitoon his liberty of choice.

"Why do they call you the Eye of Zeitoon?" I asked, when time enough had elapsed to preclude his imagining that we regarded him seriously. One has to be careful about beginnings in the Near East, even as elsewhere.

"I keep watch!" he answered proudly, but also with a deeply-grounded consciousness of cunning. There were moments when I felt such strong repugnance for the man that I itched to open the door and thrust him through—other moments when compassion for him urged me to offer money—food—influence—anything. The second emotion fought all the while against the first, and I found out afterward it had been the same with Will.

Why should Zeitoon need such special watching?" I demanded. "How do you watch? Against whom? Why?"

He laughed with a pair of lawless eyes, and showed his yellow teeth.

"Ha! Shall I speak of Zeitoon? This, then: the Turks never conquered it! They came once and built a fort on the opposite mountain-side, with guns to overawe us all. We took their fort by storm! We threw their cannon down a thousand feet into the bed of the torrent, and there they lie to-day! We took prisoner as many of their Arab *zaptiehs* as still were living—aye, they even brought Arabs against us—poor fools who had not yet heard of Zeitoon's defenders! Then we came down to the plains for a little vengeance, leaving the Arabs for our wives to guard. They are women of spirit, the Zeitoonli wives!

"Word reached Zeitoon presently that we were being hard pressed on the plains. It was told to the Zeitoonli wives that they might arrange to have pursuit called off from us by surrendering those Arab prisoners. They answered that Zeitoon-fashion. How? I will tell. There is a bridge of wood, flung over across the mountain torrent, five hundred feet above the water, spanning from crag to crag. Those Zeitoonli wives of ours bound the Arab prisoners hand and foot. They brought them out along the bridge. They threw them over one at a time, each man looking on until his turn came. That was the answer of the brave Zeitoonli wives!"

"And you on the plains?"

"Ah! It takes better than Osmanli to conquer the men of Zeitoon!" he gave the Turks their own names for themselves with the air of a brave fighting man conceding his opponent points. "We heard what our wives had done. We were encouraged. We prevailed! We fell back to-ward our mountain and prevailed! There in Zeitoon we have weapons—numbers—advantage of position, for no roads come near Zeitoon that an *araba,* or a gun, or anything on wheels can use. The only thing we fear is treachery, leading to surprise in overwhelming force. And against these I keep watch!"

"Why should you tell us all this?" demanded

Will. "How do you know we are not agents of the Turkish government?"

He laughed outright, throwing out both hands toward us. "Eenglis sportsmen!" he said simply.

"What's that got to do with it?" Will retorted. He has the unaccountable American dislike of being mistaken for an Englishman, but long ago gave up arguing the point, since foreigners refuse, as a rule, to see the sacred difference.

"I am, too, sportsman. At Zeitoon there is very good sport. Bear. Antelope. Wild boar. One sportsman to another—do you understand?"

We did, and did not believe.

"How far to Zeitoon?" I demanded.

"I go in five days when I hurry. You—not hurrying—by horse—seven—eight—nine days, depending on the roads."

"Are they all Armenians in Zeitoon?"

"Most. Not all. There are Arabs—Syrians—Persians—a few Circassians—even Kurds and a Turk or two. Our numbers have been reinforced continually by deserters from the Turkish Army. Ninety-five per cent., however, are Armenians," he added with half-closed eyes, suddenly suggesting that masked meekness that disguises most outrageous racial pride.

"It is common report," I said, "that the Turks settled all Armenian problems long ago by process of massacre until you have no spirit for revolt left."

"The report lies, that is all!" he answered. Then suddenly he beat on his chest with clenched fist. "There is spirit here! There is spirit in Zeitoon! No Osmanli dare molest my people! Come to Zeitoon to shoot bear, boar, antelope! I will show you! I will prove my words!"

"Were those six *jingaan* in the common room your men?" I asked him, and he laughed as suddenly as he had stormed, like a teacher at a child's mistake.

"*Jingaan* is a bad word," he said. "I might kill a man who named me that—depending on the man. My brother I would kill for it—a stranger perhaps not. Those men are Zingari, who detest to sleep between brick walls. They have a tent pitched in the yard."

"Are they your men?"

"Zingari are no man's men."

The denial carried no conviction.

"Is there nothing but hunting at Zeitoon?" Will demanded.

"Is that not much? In addition the place itself is wonderful—a mountain in a mist, with houses clinging to the flanks of it, and scenery to burst the heart!"

"What else?" I asked. "No ancient buildings?"

He changed his tactics instantly.

"*Effendi,*" he said, leaning forward and pointing a forefinger at me by way of emphasis, "there are castles on the mountains near Zeitoon that have never been explored since the Turks—may God destroy them!—overran the land! Castles hidden among trees where only bears dwell! Castles built by the Seljuks—Armenians—Romans—Saracens—Crusaders! I know the way to every one of them!"

"What else?" demanded Will, purposely incredulous.

"Beyond Zeitoon to north and west are cave-dwellers. Mountains so hollowed out that only a shell remains, a sponge—a honeycomb! No man knows how far those tunnels run! The Turks have attempted now and then to smoke out the inhabitants. They were laughed at! One mountain is connected with another, and the tunnels run for miles and miles!"

"I've seen cave-dwellings in the States," Will answered, unimpressed. "But just where do you come in?"

"I do not understand."

"What do you propose to get out of it?"

"Nothing! I am proud of my country. I am sportsman. I am pleased to show."

We both jeered at him, for that explanation was too outrageously ridiculous. Armenians love money, whatever else they do or leave undone, and can wring a handsome profit out of business whose very existence the easier-going Turk would not suspect.

"See if I can't read your mind," said Will. "You'll guide us for some distance out of town, at a place you know, and your *jingaan*-gipsy brethren will hold us up at some point and rob us to a fare-you-well. Is that the pretty scheme?"

Some men would have flown into a fury. Some would have laughed the matter off. Any and every crook would have been at pains to hide his real feelings. Yet this strange individual was at a loss how to answer, and not averse to our knowing that.

For a moment a sort of low cunning seemed to creep over his mind, but he dismissed it. Three times be raised his hands, palms upward, and checked himself in the middle of a word.

"You could pay me for my services," he said at last, not as if that were the real reason, nor as if he hoped to convince us that it was, but as if he were offering an excuse that we might care to accept for the sake of making peace with our own compunctions.

"There are four in our party," said Will, apropos apparently of nothing. The effect was unexpected.

"Four?" His eyes opened wide, and be made the knuckle-bones of both hands crack like caps going off. "Four Eenglis sportsman?"

"I said four. If you're willing to tell the naked truth about what's back of your offer, I'll undertake to talk it over with my other friends. Then, either we'll all four agree to take you up, or we'll give you a flat refusal within a day or two. Now—suit yourself."

"I have told the truth—Zeitoon—caves—boar—antelope—wild boar. I am a very good guide. You shall pay me handsomely."

"Sure, we'll ante up like foreigners. But why do you make the proposal? What's behind it?"

"I never saw you until this afternoon. You are Eenglis sportsmen. I can show good sport. You shall pay me. Could it be simpler?"

It seemed to me we had been within an ace of discovery, but the man's mind had closed again against us in obedience to some racial or religious instinct outside our comprehension. He had been on the verge of taking us into confidence.

"Let the sportsmen think it over," he said, getting up. *"Jannam!* (My soul!) *Effendi,* when I was a younger man none could have made me half such a sportsmanlike proposal without an answer on the instant! A man fit to strike the highway with his foot should be a judge of men! I have judged you fit to be invited! Now you judge me—the Eye of Zeitoon!"

"What is your real name?"

"I have none—or many, which is the same thing! I did not ask your names; they are your own affair!"

He stood with his hand on the door, not irresolute, but taking one last look at us and our belongings.

"I wish you comfortable sleep, and long lives, *effendim!"* he said then, and swung himself out, closing the door behind him with an air of having honored us, not we him particularly. And after he had gone we were not at all sure that summary of the situation was not right.

We lay awake on our cots until long after midnight, hazarding guesses about him. Whatever else he had done he had thoroughly aroused our curiosity.

"If you want my opinion that's all he was after anyway!" said Will, dropping his last cigarette-end on the floor and flattening it with his slipper. "Cut the cackle, and let's sleep!"

We fell asleep at last amid the noise of wild carousing; for the proprietor of the Yeni Khan, although a Turk, and therefore himself presumably abstemious, was not above dispensing at a price *mastika* that the Greeks get drunk on, and the viler raki, with which Georgians, Circassians, Albanians, and even the less religious Turks woo imagination or forgetfulness.

There was knife-fighting as well as carousal before dawn, to judge by the cat-and-dog-fight swearing in and out among the camel pickets and the wheels of *arabas.* But that was the business of the men who fought, and no one interfered.

A TIME AND TIMES AND HALF A TIME

When Cydnus bore the Taurus snows
To sweeten Cleopatra's keels,
And rippled in the breeze that sings
From Kara Dagh, where leafy wings
Of flowers fall and gloaming steals
The colors of the blowing rose,
Old were the wharves and woods and ways—
Older the tale of steel and fire,
Involved intrigue, envenomed plan,
Man marketing his brother man
By dread duress to glut desire.
No peace was in those olden days.
Hope like the gorgeous rose sun-warmed
Blossomed and blew away and died,
Till gentleness had ceased to be
And Tarsus knew no chivalry
Could live an hour by Cydnus' side
Where all the heirs of evil swarmed.
And yet—with every swelling spring
Each pollen-scented zephyr's breath
Repeats the patient news to ears
Made dull by dreams of loveless years,
"It is of life, and not of death
That ye shall hear the Cydnus sing!"

II
"HOW DID SUNSHINE GET INTO THE GARDEN? BY WHOSE LEAVE CAME THE WIND?"

WE AWOKE amid sounds unexplainable. Most of the Moslems had finished their noisy ritual ablutions, and at dawn we had been dimly conscious of the strings of camels, mules and donkeys jingling out under the arch beneath us. Yet there was a great din from the courtyard of wild hoofs thumping on the dung, and of scurrying feet as if a mile-long caravan were practicing formations.

So we went out to yawn, and remained, oblivious of everything but the cause of all the noise, we leaning with elbows on the wooden rail, and she laughing up at us at intervals.

The six Zingari, or gypsies, had pitched their tent in the very middle of the yard, ambitious above all other considerations to keep away from walls. It was a big, low, black affair supported on short poles, and subdivided by them into several compartments. One could see unshapely bulges where women did the housekeeping within.

But the woman who held us spell-bound cared nothing for Turkish custom—a girl not more than seventeen years old at the boldest guess. She was breaking a gray stallion in the yard, sitting the frenzied beast without a saddle and doing whatever she liked with him, except that his heels made free of the air, and he went from point to point whichever end up best pleased his fancy.

Travelers make an early start in Asia Minor, but the yard was by no means empty yet; some folk were still waiting on the doubtful weather. Her own people kept to the tent. Whoever else had business in the yard made common cause and cursed the girl for making the disturbance, frightening camels, horses, asses and themselves. And she ignored them all, unless it was on purpose that she brought her stallion's heels too close for safety to the most abusive.

It was only for us two that she had any kind of friendly interest; she kept looking up at us and laughing as she caught our eyes, bringing her mount uprearing just beneath us several times. She was pretty as the peep o' morning, with long, black wavy hair all loose about her shoulders, and as light on the horse as the foam he tossed about, although master of him without a second's doubt of it.

When she had had enough of riding—long before we were tired of the spectacle—she shouted with a voice like a mellow bell. One of the gypsies ran out and led away the sweating stallion, and she disappeared into the tent throwing us a laugh over her shoulder.

"D'you suppose those gypsies are really of that Armenian's party?" Will wondered aloud. "Now, if she were going to Zeitoon—!"

Feeling as he did, I mocked at him to hide my feelings, and we hung about for another hour in hope of seeing her again, but she kept close. I don't doubt she watched us through a hole in the tent. We would have sat there alert in our chairs until evening only Fred sent a note down to say he was well enough to leave the hospital.

We found him with his beard trimmed neatly and his fevered eyes all bright again, sitting talking to the nurse on the veranda about a niece of hers—Gloria Vanderman.

"Chicken in this desert!" Will wondered irreverently, and Fred, who likes his English to have dictionary meanings, rose from his chair in wrath. The nurse made that the cue for getting rid of us.

"Take Mr. Oakes away!" she urged, laughing. "He threatened to kill a man this morning. There's too much murder in Tarsus now. If he should add to it—"

"You know it wasn't on my account," Fred objected. "It was what he wrote—and said of you. Why, he has had you prayed for publicly by name, and you washing the brute's feet! Let me back in there for just five minutes, and I'll show what a hospital case should really look like!"

"Take him away!" she laughed. "Isn't it bad enough to be prayed for? Must I get into the papers, too, as heroine of a scandal?"

The head missionary was not there to say good-by to, life in his case being too serious an affair to waste minutes of a precious morning on farewells, so we packed Fred into the waiting carriage and drove all the way to Mersina, where we interrupted Monty's mid-afternoon game of chess.

Fred Oakes and Monty were the closest friends I ever met—one problem for an enemy—one stout, two-headed, most dependable ally for the lucky man or woman they called friend.

"Oh, hullo!" said Monty over his shoulder, as our names were called out by the stately consular *kavass.*

"Hullo!" said Fred, and shook hands with the consul.

"Thought you were due to be sick for another week?" said Monty, closing up the board.

"I was. I would have been. Bed would have done me good, and the nurse is a darling, old enough to be Will's mother. But they put a biped by the name of Peter Measel in the bed next mine. He's a missionary on his own account, and keeps a diary. Seems be contributes to the funds of a Welsh mission in France, and they do what he says. He has all the people he disapproves of prayed for publicly by name in the mission hall in Marseilles, with extracts out of his diary by way of explanation, so that the people who pray may know what they've got on their hands. The special information I gave him about you, Monty, will make Marseilles burn! He's got you down as a drunken pirate, my boy, with no less than eleven wives. But be asked me one night whether I thought what he'd written about the nurse was strong enough, and he read it aloud to me. You'd never believe what the reptile had dared suggest in his devil's log-book! I'm expelled for threatening to kill him!"

"The nurse was right," said the consul gloomily. "There'll be murder enough hereabouts—and soon!"

He was a fairly young man yet in spite of the nearly white hair over the temples. He measured his words in the manner of a man whose speech is taken at face value.

"The missionaries know. The governments won't listen. I've been appealed to. So has the United States consul, and neither of us is going to be able to do much. Remember, I represent a government at peace with Turkey, and so does he. The Turk has a side to his character that governments ignore. Have you watched them at prayer?"

We told him how close we had been on the previous night, and he laughed.

"Did you suppose I couldn't smell camel and khan the moment you came in?"

"That was why Sister Vanderman hurried you off so promptly!" Fred announced with an air of outraged truthfulness. "Faugh! Slangy talk and stink of stables!"

"I was talking of Turks," said the consul. "When they pray, you may have noticed that they glance to right and left. When they think there is nobody looking they do more, they stare deliberately to the right and left. That is the act of recognition of the angel and the devil who are supposed to attend every Moslem, the angel to record his good deeds and the devil his bad ones. To my mind there lies the secret of the Turk's character. Most of the time he's a man of his word—honest—courteous—considerate—good-humored—even chivalrous—living up to the angel. But once in so often he remembers the other shoulder, and then there isn't any limit to the deviltry he'll do. Absolutely not a limit!"

"I suppose we or the Americans could land marines at a pinch, and protect whoever asked for protection?" suggested Monty.

"No," said the consul deliberately. "Germany would object. Germany is the only power that would. Germany would accuse us of scheming to destroy the value of their blessed Baghdad railway."

A privy councilor of England, which Monty was, is not necessarily in touch with politics of any sort. Neither were we; but it happened that more than once in our wanderings about the world things had been forced on our attention.

"They would rather see Europe burn from end to end!" Monty agreed.

"And I think there's more than that in it," said the consul. "Armenians are not their favorites. The Germans want the trade of the Levant. The Armenians are business men. They're shrewder than Jews and more dependable than Greeks. It would suit Germany very nicely, I imagine, to have no Armenians to compete with."

"But if Germany once got control of the Near East," I objected, "she could impose her own restrictions."

The consul frowned. "Armenians who thrive in spite of Turks—"

"Would skin a German for hide and tallow," nodded Will.

"Exactly. Germany would object vigorously if we or the States should land marines to prevent the Turks from applying the favorite remedy, *vukuart*—that means 'events,' you know—their euphemism for 'massacre at rather frequent intervals.' Germany would rather see the Turks finish the dirty work thoroughly than have it to do herself later on."

"You mean," said I, "that the German government is inciting to massacre?"

"Hardly. There are German missionaries in the country, doing good work in a funny, fussy, rigorous fashion of their own. They'd raise a dickens of a hocus-pocus back in Germany if they once suspected their government of playing that game. No. But Germany intends to stand off the other powers, while Turks tackle the Armenians; and the Turks know that."

"But what's the immediate excuse for massacre?" demanded Fred.

The consul laughed.

"All that's needed is a spark. The Armenians haven't been tactful. They don't hesitate to irritate the Turks—not that you can blame them, but it isn't wise. Most of the money-lenders are Armenians; Turks won't engage in that business themselves on religious grounds, but they're ready borrowers, and the Armenian money-lenders, who are in a very small minority, of course, are grasping and give a bad name to the whole nation. Then, Armenians have been boasting openly that one of these days the old Armenian kingdom will be reestablished. The Turks are conquerors, you know, and don't like that kind of talk. If the Armenians could only keep from quarreling among themselves they could win their independence in half a jiffy, but the Turks are deadly wise at the old trick of *divide et impera*; they keep the Armenians quarreling, and nobody dares stand in with them because sooner—or later—sooner, probably—they'll split among themselves, and leave their friends high and dry. You can't blame 'em. The Turks know enough to play on their religious prejudices and set one sect against another. When the massacres begin scarcely an Armenian will know who is friend and who enemy."

"D'you mean to say," demanded Fred, "that they're going to be shot like bottles off a wall without rhyme or reason?"

"That's how it was before," said the consul. "There's nothing to stop it. The world is mistaken about Armenians. They're a hot-blooded lot on the whole, with a deep sense of national pride, and a hatred of Turkish oppression that rankles. One of these mornings a Turk will choose his Armenian and carefully insult the man's wife or daughter. Perhaps he will crown it by throwing dirt in the fellow's face. The Armenian will kill him or try to, and there you are. Moslem blood shed by a dog of a *giaour*—the old excuse!"

"Don't the Armenians know what's in store for them?" I asked.

"Some of them know. Some guess. Some are like the villagers on Mount Vesuvius—much as we English were in '57 in India, I imagine—asleep—playing games—getting rich on top of a volcano. The difference is that the Armenians will have no chance."

"Did you ever hear tell of the Eye of Zeitoon?" asked Will, apropos apparently of nothing.

"No," said the consul, staring at him.

Will told him of the individual we had talked with in the khan the night before, describing him rather carefully, not forgetting the gypsies in the black tent, and particularly not the daughter of the dawn who schooled a gray stallion in the courtyard.

The consul shook his head.

"Never saw or heard of any of them."

We were sitting in full view of the roadstead where Anthony and Cleopatra's ships had moored a hundred times. The consul's garden sloped in front of us, and most of the flowers that Europe reckons rare were getting ready to bloom.

"Would you know the man if you saw him again, Will?" I asked.

"Sure I would!"

"Then look!"

I pointed, and seeing himself observed a man stepped out of the shadow of some oleanders. There was something suggestive in his choice of lurking place, for every part of the oleander plant is dangerously poisonous; it was as if he had hidden himself among the hairs of death.

"Him, sure enough!" said Will.

The man came forward uninvited.

"How did you get into the grounds?" the consul demanded, and the man laughed, laying an unafraid hand on the veranda rail.

"My *teskere* is a better than the Turks give!" he answered in English. (A *teskere* is the official permit to travel into the interior.)

"What do you mean?"

"How did sunshine come into the garden? By whose leave came the wind?"

He stood on no formality. Before one of us could interfere (for he might have been plying the assassin's trade) he had vaulted the veranda rail and stood in front of us. As he jumped I heard the rattle of loose cartridges, and the thump of a hidden pistol against the woodwork. I could see the hilt of a dagger, too, just emerging from concealment through the opening in his smock. But he stood in front of us almost meekly, waiting to be spoken to.

"You are without shame!" said the consul.

"Truly! Of what should I be ashamed!"

"What brought you here?"

"Two feet and a great good will! You know me."

The consul shook his head.

"Who sold the horse to the German from Bitlis?"

"Are you that man?"

"Who clipped the wings of a kite, and sold it for ten pounds to a fool for an eagle from Ararat?"

The consul laughed.

"Are you the rascal who did that?"

"Who threw Olim Pasha into the river, and pushed him in and in again for more than an hour with a fishing pole—and then threw in the gendarmes who ran to arrest him—and only ran when the Eenglis consul came?"

"I remember," said the consul.

"Yet you don't look quite like that man."

"I told you you knew me."

"Neither does to-day's wind blow like yesterday's!"

"What is your name?"

"Then it was Ali."

"What is it now?"

"The name God gave me?"

"Yes."

"God knows!"

"What do you want here?"

He spread out his arms toward us four, and grinned.

"Look—see! Four Eenglis sportsman! Could a man want more?"

"Your face is hauntingly familiar," said the consul, searching old memories.

"No doubt. Who carried your honor's letter to Adrianople in time of war, and received a bullet, but brought the answer back?"

"What—are you that man—Kagig?"

Instead of replying the man opened his smock, and pulled aside an undershirt until his hairy left breast lay bare down to where the nipple should have been. Why a bullet that drilled that nipple so neatly had not pierced the heart was simply mystery.

"Kagig, by Jove! Kagig with a beard! Nobody would know you but for that scar."

"But now you know me surely? Tell these Eenglis sportsman, then, that I am good man—good guide! Tell them they come with me to Zeitoon!"

The consul's face darkened swiftly, clouded by some notion that he seemed to try to dismiss, but that refused to leave him.

"How much would you ask for your services?" he demanded.

"Whatever the *effendim* please."

"Have you a horse?"

He nodded.

"You and your horse, then, two piasters a day, and you feed yourself and the beast."

The man agreed, very bright-eyed. Often it takes a day or two to come to terms with natives of that country, yet the terms the consul offered him were those for a man of very ordinary attainments.

"Come back in an hour," said the consul.

Without a word of answer Kagig vaulted back across the rail and disappeared around the corner of the house, walking without hurry but not looking back.

"Kagig, by Jove! It would take too long now to tell that story of the letter to Adrianople. I've no proof, but a private notion that Kagig is descended from the old Armenian kings. In a certain sort of tight place there's not a better man in Asia. Now, Lord Montdidier, if you're in earnest about searching for that castle of your Crusader ancestors, you're in luck!"

"You know it's what I came here for," said Monty. "These friends of mine are curious, and I'm determined. Now that Fred's well—"

"I'm puzzled," said the consul, leaning back and looking at us all with half-closed eyes. "Why should Kagig choose just this time to guide a hunting party? If any man knows trouble's brewing, I suspect be surely does. Anything can happen in the interior. I recall, for instance, a couple of Danes, who went with a guide not long ago, and simply disappeared. There are outlaws everywhere, and it's more than a theory that the public officials are in league with them."

"What a joke if we find the old family castle is a nest of robbers," smiled Monty.

"Still!" corrected Fred.

I was watching the consul's eyes. He was troubled, but the prospect of massacre did not account for all of his expression. There was debate, inspiration against conviction, being fought out under cover of forced calm. Inspiration won the day.

"I was wondering," he said, and lit a fresh cigar while we waited for him to go on.

"I vouch for my friends," said Monty.

"It wasn't that. I've no right to make the proposal—no official right whatever—I'm speaking strictly unofficially—in fact, it's not a proposal at all—merely a notion."

He paused to give himself a last chance, but indiscretion was too strong.

"I was wondering how far you four men would go to save twenty or thirty thousand lives."

"You've no call to wonder about that," said Will.

"Suppose you tell us what you've got in mind," suggested Monty, putting his long legs on a chair and producing a cigarette.

The consul knocked out his pipe and sat forward, beginning to talk a little faster, as a man who throws discretion to the winds.

"I've no legal right to interfere. None at all. In case of a massacre of Armenians—men, women, little children—I could do nothing. Make a fuss, of course. Throw open the consulate to refugees. Threaten a lot of things that I know perfectly well my government won't do. The Turks will be polite to my face and laugh behind my back, knowing I'm helpless. But if you four men—"

"Yes—go on—what?"

"Spill it!" urged Will.

"—should be up-country, and I knew it for a fact, but did not know your precise whereabouts, I'd have a grown excuse for raising most particular old Harry! You get my meaning?"

"Sure!" said Will. "Monty's an earl. Fred's related to half the peerages in Burke. Me and him"—I was balancing my chair on one leg and he pushed me over backward by way of identification—"just pose as distinguished members of society for the occasion. I get you."

"It might even be possible, Mr. Yerkes, to get the United States Congress to take action on your account."

"Don't you believe it!" laughed Will. "The members for the Parish Pump, and the senators from Ireland would howl about the Monroe Doctrine and Washington's advice at the merest hint of a Yankee in trouble in foreign parts."

"What about the United States papers?"

"They'd think it was an English scheme to entangle the United States, and they'd be afraid to support action for fear of the Irish. No, England's your only chance!"

"Well," said the consul, "I've told you the whole idea. If I should happen to know of four important individuals somewhere up-country, and massacres should break out after you had started, I could supply our ambassador with something good to work on. The Turkish government might have to stop the massacre in the district in which you should happen to be. That would save lives."

"But could they stop it, once started?" I asked.

"They could try. That 'ud be more than they ever did yet."

"You mean," said Monty, "that you'd like us to engage Kagig and make the trip, and to remain out in case of—ah—*vukuart* until we're rescued?"

"Can't say I like it, but that's what I mean. And as for rescue, the longer the process takes the better, I imagine!"

"Hide, and have them hunt for us, eh?"

"Would it help," I suggested, "if we were to be taken prisoner by outlaws and held for ransom?"

"It might," said the consul darkly. "I'd take to the hills myself and send back a wail for help, only my plain duty is here at the mission. What I have suggested to you is mad Quixotism at the best, and at the worst—well, do you recall what happened to poor Vyner, who was held for ransom by Greek brigands? They sent a rescue party instead of money, and—"

"Charles Vyner was a friend of mine," said Monty quietly.

Fred began to look extremely cheerful and Will nudged me and nodded.

"Remember," said the consul, "in the present state of European politics there's no knowing what can or can't be done, but if you four men are absent in the hills I believe I can give the Turkish government so much to think about that there'll be no massacres in that one district."

"Whistle up Kagig!" Monty answered, and that was the end of the argument as far as yea or nay had anything to do with it. Prospect of danger was the last thing likely to divide the party.

"How about permits to travel?" asked Will. "The United States consul told me none is to be had at present."

The consul rubbed his thumb and forefinger together.

"It may cost a little more, that's all," he said. "You might go without, but you'd better submit to extortion."

He called the *kavass,* the uniformed consular attendant, and sent him in search of Kagig. Within two minutes the Eye of Zeitoon was grinning at us through a small square window in the wall at one end of the veranda. Then he came round and once more vaulted the veranda rail, for he seemed to hold ordinary means of entry in contempt. His eye looked very possessive for that of one seeking employment as a guide, but he stood at respectful attention until spoken to.

"These gentlemen have decided to employ you," the consul announced.

"Mashallah!" (God be praised!) For a Christian he used unusual expletives.

"They want to find a castle in the mountains, to hunt bear and boar, and to see Zeitoon."

"I shall lead them to ten castles never seen before by Eenglismen! They shall kill *all* the bears and pigs! Never was such sport as they shall see!"

He exploded the word pigs as if he had the Osmanli prejudice against that animal. Yet he wore a pig-skin cartridge belt about his middle.

"They will need enormous lots of ammunition!" he announced.

"What else would the roadside robbers like them to bring?"

"No Turkish servants! They throw Turks over a bridge-side in Zeitoon! I myself will provide servants, who shall bring them back safely!"

It seemed to me that he breathed inward as he said that. A Turk would have added *"Inshallah!"*—if God wills!

"Make ready for a journey of two months," he said.

"When and where shall the start be?"

It would obviously be unwise to start from the consulate.

"From the Yeni Khan in Tarsus," said Will.

"That is very good—that is excellent! I will send Zeitoonli servants to the Yeni Khan at once. Pay them the right price. Have you horses? Camels are of no use, nor yet are wheels—you shall know why later! Mules are best."

"I know where you can hire mules," said the consul, "with a Turkish muleteer to each pair."

"Oh, well!" laughed Kagig, leaning back against the rail and moving his hands palms upward as if he weighed one thought against another. "What is the difference? If a few Turks move or less come to an end over Zeitoon bridge—"

It was only for moments at a time that he seemed able to force himself to speak as our inferior. A Turk of the guide class would likely have knelt and placed a foot of each of us on his neck in turn as soon as he knew we had engaged him. This Armenian seemed made of other stuff.

"Then be on hand to-morrow morning," ordered Monty.

But the Eye of Zeitoon had another surprise for us.

"I shall meet you on the road," he announced with an air of a social equal. "Servants shall attend you at the Yeni Khan. They will say nothing at all, and work splendidly! Start when you like; you will find me waiting for you at a good place on the road. Bring not plenty, but too much ammunition! Good day, then, gentlemen!"

He nodded to us—bowed to the consul—vaulted the rail. A second later he grinned at us again through the tiny window. "I am the Eye of Zeitoon!" he boasted, and was gone. A servant whom the consul sent to follow him came back after ten or fifteen minutes saying he had lost him in a maze of narrow streets.

His latter, offhanded manner scarcely auguring well, we debated whether or not to search for some one more likely amenable to discipline to take his place. But the consul spent an hour telling us about the letter that went to Adrianople, and the bringing back of the answer that hastened peace.

"He was shot badly. He nearly died on the way back. I've no idea how he recovered. He wouldn't accept a piaster more than the price agreed on."

"Let's take a chance!" said Will, and we were all agreed before he urged it.

"There's one other thing," said the consul. "I've been told a Miss Gloria Vanderman is on her way to the mission at Marash—"

"Gee whiz!" said Will.

The consul nodded. "She's pretty, if that's what you mean. It was very unwise to let her go, escorted only by Armenians. Of course, she may get through without as much as suspecting trouble's brewing, but—well—I wish you'd look out for her."

"Chicken, eh?"

Will stuck both hands deep in his trousers pockets and tilted his chair backward to the point of perfect poise.

"Cuckoo, you ass!" laughed Fred, kicking the chair over backward, and then piling all the veranda furniture on top, to the scandalized amazement of the stately *kavass,* who came at that moment shepherding a small boy with a large tray and perfectly enormous drinks.

WHERE TWO OR THREE

Oh, all the world is sick with hate,
And who shall heal it, friend o' mine?
And who is friend? And who shall stand
Since hireling tongue and alien hand
Kill nobleness in all this land?
Judas and Pharisee combine
To plunder and proclaim it Fate.

Days when the upright dared be few
Are they departed, friend o' mine?
Are bribery and rich largesse
Fair props for fat forgetfulness,
Or anodynous of distress?
Oh, would the world were drunk with wine
And not this last besotting brew!

Oh, for the wonderful again—
The greatly daring, friend o' mine!
The simply gallant blade unbought,
The soul compassionate, unsought,
With no price but the priceless thought
Nor purpose than the brave design
Of giving that the world may gain!

III
"SAHIB, THERE IS ALWAYS WORK FOR REAL SOLDIERS!"

SO WE took two rooms at the Yeni Khan instead of one, not being minded to sleep as closely as the gentry of Asia Minor like to. Will hurried us down there for a look at the gipsy girl. But the tent was gone and the gypsies with it, and when we asked questions about them people spat.

Your good Moslem—and a Moslem is good in those parts who makes a mountain of observances, regarding mole-hills of mere morals not at all—affects to despise all *giaours;* but a *giaour,* like a gipsy, who has no obvious religion of any kind, he ranks below the pig in order of reverence. It did not redound to our credit that we showed interest in the movements of such people.

Monty brought an enormous can of bug-powder with him, and restored our popularity by lending generously after he had treated our quarters sufficiently for three days' stay. Fred did nothing to our quarters—stirred no finger, claiming convalescence with his tongue in his cheek, and strolling about until he fell utterly in love with the khan and its crowd, and the khan with him. That very first night he brought out his concertina on the balcony, and yowled songs to its clamor; and whether or not the various crowd agreed on naming the noise music, all were delighted with the friendliness.

Fred talks more languages fluently than he can count on the fingers of both hands. He began to tell tales in a sing-song eastern snarl—a tale in Persian, then in Turkish, and the night grew breathless, full of listening, until pent-up interest at intervals burst bonds and there were "Ahs" and "Ohs" all amid the dark, like little breaths of night wind among trees.

He found small time for sleep, and when dawn came, and four Zeitoonli servants according to Kagig's promise, they still swarmed around him begging for more. He went off to eat breakfast with a khan from Bukhara, sitting on a bale of nearly priceless carpets to drink overland tea made in a thing like a samovar.

All the rest of that day, and the next, sleeping only at intervals, while Monty and Will and I helped the Zeitoonli servants get our loads in shape, Fred sharpened his wonder-gift of tongues on the fascinated men of many nations, giving them London ditties and tales from the *Thousand Nights and a Night* in exchange for their news of caravan routes. He left them well pleased with their bargain.

Monty went off alone the second day to see about mules. The Turk with a trade to make believes that of several partners one is always "easier" than the rest; consequently, one man can bring him to see swifter reason than a number can. He came back that evening with twelve good mules and four attendants.

"One apiece to ride, and two apiece to carry everything. Not another mule to be had. Unpack the loads again and make them smaller!"

Fred came and sat with us that night before

the charcoal brazier in his and Monty's room.

"They all talk of robbers on the road," he said. "Northward, through the Circassian Gates, or eastward it's all the same. There's a man in a room across the way who was stripped stark naked and beaten because they thought he might have money in his clothes. When he reached this place without a stitch on him he still had all his money in his clenched fists! Quite a sportsman—what? Imagine his juggling with it while they whipped him with knotted cords!"

"What have you heard about Kagig?"

"Nothing. But a lot about *vukuart.* It's vague, but there's something in the air. You'll notice the Turkish muleteers are having nothing whatever to say to our Zeitoonli, although they've accepted the same service. Moslems are keeping together, and Armenians are getting the silence cure. Armenians are even shy of speaking to one another. I've tried listening, and I've tried asking questions, although that was risky. I can't get a word of explanation. I've noticed, though, that the ugly mood is broadening. They've been polite to me, but I've heard the word *shapkali* applied more than once to you fellows. Means hatted man, you know. Not a serious insult, but implies contempt."

"When sleepless on Eternal hills—"

Nothing but comfort and respectability ever seemed able to make Fred gloomy. He discussed our present prospects with the air of an epicure ordering dinner. And Monty listened with his dark, delightful smile—the kindliest smile in all the world. I have seen unthoughtful men mistake it for a sign of weakness.

I have never known him to argue. Nor did he then, but strode straight down into the khan yard, we sitting on the balcony to watch. He visited our string of mules first for an excuse, and invited a Kurdish chieftain (all Kurds are chieftains away from home) to inspect a swollen fetlock. With that subtle flattery he unlocked the man's reserve, passed on from chance remark to frank, good-humored questions, and within an hour had talked with twenty men. At last he called to one of the Zeitoonli to come and scrape the yard dung from his boots, climbed the stairs leisurely, and sat beside us.

"You're quite right, Fred," he said quietly.

Then there came suddenly from out the darkness a yell for help in English that brought three of us to our feet. Fred brushed his fierce mustaches upward with an air of satisfaction, and sat still.

"There's somebody down there quite wrong, and in line at last to find out why!" he said. "I've been waiting for this. Sit down."

We obeyed him, though the yells continued. There came blows suggestive of a woman on the housetops beating carpets.

"D'you recollect the man I mentioned at the consulate—the biped Peter Measel, missionary on his own account, who keeps a diary and libels ladies in it? Well, he's foul of a *thalukdar* from Rajputana, and of a Prussian contractor, recruiting men for work on the Baghdad railway. I wasn't allowed to murder him. I see why now—finger of justice—I'd have been too quick. Sit down, you idiots! You've no idea what he wrote about Miss Vanderman. Let him scream, I like it!"

"Come along," said Monty. "If he were a bad-house keeper he has had enough!"

But Will had gone before us, headlong down the stairs with the speed off the mark that they taught him on the playing field at Bowdoin. When we caught up he was standing astride a prostrate being who sobbed like a cow with its throat cut, and a Rajput and a German, either of them six feet tall, were considering whether or not to resent the violence of his interference. The German was disposed to yield to numbers. The Rajput not so.

"Why are you beating him?" asked Monty.

"*Gott im Himmel,* who would not! He wrote of me in his diary—*der Limmel!*—that I shanghai laborers."

"Do you, or don't you?" asked Monty sweetly.

"*Kreuz-blitzen!* What is that to do with you—or with him? What right had he to write that people in France should pray for me in church?"

The Rajput all this while was standing simmering, as ready as a boar at bay to fight the lot of us, yet I thought with an air about him, too, of half-conscious surprise. Several times he took a half-pace forward to assert his right of chastisement, looked hard at Monty, and checked mid-stride.

"You've done enough," said Monty.

"Who are you that says so?" the German retorted.

"He - who - will - attend - to - it - that - you - do - no - more!" Monty's smooth voice had become without inflection.

"Bah! That is easy, isn't it? You are four to one!"

"Five to one!"

The Rajput's gruff throat thrilled with a new emotion. He sprang suddenly past me, and thrust himself between Monty and the German, who took advantage of the opportunity to walk away.

"Lord Montdidier, colonel sahib bahadur, burra salaam!"

He made no obeisance, but stood facing Monty eye to eye. The words, as be rolled them out, were like an order given to a thousand men. One almost heard the swish of sabers as the squadrons came to the general salute.

"I knew you, Rustum Khan, the minute I set eyes on you. Why were you beating this man?"

"Sahib bahadur, because he wrote in his book that people in France should pray for me in church, naming my honorable name, because, says he—but I will not repeat what he says. It is not seemly."

"How do you know what is in his diary?" Monty asked.

"That German read it out to me. We were sitting, he and I, discussing how the Turks intend to butcher the Armenians, as all the world knows is written. They say it shall happen soon. Said he to me—the German said to me—'I know another,' said he, 'who if I had my way should suffer first in that event.' Saying which he showed the written book that he had found, and read me parts of it. The German was for denouncing the fellow as a friend of Armenians, but I was for beating him at once, and I had my way."

"Where is the book?" demanded Monty.

"The German has it."

"The German has no right to it."

"I will bring it."

Rustum Khan strode off into the night, and Monty bent over the sobbing form of the self-appointed missionary. We were all alone in the midst of the courtyard, not even watched from behind the wheels of *arabas,* for a fight or a thrashing in the khans of Asia Minor is strictly the affair of him who gets the worst of it.

"Will you burn that book of yours, Measel, if we protect you from further assault?"

The man sobbed that he would do anything, but Monty held him to the point, and at last procured a specific affirmative. Then Rustum Khan came back with the offending tome. It was bulky enough to contain an account of the sins of Asia Minor.

Fred and I picked the poor fellow up and led him to where the cooking places stood in one long row. Will carried the book, and Rustum Khan stole wood from other folks' piles, and fanned a fire. We watched the unhappy Peter Measel put the book on the flames with his own hands.

"You're old enough to have known better than keep such a diary!" said Monty, stirring the charred pages.

"I am at any rate a martyr!" Measel answered.

The man could walk by that time—he was presumably abstemious and recovered from shock quickly. Monty sent me to see him to his room, which turned out to be next the German's, and until Will came over from our quarters with first-aid stuff from our chest I spent the minutes telling the German what should happen to him in case he should so far forget discretion as to resume the offensive. He said nothing in reply, but sat in his doorway looking up at me with an expression intended to make me feel nervous of reprisals without committing him to deeds.

Later, when we had done our best for "the martyred biped Measel," as Fred described him, Will and I found Rustum Khan with Fred and Monty seated around the charcoal brazier in Monty's room, deep in the valley of reminiscences. Our entry rather broke the spell, but Rustum Khan was not to be denied.

"You used to tell in those days, Colonel sahib bahadur," he said, addressing Monty with that full-measured compliment that the chivalrous, old East still cherishes, "of a castle of your ancestors in these parts. Do you remember, when I showed you the ruins of my family place in Rajputana, how you stood beside me on the heights, sahib, and vowed some day to hunt for that Crusaders' nest, as you called it?"

"That is the immediate purpose of this trip of ours," said Monty.

"Ah!" said the Rajput, and was silent for about a minute. Fred Oakes began to hum through his nose. He has a ridiculous belief that doing that throws keen inquirers off a scent.

"Colonel sahib, since I was a little *butcha* not as high as your knee I have spoken English and sat at the feet of British officers. Little enough I know, but by the beard of God's prophet I know this: when a British colonel sahib speaks of 'immediate purposes,' there are hidden purposes of greater importance!"

"That well may be," said Monty gravely. "I remember you always were a student of significant details, Rustum Khan."

"There was a time when I was in your honor's confidence."

Monty smiled.

"That was years ago. What are you doing here, Rustum Khan?"

"A fair enough question! I hang my head. As you know, sahib, I am a rangar. My people were all Sikhs for several generations back. We converts to Islam are usually more thorough-going than born Moslems are. I started to make the pilgrimage to Mecca, riding overland alone by way of Persia. As I came, missing few opportunities to talk with men, who should have been the lights of my religion, I have felt enthusiasm waning. These weeks past I have contemplated return without visiting Mecca at all. I have wandered to and fro, hoping for the fervor back again, yet finding none. And now, sahib, I find you—I, Rustum Khan, at a loose end for lack of inspiration. I have prayed. Colonel sahib bahadur, I believe thou art the gift of God!"

Monty sought our eyes in turn in the lantern-lit darkness. We made no sign. None of us but he knew the Rajput, so it was plainly his affair.

"Suit yourself," said Will, and the rest of us nodded.

"We are traveling into the interior," said Monty, "in the rather doubtful hope that our absence from a coast city may in some way help Armenians, Rustum Khan."

The Rajput jumped to his feet that instant, and came to the salute.

"I might have known as much. Colonel Lord Montdidier sahib, I offer fealty! My blood be thine to spill in thy cause! Thy life on my head—thine honor on my life—thy way my way, and God be my witness!"

"Don't be rash, Rustum Khan. Our likeliest fate is to be taken prisoner by men of your religion, who will call you a renegade if you defend Armenians. And what are Armenians to you?"

"Ah, sahib! You drive a sharp spur into an open sore! I have seen too much of ill-faith—cruelty—robbery—torture—rapine—butchery, all in the name of God! It is this last threat to the Armenians that is the final straw! I took the pilgrimage in search of grace. The nearer I came to the place they tell me is on earth the home of grace, the more unfaith I see! Three nights ago in another place I was led aside and offered the third of the wealth of a fat Armenian if I would lend my sword to slit helpless throats—in the name of God, the compassionate, be merciful! My temper was about spoilt forever when that young idiot over the way described me in his book as—never mind how he described me—he paid the price! Sahib bahadur, I take my stand with the defenseless, where I know thou and thy friends will surely be! I am thy man!"

"It is not included in our plans to fight," said Monty.

"Sahib, there is always work for real soldiers!"

"What do you fellows say? Shall we let him come with us?"

"I travel at my own charges, sahib. I am well mounted and well armed."

"Sure, let him come with us!" said Will. "I like the man."

"He has my leave to come along to England afterward," said Fred, "if he'll guarantee to address me as the 'gift of God' in public!"

I left them talking and returned to see whether the "martyred biped Measel" needed further help. He was asleep, and as I listened to his breathing I heard voices in the next room. The German was talking in English, that being often the only tongue that ten men have in common. Through the partly opened door I could see that his room was crammed with men.

"They are spies, every one of them!" I heard him say. "The man I thrashed is of their party. You yourselves saw how they came to his rescue, and seduced the Indian by means of threats. This is the way of the English. ("Curse them!" said a voice.) They write notes in a book, and when that offense is detected they burn the book in a corner, as ye saw them do. I saw the book before they burned it. I thrashed the spy who wrote in the book because he had written in it reports on what it is proposed to do to infidels at the time ye know about. I tell you those men are all spies—one is as bad as the other. They work on behalf of Armenians, to bring about interference from abroad."

That he had already produced an atmosphere of danger to us I had immediate proof, for as I crossed the yard again I dodged behind an *araba* in the nick of time to avoid a blow aimed at me with a sword by a man I could not see.

"All your charming is undone!" I told Fred, bursting in on our party by the charcoal brazier. Almost breathless I reeled off what I had overheard. "They'll be here to murder us by dawn!" I said.

"Will they?" said Monty.

We were up and away two hours before dawn, to the huge delight of our Turkish muleteers, who consider a dawn start late, yet not too early for the servants of the khan, who knew enough European manners to stand about the gate and beg for tips. Nor were we quite too early for the enemy, who came out into the open and pelted us with clods of dung, the German encouraging from the roof. Fred caught him unaware full in the face with a well-aimed piece of offal. Then the khan keeper slammed the gate behind us and we rode into the unknown.

THE ROAD

There is a mystery concerning roads
And he who loves the Road shall never tire.
For him the brooks have voices and the breeze
Brings news of far-off leafiness and leas
And vales all blossomy. The clinging mire
Shall never weary such an one, nor yet their loads
O'ercome the beasts that serve him. Rock and rill
Shall make the pleasant league go by as hours
With secret tales they tell; the loosened stone,
Sweet turf upturned, the bees' full-purposed drone,
The hum of happy insects among flowers,
And God's blue sky to crown each hill!
Dawn with her jewel-throated birds
To him shall be a new page in the Book
That never had beginning nor shall end,
And each increasing hour delights shall lend—
New notes in every sound—in every nook

New sights—new thoughts too wide for words,
Too deep for pen, too high for human song,
That only in the quietness of winding ways
From tumult and all bitterness apart
Can find communication with the heart—
Thoughts that make joyous moments of the days,
And no road heavy, and no journey long!

IV
"WE ARE THE ROBBERS, EFFENDI!"

THE SNOW threatened in the mountains had not materialized, and the weather had changed to pure perfection. About an hour after we started the khan emptied itself behind us in a long string, jingling and clanging with horse and camel bells. But they turned northward to pass through the famed Circassian Gates, whereas we followed the plain that paralleled the mountain range—our mules' feet hidden by eight inches of primordial ooze.

"Wish it were only worse!" said Monty. "Snow or rain might postpone massacre. Delay might mean cancellation."

But there was no prospect whatever of rain. The Asia Minor spring, perfumed and amazing sweet, breathed all about us, spattered with little diamond-bursts of tune as the larks skyrocketed to let the wide world know how glad they were. Whatever dark fate might be brooding over a nation, it was humanly impossible for us to feel low-spirited.

Our Zeitoonli Armenians trudged through the mud behind us at a splendid pace—mountain-men with faces toward their hills. The Turks—owners of the animals another man had hired to us—rode perched on top of the loads in stoic silence, changing from mule to mule as the hours passed and watching very carefully that no mule should be overtaxed or chilled. In fact, the first attempt they made to enter into conversation with us was when we dallied to admire a view of Taurus Mountain, and one of them closed up to tell us the mules were catching cold in the wind. (If they had been our animals it might have been another story.)

Their contempt for the Zeitoonli was perfectly illustrated by the difference in situation. They rode; the Armenians walked. Yet the Armenians were less afraid; and when we crossed a swollen ford where a mule caught his forefoot between rocks and was drowning, it was Armenians, not Turks, who plunged into the icy water and worked him free without straining as much as a tendon.

The Turks were obsessed by perpetual fear of robbers. That, and no other motive, made them tolerate the hectoring of Rustum Khan, who had constituted himself officer of transport, and brought up the rear on his superb bay mare. As he had promised us he would, he rode well armed, and the sight of his pistol holsters, the rifle protruding stock-first from a leather case, and his long Rajput saber probably accomplished more than merely keeping Turks in countenance; it prevented them from scattering and bolting home.

His own baggage was packed on two mules in charge of an Armenian boy, who was more afraid of our Turks than they of robbers. Yet, when we demanded of our muleteers what sort of men, and of what nation the dreaded highwaymen might be they pointed at Rustum Khan's lean servant. At the khan the night before one of them had pointed out to Monty two Circassians and a Kurd as reputed to have a monopoly of robbery on all those roads. Nevertheless, they made the new accusation without blinking.

"All robbers are Armenians—all Armenians are robbers!" they assured us gravely.

When we halted for a meal they refused to eat with our Zeitoonli, although they graciously permitted them to gather all the firewood, and accepted pieces of their *pasderma* (sun-dried meat) as if that were their due. As soon as they had eaten, and before we had finished, Ibrahim, their grizzled senior, came to us with a new demand. On its face it was not outrageous, because we were doing our own cooking, as any man does who has ever peeped into a Turkish servant's behind-the-scene arrangements.

"Send those Armenians away!" he urged. "We Turks are worth twice their number!"

"By the beard of God's prophet!" thundered Rustum Khan, "who gave camp-followers the right to impose advice?"

"They are in league with highwaymen to lead you into a trap!" Ibrahim answered.

Rustum Khan rattled the saber that lay on the rock beside him.

"I am hunting for fear," he said. "All my life I have hunted for fear and never found it!"

"Pekki!" said Ibrahim dryly. The word means "very well." The tone implied that when the emergency should come we should do well not to depend on him, for he had warned us.

We were marching about parallel with the course the completed Baghdad railway was to take, and there were frequent parties of surveyors and engineers in sight. Once we came near enough to talk with the German in charge of a party, encamped very sumptuously near his work. He had a numerous armed guard of Turks.

"A precaution against robbers?" Monty asked, and I did not hear what the German answered.

Rustum Khan laughed and drew me aside.

"Every German in these parts has a guard to protect him from his own men, sahib! For a while on my journey westward I had charge of a camp of recruited laborers. Therefore I know."

The German was immensely anxious to know all about us and our intentions. He told us his name was Hans von Quedlinburg, plainly expecting us to be impressed.

"I can direct you to good quarters, where you can rest comfortably at every stage, if you will tell me your direction," he said.

But we did not tell him. Later, while we ate a meal, he came and questioned our Turks very closely; but since they were in ignorance they did not tell him either.

"Why do you travel with Armenian servants?" he asked us finally before we moved away.

"We like 'em," said Monty.

"They'll only get you in trouble. We've dismissed all Armenian laborers from the railway works. Not trustworthy, you know. Our agents are out recruiting Moslems."

"What's the matter with Armenians?"

"Oh, don't you know?"

"I'm asking."

The German shrugged his shoulders.

"I'll tell you one thing. This will illustrate. I had an Armenian clerk. He worked all day in my tent. A week ago I found him reading among my private papers. That proves you can't trust an Armenian."

"Ample evidence!" said Monty without a smile, but Fred laughed as we rode away, and the German stared after us with a new set of emotions pictured on his heavy face.

Late in the afternoon we passed through a village in which about two hundred Armenian men and women were holding a gathering in a church large enough to hold three times the number. One of them saw us coming, and they all trooped out to meet us, imagining we were officials of some kind.

"Effendi," said their pastor with a trembling hand on Monty's saddle, "the Turks in this village have been washing their white garments!"

We had heard in Tarsus what that ceremony meant.

"It means, *effendi,* they believe their purpose holy! What shall we do—what shall we do?"

"Why not go into Tarsus and claim protection at the British consulate?" suggested Fred.

"But our friends of Tarsus warn us the worst fury of all will be in the cities!"

"Take to the hills, then!" Monty advised him.

"But how can we, sir? How can we? We have homes—property—children! We are watched. The first attempt by a number of us to escape to the hills would bring destruction down on all!"

"Then escape to the hills by twos and threes. You ask my advice—I give it."

It looked like very good advice. The slopes of the foot-hills seemed covered by a carpet of myrtle scrub, in which whole armies could have lain in ambush. And above that the cliffs of the Kara Dagh rose rocky and wild, suggesting small comfort but sure hiding-places.

"You'll never make me believe you Armenians haven't hidden supplies," said Monty. "Take to the hills until the fury is over!"

But the old man shook his head, and his people seemed at one with him. These were not like our Zeitoonli, but wore the settled gloom of resignation that is poor half-brother to Moslem fanaticism, caught by subjection and infection from the bullying Turk. There was nothing we could do at that late hour to overcome the inertia produced by centuries, and we rode on, ourselves infected to the verge of misery. Only our Zeitoonli, striding along like men on holiday, retained their good spirits, and they tried to keep up ours by singing their extraordinary songs.

During the day we heard of the chicken, as Will called her, somewhere on ahead, and we spent that night at a *kahveh,* which is a place with all a khan's inconveniences, but no dignity whatever. There they knew nothing of her at all. The guests, and there were thirty besides ourselves, lay all around the big room on wooden platforms, and talked of nothing but robbers along the road in both directions. Every man in the place questioned each of us individually to find out why we had not been looted on our way of all we owned, and each man ended in a state of hostile incredulity because we vowed we had met no robbers at all. They shrugged their shoulders when we asked for news of Miss Gloria Vanderman.

There was no fear of Ibrahim and his friends decamping in the night, for the Zeitoonli kept too careful watch, waiting on them almost as thoughtfully as they fetched and carried for us, but never forgetting to qualify the service with a smile or a word to the Turks to imply that it was done out of pity for brutish helplessness.

These Zeitoonli of ours were more obviously every hour men of a different disposition to the meek Armenians of the places where the Turkish heel had pressed. But for our armed presence and the respect accorded to the Anglo-Saxon they would have had the whole mixed company down on them a dozen times that night.

"I'm wondering whether the Armenians within reach of the Turks are not going to suffer for the sins of mountaineers!" said Fred, as we warmed ourselves at the great open fire at one end of the room.

"Rot!" Will retorted. "Sooner or later men begin to dare assert their love of freedom, and you can't blame 'em if they show it foolishly. Some folk throw tea into harbors—some stick a king's head on a pole—some take it out for the present in fresh-kid stuff. These Zeitoonli are men of spirit, or I'll eat my hat!"

But if we ourselves had not been men of spirit, obviously capable of strenuous self-defense, our Zeitoonli would have found themselves in an awkward fix that night.

We supped off *yoghurt*—the Turkish concoction of milk—cow's, goat's, mare's, ewe's or buffalo's (and the buffalo's is best)—that is about the only food of the country on which the Anglo-Saxon thrives. Whatever else is fit to eat the Turks themselves ruin by their way of cooking it. And we left before dawn in the teeth of the owner of the *kahveh's* warning.

"Dangerous robbers all along the road!" he advised, shaking his head until the fez grew insecure, while Fred counted out the coins to pay our bill. "Armenians are without compunction—bad folk! Ay, you have weapons, but so have they, and they have the advantage of surprise! May Allah the compassionate be witness, I have warned you!"

"There will be more than warnings to be witnessed!" growled Rustum Khan as he rode away. "Those others, who sharpened weapons all night long, and spoke of robbers, have been waiting three days at that *kahveh* till the murdering begins!"

That morning, on Rustum Khan's advice, we made our Turkish muleteers ride in front of us. The Zeitoon men marched next, swinging along with the hillman stride that eats up distance as the ticked-off seconds eat the day. And we rode last, admiring the mountain range on our left, but watchful of other matters, and in position to cut off retreat.

"The last time a Turk ran away from me he took my Gladstone bag with him!" said Fred. "No, only Armenians are dishonest. It was obedience to his prophet, who bade him take advantage of the *giaour*—quite a different thing! Ibrahim's sitting on my kit, and I'm watching him. You fellows suit yourselves!"

We passed a number of men on foot that morning all coming our way, but no Armenians among them. However, we exchanged no wayside gossip, because our Zeitoonli in front availed themselves of privilege and shouted to every stranger to pass at a good distance.

That is a perfectly fair precaution in a land where every one goes armed, and any one may be a bandit. But it leads to aloofness. Passers-by made circuits of a half-mile to avoid us, and when we spurred our mules to get word with them they mistook that for proof of our profession and bolted. We chased three men for twenty minutes for the fun of it, only desisting when one of them took cover behind a bush and fired a pistol at us with his eyes shut.

"Think of the lies he'll tell in the *kahveh* to-night about beating off a dozen robbers single-handed!" Will laughed. "Let's chase the next batch, too, and give the *kahveh* gang an ear-full!"

"I rather think not," said Monty. "They'll say we're Armenian criminals. Let's not be the spark."

He was right, so we behaved ourselves, and within an hour we had trouble enough of another sort. We began to meet dogs as big as Newfoundlands, that attacked our unmounted Zeitoonli, refusing to be driven off with sticks and stones, and only retreating a little way when we rode down on them.

"Shoot the brutes!" Will suggested cheerfully, and I made ready to act on it.

"For the lord's sake, don't!" warned Monty, riding at a huge black mongrel that was tearing strips from the smock of one of our men. The owner of the dog, seeing its victim was Armenian, rather encouraged it than otherwise, leaning on a long pole and grinning in an unfenced field near by.

"The consul warned me they think more of a dog's life hereabouts than a man's. In half an hour there'd be a mob on our trail. Take the Zeitoonli up behind us."

Rustum Khan was bitter about what he called our squeamishness. But we each took up a man on his horse's rump, and the dogs decided the fun was no longer worth the effort, especially as we had riding whips. But skirmishing with the dogs and picking up the Armenians took time, so that our muleteers were all alone half a mile ahead of us, and had disappeared where the road dipped between two hillocks, when they met with the scare they looked for.

They came thundering back up the road, flogging and flopping on top of the loads like the wooden monkeys-on-a-stick the fakers used to sell for a penny on the curb in Fleet Street, glancing behind them at every second bound like men who had seen a thousand ghosts.

We brought them to a halt by force, but take them on the whole, now that they were in contact with us, they did not look so much frightened as convinced. They had made up their minds that it was not written that they should go any farther, and that was all about it.

"Ermenie!" said Ibrahim. And when we laughed at that he stroked his beard and vowed there were hundreds of Armenians ambushed by the roadside half a mile ahead. The others corrected him, declaring the enemy were thousands strong.

Finally Monty rode forward with me to investigate. We passed between the hillocks, and descended for another hundred yards along a gradually sloping track, when our mules became aware of company. We could see nobody, but their long ears twitched, and they began to make preparations preliminary to braying recognition of their kin.

Suddenly Monty detected movement among the myrtle bushes about fifty yards from the road, and my mule confirmed his judgment by braying like Satan at a side-show. The noise was answered instantly by a chorus of neighs and brays from an unseen menagerie, whereat the owners of the animals disclosed themselves—six men, all smiling, and unarmed as far as we could tell—the very same six gypsies who had pitched their tent in the midst of the khan yard at Tarsus.

Then in a clearing at a little distance we saw women taking down a long low black tent, and between us and them a considerable herd of horses, mostly without halters but headed into a bunch by gipsy children. Somebody on a gray stallion came loping down toward us, leaping low bushes, riding erect with pluperfect hands and seat.

"I've seen that stallion before!" said I.

"And the girl on his back is looking for somebody who owns her heart!" smiled Monty. "Hullo! Are you the lucky man?"

She reined the stallion in, and took a good, long look at us, shading her eyes with her hand but showing dazzling white teeth between coral lips. Suddenly the smile departed, and a look of sullen disappointment settled on her face, as she wheeled the stallion with a swing of her lithe body from the hips, and loped away. Never, apparently, did two men make less impression on a maiden's heart. The six gypsies stood staring at us foolishly, until one of them at last held his hand up palm outward. We accepted that as a peace signal.

"Are you waiting here for us?" Monty asked in English, and the oldest of the six—a swarthy little man with rather bow legs—thought he had been asked his name.

"Gregor Jhaere," be answered.

For some vague reason Monty tried him next in Arabic and then in Hindustani, but without result. At last he tried halting Turkish, and the gipsy replied at once in German. As Monty used to get two-pence or three-pence a day extra when he was in the British army, for knowing something of that tongue, we stood at once on common ground.

"Kagig told us to wait here and bring you to him," said Gregor Jhaere.

"Where is Kagig?" Monty asked, and the man smiled blankly—much more effectively than if he had shrugged his shoulders.

"We obey Kagig at times," he said, as if that admission settled the matter. Then there was interruption. Rustum Khan came spurring down the road with his pistol holsters unbuttoned and his saber clattering like a sutler's pots and pans, to see whether we needed help. He had no sooner reined in beside us than I caught sight of Will, drawn between curiosity and fear lest the muleteers might bolt, standing in his stirrups to peer at us from the top of the track between the hillocks. Somebody else caught sight of him too.

There came a shrill about from over where the women were packing up, and everybody turned to look, Gregor Jhaere included. As hard as the gray stallion could take her in a bee line toward Will the daughter of the dawn with flashing teeth and blazing eyes was riding *ventre à terre*.

"Maga!" Gregor shouted at her, and then some unintelligible gibberish. But she took no more notice of him than if he had been a crow on a branch. In a minute she was beside Will, talking to him, and from over the top of the rise we could hear Fred shouting sarcastic remonstrance.

"She is bad!" Gregor announced in English. It seemed to be all the English he knew.

"Are you her father?" Monty asked, and Gregor answered in very slipshod German:

"She is the daughter of the devil. She shall be soundly thrashed! The *chalana!* And he a *Gorgio!*"

Suddenly Fred began to shout for help then, and we rode back, the gypsies following and Rustum Khan remaining on guard between them and their camp with his upbrushed black beard bristling defiance of Asia Minor. Our Turkish muleteers had decided to make a final bolt for it, and were using their whips on the Zeitoonli, who clung gamely to the reins. As soon as we got near enough to lend a hand the Turks resigned themselves with a kind of opportune fatalism. The Zeitoonli promptly turned the tables on them by laying hold of a leg of each and tipping them off into the mud. Ibrahim showed his teeth, and reached for a hidden weapon as he lay, but seemed to think better of it. It looked very much as if those four Zeitoonli knew in advance exactly what the interruption in our journey meant.

Will was out of the running entirely, or else the rest of us were, depending on which way one regarded it. He had eyes for nobody and nothing but the girl, nor she for any one but him, and nobody could rightfully blame either of them. Yankee though he is, Will sat his mule in the western cowboy style, and he was wearing a cowboy hat that set his youth off to perfection. She looked fit to flirt with the lord of the underworld, answering his questions in a way that would have made any fellow eager to ask more. Strangely enough, Gregor Jhaere, presumably father of the girl appeared to have lost his anger at her doings and turned his back.

Fred, smiling mischief, started toward them to horn in, as Will would have described it, but at that moment about a dozen of the gipsy women came padding uproad, fostered watchfully by Rustum Khan, who seemed convinced that murder was intended somehow, somewhere. They brought along horses with them—very good horses—and Fred prefers a horse trade to triangular flirtation on any day of any week.

The gypsies promptly fell to and off-saddled our loads under Gregor Jhaere's eye, transferring them to the meaner-looking among the beasts the women had brought, taking great care to drop nothing in the mud. And at a word from Gregor two of the oldest hags came to lift us from our saddles one by one, and hold us suspended in mid-air while the saddles were transferred to better mounts. But there is an indignity in being held out of the mud by women that goes fiercely against the white man's grain, and I kicked until they set me back in the saddle.

Monty solved the problem by riding to higher, clean ground near the roadside, where we could stand on firm grass.

Seeing us dismounted, the gypsies underwent a subtle mental change peculiar to all barbarous people. To the gipsy and the Cossack, and all people mainly dependent on the horse, to be mounted is to signify participation in affairs. To be dismounted means to stand aside and "let George do it."

Gregor Jhaere became a different man. He grew noisy and in response to his yelped commands they swooped in unprovoked attack on our unhappy muleteers. Before we could interfere they had thrown each Turk face downward, our Zeitoonli helping, and were searching them with swift intruding fingers for knives, pistols, money.

The Turk leaves his money behind when starting on a journey at some other man's expense; but they did draw forth a most astonishing assortment of weapons. They were experts in disarmament. Maga Jhaere lost interest in Will for a moment, and pricked her stallion to a place where she could judge the assortment better. Without any hesitation she ordered one of the old women to pass up to her a mother-o'-pearl ornamented Smith & Wesson, which she promptly hid in her bosom. Judging by the sounds he made, that pistol was the apple of Ibrahim's old eye, but he had seen the last of it. When we interfered, and he could get to her stirrup to demand it back, Maga spat in his face; which was all about it, except that Monty made generous allowance for the thing when paying the reckoning presently. As our servants, those Turks were, of course, entitled to our protection, and besides that weapon we had to pay for five knives that were gone beyond hope of recovery.

Monty paid our Turks off (for it was evident that even had they been willing they would not have been allowed to proceed with us another mile). Then, as Ibrahim mounted and marshaled his party in front of him, he forgot manners as well as the liberal payment.

"Mashallah!" (God be praised!) he shouted, with the slobber of excitement on his lips and beard. "Now I go to make Armenians pay for this! Let the *shapkali,* too, avoid me! *Ya Ali, ya Mahoma, Alahu!"* (Oh, Ali, oh, Mohamet, God is God!)

"Let's hope they haven't a spark of honesty!" said Monty cryptically, watching them canter away.

"Why on earth—?"

"Let's hope they ride back to the consul and swear they haven't received one piaster of their pay. That would let him know we're clear away!"

"Optimist!" jeered Will. "That consul's a Britisher. He'd take their lie literally, and deduce we're no good!"

For the moment the girl on the gray stallion had ridden away from Will and was giving regal orders to the mob of women and shrill children, who obeyed her as if well used to it. Gregor Jhaere and his men stood staring at us, Gregor shaking his head as if our letting the Turks go free had been a bad stroke of policy.

"Aren't you afraid to travel with all that mob of women and cattle?" asked Monty. "We've heard of robbers on the road."

"We are the robbers, *effendi!"* said Gregor with an air of modesty. The others smirked, but he seemed disinclined to over-insist on the gulf between us.

"Hear him!" growled Rustum Khan. "A thief, who boasts of thieving in the presence of sahibs! So is corruption, stinking in the sun!"

He added something in another language that the gypsies understood, for Gregor started as if stung and swore at him, and Maga Jhaere left her womenfolk to ride alongside and glare into his eyes. They were enemies, those two, from that hour forward. He, once Hindu, now Moslem, had no admiration whatever to begin with for unveiled women. And, since the gipsy claims to come from India and may therefore be justly judged by Indian standards, and has no caste, but is beneath the very lees of caste, he loathed all gypsies with the prejudice peculiar to men who have deserted caste in theory and in self-protection claim themselves above it. It was a case of height despising deep in either instance, she as sure of her superiority as he of his.

There might have been immediate trouble if Monty had not taken his new, restless, fresh horse by the mane and swung into the saddle.

"Forward, Rustum Khan!" he ordered. "Ride ahead and let those keen eyes of yours keep us out of traps!"

The Rajput obeyed, but as he passed Will he checked his mare a moment, and waiting until Will's blue eyes met his he raised a warning finger.

"Kubadar, sahib!"

Then he rode on, like a man who has done his duty.

"What the devil does he mean?" demanded Will.

"Kubadar means, 'Take care!'" said Monty. "Come on, what are we waiting for?"

That was the beginning, too, of Will's feud with the Rajput, neither so remorseless nor so sudden as the woman's, because he had a different code to guide him and also had to convince himself that a quarrel with a man of color was compatible with Yankee dignity. We could have wished them all three either friends, or else a thousand miles apart two hundred times before the journey ended.

As we rode forward with even our Zeitoonli mounted now on strong mules, Maga Jhaere sat her stallion beside Will with an air of owning him. She was likely a safer friend than enemy, and we did nothing to interfere. Monty pressed forward. Fred and I fell to the rear.

"Haide!" shouted Gregor Jhaere, and all the motley swarm of women and children caught themselves mounts—some already loaded with the gipsy baggage, some with saddles, some without, some with grass halters for bridles. In another minute Fred and I were riding surrounded by a smelly swarm of them, he with big fingers already on the keys of his beloved concertina, but I less enamored than he of the company.

Women and children, loaded, loose and led horses were all mixed together in unsortable confusion, the two oldest hags in the world trusting themselves on sorry, lame nags between Fred and me as if proximity to us would solve the very riddle of the gipsy race. And last of all came a pack of great scrawny dogs that bayed behind us hungrily, following for an hour until hope of plunder vanished.

"That little she-devil who has taken a fancy to Will," said Fred with a grin, "is capable of more atrocities than all the Turks between here and Stamboul! She looks to me like Santanita, Cleopatra, Salome, Caesar's wife, and all the Borgia ladies rolled in one. There's something added, though, that they lacked."

"Youth," said I. "Beauty. Athletic grace. Sinuous charm."

"No, probably they all had all those."

"Then horsemanship."

"Perhaps. Didn't Cleopatra ride?"

"Then what?" said I, puzzled.

"Indiscretion!" he answered, jerking loose the catch of his infernal instrument.

"Don't be afraid, old ladies," he said, glancing at the harridans between us. "I'm only going to sing!"

He makes up nearly all of his songs, and some of them, although irreverent, are not without peculiar merit; but that was one of his worst ones.

The preachers prate of fallen man
And choirs repeat the chant,
While unco' guid with unction urge
Repression of the joys that surge,
And jail for those who can't.
The poor deluded duds forget
That something drew the sting
When Adam tiptoed to his fall,
And made it hardly hurt at all.
Of Mother Eve I sing!

Chorus:

Oh, Mother Eve, dear Mother Eve,
The generations come and go,
But daughter Eve's as live as you
Were back in Eden years ago!

Oh, hell's not hell with Eve to tell
Again the ancient tale,
But Eden's grassy ways and bowers
Deprived of Eve to ease the hours
Would very soon grow stale!
Red cherry lips that leap to laugh,
And chic and flick and flair
Can make black white for any one—
The task of Sisyphus good fun!
So what should Adam care!

Chorus:

Oh, daughter Eve, dear daughter Eve,
The tribulations go and come,
But no adventure's ever tame
With you to make surprises hum!

THE PATTERAN

Aye-yee—I see—a cloud afloat in air of amethyst
I know its racing shadow falls on banks of gold
Where rain-rejoicing gravel warms the feeding roots
And smells more wonderful than wine.
I know the shoots of myrtle and of asphodel now stir the mould
Where wee cool noses sniff the early mist.
Aye-yee—the sparkle of the little springs I see
That tinkle as they hunt the thirsty rill.
I know the cobwebs glitter with the jeweled dew.
I see a fleck of brown—it was a skylark flew
To scatter bursting music, and the world is still
To listen. Ah, my heart is bursting too—Aye-yee!

Chorus:

(It begins with a swinging crash, and fades away.)

Aye-yee, aye-yah—the kites see far
(But also to the foxes views unfold)—
No hour alike, no places twice the same,
Nor any track to show where morning came,
Nor any footprint in the moistened mould
To tell who covered up the morning star.
Aye-yee—aye-yah!

Aye-yee—I see—new rushes crowding upwards in the mere
Where, gold and white, the wild duck preens himself
Safe hidden till the sun-drawn, lingering mists melt.

I know the secret den where bruin dwelt.
I see him now sun-basking on a shelf
Of windy rock. He looks down on the deer,
Who flit like flowing light from rock to tree
And stand with ears alert before they drink.
I know a pool of purple rimmed with white
Where wild-fowl, warming for the morning flight,
Wait clustering and crying on the brink.
And I know hillsides where the partridge breeds.
Aye-yee!

Chorus:

Aye-yee, aye-yah—the kites see far
(But also to the owls the visions change)—
No dawn is like the next, and nothing sings
Of sameness—very hours have wings
And leave no word of whose hand touched the range
Of Kara Dagh with opal and with cinnabar.
Aye-yee, aye-yah!

Aye-yee—I see—new distances beyond a blue horizon flung.
I laugh, because the people under roofs believe
That last year's ways are this!
No roads are old! New grass has grown!
All pools and rivers hold New water!
And the feathered singers weave
New nests, forgetting where the old ones hung!
Aye-yah—the muddy highway sticks and clings,
But I see in the open pastures new
Unknown to busné in the houses pent!
I hear the new, warm raindrops drumming on the tent,
I feel already on my feet delicious dew,
I see the trail outflung! And oh, my heart has wings!

Chorus:

Aye-yee, aye-yah—the kites see far
(But also on the road the visions pass)—
The universe reflected in a wayside pool,
A tinkling symphony where seeping waters drool,
The dance, more gay than laughter, of the wind-swept grass—
Oh, onward! On to where the visions are!
Aye-yee—aye-yah!

V
"EFFENDI, THAT IS THE HEART OF ARMENIA BURNING!"

RUSSIA, RUMANIA, Bulgaria, Bohemia, Persia, Armenia were all one hunting-ground to the troupe we rode with. Even the children seemed to have a smattering of most of the tongues men speak in those intriguing lands. Will and the girl beside him conversed in German, but the old hag nearest me would not confess acquaintance with any language I knew. Again and again I tried her, but she always shook her head.

Fred, with his ready gift of tongues, attempted conversation with ten or a dozen of them, but whichever language he used in turn appeared to be the only one which that particular individual did not know. All he got in reply was grins, and awkward silence, and shrugs of the shoulders in Gregor's direction, implying that the head of the firm did the talking with strangers. But Gregor rode alone with Monty, out of ear-shot.

Maga (for so they all called her) flirted with Will outrageously, if that is flirting that proclaims conquest from the start, and sets flashing white teeth in defiance of all intruders. Even the little children had hidden weapons, but Maga was better armed than any one, and she thrust the new mother-o-pearl-plated acquisition in the face of one of the men who dared drive his horse between hers and Will's. That not serving more than to amuse him, she slapped him three times back-handed across the face, and thrusting the pistol back into her bosom, drew a knife. He seemed in no doubt of her willingness to use the steel, and backed his horse away, followed by language from her like forked lightning that disturbed him more than the threatening weapon. Gipsies are great believers in the efficiency of a curse.

Nothing could be further from the mark than to say that Will tried to take advantage of Maga's youth and savagery. Fred and I had shared a dozen lively adventures with him without more than beginning yet to plumb the depths of his respect for Woman. Only an American in all the world knows how to meet Young Woman eye to eye with totally unpatronizing frankness, and he was without guile in the matter. But not so she. We did not know whether or not she was Gregor Jhaere's daughter;

whether or not she was truly the gipsy that she hardly seemed. But she was certainly daughter of the Near East that does not understand a state of peace between the sexes. There was nothing lawful in her attitude, nor as much as the suspicion that Will might be merely chivalrous.

"America's due for sex-enlightenment!" said I.

"Warn him if you like," Fred laughed, "and then steer clear! Our America is proud besides imprudent!"

Fred off-shouldered all responsibility and forestalled anxiety on any one's account by playing tunes, stampeding the whole cavalcade more than once because the horses were unused to his clanging concertina, but producing such high spirits that it became a joke to have to dismount in the mud and replace the load on some mule who had expressed enjoyment of the tune by rolling in slime, or by trying to kick clouds out of the sky.

And strangely enough he brought about the very last thing he intended with his music—stopped the flirtation's immediate progress. Maga seemed to take to Fred's unchastened harmony with all the wildness that possessed her. Some chord he struck, or likelier, some abandoned succession of them touched off her magazine of poetry. And so she sang.

The only infinitely gorgeous songs I ever listened to were Maga's. Almighty God, who made them, only really knows what country the gypsies originally came from, but there is not a land that has not felt their feet, nor a sorrow they have not witnessed. Away back in the womb of time there was planted in them a rare gift of seeing what the rest of us can only sometimes hear, and of hearing what only very few from the world that lives in houses can do more than vaguely feel when at the peak of high emotion. The gypsies do not understand what they see, and hear, and feel; but they are aware of infinities too intimate for ordinary speech. And it was given to Maga to sing of all that, with a voice tuned like a waterfall's for open sky, and trees, and distances—not very loud, but far-carrying, and flattened in quarter-tones where it touched the infinite.

Fred very soon ceased from braying with his bellowed instrument. Her songs were too wild for accompaniment—interminable stanzas of unequal length, with a refrain at the end of each that rose through a thousand emotions to a crash of ecstasy, and then died away to dreaminess, coming to an end on an unfinished rising scale.

All the gypsies and our Zeitoonli and Rustum Khan's lean servant joined in the refrains, so that we trotted along under the snow-tipped fangs of the Kara Dagh oblivious of the passage of time, but very keenly conscious of touch with a realm of life whose existence hitherto we had only vaguely guessed at.

The animals refused to weary while that singing testified of tireless harmonies, as fresh yet as on the day when the worlds were born. We rattled forward, on and upward, as if the panorama were unrolling and we were the static point, getting out of nobody's way for the best reason in the world—that everybody hid at first sight or sound of us, except when we passed near villages, and then the great fierce-fanged curs chased and bayed behind us in short-winded fury.

"The dogs bark," quoted Fred serenely, "but the caravan moves on!"

An hour before dark we swung round a long irregular spur of the hills that made a wide bend in the road, and halted at a lonely *kahveh*—a wind-swept ruin of a place, the wall of whose upper story was patched with ancient sacking, but whose owner came out and smiled so warmly on us that we overlooked the inhospitable frown of his unplastered walls, hoping that his smile and the profundity of his salaams might prove prophetic of comfort and cleanliness within. Vain hope!

Maga left Will's side then, for there was iron-embedded custom to be observed about this matter of entering a road-house. In that land superstition governs just as fiercely as the rest those who make mock of the rule-of-rod religions, and there is no man or woman free to behave as be or she sees fit. Every one drew aside from Monty, and he strode in alone through the split-and-mended door, we following next, and the gypsies with their animals clattered noisily behind us. The women entered last, behind the last loaded mule, and Maga the very last of all, because she was the most beautiful, and beauty might bring in the devil with it only that the devil is too proud to dawdle behind the old hags and the horses.

We found ourselves in an oblong room, with stalls and a sort of pound for animals at one end and an enormous raised stone fireplace at the other. Wooden platforms for the use of guests faced each other down the two long sides, and the only promise of better than usual comfort lay in the piles of firewood waiting for whoever felt rich and generous enough to foot the bill for a quantity.

But an agreeable surprise made us feel at home before ever the fire leaped up to warm the creases out of saddle-weary limbs. We had given up thinking of Kagig, not that we despaired of him, but the gypsies, and especially Maga, had replaced his romantic interest for the moment with their own. Now all the man's own exciting claim on the imagination returned in full flood, as he arose leisurely from a pile of skins and blankets near the hearth to greet Monty, and shouted with the manner of a chieftain for fuel to be piled on instantly.

"For a great man comes!" he announced to the rafters. And the *kahveh* servants, seven sons of the owner of the place, were swift and abject in the matter of obeisance. They were Turks. All Turks are demonstrative in adoration of whoever is reputed great. Monty ignored them, and Kagig came down the length of the room to offer him a hand on terms of blunt equality.

"Lord Montdidier," he said, mispronouncing the word astonishingly, "this is the furthest limit of my kingdom yet. Kindly be welcome!"

"Your kingdom?" said Monty, shaking hands, but not quite accepting the position of blood-equal. He was bigger and better looking than Kagig, and there was no mistaking which was the abler man, even at that first comparison, with Kagig intentionally making the most of a dramatic situation.

Kagig laughed, not the least nervously.

"Mirza," he said in Persian, *"duzd ne giriftah padshah ast!"* (Prince, the uncaught thief is king.)

He was wearing a *kalpak*—the head-gear of the Cossack, which would make a high priest look outlawed, and a shaggy goat-skin coat that had seen more than one campaign. Unmistakably the garment had been slit by bullets, and repaired by fingers more enthusiastic than adept. There was a pride of poverty about him that did not gibe well with his boast of being a robber.

"That's the first gink we've met in this land who didn't claim to be something better than he looked!" Will whispered.

"Hopeless, I suppose!" Fred answered. "Never mind. I like the man."

It was evident that Monty liked him, too, for all his schooled reserve. Kagig ordered one of the owner's sons to sweep a place near the fire, and there he superintended the spreading of Monty's blankets, close enough to his own assorted heap for conversation without mutual offense. Will cleaned for himself a section of the opposite end of the platform, and Fred and I spread our blankets next to his. That left Rustum Khan in a quandary. He stood irresolute for a minute, eying first the gypsies, who had stalled most of their animals and were beginning to occupy the platform on the other side; then considering the wide gap between me and Monty. The dark-skinned man of breeding is far more bitterly conscious of the color-line than any white knows how to be.

We watched, disinclined to do the choosing for him, racial instinct uppermost. Rustum Khan strolled back to where his mare was being cleaned by the lean Armenian servant, gave the boy a few curt orders, and there among the shadows made his mind up. He returned and stood before Monty, Kagig eying him with something less than amiability. He pointed toward the ample room remaining between Monty and me.

"Will the sahib permit? My *izzat* (honor) is in question."

"Izzat be damned!" Monty answered.

Rustum Khan colored darkly.

"I shared a tent with you once on campaign, sahib, in the days before—the good days before—those old days when—"

"When you and I served one Raj, eh? I remember," Monty answered. "I remember it was your tent, Rustum Khan. Unless memory plays tricks with me, the Orakzai Pathans had burned mine, and I had my choice between sharing yours or sleeping in the rain."

"Truly, *huzoor.*"

"I don't recollect that I mouthed very much about honor on that occasion. If anybody's honor was in question then, I fancy it was yours. I might have inconvenienced myself, and dishonored you, I suppose, by sleeping in the wet. You can dishonor the lot of us now, if you care to, by—oh, tommyrot! Tell your man to put your blankets in the only empty place, and behave like a man of sense!"

"But, *huzoor*—"

Monty dismissed the subject with a motion of his hand, and turned to talk with Kagig, who shouted for *yoghourt* to be brought at once; and that set the sons of the owner of the place to hurrying in great style. The owner himself was a true Turk. He had subsided into a state of *kaif* already over on the far side of the fire, day-dreaming about only Allah knew what rhapsodies. But the Turks intermarry with the subject races much more thoroughly than they do anything else, and his sons did not resemble him. They were active young men, rather noisy in their robust desire to be of use.

The gypsies, with Gregor Jhaere nearest to the owner of the *kahveh* and the fireplace, occupied the whole long platform on the other side, each with his women around him—except that I noticed that Maga avoided all the men, and made herself a blanket nest in deep shadow almost within reach of a mule's heels at the far end. I believed at the moment that she chose that position so as to be near to Will, but changed my mind later. Several times Gregor shouted for her, and she made no answer.

The place had no other occupants. Either we were the only travelers on that road that night or, as seemed more likely, Kagig had exercised authority and purged the *kahveh* of other guests. Certainly our coming had been expected, for there was very good *yoghourt* in ample quantity, and other food besides—meat, bread, cheese, vegetables.

When we had all eaten, and lay back against the stone wall looking at the fire, with great fanged shadows dancing up and down that made the scene one of almost perfect savagery, Gregor called again for Maga. Again she did not answer him. So be rose from his place and reached for a rawhide whip.

"I said she shall be thrashed!" he snarled in Turkish, and he made the whip crack three times like sudden pistol-shots. Will did not catch the words, and might not have understood them in any case, but Rustum Khan, beside me, both heard and understood.

"Atcha!" he grunted. "Now we shall see a kind of happenings. That girl is not a true gipsy, or else my eyes lie to me. They stole her, or adopted her. She lacks their instincts. The *gitanas,* as they call their girls, are expected to have aversion to white men. They are allowed to lure a white man to his ruin, but not to make hot love to him. She has offended against the gipsy law. The *attaman* must punish. Watch the women. They take it all as a matter of course."

"Maga!" thundered Gregor Jhaere, cracking the great whip again. I thought that Kagig looked a trifle restless, but nobody else went so far as to exhibit interest, except that the old Turk by the fire emerged far enough out of kaif to open one eye, like a sly cat's.

The *attaman* shouted again, and this time Maga mocked him. So he strode down the room in a rage to enforce his authority, and dragged her out of the shadow by an arm, sending her whirling to the center of the floor. She did not lose her feet, but spun and came to a stand, and waited, proud as Santanita while he drew the whip slowly back with studied cruelty. The old Turk opened both eyes.

Nothing is more certain than that none of us would have permitted the girl to be thrashed. I doubt if even Rustum Khan, no admirer of gypsies or unveiled women, would have tolerated one blow. But Will was nearest, and he is most amazing quick when his nervous New England temper is aroused. He had the whip out of Gregor's hand, and stood on guard between him and the girl before one of us had time to move. The old Turk closed his eyes again, and sighed resignedly.

"Our preux chevalier—preux but damned imprudent!" murmured Fred. "Let's hope there's a gipsy here with guts enough to fight for title to the girl. It looks to me as if Will has claimed her by *patteran* law. The only man with right to say whether or not a woman shall be thrashed is her owner. Once that right is established—"

"Touch her and I'll break your neck!" warned Will, without undue emotion, but truthfully beyond a shadow of a doubt.

The gipsy stood still, simmering, and taking the measure of the capable American muscles interposed between him and his legal prey. Every gipsy eye in the room was on him, and it was perfectly obvious that whatever the eventual solution of the impasse, the one thing he could not do was retreat. We were fewer in number, but much better armed than the gipsy party, so that it was unlikely they would rally to their man's aid. Kagig was an unknown quantity, but except that his black eyes glittered rather more brightly than usual he made no sign; and we kept quiet because we did not want to start a free-for-all fight. Will was quite able to take care of any single opponent, and would have resented aid.

Suddenly, however, Gregor Jhaere reached inside his shirt. Maga screamed. Rustum Khan beside me swore a rumbling Rajput oath, and we all four leapt to our feet. Maga drew no weapon, although she certainly had both dagger and pistol handy. Instead, she glanced toward Kagig, who, strangely enough, was lolling on his blankets as if nothing in the world could interest him less. The glance took as swift effect as an electric spark that fires a mine. He stiffened instantly.

"Yok!" he shouted, and at once there ceased to be even a symptom of impending trouble. *Yok* means merely no in Turkish, but it conveyed enough to Gregor to send him back to his place between his women and the Turk unashamedly obedient, leaving Maga standing beside Will. Maga did not glance again at Kagig, for I watched intently. There was simply no understanding the relationship, although Fred affected his usual all-comprehensive wisdom.

"Another claimant to the title!" he said. "A fight between Will and Kagig for that woman ought to be amusing, if only Will weren't a friend of mine. Watch America challenge him!"

But Will did nothing of the kind. He smiled at Maga, offered her a cigarette, which she refused, and returned to his place beyond Fred, leaving her standing there, as lovely in the glowing firelight as the spirit of bygone romance. At that Kagig shouted suddenly for fuel, and three of the Turk's seven hoydens ran to heap it on.

Instantly the leaping flames transformed the great, uncomfortable, draughty barn into a hall of gorgeous color and shadows without limit. There was no other illumination, except for the glow here and there of pipes and cigarettes, or matches flaring for a moment. Barring the tobacco, we lay like a baron's men-at-arms in Europe of the Middle Ages, with a captive woman to make sport with in the midst, only rather too self-reliant for the picture.

Feeling himself warm, and rested, and full enough of food, Fred flung a cigarette away and reached for his inseparable concertina. And with his eyes on the great smoked beams that now glowed gold and crimson in the firelight, he grew inspired and made his nearest to sweet music. It was perfectly in place—simple as the savagery that framed us—Fred's way of saying grace for shelter, and adventure, and a meal. He passed from *Annie Laurie* to *Suwannee River,* and all but made Will cry.

During two-three-four tunes Maga stood motionless in the midst of us, hands on her hips, with the fire-light playing on her face, until at last Fred changed the nature of the music and seemed to be trying to recall fragments of the song she had sung that afternoon. Presently he came close to achievement, playing a few bars over and over, and leading on from those into improvisation near enough to the real thing to be quite recognizable.

Music is the sure key to the gipsy heart, and Fred unlocked it. The men and women, and the little sleepy children on the long wooden platform opposite began to sway and swing in rhythm. Fred divined what was coming, and played louder, wilder, lawlessly. And Maga did an astonishing thing. She sat down on the floor and pulled her shoes and stockings off, as unself-consciously as if she were alone.

Then Fred began the tune again from the beginning, and he had it at his finger-ends by then. He made the rafters ring. And without a word Maga kicked the shoes and stockings into a corner, flung her outer, woolen upper-garment after them, and began to dance.

There is a time when any of us does his best. Money—marriage—praise—applause (which is totally another thing than praise, and more like whisky in its workings)—ambition—prayer—there is a key to the heart of each of us that can unlock the flood-tides of emotion and carry us *nolens volens* to the peaks of possibility. Either Will, or else Fred's music, or the setting, or all three unlocked her gifts that night. She danced like a moth in a flame—a wandering woman in the fire unquenchable that burns convention out of gipsy hearts, and makes the *patteran*—the trail—the only way worth while.

Opposite, the gypsies sprawled in silence on their platform, breathing a little deeper when deepest approval stirred them, a little more quickly when her Muse took hold of Maga and thrilled her to expression of the thoughts unknown to people of the dinning walls and streets.

We four leaned back against our wall in a sort of silent revelry, Fred alone moving, making his beloved instrument charm wisely, calling to her just enough to keep a link, as it were, through which her imagery might appeal to ours. Some sort of mental bridge between her tameless paganism and our twentieth-century twilight there had to be, or we never could have sensed her meaning. The concertina's wailings, mid-way between her intelligence and ours, served well enough.

My own chief feeling was of exultation, crowing

over the hooded city-folk, who think that drama and the tricks of colored light and shade have led them to a glimpse of the hem of the garment of Unrest—a cheap mean feeling, of which I was afterward ashamed.

Maga was not crowing over anybody. Neither did she only dance of things her senses knew. The history of a people seized her for a reed, and wrote itself in figures past imagining between the crimson firelight; and the shadows of the cattle stalls.

Her dance that night could never have been done with leather between bare foot and earth. It told of measureless winds and waters—of the distances, the stars, the day, the night-rain sweeping down—dew dropping gently—the hundred kinds of birds-the thousand animals and creeping things—and of man, who is lord of all of them, and woman, who is lord of man—man setting naked foot on naked earth and glorying with the thrill of life, new, good, and wonderful.

One of the Turk's seven sons produced a *saz* toward the end—a little Turkish drum, and accompanied with swift, staccato stabs of sound that spurred her like the goads of overtaking time toward the peak of full expression—faster and faster—wilder and wilder—freer and freer of all limits, until suddenly she left the thing unfinished, and the drum-taps died away alone.

That was art—plain art. No human woman could have finished it. It was innate abhorrence of the anticlimax that sent her, having looked into the eyes of the unattainable, to lie sobbing for short breath in her corner in the dark, leaving us to imagine the ending if we could.

And instead of anticlimax second climax came. Almost before the echoes of the drum-taps died among the dancing shadows overhead a voice cried from the roof in Armenian, and Kagig rose to his feet.

"Let us climb to the roof and see, *effendim,*" he said, pulling on his tattered goat-skin coat.

"See what, Ermenie?" demanded Rustum Khan. The Rajput's eyes were still ablaze with pagan flame, from watching Maga.

"To see whether thou hast manhood behind that swagger!" answered Kagig, and led the way. No man ever yet explained the racial aversions.

"Kopek!—dog, thou!" growled the Rajput, but Kagig took no notice and led on, followed by Monty and the rest of us. Maga and the gypsies came last, swarming behind us up the ladder through a hole among the beams, and clambering on to the roof over boxes piled in the draughty attic. Up under the stars a man was standing with an arm stretched out toward Tarsus.

"Look!" he said simply.

To the westward was a crimson glow that mushroomed angrily against the sky, throbbing and swelling with hot life like the vomit of a crater. We watched in silence for three minutes, until one of the gipsy women began to moan.

"What do you suppose it is?" I asked then.

"I know what it is," said Kagig simply.

"Tell then."

"Effendi, that is the heart of Armenia burning. Those are the homes of my nation—of my kin!"

"And good God, where d'you suppose Miss Vanderman is?" Fred exclaimed.

Will was standing beside Maga, looking into her eyes as if he hoped to read in them the riddle of Armenia.

LAUS LACHRIMABILIS

So now the awaited ripe reward—
Your cactus crown! Since I have urged
"Get ready for the untoward"
Ye bid me reap the wrath I dirged;
And I must show the darkened way,
Who beckoned vainly in the light!
I'll lead. But salt of Dead Sea spray
Were sweeter on my lips to-night!

Oh, days of aching sinews, when I trod the choking dust
With feet afire that could not tire, atremble with the trust
More mighty in my inner man than fear of men without,
The word I heard on Kara Dagh and did not dare to doubt—
Timely warning, clear to me as starlight after rain
When, sleepless on eternal hills, I saw the purpose plain
And left, swift-foot at dawn, obedient, to break
The news ye said was no avail—advice ye would not take!

Oh, nights of tireless talking by the hearth of hidden fires—

On roofs, behind the trade-bales, among oxen in the byres—
Out in rain between the godowns, where the splashing puddles warn
Of tiptoeing informers; when I faced the freezing dawn
With set price on my head, but still the set resolve untamed,
Not melted by the mockery, by no suspicion shamed,
To hide by day in holes, abiding dark and wind and rain
That loosed me straining to the task ye ridiculed again!

Oh, weeks of empty waiting, while the enemy designed
In detail how to loot the stuff ye would not leave behind!
Worse weeks of empty agony when, helpless and alone,
I watched in hiding for the crops from that seed I had sown;

For dust-clouds that should prove at last Armenia awake—
A nation up and coming! I had labored for your sake,
I had hungered, I had suffered. Ye had well rewarded then
If ye had come, and hanged me just to prove that ye were men!

But all the pride was promises, the criticism jeers;
Ye had no heart for sacrifice, and I no time for tears.
I offered—nay, I gave! I squandered body and breath and soul,
I bared the need, I showed the way, I preached a goodly goal,
I urged you choose a leader, since your faith in me was dim,
I swore to serve the chief ye chose, and teach my lore to him,
So he should reap where I had sown. And yet ye bade me wait—
And waited till, awake at last, ye bid me lead too late!

And so, in place of ripe reward,
Your cactus crown! And I, who urged
"Get ready for the untoward"
Must drink the dregs of wrath I dirged!
Ye bid me set time's finger back!
And stage anew the opened fight!
I'll lead. But slime of Dead Sea wrack
Were sweeter on my lips this night!

VI
"PASSING THE BUCK TO ALLAH!"

THE FIRST thought that occurred to each of us four was that Kagig had probably lied, or that he had merely voiced his private opinion, based on expectation. The glare in the distance seemed too big and solid to be caused by burning houses, even supposing a whole village were in flames. Yet there was not any other explanation we could offer. A distant cloud of black smoke with bulging red under-belly rolled away through the darkness like a tremendous mountain range.

We stood in silence trying to judge how far away the thing might be, Kagig standing alone with his foot on the parapet, his goat-skin coat hanging like a hussar's dolman, and Monty pacing up and down along the roof behind us all. The gypsies seemed able to converse by nods and nudges, with now and then one word whispered. After a little while Maga whispered in Will's ear, and he went below with her. All the gypsies promptly followed. Otherwise in the darkness we might not have noticed where Will went.

"That proves she is no gipsy!" vowed Rustum Khan, standing between Fred and me. "They, would have trusted one of their own kind."

"They call her Maga Jhaere," said I. "The *attaman's* name is Jhaere. Don't you suppose he's her father?"

"If he were her father he would have no fear," the Rajput answered. "All gypsies are alike. Their women will dance the nautch, and promise unchastity as if that were a little matter. But when it comes to performance of promises the *gitana* is true to the *Rom.* It is because she is no gipsy that they follow her now to watch. And it is because men say that Americans are Mormons and polygamous, and very swift in the use of revolvers, that all follow instead of one or two!"

"Go down then, and make sure they don't murder him!" commanded Monty, and Rustum Khan turned to obey with rather ill grace. He contrived to convey by his manner that he would do anything for Monty, even to the extent of saving the life of a man he disliked. At the moment when he turned there came the sound of a troop of horses galloping toward us.

"I will first see who comes," he said.

"The blood of Yerkes sahib on your head, Rustum Khan!" Monty answered. At that he went below.

But neither were we destined to remain up there very long. We heard colossal thumping in the *kahveh* beneath us and presently the Rajput's head reappeared through the opening in the roof.

"The fools are barricading the door," he shouted. "They make sure that an enemy outside could burn us inside without hindrance!"

At that Kagig came along the roof to our corner and looked into Monty's eyes. Fred and I stood between the two of them and the parapet, because for the first few seconds we were not sure the Armenian did not mean murder. His eyes glittered, and his teeth gleamed. It was not possible to guess whether or not the hand under his goat-skin coat clutched a weapon.

"It is now that you Eenglis sportsmen shall endure a test!" he remarked.

Exactly as in the Yeni Khan in Tarsus when we first met him there was a moment now of intense repulsion, entirely unaccountable, succeeded instantly by a wave of sympathy. I laughed aloud, remembering how strange dogs meeting in the street to smell each other are swept by unexplainable antipathies and equally swift comradeship. He thought I laughed at him.

"Neye geldin?" he growled in Turkish. "Wherefore didst thou come? To cackle like a barren hen that sees another laying? *Nichevo*," he added, turning his back on me. And that was insolence in Russian, meaning that nobody and nothing could possibly be of less importance. He seemed to keep a separate language for each set of thoughts. "Let us go below. Let us stop these fools from making too much trouble," he added in English. "One man ought to stay on the roof. One ought to be sufficient."

Since he had said I did not matter, I remained, and it was therefore I who shouted down a challenge presently in round English at a party who clattered to the door on blown horses, and thundered on it as if they had been *shâtirs* hurrying to herald the arrival of the sultan himself. There was nothing furtive about their address to the decrepit door, nor anything meek. Accordingly I couched the challenge in terms of unmistakable affront, repeating it at intervals until the leader of the new arrivals chose to identify himself.

"I am Hans von Quedlinburg!" he shouted. But I did not remember the name.

"Only a thief would come riding in such a hurry through the night!" said I. "Who is with you?"

Another voice shouted very fast and furiously in Turkish, but I could not make head or tail of the words. Then the German resumed the song and dance.

"Are you the party who talked with me at my construction camp?"

"We talk most of the time. We eat food. We whistle. We drink. We laugh!" said I.

"Because I think you are the people I am seeking. These are Turkish officials with me. I have authority to modify their orders, only let me in!"

"How many of you?" I asked. I was leaning over at risk of my life, for any fool could have seen my head to shoot at it against the luminous dark sky; but I could not see to count them.

"Never mind how many! Let us in! I am Hans von Quedlinburg. My name is sufficient."

So I lied, emphatically and in thoughtful detail.

"You are covered," I said, "by five rifles from this roof. If you don't believe it, try something. You'd better wait there while I wake my chief."

"Only be quick!" said the German, and I saw him light a cigarette, whether to convince me he felt confident or because he did feel so I could not say. I went below, and found Monty and Kagig standing together close to the outer door. They had not heard the whole of the conversation because of the noise the owner's sons had made removing, at their orders, the obstructions they had piled against the door in their first panic. Every one else had returned to the sleeping platforms, except the Turkish owner, who looked awake at last, and was hovering here and there in ecstasies of nervousness.

I repeated what the German had said, rather expecting that Kagig at any rate would counsel defiance. It was he, however, who beckoned the Turk and bade him open the door.

"But, *effendi*—"

"Chabuk! Quickly, I said!"

"Che arz kunam?" the Turk answered meekly, meaning "What petition shall I make?" the inference being that all was in the hands of Allah.

"Of ten men nine are women!" sneered Kagig irritably, and led the way to our place beside the fire. The Turk fumbled interminably with the door fastenings, and we were comfortably settled in our places before the new arrivals rode in, bringing a blast of cold air with them that set the smoke billowing about the room and made every man draw up his blankets.

"Shut that door behind them!" thundered Kagig. "If they come too slowly, shut the laggards out!"

"Who is this who is arrogant?" the German demanded in English.

He was a fine-looking man, dressed in civilian clothes cut as nearly to the military pattern as the tailor could contrive without transgressing law, but with a too small fez perched on his capable-looking head in the manner of the Prussian who would like to make the Turks believe he loves them. Rustum Khan cursed with keen attention to detail at sight of him. The man who had entered with him became busy in the shadows trying to find room to stall their horses, but Von Quedlinburg gave his reins to an attendant, and stood alone, akimbo, with the firelight displaying him in half relief.

"I am a man who knows, among other things, the name of him who bribed the *kaimakam* on Chakallu," Kagig answered slowly, also in English.

The German laughed.

"Then you know without further argument that I am not to be denied!" he answered. "What I say to-night the government officials will confirm to-morrow! Are you Kagig, whom they call the Eye of Zeitoon?"

"I am no jackal," said Kagig dryly, punning on the name Chakallu, which means "place of jackals."

The German coughed, set one foot forward, and folded both arms on his breast. He looked capable and bold in that attitude, and knew it. I knew at last who he was, and wondered why I had not recognized him sooner—the contractor who had questioned us near the railway encampment along the way, and had offered us directions; but his manner was as different now from then as a bully's in and out of school. Then he had sought to placate, and had almost cringed to Monty. Everything about him now proclaimed the ungloved upper hand.

His party, finding no room to stall their horses, had begun to turn ours loose, and there was uproar along the gipsy side of the room—no action yet, but a threatening snarl that promised plenty of it. Will was half on his feet to interfere, but Monty signed to him to keep cool; and it was Monty's aggravatingly well-modulated voice that laid the law down.

"Will you be good enough," be asked blandly, "to call off your men from meddling with our mounts?" He could not be properly said to drawl, because there was a positive subacid crispness in his voice that not even a Prussian or a Turk on a dark night could have over-looked.

The German laughed again.

"Perhaps you did not hear my name," he said. "I am Hans von Quedlinburg. As over-contractor on the Baghdad railway I have the privilege of prior accommodation at all road-houses in this province—for myself and my attendants. And in addition there are with me certain Turkish officers, whose rights I dare say you will not dispute."

Monty did not laugh, although Fred was chuckling in confident enjoyment of the situation.

"You need a lesson in manners," said Monty.

"What do you mean?" demanded Hans von Quedlinburg.

Monty rose to his feet without a single unnecessary motion.

"I mean that unless you call off your men—at once this minute from interfering with our animals I shall give you the lesson you need."

The German saluted in mock respect. Then he patted his breast-pocket so as to show the outline of a large repeating pistol. Monty took two steps forward. The German drew the pistol with an oath. Will Yerkes, beyond Fred and slightly behind the German, coughed meaningly. The German turned his head, to find that he was covered by a pistol as large as his own.

"Oh, very well," he said, "what is the use of making a scene?" He thrust his pistol back under cover and shouted an order in Turkish. Monty returned to his place and sat down. The newcomers at the rear of the room tied their horses together by the bridles, and Hans von Quedlinburg resumed his well-fed smile.

"Let it be clearly understood," he said, "that you have interfered with official privilege."

"As long as you do your best in the way of

manners you may go on with your errand," said Monty.

Suddenly Fred laughed aloud.

"The martyred biped!" he yelped.

He was right. Peter Measel, missionary on his own account, and sometime keeper of most libelous accounts, stepped out from the shadows and essayed to warm himself, walking past the German with a sort of mincing gait not calculated to assert his manliness. Hans von Quedlinburg stretched out a strong arm and hurled him back again into the darkness at the rear.

"Tchuk-tchuk! Zuruek!" he muttered.

It clearly disconcerted him to have his inferiors in rank assert themselves. That accounted, no doubt, for the meek self-effacement of the Turks who had come with him. Peter Measel did not appear to mind being rebuked. He crossed to the other side of the room, and proceeded to look the gypsies over with the air of a learned ethnologist.

"You speak of my errand," said Hans von Quedlinburg, "as if you imagine I come seeking favors. I am here incidentally to rescue you and your party from the clutches of an outlaw. The Turkish officials who are with me have authority to arrest everybody in this place, yourselves included. Fortunately I am able to modify that. Kagig—that rascal beside you—is a well-known agitator. He is a criminal. His arrest and trial have been ordered on the charge, among other things, of stirring up discontent among the Armenian laborers on the railway work. These gypsies are all his agents. They are all under arrest. You yourselves will be escorted to safety at the coast."

"Why should we need an escort to safety?" Monty demanded.

"Were you on the roof?" the German answered. "And is it possible you did not see the conflagration? An Armenian insurrection has been nipped in the bud. Several villages are burning. The other inhabitants are very much incensed, and all foreigners are in danger—yourselves especially, since you have seen fit to travel in company with such a person as Kagig."

"What has Peter Measel got to do with it?" demanded Fred. "Has he been writing down all our sins in a new book?"

"He will identify you. He will also identify Kagig's agents. He brings a personal charge against a man named Rustum Khan, who must return to Tarsus to answer it. The charge is robbery with violence."

Rustum Khan snorted.

"The violence was only too gentle, and too soon ended. As for robbery, if I have robbed him of a little self-conceit, I will answer to God for that when my hour shall come! How is it your affair to drag that whimpering fool through Asia at your tail—you a German and he English?"

The German had a hot answer ready for that, but the Turks had discovered Maga Jhaere in hiding in the shadows between two old women. She screamed as they tried to drag her forth, and the scream brought us all to our feet. But this time it was Kagig who was swiftest, and we got our first proof of the man's enormous strength. Fred, Will and I charged together round behind the newcomers' horses, in order to make sure of cutting off retreat as well as rescuing Maga. Monty leveled a pistol at the German's head. But Kagig did not waste a fraction of a second on side-issues of any sort. He flew at the German's throat like a wolf at a bullock. The German fired at him, missed, and before he could fire again he was caught in a grip he could not break, and fighting for breath, balance and something more.

One of the gypsies, who had not seen the need of hurrying to Maga's aid, now proved the soundness of his judgment by divining Kagig's purpose and tossing several new faggots on the already prodigious fire.

"Good!" barked Kagig, bending the struggling German this and that way as it pleased him.

Seeing our man with the upper hand, Monty and Rustum Khan now hurried into the mêlée, where two Turkish officers and eight *zaptieh* were fighting to keep Maga from four gypsies and us three. Nobody had seen fit to shoot, but there was a glimmering of cold steel among the shadows like lightning before a thunder-storm. Monty used his fists. Rustum Khan used the flat of a Rajput saber. Maga, leaving most of her clothing in the Turk's hands, struggled free and in another second the Turks were on the defensive. Rustum Khan knocked the revolver out of an officer's hand, and the rest of them were struggling to use their rifles, when the German shrieked. All fights are full of pauses, when either side could snatch sudden victory if alert enough. We stopped, and turned to look, as if our own lives were not in danger.

Kagig had the German off his feet, face toward the flames, kicking and screaming like a madman. He whirled him twice—shouted a sort of war-cry—hove him high with every sinew in his tough frame cracking—and hurled him head-foremost into the fire.

The Turks took the cue to haul off and stand staring at us. We all withdrew to easier pistol range, for contrary to general belief, close quarters almost never help straight aim, especially when in a hurry. There is a shooting as well as a camera focus, and each man has his own.

Pretty badly burnt about the face and fingers, Hans von Quedlinburg crawled backward out of the fire, smelling like the devil, of singed wool. Kagig closed on him, and hurled him back again. This time the German plunged through the fire, and out beyond it to a space between the flames and the back wall, where it must have been hot enough to make the fat run. He stood with a forearm covering his face, while Kagig thundered at him voluminous abuse in Turkish. I wondered, first, why the German did not shoot, and then why his loaded pistol did not blow up in the heat, until I saw that in further proof of strength Kagig had looted his pistol and was standing with one foot on it.

Head foremost into the fire.

Finally, when the beautiful smooth cloth of which his coat was made bad taken on a stinking overlay of crackled black, the German chose to obey Kagig and came leaping back through the fire, and lay groaning on the floor, where the *kahveh's* owner's seven sons poured water on him by Kagig's order. His burns were evidently painful, but not nearly so serious as I expected. I got out the first-aid stuff from our medicine bag, and Will, who was our self-constituted doctor on the strength of having once attended an autopsy, disguised as a reporter, in the morgue at the back of Bellevue Hospital in New York City, beckoned a gipsy woman, and proceeded to instruct her what to do.

However, Hans von Quedlinburg was no nervous weakling. He snatched the pot of grease from the woman's hands, daubed gobs of the stuff liberally on his face and hands, and sat up—resembling an unknown kind of angry animal with his eyebrows and mustache burned off except for a stray, outstanding whisker here and there. In a voice like a bull's at the smell of blood he reversed what he had shouted through the flames, and commanded his Turks to arrest the lot of us.

Kagig laughed at that, and spoke to him in English, I suppose in order that we, too, might understand.

"Those Turks are my prisoners!" he said. "And so are you!"

It was true about the Turks. They had not given up their weapons yet, but the gypsies were between them and the door, and even the gipsy women were armed to the teeth and willing to do battle. I caught sight of Maga's mother-o'-pearl plated revolver, and the Turkish officer at whom she had it leveled did not look inclined to dispute the upper hand.

"You Germans are all alike," sneered Kagig. "A dog could read your reasoning. You thought these foreigners would turn against me. It never entered your thick skull that they might rather defy you than see me made prisoner. Fool! Did men name me Eye of Zeitoon for nothing? Have I watched for nothing! Did I know the very wording of the letters in your private box for nothing? Are you the only spy in Asia? Am I Kagig, and do I not know who advised dismissing all Armenians from the railway work? Am I Kagig, and do I not know why? *Kopek!* (Dog!) You would beggar my people, in order to curry favor with the Turk. You seek to take me because I know your ways! Two months ago you knew to within a day or two when these new massacres would begin. One month, three weeks, and four days ago you ordered men to dig my grave, and swore to bury me alive in it! What shall hinder me from burning you alive this minute?"

There were five good hindrances, for I think that Rustum Khan would have objected to that cruelty, even had he been alone. Kagig caught Monty's eye and laughed.

"Korkakma!" he jeered. "Do not be afraid!" Then be glanced swiftly at the Turks, and at Peter Measel, who was staring all-eyes at Maga on the far side of the room.

"Order your pigs of *zaptieh* to throw their arms down!"

Instead, the German shouted to them to fire volleys at us. He was not without a certain stormy courage, whatever Kagig's knowledge of his treachery.

But the Turks did not fire, and it was perfectly plain that we four were the reason of it. They had been promised an easy prey—captured women—loot—and the remunerative task of escorting us to safety. Doubtless Von Quedlinburg had promised them our consul would be lavish with rewards on our account. Therefore there was added reason why they should not fire on Englishmen and an American. We had not made a move since the first scuffle when we rescued Maga, but the Turkish lieutenant had taken our measure. Perhaps he had whispered to his men. Perhaps they reached their own conclusions. The effect was the same in either case.

"Order them to throw their weapons down!" commanded Kagig, kicking the German in the ribs. And his coat had been so scorched in the fierce heat that the whole of one side of it broke off, like a cinder slab.

This time Hans von Quedlinburg obeyed. For one thing the pain of his burns was beginning to tell on him, but he could see, too, that he had lost prestige with his party.

"Throw down your weapons!" he ordered savagely.

But he had lost more prestige than he knew, or else he had less in the beginning than be counted on. The Turkish lieutenant—a man of about forty with the evidence of all the sensual appetites very plainly marked on his face—laughed and brought his men to attention. Then he made a kind of half-military motion with his hand toward each of us in turn, ignoring Kagig but intending to convey that we at any rate need not feel anxious.

It was Maga Jhaere who solved the riddle of that impasse. She was hardly in condition to appear before a crowd of men, for the Turks bad torn off most of her clothes, and she had not troubled to find others. She was unashamed, and as beautiful and angry as a panther. With panther suddenness she snatched the lieutenant's sword and pistol.

It suited neither his national pride nor religious prejudices to be disarmed by a gipsy woman; but the Turk is an amazing fatalist, and unexpectedness is his peculiar quality.

"Che arz kunam?" he muttered—the perennial comment of the Turk who has failed, that always made Kagig bare his teeth in a spasm of contempt. "Passing the buck to Allah," as Will construed it.

But disarming the mere conscript soldiers was not quite so simple, although Maga managed it. They had less regard for their own skins than handicapped their officer, and yet more than his contempt for the female of any human breed.

They refused point-blank to throw their rifles down, bringing a laugh and a shout of encouragement from the German. But she screwed the muzzle of her pistol into the lieutenant's ear, and bade him enforce her orders, the gipsy women applauding with a chorus of "Ohs" and "Ahs." The lieutenant succumbed to *force majeure,* and his men, who were inclined to die rather than take orders from a woman, obeyed him readily enough. They laid their rifles down carefully, without a suggestion of resentment.

"So. The women of Zeitoon are good!" said Kagig with a curt nod of approval, and Maga tossed him a smile fit for the instigation of another siege of Troy.

The gipsy women picked the rifles up, and Maga went to hunt through the mule-packs for clothing. Then Kagig turned on us, motioning with his toe toward Hans von Quedlinburg, who continued to treat himself extravagantly from our jar of ointment.

"You do not know yet the depths of this man's infamy!" he said. "The world professes to loathe Turks who rob, sell and murder women and children. What of a German—a foreigner in Turkey, who instigates the murder—and the robbery—and the burning—and the butchery—for his own ends, or for his bloody country's ends? This man is an instigator!"

"You lie!" snarled Von Quedlinburg. "You dog of an Armenian, you lie!" Kagig ignored him.

"This is the German sportsman who tried once to go to Zeitoon to shoot bears, as he said. But I knew he was a spy. I am not the Eye of Zeitoon merely because that title rolls nicely on the tongue. He has—perhaps he has it in his pocket now—a concession from the politicians in Stamboul, granting him the right to exploit Zeitoon—a place he has never seen! He has encouraged this present butchery in order that Turkish soldiers may have excuse to penetrate to Zeitoon that he covets. He wants you Eenglis sportsmen out of the way. You were to be sent safely back to Tarsus, lest you should be witnesses of what must happen. Perhaps you do not believe all this?"

He stooped down and searched the German's coat pockets with impatient fingers that tugged and jerked, tossing out handkerchief and wallet, cigars, matches that by a miracle had not caught in the heat, and considerable money to the floor. He took no notice of the money, but one of the old gipsy women crept out and annexed it, and Kagig made no comment.

"He has not his concession with him. I can prove nothing to-night. I said you shall stand a test. You must choose. This German and those Turks are my prisoners. You have nothing to do with it. You may go back to Tarsus if you wish, and tell the Turks that Kagig defies them! You shall have an escort as far as the nearest garrison. You shall have fifty men to take you back by dawn to-morrow."

At that Rustum Khan turned several shades darker and glared truculently.

"Who art thou, Armenian, to frame a test for thy betters?" he demanded, throwing a very military chest. And Will promptly bridled at the Rajput's attitude.

"You've no call to make yourself out any better than he is!" he interrupted. And at that Maga Jhaere threw a kiss from across the room, but one could not tell whether her own dislike of Rustum Khan, or her approval of Will's support of Kagig was the motive.

Fred began humming in the ridiculous way he has when be thinks that an air of unconcern may ease a situation, and of course Rustum Khan mistook the nasal noises for intentional insult. He turned on the unsuspecting Fred like a tiger. Monty's quick wit and level voice alone saved open rupture.

"What I imagine Rustum Khan means is this, Kagig: My friends and I have engaged you as guide for a hunting trip. We propose to hold you strictly to the contract."

Kagig looked keenly at each of us and nodded.

"In my day I have seen the hunters hunted!" he said darkly.

"In my day I have seen an upstart punished!" growled the Rajput, and sat down, back to the wall.

"Castles, and bears!" smiled Monty.

Kagig grinned.

"What if I propose a different quarry?"

"Propose and see!" Monty was on the alert, and therefore to all outward appearance in a sort of well-fed, catlike, dallying mood.

"This dog," said Kagig, and he kicked the German's ribs again, "has said nothing of any other person he must rescue. Bear me witness."

We murmured admission of the truth of that.

"Yet I am the Eye of Zeitoon, and I know. His purpose was to leave his prisoners here and hurry on to overtake a lady—a certain Miss Vanderman, who he thinks is on her way to the mission at Marash. He desired the credit for her rescue in order better to blind the world to his misdeeds! Nevertheless, now that she can be no more use to him, observe his chivalry! He does not even mention her!"

The German shrugged his shoulders, implying that to argue with such a savage was waste of breath.

"What do you know of Miss Vanderman's whereabouts?" demanded Will, and Maga Jhaere, at the sound of another woman's name, sat bolt upright between two other women whose bright eyes peeped out from under blankets.

"I had word of her an hour before you came, *effendi,"* Kagig answered. "She and her party took fright this afternoon, and have taken to the hills. They are farther ahead than this pig dreamed"—once more he kicked Von Quedlinburg—"more than a day's march ahead from here."

"Then we'll hunt for her first," said Monty, and the rest of us nodded assent.

Kagig grinned.

"You shall find her. You shall see a castle. In the castle where you find her you shall choose again! It is agreed, *effendi!"*

Then he ordered his prisoners made fast, and the gypsies and our Zeitoonli servants attended to it, he himself, however, binding the German's hands and feet. Will went and put bandages on the man's burns, I standing by, to help. But we got no thanks.

"Ihr seit verruekt!" he sneered. "You take the side of bandits. *Passt mal auf...* there will be punishment!"

The Zeitoonli were going to tie Peter Measel, but he set up such a howl that Kagig at last took notice of him and ordered him flung, unbound, into the great wooden bin in which the horse-feed was kept for sale to wayfarers. There he lay, and slept and snored for the rest of that session, with his mouth close to a mouse-hole.

Then Kagig ordered our Zeitoonli to the roof on guard, and bade us sleep with a patriarchal air of authority.

"There is no knowing when I shall decide to march," be explained.

Given enough fatigue, and warmth, and quietness, a man will sleep under almost any set of circumstances. The great fire blazed, and flickered, and finally died down to a bed of crimson. The prisoners were most likely all awake, for their bonds were tight, but only Kagig remained seated in the midst of his mess of blankets by the hearth; and I think he slept in that position, and that I was the last to doze off. But none of us slept very long.

There came a shout from the roof again, and once again a thundering on the door. The move—unanimous—that the gypsies' right hands made to clutch their weapons resembled the jump from surprise into stillness when the jungle is caught unawares. A second later when somebody tossed dry fagots on the fire the blaze betrayed no other expression on their faces than the stock-in-trade stolidity. Even the women looked as if thundering on a *kahveh* door at night was nothing to be noticed. Kagig did not move, but I could see that he was breathing faster than the normal, and he, too, clutched a weapon. Von Quedlinburg began shouting for help alternately in Turkish and in German, and the owner of the place produced a gun—a long, bright, steel-barreled affair of the vintage of the Comitajes and the First Greek War. He and his sons ran to the door to barricade it.

"Yavash!" ordered Kagig. The word means slowly, as applied to all the human processes. In that instance it meant "Go slow with your noise!" and mine host so understood it.

But the thundering on the great door never ceased, and the *kahveh* was too full of the noise of that for us to hear what the Zeitoonli called down from the roof. Kagig arose and stood in the middle of the room with the firelight behind him. He listened for two minutes, standing stock-still, a thin smile flickering across his lean face, and the sharp satyr-like tops of his ears seeming to prick outward in the act of intelligence.

"Open and let them in!" he commanded at last.

"I will not!" roared the owner of the place. "I shall be tortured, and all my house!"

"Open, I said!"

"But they will make us prisoner!"

Kagig made a sign with his right hand. Gregor Jhaere rose and whispered. One by one the remaining gypsies followed him into the shadows, and there came a noise of scuffling, and of oaths and blows. As Gregor Jhaere had mentioned earlier, they did obey Kagig now and then. The Turks came back looking crestfallen, and the fastenings creaked. Then the door burst open with a blast of icy air, and there poured in nineteen armed men who blinked at the firelight helplessly.

"Kagig—where is Kagig?"

"You cursed fools, where should I be!"

"Kagig? Is it truly you?" Their eyes were still blinded by the blaze.

"Shut that door again, and bolt it! Aye—Kagig, Kagig, is it you!"

"It is Kagig! Behold him! Look!"

They clustered close to see, smelling infernally of sweaty garments and of the mud from unholy lurking places.

"Kagig it is! And has all happened as I, Kagig, warned you it would happen?"

"Aye. All. More. Worse!"

"Had you acted beforehand in the manner I advised?"

"No, Kagig. We put it off. We talked, and disagreed. And then it was too late to agree. They were cutting throats while we still argued. When we ran into the street to take the offensive they were already shooting from the roofs!"

"Hah!"

That bitter dry expletive, coughed out between set teeth, could not be named a laugh.

"Kagig, listen!"

"Aye! Now it is 'Kagig, listen!' But a little while ago it was I who was saying 'Listen!' I walked myself lame, and talked myself hoarse. Who listened to me? Why should I listen to you?"

"But, Kagig, my wife is gone!"

"Hah!"

"My daughter, Kagig!"

"Hah!"

A third man thrust himself forward and thumped the butt of a long rifle on the floor.—"They took my wife and two daughters before my very eyes, Kagig! It is no time for talking now—you have talked already too much, Kagig,—now prove yourself a man of deeds! With these eyes I saw them dragged by the hair down street! Oh, would God that I had put my eyes out first, then had I never seen it! Kagig—"

"Aye—Kagig!"

"You shall not sneer at me! I shot one Turk, and ten more pounced on them. They screamed to me. They called to me to rescue. What could I do? I shot, and I shot until the rifle barrel burned my fingers. Then those cursed Turks set the house on fire behind me, and my companions dragged me away to come and find others to unite with us and make a stand! We found no others! Kagig—I tell you—those bloody Turks are auctioning our wives and daughters in the village church! It is time to act!"

"Hah! Who was it urged you in season and out of season—day and night—month in, month out—to come to Zeitoon and help me fortify the place? Who urged you to send your women there long ago?"

"But Kagig, you do not appreciate. To you it is nothing not to have women near you. We have mothers, sisters, wives—"

"Nothing to me, is it? These eyes have seen my mother, ravished by a Kurd in a Turkish uniform!"

"Well, that only proves you are one with us after all! That only proves—"

"One with you! Why did you not act, then, when I risked life and limb a thousand times to urge you?"

"We could not, Kagig. That would have precipitated—"

He interrupted the man with an oath like the aggregate of bitterness.

"Precipitated? Did waiting for the massacre like chickens waiting for the ax delay the massacres a day? But now it is 'Come and lead us, Kagig!' How many of you are there left to lead?"

"Who knows? We are nineteen—"

"Hah! And I am to run with nineteen men to the rape of Tarsus and Adana?"

"Our people will rally to you, Kagig!"

"They shall."

"Come, then!"

"They shall rally at Zeitoon!"

"Oh, Kagig—how shall they reach Zeitoon? The cursed Turks have ordered out the soldiers and are sending regiments—"

"I warned they would!"

"The cavalry are hunting down fugitives along the roads!"

"As I foretold a hundred times!"

"They were sent to protect Armenians—"

"That is always the excuse!"

"And they kill—kill—kill! A dozen of them hunted me for two miles, until I hid in a watercourse! Look at us! Look at our clothes! We are wet to the skin—tired—starving! Kagig, be a man!"

He went back to his mess of blankets and sat down on it, too bitter at heart for words. They reproached him in chorus, coming nearer to the fire to let the fierce heat draw the stink out of their clothes.

"Aye, Kagig, you must not forget your race. You must not forget the past, Kagig. Once Armenia was great, remember that! You must not only talk to us, you must act at last! We summon you to be our leader, Kagig, son of Kagig of Zeitoon!"

He stared back at them with burning eyes -raised both bands to beat his temples—and then suddenly turned the palms of his hands toward the roof in a gesture of utter misery.

"Oh, my people!"

That glimpse he betrayed of his agony was but a moment long. The fingers closed suddenly, and the palms that had risen in helplessness descended to his knees clenched fists, heavy with the weight of purpose.

"What have you done with the ammunition?" he demanded.

"We had it in the manure under John Zimisces' cattle."

"I know that. Where is it now?"

"The Turks discovered it at dawn to-day. Some one had told. They burned Zimisces and his wife and sons alive in the straw!"

"You fools! They knew where the stuff was a week ago! A month ago I warned you to send it to Zeitoon, but somebody told you I was treacherous, and you fools listened! How much ammunition have you left now?"

"Just what we have with us. I have a dozen rounds."

"I ten."

"I nine."

"I thirty-three."

Each man had a handful, or two handfuls at the most. Kagig observed their contributions to the common fund with scorn too deep for expression. It was as if the very springs of speech were frozen.

"We summon you to lead us, Kagig!"

Words came to him again.

"You summon me to lead? I will! From now I lead! By the God who gave my fathers bread among the mountains, I will, moreover, be obeyed! Either my word is law—"

"Kagig, it is law!"

"Or back you shall go to where the Turks are wearing white, and the gutters bubble red, and the beams are black against the sky! You shall obey me in future on the instant that I speak, or run back to the Turks for mercy from my hand! I have listened to enough talk!"

"Spoken like a man!" said Monty, and stood up.

We all stood up; even Rustum Khan, who did not pretend to like him, saluted the old warrior who could announce his purpose so magnificently. Maga Jhaere stood up, and sought Will's eyes from across the room. Fred, almost too sleepy to know what he was doing (for the tail end of the fever is a yearning for early bed) undid the catch of his beloved instrument, and made the rafters ring. In a minute we four were singing "For he's a jolly good fellow," and Kagig stood up, looking like Robinson Crusoe in his goat-skins, to acknowledge the compliment.

The noise awoke Peter Measel, and when we had finished making fools of ourselves I walked over to discover what he was saying. He was praying aloud—nasally—through the mouse-hole—for us, not himself. I looked at my watch. It was two hours past midnight.

"You fellows," I said, "it's Sunday. The martyred biped has just waked up and remembered it. He is praying that we may be forgiven for polluting the Sabbath stillness with immoral tunes!"

My words had a strange effect. Monty, and Fred, and Will laughed. Rustum Khan laughed savagely. But all the Armenians, including Kagig, knelt promptly on the floor and prayed, the gypsies looking on in mild amusement tempered by discretion. And out of the mouse-hole in the horse-feed bin came Peter Measel's sonorous, overriding periods:

"And, O Lord, let them not be smitten by Thine anger. Let them not be cut down in Thy wrath! Let them not be cast into hell! Give them another chance, O Lord! Let the Ten Commandments be written on their hearts in letters of fire, but let not their souls be damned for ever more! If they did not know it was the Sabbath Day, O Lord, forgive them! Amen!"

It was a most amazing night.

LIBERA NOS, DOMINE!

A priest, a statesman, and a soldier stood
Hand in each other's hand, by ruin faced,
Consulting to find succor if they could,
Till soon the lesser ones themselves abased,
Their sword and parchment on an altar laid
In deep humility the while the priest he prayed.

He prayed first for his church, that it might be
Upholden and acknowledged and revered,
And in its opal twilight men might see
Salvation if in truth enough they feared,
And if enough acknowledgment they gave
To ritual, and rosary, and creed that save.

Then prayed he for the state, that it should wean
Well-tutored counselors to do their part
Full profit and prosperity to glean

With dignity, although with contrite heart
And wisdom that Tradition wisdom ranks,
That church and state might stand and men give thanks.

Last prayed he for the soldier—longest, too,
That all the honor and the aims of war
Subserving him might carry wrath and rue
Unto repentance, and in trembling awe
The enemy at length should fault confess
And yield, to crave a peace of righteousness.

Behind them stood a patriot unbowed,
Not arrogant in gilt or goodly cloth,
Nor mincing meek, and yet not poorly proud;
With eyes afire that glittered not with wrath;
Aware of evil hours, and undismayed
Because he loved too well. He also prayed.

"Oh, Thou, who gavest, may I also give,
Withholding not—accepting no reward;
For I die gladly if the least ones live.
Twice righteous and two-edged be the sword,
'Neath freedom's banner drawn to prove Thy word
And smite me if I'm false!" His prayer was heard.

VII "WE HOLD YOU TO YOUR WORD!"

THE REMAINDER of that night was nightmare pure and simple—mules and horses squealing in instinctive fear of action they felt impending—gypsies and Armenians dragging packs out on the floor, to repack everything a dozen times for some utterly godless reason—Rustum Khan seizing each fugitive Armenian in turn to question him, alternating fierce threats with persuasion—Kagig striding up and down with hands behind him and his scraggly black beard pressed down on his chest—and the great fire blazing with reports like cannon shots as one of the Turk's sons piled on fuel and the resinous wet wood caught.

The Turk and his other six sons ran away and hid themselves as a precaution against our taking vengeance on them. With situations reversed a Turk would have taken unbelievable toll in blood and agony from any Armenian he could find, and they reasoned we were probably no better than themselves. The marvel was that they left one son to wait on us, and take the money for room and horse-feed.

"Remember!" warned Monty, as we four sidled close together with our backs against the wall. "Until we're in actual personal danger this trouble is the affair of Kagig and his men!"

"I get you. If we horn in before we have to we'll do more harm than good. Give the Turks an excuse to call us outlaws and shoot instead of rescue us. Sure. But what about Miss Vanderman?" said Will.

"I foresee she's doomed!" Fred stared straight in front of him. "It looks as if we'll lose our little Willy too! One woman at a time, especially when the lady totes a mother-o'-pearl revolver and about a dozen knives! If you come out of this alive, Bill, you'll be wiser!"

"Fond of bull, aren't you! You'd jest on an ant-heap."

"There's nothing to discuss," said I. "If there's a lady in danger somewhere ahead, we all know what we're going to do about it."

Monty nodded.

"If we can find her and get word to the consul, that 'ud be one more lever for him to pull on."

"D'you suppose they'd dare molest an Englishwoman?" I asked, with the sudden goose-flesh rising all over me.

"She's American," said Will between purposely set lips. But I did not see that that qualified the unpleasantness by much.

One of the Armenians, whom Rustum Khan had finished questioning, went and stood in Kagig's way, intercepting his everlasting sentry-go.

"What is it, Eflaton?"

"My wife, Kagig!"

"Ah! I remember your wife. She fed me often."

"You must come with me and find her, Kagig—my wife and two daughters, who fed you often!"

"The daughters were pretty," said Kagig. "So was the wife. A young woman yet. A brave, good woman. Always she agreed with me, I remember. Often I heard her urge you men to follow me to Zeitoon and help to fortify the place!"

"Will you leave a good woman in the hands of Turks, Kagig? Come—come to the rescue!"

"It is too bad," said Kagig simply. "Such women suffer more terribly than the hags who merely die by the sword. Ten times by the count—during ten succeeding massacres I have seen the Turks sell Armenian wives and daughters at auction. I am sorry, Eflaton."

"My God!" groaned Will. "How long are we four loafers going to sit here and leave a white woman in danger on the road ahead?" He got up and began folding his blankets.

The Armenian whom Kagig had called Eflaton threw himself to the floor and shrieked in agony of misery. Rustum Khan stepped over him and came and stood in front of Monty.

"These men are fools," he said. "They know exactly what the Turks will do. They have all seen massacres before. Yet not one of them was ready when the hour set for this one came. They say—and they say the truth, that the Turks will murder all Europeans they catch outside the mission stations, lest there be true witnesses afterward whom the world will believe."

"But a woman—scarcely a white woman?" This from Will, with the tips of his ears red and the rest of his face a deathly white.

"Depending on the woman," answered Rustum Khan. "Old—unpleasing—" He made an upward gesture with his thumb, and a noise between his teeth suggestive of a severed wind-pipe. "If she were good-looking—I have heard say they pay high prices in the interior, say at Kaisarieh or Mosul. Once in a harem, who would ever know? The road ahead is worse than dangerous. Whoever wishes to save his life would do best to turn back now and try to ride through to Tarsus."

"Try it, then, if you're afraid!" sneered Will, and for a moment I thought the Rajput would draw steel.

"I know what this lord sahib and I will do," he said, darkening three or four shades under his black beard. "It was for men bewitched by gipsy-women that I feared!"

Will was standing. Nothing but Monty's voice prevented blows. He rapped out a string of sudden rhetoric in the Rajput's own guttural tongue, and Rustum Khan drew back four paces.

"Send him back, Colonel sahib!" he urged. "Send that one back! He and Umm Kulsum will be the death of us!"

Fred went off into a peal of laughter that did nothing to calm the Rajput's ruffled temper.

"Who was Umm Kulsum?" I asked him, divining the cause.

"The most immoral hag in Asian legend! The aggregated essence of all female evil personified in one procuress!"

"Say, I'll have to teach that gink—"

Monty got up and stood between them, but it was a new alarm that prevented blows. A fist-blow in the Rajput's face would have meant a blood-feud that nothing less than a man's life could settle, and Monty looked worried. There came a new thundering on the door that brought everybody to his feet as if murder were the least of the charges against us. Only Kagig appeared at ease and unconcerned.

"Open to them!" he shouted, and resumed his pacing to and fro.

Our Armenian servants ran to the door, and in a minute returned to say that fifty mounted men from Zeitoon were drawn up outside. Kagig gave a curt laugh and strode across to us.

"I said you Eenglis sportsmen should see good sport."

Monty nodded, with a hand held out behind him to warn us to keep still.

"I said you shall shoot many pigs!"

"Lead on, then."

"Turks are pigs!"

Monty did not answer. To have disagreed would have been like flapping a red cloth at a tiger. Yet to have agreed with him at once might have made him jump to false conclusions. The consul's last words to us had been insistent on the unwisdom of posing as anything but hunters, legitimately entitled to protection from the Turkish government.

"I would like you gentlemen for allies!"

"You are our servant at present."

"Would you think of holding me to that?" demanded Kagig with a gesture of extreme irritation. It is only the West that can joke at itself in the face of crisis.

"If not to that," said Monty blandly, "then what agreements do you keep?"

Kagig saw the point. He drew a deep impatient breath and drove it out again hissing through his teeth. Then he took grim hold of himself.

"Effendi," he said, addressing himself to Monty, but including all of us with eyes that seemed to search our hearts, "you are a lord, a friend of the King of Eengland. If I were less than a man of my word I could make you prisoner and oblige your friend the King of Eengland to squeeze these cursed Turks!"

Rustum Khan heard what he said, and made noise enough drawing his saber to be heard outside the *kahveh,* but Kagig did not turn his head. Three gypsies attended to Rustum Khan, slipping between him and their master, and our four Zeitoonli servants cautiously approached the Rajput from behind.

"Peace!" ordered Monty. "Continue, Kagig."

Kagig held both hands toward Monty, palms upward, as if he were offering the keys of Hell and Heaven.

"You are sportsmen, all of you. Shall I keep my word to you? Or shall I serve my nation in its agony?"

Monty glanced swiftly at us, but we made no sign. Will actually looked away. It was a rule we four had to leave the playing of a hand to whichever member of the partnership was first engaged; and we never regretted it, although it often called for faith in one another to the thirty-third degree. The next hand might fall to any other of us, but for the present it was Monty's play.

"We hold you to your word!" said Monty.

Kagig gasped. "But my people!"

"Keep your word to them too! Surely you haven't promised them to make us prisoner?"

"But if I am your servant—if I must obey you for two piasters a day, how shall I serve my nation?"

"Wait and see!" suggested Monty blandly.

Kagig bowed stiffly, from the neck.

"It would surprise you, *effendi,*" he said grimly, "to know how many long years I have waited, in order that I may see what other men will do!"

Monty never answered that remark. There came a yell of "Fire!" and in less than ten seconds flames began to burst through the door that shut off the Turks' private quarters, and to lick and roar among the roof beams. The animals at the other end of the room went crazy, and there was instant panic, the Armenians outside trying to get in to help, and fighting with the men and animals and women and children who choked the way. Then the hay in the upper story caught alight, and the heat below became intolerable. Monty saw and instantly pounced on an ax and two crow-bars in the corner.

"Through the wall!" he ordered.

Fred, Will and I did that work, he and Kagig looking on. It was much easier than at first seemed likely. Most of the stones were stuck with mud, not plaster, and when the first three or four were out the rest came easily. In almost no time we had a great gap ready, and the extra draft we made increased the holocaust, but seemed to lift the heat higher. Then some of the Zeitoonli saw the gap, and began to hurry blindfolded horses through it and in a very little while the place seemed empty. I saw the Turkish owner and several of his sons looking on in fatalistic calm at about the outside edge of the ring of light, and it occurred to me to ask a question.

"Hasn't that Turk a harem?" I asked.

In another second we four were hurrying around the building, and Will and I burst in the door at the rear with our crow-bars. Monty and Fred rushed past us, and before I could get the smoke out of my eyes and throat they were hurrying out again with two old women in their arms—the women screaming, and they laughing and coughing so that they could hardly run. Then Will made my blood run cold with a new alarm.

"The biped!" he shouted. "The Measel in the corn-bin!"

They dropped the old ladies, and all four of us raced back to our hole in the wall—plunged into the hell-hot building, pulled the lid off the corn-bin (it was fastened like an ancient Egyptian coffin-lid with several stout Wooden pegs), dragged Measel out, and frog-marched him, kicking and yelling, to the open, where Fred collapsed.

"Measel," said Will, stooping to feel Fred's heart, "if you're the cause of my friend Oakes' death, Lord pity you!"

Fred sat up, not that he wished to save the "biped" any anguish, but the wise man vomits comfortably when he can, the necessity being bad enough without additional torment.

"See!" said a voice out of darkness. "He empties himself! That is well. It is only the end of the fever. Now he will be a man again. But the sahibs should have left that writer of characters in the corn-bin, where he could have shared the fate of his master without troubling us again!"

Rustum Khan strode into the light, with half his fierce beard burned away from having been the last to leave by the front entrance, and a decided limp from having been kicked by a frantic mule.

"What have you done with the German?" demanded Monty.

"I, sahib? Nothing. In truth nothing. It was the seven sons of the Turk—abetted I should say by gypsies. It was the German who set the place alight. The girl, Maga Jhaere they call her, saw him do it. She watched like a cat, the fool, hoping to amuse herself, while he burned off his ropes with a brand that fell his way out of the fire. When another brand jumped half across the room he set the place alight with it, tossing it over the party wall. He was an able rascal, sahib."

"Was?" demanded Monty.

"Aye, sahib, was! In another second he released the Turkish lieutenant and shouted in his ear to escape and say that Armenians burned this *kahveh!* Gregor Jhaere slew the Turk, however. And Maga followed the German into the open, where she denounced him to some of the Zeitoonli who recently arrived. They took him and threw him back into the fire—where he remained. I begin to like these Zeitoonli. I even like the gypsies more than formerly. They are men of some discernment, and of action!"

"Man of blood!" growled Monty. "What of the Turkish owner and his seven sons?"

"They shall burn, too, if the sahib say so!"

"If they burn, so shall you! Where is Kagig?"

"Seeing that the sahibs' horses are packed and saddled. I came to find the sahibs. According to Kagig it is time to go, before Turks come to take vengeance for a burned road-house. They will surely say Armenians burned it, whether or not there is a German to support their accusation!"

Then we heard Kagig's high-pitched *"Haide—chabuk!"* and picked up Peter Measel, and ran around the building to where the horses were already saddled, and squealing in fear of the flames. We left the Turk, and his wives and seven sons, to tell what tale they pleased.

LO HERE! LO THERE!

Ye shall not judge men by the drinks they take,
Nor by unthinking oath, nor what they wear,
For look! the mitered liars protest make
And drinking know they lie, and knowing swear.
No oath is round without the rounded fruit,
Nor pompous promise hides the ultimate.
In scarlet as in overalls and tailored suit
To-morrow's true men and the traitors wait
Untold by trick of blazonry or voice.
But harvest ripens and there come the reaping days
When each shall choose one path to bide the choice,
And ye shall know men when they face dividing ways.

VIII
"I GO WITH THAT MAN!"

TO THOSE who have never ridden knee to knee with outlaws full pelt into unknown darkness, with a burning house behind, and a whole horizon lit with the rolling glow of murdered villages, let it be written that the sensation of so doing is creepy, most amazing wild, and not without unrighteous pleasure.

There was a fierce joy that burned without consuming, and a consciousness of having crossed a Rubicon. Points of view are left behind in a moment, although the proof may not be apparent for days or weeks, and I reckon our mental change from being merely hunters of an ancient castle and big-game-tourists-trippers, from that hour. As we galloped behind Kagig the mesmerism of respect for custom blew away in the wind. We became at heart outlaws as we rode—and one of us a privy councilor of England!

The women, Maga included, were on in front. The night around and behind us was full of the thunder of fleeing cattle, for the Zeitoonli had looted the owner of the *kahveh's* cows and oxen along with their own beasts and were driving them helter-skelter. The crackling flames behind us were a beacon, whistling white in the early wind, that we did well to hurry from.

It was Monty who called Kagig's attention to the idiocy of tiring out the cattle before dawn, and then Kagig rode like an arrow until he could make the gypsies hear him. One long keening shout that penetrated through the drum of hoofs brought them to a walk, but they kept Maga in front with them, screened from our view until morning by a close line of mounted women and a group of men. The Turkish prisoners were all behind among the fifty Armenians from Zeitoon, looking very comfortless trussed up on the mounts that nobody else had coveted, with hands made fast behind their backs.

A little before dawn, when the saw-tooth tips of the mountain range on our left were first touched with opal and gold, we turned off the *araba* track along which we had so far come and entered a ravine leading toward Marash. Fred was asleep on horseback, supported between Will and me and snoring like a throttled dog. The smoke of the gutted *kahveh* had dwindled to a wisp in the distance behind us, and there was no sight or sound of pursuit.

No wheeled vehicle that ever man made could have passed up this new track. It was difficult for ridden horses, and our loaded beasts had to be given time. We seemed to be entering by a fissure into the womb of the savage hills that tossed themselves in ever-increasing grandeur up toward the mist-draped heights of Kara Dagh. Oftener than not our track was obviously watercourse, although now and then we breasted higher levels from which we could see, through gaps between hill and forest, backward along the way we had come. There was smoke from the direction of Adana that smudged a whole sky-line, and between that and the sea about a dozen sooty columns mushroomed against the clouds.

There was not a mile of the way we came that did not hold a hundred hiding-places fit for ambuscade, but our party was too numerous and well-armed to need worry on that account. Monty and Kagig drew ahead, quite a little way behind the gypsies still, but far in front of us, who had to keep Fred upright on his horse.

"My particular need is breakfast," said I.

"And Will's is the woman!" said Fred, admitting himself awake at last. Will had been straining in the stirrups on the top of every rise his horse negotiated ever since the sun rose. It certainly was a mystery why Maga should have been spirited away, after the freedom permitted her the day before.

"Rustum Khan has probably made off with her, or cut her head off!" remarked Fred by way of offering comfort, yawning with the conscious luxury of having slept. "I don't see Rustum Khan. Let's hope it's true! That 'ud give the American lady a better chance for her life in case we should overtake her!"

Will and Fred have always chosen the most awkward places and the least excuse for horseplay, and the sleep seemed to have expelled the last of the fever from Fred's bones, so that he felt like a schoolboy on holiday. Will grabbed him around the neck and they wrestled, to their horses' infinite disgust, panting and straining mightily in the effort to unseat each other. It was natural that Will should have the best of it, he being about fifteen years younger as well as unweakened by malaria. The men of Zeitoon behind us checked to watch Fred rolled out of his saddle, and roared with the delight of fighting men the wide world over to see the older campaigner suddenly recover his balance and turn the tables on the younger by a trick.

And at that very second, as Will landed feet first on the gravel panting for breath, Maga Jhaere arrived full gallop from the rear, managing her ugly gray stallion with consummate ease. Her black hair streamed out in the wind, and what with the dew on it and the slanting sun-rays she seemed to be wearing all the gorgeous jewels out of Ali Baba's cave. She was the loveliest thing to look at—unaffected, unexpected, and as untamed as the dawn, with parted lips as red as the branch of budding leaves with which she beat her horse.

But the smile turned to a frown of sudden passion as she saw Will land on the ground and Fred get ready for reprisals. She screamed defiance—burst through the ranks of the nearest Zeitoonli—set her stallion straight at us—burst between Fred and me—beat Fred savagely across the face with her sap-softened branch—and wheeled on her beast's haunches to make much of Will. He laughed at her, and tried to take the whip away. Seeing he was neither hurt nor indignant, she laughed at Fred, spat at him, and whipped her stallion forward in pursuit of Kagig, breaking between him and Monty to pour news in his ear.

"A curse on Rustum Khan!" laughed Fred, spitting out red buds. "He didn't do his duty!"

He had hardly said that when the Rajput came spurring and thundering along from the rear. He seemed in no hurry to follow farther, but drew rein between us and saluted with the semi-military gesture with which he favored all who, unlike Monty, had not been Colonels of Indian regiments.

"I tracked Umm Kulsum through the dark!" he announced, rubbing the burned nodules out of his singed beard and then patting his mare's neck. "I saw her ride away alone an hour before you reached that fork in the road and turned up this watercourse. 'By the teeth of God,' said I, 'when a good-looking woman leaves a party of men to canter alone in the dark, there is treason!' and I followed."

I offered the Rajput my cigarette case, and to my surprise he accepted one, although not without visible compunction. As a Mohammedan by creed he was in theory without caste and not to be defiled by European touch, but the practices of most folk fall behind their professions. A hundred yards ahead of us Maga was talking and gesticulating furiously, evidently railing at Kagig's wooden-headedness or unbelief. Monty sat listening, saying nothing.

"What did you see, Rustum Khan?" asked Fred.

"At first very little. My eyes are good, but that gipsy-woman's are better, and I was kept busy following her; for I could not keep close, or she might have heard. The noise of her own clumsy stallion prevented her from hearing the lighter footfalls of my mare, and by that I made sure she was not expecting to meet an enemy. 'She rides to betray us to her friends!' said I, and I kept yet farther behind her, on the alert against ambush."

"Well?"

"She rode until dawn, I following. Then, when the light was scarcely born as yet, she suddenly drew rein at an open place where the track she had been following emerged out of dense bushes, and dismounted. From behind the bushes I watched, and presently I, too, dismounted to hold my mare's nostrils and prevent her from whinnying. That woman, Maga Jhaere, knelt, and pawed about the ground like a dog that hunts a buried bone!"

In front of us Maga was still arguing. Suddenly Kagig turned on her and asked her three swift questions, bitten off like the snap of a closing snuff-box lid. Whether she answered or not I could not see, but Monty was smiling.

"I suspect she was making signals!" growled Rustum Khan. "To whom—about what I do not know. After a little while she mounted and rode on, choosing unerringly a new track through the bushes. I went to where she had been, and examined the ground where she had made her signals. As I say, my eyes are good, but hers are better. I could see nothing but the hoof-marks of her clumsy gray brute of a stallion, and in one place the depressions on soft earth where she had knelt to paw the ground!"

Monty was beginning to talk now. I could see him smiling at Kagig over Maga's head, and the girl was growing angry. Rustum Khan was watching them as closely as we were, pausing between sentences.

"It may be she buried something there, but if so I did not find it. I could not stay long, for when she rode away she went like wind, and I needed to follow at top speed or else be lost. So I let my mare feel the spurs a time or two, and so it happened that I gained on the woman; and I suppose she heard me. Whether or no, she waited in ambush, and sprang out at me as I passed so suddenly that I know not what god of fools and drunkards preserved her from being cut down! Not many have ridden out at me from ambush and lived to tell of it! But I saw who she was in time, and sheathed my steel again, and cursed her for the gipsy that she half is. The other half is spawn of Eblis!"

A hundred yards ahead of us Kagig had reached a decision, but it seemed to be not too late yet in Maga's judgment to try to convert him. She was speaking vehemently, passionately, throwing down her reins to expostulate with both hands.

"Kagig isn't the man you'd think a young woman would choose to be familiar with," Fred said quietly to me, and I wondered what he was driving at. He is always observant behind that superficial air of mockery he chooses to assume, but what he had noticed to set him thinking I could not guess.

Rustum Khan threw away the cigarette I had given him, and went on with his tale.

"That woman has no virtue."

"How do you know?" demanded Will.

"She laughed when I cursed her! Then she asked me what I had seen."

"What did you say?"

"To test her I said I had seen her lover, and would know him again by his smell in the dark!"

"What did she say to that?"

"She laughed again. I tell you the woman has no shame! Then she said if I would tell that tale to Kagig as soon as I see him she would reward me with leave to live for one whole week and an extra hour in which to pray to the devil—meaning, I suppose, that she intends to kill me otherwise. Then she wheeled her stallion—the brute was trying to tear out the muscles of my thigh all that time—and rode away—and I followed—and here I am!"

"How much truth is there in your assertion that you saw her lover?" Will demanded.

"None. I but said it to test her."

"Why in thunder should she want it believed?"

"God knows, who made gypsies!"

At that moment the advance-guard rode into an open meadow, crossed by a shallow, singing stream at which Kagig ordered a halt to water horses. So we closed up with him, and he repeated to us what he had evidently said before to Monty.

"Maga says—I let her go scouting—she says she met a man who told her that Miss Gloria Vanderman and a party of seven were attacked on the road, but escaped, and now have doubled on their tracks so that they are far on their return to Tarsus."

Rustum Khan met Monty's eyes, and his lips moved silently.

"What do you know, sirdar?" Monty asked him.

"The woman lies!"

Maga was glaring at Rustum Khan as a leopardess eyes an enemy. As he spoke she made a significant gesture with a finger across her throat, which the Rajput, if he saw, ignored.

"To what extent?" demanded Kagig calmly.

"Wholly! I followed her. She met no man, although she pawed the ground at a place where eight ridden horses had crossed soft ground a day ago."

Kagig nodded, recognizing truth—a rather rare gift.

If the Rajput's guess was wrong and Maga did know shame, at any rate she did not choose that moment to betray it.

"Oh, very well!" she sneered. "There were eight horses. They were galloping. The track was nine hours old."

Kagig nodded without any symptom of annoyance or reproach.

"There is an ancient castle in the hills up yonder," he said, "in which there may be many Armenians hiding."

He took it for granted we would go and find out, and Maga recognized the drift.

"Very well," she said. "Let that one go, and that one," pointing at Fred and me.

"You'll appreciate, of course," said Monty, "that it's out of the question for us to go forward until we know where that lady is."

Kagig bowed gravely.

"I am needed at Zeitoon," he answered.

Then Maga broke in shrilly, pointing at Will:

"Take that one for hostage!" she advised. "Bring him along to Zeitoon. Then the rest will follow!"

Kagig looked gravely at her.

"I shall take this one," he answered, laying a respectful hand on Monty's sleeve. *"Effendi,* you are an Eenglis lord. Be your life and comfort on my head, but I need a hostage for my nation's sake. You others—I admit the urgency—shall hunt the missionary lady. If I have this one"—again he touched Monty—"I know well you will come seeking him! You, *effendi,* you understand my—necessity?"

Monty nodded, smiling gravely. There was a fire at the back of Monty's eyes and something in his bearing I had never seen before.

"Then I go with my colonel sahib!" announced Rustum Khan. "That gipsy woman will kill him otherwise!"

"Better help hunt for the lady, Rustum Khan."

"Nay, colonel sahib bahadur—thy blood on my head! I go with thee—into hell and out beyond if need be!"

"You fellows agreeable?" asked Monty. "There is no disputing Kagig's decision. We're at his mercy."

"We've got to find Miss Vanderman!" said Will.

"You are not at my mercy, *effendi,*" grumbled Kagig. The man was obviously distressed. "You are rather at my discretion. I am responsible. For my nation's sake and for my honor I dare not lose you. Who has not seen how a cow will follow the calf in a wagon? So in your case, if I hold the one—the chief one—the noble one—the lord—the cousin of the Eenglis king" (Monty's rank was mounting like mercury in a tube as Kagig warmed to the argument)—"you others will certainly hunt him up-hill and down-dale. Thus will my honor and my country's cause both profit!"

Monty smiled benignantly.

"It's all one, Kagig. Why labor the point? I'm going with you. Rustum Khan prefers to come with me." Kagig looked askance at Rustum Khan, but made no comment. "One hostage is enough for your purpose. Let me talk with my friends a minute."

Kagig nodded, and we four drew aside.

"Now," demanded Fred, who knew the signs, "what special Quixotry do you mean springing?"

"Shut up, Fred. There's no need for you fellows to follow Kagig another yard. He'll be quite satisfied if he has me in keeping. That will serve all practical purposes. What you three must do is find Miss Vanderman if you can, and take her back to Tarsus. There you can help the consul bring pressure to bear on the authorities."

"Rot!" retorted Fred. "Didums, you're drunk. Where did you get the drink?"

Monty smiled, for he held a card that could out-trump our best one, and he knew it. In fact he led it straight away.

"D'you mean to say you'd consider it decent

to find that young woman in the mountains and drag her to Zeitoon at Kagig's tail, when Tarsus is not more than three days' ride away at most? You know the Turks wouldn't dare touch you on the road to the coast."

"For that matter," said Fred, "the Turks 'ud hardly dare touch Miss Vanderman herself."

"Then leave her in the hills!" grinned Monty. "Kagig tells me that the Kurds are riding down in hundreds from Kaisarich way. He says they'll arrive too late to loot the cities, but they're experts at hunting along the mountain range. Why not leave the lady to the tender ministrations of the Kurds!"

"One 'ud think you and Kagig knew of buried treasure! Or has he promised to make you Duke of Zeitoon?" asked Will. "Tisn't right, Monty. You've no call to force our band in this way."

"Name a better way," said Monty.

None of us could. The proposal was perfectly logical.

Three of us, even supposing Kagig should care to lend us some of his Zeitoonli horsemen, would be all too few for the rescue work. Certainly we could not leave a lady unprotected in these hills, with the threat of plundering Kurds overhanging. If we found her we could hardly carry her off up-country if there were any safer course.

"Time—time is swift!" said Kagig, pulling out a watch like a big brass turnip and shaking it, presumably to encourage the mechanism.

"The fact is," said Monty, drawing us farther aside, for Rustum Khan was growing restive and inquisitive, "I've not much faith in Kagig's prospects at Zeitoon. He has talked to me all along the road, and I don't believe he bases much reliance on his men. He counts more on holding me as hostage and so obliging the Turkish government to call off its murderers. If you men can rescue that lady in the hills and return to Tarsus you can serve Kagig best and give me my best chance too. Hurry back and help the consul raise Cain!"

That closed the arguments, because Maga Jhaere slipped past Kagig and approached us with the obvious intention of listening. She had discovered a knowledge of English scarcely perfect but astonishingly comprehensive, which she had chosen to keep to herself when we first met—a regular gipsy trick. Fred threw down the gauntlet to her, uncovering depths of distrust that we others had never suspected under his air of being amused.

"Now, miss!" he said, striding up to her. "Let us understand each other! This is my friend." He pointed to Monty. "If harm comes to him that you could have prevented, you shall pay!"

Maga tossed back her loose coils of hair and laughed.

"Never fear, sahib!" Rustum Khan called out. "If ought should happen to my Colonel sahib that Umm Kulsum shall be first to die. The women shall tell of her death for a generation, to frighten naughty children!"

"You hear that?" demanded Fred.

Maga laughed again, and swore in some outlandish tongue.

"I hear! And you hear this, you old—" She called Fred by a name that would make the butchers wince in the abattoirs at Liverpool. "If anything happens to that man,—she pointed to Will, and her eyes blazed with lawless pleasure in his evident discomfort—"I myself—me—this woman—I alone will keel—keel—keel—torture first and afterwards keel your friend 'at you call Monty! I am Maga! You have heard me say what I will do! As for that Rustum Khan—you shall never see him no more ever!"

Kagig pulled out the enormous watch again. He seemed oblivious of Maga's threats—not even aware that she had spoken, although she was hissing through impudent dazzling teeth within three yards of him.

"The time," he said, "has fleed—has fled—has flown. Now we must go, *effendi!*"

"I go with that man!" announced Maga, pointing at Will, but obviously well aware that nothing of the kind would be permitted.

"Maga, come!" said Kagig, and got on his horse. "You gentlemen may take with you each one Zeitoonli servant. No, no more. No, the ammunition in your pockets must suffice. Yes, I know the remainder is yours; come then to Zeitoon and get it! *Haide—Haide!* Mount! Ride! *Haide,* Zeitoonli! To Zeitoon! *Chabuk!*"

WITH NEW TONGUES

Oh, bard of Avon, thou whose measured muse
Most sweetly sings Elizabethan views
To shame ungentle smiths of journalese
With thy sublimest verse, what words are these
That shine amid the lines like jewels set

But ere thine hour no bard had chosen yet?
Didst thou in masterly disdain of too much law
Not only limen the truths no others saw
But also, lord not slave of written word,
Lend ear to what no other poet heard
And, liberal minded on the Mermaid bench
With bow for blade and chaff for serving wench
Await from overseas slang-slinging Jack
Who brought the new vocabulary back?

IX
"AND YOU LEFT YOUR FRIEND TO HELP ME?"

SO WE three stood still in a row disconsolate, with three ragged men of Zeitoon holding our horses and theirs, and watched Monty ride away in the midst of Kagig's motley command, he not turning to wave back to us because he did not like the parting any better than we did, although he had pretended to be all in favor of it.

Kagig had left us one mule for our luggage, and the beast was unlikely to be overburdened, for at the last minute he had turned surly, and as he sat like a general of division to watch his patch-and-string command go by he showed how Eye of Zeitoon only failed him for a title in giving his other eye—the one he kept on us—too little credit. It was a good-looking crowd of irregulars that he reviewed, and every bearded, goat-skin clad veteran in it had a word to say to him, and he an answer—sometimes a sermon by way of answer. But he saw every item that we removed from the common packs, and sternly reproved us when we tried to exceed what he considered reasonable. At that he based our probable requirements on what would have been surfeit of encumbrance for himself.

"Empty your pockets, *effendim!*" he ordered at last. "Six cartridges each for rifle, and six each for pistol must be all. Your cartridges I know they are. But my people are in extremity!"

When he rode away at last, sitting his horse in the fashion of a Don Cossack and shepherding Maga in front of him because she kept checking her gray stallion for another look at Will, he left us no alternative than to take to the mountains swiftly unless we cared to starve. We watched Monty's back disappear over a rise, with Rustum Khan close behind, and then Fred signed to one of the three Zeitoonli to lead on.

All three of the men Kagig had left with us were surly, mainly, no doubt, because they disliked separation from their friends. But there was fear, too, expressed in their manner of riding close together, and in the fidgety way in which they watched the smoke of burning Armenian villages that smudged the sky to our left.

"If they try to bolt after Kagig and leave us in the lurch I'm going to waste exactly one cartridge as a warning," Fred announced. "After that—!"

"Probably Kagig 'ud skin them if they turned up without us," remarked Will.

There was something in that theory, for we learned later what Kagig's ferocity could be when driven hard enough. But from first to last those men of Zeitoon never showed a symptom of treachery, although their resentment at having to turn their backs toward home appeared to deepen hourly.

With strange unreason they made no haste, whereas we were in a frenzy of impatience; and when Fred sought to improve their temper by singing the songs that had hitherto acted like charms on Kagig's whole command, they turned in their saddles and cursed him for calling attention to us.

"Inch goozek?" demanded one of them (What would you like?), and with a gesture that made the blood run cold he suggested the choice between hanging and disembowelment.

Will solved the speed problem by striving to push past them along the narrow track; and they were so determined to keep in front of us that within half an hour from the start our horses were sweating freely. Then we began to climb, dismounting presently to lead our horses, and all notions of speed went the way of other vanity.

Several times looking back toward our right hand we caught sight of Kagig's string threading its way over a rise, or passing like a line of ants under the brow of a gravel bank. But they were too far away to discern which of the moving specks might be Monty, although Kagig was now and then unmistakable, his air of authority growing on him and distinguishing him as long as he kept in sight.

We saw nothing of the footprints in soft earth that Maga had read so offhandedly. In fact we took another way, less cluttered up with roots and bushes, that led not straight, but persistently toward an up-towering crag like an eye-tooth. Below it was thick forest, shaped like a shovel beard, and the crag stuck above the beard like an old man's last tooth.

But mountains have a discouraging way of folding and refolding so that the air-line from point to point bears no relation to the length of the trail. The last kites were drooping lazily toward their perches for the night when we drew near the edge of the forest at last, and were suddenly brought to a halt by a challenge from overhead. We could see nobody. Only a hoarse voice warned us that it was death to advance another yard, and our tired animals needed no persuasion to stand still.

There, under a protruding lock as it were of the beard, we waited in shadow while an invisible somebody, whose rifle scraped rather noisily against a branch, eyed every inch of us at his leisure.

"Who are you?" he demanded at last in Armenian, and one of our three men enlightened him in long-drawn detail.

The explanation did not satisfy. We were told to remain exactly where we were until somebody else was fetched. After twenty minutes, when it was already pitch-dark, we heard the breaking of twigs, and low voices as three or four men descended together among the trees. Then we were examined again from close quarters in the dark, and there are few less agreeable sensations. The goose-flesh rises and the clammy cold sweat takes all the comfort out of waning courage.

But somebody among the shadowy tree-trunks at last seemed to think he recognized familiar attitudes, and asked again who we might be. And, weary of explanations that only achieved delay our man lumped us all in one invoice and snarled irritably:

"These are Americans!"

The famous "Open sesame" that unlocked Ali Baba's cave never worked swifter then. Reckless of possible traps no less than five men flung themselves out of Cimmerian gloom and seized us in welcoming arms. I was lifted from the saddle by a man six inches shorter than myself, whose arms could have crushed me like an insect.

"We might have known Americans would bring us help!" he panted in my ear. His breath came short not from effort, but excitement.

Fred was in like predicament. I could just see his shadow struggling in the embrace of an enthusiastic host, and somewhere out of sight Will was answering in nasal indubitable Yankee the questions of three other men.

"This way! Come this way! Bring the horses, oh, Zeitoonli! Americans! Americans! God heard us—there have come Americans!"

Threading this and that way among tree-trunks that to our unaccustomed eyes were simply slightly denser blots on blackness, Will managed to get between Fred and me.

"We're all of us Yankees this trip!" he whispered, and I knew he was grinning, enjoying it hugely. So often he had been taken for an Englishman because of partnership with us that he had almost ceased to mind; but he spared himself none of the amusement to be drawn out of the new turn of affairs, nor us any of the chaff that we had never spared him.

"Take my advice," he said, "and try to act you're Yanks for all you've got. If you can make blind men believe it, you may get out of this with whole skins!"

I expected the retort discourteous to that from Fred, who was between Will and me, shepherded like us by hard-breathing, unseen men. But he was much too subtly skillful in piercing the chain-mail of Will's humor—even in that hour.

"Sure!" he answered. "I guess any gosh-durned rube in these parts 'll know without being told what neck o' the woods I hail from. Schenectady's my middle name! I'm—"

"Oh, my God!" groaned Will. "We don't talk that way in the States. The missionaries—"

"I'm the guy who put the 'oh!' in Ohio!" continued Fred. "I'm running mate to Colonel Cody, and I've ridden herd on half the cows in Hocuspocus County, Wis.! I can sing *The Star-Spangled Banner* with my head under water, and eat a chain of frankfurters two links a minute! I'm the rip-roaring original two-gun man from Tabascoville, and any gink who doubts it has no time to say his prayers!"

There were paragraphs more of it, delivered at uneven intervals between deep gasps for breath as we made unsteady progress up-hill among roots and rocks left purposely for the confusion of an enemy. At first it filled Will with despair that set me laughing at him. Then Will threw seriousness to the winds and laughed too, so that the spell of impending evil, caused as much as anything by forced separation from Monty, was broken.

But it did better than put us in rising spirits. It convinced the Armenians! That foolish jargon, picked up from comic papers and the penny dreadfuls, convince more firmly than any written proof the products of the mission schools, whose one ambition was to be American themselves, and whose one pathetic peak of humor was the occasional glimpse of United States slang dropped for their edification by missionary teachers!

"By Jiminy!" remarked an Armenian near me.

"Gosh-all-hemlocks!" said another.

Thenceforward nothing undermined their faith in us. Plenty of amused repudiation was very soon forthcoming from another source, but it passed over their heads. Fred and I, because we used fool expressions without relation to the context or proportion, were established as the genuine article; Will, perhaps a rather doubtful quantity with his conservative grammar and quiet speech, was accepted for our sakes. They took an arm on either side of us to help us up the hill, and in proof of heart-to-heart esteem shouted "Oopsidaisy!" when we stumbled in the pitchy dark. When we were brought to a stand at last by a snarled challenge and the click of rifles overhead, they answered with the chorus of *Ta-ra-ra-boom-de-ay,* a classic that ought to have died an unnatural death almost a quarter of a century before.

Suddenly we smelt Standard oil, and a man emerged through a gap in ancient masonry less than six feet away carrying a battered, cheap "hurricane" lantern whose cracked glass had been reinforced with patches of brown paper. He was armed to the teeth—literally. He had a long knife in his mouth, a pistol in his left hand, and a rifle slung behind him, but after one long look at us, holding the lantern to each face in turn, he suddenly discarded all appearances of ferocity.

"You know about pistols?" he demanded of me in English, because I was nearest, and thrust his Mauser repeater under my nose. "Why won't this one work? I have tried it every way."

"Lordy!" remarked Will.

"Lead on in!" I suggested. Then, remembering my new part, "It'll have to be *some* defect if one of us can't fix it!"

The gap-guard purred approval and swung his lantern by way of invitation to follow him as he turned on a naked heel and led the way. We entered one at a time through a hole in the wall of what looked like the dungeon of an ancient castle, and followed him presently up the narrow stone steps leading to a trap-door in the floor above. The trap-door was made of odds and ends of planking held in place by weights. When he knocked on it with the muzzle of his rifle we could hear men lifting things before they could open it.

When a gap appeared overhead at last there was no blaze of light to make us blink, but a row of heads at each edge of the hole with nothing but another lantern somewhere in the gloom behind them. One by one we went up and they made way for us, closing in each time to scan the next-comer's face; and when we were all up they laid the planks again, and piled heavy stones in place. Then an old man lighted another lantern, using no match, although there was a box of them beside him on the floor, but transferring flame patiently with a blade of dry grass. Somebody else lit a torch of resinous wood that gave a good blaze but smoked abominably.

"What has become of our horses?" demanded Fred, looking swiftly about him.

We were in a great, dim stone-walled room whose roof showed a corner of star-lit sky in one place. There were twenty men surrounding us, but no woman. Two trade-blankets sewn together with string hanging over an opening in the wall at the far end of the room suggested, nevertheless, that the other sex might be within ear-shot.

"The horses?" Fred demanded again, a bit peremptorily.

One of the men who had met us smirked and made apologetic motions with his hands.

"They will be attended to, *effendi*—"

"I know it! I guarantee it! By the ace of brute force, if a horse is missing—! Arabaiji!"

One of our three Zeitoonli stepped forward.

"Take the other two men, Arabaiji, and go down to the horses. Groom them. Feed them. If any one prevents you, return and tell me." Then he turned to our hosts. "Some natives of Somaliland once ate my horse for supper, but I learned that lesson. So did they! I trust I needn't be severe with you!"

There was no furniture in the room, except a mat at one corner. They were standing all about us, and perfectly able to murder us if so disposed, but none made any effort to restrain our Zeitoonli.

"Now we're three to their twenty!" I whispered, and Will nodded. But Fred carried matters with a high hand.

"Send a man down with them to show them where the horses are, please!"

There seemed to be nobody in command, but evidently one man was least of all, for they all began at once to order him below, and he went, grumbling.

"You see, *effendi,* we have no meat at all," said the man who had spoken first.

"But you don't look hungry," asserted Fred.

They were a ragged crowd, unshaven and not too clean, with the usual air of men whose only clothes are on their backs and have been there for a week past. All sorts of clothes they wore—odds and ends for the most part, probably snatched and pulled on in the first moment of a night alarm.

"Not yet, *effendi.* But we have no meat, and soon we shall have eaten all the grain."

"Well," said Fred, "if you need horse-meat, gosh durn you, take it from the Turks!"

"Gosh durn you!" grinned three or four men, nudging one another.

They were lost between a furtive habit born of hiding for dear life, a desire to be extremely friendly, and a new suspicion of Fred's high hand. Fred's next words added disconcertment.

"Where is Miss Vanderman?" he demanded, suddenly.

Before any one had time to answer Will made a swift move to the wall, and took his stand where nobody could get behind him. He did not produce his pistol, but there was that in his eye that suggested it. I followed suit, so that in the event of trouble we stood a fair chance of protecting Fred.

"What do you mean?" asked three Armenians together.

"Did you never see men try to cover a secret before?" Will whispered.

"Or give it away?" I added. Six of the men placed themselves between Fred and the opening where the blankets hung, ostentatiously not looking at the blankets.

"Have you an American lady with you?" Fred asked, and as he spoke he reached a hand behind him. But it was not his pistol that he drew. He carries his concertina slung to him by a strap with the care that some men lavish on a camera. He took it in both hands, and loosed the catch.

"Have you an American lady named Miss Vanderman with you?" he repeated.

"Effendi, we do not understand."

He repeated in Armenian, and then in Turkish, but they shook their heads.

"Very well," he said, "I'll soon find out. A mission-school pupil might sing *My Country, 'Tis of Thee* or *Suwannee River* or *Poor Blind Joe.* You know *Poor Blind Joe,* eh? Sung it in school? I thought so. I'll bet you don't know this one."

He filled his impudent instrument with wind and forthwith the belly of that ancient castle rang to the strains of a tune no missionaries sing, although no doubt the missionary ladies are familiar with it yet from where the Arctic night shuts down on Bering Sea to the Solomon Islands and beyond—a song that achieved popularity by lacking national significance, and won a war by imparting recklessness to typhus camps. I was certain then, and still dare bet to-day that those ruined castle walls re-echoed for the first time that evening to the clamor of "A Hot Time in the Old Town To-night!"

Seeing the point in a flash, we three roared the song together, and then again, and then once more for interest, the Armenians eying us spell-bound, at a loss to explain the madness. Then there began to be unexplained movements behind the blanket hanging; and a minute later a woman broke through -an unmistakable Armenian, still good-looking but a little past the prime of life, and very obviously mentally distressed. She scarcely took notice of us, but poured forth a long flow of rhetoric interspersed with sobs for breath. I could see Fred chuckling as he listened. All the facial warnings that a dozen men could make at the woman from behind Fred's back could not check her from telling all she knew.

Nor were Will and I, who knew no Armenian, kept in doubt very long as to the nature of her trouble. We heard another woman's voice, behind two or three sets of curtains by the sound of it, that came rapidly nearer; and there were sounds of scuffling. Then we heard words.

"Please play that tune again, whoever you are! Do you hear me? Do you understand?"

"Boston!" announced Will, diagnosing accents.

"You bet your life I understand!" Fred shouted, and clanged through half a dozen bars again.

That seemed satisfactory to the owner of the voice. The scuffling was renewed, and in a moment she had burst through the crude curtains with two women clinging to her, and stood there with her brown hair falling on her shoulders and her dress all disarrayed but looking simply serene in contrast to the women who tried to restrain her. They tried once or twice to thrust her back through the curtain, although clearly determined to do her no injury; but she held her ground easily. At a rough guess it was tennis and boating that had done more for her muscles than ever strenuous housework did for the Armenians.

"Who are you?" she asked, and Will laughed with delight.

"I reckon you'll be Miss Vanderman?" suggested Fred in outrageous Yankee accent. She stared hard at him.

"I am Miss Vanderman. Who are you, please.

I sat down on the great stone they had rolled over the trap, for even in that flickering, smoky light I could see that this young woman was incarnate loveliness as well as health and strength. Will was our only ladies' man (for Fred is no more than random troubadour, decamping before any love-affair gets serious). The thought conjured visions of Maga, and what she might do. For about ten seconds my head swam, and I could hardly keep my feet.

Will left the opening bars of the overture to Fred, with rather the air of a man who lets a trout have line. And Fred blundered in contentedly.

"I'll allow my name is Oakes—Fred Oakes," he said.

"Please explain!" She looked from one to the other of us.

"We three are American tourists, going the grand trip." (Remember, a score of Armenians were listening. Fred's intention was at least as much to continue their contentment as to extract humor from the situation.) "You being reported missing we allowed to pick you up and run you in to Tarsus. Air you agreeable?"

The women were still clinging to her as if their whole future depended on keeping her prisoner, yet without hurt. She looked down at them pathetically, and then at the men, who were showing no disposition to order her release.

"I don't understand in the least yet. I find you bewildering. Can you contrive to let us talk for a few minutes alone?"

"You bet your young life I can!"

Fred stepped to the wall beside us, but we none of us drew pistol yet. We had no right to presume we were not among friends.

"Thirty minutes interlude!" he announced. "The man who stands in this room one minute from now, or who comes back to the room without my leave, is not my friend, and shall learn what that means!"

He repeated the soft insinuation in Armenian, and then in Turkish because he knows that language best. There is not an Armenian who has not been compelled to learn Turkish for all official purposes, and unconsciously they gave obedience to the hated conquerors' tongue, repressing the desire to argue that wells perennially in Armenian breasts. They had not been long enough enjoying stolen liberty to overcome yet the full effects of Turkish rule.

"And oblige me by leaving that lady alone with us!" Fred continued. "Let those dames fall away!"

Somebody said something to the women. Another Armenian remarked more or less casually that we should be unable to escape from the room in any case. The others rolled the great stone from the trap and shoved the smaller stones aside, and then they all filed down the stone stairs, leaving us alone—although by the trembling blankets it was easy to tell that the women had not gone far. The last man who went below handed the spluttering torch to Miss Vanderman, as if she might need it to defend herself, and she stood there shaking it to try and make it smoke less until the planks were back in place. She was totally unconscious of it, but with the torch-light gleaming on her hair and reflected in her blue eyes she looked like the spirit of old romance come forth to start a holy war.

"Now please explain!" she begged, when I had pushed the last stone in place. "First, what kind of Americans can you possibly be? Do you all use such extraordinary accents, and such expressions?"

"Don't I talk American to beat the band?" objected Fred. "Sit down on this rock a while, and I'll convince you."

She sat on the rock, and we gathered round her. She was not more than twenty-two or three, but as perfectly assured and fearless as only a well-bred woman can be in the presence of unshaven men she does not know. Fred would have continued the tomfoolery, but Will oared in.

"I'm Will Yerkes, Miss Vanderman."

"Oh!"

"I know Nurse Vanderman at the mission."

"Yes, she spoke of you."

"Fred Oakes here is—"

"Is English as they make them, yes, I know! Why the amazing efforts to—"

"I stand abashed, like the leopard with the spots unchangeable!" said Fred, and grinned most unashamedly.

"They're both English."

"Yes, I see, but why—"

"It's only as good Americans that we three could hope to enter here alive. They're death on all other sorts of non-Armenians now they've taken to the woods. We supposed you were here, and of course we had to come and get you."

She nodded. "Of course. But how did you know?"

"That's a long story. Tell us first why you're here, and why you're a prisoner."

"I was going to the mission at Marash—to stay a year there and help, before returning to the States. They warned me in Tarsus that the trip might be dangerous, but I know how short-handed they are at Marash, and I wouldn't listen. Besides, they picked the best men they could find to bring me on the way, and I started. I had a Turkish permit to travel—a *teskere* they call it—see, I have it here. It was perfectly ridiculous to think of my not going."

"Perfectly!" Fred agreed. "Any young woman in your place would have come away!"

She laughed, and colored a trifle. "Women and men are equals in the States, Mr. Oakes."

"And the Turk ought to know that! I get you, Miss Vanderman! I see the point exactly!"

"At any rate, I started. And we slept at night in the houses of Armenians whom my guides knew, so that the journey wasn't bad at all. Everything was going splendidly until we reached a sort of crossroads—if you can call those goat-tracks roads without stretching truth too far—and there three men came galloping toward us on blown horses from the direction of Marash. We could hardly get them to stop and tell us what the trouble was, they were in such a hurry, but I set my horse across the path and we held them up."

"As any young lady would have done!" Fred murmured.

"Never mind. I did it! They told us, when they could get their breath and quit looking behind them like men afraid of ghosts, that the Turks in Marash—which by all accounts is a very fanatical place—had started to murder Armenians. They yelled at me to turn and run.

" 'Run where?' I asked them. 'The Turks won't murder me!'

"That seemed to make them think, and they and my six men all talked together in Armenian much too fast for me to understand a word of it. Then they pointed to some smoke on the sky-line that they said was from burning Armenian homes in Marash.

" 'Why didn't you take refuge in the mission?' I asked them. And they answered that it was because the mission grounds were already full of refugees.

"Well, if that were true—and mind you, I didn't believe it—it was a good reason why I should hurry there and help. If the mission staff was overworked before that they would be simply overwhelmed now. So I told them to turn round and come to Marash with me and my six men."

"And what did they say?" we demanded together.

"They laughed. They said nothing at all to me. Perhaps they thought I was mad. They talked together for five minutes, and then without consulting me they seized my bridle and galloped up a goat-path that led after a most interminable ride to this place."

"Where they hold you to ransom?"

"Not at all. They've been very kind to me. I think that at the bottom of their thoughts there may be some idea of exchanging me for some of their own women whom the Turks have made away with. But a stronger motive than that is the determination to keep me safe and be able to produce me afterward in proof of their bona fides. They've got me here as witness, for another thing. And then, I've started a sort of hospital in this old keep. There are literally hundreds of men and women hiding in these hills, and the women are beginning to come to me for advice, and to talk with me. I'm pretty nearly as useful here as I would be at Marash."

"And you're—let's see—nineteen-twenty—one—two—not more than twenty-two," suggested Fred.

"Is intelligence governed by age and sex in England," she retorted, and Fred smiled in confession of a hit.

"Go on," said Will. "Tell us."

"There's nothing more to tell. When I started to run toward the—ah—music, the women tried to prevent me. They knew Americans had come, and they feared you might take me away."

"They were guessing good!" grinned Will.

She shook her head, and the loosened coils of hair fell lower. One could hardly have blamed a man who had desired her in that lawless land and sought to carry her off. The Armenian men must have been temptation proof, or else there had been safety in numbers.

"I shall stay here. How could I leave them? The women need me. There are babies—daily—almost hourly—here in these lean hills, and no organized help of any kind until I came."

"How long have you been here?" I asked.

"Nearly two days. Wait till I've been here a week and you'll see."

"We can't wait to see!" Will answered. "We've a friend of our own in a tight place. The best we can do is to rescue you—"

"I don't need to be rescued!"

"—to rescue you—take you back to Tarsus, where you'll be safe until the trouble's over—and then hurry to the help of our own man."

"Who is your own man? Tell me about him."

"He's a prince."

"Really?"

"No, really an earl—Earl of Montdidier. White. White all through to the wish-bone. Whitest man I ever camped with. He's the goods."

"If you'd said less I'd have skinned you for an ingrate!" Fred announced. "Monty is a man men love."

Miss Vanderman nodded. "Where is he?"

"On the way to a place called Zeitoon," answered Will.

"He's a hostage, held by Armenians in the hope of putting pressure on the Turks. Kagig—the Armenians, that's to say—let us go to rescue you, knowing that he was sufficiently important for their purpose."

"And you left your friend to help me?"

"Of course. What do you suppose?"

"And if I were to go with you to Tarsus, what then?"

"He says we're to ride herd on the consulate and argue."

"Will you?"

"Sure we'll argue. We'll raise particular young hell. Then back we go to Zeitoon to join him!"

"Would you have gone to Tarsus except on my account?"

Will hesitated.

"No. I see. Of course you wouldn't. Well. What do you take *me* for? You did not know me then. You do now. Do you think I'd consent to your leaving your fine friend in pawn while you dance attendance on me? Thank you kindly for your offer, but go back to him! If you don't I'll never speak to one of you again!"

THESE LITTLE ONES

If Life were what the liars say
And failure called the tune
Mayhap the road to ruin then
Were cluttered deep wi' broken men;
We'd all be seekers blindly led
To weave wi' worms among the dead,
If Life were what the liars say
And failure called the tune.

But Life is Father of us all
(Dear Father, if we knew!)
And underneath eternal arms
Uphold. We'll mock the false alarms,
And trample on the neck of pain,
And laugh the dead alive again,
For Life is Father to us all,
And thanks are overdue!

If Truth were what the learned say
And envy called the tune
Mayhap 'twere trite what treason saith
That man is dust and ends in death;
We'd slay with proof of printed law
Whatever was new that seers saw,
If Truth were what the learned say
And envy called the tune.

But Truth is Brother of us all
(Oh, Brother, if we knew!)
Unspattered by the muddied lies
That pass for wisdom of the wise—
Compassionate, alert, unbought,
Of purity and presence wrought,—
Big Brother that includes us all
Nor knows the name of Few!

If Love were what the harlots say
And hunger called the tune
Mayhap we'd need conserve the joys
Weighed grudgingly to girls and boys,
And eat the angels trapped and sold
By shriven priests for stolen gold,
If Love were what the harlots say
And hunger called the tune.

But Love is Mother of us all
(Dear Mother, if we knew!)—
So wise that not a sparrow falls,
Nor friendless in the prison calls
Uncomforted or uncaressed.
There's magic milk at Mercy's breast,
And little ones shall lead us all
When Trite Love calls the tune!

X
"WHEN I FIRE THIS PISTOL—"

NATURALLY, BEING what we were, with our friend Monty held in durance by a chief of outlaws, we were perfectly ready to kidnap Miss Vanderman and ride off with her in case she should be inclined to delay proceedings. It was also natural that we had not spoken of that contingency, nor even considered it.

"We never dreamed of your refusing to come with us," said Will.

"We still don't dream of it!" Fred asserted, and she turned her head very swiftly to look at him with level brows. Next she met my eyes. If there was in her consciousness the slightest trace of doubt, or fear, or admission that her sex might be less responsible than ours, she did not show it. Rather in the blue eyes and the athletic poise of chin, and neck, and shoulders there was a dignity beyond ours.

Will laughed.

"Don't let's be ridiculous," she said. "I shall do as I see fit."

Fred's neat beard has a trick of losing something of its trim when he proposes to assert himself, and I recognized the symptoms. But at the moment of that impasse the Armenians below us had decided that self-assertion was their cue, and there came great noises as they thundered with a short pole on the trap and made the stones jump that held it down.

At that signal several women emerged from behind the hanging blankets—young and old women in various states of disarray—and stood in attitudes suggestive of aggression. One did not get the idea that Armenians, men or women, were sheeplike pacifists. They watched Miss Vanderman with the evident purpose of attacking us the moment she appealed to them.

"If you don't roll the stones away I think there'll be trouble," she said, and came and stood between Will and me. Fred got behind me, and began to whisper. I heard something or other about the trap, and supposed he was asking me to open it, although I failed to see why the request should be kept secret; but the women forestalled me, and in a moment they had the stones shoved aside and the men were emerging one by one through the opening.

Then at last I got Fred's meaning. There was a second of indecision during which the Armenians consulted their women-folk, in two minds between snatching Miss Vanderman out of our reach or discovering first what our purpose might be. I took advantage of it to slip down the stone stairs behind them.

The opening in the castle wall was easy to find, for the star-lit sky looked luminous through the hole. Once outside, however, the gloom of ancient trees and the castle's shadow seemed blacker than the dungeon had been. I groped about, and stumbled over loose stones fallen from the castle wall, until at last one of our own Zeitoonli discovered me and, thinking I might be a trouble-maker, tripped me up. Cursing fervently from underneath his iron-hard carcass I made him recognize me at last. Then he offered me tobacco, unquestionably stolen from our pack, and sat down beside me on a rock while I recovered breath.

It took longer to do that than he expected, for he had enjoyed the advantage of surprise while hampered by no compunctions on the ground of moderation. When the agony of windlessness was gone and I could question him he assured me that the horses were well enough, but that he and his two companions were hungry. Furthermore, he added, the animals were very closely watched—so much so that the other two, Sombat and Noorian, were standing guard to watch the watchers.

"But I am sure they are fools," he added.

This man Arabaiji had been an excellent servant, but decidedly supercilious toward the others from the time when he first came to us in the khan at Tarsus. Regarding himself as intelligent, which he was, he usually refused to concede that quality, or anything resembling it, to his companions.

"That is why I was looking for you when you hit me in the dark with that club of a fist of yours,"

I answered. "I wanted to speak with you alone because I know you are not a fool."

He felt so flattered that he promptly let his pipe go out.

"While Sombat and Noorian are keeping an eye on the horses, I want you to watch for trouble up above here," I said. "In case the people of this place should seek to make us prisoner, then I want you to gallop, if you can get your horse, and run otherwise, to the nearest—"

He checked me with a gesture and one word.

"Kagig!"

"What about him?" I demanded.

"If I were to bring Turks here, Kagig would never rest until my fingers were pulled off one by one!"

"If you were to bring Turks here, or appeal to Turks," said I, "Kagig would never get you."

"How not?"

"Unless he should find your dead carcass after my friends and I had finished with it!"

"What then?"

He lighted his pipe again by way of reestablishing himself in his own esteem, and it glowed and crackled wetly in the dark beside me in response to the workings of his intelligence.

"In case of trouble up here, and our being held prisoner, go and find other Armenians, and order them in Kagig's name to come and rescue us."

"Those who obey Kagig are with Kagig," he answered.

"Surely not all?"

"All that Kagig could gather to him after eleven years!"

"In that case go to Kagig, and tell him."

"Kagig would not come. He holds Zeitoon."

"Are you a fool?"

"Not I! The other two are fools."

"Then do you understand that in case these people should make us prisoner—"

He nodded. "They might. They might propose to sell you to the Turks, perhaps against their own stolen women-folk."

"Then don't you see that if you were gone, and I told them you had gone to bring Kagig, they would let us go rather than face Kagig's wrath?"

"But Kagig would not come."

"I know that. But how should they know it?"

I knew that be nodded again by the motion of the glowing tobacco in his pipe. It glowed suddenly bright, as a new idea dawned on him. He was an honest fellow, and did not conceal the thought.

"Kagig would not send me back to you," he said. "He is short of men at Zeitoon."

"Never mind," said I. "In case of trouble up above here, but not otherwise, will you do that?"

"Gladly. But give it me in writing, lest Kagig have me beaten for running from you without leave."

That was my turn to jump at a proposal. I tore a sheet from my memorandum book, and scribbled in the dark, knowing be could not read what I had written.

"This writing says that you did not run away until you had made quite sure we were in difficulties. So, if you should run too soon, and we should not be in difficulties after all, Kagig would learn that sooner or later. What would Kagig do in that case?"

"He would throw me over the bridge at Zeitoon—if he could catch me! Nay! I play no tricks."

"Good. Then go and hide. Hide within call. Within an hour, or at most two hours we shall know how the land lies. If all should be well I will change that writing for another one, and send you to Kagig in any case. No more words now—go and hide!"

He put his pipe out with his thumb, and took two strides into a shadow, and was gone. Then I went back through the gap in the dungeon wall, and stumbled to the stairs. Apparently not missing me yet, they had covered up the trap, and I had to hammer on it for admission. They were not pleased when my head appeared through the hole, and they realized that I had probably held communication with our men. I suppose Fred saw by my face that I had accomplished what I went for, because he let out a laugh like a fox's bark that did nothing toward lessening the tension.

On the other hand it was quite clear that during my absence Miss Vanderman had not been idle. Excepting the two men who had admitted me, every one was seated—she on the floor among the women, with her back to the wall, and the rest in a semicircle facing them. Two of the women had their arms about her, affectionately, but not without a hint of who controlled the situation.

"What have you been doing?" Fred demanded, and be laughed at Gloria Vanderman with an air of triumph.

"Making preparations," I said, "to take Miss Vanderman to Tarsus."

I wish I could set down here a chart of the mixed

emotions then expressed on that young lady's face. She did not look at Will, knowing perhaps that she already had him captive of her bow and spear. Neither did Will look at us, but sat tracing figures with a forefinger in the dust between his knees, wondering perhaps how to excuse or explain, and getting no comfort.

If my guess was correct, Gloria Vanderman was about equally distracted between the alternative ignominy of submitting her free will to Armenians or else to us. Compassion for the women in their predicament weighed one way—knowledge that our friend Monty was in durance vile contingent on her actions pulled heavily another Fred was frankly enjoying himself, which influenced her strongly toward the Armenian side, she being young and, doubtless the idol of a hundred heart-sick Americans, contemptuous of forty-year-old bachelors.

"Of course we shall not let you go!" one of the Armenians assured her in quite good English, and I began fumbling at the pistol in my inner pocket, for if Arabaiji was to run to Zeitoon, then the sooner the better. But it needed only that imputation of helplessness to tip the beam of Miss Gloria's judgment.

"You can attend to the sick ones. You can play music for us all. Doubtless these other two have qualifications."

I was too busy admiring Gloria to know what effect that announcement had on Fred and Will. She shook herself free from the women, and stood up, splendid in the flickering yellow light. There was a sort of swift move by every one to be ready against contingencies, and I judged it the right moment to spring my own surprise.

"When I fire this pistol," I said, producing it, "a man will start at once for Zeitoon to warn Kagig. He has a note in his pocket written to Kagig. Judge for yourselves how long it will take Kagig and his men to reach this place!"

The nearest man made a very well-judged spring at me and pinned my elbows from behind. Another man knocked the pistol from my hand. The women seized Gloria again. But Fred was too quick—drew his own pistol, and fired at the roof.

"Twice, Fred!" I shouted, and he fired again.

"There!" said I. "Do what you like. The messenger has gone!"

And then Gloria shook herself free a last time, and took command.

"Is that true?" she demanded.

I nodded. "The best of our three men was to start on his way the minute he heard the second shot."

Then I was sure she was Boadicea reincarnate, whether the old-time British queen did or did not have blue eyes and brown hair.

"I will not have brave men brought back here on my account! Kagig must be a patriot! He needs all his men! I don't blame him for making a hostage of Lord Montdidier! I would do the same myself!"

Will had evidently given her a pretty complete synopsis of our adventure while I was outside talking with Arabaiji. It is always a mystery to the British that Americans should hold themselves a race apart and rally to each other as if the rest of the Anglo-Saxon race were foreigners, but those two had obeyed the racial rule. They understood each other—swiftly—a bar and a half ahead of the tune.

"This old castle is no good!" she went on, not raising her voice very high, but making it ring with the wholesomeness of youth, and youth's intolerance of limits. "The Turks could come to this place and burn it within a day if they chose!"

"The Turks won't trouble. They'll send their friends the Kurds instead," Fred assured her.

"Ah-h-h-gh!" growled the Armenians, but she waved them back to silence.

"How much food have you? Almost none! How much ammunition?"

"Ah-h-h-h!" they chorused in a very different tone of voice.

"D'you mean you've got cartridges here?" Fred demanded.

"Fifty cases of cartridges for government Mauser rifles!" bragged the man who was nearest to Will.

"Gee! Kagig 'ud give his eyes for them!" (Will devoted his eyes to the more poetic purpose of exchanging flashed encouragement with Gloria.)

"Men, women and children—how many of you are there?"

"Who knows? Who has counted? They keep coming."

"No, they don't. You've set a guard to keep any more away for fear the food won't last—I know you have! Well—what does it matter how many you are? I say let us all go to Zeitoon and help Kagig!"

"Oh, bravo!" shouted Fred, but it was Will's praise that proved acceptable and made her smile.

"Second the motion!"

I added a word or two by way of make-weight,

that did more as a matter of fact than her young ardor to convince those very skeptical men and women. No doubt she broke up their determination to sit still, but it was my words that set them on a course.

"Kagig will be angry when he comes. He's a ruthless man," said I, and the Armenians, men as well as women, sought one another's eyes and nodded.

"Kagig must be more of a ruthless bird than we guessed!" Will whispered.

Counting women, there was less than a score of refugees in the room, and if we had only had them to convince, our work was pretty nearly done. There was the guard among the trees down-hill that we knew about still to be converted, or perhaps coerced. But just at the moment when we felt we held the winning hand, there came a ladder thrust down through the hole in the corner of the roof, and a man whom they all greeted as Ephraim began to climb down backward. He was so loaded with every imaginable kind of weapon that he made more noise than a tinker's cart.

Nor was Ephraim the only new arrival. Man after man came down backward after him, each man cursed richly for treading on his predecessor's fingers—a seeming endless chain of men that did not cease when the room was already uncomfortably overcrowded. Some of these men wore clothes that suggested Russia, but the majority were in rags. The ladder swayed and creaked under them, and finally, at a word from Ephraim, the last-comers sat on the upper rungs, bending the frail thing with their weight into a complaining loop.

Several of the newcomers had torches, and their acrid smoke turned the twice-breathed air of the place into evil-tasting fog.

Three men put their faces close to Ephraim's and proceeded to enlighten him as to what had passed. He seemed to be recognized as some sort of chieftain, and carried himself with a commanding air, but so many men talked at once, and all in Armenian, that we could not pick out more than a word or two here and there. Even Fred, with his gift of tongues, could hardly make head or tail of it.

We three pressed through the swarm and took our stand beside Gloria, not hesitating to thrust the other women aside. They dragged at their men-folk to call attention to us, but the argument was too hot to be missed, and the women clawed and screamed in vain.

"I believe we could get out!" I shouted in Will's ear. But he shook his head. At least six men were standing on the trap, and we could not have driven them off it because there was no other space on the floor that they could occupy. So I turned to Fred.

"Couldn't we shake those ruffians off the ladder, and climb up it and escape?" I shouted. But Fred shook his head, and went on listening, trying to follow the course of the dispute.

At last somebody with louder lungs than any other man made Ephraim understand that it was I who sent the messenger to Zeitoon. Instantly that solved the problem to his mind. I should be hanged, and that would be all about it. He gesticulated. The men swarmed down off the ladder to the already overcrowded floor, and mistaking Will for me several men started to thrust him forward. A face appeared through the hole in the roof and its owner was sent running for a rope. I had not recovered my pistol, and my rifle was slung at my back where I could not possibly get at it for the crowd. But Fred had a Colt repeater handy in his hip-pocket and he promptly screwed the muzzle of it into Ephraim's ear. What he said to him I don't know, but Ephraim's convictions underwent a change of base and he began to yell for silence. The men who had seized Will let go of him just as the rope with a disgusting noose in the end was lowered through the roof. And then Ossa was imposed on Pelion.

A new face appeared at the hole. Not that we could see the face. We could only see the form of a man who shook the bloody stump of a forearm at us, and shrieked unintelligible things. After thirty seconds even the men in the far corner were aware of him, and then there was stony silence while he had his say. He repeated his message a dozen times, as if he had it by heart exactly, spitting foam out of his mouth and never ceasing to shake the butchered stump of an arm. At about the dozenth time he fainted and fell headlong down the ladder bringing up on the shoulders of the men below.

"What does he say?" I bellowed in Fred's car. But Fred was forcing his way closer to Gloria, to tell her.

"He says the Kurds are coming! He says two regiments of Kurdish cavalry have been turned loose by the Turks with orders to 'rescue' Armenians. They are on their way, riding by night for a wonder. They cut both his hands off, but he got away by shamming dead.

He says they are cutting off the feet of people and bidding them walk to Tarsus. They are taking the women and girls for sale. Old women and very little children they are making what they call sport with. Have you heard of Kurds? Their ideas of sport are worse than the Red-man's ever were."

Every tongue in the room broke loose. In another second every man was still. They looked toward Ephraim. He who could order a hanging so glibly should shoulder the new responsibility.

But Ephraim was not ready with a plan, and could not speak English. Wild-eyed, he seized the lapel of my coat in trembling fingers, and with a throat grown suddenly parched, crackled a question at me in Armenian. I could have understood Volopuk easier.

"What does he say, Fred?"

"He wants to know how soon Kagig can be here."

"Kagig!" Ephraim echoed, clutching at my collar. "Yes, yes, yes! Kagig! Come—how soon?"

"We shall be all right," said another man in English over on the far side of the room. His hoarse voice sounded like a bellow in the silence. "Kagig will come presently. Kagig will butcher the Kurds. Kagig will certainly save us."

"Kagig!" Ephraim insisted. "Come—how soon?"

But I knew Kagig would not come, that night or at any time, and Ephraim shook me in frenzied impatience for an answer.

"MALE AND FEMALE CREATED HE THEM"

The ancient orders pass. The fetters fall.
All-potent inspiration stirs dead peoples to new birth.
And over bloodied fields a new, clear call
Rings kindlier on deadened ears of earth.
Man—male—usurping—unwise overlord,
Indoctrinated, flattered, by himself betrayed
And all-betraying since with idiot word
He bade his woman bear and be afraid,
Awakes to see delusion of the past
Unmourned along with all injustice die,
Himself by woman wisdom blessed at last
And her unchallenged right the reason why.

XI
"THAT MAN'S DOSE IS DEATH, AND HE DIES UNSHRIVEN!

NOW FOR a moment I became the unwilling vortex of that mob of anxious men and women—I who by, my own confession knew Kagig, I who had sent Kagig a message, I who five minutes ago was on the verge of being hanged in the greasy noose that still swung above the ladder through the hole in the roof—I who therefore ought to be thoroughly plastic-minded and obedient to demands.

The place had become as evil smelling as the Black Hole of Calcutta. Everybody was sweating, and they shoved and milled murderously in the effort to get near me and learn, each with his own ears from my lips, just when Kagig might be expected. Ephraim, their presumptive leader, got shuffled to the outside of the pack—the only silent man between the four walls, watchful for new opportunity.

With my clothing nearly torn off and cars in agony from bellowed questions, the only remedy I could think of was to yell to Fred to start up a tune on his concertina; I had seen him change a crowd's temper many a time in just that way. But even supposing my advice had been good, he could not get his arms free, and it was Gloria Vanderman who saved that day.

Whoever has tried to write down the quality that makes the college girl, United States or English, what she is has failed, just as whoever has tried to muzzle or discredit her has failed. She is something new that has happened to the world, not because of men and women and the priests and pundits, but in spite of them. Part of the reason can be given by him who knows history enough, and commands almost unlimited leisure and page; but that would only be the uninteresting part that we could easily dispense with. The college girl has happened to the world, as light did in Genesis 1:3.

Gloria Vanderman, with her back against the wall, struggled and contrived to get her foot on Will's bent knee. Another struggle sent her breast-high above the sea of sweating faces. There was fitful light enough to see her by, because the man who held a pine torch was privileged. If there had not been hot sparks scattering from the thing doubtless they would have closed in on him and crushed it down, and out, but he had elbow-room, and accordingly Gloria's face glowed golden in its frame of disordered chestnut hair. One heard her voice because it was clear, and sweet with reasonableness, so that it vibrated in an unobstructed orbit.

"Surely you are not cowards?" she began, and they grew silent, because that idea called for consideration.

"Kagig is a patriot. Kagig is fighting for all Armenia. Surely you are not the men to let brave Kagig be tempted away from his post of danger at Zeitoon? If I know you men and women you will hasten to meet Kagig, taking your food, and weapons, and children with you. You will hurry—hurry—hurry to meet him—to meet him as near Zeitoon as possible, so as to turn him back to his post of duty!"

Then Ephraim saw his chance. Some whisperer translated to him and he owned a voice that was worth gold for political purposes.

He took up the tale in Armenian, working himself up into a splendid fervor, and so amplifying the argument that he could almost fairly claim it as his own before he was half-done. She had introduced the light, but he exploited it, and he knew his nation—knew the tricks of speech most likely to spur them into action.

Within five minutes they were shoving the stones off the trap at imminent risk of anybody's legs, and the ladder bent groaning under the weight of twice as many as it ought to bear, as half of them essayed the short cut over the roof. A blast of sweet air through the opened trap ejected most of the smoky ten-times-breathed stuff out with the climbers; and as the room emptied and we wiped the grimy sweat from our faces I heard Will talking to Gloria Vanderman in a new tongue—new, that is to say, to the old world.

"Good goods! Stampeded 'em! They'll vote for you for any office—your pick! If that guy Ephraim plans buttering the slide we'll set him on it—watch!"

"You bet," she answered sentimentally. "I wasn't cheer leader for nothing. Besides, I delivered the valedictory—say, what are we waiting here for?"

"Come on, then!" I urged her. "We'll leave our mule-load behind in case they've eaten your horse. Come with us to the stables and—"

But she interrupted me.

"You men go down and get the horses. Do what you can with the crowd. I'll get the women into something like order if that's possible, and we'll all meet wherever there's open ground and moonlight at the foot of the hill."

"I'll come with you," Will proposed. "You'll need—"

"No you won't! The women are easy. They've been taught to obey orders! It'll take all the wit you three men own between you to get the men in line! Let's get busy!"

The men had treated the hanging blankets with the respect the ancient Jews accorded to the veil of the Holy of Holies. (We learned afterward that there was an Armenian man of the party who had followed a circus one summer all across the States, and had brought that sensible precaution home with him as rule number one for successful management of mixed assemblies.) Gloria Vanderman made a run for the curtain and dived behind it. We heard the women welcome her.

"Let's go!" said Will.

Will had ever been our ladies' man in all our wanderings, because women could never resist his unaffected comradeship. Even among Americans he was rare in his gift of according to women equality not only of liberty, but of understanding and good sense, and it went like wine to the heads of some we had met, so that Will was seldom without a sex-problem on his hands and ours. But Will was too good a comrade to be surrendered to any woman lightly.

"Damn that chicken!" murmured Fred by way of praying fervently, pausing in the breach in the wall to rub his shin. "Feel that bruise, will you! No young woman ever brought me luck yet!"

"What are you waiting for?" complained a voice from outer darkness. "Come on, you rummies!"

Fred sat down on the protruding stone that had injured his shin, and detained me with his arm across the opening.

"Mark my words! In order that young woman may be educated to consider Will Yerkes a paragon of unimaginable virtues, we—you and I—are going to have to do what he calls 'hustle.' We're going to see speed, and we're going to sweat, trying to catch up. There isn't a scatterbrained adventure conceivable that we're not going to be forced into, nor an imaginable peril that we're not going to have to pull him out of. We're going to be cursed for our trouble, and ridiculed to make amusement for her majesty. And at the end of it all we're going to be patronized for a couple of ignorant damned fools who don't know better than be bachelors. What's worse, we're going to submit tamely. What is infinitely worse, we're going to like it! There are times when I doubt the sanity of my whole sex!"

"Have you guys taken root?" demanded the familiar voice and we heard Will's returning footsteps.

"No, America. But I have to sit down when my shin hurts and I'm seized with the gift of prophecy."

"Huh! We'll find Miss Vanderman tired of waiting for us with the women. Since when has a crack on the shin made a baby of you? You used to be tough enough!"

"D'you get the idea?" chuckled Fred. "We're coming, Will, we're coming."

Perfectly unconsciously Will took the lead, and most outrageously he drove us. Not that his driving was not shrewd, for his usually practical and quick mind seemed to take on added brilliancy. And since we first joined partnership—he and Monty and Fred and I—we had always been contented to follow the lead of whichever held it at the moment. But there was new efficiency, and impatience of a brand-new kind that would not rest until every man and animal had been rummaged in darkness out of that old ruin, and men, horses, cows, goats, bags of grain, and fifty cases of cartridges were driven down through the forest like water forced through a sieve, and were gathered in the only open space discoverable.

There we cooled our heels, fearful and full of vague imaginings until Miss Vanderman should bring the women, not at all encouraged by shouts in the distance that well might be the exulting of plundering Kurds, nor by occasional rifle-shots that sounded continually nearer, nor by the angry crimson glow of burning roofs that lighted half the horizon.

We waited an hour, Will objecting whenever either of us proposed to return and speed Miss Vanderman.

"Aw, what's the use? D'you suppose she doesn't know we're waiting?"

At last Fred proposed that Will himself go and investigate. He went through the form of demurring, but yielded gracefully.

"The spirit," Fred chuckled, "is weak, and the flesh is willing!"

Will handed his mule's reins to an Armenian and started alone up-hill through the pitch-dark forest; and because the world is mixed of unexpectedness and grim jest in fairly equal proportions, five minutes after he left us Gloria Vanderman came leading the women by another path.

To avoid confusion with our part, and for sake of silence, she had led them a circuit, and except for the occasional wail of a child and a little low talking that blended like the hum of insects with the night, they made very little noise. The rear was brought up by the strongest women carrying the sick and wounded on litters that had been improvised in a hurry, and like most things of the sort were much too heavy.

"Your mule is ready," said I. But she shook her head.

"You gentlemen must give your mules up to the sick and wounded. We well ones can walk."

I did not know how to answer her, although I knew she was wrong. The way to organize a marching column is not to level down to the ability of the weakest, although the pace of the weakest may have to be the measure of speed. We, who had to protect the column and shepherd it, would need our mounts; without them we should all be at the mercy of any enemy, with no corresponding gain to any one except the litter-bearers. All the same, I did not care to take issue with that capable young woman then and there. She would have put me in the wrong and left me speechless and indignant, after the fashion that is older than poor Shylock's tale.

But Fred is made of sterner stuff than I, and was never above amusing himself at the expense of anybody's dignity.

"Will is the youngest," he answered. "Besides, he's keeping us all waiting with his love-affairs! He ought to be made to walk!"

"His love-affairs?"

"He went into the woods to see a woman," Fred answered imperturbably. "Let him forfeit his mule. Here he comes. Did you find her, America?"

Will emerged out of gloom with a grin on his face.

"Just my luck!" he said simply. "What are we waiting for? I can hear the Kurds. Let's start."

At that Gloria got excited.

"D'you mean you're willing to leave a woman

behind alone in that forest?" she demanded, and Will's jaw dropped.

Fred nudged my ribs.

"Come on! We've given 'em a ground for their first quarrel. They'll never thank us if we wait a week. Mount! Walk—ride!"

We sent our two Zeitoonli in advance to show the way. True to his word, Arabaiji had left us, mule and all, and we missed him as we strove to get the unwieldy column marshaled and moving in line. We did not see Will and Gloria again that night, except when they passed between us, walking, arguing—Will explaining—we sitting on our mules on either side of the track until the last of the swarm tailed by. Then we brought up the rear together, to drive the stragglers and look out for pursuit.

"Not that I know what the devil we'll do if the Kurds get after us!" said Fred.

"Let's hope they make for the castle to-night, and waste time plundering that."

"Piffle!" he answered.

"Why?"

"Because, you ass, if they get to the place and find if empty they'll deduce, being less than idiots, that we're not far off and that we're at their mercy in the open! Let's hope to God they funk attacking in the dark, and wait out of range of the walls until daylight. In that case we've a chance. Otherwise—I've still got six rifle cartridges, and four for my pistol. How many have you?"

"Six of each."

"Then you owe me one for my pistol."

I passed it to him.

"So. Now we're good for exactly twenty-two Kurds between us. If we're pursued I propose to give those two young lovers a chance by making every cartridge count from behind cover."

"They'd hear the shooting and—"

"Not if we drop far enough behind."

"They'd hear shooting and Will, at any rate, would ride back."

"He couldn't! He'd have to look after the girl and the column."

"All the same—Will's—"

"I know he is. Very well. I'll arrange it another way. You wait behind here."

So I rode along slowly, and he spurred his horse to a trot. But he did not hold the trot long. I could hear him objurgating, coaxing, encouraging, explaining, and the shrill voices of women answering, as he tried at one and the same time to pass the unfortunates in the dark and to make them see the grim necessity for speed. Soon I grew as busy as he, bullying litter-bearers and mothers burdened with crying babies. In times of massacre and war, survivors are not necessarily those who enjoyed the best of it. Nearly-drowned men brought to life again would forego the process if the choice were theirs, and there were nearly twenty women who would have preferred death to that night's march. But I did not dare load my horse with babies, since it would likely be needed before dawn for sterner work.

It was more than an hour before Fred loomed in sight again, standing beside his horse in wait for me. He, too, had resisted the temptation to relieve mothers of their living loads (not that they ever expected it).

"How did you manage?" I asked, for I could tell by his air that the errand had been successful.

"I lied to him."

"Of course. What did you say?"

"Said if the straggling got bad you and I might fall a long way behind and fire our pistols, so as to give the impression Kurds are in pursuit. That would tickle up the rear-end to a run!"

"And he believed that?" Will knew as well as I Fred's not exactly subtle way of maneuvering to get the post of greatest danger for himself.

"He'd have believed anything! He's head-, heart- and heels-over-end in love with the girl, and she's as bad as he is. They're talking political economy and international jurisprudence. When I reached 'em they'd just arrived at the conclusion that the United States can save the world, maybe—maybe not, but nothing else can. I was decidedly *de trop.* They're pretty to watch. No, he hasn't kissed her yet—you could tell that even in the dark. It's my belief he won't for a long time; America's way with women is beyond belief. They're telling each other all they know, and like, and dislike, and believe, and hope. It 'ud take a bullet to divide their destinies. I delivered my message, and they were so devilish polite you'd think I was the parson come to marry 'em. They'd forgotten my very existence. When it dawned on 'em who I was they were so keen to be rid of me they'd have agreed to anything at all. So it was easy."

"Good."

"No, it's bad. Will's a friend of mine. I hate to

see him squandered on a woman. However, I did better than that."

"How so?"

As I spoke there loomed out of the darkness just ahead of us eight men surrounding something on the track, their rifles sticking up above their shoulders.

"I've found eight men with rifles all alike that fit the ammunition in the boxes. It's stolen Turkish government ammunition, by the way. The rifles come from the same source. The point is that a man caught with a stolen government rifle and ammunition in his possession would be tortured. Incidentally the men seem game. Therefore, if we have to fight a rear-guard action we can reasonably count on them. *Haide!"* he called to the eight men, and they picked up the case of cartridges, and resumed the march just ahead of us.

Fred lit his pipe contentedly, as he always is contented when he can make satisfactory arrangements to sacrifice himself unselfishly and pretend to himself he is a cynic. Whether because the armed guard of their own people put new courage in them, or because rifles at their rear made them more afraid, the stragglers gave less trouble for the next few hours. Perhaps they were growing more used to the march, and some of them were numb with anxiety, while not so weary yet that feet would not carry them forward.

Somewhere in advance a man with a high tenor voice began to sing a wild folk-song, of the sort that is common to all countries whose heritage is hope unstrangled. He and others like him with love and music in their brave hearts sang the tortured column through its night of agony, keeping alive faint hope that hell must have an end. Dawn broke sweet and calm. For it makes no matter if a nation writhes in agony, or man wreaks hate on man, the wind and the sky still whisper and smile; and the scent of wild flowers is not canceled by the stench of tired humanity.

Fred knocked his pipe out and rode to the top of shoulder of rock beside the track, beckoning to me to follow. We could see our column, astonishingly long drawn, winding like a line of ants in and out and over, following the leaders in a dream because there seemed nothing else to do or dream about. Once I thought I caught sight of Will on his horse, passing between trees, but I was not sure. Fred turned his horse about and looked in the direction we had come from. Presently, be nudged me.

"That smoke might be the castle we were in last night. See—it's red underneath. What'll you bet me Kurds don't show up in pursuit before the day's an hour old?"

That was nothing to bet about, and that kind of dawn is not the hour for roseate optimism.

"If they come," said I, "I hope I don't live to see what they'll do to the women."

Fred met my eyes and laughed.

"That's all right," he said. "You ride on. This rock commands the track. I'll follow later when pursuit's called off."

"Ride on yourself!" I answered, and he chuckled as he lighted his pipe again.

One of the men had a kerosene can filled with odds and ends of personal belongings. I turned them out in a hollow of the rock, and sent him to fill the can with drinking water at a spring. Then Fred and I chose stations, and Fred went to vast pains lecturing every one of us on how to keep cover. We had nothing to eat, and therefore no notion of putting up anything but a short fight. Our best point was the surprise that unexpected, organized resistance would be likely to produce on plundering Kurds.

It was pleasant enough where we lay, and reminded both of us of far less strenuous days. The little animals that are always curious to the point of their undoing came out and investigated our tracks as soon as the noise of the stragglers had ceased. The Armenians took no notice of the wild life; persecuted people seldom do, having their own hard case too much in mind; but Fred knew the name of nearly every bird and animal that showed itself, and even ceased smoking as his interest increased.

"Ever go fishing as a boy?" he asked.

"Didn't I!"

"Get up before daylight and escape from the house by the back way—"

"Stealing bread and cheese from the pantry on the way out—"

"And stopping where the grass was long near the watering place to dig worms—"

"And unchain the dog with frantic efforts to keep him from barking—"

"Yes, but the rascal always would do it—bark and wake everybody! Lucky if nobody saw you as you slipped through the gate into the fields!"

"Ah! But then what a time the dog had—it was almost as good fun as the fishing to watch him scamper. And how hungry he got—and he ate more than his share of the bread and cheese, so that you'd have had to go home early because of the aching void if it hadn't been for the cottage where they gave a fellow milk out of a brown dish."

"Yumm! Didn't that country milk taste good! Snff—snff—they were mornings just like this at home when I went fishing. Cool and sweet and full of scent. Snff—snff!"

We sat still behind the ledge and let the air and scenery revive kind memories. The only noise was what our horses made cropping the grass in a hollow behind us, for the Armenians were well content to ruminate. Most likely they would have fallen asleep if we had not been there to keep an eye on them, for prolonged subjection to too much fear is soporific, so that tortured poor wretches sleep on the tightened rack.

I was very nearly asleep myself, having had practically none of it for two nights in succession, and had taken to watching the horses to keep my mind busy, when the movement of my horse's ears struck me as peculiar. Presently he ceased grazing and raised his head. I thought he was going to whinny, and turned to see Fred squinting down his rifle at something that was not in the range of my vision.

"Here they come!" he whispered.

As he spoke a Kurd stepped out from between the trees, and we could see that he had tied his horse to a branch in the gloom behind him. He had the long sleeves reaching nearly to the ground peculiar to his race, and the unmistakable sheeny nose and cruel lips. From the rifle that he carried cavalierly over his shoulder hung a woman's undergarment, with a dark stain on it that looked suspiciously like blood. My horse whinnied then, and his beast answered. At that he brought his rifle to the "ready" and nearly jumped out of his skin.

"I'm judge, jury, witness, prosecutor and executioner!" Fred whispered. "That man's dose is death, and he dies unshriven!"

Then he fired, and Fred could not miss at that range if he tried. The Kurd clapped a hand to his throat and fell backward, and one of our Armenians ran before we could stop him to seize the tied horse, and any other plunder. One of the things he brought back with him, besides the horse and rifle and ammunition belt, was a woman's finger with the ring not yet removed. He said he found it in the cartridge pouch.

In proof that organized defense was the last thing they reckoned on, nine more Kurds came galloping down the track pell-mell toward the place where they had heard the solitary rifle-shot, doubtless supposing their own man had come upon the quarry. We fired too fast, for the Armenians were not drilled men, but we dropped two horses and five Kurds, and the remaining four fled, with the riderless animals stampeding in their wake.

"What next?" said I, as Fred wiped out his rifle-barrel.

"They'll return in greater force. We'd better change ground. D'you notice how this rock is covered by that other one a quarter of a mile to the right? Higher ground, too, and the last place they'll look—come on!"

The man with the water-can spilled it all, for the sake of his medley of possessions, and I had to send him all the way back for more. But we took up our new stand at last with the horses well hidden and enough to drink to last the day out, and then had to wait half an hour before any Kurds came back to the attack.

They came on the second time with infinite precaution, lurking among the trees on the outskirts of the clearing and firing several random shots at our old position in the hope of drawing our fire. Finally, they emerged from the forest thirty strong and rushed our supposed hiding-place at full gallop.

They were not even out of pistol range. Fred used the Mauser rifle taken from the dead Kurd, and then we both emptied our pistols at the fools, the Armenians meanwhile keeping up a savage independent fire so ragged and rapid that it might have been the battle of Waterloo.

The Kurds never knew whether or not we were another party or the first one. They never discovered whether our former post was deserted or not. We never knew how many of them we hit, for after about a dozen had tumbled out of the saddle the remainder galloped for their lives. For minutes afterward we heard them crashing and pounding away in the distance to find their friends.

Our loot consisted of two wounded prisoners and four good horses, in addition to rifles and cartridges. We let the dead lie where they were for a warning to other scoundrels, and we looked on while our Armenians searched the bodies for anything likely to be of slightest use. They found almost nothing originally Kurdish, but more Armenian trinkets than would have stocked a traveling merchant's show-case, including necklaces and earrings.

Fred took the two prisoners aside and in Persian, which every Kurd can understand and speak after a fashion, offered them their choice between telling the whole truth or being handed over to Armenians. And as there isn't a bloody rascal in the world but suspects his intended victims of worse hankerings than his own, they loosed their tongues and told more than the truth, adding whatever they thought likely to please Fred.

"They say there were only about fifty of them in this raiding party to begin with, and several came to trouble before they met us. Seems there are Armenians hidden here and there who are able to give an account of themselves. Ten or twelve elected to stay near the castle we were in last night. They've burned it, but they have some captured women and propose to enjoy themselves. Shall we ride back and break in on the party?"

He meant what he said, but it was out of the question. "The party we've just trounced will give the alarm," I objected. "We'd only ride into a trap. Besides, you've no proof these prisoners are not lying to you."

"They say their raiding party is the only one within thirty miles. They rode ahead of the regiments to get first picking."

"We're none of us fit for anything but food and sleep," said I, and Fred had to concede the point.

Fortunately the food problem was solved for the moment by the Kurds, who had a sort of cheese with them whose awful taste deprived one of further appetite. We ate, and tied our two wounded prisoners on one horse; and as we had nothing to treat their wounds with except water they finished their trip in exquisite discomfort. Surprise that we should attend to their wounds at all, added to their despondency after they had time to consider what it meant. There was only one burden to their lamentation:

"What are you going to do with us? We will tell what we know! We will name names! We are your slaves! We kiss feet! Ask, and we will answer!"

They thought they were being kept alive for torture, and we let them keep on thinking it. Fred tied their horse to his own saddle and towed them along, singing at the top of his lungs to keep the rest of us awake; and for all his noise I fell asleep until he reached for his concertina and, the humor of the situation dawning on him, commenced a classic of his own composition, causing the morning to re-echo with irreverence, and making all of us except the prisoners aware of the fact that life is not to be taken seriously, even in Armenia. The prisoners intuitively guessed that the song had reference to ways and means they would rather have forgotten.

"Ow! My name it is 'orrible 'Enery 'Emms,
And I 'ails from a 'ell of a 'ole!
The things I 'ave thought an' the deeds I 'ave did
Are remarkable lawless an' better kept 'id,
So if Morgan you think of, an' Sharkey, an' Kidd,
Forget 'em! To name such beginners as them's
An insult, so shiver my soul!
Yow! In every port o' the whole seven seas
I 'ave two or three wives on the rates,
For I'm free wi' my fancy an' fly wi' my picks,
And I've promised 'em plenty, an' given 'em nix,
But have left ev'ry one in a 'ell of a fix!
'Ooever said Bluebeard was brother to me's
Either jealous or misunderstates!

"Wow! For awful atrocity, murder an' theft,
For battery, arson and 'ate,
From breakin' the Sabbath to covetin' cows,
An' false affidavits an' perjurin' vows,
I'm adept at whatever the law disallows,
And the gallowsmen gape at the noose that I left,
For I flit while the bally fools wait!"

Fred kept us awake all right. Like most of his original songs, that one had sixty or seventy verses.

CUI BONO?

Did caution keep the gates of Greece,
Ye saints of "safety first!"
Twixt Thessaly and Locris when
Leonidas' thousand men
Died scornful of the proffered peace
Of Xerxes the accurst?
Watch ye have kept, ward ye have kept,

But watch and ward were vain
If love and gratitude have slept
While ye stood guard for gain.

Or ye, who count the niggard cost
In time and coin and gear
Of succoring the under-dog,
How often have ye seen a hog,
Establishing his glutton boast,
Survive a famine year?
Fast ye have kept, feast ye have made;
Vain were the deeds and doles
If it was fear that ye obeyed
To save your coward souls.

Ye banish beauty to the stews
For lack of eyes that see,
And stifle joy with deadly rote
As empty as the texts ye quote,
The while forgiveness ye refuse
Lest wrath dishonored be.
Gray are your days, drab are your ways,
Strong are your fashioned bars,
But, ye who ask if service pays—
Who polishes the stars?

XII
"AMERICA'S WAY WITH A WOMAN IS BEYOND BELIEF!

SPRING IN Armenia is almost as much like heaven as heaven itself could be, if it were not for the unspeakable Turk, but his blight rests on everything. I could have kept awake that morning without Fred's irreverent music, simply for sake of the scenery, if its freshness had been untainted. But there hung a sickly, faint pall of smoke that robbed the green landscape of all liveliness. One breathed weariness instead of wine.

We could not possibly have lost the way, because our crawling column had left a swath behind it of trampled grass and trodden crossing-places where the track wound and rewound in a game of hide-and-seek with tinkling streams. But we began to wonder, nevertheless, why we caught up with nobody.

It was drawing on to ten in the morning, and I had dozed off for about the dozenth time, with my horse in pretty much the same condition, when I heard Will's voice at last, and looked up. He was standing alone on a ledge overlooking the track, but I could see the ends of rifles sticking up close by. If we had been an enemy, we should have stood small chance against him.

"Where are the rest of you?" I asked, and he laughed!

"Women, kids and wounded all swore a pitched battle was raging behind them. Most of them wanted to turn back and lend a hand. I thought you guys mighty cruel to put all that scare into a crowd in their condition—but I see—"

"Guests, America! My country's at peace with Turkey! Where shall we stow our guests?"

"There's a village below here."

He jerked a thumb over his shoulder. But behind him was the apex of a spur thrust out in mid-curve of the mountainside, and one could not see around that. We had emerged out of the straggling outposts of the forest high above the plain, and to our right the whole panorama lay snoozing in haze. The path by which we had turned our backs on Monty and Kagig went winding away and away below, here and there an infinitesimal thin line of slightly lighter color, but more often suggested by the contour of the hills. Our Zeitoonli in their zeal to return to their leader had been evidently cutting corners. If the smudge of smoke to the right front overhung Marash, then we were probably already nearer Zeitoon than when we and Kagig parted company.

"Come up and see for yourselves," said Will.

Fred passed the line that held his prisoners in tow to an Armenian, and we climbed up together on foot. Around the corner of the spur, within fifty feet of where Will stood, was an almost sheer escarpment, and at the foot of that, a thousand feet below us, with ramparts of living rock on all four sides, crouched a little village fondled in the bosom of the mountains.

"They've piled down there and made 'emselves at home. The place was deserted, prob'ly because it 'ud be too easy to roll rocks down into it. But I can't make 'em listen. Ours is a pretty chesty lot, with guts, and our taking part with 'em has stiffened their courage. They claim they're goin' to hold this rats' nest against all the Turks and Kurds in Asia Minor!"

"That's where the rest of us are," said Will

"Where's Miss Vanderman?"

"Asleep—down in the village. They're all asleep.

You guys go down there and sleep, too. I'll follow, soon as I've posted these men on watch. That small square hut next the big one in the middle is ours. She's in the big one with a crowd of women. Now don't make a fool row and wake her! Tie your horses in the shade where you see the others standing in line; there's a little corn for them, and a lot of hay that the owners left behind."

So we undertook not to wake the lady, and left Will there carefully choosing places, in which the men fell fast asleep almost the minute his back was turned. Sleep was in the air that morning—not mere weariness of mind and limb that a man could overcome, but inexplicable coma. Whole armies are affected that way on occasion. There was a man once named Sennacherib.

"Sleepy hollow!" said Fred, and as he spoke his horse pitched forward, almost spilling him; the rope that held the prisoners in tow was all that saved the lot of them from rolling down-hill. Fred dismounted, and drove the horse in front of him with a slap on the rump, but the beast was almost too sleepy to make the effort to descend.

There was no taint of gas or poison fumes. The air tasted fresh except for the faint smoke, and the birds were all in full song. Yet we all had to dismount, and to let the prisoners walk, too, because the horses were too drowsy to be trusted. The path that zig-zagged downward to the village was dangerous enough without added risk, and the eight Armenian riflemen refused point-blank to lead the way unless they might drive the animals ahead of them.

Even so, neither we nor they were properly awake when we reached the village. We tied up the horses in a sort of dream—fed them from instinct and habit—and made our way to the hut Will had pointed out like men who walked in sleep.

Nobody was keeping watch. Nobody noticed our arrival. Men and women were sleeping in the streets and under the eaves of the little houses. Nothing seemed awake but the stray dogs nosing at men's feet and hunting hopelessly among the bundles.

The little house Will had reserved for our use contained a stool and a string-cot. On the stool was food—cheese and very dry bread; and because even in that waking dream we were conscious of hunger, we ate a little of it. Then we lay down on the floor and fell asleep—we, and the prisoners, and the eight Armenian riflemen. Within a quarter of an hour Will followed us into the house, but we knew nothing about that. Then he, too, fell asleep, and until two or three hours after dark we were a village of the dead.

To this day there is no explaining it. Certainly no human watch or ward saved us from destruction at the hands of roving enemies. I was awakened at last by a brilliant light, and the effort made by our two prisoners, still tied together, to crawl across my body. I threw them off me, and sat up, rubbing my eyes and wondering where I was.

In the door stood Kagig, with a lantern in his right hand thrust forward into the room. His eyes were ablaze with excitement, and between black beard and mustache his teeth showed in a grin mixed of scorn and amusement.

Next I beard Will's voice: "Jiminy!" and Will sat up. Then Fred gave tongue:

"That you, Kagig? Where's Monty? Where's Lord Montdidier?"

Kagig strode into the room, set the lantern on the floor, struck the remnants of the food from off the little stool, and sat down. I could see now that he was deathly tired.

"He is in Zeitoon," he answered.

Noises from outside began then to assert themselves in demonstration that the village was awake at last—also that the population had swollen while we slept. I could hear the restless movement of more than twice the number of horses we had had with us.

Kagig began to laugh—a sort of dry cackle that included wonder as well as rebuke. He threw both hands outward, palms upward, in a gesture that complemented the motion of shoulders shrugged up to his ears.

"All around—high hills! From every side from fifty places rocks could have been rolled upon you! So—and so you sleep!"

"I set guards!" Will exploded.

"Eleven guards I found—all together in one place—fast asleep!"

He showed his splendid teeth and the palms of his hands again in actual enjoyment of the situation. For the first time then I saw there was wet blood on his goat-skin coat.

"Kagig—you're wounded!"

He made a gesture of impatience.

"It is nothing—nothing. My servant has attended to it."

So Kagig had a servant. I felt glad of that. It meant a rise from vagabondage to position among his people.

Of all earthly attainments, the first and most desirable and last to let go of is an honest servant—unless it be a friend. (But the difference is not so distinct as it sounds.)

A huge fear suddenly seized Fred Oakes.

"You said Monty is in Zeitoon—alive or dead? Quick, man! Answer!"

"Should I leave Zeitoon," Kagig answered slowly, unless I left a better man in charge behind me? He is alive in Zeitoon—alive—alive! He is my brother! He and I love one purpose with a strong love that shall conquer! You speak to me of Lord what-is-it? Hah! To me forever he is Monty, my brother—my—"

"Where's Miss Vanderman?" I interrupted.

"Here!" she said quietly, and I turned my head to discover her sitting beside Will in the shadow cast by Kagig's lantern. She must have entered ahead of Kagig or close behind him, unseen because of his bulk and the tricky light that he swung in his right hand.

Kagig went on as if he had not heard me.

"There is a castle—I think I told you?—perched on a crag in the forest beside Zeitoon. My men have cut a passage to it through the trees, for it had stood forgotten for God knows how long. Later you shall understand. There came Arabaiji, riding a mule to death, saying you and this lady are in danger of life at the hands of my nation. I did not believe that, but Monty—he believed it."

"And I'll wager you found him a hot handful!" laughed Fred. "Not so hot. Not so hot. But very determined. Later you shall understand. He and I drove a bargain."

"Dammit!" Fred rose to his feet. "D'you mean you used our predicament as a club to drive him with?"

Kagig laughed dryly.

"Do you know your friend so little, and think so ill of me? He named terms, and I agreed to them. I took a hundred mounted men to find you and bring you to Zeitoon, spreading them out like a fan, to scour the country. Some fell in with a thing the Turks call a *hamidieh* regiment; that is a rabble of Kurds under the command of Tenekelis."

"What are they?"

"Tenekelis? The word means 'tin-plate men.' We call them that because of the tin badges given them to wear in their head-dress. In no other way do they resemble officers. They are brigands favored by official recognition, that is all. Their purpose is to pillage Armenians. While you slept in this village, and your watchmen slept up above there, that whole rabble of bandits with their tin-plate officers passed within half a mile, following along the track by which you came! If you had been awake—and cooking—or singing—or making any sort of noise they must have heard you! Instead, they turned down toward the plain a little short distance too soon—and my men met them—and there was a skirmish—and I rallied my other men, and attacked them suddenly. We accounted for two of the tin-plate men, and so many of the thing they call a regiment that the others took to flight. *Jannam!* (My soul!) But you are paragons of sleepers!"

"Do you never sleep?" I asked him.

"Shall a man keep watch over a nation, and sleep?" he answered. "Aye—here a little, there a little, I snatch sleep when I can. My heart burns in me. I shall sleep on my horse on the way back to Zeitoon, but the burning within will waken me by fits and starts."

He got up and stood very politely in front of Gloria Vanderman, removing his Cossack *kalpak* for the first time and holding it with a peculiar suggestion of humility.

"You shall be put to no indignity at the hands of my people," he said. "They are not bad people, but they have suffered, and some have been made afraid. They would have kept you safe. But now you shall have twenty men if you wish, and they shall deliver you safely into Tarsus. If you wish it, I will send one of these gentlemen with you to keep you in countenance before my men; they are foreigners to you, and no one could blame you for fearing them. The gentleman would not wish to go, but I would send him!"

She shook her head, pretty merrily for a girl in her predicament.

"I was curious to meet you, Mr. Kagig, but that's nothing to the attraction that draws me now. I must meet the other man—is it Monty you all call him—or never know a moment's peace!"

"You mean you will not go to Tarsus?"

"Of course I won't!"

"Of course!" laughed Fred. "Any young woman—"

"Of course?" Kagig repeated the extravagant gesture of shrugged shoulders and up-turned palms. "Ah, well. You are American. I will not argue. What would be the use?"

He turned his back on us and strode out with that air that not even the great stage-actors can ever acquire, of becoming suddenly and utterly oblivious of present company in the consciousness of deeds that need attention. Generals of command, great captains of industry, and a few rare statesmen have it; but the statesmen are most rare, because they are trained to pretend, and therefore unconvincing. The generals and captains are detested for it by all who have never humbled themselves to the point where they can think, and be unselfishly absorbed. Kagig stepped out of one zone of thought into the next, and shut the door behind him.

A minute later we heard his voice uplifted in command, and the business of shepherding those women and children was taken out of our hands by a man who understood the business. The intoxicating sounds that armed men make as they evolve formation out of chaos in the darkness came in through open door and windows, and in another moment Kagig was back again with a hand on each door-post.

"You have brought all those cartridges!"

He thrust out both hands in front of him, and made the knuckles of every finger crack like castanets. In another second he was gone again. But we knew we were now forgiven all our sins of omission.

Somewhere about midnight, with a nearly full moon rising in a golden dream above the rim of the ravine, we started. And no wheeled vehicle could have followed by the track we took. It was no mean task for men on foot, and our burdened animals had to be given time. Whether or not Kagig slept, as he had said he would, on horse-back, he kept himself and our prisoners out of sight somewhere in the van; and this time the rear was brought up by a squadron of ragged irregular horse that would have made any old campaigner choke with joy to look at them.

Drill those men knew very little of—only sufficient to make it possible to lead them. No two men were dressed alike, and some were not even armed alike, although stolen Turkish government rifles far predominated. But they wore unanimously that dare-devil air, not swaggering because there is no need, that has been the key to most of the sublime surprises of all war. The commander, whose men sit that way in the saddle and toss those jokes shoulder over shoulder down the line, dare tackle forlorn hopes that would seem sheer leap-year lunacy to the martinet with twenty times their number.

"Who'd have thought it?" said Fred. "We've all heard the Turk was a first-class fighting man, but I'd rather command fifty of these, than any five hundred Turks I ever saw.

There was no gainsaying that. Whoever had seen armies with an understanding eye must have agreed.

"Turks don't hate Armenians for their faults," I answered. "From what I know of the Turk he likes sin, and prefers it cardinal. If Armenians were mere degenerates, or murdering ruffians like the Kurds, the Turk would like them."

Fred laughed.

"Then if a Turk liked me, you'd doubt my social fitness?"

"Sure I would, if he liked you well enough to attract attention. The fact that the Turk hates Armenians is the best advertisement Armenians have got."

We were entering the heart of savage hills that tossed themselves in ever increasing grandeur up toward the mist-draped crags of Kara Dagh, following a trail that was mostly watercourse. The simple savagery of the mountains laid naked to view in the liquid golden light stirred the Armenians behind us to the depths of thought; and theirs is a consciousness of warring history; of dominion long since taken from them, and debauched like pearls by swine; of hope, eternally upwelling, born of love of their trampled fatherland. They began to sing, and the weft and woof of their songs were grief for all those things and a cherished, secret promise that a limit had been set to their nation's agony.

In his own way, with his chosen, unchaste instrument Fred is a musician of parts. He can pick out the spirit of old songs, even when, as then, he hears them for the first time, and make his concertina interpret them to wood and wind and sky. Indoors he is a mere accompanist, and in polite society his muse is dumb. But in the open, given fair excuse and the opportunity, he can make such music as compels men's ears and binds their hearts with his in common understanding.

Because of Fred's concertina, quite without knowing it, those Armenians opened their hearts to us that night, so that when a day of testing came they regarded us unconsciously as friends. Taught by the atrocity of cruel centuries to mistrust even one another, they would surely have doubted us otherwise, when crisis came. Nobody knows better than the Turk how to corrupt morality and friendship, and Armenia is honeycombed with the rust of mutual suspicion. But real music is magic stuff. No Turk knows any magic.

At dawn, twisting and zigzagging in among the ribs of rock-bound hills, we sighted the summit of Beirut Dagh all wreathed in jeweled mist. Then the only life in sight except ourselves was eagles, nervously obsessed with goings-on on the horizon. I counted as many as a dozen at one time, wheeling swiftly, and circling higher for a wider view, but not one swooped to strike.

Once, as we turned into a track that they told us led to El Oghlu, we saw on a hill to our left a small square building, gutted by fire. Twenty yards away from it, on top of the same round hill, strange fruit was hanging from a larger oak than any we had seen thereabouts—fruit that swung unseemly in the tainted wind.

"Turks!" announced one of Kagig's men, riding up to brag to us. "That square building is the guardhouse for the *zaptieh,* put there by the government to keep check on robbers. They are the worst robbers!"

The man spoke English with the usual mission-school air suggestive of underdone pie. As a rule they go to school at such great sacrifice, and then so limited for funds, that they have to get by heart three times the amount an ordinary, undriven youth can learn in the allotted time. But by heart they have it. And like the pie they call to mind, only the surface of their talk is pale. Because their heart is in the thing, they under-stand.

"By hanging Turkish police," said Fred, "you only give the Turks a good excuse for murdering your friends."

"Come!" said the man of Zeitoon. "See."

He led the way down a path between young trees to a clearing where a swift stream gamboled in the sun. Down at the end of it, where the grass sloped gently upward toward the flanks of a great rock was a little row of graves with a cross made of sticks at the head of each—clearly not Turkish graves.

"Three men—eleven women," our guide said simply.

"You mean that the Turkish police—"

"There were fifteen on their way to Zeitoon. One survived, and reached Zeitoon, and told. Then he died, and we rode down to avenge them all. The Turks took the three men and beat them on the feet with sticks until the soles of their feet swelled up and burst. Then they made them walk on their tortured feet. Then they beat them to death. Shall I say what they did to the women?"

"What did you do to the Turks?" said I.

"Hanged them. We are not animals—we simply, hanged them."

Somewhere about noon we rode down a gorge into the village of El Oghlu. It was a miserable place, with a miserable, tiny *kahveh* in the midst of it, and Kagig set that alight before our end of the column came within a quarter of a mile of it. We burned the rest of the village, for he sent back Ephraim to order no shelter left for the regiments that would surely come and hunt us down. But the business took time, and we were farther than ever behind Kagig when the last wooden roof began to cockle and crack in the heat.

Will and Gloria were somewhere on in front, and Fred and I began to put on speed to try to overtake them. But from the time of leaving the burned village of El Oghlu there began to be a new impediment.

"We are not taking the shortest way," said Ephraim. "The shortest way is too narrow—good for one or two men in a hurry, but not for all of us."

We were gaining no speed by taking the easier road. There began to be vultures in evidence, mostly half-gorged, flopping about from one orgy to the next. And out from among the rocks and bushes there came fugitive Armenians—famished and wounded men and women, clinging to our stirrups and begging for a lift on the way to Zeitoon. Zeitoon was their one hope. They were all headed that way.

Fred detached a dozen mounted men to linger behind on guard against pursuit, and the rest of us overloaded our horses with women and children, giving up all hope of overtaking Gloria and Will, forgetting that they had come first on the scene. In my mind I imagined them riding side by side, Will with his easy cowboy seat, and Gloria looking like a boy except for the chestnut hair. But that imagination went the way of other vanities.

There was neither pleasure nor advantage in striding slowly beside my laboring horse, nor any hope of mounting him again myself. So I walked ahead and, being now horseless, ceased to be mobbed by fugitives. At the end of an hour I overtook two horses loaded with little children; but there was no sign of Gloria and Will, and losing zest for the pursuit as the sun grew stronger I sat down by the ways-side on a fallen tree.

It was then that I heard voices that I recognized. The first was a woman's.

"I'm simply crazy to know him."

A man's, that I could not mistake even amid the roar of a city, answered her.

"You've a treat in store. Monty is my idea of a regular he-man."

"Is he good-looking?"

"Yes. Stands and looks like a soldier. I've seen a plainsman in Wyoming who'd have matched him to a T all except the parted hair and the mustache."

"I like a mustache on a tall man."

"It suits Monty. The first idea you get of him is strength—strength and gentleness; and it grows on you as you know him better. It's not just muscles, nor yet will-power, but strength that makes your heart flutter, and you know for a moment how a woman must feel when a fellow asks her to be his wife. That's Monty."

I got up and retraced a quarter of a mile, to wait for Fred where I could not accuse myself of "listening in."

"Fred," I said, when he overtook me at last and we strode along side by side, "you were right. America's way with a woman is beyond belief!"

I told him what I had heard, and he thought a while.

"How about Maga Jhaere's way, when she and Will and the Vanderman meet?" he said at last, smiling grimly.

"TO-MORROW WE DIE"

All that is cynical; all that refuses
Trust in an altruist aim;
Every specious plea that excuses
Greed in necessity's name;
Studied indifference; scorn that amuses;
Cleverness, shifting the blame;
Selfishness, pitying trust it abuses—
Treason and these are the same.
Finally, when the last lees ye shall turn from
(E'en intellectuals flinch in the end!)
Ashes of loneliness then ye shall learn from—
All that's worth keeping's the faith of a friend.

XIII
"'TAKE YOUR SQUADRON AND GO FIND HIM, RUSTUM KHAN!' AND I, SAHIB, OBEYED MY LORD BAHADUR'S ORDERS."

NEVER TO be forgotten is that journey to Zeitoon. We threaded toward the heart of opal mountains along tracks that nothing on wheels—not even a wheel-barrow—could have followed. Perpetually on our right there kept appearing brilliant green patches of young rice, more full of livid light than flawless emeralds. And, as in all rice country, there were countless watercourses with frequently impracticable banks along which fugitives felt their way miserably, too fearful of pursuit to risk following the bridle track.

There is a delusion current that fugitives go fast. But it stands to reason they do not; least of all, unarmed people burdened with children and odds and ends of hastily snatched household goods. We found them hiding everywhere to sleep and rest lacerated feet, and there was not a mile of all that distance that did not add twenty or thirty stragglers to our column, risen at sight of us out of their lurking places. We scared at least as many more into deeper hiding, without blame to them, for there was no reason why they should know us at a distance from official murderers. *Hamidieh* regiments, the militia of that land, wear uniforms of their own choosing, which is mostly their ordinary clothes and weapons added.

With snow-crowned Beirut Dagh frowning down over us, and the track growing every minute less convenient for horse or man, word came from the rear that the *hamidieh* were truly on our trail. Then we had our first real taste of what Armenians could do against drilled Turks, and even before Fred and I could get in touch with Will and Gloria we realized that whether or not we took part with them there was going to be no stampede by the men-folk.

Nothing would persuade Gloria to go on to Zeitoon and announce our coming. Kagig came galloping back and found us four met together by a little horsetail waterfall. He ordered her peremptorily to hurry and find Monty, but she simply ignored him. In another moment he was too bent on shepherding the ammunition cases to give her a further thought.

Men began to gather around him, and he to issue orders. They had either to kill him or obey. He struck at them with a rawhide whip, and spurred his horse savagely at every little clump of men disposed to air their own views.

"You see," he laughed, "unanimity is lacking!" Then his manner changed back to irritation. "In the name of God, *effendim,* what manner of sportsmen are you? Will not each of you take a dozen men and go and destroy those cursed Turks?" (They call every man a Turk in that land who thinks and acts like one, be he Turk, Arab, Kurd or Circassian.)

It was all opposed to the consul's plan, and lawless by any reckoning. To attack the troops of a country with which our own governments were not at war was to put our heads in a noose in all likelihood. Perhaps if he had called us by any other name than "sportsmen" we might have seen it in that light, and have told him to protect us according to contract. But he used the right word and we jumped at the idea, although Gloria, who had no notions about international diplomacy, was easily first with her hat in the ring.

"I'll lead some men!" she shouted. "Who'll follow me?" Her voice rang clear with the virtue won on college playing fields.

"Nothing to it!" Will insisted promptly. "Here, you, Kagig—I'll make a bargain with you!"

"Watch!" Fred whispered. "Will is now going to sell two comrades in the market for his first love! D'you blame him? But it won't work!"

"Send Miss Vanderman to Zeitoon with an escort and we three—"

"What did I tell you?" Fred chuckled.

"—will fight for you all you like!"

But Gloria had a dozen men already swarming to her, with never a symptom of shame to be captained by a woman; and others were showing signs of inclination. She turned her back on us, and I saw three men hustle a fourth, who had both feet in bandages, until he gave her his rifle and bandolier. She tossed him a laugh by way of compensation, and be seemed content, although he had parted with more than the equivalent of a fortune.

"That girl," said Kagig, from the vantage point of his great horse, "is like the brave Zeitoonli wives! They fight! They can lead in a pinch! They are as good as men—better than men, for they think they know less!"

Fred swiftly gathered himself a company of his own, the older men electing to follow his lead. Gloria had the cream of the younger ones—men who in an earlier age would have gone into battle wearing a woman's glove or handkerchief—twenty or thirty youths blazing with the fire of youth. Will went hot-foot after her with most of the English-speaking contingent from the mission schools. Kagig had the faithful few who had rallied to him from the first—the fighting men of Zeitoon proper, including all the tough rear-guard who had sent the warning and remained faithfully in touch with the enemy until their chief should come.

That left for me the men who knew no English, and Ephraim was enough of a politician to see the advantage to himself of deserting Fred's standard for mine; for Fred could talk Armenian, and give his own orders, but I needed an interpreter. I welcomed him at the first exchange of compliments, but met him eye to eye a second later and began to doubt.

"I'm going to hold these men in reserve," I told him, "until I know where they'll do most good. You know this country? Take high ground, then, where we can overlook what's going on and get into the fight to best advantage."

"But the others will get the credit," he began to object.

"I'll ask Kagig for another interpreter. Wait here."

At that he yielded the point and explained my orders to the men, who began to obey them willingly enough. But he went on talking to them rapidly as we diverged from the path the others had taken and ascended a trail that wild goats would have reveled in, along the right flank of where fighting was likely to take place. I did not doubt be was establishing notions of his own importance, and with some success.

Firing commenced away in front and below us within ten minutes of the start, but it was an hour before I could command the scene with field-glasses, and ten minutes after that before I could make out the positions of our people, although the enemy were soon evident—a long, irregular, ragged-looking line of cavalry thrusting lances into every hole that could possibly conceal an Armenian, and an almost equally irregular line of unmounted men in front of them, firing not very cautiously nor accurately from under random cover.

It became pretty evident, after studying the positions for about fifteen minutes and sweeping every contour of the ground through glasses, that the enemy had no chance whatever of breaking through unless they could outflank Kagig's line. I held such impregnable advantage of height and cover and clear view that the men I had with me were ample to prevent the turning of our right wing. Our left flank rested on the brawling Jihun River that wound in and out between the rice fields and the rocky foot-hills. There lay the weakness of our position, and more than once I caught sight of Kagig spurring his horse from cover to cover to place his men. Once I thought I recognized Fred, too, over near the river-bank; but of Will or of Gloria I saw nothing.

It was obvious that if reserves were needed anywhere it would be over on that left flank by the fordable Jihun. Ephraim saw that, and proceeded to preach it like gospel to the men before consulting me. Then, arrogant in the consciousness of majority approval, he came and advised me.

"Those—ah—*hamidieh* not coming this—ah—way. We cross over to—ah—other side. Then Kagig is being pleased with us. I give orders—yes?"

He did not propose to wait for my consent, but I detained him with a hand on his shoulder. It would have taken us two hours to get into position by the river-bank.

"Find out how many of the men can ride," I ordered.

Taken by surprise he called out the inquiry without stopping to discover my purpose first. It transpired there were seventeen men who had been accustomed to horseback riding since their youth. That would leave nine men for another purpose. I separated sheep from goats, and made over the nine to Ephraim.

"You and these nine stay here," I ordered, "and hold this flank until Kagig makes a move." I did not doubt Kagig would fall back on Zeitoon as soon as he could do that with advantage. Neither did I doubt Ephraim's ability to spoil my whole plan if be should see fit. Yet I had to depend on his powers as interpreter.

There are two ways of relieving a weak wing, and the obvious one of reinforcing it is not of necessity the best. I could see through the glasses a bowl of hollow grazing ground in which the dismounted Kurds had left their horses; and I could count only five men guarding them. Most of the horses seemed to be tied head to head by the reins, but some were hobbled and grazing close together.

"Tell these seventeen men I have chosen that I propose to creep up to the enemy's horses and steal or else stampede them," I ordered.

Ephraim hesitated. Glittering eyes betrayed fear to be left out of an adventure, disgust to see his own advice ignored, and yet that he was alert to the advantage of being left with a lone command.

"But we should—ah—cross to the—ah—other side and—ah—help Kagig," he objected. Perhaps he hoped to build political influence on the basis of his own account to Kagig afterward of how be had argued for the saner course.

"Please explain what I have said—exactly!"

He continued to hesitate. I could see the Kurdish riflemen responding to orders from their rear and beginning to concentrate in the direction of our left wing. Our center, where Gloria and Will were probably concealed by rocks and foliage, poured a galling fire on them, and they had to reform, and detach a considerable company to deal with that; but two-thirds of their number surged toward our left, and if my plan was to succeed almost the chief element was time.

"But Kagig will—"

One of the men had a hide rope, very likely looted from the village we had burned. I took it from him and tied a running noose in the end. Then I made the other end fast to the roots of a tree that had been rain-washed until they projected naked over fifty feet of sheer rock.

"Now," I said, "explain what I said, or I'll hang you in sight of both sides!"

I wondered whether he would not turn the tables and hang me. I knew I would not have been willing to lessen Kagig's chances by shooting any of them if they had decided to take Ephraim's part. But the politician in the man was uppermost and he did not force the issue.

"All right, *effendi*—oh, all right!" he answered, trying to laugh the matter off.

"Explain to them, then!"

I made him do it half a dozen times, for once

we were on our way along the precipitous sides of the hills the only control I should have would be force of example, aided to some extent by the sort of primitive signals that pass muster even in a kindergarten. If they should talk Turkish to me slowly I might understand a little here and there, but to speak it myself was quite another matter; and in common with most of their countrymen, though they understood Turkish perfectly and all that went with it, they would rather eat dirt than foul their months with the language of the hated conqueror.

But, once explained, the plan was as obvious as the risk entailed, and they approved the one as swiftly as they despised the other. The Kurds below were not oblivious to the risk of reprisals from the hills, and we spent five minutes picking out the men posted to keep watch, making careful note of their positions. At the point where we decided to debouch on to the plain there were two sentries taking matters fairly easy, and I told off four men to go on ahead and attend to those as silently as might be.

Then we started—not close together, for the Kurds would certainly be looking out for an attack from the hills in force, and would not be expecting individuals—but one at a time, two Armenians leading, and the rest of them following me at intervals of more than fifty yards.

At the moment of starting I gave Ephraim another order, and within two hours owed my life and that of most of my men to his disobedience.

"You stay here with your handful, and don't budge except as Kagig moves his line! Few as you are, you can hold this flank safe if you stay firm."

He stayed firm until the last of my seventeen had disappeared around the corner of the cliff; and five minutes later I caught sight of him through the glasses, leading his following at top speed downward along a spur toward the plain. The Kurds on the lookout saw him too and, concentrating their attention on him, did not notice us when we dodged at long intervals in full sunlight across the face of a white rock.

There was little leading needed; rather, restraining, and no means of doing it. Instead of keeping the formation in which we started off, those in the rear began to overtake the men in front and, rather than disobey the order to keep wide intervals, to extend down the face of the hill, so that within fifteen minutes we were in wide-spaced skirmishing order. Then, instead of keeping along the hills, as I had intended, until we were well to the rear of the Kurdish firing-line, they turned half-left too soon, and headed in diagonal bee line toward the horses, those who had begun by leading being last now, and the last men first. Being shorter-winded than the rest of them and more tired to begin with, that arrangement soon left me a long way in the rear, dodging and crawling laboriously and stopping every now and then to watch the development of the battle. There was little to see but the flash of rifles; and they explained nothing more than that the Kurds were forcing their way very close to our center and left wing.

Not all the fighting had been done that day under organized leadership. I stumbled at one place and fell over the dead bodies of a Kurd and an Armenian, locked in a strangle-hold. That Kurd must have been bold enough to go pillaging miles in advance of his friends, for the two had been dead for hours. But the mutual hatred had not died off their faces, and they lay side by side clutching each other's throats as if passion had continued after death.

The sight of Ephraim and his party hurrying across their front toward Kagig's weak left wing had evidently convinced the Kurds that no more danger need be expected from their own left. There can have been no other possible reason why we were unobserved, for the recklessness of my contingent grew as they advanced closer to the horses, and from the rear I saw them brain one outpost with a rock and rush in and knife another with as little regard for concealment as if these two had been the only Kurds within eagle's view. Yet they were unseen by the enemy, and five minutes later we all gathered in the shelter of a semicircle of loose rocks, to regain wind for the final effort.

"Korkakma!" I panted, using about ten per cent of my Turkish vocabulary, and they laughed so loud that I cursed them for a bunch of fools. But the man nearest me chose to illustrate his feeling for Turks further by taking the corner of his jacket between thumb and finger and going through the motions of squeezing off an insect—the last, most expressive gesture of contempt.

The horses were within three hundred yards of us. On rising ground between us and the Kurdish firing-line was a little group of Turkish officers, and to our right beyond the horses was miscellaneous baggage under the guard of Kurds, of whom more than half were wounded. I could see an obviously Greek doctor bandaging a man seated on an empty ammunition box.

But our chief danger was from the mounted scoundrels who were so busy murdering women and children and wounded men half a mile away to the rear. They had come along working the covert like hunters of vermin, driving lances into every possible lurking place and no doubt skewering their own wounded on occasion, for which Armenians would afterward be blamed. We could hear them chorusing with glee whenever a lance found a victim, or when a dozen of them gave chase to some panic-stricken woman in wild flight. Through the glasses I could see two Turkish officers with them, in addition to their own nondescript "tin-plate men"; and if officers or men should get sight of us it was easy to imagine what our fate would be.

That thought, and knowledge that Gloria Vanderman and Will and Fred were engaged in an almost equally desperate venture within a mile of me (evidenced by dozens of wild bullets screaming through the air) suggested the idea of taking a longer chance than any I had thought of yet. A moment's consideration brought conviction that the effort would be worth the risk. Yet I had no way of communicating with my men!

I pointed to the Turkish officers clustered together watching the effort of their firing-line. From where we lay to the horses would be three hundred yards; from the horses to those officers would be about two hundred and fifty yards farther at an angle of something like forty degrees. Counting their orderlies and hangers-on we outnumbered that party by two to one; and "the fish starts stinking from the head" as the proverb says. With the head gone, the whole Kurdish firing-line would begin to be useless.

I tried my stammering Turkish, but the men were in no mood to be patient with efforts in that loathly tongue. None of them knew a word in English. I tried French—Italian—smattering Arabic—but they only shook their heads, and began to think nervousness was driving me out of hand. One of them laid a soothing hand on my shoulder, and repeated what sounded like a prayer.

To lose the confidence of one's men under such circumstances at that stage of the game was too much. I grew really rattled, and at random, as a desperate man will I stammered off what I wanted to say in the foreign tongue that I knew best, regardless of the fact that Armenians are not black men, and that there is not even a trace of connection between their language and anything current in Africa. Zanzibar and Armenia are as far apart as Australia and Japan, with about as much culture in common.

To my amazement a man answered in fluent Kiswahili! He had traded for skins in some barbarous district near the shore of Victoria Nyanza, and knew half a dozen Bantu languages. In a minute after that we had the plan well understood and truly laid; and, what was better, they had ceased to believe me a victim of nerves—a fact that gave me back the nerve that had been perilously close to vanishing.

We paid no more attention to the firing-line, nor to the mounted Kurds who were drawing the coverts nearer and nearer to us. It was understood that we were to sacrifice ourselves for our friends, and do the utmost damage possible before being overwhelmed. We shook hands solemnly. Two or three men embraced each other. The five who by common consent were reckoned the best rifle shots lay down side by side with me among the rocks, and the remainder began crawling out one by one on their stomachs toward the horses, with instructions to take wide open order as quickly as possible, with the idea of making the Kurds believe our numbers were greater than they really were.

When I judged they were half-way toward the horses we six opened fire on the Turkish officers. And every single one of us missed! At the sound of our volley the devoted horse-thieves rose to their feet and rushed on the horse-guards, forgetting to fire on them from sheer excitement, and as a matter of fact one of them was shot dead by a horse-guard before the rest remembered they had deadly weapons of their own.

I remedied the first outrageous error to a slight extent by killing the Turkish colonel's orderly, missing the commander himself by almost a yard. My five men all missed with their second shots, and then it was too late to pull off the complete coup we had dared to hope for. The entire staff took cover, and started a veritable hail of fire with their repeating pistols, all aimed at us, and aimed as wildly as our own shots had been.

Meanwhile the mounted Kurds at the rear had heard the firing and were coming on full pelt, yelling like red Indians. I could see, in the moment I snatched for a hurried glance in that direction, that the purpose of cutting loose and stampeding the horses was being accomplished; but even that comparatively simple task required time, and as the Kurds galloped nearer, the horses grew as nervous as the men who sought to loose them.

But conjecture and all caution were useless to us six bent on attacking the colonel and his staff. We crawled out of cover and advanced, stopping to fire one or two shots and then scrambling closer, giving away our own paucity of numbers, but increasing the chance of doing damage with each yard gained. And our recklessness had the additional advantage of making the staff reckless too. The colonel kept in close hiding, but the rest of them began dodging from place to place in an effort to outflank us from both sides, and I saw four of them bowled over within a minute. Then the remainder lay low again, and we resumed the offensive.

The next thing I remember was hearing a wild yell as our party seized a horse apiece and galloped off in front of the oncoming Kurds—straight toward Kagig's firing-line. That, and the yelling of the horsemen in pursuit drew the attention of the riflemen attacking Kagig to the fact that most of their horses were running loose and that there was imminent danger to their own rear. I only had time to get a glimpse of them breaking back, for the Turkish colonel got my range and sent a bullet ripping down the length of the back of my shooting jacket. That commenced a duel—he against me—each missing as disgracefully as if we were both beginners at the game of life or death, and I at any rate too absorbed to be aware of anything but my own plight and of oceans of unexplained noise to right and left. I knew there were galloping horses, and men yelling; but knowledge that the Turkish military rifle I was using must be wrongly sighted, and that my enemy had no such disadvantage, excluded every other thought.

I had used about half the cartridges in my bandolier when a Kurd's lance struck me a glancing blow on the back of the head. His horse collapsed on top of me, as some thundering warrior I did not see gave the stupendous finishing stroke to rider and beast at once.

There followed a period of semi-consciousness filled with enormous clamor, and upheavings, and what might have been earthquakes for lack of any other reasonable explanation, for I felt myself being dragged and shaken to and fro. Then, as the weight of the fallen horse was rolled aside there surged a tide of blissful relief that carried me over the border of oblivion.

When I recovered my senses I was astride of Rustum Khan's mare, with a leather thong around my shoulders and the Rajput's to keep me from falling. We were proceeding at an easy walk in front of a squadron of ragged-looking irregulars whom I did not recognize, toward the center of the position Kagig had held. Kagig's men were no longer in hiding, but standing about in groups; and presently I caught sight of Fred and Will and Kagig standing together, but not Gloria Vanderman. A cough immediately behind us made me turn my head. The Turkish colonel, who had fought the ridiculously futile duel with me, was coming along at the mare's tail with his hands tied behind him and a noose about his neck made fast to one of the saddle-rings.

"Much obliged, Rustum Khan!" I said by way of letting him know I was alive. "How did you get here?"

"Ha, sahib! Not going to die, then? That is good! I came because Colonel Lord Montdidier sahib sent me with a squadron of these mountain horsemen—fine horsemen they are—fit by the breath of Allah to draw steel at a Rajput's back!"

"He sent you to find me?"

"Ha, sahib. To rescue you alive if that were possible."

"How did he know where I was?"

"An Armenian by name of Ephraim came and said you had gone over to the Turks. Certain men he had with him corroborated, but three of his party kept silence. My lord sahib answered 'I have hunted, and camped, and fought beside that man—played and starved and feasted with him. No more than I myself would he go over to Turks. He must have seen an opportunity to make trouble behind the Turks' backs. Take your squadron and go find him, Rustum Khan!' And I, sahib, obeyed my lord bahadur's orders."

"Where is Lord Montdidier now?"

"Who knows, sahib. Wherever the greatest need at the moment is."

"Tell me what has happened."

"You did well, sahib. The loosing of the horses and the shooting behind their backs put fear into the Kurds. They ceased pressing on our left wing. And I—watching from behind cover on the right wing—snatched that moment to outflank them, so that they ran pell-mell. Then I saw the mounted Kurds charging up from the rear, and guessed at once where you were, sahib. The Kurds were extended, and my men in close order, so I charged and had all the best of it, arriving by God's favor in the nick of time for you, sahib. Then I took this colonel prisoner. Only once in my life have I seen a greater pile than his of empty cartridge cases beside one man. That was the pile beside you, sahib! How many men did you kill, and he kill? And who buried them?"

"Where is Miss Vanderman?" I asked, turning the subject.

"God knows! What do I know of women? Only I know this: that there is a gipsy woman bred by Satan out of sin itself, who will make things hot for any second filly in this string! Woe and a woman are one!"

Not caring to listen to the Indian's opinions of the other sex any more than he would have welcomed mine about the ladies of his own land, I made out my injuries were worse than was the case, and groaned a little, and grew silent.

So we rode without further conversation up to where Fred and Will were standing with Kagig, and as I tumbled off into Fred's arms I was greeted with a chorus of welcome that included Gloria's voice.

"That's what I call using your bean!" she laughed, in the slangy way she had whenever Will had the chance to corrupt her Boston manners.

"It feels baked," I said. "I used it to stop a Kurd's lance with. Hullo! What's the matter with you?"

"I stopped a bullet with my forearm!"

She was sitting in a sort of improvised chair between two dwarfed tree-trunks, and if ever I saw a proud young woman that was she. She wore the bloody bandage like a prize diploma.

"And I've seen your friend Monty, and he's better than the accounts of him!"

I glanced at Will, alert for a sign of jealousy.

"Monty is the one best bet!" he said. And his eyes were generous and level, as a man's who tells the whole truth.

"LO, THIS IS THE MAN..."

(PSALM 52)

Choose, ye forefathers of to-morrow, choose!
These easy ways there be
Uncluttered by the wrongs each other bears,
And warmly we shall walk who can not see
How thin some other fellow's garment wears,
Nor need to notice whose.

Choose, ye stock-owners in to-morrow, choose!
The road these others tread
Is littered deep with jetsam and the bones
Of their dishonored dead.
What altruism for defeat atones?
Have ye not much to lose?

Choose, ye inheritors of ages, choose!
What owe ye to the past?
The burly men who Magna Charta wrung
From tyranny entrenched would stand aghast
To see the ripples from that stone they flung,
They, too, had selfish views.

Choose, ye investors in the future, choose!
Ye need pick cautious odds;
To-morrow's fruit is seeded down to-day,
And unwise purpose like the unknown gods
Tempts on a wasteful way.
'Ware well what guide ye use!

XIV
"RAJPUT, I SHALL HANG YOU IF YOU MAKE MORE TROUBLE!"

WE WENT and bivouacked by the brawling Jihun under a roof of thatch, whose walls were represented by more or less upright wooden posts and débris; for Kagig would not permit anything to stand even for an hour that Turks could come and fortify. None of us believed that the repulse of that handful of Kurdish plunderers and the capture of a Turkish colonel would be the end of hostilities—rather the beginning.

Kagig, when Gloria asked him what he proposed to do with Rustum Khan's prisoner, smiled cynically and ordered him searched by two of the Zeitoonli standing guard. Rustum Khan was standing just out of low ear-shot absorbed in contemplation of the lie of the country. I noticed that Fred began to look nervous, but he did not say anything. Will was too busy fussing with Gloria's wound, making a new bandage for it and going through the quite unnecessary motions of keeping up her spirits, to observe any other phenomena. An Armenian woman named Anna, who had attached herself to Gloria because, she said, her husband and children had been killed and she might as well serve as weep, sat watching the two of them with quiet amusement.

The Turk offered no further objection than a shrug of his fatalist shoulders and a muttered remark about Ermenie and bandits. Even when the mountaineers laughed at the chink of stolen money in all his pockets he did not exhibit a trace of shame. They shook him, and pawed him, and poured out gold in little heaps on the ground (out of the magnanimity of his official heart he had doubtless left all silver coin for his *hamidieh* to pouch); but Kagig only had eyes for the papers they pulled out of his inner pocket and tossed away. He pounced on them.

"Hah!" he laughed. "There! Did I tell you? These are his orders—signed by a governor's secretary—countersigned by the governor himself—to 'set forth with his troops and rescue Armenians in the Zeitoon district.' Rescue them! Have you seen? Did you observe his noble rescue work? Here—see the orders for yourselves! Observe how the Stamboulis propose to prove their innocence after the event!"

Since they were written in Turkish they were of no conceivable use to any one but Fred and Rustum Khan. Fred glanced over them, and shouted to Rustum Khan to come and look. That was a mistake, for it called the Rajput's attention to what had been happening to his prisoner. He came striding toward us with his black beard bristling and eyes blazing with anger.

"Who searched him?" he demanded.

"He was searched by my order," Kagig answered in the calm level voice that in a man of such spirit was prophetic of explosion.

"Who gave thee leave to order him searched, Armenian?"

"I left you his money," Kagig answered with biting scorn, pointing to the little heaps of gold coin on the ground.

I had no means of knowing what peaks of friction had already been attained between the two, and it was not likely that I should instantly choose sides against the man who within the hour had saved my life at peril of his own. But Will saw matters in another light, and Fred began humming through his nose. Will left Gloria and walked straight up to Rustum Khan. He had managed to shave himself with cold Jihun water and some laundry soap, and his clean jaw suggested standards set up and sworn to since ever they gave the name of Yankee to men possessed by certain high ideals.

"Kagig needs no leave from any one to order prisoners searched!" he said, shaping each word distinctly.

Rustum Khan spluttered, and kicked at a heap of coin.

"Perhaps you have bargained for your share of all loot? I have heard that in America men—"

"Rajput!" said Kagig, looking down on him from slightly higher ground, "I will hang you if you make more trouble!"

At that I interfered. I was not the only one in Rustum Khan's debt; it was likely his brilliant effort at the critical moment had saved our whole fighting line. Besides, I saw the Turk grinning to himself with satisfaction at the rift in our good will.

"Suppose we refer this dispute to Monty," I proposed, reasoning that if it should ever get as far as Monty, tempers would have died away meanwhile. Not that Monty could not have handled the problem, tempers and all.

"I refer no points of honor," growled the Rajput. "I have been insulted."

"Rot!" exclaimed Fred, getting to his feet. When his usually neat beard has not been trimmed for a day or two he looks more truculent than he really is. "I've been listening. The insolence was on the other side."

"Do you deny Kagig's right to question prisoners?" I asked, thinking I saw a way out of the mess.

"Can I not question him?" Rustum Khan turned on me with a gesture that made it clear he held me to no friendship on account of service rendered.

He strode toward his prisoner, with heaven knows what notion in his head, but Fred interposed himself. The likeliest thing at that moment was a blow by one or the other that would have banished any chance of a returning reign of reason. Rustum Khan turned his back to the Turk and thrust out his chest toward Fred as if daring him to strike.

Even the kites seemed to expect bloodshed and circled nearer.

It was Gloria who cut the Gordian knot. It was her unwounded hand, not Fred's, that touched the Rangar's breast.

"Rustum Khan," she said, "I think better of you than to believe you would take advantage of our ignorance. You're a soldier. We are only civilians trying to help a tortured nation. We know nothing of Rajput customs. Won't you go to Lord Montdidier and tell him about it, and ask him to decide? We'll all obey Monty, you know."

Rustum Khan looked down at her bandaged wrist, and then into violet eyes that were not in the least degree afraid of him but only looking diligently for the honor he so boasted.

"Who can refuse a beautiful young woman?" he said, beginning to melt. But he refused to meet her eyes again, or even to acknowledge our existence.

"I give you the prisoner!" He made her a motion of arrogant extravagance with his right hand as if performing the act of transfer. Then he turned on his heel with a little simultaneous mock salute, and striding to his bay mare, mounted and rode away.

Kagig took over the prisoner at once without comment and began to question him under a tree twenty yards away, paying no attention to the riflemen who matched one another, laughing, for the plundered money. We four went back to the shelter of the thatch roof, for the plan was to remain behind with the company of Zeitoonli whom Kagig had placed carefully at vantage points, and give stragglers a chance to save themselves before we resumed the journey to Zeitoon.

Naturally enough, Rustum Khan and his fiery unreason was the subject we discussed, and Fred laid law down as to how he should be dealt with whenever the chance should come to bring him to book. But Rustum Khan was a bagatelle compared to what was coming, if we had only known it. While we talked I saw Gregor Jhaere, the *attaman* of gypsies, ride down the track on a brown mule and dismount within ten yards of Kagig. He hobbled his mule, and went and sat close by Kagig and the Turk, engaging in a three-cornered talk with them. Kagig seemed to have expected him, for there was no sign of greeting or surprise.

There was nothing disturbing about Gregor's arrival on the scene; he was evidently helping Kagig to cross-examine the Turk and check up facts. Within their limits gypsies are about the best spies obtainable because of their ability to take advantage of credulity and their own immeasurable unbelief in protest or appearances. It was the individual who followed Gregor at a distance, and dismounted from a gray stallion quite a long way off in order not to draw attention to herself, who made my blood turn cold. I caught sight of Maga Jhaere first because the others had their backs toward her. Then the expression of my face brought Fred to his feet. By that time Magi had vanished out of view unaware that any one had seen her, creeping like a pantheress from rock to rock.

"What's the matter?" Fred demanded, sitting down again, ill-tempered with himself for being startled.

"Maga Jhaere!"

"How exciting!" said Gloria. "I'm crazy to meet her."

But Will looked less excited and more anxious than I had ever seen him, and we all three laughed.

"All right!" he said. "I tell you it's no joke. That woman believes she's got her hooks in."

We tried to go on talking naturally, but lapsed into uncomfortable silence as the minutes dragged by and no Maga put in her appearance. Fred began humming through his nose again in that ridiculous way that he thinks seems unconcerned, but that makes his best friends yearn to smite him hip and thigh.

"I guess you were mistaken," Will said at last, spreading out his shoulders with relief at the mere suggestion. But I was facing the direction of Zeitoon, as he was not, and again the expression of my face betrayed the facts.

There were two large stones leaning together, with a small triangular gap between them, less than thirty feet from where we sat. In that gap I could see a pair of eyes, and nothing else. They had almost exactly the expression of a panther's that is stalking, not its quarry, but its mortal foe. In spite of having seen Maga approaching, I would have believed them an animal's eyes, only that from experience I knew an animal's eyes betray fear and anger without reason, whereas these blazed with the desperate reasoning that holds fear in contempt. Panthers can hate, be afraid, sweep fear aside with anger, and plan painstakingly for murderous attack; but it is only behind human eyes that one may recognize the murder—purpose based on argument.

"I see her," I said. "I suspect she's got a pistol, and—"

I had not known until that moment that the short hair was standing up the back of my head, but I felt it go down with a creepy cold chill as I spoke. Then once more it rose. Knowing she was seen and recognized, Maga got to her feet and stood on the larger of the two stones, looking down on us. Her hands were on her hips, and I could see no weapon, but her lips moved in voiceless imprecation.

"Are you Maga Jhaere?" asked Gloria, first of us all to recover some measure of self-command.

Maga nodded. She was barefooted, clothed only in bodice and leather jacket and a rather short ocher-colored skirt that blew in the gaining wind and showed the outline of her lithe young figure. Her long black hair billowed and galloped in the wind behind her.

"I am Maga Jhaere," she said slowly, addressing Gloria. "Who are you?"

"My name is Gloria Vanderman."

"And that man beside you—who is he?"

Gloria did not answer. Will looked more embarrassed than the devil caught in daylight, and Fred recovered his mental equilibrium sufficiently to chuckle.

"Is he your husband?"

"No."

"Then what you want with 'im?"

No one said a word. Only, Fred made a movement with his hand behind him that Maga noticed and spurned with a toss of her chin.

"You coming to Zeitoon?"

Gloria nodded. Glancing over toward Kagig I saw that he was aware of Maga and was watching her out of the corner of his eye while he talked with Gregor and the Turk. They were both getting angry with the Turk and using gestures suggestive of impending agony by way of emphasis. The Turk was growing fidgety.

Maga spread her arms out as if she were embracing all the universe and called it hers.

"Then—if you ar-re coming to Zeitoon—you choose first a 'usband. There are—many 'usbands. Some 'ave lost a wife—some 'ave sick wife—some not yet never 'ad no wife. Plenty Armenians—also two other men there—but you let that one—Will—alone! Choose a 'usband—marry 'im—then you come to Zeitoon! If you come without a 'usband—I will keel you—do you understand?"

"Now then, America!" grinned Fred in a stage aside that Maga could hear as clearly as if it had been intended for her. "Let's see the eagle scream for liberty!"

"Eagle scream?" said Maga, almost screaming herself. "What you know about eagles? You ol' fool! That man Will is thinking you ar-re 'is frien'. You ar-re not 'is frien'! Let 'im come with me, an' I will show 'im what are eagles—what is freedom—what is knowledge—what is life! I know. You ol' fool, you not know! You ol' fool, you marry that woman—then you can bring 'er to Zeitoon an' she is safe! Otherwise—"

She reached in the bosom of her blouse and drew out, not the mother-o'-pearl-plated pistol that I feared, but a knife with an eighteen-inch blade of glittering steel. Instantly Fred covered her with his own repeater, but she laughed in his face.

"You ol' fool, you ar-re afraid to shoot me!"

If she meant that Fred would feel squeamish about shooting before she hurled the knife, then she was certainly right. But she knew better than to make one preliminary motion. And Kagig knew better than to permit further pleasantries. I saw him whisper to Gregor, and the gipsy *attaman* started on hands and knees to creep round behind her. But Maga's eyes were practiced like those of all other wild creatures in detecting movement behind her as well as in front. She spat, and gave vent to a final ultimatum.

"You 'ave 'eard. I said—you let that man Will Yerr-kees alone! An' don't you dare come to Zeitoon without a 'usband!"

Then she turned and dodged Gregor, and ran for her gray stallion—mounted the savage brute with a leap from six feet away, and rode like the wind toward the gut of the pass that shut off Zeitoon from our view. A minute later a shell from a small-bore cannon screamed overhead, and burst a hundred yards beyond us on a sheet of rock.

"Not bad for a ranging shot!" said Fred, suddenly as self-possessed as if the world never held such a thing as an untamed woman.

"Observe, you sportsmen all!" Kagig exclaimed, getting to his feet. "The Turkish nobility are proceeding to rescue poor Armenians. Behold, their charity comes even from the cannon's mouth! It is time to go now, lest it overtake us! No cannon can come in sight of Zeitoon. Follow me."

With his usual sudden oblivion of everything

but the main objective Kagig mounted and rode away, followed by Gregor in charge of the prisoner, and by a squadron or so of mounted Zeitoonli who attempted no formation but came cantering as each detachment realized that their leader was on the move. We found ourselves last, without an armed man between us and the enemy, although without a doubt there were still dozens of fugitive poor wretches who had not had the courage or perhaps the strength to overtake us yet.

Kagig had had the forethought to leave comparatively fresh mules for us to ride, and there was not any particular reason for hurry. Will went ahead, with Gloria and Anna beside him on one mule—Gloria laughing him out of countenance because of his nervousness on her account, but he insistent on the danger in case of repeated gun-fire. Fred rode slowly beside me in the rear, for we still hoped to encourage a few stray fugitives to come out of their hiding holes and follow us to safety.

A second cannon shot, not nearly so well aimed as the first had been, went screaming over toward our left and landed without bursting among low bushes. A third and a fourth followed it, and the last one did explode. That was plainly too much for some one who had dodged into hiding when the second shot fell; we saw him come rushing out from cover like a lunatic, unconscious of direction and only intent on shielding the top of his head with his hands.

"Is the poor devil hurt?" I said, wondering. But Fred broke into a roar of laughter; and he is not a heartless man—merely gifted more than usual with the hunter's eye that recognizes sex and species of birds and animals at long range. I can see farther than Fred can, but at recognizing details swiftly I am a blind bat compared to him.

"The martyred biped!" he laughed. "Peter Measel by the God of happenings!"

We rode over toward him, and Peter it was, running with his eyes shut. He screamed when we stopped him, and sobbed instead of talking when we pulled him in between our mules and offered him two stirrup leathers to hold. He seemed to think that standing between the mules would protect him from the artillery fire, and as we were not in any hurry we took advantage of that delusion to let him recover a modicum of nerve.

And the moment that began to happen he was the same sweet Peter Measel with the same assurance of every other body's wickedness and his own divinity, only with something new in his young life to add poignancy.

"What were you doing there?" demanded Fred, as we got him to towing along between us at last.

"I was looking for her."

"For whom?"

"For Maga Jhaere."

Fred allowed his ribs to shake in silent laughter that annoyed the mule, and we had to catch Measel all over again because the beast's crude objections filled the martyred biped full of the desire to run.

"Somebody must save that girl!" he panted. "And who else can do it? Who else is there?"

"There's only you!" Fred agreed, choking down his mirth.

"I'm glad you agree with me. At least you have that much blessedness, Mr. Fred. D'you know that girl was willing to be a murderess? Yes! She tried to murder Rustum Khan. Rustum Khan ought to be hanged, for he is a villain—a black villain! But she must not have blood on her hands—no, no!"

"Why didn't she murder him?" demanded Fred. "Qualms at the last moment?"

"No. I'm sorry to say no. She has no God-likeness yet. But that will come. She will repent. I shall see to that. It was I who prevented her, and she all but murdered me! She would have murdered me, but Kagig held her wrist; and to punish her he gave an order that I should preach to her morning, afternoon, and evening—three times a day. So I had my opportunity. There was a guard of gipsy women set to see that she obeyed."

"Continue," said Fred. "What happened?"

"She broke away, and came down to see the fighting."

"Why did you follow her? Weren't you afraid?"

"Oh, Mr. Fred, if you only knew! Yet I felt impelled to find her. I could not trust her out of sight."

"Why not? She seems fairly well able to look after herself."

"Oh, I can not allow wickedness. I must make it to cease! It entered my head that she intended to find Kagig!"

"Well? Why not?"

"Oh, Mr. Fred—tell me! You may know—you perhaps as well as any one, for you are such an ungodly man! What are her relations with Kagig? Does he—is he—is there wickedness between them?"

"Dashed if I know. She's a gipsy. He's a fine half-savage. Why should it concern you?"

"Oh, I could not endure it! It would break my heart to believe it!"

"Then why think about it?"

"How can I help it? I love her! Oh, I love her, Mr. Fred! I never loved a woman in all my life before. It would break my heart if she were to be betrayed into open sin by Kagig! Oh, what shall I do? What shall I do? I love her! What shall I do?"

"Do?" said Fred, looking forward in imagination to new worlds of humor, "why—make love, if you love her! Make hot love and strong!"

"Will you help me, Mr. Fred?" the biped stammered. "You see, she's rather wild—a little unconventional—and I've never made love even to a sempstress. Will you help me?"

"Certainly!" Fred chuckled. "Certainly. I'll guarantee to marry her to you if you'll dig up the courage. Have you a ring?"

Peter Measel produced a near-gold ring with a smirk almost of recklessness, a plain gold ring whose worn appearance called to mind the finger taken from a dead Kurd's cartridge pouch. It may be that Measel bought it, but neither Fred nor I spoke to him again, for half an hour.

THE REBEL'S HYMN

The seeds that swell within enwrapping mould,
Gray buds that color faintly in the northing sun,
Deep roots that lengthen after winter's rest,
The flutter of year's youth in April's breast
As young leaves in the warming hour unfold—
These and my heart are one!

Go dam the river-course with carted earth;
Or bind with iron bands that riven stone
That century on century has slept
Until into its heart a tendril crept,
And in the quiet majesty of birth
New nature broke into her own!
Or bid the sun stand still! Or fashion wings
To herd the heaven's stars and make them be
Subservient to will and rule and whim!
Or rein the winds, and still the ocean's hymn!
More surely ye shall manage all these things
Than chain the Life in me!

Great mountains shedding the reluctant snow,
Vision of the finish of the thing begun,
Spirit of the beauty of the torrent's song,
Unconquerable peal of carillon,
And secrets that in conquest overflow—
These and my heart are one!

XV
"SCENERY TO BURST THE HEART!"

YET ANOTHER night we were destined to spend on the Zeitoon road, for we had not the heart to leave behind us the stragglers who balked fainting in the gut of the pass. Some were long past the stage where anything less than threats could make impression on them, and only able to go forward in a dull dream at the best. But there were numbers of both men and women unexpectedly capable of extremes of heroism, who took the burden of misery upon themselves and exhibited high spirits based on no evident excuse. Nothing could overwhelm those, nothing discourage them.

"To Zeitoon!" somebody shouted, as if that were the very war-cry of the saints of God. Then in a splendid bass voice he began to sing a hymn, and some women joined him. So Fred Oakes fell to his old accustomed task, and played them marching accompaniments on his concertina until his fingers ached and even he, the enthusiast, loathed the thing's bray. In one way and another a little of the pall of misery was lifted.

Kagig sent us down bread and *yoghourt* at nightfall, so that those who had lived thus far did not die of hunger. Women brought the food on their heads in earthen crocks—splendid, good-looking women with fearless eyes, who bore the heavy loads as easily as their mountain men-folk carried rifles. They did not stay to gossip, for we had no news but the stale old story of murder and plunder; and their news was short and to the point.

"Come along to Zeitoon!" was the burden of it, carried with a singsong laugh. "Zeitoon is ready for anything!"

Before we had finished eating, each two of them gathered up a poor wretch from our helpless crowd and strode away into the mountains with a heavier load than that they brought.

"Come along to Zeitoon!" they called back to us. But even Fred's concertina, and the hymns of the handful who were not yet utterly spent, failed to get them moving before dawn.

We did not spend the night unguarded, although no armed men lay between us and the enemy. We could hear the Kurds shouting now and then, and once, when I climbed a high rock, I caught sight of the glow of their bivouac fires. Imagination conjured up the shrieks of tortured victims, for we had all seen enough of late to know what would happen to any luckless straggler they might have caught and brought to make sport by the fires. But there was no imagination about the calls of Kagig's men, posted above us on invisible dark crags and ledges to guard against surprise. We slept in comfortable consciousness that a sleepless watch was being kept—until fleas came out of the ground by battalions, divisions and army corps, making rest impossible.

But even the flea season was a matter of indifference to the hapless folk who lay around us, and although we fussed and railed we could not persuade them to go forward before dawn broke. Then, though, they struggled to their feet and started without argument. But an hour after the start we reached the secret of the safety of Zeitoon, without which not even the valor of its defenders could have withstood the overwhelming numbers of the Turks for all those scores of years; and there was new delay.

The gut of the pass rose toward Zeitoon at a sharp incline—a ramp of slippery wet clay, half a mile long, reaching across from buttress to buttress of the impregnable hills. It was more than a ridden mule could do to keep its feet on the slope, and we had to dismount. It was almost as much as we ourselves could do to make progress with the aid of sticks, and we knew at last what Kagig had meant by his boast that nothing on wheels could approach his mountain home. The poor wretches who had struggled so far with us simply gave up hope and sat down, proposing to die there. The martyred biped copied them, except that they were dry-eyed and he shed tears. "To think that I should come to this—that I should come to this!" he sobbed. Yet the fool must have come down by that route, and have gone up that way once.

We should have been in a quandary but for the sound of axes ringing in the mountain forest on our left—a dense dark growth of pine and other evergreens commencing about a hundred feet above the naked rock that formed the northerly side of the gorge. Where there were axes at work there was in all likelihood a road that men could march along, and our refugees sat down to let us do the prospecting.

"It would puzzle Napoleon to bring cannon over this approach, and the Turks don't breed Napoleons nowadays!" Fred shouted cheerily. "Give me a hundred good men and I'll hold this pass forever! Wait here while I scout for a way round."

He tried first along the lower edge of the line of timber, encouraged by ringing axes, falling trees, and men shouting in the distance.

"It looks as if there once had been a road here," he shouted down to us, "but nothing less than fire would clear it now, and everything is sopping wet. I never saw such a tangle of roots and rocks. A dog couldn't get thought!"

Will volunteered to cross to the right-hand side and hunt over there for a practicable path. Gloria stayed beside me, and I had my first opportunity to talk with her alone. She was very pale from the effects of the wound in her wrist, which was painful enough to draw her young face and make her eyes burn feverishly. Even so, one realized that as an old woman she would still be beautiful.

I watched the eagles for a minute or two, wondering what to say to her, and she did not seem to object to silence, so that I forced an opening at last as clumsily as Peter Measel might have done it.

"What is it about Will that makes all women love him?" I asked her.

"Oh, do they all love him?"

"Looks like it!" said I.

She still wore the bandolier they had stripped from the man with the bandaged feet, although Will had relieved her of the rifle's weight. To the bottom of the bandolier she had tied the little bag of odds and ends without which few western women will venture a mile from home. Opening that she produced a small round mirror about twice the size of a dollar piece, and offered it to me with a smile that disarmed the rebuke.

"Perhaps it's his looks," she suggested.

I took the mirror and studied what I saw in it. In spite of a cracking headache due to that and the gaining sun (for I had lost my hat when the Kurd rode me down with his lance) the episode of Rustum Khan carrying me back out of death's door on his bay mare had not lingered in memory. There had been too much else to think about. Now for the first time I realized how near that lance-point must have come to finishing the chapter for me. I had washed in the Jihun when we bivouacked, but had not shaved; later on, my scalp had bled anew, so that in addition to unruly hair tousled and matted with dry blood I had a week-old beard to help make me look like a graveyard ghoul.

"I beg pardon!" I said simply, handing her the mirror back.

At that she was seized with regret for the unkindness, and utterly forgot that I had blundered like a bullock into the sacred sanctuary of her newborn relationship to Will.

"Oh, I don't know which of you is best!" she said, taking my hand with her unbandaged one. "You are great unselfish splendid men. Will has told me all about you! The way you have always stuck to your friend Monty through thick and thin—and the way you are following him now to help these tortured people—oh, I know what you are—Will has told me, and I'm proud—"

The embarrassment of being told that sort of thing by a young and very lovely woman, when newly conscious of dirt and blood and half-inch-long red whiskers, was apparently not sufficient for the mirth of the exacting gods of those romantic hills. There came interruption in the form of a too-familiar voice.

"Oh, that's all right, you two! Make the most of it! Spoon all you want to! My girl's in the clutches of an outlaw! Kiss her if you want to—I won't mind!"

I dropped her hand as if it were hot lead. As a matter of fact I had hardly been conscious of holding it.

"Oh, no, don't mind me!" continued the "martyred biped" in a tone combining sarcasm, envy and impudence.

"Shall I kill him?" I asked.

"No! no!" she said. "Don't be violent—don't—"

Peter Measel, whom we had inevitably utterly forgotten, was sitting up with his back propped against a stone and his legs stretched straight in front of him, enjoying the situation with all the curiosity of his unchastened mind. I hove a lump of clay at him, but missed, and the effort made my headache worse.

"If you think you can frighten me into silence you're mistaken!" he sneered, getting up and crawling behind the rock to protect himself. But it needed more than a rock to hide him from the fury that took hold of me and sent me in pursuit in spite of Gloria's remonstrance.

Viewed as revenge my accomplishment was pitiful, for I had to chase the poor specimen for several minutes, my headache growing worse at every stride, and he yelling for mercy like a cur-dog shown the whip, while the Armenians—women and little children as well as men—looked on with mild astonishment and Gloria objected volubly. He took to the clay slope at last in hope that his light weight would give him the advantage; and there at last I caught him, and clapped a big gob of clay in his mouth to stop his yelling.

Even viewed as punishment the achievement did not amount to much. I kicked him down the clay slope, and he was still blubbering and picking dirt out of his teeth when Will shouted that he had found a foot-track.

"Do you understand why you've been kicked?" I demanded.

"Yes. You're afraid I'll tell Mr. Yerkes!"

"Oh, leave him!" said Gloria. "I'm sorry you touched him. Let's go!"

"It was as much your fault as his, young woman!" snarled the biped, getting crabwise out of my reach. "You'll all be sorry for this before I'm through with you!"

I was sorry already, for I had had experience enough of the world to know that decency and manners are not taught to that sort of specimen in any other way than by letting him go the length of his disgraceful course. Carking self-contempt must be trusted to do the business for him in the end. Gloria was right in the first instance. I should have let him alone.

However, it was not possible to take his threat seriously, and more than any man I ever met he seemed to possess the knack of falling out of mind. One could forget him more swiftly than the birds forget a false alarm. I don't believe any of us thought of him again until that night in Zeitoon.

The path Will had discovered was hardly a foot wide in places, and mules could only work their way along by rubbing hair off their flanks against the rock wall that rose nearly sheer on the right hand. From the point of view of an invading army it was no approach at all, for one man with a rifle posted on any of the overhanging crags could have held it against a thousand until relieved. It was a mystery why Kagig, or some one else, had not left a man at the foot of the clay slope to tell us about this narrow causeway; but doubtless Kagig had plenty to think about.

He and most of his men had gone struggling up the clay slope, as we could tell by the state of the going. But they were old hands at it and knew the trick of the stuff. We had all our work cut out to shepherd our poor stragglers along the track Will found, and even the view of Zeitoon when we turned round the last bend and saw the place jeweled in the morning mist did not do much to increase the speed.

As Kagig had once promised us, it was "scenery to burst the heart!" Not even the Himalayas have anything more ruggedly beautiful to show, glistening in mauve and gold and opal, and enormous to the eye because the summits all look down from over blowing cloud-banks.

There were moss-grown lower slopes, and waterfalls plunging down wet ledges from the loins of rain-swept majesty; pine trees looming blue through a soft gray fog, and winds whispering to them, weeping to them, moving the mist back and forth again; shadows of clouds and eagles lower yet, moving silently on sunny slopes. And up above it all was snow-dazzling, pure white, shading off into the cold blue of infinity.

Men clad in goat-skin coats peered down at us from time to time from crags that looked inaccessible, shouting now and then curt recognition before leaning again on a modern rifle to resume the ancient vigil of the mountaineer, which is beyond the understanding of the plains-man because it includes attention to all the falling water voices, and the whispering of heights and deeps.

We came on Zeitoon suddenly, rising out of a gorge that was filled with ice, or else a raging torrent, for six months of the year. Over against the place was a mountainside so exactly suggesting painted scenery that the senses refused to believe it real, until the roar and thunder of the Jihun tumbling among crags dinned into the ears that it was merely wonderful, and not untrue.

The one approach from the southward—that gorge up which we trudged—was overlooked all along its length by a hundred inaccessible fastnesses from which it seemed a handful of riflemen could have disputed that right of way forever. The only other line of access that we could see was by a wooden bridge flung from crag to crag three hundred feet high across the Jihun; and the bridge was overlooked by buildings and rocks from which a hail of lead could have been made to sweep it at short range.

Zeitoon itself is a mountain, next neighbor to the Beirut Dagh, not as high, nor as inaccessible; but high enough, and inaccessible enough to give further pause to its would-be conquerors. Not in anything resembling even rows, but in lawless disorder from the base to the shoulder of the mountain, the stone and wooden houses go piling skyward, overlooking one another's roofs, and each with an unobstructed view of endless distances. The picture was made infinitely lovely by wisps of blown mist, like hair-lines penciled in the violet air.

Distances were all foreshortened in that atmosphere, and it was mid-afternoon before we came to a halt at last face to face with blank wall. The track seemed to have been blocked by half the mountain sitting down across it. We sat down to rest in the shadow of the shoulder of an overhanging rock, and after half an hour some one looked down on us, and whistled shrilly. Kagig with a rifle across his knees looked down from a height of a hundred and fifty feet, and laughed like a man who sees the bitter humor of the end of shams.

"Welcome!" he shouted between his hands. And his voice came echoing down at us from wall to wall of the gorge. Five minutes later he sent a man to lead us around by a hidden track that led upward, sometimes through other houses, and very often over roofs, across ridiculously tiny yards, and in between walls so closely set together that a mule could only squeeze through by main force.

We stabled the mules in a shed the man showed us, and after that Kagig received us four, and Anna, Gloria's self-constituted maid, in his own house. It was bare of nearly everything but sheer necessities, and he made no apology, for he had good taste, and perfect manners if you allowed for the grim necessity of being curt and the strain of long responsibility.

A small bench took the place of a table in the main large room. There was a fireplace with a wide stone chimney at one end, and some stools, and also folded skins intended to be sat on, and shiny places on the wall where men in goat-skin coats had leaned their backs.

Two or three of the gipsy women were hanging about outside, and one of the gypsies who had been with him in the room in the khan at Tarsus appeared to be filling the position of servitor. He brought us yoghurt in earthenware bowls—extremely cool and good it was; and after we had done I saw him carry down a huge mess more of it to the house below us, where many of the stragglers we had brought along were quartered by Kagig's order.

"Where's Monty?" Fred demanded as soon as we entered the room.

"Presently!" Kagig answered—rather irritably I thought. He seemed to have adopted Monty as his own blood brother, and to resent all other claims on him.

The afternoon was short, for the shadow of the surrounding mountains shut us in. Somebody lighted a fire in the great open chimney-place, and as we sat around that to revel in the warmth that rests tired limbs better than sleep itself, Kagig strode out to attend to a million things—as the expression of his face testified.

Then in came Maga, through a window, with self-betrayal in manner and look of having been watching us ever since we entered. She went up to Will, who was squatted on folded skins by the chimney corner, and stood beside him, claiming him without a word. Her black hair hung down to her waist, and her bare feet, not cut or bruised like most of those that walk the hills unshod, shone golden in the firelight. I looked about for Peter Measel, expecting a scene, but he had taken himself off, perhaps in search of her.

She had eyes for nobody but Gloria, and no smile for any one. Gloria stared back at her, fascinated.

"You married?" she asked; and Gloria shook her head. "You 'eard me, what I said back below there!"

Gloria nodded.

"You sing?"

"Sometimes."

"You dance?"

"Oh, yes. I love it."

"Ah! You shall sing—you shall dance—against me! First you sing—then I sing. Then you dance—then I dance—to-night—you understan'? If I sing better as you sing—an' if I dance better as you dance—then I throw you over Zeitoon bridge, an' no one interfere! But if you sing better as I sing—an' if you dance better as I dance—then you shall make a servant of me; for I know you will be too big fool an' too chicken 'earted to keel me, as I would keel you! You understan'?"

It rather looked as if an issue would have to be forced there and then, but at that minute Gregor entered, and drove her out with an oath and terrific gesture, she not seeming particularly afraid of him, but willing to wait for the better chance she foresaw was coming. Gregor made no explanation or apology, but fastened down the leather window-curtain after her and threw more wood on the fire.

Then back came Kagig.

"Where the devil's Monty?" Fred demanded.

"Come!" was the only answer. And we all got up and followed him out into the chill night air, and down over three roofs to a long shed in which lights were burning. All the houses—on every side of us were ahum with life, and small wonder, for Zeitoon was harboring the refugees from all the district between there and Tarsus, to say nothing of fighting men who came in from the hills behind to lend a hand. But we were bent on seeing Monty at last, and had no patience for other matters.

However, it was only the prisoners he had led us out to see, and nothing more.

"Look, see!" he said, opening the heavy wooden door of the shed as an armed sentry made way for him. (Those armed men of Zeitoon did not salute one another, but preserved a stoic attitude that included recognition of the other fellow's right to independence, too.) "Look in there, and see, and tell me—do the Turks treat Armenian prisoners that way?"

We entered, and walked down the length of the dim interior, passing between dozens of prisoners lying comfortably enough on skins and blankets. As far as one could judge, they had been fed well, and they did not wear the look of neglect or ill-treatment. At the end, in a little pen all by himself, was the colonel whom Rustum Khan had made a present of to Gloria.

"What's the straw for?" Fred demanded.

"Ask him!" said Kagig. "He understands! If there should be treachery the straw will be set alight, and he shall know how pigs feel when they are roasted alive! Never fear—there will be no treachery!"

We followed him back to his own house, he urging us to make good note of the prisoners' condition, and to bear witness before the world to it afterward.

"The world does not know the difference between Armenians and Turks!" he complained again and again.

Once again we arranged ourselves about his open chimney-place, this time with Kagig on a foot-stool in the midst of us. Heat, weariness, and process of digestion were combining to make us drowsily comfortable, and I, for one, would have fallen asleep where I sat. But at last the long-awaited happened, and in came Monty striding like a Norman, dripping with dew, and clean from washing in the icy water of some mountain torrent.

"Oh, hello, Didums!" Fred remarked, as if they had parted about an hour ago. "You long-legged rascal, you look as if you'd been having the time of your life!"

"I have!" said Monty. And after a short swift stare at him Fred looked glum. Those two men understood each other as the clapper understands the bell.

"IT WAS VERY GOOD"

(GENESIS 1:31)

I saw these shambles in my youth, and said
There is no God! No Pitiful presides
Over such obsequies as these. The end
Alike is darkness whether foe or friend,
Beast, man or flower the event abides.
There is no heaven for the hopeful dead—
No better haven than forgetful sod
That smothers limbs and mouth and ears and eyes,
And with those, love and permanence and strife
And vanity and laughter that they thought was life,
Making mere compost of the one who dies.
To whose advantage? Nay, there is no God!
But He, whose other name is Pitiful, was pleased
By melting gentleness whose measures broke
The ramps of ignorance and keeps of lust,
Tumbling alike folly and the fool to dust,
To teach me womanhood until there spoke
Still voices inspiration had released,
And I heard truly. All the voices said:
Out of departed yesterday is grown to-day;
Out of to-day to-morrow surely breaks;
Out of corruption the inspired awakes;
Out of existence earth-clouds roll away
And leave all living, for there are no dead!

XVI
"WHAT CARE I FOR MY BELLY, SAHIB, IF YOU BREAK MY HEART?"

After we had made room for Monty before the fire and some one had hung his wet jacket up to dry, we volleyed questions at him faster than he could answer. He sat still and let us finish, with fingers locked together over his crossed knee and, underneath the inevitable good humor, a rather puzzled air of wishing above all things to understand our point of view. Over and over again I have noticed that trait, although he always tried to cover it under an air of polite indifference and easy tolerance that was as opaque to a careful observer as Fred's attempts at cynicism.

In the end he answered the last question first.

"My agreement with Kagig?"

"Yes, tell them!" put in Kagig. "If I should, they would say I lied!"

"It's nothing to speak of," said Monty offhandedly. "It dawned on our friend here that I have had experience in some of the arts of war. I proposed to him that if he would take a force and go to find you, I would help him to the limit without further condition. That's all."

"All, you ass? Didums, I warned you at the time when you let them make you privy councilor that you couldn't ever feel free again to kick over traces! Dammit, man, you can be impeached by parliament!"

"Quite so, Fred. I propose that parliament shall have to do something at last about this state of affairs."

"You'll end up in an English jail, and God help you!—social position gone—milked of your last pound to foot the lawyers' bills—otherwise they'll hang you!"

"Let 'em hang me after I'm caught! I've promised. Remember what Byron did for Greece? I don't suppose his actual fighting amounted to very much, but he brought the case of Greece to the attention of the public. Public opinion did the rest, badly, I admit, but better badly and late than never. I'm in this scrimmage, Fred, until the last bell rings and they hoist my number."

"Fine!" exclaimed Gloria, jumping to her feet. "So am I in it to a finish!"

Monty smiled at her with understanding and approval.

"Almost my first duty, Miss Vanderman," he said kindly, "will be to arrange that you can not possibly come to harm or be prejudiced by any course the rest of us may decide on."

"Quite so!" Will agreed with a grin, and Fred began chuckling like a schoolboy at a show.

"Nonsense!" she answered hotly. "I've come to harm already—see, I'm wounded—I've been fighting—I'm already prejudiced as you call it! If you're an outlaw, so am I!"

She flourished her bandaged wrist and looked like Joan of Arc about to summon men to sacrifice. But the argument ready on her lips was checked suddenly. The night was without wind, yet the outer door burst open exactly as if a sudden hurricane had struck it, and Maga entered with a lantern in her hand. She tried to kick the door shut again, but it closed on Peter Measel who had followed breathlessly, and she turned and banged his head with the bottom of the lantern until the glass shattered to pieces.

"That fool!" she shouted. "Oh, that fool!" Then she let him come in and close the door, giving him the broken lantern to hold, which he did very meekly, rubbing the crown of his head with the other hand; and she stood facing the lot of us with hands on her hips and a fine air of despising every one of us. But I noticed that she kept a cautious eye on Kagig, who in return paid very little attention to her.

"Fight?" she exclaimed, pointing at Gloria. "What does she know about fighting? If she can fight,—let her fight me! I stand ready—I wait for 'er! Give 'er a knife, an' I will fight 'er with my bare 'ands!"

Gloria turned pale and Will laid a hand on her shoulder, whispering something that brought the color back again.

"Maga!"

Kagig said that one word in a level voice, but the effect was greater than if he had pointed a pistol. The fire died from her eyes and she nodded at him simply. Then her eyes blazed again, although she looked away from Gloria toward a window. The leather blind was tied down at the corners by strips of twisted hide.

She began to jabber in the gipsy tongue—then changed her mind and spat it out in English for our joint benefit.

"All right. She is nothing to do with me, that woman, and she shall come to a rotten end, I know, an' that is enough. But there is some one listening! Not a woman—not with spunk enough to be a woman! That dirty horse-pond drinking unshaven black bastard Rustum Khan is outside listening! You think 'e is busy at the fortifying? Then I tell you, No, 'e is not! 'E is outside listening!"

The surprising answer to that assertion was a heavy saber thrust between the window-frame and blind and descending on the thong. Next followed Rustum Khan's long boot. Then came the man himself with dew all over his upbrushed beard, returning the saber to its scabbard with an accompanying apologetic motion of the head.

"Aye, I was listening!" He spoke as one unashamed. "Umm Kulsum" (that was his fancy name for Maga) "spoke truth for once! I came from the fortifying, where all is finished that can be done to-night. I have been the rounds. I have inspected everything. I report all well. On my way hither I saw Umm Kulsum, with that jackal trotting at her heel—he made a scornful gesture in the direction of Peter Measel, who winced perceptibly, at which Fred Oakes chuckled and nudged me—"and I followed Umm Kulsum, to observe what harm she might intend."

"Black pig!" remarked Maga, but Rustum Khan merely turned his splendid back a trifle more toward her. His color, allowing for the black beard, was hardly darker than hers.

"Why should I not listen, since my heart is in the matter? Lord sahib—Colonel sahib bahadur!—take back those words before it is too late! Undo the promise made to this Armenian! What is he to thee? Set me instead of thee, sahib! What am I? I have no wives, no lands any longer since the money-lenders closed their clutches on my eldest son, no hope, nor any fellowship with kings to lose! But I can fight, as thou knowest! Give me, sahib, to redeem thy promise, and go thou home to England!"

"Sit down, Rustum Khan!"

"But, sahib—"

"Sit down!" Monty repeated.

"I will not see thee sacrificed for this tribe of ragged people, Colonel sahib!"

Monty rose to his feet slowly. His face was an enigma. The Rajput stood at attention facing him and they met each other's eyes—East facing West—

in such fashion that manhood seemed to fill the smoky room. Every one was silent. Even Maga held her breath. Monty strode toward Rustum Khan; the Rajput was the first to speak.

"Colonel sahib, I spoke wise words!"

It seemed to me that Monty looked very keenly at him before he answered.

"Have you had supper, Rustum Khan? You look to me feverish from overwork and lack of food."

"What care I for my belly, sahib, if you break my heart?" the Rajput answered. "Shall I live to see Turks fling thy carcass to the birds? I have offered my own body in place of thine. Am I without honor, that my offer is refused?"

Monty answered that in the Rajput tongue, and it sounded like the bass notes of an organ.

"Brother mine, it is not the custom of my race to send substitutes to keep such promises. That thou knowest, and none has reason to know better. If thy memories and honor urge thee to come the way I take, is there no room for two of us?"

Maga Yaki

"Aye, sahib!" said the Rajput huskily. "I said before, I am thy man. I come. I obey!"

"Obey, do you?" Monty laid both hands on the Rajput's shoulders, struck him knee against knee without warning and pressed him down into a squatting posture. "Then obey when I order you to sit!"

The Rajput laughed up at him as suddenly sweet-tempered as a child.

"None other could have done that and not fought me for it!" he said simply. "None other would have had the strength!" he added.

Monty ignored the pleasantry and turned to Maga, so surprising that young woman—that she gasped.

"Bring him food at once, please!"

"Me? I? I bring him food? I feed that black—"

"Yes!" snapped Kagig suddenly. "You, Maga!"

Maga's and Kagig's eyes met, and again he had his way with her instantly. Peter Measel, standing over by the door, looked wistful and sighed noisily.

"Why should you obey him?" he demanded, but Maga ignored him as she passed out, and Fred nudged me again.

"A miracle!" he whispered. "Did you hear the martyred biped suggest rebellion to her? He'll be offering to fight Kagig next! Guess what is Kagig's hold over the girl—can you?"

But a much greater miracle followed. Rather than disobey Monty again; rather than seem to question his authority, or differ from his judgment in the least, Rustum Khan forbore presently from sending for his own stripling servant and actually accepted food from Maga's hands.

As a Mohammedan, he made in theory no caste distinctions. But as a Rajput be had fixed Hindu notions without knowing it, and almost his chief care was lest his food should be defiled by the touch of outcasts, of whom he reckoned gypsies lowest, vilest and least cleansible. Nevertheless he accepted curds that had been touched by gipsy fingers, and ate greedily, in confirmation of Monty's diagnosis; and after a few minutes he laid his head on a folded goat-skin in the corner, and fell asleep.

Then Monty sent a servant to his own quarters for some prized possession that he mentioned in a whisper behind his hand. None of us suspected what it might be until the man returned presently with a quart bottle of Scotch whisky. Kagig himself got mugs down from a shelf three inches wide, and Monty poured libations. Kagig, standing with legs apart, drank his share of the strong stuff without waiting; and that brought out the chief surprise of the evening.

"Ah-h-h!" he exclaimed, using the back of his hand to wipe mobile lips. "Not since I drank in Tony's have I tasted that stuff! The taste makes me homesick for what never was my home, nor ever can be! Tony's—ah!"

"What Tony's?" demanded Will, emerging from whispered interludes with Gloria like a man coming out of a dream.

"Tony's down near the Battery."

"What—the Battery, New York—?"

"Where else? Tony was a friend of mine. Tony lent me money when I landed in the States without a coin. It was right that I should take a last drink with Tony before I came away forever."

Fred reached into the corner for a lump of wood and set it down suggestively before the fire. Kagig accepted and sat down on it, stretching his legs out rather wearily.

"I noticed you've been remembering your English much better than at first," said Will. "Go on, man, tell us!"

Kagig cleared his throat and warmed himself while his eyes seemed to search the flames for stories from a half-forgotten past.

"Weren't the States good enough for you?" Will suggested, by way of starting him off.

"Good enough? Ah!" He made all eight fingers crack like castanets. "Much too good! How could I live there safe and comfortable—eggs and bacon—clean shirt—good shoes—an apartment with a bath in it—easy work—good pay—books to read—kindness—freedom—how could I accept all that, remembering my people in Armenia?"

He ran his fingers through his hair, and stared in the fire again—remembering America perhaps.

"There was a time when I forgot. All young men forget for a while if you feed them well enough. The sensation of having money in my pocket and the right to spend it made me drunk. I forgot Armenia. I took out what are called first papers. I was very prosperous—very grateful."

He lapsed into silence again, holding his head bowed between his hands.

"Why didn't you become a citizen?" asked Will.

"Ah! Many a time I thought of it. I am citizen of no land—of no land! I am outlaw here—outlaw in the States! I slew a Turk. They would electrocute me in New York—for slaying the man who—have you heard me tell what happened to my mother, before my very eyes? Well—that man came to America, and I slew him!"

"Why did you leave Armenia in the first place?" asked Gloria, for he seemed to need pricking along to prevent him from getting off the track into a maze of silent memory.

"Why not? I was lucky to get away! That cursed Abdul Hamid had been rebuked by the powers of Europe for butchering Bulgars, so he turned on us Armenians in order to prove to himself that he could do as he pleased in his own house. I tell you, murder and rape in those days were as common as flies at midsummer! I escaped, and worked my passage in the stoke-hole of a little merchant steamer—they were little ships in those days. And when I reached America without money or friends they let me land because I had been told by the other sailors to say I was fleeing from religious persecution. The very first day I found a friend in Tony. I cleaned his windows, and the bar, and the spittoons; and he lent me money to go where work would be plentiful. Those were the days when I forgot Armenia."

He began to forget our existence again, laying his face on his forearms and staring down at the floor between his feet.

"What brought it back to memory?" asked Gloria.

"The Turk brought it back—Fiamil—who bought my mother from four drunken soldiers, and ill-treated her before my eyes. He came to the Turkish consulate, not as consul but in some peculiar position; and by that time I was thriving as head-waiter and part-owner of a New York restaurant. Thither the fat beast came to eat daily. And so I met him, and recognized him. He did not know me.

"Remember, I was young, and prosperous for the first time in all my life. You must not judge me by too up-right standards. At first I argued with myself to let him alone. He was nothing to me. I no longer believed in God. My mother was long dead, and Armenia no more my country. My money was accumulating in a savings bank. I was proud of it, and I remember I saw visions of great restaurants in every city of America, all owned by me! I did not like to take any step that should prevent that flow of money into the savings bank.

"But Fiamil inflamed my memory, and I saw him every day. And at last it dawned on me what his peculiar business in America must be. He was back at his old games, buying women. He was buying American young women to be shipped to Turkey, all under the seal of consular activity. One day, after he had had lunch and I had brought him cigarettes and coffee, he made a proposal. And although I did not care very deeply for the women of a free land who were willing to be sold into Turkish harems, nevertheless, as I said, he inflamed my memory. A love of Armenia returned to me. I remembered my people, I remembered my mother's shame, and my own shame.

"After a little reflection I agreed with Fiamil, and met him that night in an up-stairs room at a place he frequented for his purposes. I locked the door, and we had some talk in there, until in the end he remembered me and all the details of my mother's death. After that I killed him with a corkscrew and my ten fingers, there being no other weapon. And I threw his body out of the window into the gutter, as my mother's body had been thrown, myself escaping from the building by another way.

"Not knowing where to hide, I kept going—kept going; and after two days I fell among sportsmen—cow-punchers they called themselves, who had come to New York with a circus, and the circus had gone broke. To them I told some of my story, and they befriended me, taking me West with them to cook their meals; and for a year I traveled in cow camps. In those days I remembered God as well as Armenia, and I used to pray by starlight.

"And Armenia kept calling—calling. Fiamil had wakened in me too many old memories. But there was the money in the savings bank that I did not dare to draw for fear the police might learn my address, yet I had not the heart to leave behind.

"So I took a sportsman into my confidence, and told him about my money, and why I wanted it. He was not the foreman, but the man who took the place of foreman when the real foreman was too drunk—the hungriest man of all, and so oftenest near the cook-fire. When I had told him, he took me to a township where a lawyer was, and the lawyer drew up a document, which I signed.

"Then the sportsman—his name was Larry Atkins, I remember—took that document and went to draw the money on my behalf. And that was the last I saw of him. Not that he was not sportsman—all through. He told me in a letter afterward that the police arrested him, supposing him to be me, but that he easily proved he was not me, and so got away with the money. Enclosed in the package in which the letter came were his diamond ring and a watch and chain, and he also sent me an order to deliver to me his horse and saddle.

"He explained he had tried to double my money by gambling, but had lost. Therefore he now sent me all he had left, a fair exchange being no robbery. Oh, he was certainly sportsman!

"So I sold his watch and chain and the horse—but the diamond ring I kept—behold it!—see, on Maga's hand!—it was a real diamond that a woman had given him; and with the proceeds I came back to Armenia. In Armenia I have ever since remained, with the exception of one or two little journeys in time of war, and one or two little temporary hidings, and a trip into Persia, and another into Russia to get ammunition.

"How have I lived? Mostly by robbery! I rob Turks and all friends of Turks, and such people as help make it possible for Turks as a nation to continue to exist! I—we—I and my men—we steal a cartridge sooner than a piaster—a rifle sooner than a thousand rubles! Outlaws must live, and weapons are the chief means! I am the brains and the Eye of Zeitoon, but I have never been chieftain, and am not now. Observe my house—is it not empty? I tell you, if it had not been for my new friend Monty there would have been six or seven rival chieftains in Zeitoon to-night! As it is, they sulk in their houses, the others, because Monty has rallied all the fighting men to me! Now that Monty has come I think there will be unity forever in Zeitoon!"

He turned toward Monty with a gesture of really magnificent approval. Caesar never declined a crown with greater dignity.

"You, my brother, have accomplished in a few days what I have failed to do in years! That is because you are sportsman! Just as Larry Atkins was sportsman! He sent me all he had, and could not do more. I understood him. Why did he do it? Simply sportsman—that is all! Why do you do this? Why do you throw your life into the hot cauldron of Zeitoon? Because you are sportsman! And my people see, and understand. They understand, as they have never understood me! I will tell you why they have never understood me. This is why:

"I have always kept a little in reserve. At one time money in a bank. At another time money buried. Sometimes a place to run and hide in. Now and then a plan for my own safety in case a defense should fail. Never have I given absolutely quite all, burning all my bridges. Had I been Larry Atkins I would not have gambled with the money of a man who trusted me; but, having lost the money, I would not have sent my diamond and the watch and chain! Neither, if the horse and saddle bad been within my reach would I have sent an order to deliver those! That is why Zeitoon has never altogether trusted me! Some, but never all, until to-night!

"My brother—"

He stood up, with the motions of a man who is stiff with weariness.

"I salute you! You have taught me my needed lesson!"

"I wonder!" whispered Fred to me. "Remember Peter at the fireside? Methinks friend Kagig doth too much protest! We'll see. Nemesis comes swiftly as a rule."

I shoved Fred off his balance, rolled him over, and sat on him, because cynicism and iconoclasm are twin deities I neither worship nor respect. But at times Fred Oakes is gifted with uncanny vision. While he struggled explosively to throw me off, the door began resounding to steady thumps, and at a sign from Kagig, Maga opened it.

There strode in nine Armenians, followed closely by one of the gypsies of Gregor Jhaere's party, who whispered to Maga through lips that hardly moved, and made signals to Kagig with a secretive hand like a snake's head. I got off Fred's stomach then, and when he had had his revenge by emptying hot pipe ashes down my neck he sat close beside me and translated what followed word for word. It was all in Armenian, spoken in deadly earnest by hairy men on edge with anxiety and yet compelled to grudging patience by the presence of strangers and knowledge of the hour's necessity.

When the gipsy had finished making signals to Kagig be sat down and seemed to take no further interest. But a little later I caught sight of him by the dancing fire-light creeping along the wall, and presently he lay down with his head very close to Rustum Khan's. Nothing points more clearly to the clarifying tension of that night than the fact that Rustum Khan with his notions about gypsies could compel himself to lie still with a gipsy's head within three inches of his own, and sham sleep while the gipsy whispered to him. I was not the only one who observed that marvel, although I did not know that at the time.

The nine Armenians who had entered were evidently influential men. Elders was the word that occurred as best describing them. They were smelly with rain and smoke and the close-kept sweat beneath their leather coats—all of them bearded—nearly all big men—and they strode and stood with the air of being usually heard when they chose to voice opinion. Kagig stood up to meet them, with his back toward the fire—legs astraddle, and hands clasped behind him.

"Ephraim says," began the tallest of the nine, who had entered first and stood now nearest to Kagig and the firelight, "that you will yourself be king of Armenia!"

"Ephraim lies!" said Kagig grimly. "He always does lie. That man can not tell truth!"

Two of the others grunted, and nudged the first man, who made an exclamation of impatience and renewed the attack.

"But there is the Turk—the colonel whom your Indian friend took prisoner—he says—"

"Pah! What Turk tells the truth?"

"He says that the Indian—what is his name? Rustum Khan—was purposing to use him as prisoner-of-war, whereas in accordance with a private agreement made beforehand you were determined to make matters easy for him. He demands of us better treatment in fulfillment of promise. He says that the army is coming to take Zeitoon, and to make you governor in the Sultan's name. He offered us that argument thinking we are your dupes. He thought to—"

"Dupes?" snarled Kagig. "How long have ye dealt with Turks, and how long with me, that ye take a Turk's word against mine?"

"But the Turk thought we are your friends," put in a harsh-voiced man from the rear of the delegation. "Otherwise, how should he have told us such a thing?"

"If he had thought you were my friends," Kagig answered, "he would never have dared. If you had been my friends, you would have taken him and thrown him into Jihun River from the bridge!"

"Yet he has said this thing," said a man who had not spoken yet.

"And none has heard you deny it, Kagig!" added the man nearest the door.

"Then hear me now!" Kagig shouted, on tiptoe with anger. Then he calmed himself and glanced about the room for a glimpse of eyes friendly to himself. "Hear me now. Those Turks—truly come to set a governor over Zeitoon. I forgot that the prisoner might understand English. I talked with this friend of mine—he made a gesture toward Monty. "Perhaps that Turk overheard, he is cleverer than he looks. I had a plan, and I told it to my friend. The Turk was near, I remember, eating the half of my dinner I gave him."

"Have you then a plan you never told to us?" the first man asked suspiciously.

"One plan? A thousand! Am I wind that I should babble into heedless ears each thought that comes to me for testing? First it was my plan to arouse all Armenia, and to overthrow the Turk. Armenia failed me. Then it was my plan to arouse Zeitoon, and to make a stand here to such good purpose that all Armenia would rally to us. Bear me witness whether Zeitoon trusted me or not? How much backing have I had? Some, yes; but yours?

"So it was plain that if the Turks sent a great army, Zeitoon could only hold out for a little while, because unanimity is lacking. And my spies report to me that a greater army is on the way than ever yet came to the rape of Armenia. These handful of *hamidieh* that ye think are all there is to be faced are but the outflung skirmishers. It was plain to me that Zeitoon can not last. So I made a new plan, and kept it secret."

"Ah-h-h! So that was the way you took us into confidence? Always secrets behind secrets, Kagig! That is our complaint!"

"Listen, ye who would rather suspect than give credit!" He used one word in the Armenian. "It was my plan—my new plan, that seeing the Turks insist on giving us a governor, and are able to overwhelm us if we refuse, then I would be that governor!"

"Ah-h-h! What did we say! Unable to be king, you will be governor!"

"I talked that over with my new friend, and he did not agree with me, but I prevailed. Now hear my last word on this matter: I will not be governor of Zeitoon! I will lead against this army that is coming. If you men prevent me, or disobey me, or speak against me, I will hang you—every one! I will accept no reward, no office, no emolument, no title—nothing! Either I die here, fighting for Zeitoon, or I leave Zeitoon when the fighting is over, and leave it as I came to it—penniless! I give now all that I have to give. I burn my bridges! I take inviolable oath that I will not profit! And by the God who fed me in the wilderness, I name my price for that and take my payment in advance! I will be obeyed! Out with you! Get out of here before I slay you all! Go and tell Zeitoon who is master here until the fight is lost or won!"

He seized a great fire-brand and charged at them, beating right and left, and they backed away in front of him, protesting from under forearms raised to protect their faces. He refused to hear a word from them, and drove, them back against the door.

Strange to say, it was Rustum Khan who gave up all further pretense at sleeping and ran round to fling the door open—Rustum Khan who took part with Kagig, and helped drive them out into the dark, and Rustum Khan who stood astraddle in the doorway, growling after them in Persian—the only language he knew thoroughly that they likely understood:

"Bismillah! Ye have heard a man talk! Now show yourselves men, and obey him, or by the beard of God's prophet there shall be war within Zeitoon fiercer than that without! Take counsel of your women-folk! Ye—" (he used no drawing-room word to intimate their sex)—"are too full of thoughts to think!"

Then he turned on Kagig, and held out a lean brown hand. Kagig clasped it, and they met each other's eyes a moment.

"Am I sportsman?" Kagig asked ingenuously.

"Brother," said Rustum Khan, "next after my colonel sahib I accept thee as a man fit to fight beside!"

We were all standing. A free-for-all fight had seemed too likely, and we had not known whether there were others outside waiting to reinforce the delegation. Rustum Khan sought Monty's eyes.

"You have the news, sahib?"

Kagig laughed sharply, and dismissed the past hour from his mind with a short sweep of the hand.

"No. Tell me," said Monty.

"The gipsy brought it. A whole division of the Turkish regular army is on the march. Their rear-guard camps to-night a day's march this side of Tarsus. Dawn will find the main body within sight of us. Half a brigade has hurried forward to reinforce the men we have just beaten. Are there any orders?"

Fred's face fell, and my heart dropped into my boots. A division is a horde of men to stand against.

"No," said Monty. "No orders yet."

"Then I will sleep again," said Rustum Khan, and suited action to the word, laying his head on the same folded goat-skin he had used before and breathing deeply within the minute.

Nobody spoke. Rustum Khan's first deep snore had not yet announced his comment on the situation, and we all stood waiting for Kagig to say something. But it was Peter Measel who spoke first.

"I will pray," he announced. "I saw that gipsy whispering to the Indian, and I know there is treachery intended! O Lord—O righteous Lord—forgive these people for their bloody and impudent plans! Forgive them for plotting to shed blood! Forgive them for arrogance, for ambition, for taking Thy name in vain, for drinking strong drink, for swearing, for vanity, and for all their other sins. Forgive above all the young woman of the party, who is not satisfied with a wound already but looks forward with unwomanly zest to further fighting! Forgive them for boasting and—"

"Throw that fool out!" barked Kagig suddenly.

"O Lord forgive—"

Fred was nearest the door, and opened it. Maga laughed aloud. I was nearest to Peter Measel, so it was I who took him by the neck and thrust him into outer darkness. Kagig kicked the door shut after him; but even so we heard him for several minutes grinding out condemnatory prayers.

"Now sleep, sportsmen all!" said Kagig, blessing us with both hands. "Sleep against the sport to-morrow!"

"AND DELILAH SAID—"

Always at fault is the fellow betrayed
(Majorities murder to prove it!)
As Samson discovered, Delilah lies,
The stigma's stuck on by the cynical wise,
And nothing can ever remove it.
We'll cast out Delilah and spit on her dead,
(That revenge is remarkably human),
And pity the victim of underhand tricks
So be that it's moral (the sexes don't mix);
But, oh, think what the cynical wise would have
said
If Judas were only a woman!

XVII
"I KNEW WHAT TO EXPECT OF THE WOMEN!"

WE SLEPT until Monty called us, two hours before dawn, although I was conscious most of the night of stealthy men and women who stepped over me to get at Kagig and whisper to him. His marvelous spy system was working full blast, and he seemed to run no risks by letting the spies report to any one but himself. Fred, who slept more lightly than I did, told me afterward that the women principally brought him particulars of the workings of local politics; the men detailed news of the oncoming concrete enemy.

There was breakfast served by Maga in the dark—hot milk, and a strange mess of eggs and meat. For some reason no one thought of relighting the fire, and although the ashes glowed we shivered until the food put warmth in us.

By the light of the smoky lamp I thought that Monty wore a strangely divided air, between gloom and exultation. Fred had been wide awake and talking with him since long before first cock-crow and was obviously out of sorts, shaking his head at intervals and unwilling more than to poke at his food with a fork. I crossed the room to sit beside them, and came in for the tail end of the conversation.

"I might have known it, Didums, when I let you go on alone. I'll never forgive myself. I had a premonition and disobeyed it. You pose as a cast-iron materialist with no more ambition than money enough to retrieve your damned estates, and all the while you're the most romantic ass who ever wore out saddle-leather! Found it, have you? Then God help us all! I know what's coming! You're about to 'vert back to Crusader days, and try to do damn silly deeds of chivalry without the war-horse or the suit of mail!"

"No need for you to join me, Fred. You take charge of the others and get them away to safety."

"Take charge of hornets! I'd leave you, *of course*, like a shot! But can you see Will Yerkes, for instance, riding off and leaving you to play Don Quixote? Damn you, Didums, can't you see—?"

"Destiny, Fred. Manifest destiny."

"Can't you see crusading is dead as a dead horse?"

"So am I, old man. I'm no use but to do this very thing. I can serve these people. If I'm killed, there'll be a howl in the papers. If I'm taken, there'll be a row in parliament."

"You don't intend to be taken—I know you!"

"Honest, Fred, I—"

"Have I known you all these years to be fooled now? Smelling rats 'ud be subtle to it—I can feel the air bristling! You mean to raise the Montdidier banner and die under it, last of your race. But you're not last, you bally ass!"

"Last in the direct line, Fred."

"Yes, but there's that rotter Charles ready to inherit! If you're bent on suicide—"

"I'm not. You know I'm not."

"—you might have the decency to kill that miserable cousin first and bring the line to an end in common honor! He'll survive you, and as sure as I sit here and swear at you, he'll bring the Montdidier name into worse disgrace than Judas Iscariot's!"

"I've no intention of suicide, Fred. I assure you—"

But Fred waved the argument aside contemptuously, and stood up to gather our attention.

"Listen!" He thrust forward his Van Dyke beard that valiantly strove to hide a chin like a piece of flint. "Monty has found the robbers' nest that used to belong to his infernal ancestors. I charge any of you who count yourselves his friends to help me prevent him from behaving like an idiot!"

"That'll do, Fred!" said Monty, pressing him back against the wall. "The fact is," he twisted at his black mustache and eyed us each for a second in turn, looking as handsome as the devil, "that I have found what I originally set out to look for. It overlooks Zeitoon, hidden among trees. I propose to use it. As for Quixotism—is there any one here not willing to fight in the last ditch to help Kagig and these Armenians?"

"I'm with you!" laughed Gloria, and she and Will had a scuffle over near the fireplace.

"I knew what to expect of the women," said Monty rather bitterly. "I'm speaking to Fred and the men!"

"Where's Peter Measel?" I asked. But the others did not see the connection.

"Come along," said Monty. "Seems to me we're wasting time," and he strode out through the window on to the roof of the house below—usually the shortest way from point to point in Zeitoon. Kagig followed him, and then Rustum Khan. The stars were no longer shining in the pale sky overhead, but it was dark where we were because of the mountains that shut out the dawn. Fred came last, grumbling and stumbling, too disturbed to look where he was going.

"Fancy me acting Cassandra at my time of life and none to believe me!" he muttered. Then, louder: "I warn you all! I know that fellow Monty. If he comes out of this alive it'll be because we haul him out by the hair! Won't you listen?"

Outside the window I remembered the field-glasses I had laid down in a corner, and returned to get them. In the room were Maga and the woman Anna, who had appointed herself Gloria Vanderman's maid; they were apparently about to sweep the floor and tidy the place, but as I crossed the room an older gipsy woman entered by the door, and she and Maga promptly drove Anna out through the window after my party. Then the old woman came close to me, her beady bright eyes fixed on mine, and went through the suggestive gipsy motions that invite the crossing of a palm with silver.

There seemed at first no excuse for listening to her. Every gipsy will beg, whether there is need or not, and knowledge of their habits did not make me less short-tempered; besides I had no silver within reach, nor time to waste.

"Not now!" I said, pushing her aside.

But Maga came to her rescue, and clutched my arm.

"See!" she said, and took a Maria Theresa dollar from some hiding-place in her skirt. "I give silver for you. So." The old hag pouched the coin with exactly the same avidity with which she would have taken it from me. "Now she will make magic. Then I see. Then I tell you something. You listen!"

It began to dawn on me that I would better listen after all. Every human is superstitious, whether or not he admits if to himself; but the particular fraud of pretending to tell fortunes never did happen to find the joint in my own armor. It seemed likely these two women had some plan that included the preliminary deception of myself, and the sooner I knew something about it the better. So I sat down on Kagig's stool, to give them a better opinion of their advantage over me, there being nothing like making the enemy too confident. Then I held out the palm of my hand for inspection and tried to look like a man pretending he does not believe in magic. Whatever Maga thought, the old hag was delighted. She began to croak an incantation, shuffling first with one foot, then with the other, and finally with both together in a weird dance that almost shook her old frame apart. Then she went through a pantomime of finger-pointing, as if transferring from herself to Maga the gift of divining about me.

Presently, standing a little to one side of me, with eyes on the old hag's and my hand held between her two, Maga began chanting in English. The fact that her voice was musical and low where the bag's had been high-pitched and rasping heightened interest, if nothing else.

"You now four men," she began, with a little pause, and something like a swallow between each sentence. "You all love one another ver' much. You all like Kagig. Kagig is liking you. But Turks are coming presently, and they keel Kagig—keel heem, you understan'? That man Monty is also keel—keel dead. That man Fred—I not know—I not see. You I see—you I see two ways. First way, you marry that woman Gloria—you go away—all well—all good. Second way—you not marry her. Then you all die—dam' quick—Monty, Fred, Will, you, Gloria, everybody—an' Zeitoon is all burn' up by bloody Turks!"

She paused and looked at me sidewise under lowered eyelids. I stared straight in front of me, as if in the state of self-hypnotism that is the fortune-teller's happy hunting-ground.

"You understan'?"

"Yes," I said. "I think I see. But how shall I marry Miss Gloria? Suppose she does not want me?"

"You must! Never mind what she want! Listen! This is only way to save your frien's and Zeitoon! I am giving men—four—five—six men. They are seizing Gloria. You go with them. They take you safe away. Then Zeitoon is also safe, an' your frien's are also safe."

"Monty, too?" I asked.

"Yes, then he is also safe." But—I felt her hands tremble slightly as she said that.

"Do you mean I should leave him?" I asked.

"You must! *You must!*" She almost screamed at me, and shook my hand between her two palms as if by that means to drive the fact into my consciousness. The old hag had her eyes fixed on my right temple as if she would burn a hole there, and between them they were making a better than amateur effort to control me by suggestion. It seemed wise to help them deceive themselves. Maga let go my hand gently, and began passing her ten fingers very softly through my hair, and there are other men who will bear me witness that there exists sensation less appealing than when a pretty girt does that.

"You must!" she said again more quietly. "That is the only way to save Zeitoon. God is angry."

"What do you know about God?" I asked unguardedly, knowing well that whatever their open pretenses, gypsies despise all religion except diabolism. They study creeds for the sake of plunder, just as hunters study the habits of the wild.

"Maybe nothing—maybe much! Peter Measel, he say—"

She paused, as if in doubt whether she was using the right argument. And in that moment I recalled what Rustum Khan had once said about her being no true gipsy.

"Go on," I urged her. "Peter Measel is an expert. He's a high priest. He knows it all."

"Peter Measel is saying, God is ver' angry with Zeitoon and is sending to destroy such bloody people what plan fighting and rebellion."

"I'll think it over," I said, moving to get up. But independent thinking was the last thing that Maga intended to permit me.

"No, no! No, no, no! You must dee-cide now—at once! There is no time. Now—now I give you five—six mens—now they seize that woman Gloria—now you carry 'er away into the mountains—now you make 'er yours—your own, you understan', so as she is ashamed to deny it afterward—yes?—you see?"

"Where are the men?" I demanded.

"I fetch them quick!"

I could see the hilt of her knife, and the bulge of her repeating pistol, but I could also feel the weight of my own loaded Colt against my hip. I did not doubt I could escape before her men could arrive on the scene, but that would have been to leave some secret only part uncovered. There was obviously more behind this scheme than met the ear. It is my experience that if we throw fear to the winds, and are willing to wait in tight places for the necessary inspiration, then we get it.

"Very well," I said. "I agree. Bring your men."

"You wait. I get 'em."

I nodded, and she said something in the gipsy language to the old hag, who went out through the door in a hurry. Alone with Maga I felt less than half as safe as I had been. She proceeded to make use of every moment in the manner they say makes millionaires.

"Gloria, she is ver' nice girl!" She made a wonderful gesture of both hands that limned in empty air the curves of her detested rival. "You will love her. By-and-by she love you—also ver' much."

The thought flashed through my head again that I ought to escape whole while I had the chance; but the answer to that was the certainty that she would thence-forward be on guard against me without having given me any real information. I was perfectly convinced there was a deep plot underlying the foolishness she had proposed. The fact that she considered me so venial and so gullible was no proof that the hidden purpose was not dangerous. The mystery was how to seem to be fooled by her and yet get in touch with my friends. Then suddenly I recalled that she and the hag had been trying to use the gipsy's black art. Unless they can trick their victim into a mental condition in which innate superstition becomes uppermost, players of that dark game are helpless.

Yet gypsies are more superstitious than any one else. Hanging to her neck by a skein of plaited horse-hair was the polished shell of a minute turtle—smaller than a dollar piece.

"Give me that," I said, "for luck," and she jumped at the idea.

"Yes, yes—that is to bring you luck—ver' much luck!"

She snatched it off and hung it around my neck, pushing the turtle-shell down under my collar out of sight.

"That is love-token!" she whispered. "Now she love you immediate'! Now you 'ave ver' much luck!"

The last part of her prophecy was true. The luck seemed to change. That instant the key was given me to escape without making her my relentless enemy, a voice that I would know among a million began shouting for me petulantly from somewhere half a dozen roofs away.

"What in hell's keeping you, man? Here's Monty getting up a tourist party to his damned ancestral nest and you're delaying the whole shebang! Good lord alive! Have you fallen in love with a woman, or taken the belly-ache, or fallen down a well, or gone to sleep again, or all of them, or what?"

"Coming, Fred!" I shouted. "Coming!"

"You'd better!"

He began playing cat-calls on his concertina—imitation bugle-calls, and fragments of serenades. For a second Maga looked reckless—then suspicious—then, as it began to dawn on her from studying my face that I, too, was afraid of Fred, relieved.

"Does he know anything?" I asked her.

"He? That Fred? No! No, no, no! An' you no tell 'im. You 'ear me? You no tell 'im! You go now—go to 'im, or else 'e is get suspicious—understan'? My men—they go an' get that woman. When they finish getting that woman, then I send for you an' you come quick—understan'?"

I nodded.

"Listen! If you tell your frien's—if you tell that Frrred, or those others—then I not only keel you, but my men put out your eyes first an' then pull off your toes an' fingers—understan'?"

I shrugged my shoulders, suggesting an attempt to seem at ease.

"Besides—I warn you! You tell Kagig anything against me an' Kagig is at once your enemy!"

I nodded, and tried to look afraid. Perhaps the speculation that the last boast started in my mind helped give me a look that convinced her.

Fred began calling again.

"You go!" she ordered imperiously, with a last effort to impress me with her mental predominance. "Go quickly!"

I made motions of hand and face as nearly suggestive of underhanded cunning as I could compass, and climbed out through the window without further invitation. Seeing me emerge, Fred beckoned from fifty yards away and turned his back. Morning was just beginning to descend into the valley, suddenly bright from having finished all the dawn delays among the crags higher up; but there were deep shadows here and especially where one roof overhung another.

Jumping from roof to roof to follow Fred, I was suddenly brought up short by a figure in shadow that gesticulated wildly without speaking. It was below me, in a narrow, shallow runway between two houses, and I had been so impressed by my interview with Maga that assassination was the first thought ready to mind. I sprang aside and tried to check myself, missed footing, and fell into the very runway I had tried to avoid.

A friend unmistakable, Anna—Gloria's self-constituted maid—ran out of the darkest shadow and kept me from scrambling to my feet.

"Wait!" she whispered. "Don't be seen talking to me. Listen!"

My ankle pained considerably and I was out of breath. I was willing enough to lie there.

"Maga has made a plot to betray Zeitoon! She has been talking with that Turkish colonel who was captured. I don't know what the plot is, but I listened through a chink in the wall of the prison, and I heard him promise that she should have Will Yerkes!"

"What else did you hear?"

"Nothing else. There was wind whistling, and the straw made a noise."

At that moment Fred chose to turn his head to see whether I was following. Not seeing me, he came back over the roofs, shouting to know what had happened. I got to my feet but, although he hardly looks the part, he is as active as a boy, and he had scrambled to a higher roof that commanded a view of my runway before my twisted ankle would permit me to escape.

"So that's it, eh? A woman!"

"Keep an eye on Miss Gloria!" I whispered to Anna, and she ducked and ran.

If I had had presence of mind I would have accepted the insinuation, and turned the joke on Fred. Instead, I denied it hotly like a fool, and nothing could have fed the fires of his spirit of raillery more surely.

"I've unearthed a plot," I began, limping along beside him.

"No, sir! It was I who unearthed the two of you!"

"See here, Fred—"

"Look? I'd be ashamed! No, no—I wasn't looking!"

"Fred, I'm serious!"

"Entanglements with women are always serious!"

"I tell you, that girl Maga—"

"Two of 'em, eh? Worser and worser! You'll have Will jealous into the bargain!"

"Have it your own way, then!" I said, savage with pain (and the reasons he did not hesitate to assign to my strained ankle were simply scandalous). "I'll wait until I find a man with honest ears."

"Try Kagig!" he advised me dryly.

And Kagig I did try. We came on him at our end of the bridge that overhung the Jihun River. Our party were waiting on the far side, and Fred hurried over to join them. Kagig was listening to the reports of a dozen men, and while I waited to get his ear I could see Fred telling his great joke to the party. It was easy to see that Gloria Vanderman did not enjoy the joke; nor did I blame her. I did not blame her for sending word there and then to Anna that her services would not be required any more.

As soon as Kagig saw me he dismissed the other men in various directions and made to start across the bridge. I called to him to wait, and walked beside him.

"I've uncovered a plot, Kagig," I began. "Maga Jhaere has been talking with the Turkish prisoner."

"I know it. I sent her to talk with him!"

"She has bargained with him to betray Zeitoon!"

For answer to that Kagig turned his head and stared sharply at me—then went off into peals of diabolic laughter. He had not a word to offer. He simply utterly, absolutely, unqualifiedly disbelieved me—or else chose to have it appear so.

AND HE WHO WOULD SAVE HIS LIFE SHALL LOSE IT

The fed fools beat their brazen gong
For gods' ears dulled by blatant praise,
Awonder why the scented fumes
And surplices at evensong Avail not as in other days.
Shrunken and mean the spirit fails
Like old snow falling from the crags

And priest and pedagogue compete
With nostrums for the age that ails,
But learn not why the spirit lags.
Tuneless and dull the loose lyre thrums
Ill-plucked by fingers strange to skill
That change and change the fever'd chords,
But still no inspiration comes
Though priest and pundit labor still.
Lust-urged the clamoring clans denounce
Whate'er their sires agreed was good,
And swift on faith and fair return
With lies the feud-leaders pounce
Lest Truth deprive them of their food.
Dog eateth dog and none gives thanks;
All crave the fare, but grudge the price
Their nobler forbears proudly paid,
That now for moonstruck madness ranks—
The only true coin—Sacrifice!

XVIII
"PER TERRAM ET AQUAM."

THE MAN who is a hero to himself perhaps exists, but the surface indications are no proof of it. I don't pretend to be satisfied, and made no pretense at the time of being satisfied with my share in Maga's treachery. But I claim that it was more than human nature could have done, to endure the open disapproval of my friends, begun by Fred's half-earnest jest, and continued by my own indignation; and at the same time to induce them to take my warning seriously.

Will avoided me, and walked with Gloria, who made no particular secret of her disgust. Fred naturally enough kept the joke going, to save himself from being tripped in his own net. He had probably persuaded himself by that time that the accusation was true, and therefore equally probably regretted having made it; for he would have been the last man in the world to give tongue about an offense that he really believed a friend of his had committed.

Monty, who believed from force of habit every single word Fred said, walked beside me and was good enough to give me fatherly advice.

"Not the time, you know, to fool with women. I don't pretend, of course, to any right to judge your private conduct, but—you can be so awfully useful, you know, and all that kind of thing, when you're paying strict attention. Women distract a man."

All, things considered, I might have done worse than decide to say no more about the plot, but to keep my own eyes wide open. (I was particularly sore with Gloria, and derived much unwise consolation from considering stinging remarks I would make to her when the actual truth should out.)

Monty began making the best of my, in his eyes, damaged character by explaining the general dispositions he and Kagig had made for the defense of Zeitoon.

"According to my view of it," he said, "this bridge we've just crossed is the weakest point—or was. I think we can hold that clay ramp you came up yesterday against all comers. But there's a way round the back of this mountain that leads to the dismantled fort you see on this side of the river. That is the fort built by the Turkish soldiers whom Kagig told us the women of Zeitoon threw one by one over the bridge."

He stopped (we had climbed about two hundred feet of a fairly steep track leading up the flank of Beirut Dagh) and let the others gather around us.

"You see, if the enemy can once establish a footing on this hill, they'll then command the whole of Zeitoon opposite with rifle fire, even if they don't succeed in bringing artillery round the mountain."

Between us and Zeitoon there now lay a deep, sheer-sided gash, down at the bottom of which the Jihun brawled and boiled. I did not envy any army faced with the task of crossing it, even supposing the bridge should not be destroyed. But they would not need to cross in order to make the town untenable.

"The Zeitoonli are, you might say, superstitious about that bridge," Monty went on. "They refuse as much as to consider making arrangements to blow it up in case of need. Another remarkable thing is that the women claim the bridge defense as their privilege. That doesn't matter. They look like a crowd of last-ditch fighters, and we're awfully short of men. But we're almost equally short of ammunition; and if it ever gets to the point where we're driven in so that we have to hold that bridge, we shall be doling out cartridges one by one to the best shots! I have tried to persuade the women to leave the bridge until there's need of defending it, and to lend us a hand elsewhere meanwhile; but they've always held the bridge, and they propose to do the same again. Even Kagig can't shift them, although the women have been his chief supporters all along."

Fred interrupted, pointing toward a few acres of level land to our left, below Zeitoon village but still considerably above the river level.

"Is that Rustum Khan?"

"He it is," said Kagig. "A devil of a man—a wonder of a devil—no friend of mine, yet I shook hands with him and I salute him! A genius! A cavalryman born. Our people are not cavalrymen. No place for horses, this. Yet, as you have seen, there are some of us who can ride, and that Rustum Khan found many others—refugees from this and that place. See how he drills them yonder—see! It was the gift of God that so many horses fell into our hands. Some of the refugees brought horses along for food. Instead, Rustum Khan took men's corn away, to feed the hungry horses!"

"We could never have held the place without Rustum Khan," said Monty. "As it is we've a chance. The last thing the Turks will expect from us is mounted tactics. Allowing for plenty of spare horses, we shall have two full squadrons—one under Rustum Khan, and one I'll lead myself. From all accounts they're bringing an awful number of men against us, and we expect them to try to force the clay ramp. In that case—but come and see."

He led on up-hill, and after a few minutes the well-worn track disappeared, giving place to a newly cleared one. Trees had been cut down roughly, leaving stumps in such irregular profusion that, though horses could pass between them easily, no wheeled traffic could have gone that way. The undergrowth and the tree-trunks had been piled along either side, so that the new path was fenced in. It was steep and crooked, every section of it commanded by some other section higher up, with plenty of crags and boulders that afforded even better cover than the trees.

"Discovered this the first day I got here," said Monty. "Asked about bears, and a man offered to show me where a dozen of them lived. I was curious to see where a dozen bears could live in amity together—didn't believe a word of it. We set out that afternoon, and didn't reach the top until midnight. Worst climb I ever experienced. Lost ourselves a hundred times. Next day, however, Kagig agreed to let me have as many men as could be crowded together to work, and I took a hundred and twenty. Set them to cutting this trail and another one. They worked like beavers. But come along and look."

"How about the bears?" Fred demanded. "Did you get them?"

"Smelt 'em. Saw one—or saw his shadow, and heard him. Followed him up-hill by the smell, and so found the castle wall. Haven't seen a bear since."

"Hssh!" said Kagig, and sprang up-hill ahead of us to take the lead. "There are guards above there, and they are true Zeitoonli—they will shoot dam' quick!"

They did not shoot, because we all lay in the shadow of a great rock as soon as we could see a ragged stone wall uplifted against the purple sky, and Kagig whistled half a dozen times. We plainly heard the snap of breech-blocks being tested.

"They are weary of talking fight!" Kagig whispered.

But the sixth or seventh whistle was answered by a shout, and we began to climb again. Close to the castle the tree-cutters had been able to follow the line of the original road fairly closely, and there were places underfoot that actually seemed to have been paved. Finally we reached a steep ramp of cemented stone blocks, not one of which was out of place, and went up that toward an arch—clear, unmistakable, round Roman that had once been closed by a portcullis and an oak gate. All of the woodwork had long ago disappeared, but there was little the matter with the masonry.

Under the echoing arch we strode into a shadowy courtyard where the sun had not penetrated long enough to warm the stones. In the midst of it a great stone keep stood as grim and almost as undecayed as when Crusaders last defended it. That castle had never been built by Crusaders; they had found it standing there, and had added to it, Norman on to Roman.

The courtyard was littered with weeds that Kagig's men had slashed down, and here and there a tree had found root room and forced its way up between the rough-hewn paving stones. Animals had laired in the place, and had left their smell there together with an air of wilderness. But now a new-old smell, and new-old sounds were awakening the past. There were horses again in the stables, whose roof formed the fighting-platform behind the rampart of the outer wall.

Monty led the way to the old arched entrance of the keep, and pointed upward to a spot above the arch where some one had been scraping and scrubbing away the stains of time. There, clean white now in the midst of rusty stonework, was a carved device—shield-shaped—two ships and two wheat-sheaves; and underneath on a scroll the motto in Latin—*Per terram et aquam*—By Land and Sea—in token that the old Montdidiers held themselves willing to do duty on either element. The same device and the same motto were on the gold signet ring on Monty's little finger.

"What's happening on top of the keep?" demanded Will.

Fred laughed aloud. We could not see up from inside, for at least one of the stone floors remained intact.

"Can't you guess?" demanded Fred. "Didn't I tell you the man has 'verted to Crusader days?"

But Monty explained.

"There's an old stone socket up there that used to hold the flag-pole. Two or three fellows have been kind enough to haul a tree up there, and they're trimming it to fit."

"If we were wise we'd hang you to it, Didums, and save you from a lousy Turkish jail!"

"Thank you, Fred," Monty answered. "There are capitulations still, I fancy. No Turk can legally try me, or imprison me a minute. I'm answerable to the British consul."

"They're fine, legal-minded sticklers for the rules, the Turks are!" Fred retorted.

"But we've a net laid for the Turks!" smiled Monty.

Fred shook his head. Monty led the way toward stone steps, whose treads bad been worn into smooth hollows centuries before by the feet of men in armor.

Up above on the outer rampart we could see Kagig's sentries outlined against the sky, protected against the chilly mountain air by goat-skin outer garments and pointed goat-skin hats. We mounted the stone stair, holding to a baluster worn smooth by the rub of countless forgotten hands, as perfect yet as on the day when the masons pronounced it finished; and emerged on to a wide stone floor above the stables, guarded by a breast-high parapet pierced by slits for archers.

From below the breathing of the pines came up to us, peculiarly audible in spite of the Titan roar of Jihun River. Immediately below us was a ledge of forest-covered rock, and beyond that we could see sheer down the tree-draped flank of Beirut Dagh to the foaming water. We leaned our elbows on the parapet, and stared in silence all in a row, stared at in turn by the more than half-suspicious sentries.

"How does it feel, old man" asked Will at last, "standing on ramparts where your ancestors once ruled the roost?"

"Stranger than perhaps you think," Monty answered, not looking to right or left, or downward, but away out in front of him toward the sky-line on top of the opposite hills.

"I bet I know," said Will. "You hate to see the old order passing. You'd like the old times back."

"You're wrong for once, America!" Monty turned his back on the parapet and the view, and with hands thrust deep down in his pockets sought for words that could explain a little of his inner man. Fred had perhaps seen that mood before, but none of the rest of us. Usually he would talk of anything except his feelings. He felt the difficulty now, and checked.

"How so?" demanded Will.

"I've watched the old order passing. I'm part of it. I'm passing, too."

Gloria watched him with melting eyes. Fred turned his back and went through the fruitless rigmarole of trying to appear indifferent, going to the usual length at last of humming through his nose.

"That's what I said. You'd like these castle days back again."

"You're wrong, Will. I pray they never may come back. The place is an anachronism. So am I!—useless for most modern purposes. You'd have to tear castle or me so to pieces that we'd be unrecognizable. The world is going forward, and I'm glad of it. It shall have no hindrance at my hands."

"If men were all like you—" began Gloria, but he checked her with a frown.

"You can call this castle a robbers' nest, if you like. It's easy to call names. It stood for the best men knew in those days—protection of the countryside, such law and order as men understood, and the open road. It was built primarily to keep the roads safe. There are lots of things in England and America to-day, Will, that your descendants (being fools) will sneer at, just as it's the fashion to-day to sneer at relics of the past like this—and me!"

"Who's sneering? Not I! Not we!"

"This castle was built for the sake of the countryside. I've a mind to see it end as it began—that's all."

"Aw—what's eating you, Monty?"

"Shut up croaking, you old raven!" grumbled Fred.

"Show us the view you promised. This isn't it, for there isn't a Turk in sight."

Monty knew better than mistake Fred's surliness for anything but friendship in distress. Without another word he led the way along the parapet toward a ragged tower at the southern corner. It had been built by Normans, evidently added to the earlier Roman wall.

"Now tell me if the old folk didn't know their business," said Monty. "Very careful, all! The steps inside are rough. The roof has fallen in, and the ragged upper edge that's left probably accounts for the castle remaining undetected from below all these years—looks like fangs of discolored rock."

We followed him through the doorless gap in the tower wall, and up broken stone stairs littered with fragments of the fallen roof, until we stood at last in a half-circle around the jagged rim, our feet wedged between rotten masonry, breasts against the saw-edge parapet, and heads on a level with the eagles. From that dizzy height we had a full view between the mountains, not only of the immediate environs of Zeitoon, but of most of the pass—up which we ourselves had come, and of some of the open land beyond it.

"D'you see Turks now?"

Monty pointed, but there was no need. Dense masses of men were bivouacked beyond the bottom of the wide clay ramp. Through the glasses I could see artillery and supply wagons. They were coming to make a thorough job of "rescuing" Zeitoon this time! After a while I was able to make out the dark irregular line of Kagig's men, and here and there the lighter color of freshly dug entrenchments. None of Zeitoon's defenders appeared to be thrown out beyond the clay ramp, but they evidently flanked it on the side of the pass that was farthest from us.

"Now look this way, and you'll understand."

Monty pointed to our right, and the significance of the voices we had heard so close to us when Fred was searching for a path around the clay on the morning of our arrival, was made plain instantly. Down from the ledge on which the castle stood to a point apparently within a few yards of the clay ramp there had been cut a winding swath through the forest, along which four horses abreast could be ridden, or as many men marched.

"How did you do all that in time?" demanded Will. "It looks like one of those contractor's jobs in the States—put through while you wait and to hell with everything!"

"It follows the old road," Monty answered. "There was too much cobble-paving for the trees to take hold, and most of what they had to cut was small stuff. That accounts, too, for the freedom from stumps. But, do you get the idea? The trees between the end of the cutting and the clay ramp are cut almost through—ready to fall, in fact. I'm afraid of a wind. If it blows, our screen may fall too soon! But if the Turks try to storm the ramp, we'll draw them on. Then, hey—presto! Down go the remaining trees, and into the middle of 'em rides our cavalry!"

"What's the use of cavalry four abreast?" demanded Fred, in no mood to be satisfied with anything.

"Rustum Khan is concentrating all his energy on teaching that one maneuver," Monty answered. "We come—"

"Thought it 'ud be 'we!' Your place is at the rear, giving orders!"

"We come down the track at top speed, and the impetus will carry us clear across the ramp. Some of the horses'll go down, because the slope is slippery. But the remainder will front form squadron, and charge down hill in line. Then watch!"

"All right," Fred grumbled. "But how about you rear while all that's going on? The Turk must have worked his way around Beirut Dagh on former occasions—or how else could he ever have built and held that dismantled fort? What's to stop him from doing it again?"

"It's a fifteen-mile fight ahead of him," Monty answered, "with riflemen posted at every vantage-point all the way—"

"Who is in charge of the riflemen?"

Kagig leaned back until he looked in danger of falling, and tapped his breast significantly three times.

"I—I have picked the men who will command those riflemen and women!"

"Well," Fred grumbled, "what are your plans for us?"

"For the last time, Fred, I want you, old man, to help me to persuade these others to escape into the hills while there's still a chance, and I want you to go with them."

"I also!" exclaimed Kagig. "I also desire that!"

"Now you've got that off your chest, Didums, suppose you talk sense," suggested Fred. "What are your plans?"

Monty recognized the unalterable, and set his face.

"You first, Miss Vanderman. There's one way in which we can always use a gentlewoman's services."

"Mayn't I fight?" she begged, and we all laughed.

" 'Fraid not. No. The women have cleared out several houses for a hospital. Please go and superintend."

"Damn!" exclaimed Gloria, Boston fashion, not in the least under her breath.

"I am sending word," said Kagig, "that they shall obey you or learn from me!"

"The rest of us," Monty went on, "will know better what to do when we know what the Turk intends, but I expect to send all of you from time to time to wherever the fighting is thickest. Kagig, of course, will please himself, and my orders are subject to his approval."

"I'll go, then," said Gloria. "Good-by!" And she kissed Will on the mouth in full view of all of us, he blushing furiously, and Kagig cracking all his finger-joints.

"Go with her, Will!" urged Monty, as she disappeared down the steps. "Go and save yourself. You're young. I've notions of my own that I've inherited, and the world calls me a back number. You go with Miss Vanderman!"

I seconded that motion.

"Go with her, Will! I've warned you she's unsafe alone! Go and protect her!"

Will grinned, wholly without malice.

"Thanks!" he said. "She's a back number, too. So'm I! If I left Monty in this pinch she'd never look at me, and I'd not ask her to! Inherited notions about merit and all that kind of thing, don't you know, by gosh! No, sir! She and I both sat into this game. She and I both stay! Wish Esau would open the ball, though. I'm tired of talking."

ICH DIEN

Is honor out of fashion and the men she named
Fit only to be buried and defamed
Who dared hold service was true nobleness
And graced their service in a fitting dress?
Are manners out of date because the scullions
  scoff
At whosoever shuns the common trough
Liking dry bread better than the garbled stew
Nor praising greed because the style is new?
Let go the ancient orders if so be their ways
Are trespassing on decency these days.
So I go, rather than accept the trampled spoil
Or gamble for what great men earned by toil.
For rather than trade honor for a mob's foul
  praise
I'll keep full fealty to the ancient ways
And, hoisting my forebear's banner in the face of
  hell,
Will die beneath it, knowing I die well!

XIX
"SUCH DRILLING AS THEY HAVE HAD—SUCH LITTLE DRILLING!"

FIFTEEN MINUTES after Gloria Vanderman left us I saw a banner go jerkily mounting up the newly placed flag-pole on the keep. A man blew a bugle hoarsely by way of a salute. I raised my hat. Monty raised his. In a moment we were all standing bareheaded, and the great square piece of cloth caught the wind that whistled between two crags of Beirut Dagh.

Fred, our arch-iconoclast, stood uncovered longest.

"Who the devil made it for you?" he inquired.

Stitched on the banner in colored cloth were the two wheat-sheaves and two ships of the Montdidiers, and a scroll stretched its length across the bottom, with the motto doubtless, although in the wind one could not read it.

"The women. Good of 'em, what? Miss Vanderman drew it on paper. They cut it out, and sat up last night sewing it."

"I suppose you know that's filibustering, to fly your private banner on foreign soil?"

"They may call it what they please," said Monty. "I can't well fly the flag of England, and Armenia has none yet. Let's go below, Fred, and see if there's any news."

"Yes, there is news," said Kagig, leading the

way down. "I did not say it before the lady. It is not good news."

"That's the only kind that won't keep. Spit it out!" said Will.

Kagig faced us on the stable roof, and his finger-joints cracked again.

"It is the worst! They have sent Mahmoud Bey, against us. I would rather any six other Turks. Mahmoud Bey is not a fool. He is a young successful man, who looks to this campaign to bolster his ambition. He is a ruthless brute!"

"Which Turk isn't?" asked Will.

"This one is most ruthless. This Mahmoud is the one who in the massacres of five years ago caused Armenian prisoners to have horse-shoes nailed to their naked feet, in order, he said, that they might march without hurt. He will waste no time about preliminaries!"

Kagig was entirely right. Mahmoud Bey began the overture that very instant with artillery fire directed at the hidden defenses flanking the clay ramp. Next we caught the stuttering chorus of his machine guns, and the intermittent answer of Kagig's riflemen.

"Now, *effendim,* one of you down to the defenses, please! There is risk my men may use too many cartridges. Talk to them—restrain them. They might listen to me, but—" His long fingers suggested unhappy fragments of past history.

"You, Fred!" said Monty, and Fred hitched his concertina to a more comfortable angle.

Fred was the obvious choice. His gift of tongues would enable him better than any of us to persuade, and if need were, compel. We had left our rifles leaning by the wall at the castle entrance, and in his cartridge bag was my oil-can and rag-bag. I asked him for them, and he threw them to me rather clumsily. Trying to catch them I twisted for the second time the ankle I had hurt that morning. Fred mounted and rode out through the echoing entrance without a backward glance, and I sat down and pulled my boot off, for the agony was almost unendurable.

"That settles your task for to-day," laughed Monty. "Help him back to the top of the tower, Will. Keep me informed of everything you see. Will—you go with Kagig after you've helped him up there."

"All right," said Will. "Where's Kagig bound for?"

"Round behind Beirut Dagh," Kagig announced grimly. "That's our danger-point. If the Turks force their way round the mountain—" He shrugged his expressive shoulders. Only he of all of us seemed to view the situation seriously. I think we others felt a thrill rather of sport than of danger.

I might have been inclined to resent the inactivity assigned to me, only that it gave me a better chance than I had hoped for of watching for signs of Maga Jhaere's promised treachery. Will helped me up and made the perch comfortable; then he and Kagig rode away together. Presently Monty, too, mounted a mule, and rode out under the arch, and fifteen minutes later fifty men marched in by twos, laughing and joking, and went to saddling the horses in the semicircular stable below me. After that all the world seemed to grow still for a while, except for the eagles, the distant rag-slitting rattle of rifle-fire, and the occasional bursting of a shell. Most of the shells were falling on the clay ramp, and seemed to be doing no harm whatever.

Away in the distance down the pass, out of range of the fire of our men, but also incapable of harm themselves until they should advance into the open jaws below the clay ramp, I could see the Turks massing in that sort of dense formation that the Germans teach. Even through the glasses it was not possible to guess their numbers, because the angle of vision was narrow and cut off their flanks to right and left; but I sent word down to Monty that a frontal attack in force seemed to be already beginning.

For an hour after that, while the artillery fire increased but our rifle-fire seemed to dwindle under Fred's persuasive tongue, I watched Monty mustering reinforcements in the gorge below the town. He overcame some of the women's prejudice, for it was a force made up of men and women that he presently led away. I was rather surprised to see Rustum Khan, after a talk with Monty, return to his squadron and remain inactive under cover of the hill; that fire-eater was the last man one would expect to remain willingly out of action. However, twenty minutes later, Rustum Khan appeared beside me, breathing rather hard. He begged the glasses of me, and spent five minutes studying the firing-line minutely before returning them.

"The lord sahib has more faith in these undrilled folk than I have!" he grumbled at last. "Observe: he goes with that bullet-food of men and women mixed, to hide them in reserve behind the narrow gut at the head of the ramp. The Turks are fools, as Kagig said, and their general is also a fool, in spite of Kagig. They propose to force that ramp. You see that by Frredd sahib's orders the firing on our side has grown greatly less. That is to draw the Turks on. See! It has drawn them! They are coming! The lord sahib will send for Frredd sahib to take command of that reserve, to man the top of the ramp in case the Turks succeed in climbing too far up it. Then he himself will gallop back to take charge of my squadron below there; and I take charge of his squadron up here. He and I are interchangeable, I having drilled all the men in any case—such drilling as they have had—such little, little drilling!"

The Turks began their advance into the jaws of that defile with a confidence that made my heart turn cold. What did they know? What were they depending on in addition to their weight of numbers? Mahmoud Bey had evidently hurried up almost his whole division, and was driving them forward into our trap as if he knew he could swallow trap and all. Not even foolish generals act that way. It needs a madman. Kagig had said nothing about Mahmoud being mad.

"Listen, Rustum Khan!" I said. "Go with a message to Lord Montdidier. Tell him the whole Turkish force is in motion and coming on as if their general knows something for certain that we don't know at all. Tell him that I suspect treachery at our rear, and have good reason for it!"

Rustum Khan eyed me for a minute as if he would read the very middle of my heart.

"Can you ride?" he asked.

"Of course," I answered. "It's only walking that I can't do."

"Then leave those glasses with me, and go yourself!"

"Why won't you go?" I asked.

"Because here are fifty men who would lack a leader in that case."

The answer was honest enough, yet I had my qualms about leaving the post Monty had assigned to me. The thought that finally decided me was that I would have opportunity to gallop past the hospital, two hundred yards over the bridge on the Zeitoon side, and make sure that Gloria was safe.

"Have you seen Maga Jhaere anywhere?" I asked.

"No," said the Rajput, swearing under his breath at the mere mention of her name.

"Then help me down from here. I'll go."

He muttered to himself, and I think he thought I was off to make love to the woman; but I was past caring about any one's opinion on that score. Five minutes later I was trotting a good horse slowly down the upper, steeper portion of the track toward Zeitoon, swearing to myself, and dreading the smoother going where I should feel compelled to gallop whether my ankle hurt or not. As a matter of fact I began to suspect a broken bone or ligament, for the agonizing pain increased and made me sit awkwardly on the horse, thus causing him to change his pace at odd intervals and give me more pain yet. However, gallop I had to, and I reached the bridge going at top speed, only to be forced to rein in, chattering with agony, by a man on foot who raced to reach the bridge ahead of me, and made unmistakable signals of having an important message to deliver.

He proved to be from Kagig, with orders to say that every man at his disposal was engaged by a very strong body of Turks who had spent the night creeping up close to their first objective, and had rushed it with the bayonet shortly after dawn.

"Order the women to stand ready by the bridge!" were the last words (the man had the whole by heart), and then there was a scribbled note from Will by way of make-weight.

"This end of the action looks pretty serious to me. We're badly outnumbered. The men are fighting gamely, but—tell Gloria for God's sake to look out after herself!"

I could hear no firing from that direction, for the great bulk of Beirut Dagh shut it off.

"How far away is the fighting?" I demanded.

"Oh, a long way yet."

I motioned to him to return to Kagig, and sent my horse across the bridge, catching sight of Gloria outside the hospital directly after I had crossed it. She waved her hand to me; so, seeing she was safe for the present, I let the message to her wait and started down the valley toward Monty as fast as the horse could go. I had my work cut out to drive him into the din of firing, for it was evidently his first experience of bursting shells, and even at half-a-mile distance he reared and plunged, driving me nearly crazy with pain. I found Monty shepherding the reserves he had brought down, watching through glasses from over the top of the spur that formed the left-hand wall of the gut of the pass.

"I left Rustum Khan in my place," I began, expecting to be damned at once for absenting without leave.

"Glad you came," he said, without turning his head.

I gave him my message, he listening while he watched the pass and the oncoming enemy.

"I tried to warn you of treachery this morning!" I said hotly. Pain and memory did nothing toward keeping down choler. "Where's Peter Measel? Seen him anywhere? Where's Maga Jhaere? Seen her, either? Those Turks are coming on into what they must know is a trap, with the confidence that proves their leaders have special information! Look at them! They can see this pass is lined, with our riflemen, yet on they come! They must suspect we've a surprise in store—yet look at them!"

They were coming on line after line, although Fred had turned the ammunition loose, and the rifle-fire of our well-hidden men was playing havoc. Monty seemed to me to look more puzzled than afraid. I went on telling him of the message Kagig had sent, and offered him Will's note, but he did not even look at it.

"Ah!" he said suddenly. "Now I understand! Yes, it's treachery. I beg your pardon for my thoughts this morning."

"Granted," said I, "but what next?"

"Look!" he said simply.

There were two sudden developments. What was left of the first advancing company of Turks halted below the ramp, and with sublime effrontery, born no doubt of knowledge that we had no artillery, proceeded to dig themselves a shallow trench. The Zeitoonli were making splendid shooting, but it was only a question of minutes until the shelter would be high enough for crouching men.

The second disturbing factor was that in a long line extending up the flank of the mountain, roughly parallel to the lower end of the track that Monty had caused to be cut from the castle, the trees were coming down as if struck by a cyclone! There must have been more than a regiment armed with axes, cutting a swath through the forest to take our secret road in flank!

That meant two things clearly. Some one had told Mahmoud of our plan to charge down from the height and surprise him, thus robbing us of all the benefit of unexpectedness; and, when the charge should take place, our men would have to ride down four abreast through ambush. And, if Mahmoud had merely intended placing a few men to trap our horsemen, he would never have troubled to cut down the forest. Plainly, he meant to destroy our mounted men at point-blank range, and then march a large force up the horse-track, so turning the tables on us. Considering the overwhelming numbers he had at his disposal, the game to me looked almost over.

Not so, however, to Monty. He glanced over his shoulder once at the men and women waiting for his orders, and I saw the women begin inspiriting their men. Then he turned on me.

"Now damn your ankle," he said. "Try to forget it! Climb up there and tell Fred to choose a hundred men and bring them down himself to oppose the enemy in front if he comes over the top of that ditch. Then you gallop back and get word to Rustum Khan to bring both squadrons down here. Tell him to stay by Fred and hold his horses until the last minute. Then you get all the women you can persuade to follow you, and man the castle walls! Hurry, now—that's all!"

There was a man holding my horse. I tied the horse securely to a tree instead, and told the man to help me climb, little suspecting what a Samson I had happened on. He laughed, seized me in his arms, and proceeded to carry me like a baby up the goat-track leading to the hidden rifle-pits and trenches. I persuaded him to let me get up on his shoulders, and in that way I had a view of most of what was happening.

Monty led his men and women at a run across the top of the ramp flanked by the full fire of the entrenched company below; and his action was so unexpected that the Turks fired like beginners. There were not many bodies lying quiet, nor writhing either when the last woman had disappeared among the trees on the far side. Those that did writhe were very swiftly caused to cease by volleys aimed at them in obedience to officers' orders. It began to look as if Gloria's hospital would not be over-worked.

The tables were now turned on the Turks, except in regard to numbers. In the first place, as soon as Monty's command had penetrated downward through the trees parallel with the side of the ramp, he had the entrenched company in flank. It did not seem to me that he left more than ten or fifteen men to make that trench untenable, but the Turks were out of it within five minutes and in full retreat under a hot fire from Fred's men.

Then Monty pushed on to the far side of the castle road and held the remaining fringe of trees in such fashion that the Turks could not guess his exact whereabouts nor what number he had with him. Cutting down trees in a hurry is one thing, but cutting them down in face of hidden rifle-fire is most decidedly another, especially when the ax-men have been promised there will be no reprisals.

The tree-felling suddenly ceased, and there began a close-quarters battle in the woods, in which numbers had less effect than knowledge of the ground and bravery. The Turk is a brave enough fighter, but not to be compared with mountain-Armenians fighting for their home, and it was easy to judge which held the upper hand.

I found Fred smoking his pipe and enjoying himself hugely, with half a dozen runners ready to carry word to whichever section of the defenses seemed to him to need counsel. He could see what Monty had done, and was in great spirits in consequence.

"I've bagged two Turk officers to my own gun," he announced. "Murder suits me to a T."

I gave him the message.

"Piffle!" he answered. "They can never take the ramp by frontal attack! The right thing to do is hold the flanks, and wither 'em as they cone!"

"Monty's orders!" I said, "and I've got to be going."

"Damn that fellow Didums!" he grumbled. "All right. But it's my belief he's turning a classy little engagement into a bloody brawl! Cut along! I'll pick my hundred and climb down there."

Cutting along was not so easy. My magnificent human mount was hit by a bullet—a stray one, probably, shot at a hazard at long range. He fell and threw me head-long; and the agony of that experience pretty nearly rendered me unconscious. However, he was not hit badly, and essayed to pick me up again. I refused that, but he held on to me and, both of us being hurt in the leg on the same side, we staggered together down the goat-track.

Down below we found the horse plunging in a frenzy of fear, and he nearly succeeded in breaking away from both of us, dragging us out into full view of the enemy, who volleyed us at long range. Fortunately they made rotten shooting, and one ill-directed hail of lead screamed on the far side, causing the horse to plunge toward me. The Armenian took me by the uninjured foot and flung me into the saddle, and I left up-pass with a parting volley scattering all around, and both hands locked into the horse's mane. He needed neither whip nor spur, but went for Zeitoon like the devil with his tail on fire.

I suppose one never grows really used to pain, but from use it becomes endurable. When Anna ran out to stop me by the great rock on which the lowest Zeitoon houses stand, and seized me by the foot, partly to show deference, partly in token that she was suppliant, and also partly because she was utterly distracted, I was able to rein the horse and listen to her without swearing.

"She is gone!" she shouted. "Gone, I tell you! Gloria is gone! Six men, they come and take her! She is resisting, oh, so hard—and they throw a sack over her—and she is gone, I tell you! She is gone!"

"Where is Maga?"

"Gone, too!"

"In which direction did they take Miss Gloria?"

"I do not know!"

I rode on. There were crowds of women near the bridge, all armed with rifles, and I hurried toward them.

But they refused to believe that any one in Zeitoon would do such a thing as kidnap Gloria, and while I waited for Anna to come and convince them a man forced himself toward me through the crowd. He was out of breath. One arm was in a bloody bandage, but in the other hand he held a stained and crumpled letter.

It proved to be from Will, addressed to all or any of us.

> "Kagig is a wonder!" it ran, "He has put new life into these men and we've thrashed the Turk soundly. How's Gloria? Kagig says, 'Can you send us reinforcements?' If so we can follow up and do some real damage. Send 'em quick! Make Gloria keep cover!
>
> Will."

THOU LAND OF THE GLAD HAND

Thou land of the Glad Hand, whose frequent
boast

Is of the hordes to whom thou playest host!
Whose liberty is full! whose standard high
Has reached and taken stars from out the sky!
Whose fair-faced women tread the streets
unveiled,
Unchallenged, unaffronted, unassailed!
Whose little ones in park and meadow laugh,
Nor know what cost that precious cup they
quaff,
Nor pay in stripes and bruises and regret
Ten times each total of a parent's debt!
Thou nation born in freedom—land of kings
Whose laws protect the very feathered things,
Uplifting last and least to high estate
That none be overlooked—and none too great!
Is all thy freedom good for thee alone?
Is earth thy footstool? Are the clouds thy throne?
Shall other peoples reach thy hand to take
That gladdens only thee for thine own sake?

XX
"SO FEW AGAINST SO MANY! I SEE DEATH, AND I AM NOT SORRY!"

TO GET word to Rustum Khan was simple enough, for he himself came riding down to get news. The minute he learned what Monty wanted of him he turned his horse back up-hill at a steady lope, and I began on the next item in the program.

Nor was that difficult. The reading aloud of Will's letter, translated to them by Anna, convinced the women that their beloved bridge was in no immediate danger, and no less than three hundred of them marched off to reinforce Kagig's men behind Beirut Dagh. I reckoned that by the time they reached the scene of action we would have a few more than three thousand men and women in the field under arms—against Mahmoud Bey's thirty thousand Turks!

There remained to scrape together as many as possible to man the castle walls; and what with wounded, and middle-aged women, and men whose weapons did not fit the plundered Turkish ammunition, I had more than a hundred volunteers in no time. The only disturbing feature about this new command of mine was that it contained more than a sprinkling of the type of malcontents who had bearded Kagig in his den the night before. Those looked like thoroughly excellent fighting men, if only they could have been persuaded to agree to trust a common leader.

Not one of them but knew a thousand times more of Zeitoon, and their people, and the various needs of defense than, for instance, I did. Yet they clustered about me for lack of confidence in one another, and shouted after the women who marched away advice to watch lest Kagig betray them all. Not for nothing had the unspeakable Turk inculcated theories of misrule all down the centuries!

I led them up to the castle, they carrying with them food enough for several days. We passed Rustum Khan coming down with the horsemen, and I fell behind to have word with him.

"Which of these men shall I pick to command the rest?" I asked him. "You've more experience of them."

"Any that you choose will be pounced on by the rest as wolves devour a sheep!" the Rajput answered.

"Should I have them vote on it?"

"They would elect you," he answered.

"I've got to be free to look for Miss Gloria. She's kidnapped—disappeared utterly!"

Rustum Khan swore under his breath, using a language that I knew no word of.

"A woman again, and more trouble!" he said at last grimly. "Let like cure like then! Choose a woman herdsman!" he grinned. "It may be she will surprise them into obedience!"

"I'll take your advice," said I, although I resented his insinuation that they were a herd—so swiftly does command make partisans.

"The last thing you may take from me, sahib!" he answered.

"How so?"

"So few against so many! I see death and I am not sorry. Only may I die leading those good mountain-men of mine!"

It was part and parcel of him to praise those he had drilled and scorn the others. I shook hands and said nothing. It did not seem my place to contradict him.

"Let us hope these people are the gainers by our finish!" he called over his shoulder, riding on after his command. "They are not at all bad people—only un-drilled, and a little too used to the ways of the Turk! Good-by, sahib!"

Within the castle gate I found a woman, whom they all addressed as Marie, very busy sorting out the bundles they had thrown against the wall. She was putting all the food together into a common fund, and as I entered she shouted to her own nominees among the other women to get their cooking pots and begin business.

Still pondering Rustum Khan's advice, in the dark whether or not be meant it seriously, I chose Marie Chandrian to take command. She made no bones about it, but accepted with a great shrill laugh that the rest of them seemed to recognize—and to respect for old acquaintance' sake. She turned out to have her husband with her—an enormous, hairy man with a bull's voice who ought to have been in one or other of the firing-lines but had probably held back in obedience to his better half. She made him her orderly at once, and it was not long before every soul in the castle had his or her place to hold.

Then I mounted once more and rode at top speed down the new road that Monty was defending, taking another horse this time, not so good, but much less afraid of the din of battle.

I found Monty scarcely fifty paces from the track, on the outside edge of the fringe of trees that the Turks had been unable to cut down. There were numbers of wounded laid out on the track itself, with none to carry them away; and the Turks were keeping up a hot fire from behind the shelter of the felled trees and standing stumps. The outside range was two hundred yards, and there were several platoons of the enemy who had crept up to within thirty or forty yards and could not be dislodged.

I pulled Monty backward, for he could not hear me, and he and I stood behind two trees while I told him what I had done, shouting into his ear.

"I've got to go and find Gloria!" I said finally, and he frowned, and nodded.

"Go first and take a look at the ramp through the trees. Tell me what's happening."

So I limped down to the end of the track and made my way cautiously through the lower fringe of trees that had been cut three-parts through in readiness for felling in a hurry. Just as I got there the Turks began a new massed advance up the ramp, as if in direct proof of Monty's mental alertness.

The men posted on the opposite flank to where I was opened a terrific fire that would have made poor Kagig bite his lips in fear for the waning ammunition. Then Fred came into action with his hundred, throwing them in line into the open along the top, where they lay down to squander cartridges—squandering to some purpose, however, for the Turkish lines checked and reeled.

But Mahmoud Bey had evidently given orders that this advance should be pressed home, and the Turks came on, company after company, in succeeding waves of men. There were some in front with picks and shovels, making rough steps in the slippery clay; and I groaned, hating to go and tell Monty that it was only a matter of minutes before the frontal attack must succeed and the pass be in enemy hands.

"Here goes Armenia's last chance!" I thought; and I waited to see the beginning of the end before limping back to Monty.

And it was well I did wait. I had actually forgotten Rustum Khan and his two squadrons. Nor would I ever have believed without seeing it that one lone man could so inspirit and control that number of aliens whom he had only as much as drilled a time or two. It said as much for the Zeitoonli as for Rustum Khan. Without the very ultimate of bravery, good faith, and intelligence on their part he could never have come near attempting what he did.

He brought his two squadrons in line together suddenly over the brow of the ramp, galloped them forward between Fred's extended riflemen, and charged down-hill, the horses checking as they felt the slippery clay under foot and then, unable to pull up, careering head-long, urged by their riders into madder and madder speed, with Rustum Khan on his beautiful bay mare several lengths in the lead.

Cavalry usually starts at a walk, then trots, and only gains its great momentum within a few yards of the enemy. This cavalry started at top speed, and never lost it until it buried itself into the advancing Turks as an avalanche bursts into a forest! No human enemy could ever have withstood that charge. Many of the horses fell in the first fifty yards, and none of these were able to regain their feet in time to be of use. Some of the riders were rolled on and killed. And some were slain by the half-dozen volleys the astonished Turks found time to greet them with. But more than two-thirds of Rustum Khan's men, armed with swords of every imaginable shape and weight, swept voiceless into an enemy that could not get out of their way; and regiments in the rear that never felt the shock turned and bolted from the wrath in front of them.

I climbed out to the edge of the trees, and yelled for Fred, waving both arms and my hat and a branch. He saw me at last, and brought his hundred men down the ramp at a run.

"Join Monty," I shouted, "and help him clear the woods."

He led his men into the trees like a pack of hounds in full cry, and I limped after them, arriving breathless in time to see the Turks in front of Monty in full retreat, fearful because the Rajput's cavalry had turned their flank. Then Monty and Fred got their men together and swung them down into the pass to cover Rustum Khan's retreat when the charge should have spent itself.

The Rajput had managed to demoralize the Turkish infantry, but Mahmoud's guns were in the rear, far out of reach. Bursting shells did more destruction as he shepherded the squadrons back again than bullet, bayonet and slippery clay combined to do in the actual charge itself. Monty gave orders to throw down the fringe of trees and let them through to the castle road, so saving them from the total annihilation in store if they had essayed to scramble up the slippery ramp. And then Fred's men joined Monty's contingent, helping them fortify the new line—deepening and reversing the trench the Turks had dug below the ramp, and continuing that line along through the remaining edge of trees that still stood between the enemy and the castle road.

But by cutting down the fringe at the end of the road to let Rustum Khan through we had forfeited the last degree of secrecy. If the Turks could come again and force the gut of the pass, nothing but the hardest imaginable fighting could prevent them from swinging round at that point and making use of our handiwork.

"That castle has become a weakness, not a strength, Colonel sahib!" said Rustum Khan, striding through the trees to where Monty and Fred and I were standing. "I have lost seven and thirty splendid men, and three and forty horses. One more such charge, and—"

"No, Rustum Khan. Not again," Monty answered.

"What else?" laughed the Rajput. "That castle divides our forces, making for weakness. If only—"

"We must turn it to advantage, then, Rustum Khan!"

"Ah, sahib! So speaks a soldier! How then?"

"Mahmoud knows by now that the trees are down," said I. "His watchers must have seen them fall. Some of the trees are lying outward toward the ramp."

"Exactly," said Monty. "His own inclination will lead him to use our new road, and we must see that he does exactly that. The guns are making the ramp too hot just now for amusement, but let some one—you, Fred—run a deep ditch across the top of the ramp; and if we can hold them until dark we'll have connected ditches dug at intervals all the way down."

Looking over the top of the trees I could just see the Montdidier standard bellying in the wind.

"I'll bet you Mahmoud can see that, too!" said I, drawing the others' attention to it.

"Let's hope so," Monty answered quietly. "Now, Rustum Khan, find one of those brave horsemen of yours who is willing to be captured by the enemy and give some false information. I want it well understood that our only fear is of a night attack!"

"You say, Colonel sahib, there will be no further use for cavalry?"

"Not for a charge down that ramp, at any rate!"

"Then send me! My word will carry conviction. I can say that as a Moslem I will fight no longer on the side of Christians. They will accept my information, and then hang me for having led a charge into their infantry. Send me, sahib!"

Monty shook his head. Rustum Khan seemed inclined to insist, but there came astonishing interruption. Kagig appeared, with arms akimbo, in our midst.

"Oh, sportsmen all!" he laughed. "This day goes well!"

"Thank God you're here!" said Monty. "Now we can talk."

"That Will—what is his name?—Will Yerkees is a wonderful fighter!" said Kagig, snapping his fingers and making the joints crack.

"He accuses you of that complaint," said I.

"Me? No. I am only enthusiast. The road behind Beirut Dagh is rough and narrow. The Turks had hard work, and less reason for eagerness than we. So we overcame them. They have fallen back to where they were at dawn, and they are discouraged"—he made his finger-joints crack again—"discouraged! The women feel very confident. The men feet exactly as the women do! The Turks are preparing to bivouac where they lie. They will attack no more to-day—I know them!"

"Listen, Kagig!" Monty drew us all together with a gesture of both hands. "These Turks are too many for us, if we give them time. Our ammunition won't last, for one thing. We must induce Mahmoud to attack to-night—coax him up this castle road, and catch him in a trap. It can be done. It must be done!"

"I know the right man to send to the Turk to tell him things!" Kagig answered slowly with relish.

"That is my business!" growled Rustum Khan, but Kagig laughed at him.

"No Turk would believe a word you say—not one leetle word!" he said, snapping his fingers. "You are a good fighter. I saw your charge from the castle tower; it was very good. But I will send an Armenian on this errand. Go on, Lord Monty; I know the proper man."

"That's about the long and short of it," said Monty. "If we can induce Mahmoud to attack to-night, we've a fair chance of hitting him so hard that he'll withdraw and let us alone. Otherwise—"

Kagig's finger-joints cracked harder than ever as his quick mind reviewed the possibilities.

"Have you any idea what can have happened to Miss Vanderman?" I asked him.

"Miss Vanderman? No? What? Tell me!"

He seemed astonished, and I told him slowly, lest he miss one grain of the enormity of Maga's crime. But instead of appearing distressed he shook his bands delightedly and rattled off a very volley of cracking knuckles.

"That is the idea! We have Mahmoud caught! I know Mahmoud! I know him! The man I shall choose shall tell Mahmoud that Gloria Vanderman—the beautiful American young lady, who is outlawed because of her fighting on behalf of Armenians—who—who could not possibly be claimed by the American consul, on account of being outlawed—is in the castle to-night and can be taken if he only will act quickly! Oh, how his eyes will glitter! That Mahmoud—he buys women all the time! A young—beautiful—athletic American girl—Mahmoud will sacrifice three thousand men to capture her!"

Monty ground his teeth. Fred turned his back, and filled his pipe. Rustum Khan brushed his black beard upward with both hands.

"Suppose you go now and try to find Miss Vanderman," said Monty rather grimly to me. "If you find her, hide her out of harm's way and communicate with Will!"

So Fred helped me on the horse and I rode back to the castle, where I explained the details of the fighting below to the defenders, and then rode on down to Zeitoon by the other road. It was wearing along into the afternoon, and I had no idea which way to take to look for Gloria; but I did have a notion that Maga Jhaere might be looking out for me. There was a chance that she might have been in earnest in persuading me to elope, and that if I rode alone she might show herself—she or else Gloria's captors.

Failing signs of Maga Jhaere or her men, I proposed to ride behind Beirut Dagh in search of Will, and to get his quick Yankee wit employed on the situation.

So, instead of crossing the bridge into Zeitoon I guided my horse around the base of the mountain, riding slowly so as to ease the pain in my foot and to give plenty of opportunity to any one lying in wait to waylay me.

It happened I guessed rightly. The track swung sharp to the left after a while, and passed up-hill through a gorge between two cliffs into wilder country than any I had yet seen in Armenia. From the top of the cliff on the right-hand side a pebble was dropped and struck the horse—then another—then a third one. I thought it best to take no notice of that, although the horse made fuss enough.

The third pebble was followed by a shrill whistle, which I also decided to ignore, and continued to ride on toward where a clump of scrawny bushes marked the opening out of a narrow valley. I heard the bushes rustle as I drew near them, and was not surprised to see Maga emerge, looking hot, impatient and angry, although not less beautiful on that account.

"Fool!" she began on me. "Why you wait so long? Another half-hour and it is too late altogether! Come now! Leave the horse. Come quick!"

Wondering what important difference half an hour should make, it occurred to me that Will was probably impatient long ago at receiving no news of Gloria. If I judged Will rightly, he would be on his way to look for her.

"Come quick!" commanded Maga.

"I can't climb that cliff," said I. "I've hurt my foot."

"I help you. Come!"

She stepped up close beside me to help me down, but that instant it seemed to me that I heard more than one horse approaching.

"Quick!" she commanded, for she heard them, too, and held out her arms to help me. "Quick! I have two men to help you walk!"

I could have reached my pistol, but so could she have reached hers, and her hand and eye were quicker than forked lightning. Besides, to shoot her would have been of doubtful benefit until Gloria's whereabouts were first ascertained. She put an arm round me to pull me from the saddle, and that settled it. I fell on her with all my weight, throwing her backward into the bushes, and kicking the horse in the ribs with my uninjured foot. The horse took fright as I intended, and went galloping off in the direction of the approaching sounds.

I had not wrestled since I was a boy at school, and then never with such a spitting puzzle of live wires as Maga proved herself. I had the advantage of weight, but I had told her of my injured foot, and she worked like a she-devil to damage it further, fighting at the same time with left and right wrist alternately to reach pistol and knife.

I let go one wrist, snatched the pistol out of her bosom and threw it far away. But with the free and she reached her knife, and landed with it into my ribs. The pain of the stab sickened me; but the knowledge that she had landed fooled her into relaxing her hold in order to jump clear. So I got hold of both wrists again, and we rolled over and over among the bushes, she trying like an eel to wriggle away, and I doing my utmost to crush the strength out of her. We were interrupted by Will's voice, and by Will's strong arms dragging us apart.

"Catch her!" I panted. "Hold her! Don't let her go!"

"Never fear!" he laughed.

"Her men have kidnapped Gloria! Tie her hands!"

Will had two men with him, one of whom was leading my runaway horse. They gazed open-eyed while Will tied Maga's wrists behind her back.

"Kagig—what will he say?" one of them objected, but Will laughed.

"What you do with me?" demanded Maga.

"Take you to Kagig, of course. Where's Miss Vanderman?"

Then suddenly Maga's whole appearance changed. The defiance vanished, leaving her as if by magic supple again, subtle, suppliant, conjuring back to memory the nights when she had danced and sung. The fire departed from her eyes and they became wet jewels of humility with soft love lights glowing in their depths.

"You do not want that woman!" she said slowly, smiling at Will. "You give 'er to this fool!" She glanced at my bleeding ribs, as if the blood were evidence of folly. "You take me, Will Yerkees! Then I teach you all things—all about people—all about land, and love, and animals, and water, and the air—I teach you all!"

She paused a moment, watching his face, judging the effect of words. He stood waiting with a look of puzzled distress that betrayed regret for her tied wrists, but accepted the necessity. Perhaps she mistook the chivalrous distress for tenderness.

"I 'ave tried to make that man Kagig king! I 'ave tried, and tried! But 'e is no good! If 'e 'ad obeyed me, I would 'ave made 'im king of all Armenia! But 'e is as good as dead already, because Mahmoud the Turk is come to finish 'im—so!" She spat conclusively. "So now I make you king instead of 'im! You let that Gloria Vanderman go to this fool, an' I show you 'ow to make all Armenians follow you an' overthrow the Turks, an' conquer, an' you be king!"

Will laughed. "Better stick to Kagig! I'm going to take you to him!"

"You take me to 'im?"

She flashed again, swift as a snake to illustrate resentment.

"Yes."

"Then I tell 'im things about you, an' 'e believe me!"

"Let's bargain," laughed Will. "Show me Miss Vanderman, alive and well, and—"

"Steady the Buffs!" I warned him. "Gloria's not far away. There were pebbles dropped on my horse. There may be a cave above this cliff—or something of the sort."

Will nodded. "—and I won't tell Kagig you made love to me!" he continued.

"Poof! Pah! Kagig, 'e know that long ago!"

Will turned to his two men and bade them tie the horses to a bush.

"How are the ribs?" he asked me.

"Nothing serious," said I.

"Do you think you can watch her if I tie her feet?"

"She's slippery and strong! Better tie her to a tree as well!"

So between them Will and the two men trussed her up like a chicken ready for the market, making her bound ankles fast to the roots of a bush. Then he led the two men up the cliff-side, and Maga lay glaring at me as if she hoped hate could set me on fire, while I made shift to stanch my wound.

But she changed her tactics almost before Will was out of sight beyond a boulder, beginning to scream the same words over and over in the gipsy tongue and struggling to free her feet until I thought the thongs would either burst or strip the flesh from her.

The screams were answered by a shout from up above. Then I heard Will shout, and some one fired a pistol. There came a clatter of loose stones, and I got to my feet to be ready for action—not that my hurts would have let me accomplish much.

A second later I saw three of Gregor Jhaere's gypsies scurrying along the cliff-side, turning at intervals to fire pistols at some one in pursuit. So I joined in the fray with my Colt repeater, and flattered myself I did not do so badly. The first two shots produced no other effect than to bring the runaways to a halt. The next three shots brought all three men tumbling head over heels down the cliff-side, rolling and sliding and scattering the stones.

One fell near Maga's feet and lay there writhing. The other two came to a standstill in a hideous heap beside me, and I stooped to see if I could recognize them.

What happened after that was almost too quick for the senses to take in. One of the gypsies came suddenly to life and seized me by the neck. The other grasped my feet, and as I fell I saw the third man slash loose Maga's thongs and help her up.

My two assailants rolled me over on my back, and while one held me the other aimed blows at my head with the butt of his empty pistol. Once he hit me, and it felt like an explosion. Twice by a miracle I dodged the blows, growing weaker, though, and hopeless. He aimed a fourth blow, taking his time about it and making sure of his aim, and I waited in the nearest approach to fatalistic calm I ever experienced.

In a strange abstraction, in which every movement seemed to be slowed down into unbelievable leisureliness, I saw the butt of the pistol begin to approach my eye—near—nearer. Then suddenly I heard a woman scream, and a shot ring out.

Instead of the pistol butt the gipsy's brains splashed on my face, and the man collapsed on top of me. Next I realized that Gloria Vanderman was wiping my face with a cloth of some kind, holding a hot pistol in her other hand, while Will was standing laughing over me, and Maga Jhaere with the other gipsy had disappeared altogether.

"Did you shoot Maga?" I mumbled.

"No," Will laughed. "I'd hate to shoot a woman who'd offered to make me king! She ought to be hung, though, for a horse-thief! She and that other gipsy got away with the mounts! Never mind—there are four of us to carry you, if Gloria lends a hand!"

But I have no notion how they carried me. All I remember is recovering consciousness that evening in the castle, to discover myself copiously bandaged, and painfully stiff, but not so much of an invalid after all.

FRAGMENT

Oh, fear and hate shall have their spate
(For both of the twain are one)
And lust and greed devour the seed
That else had growth begun.
Fiercely the flow of death shall go
And short the good man's shrift!
All hell's awake full toll to take,
And passions hour is swift.

But there be cracks in evil's tracks
Where seed shall safe abide,
And living rocks shall breast the shocks
Of overflowing tide.
Castle and wall and keep shall fall,
Prophet and plan shall fail,
And they shall thank nor wit nor rank
Who in the end prevail.

XXI
"THOSE WHO SURVIVE THIS NIGHT SHALL HAVE BRAVE MEMORIES!"

LOOKING BACK after this lapse of time there seems little difference between the disordered dreams of unconsciousness and the actual waking turmoil of that night. At first as I came slowly to my senses there seemed only a sea of voices all about me, and a constant thumping, as of falling weights.

There were great pine torches set in the rusty old rings on the wall, and by their fitful light I saw that I lay on a cot in the castle keep. Monty, Fred, Will, Kagig and Rustum Khan were conversing at a table. Gloria sat on an up-ended pine log near me. A dozen Armenians, including the "elders" who had disagreed with Kagig, stood arguing rather noisily near the door.

"What is the thumping?" I asked, and Gloria hurried to the cot-side. But I managed to sit up, and after she had given me a drink I found that my foot was still the most injured part of me. It was swollen unbelievably, whereas my bandaged head felt little the worse for wear, and the knife-wound did not hurt much.

"They're bringing in wood," she answered.

"Why all that quantity?"

The thumping was continuous, not unlike the noise good stevedores make when loading against time.

"To burn the castle!"

At that moment Rustum Khan left the table, and seeing me sitting up strode over.

"Good-by, sahib!" he said, reaching out for my hand.

"The lord sahib has given me a post of honor and I go to hold it. Those who survive this night shall have brave memories!"

I got to my feet to shake hands with him, and I think he appreciated the courtesy, for his stern eyes softened for a moment. He saluted Gloria rather perfunctorily as became his attitude toward women, and strode away to a point half-way between the door and Monty. There he turned, facing the table.

"Lord sahib bahadur!" he said sonorously.

Monty got up and stood facing him.

"Salaam!"

"Salaam, Rustum Khan!" Monty answered, returning the salute, and the others got to their feet in a hurry, and stood at attention.

Then the Rajput faced about and went striding through the doorless opening into the black night—the last I was destined to see of him alive.

"May we all prove as faithful and brave as that man!" said Monty, sitting down again, and Kagig cracked his knuckles.

Gloria and I went over and sat at the table, and seeing me in a state to understand things Monty gave me a précis of the situation.

"We're making a great beacon of this castle," he said. "Three hundred men and women are piling in the felled logs and trees and downwood—everything that will burn. We shall need light on the scene. Rustum Khan has gone to hold the clay ramp and make sure the Turks turn up this castle road. Fred is to hold the corner; we've fortified the Zeitoon side of the road, and Fred and his men are to make sure the Turks don't spread out through the trees. Kagig, Will and I, with twenty-five very carefully picked men for each of us, wait for the Turks at the bottom of the road and put up a feint of resistance. Our business will be to make it look as little like a trap and as much like a desperate defense as possible. We hope to make it seem we're caught napping and fighting in the last ditch."

"Last ditch is true enough!" Fred commented cheerfully. Fred was obviously in his best humor, faced by a situation that needed no cynicism to discolor it—full of fight and perfectly contented.

"Practically all of the rest of the men and women who are not watching the enemy on the other side of Beirut Dagh," Monty went on, "are hidden, or will be hidden in the timber on either side of the road. We're hoping to God they'll have sense enough to keep silent until the beacon is lighted. You're to light the beacon, since you're recovering so finely—you and Miss Vanderman."

"Yes, but when?" said I.

"When the bugles blow. We've got six bugles—"

"Only two of them are cornets and one's a trombone," Fred put in.

"And when they all sound together, then set the castle alight and kill any one you see who isn't an Armenian!"

"Or us!" said Fred. "You're asked not to kill one of us!"

"As a matter of fact," said Monty, "I rather expect to be near you by that time, because we don't want to give the signal until as many Turks as possible are caught in the road like rats. At the signal we dose the road at both ends; Rustum Khan and Fred from the bottom end, and we at the top."

"Most of the murder," Fred explained cheerfully, "will be done by the women hidden in the trees on either flank. As long as they don't shoot across the road and kill one another it'll be a picnic!"

"How do you know the Turks will walk into the trap?" I asked.

"Ten 'traitors,' " said Monty, "have let themselves get caught at intervals since noon. One of Kagig's spies has got across to us with news that Mahmoud means to finish the hash of Zeitoon to-night. His men have been promised all the loot and all the women."

"Except one!" Fred added with a glance at Gloria.

"Two! Except two!" remarked Kagig with a glance at the door. We looked, and held our breath.

Maga Jhaere stood there, with a hand on the masonry on each side!

"You fool, Kagig, what you fill this castle full of wood for?" she demanded.

Kagig beckoned to her.

"To burn little traitresses!" he answered tenderly. "Come here!"

She walked over to him, and he put his arm around her waist, looking up from his seat into her face as if studying it almost for the first time. She began running her fingers through his hair.

"Is she not beautiful?" he asked us naively. Then, not waiting for an answer: "She is my wife, *effendim.* You would not have me be revengeful—not toward my wife, I think?"

"Your wife? Why didn't you tell us that before?" Gloria seemed the most surprised, as well as the most amused, although we were all astonished.

"Not tell you before? Oh—do you remember Abraham—in the Bible—yes? She has been my best spy now and then. As Kagig's wife what good would she be?" Yet, had I not married her, I should have lost the services of most of my best spies—Gregor Jhaere for one. He is not her father, no. They call her their queen. She is daughter of another gipsy and of an Armenian lady of very good family. She has always hoped to see me a monarch!"

He laughed, and cracked his finger-joints.

"To make of me a monarch, and to reign beside me! Ha-ha-ha! I did those gypsies a favor by marrying her, for she was something of a problem to them, no gipsy being good enough in her eyes, and no busne caring for the honor until I saw and fell in love! Oh, yes, I fell in love! I, Kagig, the old adventurer, I fell in love!"

He drew her down and kissed her as tenderly as if she were a little child; then rose to his feet.

"You forgive her, *effendim?"* he asked. "You forgive her for my sake?"

None answered him. Perhaps he asked too much.

"Never mind me, then, *effendim.* Not for my sake, but for the good work she has so often done, and for the work she shall do—you forgive her?"

We all looked toward Gloria. It was her prerogative. Gloria took Maga's left hand in her right.

"I don't blame you," she said, "for coveting Will. I've coveted him myself! But you needn't have let your men handle me so roughly!"

"No?" said Maga blandly. "Then why did you 'urt two of them so badly that they run away? Did not you shoot that other one? So—I give 'im to you. I give you that Will Yerkees—"

"Thanks!" put in Will, but Maga ignored the interruption.

"—not because you are cleverer than me—or more beautiful. You are uglee! You can not dance, and as for fighting, I could keel you with one 'and! But because I like Kagig better after all!"

At that Kagig suddenly dismissed all such trivialities as treachery and matrimony from his mind with one of his Napoleonic gestures.

"It is time, *effendim,* to be moving!" He led the way out without another word, I limping along last and the Armenian "elders" following me.

It was pitchy dark in the castle courtyard, and without the light from numerous kerosene lanterns it would not have been possible to find the way between the heaped-up logs. There was only a crooked, very narrow passage left between the keep and the outer gate, and they had long ago left off using the gate for the lumber, but were hoisting it over the wall with ropes. One improvised derrick squealed in the darkness, and the logs came in by twos and tens and dozens. No sooner were we out of the keep than women came and tossed in logs through the door and windows, until presently that building, too, contained fuel enough to decompose the stone. And over the whole of it, here, there and everywhere, men were pouring cans and cans of kerosene, while other men were setting dry tinder in strategic places.

There was no moon that night. Or if there was a moon, then the dark clouds hid it. No doubt Mahmoud thought he had a night after his own heart for the purpose of overwhelming our little force; for how should he know that we were ready for the massed battalions forming to storm the gorge again. At a little after eight o'clock Mahmoud resumed the offensive with his artillery, and a messenger that Monty sent down to watch returned and reported the shells all bursting wild, with Rustum Khan's men taking careful cover in the ditches they had zigzagged down the whole face of the ramp.

An hour later the Turk's infantry was reported moving, and shortly before ten o'clock we heard the opening rattle of Rustum Khan's stinging defense. There was intended to be no deception about that part of our arrangements; nor was there. The oncoming enemy was met with a hail of destruction that checked and withered his ranks, and made the succeeding companies only too willing to turn at the castle road instead of struggling straight forward.

Nor was the turn accomplished without further loss; for our Zeitoonli, still entrenched on the flank of the pass, loosed a murderous storm of lead through the dark that swept every inch of the open castle road, and the turn became a shambles.

But Mahmoud had reckoned the cost and decided to pay it. Company after company poured up the gorge in the rear of the front ones, and turned with a roar up the road, butchered and bewildered, but ever adding to the total that gained shelter beyond the first turn in the road.

Those, however, had to deal at once with Monty, Will and Kagig, who opened on them guerrilla warfare from behind trees—never opposing them sufficiently to check them altogether, but leading them steadily forward into the two-mile trap. From where I stood on the top of the castle wall I could judge pretty accurately how the fight went; and I marveled at the skill of our men that they should retire up the road so slowly, and make such a perfect impression of desperate defense. Gloria refused from the first to remain inactive beside me, but went through the trees down the line of the road, crossing at intervals from side to side, urging and begging our ambushed people to be patient and reserve their fire until the chorus of bugles should blow.

About eleven o'clock a breathless messenger came to say that the Turks had renewed the attack on the other side of Beirut Dagh; but I did not even send him on to Kagig. If the attack was a feint, as was probable, intended to distract us from the main battle, then there were men enough there to deal with it. If, on the other hand, Mahmoud had divided forces and sent a formidable number around the mountain, then our only chance was nevertheless to concentrate on our great effort, and defeat the nearest first. There was not the slightest wisdom in sending down a message likely to distract Monty or Will or Kagig from their immediate task.

The women kept piling in the pine trees, until I thought the very weight of lumber might defeat our purpose by delaying the blaze too long. But Kagig had requisitioned every drop of kerosene in Zeitoon, and the stuff was splashed on with the recklessness that comes of throwing parsimony to the winds. Then I grew afraid lest they should fire the stuff too soon, or lest some stray spark from a man's pipe or an overturned lantern should do the work. Every imaginable fear presented itself, because, having no active part in the fighting, I had nothing to distract me from self-criticism. It became almost a foregone conclusion after a while that the night's work was destined to be spoiled entirely by some oversight or stupidity of mine.

The battle down in the valley dinned and screamed like the end of the world, although the Turks could not use their artillery for fear of slaughtering their own men. I could hear Fred hotly engaged, holding the corner of the turn where the Turks were seeking in vain to widen it. Probably the Turks supposed he was put there with a hundred men to defend the road, instead of to drive their thinned battalions up it.

In the end it was an accident that set the bugles blowing, and probably that accident saved our fortunes. Monty shouted to a man to run and ask for news of the fighting below. Mistaking the words in the din, the messenger ran to the rock in the clearing on which the musicians waited, and a minute later the first bars of the *Marseillaise* rang clearly through the trees.

The almost instant answer was a volley from each side of the road that sounded like the explosion of the whole world. And the Turks hardly half into the trap yet! Monty and Will and Kagig brought their men back up the road at the double, as the only way to escape the fire of our ambushed friends. I was two minutes fumbling with matches in the wind before I could light the kindling set ready in the entrance arch; and it was about three minutes more before the first long flame shot skyward and the beacon we had set began to do its appointed work.

Then, though, that castle proved to be a very

Vesuvius, for the draught poured in through the doorless arch and hurried the hot flames skyward to be mushroomed roaring against the belly of black clouds. None of us knew then where Mahmoud was, nor that he had given the order that minute to his trapped battalions to halt, face the trees on either side, and advance in either direction in order to widen their front.

The firing of the castle, for some mad reason of the sort that mothers every catastrophe, caused them to disobey that order and, instead, to charge forward at the double. In a moment the new fury (for it was not panic, nor yet exactly the reverse) communicated itself all along the road, and the regiments at the rear, in spite of the murderous fire from our ambush, yelled and milled to drive the men in front more swiftly.

Then Fred saw the castle flames, and led his men forward to plug up the lower end of the road. Next Rustum Khan saw it, and advanced three hundred down the ramp to hold the ditch at the bottom and prevent reserves from coming to the rescue.

It was then, so he told us afterward, that Fred realized who was the person in authority who had sought to change the line of battle at the critical moment. Mahmoud himself, surrounded by his staff, had ridden forward to see what the true nature of the difficulty might be, and had got caught in the trap when Fred closed it and Rustum Khan cut off the flow of men!

Fred did his best by rapid fire to put an end to Mahmoud, staff and all. But the light from the castle did not reach down in among the trees, and when he told the nearest men who the target was that only made the shooting wilder. Nor was Mahmoud a man without decision. Realizing that he was trapped, at any rate from behind, he galloped forward with his staff, scattering bewildered men to right and left of him, to find out whether the trap could not be forced from the upper end, knowing that there were plenty of men on the road already to account for any possible total we could bring against them, if only they could be led forward and deployed.

So it came about that Mahmoud on a splendid war-horse, and five of his mounted staff, arrived at the head of the oncoming column; and Kagig saw them in a moment when the flare from the castle roared like a rocket hundreds of feet high and scattered all the shadows on that section of the road. Kagig passed the word along, but it was Monty who devised the instant plan, and one of Will's men who came running to find me.

So I forgot pain and disability in the excitement of having a part to play. Gloria had found her way back to the castle, and it was she who rallied all the men and women who had worked at piling fuel, and brought them to where I lay. Then I begged her to get back somewhere and hide, but she laughed at me.

Our business was to burry down the road and plug it against Mahmoud and his men, while Kagig got behind him by sheer hand-to-hand fighting, and Monty and Will approached him from the flanks. We had to be cautious about shooting, because of Kagig, for one thing, but for another, Will had sent the message, "Don't kill Mahmoud." And that, of course, was obvious. Mahmoud alive would be worth a thousand to us of any Mahmoud dead.

Gloria ran down the road beside me, and Will caught sight of her in the dancing light. I heard him shout something in United States English about women and hell-fire and burned fingers, but beyond that it was not polite, and was intended for me as much as for Gloria, I did not get the gist of it. Then the battle closed up around us, and we all fought hand to hand—women harder than the men—to close in on Mahmoud and drag him from his horse.

Three times in the fitful dark and even more deceptive dancing light we almost had him. But the first time he fought free, and his war-horse kicked a clear way for him for a few yards through the scrimmage. Then Kagig closed in on him from the rear. But three of the staff engaged Kagig alone, and twenty or thirty of Mahmoud's infantry drove Kagig's men back on the still advancing column. Kagig went down, fighting and shouting like a Berserker, and Monty let Mahmoud go to run to Kagig's rescue.

Monty did not go alone, for his men leapt after him like hounds. But he fought his way in the lead with a clubbed rifle, and stood over Kagig's body working the weapon like a flail. That was all I saw of that encounter, for Mahmoud decided to attempt escape by the upper way again, and it was I who captured him. I landed on him through the darkness with my clenched fist under the low hung angle of his jaw and, seizing his leg, threw him out of the saddle. There Gloria helped me sit on him; and the greater part of what we had to do was to keep the women from tearing him to pieces.

At last Gloria and I, with a dozen of them, took Mahmoud up-hill and made him sit down in full firelight with his back against a rock. He had nothing to say for himself, but stared at Gloria with eyes that explained the whole philosophy of all the Turks; and she, for sake of the decency that was her birthright, went and stood on the far side of the rock and kept the bulge of it between them.

Then I sent for Kagig, and Monty, and Will; And after they had seen to the barricading of the upper end of the road with fallen trees and a fairly wide ditch, Kagig and Will came, followed by half a dozen of the elders, who had been lending a stout hand during that part of the night's work. Kagig was out of breath, but apparently not hurt much.

They came so slowly that I wondered. Gloria, who could see much farther through the dark than I, gave a little scream and ran forward. I saw then by a sudden burst of flame from the castle that they were carrying something heavy, and I guessed what it was although my heart rebelled against belief; but I did not dare leave Mahmoud, who seemed inclined to take advantage of the first stray opportunity. I stuck my pistol into his ear and dared him to move hand or foot.

Gloria came back in tears, and took Mahmoud's cape and my jacket, and spread them on the ground. On these they laid Monty very tenderly, Kagig looking on with cracking finger-joints that I could hear quite plainly in spite of the awful rage of battle that thundered and crashed and screamed among the woods. It was as one sometimes hears the ticking of a watch beneath the pillow in a nightmare.

Monty was alive, but in spite of what Gloria could do the dark blood was welling out from a sword gash on his right side, and we had not a surgeon within miles of us. From somewhere out of the darkness Maga appeared, bringing water, her face all black with the filth of fighting among trees, and her eyes on fire.

Monty seemed to be listening to the noise of battle—Kagig to think of nothing but his loss. He pointed at Mahmoud, who was eying Monty curiously.

"See the prisoner!" he said. "Ha! I would give a hundred of him a hundred times for Monty, my brother!"

Monty turned his head to see Mahmoud, and appeared partly satisfied.

"You hold the key," he said painfully. "Mahmoud will make terms. But it will take time to stop the fighting. You must send down reserves to Fred and Rustum Khan—that is where the strain is—you must see that surely—the enemy from below will be trying to come forward, and those in the trap to return. Fred and Rustum Khan are bearing all the brunt. Relieve them!"

It did not look good to me that Will should leave Gloria again; and Kagig must surely stay there to do the bargaining. So I took Monty's hand to bid him good-by, and limped off through the dark to try to find men who would come with me to the shambles below. It wag Kagig and Will together who overtook me, picked me off my feet, and dragged me back, and Will went down alone, with a wave of the hand to Gloria, and a laugh that might have made the devil think he liked it.

Then began the conference, I holding a mere watching brief with a pistol reasonably close to Mahmoud's ear. And for a time, while Monty lived, the elders supported Kagig and insisted on the full concession of his demands. But Monty, with his head on Gloria's lap, died midway of the proceedings; and after that the elders' suspicion of Kagig reawoke, so that Mahmoud took courage and grew more obstinate. Kagig called them aside repeatedly to make them listen to his views.

"You fools!" he swore at them, cracking his knuckles and twisting at his beard alternately. "Do you not realize that Mahmoud is ambitious! Do you not understand that he must yield all, if you insist! Otherwise we hang him here to a tree in sight of the burning castle and his own men! No ambitious rascal is ever willing to be hanged! Insist! Insist!"

"Ah, Kagig!" one of them answered. "Speak for yourself. You would not like to be hanged perhaps! But we must concede him something, or how shall he satisfy ambition? He must be able to go back with something to his credit in order to satisfy the politicians."

"Oh, my people! Oh, my people!" grumbled Kagig. "Can you never see?"

But they went back to Mahmoud with a fresh proposal, milder than the first; and eventually, after yielding point by point, until Kagig begged them kindly to blow his brains out and bury him with

Monty, they reached a basis on which Mahmoud was willing to capitulate—or to oblige them, as he expressed it.

He won his main point: Zeitoon was to accept a Turkish governor. They won theirs, that the governor was to bring no troops with him, but to be contented with a body-guard of Zeitoonli. For the rest: Mahmoud was to go free, taking his wounded with him, but surrendering all the uninjured Turkish soldiers in the trap as hostages for the release of all Armenian prisoners taken anywhere between Tarsus and Zeitoon. It was agreed there were to be no subsequent reprisals by either side, and that hostages were not to be released until after Mahmoud's army corps should have returned to whence it came.

Kagig wrote the terms in Turkish by the light of the holocaust in Monty's ancestral keep, and Mahmoud signed the paper in the presence of ten witnesses. But whether he, or his brother Turks, have kept, for instance, the last clause of the agreement, history can answer.

ARMENIA

First of the Christian nations; the first of us all
to feel
The fire of infidel hatred, the weight of the
pagan heel;
Faithfullest down the ages tending the light that
burned,
Tortured and trodden therefore, spat on and
slain and spurned;
Branded for others' vices, robbed of your rightful
fame,
Clinging to Truth in a truthless land in the name
of the ancient Name;
Generous, courteous, gentle, patient under the
yoke,
Decent (hemmed in a harem land ye were ever a
one-wife folk);
Royal and brave and ancient—haply an hour
has struck
When the new fad-fangled peoples shall weary
of raking muck,
And turning from coward counsels and loathing
the parish lies,
In shame and sackcloth offer up the only
sacrifice.
Then thou who hast been neglected, who hast
called o'er a world in vain
To the deaf deceitful traders' ears in tune to the
voice of gain,
Thou Cinderella nation, starved that our
appetites might live,
When we come with a hand outstretched at
last—accept it, and forgive!

XXII
"GOD GO WITH YOU TO THE STATES, EFFENDIM!"

THE FIGHTING lasted nearly until dawn, because of the difficulty of conveying Mahmoud's orders to the Turks, and Kagig's orders to our own tree-hidden firing-line. But a little before sunrise the last shot was fired, at about the time when most of the castle walls fell in and a huge shower of golden sparks shot upward to the paling sky. The cease fire left all Zeitoon's defenders with scarcely a thousand rounds of rifle ammunition between them; but Mahmoud did not know that.

An hour after dawn Fred joined us. He had the news of Monty's death already, and said nothing, but pointed to something that his own men bore along on a litter of branches. A minute or two later they laid Rustum Khan's corpse beside Monty's, and we threw one blanket over both of them.

I don't remember that Fred spoke one word. He and Monty had been closer friends than any brothers I ever knew. No doubt the awful strain of the fighting at the corner of the woods had left Fred numb to some extent; but he and Monty had never been demonstrative in their affection, and, as they had lived in almost silent understanding of each other, hidden very often for the benefit of strangers by keen mutual criticism, so they parted, Fred not caring to make public what he thought, or knew, or felt.

Kagig, not being in favor with the elders, vanished, Maga following with food for him in a leather bag, and we saw neither of them again until noon that day, by which time we ourselves had slept a little and eaten ravenously. Then he came to us where we still sat by the great rock with Mahmoud under guard (for nobody would trust him to fulfill his agreement until all his troops had retired from the district, leaving behind them such ammunition and supplies as they had carried to the gorge below the ramp).

We had laid both bodies under the one blanket in the shade, and Kagig pointed to them.

"I have found the place—the proper place, *effendim!*" he said simply. "Maga has made it fit."

Not knowing what he meant by that last remark, we invited some big Armenians to come with us to carry our honored dead, and followed Kagig one by one up a goat track (or a bear track, perhaps it was) that wound past the crumbled and blackened castle wall and followed the line of the mountain. Here and there we could see that Kagig had cleared it a little on his way back, and several times it was obvious that there had been a prepared, frequented track in ancient days.

"It took time to find," said Kagig, glancing back, "but I thought there must be such a place near such a castle."

Presently we emerged on a level ledge of rock, from a square hole in the midst of which a great slab had been levered away with the aid of a pole that lay beside it. All around the opening Maga had spread masses of wild flowers, and either she or Kagig had spread out on the rock the great banner with its ships and wheat-sheaves that the women had made by night in Monty's honor.

By Land and Sea.

We could read the motto plainly now—*Per terram et aquam*—By land and sea; and Kagig pointed to some marks on the stone slab. Moss had grown in them and lichens, but he or else Maga had scraped them clean; and there on the stone lay the same legend graven bold and deep, as clear now as when the last crusader of the family was buried there, lord knew how many centuries before.

The tomb was an enormous place—part cave, and partly hewn—twenty feet by twenty by as many feet deep at the most conservative guess; and on four ledges, one on each side, not in their armor, but in the rags of their robes of honor, lay the bones of four earlier Montdidiers—all big men, broad-shouldered and long of shin and thigh.

We did not need to go down into the tomb and break the peace of centuries. Under the very center of the opening was a raised table of hewn rock, part of the cavern floor, about eight feet by eight that seemed to have been left there ready for the next man, or next two men when their time should come.

Down on to that we lowered Monty's body carefully with leather ropes, and then Rustum Khan's beside him, Rustum Khan receiving Christian burial, as neither he nor his proud ancestors would have preferred. But his line was as old as Monty's, and he died in the same cause and the selfsame battle, so we chose to do his body honor; and if the prayers that Fred remembered, and the other cheerfuller prayers that Gloria knew, were an offense to the Rajput's lingering ghost, we hoped he might forgive us because of friendship, and esteem, and the homage we did to his valor in burying his body there.

We covered Monty's body with the banner the women had made, and Rustum Khan's with flowers, for lack of a better shroud; then levered and shoved the great slab back until it rested snugly in the grooves the old masons had once cut so accurately as to preserve the bones beneath.

Then, when Gloria had said the last prayer:

"What next, Kagig?" Will demanded.

Kagig was going to answer, but thought better of it and strode away in the lead, we following. He did not stop until we reached the open and the smoking ruins of the castle walls. When he stopped:

"Has any one seen Peter Measel?" I asked.

"Forget him!" growled Will.

"Why?" demanded Maga. "Will you bury him in that same hole with them two?"

"Has any one seen him?" I asked again, uncertain why I asked, but curious and insistent.

"Sure!" said Maga. "Yes. Me I seen 'im. I keel 'im—so—with a knife—las' night! You not believe?"

Whether we believed or not, the news surprised us, and we waited in silence for an explanation.

"You not believe? Why not? That dog! 'E make of me a damfool! 'E tell me about God. 'E say God is angry with Zeitoon, an' Kagig is as good as a dead man, an' I shall take advantage. 'E 'ope 'e marry me. I 'ope if Kagig die I marry Will Yerkees, but I agree with Measel, making pretend, an' 'e run away to talk 'is fool secrets with the Turks. Then I make my own arrangements! But Mahmoud is not succeeding, and I like Kagig better after all. An' then last night in the darkness Peter Measel he is coming on a 'orse with Mahmoud because Mahmoud is not trusting him out of sight. An' I see him, an' 'e see me, an' 'e call me, an' I go to 'im through all the fighting, an' 'e get off the 'orse an' reach out 'is arms to me, an' I keel 'im with my knife—so! An' now you know all about it!"

"What next?" Will demanded dryly.

"Next?" said Kagig. "You *effendim* make your escape! The Turks will surely seek to be revenged on you. I will show you a way across the mountains into Persia."

"And you?" I asked.

"Into hiding!" he answered grimly. "Maga—little Maga, she shall come with me, and teach me more about the earth and sky and wind and water! Perhaps at last some day she shall make me—no, never a king, but a sportsman."

"Come with us," said Will. "Come to the States."

"No, no, *effendi*. I know my people. They are good folk. They mistrust me now, and if I were to stay among them where they could see me and accuse me, and where the Turks could make a peg of me on which to hang mistrust, I should be a source of weakness to them. Nevertheless, I am ever the Eye of Zeitoon! I shall go into hiding, and watch! There will come an hour again—infallibly—when the Turks will seek to blot out the last vestige of Armenia. If I hide faithfully, and watch well, by that time I shall be a legend among my people, and when I appear again in their desperation they will trust me."

Will met Gloria's eyes in silence for a moment.

"I've a mind to stay with you, Kagig, and lend a hand," he said at last.

"Nay, nay, *effendi!*"

"We can attach ourselves to some mission station, and be lots of use," Gloria agreed.

"Use?" said Kagig, cracking his fingers. "The missions have done good work, but you can be of much more use—you two. You have each other. Go back to the blessed land you come from, and be happy together. But pay the price of happiness! You have seen. Go back and tell!"

"Tell about Armenian atrocities?" said Will. "Why, man alive, the papers are full of them at regular intervals!"

Kagig made a gesture of impatience.

"Aye! All about what the Turks have done to us, and how much about us ourselves? America believes that when a Turk merely frowns the Armenian lies down and holds his belly ready for the knife! Who would care to help such miserable-minded men and women? But you have seen otherwise. You know the truth. You have seen that Armenia is undermined by mutual suspicion cunningly implanted by the Turk. You have also seen how we rally around one man or a handful whom we know we dare trust!"

"True enough!" said Will. "I've wondered at it."

"Then go and tell America," Kagig almost snarled with blazing eyes, "to come and help us! To give us a handful of armed men to rally round! Tell them we are men and women, not calves for the shambles! Tell them to reach us out but one finger of one hand for half a dozen years, and watch us grow into a nation! Preach it from the house-tops! Teach it! Tell it to the sportsmen of America that all we need is a handful to rally round, and we will all be sportsmen too! Go and tell them—tell them!"

"You bet we will!" said Gloria.

"Then go!" said Kagig. "Go by way of Persia, lest the Turks find ways of stopping up your mouths. Monty has died to help us. I live that I may help. You go and tell the sportsmen all. Tell them we show good sport in Zeitoon—in Armenia! God go with you all, *effendim!*"

CORRESPONDENCE

IT WILL be good news to you that his tale in this number is only the first of a series that Talbot Mundy is writing for us. Time was when he turned out his stories briskly and in large number, and you liked them better than any others of our tales. Nowadays he works more slowly and though his stories come at longer intervals I think you'll find them even more worth waiting for.

Here is a word to you from him. In it he fails to mention that many of at least the minor incidents are bits out of his own life. For example, the landing at Lourenço Marques.

New York.

This, and the stories that will follow, are all more or less reminiscent. The names of people have been so entirely changed that the originals are unrecognizable, except that the man Charles du Maurier under his real name made such a reputation on that countryside as to be undisguisable anyhow. Any one who lived in Lourenço Marques in the bad old days of monarchical government would need no spirit of divination to help him identify the original of du Maurier and his family, even if I had called him Jones.

As for the Portuguese and their government of those days, there is this to be said for them: they were human. Murder was frequent, "justice" was purchasable and not to be had by any other means unless a man took law into his own hands—as he very well could do, if man enough, at almost any point thirty miles back from the sea. Where the coconut trees ceased from bearing fruit there ceased all but the shadow of the King of Portugal's authority. But the Portuguese, unofficial and official, were hospitable folk, as far as I was able to observe and quite devoid of the Spanish element of cruelty, very often brave, and frequently generous. They were frankly ashamed of their own misgovernment and ready at any time to talk of a republic with any one, but in almost every instance unwilling, or unable, to forego the chance of looting while the chance remained.

Of course this utter corruption of their government attracted to Lourenço Marques and the other towns (such as Inhambane, Beira and so on) all the undesirables from British territory and not a few from Madagascar; and their crimes were naturally credited to the Portuguese. That was not so unjust after all, for it was the Portuguese who made the rascality possible and whose highest officials set the worst example in the first place.

There were two or three peculiarities I especially noticed that are worth preserving from oblivion; and there is one conjecture I would like to offer. They were much more capable of deliberate cruelty toward a white man than a black. It is true that they were guilty of the most atrocious conduct toward natives, but they fed them, whereas they would let a white man starve (and frequently did) without compunction. They recruited slave-gangs on the East Coast for the West, and vice versa, and the cruelty inflicted on the "laborers" is best unwritten. Yet the Portuguese themselves were often the severest critics of the system and the guilty officials responsible for its continuance were a minority held in unqualified contempt. They did not permit flogging of natives by planters and private citizens.

The lower-class Portuguese invariably loathed the English. The better class invariably liked them. (I found the exact contrary to be the case in German territory.) The reason, I suppose, was that the riffraff of the population and the corrupt officials came in contact almost exclusively with blackguard Englishmen, as corrupt, as greedy and degraded as themselves; whereas the Portuguese gentlemen met English gentlemen and discovered ideas in common. Unhappily, the gentlemen of either race were rare in that afflicted land.

My conjecture is that the reason why the Portuguese find themselves fighting on the side of the Allies in this war is that the Portuguese, as a nation, were conscious of the shortcomings of their government and had not a good word to say for it. The German people, of course, have endorsed every action of their government; the more scoundrelly the atrocity, the louder their paeans of praise. Whereas I never once heard a Portuguese—not even a Portuguese official—praise his government. They denounced it first, last and all the time; and, although they took advantage of it with almost unbelievable cynicism, when their chance came at last they overthrew it. They were human. They did not care ten *reis* for efficiency without humanity, and they made no pretense at all to be supermen or demigods.

WHEN I first read Talbot Mundy's "Up and Down the Earth Tales" I wrote him that I didn't like Monty, that he got on my nerves just as he got on the nerves of Yerkes the American, and couldn't he tone Monty down a bit? I figured Monty would rile other democratic Americans as he had Yerkes and me.

Here is the letter in which Mr. Mundy knocks me out of the ring so hard and far that no undertaker is needed. It sounds as if he were mad. He wasn't. He and I have a pleasant little habit of pounding each other over the head and like each other the better for it. In this case I might dig up a small comeback or two but the honors are all his, and I'm pleased as he is.

Born an Englishman, he has become an American citizen. If you want to know how good an American he makes, read a certain article in a back *Everybody's* that tells what he and Hugh Pendexter and a few others did to make Oxford County, Maine, one of the banner counties of the whole United States in all kinds of practical accomplishments toward winning the war. I wish we had a million more Americans like him.

Yarmouth, Maine.

Don't consider my feelings; I simply haven't any left after reading what you say about my friend Monty.

See here—from first to last I have never pretended Monty is a democrat. I don't pretend he's right. He's a character; and the proof he is one lies in the fact that you hate him. You wouldn't hate a nonentity, would you?

(As a matter of fact Lenin and Trotsky call themselves democrats—so does Hylan—so does Hearst. I'm not in love with the word.)

Monty is the type of man who led the men who died in Flanders. Under the mellowing influence of Yerkes I rather expect he will undergo a lot of transmogrification, if that's the proper word.

But the point of the story, which you say you get, and which I observe with gratitude that you consider makes good reading, is—when free men and true have elected a leader, then they shall obey him!

In course of my observations of the development of this great and greater growing land I have seen many a fine fellow in khaki wrestling with this question, put to himself by himself: "Why should I, a free man in a free land, submit my free mind and body to the absolute discretion of a man with whom I often don't agree, whom I regard on many points as a damphule, and whose personal attitude toward life's problems is not at all my notion of democracy? Here I am—in khaki—bound to obey! How do I justify it?"

You ask me to think it over. Gosh! Did I do no thinking before I took out final papers? I'm an American from choice, because I'm convinced that this America of ours begins to think at about the point where the rest of the world leaves off.

So if your readers are able to be perverted from the true path by the story of the views and unregeneracy of an imaginary "English nobleman, then their democracy is slack in the back—and to —— with 'em!

Democracy is not "my will be done." Democracy is "Thy will be done, as in heaven, so on earth!"

An English nobleman who takes his election to be gang leader so seriously that he actually dares to imitate Abe Lincoln's method is no argument against democracy, but PROOF OF IT! Hurrah!

As Whistler said, I'm not arguing, I'm telling you!

Besides—do get this: I'm no lay preacher. I'm merely a recorder of what I see, using "fiction" for a method. If I can write good reading, yet preach no heresy—can a man do better?—TALBOT MUNDY.

SOME FIVE or six years ago, when our Camp-Fire was just starting, I asked some of the men who were giving us our stories in those days to tell us rather fully about their own adventures. Some of these got published; one or two, because of those famous "exigencies of space," never saw print. Here is Talbot Mundy's; with his present series of stories now running in our magazine, it had an added interest.

Since it was written he has, as you know, become an American citizen and a very good one, spending most of his time in Maine but now in New York again, and adding no chapters to the record of his outland adventures.

IT HAPPENS very seldom in a man's life that he gets the opportunity to talk about himself to the people who are going to read his stories; and it happens still less frequently that he can do it without his victims being able to talk back. So I'm going to make the most of this. Sit still, and suffer!

Why shouldn't a man talk about himself? I know when I read a story I always wonder whether the writer of it has lived through the fear and the joy and the various mixed emotions that he portrays, or whether he is only guessing. If I know that he has seen it all, or something very like it, I enjoy the story; otherwise I don't. And I dare say I am not at all unusual in that respect.

Standing at my own grave-side, and looking down into the grave that had been dug for me, was what actually started me at the writing game. Though I did not actually begin just at that time, it put the notion into my head that some of my experiences might make valuable copy. I made the usual beginner's mistake at first of writing the bald narrative of what had happened instead of inventing new episodes and fitting men I had met into them.

Naturally nobody wanted to read the unvarnished experiences of a rolling stone, strung into paragraphs but quite devoid of plot; in fact the only excuse for talking about them now is to prove that I know more or less what I write about, for a man who has knocked about the world for fifteen years or so without getting rich has very little to boast of.

But I was born with a thirst for adventure, or at all events I developed it at a very early age; and along with it came an insatiable passion for finding out how people would act under given circumstances. For instance, one of the earliest things I can remember is sticking a pin into a man to find out what he would do; and what he did to me was a very small matter when compared to the satisfaction of finding out something for myself.

My people destined me for the church or the law, I forget which, but I know they gave me the choice of two evils and that I chose a third that they never even dreamed of. They cut off supplies to enforce obedience, and I went without supplies to Germany. The method of choosing my destination was my own idea, though I have no doubt that many people have used it before and since; but it is so delightfully simple and devoid of detail, and I have used it with desirable results so frequently, that it is worth mentioning.

The plan is to first count all your money and then, by consulting railway time-tables and shipping lists, to find out just how far it will take you in any direction. Then put just so much of a map of the world on the table as your money will cover, shut your eyes and make a jab at the map with something sharp. Make a note of the town or village nearest to where the pricker lands, and go there without further argument. My pricker landed on a place called Quedlinburg in the Harz Mountains, and I arrived there a couple of days later with an English five-shilling piece in my pocket, a fox terrier dog on a leash, and a portmanteauful of clothes somewhere on the line behind me. I have often wondered who got the portmanteau.

There was a sort of mechanic person in Quedlinburg just then; his job was driving a traction engine that towed some vans belonging to a circus. He talked tolerable English, and, as I couldn't talk German, I was glad to make friends with him. He had only two ambitions. One was to keep his job, and the other was to get drunk—very drunk, and very often. I helped him to satisfy one of them the first night with my five shillings. The next morning he gave me a job. In future I was to drive the engine and he was to drink the beer; I was to get ten marks a week from the proprietor and eight more from him, but on the other hand I was to do all the work, take all the blame if anything went wrong, and sleep under the engine in all weathers, so as to be "Johnny on the spot," so to speak.

It turned out to be a good job, and I liked it, and I found out all there was to know about that traction engine in a very short time. We had a steam roundabout and swings and boxing-booths, and some wild animals in cages along with the circus; in fact, it was almost a traveling fair. My job at night was to drive the dynamo that was fixed on to the front of the engine, and I used to sit up on the driver's seat and watch the crowd and absolutely revel in the noise and glamor and confusion.

But one day my mechanic friend got more than usually drunk and killed my dog; and he got the worst of the battle royal that followed. Of course that ended our gentleman's agreement and I had to quit; and I tried my luck from end to end of Germany after that, working at any sort of job I could get, and usually hungry.

I got a good job at last—back close to Quedlinburg where I started. But it seems that in this extraordinary world a good job always has a handle to it; you've got to give your whole time and thought and energy to your boss. I was hired distinctly on those terms, and I made good, but I didn't like it. A man back in England happened to hear that I had made good and hired me at a salary that was absolutely enormous for a boy of seventeen, but on absolutely the same stipulation.

My new employer had a peculiarity that is not at all uncommon among men of his type in England; he loved buying expensive hunters, but he had not always the nerve to ride them; so quite a large part of my duties consisted in riding his hunters for him three days a week or so during the season. Besides being splendid sport and keeping me in excellent condition, the experience gave me a knowledge of horsemanship and wood-craft that has been invaluable since. I piled up money, though, because I hadn't a chance to spend it. As a matter of fact I piled up too much money, and that, and the fact that I was barely twenty-one and that my job had grown monotonous, got me going with the map of the world and the sticker again.

This time, though, I could afford steamboat fares, so I hadn't got to cut the map. I had the whole wide world to choose from at random, and the compass point came down bang in the middle of India. I asked my employer whether he hadn't any kind of pull that would secure me a job in that country, and as good luck would have it, he had; he secured me a sort of hybrid Government job in a Native State, and I started off for India feeling something as Alexander must have done.

The first thing I saw in India was a bullock-cart loaded up with corpses—legs and arms sticking out from every side of it, and a fetid mixture of flies and aroma floating up above. That looked good to me; I thought that maybe I might really get interested before long, and I left Bombay with a heart full of hope and a boxful of Kipling's books in the railway carriage with me. Plague, of course, was the cause of the corpses in the bullock-cart; they were on their way to be disposed of at the burning ghat; and though I hadn't bargained for it, I had to spend the next fifteen months fighting plague and cholera and famine in turn—single-handed a good part of the time—in a temperature in the shade of anything from one hundred and twelve upward.

The only compensation that made the job in any way worth while was the pig-sticking; that, and foxhunting, are the two finest land sports in the world, and I got nearly all I wanted of it, though I could not always get away. There was a sort of permanent tent club not far away; it was the one common meeting ground for the white men scattered through the district, and when the morning's sport was over and we were lounging under the double flies I had the privilege of talking to some of the most interesting men I have ever met—men who were giving up their lives out of absolutely unselfish devotion to their country.

I found out no end of things of course, and it was very interesting, but I can't say that I enjoyed it. No doubt the impression that the experience made on me has come in very useful since, but I don't like to think about the details for very long at a time; the sight of all those thousands of people, good decent people, too, for the most part, rotting to death from various causes and suffering unspeakably would be likely to have a sobering effect on any one. The worst part of it was being able to do so little for them.

I went down pretty badly from malaria and over-work, and a sort of temperamental nausea, so when the plague had retired under cover and the famine had lessened sufficiently to give the

Government time to breathe, I asked to be relieved, and another man was sent to take my job. I could have had another job straight away had I wanted it; but I had a sort of notion that I had been deep down into hell, and I had no desire just then to take the trip again. The prospect of a trip to Europe with a pocketful of money was much more alluring, and off to Europe I went to luxuriate and loaf and breathe clean cool air for six months.

But six months of Europe are enough for anybody at one time, and I soon got hungry for India again, for, after all, I had seen only a little corner of it, and that from only one point of view. This time I was lucky enough to arrange with a big firm of publishers to act as their occasional correspondent, and I walked on board the P. & O. steamer at Tilbury docks with the idea firmly planted in my head that I was going to set the Thames on fire at last. I didn't do it, of course; but I had a durned hard try.

A little native war broke out almost directly; after I landed, and on the strength of the credentials I had with me I hadn't very much difficulty getting to the front as a sort of junior war correspondent. My word! When I walked out of the Government office at last with the signed permit in my pocket I wouldn't have traded jobs with anybody in all the wide world! I could see fame in the offing already, and fortune coupled to it. Even now I would rather make a reputation as a war correspondent than in any other way, so you can imagine what I felt like then with what looked like the chance in front of me. I remember I felt awfully sorry for all the unfortunate writer-men who hadn't got my opportunity.

But I started in to make a whole lot too much of the opportunity. The thing wasn't so good as I thought it was anyhow, and besides that I was much too keen. The General commanding the British forces was enjoying his first experience of the war game too; he hadn't felt his feet yet, and he didn't believe in war correspondents on any terms; but he particularly didn't want anybody there to criticize him during the early stages of the campaign. Of course his object of it was perfectly natural under the circumstances, but it didn't suit me; he issued an order forbidding any one to leave the lines after dark; or at any time without permission; and as he never once gave his permission I disobeyed the order. Or, at least, he said I disobeyed the order.

What actually happened was this. I kept pestering him for permission to visit the advanced posts, and he kept on refusing; and each time he refused he did it more violently and with less command of his temper. At last one afternoon I was particularly insistent, and he turned round and told me to "go to ——!" Well, I took that for verbal permission to go just where I pleased; a fellow can't go to —— until he knows where it is, and I set out to find it.

I didn't get back to camp until two hours after dawn the following morning because a Ghoorka picket happened to hear me, and they amused themselves by firing volleys at me at intervals from midnight onward, and I had to wait until the mist lifted and they could see who I was. I hid behind a rock, but they made awfully good shooting in the dark, and chipped pieces off the rock all round me. Even when you know you can't be hit, the experience of being fired at is not pleasant, and it is still less so when you are wet through and shivering with cold.

So I lay there and tried to console myself with the knowledge that I had secured some quite important information. It was important, too, because the General pumped me dry and made use of it. But he didn't say thank you. He censored my despatches out of existence, and ordered me back to the base for disobedience to orders. And back to the base I had to go, having seen both the beginning and the end of my career as war correspondent within a month.

I went tiger shooting after that; and then on a trip up to Afghanistan, though I hadn't gone very far over the Himalayas before the Government turned me back. I had come to the conclusion by that time that the Government of India was a pretty difficult outfit to fool, so I had a look at China and Singapore and the Straits Settlements and gave them time to forget me. I thought that wouldn't take long. Then I took a trip up the Persian Gulf on a tramp steamer with a black skipper; we broke down half-way up the Gulf, and then I really did know what —— was like. On that trip I saw oxen being fed on dried fish. It sounds improbable, but I saw it with my two eyes.

I cooked up a gorgeous scheme then for a trip with another man up through India to Siberia, but the South African war broke out and that put quite another complexion on things. Of course I hadn't seen anything like the whole of India;

a man couldn't do that in a life-time. But I had seen and got to know Tommy Atkins at his best, and the men who lead Tommy Atkins "when the guns wheel into line," and my head was already cramfull of facts and fragments of facts that have since formed the foundation for such stories as "The Phantom Battery." If I have the ill-luck to live a hundred years, and keep on writing all the time, I may be able to exhaust half the stories that I know I can write about India; and though I have dived down deep into it, and seen it from several points of view, I know no more of if than a crab knows of the ocean. India is some country.

I wasn't tired of it yet by any means; in fact I have always meant to go back there again some day; but for the present there was a real live war to go to, and there were quite a lot of men in India besides myself who imagined that war was the one big picnic that should on no account be missed; so we made quite a strong regiment. We spent our own money on accouterments, and landed in Africa with only one regret among the lot of us—that it wasn't going to be a real war. It seemed to us an awful pity that such a fine regiment as we were should be wasted on a coconut-shy campaign against an enemy that hadn't any cavalry. We were cavalry—to begin with.

Barring a few prisoners, and mighty few of those, I never saw a live Boer the whole time. The picnic consisted for the most part of lying in the rain and being fired at, or lying in the scorching sun and being fired at. The rations were usually dead trek-ox or dead horse, dry biscuit, nice green water to wash it down with, and as a general rule no salt. There was no smoke to speak of, but every now and then you could see a flash somewhere on the hillside in front of you, and sometimes the man next to you would give a short sudden sob and lie very still. Or then again, sometimes he would sit up and scream, and go rolling over and over in agony. When the ground wasn't wet it was swarming with vermin, and most of the men who weren't shot went sick either from the vermin or the flies; or the bad water or else exposure. I had the good luck to get hurt with a piece of shell before the relief of Ladysmith, and that meant Cape Town for me, and nothing more to do.

The people in Cape Town who weren't talking treason were all full of schemes for getting suddenly rich. I thought out a scheme too. So two months later I left Cape Town, broke to the world and very glad indeed to get a job before the mast on a big steel sailing ship. I did the same thing again not long afterward, but not from choice, and I have since left off wondering why men can be found who are fools enough to go to sea at all—I mean on merchant ships. We were short-handed, fed on offal that would not be good for pigs, ill-treated, struck, sworn at, overworked all the time, housed in a fo'castle that was swarming with rats and vermin, deprived of any kind of privacy, and, in fact, treated like animals. Only animals are never worked so hard.

By the time that we reached Australia another Englishman and myself had had enough of it, so we ran away from the ship, leaving our kit and our wages behind us. We neither of us had any qualifications that were likely to get us a job up country, but we hadn't any money either, so we couldn't stay in Sydney; we had either to walk or go to sea again. We walked.

The two of us tramped all the way to Brisbane together asking for work at every place we came to, and never getting it. We got food, though, because of Australia they have to feed all "sun-downers," as hoboes are called; if they didn't, nobody would ever go on the road to look for work. Now and then we eked out a little money by singing songs in wayside pubs, but we arrived in Brisbane just as broke as when we set out.

There seemed nothing else for it but the sea again, and we finally reached Hobart, Tasmania, in the stokehold of a small steamer. The work was hard, but the grub was good, and the pay (ten pounds a month) was quite excellent. Hobart is a lovely little place but I couldn't see any chance of getting rich there. Charlie (the other fellow) elected to stop, though, and I pulled out alone, before the mast again on a three-masted barque: loaded up with blue-gum piles for the new pier at Delagoa Bay.

There is no need to describe that ship; it is sufficient to say that she was worse than the first one. We were very nearly wrecked on the way across, and the crew went sick from being fed on salt fish; every man Jack deserted, including myself, at Lourenço Marques.

Lourenço Marques is a pretty easy place to go broke in; and when you are broke it must be nearly the hardest place in the world in which to get on your feet again. Before I succeeded in getting a job I got so low with fever, and so absolutely busted, that I was glad to accept the hospitality of a Chinese laundryman; he put me to bed between clean sheets, and fed me back to health again. Then he told me where to go and get a job! I landed the job at the first try, and it was a good one, too, if you reckon without the climate.

I had to run a big estate up the Limpopo River, and while doing it I am glad to say that I was able to help my friend the Chinaman. It seems that he was getting too prosperous, and the local officials came down on him for an extra big rake-off. He refused, so they trumped up two or three changes against him and put him out of business, fining him every cent of money he had and turning him out on the street penniless. Then he remembered me, and one day he arrived at my hut on the bank of the Limpopo, much more dead than alive. It was turn about then; I gave him a bed and fed him back to health, and then lent him money, and in about three months time he was in a fair way to becoming a prosperous trader, buying corn from the natives and shipping it to the coast.

Then I went down with fever so badly that I had either to chuck my job or die, and, not being at all anxious to die, I did the other thing. The British East African Government had just finished the railway to the Lake, and the country was being boomed like wild-fire, so I decided to go there and took the very first steamer with the idea of getting well again on the way up. Of course every body knows now that British East Africa is a very much overrated country; there is neither mineral there nor anything else of much value except wild game; but I was one of the comparatively early birds who helped to find it out.

There were no jobs to be had, but there was some money to be made shooting elephants, although one had to ignore the Government regulations in order to do it. Off the beaten track, though, it was not very difficult at that time to keep out of the Government's reach; the job was to slip through into the open and, once outside the pale, to stay there until you had cleaned up what you were after. So I hired a native named Kazi Moto, who had just come out of jail, as my personal servant and took the train up country. Kazi Moto means "Work like ——," and he certainly did fill the bill. With his help I got a *safari* together and slipped through into the elephant country, where I joined a Greek of most blazing amazing courage but very doubtful reputation.

The hunting that followed was the hardest and most dangerous work I ever tackled; for excitement it beat war all to smithereens, and among other things it gave me an insight into the meaning of the word fear. I will take off my hat at any time to a man who can truthfully say that he is not afraid of a charging elephant.

I didn't get rich at the game, but I made enough money to pay my men and I got hold of a good big mob of cattle, which I drove down over the border into German territory. A marauding band of Masai tackled me not far from Shirati and drove off the whole lot. Naturally I resented it and, in the process of doing so, I received a spear-wound in my right leg. Kazi Moto killed my assailant with the butt end of a gun and then proceeded to suck my wound. He said he was sucking out poison and that he wasn't sure that he had got it all out. I didn't believe him, but he called up six other of my men, and among them they threw me on the ground and cauterized the wound thoroughly with firebrands. During the proceeding I bit Kazi Moto, who was sitting on my head, rather severely, but he never bore any malice about it.

The cattle being my only visible wealth and the cattle being all gone, all my men except Kazi Moto ran away, taking their loads with them in lieu of wages; and Kazi Moto and I set out to reach Muanza, a place nearly two hundred miles away, where the nearest doctor was. By the time I reached there I was naturally about all in, although, but for the fact that it was full of insects, my wound was not so bad as might have been expected.

The Germans were not at all pleased to see me, but, as I had developed black-water fever, they gave me a place to go away and die in. It was a dark and very dirty shed with a grass roof, which, besides me and Kazi Moto, had to shelter nearly all the rats in East Africa. Kazi Moto used to go out every day and steal things for me to eat, and once a day the doctor would come, look at me, give me a bottle of physic, grunt and go out again.

One morning he brought a sergeant with him and I heard him say to the sergeant, "All right... he'll be dead by this afternoon... you'd better send the chain-gang over to the burial-ground and get his grave dug, then we can get him out of the way before dark."

He didn't come in that morning, but just looked at me through the door; what he said to the sergeant, though, did me more good than all his physic. Up to that time I had not particularly wanted to get well; I had neither money nor prospects and was feeling much too ill to care, and I haven't the least doubt that if he had said nothing I would have died either that day or the day following, But I hated the man so, and was so utterly disgusted with his treatment of me, that I made up my mind to disappoint him, and from that minute I began to get better. When the chain-gang came with a sack to tie me up in I was sitting up with the aid of Kazi Moto. Two days later I leaned on Kazi Moto's shoulder and walked out to have a look at the grave; I was so weak that I very nearly tumbled into it.

Until then it had never once occurred to me that I had found out nearly enough for a young man of my age; but, looking into it, and back across it, I realized that, although I had done absolutely nothing to be proud of I had really acquired quite a lot of information. I sat there for about an hour, thinking; and at the end of it I pushed some dirt down into the grave as a sort of concrete sign that I had buried the old wanderlust at the bottom of it and would try henceforward to put my garnered knowledge to some use, I have not wandered more than twelve or thirteen thousand miles since.

I did a good bit of trekking about German East Africa after I got better, but this time always with a view to making money; and when I found that I could not make more than enough to live on, I decided to go up to British East again. So I took passage on a dhow, and that was another choice experience. The dhow was about thirty-five feet long over all and was loaded down with cargo. The cargo was covered with a sort of thatched roof, under which, and on top of the sacks of peanuts and drums of ghee, I and Kazi Moto, two native women, two babies, two goats, some chickens and eleven other natives including the crew had to exist. The voyage lasted ten days and it rained in torrents the whole time. When we made a smudge to drive out the mosquitoes the smoke was intolerable, and when we threw the smudge overboard the mosquitoes swarmed in like a hungry army.

One night the native who was sleeping next to me died (of pneumonia I think); I felt his back getting colder and colder but I had no idea that he was dead until the morning. They carried him ashore, and buried him in my blanket.

I did all right up in British East, for I secured a road contract, and, when I made good on that, the Government gave me an official job. But the climate where I was was awfully unhealthy; I had made up my mind by that time to write stories, and I had to work too hard to be able to find time for writing. In addition to that, people had a distressing habit of committing suicide there; they did it one after another, and that kind of thing gets on your nerves after a while.

I saw two native campaigns, but they weren't sufficiently exciting to make up for the depressing surroundings during all the rest of the time. A final dose of black-water fever convinced me that I had had enough of Africa, so I paid off Kazi Moto and sailed for Europe. Before I left, Kazi Moto stole my razors, watch, camp-kit and some of my money, but I don't grudge him any or it. I had intended to give him everything except the watch, so he didn't get much more than he was entitled to anyhow. He was a good man, and he saved my life four separate times.

Europe turned out to be as amusing and as comfortable and as unsatisfactory as ever when I got there. So I held the map and used the pricker. Others maintained that I made it come down in the U.S.A. on purpose. At all events I am glad that it did so.

Now that's a deuce of a long talk about very little, isn't it! But I've left a whole lot out. What I've tried to do is to prove that I've met real live men and seen them behave under all sorts of conditions, and that I've suffered with them and seen what they've seen and laughed with them sufficiently to be able to understand them and their motives. And consequently claim that the people in my stories are real people who are worth writing about.

That is the only claim that a writer-man has any right to make. He himself, his private life, and his present possessions are matters of absolutely no importance; but his experience does count, because that is his only qualification, barring of course the technical knowledge that he can learn at school.

It goes without saying that there are different sorts of experience which are suitable for different styles of writing. Mine has been mixed and varied, and I try to write various stories. I have dined with a prince, who was afterward a king, and also at a Chinaman's table between my host and a buck

Zulu; it doesn't matter which experience I liked best; the point is that I have sampled both. I have earned my living carrying sacks of potatoes at the wharf-side, and I have also had a very good time indeed in certain London clubs; and in between those two walks in life are an unnumbered host of others, many of which I have come into contact with at one time or another.

I claim to be nothing but a lineal descendant of the old-time story-teller, who spun his yarn and passed the hat round. Nowadays it is the editor who passes round the hat, and he is rather more particular than the old-time capper used to be; but the effect is just the same. The public pays, and the public calls the tune. I believe, too, that the public likes to know now, just as much as it did then, that the man who spins the yarn has seen the things he writes about. I have no other excuse for discussing myself and my wanderings over so many pages.—TALBOT MUNDY.

ENDNOTES

1 Here I give a brief overview of the known facts of this time, as relevant to Mundy's later writing; the reader is advised to handle with care sensationalized allegations about the period, many of them based on hearsay, and unverified sources—most prominently a later literary rival who was jealous of Mundy's greater success.

2 Archie Kilpatrick, "Talbot Mundy Is Dead, Writer, Resident Here," *Manchester Evening Herald,* August 6, 1940, p. 2.

3 Talbot Mundy, "A Jungle Sage," *Adventure,* 82 (March 15, 1932), 113.

4 Talbot Mundy, "On the Trail of Sindbad the Sailor," *The Frontier,* 1 (February 1925), 106.

5 Talbot Mundy, "Autobiography," in "The Camp-Fire," *Adventure,* 21 (April 1, 1919).

6 Kilpatrick, p. 2.

7 Marguerite Mooers Marshall, "Treasure of Tippoo Tib, 100,000,000 Pounds Ivory, Awaits Finder in Africa," *New York Evening World,* 60, no. 21, 169, undated newspaper clipping in Talbot Mundy Promotional File, Bobbs-Merrill mss.

8 Mundy, "Autobiography." He fictionalized the experience in chapters 6–9 of *The Ivory Trail.*

9 Brian Taves, *Thomas Ince: Hollywood's Independent Pioneer* (Lexington, KY: University Press of Kentucky, 2011).

10 Talbot Mundy, *Solomon's HalfWay House, Maclean's,* 47 (August 15, 1934), 39.

11 Talbot Mundy, "Oakes Respects an Adversary," *Adventure,* 19 (December 3, 1918), 3.

12 Mundy, "Oakes Respects an Adversary," 6.

13 Talbot Mundy, letter to H.H. Howland, November 7, 1918, p. 2, Bobbs-Merrill mss.

14 Mundy, letter to H.H. Howland, pp. 1–2, Bobbs-Merrill mss. For a publishing history of the novel, see Louis E. Lambert, "Episodes in the Publishing of Talbot Mundy's *The Ivory Trail,*" *The Indiana University Bookman,* No. 8 (March 1967), 57–62.

15 Talbot Mundy, *The Ivory Trail* (Indianapolis: Bobbs-Merrill, 1919), 84.

16 Talbot Mundy, letter to H.H. Howland, April 2, 1919, p. 1, Bobbs-Merrill mss. See also "Watu," *Adventure,* 82 (April 1, 1932), 52–53.

17 Mundy, *The Ivory Trail,* 379, 32.

18 Mundy, *The Ivory Trail,* 201–202.

19 Mundy, *The Ivory Trail,* 221.

20 Mundy, *The Ivory Trail,* 265.

21 Fred F. Fleischer, Letter in "The Camp-Fire" on propaganda and *The Ivory Trail, Adventure,* 42 (April 20, 1923), 183.

22 "The Ivory Trail," *New York Times Book Review,* July 13, 1919, p. 355.

23 Mundy, *The Ivory Trail,* 404.

24 Mundy, *The Ivory Trail,* 353.

25 Mundy would return to the Red Sea with a gunrunning tale in the August 1933 issue of *Adventure* and the race horse novelette *Odds on the Prophet,* published posthumously in the August 10, 1941 issue of *Short Stories.*

26 "Mission Board Told of Turkish Horrors," *New York Times,* September 17, 1915, www.cilicia.com/armo10cnyt19150917.html.

27 Talbot Mundy, letter to Mr. Bobbs, October 18, 1919, Bobbs-Merrill mss.

28 *The Eye of Zeitoon* was translated into Armenian for a Boston ethnic newspaper, *Hairenik,* and certainly had an impact within that community.

29 D.L. Chambers to Talbot Mundy, June 8, 1920, p. 1, Bobbs-Merrill mss. Such poor sales were especially disappointing considering the popularity of *The Ivory Trail,* but Mundy was disillusioned with the book even before publication; in November 1919 he wrote Sally Ames that he regarded it as "a very bad book." Talbot Mundy to Sally Ames, November 13, 1919, p. 6, Richards Ames collection.
An unusual approach was taken to illustrating Bobbs-Merrill's edition of *The Eye of Zeitoon.* Dwight Franklin created wax figurines of the characters against realistic backgrounds, which were then photographed in color. Mundy was enthusiastic about Franklin's work, believing that these expensive illustrations and his frequently vague poems (which had not appeared in the *Romance* serialization) would be major selling points. Sadly, he was wrong at least regarding Franklin's four illustrations, and the Bobbs-Merrill campaign built around them failed dismally: the plaster casts proved too difficult to be shipped for display without suffering damage.

30 Curtis Brown to Howland, April 15, 1920, Curtis Brown mss.

31 Monthly Statement to Talbot Mundy, April 28, 1924, Bobbs-Merrill mss. In the last half of 1921, only eleven copies of *The Eye of Zeitoon* had sold, insufficient for royalty payment. Statement December 31, 1921, *The Eye of Zeitoon* Talbot Mundy in account with Hutchinson & Co., Curtis Brown mss.; Statement May 18, 1922, *The Eye of Zeitoon* Talbot Mundy in account with Hutchinson & Co., Curtis Brown mss.

32 Cape Dutch word—foreigners. Invariably a term of reproach.

33 *Baas*—master. The Bantu word from which the American "boss" may possibly be derived.

34 The words *"Njo hapa"* in the Kiswahili tongue are the equivalent of "come hither!"

35 *Bwana,* Swahili word meaning *master.*

36 *Mali,* Swahili word meaning *possessions, property.*

37 Slavery was not absolutely and finally abolished in Zanzibar until 1906, during which year even the old slaves, hitherto unwilling to be set free, had to be pensioned off.

38 *Jambo,* good day.

39 *Wapagazi,* plural of *pagazi,* porter.

40 *Safari,* journey, and, by inference, outfit for a journey.

41 *Imshi* (Arabic), get to hell out of here!

42 *Voetsak* (Cape Dutch), ditto.

43 *Enenda zako* (Kiswahili), ditto.

44 *Kuma nina* (Kiswahili). An opprobrious, and perhaps the commonest expletive in the language, amounting to a request for details of the objurgee's female ancestry. By no means for use in drawing-rooms.

45 *Melikani,* the unbleached calico made in America that is the most useful trade goods from sea to sea of Central Africa.

46 *Kanga,* cotton piece goods.

47 *Askari,* native soldier.

48 The principal hotel In Zanzibar was formerly Tippoo Tib's residence, quite a magnificent mansion for that period and place.

49 *Gefaehrlich,* dangerous.

50 In 1914 there were still thousands of slaves in German East, although the German press and public were ever loudest in their condemnation of British conditions.

51 *Askari,* soldier.

52 *Bwana makubwa,* lit. big master, senior government officer.

53 *Monumme* (Kiswahili)—lit. male—man in his prime.

54 It was the cheerful Arab rule never to release one slave from the yoke if the other failed on the journey, on the principle that then the stronger would be more likely to care for, encourage, and drive the weaker.

55 *Sijui,* I don't know: the most aggravating word in Africa, except perhaps *bado kidogo,* which means "presently," "bye and bye," "in a little while."

56 *Gali,* same as Hindustani *kali*—cruel, hard, fierce, terrible.

57 *Karibu,* enter, come in.

58 *Fundis*—skilled workmen.

59 *Ruksa,* you have leave to go.

60 You want to be popular, don't you!

61 Now, hit good and hard!

62 *Cadi*—judge.

63 Literally, pig-play.

64 Plural of *machenzie,* "man from 'way back," "rube," "simp."

65 It is a characteristic of the so-called Sleeping Sickness that is decimating the tribes around Victoria Nyanza that the victim, although he goes into a coma, never actually sleeps from the time of taking the disease until the end, usually more than a year later. The natives, a tribe that came originally down from Egypt, themselves say that the dreaded sickness is a "visitation" by way of revenge on them for former sins, although what sins, and whose vengeance, they are at a total loss to explain.

66 *Hodi!* Equivalent to "May I come in?"

67 *Jambo!* Kiswahili equivalent of "How d'you do?"

68 The legendary place that every Ivory hunter hopes some day to stumble on, where elephants are said to have gone away to die of old age, and where there should therefore be almost unimaginable wealth of ivory. The legend, itself as old as African speech, is probably due to the rarity of remains of elephants that have died a natural death.

69 *Ngumu sana,* very severely.

70 Turkish word: happenings, a euphemism for massacre.

71 Punjabi word—landholder.

72 *Chalana*—She-jockey (a compliment).

73 *Gorgio*—Gentile (an insult).

74 *Shapkali*—hatted man—foreigner.

75 *Haide!*—Turkish, "Come on!"

76 *Busné*—Gipsy word—Gentile, or non-gipsy.

77 *Attaman,* gipsy headman.

78 *Patteran,* a gipsy word: trail.

79 *Gitana,* gipsy young woman.

80 *Rom*—Gipsy husband, or family man.

81 *Shâtir,* the man who runs before a personage's horse.

82 *Kaimakam,* headman (Turkish).

www.ingramcontent.com/pod-product-compliance
Lightning Source LLC
Chambersburg PA
CBHW081132300726
48982CB00005B/943

* 9 7 8 1 6 1 8 2 7 3 5 6 7 *